THE ELITE KINGS
BOX SET

VOL II

AMO JONES

THE
SILVER
SWAN

THE ELITE KING'S CLUB BOOK ONE

DEDICATION

To stories that fuck you so good you'll need a cigarette.

This is one of those stories.

CHAPTER I

The school hallways cave in on me as I walk through what would be my first day at Riverside Preparatory Academy. The sound of closing lockers and snickering voices surround me, and all I want to do is go visit my mom's grave. My dad moved us across the state, because he had found "the one." I'm beginning to think he can't count. This would be his third "the one" since my mom's passing.

Reaching my locker, I pull it open and place my brand-new textbooks inside before taking out my class schedule. *Calculus.* Great. My leather bangles jingle as I close my locker door and make my way to calculus. It's September, so at least I'm starting at the beginning of the school year.

Halting at the threshold of the classroom, I look down to my paper to check the numbers before looking at the ones mounted above the door. Ignoring the twenty or so eyes gawking at me, I manage to slip out, "Is this 1DY for calculus?"

The teacher, I assume, walks up to me, his black-rimmed glasses shielding his tired eyes and his gray hair illustrating his age. "Yes, Madison Montgomery?"

Swallowing, I nod. "Yes, that's me."

"Welcome to Riverside Prep. I'm Mr. Warner. Why don't you take a seat?"

I smile at him, clutching my books, and walk toward the crowd of students who are all sitting in their chairs, and that's when the whispering starts.

"Madison Montgomery? Isn't that the girl whose mom murdered her dad's girlfriend before killing herself?"

"Are you sure?" her friend asks, eyeing me skeptically. *"She seemed so much prettier in the newspapers."*

"No, that's definitely her. Her dad is loaded too. They're from old money, and her mom was a bored housewife who caught her husband cheating. So she stabbed the woman to death before shooting herself in the head—with Madison's shotgun." The air begins to thicken as I drop down to my seat.

"Her shotgun? She owns a shotgun? Ew. Better stay away from her. She might be as crazy as her mother."

They laugh before Mr. Warner clicks his fingers, demanding their attention. I close my eyes briefly, swallowing down any hope I had at getting a fresh start at a new school. Nothing and no one could give me a new beginning. Who was I kidding?

At first break, I walk to the outside entrance and take a seat on one of the steps.

The way the school is laid out allows students to use the front steps to eat their lunch or the cafeteria. The atrium is filled with students, so I opt to eat out here where the sun is shining and where it's less... people-y.

"Hi!" a chirpy voice bellows, and I look up behind me to find a girl who's as small as a pixie. Her tiny body is covered in the finest labeled clothes, and her white-blonde hair has the sun bouncing off it. I also can't help but notice that where my wrists are bound by black metal and leather bangles, hers are silver and gold. I know instantly we can't be friends.

"Hi." I tuck my brown hair behind my ear.

She sits down beside me anyway, taking a bite out of her sandwich. "I'm Tatum. You're new, right?"

I nod, sucking the juice from my apple off my thumb. "Yup. Sorry, you probably don't want to be seen with me."

She waves my comment away. "I know all about you. Madison Montgomery, seventeen years old. Daughter of a murderer who then shot herself. Dad has money coming out his butt. Came from Beverly Hills to the Hamptons. Have I missed anything?"

I blink slowly before narrowing my eyes. "You forgot the part where it was my gun."

She laughs nervously. "I know. I was just hoping that wasn't true."

"My point. You probably don't want to be seen with me." I turn my attention back to my apple.

She shakes her head. "Nope, you and I are going to be great friends."

After break, I carry on to my next class, and before I know it, the bell rings for lunch. Tatum insists on showing me around the school the best she can, pointing out all the different classrooms and where I can sign up for what. During lunch, the boys come from their side of the school, and we all join in the cafeteria, which splits the girl and boy sides of the school. On the rich side, it's up there on Bill Gates's status, and I'm seriously wondering how the hell my father managed to get me in. We're rich, yes, but there's something else about this school. You need a high level of pedigree to get in, too.

We walk into the cafeteria, and Tatum points down to my skirt. "You can accessorize your school uniform. We can hem it higher if we want." My plaid school skirt sits just above my knees, and I'm okay with the length. I don't want to attract any more attention, so I brush off her suggestion.

"Thanks," I answer dryly, before bringing my eyes to the doors that open out to the boy's side. A handful of guys push through the doors, talking and laughing with each other. They commanded the atmosphere instantly. Their grins are cocky with self-assurance.

"Who're they?" I ask, nudging my head toward the group walking toward the garden wall at the far side of the right wing.

"*They* are trouble," Tatum mumbles, taking a seat on one of the picnic tables. I watch them closely. They're all hot, *really* hot. Tatum turns around, following my line of sight. "And *that's* slut trouble," she mutters, pointing toward the girls who were babbling off earlier in calculus.

"What do you mean by trouble?" I ask, ignoring her reference to the girls and taking my eyes away from the commotion.

"I mean, not only are they advantaged assholes who own this school, and when I say own, I mean literally—at least for Nate anyway. But around here? They call the shots. The students of Riverside Prep are just pawns in their sick and twisted games. They own this school, Madison."

"You say that like they're in a gang." I peel open my yogurt.

"They may as well be," she replies, opening her carton of juice. "Apparently, they're members of this super-secret club." She leans in closer and smiles. "The Elite Kings Club."

CHAPTER 2

"The Elite Kings Club?" I ask, taking a bite out of my sandwich. Jimmy, our cook, made my favorite. Chicken salad with diced tomatoes and chopped lettuce mixed together with mayonnaise. He's so good at his job that my father uproots and brings him wherever we end up living.

Tatum waves her hand around, rolling her eyes. "They're like this undercover exclusive club. No one really knows what happens in this club, or who all the members really are, but it has to do with blood and your family lineage, apparently."

I continue eating my sandwich. The bell rings to signal that break is over once again, so I collect my books from the table.

"What do you have now?" Tatum asks, shoving an apple in her mouth so she can have a free hand to collect her books. I laugh under my breath as she takes the apple out of her mouth. "What?"

I shake my head. "Nothing, and I have PE."

She scrunches her face. "You do know that was optional, right?"

I nod, helping her pick up her books when I see she's taking too long. "I like sports."

We turn to walk back into the girls' hall, and just when I hit the doorway, something urges me to turn back around.

You know that feeling you get when you can feel someone watching you? Yeah, I had that times seven. When I pause in my step, Tatum halts her yapping about some game that's happening on Friday night, her eyes going over my shoulder before her face pales and her eyebrows pinch together. I slowly turn back around to look in the cafeteria to find all—seven, there's seven—boys staring right at me. I scan over each of them, lingering a little too long on the one with messy dark brown hair who's sitting slouched over a chair. He has wide shoulders and a strong, angular jaw. His eyes continue to summon mine when suddenly I feel as though I'm locked in a trance. Knowing I should pull away, I swallow and turn back around to go to my next class.

"Whoa! Hold up!" Tatum runs up behind me. "What the hell was that about?"

I shrug, pulling out my schedule from my pocket. "They've probably heard about my mom."

Tatum scoffs. "They wouldn't care about that, I'm sure. That was something else. But hey"—her firm grip on my arm halts my forward momentum—"you don't want *them* to notice you, Madison. They're not good people."

"Well, seems it's a little late for that." I shove past her and carry on toward the back doors that lead to the gym. I'm walking down the long corridor and am about to round the corner into the girls' locker room when I walk into a rock-hard chest.

"Holy shit," I whisper, pulling my hand back from his pec. "I'm so sorry." I look up to honey-brown eyes shaped by thick eyelashes. *Pretty boy.*

"Hey, no worries." He collects his duffle bag from the ground before reaching his hand out to me. "Carter. And you must be Madison Montgomery."

"Great," I mutter. "You've heard all about me." I drop my eyes to his chest, remembering how hard it felt under my palm.

He chuckles. "Which story?" he teases, winking at me.

I smile at his attempt to lighten up the mood, shaking my head. "I thought this was the girls' side?"

"The gym is co-ed. How're you liking your first day?" he asks, leaning against the wall.

"Well," I begin, my eyes darting around the long corridor, "a little intense."

"Carter! Get your ass in here!" an older man wearing a whistle around his neck and a baseball cap calls out from the other end of the corridor.

Carter's eyes stay on mine, a small smirk appearing on his mouth. "I'll see you around, Madison." He pushes off the wall with a grin, strolling past me.

"Yeah," I answer, once he's already gone. "I'll see you around." Turning back around to peer over my shoulder, I catch him watching me, so I wave lightly at him before carrying on toward PE.

That's two nice people I've met on my first day, and I didn't see him sitting with the Elite-whatever boys, so I'm hoping he isn't friends with them.

I'm waiting outside the front gate of the school for my driver when Tatum comes running up to me. "So, Carter Mathers." She wiggles her eyebrows.

I tilt my head. "How do you even know about that? It literally happened not one hour ago."

"News travels fast around here." She picks at her nails, unfazed.

"I'm starting to get that," I mutter.

"So anyway," she continues, hooking her arm in mine. "I need your number so we can plan this weekend." I see my black limo pull up to the curb, and Harry, my dad's driver, steps out of the driver side. Tatum pulls out her phone, and I ramble off the numbers to her while making my way to my ride. "Okay! I'll text you!" she yells out, as Harry opens my door and I clutch it in my hand.

"Do you have a driver?" I ask her, one foot inside the car.

She shakes her head. "I drive."

I wave her off and slide into the back of the car. Today was truly interesting. I'm not sure how to take the events that have happened, but if every day is going to be like today, I'm in for a long ride.

CHAPTER 3

After pushing open the double front doors to our colonial home, I drop my bag in the foyer and make my way into the kitchen. Our house is exactly what you'd expect someone like my father to own. All neutral milky whites on the walls, with a crystal white staircase that leads up to the second level. I take a can of Coke out of the fridge before making my way upstairs. My dad and his new bride will be back on Monday, and I've only met her once or twice, but from what I've seen, she seems nice. Nicer than his last money-hungry broad, who he brought home anyway. I'm walking up the stairs when my phone vibrates in my back pocket. I fish it out quickly and slide it open when I see it's my dad.

"Hey."

"Madi, sorry, honey. We forgot to tell you that Elena's son will be moving into the manor as well."

I pause, scanning the long hallway once I reach the top of the staircase. "Okaaay. I didn't know she had a son."

"She does. He attends your school. I need you to keep him at arm's length."

"What does that mean?"

He sighs. "Just wait until we get home, Madi."

"Dad, you're being cryptic. I'll see you when you get home, and I'm sure I'll be fine."

I hang up the phone before he can continue to badger me, or worse, give me "the talk." After shoving my phone into the back pocket of my jeans, I walk to my bedroom door, halting when I hear sounds coming from the bedroom next to mine. Is he already here? Fighting my nosey tendencies, I push through my door and sigh with the relief of being back in my safe bubble. Kicking my door closed, I walk toward the Victorian-style glass doors that open out onto the little balcony that hangs over the pool. I push open the white net curtains and unlock the latch to let some air in. The light afternoon breeze brushes over me, sending my long brown hair swishing over my shoulder.

My safe bubble of relaxation is short-lived as Ludacris's "What's Your Fantasy" shakes the vintage art I have hanging on my walls with its deep-sounding bass. I shake my head, walking back into the room, which continues to house boxes of all my items I haven't unpacked yet. I pull open the bathroom door that's joined onto my room and close it before wiggling out of the clothes I wore to school. Slipping into the scorching yet soothing spray of water, I work double time at washing myself before turning off the faucet and wrapping a towel around my body.

I'm stepping out of the shower when I see someone leaning against the doorframe of the other room that's connected to the bathroom. A loud scream erupts from me, and I clutch the towel around my body. *I forgot about that damn door.* Genuine's "Pony" is playing now, and my eyes narrow on the tall, lean guy standing in front of me with his arms crossed in front of himself.

"Get out!" I point to his room.

He chuckles, his eyes traveling down my body, and his head tilts. "Oh, don't be shy, little sis. I don't bite…" He grins. "*Hard.*"

I clutch the towel tighter, scanning down his naked chest to where a tight six-pack sits proudly, with two muscular arms framing his torso. A large Celtic cross tattoo sits over his left pec, and on the right of his ribcage, he has a scripted tattoo sprawled out over it.

I look up to his face, where the corner of his mouth kicks up in a smirk. A lip ring sits to the side, and his eyes zone in on me, glistening with mischief. "You done eye-fucking me, little sis?"

"I'm not your little sister," I hiss, narrowing my eyes. "Get out. I need to get changed."

"You not gonna ask my name?" he questions, his smooth, sun-kissed skin glowing in the bathroom light, his blue eyes laced with mischief. He pushes off the doorframe he was leaning on, walking toward me with so much swagger he could give 50 Cent a run for his money. His dark blond hair sits messily all over his head, and his torn jeans hang nicely off his hips, showcasing the rim of his Phillip Plein briefs. He pauses when his chest is almost flush with mine.

Reaching for his toothbrush, he grins. "The name's Nate, little sis." He winks at me, squirting toothpaste onto his brush before his smile flicks to the mirror. He pops the toothbrush into his mouth and smirks.

Spinning around, I quickly dash out my door. What the fuck was that about? And there's no way I'm sharing a bathroom with him. Picking up my phone from the bed, I dial my dad. When it goes straight to his voice mail, I growl lightly. "Dad, we need to talk about my living situation—STAT!"

Shuffling into some skinny jeans and a checkered top, I brush my hair out and tie it into a messy high ponytail. Shoving on my Converse sneakers, I head for the door. Just as I open up my bedroom, Nate is walking out of his, still with no top on, and still with those sinful jeans hanging off him. He annoys me instantly. His cocky smirk is spread out over his mouth, and his baseball cap is flipped backward. "Where you off to?"

"None of your business," I answer, slamming my bedroom door and wondering whether I should have locks put on it. I continue toward the stairs when he races up behind me.

"Sure it is. Big brothers are supposed to look out for the little ones."

I halt, spinning around on the fourth step and glaring up at him. "We"—I gesture between the two of us—"are not related, Nate." That only makes his grin go wider. He leans on the rail of the stairs, and my eyes flick under his bicep, where there's a scar embossed into his skin. He sees where my eyes go and quickly crosses his arms in front of himself. "But since you're asking," I say, walking the rest of the way down the steps. I turn to face him and tilt my head once I hit the bottom. "I'm going shooting."

CHAPTER 4

Arriving home later that night, I thank Harry and make my way up the large cobblestone entryway, up to the front door. I can hear the music before I hit the entrance, so when I swing the door open and see a house party in full swing, I'm not even slightly surprised. Slamming the door shut—rather dramatically—I scan over the drunken crowd. Where our marble kitchen is, there are teenagers playing beer pong, and dancing and grinding on each other in the background.

Swinging my eyes to the sitting room that leads off to our outdoor pool and pool house, I see another crowd dancing in strobe lights, with Akon's "Ain't Saying Nothing" blasting from the DJ booth set up where our couch once sat. I look back outside and see the party lights on inside our pool, and half-naked people cannon-balling into it, with a few others making out in our Jacuzzi.

Motherfucker!

Narrowing my eyes, I can almost make out another crowd behind the pool, on the grass area where our backyard leads to the beach. *Oh, man, I'm going to kick his fucking ass.* When I see the black baseball cap with blond hair peeking out slightly from underneath, and the same lean, tan build—still wearing no shirt—I know I've found Nate. I walk toward the couch, where he lounges with a few other guys, his head bobbing to the beat of "Nightmare on My Street" by DJ Jazzy Jeff, as he loads up the tip of a bong with weed.

I recognize all of them from school today—the guys Tatum referred to as "The Elite Kings Club." Nate is apparently the one whose great-great-grandparents were the founders of Riverside Prep. I'm not sure if that was from his mother or father. Elena is lovely and is as rich as my father. That's probably why I like her more than anyone else he's introduced me to. I know she isn't just after his money. So I guess it's her side. My dad is good-looking for an old man. He isn't really old though, sitting at forty-seven. I guess there are fathers with kids my age who are older. He trains daily and eats well, and Elena is the same. She's fit for her age and takes care of herself. Though I have only met her twice—the first time was when we moved here a few days ago, and the second time was before they flew to Dubai for a business meeting—she was nothing but nice to me. How she managed to have a shithead son like Nate, I don't know.

"Nate!" I snap, rounding the couch until I'm standing in front of him. His arms are stretched wide over the sofa, his legs spread in front of himself, his lips forming an O before he slowly blows out a thick cloud of smoke, while his eyes stare straight through me.

"Shut this down—now." The blur of movement catches my attention in my peripheral vision, but I ignore it.

He smirks. "Little sis, might want to go put that gun in the cabinet before you freak everyone out."

I clutch the straps to my 12-gauge around my shoulders. "Shut it down, Nate. I'm serious."

He shoots up off the couch with a red cup in one hand. "Wait! Come here." He pulls me under his shoulder, his mouth dropping down to my ear. He points to the first guy who was sitting beside him on the couch. "That's Saint, Ace, Hunter, Cash, Jase, Eli, Abel, Chase, and Bishop." My eyes drift over them dismissively. I recall a few of them from school, but there're a couple older-looking guys who I don't recognize.

"Hi," I manage to say—awkwardly, I might add. I turn back to Nate. "I'm serious. You will get us both into trouble. Close it down." I turn around, and just as I'm about to hit the entryway to exit the lounge, I spin back around and catch them all watching me. Nate is smiling from behind his cup, while the rest of them have a mixture of emotions sprawled across their faces. When I settle on... I think Nate said his name was Bishop, the same guy I had a stare down with at school today, who is now sitting on a kitchen chair with his legs spread out in front of him, my cheeks flare to life. His eyes burn into my skull, and if guys had a resting bitch face, then that would be it.

Shivers creep up my spine; I don't even know why. Maybe it's because he seems just so... unapproachable. I scoff inwardly. *Typical fucking prep school students.* Walking back up the stairs, leaving Nate to shut it down on his own, I walk into my room, placing my shotgun at the top of my closet, and take out some clothes while I'm there. Slipping into the bathroom, double checking the locks on both doors this time, and taking hold of the faucet, I turn it on to scorching hot before stepping into the cascading waters. I let the harsh pounding of the water drown out the bass of the music. I stay under the water until the warmth prunes my skin slightly.

Quickly drying my body and stepping into my silk pajama shorts and a tank top, I hang up the towel after ruffling it through my hair. Unlatching the lock to Nate's room, I then turn and step into the cool air of my own. The music has stopped, and I can hear distant shouting slowly descend outside with cars skidding off and girls screaming. I crank open the door to my little patio, opening it wide. Once the house sounds safe enough to set foot out again, I walk across my room and pull open my bedroom door, making my way down the stairs slowly. I'm halfway to the kitchen when I notice Nate and his friends still in the same position in the lounge. They pause their talking, right along with my steps.

I look at them. "Don't stop on my account," I murmur before I continue my trek to the kitchen. After shooting, I'm always hungry, and I'm not about to stop my routine because some "elite boys" were in my house. I woke up this morning an only child. How did I manage to gain not only a stepbrother but someone like Nate as a said stepbrother?

I pull open the fridge, taking out some eggs, milk, and butter, before going to the pantry for the flour and sugar. Placing all the ingredients on the kitchen counter, Nate walks in with his arms crossed over his chest as he leans against the entryway. I bend down and take out a bowl from under the breakfast bar along with a wooden spoon.

I point to him. "Do you ever wear a shirt?"

He snorts. "Girls rather I didn't." He winks before moving toward me as Cash, Jase, Eli, Saint, and Hunter walk into the kitchen, all eyeing me skeptically.

"What're you making?" Nate asks, watching me closely.

"Waffles." I look toward the other boys, who are all spread out in different spots in the kitchen. The air is a little uncomfortable.

I clear my throat and look to Nate. "How come I've never heard of you? My dad didn't tell me Elena had a son." I pour in all the ingredients as Nate walks toward one of the cupboards and pulls out the waffle maker, plugging it into the wall.

He shrugs, leaning back against the counter. "Don't know. Maybe because I'm such a rebel." He grins.

"Are the stories about you true?" Hunter questions, his eyes darkening on me.

"What stories might those be? There are a few," I retort, walking up to the waffle maker. Nate takes the bowl from me and begins pouring the batter into the maker.

"About your mom." A little blunt, but I'm used to it.

"The part about her killing herself, or the part about her murdering my father's side chick beforehand?" I throw back, my head tilting.

Hunter has what I'd call rough features. I'm not sure how to place his ethnicity. He has dark eyes, olive skin, and a scruffy but clean five o'clock shadow over his jaw.

He leans against his chair more, eyeing me closely. "Both."

"Yes and yes," I answer flatly. "And yes it was my gun."

I turn around to catch Nate glaring at Hunter. "Move," I order, pointing toward the waffle maker. Nate steps aside to let me in, and my arm brushes against his. I pause, my eyes going up to his face to catch him smirking down at me. Before I can tell him to wipe the smile off his face, Eli comes up beside me.

"I'm Eli, and I'm the eyes and ears of our group. I'm also the little brother to Ace." He points over his shoulder to an older and bulkier version of himself.

I smile politely at Ace, not gaining a smile in return. Whatevs.

"You mean *club*?" I reply without looking at him. I pour more batter into the maker before noticing everyone is quiet.

"Tsk, tsk. I see rumors have already made it to you on your first day. Who told you?" Nate asks.

I step away from him, putting the waffle on my plate and deciding I want out of this kitchen because it's a little too crowded with testosterone.

"Tatum." I squirt maple syrup onto my waffle. "I'm going to go." Then I snatch my plate and make my way toward the stairs. On my passing, I see Bishop and Brantley talking in the living room, still in their same seats.

I pause, gripping onto the stairwell, and turn my head toward them, only to find Bishop looking straight through me. I'm not sure what these boys' deal is, but it's a little intense. Bishop has an angular face with high cheekbones and a jaw that could be sculpted for a Greek god. He has loose dark hair that makes my fingers twitch to run them through it, and piercing, dark, army green eyes. His thick dark lashes fan out across his perfect skin. His shoulders are lean yet are set with confidence. The dominance that surrounds him is evident, and once I realize I'm still ogling, my eyes widen in horror before I spin around and dash back up the stairs.

Closing my bedroom door, I place my plate on my study desk that sits beside the balcony door and sigh. There's no way I'll be able to stomach eating anything now. Climbing under my crisp linen sheets, I turn on the television that hangs on the wall opposite my bed and push Play on the next episode of *Banshee* before sinking into my pillow, my body finally relaxing after one long-ass day.

CHAPTER 5

I'm coming down the stairs the next morning with an apple jammed in my mouth, and my books clutched in my arm when I walk straight into Nate's back. I take the apple out of my mouth. "Shit, sorry, I'm so late."

"I know. How many episodes of *Banshee* did you watch last night?" he asks, collecting his keys off the kitchen table.

"I don't know. I lost cou— Wait!" I throw my hand up. "How'd you know I was watching *Banshee*?" I hop up and down, trying to shove my foot into my Converse.

"I came in to see if you were okay when I saw light was shining under your door. You were crashed out by then. By the way, nice pick of TV show. Is Harry taking you to school?" He takes hold of my arm so I can lean on him to balance my footing before finally getting my foot into the damn shoe.

I hand him my books to hold and bend down to tie up my laces. "Yeah, he does every morning."

I stand back up as he passes me my books and we make our way out the front door. "I'll drive you. Doesn't make sense not to. We go to the same school."

I look down the driveway to see Harry not here. Crap. Chewing on my lip nervously, I nod. "Okay."

He gives me a cheesy grin, his dimples popping out as he takes my hand and we walk toward his Porsche 918 Spyder. He beeps her, and I slip into the passenger seat, clicking my seatbelt on.

Sparking the car to life, he smiles. "You know… you made a little bit of an impression on the boys last night."

"What?" I ask, shocked. "That was one of the most awkward moments of my life, and that's saying something, because my life is made up of awkward moments."

He laughs as I reach for the stereo. When it switches on, Dr. Dre's "Forgot about Dre" shakes the inside of the car, and I quickly turn it down. "Jesus!"

He chuckles from his seat, watching me closely. "What? Don't like old school hip-hop, sis?"

"Nothing wrong with hip-hop, but having it that loud will blow your eardrums. You should look at getting them checked, just in case you've already done damage."

"If I had a hearing problem…" he smirks, dropping down gears and jolting us forward so fast my head slams back into the headrest, "…it wouldn't be from loud music.

It'd be from Little Nate penetrating women so good that it has them screaming bloody murder."

I jerk away from him in disbelief. "Little Nate?"

His face drops. "What's wrong with naming it Little Nate?" He almost looks offended that I laughed. I feel a little bad about that. Nate has a twisted bad boy feel about him, with added cockiness. But now he's not playing fair, because when he pouts, it looks cute on him.

"Uhhh… the fact that you actually *named* it. And anyway, why would you want to name…" I point down to his crotch, and when my eyes travel back up to his face, I'm greeted by his cocky all-boy grin. His hand travels down the front of his ripped jeans as he clutches his junk. *Oh, Lord.* "Y-your…" I stutter. "For the love of God," I whisper, shaking my head.

He teases, "Cock? Dick? Magic stick? The power shaft? The womb raider? The yogurt—"

I shake my head, cutting him off, "Elena is a sweet woman. How the fuck did you come from her?"

We pull into the private underground parking lot under the school, and I climb out of the car, shutting the door behind me.

"What's your last class?" he asks, rounding the car and hooking his arm around my waist. I wiggle out of it. I've become aware over the last twenty-four hours how smooth things are around Nate, but I still can't have his arm around me. I've never had many friends at other schools. He and Tatum are the first people, since before my mom snapped, to not have my past bother them as much.

"Um, I think I have PE."

He nods as we begin walking toward the elevator that takes you to the school's first floor. "I'll pick you up from there. What do you have now?"

"Calculus." I cringe, knowing Ally Parker and Lauren Bentley are in that same class.

"I'll take you there now." He nods toward the corridor.

I smile. Maybe I threw him off the boat a little too early. He's only being nice to me. Nicer than most people are, anyway. "You don't need to do that, Nate. I'm fine."

He wraps his arm around my neck and pulls me into his embrace. "Well, since we're siblings and all, it's my duty to look after you."

"Nate," I groan, as we continue walking down the corridor that leads to my first class. The walls are painted in classic whites and neutral colors, with all the rooms leading off it in similar hues. The gym sits at the end of the corridor toward the fire exit, and although I haven't seen the boy's hall yet, I have a feeling it is similar to ours. "You really don't. I'll be fine."

"I just wanna get to know my new sister. That's all." He winks down at me just as we reach the doorway to my class.

"Fine," I say, crossing my arms in front of my chest. "But I'm not good with people, just giving you a warning. I'm more the loner type." He watches me carefully, his head tilting while he studies me closely.

"I can dig the lonely girl thing." He winks at me again before turning around and heading toward the boys' hall.

Why? Why did I have to get someone annoying like Nate as a stepbrother?

CHAPTER 6

The bell ringing breaks the concentrated silence in the classroom as we all gather up our books. Tatum bumps my hip with hers, flicking her long blonde hair over her shoulder. "Lunchtime! That class almost killed me."

I smile, collecting my pens and placing them on top of my books. "You say that in every class." I roll my eyes as we begin retreating from the room.

She snorts. "That's true. So, what's your plan for after school? Nate Riverside is throwing a party this weekend, and I'm not usually one for going to any of these parties, and we might get kicked out, because we don't hold the same status, but I feel like crashing. You in?" she asks, as we make our way to the cafeteria.

I roll my eyes again as we push through the doors. "That means it will most likely be at my house then."

She pauses, her little hand wrapping around my arm. "Elaborate, Montgomery. What does that mean?"

"Nate," I say flatly. "His mom and my dad are married. We live together, and before you jump down my throat, I only just found out yesterday." Yesterday feels like a century ago, because of how easygoing Nate has been with me.

Her mouth drops to the ground. "Shut. Up."

"What?" I reply, turning her toward the buffet. My stomach is grumbling, and because of skipping dinner last night, all I had in my stomach was the apple I power-ate this morning.

"Holy shit," she whispers in shock. Her eyes lock back onto mine. "This is fucking awesome! We're so crashing," she squeals out in excitement.

"Um, Tatum? It's not crashing if we're in my house. He's doing it on purpose, because our parents don't get back until Monday." We both pile our plates with the different variety of foods they have available. Sushi and exotic fruits? Am I in school or at a five-star restaurant?

"Holy shit. No, Madison, you don't understand. These boys never—"

Fingers slide over my eyes, blacking out my vision. Tatum sucks in a breath. Lips skim over the back of my ears as a deep growl sounds. "How do you feel about incest, little sis?" Before his hands drop from my eyes, he laughs, stumbling backward. Tatum's jaw is about to be permanently dislocated if she isn't careful, and when I spin around to evil eye Nate, I'm cut off by the entire cafeteria and how it had grown almost silent, watching our exchange

"The students of Riverside Prep are just pawns in their sick and twisted games. They own this school, Madison."

"Nate," I hiss at him. I haven't managed to tell him yet, but I'd really appreciate keeping a low profile.

His smile drops. "What?" he asks innocently, much like a toddler who didn't know he wasn't supposed to eat a cookie before dinner.

I nod toward everyone watching us, and he shrugs, locking his arm around mine. "Come sit with us." He looks toward Tatum. "You too, Masters." Then he pulls me down beside him.

I drop my tray on the table, moving over for Tatum to take a seat beside me. Her arm brushes against mine stiffly. I can sense her discomfort and unanswered questions, but I can answer them later. Opposite me to the left, Bishop and then Brantley sit opposite Tatum. Beside Brantley are Abel, Hunter, Eli, and Cash.

I pick up one of my sushi rolls and bite down on it, trying really hard not to make a mess, but sushi being sushi, rice ends up on my lap. Nate's talking about the party this weekend, and when I raise my eyes up to look in front of me, I'm instantly imprisoned by Bishop's glare. His face is blank, filled with—nothing. His strong, chiseled jaw sits taut, and his green eyes remain glued on mine. I squirm in my seat, and Tatum looks at me sideways. Her hand goes under the table, and a second later, my phone vibrates in my pocket. I reach in to take it out when Nate looks toward me. "What do you think, sis?"

"Hmm?" I ask, annoyed that he's interfered with whatever Tatum was about to say to me.

"What kind of alcohol do you want this weekend?" he prompts, his eyes drifting between both of mine.

Damn it, he's hella fine.

I scowl at my inner self. The hell is wrong with me? *He's basically your brother, you fuckwad.*

"Oh!" I smile, my cheeks heating. "I don't really drink." I clutch my phone in my hand, ignoring the dark green eyes that are still peering at me from across the table.

Nate scoffs, taking one of my sushi rolls and popping the whole thing in his mouth. "That changes this weekend. It's Brantley's birthday. We don't usually throw parties"—the corner of his lip kicks up as a mischievous glint darkens in his eyes—"but we do birthdays."

I swallow past the lump that has now formed in my throat. My eyes flutter to Bishop again to find him looking down at his phone. Dropping my eyes to my lap, I slide my phone unlocked to see Tatum's message.

Tatum – *No way*
Me – *What?*

I glance at Tatum, who has a shit-eating grin on her face. Her eyes drop down to her lap, and I wait impatiently for her text. Stretching my feet out, they collide with someone else's under the table, so I quickly pull them back. *Shit.* My phone vibrates, and I look back down.

Tatum – *You have a particular set of eyes on you that every girl at this school would plead for. That's what.*

Me – *What the hell are you talking about, Tatum?*

"Hey!" Nate bumps my arm playfully. "Who're you texting?"

Brantley and Bishop begin talking about something in hushed tones. If my observations are correct, Brantley and Bishop seem like the quieter ones. I think Nate likes me, but the other guys, I'm undecided still. Apart from that little talk in the kitchen last night, I don't have much to go on, but they all make me extremely uncomfortable.

I look to Nate pleadingly. "Can I talk to you?"

His face sobers. "Yeah, come on." He takes my hand in his as I smile down to Tatum. "Won't be long." My eyes drift to Bishop, who's watching Nate's fingers lock around my hand. I don't know why, but I pull out of Nate's hold. He falters for a second, but when I look back down to Bishop, he's scowling at me.

What the fuck?

We begin walking out of the cafeteria and toward the front doors, where there are concrete stairs sprawled out to accommodate more than enough people to sit on. Some are eating lunch out here, not many though. They look like the type of people I should be eating with, not Nate and his damn club.

"What's up?" he asks, once we get outside.

I sigh. "Nothing, I just… really, it's a little much," I answer truthfully. "What's the deal with you guys?" We continue walking down the steps as Nate shoves his hands into his pockets.

"What have you heard?" His eyes remain ahead.

I look to him every two seconds while watching my step. "Well, only from Tatum about some Elite Kings Club?" I quiz him.

He laughs, throwing his head back. "Madi, that club is merely a legend. It's all fueled by teenage drama queen bullshit." His laugh is forced and his smile doesn't reach his eyes.

"Okay," I say. "Tell me more about this legend."

He smirks, pausing his step. "Maybe one day, just… not today."

"What?" I grin playfully. "Why not today?"

His eyes flick over my shoulder, his face turning serious. He looks back to me. "Not yet, I'll tell you when I think you can handle it."

He winks at me before walking past and back toward the doors again. When I turn around to see where his eyes drifted to, I catch the back of Bishop walking back inside. Sighing, I shake my head, wondering when the exact moment was my life had become so damn eventful.

CHAPTER 7

I'm piling my hair into a high ponytail when Nate walks into my room. I rode with him on the way home today, and it wasn't that bad. After we both battled over the music selection, eventually Nate told me if I touched it again, I would have to walk home. The way he smirked when he told me that had me thinking otherwise though.

"Hey!" I pull my leather jacket over my white tank, opting for skinny jeans and my Chucks to go with it.

He leans against the doorframe, a bag of chips in one hand, again with no shirt on, low-riding jeans, and his cap flipped on backward. He points down to me. "Where're you going?"

"Hmmm?" I ask, picking up my phone from my bed. "To the mall with Tatum."

"Tatum, huh?" he teases, sucking the excess flavor off his fingers. "She single?" His sucking halts before he slowly pulls his finger out of his mouth. "Not that the relationship status bothers me."

I stop him, my hand going up to his chest. "I don't know. I think so. Are you going to move?" I ask, pointing down the hallway to let me through.

He looks down at me smugly before Chamillionaire's "Rockstar" starts playing in his pocket. His smile falls as he quickly walks back to his bedroom, closing the door behind himself.

"Everyone is weird at this school," I mumble under my breath, pulling my door closed. Taking a step forward, I crash into a solid body. Just as solid as Nate's but... a little bigger.

"Shit," I mutter, my hand coming up to my forehead. When I drag my eyes up the body, they fall on Brantley. "Nate's in his room. Sorry," I apologize again for bumping into him.

His eyes darken, a snarl bringing up the corner of his mouth, which he opens, ready to say something—

"Brantley!" a low growl snaps from behind him. The air suddenly thickens, and when I look behind him, I see Bishop standing there, his eyes glued on the back of Brantley's head. "Go to Nate's room." Brantley narrows his eyes on me again before he continues down the hallway and into the bedroom.

Once the door closes, I huff and look to Bishop. "Who stole his toys?"

Bishop's eyes stay on Nate's door, refusing to acknowledge me.

I curse under my breath. "Sorry, hi, I'm Madison."

His eyes finally drop down to mine. He has really amazing eyes, not only the deep jade army color, but how they're shaped. And when they look at you? They look through you, as if they're summoning your soul and calling the reaper.

"Wish I could say I was sorry about that," he mutters his reply, his eyes going back to Nate's door.

I turn to follow his line of sight before looking back at him. "Don't worry about it," I whisper softly. "I'm used to it." I step to the side to walk around him, when he matches my step, blocking my way.

He searches my eyes intently before dropping them to my lips then back to my eyes.

I tilt my head. "Can I leave?"

He doesn't say anything, just stares blankly at me for a few seconds before finally walking down to Nate's room.

Shaking my head, I pull open the door when Tatum drives up in her baby blue Ferrari, complete with black rims and black tint. It's the nicest Ferrari I've ever seen, and fits Tatum to a T. Her parents are always away for work, and Tatum jokes that her "family time" is watching the latest box office movies. I wish I could sympathize with her, but I don't think she worries that much. I clutch the door handle and turn to slide inside the passenger seat of the car before I turn around and look up to Nate's bedroom window, finding all three of them staring down at me, watching carefully. My smile falters before I slide into the compact car.

"Hey, sugar!" Tatum claps in excitement. "Let's splash some cash!"

The drive to the mall is short, because Tatum has a seriously heavy foot. We scan the stores, while, more Tatum than I, looks for the perfect outfit. By the fourth store, I give up and hand her my dad's platinum card to just buy whatever she wants me to wear, because if there's one thing I hate, it's shopping. She exits one of the boutique stores with a shit-eating grin on her beautiful face, and I wince. I can almost feel my tits shrivel up from how tight whatever it is she chose for me. Pulling me up by my hand, she drags me toward a little quirky ornament shop, tucking the dress away.

"Your new room. I thought maybe we could get something. I mean, I know I haven't seen your room yet, but I figure, because you just moved here, it'd be a little empty."

Understanding the kindness in her suggestion, and still trying to not find someone being nice to me as something awkward, I nod.

"I could always do with something else. I love décor."

"Good!" She claps her hands. "I didn't really feel like dragging you in on my own." We walk into the dark purple shop that's surrounded by hot lava lamps and smells of incense. I'm instantly drawn to a little light that is turned on and showcasing its colors against the blank white wall at the back of the store. Walking toward it, I smile. "I want that!"

Tatum's eyebrow quirks. "You sure? I mean, it's cool, but where would you put it?"

I step toward it and drop down to my knees, tilting the bulb upward. "You can move it so it's on the ceiling." I shift the bulb to tilt it higher, and instantly, all the stars light up.

"Wow!" Tatum whispers. "That looks much better."

I nod. "It reminds me of when my parents used to take me out on hunting trips and we'd camp out in the forest."

Her eyes narrow. "Hunt what exactly?"

I stand back to my feet. "Just deer. Or we would go duck shooting."

Her features relax. "That sounds... nice, I guess."

I laugh. "It is! We'll have to go sometime."

"Yeah," she says, looking to the side. "Maybe."

"Hey," I swat her, "I came shopping, so you come hunting."

She gulps. I laugh, just as I see one of the workers walk toward us.

"Ohhh," the member of staff says, looking up to the ceiling. "That's how I was supposed to set it up."

I laugh again, looking up to the stars once more. "Yeah, I think. I'm not sure."

The worker looks back to me. She has to be around our age. She has long, pastel pink hair that's braided in a fishtail over her shoulder, and bright green eyes. Her little pixie nose sits on her olive face, crinkling as she laughs. "I better change that." Stepping forward, she leaves it how I had it. "Thanks. You probably saved my ass from my boss."

"Oh," I reply. "No problem."

She picks up one of the boxes and hands it to me, then we follow her back to the counter. She beeps it through and smiles. "This is pretty cool, right?"

"Yeah." I return her smile. "I'm new here, so Tatum thought I needed something to spice up my room."

"Oh, you're new?" Her gaze falls on us. "I probably don't need to ask what school you go to." She says it politely enough.

"Riverside."

She nods with a small smile.

"What school do you got to?" I ask, leaning on the counter.

"Hampton Beach High."

"Oh!" Public? That's a school I'd feel more comfortable in.

She gestures toward the lamps. "We have these lamps that have like, ambient sounds that play and make it feel like you're in the forest."

I spin around to look at where she's pointing, getting far too excited.

"Seriously?" Tatum mutters under her breath.

"Ignore her." I walk toward the lamps and snatch one greedily. "Thank you! My stepbrother is having a party this weekend, so when I decide to ditch and go to bed, I can use this. Might save his life." I grin at her. She bursts out laughing, and I tilt my head. "Hey, do you like parties?"

After switching numbers with the worker girl, whose name is Tillie, we sit down at a café and eat our weight in fried food and chocolate brownies.

"I can't believe you invited her off the bat." Tatum pops a chicken tender in her mouth. "Mmm, but she seems nice, right?"

"Right," I agree. "So be nice."

"Hey!" she scolds me. "I'm always nice."

That wasn't fair of me to say. She has been nothing but nice to me. I smile, shoveling another piece of brownie into my mouth, where it melts on my tongue, mixing with a spoonful of ice cream. It turns out Tatum has as much of a sweet tooth as I do, and we make plans to have a girls' movie night tomorrow night with buckets of candy. Tatum said she wants to watch a chick flick, but I cut her off by declaring my dislike for corny romcoms. So we agreed that I'll pick the movies and she'll bring the candy. Win-win.

"So what's it like being Nate Riverside's little sister?" Tatum asks, driving us back to my place.

"I'm not really his little sister," I deadpan. "I don't know why, but he's taken it upon himself to torment me at his every turn."

She giggles, dropping gears, and my head slams against the headrest from the force. "Honey, if Nate took it upon himself to torment me, I'd welcome it. He's the biggest manwhore of Riverside Prep though. He's even slept with Sasha Van Halen."

"I'm not even surprised," I mutter under my breath as we pull into our private driveway.

Sasha Van Halen is the daughter of the biggest tycoon in the United States. She's splashed all over the tabloids—hot mess and all that.

"One last thing," she says, pulling up the emergency brake. "I want to talk to you about them." She gestures toward Nate's window and my eyes follow. "You gained Bishop's attention today at lunch."

"Hardly," I scoff, shaking my head.

"I need to educate you on Bishop Vincent Hayes," she begins, and I tilt my head toward her. "He's only ever been seen with one other girl more than once, that I know of. One, and she meant a lot to him. They were together for years. Everyone would say it was fate, Bishop and Khales; they were this match made in heaven. She moved, he moved. They knew each other since they were little, because Khales's mom was a junkie and would leave Khales in the house on her own for hours on end. Khales went to Hampton Beach High School, which is on the rough side of town. Anyway, Bishop tried to save her. He tried so hard, but eventually, Khales followed her mother's footsteps and picked up the needle." She took a breath.

"She died?" I ask, my heart sinking. I know what it's like losing someone you love.

"No, we don't know where she is. About two years ago, she sort of just disappeared. No one whispers her name. The week she went missing, all the boys weren't at school, and then suddenly they're all walking back into the cafeteria like they own the place, as if she didn't exist. Someone tried to ask Bishop about her, but he almost snapped the guy's neck, so everyone took that as a sensitive subject and never asked questions again."

She pauses again, her bright blue eyes twinkling on mine. "I'm only telling you because so many girls have tried to fill the spot that Khales left. As far as I know, Bishop hasn't had another girlfriend since. That's two years. Anyway, that brings me to the next subject." My mind is still swimming with the mass of information she just unloaded on me. Two years ago? People don't just disappear into thin air. There's always a reason why people go missing. She clears her throat. "The Elite Kings Club—"

"I asked Nate about it, and he said it's all based on legend and false assumptions."

She shakes her head, her blonde waves falling over her slender shoulders. "They won't tell you. It may sound like gossip, but it's very true. I've seen the mark."

"Mark?" My brain is about to explode from the information that is being shoved inside it.

"Yeah, they're branded when they're babies. It's a ritual all the parents perform."

"That's crazy." My shoulders go slack. "I've heard enough. Anything else?"

"Yes! Be careful. I only know so much about them because I've studied them for as long as I've known them. I've never shared my thoughts with anyone else, because no one else has become close to them, but I can see that's going to be changing with you. You need to be careful, Madi."

I clutch the door handle and push it open, taking my bags out of the backseat. "Okay, I'll be careful, but I think you're being paranoid."

She offers a small smile before I close the passenger door, and then she skids out of my driveway.

This kind of stuff just doesn't happen, not in this world.

CHAPTER 8

Slamming the front door closed, I walk into the kitchen with all the information Tatum just fed me brewing in my brain. Pulling a Coke from the fridge, I close the door when my heart leaps at the sight of Hunter leaning against the entryway.

"Shit!" My hand flies up to my chest.

"Sorry." He smirks. "Nate has training, so he has me on babysitting duties."

"Babysitting duties?" I ask, offended. "I don't need a babysitter."

He shrugs. "Brantley is here. You need someone near you when he's around."

I cock my head, running my eyes over him. Standing at around six-foot-two, he towers over my five-foot-three.

"Why?" I ask, my eyes diverting to the wall. "What did I do to him?"

Hunter pauses, his finger running across his upper lip. "That's not something you need to worry about yet."

"I'm sure I could just get the full lowdown if I ask Tatum," I mumble from the rim of my Coke.

"Tatum?" He barks out a laugh. "Tatum lives for drama and bullshit. Nothing she says holds any substance." His eyes narrow on me briefly.

"And your words do?" I cock my head. "I don't need a sitter," I mutter bitterly, as I head toward the stairs—only for a wall of muscle to slam into my face yet again. "Jesus!" I cuss, getting annoyed at how my house has been taken over by mysterious boys who can never give me any answers. My eyes travel up a broad chest and land on Brantley's dark, beady eyes. He has a bit of scruff around his jaw—not much, just enough it'll scratch you lightly—and his eyes are as dark as a bottomless pit leading to the gates of hell. And when he opens his mouth, I find his words are much like his eyes.

"You'd do good to stay the fuck outta my way."

Having about enough of all this bullshit, I cross my arms in front of myself. *'Cause I'm a badass.* "What the fuck did I ever do to you?"

I can feel Hunter's presence behind me, silently watching.

Brantley's eyes snap to mine, burning into me like a hot knife through cold butter. "How about just existing? Everything was fine until you came back," he mutters, before shoving me out of the way and walking toward the door. He pauses with his hand on the handle and peers at me over his shoulder briefly. His dark jeans hang off his narrow hips, and the white tee he's sporting clings to him effortlessly. He mumbles something before storming out the door.

"Back?" I ask Hunter. "I've never been here in my life."

He watches me, pushing off the side of the wall. "He didn't mean back. He just meant when you got here." He walks toward the front door, dismissing me. "I'm out. My duties are no longer needed."

I stay there, staring at the door absently for a couple of breaths. "What in the world?" Immensely confused by everything that has shifted in my world in such a short amount of time, I walk up the stairs and into my room, pulling out my sketchbook and sitting down at my desk. Taking the remote off my table, I push Play on my sound dock. Picking up my pencil, I then press it into the corner of the blank white page and start scribbling.

Banging on my door somehow breaks through my drawing and music haze.

Thud thud thud. "Madi!"

Sliding my chair back, I glance at my alarm clock that sits on top of my bedside table. "Fuck." It's 5:30 p.m. I have been sketching for three hours flat without so much as a break for fresh air. Before my mom passed, I would draw like this at least three times a week, if not more, but since she died, I find it more difficult to completely let go of my surroundings and engross myself into my pencil and pad. Music has always been an outlet for me, but sketching was something personal that my mom and I used to do together.

Pulling on my bedroom door, I open it to Tatum. "I'm sorry," I murmur. "I got a little carried away in my drawing."

Tatum strolls past me, a paperback clutched in one hand and a pink duffel bag in the other. "I see that." She waves her hands around my head, referring to my wayward bun that's messily scrunched up and sitting lopsided on the side of my skull.

"Hey!" I scold her, giggling as I point to the bed. "This is nothing. You should see it in the morning." This is true, because my hair game is atrocious in the morning. Not only is it thick and long, but it also has a natural bouncy wave to it too, coming from my mom's Spanish background. "Relax." I eye her suspiciously. "Where're your pajamas?"

She looks at me with a smile, pulling out a pack of Twizzlers. "In my bag."

I bend over, snatching candy from the pack, and walk toward my closet, taking out my cotton pajama shorts and a light tank. "I'll take a shower. I came straight home and didn't get a chance to clean up."

"Oh," Tatum clutches her chest in mock awe, "you're getting pretty for me?"

I scoff, walking toward the en suite bathroom. "Definitely not."

After scrubbing up in the shower, I brush my teeth quickly, just in case I fall asleep during the movie, and flick Nate's door unlocked before slipping into my room.

I look down at the mountain of sweets around her legs. "Holy mother of f—"

"What?" she asks innocently. "Did you underestimate my sweet tooth?" I look down at the cheesecake, potato chips, M&M's, packaged donuts, gummy bears, and soda. "I think I'm about to get diabetes."

She tosses a handful of M&M's into her mouth. "Possibly."

"I'll go down and get some spoons for that." I flick my fingers toward the cheesecake. Leaving her unattended with the goods, I fly down the stairs and run into the kitchen, my head bobbing as I hum the tune to "Simple Man" by Lynyrd Skynyrd—it's still stuck in my head from my sketching. With two spoons clutched in my hand safety, I fly out of the kitchen, but pause at the foot of the stairwell, backing up until I'm in clear vision of the sitting room, where all the boys are sitting around on the large L-shaped sofa.

Nate is leaning back, his hand hiding his mouth, but the smile lines around his eyes show how much he's trying to hold back a laugh.

"What?" I snap at him, ignoring the rest of the boys. God, he annoys me.

Uncovering his mouth, he shakes his head. "Nothing."

My eyes narrow. "Yeah, sure." I look to his left to see Bishop sitting there, his arms sprawled out over the couch. His dark T-shirt hugs him in all the right places, and his dark jeans sit on him casually. He has white Air Force Ones on his feet, and by the time my gaze travels back up his body, landing on his eyes again, his features have changed. Wiped clean of anything else but the resting bitch face he gives like a pro.

"Don't you guys have a place where you can all meet? Why here?" I tilt my head, looking at all of them.

"Calm down, kitten. I'm on babysitting duty, so we have to come here." Nate pauses, his grin kicking up. "Unless, of course, you would like to come with us?" I look back to Bishop to see his eyes, which still haven't moved themselves off me, darken. Ace whips his attention to Nate, scolding him.

"First of all," I say calmly, "don't ever call me kitten—ever again. Or I'll shoot you." I pause, laughing inwardly at his change of facial expressions. That probably wasn't very nice, considering everyone already thinks I'm crazy because of my mom. "Second of all," I add, "I'm not a child. I can take care of myself." The end is more of a mutter, as I turn on my feet and walk up the stairs. I have just landed at the top, when I glance over my shoulder, feeling eyes on me. Bishop is at the bottom, staring up at me.

I turn to face him. "What?" He hasn't spoken much to me, except for that day with Brantley. Tatum warned me about his reputation, and if that wasn't a dead giveaway of how completely standoffish and uptight he is, not to mention unapproachable—have I said that yet? It deserves to be stated a second time—his personality in general would make you want to run. He reminds me of a king cobra. Silent, deadly, and leaving you guessing about what lies beneath his bite.

His blank face remains stoic, his strong jaw tensing, until eventually, I spin around and walk into my room. My heart pounds against my chest until my throat feels bruised and my saliva has run dry. Smashing my head against the back of my door, I watch Tatum scoot off the bed, now in her pajamas.

"You okay?"

"Yeah," I answer, handing her a spoon and walking toward the bed. "Let's just eat all the sugar."

I spoon a huge chunk of chocolate cheesecake into my mouth, groaning in approval at the soft, sweet crumble touching my taste buds.

"So tell me," Tatum states, wrapping her long hair into a bow bun on the top of her head and removing her slim-rimmed glasses. "How did you manage to catch the eye of the one and only Bishop Vincent Haynes?"

"Oh, God, not this again," I utter under my breath, going for another spoonful to fill my mouth. The movie has long since started, and the gunshots in the background are pitched low.

"He stared. That doesn't exactly mean he's interested—or me, for that matter. Because I'm not."

"Mmmm." She sucks the cheesecake off her spoon. "Now, say it again. This time with more conviction!"

I snatch my pillow and throw it at her head, but she catches it, falling onto her back and laughing.

"Okay, okay, I'm sorry, but for the record, that little eye"—she gestures between our eyes—"fuckery that you two had going on was more than I had seen out of him—ever. No one at RSPA is good enough for his royal highness." She rolls her eyes, opening a bag of gummy bears.

"How do you know? Maybe he's just discreet about it."

She shakes her head. "Oh no, he has been with other girls, but they don't attend RSPA. They're like—" She pauses, mulling over the word she wanted to use. "—famous and stuff."

Disappointed at her lack of a better word, I ask for clarification, "Famous—*and stuff?*"

She nods, oblivious to my stab at her wording. "Yeah. But those are all rumors though. No one has seen him with any of the girls who have apparently been with him. I'm talking like tycoon daughters, heiresses, that sort of boring crap. The only girl I know with 100 percent certainty was Khales, and that's because, yeah, they were always together when they weren't at school. It was like a modern-day Cinderella, where the poor princess found her prince."

"Oh! That's just being mean."

Shaking her head, she pops another gummy bear in her mouth, and I reach for one before she eats them all. "Truth. Shame really. He was still unapproachable back then, but at least he had a smile on his face when she was around, and he didn't tell people to 'fuck off' if they got too close to him."

I let out a breath. "Well… lucky girl then, I guess. Maybe. Because he sounds like an asshole."

Tatum laughs, throwing a bear at me. "See… I knew we would be great friends."

She was right.

CHAPTER 9

My cell phone's annoying ringtone sounds off on my bedside table, waking me from my deep sleep. Grunting, I sit up off the bed and blindly reach for it, accidently hitting Tatum's sleeping form.

"I don't want to go to Candy Land," she mutters sleepily, flipping onto her side. I stifle a laugh, sliding my phone unlocked and pressing it to my ear.

"Hello?" I whisper, careful not to wake Tatum.

"Sis...."

I look down at the screen of my phone, squinting my eyes from the bright light assaulting my vision. Pressing it back to my ear, I whisper loudly, "Nate! What do you want?"

"Why are you whispering?" he murmurs, almost whispering himself. "Ouch!" I hear him growl, and in the background, someone else says, "That's not why you're calling, fucker."

Walking into the bathroom, I flick the light on and close the door, careful to do it quietly. "What, why? *What*? Why the hell are you calling me at..." I look down at my phone again. "Fucking 3:00 a.m.?" My voice gets a little loud toward the end.

"I need your help."

"Why would I help you? I'm not even sure I like you!"

"What? Why? I've been nice to you. I thought we had a—ouch! Fuck! Okay." He takes a breath. "For real, Madi. I need your help." His change in tone jolts me, my eyebrows rising instead of pinching together.

Closing my eyes, I lean over the sink, massaging my temple with my free hand. "What is it?"

"I cannot believe I'm fucking doing this," I mutter to myself, no longer caring if I wake Tatum. Walking into my closet, I leave my pajama shorts and tank on but pull a zip-up hoodie off a hook, sliding it on before throwing my hair into a tight, high ponytail and slipping on my Chucks. Walking out of my closet, I flick the light off, noticing how Tatum hasn't moved, then walk out my bedroom and trek down our double stairs. The pitter-patter of my rubber soles squeaking over the tiles in the foyer is the only proof I'm making my way to our underground garage. After passing the theater, I push open the door onto the clean white space of the ten-car garage, which looks more like a showroom

Seeing the midnight black Escalade, I unhook the keys that are hanging on the hook and beep it unlocked. Adding up the numbers in my head, I growl in frustration. Stupid Nate obviously wasn't thinking. How the hell am I supposed to fit them all into the SUV that only has seven passenger seats? Popping the trunk, I lay the seats in the back down flat and then slam it shut, walking back to the driver seat. Starting the car, I place my phone into the holder and speaker dial Nate.

"You good?" he answers.

"No, Nate, I'm not fucking good. It's 3:00 a.m. and you call me to pick you guys up from God knows where in a fucking seven-seated car. By the way, I usually need caffeine in the mornings before I can even function, and I'm not a fucking morning person. Let alone a 3:00 a.m. person!"

"You done?" he questions casually.

"I'm going to kill you."

"Sis, you're on speaker."

"I don't care."

He laughs.

"Tell me where I'm going," I snap.

He yaps off the directions as I drive. As more time passes and more directions get spoken, it sends me deeper and deeper into the outskirts of town. "So you'll get to a dark gravel private road to the left. Do you see it?"

Chills creep down my spine. "What? Yes." I look from left to right, and I'm pretty sure I'm seeing shadows whip past my windows and weaving into the trees on the side of the road.

"Good girl." He pauses. "Take that turn."

Something doesn't sit right with what he's saying and his tone, but it better be worth it, and they better be in trouble, or I will so be telling on him.

If I'm still alive, that is. If not, I'll just come back in ghost form and tear up their lives.

Pulling down the dark, eerie, bumpy gravel road, with nothing but the bright head-lights of the SUV guiding my way, I swallow down my nerves. What the fuck is he doing, and why the hell did he tell me to come down here?

"Nate?" I whisper. "Maybe I took the wrong turn."

Silence.

"Nate!" I yell at the phone. "This isn't funny."

"I'm not laughing, sis. Keep going. We can see your headlights." What am I doing? I'm basically relying on the fact that Nate and I had bonded a little and our parents are together. I'm not sure those facts are worth my life. *No, he wouldn't.* I'm just being paranoid. The only time, except for school, when I didn't bring my fucking pistol either. I sag in defeat. My dad will not be impressed with my not carrying, and my mom will no doubt be screaming at me from the other side about how these are the reasons why she and my dad educated me so much on firearms. I've failed as a fucking daughter. I scoot up in my seat.

"Nate, I don't fucking see anything up here, but ja— *oh my God!*" I slam on the breaks, all four tires locking up in a skid. I squeeze the steering wheel tightly, banging down the locks on the doors. "Nate!" I yell into the phone.

Silence.

Slowly, I look up out the front windshield, the thick dust from my tires interrupting the dust still floating in the air, and that's when I see it again.

Ten men.

Ten dark hoodies covering their faces.

Ten—

"Nate?" Understanding sets in. *Ten.*

Slamming the gear into reverse, I'm just about to floor it backward—to hell with anything or anyone behind me—when my driver window smashes into a million pieces, the tiny shards of glass falling onto my lap. I scream, my hands coming up to shield my face just as an arm slips inside and pops up the lock.

A deep chuckle breathes over the back of my neck as a leather gloved hand wraps around my mouth. "Hello, Madison. You may not know us, but we know you. We want to play a game. Here's what happens if you lose...."

CHAPTER 10

I bite down on his palm, knowing it won't do anything with the glove protecting it, but I refuse to go down without a fight. He laughs, pulling me out until the air is dragged out of my lungs, and then he drops me. My back slams against the gravel road. Hair flies across my face as dark hands come down toward me again. Fear drives my body into auto-pilot mode, so I launch my foot out, kicking, lunging, and tossing myself around. I won't go down without a fight, that's for damn sure.

"What the fuck are you doing?" I scream at them.

Scooping my legs under his arms, he swings me over his shoulder effortlessly.

"Nate!" I scream for him. "I'll kill you. I swear to fucking God, you're dead!"

"Not if we kill you first. Shut the fuck up." Big shoulders continue to carry me down the dead road until he stops.

I raise my head, finding four dark shadows following behind us, all wearing hoodies to cover their faces. Scanning my eyes over each one, they land on who I'm pretty sure is Nate. "Why?"

He pauses, walking toward me just as whoever is holding me drops me to the ground. "Why, Nate?" I scream, my butt aching from being slammed onto the gravel.

Nate—I think— walks toward me, dropping to the ground until he's kneeling in front of me. He leans forward, and if the ski mask wasn't covering his face, I'd be able to see what I'm guessing is the smirk on his face. "You act like you don't know."

"What?" I turn and watch as he gets to his feet and opens up the back door of a long stretch limo.

"Blindfold her," another voice says.

"*What?*" I whip my head from side to side, watching each of them. "No!" I shake my head, stepping back until my butt hits the car. A strong arm wraps around my waist from inside the limo and pulls me inside. I scream—a full girly scream—just as a blindfold is being tugged around my eyes, shutting off my vision.

Silence.

With no vision.

All I have are my listening skills, which, if I'm being honest, doesn't have a very good track history. Breathing, deep breathing, in and out. That's all I can hear as the car dips with people piling into the back. My chest rises and falls, my anger beginning to boil to the surface. I hear a door shut just before we start pulling out of wherever the hell we are.

"Why the fuck is this happening?" I decide to be the first person to break the silence.

"Stop the act, sis." Nate. And he's sitting beside me. Whoever pulled me into the car is sitting on the other side.

My head whips to where Nate is. "What fucking act? You're truly starting to piss me off. I don't know what the fuck you're talking about. I came here because I thought the rest of you pieces of shit were in trouble! So you mean to tell m—"

"Jesus fuck, someone shut it up." That came from the voice beside me. Nate chuckles, but I ignore him. My head turns to the other voice. "Oh, I'm sorry. I truly am. I'm so fucking sorry for actually leaving my warm bed and coming to make sure the rest of you are fucking safe and to bail you out of whatever the fuck you were all doing!"

"Nate, man, is your old lady serious about her dad? 'Cause I feel sorry for you." That came from someone opposite me.

I flip whoever that was the bird, not knowing whether they can see me or not.

"Sis, play nice. You do as you're told, and this will end fine."

"Yeah, except for the fact I don't think she's very good at doing what she's fucking told." That was the voice beside me again. Deep, domineering, and—

"Well, fuck!" Nate gripes beside me. "Tell me what the fuck to do 'cause I got nothing! She is a *girl!*"

"Are you sure?" a voice opposite me asks. "I mean, she's into guns, and has a smart fucking mouth on her. Maybe she's not. Maybe I should check?"

"Fuck off, Hunter." That was Nate.

I turn rigid. "No one will be checking anything."

Nate shuffles beside me. "I'm going to ask you something, sis. Answer me truthfully, because where we're taking you, you won't make it out alive if you can't be honest."

"Where are you taking me?" I ask, mimicking his tone. "And who the fuck is that?" I bite out.

"Here we go," the other voice beside me mutters.

"I'm sorry, would you like to wear the fucking blindfold?" I ask him, annoyed.

"I volunteer!" another voice says.

"Shut the fuck up, Cash!" Nate's hackles rise again.

"Cash?" I scoff.

"You too!" Nate yells toward me. "Shut up."

"Can someone please remove this blindfold?"

"I like it on you," that same voice murmurs across from me.

Nate growls. "Back to my question!" he yells, though I get the feeling he's not yelling at me this time. "Listen, we need to know if you've been here before."

"Where?" I ask.

"To the Hamptons."

Instant. "No."

"This makes no fucking sense," the voice beside me mutters again.

"Are you a virgin?" Nate asks.

That earns him a scowl. "What?" I sputter. "What sort of question is that?"

"Answer the fucking question."

"She is," the one beside me says.

"Oh, I'm sorry!" I scoff. "Would you like to answer all my questions for me? And I'd rather not talk about that."

"Are you going to keep delaying your answers?" he retorts.

"I'm not—" A hand skims up my right thigh, on Nate's side. "What are you doing?" I shove his hand off my leg, only for it to come straight back. "Go with it, sis."

"Okay, first of all, if you're going to be feeling me up, could you keep 'sis' out of your mouth?"

He laughs, then his hand skims higher. "But I'd rather not." Nate pulls away. "No, you're right. This is too weird. Bishop." He must lean over because his breath falls over my face.

"Yeah, no, that's not what I meant!"

Bishop growls. *Straight up growls.* "Move, Nate."

Nate's leg that was brushing against me is now gone, and I turn my head toward where Bishop is, to ask what the fuck is going on, when I'm suddenly on my back and a hard body is hovering over me.

"What are you doing?" I whisper, feeling a little claustrophobic with my lack of vision and with him lying on top of me. Although he isn't resting his whole body on me, his waist pins me down.

"Bishop," someone warns opposite me.

His body brushes over me, and I slam my mouth shut. Warm, misty breath falls over my mouth in shallow pants. "Answer me when I ask you a question. If you lie, I'll do something you may find inappropriate. Do you understand?"

"Um, honestly? No, I don—"

His mouth presses against mine, warm, soft lips heavy on my own. My blood heats and my ears begin to pound. He lifts lightly. "Do you—" He brings his mouth down to my ear. "—understand?" he growls into the thin flesh of my neck.

"Ye—" I clear my throat. "Yes."

"All we had to do was kiss her to shut her up?" a voice says, then I hear a whack, and then he grunts, "Ouch!"

"Have you ever lied?"

What kind of question is that?

"Yes."

"Are you a virgin?"

"That's a tricky question."

"How so?" he asks. I can almost imagine the head tilt.

"Well…" I clear my throat. *You will not remember.* "It just is."

Pause. Silence.

"She's not lying," Bishop whispers.

"Yeah, we'll be talking about that," Nate says from the other side of the car.

"I doubt that, brother. The only thing you'll be talking about is how you missed a flying bullet."

Silence, and then laughter from everyone but Nate and Bishop.

"Do you trust me?" Bishop asks.

"No."

"You're smart."

"Debatable, considering my current circumstances." He lifts off me, and I scoot up from my position.

"Take off the blindfold." I grip onto it, pushing it up my forehead. There are gold neon lights lining the inside of the... stretched Hummer? No wonder so many people could fit in it.

"Holy shit," I whisper, looking around and out the windows. "Where the fuck am I?"

I look to Bishop, finding him every bit as delicious as I found him at school. Even though he and I had only spoken once before this, it's still hard to realize it's the same guy. Before tonight, I only had stare-downs to compare anything to besides the night he made Brantley leave me alone.

"Take her home." Bishop doesn't look at me; he looks straight at Nate.

"We can't do that," Brantley growls from a dark corner, his hoodie still over his face. Bishop still has his on too, along with his loose expensive-looking destroyed jeans.

Bishop looks directly at Brantley this time. "We're taking her home."

"Um, not to be a pain in the ass or anything, but you guys owe me an explanation. You pulled me out of bed at three in the morning, kidnap me, and then..." I look directly at Bishop this time, his eyes peering straight back from under his hood. *Damn. Focus.* "... kiss me. What the hell is going on?"

"Nothing that concerns you," Bishop says, his eyes not moving from me. "At least not now."

"Hmm, see, I have a problem with tha—"

His hand comes out to mine, and then he tugs on me roughly until I'm on his lap, straddling him.

"What are you doing?" I push on his chest. *Hard chest—check!* One of his hands snakes up my spine and then toward the back of my neck, while his other remains clenched on my hip. He pulls my face down to meet his until his lips are skimming over mine. "Whatever the fuck I want to do. Now, do us all a favor, and shut your fucking mouth."

I slam my mouth shut, my teeth pulling in my bottom lip. His eyes drop to my mouth before coming back to my eyes.

"I just realized I'm still in my pajamas. Yes, I want to go home. Take me home." I climb off his lap and his grip on me loosens after a few seconds. Plopping down beside him, I look at Nate. "Fuck you."

"Oh, you love me."

"No, I'm pretty sure I don't."

"Sure you do." He grins at me. "I'm sorry, kitten."

"Nope." I shake my head, pulling my hair out of its ponytail before raking my fingers through and pulling it back to the top of my head. "I'm not cool with kitten either."

"But it's cute." Nate grins.

"Exactly, and I'm not."

"Truth," Brantley murmurs. "She's fucking annoying. Call her... *rat.*"

I flip him off, and his eyes darken, but not in the way Bishop's do. In a way that would probably send chills down my spine, because I'm 100 percent certain he hates me.

We're pulling back up our private driveway, and when the car stops, I go to launch out the door.

"Wait!" Nate halts me. "I'm serious, sis. You can't tell anyone about what happened tonight."

"What the fuck did happen tonight?" I ask, looking at all of them.

"We—I can't talk about it with you."

"Well, why fucking kidnap me then?" I'm looking directly at Nate now. "Why not just say to me, 'Oh hey, wanna play Truth or Dare?' Like, fuck, Nate!"

"Fuck," he grunts and then looks to Bishop. "We should have done that."

Bishop shrugs. "Never played that fucking game, and ain't about to start." Bishop then looks to me. "And that ain't what we're about, *Kitty*."

"Oh! No you—"

Nate pushes me out and then slams the door. My mouth drops open at the closed door just as the stretched Hummer starts to pull out. I bring my hand up and flip them off, not doubting they'd be able to see, before I stomp up the marble stairs and then to the heavy double doors. A yawn slips past my mouth, and when I see the large clock that hangs on the feature wall inside the sitting room, I know why. The sun is about to come up, and I don't want to risk waking Tatum or having her inquire where I've been, so I walk into the living room. After removing my shoes, I pull down the throw from the back of the couch and curl into the warm, soft blanket.

CHAPTER 11

My leg feels heavy, and the first thing I smell is—
"Bacon!" My eyes pop open.

Tatum walks into the sitting room with a frying pan in her hand and her hair already flat-ironed dead straight. "Get up, we need to have breakfast and then we need to leave."

I groan, leaning back into the couch. "School."

"Yes!" she hisses. "School! And by the way, if my snoring annoyed you so bad, you should have kicked me out. You didn't have to sleep out here."

"No!" I shake my head. "That wasn't it. I just struggle to sleep with other people." Not entirely a lie. I'm actually not the best sleeper when it comes to sleeping around other people. I get anxiety. Am I breathing too much? What if I accidently touch them in my sleep? Not in a sexual way, but yes, what if in a sexual way? I don't do well with it. I'm much more comfortable sleeping on my own. Also, I don't share covers. Ever.

Tatum rolls her eyes, sensing my lie, but not knowing what part or why. "Come on. Breakfast time."

I push up off the couch. "I'll be out in a second. I'm going to jump in the shower." Climbing the stairs, I walk into my room and consider checking to see if Nate is in his room, but think better of it. Asshole. I don't know what the hell that was about this morning. Do I want to know more? Yes, probably. But am I angry more than anything? Yes. I've also come to the conclusion—between my trip from the couch to my room— that they're a seriously fucked up group of friends. Not only are they edgy, mysterious, and bossy, but they're... alluring. Exactly why I must stay away from them at all cost. Especially Bishop Vincent fucking Hayes. Motherfucker kissed me! And... and I loved it.

Cursing at myself under my breath, I make a mental note to go shooting after school. Since it is Friday and no doubt Tatum will want to do something this weekend, it'll be better if I get it out of the way early. I pull down some army green skinny pants and a white tank before slipping into the shower and rinsing off all of last night's fuckery.

Massaging the conditioner into my hair and taking in the silence of Nate's room, I'd say he didn't come home last night. So much for "I have to look after you." Lying ass. Stepping out of the shower, I pull down my towel and dry off quickly before getting dressed. Blowing out my hair, I brush on some light makeup, let my dark waves hang down my back, and then slip on my leather bangles plus the one my mom gave me before she passed. It's a leather Pandora charm bracelet. We would get new charms for it for every defining moment in my life. According to Mom, even dying my hair was a defining moment, so yup, we had a charm for that too. Wiping away the condensation on the mirror, I scan my face, gliding the wand of my lip balm over my lips. I have an angular, sharp jaw, cherubic pouty lips, and hazel eyes. My eyelashes are long and thick and natural, and my skin holds a natural shimmer of gold in it from my mother's Spanish heritage. I don't think I'm bad to look at, but I'm not anything special either. Especially if you stand me next to someone like Tatum or Tillie.

Walking back down to the kitchen, I see Tatum is already sitting on the barstool, digging into her breakfast.

"Good to know you make yourself at home." I laugh, going to where she placed my plate.

"Well, you know. All this food and no one eats it? It's criminal."

I snort, picking up half of a bagel. "My dad will be home this Monday."

"Mmm," Tatum says, licking mayonnaise off her finger. "Your house feels as empty as mine. No offense."

"None taken, and it never used to be like this." I bite into the greasy breakfast. "Anyway," I mutter, swallowing my food and taking a swig of juice. "I wouldn't have pegged you as someone who eats this sort of food."

"I never used to," she says shyly. I don't want to pursue what she meant by that, so I just concentrate on eating the rest of my food. After eating, we empty our plates and walk out the house, the direct morning sun hitting both of us. I pull down my glasses as she beeps her car. "Guess it's school time! Oh, hey, about tonight's party, are you going to text Tillie to give her the deets?"

"Shit!" I gasp, remembering that I had left my phone in my dad's Caddy, which was still not home. I'd have to talk to Nate about that when, or if, I see him. "Erm," I answer, noticing Tatum watching me as she slides up her scissor door. "Yeah, I'll text her later today about it." I want to ask her more questions about The Elite Kings Club too, but I'm afraid my newfound interest in the group would make Tatum suspicious.

We pull up to school not long after that. Tatum directs us into the private student parking, and we get out, walking toward the elevators that take us to the main lobby of the school. We're late—no surprise there. Running down the hallway, I push open the door to English, and the professor looks up at me, startled from his scribbling on the chalkboard. "So nice of you to join us, Montgomery. Take a seat, and don't make a pattern out of this." I nod, mouthing an apology, and then look toward the only free space there is left beside Ally. She stares at me with a snarl, and I drop my books on my desk, sinking into my chair in an attempt to focus on my schoolwork.

"Madison!" a voice yells out from behind me, as I walk toward the buffet, picking up a tray.

Carter smiles, taking a tray and falling into step beside me. "So, ah, I didn't know you were Nate's new stepsister."

"Oh no." I roll me eyes, picking up an apple. "Don't tell me you hang with them?"

He flashes me a boyish grin, and I take this brief minute to scan over his body. Strong, athletic, you can see he spends his extra time playing football. His floppy blond hair hangs short over his forehead, and his baby blues sparkle with a gleam. "Well, no... we roll in different circles."

I take a bite out of my apple and point to his varsity jacket. "I see that." I didn't mean that in an offensive way, just... Nate and those boys dress with swagger. Their bodies are built like athletes, but I'd bet my last dollar that none of them would be throwing balls.

"So you'll be at his party tonight, then?" he asks, as we reach the end of the line.

I spin around and face him. "Yup. Are you going to be there?" I ask as we head back to our tables.

He flashes me another boyish grin. "I think I've found my reason to be there." Then he winks at me and saunters back to his table.

I'm still grinning from ear to ear and laughing under my breath when my eyes fall on a scowling Bishop. My smile instantly drops, and then Nate is pushing through people, heading straight toward me. "What was that about?"

"What?" I shove past him, my mood instantly changing. "Nothing."

"Bullshit, Madi." I ignore him and go to step toward my table, when his hand catches my arm, halting any movement. "Stay away from him."

I shove out of his grip. "I should be staying away from you," I hiss. "And by the way, where is my phone and my SUV?"

"Caddy is at home, and here's your phone." He tosses my cell toward me, and I catch it quickly before taking a seat on my chair.

"What the hell is that about?" Tatum mutters under her breath.

Nate comes next to me in a flash. "Come sit with us."

"No." I pick up my sandwich, unfazed by his presence, but fazed by all the attention he's bringing to me.

"Fine." He scowls at me, and then looks up to the rest of his hounds, letting out a loud whistle and then nudging his head.

No. Fucking. Way.

All seven of them drop their shit at the table, Nate resting comfortably beside me and Bishop sitting directly opposite me.

"I can't do this," I murmur to myself, shaking my head.

"Do what?" Bishop asks, eyebrow cocked. He leans forward, and whispers, "Wanna play a game?"

Tatum tenses and then looks to me. I ignore everything that's going on behind me, my eyes remaining locked on Bishop's dark, murky green ones. My jaw clenches. He leans back into the chair, and I stretch my leg out under the table, only for it to connect with his leg. His eyes twitch slightly before a grin appears.

Tatum clears her throat. "Um." I look at her, leaving Bishop to continue his stare-down on his own. "Are you going to text Tillie?"

I pull my phone out of my pocket, sliding it unlocked. "Yeah, I'll text her now."

"Two questions," Nate starts, taking my sandwich and biting into it. I whack his arm with the back of my hand. "What?" He looks at me annoyed.

"Can you fucking not? I'm hungry. Eat this." I throw him an energy bar.

"I didn't eat this morning!"

"Well, that's your own fault for not coming home last night. Eat. Give this—" I take the sandwich from his grabby hands. "—back." He looks longingly at my sandwich, and I chuckle.

"Mmm." I curve my mouth around it slowly, biting down on it. "So..." I chew slowly until I swallow. Swiping a drop of mayonnaise of the corner of my mouth with my thumb, I suck it off. "Good." I laugh again, taking another normal bite, and then look around the table at everyone's silence. They're all watching me with mixed expressions. I look back to Nate, about to ask what the hell is going on, only his mouth is hanging open.

"Yeah." He takes the sandwich from me. "No more mayonnaise sandwiches for you. Mmkay?" Then he shovels the remainder of what was left into his fat gob. I flip him off, looking back down at my phone. I scroll through the contacts until I've find Tillie, and send her a quick message.

Me – *Hey, it's Madison. Are you still on for tonight?*
Tillie – *Hey! I was wondering when you'd text. Sure, what time?*
Me – *Tatum and I will come pick you up after school if you want?*
Tillie – *Um, I can get dropped off.*
Me – *Are you sure?*
Tillie – *Yeah. Just send me your address and I'll be there.*

After sending Tillie my address, I look back up to Tatum. "She'll get dropped off after school."

"Back to my questions. Who is Tillie, and is she single?"

I throw a carrot stick at Nate and then go back to eating whatever is left on my plate. My eyes fall on Brantley, who has gone from scowling at me to flat out ignoring me, and then drift down to the rest of the guys, who seem to be eating and conducting small talk among themselves. My eyes eventually fall on Bishop... and... he's staring at me again.

"You know," I whisper, inching toward him with a teasing grin, "it's rude to stare."

He clenches his jaw, his eyes and face hard and unfazed. Then his mouth tips as he leans forward until his lips are a mere breath away from mine. "You know," he whispers back, cocking his head, "I think you know how poor my manners are."

I look from his eyes, down to his mouth, and then back to his eyes. Narrowing my glare, I slide out of my seat.

"Oh, come on, kitty," Bishop taunts as I walk toward the trash can, dumping the rest of my food. "I know how you like games."

I flip him off over my shoulder and walk toward the girls' side of the school, Tatum quickly catching up to me breathlessly.

"What the ever-loving fuck is going on with you and Bishop?" she asks loudly, gaining the attention of Ally and Lauren, who are stashing their books into their lockers.

"Shh!" I scold her, walking toward my next class. "I'll tell you later."

She stops, letting me carry on my walk toward my next subject alone. "You better!" she yells to my back.

I look down at my watch, seeing I still have some time to burn, so I decide to take a detour to the library. I haven't checked it out yet, but it has been on my list of things to do.

Pushing open the double doors, I walk into the smell of worn paper, sound knowledge, and history, and it instantly warms my heart. Pulling in a deep breath, I close my eyes and exhale softly, unleashing any bad juju I had by leaving it at the library's door. There's just something magical about a library. It's like a portal to many different worlds. We have one ready to be set up at home. My dad at least made sure to get a house with a library in it, so all I have to do is fill it and furnish the place. I'm sure I could do it anytime I want, with my dad's little plastic friend, but I want to make sure we really are staying here before I put down roots like that, and also without getting too attached. I've never let myself get too attached or too comfortable with where we have been, because I've been afraid. Afraid, because anytime I start getting comfortable, Dad would uproot our life and we'd be moving somewhere else. Do I know what Dad does for work? I mean, we all knew he is wealthy and came from old oil money, but he also has shares in different establishments, not only in the United States but in Europe as well. Money has never been an issue for me, but having an actual home has.

After giving the librarian a polite wave, I head toward a dark, cozy corner tucked away behind History. After dropping my bag to the table that sits in front of the plush LazyBoy, I start on my trek of finding something to humor me for the remainder of lunch. After doing big circles around, I find myself down the Historical Folklore aisle.

Tilting my head, my eyes run over all the worn brown spines until I'm drawn to one with a circle symbol on. I don't know why, but I feel like it's familiar. I just can't pinpoint anything I have ever seen before. Slipping my finger on the top, I slide the heavy, long book out and carry it back to my seat. Crossing my legs underneath me, I run my fingertips over the cover of the book. The embroidered circle emblem with a double infinity inside of it. So simple, yet so familiar.

Opening the cover, the title page reads, *Secrets are weapons, and silence is the trigger.* – V. S. H.

I read over that phrase a couple more times. So vague. With a roll of my eyes, I flip the page, skipping the table of contents.

1

The Calling.

The somber side of me knew what was to come. When I felt my baby's first kick, I knew. Knowledge wasn't one we liked to hold onto very well in our world, not when The Chosen go by facts alone, not knowledge. Impulse actions, not knowledge. Consequences be damned. My child was to be one of The Chosen. He would be one of the originals. This corrupt pact that Joseph had begun was only the beginning for generations to come. The firstborn sons of each chosen family. Dirty, spilled blood would then be passed down on to their hands.

The Calling. This was the calling.

"Madison, is it?" The librarian looks down at me, and I snap the book closed as if I had done something wrong.

"Yes, sorry."

She points down to her watch. "Lunch is over. It's time to head to class."

"Oh!" I gather up my bag. "Can I borrow this?"

She looks at me, the sides of her eyes crinkling. "Sorry, honey, that's a part of the section we don't allow to check out. You can come in and read it anytime you like, though." I hand it to her, and she walks over and slides it back into its slot.

Damn. I really wanted to read the rest of that book and I don't even know why. It's not a genre I usually read, far away from dystopian or vampire romances, but I really want to read whatever the hell is in that book. Slinging my bag over my shoulder, I nod. "Thanks." And then I walk out of the library. As soon as the doors swing closed, I inhale my problems I had left at the door.

Great.

CHAPTER 12

"So she said she would be here?" Tatum quizzes, rummaging through my closet with a bottle of Moet in her other hand. It's 5:00 p.m. and she's already started drinking. I fear she might be going to bed early tonight.

"Yes!" I hit my phone, dialing Tillie again. This time, she picks up.

"Sorry! I got caught up and I had to do…." She pauses, brushing me off. "Shit. I'm almost there."

Hanging up my phone, I toss it onto the bed and buzz Sam to let her in as soon as he gets here, just in case we don't hear her knock. Nate hasn't come home, again, but he did text to say that they'll be here soon to set up whatever it is they need to set up. My dad is going to kill us. I made it my duty, this time, to go around the house and put away any expensive items. Our house is still rather empty, even though Dad hired a few people to come out and unload boxes to make it more homey for me, which I'm used to. He's never been a home parent; Sam practically raised me. Even when my mom was alive, they were both almost always away on business, and now that I look back on it, my mom probably followed him around like a lost puppy in hopes to keep him on a leash.

It's true, my dad has never been one for commitment, and I'm surprised he hasn't already found another mistress, but that side of him has never impacted me or how he parented me. Yes, he's an absent parent, but I'm not bratty enough to give him a hard time about it. I'm well aware of his hard work and how I wouldn't have the life I have if he didn't. But if I'm honest, I always wondered what it would be like for my dad to be a middle-class working man. One who fishes on the weekends, is always home by 5:00 p.m., and watches the game on TV while tossing back a cold beer.

I stand to my feet, brushing off my pants, and walk into the closet to help Tatum find something to wear before she has a breakdown.

"Why don't you just wear the dress you bought at the mall?"

"Because," she whines, "I'm almost certain I've gained three pounds since then."

"Tatum?"

"Yes?" She groans into her hands, looking all distressed. I almost laugh. Almost.

"That was two days ago. Not possible."

"Maybe not for you." She eyes me up and down.

"Hey!" I whack her with the back of my hand. "I'll have you know that if I didn't watch what I eat, I would be the size of a house. Dude…" I grab onto my hips, "—they jiggle a bit."

She pouts, and then we both burst out laughing. "Well...," she says, handing me the bottle of champagne, "let's just do the alcohol diet."

I take the bottle from her, slipping out of my skinny jeans and hoodie. "And what's that diet?" I ask, standing in my bra and lace panties, bringing the rim to my mouth and tossing it back until the bubbles are enticing my taste buds.

She waves her hands, freaking out over a black sequin dress. "Well, we get so drunk that we no longer care about our weight."

I laugh, taking another swig and pointing to the dress she's holding and contemplating. "Deal. By the way, wear that dress."

She nods and then spins to look me up and down. "By the way," she mimics my tone, her eyes eating up my skin, "you have a fucking banging body, Madi. What the fuck?"

I turn beat red and change the subject. "Wear the dress." I bring the wine back to my lips.

My bedroom door swings open, and I turn around with the bottle of wine pressed to my mouth, expecting Tillie to walk through.

It is Tillie. But she is not alone. *Fuck.*

"Holy shit!" Hunter gasps. Nate halts the door from opening any more, and then Bishop strolls in, his eyes licking all over my skin, making me feel even more naked than what I already do.

I squeal, dropping to the ground and ducking behind my bed. "Oh my God! Everyone but Tillie, get the fuck out!"

Bishop watches me, his head tilting until his eyes twinkle in mischief.

"Hey!" I point at the door. "Get. Out!"

They leave, but not before Hunter halts, his fingers gripping the edge of the door. "Just for, you know, future reference, what were you two—"

Bishop drags him out of my room by the back of his collar, and Tillie slams the door in all their faces.

"Jesus," I mumble, getting back to my feet. "Fucking pack of unruly wolves." Tillie is still watching the door when I burst out laughing.

"Sorry about that. I should have warned you about my stepbrother and his pack of..." I pause, attempting to find the appropriate word for them. "Of exactly that—wolves."

Tillie turns to me and smiles. "No problem at all." She looks down my body. "But seriously, can I have your boobs, because mine are like tiny lemons compared to those scrumptious things."

We all laugh as she steps in closer with her bag propped over her shoulder. "I'll get ready here."

I nod, handing her the bottle of wine. "As you can see... we are far from dressed."

Tatum nudges my hip with hers. "Ignore Madi. She's a little..." She circles her index finger up near her temple to emphasize my edginess. "...crazy, because she didn't get to go shooting after school."

"Shooting?" Tillie asks, pulling out some clothes from her backpack.

"It's a sort of hobby of mine." I smile at her, and she grins at me.

"That's badass. I'd love to learn one day."

My back straightens at the opportunity to find someone, a friend, who is maybe interested in something I do. I know Tatum and I have grown extremely close in the short amount of time we've known each other, despite my thinking we couldn't be friends, but Tillie seems like the center of Tatum and me. Sort of like... a bit of each of us.

I'm obviously a little buzzed, because my train of thought is heading into the emotional tunnel, and I need to derail that right now. Swallowing, I nod. "I'd love to take you! Get changed and drink!"

She laughs, pulling out a long-sleeved short dress that looks tight. She hitches her thumb over her shoulder. "I'll slip into the bathroom."

Modest... far more modest than I'm being right now, which, now that I think about it, is a lot worse. At my revelation, I place the bottle of Moet down on my bedside table and turn to face her. "Of course." *Sober up right now, Madi, or you'll be joining Tatum facedown before 9:00 p.m.*

I spin back around to face my closet when I catch Tatum looking at the closed door. "Why would she be shy around us?" she whispers.

"Shh!" I bring my finger up to my mouth. "Maybe," I say, scolding her and pulling my new—or Tatum's—choice of dress off the rack, "because she's been around us for all of five minutes."

Tatum narrows her eyes. "Hmmm, maybe."

"Stop!" I point my finger against the tip of her nose. "Don't dig or anything. Just leave it." Shit. I'm a little buzzed. "What the hell is in that wine, anyway?"

"Uhh, wine? Wine is what's in that wine, and not the cheap kind. Live and learn, my love." She steps into her dress, every inch of the sequined material pushing against her tiny frame. "Do me up!" I zip her up and she turns. "How do I look?"

"Holy shit, you look incredible!" Tillie says, walking out of the bathroom.

I halt, scanning her curvy frame filling her tiny little dress. "So do you!" I point. "You two are going to make me look like the ugly stepsister." Tatum looks at me like I've lost my mind, and Tillie scrunches up her face. "Better continue my drinking," I half joke under my breath.

I don't have that high of a self-esteem, but that came from years and years of just never fitting in. All the pretty girls hang together; they all gravitate toward each other and all feed off each other's beauty and what not, but that's never been me. I've always been the tomboy loner who likes to shoot guns and wear Keds or Chucks. Tatum? She's a heels-and-diamonds kind of girl—always looks stunning—and has the kind of confidence that could only come from being told "you're the shit" for most of your life. Tillie, on the other hand, I'm still trying to work out. She has this retro hippie feel about her, what with her pastel pink hair and earthy, naturally beautiful, in-line-with-the-universe thing going on, if that even makes sense—which I'm sure it doesn't, because *fucking wine.*

Jesus, I need to pull my shit together. *Deep breathing, in and out.* But every intake of breath I take, I get hit with a rich tang on the back of my throat from the after taste of the expensive alcohol.

"Hello?" Tatum waves her hands in front of my face. "Earth to Madi, get changed!"

"Shit." I snap out of my lingering thoughts of self-pity and tipsy ramblings. "I'll get changed. Fire up the curlers." I slip into my closet, unclip my current bra, and snap on a strapless. When I step back out, I say, "Tatum, did I tell you how much I hate you for choosing this dress? I don't do dresses."

"Good thing I gave you wine beforehand then." She winks, curling her hair, as Tillie leans over the sink in the bathroom, doing her makeup.

"This was your plan?" I look at her with fresh eyes. She's sneakier than I ever imagined. Tatum taps her head. "You'll never know."

Hmm, sure I won't.

"So," Tillie says from the bathroom, "I've never been to an elite party before."

I halt, dress clutched in my hand. "What?" I ask lightly.

"You know," Tillie lines her eyes with black, "an elite party."

"You mean figuratively?"

Tatum rolls her eyes, letting her long, blonde fresh curls drop over her slender shoulders. "No. She means Elite, Madi. We've had this discussion."

"Wait, how do you even know about that?" I look back toward Tillie.

She stops what she's doing. "We've all heard of them, Madi. I didn't realize your stepbrother was Nate Riverside, though."

"Are you judging me?"

She stops and spins to face me, horror flashing over her freshly marked face. "God, no, Madi. No. I was just surprised when I pulled up here. That's all."

I nod, turning back to hold my dress. If Nate and his boys cost me a friendship, I'll have to kill him for real. I have a hard enough time making friends—not that I actually care—but I happen to like Tillie, so I don't want to lose her friendship. "By the way, whatever you heard about them, it's not true."

"Is so."

"Tatum, shut up." I look back to Tillie with a smile. "It's really not. They're not all that interesting." I don't know why I feel the need to protect whatever the fuck I'm protecting, but I'll blame it on the wine again.

Tillie shrugs. "I don't know much, only rumors, and of course, Bishop Hayes used to date a girl from my school." My heartbeat slows, thickening my blood. "And everyone knows who The Elite Kings are. Also," she adds casually, "Nate and Cash are always at Backyard Bucks, and as usual," she says casually, lining her lips, "Bishop is always ripping through the streets."

"What, what, and what?" I ask, stepping closer to her and shimmying into the tight red strapless dress. It's thin, snug, and has a deep dip over my sternum, showcasing my cleavage.

"You know, Backyard Bucks Octagon, and Bishop, racing?" She looks at me, waiting for me to catch on.

Tatum looks at me sideways. "She's new. She'll figure it out."

"I'm sorry." I clear my throat, signaling for Tatum to zip up my back. "Did I get this right? Nate in an octagon, and Bishop races what? Cars?"

Tatum starts applying makeup and acting like she isn't inhaling all the drama and new information. I know this is news to her too, because her mouth is shut and she has her ears tuned in to our convo.

"The races," Tillie says ashamedly, almost like she thinks she's not allowed to put her foot in it. Tatum starts applying makeup to my face and fluffing up my natural waves. "I assumed you knew, because, well…." She gestures around the place. "I only know because my sister occasionally sleeps with Jase, Hunter's older brother. I heard them talking about it, so I snuck out and followed them one day."

My breathing slows, the information sinking into me. I whack Tatum's hands away from my face. *What the fuck is with these boys?*

"Because otherwise, that's super confidential information. I don't even know why Jase would've told my stupid sister, and please forget I ever told you."

Tatum holds up a pair of hoop earrings in front of my face. "Earrings?"

My face falls in a death glare. "Hold them." I get to my feet and storm out my bedroom door. I don't care that my makeup is only half done and my hair is in a thick mane of soft waves down my back, or that I have no shoes on. This is my fucking house anyway. I fly down the stairs, the deep, slow, dark bass of "Devil's Night" by D12 already shaking the chandelier that hangs in the foyer. I round the corner to the living room, so fucking angry I want to hit something, preferably all of them, until they tell me what the fuck is going on.

I halt at the opening. They are all lounging around already, with Ally and Lauren stretched over their laps—or should I say, Ally stretched out over Bishop's lap. Awesome. I needed to hit Tatum for saying he isn't a manwhore and that he is fussy. Lies. No fussy man would have that dirty slut stretched out across his lap.

Okay, angry Madi is about to rear her ugly head. Maybe another glass? Or bottle... because you're classy like that. Nate is stretched out, with a bong in one hand and a cigarette in the other, grinning at me. Looking beside him, Hunter's chopping up white powder on the coffee table and rolling up a hundred-dollar bill. I shiver, not wanting to touch that subject right now.

Bringing my eyes back to Bishop, I see Ally purr against his chest. "Why's she coming?"

Bishop's jaw clenches, his eyes staying on mine as he strokes Ally's hair. He wraps her long mane around his fist, yanking her head up to face him, all while his eyes remain on mine. Locked, entranced, and fucking hypnotic.

He slowly drawls his tongue out and licks her across her bottom lip. "I don't know, babe. Maybe you should ask Nate why his annoying little sister is coming tonight with her annoying little friends." He sucks her bottom lip into his mouth, catching it between his teeth, before pulling back roughly. She moans shamelessly—fuck everyone else in the room.

Heat mixed with anger pulses through me. *Calm breathing, Madi. Fuck him.*

I look to Ally, a grin slithering onto my mouth. "Oh now, now," I tsk, my poker face game strong. "Don't act like his kisses are that good." I roll my eyes with a smirk, narrowing them onto Bishop and cocking my head. "He tastes like washed up whores strung out on crack." Then I look to Ally. "But I guess, now that I know who he has been kissing"—my smirk deepens—"it actually makes sense."

"You bi—"

She goes to launch off the couch when a laugh erupts out of me. Nate snatches her arm, shoving her back onto Bishop's lap. Bishop, who has hunger and hate mixed in his eyes, watches me carefully. I smirk at him, chuckling devilishly. If he thinks I'll lay back and let him make a fool out of me with his little toy, he's mistaken. I've spent most of my life being made a fool of, and I've come to realize, as of recently, I don't much like feeling that way. Of course, this is because *wine*.

"You!" Nate points to me. "Need to change. You cannot dress like that here tonight."

"He's right." Cash nods. Cash never says much of anything, so him even adding his two cents is odd.

"First of all, fuckers, I'm not changing. Do you know how long it took to get into this dress?" I ask sweetly, a smile still on my face. "I mean, one can only hope that, whoever the lucky guy is that I find myself with tonight, he finds it easier to take it off than I did putting it on."

"Shut up. Get changed." Nate points toward the stairs.

"No," I hiss, offended and looking him up and down.

"Jesus," Brantley scoffs. "She's already buzzed."

Ally laughs, wrapping Bishop's hands around her waist as she wiggles on his lap. "Oh, this is comical."

I flip them both off. "Not as funny as your breath, which tastes like ass, by the way."

"Oh?" she asks, laughing and getting ready to shame me in front of everyone. Someone like Ally Parker doesn't go down without a fight. "And you know what ass tastes like?" She and Lauren smirk at each other in triumph.

"Of course I do," I say stiffly. "I've had my lips wrapped around Bishop's tongue."

Their laughing instantly stops, and she goes to launch off the couch again, but this time it's Bishop who halts her movements.

"That was the last time you threaten me, in my fucking house too, by the way," I say snidely, my shoulders squaring. Fuck her, and fuck these boys.

I turn around, forgetting why I even came down to see them.

"Oh, sis, come on," Nate moans behind me. I flip him off and run up the stairs to continue getting changed.

New goals: look hot as fuck tonight, get drunk, and hopefully find someone to rub my ass against.

CHAPTER 13

"Jesus." I glance at the stranger in the mirror. "That's me?" I smirk, brushing myself off.

Tatum and Tillie burst out laughing, both of them nice and tipsy, and me a little bit past tipsy, but still sober enough to walk, talk, and act straight. I'm in that zone where everything is warm, when your blood is pumping, and you just know that tonight is going to be a good night. I can feel it in my bones and in my blood.

I touch my nude lips. "Damn. I look decent."

"Decent?" Tatum mocks, offended. "Oh, honey, I don't create decent. I create daaaymn,'" she mocks Smokey and Ice Cube's voices from the movie *Friday*.

I burst out laughing. Tatum did fucking good. My brunette hair is dead straight, hanging to my tailbone, my eyes smoked out in black, and my skin dusted in golden bronzer. My cheeks are brushed with peach blush, and my dress has been replaced with a more revealing one. Yup, I ditched the modest tight red dress, which Nate already tried to tell me to change out of, and replaced it with a thin spaghetti strap nude leather-like dress. It clings to my body like a second skin, accentuating my narrow waist and how my hips flare out slightly. It also showcases my bubble butt and D-sized breasts, both of which I always attempt to hide.

Not tonight though. Oh no.

I've always been self-conscious of my body. Because I don't have that nice small butt or the perky small boobs that just sit there and look perfect. I'm not big. I'm actually petite, but my curves are most definitely not. The dress shows most of my boobs and a whole lot of my figure. I've done a good job at hiding it—up until now. Ally got to me. Bishop got to me. They all got to me. Now I'm out to fuck them all over, in a small package of a dress.

"Wear the heels." Tatum throws the black pumps at me.

"I really don't wanna."

"I don't care." She giggles, taking another drink.

The party downstairs is obviously in full swing, what with the loud pumping music, glasses clinking, and the roar of laughter. The squeals of annoying fucking drunk girls— *you're a drunk girl right now*—and the coming and leaving of headlights lighting up my dim bedroom further proves that tonight is going to be a messy night. We spent most of the night up here getting drunk and ready, and it was nice. I feel like I've known and Tatum all my life, almost like we're all soul mates but the friend kind. Or maybe girls are supposed to find their soul mates in their friends, and guys are just there for the D.

After I relayed everything that happened in the living room back to the girls, we all decided to switch up my outfit and go a little over the top—which is why I am looking like I am right now.

"Are we ready, girls?" Tillie wiggles her eyebrows from the doorway.

"Wait, wait!" Tatum stops. "Are we getting ass tonight?"

I laugh. "I hope so."

They both look at me. "Are you a virgin?"

"What?" I'm just about to give them a small fib when I decide I don't need to lie to these girls. They're my friends, real ones. "No." My laughing turns serious. "I'm not kidding. I'm not a virgin. But I'd rather not go there right now." I pause, looking back to them. "Are either of you?"

Tatum nods.

"No way!" I breathe, but then feel instantly bad that I assumed she wasn't. "Sorry."

She shakes her head. "It's fine. Most people think I'm a slut."

"We can talk about this later," I say to her. That wasn't a question; it was a promise. I look to Tillie. "What about you?"

She shakes her head. "No." Then she adds, "Far from it."

"Oh?" I smile at her. "Like that, huh?"

"Oh, I'm all about women's sexuality. We have every right to enjoy it just like guys do."

I hold my fist out to her. "Word!"

We fist-bump, and then Tatum looks at us. "I feel left out. New plan: Get Tatum laid."

We all laugh, and Tillie swings the door open all the way, letting the bass stream through loudly. There is no one upstairs, which is a relief, but I gather that no one would step up to Nate and the boys by trying to cross them and invading our personal space. No one but me, because fuck them, basically.

We walk down the stairs, laughing and clutching a bottle of champagne each. I'm still not too hot on these heels, but hey, I can blame wine if I fall on my face. Yin Yang Twins' "Shake" starts playing through the beefy speakers, and Tatum starts dancing and hopping down the stairs, our hair flying around the place. Yup, we are all very much drunk. Dragging us to the living room, where bodies are crushing against each other to the music, we ignore all the staring eyes glued on us as we continue dancing around, blocking everyone out.

I laugh, twisting in Tillie's grasp. When my eyes land on the boys, who are standing on the other side of the room, I drop down to the floor and grin at them before snaking back up, pressing my butt into Tillie. Not all of them are here, but Nate, Bishop, Brantley, Ace, and Saint are. Ally and Lauren are way past drunk, falling all over the place and rubbing up on each other. A giggle escapes me as my head swings back. They probably think they look sensual. *Yeah, if sensual was two drowned raccoons who look like they just got smashed seven ways from Sunday with Charlie Sheen.*

Bishop's eyes slowly lick all over my body, his lip twitching at the corner of his mouth. *Psh, yeah right.* I look to Nate, who's already storming up to me, his face red and angry, followed closely by the rest of them.

"Get. Fucking. Changed, Madi. Tonight is not the night to be dressed and acting like this."

"Oh, I'm sorry." I smirk, turning around and dancing against his chest, my ass pressing into him. *Gag.* "You're mistaking me for someone who gives a fuck."

"Tillie!" Saint snaps at my friend.

"Hey!" I click my fingers in his face, stepping between the two of them and narrowing my eyes. "Leave her alone, bud."

He grins, finding me amusing. "Step away, kitty. You already know we don't play fair."

"Oh," I say, matching his fight, "neither do I. You boys just caught me off guard that night."

I look to all of them. "Now, if you don't mind, you're kind of cock blocking us." Then I take the girls' hands and walk them outside to where the music is pouring out, and the moon is shining over the bright fairy lights, the colored neons inside the pool, and all the half-naked drunk teens walking around.

I tip my head back, swallowing more wine. "That was fucking awesome."

A young guy is tilted over one of the lawn chairs, his bottle of tequila hanging between his fingers loosely. Tillie walks up to him, snatching the bottle quickly, and then comes back to us. "Time to really get shit started."

We drink, dance, and rub against each other until sweat is beading on our skin and the smile lines are permanently imprinted on our faces.

We're dancing to "Dangerous" by Akon when my eyes land on Carter. He's walking through the opening doors that lead out to where we are beside the pool. He's with three or four friends, all wearing their varsity jackets. *Damn.* I lick my lips. He's looking a little more delicious than he usually does. *Wine.* Oh no, *Tequila.* He's searching for someone in the crowd, and when his eyes land on me, a smile lights up his face, and probably the rest of outside, because he is just that damn beautiful right now. After being surrounded by asshole moody guys for the past couple of nights, I need this. I need to see a friendly face. Someone who makes me feel good. I wave. *Oh God, I just waved.*

"Did you just fucking wave?" Tatum hisses from beside me.

"Shut up." I keep the smile on my face as he walks toward us, drinking in what I'm wearing.

"Well, damn." He pulls me into his chest, where I instantly melt against him.

I look up at him and smile. "Nice to see you. I'm a bit drunk. Not enough to look like that." I wave over to Ally and Lauren. *Ha ha.* "Albeit, still drunk."

"Did you just say albeit?" Tatum scolds me through a whisper. Jesus, anyone would think *I'm* the virgin and she's the cock expert. I discretely shove her away.

Worst. Wingwoman. Ever.

Looking over to Tillie, I see her dancing in one of Carter's friends' arms, her eyes rolling to the back of her head, lost in the beat of the song.

Best. Wingwoman. Ever.

Tatum is fired.

He grins, hooking his finger under my chin. "You're cute as shit. You know that?"

"Hmm." My eyes narrow as I ponder his words. "Not exactly the best line I've heard—"

He kisses me. His warm lips press against mine as his slick tongue slips between my lips. I freeze slightly, but then images of Bishop and Ally come through my brain like a bad romance movie, and my hands wrap around the back of his neck instinctively as I grind into him.

He pulls back, searching my eyes. "Wanna get out of here?" He waits for me to answer and must sense my hesitation. "Your friends can come." He gestures to Tillie, where she's locking lips with his friend.

"Okay." I would not have been this easy had I been sober, and although I'm getting cold feet about this getting laid business, it's not like anything could happen if Tillie is with me. And besides all of that, Carter's cool. I'm comfortable enough with him to go with him. Or maybe this is another thing I can blame on wine and bad experiences. Only, I have enough of those to last two lifetimes.

"To where?" I ask.

"To a good time?" he replies with a grin.

I look at Tillie, who is looking back at me pleadingly; she obviously isn't having second thoughts about getting ass tonight.

"Okay." He takes my hand, and I stop, looking back inside the house.

"Nate and Bishop left if you're worried about slipping past them?" Carter searches my eyes.

"But Hunter and Saint are...." I look to the side of the house, pulling on his arm and turning to face Tatum. "Come on!"

Tatum looks at us reluctantly. "Fine, fuck it. YOLO and all that shit."

I laugh, tugging Carter with me, his strong body brushing against my back. "You give me shit about using 'albeit,' and then you go and drop something like YOLO?" I unlatch the lock on the side gate and drag them through the finely trimmed gardens until we're eventually out front of the house.

"Tada!" I laugh, stretching my arms wide.

Carter points to a Porsche. "You're riding shotgun." He slaps my ass as he passes me, slipping into the driver seat. The guy Tillie is with gets into the back, and then I shove Tatum in after Tillie.

"Oh, stop complaining." I smirk at Tatum, who is in the back pressed against the car, trying to escape Tillie sucking face with... "What's your name?" I ask the hottie in the back.

"Pauly."

Then I look back to Tatum, only to find her scowling at me. "What kind of car does Bishop have?" I ask, pondering over what Tillie told us earlier tonight.

Carter snickers. "A matte black GranTurismo Maserati, why?" He looks at me over his arm.

I shrug. Of course he owns a Maserati. "Just wondering." I look back at Carter. "And how do you know what he drives?"

He grins at me from the side. "You're about to find out." Then he drops the car into second gear as we zoom onto the highway, the tires eating up the asphalt.

CHAPTER 14

The Chainsmokers' "Closer" is pulsing through the small enclosure of the car, and I spin around, dancing in my seat while watching Tatum, who has loosened up a lot more since leaving the house, dance in her seat. *Thank you, tequila.*

"So where're we going?" We've been driving for half an hour now, the distant lights of the town long gone.

Carter grins, putting his headlights on high beam and then yanking up the emergency brake until the back wheels are latching onto the road. Suddenly, we're sliding into a private long driveway, leaving a thick dust of smoke behind us.

Tatum scolds him, "Not cool, Dominic Toretto."

I'm too busy smiling from ear to ear. "I want to do that again."

Tatum kicks the back of my seat. I look at Carter, ignoring my tantrum-throwing bestie in the back. "I'm serious." He smiles and then puts his eyes back to the road ahead. Upscale fencing encases the endless driveway. "What?" I grumble under my breath. We finally come to the end of the driveway, and I look at the half circle of cars lined up with people crowding around. And when I say cars, I mean *cars*. I narrow my eyes. "Is this the rich boys' playground?"

Carter chuckles, pulling up to a stop. I'm not oblivious to how everyone has stopped what they're doing, watching us in the car. "You could say that," he says, winking at me and clutching his door handle. "Let's go."

Tillie grumbles, sitting forward, "I guess we're going to see firsthand what Bishop does when he races."

Wait, what?

Shit.

I push my door open, and Carter is already rounding my side. He places his hand out and I take it, standing to my feet. All eyes are on us. Great. I think I need more tequila. Snatching the bottle out of a very drunk Tatum's hands, I bring the rim to my lips and pound it back.

"Hey," he pulls me into his body, "you can ride with me."

I swallow the potent liquid. "Really?"

He looks down at me, his eyes searching mine. "Really, really."

Hooking my hands around his neck, I pull his lips down to mine. His warm breath falls over my lips and my heart pounds in my chest. I lean forward, about to kiss him—

A strong arm wraps around my waist, tugging me out of his grip. "Yeah, not gonna happen."

I'm pushed behind Bishop's body, with both him and Nate standing in front of me.

"Uh yeah, I'm pretty sure she rolled up with me, so she's riding with me." Carter reaches out to my arm, and he barely touches me, when Bishop steps up to him, chest to chest, nose to nose.

"Yeah," Bishop murmurs, his eyes searching Carter's and his square jaw clenching. "And I said it's not gonna happen." The entire crowd of people here are watching this epic pissing contest, Tatum and Tillie both awkwardly silent behind me.

"Bishop," I whisper, but he doesn't move. I look to Nate for help, only finding him watching Bishop with a questioning glare, and then looking back to Carter, who seems like he's not going to back down anytime soon. *Fuck. I'm on my own.*

Bishop doesn't move, so I raise my hand, grabbing hold of his thick arms. I could swear goose bumps break out over his arms at the connection of our skin. "Bishop?" I repeat, looking around nervously at everyone who is watching.

"Nah, it's cool," Carter says, brushing me off while his eyes search Bishop's with venom. "You can take her for a ride. But make no mistake, she will be with me after, and..." He pauses, pretending to think over his next words. "...after that too."

Oh, Jesus Christ.

He pushes away from Bishop, all of them still watching as Carter gets back into his car. Tatum clears her throat. "Um, well that was awkward."

Bishop spins around to face me, both he and Nate obviously pissed at me. "What the fuck are you doing getting in the car with him? You were supposed to stay the fuck home!"

"Last I checked," I said, looking directly at Bishop, "you don't tell me what the fuck to do!" I really hope I didn't slur in that sentence.

Bishop points toward his beautiful—*fucking beautiful*—Maserati. "Get in the fucking car, kitty, and don't fucking move unless I tell you otherwise." My mouth damn near drops open as I look to Nate, waiting for him to help me out here.

But my stepbrother is trying to hold in his laugh, his face turning purple. "Nate!" I hiss.

"Okay, okay, sorry, sis, but he's right. I was going to lose my shit at you, but he did it for the both us. Get in the car." He looks behind me, directly at Tatum. "You get in the fucking car too." Then he looks to Tillie, who is now pushing Carter's friend away. "And you, too."

"Fuck." Bishop shakes his head. "I can't be carrying too much weight. I'll take Madison."

"Like fuck!" I blurt out. Bishop's eyes narrow on me. I point. "Take Nate!"

"No!" Bishop orders, stepping closer. "Someone needs to keep an eye on you." He snatches the bottle of tequila out of my hands and tosses it to the ground. "And since pussy doesn't ride shotgun in my car..." He looks to Tatum and Tillie with a curled lip. *Rude!* "You will have to fucking do. Get. In."

"You just said pussy doesn't ride shotgun in your car!" I'm well aware people are still watching us, but because of tequila, I no longer care. I think I'll give lots of fucks come Monday, though. "Last I checked, I have a pussy."

Bishop grins, walking up to me. He tilts his head. "Hmm, want me to check? 'Cause I'm not so sure."

I flip him off. "Fuck you." Then I storm off toward his car, yanking the door open...
and then failing, because they're fucking scissor doors, before sliding inside. Bishop is
still scowling at me from the same spot before he finally turns to talk with Nate, who has
tucked both Tillie and Tatum under each arm with a sly smirk on his face. Both girls look
up at him like he's God's gift to women. *Oh, ew.*

Why the hell are they racing, anyway? It's not like they need money or cars, so
why? Bishop turns and walks back toward me, sliding up his door and getting in.

"I don't know why the fuck you're doing this. Why couldn't you and Nate just ride
around your little circuit? I'd still be here when you got back."

"First of all, it's not a little circuit. It's a forty-minute race across town. Second of
all, you're drunk, and there's no way Nate would leave you unattended."

Nate? It's more like *he* has a lot to say about where or who I'm with tonight, but
admitting I noticed would be about as useful as telling him I think he's hot. It would
embarrass me, because he would know I noticed, and then the ball would be in his court,
which I'm not cool with.

"A forty-minute circuit?" He pulls my belt on and I ignore the way his strong arm
brushes against my own.

Firing up his car, he hits his headlights and puts it into first gear. "Yes." He pushes
buttons on the GPS that sits on his dashboard until a map comes up with a trail of green.

"Why?" I ask, looking back to his chiseled profile. He really is that fine. I need to
stop looking or sober up, or both.

"Why what?" he asks, revving the car until the rumble of the whatever-cylinder
engine shakes under our weight.

"Why do you do it?"

"Ahh." He grins at me from the side and taps his temple. "That's the million-dollar
question though, isn't it?" Then he slams it into first gear, the tires kicking up the gravel
before we're skidding down the driveway.

"Holy shit!" I spin in my chair to see the headlights behind us disappear as Bishop
drops it into third gear and then back to second just as he reaches the end of the
driveway, ripping up the emergency brake. The car's ass end slides out sideways, and we
drift around back, onto the quiet road that leads to the highway. A very girly scream
leaps out of my mouth, and I quickly slam my hand over my lips, unable to contain my
laughter.

The passing streetlights flash across Bishop's face, showcasing shadows over his
finely cut features. "Take a right turn at the next intersection," the GPS's electronic voice
instructs from the dash. Bishop swerves into the right lane and pounds it until we're
clocking in at around 100 mph. I thought I'd be scared. I mean, I have no experience
when it comes to Bishop and his driving, but I not, and this may be the sole reason as to
why so many young people are killed during illegal races—pure stupidity. I don't feel anything but the sheer adrenaline pulsing through me.

"You and Carter?" he asks, his eyes staying on the road ahead of us.

"Are about as friendly as you and Ally." My answer is clipped, but regardless of
whether I'm enjoying this ride or not, I didn't ask for it. Bishop is an asshole and stuck-up.
Everything I dislike in a male, or in a person in general.

He laughs, but it's more like a snark. "Ally means less than shit to me."

"Charming," I reply, deadpan.

He looks at me, a dark smirk coming onto his mouth. "Never." Then he slams it into third gear, and we shoot forward onto the highway. He rips up the brake as we drift onto a right turn effortlessly.

For the most part, the trip is quiet and uneventful. Bishop, being Bishop—all broody and silent. It's unsettling, and I don't really know what to fill the awkward silence with, so I just keep quiet. Bishop eventually hooks into an underground industrial parking lot, the deep pulsing vibrations of the car echoing through the vast empty space.

"Stay in the car."

We pull around a corner, where a long stretched limo waits. A man dressed in a finely pressed suit, gray hair slicked back, and a cigar hanging out his mouth is leaning against it. To the left of him stand his two bodyguards, both in matching black suits, and both their eyes covered by dark sunglasses. Bishop pulls to a stop and gets out of the car. I contemplate getting out just to spite him, but then I look back at the man with the cigar and think better of it. He grins at Bishop in a way that has my skin prickling. Handing him a cigar, Bishop takes it then pushes it into his pocket.

What the hell?

Looking over my shoulder, I see how there's no one behind us. Surely, the guys wouldn't be that far behind. Bishop turns on his feet and walks back to the car, his eyes catching mine. I squirm, sliding down lower in my seat. Just as his hand falls on the door handle, I look back up to the man who is dressed in a suit to find him looking right at me. I need to look away from his gaze, but I can't. His eyes skillfully laser into mine with an unreadable expression. He tilts his head then looks up at Bishop, who has paused with his hand on the door handle. I look away from the suit man and look back to Bishop, before the door swings open, and he slides in beside me. Firing up the car, Bishop snarls at the man and then floors it backward, snaking out of the compact underground parking lot.

"Fuck!" Bishop slams his hand on the steering wheel.

"What?" I look around us, wondering what could be bothering him. I mean, he won, right? That's what this was for. I look back to him, and he reaches into his pocket, pulling out his phone.

"Bishop?"

He ignores me, pressing the phone to his ear. "Yeah, we have a problem. She did stay in the car! It doesn't matter. I saw it. Yeah, I'll go there now."

He hangs up the phone and then drops it into fourth, slowing his speed.

"What's going on?" I ask, leaning on the door. "Bishop, for fuck's sake!"

"Nothing you need to worry about."

"Oh?" I say, my eyebrows quirking up. "If that's the case, then what was that about?"

We turn down a street that isn't far from my place. If my memory serves correctly, it's one street over from my house, which relaxes me somewhat. I hope Nate was right and we can trust Hunter and Saint to watch over the party, though I'm sure he's not lying. I've noticed how everyone moves around them. Careful, scared, but respectful. Those are all things that come to mind. I already know Bishop is the ringleader. If Tatum telling me wasn't enough, anyone could pin it with his air of command.

We pull into a high-gated driveway, and he rolls down his window, punching in a code. After a few seconds, the high wired fence separates and we drive down the cobblestone private road. Trees line our way, and tea lights hang amongst the leaves. We come to a large, round entryway, and—holy crap. When coming down the driveway, I assumed we'd be met with an old Victorian-style mansion, but that's not the case. A massive glass house greets me, and I mean glass everywhere. The executive-style home is beautiful, but cold. I look around to the back and see a huge backyard, where a river flows on the edge of the property. Bishop pulls up the brake and gets out of the car. I take that as my cue to get out, so I slip out, my head spinning lightly. I think I'm past the drunk phase now, and head straight into the hung-over phase, except I should be sleeping through this, not awake. Damn.

"Where are we?" I ask, looking back to the house. The square glass that sits on the top of a slightly smaller glass where the front metal doors are.

Bishop walks around to my side of the car, taking my hand and tugging me forward. "Come on."

"Where are we?"

"Do you ever shut up?"

"Honestly? No."

He ignores me by pulling me forward. In return, I ignore the way his hand feels intertwined with mine, but sweat beads on my temple anyway. I quickly swipe it away with my other hand. He walks us toward the side of the house, through the garden, and then toward the backyard. I almost stop in my tracks. The pool is twice the size of ours and has a glass bar that sits in the middle of it. Jesus. Who are these people? There are neon lights that light up the floating stools that round the bar, and more that light up inside the pool. Toward the back of the pool, there's a mini house that looks exactly like the main home, only smaller.

"Whose place is this? And why am I here?"

Bishop ignores me yet again, because he's good at that, and then pulls me toward the smaller guest house. Walking up the few steps, he slides the floor-to-ceiling door open and pushes the black net curtain out of the way.

Holy fuck. I'm in Bishop Vincent Hayes' bedroom.

CHAPTER 15

He slides the door closed and I pause, looking around the dark room. The walls are glossed with black paint, all except the wall his bed's headboard is against. That one is red marble with black swirls messily woven into it. There's no trashy posters, no naked woman—unlike Nate's. It's clean, yet disturbingly dark. His bed covers are red and black silk, his dresser black marble, and there's a large L-shaped black leather living room suite opposite his bed on the other side of the huge room. I thought this was a guesthouse, but it looks like it's just one huge room with maybe… a bathroom? No kitchen. There's a red and black rug sprawled out on the dark carpet, and the biggest TV I have ever seen hangs on the wall.

Yet, there're no personal touches to it. It's as though he doesn't spend that much time here. There're no pictures, no nothing. It's… *empty.* I step forward, toward the back wall, which is all glass and looks over the river that flows down his backyard. It's stunning. This room is stunning. Reaching out to touch the glass, I turn around to find him watching me closely. This is the first time we've been together alone in a room. I thought the car ride would have been awkward, but we somehow fell into an easy silence. Being in his room, though, this is strange.

His eyes run over my body. "We're just waiting for Nate and the boys. They're shutting down the party." He walks toward the black mini fridge he has in the corner of the room and pulls out a bottle of water then walks up to me, popping the cap off. "Drink."

"I'm not thirsty."

"Drink the water, Madison. You look like you're about to drop into a coma."

I take it from him. "Thanks." I sip the cool water, letting it soothe my dry mouth and throat. Jesus, I need to go to bed. My eyes stay on Bishop's as I take another drink. His mouth opens to say something but is interrupted when the door slides open, showing Nate, Hunter, Brantley, and Saint.

Nate stops at the threshold, eyeing both Bishop and me before a sly grin comes onto his mouth. "Interrupting?"

I roll my eyes, but Bishop ignores him. They all step inside, closing the door behind themselves. Nate walks toward me, pulling me into his arms. I look down at his white tee and scowl. "Jeez, Nate," I murmur into his shirt. It smells of his cologne and Tatum's perfume. "Leave my friends alone."

"Hey!" He feigns innocence, dragging me toward the large sofa and pulling me down beside him. Tucking me under his arm, he grins. "She was all over my dick, and she's hot."

I pinch his arm. "Leave my friends alone. The last thing I need is them not wanting to hang with me because my slut stepbrother can't keep his dick in one hole for longer than twenty-four hours."

He pauses, his mouth hanging open, but collects himself quickly with one of his sly smirks. "Well, now, that's not fair. I've been known to hit it more than once."

"No, you haven't," Hunter scoffs at him.

"Ah-ha!" I point to Nate, his mouth open again and his eyes narrow on Hunter.

"Why are we even here?" He changes the subject by looking back to Bishop.

"We need to talk about the pick-up." Bishop leans forward.

"You got there. So what's the issue?" Nate asks. I thought Bishop called him in the car, but I'm guessing it wasn't him. My eyes start to get heavy, so I press into Nate more, tucking myself under his arm. Their chatting drifts off into the back of my brain as sleep slowly takes over.

I wake to someone carrying me, and the chilly outside air skimming over my cheek. "Nate?"

"Bishop." He pauses, and my arm hooks harder around his neck. "Nate had to leave. I'll take you home."

What? Nate had to leave? He left me here? *Piece of shit.*

"You don't need to." I clear my eyes as we get closer to Bishop's car.

"What? Would you rather sleep here?" I don't miss the laugh in his tone.

I pause. "You're right. Just put me down." He puts me back to my feet and pops open the door for me. I slide in, looking down at my phone, and I notice it's 4:00 a.m. The sun is sure to come out soon. Bishop slips into his seat and fires up the car.

"I was out for a couple hours."

"You were," he confirms, driving us out the long driveway.

"What did I miss?"

He chuckles. "Just Nate losing his shit."

"Do I want to know?"

He shakes his head. "Probably not, no." He takes the left onto my street, and I was correct; it's literally a two-minute drive from Bishop's. After pulling into our driveway, he stops at the front of my house.

I turn to him. "Why are there so many secrets?"

He looks at me sideways, his hand running over his upper lip. "In this world, secrets are weapons, kitty. It's what stands between us and six feet underground."

I chuckle lightly, clearing my throat while swiping my hair away from my face. "You say that like you live a different life."

His head tilts. "Not everything is as it seems."

"Hmm, cliché."

He grins. "Come on, I'll walk you in. Nate said your dad will be back on Monday?"

"Yeah." I clear my throat and get out of the car. "I almost forgot. I've only been at this school for a week and it feels like a month."

He laughs, taking my hand and walking me to the front door. "You say that like it's a bad thing."

"It's a confusing thing."

He nods, pushing the front door open and displaying the littered floor. Red cups are scattered everywhere. "Well, luckily I have a cleaner on speed dial."

Bishop closes the door, and I make my way up the stairs. "You don't have to walk me up."

"Yeah, pretty sure I do." Cryptic again. Nice.

"Why are you being nice to me all of a sudden?" I ask, hitting the top of the stairs. I stroll toward my room, with him close behind. I walk in then drop to my bed, and he follows, kicking the door shut behind him.

"It's not for you."

"Oh, and just when I thought we were getting along."

He shrugs. "I'm not doing it for you."

I don't know why, but that hurts. Because I'm stupid, that's why. I swallow, my throat swollen and hoarse. "You can leave then."

"If I said it was for you—" He walks toward my balcony door and looks out the curtain. "—would you say stay?"

I turn toward him, my hair sprawling out underneath me. "I don't know. I don't think so. Why are you looking out my door?"

"Why do you ask so many fucking questions?" he shoots back, stepping away from the door.

"You can leave," I repeat.

"I'll leave when Nate gets here."

"That could be two minutes, or it could be days. Depending on how many women he's found."

Bishop drops down onto the chair that sits beside my bed, his legs spread out and his finger running over his upper lip. His eyes rake over my body in a way that makes my heartbeat speed up and butterflies erupt.

"We could make this more fun?" He grins.

My mouth snaps shut. "You confuse me. I thought you hated me." I roll my eyes, kick off my shoes, and then get to my feet. Dying to get out of this damn dress, I walk into my closet, closing the door slightly, and reach for my zipper. Then I laugh under my breath. "Of fucking course." Peeking around the door, I smile at Bishop. "Can you help me?"

He doesn't say anything, just gets to his feet and walks toward me. Turning around, I scoop my hair out of the way and close my eyes. He takes the zipper and slides it down slowly, his rough knuckles skimming over my spine in the progress. Pulling my bottom lip into my mouth, I bite down hard to try to distract myself from the amazing feel of his skin on mine.

"Thanks," I whisper breathlessly once he's hit the bottom of my dress. I let the straps fall off my shoulders and then shimmy it down to pool at my feet. Laughing, I spin around, ready to tell him to get out, but as soon as his eyes lock onto mine, his arm wraps around my waist, and he pulls me into him. His lips smash against mine, and all oxygen and sense leave at his invasion. I fight it at first, confusion cloaking me, until he walks me backward and my back smashes against the wall, our kiss never breaking.

I open my mouth, allowing his tongue to slip in. He licks the inside of my mouth skillfully, expertly, enough to blow my fucking mind, and that's when I tap out and my hormones take charge. I wrap my hands around the back of his tanned, muscled neck, my tongue caressing his gently. He groans into my mouth while his hands clench around my upper thighs and lift me off the ground. I squeeze my legs around his waist as his hands come up to either side of my face, while his groin pushes me harder against the wall. *Shit*. I feel my stomach clench with unease and uncertainty, fueled by fire. Pure, hot, untouched, and lit-the-fuck-up fire.

His tongue slides across my bottom lip before he sucks it into his mouth and bites down on it roughly, pulling on it until it pops out of his mouth. He looks at me, his dark green eyes searching both of mine. "Fuck." He stops, looking down to my mouth and then back to my eyes.

"Don't." I shake my head. "Don't think about it." *What the hell am I saying?* I circle the back of his neck like a needy fucking cat would caress its owner to get attention. *Jesus, I need help.*

He groans again, shutting his eyes. "We had a rule."

"A rule?" I bait, my head tilting.

"Yeah. Actually, more like a pact."

"This pact." I gesture with my fingers. "Does it involve me?"

He looks at me. "Don't try to be cute, Madison. You know damn well it involves you."

"What is it?"

"Fuck," he whispers. "There's so much you don't fucking know, and you *won't* fucking know. This is already thin ice we're walking on."

I look into his eyes, studying them. The way his dark green eyes have an even darker ring around the lighter color, and how his tanned skin glistens under my dim closet light. How his lips are slightly plump, delicious, and enough to make you fight a strong inner urge to bite down on them. Or his damn just-fucked hair. Bishop is intense and drop-dead gorgeous, but has an air of danger that hovers over him—and his damn Maserati. If that isn't enough to fuck with your morals, the fact he's an unattainable asshole would.

I grind over him slightly, lean down to his ear, and whisper, "Then we'll *run*." I lean back, seeing the shift in his eyes. Shit, I might still be drunk, but there's—

His lips smash back onto mine as he lifts me off the wall and walks me into the room. His palm skims down my spine until it gets to my bra clasp, and then he flicks it off with one simple twist of his wrist. Spinning me around, he throws me onto my bed, with nothing covering me expect for my lace panties.

He tilts his head as he pulls off his shirt. "You a virgin? And be honest."

"Does it matter?"

He shrugs. "Not really. But answer the question, because I don't feel like being gentle." He throws his shirt onto the ground while walking up to me, a smirk plastered on his mouth. A mouth I want to chew on, and a chest I want to scratch. Running my eyes up his beautiful body, every muscle trained, every single inch of Bishop Vincent Hayes is perfect. If I weren't so horny, I'd want to punch him for being so flawless.

My eyes lock onto his as I smile sweetly. Shaking my head slowly, I mouth, "I'm not."

"Fuck." He loosens his belt and crawls up the bed with it dangling off his loose ripped jeans. Each crawl he takes toward me, I lie back farther onto my back, until eventually he's hovering over me. Gripping onto my wrists, he slams them above my head, his legs coming between mine to stretch them wider. I close my eyes briefly, inhaling his scent as his flesh gently rubs over mine. He drops his lips down to mine, and as soon as his tongue dives into my mouth, I suck on it and twirl my tongue around him. He groans again, pulling back and running his tongue over my jaw.

"Shit," I whisper, the way his smooth tongue and kisses are trailing over my sensitive flesh becoming overwhelming. Dragging his tongue down, he pulls my nipple into his mouth until the cool air is replaced with warm, needy saliva. My back arches into him, and his grip around my wrists above my head tightens.

"Keep still."

Jesus, what? I loosen, attempting to harbor my breathing, but failing because of the trickery his tongue is playing with my nipple. He drags it down the flesh of my breast, dipping it into my sternum. Licking lower, he looks up at me from below as he sucks all over my flat stomach, until he reaches the elastic of my panties. His other hand comes down and tears them off, flicking them across the room. He leans back and stares at me intensely.

I squirm silently. I'm not that shy when it comes to sex, and I've only had it a couple of times. My first time doesn't count, but the only other guy I've ever had sex with was a guy from my last school. We were together for three months. I had no friends, as usual, but he took me under his wing anyway, introduced me to the football team. None of the girls liked me. I wasn't a cheerleader and wasn't on the same social level as Jacob, so in their eyes, I was nowhere near good enough for him. We were together for those awesome three months and were quite sexually active. Until I found him in bed with Stacey Chance, the biggest slut of the school. It ended instantly.

But the way Bishop is staring at me, down there, has me fighting to squirm.

"Damn." He licks his bottom lip, and my eyes blaze open, landing on his instantly. "That right there is the sexiest little pussy I've ever seen." *Oh, Jesus.* His dirty words shouldn't turn me on, but they do. He drops his head forward while his eyes stay on mine. "Keep your eyes open, kitty," he growls from between my thighs, the vibration shaking my clit. Then he presses his tongue against my folds, circling my entrance slowly, then looks down to what he's doing before running his tongue up my slit, finding my clit.

My chest rises and falls as my breathing rattles, and my eyes fight to stay open. I keep them on him and watch as his lips wrap around my clit, cloaking me with his warm, needy mouth. "Oh shit," I whisper, my pussy clenching, tingling, aching, and pleading for him to go harder and faster, but he doesn't. He kisses me down there, and then drags his tongue back down to my opening, slipping it inside before hitting my neediest spot. My head swings back as my hands curl into his hair and my hips rise, grinding against his face. Moaning, I lick my lips as my grip tightens, but then it's gone, and all I'm left with is the cold air brushing over where his mouth was.

I look back down at him, wondering what the fuck caused him to stop. He swings my leg over so I'm on all fours, slaps my ass, and pulls his cock out. "I told you to keep your eyes on me." I peek at him over my shoulder, hiding my smile. He grins at me, pumping his sexy, thick length, his eyes rolling to the back of his head sensually before coming back to mine, this time with dark undiluted heat. "Bad kitty."

I think I bit off more than I could chew with Bishop. He slaps my ass again, this time harder, the sting belting across my sensitive cheek. "Ouch!" I squeal, my back arching and my ass pushing against his cock. He wraps his hands around my sharp hipbones, the tip of him lining up against my channel. Running his hand over my tailbone before going up my spine, he eventually rests his hand on the back of my neck. He squeezes it tightly and then sinks into me. I squirm at the invasion of his length, allowing myself to slowly open for him, clenching around him. "Fuck, you're tight."

Once he's in me, I push back against him. "Harder."

He pulls back and then slams into me. A loud moan escapes me at the feel of his tip hitting my cervix. Arching my back, he wraps my hair around his wrist, tugging on it until my head bends backward. He wraps his other hand around the front of my throat, his cock continuing its brutal assault on my pussy. He runs his tongue down my temple, his grip around my throat tightening. His other hand comes down between my legs, and I moan again as his thumb presses circles against my clit. My thighs clench, my stomach filled with heat so hot it could be lit in blue, and then I explode around him, my body wracking, my vision shaking so badly colorful dots dance around my room. He pulls out, flips my sweaty body around, and then lies on top of me, his heavy body pressing mine into the bed.

"Fuck," I whisper hoarsely.

"Yeah, babe, you just got fucked." He runs his nose down from my forehead, over my nose, and then his mouth drops onto mine, leaving the taste of myself on the back of my throat. He squeezes my breast, his legs opening me wide, his thick cock rubbing over my clit as he grinds into me in slow circles, slowly working my body up again. His hand comes to my inner thigh as he stretches me wide before slipping inside of me. His mouth comes back to mine, his tongue clashing, rubbing, and licking everywhere. Owning every single inch of me without being too much.

He groans, pulling back and then slamming into me again, my boobs bouncing and my head smashing against the headboard as he rides my body like a wave. His hand comes to my throat as his other comes to my hair, wrapping it around his fist and tugging on it. That sets me off even more as I push up, meeting his every thrust. He grinds himself back into me, all while his mouth never leaves mine, his tongue not stopping its intense caresses. His pelvic bone hits my clit every time he descends back inside me. Picking up his pace, he pounds into me harder until I'm screaming his name through my sore throat and I'm exploding all over him again, his cock pulsing its release. I grind against him, milking every single drop of him. A side of me, a side I haven't ever opened before, wants to fuck the soul out of him.

He drops down on top of me, his lips brushing over the side of my slippery neck. My eyes slowly shut as I turn, taking the sheet with me, and lay into his arms, where I fall asleep.

CHAPTER 16

"Madi!" Tatum waves in front of my face as I close my locker.

"Oh, what?" I ask, locking it and tucking my books under my arm.

"I said, did your dad know about the party when he got home this morning?"

We head down the hallway on our way to English. It's the only class Tatum and I share together.

"Um, no," I answer, trying to avoid her eyes. "Truthfully, Dad wouldn't care. As long as we stay away from his liquor cabinet and my gun cabinet, we're good."

"Oh!" Tatum replies, running her hand through her hair. "So how was the rest of your night, anyway? I haven't seen you since Bishop whisked you off in his car and you avoided my texts all weekend. Did I do something wrong?"

Huh, what? I stop outside our next class. "Why would you have done something wrong?"

A guilty flush flashes over her face and recognition comes to me. "You and Nate."

"I mean..." she corrects, "we sort of...."

"*What?*" I whisper-yell, gripping onto her arm and dragging her to a private corner. "You did not."

She nods, a puppy-like smile on her face. "I did."

"Tatum...."

Her hand comes to my arm. "It's okay, Madi. I know who Nate is. I'm not stupid. I wanted to get rid of it, and he was obviously the perfect guy to do it with."

My eyes narrow. "Yeah, I wouldn't be so sure of that, T."

She waves my comment away. "Oh please, I know I'm just another notch on his belt. It's fine. It's why I chose him."

I relax a little, yet not enough to trust what she's saying. Not that I know anything about good—or halfway decent—first times. We start walking back to class.

"Anyway..." She grins. "...so what happened with you?"

What happened with me? Oh you know, got fucked seven ways from Sunday, and then the said person who did all the fucking left in the middle of the night and I haven't heard from him since.

"Nothing."

We walk into class and drop down into two of the back desks.

Lunch bell rings, and I gather up my books, tucking my hair behind my ear as I walk toward the door, when Ally shoulder barges me. "Oops." Her hand comes up to her mouth, hiding her grin. "So sorry, I thought they took the trash out early today." She looks to Lauren, and they both laugh, flicking their hair behind their shoulders.

"Wow," I say flatly. "Didn't think I could think any lower of you, but it turns out your lack of creativity when it comes to comebacks changed my mind." Then I turn and leave them with their lips curled and their scowls carved into their faces.

"Hey!" Ally halts me. I stop just short of the door, and Mrs. Robinson stops stacking her paperwork on her desk. "Bishop is mine."

I laugh. "You can have him." When I finally leave, I walk out the door and toward my locker. Punching in my code, I slide my books in, obviously in a huff. I shouldn't let Ally wind me up, but I do. I let her get to me, which isn't a good sign. It means I'm starting to feel for the people I keep around me. *Hello, Bishop.*

"Hey." A voice from behind me stops my deep breathing, but it's not the voice I want to hear.

"Carter, hey!" I close my locker and start toward the entry to the cafeteria.

He follows closely behind me. "Hey, I wanted to talk to you about that kiss."

And I want to laugh. That kiss had long since been replaced and stolen and then shattered into tiny little shards of nothingness by Bishop.

"We really don't need to go there," I assure him, brushing it off as we enter the lunchroom. I'm not deluded. I know how exclusive Bishop is, and I know he doesn't just sleep with and get with just anyone—well, so I've been told—plus, I know I'm nothing special. But being left cold while you're sleeping is a whole new level of rejection. *Asshole.*

Thinking about it just makes me mad, and instinctively, I lean into Carter. Not to spite Bishop, because I know he won't care, but to seek comfort in someone who maybe does want me. No, I couldn't do that. Squashing my thoughts, I grab a tray.

"So what do you think?" he asks as we get in line.

"About?" I raise an eyebrow, putting an apple and a salad onto my tray.

"About camping. We're all thinking of hitting the mountains for Halloween."

"Oh," I say, suddenly interested. I love camping and the outdoors as much as I enjoy recreational sports. "When?"

He loads up his plate, smiling at me as he tosses a carrot stick into his mouth, his two dimples popping in his cheeks. He's cute; I could do a lot worse where rebounds are concerned, but at the same time, I don't want to lead him on, because truthfully, I'm not interested in jumping into anything sexual or even halfway serious with Carter. Bishop was a wake-up call. Our one-night stand set off the alarm in my head.

"Who will be coming?" I continue, coming to the end of the table and taking a bottle of water.

"Pauly and Alias will be coming, with their girls, but you could bring Tatum if you want."

I take a bite of my apple, my eyes going over his shoulder and landing on Bishop and the rest of the guys that are there, Nate included.

"One problem," I interject, squirming under the daggers Bishop is aiming at me. "My aggro stepbrother and his pack of hounds? They won't let me out of their sight." *Please let this go. Please let this go...* I chant my prayer, hoping he'll tell me to forget it.

No such luck.

He shrugs. "It'll be a party."

I look over his shoulder again, catching Ally on Bishop's lap and playing with his hair. But his eyes are still on mine, boring holes into me.

"Good." I smile sweetly, looking directly at Bishop. "It should be fun." Two can play this game. I know I have no right to get angry or upset about him and Ally, but I'd be lying if I said it didn't sting a little seeing her so cozy on his lap—and him doing nothing to move her. But I'm not naïve enough to say we had a connection and that we were deeply into each other now. This isn't a fairy tale, and that's just not how things go. At least not for me, anyway.

"So when is it?" I ask, looking back to Carter and letting him lead me to the table where Tatum is sitting.

"Next weekend." He surprises me by sitting beside us at the table, a couple of his friends who were waiting for him at theirs following suit, scattering themselves around our group.

"What's next weekend?" Tatum asks, peeling off her yogurt lid.

"Camping!" I answer her cheerfully, knowing full well she's going to scold me.

She kicks me under the table. "Great! Should be fun."

I laugh, taking another bite out of my apple, and go back to ignoring Bishop. That is, until Nate comes to our table, leaning down and grinning at me, right before winking at Tatum. "Hey, sis, you need a ride after school?"

I nod happily, wiping my mouth. "Yeah, thanks." He nods too, a small smile coming onto his mouth, and then he goes to push off the table and walk away. "Wait!" I holler, and he stops, turning back to face me. Nudging my thumb to Carter, I say, "Carter invited us to this camping trip this weekend. You wanna come with?"

"What, you think you can take my new baby sister without me, fucker?" Nate grins at Carter, but the grin isn't the playful one Nate usually displays. This one is edgy, filled with warning bells and sirens. Nate continues to walk backward. "Of course we'll be there." Then he turns and goes back to where he was. Great. I could cut the tension in the air between these two.

I look at Carter, searching his eyes. "Hey," I prompt, shoving his arm. I can't be mad at Carter. He's done nothing but make me feel wanted every time he's around me. He looks back at me, his frown slowly disappearing. "You okay?"

He smiles. "Of course."

"Is there something I should know between you guys?" I search his eyes, his breath a mere centimeter away from me. If he leaned forward, he could kiss me. *Please don't.* I like Carter, but I think I've put him in the friend zone without knowing it.

"Yeah," he whispers, his eyes falling onto my lips.

Oh no. Oh no, oh no.

Standing to my feet quickly, I tell him, "Great!" and pick up my tray.

"You didn't eat much." He points down to my food, and I pause, looking back up to Bishop to see Ally sitting beside him now, not on him. Progress, I suppose, but I still hate him. I drag my eyes away from Bishop and smile down at Carter. "Sort of lost my appetite." Then I take my tray and walk toward the doors, emptying my trash and placing it onto the table.

Tatum runs up behind me. "Hey!" She takes my hand but I pull away from her, picking up my run. I'm not used to being around so many people, or even so many people being interested in me and my life. It's all starting to overwhelm me, and I'm confused about Bishop and his mind games.

Why would he just leave? Was I not good enough?

Of course you weren't! You're a disgusting little girl who likes to do bad things.

My eyes shut as I attempt to push the ugly voice out of my head. It's been a long time since I've heard that voice, and I don't know what triggered hearing it today, but there it is. Opening my eyes, I see the bathrooms and run toward them, ignoring Tatum cursing behind me. My tears partly blind me, and the blue sign that shows it's the girls' bathroom looks all distorted and warped. I push through the door and fly into one of the stalls, slamming it closed and sliding the lock over. A second later, the door opens again.

"Madi?" Tatum whispers. "Can you talk to me?"

I've begun to like these people. Nate and Tatum, and maybe Hunter, anyway. I'm not sure about the rest of the Kings. Carter, too, he's not bad. But it's overwhelming. I've never had so many people show they give a fuck so much. I can't help but think this is all some sort of sick game. Why did Nate and Bishop take me that night? What did they mean when they said games, and why did they stop? Why? So many questions, it's making my head swim in confusion.

"Madi, talk to me, babe," Tatum whispers, leaning her head on the other side of the stall. "What happened?"

It's not Bishop and Ally who even triggered this, or triggered *the voice*. It's my own insecurities from my fucked up past. A past I've lived with on my own with fears of stressing my father out so close after my mother's death. But I blurt out Bishop anyway, because that's the easiest of the two to talk about, and it's believable.

"I slept with Bishop."

She sucks in a breath. "Well, I can't say I'm that surprised. So you're upset about him and Ally?"

Swallowing and swiping the tears from my cheeks, I lie, "A little."

I have to open up to someone, and if it's going to be anyone, it will be Tatum. She and I have hit it off since day one, regardless of our differences. She's become the yin to my yang, and above all, I trust her. Leaning forward, I flick the lock and the door opens to Tatum's worried face. She steps inside the small stall, closes the door, and then locks it again. Dropping to her knees, she ignores the filthy ground, which is so unlike Tatum, the clean freak, but it also shows how much of a loyal friend she is.

"She means nothing to Bishop, honey. But I should have warned you about him. He's never been exclusive to anyone except Khales." She pauses and then pats my knee. "Don't get me wrong," she says with a laugh, "there have been a few others since her, but they've all been socialites, dosed in fame. No one has ever come close to bedding him from this school, or even college. And when I say there has been some, I mean, like, two girls that I know of. Well"—she tilts her head—"that the paparazzi have shot him with."

"Paparazzi?" I question, a little horrified at why a paparazzi would take pictures of him.

"Well, aside from the girls he was with being famous, Bishop's mom is famous too."

"Huh," I huff, swiping away my final tears. "How so?"

She smiles, her lips pulling into her mouth. "Well, his dad is well respected in New York. They own most of the Upper East Side. Real estate market and all that. And his mom is Scarlett Blanc."

"Scarlett Blanc is his mom?"

Tatum nods. "Yeah. So as you can see...."

I do see. Scarlett Blanc is a very famous actress. "Interesting." My tears have long since dried.

"Was that all? There's nothing else causing this?" she asks.

I shake my head. "No, nothing else," I lie, because truthfully, I don't want her to know I care. I don't want anyone to know I care about how Bishop had Ally on his lap. That shows weakness, and I've never been good at showing vulnerability.

She takes my hand, pulling me up off the toilet seat. "Okay, so this is what we're going to do." She swipes the tears off my cheeks. "We're going to never cry about Bishop Vincent Hayes again. Deal?"

I laugh, nodding. "Deal."

We walk out of the bathroom, and Tatum turns to face me. "So Tillie wants to meet with us after school. Shall I catch a ride with you?"

I hitch up my books. "Yeah. I just have to head home and face Dad first, but you can come."

"First time home since you got here?" she asks, an eyebrow quirked. To other people, the absentness of our parents is probably a foreign thing, but with me and Tatum, it's all we've known. It's a part of the package, whether we like it or not.

"Yeah, not that that's the issue."

"What is?" she asks, as we walk down the long corridor.

"Just the fact he told me to keep Nate at arm's length for God knows what reason."

Tatum smiles. "The club, that's why. He would have heard all the stories, no doubt."

I scoff. "I doubt it. My dad isn't even from here. He's from New Orleans, anyway." I look toward the library longingly. "I'll see you after school." Then I power walk toward the library, leaving Tatum behind.

Swinging open the doors, I walk in and head straight toward where the book I picked up was.

"Madison?" the librarian, who I still haven't caught her name, prompts, standing from her chair. She looks to be around mid-to-late thirties and doesn't look like your typical cliché librarian. She's funky, young-looking, and vibrant. No pantyhose and glasses on this one, nope. She has naturally red hair, pale skin, and a light sprinkle of freckles under her bright green eyes. Her skin is something to envy; it looks like silk. I try not to get too envious as I battle down my third zit this week.

"Hi." I smile at her, clutching my books in my hand. "Sorry, I'm just going back to reading that book."

She shakes her head. "No need to apologize. But can I ask what your fascination is with that particular book?" She quirks one eyebrow and leans against the desk, crossing her legs in front of herself.

"Honestly?" I scoff. "I couldn't tell you. No idea."

She watches me carefully, as if she's trying to read between my words, and then exhales, her shoulders relaxing. "Go ahead. Just don't be late to class."

"Yes, ma'am," I answer, walking back toward the little corner in the library I was in a couple of days ago. Dumping my books on the table, I start scanning through all the old spines until I find the one I want. Exhaling out a long breath, I slip it out of its slot and walk back to my chair. The sun hits the old leather cover as I run the palm of my hand over it, over the circle emblem with the double infinity inside. *What is with this book?* Why do I feel so drawn to it, like a magnetic field? Shivers erupt over my spine as I flip it open, picking up where I left off.

2.

The Decision

The sweat trickled over my head as I pushed for what felt like the one-hundredth time. I squeezed my husband's hand, the hand I took when we said our vows, the hand I trusted with my life, my child's life. The hand that would ultimately be the death of me. The hand that would wrap around my neck like the perfect brace, as the eyes, the eyes I looked up to now, admiring, the love and my future, would be the last thing to close the devil's door in my death.

With all my might, I pushed harder, until I felt as though my pelvic bone was being yanked out of me, until I saw stars exploding in pain behind my shut lids, until my legs were convulsing and sweat drowned my flesh, until the little howl of my baby boy's cry reverberated around the cold atmosphere. Just as quickly as he arrived into this world, he was taken away. With a wrap of a blanket and a snip of the umbilical cord, my husband took my baby away from me.

My head fell back on my bed as the flames from the open fire pit flicked over my hot skin. Warm, sticky wetness slithered out from between my legs as my eyes began to drop, weaken. I opened them slowly, watching the flames as they flickered under the kettle that hung over it, warming the water. A dark shadow came over the side of my bed as my husband, cradling my son, looked down at me.

"This is the decision, wife. You know what this means for him, what our cause is."

I struggled to gather words, my mouth closing and opening as my tongue licked my upper mouth, seeking moisture. I nodded, knowing this was what had to happen. I had no say in the matter, and if I did disagree, there wasn't a lot I could do about it. So I nodded and watched as my husband and his three friends took my newborn son and laid him flat on the blank stone.

His piercing scream rippled through me and tears fell from my eyes. My husband took the small branding iron, laid it over the hot flame, and then walked back to my son. He pressed it onto his little upper arm. The scream turned violent, and my tears rippled through me as my heart broke. My husband wrapped him back up in his little blanket and then brought him back to me, placing him in my arms.

I cooed to my baby, moving up onto my elbows as one of our maids came rushing in, holding a warm bucket of water and rags. I rocked my baby, looking up to my husband with newfound hate, and then looked back down to my son, the Circle of Infinity now embossed into his innocent fresh skin.

The decision was made, and a new world order was about to begin.

Goose bumps break out over me.

"Madison? It's time for class, hon."

"Oh, okay." I shut the book and clutch it under my arm.

"I'm Miss Winters, just so you know next time you come in." She leans on one of the bookshelves.

"Will most likely be handy to know," I say, walking toward where I picked up the book.

She watches me carefully. Her mouth opens and then closes, as if she wants to say something. I pick up my books from the small table and smile at her. "Thanks for letting me slip in here real quick."

"No problem." She smiles weakly. I turn to walk out the door, when a word stops me. "Ten."

I turn around to face her. "Pardon?"

She clears her throat. "We close at 10:00 p.m. on Fridays. I mean, just the library and the gym. You have to access from the side door with your student ID card, but we're open until then."

She walks to where the titleless book is pushed in, her finger brushing over the spine. "Do you know why this book has no title?" she asks me softly, looking back to me.

I shake my head slowly. "No. I'm only up to chapter two."

She smiles. "Those aren't chapters, and this isn't a book."

Huh? Without wanting to sound like an idiot, I don't say anything at all, hoping she'll elaborate. She does.

"It's all myth and legend, old folklore." She smiles at me. "But this wasn't written to be a book. The women who wrote it...." She opens the first page, running her fingers over the fine cursive writing. Every stroke of the crow quill done with perfect precision. "She wasn't writing a book."

"What was she writing, then?" I clear my throat.

"Her suicide note."

CHAPTER 17

The rest of the day goes painfully slow. After that talk with Miss Winters, I left. I'm going to go back in there on Friday though. I want to read as much of that book as possible, even if it is a very long one. Or a suicide note, as Miss Winters said. That thought gives me the heebie-jeebies.

Suicide note? If it was her suicide note, then what is with her comments about her husband's hand wrapped around her throat? Maybe they just liked kinky sex. But even as my dry sense of humor tries to make light of an obviously very dark subject and situation, my heart sinks. I felt everything that the woman had written. I was there with her through the birth of her son, as if I was watching a live show. With thoughts of the book, which I've decided to name *The Book*, since it doesn't have a title, the final bell rings and school is over for the day.

Walking out my classroom, I'm making my way down the rowdy corridor, when Nate hooks his arm around me. "Hey, you."

"Hi." I smile up at him. I had forgotten all about Bishop and Ally, and now I'm reminded why I love books so much—the escape. "How was your day?"

He shrugs. "It's school. What do you expect?"

"Truth!" I say, letting him lead me down to the underground parking lot. "Ready to face your mom and my daddy dearest?"

He grins, slipping his aviators over his eyes. "Nope."

I stop. "Crap! I forgot. Tatum is coming with us."

Nate shrugs. "Text her and tell her to hurry up."

"Is this going to be weird?" I ask him with skeptical eyes.

"What, 'cause I fucked her?"

"Well, yes."

"No." He watches me and then exhales, walking up and lacing his hands with mine. "I promise it's not weird. I'm used to clingy. I know how to handle girls like Tatum."

I scoff, reaching into my pocket to get my phone out. "Oh," I grunt, punching in a quick text to her. "I'm not worried about Tatum, trust me." His smile drops. I roll my eyes. How can he be offended by that? But then it's Nate. Under the tough, bad-boy exterior, he has a very large ego. Shocker. He cares about himself, so me insinuating that Tatum isn't interested hurt his little feelings. Hitting Send on her text, I clarify, "What I mean is that she's not clinging. She used you like you did her."

Tatum texts back almost instantly, saying she'll meet me at my place.

Nate laughs freely, brushing me off. "See? Perfect. Maybe I should hit it again if she understands the deal."

I nudge my head. "First of all, no. Leave her alone. Second of all, she'll meet us at home."

"Do I need to have the talk with you about my friends?" He looks at me under his arm as we start walking toward the elevator that leads to his vehicle.

I scoff. "No, definitely not."

Because it's too late.

CHAPTER 18

You know that part in movies where you see the two toddlers who got caught drawing on the walls, or cutting up their mother's new Egyptian cotton sheets, sitting on the sofa, attempting to look innocent as their parents sit opposite them, disappointed and deciding what they're going to do as punishment?

Yeah, Nate and I are the toddlers right now.

"Madi?" my father asks, looking down at Nate's arm that is snaked around my waist casually as we sit on the L-shaped couch. I shuffle anxiously, not liking the way my dad's obviously uncomfortable with Nate's arm around me.

"Hmm? Yes?" I decide to aim for innocence. Innocence always works with my dad. He actually thinks I'm naïve and probably thinks I'm still a virgin. Technically speaking, that wouldn't be a hard thing to admit when you're seventeen, but not all girls have my life or *had* my life.

Elena exhales, standing from the leather couch. "Michael, it's fine. They're kids. It's what they do." She pauses. "At least they get along enough to throw a party."

I honestly didn't think my dad would mind, not that I've ever thrown a party before, but he's an absent-ish parent. I'm almost certain his punishment card is void. He punched that ticket when he left me the week of my fifth birthday.

Dad gets up from the couch, his eyebrows drawn in and the wrinkles around his eyes deep. He looks to Nate. "No more." Then he disappears down the hallway with Elena on his trail.

"Whoa!" Nate laughs, leaning back on the couch and tilting his cap lower to hide his eyes.

"Whoa?" I whisper-hiss. "Are you kidding me?" I elbow him and get off the couch. "This is your fault."

He chuckles, the unfazed asshole that Nate is. "I'll take that."

"Nate!" I pinch his arm.

"Ouch!" He whacks his hat up higher until his eyes zero in on me. "What?"

"You were supposed to take care of the garbage bins!"

"No." He shakes his head. "I specifically remember doing them. Me and Tatum went around...." He trails off, his eyes gazing off into the distance.

"Hmm? You and Tatum went around where?" I tap my foot in frustration.

Nate laughs. "Okay, I'm sorry!" He gets up off the sofa, wrapping his arm around me and pulling me into his body.

I fight against his hard chest for a second before giving up with a huff, melting into his arms. "Don't do that again. We had a plan, and if we want any freedom around here, we need to stick to the plan."

"Yeah." His voice vibrates against my cheek, his sweet cologne hitting my nostrils. "But we don't need to throw parties here anyway. We have Brantley's house."

"Brantley doesn't like me very much, and it doesn't matter. I shouldn't be attending parties."

"Brantley doesn't *not* like you."

"Oh, really?" I step away from his embrace, just enough to be able to see his face but still be in his arms. "The man's lip is curled at me constantly. I think he hates me more than Bishop does."

Nate's arm tightens around me. "Bishop doesn't hate you."

"I'm pretty sure he does. In fact, I don't think any of your pack are entirely happy about my existence."

"They just don't know you."

"You all kidnapped me. They'd be fucking lucky to know me, which, by the way, why am I hugging you? I'm still pissed about that." I push out of his embrace, only for him to tighten his grip. He hooks his finger under my chin and tilts my head up so I'm facing him. His eyes search mine, his lips so close that if I inched forward, we'd be kissing.

"You don't get a say in what happened that night." He's serious, and that makes me nervous. I've never seen Nate like this often. "I'm serious, Madi. We didn't and don't have much choice, except for probably Bishop."

"Why do *you* like me?" I ask. He narrows his eyes. "I mean," I whisper, my eyes dropping to his mouth, "you didn't have to like me. We're stepsiblings. We should hate each other."

He inches forward, his arm clenching around my waist, pulling me in closer so I can feel his hard erection pressing into my tummy. He drops his lips softly, so they're brushing over mine. "It was either I warm up to you..." He grins against my lips, but I don't move. I should move; if I was smart, I'd move. But I've not been very smart lately. "Or I fuck you." He sucks my bottom lip into his mouth.

Just as he's about to pull away, I grip onto the back of his neck and pull him into me until I'm kissing him. I open my mouth and let his tongue slide in. *Nate has his tongue pierced?* The ball of his piercing glides over my tongue expertly, and holy hell, he's a great kisser. He pushes my body down onto the sofa with his until my back hits the soft cushions. I inch my legs open until his knee is resting in between mine, not breaking the kiss. He tilts his head, giving me more access, and I lick his tongue, pulling it into my mouth while sucking on it.

"Madi, we're going out for dinner tonight!" My father's distant yell is like a bucket of ice-cold water. Nate and I both pull back, my hand coming up to my mouth and his eyes wide on mine, both of us in shock. I push him off me, and we both land on our feet just as my dad walks into the living room, doing up his cufflinks. "You'll both come."

"Sorry," Nate deadpans. "I have plans tonight." Then he looks to me. "And weren't you saying that Tatum is coming over?"

I look between Nate and my dad nervously. "Yeah, but I can cancel."

Nate looks at me with widened eyes. I widen mine back, because he's being rude. I know my dad is blunt, but that's how he has always been, and he may not be a great father, but he's always tried. "Good. It's settled. I'll meet you both out in the car in half an hour."

Half an hour later, Nate and I are both in the back of my dad's Range Rover, both scowling at each other, and neither has spoken since "the mistake." I would call it the kiss, but mistake sounds more fitting. Nate is dressed in casual dark jeans, a polo shirt, and black boots. I'm casual like him too, but not quite able to get away with jeans. I decided on a pant jumpsuit. It's black and plain, but has two slight slits on either side of my ribcage, showing a whisper of skin. It's one of the many clothes I have in my closet that I don't particularly like wearing, but because of status, I have to own it in case, I don't know... my dad decides to spring it on me that he's taking us out to The Plaines, the most elite restaurant there is on this side of town. I only know this, because when I texted Tatum to tell her I couldn't do tonight and that she and Tillie were on their own, she told me so. Right after cursing me out.

"So, Madison, how has school been?" Elena asks from the passenger seat.

"It's been good."

"Madi has settled right in." Nate smirks from his seat. "Haven't you, sis?"

The fact the same lips I was just kissing called me sis makes me gag. The hell was I thinking? My father looks at me in the rearview mirror.

"Yeah, I've found one or two great friends."

My phone vibrates in my pocket as Elena shoots her questions at Nate. I slide my phone unlocked.

Bishop – *we need to talk.*

Is he serious?

Me – *We really don't.*
Bishop – *I'm not Nate, Madison. I don't just stick my dick in every girl I see. We. Need. To. Talk.*
Me – *The way Ally paws at you, you could have fooled me.*
Bishop – *Jealous?*
Me – *No. And no, I don't want to or need to talk. Just forget it happened. I'm pretty much with Carter now.*

Lies. Why the fuck did I just say that? It's the year 2017. We have drones, cars that can go in water, and men who walk on the moon. Why the hell haven't they figured out how to unsend a text message? I don't know who "they" are, but I'm blaming it on Apple.

Bishop – *Careful, kitty...*

I roll my eyes and push my phone back into my pocket. Nate's leg nudges mine, and I look up at him, the passing streetlights illuminating his sharp features. "What?" I ask.

"Who was that?"

"No one."

I look out the window, ignoring his gaze. How is it that, in a matter of weeks, I've woven this messy web? Suddenly, I'm wanting to be that new girl again, the one who was walking the halls for the first time ever.

"Dad?" I prompt, pressing my forehead against my cool window.

"Yeah?"

I exhale. "Can you fit in a round tomorrow before you leave?"

There's a long pause, and I close my eyes. If he says no, I might break. After everything that's happening around me, I want my dad with me, shooting like we used to. I need it to bring me back down from whatever cloud I've drifted off on.

"Sure, baby girl." I exhale at his answer, my shoulders slacking and my stress already lifting somewhat.

Once we've pulled into the restaurant parking lot, I get out my side of the SUV and Elena looks at me. "For what it's worth, I'm glad you and Nate get along."

"I wouldn't exactly say get along."

"He cares about you," she assures, closing her door. "That counts for something, because Nate cares about very little. Apart from his friends."

I close my door and nod. "I guess we get along a little bit."

Elena smiles and hooks her arm into mine. "So tell me. You like guns?"

After a surprisingly normal dinner, we came home, and Nate left almost instantly. We hardly spoke through dinner, as though the mistake was already forgotten. Works for me, because it won't be happening again. There's a light knock on my door just as I'm about to get into my pajamas and start on my English paper.

"Come in!" I yell out, rummaging through my closet. It's still a mess from the party, and in other cases, I would be the first to clean it, but I've found myself more relaxed lately, sedated almost.

"Hey, sugar!" Tatum walks in, with Tillie following closely behind her.

"Hey!" I smile at both of them. "What are you two doing?"

"We thought we'd come see you, since you pulled a sicky on us and bailed." Tatum takes a seat on my bed, and Tillie slips onto the chair beside my white study desk.

"Yeah," I mutter, finding my tank top and pulling it on. "Sorry about that."

This is awkward; even though the mistake meant nothing to me, I don't know if it would mean anything to Tatum. She says that Nate was just a "nothing" to her, but don't we all say that?

"I brought my favorite friend." Tatum whips out a blue book-style box with gold trimming.

"No way!" I gush, walking toward her. "Debauve & Gallais's Le Livre?" I blurt out excitedly.

"Geez," Tatum mutters. "Your French is more immaculate than mine, and I lived there for a year."

I wave her off. "I've studied the language, and the culture, and in this case… the chocolates!" I open the gold-embossed leather box and inhale the sweet, rich smell of ganaches and pralines. "Mmm." I take one out. "I haven't had these in years."

Tatum looks toward Tillie and rolls her eyes. "Don't let this pig eat them all. Come taste."

Tillie swallows nervously and then steps toward us. I fight the urge to snatch the box and run away like a cavewoman.

"What's so great about it? It's just chocolate, right?" Tillie asks, picking up one of the pralines. I pause my chewing, narrowing my eyes. Insult chocolate, you should not. Especially Sulpice Debauve's fine work.

"Aside from the fact that you have to be on a waitlist to order a box and it's five-hundred or so dollars? Not much." Tatum shrugs.

Tillie blushes. "You guys are way too rich. I feel like the lost girl."

"You're not a lost girl. You're perfectly within your element with us."

Tillie smiles softly, tucking her hair behind her ear. "Yeah, I guess."

I lick the chocolate off the top of my mouth, looking at how Tillie has gone quiet. "What's wrong? Are you okay?"

She looks at me. "Yeah!" She smiles fakely. "Everything is fine. What are we doing this weekend?"

Tatum kicks off her shoes, and Tillie removes hers, shuffling beside Tatum. "I don't know. We've all, you included"—Tatum looks at Tillie—"have been invited to a campout with Madi's new man for Halloween."

"He's not my man," I say to Tillie.

"He's totally her man," Tatum retorts casually.

I shake my head and mouth "He's not" to Tillie.

"Anyway," Tatum interjects loudly. "I think we should do it."

"I don't know," I mutter, standing from my bed. I wanted to go camping for so long, but now that I know Carter has other feelings toward me, I'm a little scared he might get the wrong idea about my saying yes.

"What's there to not know about?" Tatum asks, wriggling up to my headboard and slipping under my covers. Her ash blonde hair is up in a perfect bow bun on the top of her head, and her face is fresh from makeup. She definitely has that deflowered glow about her. *Fucking Nate.*

"Lots!" I say, waving my hands in the air. Tillie scoots up beside Tatum and slips under with her, following the chocolates.

"Madi!" my dad yells from downstairs. I walk toward the girls, snatching the expensive box of chocolate from them, tucking it under my arm. I evil eye them, walking toward my door.

"Coming!" I yell back, opening my door. I turn around to face them and point my finger. "This conversation is not over."

Walking down the long stairwell, I see Dad is standing beside the opened front door. His face is blank, his jaw taut, and his eyes hard. *Oh no, now what have I done?*

"What's up, Daddy?" I coo, coming to the door. He looks outside and I follow his vision until I'm looking directly at Bishop, who is standing there in ripped jeans and a white T-shirt, with combat boots on his feet. My mouth waters, and it's not from the chocolates.

"Hi," I say to him, ignoring how his hair still looks damp and how relaxed his stance is. Both legs spread casually, his jaw tense, his eyes hard, but his mouth inching toward a smirk.

"I got this, Dad."

My dad stalls, looking to me and then to Bishop and then back to me. He kisses my forehead and then looks into my eyes. "We'll talk tomorrow."

Of course we will.

I smile. "Sure thing." I'm not looking forward to this chat.

"What are you doing here?" I ask Bishop, stepping outside into the dark night and closing the heavy wooden door behind myself. He steps backward and takes a seat on one of the steps. His car is parked directly in front of the stairs, and I'm even more annoyed at how distracted I must have been to not hear his car pull up.

"I told you," he says casually. "We need to talk." Ignoring the fact I'm in tiny little booty shorts and a tight tank that rides up my tummy, I take a seat beside him. Thank God my feet are covered by my socks. Bishop looks down to my feet. "Is that Banksy's work?"

"I'm shocked," I scoff sarcastically. "You know Banksy?"

"I know his artwork."

Trying not to look at him, I flip open the box of chocolates and sit them in the middle. "I can share."

I give in and look at his face, catching his eyes piercing into mine. His mouth is behind his shoulder and he's studying me like I'm the most important test in history.

When the silence becomes too much and my face feels like it's going to burst into flames, I pop a chocolate into my mouth. "What?"

He pauses and then shakes his head, looking ahead of himself by breaking our eye contact. I instantly miss his demanding glare. "You're different."

"I've been told that all my life," I snark. His jaw tenses. "Is that what you wanted to talk about?"

"You and Carter?" he counters.

"Are none of your business."

"Really?" He scoffs, swinging his attention back to me, and when his eyes lock onto mine, my breath catches at the intensity of it. "Pretty sure you made it my business the second you were screaming my name and clawing up my back."

"I don't scratch," I correct him casually, sucking the chocolate off my fingers.

His eyebrow quirks. "Sure about that, *kitty*? I can show you the marks if you want? Pretty sure they're still there."

"You don't get to ask about me and Carter when you had Ally on your lap." I keep the jealousy down, because that's exactly what I am. Jealous.

"Ally is nothing. It's what she's always done. She hangs around us like a fly does to shit. It's nothing, never has been. I thought you would know this, but then I forgot you were new."

"So if that's true, what? What did you want to talk about?"

He exhales. "I don't fucking know, Madi. Jesus."

"Call me when you figure it out." I go to stand, when his hand catches mine. I look at him and he stands, towering over me. "All I know is that I fucking hate when Carter has his hands on you, and I'm not familiar with this feeling." I'm guessing this is a shit time to bring up his ex, so I swallow my nosy questions.

"But?" I ask, because... I don't know why. I'm a girl with fully functioning lady parts, and Bishop is hotter than sin, and that's all I got.

"But this can't ever work, and I don't know what the fuck to do about it. I'm not used to not getting what I want."

"I see that."

He chuckles, his finger running down the side of my face. "Fuck, kitten, you have no idea the kind of crazy shit you have me feeling." His smile falls and his jaw tenses. "But we can't."

"Why?" I whisper, looking to his mouth. "Why can't this happen?"

"That's the shit part," he replies. "I can't even tell you why."

"Then you already know this discussion is over." I've come to realize there are secrets upon secrets, and no one is telling me anything. I've brought it down to it not being any of my business, but it's getting old real fast. I'm not one to pry into other people's business, but these secrets he, Nate, and the guys have are starting to itch at the back of my brain.

"Yeah," he replies, looking down at me and stepping backward. "I just wanted you to know that I wish it could've been different between us, and shit is about to get worse."

"Yeah," I whisper, as he walks back to his car and gets into the driver seat. "Me too."

I go back to my room, slamming my bedroom door to find the girls snuggled in my bed and watching Netflix. "We're fucking going camping."

CHAPTER 19

"I just want you to be careful, baby," Dad assures me, loading up his third round. He points toward the cutout target, then squeezes the trigger, emptying out.

I point toward mine, closing one eye and zoning in to the bull's-eye. I squeeze the trigger on the pistol and fire. The kickback isn't as bad as it should be with someone light like me firing a Desert Eagle, but it's Daddy's, and he's had me shooting this since I started out. It may sound dangerous to some people, but our home has always been a strong advocate at exercising our second amendment rights, and aside from that, we love to hunt deer. I don't own a pistol; I own shotguns, and use them often.

"I'll be fine, Daddy."

He looks at me worriedly, and we both remove our protective glasses, waiting for our targets to come up. "I don't like Nate and his friends."

I roll my eyes, unclipping my target man and seeing I shot within range. "Daddy, you don't like any boys."

"No." His tone changes, becoming stern. "Madison, I'm serious. I don't like those boys."

I take my grin away from my amazing shots and look toward Dad. He hardly ever uses that tone with me, and it sobers me some. "Okay, Dad, I'll be careful."

"Good." He smiles again and then looks at my target. "How'd you do?"

Walking into my bedroom after seeing Dad and Elena off again, I flop down onto my bed, mulling over my thoughts from today. After Bishop left last night, Tatum and Tillie ended up crashing in bed with me halfway through a *Sons of Anarchy* episode. Tatum was bored out of her brains during episode one, but Tillie and I wanted to watch it. My phone vibrates in my back pocket, and I slip it out, sliding it unlocked and answering. "Hello?"

"I'm almost home. Come out when I beep."

"Why?" I slowly rise from my bed.

"Because I'm back to babysitting duty, so you have to stay near me."

"Yeah…" I shake my head. "…about that. I don't think my dad actually put you on babysitting duty, Nate. The man doesn't like you very much."

"Fuck your dad," he mutters.

"Pardon?"

"Nothing. Get out of the house and come down when I beep, or I'll drag you down over my shoulder. And just so you know, Hunter and Brantley are here."

"Fine!" I blurt, hanging up my phone and tossing it onto my bed. I walk into my bathroom and let my hair trail down to my tailbone before shoving on a NY baseball cap. I'm still in my yoga pants and tight tank from shooting, but I slip out of my running shoes and put on a pair of Air Max 90s. I'm picking up my phone from the bed when Nate beeps from outside. Taking the steps two at a time, I walk out the front door and pause.

"I can sit in the back," I say to Brantley, as he gets out of the passenger seat of Nate's Ford Raptor. Brantley doesn't answer; he just slips into the back. "Or not," I mutter, stepping up on the running board and sliding into the seat.

"So you know how it's Halloween this weekend?" Nate grins as he pulls us out of the driveway.

"It is?" I ask sarcastically. "I didn't even realize."

"Yeah." Brantley smirks from the back. "It is."

I look to Nate. "So why am I here, anyway?"

"I told you." He looks to me, pulling down a street off ours. "I have to look after you." He pulls us into a long gravel driveway, up to an old southern-style-looking home. High ceilings, white pillars, the American flag flying proudly outside the front door.

"Do we all live down the same street?" I ask Nate.

Brantley grunts in the back, ripping off his seatbelt and getting out of the truck once we stop. I look to Nate nervously. "Nate, I don't really wanna be here if this is Brantley's house."

Hunter clears his throat from the back. "Don't worry about him."

I look to Hunter, shocked about him talking to me. "But I do worry."

Hunter rolls his eyes, taking off his belt and opening the door. "She's a lost cause if someone like Brantley scares her." Then he shuts the door and follows the way Brantley led toward the house.

I follow behind Nate as he leads us through the massive entry to the house and then downstairs into a bedroom. There's an entry door to the side that goes out to the swimming pool, and the whole back wall is floor-to-ceiling windows. I flop down on one of the single sofas in the corner of the room. Hunter and Nate slide open the door and walk out toward the pool, laughing. Fucking Nate, leaving me in here with Brantley. Brantley is brooding, over the top, and… silent. He's around six feet, dark hair, piercing dark eyes, and a sprinkle of stubble over his jaw. He's the definition of scruffy hot. Brantley leans on the door, looking out to Nate and Hunter.

Wanting to break the silence, my no-filter comes out in full effect. "Why do you hate me?"

He looks at me over his shoulder. "You're not a very likeable person."

"Really?" My eyebrow quirks. "And you think you know me well enough to make that assumption?"

He scoffs, pushing off the door and turning to face me, his arms crossed in front of his chest. "I don't have to know you to make that assumption. I've heard enough."

"You're a bit of a dick."

He looks directly at me, his eyes piercing into mine. I fight the need to squirm. "I've never claimed to be anything else, *kitty*."

"What did I do? Or what did you hear I did?"

"It's not what I heard," he says casually. "It's what I know."

"That makes no sense."

"You make no sense," he responds, walking toward me. He's wearing a dark shirt, loose jeans, and black boots. He stops directly in front of me, bringing both hands down to the armrests on either side of my chair, caging me in. Leaning down, his eyes go from my lips to my eyes and then back again. "You think because Bishop fucked you that you have a free pass?"

My heart launches in my chest, and surprise must spread over my face, because he laughs, a menacing tone in his chuckle.

"Oh what? You thought he actually wanted to fuck you?" He tilts his head and leans closer so his nose is touching mine, his lips a whisper away. I hold my breath. "Naw, kitty. That was all part of the plan." He inches forward, his lips brushing over mine. "Get you wet and needy, fuck you inside out, pretend that you meant more than an easy piece of ass." He pauses, searching my eyes. "'*I wish it didn't have to be this way,*'" Brantley mimics Bishop's last words to me from the other night.

My vision turns bleak. Everything in my peripheral turns black. "It was a trick?" I whisper, more to myself than to him.

Brantley laughs. "This is all a game, kitty. And you're in the middle of a very fucked-up board."

I snort sarcastically. "You think I care?" I brave myself to bring my eyes straight to his.

His narrow, dropping to my mouth. "Prove you don't."

"You hate me."

"I'll fuck you as hard as I hate you."

My eyes grow hooded as I run my tongue over my bottom lip. "I sort of have a boyfriend."

He laughs, his eyes still searching mine. Everything in the center of me kicks up to scorching levels. "Carter?" His hand flies up to my neck as he pushes my head back into the chair more. He tilts his face. "You and I both know he's too vanilla for the shit that goes on in your head." He pulls me up off the chair by my neck.

I match his stare. "Big words. All talk, no bite?" *What the hell am I doing?*

He laughs, the grip he has on my neck tightening, and then he pulls me into his mouth, catching my bottom lip between his teeth. He tugs on it roughly then slips his tongue into my mouth. I open it, angry at everyone. Angry at Nate, because I don't know if his caring about me is genuine. Angry at Bishop for using me like a toy. Angry at my-fucking-self for thinking Bishop was into me. *Just make it go away.*

I wrap my hands around the back of Brantley's neck, and his grip disappears from my throat as he pushes my hands away from his skin, picking me up from behind my thighs and throwing me onto the bed. He crawls up to me slowly, gripping my wrists and slamming them above my head.

"Brantley, Nate and Hunter will come back soon."

He smirks, his eyes darkening and his waist pinning me to the bed. "Yeah, sort of counting on it. I'm sure we can work out a roster."

"Not happening."

"You say it like you're the one in charge here?" he asks, running his finger down my sternum before coming back up to my throat.

He squeezes again, and my core clenches in response as my eyes roll to the back of my head. "Yeah."

His mouth drops to the side of my neck, his legs coming between mine, spreading me wide. "You like that shit, huh?" *I do.* He grinds into me, his hardness pushing against my sex.

Make it go away.

"Interrupting?" A voice breaks our embrace, but Brantley stays there, looking down at me, and then grins.

"Depends," he says, looking over his shoulder at Bishop, who just walked in the room. "Care to join? Wouldn't be the first time we've shared."

Bishop stays silent, so I inch up onto my elbows to look at him.

He looks at me and smirks. "Naw, I'm good. I've already had her. I don't feel like shoving my dick in dirt for a second time."

"Ouch," I reply deadpan. It hurt more than I care to admit, but being told I was being used has somewhat numbed any pain afterward. I hate Bishop Hayes.

"Yo! Brantley has—" Nate walks into the room, speaking directly to Bishop, when he sees me and Brantley on the bed. He rolls his eyes. "Get off her, dawg."

"What if I don't want him to get off?" I snap. If I'm dirt and mean less than nothing to these boys, then what's the point of walking out with my dignity? "Or what, Nate?" I smirk at him. "Mad it's not your tongue down my throat?" Then I push off Brantley's chest, crawling out from under him toward the edge of the bed. "I'm leaving." I walk toward the door, straightening my tank.

"Oh, come on, sis. We're just playing."

"Fine, but find a new toy." I look to Bishop. "One that doesn't feel like you're *fucking* dirt." I pull open the bedroom door.

"You fucked her?" Nate barks at Bishop.

Oops, did I let that slip? My bad.

I walk out the front door and then break out in a jog. I know my house is only a five-minute walk, but I don't feel like talking to anyone right now, and I have a feeling Nate will try to chase me. Bishop, Nate, Hunter, and Brantley have already stirred shit with me. I don't even want to see what Saint, Ace, and Jase are capable of, what with them being the older brothers. It was all a game. Bishop pretending to give a fuck, they played me like a fucking fiddle.

CHAPTER 20

The next day, I'm sitting beside Carter in the cafeteria, when Tatum drops her bag beside me. "I fucking can't wait for Halloween this weekend."

"I can't believe we're doing it in the woods," I answer, taking a bite out of my apple.

Carter nudges my arm with his. "Leave your guns at home?"

"Maybe." I look up toward Bishop. "Or maybe not."

Carter follows my eyes. "Trouble?"

"You could say that," I mutter, dragging my eyes away from them. Ally walks across to their table, and I roll my eyes. Here we go. Only this time when she goes to lower herself onto Bishop's lap, he pushes her off, and she falls to the ground in a mess. Nate laughs, Brantley grins, Hunter barks out a hyena howl, and the rest of the boys snicker, watching her with distaste. Every single one of them are assholes. I don't like Ally, and I might even go as far as to say I hate her a little bit, but that proved there is not one redeeming quality in any of those boys. They're all assholes. Usually, there's at least one in a group who isn't. But not here and not them. I've tangled a web with the school bad boys, and now I have to unleash my claws to escape.

"What's going on with you guys?" Tatum asks, taking a swig of her water.

I shake my head. "Nothing."

"You locked Nate out of your room last night. That's not nothing."

"I don't like Nate very much right now."

Carter hooks his arm around my waist and pulls me into him. I know I should pull away. Nothing good will come from me leading him on. But I can't help it. Having someone who is interested in me makes me feel wanted. That's all a girl really wants, isn't it? To feel wanted?

"Hey." I turn to face him. "I'll drive out on Friday. I just need to do a couple things beforehand."

"I can come with you," Tatum adds.

I shake my head. "It's fine. I have Google maps or whatever. Just give me the details on where we're going and I'll meet you all out there."

Carter looks to me. "You sure?"

I nod. "Yeah, positive." He pulls out a piece of paper, squiggles down the directions, and then slips it across the table to me. "It's about an hour and a half drive inland. The conditions are rough. It's called The Myriad. It's a water hole and is literally in the middle of nowhere. You have to park your car and then follow the manmade trail into the forest. You'll see everyone's cars, so it should be fine, but you don't get cell phone service out there, so I'd suggest you take someone with you."

"Carter, I'll be fine."

"I don't know." Tatum chews her lip. "What about mountain lions?"

"This isn't my first camping trip. I have my dad's compass too. I'll be fine. I'm experienced in the forest like you are at shopping in Barney's."

"Okay, fine," she exhales. "Me and Tillie will meet you there."

The lunch bell rings and I gather up all my trash, placing it onto my tray.

"Madi!" Bishop yells out to me. I ignore him, but it's obvious I heard him as the whole cafeteria pretty much stops what they're doing. Tatum looks at me, but I ignore her too. Walking to the other side of the room, I dump my tray into the garbage and push through the doors.

Fuck him. `

My phone vibrates in my pocket just as I hit my next class.

Tillie – Hey, chica! Are we still on for this weekend? How are we dressing?

Right. Halloween. Between everything else, the drama with Bishop, camping, and wanting to keep reading *The Book*, I forgot about what we're dressing as for Halloween.

Me – Still a go! You'll ride with Tatum. Dress wise, I'm not sure. I'm guessing Tatum will want to go shopping. What're you doing after school?"
Tillie – Today?
Me – Yes.
Tillie – I can come.
Me – Okay, we'll pick you up from school.

I haven't been to Tillie's school before. Never had a reason to. But suddenly, I want to see it. There's so much to Tillie I still don't know, but she fits in with Tatum and me like the missing puzzle we need. The day goes slow, and I pass my science test, even though I didn't study for it. I'm walking out of class at the end of the day, when Tatum catches up to me, clutching her books and out of breath.

"Shit, bitch, slow down next time." She huffs.

I giggle. "Maybe we should start exercising."

We both pause and look at each other, then start laughing. "Maybe not."

I nudge her. "Hey, we have to pick up Tillie. She wants to go shopping for this weekend."

"Yes!" Tatum says, rolling her shoulders like she's gearing up for war.

I stop. "What? Now you want to exercise your shoulders?"

"Of course," she mutters. "Dad's black card is about to get a workout."

Walking out the front of the school, we wait for Sam to pick us up. Sam is my dad's other driver, but she's more my driver when Dad is away and takes Harry with him.

Since yesterday, I've ignored Nate and his wanting to give me rides to school. I have nothing really to say to them, and I don't trust any of them, even less since they kidnapped me. Which Tatum still doesn't know about.

We slide in, and Sam smiles at me in the rearview mirror. "Have a good day?"

I shrug. "Could have been better."

"But...," Sam prompts, knowing what I'm like. Sam has been our driver since as long as I can remember. She's a fifty-two-year-old African American woman who has practically raised me since I was a child. Her and Jimmy both did. Jimmy is almost sixty, and I've been trying to get them together for years. If you ask me, I'd say they've been sporting a bit of a crush on each other for years now, but neither of them wants to act on it.

Tatum interrupts, "But she has boy trouble."

"Oh," Sam quips, pulling out onto the street. "What kind? The kind I'll need a shovel and an alibi for, or the kind I should make pie and threaten to cut his balls off until *he* forgives *you* kind?"

I giggle and Tatum laughs. "No, neither. I don't want you making pies for any of them."

"You be careful, baby. I know you think you don't care and you shut all your feelings out, but one of these days, it could bite you in the ass."

"What?" I snort, leaning back in my seat. "Like I might start caring too much?"

Sam shakes her head. "No, baby girl, more like you might not be able to ever switch it back on. You're too young. Live, feel, have sex—don't tell your father I said that—but don't ever *not* feel. That's what makes you Madison."

"I feel, Sam," I whisper, looking out the window. I can see Tatum staring at me out the corner of my eye, no doubt brewing her hundred and one questions she's going to slam me with. "I just try to choose where I direct my energy and who deserves it." Sam knows about my past and what happened there. She's the only person walking this earth who knows, and that's how I like to keep it. The only reason she knows is because I came home drunk from a party one time and spilled everything to her.

"Hey." Tatum nudges me. "What's up with you spending so much time in the library anyway?"

"I don't know. I've always loved books."

"Nuh-uh," Tatum says. "There's something else."

Sam looks at me with a smile. "Madi has always liked books. We used to read her everything when she was a little girl, and she was reading chapter books when she turned six. Smart girl, in some aspects."

We pull up to the house and I slide out. "Thanks, Sam. Can you tell Jimmy that me, Tatum, and Tillie will be home for dinner tonight?"

"What about Nate?" Sam asks, just as I'm getting out of the car.

"Fuck Nate."

"Madison Maree Montgomery!"

"Oh, you did not just triple-M me, Sammy!" I spin back around to face her with a grin on my face as I walk backward toward the house. "You take that back!" Triple-M is my initials. I despise the fact that my name starts with an M all three times. I think it was my mom's way of punishing me just a little bit more. I used to joke about that when she was still alive, but now that she's dead, the thought just makes me feel guilty.

"Don't swear at me, little lady!" Sammy doesn't like swearing, and her hackles go up anytime someone cusses around her. That's probably why she and Jimmy never worked, because the Italian has a foul mouth. Which is one of the many reasons why

I've always loved him. He sometimes swears in Italian, and for a long time when I was younger, we would both swear in Italian around Sam so she didn't know. *"Scopare questa merda!"* Sammy wouldn't know what the hell we were talking about. It was funny.

I walk inside with Tatum on my tail, and head into the kitchen, opening the side cupboard to get out the car keys. I take the GMC keys, and we both walk out to the garage.

"You know...," Tatum starts, as we both slip into our seats. "How was Bishop in bed?"

I laugh, firing the car up. "I don't kiss and tell, Tate."

"Ohh, sure you do."

I shake my head and laugh, pulling out of the long driveway. "I really don't."

Pulling up to the curb of Hampton Beach High, Tatum whispers, "I haven't been here in a while."

"It's not that bad. I expected a little more on the rough side."

Tatum shakes her head. "The people are a lot on the rough side, though."

Tillie comes walking out of the front gate, clutching her backpack, with another guy walking beside her.

"Hotness at four o'clock," Tatum announces, eyeing up Tillie's friend.

I shove her. "Don't be a gawker." But then I run my eyes up and down his body. "Totally hot though." He has a shaved head, tattoos mapping out all over his neck and arms. His dark eyes and olive skin have me thinking that he's a little Spanish? Maybe? But then again, he has fair features. Sharp nose, a jaw that could match Bishop's.

"You just told me not to gawk, and then you go and drool all over the center console?" Tatum shoves me.

Tillie opens the back door and cranks down her window. "Girls, this is my friend Ridge, who is annoying, by the way," she announces, evil eyeing him.

Ridge grins, and damn all hot bad boys from the wrong side of the tracks. He flashes his deep dimples and pearly white teeth at Tatum. "Naw, I'm not annoying." He looks up to Tatum and me. "She just needs to be extra careful."

Tillie rolls her eyes. "I'm always careful. You're just overbearing."

"I'm Tatum." She waves from the front.

He looks at her and nudges his head. "Sup."

I smile. "I'm Madison."

He tips his head at me. "Okay, got to go now."

"Who is that?" Tatum purrs, as we pull away from the school. "Please tell me you're hitting it."

"I am." Tillie nods. "But it's completely mutual, and we have no interest in ever going further than great sex with each other."

I look at her in my rearview mirror. It's not that I don't believe her. It's just that... yeah, I don't believe her. You don't become friends with someone who looks like Tillie and then who looks like Ridge, and not want to make babies together.

"Really?" I answer. "How does that work? You know... without becoming attached in some way." Not that I'm clingy, but even I struggle with separating my feelings with sex. It's something I've always struggled with. I've never been able to be one of those girls who could have sex with a guy and not at least feel something for him, even just a little bit. And even without knowing Bishop, I just don't think it's in me to do that. Except now I definitely feel something for Bishop. Hate.

"It just does. Ridge and I have known each other since we were kids. We're probably a little more experienced than most people our age, but that's because we've been sleeping together for a very long time."

I pull onto our highway and head toward the mall. "And what about when one of you wants to sleep with someone else? Won't the other get mad?"

She shakes her head. "No. It's seriously just sex. I know it's hard to understand for most people, and I know girls say they're cool with this kind of situation and then they get attached, but I really am cool with it. He's had lots of girlfriends since we started sleeping together." She shrugs, and I watch her in the rearview mirror, trying to catch her bluff. "Sometimes he cheats with me, or sometimes he doesn't. Either way, I get laid." She winks at me.

I shake my head and laugh, pulling into the parking lot. "Well, he's hot, just saying."

"You want his number? Certain he would be interested," Tillie says, shrugging and pushing open her door.

"What?" I scoff, getting out and walking around to the front as we start toward the mall. "I didn't mean as in I want a taste. I just mean as in he's hot."

"Well, I do!" Tatum says, linking her arm with Tillie's.

Tillie laughs and then stops when she realizes Tatum is serious. "Oh no, no, no, honey." Tillie taps her hand as we walk into the cool air-conditioned mall. "He would eat you alive."

It's funny. At first glance, you would think Tatum is the slut of the group, not me or Tillie. Not saying we're sluts, but we're the most sexually active out of the tripod.

I burst out laughing just as my phone vibrates in my pocket. Seeing it's an unknown caller, I shoo them into the closest clothing store and swipe my phone unlocked.

"Hello?" I'm still laughing when the word leaves my mouth.

"Riddle me this," an automated voice answers on the other end.

"Pardon?" I ask, taking a seat on one of the café chairs. "Who is this?"

"I am neither dead, nor alive, and I'm not something little Madison can hide. But you will be dead by the time this is done. The timer starts now. The games have just begun."

"Hello? This is not funny—" The line goes dead, and I look down to my phone, my mouth slightly open. What the hell was that about?

"Madi!" Tillie yells out from one of the clothing shops, waving a dress around.

Oh no.

"Coming!" I call out, looking back down to my phone. Who even uses that spooky voice, and who the hell was that? Some stupid kid playing with their parents' phone.

Yeah, some stupid kid who just so happens to know how to block their caller ID.

Standing to my feet, I walk toward the clothing store and push my phone back into my pocket, along with my feelings about that call.

"What. Is. That?" I ask, pointing toward the outfit Tatum is brushing down in front of the mirror.

"What?" She laughs like a hyena. "This is Harley Quinn!"

"I know it's Harley Quinn, but why are you wearing it?" I giggle, taking the costume Tillie chose for me from her.

"Because I wanna find me my puddin'."

"Oh Lord."

She starts flicking her hair around like the lunatic she is and I shake my head, looking down at the... "I am not wearing this."

"Whyyy?" Tillie moans. "It's cute!"

"Yeah, for a girl who wants her cookie hanging out." I give it back to her and flop down onto the customer chairs. "I can't even think about what I want to dress as."

"Well, you have to go as something!" Tatum exasperates, walking back into the changing room and slipping out of her outfit.

"Yeah, well...." I look to the left and see a skeleton-style masquerade mask. "Hold that thought." I walk toward it, standing on my tippy-toes to unhook it from the mannequin. Running my thumb over the embossed skeletons and lace, I smirk. "This I can work with."

"That's a little creepy," Tatum mutters from over my shoulder.

"Well, duh, it's Halloween, and I know this may come as a shock to you, but you're supposed to dress creepy, not like a skank. We save that for the weekends our boyfriends break up with us." I smile at her; adding that last part was to soften the blow. Tatum isn't a whore or a slut, but she is a bit of a skank. But aren't we all? As much as I love jeans, hoodies, and clothes that cover my butt, sometimes I like dressing up too.

Tillie laughs. "Well, I'm going as a cowgirl, Tatum is going as Harley Quinn, and Madi is going as a ballroom zombie! We're all a match made in hell."

We start laughing, and I walk away from them, going through the clothes to try and find a dress or something to wear with it. After the fifth failed attempt, I push one of the dresses back onto the hook and spin around. "I can just wear a black dress with this."

"And suspenders!" Tatum yells as we walk out of the shop.

"No, no suspenders."

"You're no fun."

"Tatum, we're going to be in the forest. I'm not dressing like a skank in the forest. By the way, who's going to set up our tents?" I ask, stopping outside a little café and dropping my bag down on the table. Tatum and Tillie take a seat. "Good question. Maybe you should ask Carter since he will be there early." One of my many problems. But he could set up our tent, and it's not an invitation or anything. But he is a male, and sometimes they expect something in return.

"I'll text him." I take a seat and look through the menu.

"So... Bishop, huh?" Tillie wiggles her eyebrows. I peek up at her from the menu.

"We don't talk about him," I reply blandly, before going back to searching between BLT bagels and potato skins with sour cream.

Tatum pours her a glass of water and giggles. "Yeah, he's a no-go zone as far as conversation starters go with Madi."

"But I haven't even had a chance to talk about it!" Tillie scolds like a burned out toddler wanting the last cookie.

"Nothing great." I drop the menu as the waiter comes to our table. "Can I get the potato skins, chicken tenders, and a Coke?"

"Why?" Tillie questions, after ordering her food.

"Because it happened, and then I found out it was all some sick fucking...." I pause, looking up at the waiter, who had to be around our age, sporting floppy brown hair and makeup that could give Tatum's a run for her money.

He notices me watching him and laughs, brushing me off. "Oh, girl, you don't have to worry about me."

"Yeah, okay." I smile at him, and he rolls his eyes, scribbling down our orders before leaving.

"Sick, what?" Tatum taunts, taking a drink of her water while smirking around the rim of her glass.

"I don't know, but it wasn't real. None of this is real."

"None of what?" Tatum asks, leaning back in her chair. I really wish she would stop asking so many fucking questions.

"I don't know, Tatum. I'm lost and confused."

"They're dangerous, Madi," Tatum whispers, leaning forward. Tillie pauses and watches our exchange closely. "Think about it. Khales went missing... no one knows where she is or what happened. All we know is that she dated Bishop." She leans back into her chair.

"So? That could mean nothing," I reply smoothly.

"And it could mean *everything*," Tatum retorts calmly.

I shrug. "So what? I'm staying away. I don't even know what happened between us."

"Nothing," Tillie announces out of nowhere.

"What?" I whisper. It's the first time I have heard her say anything since bringing up this conversation to begin with.

"Nothing happened between you. It meant nothing to him."

"And how do you know that? I mean, I know that, but how do you know that?" I ask, leaning forward and pouring another glass of water as the waiter comes back and places our food on our table.

"Just a guess. I mean... none of those guys had ever had a girlfriend before," Tillie says casually, taking one of my potato skins. "The only one who ever did was Bishop, and look how that ended." She laughs, shaking her head. "I don't mean it in a mean way, just in a real way."

"It's fine," I whisper, picking up some fries and dipping the crispy, deep-fried goodness into the sour cream. "I just wish they would forget about me."

CHAPTER 21

"So now that we have our costumes sorted for this weekend," Tatum says over the phone, as I turn on the faucet to my shower, "have you asked Carter if he can set up our tents?"

Nate walks into the bathroom, his hair all over the place and his white Calvin Klein boxers on. He doesn't spare me a second glance, just goes straight to the sink and squirts toothpaste onto his toothbrush.

"Madi?"

"What?" I ask, looking back to the floor. No smart remark from Nate? That's unlike him. I look back up to him in the mirror. He brushes his teeth, his eyes peering back, but this time they're looking through me, not at me, and when it comes to Nate, there's a huge difference. I shiver at the stare he's giving me.

"Sorry, um, yeah, Carter said he would."

"Okay, good."

Nate stops his brushing, his eyes remaining on me as he leans over and slowly spits. Rinsing his toothbrush, he puts it back on the sink.

"I gotta go." Just as I hang up the phone, Nate walks out, slamming the door behind himself. *What the fuck is his problem?* Deciding I don't want to face his bullshit, I walk over and flick the lock before shimmying out of my pajamas.

Scrubbing the sweet-smelling soap into my skin, my eyes close as vivid pictures of the night they stopped me down the dark road come back to me. My breathing picks up slowly, my chest rising and falling. *"You want to play a game, kitty?"* The rough material of their ski masks burn across my face. Fight or flight. Fight or flight. *Flight.* My hand skims over my belly ring, down to the apex of my thighs. *"You know you want this, kitty,"* Bishop's lazy voice comes into earshot. *I do.*

Slipping my fingers between my folds, I glide one of my fingers inside me. Groaning and tilting my head back, I massage the inside of myself, Bishop's grin flashing in my memories. His touch, the way he rode my body until I couldn't feel my legs and sweat was pouring out of my pores. The way he ran his tongue all over my flesh and then down to my clit.

I grab onto the soap and lather up my finger before bringing it back to my clit, imagining it's Bishop's expert tongue flicking over my nub. My eyes slam shut, my legs clench, and my core erupts in pleasure as my orgasm rips through me, owning me. Opening my eyes slowly, I blush. I can't believe I just fucking did that. I hate him, so why the fuck does he still turn me on? Even though I know nothing was real with him? Am I that screwed up?

Possibly.

Getting out of the shower, I dry myself quickly and get dressed. Walking down the stairs, the house is eerily silent, something I used to be accustomed to. But since being here, it's not something I'm used to anymore because of Nate, who is the furthest thing from silent. "So much for babysitting," I mutter to myself, as I step outside our front door and see his car is gone. Closing it, Sam opens the door behind me again. "Madi, you need a ride to school today?"

I shake my head. "It's cool. I've got that camping trip tonight, remember?" My dad and Elena will be home tonight from their trip too, so I won't be coming home after my detour to the library. I figure I'll get changed in the girls' locker rooms before leaving and get a workout in before the school gym closes at ten. By the time I get out to the site, which apparently isn't a real campsite, it will be close to midnight, but I'm hoping that it's one, easy to find, and two, it's easy to *fricking* find.

"Oh, right. Do you have everything packed?"

"Yes, Sammy, I have everything." I step down the stairs, clutching my duffel bag. "I'll see you on Sunday!" I yell out to her.

"Oh! Madi!" Sammy hollers, and I spin around.

"What?"

She rushes inside and then comes out again, tossing me some keys. "The GMC isn't here. It's getting fixed, something to do with a faulty fuel pump." She shakes her head then looks back to me. "You'll have to take your dad's Aston Martin."

I catch the keys midair. "The DB9?" I shiver. "I can't take that. He'll kill me."

"He will not, and he was the one who called me to say you needed to use that car."

I pause. "Is this a joke?" I look around my body. "Daddy loves me, but he doesn't love me that much."

Sammy laughs, spinning around and waving my dramatic ass off. "Have fun, Madison."

I grin. Dad is letting me take the DB9? That's so far past odd I can't even see the fuck-ing aliens anymore. That made no sense. I beep it unlocked, slide into the driver seat before clutching it into first gear, and drive toward the school.

I'm late. Again.

"Madison, I thought we had this discussion about your tardiness?" Mr. Barron, my physics teacher scolds, looking me up and down. Mr. Barron is one of those teachers who have an authoritative hand, but you don't mind, because he's young and handsome, so you wouldn't mind him spanking your ass while you call him Daddy.

Face palm, Madison.

Five o'clock shadow, plaid shirts, nicely fitting jeans that show his butt. Mr. Barron is hot, so I instinctively blush under his glare. "Sorry, it really wasn't my fault this time. There was traffic." His stare stays glued on mine until I'm squirming in my spot. "It won't happen again, sir."

He nods. "Very well, take a seat."

Did I mention the Irish accent? *Someone splash me with cold water.* I scramble back to my desk and pull out my notepad.

Ally turns in her seat toward me. "Hey, slut."

The whole class starts laughing.

I narrow my eyes at her. "You say it like you know, Ally. Say, don't you speak slut, too? Of course you do," I answer for her, bored with her weak jabs.

She spins around toward me. "Bishop told me about how you scratch in bed." She's digging to hit a nerve, and besides the fact I'm pissed Bishop has talked to her about our little fling, I won't give her the satisfaction of seeing it. Fuck her.

"Really?" I tease with a quirked eyebrow and a smirk. "So he told you just how sharp they are then?" My smirk deepens, and when she realizes what I'm implying, her mouth snaps shut.

"Still a slut."

"Still don't care."

The bell finally rings for the next period and I scramble out of my chair, pushing through the crowds before making my way to my next class. Please, please let this day go fast.

This day is not going fast. I drop my tray onto the lunch table just as Tatum dances over with Carter and... I forgot his name already... on her tail.

"Hey, sugar! You don't look so hot."

"Thanks, Tatum," I mutter, dropping down onto the seat. Carter slips in next to me, and I try my hardest to ignore Nate and Bishop in the corner.

"She always looks hot. What are you talking about?" Carter scolds Tatum.

"Please stop." I massage my temples slowly, taking in deep breaths. "I literally don't know how I'm going to make it past this day, let alone tonight. I feel like Ally sucks the life out of me, and I've had her in all three of my morning classes." I yank open the lid to my yogurt, tossing it onto my tray. "She's fucking—"

"Not worth your energy," Carter finishes, taking the yogurt from me. He laughs. "Calm down or you're going to get this all over your clothes."

I can't help it anymore; my attempting to not look toward Bishop and Nate fails me on epic portions, because I fucking look. Only, they're not looking at me. Nate has a new girl on his lap, and Bishop has gone back to his stone-cold self, not acknowledging anyone else's existence. Huh. I thought I'd be pleased, but because of Nate's icy-cold shoulder he threw at me this morning, I don't know. I've somehow grown accustomed to them watching me, whether it's creepy, annoying, or not.

"Thanks," I say to Carter, dragging my eyes from the group of them.

"So what time will you get out tonight?" He swings his leg over his chair so he's sitting on it backward.

"I've just got a couple things to do, but I should be there around midnight. I'll text you guys when I'm on my way."

He looks like he's mulling over my idea, but then nods. "Yeah, okay. We're going out after school so I will set up your girls' tent."

"Mmm!" Tatum wiggles on her chair. "Can you put us in the best spot?"

"What? Tatum, it's literally in the middle of the forest. There're a few flat areas where we set up, but it's black. There are no best areas." Carter chuckles.

Tatum pauses. "Wait, I thought it would like, have a lake or something pretty?"

He laughs. "No. This is a Halloween party camp out. There are no pretty things."

I giggle when I see Tatum's face fall.

"But I bought heels." She pouts.

Carter laughs again. "Take them back, baby girl. You won't be needing those."

Her lip trembles, before she takes a bite out of her apple. "I guess Harley Quinn could wear Chucks."

Someone find this girl her puddin'.

CHAPTER 22

The final bell rings and I nervously pull out my phone from my pocket, sliding it open. I'm sick of not knowing what the hell is going on with Nate, so I send him a text.

Me – What's going on with you?

Shoving my phone back into my pocket, I head toward the library. Flopping down onto the sofa, with *The Book* in one hand, I look down at my phone again. Zero new messages. Frustrated, I open a new message and type one to Bishop.

Me – Is Nate with you?

Sighing, and a little more agitated than usual, I shove my phone away and flip open to the next excerpt.

3.
The Ritual

Flames danced around the pitch-black night of nothingness like bright flickers of warmth, tormenting the sky like it had been waiting for me. For my son. Licking over my skin in faded hope, because I've come to realize… this was false hope for me. But I hoped someone somewhere would find my words one day, not for solace, and not for understanding.

I walked down the dirt path that led to the center, where the mass of flames were alight from the bundle of dry wood. Five men surrounded the pit of flames, all covered in long, hooded cloaks. They didn't have to show their faces for me to know who they were. They were my husband's soldiers. They believed in this atrocious cause just as much as my husband did. Blinded by some false perfection of what the world should be.

My husband has always been an overachiever on a larger scale. It would frighten me at times, because when he was fixated on something or someone he wanted, he stopped at absolutely nothing to get it. It was almost as though a blood thirst would start in his bones, and he wouldn't sleep until he had his feeding. His latest obsession, I knew it wouldn't pass. They never did. He always got what he wanted in the end, above all. But I had hoped he would change the plans, the rules.

*Though, he said there were no rules. "*نين‌اوق دجوت ال*" he would write, which means "There are no rules" in Aramaic. I wasn't sure what he meant by that, at least not right now, at this moment, but it wasn't long before I would learn exactly what he meant.*

I walked toward the men, my son cradled in my arms.

"Katsia, give me the boy." My husband hurried from the other side, standing near a large, flat, cold stone.

I looked down to my little boy, my throat contracting and my tears welling up behind my lids. I didn't want this. I didn't want to do this. I didn't care about building a syndicate of men who would rule for generations to come. I didn't care about riches or power. I cared about my child. But my husband swore that no harm was going to come to him, not one speck. So, slowly but gently, I headed toward the stone, the flickering of the flames lighting up the dark moonlit night like large fireflies.

"Put him down, Katsia. We will do no harm. That, I promise you."

Clutching my son in my arms, the little swaddle wrap he was tucked into flush against my chest. "Your promises don't do anything to calm my erratic thoughts, husband."

He stepped toward me, taking my baby away and placing him down onto the rock before unwrapping the cloak I had him snuggled into. "Your feelings are no business to me, Katsia. Now, leave if you can't handle this."

"I will not leave my child with you, Humphrey. Not ever. Do it fast and give my boy back."

His eye twitched, just as he drew his hand back and then pounded it across my face, a loud slap sounding out just as a sharp sting erupted over my cheekbone. I fell to the ground in a mess, clutching the damp, loose dirt ground under my fingernails. Pushing myself up slowly, I looked up at him from the earth.

"You call me Husband. Not Humphrey. Get up and stand like a real woman should. You're embarrassing me."

I stood again, squaring my shoulders. He looked down to my son, just as someone else came over clutching a metal stick.

"He has to be initiated through correctly," my husband said, looking toward David, one of his men. "Bring me the girl."

A young teenager was pulled from the forest, stuck in between two other cloaked men. She had a blindfold around her eyes, and her hands were bound behind her back. She had slits already sliced around her neck.

"What are you doing?" I asked Humphrey, watching the frantic girl pant for escape from beneath the gag in her mouth.

Humphrey smirked at me. "This is the ritual. It's what every initiation has to go through after the branding, and then once again when he hits puberty."

"What?" I whispered, because I had quite possibly lost my voice.

He walked toward me, running his rough hand down the side of my cheek. "Oh, sweet Katsia. I told you. This is the process, and you have to trust it." But I didn't. "This woman will be kept for him until he comes to puberty."

"And then what?" I muttered, holding back the bile that was rising in my throat.
"And then she will take his virginity."

I shook my head. *"No."* But even as I denied it, the snarling grin that popped up at the corner of his mouth told me that he was far from finished with revealing his sick plans.

"And then he will kill her."

With my stomach churning, the ringing of my phone interrupts my reading, and I fish it out, flicking to answer it without looking at the screen.

"Hello?"

"When the lights go out, and no one is about, will Madison scream or will she pout? Because one thing I know, that you may not so, is how you scream for me, down below."

"Who is this?" My breathing thickens again, and I stand from my chair, the book dropping to the floor.

The twisted crackle of a toned laugh blisters through my eardrums, and my pulse picks up. *"Wouldn't you like to know, my favorite little slut? Tell me... does Daddy know how fucking good you suck?"*

"This isn't funny." I look down to my phone and then bring it to my ear. "Seriously—"

They hang up. The blank dial tone rings through my ears and I shove my phone back into my pocket, bending down to pick up the book. I look around the library. When I walked in here, there were lights on down a few aisles, but now it's inky dark, with nothing but the weak lighting hovering over the reception desk where Miss Winters is sitting. Clearing my throat, I place the book back onto the bookshelf and collect my bag before swinging it over my shoulder. Whoever this caller is, he's starting to freak me out. I haven't even solved his first riddle—which, in my opinion, didn't make sense.

Walking toward the student access door, Miss Winters stops me. "Madison?"

I turn to face her, my hand on the cold metal bar of the door. She walks to where I was, and then comes back to me, clutching the book. Shoving it into my hands, she says, "Just take it."

"But I thought—"

She shakes her head. "Don't ask, just..." She looks around nervously, as if she's checking for the boogie man. "Just take it, *okay?*" Her eyes lock onto mine pleadingly.

Slipping my fingers around the old, worn leather cover, I nod. "Thank you, you didn't have to do this, though."

She looks over my shoulder, a shimmer of panic crawling over her face before she masks it with a fake smile. "It's okay. It's nothing. I noticed how much you've been coming in to read it, so I'm sure I can make up some story about it being lost and then magically finding it when you return it. It's no biggie." She brushes me off, but I still see the underlying panic beneath her words.

"Okay, well, thank you." I slip past her finally, clutching the book in my hands, and make my way to the girls' locker room near the gym.

Walking into the empty stalls, I place the book into my bag and pull out my dress, hair dryer, and flat iron. I can't believe I decided to get ready here. *Should I just brave it and go home?* No. No, that's a terrible idea. Shimmying out of my clothes, I wrap the towel around myself and walk into the scolding hot spray of water, scrubbing up in fast-forward, because, let's face it, all people get murdered in the damn shower in locker rooms.

I've watched *Scream*. I know what happens when you turn to get your shampoo. Not to me though, nope.

Turning off the faucet, I wrap the towel around my body again and slip out, drying my hair first, and then I run the flat iron through it quickly. I don't know why I'm spending so much unneeded time on this; it's not like my outfit is to die for. No pun intended. Slipping on the black strapless dress, which hugs around my butt a little more than I wanted for tonight, I brush on some makeup, going heavy on the eyes to add the effect to my zombie masquerade mask, and then slip it over my head. There. That's all I need. Gliding on a deep burgundy matte lipstick, I walk back to my bag, pull out my Keds, and shove them on my feet before putting all my clothes back into my bag, on top of the book. Now that I have it, it's all I can think about. Hopefully, the party won't last too long, and people won't notice I've snuck into my tent to read. Major regrets are rolling in now about me agreeing to do this. This isn't even my idea of what camping is.

Shoving everything inside, I swing my bag over my shoulder and then make my way down the dark corridor to the elevator that'll take me down to the basement of the student parking lot. Chills break out over my spine, and I get this overbearing feeling that someone is watching me. Someone I don't know or am familiar with. Shrugging it off, and wanting to get the fuck out of here STAT, I push the button, and then push it a few more times in an attempt to hurry it up. It dings open, so I walk inside the warm enclosure, pushing the correct button. It's a quick trip down, and once it pops open, I'm once again met with echoing silence of nothing between these concrete walls. Beeping Dad's car, I pull open the driver door with my heart pounding in my chest, swing my bag inside, and quickly slide in, locking the doors instantly.

"Holy shit," I whisper. I'm completely aware at how I'm working myself up. My pulse slowly drops and I press the button, starting the car.

"Call Tatum," I order the Bluetooth, just as I'm pulling out of the garage.

"Calling Tatum," she replies, and I hit the stereo on just as Figure's "The Exorcist" starts pumping through the speakers. Turning it down a little low so I can hear Tatum, she picks up almost instantly, and I let her and the music calm me.

Except you turned on a remix song for The Exorcist. *Who are you trying to calm? Your ninth demon?*

"Girrrl!" Tatum squeals down the phone, her voice doused in muffled drunk tones and loud music.

I laugh, pulling onto the main highway that will take me to where they are. According to my GPS, it's a thirty-minute drive into literally the middle of nowhere. "What?"

"This party is puuumping! And, oh my God!" she slurs. *Oh dear.* "Carter put us on the flattest part of the ground, you know, like sort of beside him, which is shady as fuck! But still, everyone else's tents are a little lopsided." She giggles and then burps. "Oops. 'Scuse me."

"Tate?" I laugh. "Slow down or you won't be able to meet me when I get there. Remember, I have no service. Where's Tillie?"

"She's here somewhere." She brushes me off. "Hurry up! We need you! Oh! And the Kings aren't here. You're safe!"

Shaking my head. "Okay, I'll see you in thirty minutes! Get someone sober to come with you."

She hangs up the phone. The Kings aren't there? That's odd, considering they were so hell-bent on making my life miserable. They must have found a new toy to play with. I should be happy, but another side of me—the girly side—wants to know what the fuck I did wrong.

Turning the volume to full blast on the radio, I let Disturbed's lyrics from "Tyrant" absorb all my feelings. Just as I hit the exit, my phone lights up on the seat.

Unknown – *Run*

I swerve on the road, headlights flashing ahead of me and taking my attention away from my phone. Just as I correct the car back onto the road, another text lights up.

Unknown – *Amateur move. I really hoped that would have killed you once and for all.*

Throwing my phone onto the ground, I look in my rearview mirror but see nothing. No headlights, nothing but darkness and the passing glow from the street markings. A bead of sweat forms on my forehead, so I swipe it away. Am I being stalked? What the fuck is going on? Glancing down to my phone that's on the floor on the passenger side, I ignore the incoming text and concentrate on making sure I get there in once piece.

"You have reached your destination," the GPS announces, just as I pull down a dark, bumpy gravel road.

"And where exactly is that?" I ask myself. Two seconds later, my phone lights up on the floor again and I roll my eyes, reaching over and scooping it up. Sliding it unlocked, I open it onto the recent message.

Unknown – *Hell*

My panic starts to kick in and I look in my rearview mirror again, only to find I'm all alone with no road markings. Now I'm just surrounded by inky blackness, full-on creepiness, amongst the freaking forest. Looking forward, I concentrate on what I'm doing. Leaning over, I pop the glove compartment and see my dad's pistol he keeps in there. Smiling, and feeling a lot safer than I felt two seconds ago, I pull it out and place it on my lap. My dad always said to me, *"Madi, don't ever point a gun at a man unless you have the balls to pull the trigger."* Suffice it to say, I have big balls right about now. I don't want to hurt anyone, but I've been trained to take care of myself, and this is how I do it. Guns don't kill people. People kill people. Guns are there to protect people who need to be protected from people who kill people.

Just as I pull up next to a line of cars, another text comes through. "Seriously?" I groan, picking up my phone and sliding it unlocked.

Unknown – *Naw, baby. That ain't gonna do jack shit when my hands are wrapped around your neck and your mouth is sucking on my dick.*

I spin around, looking outside, but no one has followed me this whole time. What the fuck? I notice I'm still getting service since his texts are coming through just fine, but when I look at the service bar, I can see it dropping in and out. "Shit." Taking a chance anyway, I dial Carter. There's no use in trying Tatum; she's probably already smashed, and as far as I know, Tillie doesn't actually own a phone. I mean, we text her when we're not with her, but she never has a phone when she's with us.

Carter picks up, but I can hear a girl's voices in the background. I roll my eyes. "Carter?"

"Hello? Madi? Can you hear me?"

No, I cannot hear you over all the mouthful of cock.

"Yeah, Carter—" the line goes dead, and I look down to my phone to see the service gone. "Fuck!" Picking up my bag from the passenger seat, I push my phone into the front pocket and pick up my gun.

This doesn't seem like a great idea anymore. Back at school, when I said I'd do this, it was because I was in the light of the day. Now, I'm in the dark and can't see shit. Shivering slightly, I think about throwing on a sweater, but my dad always said that the cold is what helps you stay alert. With that in my brain, I slip out of the car, ignoring the stabs of panic that erupt all over my flesh from being out in the cold, quiet open, and then slam the door shut, hiding the pistol behind my duffel bag as it slouches on my shoulder, but not far enough I can't pull it out whenever I need it. Walking forward to the breaking of the forest—what Carter said to follow—I tighten my grip on the gun. It's too silent. Why's it so silent? It's throwing me off. No birds or crickets chirping.

I kick myself. I should have bought my headphones. It would have made this trip a little less daunting, and then maybe I could have ran through the forest until I got to the site. Crunching of the dead leaves vibrates under the soles of my feet as the cold, thick air whips my hair across my face.

"I wanna play a game," a voice whispers from behind me, and I jump two feet into the air, whipping around to face whoever it is that's there, my gun drawn.

But no one is there.

"Who the fuck are you?"

A round of echoing laughter breaks through the night, swimming with the heavy gusts of wind. "Riddle me this...."

"No! Fuck you!"

They all laugh again, like a torturous cackle created from my very own nightmares. "Oh, you will," another voice growls over the back of my neck, so close I could feel his warm breath fall over the fine hairs on my back.

I swing around, but once again, I'm met with empty air.

"Weak," another voice taunts.

"Too slow!" another one laughs.

Sucking in my breath, I whip around, only to be met with the dark, inky forest, filled with the tang of pine, crisp dry leaves, and the moonlight reflecting between the broken branches of the trees. Moss blankets the thick sheet of dirt that is around my feet, and I bring my hand up, aiming my gun at nothing. "Who the fuck are you, and why the fuck are you following me?"

I feel his presence before he speaks, but when he opens his mouth, I know who it is instantly. "Riddle me this, *kitty,*" he whispers softly through his rough, lazy voice. "How many secrets do you hold within your bones? Or do I need to cut you open until your mysteries bleed out all over your home?" He steps forward, his hard chest brushing against my back muscles. I close my eyes, my grip around the gun tightening. Running his lips over the back of my earlobe, he groans, "You're not the only one who can leave scratch marks." Then he shoves me forward until I smash into a large tree trunk. The gasp of air I was holding in rushes out from my lungs as he steps between my legs, stretching me wide.

"Leave me alone, Bishop."

He laughs and grips my wrists tightly. He snatches my gun from me and then pulls cable ties around my wrist. Fuck! Panic starts to rise again. Why the hell are they doing this to me? Nothing makes sense, and nothing has made sense since I got here. "You and I both know that's not what you really want."

Loud footsteps sound out behind me, and when Bishop finally shoves me around to face him, his face catches my attention first. It's completely masked in skeleton special effects makeup, and he's wearing dark loose jeans, with a dark hoodie covering his head. His eyes peer into mine, but they're covered by white wolf contacts. "You"—he steps forward—"know what I'm talking about, kitty. Why are you acting dumb?"

I swallow. "Dumb? What the hell are you talking about?" I look over his shoulder and see more figures, with skeleton faces and dark hoodies and jeans on, scattered around the place, leaning against trees. I search for Nate, and Bishop must know what I'm doing, because he laughs again, his hand flying up to my throat. He squeezes gently. "He can't and won't save you, kitty."

His grip tightens, and my swallowing gets heavy. I look up into his eyes as he pushes me against the tree trunk again, the burning graze cutting into my back.

Stepping between my legs again, he drops his mouth to my ear, and growls, "Tell me what you know."

"What?" What does he mean what I know?

"Wrong answer, kitty. You lose round one."

"Round one?" I scoff, yanking at the cable ties that are digging into my wrists. "What the fuck do you want?" My anger is kicking up a notch. Sure, I may be timid and a quiet girl at times, but my fuse is very short. I can't be bothered with killing people with kindness; that shit takes far too long. He pushes me back, his grip tightening until my air supply is stolen.

"What do you know about the Kings, kitty?"

My eyes close, the desperation to gain more air strengthening with each passing minute. Legs! I draw my leg back and kick him straight between his.

"Fuck!" he roars, bending over but not letting go of my throat. The rest of the boys watching behind us jolt forward, but they're too slow. I kick him again, in the same spot, and his grip around my neck unlatches.

I quickly spin around and bolt. Running through all the scattered leaves, on broken sticks, and jumping over fallen logs, I run until my chest is burning and my vision is blurred. Something's wrong. *Silence.* Complete silence. Slowing my running, I suck in heavy breaths as chills break over my flesh and what feels like a hundred tiny slithering snakes crawl up my spine. *I shouldn't have stopped.* Stupid rookie move. Cranking my head over my shoulder a little, I see the shadow of someone coming up fast behind me. Just as I'm about to run, someone pushes me from behind, and I'm falling, face first. Because my hands are tied, I have nothing to break my fall.

"Fuck!" Bishop yells from behind me, and then a heavy body is pressing into my back. He digs his knee into the center of my spine, shoving my already pounding face that's shoved into the dirt deeper. His hand wraps around the back of my neck as he squeezes again. I inch backward, my shoulders coming up in an attempt to stop his assault. "Don't. Fucking. Run, kitty. You wanna know why?" he grates, dropping down to my ear, and my eyes sting with unshed tears.

"Why?" I croak through my parched throat.

He laughs, and I swear to God that laugh is enough to fuck with any demonic being. "Because I will always catch you, kitty, and trust me when I say," he murmurs into my ear, his warm breath gliding over my neck, "I'll always find you." He gets up off me and flips me over onto my back.

"Tsk, tsk, little sis." Nate walks toward me, but I focus my eyes on the sky. The branches frame my vision like a small circle, and I tilt my head, studying them closely. Nate bends down, but I can't look at him. I always knew Bishop hated me somewhat, and when we slept together, it was more of a hate fuck, but Nate straight up betrayed me. *Surprise, surprise.* Most people do, I've come to learn. "Answer the question."

"Fuck you."

He laughs, his hand coming down to my throat. He looks up at Bishop and then grins over his shoulder. I quickly look back up to the stars once he's brought his attention back down to me. Gripping me roughly, he yanks me to my feet and shoves my back up against a tree trunk. My head smashes against the hard bark and I groan, my eyes closing. That fucking hurt.

"B, come grab her legs so she can't kick..." Nate studies my face, his wolf-colored eyes looking over my body. He grins. "Or scratch us." I snap my mouth closed before opening it again.

"Nate, what the fuck are you doing?"

"I need to know the truth, kitty. And I need to know tonight." I look over his shoulder to see the other five boys there, standing in the weak mist of the foggy night. The air is thick, and I know the fog is about to get a lot worse.

"I don't know what the fuck you mean!" I scream.

Bishop steps forward, pushing Nate over slightly and grabbing onto my legs. Before I know it, they're wrapped around his narrow waist and he's pressing his groin into my center, the bark from the tree once again digging into my back. I should have worn the damn hoodie. He shoves me again, using his waist to move me. "Answer the fucking questions, kitty."

I don't ignore the way his bulge has expanded against me either, and as much as I hate him and hate what's happening, my body has a mind of its own. "I am answering the questions! You're just not listening!" I yell, pissed off at all of them. Do I think they will hurt me? Yes. But my anger trumps my fear, and that's a dangerous trait to have against Bishop and Nate, because they love the fear. I can feel it, see it in their eyes. When they know I'm afraid, they get a kick out of it.

Nate looks over his shoulder and gives the other boys a look before staring back at me. He steps aside, giving Bishop even more reign over my body. Slowly, Bishop's hips sink into me again and my throat contracts. I narrow my eyes on him.

He smirks, before groaning, "What?" innocently.

"You know *what*, and for the record, that is not happening again."

Nate laughs behind him. "We all know that's bullshit."

Bishop smirks at me again. "Unconvinced."

"I know nothing. Now let me go before my friends come find me."

"I don't buy that you don't know anything about us, kitty. In fact, I'd be willing to bet on it." He pushes into me again and my stupid core contracts.

Are you kidding me? He runs his nose down my jaw, but I fight it. I look directly at Nate. "This what you wanted?" I question him, my eyebrow quirked. "To see how hard Bishop can fuck me? Maybe learn a thing or two for the next time you're mouth-fucking me on the couch?"

Bishop stills. Every muscle in his body turns rigid against mine before he loosens. I don't know if he knows I caught that, or if he even cares that I know.

Nate comes to the side of me, running his finger down the side of my cheek. I shove away from him. "Naw, sis, don't act like you didn't mouth-fuck me back. In fact, if I remember correctly, it was your hot little tongue that slipped into my mouth first."

Bishop comes up from my neck, his hand coming to my cheeks, where he squeezes roughly. "Answer the fucking questions, kitty, before I fuck you right here and now. And trust me, what you experienced the first time was gentle up against how deep I'd fuck you right now."

"Bro? What if she's telling the fucking truth?" someone behind Nate asks, stepping toward us. When he gets closer, I see it's Cash. "I mean, it's possible that she—"

"Shut the fuck up, and no it's not. And no we can't take chances. And no I won't fucking take her word for it," Bishop snaps, looking over his shoulder. "Get back to where the fuck you came from and don't interrupt again."

Cash's jaw tenses. I think I like him a little more than I did before.

"Game time," Bishop says to me. "Every time I think you're lying—" He pulls out a Swiss Army blade from his back pocket and flicks it open. "—you lose a piece of clothing." He tilts his head. "And when you have no clothing left?" He glides the blade down my sternum to my belly button. "Then we'll have to start getting creative."

"This is bullshit!" I spit. "I fucking told you that I don't know anything!" Goose bumps break out over my flesh, and he sees it. Grinning, he grips the knife in his hand and then grabs onto my thigh again. "I'd be real honest if I were you, kitty, 'cause boundaries?" he taunts. "Those are things I don't have."

"Fine!" I splutter. "I'll answer with complete honesty, but then, you will let me go!"

Bishop searches my eyes, his bright, marble wolf ones looking into mine. Why the fuck does the whole skeleton thing do it for me? And why the fuck am I thinking about what does it for me and what doesn't right now?

"I'll be the judge of that." Then he leans forward and nips my lower lip, like he fucking owns it. I growl, the vibration pressing against his chest. "Aw, that's real cute. The kitty purrs."

"Fuck you."

"Can we get to the questions?" Nate says, looking between Bishop and me in disbelief. "Geez, your guys' hatred used to be hot foreplay, but now I'm seriously thinking I'll be needing to hide the knives."

I laugh, tilting my head back, and then look back to Nate. "Oh, you'll be needing to hide them from me, brother, and I'd be sleeping with one eye open from now on."

"Hot. Gonna come suck my dick in my sleep?"

"More like bite it off." I pause and pretend to mull over my thoughts. "Oh, but that would require me actually being able to locate it. Houston, we have a p—"

Bishop slams his hand over my mouth. "Shut the fuck up!"

I nod and he lets go, but I still manage to send a snarl toward Nate.

"Do you know about The Elite Kings?" Bishop shoots off.

"Only what Tatum has told me. Which isn't much."

He pauses, waiting for me to continue. "And what is that, exactly?"

My eyes narrow. "It's literally not much as I can't even really remember what she said. Honestly? That little race you had, told me more than what Tatum could have."

"What's that supposed to mean?" Nate snaps, his lip curled.

I giggle. *Fucking giggle.* I could slap myself, but it added to the effect of my sarcasm, so I go with it. "Nate, so you all go do a little underground racing? Big wow, I don't really care." My eyes widen at the end of my sentence.

Bishop studies me, and then slowly but surely, his grin tilts up to a full clown smile, displaying his pearly white teeth and dimples. But his eyes? Yeah, his eyes aren't smiling. They are dark, shaded with hate, and planted by anger. It's in this very moment I realize that maybe I'm wrong. My face slowly falls, which only makes Nate start grinning.

"Aw, that's cute, kitten." He brings his hand up to my dress, over my breasts, and flicks his knife open before slowly cutting down my front. Now my tight strapless dress has a jagged cut down the front, my bright yellow lace bra on full display, but thankfully, because it's tight, it doesn't fall off me.

"What the fuck?" I yell at him. "I answered your question. That wasn't part of the rules!"

Bishop smiles. "I make the rules."

"Has anyone else spoken to you about us?" he questions.

"What?" Now I'm just over it, sick of the games and the underlying bullshit they seem to put me through. This is the second time they've done some fucked up cat-and-mouse game with me, and each passing minute, my patience runs thinner. "No one has said anything! I don't know who the fuck you are, what the fuck you stand for—or don't—and I don't care! Now…" I slice my glare to Bishop. "Let. Me. Go!"

He pauses, studying me closely. "And if I don't fucking believe you?"

"Then your lie detector is shit." I stand my ground from my precarious position.

Nate throws me a wink and then walks off toward Hunter and Brantley, who are standing beside a thick tree. Bishop hasn't moved, his hands still gripping around my thighs tightly. "You fuck him?"

I scowl. "What?"

"You heard me. Answer the question," he growls, pressing into me again.

"Hang on a second. You guys stalk me, chase me through a forest, scare the shit out of me, tie me up, and cut my fucking dress, and now you're asking if I fucked Nate, like you give a shit?"

"I didn't say I give a shit." Bishop smirks. He drops his lips to my ear, his hand running down the side of my ribs. He squeezes roughly, a little too roughly. Rough enough to leave a bruise. "I just need to know if I won the bet or not," he seethes through a harsh whisper. I tilt my head back, forcing the tears back. Of course. Of course this is a fucking game to these boys. I'm such a fucking idiot.

"You lost!" Nate laughs, walking back toward us. He comes up beside us, tilting his head at me, before he says harshly, "She didn't open her gap for me."

"Fuck you, Nate. Fuck both of you."

Bishop lets me go instantly and I fall to the ground with a *humph*, the dirt and leaves grabbing onto my thighs and ass. Bishop leans down and cuts the cable ties in the middle, freeing my wrists. I stretch them out, looking up at him.

"I hate you," I snarl.

He grins. "And I still wanna fuck you, so we'll figure something out."

I snap my mouth shut, getting to my feet. He follows, standing an inch away from me. "There is no way in hell you are ever touching me again." I glare.

He steps forward, backing me against the trunk. "Nice. Now, try again, but this time"—his hands slam up against the tree, caging me in—"say it like you mean it." Then he bends down, pulling my lower lip into his mouth.

I fight a groan at how it feels to have his mouth on me again, and I can't help it. I fucking hate myself for being this easy for him, but he doesn't have to know how well my body responds to him.

He smirks against my mouth, slowly pulling back until my lip pops from his. He licks my chin leisurely. "Wanna lie to me again?"

"I hate you," I repeat.

"Yeah, I know, but we fuck so well together."

"Bishop!" Cash hollers from behind us. "Give the girl your fucking hoodie so we can get back to camp."

Bishop grins, zipping his hoodie down, exposing his white shirt that glows in the moonlight. He tosses it at me and I catch it, slipping my arms into the warmth and fighting the urge to sniff the collar where his sweet, woodsy cologne is strongest. Planted right between clean soap and pure masculinity.

Scowling at him, Nate walks up to us, taking my hand, but I pull back. "Get fucked. I'm not following you anywhere."

Nate shrugs. "Fine by me."

Asshole.

Bishop chuckles, but I turn, making my way to God knows where in the forest. "Oh, and I need my gun back!" I yell out over my shoulder.

"Where are you going, kitty?" Nate asks as they all follow me.

"Well, to the camp, of course."

"And how do you know it's this way?" Bishop asks, his voice closer behind me.

"Because I just know."

We make it to the camp, and as soon as the bonfire comes into view, I relax. It's in the middle, and there're around seven tents scattered throughout the area, but far enough away from each other to not know what's going on in the one across from you.

"Madi!" Carter yells out from a log beside the campfire. He jogs up to me, and I see his eyes go over my shoulder to the boys behind me, a hundred questions no doubt simmering through his brain. A hundred questions I don't owe him answers for. "Hey, you made it."

I smile. "Just."

Bishop snickers from behind me, and Nate leaves, snatching a bottle of whiskey off someone who has already passed out.

Carter looks back to me, his eyes glassy and lazy. Obviously, he's drunk, and obviously, I'm jealous. It's not quite midnight yet, and I need a drink. "Let me show you where your tent is."

"Ok—"

"I got this. Thanks, bumboy." Bishop hooks his arm around my waist, steering me toward a tent at the back, hidden a little deeper into the forest.

"Bishop! That was fucking rude. He set up our tent."

"So he fucking should. It's what bumboys do. Now…" We step into the junction of the tent, where two of the bedrooms join the other two bedrooms. He unzips one side, pushing me into the dark room. "Get changed into something more slutty."

"What?" I snap. He steps inside the room too, but I can't see him. I can only make out the edges of his body from the flickering fire dancing, where the party is. "Get out."

He steps closer. "No."

I step backward. "Bishop, I mean it. Get back."

He counters my footwork, stepping forward once again. "No," he whispers into the inky yet surprisingly warm enclosure of the tent. My back hits the weak wall of the tent and I gasp, closing my eyes. Fuck. I'm so totally screwed with him. I feel him before I see anything, his thumb dancing across my bottom lip. "Scared?"

"Define scared," I breathe, my eyes still closed.

His thumb moves down the rim of my jaw, slowly trickling down the side of my neck and over my jugular. His warm mouth skims over mine softly. "Of me," he whispers.

I open my eyes, the white of his skeleton mask glowing and the white of his eyes bright. "Yes," I answer honestly, because I am. I don't trust him, but I did like having sex with him. Maybe he's right; maybe we can just have sex.

"Good."

"This." I gesture between us. "What is it?"

He lets out a throaty chuckle. "It means nothing. Just sex. You seem to get my dick hard, so I'm running with it."

Swallowing past his words, I think over what this would mean for me. I've always gotten attached to the guys I sleep with. It's a fault of mine, and inside, I'd probably be labeled as a crazy girl, but I tend to feel too much.

"I've never done it before," I admit. "The whole friends-with-benefits thing."

He laughs, this time tilting his head back, and thoughts dance in my head to what it would be like smacking him upside the head in this very moment. "Baby, we are not friends, and we are most definitely not friends with benefits. You're my *nemesis*, who I always get *panty-less*. Now," he mutters, gripping the front of my dress and tearing it off. "Drop them."

Pushing my thoughts to the back of my head, I step out of my thong, kicking it away. He steps back, and I see his head tilt in the shadows.

"Fine," I mutter. "But no one is to know, and also, I'm not very good at this, because I tend to—"

"Stop fucking talking." His mouth smashes down onto mine. I groan softly, tilting my head to give his tongue more access. He works with his belt between us, yanking it off and dropping it to the ground with a clink. Bringing his hand up to my throat, he clenches roughly before slowly gliding down the front of me, squeezing one of my nipples between his fingers.

"Mmm," I moan into his mouth.

"Fucking missed this mouth," he mutters against my lips before dropping to his knees.

Clutching his hair into my fists, I yank his head up to look at me from down below.

"First of all, no one will know about us, and secondly, you will *not* fuck anyone else. Comprende?" I hiss, my eyebrows quirked, even though I know he can't see me. I tug at his hair again. "If you can't agree to not sleeping with someone else while we're fucking, Bishop, you can leave right now and I'll take care of myself for tonight," I warn.

His slick tongue presses against the inside of my thigh. "Yeah, babe, pretty sure I can do that, since I don't go sinking my dick into any fucking gap."

I tilt my head back. "I hate you."

He licks me all the way up to the junction of my thighs and then bites down on the tender flesh. "Ditto, baby." He flicks my clit softly and my heart launches in my chest, my core tensing and my knees almost buckling. "Stay up!" he orders, pulling away from me with bite in his tone. He comes back to me and wraps his delicious lips around my clit, bending down more as his tongue slides deep inside of me.

"Oh fuck!" I pant, gripping his hair again and trying to fight the need to fall to the ground.

He drags his tongue up to my clit, circling again before one of his fingers slips inside of me, and then another joins in.

"Bishop," I moan, as his pace picks up and his finger curls to hit the spot in me that has only ever been hit by him. Usually, I'm a clit orgasm kinda girl, but since Bishop, I've found out just how pleasurable it can be through penetration and when you fuck someone who knows what the hell they're doing. I arch my back, pressing myself into his mouth. "Shit," I whimper.

"Yeah, baby, let go." He groans against my clit. His arm brushes against my ankles as he pumps himself, and with that thought in my head, I explode around and on his tongue, my body jolting and my brain swimming in a deep, dark, misty haze of euphoria. With one last long lick down my slit, he stands, his finger diving back into my channel. He withdrawals and brings his finger to my mouth. I open—unwillingly, mind you—and he slips his finger into my mouth. I circle it, sucking off the sweet taste of my pleasure.

"That... is proof you lied to me, kitty," he growls, pulling his fingers out of my mouth.

"What are you going to do about it?" I taunt him, smirking.

Silence.

Then he wraps my hair around his fist and tugs my hair so hard I swear I feel strands being ripped from my scalp. Pulling my bottom lip into his mouth, he bites down on it roughly, until the tang of blood trickles down the back of my throat. "Now? Now, I'm going to play with you."

I smirk up at him, and his grip intensifies. I hiss through the snapping of my hair. "I'm not a toy, Bishop."

"Wrong answer, Madison, because you *are* my toy, and the last toy I had?" His other hand latches around my throat like a choker as his mouth skims over mine again, sailing over his bite mark. "Broke."

Khales?

Too horny to ask questions, I run my hand over his hard chest, every defined ab jolting under the soft palm of my hand. "I don't like being a toy."

"Tough shit." He twists me around by my hair, and I obey, because he has my *fucking hair*, before shoving me down onto the mattress on the floor. My hands come out to steady myself, and I arch my back, pressing into him. His fingers dig into my hip bones as he runs his hand down from the back of my neck. "Fuck, you've got a sexy fucking spine."

"What?" I whisper, looking over my shoulder, but he pushes on my head until my face is buried in the soft blankets and my ass is elevated high into the air.

"I wonder," he whispers, pressing one finger inside of me before his mouth comes to my pussy from behind. "What it would be like to take it apart."

I pause, my breath stilling. *What the hell does that mean?* And why don't I care? I grind into his mouth, ignoring the fact that my butt is probably right there in his face, but he doesn't mind. Drawing his tongue out, he licks over my slit, over the opening of my pussy, and then comes to the crack of my ass, licking over my exit. *Holy fucking shit!*

"Yeah," he murmurs, coming back up. "I'd fucking snap you, kitty." Then his hand lands on my ass cheek with a stinging slap. I scream out, because it's fucking sore. "And I look forward to watching you break in my very hands." Then he presses himself inside me until he tears through my tight entrance, the rim of his cock grazing over every inch of my wet walls. He pumps me once.

And then again.

Every single time, the head of his cock rubs deliciously against the most sensitive part of my pussy.

"And what if I let you?" I whisper into the blanket, drunk by his assault, hazy from his need. He pushes again, and then pulls out of me, flipping me over onto my back. I look up at him as he crawls over my body, his head tilted.

"Then I gave you too much credit," he mutters. *Shit. Did her hear me?* "You're stupider than I thought."

Crawling off the mattress on the floor, I swipe my sweaty hair off my sticky forehead and look over my shoulder. Bishop looks at me from his position, sprawled out on the bed, his body on full display for me. Every muscle beneath his beautiful olive skin defined, but not so he's bulky. "Are you going to go all weird on me?" I ask, our eyes entranced together, locked in some epic stare-down, and the only thing going to lose are the butterflies entrapped in my gut. He continues to stare at me with a blank expression, while his index finger works his upper lip. His eyes are dark and brooding, just like him. Intimidating yet captivating. When our eyes connect, it's like he's shoved me through the gates of hell and locked them behind himself. I'm so totally screwed with him. I've never been able to separate sex from feelings, so why did I think I could do it with the one guy who evoked feelings in me the first time I saw him?

He shakes his head slowly. "I don't go weird."

I quirk my eyebrow. "Sure about that? Mr. Went All Weird On Me After the First Time?"

His jaw tics, his eyes remaining as cold as stone. Sensing the tense silence, I get to my feet, fully naked, and drop down, picking up a new dress. I shimmy into it, not needing a bra or panties, or maybe just wanting to get out of this room, because it's claustrophobic. Fluffing my hair up, I pull my Keds on.

"Where are you going?" he asks through a raspy voice.

"To get drunk." And then I pull open the tent flap and march toward the bonfire and all the drunk screams. Regardless if I know I haven't been able to separate sex from attachment, I still want to try. And considering that when it comes to Bishop, I'm stubborn, I'm hoping that will win out and I won't let my pride get hurt by showing him I have feelings for him. Which I don't right now, unless you count hate as a feeling, but I know the possibility is there. It's always there with me.

Just as I approach the keg, Tillie walks up to me—or stumbles, rather. "I'm too drunk." Her eyes are crossed, her words slurred.

I laugh. "I see that. Do I need to take you to bed?"

She shakes her head. "No." *Burp.* "No. But I made a mistake."

Filling up my cup, I watch as the foam wraps around the rim of my red cup.

"Okay, what have you done?" I smirk around my cup, lifting the disgusting beer to my mouth. Nate walks toward us and wraps his arm around Tillie's waist.

"Tada!" she announces, stretching her arm wide toward Nate. "Introducing: my mistake." Oh no.

My smile falls instantly. "Nate!" I hiss. "She's drunk!"

He shrugs. "Needed something to take my mind off my stabby stepsister, you know, since you don't give it up."

"Give what up?" My eyes slant. He pushes Tillie away and stalks toward me. "Nate? What the fuck are you doing?"

Caging me against a tree, he tilts his head, studying me. "There's so much you don't know, sis," he snaps. "You're fucking deluded if you think you can make it out of this with your life." He bends down, running his lips over the crook of my neck. "You're going to die."

It feels as though a knife launched into my throat, and I swallow past it before shoving him away. "Leave me alone."

"Naw," he murmurs lazily, coming back to me and wrapping his hands around the backs of my thighs, lifting me up. He slams me against the tree trunk again, and I mentally slap myself for wearing no panties. "You and I both know you don't mean that." He lips skim over mine, but I move my face away from him.

"No, I mean it. Let me down, Nate. You're obviously high. Let me go." I can see it in how dilated his pupils are that he's on some heavy shit.

"Nate!" Bishop barks from behind us.

Nate grins at me but slowly rubs my body down his abs as he drops me back to the ground. "I warned you," he whispers, before bending down to my ear. "This is all a game, kitty. Bishop, me, the Kings—it's a game, but it's a *death match.*"

I watch his retreating back before looking at Bishop. "I think it's time I start asking questions."

Bishop walks toward me slowly. "Pretty sure asking questions is out of your jurisdiction."

CHAPTER 23

"I was so drunk last night." Tillie massages her temples as I strip down to my bikini. Tatum scoffs, ripping off her clothes so she's in hers as well. "No shit." She rolls her eyes and steps into the cold lake. I woke up this morning needing a bath or shower, so I woke up Tillie and Tatum and dragged their asses with me to try to find a lake, which we did. Buried in the middle of nowhere, about a forty-minute walk north from the camp. Tonight is our last night here before going home tomorrow, thank God. I don't want anyone to find out about Bishop and me sleeping together—again—so when—not if, *when*—something happens, no one can tell me they told me so.

"I can't believe you slept with Nate, Tillie." Tatum shakes her head and then dunks under the water, pushing her hair out of her face. "But seriously… how good is he?"

"Stop. Gross." I shake my head, stepping into the lake. There are rocks that surround it, so I take a step on the first one, tying my hair up into a messy ponytail. "I don't want to know about Nate and his…." I pause.

"Huge cock?" Tatum winks at me.

"Really?" I scold her. "You just had to say that?"

"Yes, really, and I'm flattered. I really am." Nate smirks, walking toward the mouth of the lake, with Bishop, Cash, Abel, Chase, Hunter and Eli following behind him.

The Kings are all here.

My frown deepens, but I turn back toward the water and dive in until I'm under the bitter glacial water. Swimming to the top, I surface and swipe my hair out of my face with a smirk of my own. The sound of birds tweeting and crickets chirping hum through the blistering silence, and it feels natural, perfect. Doggy paddling under the water to keep my body afloat, I dunk my mouth under and examine the Kings. They're all in board shorts, shirtless, blessing us all with their—what I have no doubt they call—masterpieces for bodies. Nate starts talking to Tillie, much to her dismay, and Tatum looks to be taunting Hunter and Abel, as the rest of the boys take a seat on a couple of rocks overlooking the vast area of the lake.

Still doggy paddling to keep above the water, Bishop starts walking in, headed for me. Each saunter he makes toward me, the waters separate for him, much like the human race whenever Bishop is around. He gets closer and then dives under, every muscle in his body rippling as he plunges in. He disappears. Seconds pass, and he still hasn't resurfaced. I look around, left to right, and then finally come back to where everyone is on the shoreline, all talking like they were.

Where the fu—

Arms latch around my ankles, and I scream out loudly before the glacial waters suck me under again. My hands swing out as I attempt to pull myself to the surface, but Bishop's arm locks around my waist tightly, pulling me closer to him until my body is flush against his and we're both entrapped by the water. He grabs me at the back of my neck and pulls my lips to his, his tongue slipping inside my mouth. He grabs one of my boobs, pushing my bikini down and squeezing my nipple. Deciding to take his lack of grip on me as a chance to break free, I push off his chest and struggle to the surface, sucking in a large gulp of air and swiping my hair off my face. Bishop comes up a second after me, a smirk on his mouth and water trickling over his perfect face.

I splash him. "Dick move!"

He grins, swimming up to me. "I never said I wasn't a dick, kitty." He wraps one of his arms around the back of my waist and pulls me into him. I search his eyes for something, and I don't even know what. He glares back at me, burning enough to set my body on fire despite the fact I'm in a freezing fucking cold lake.

"What?" he asks, and I keep my hand on his chest, trying to ignore how his cock presses against my stomach every few seconds as he bobs in the water.

"We're supposed to be a secret, remember?" I tilt my head. "You're not being very secretive."

He shrugs and licks the lake water off his plump lips. "I didn't get to where I am by giving a fuck what people think."

"And where is that?" I ask, sinking closer into his embrace. I'm well aware of how this would look to our friends on the shore, but I'm so entranced by Bishop that I no longer care. Black Veil Brides' "Knives and Pens" plays from Tillie's Beats sound-dock in the distance just as Bishop grins.

"God status."

I roll my eyes, swimming to the edge of one of the big rocks that are placed around the edge of the lake, pushing myself up and taking a seat on one that's tucked away slightly. Bishop follows, coming to me and climbing up. I try to ignore the way his tan skin glistens in the afternoon sun and how his muscles contract with every single movement. I notice the scripted tattoo over his ribcage and nudge my head as he takes a seat beside me. "What's the tattoo say?"

He leans over, lifting his arm to look at it, and then leans back on his elbows, shaking the water out of his hair. *"There are humans, and there are wolves, and then there is me..."* He inches up to me, his lips gliding over the thin flesh of my neck. *"A fucking god."*

I close my eyes and internally fight the urge to crawl onto his lap. Prying them open, they fall on everyone back at the mouth of the lake. "You did not get that."

He chuckles. "Yeah, I did."

"I'm not even surprised." I lie on my back, throwing my arm over my eyes to shield the sun. Little colorful dots dance behind my shut lids, and I'm just about to ask Bishop about what the whole "riddle me this" stuff was about, when I feel his fingertip glide down the side of my ribcage.

"Bishop," I warn through a whisper.

"Shh," he coos, pushing his finger up to my lips. "Just go with it."

"But what about the rules? We had rules."

"Kitty, I don't do rules—ever. In anything too, by the way. I do what the fuck I want, and if people don't like it, then it's no loss to me." His warm lips press to the crook of my neck, and I suck in a breath, my pulse picking up speed. "I want you. You want me. Stop being such a fucking girl and spread those legs."

Obeying his order, I slowly inch my legs wider, and he dips back into the water. Pulling my legs toward him, he ducks behind the rock and grips my bikini bottoms.

"Bishop!" I laugh, getting up on my elbows.

"What?" He licks his lips. "They can't see, and who the fuck cares if they could?"

"Ah, me?" I answer sarcastically. "This may come as a shock to you, but I don't go flashing my hoo-ha to just anyone."

"Don't say hoo-ha ever again."

"Oh?" I quirk my eyebrow. "Is that your cock-block?"

"What do you mean?" he asks, dunking his lips under the water and then spitting it out.

"The opposite of cock-bait."

He stops, his eyes running over my body in such a way it has me forgetting everyone that is here. "Naw, babe. Nothing can stop me from this." He presses the cushion of his thumb against my clit, and I drop down to my back, my eyes closing but the afternoon sun fighting to break through my eyelids. "Your Betrayal" by Bullet For My Valentine starts blaring in the distance, just as Bishop pulls off my bikini bottoms and the fresh forest air whips around my tender flesh.

My chest rises and falls, my breathing heavy and needy, wanting him to dull the ache he has started, the ache that seems to be on Nitric Oxide whenever he's around. His warm mouth blankets my folds and my back arches, my hand slamming down on my own mouth to stifle my moans. Spreading my legs wide, he licks me from my entry to my clit and then sucks on it softly before circling my nub in his mouth with slow, pressured rotations.

"Bishop," I moan softly.

"What do you want, kitty?" he murmurs against my needy clit. "I might give it to you."

"I... I...," I mutter hoarsely. He presses his tongue over my clit, rubbing it vigorously until my thighs are quivering and my moans are about to scream out of my body. "I want you!" I whisper-yell. "Fuck, I want you, Bishop."

"My what, kitty? You can't have it all."

Not seeing the truth in his words during my sex-drunken haze, I answer, "Your cock. I need it. I need you."

He yanks my body and I fall into the water with a loud splash, the ice-cold lake only enhancing the sensitivity of my nipples. Wrapping his arm around waist, he props me up and surfaces me on the water. I wrap my hands around his neck, squeezing my legs around him, and slowly sink myself down on top of his thick head. His eyes roll back—fucking roll back—and my pussy clenches at the sight alone, but my finger comes up to his lips, where I run it over the plumpness roughly. He hits my hand away and shoves me against one of the rocks before trying to pull out of me. I clench around him, pulling him into myself during his outward stroke.

"Fuck," he mutters. "So fucking tight." His hand comes up to my throat. "But I fucking hate you." He pumps me again. "Hate what you are." He pulls out and then pushes in roughly, so rough my back starts to sting from the friction. He kisses me urgently, sucking my bottom lip into his mouth. "Hate who you are." He pounds into me, raw and consistently, my back aching from the grazes, which is almost unbearable, but I'm so lost in our cage, a cage that's entranced by Bishop's voodoo sex magic, I don't care. His hands come to my thighs, where he spreads me wider. "I hate you, kitty, and that's why you will always just be another fuck for me."

I rub myself against him. "I'm... I'm..." I wanna say a stupid bitch, but what comes out is, "...going to come!" I let go, my body shaking, my brain fuzzy, my vision blurred, and my hearing frizzled. My orgasm takes every drop of my energy and sucks it into a hole of nothingness with empty feelings.

He follows closely, his cock pulsing inside of me as I continue to milk him.

His shoulders turn slack as he leans back, searching my eyes. "I'm flattered you hate me that much." I roll my eyes and push away from him. He lets me go, and I try to hide my disappointment. Do I want him to chase me? Possibly. I have too much pride to accept him just letting me walk away, but I also know this is Bishop. It's obvious just how unattainable he is, and him gracing me with his presence is what I should be happy with. I scoff inwardly. Fuck that.

"Hey." His hand catches mine just as I get out of the lake and back onto the rock. I look at him over my shoulder, and he stills. His eyes settle on my back. "Shit."

I look over my shoulder. "Those will heal." I shrug, stepping off the rock and walking away from him, opting for the short trek back through the tree line of the lake to get back to the girls instead of swimming back. "My feelings, on the other hand...," I whisper angrily under my breath. My feelings shouldn't even be in the equation. I know this, but he doesn't. He's made it crystal clear he doesn't want more, so I should just walk away now before I get hurt—or break.

"Madison!" he yells, jogging up to me. I ignore him, carrying on my walk. Am I being ridiculous? Yes. Do I care? No.

"Hey!" He tugs on my hand, spinning me around to face him. "What's wrong?" His eyebrows draw in. He looks genuinely confused.

I shake my head. "Nothing. Don't worry about it." Then I turn around again and start walking back toward the girls.

He tugs on my hand again, only this time I fall against his chest. He looks down at me, making me feel small with a simple glare. "What. The. Fuck. Is your problem, kitty?"

I exhale. "It's nothing. I guess I always knew you hated me, but I didn't know the severity of it."

He tilts his head. "So why are you sulking, then?"

I push at his chest, but his hand comes up and catches my wrist. "Stop the fucking bullshit, kitty. Tell me what's wrong!"

"Why do you hate me so much?" I blurt out. "Why? Why did you say you hate what I am and who I am—as if you've known me forever?"

His jaw tics, but his grip doesn't loosen. "Maybe I fucking have. Ever thought about that?"

I pause, slamming my mouth shut. "What do you mean?" I ask after a moment.

He pushes me this time. "Maybe I've known who you are for some time." He starts walking back toward the mouth of the lake.

I run up to him, falling into step behind him. "What the fuck does that mean?"

"It means you should just stay away."

"No."

"What?" He spins around to face me. "What do you mean no?"

"I won't stay away from you just because you said so!" I retort. "Tell me!"

He steps up to me, his eyes cold, his jaw stone, and his lip slightly curled. "You don't know anything."

"So fucking tell me!" I shout at him, searching his eyes and ignoring the shiver of goose bumps that have spiked over my skin. "God, Bishop," I whisper in defeat. "Be honest with me."

Silence. I look back at his face, catching him watching me closely. "You're not ready. But I will tell you this…" He pauses, licking his bottom lip. "Not everything is as it seems. We—The Kings—don't play games for shits and giggles. There's a reason why we do what we do when we have to, and trust me, kitty. You're lucky you made it out with your life intact—for now."

"What?" I whisper in shock. I told him to be honest, but now he has given me even more questions to ask.

"As much as it looks like we're trying to hurt you…" He pauses again. "As much as we have hurt you, it's all for your own good."

"What the fuck does that mean?" I rake my hair out of my face, my breath quickening. "Bishop, that's just giving me more questions."

"Do you trust me?"

Instant. "No."

He gives me one of his panty-melting smirks. "Good. Do you trust Nate?"

Hesitation. "N—no."

"Your judgment isn't as shit as you think, then." He steps up to me, gripping my fingers with his and pulling me into his body. "Believe it or not, though, we're doing this for your own good, and it could quite possibly put us in danger too."

I rub my temples. "You're giving me a headache," I murmur into his warm, hard chest.

"Well then, we're even, 'cause I have something else that's aching."

I shove him, a small smile pulling on my lips. "So you hate me that much, huh?" I ask playfully, as we walk back toward everyone.

"Yes. I won't lie about that, but that's only because I have unanswered questions, suspicions, and a whole lot of facts that are in front of me. But it just so happens… you get my dick hard."

"Hmm," I murmur, just as we step out onto the sandy area. "And men say girls are complicated? That right there, Bishop Vincent Hayes, was a grade-A clinger warning!" I mock him, my mouth open.

He stops his walk, scowling at me with his lip curled up. "Say what?" Then he charges at me, grabbing the back of my thighs firefighter-style and flinging me over his shoulder.

I scream out loudly, hitting his ass with my hand while everyone chuckles in the background. "Bishop!" I yell at him, just as he tosses me into the air. I swim around midair just as my back and butt hit the hard water with a loud splash, and little bites cover my ass.

Thirty minutes. That's how long I spent with Bishop. And he has bruised me in more places than I can see.

CHAPTER 24

"So are we just going to ignore the fact that you and Bishop Vincent fucking Hayes are obviously banging?" Tatum states, pulling on her cutoff shorts.

I tug on my little black shorts, buttoning them up, and then throw on a loose white boyfriend suit-shirt, tucking one side in. "I mean, I don't know. We're just sleeping together, but you can't say anything. And when this all blows up in my face, you're still not allowed to say anything!" I look pointedly to both Tatum and Tillie.

"I didn't say anything." Tatum shakes her head, a small smile playing on her lips. But then her smile falls. "But please be careful. They're dangerous, Madi."

"I know how to take care of myself," I reassure her with a smile. Looking to Tillie, I nudge my head. "What's up with you and Nate?"

She stills, pulling on her boyfriend jeans. "Nothing."

I narrow my eyes. "Bullshit."

She exhales. "I don't know. We slept together last night." She looks to Tatum nervously.

Tatum stops what she's doing, looking at me and Tillie. "What? Oh, please. Like I care. I was serious when I said I used him just like he used me. I wish you all the sexy times in the world, I promise."

"Okay," Tillie says relieved. "But he's... I don't know. Confusing."

"Duh, it's Nate. He's a dick," Tatum scoffs.

"No, that's not it," Tillie murmurs. "I mean, he's obviously a dick and all that, but to me, not so much."

"Hmm." I stare off into the distance. "Interesting."

Tillie laughs, tying her pastel pink hair up in a high ponytail. "It's nothing."

I bend down, pull out the bottle of Grey Goose, and then throw the red cups in the middle. "So this wasn't exactly what I had in mind when I said we should all go camping." I roll my eyes. "This isn't the camping I usually do."

"We know that." Tatum grins. "You should have brought your guns!"

A horrified expression pulls across my face. "What? No way. That's not—no. That's going against everything my dad taught me growing up."

"Well, maybe we could all go together sometime. I've never shot a gun." Tillie stares off into the distance.

"That's a better idea!" I point, widening my eyes at Tatum.

"What?" Tatum feigns innocence. "Just saying… maybe you could shoot Bishop, and people would think it was an accident." We all start laughing. Clutching my stomach, I wipe the tears off my cheeks.

"You know," I say, pouring in the vodka and then opening the orange juice. "When I started at Riverside, I had no idea what to expect. All my other schools? It was difficult."

"How so? You're probably the coolest chick I've ever met," Tillie says, and then looks to Tatum. "No offense."

Tatum clutches her heart in mock hurt and then giggles.

"Because I just didn't… fit in. Girls would just flat out hate me." I shook my head. "Anyway, the only school I sort of did fit in—but somehow still didn't—was in Minnesota. And that's only because I was dating the quarterback." I laugh. "He was popular, and everyone hated that I was the girl he chose, but they didn't voice it." I take a swig of my drink. "At least not until we broke up."

"Well, if it's any consolation," Tatum murmurs, sinking her drink, "no one has liked me as much as you two do either. But… I've never liked them either, so it worked out well."

I smile, holding up my drink. "To us!" We clink and then swallow our drinks.

Tatum lies down. "Are we being unsociable by not being out there drinking with everyone else?"

I lean back on my elbows. "Probably, but we never liked any of them before we came here, so who cares?"

"Knock, knock!"

"Don't come in. We're naked!" Tatum laughs dramatically.

The zipper rips open, and Carter steps inside with a grin. "Aw, I'm disappointed." He drops down beside me. "Why are you girls hiding out in here?"

I giggle, leaning up and pouring more vodka and orange juice into my cup. "Because we can."

"Oh, I see." Carter grins. "My beer not good enough for you?"

I look at him, noticing where Bishop's eyes are dark green and smoldering, Carter's are bright and lively. Where Bishop's bottom lip has a slight pout to it, Carter's are average at best. Where Bishop's skin is soft, tan, and glistens in the sun, Carter's is pale white but has a slight blush to his cheeks that is—undoubtedly—adorable. Carter also has a single dip in his chin too that I also find adorable.

I look back into his eyes to find him looking at me with a smug grin. "Like what you see?"

I see Tatum whips her head toward us out the corner of my eye. I take a drink. "Meh." I shrug. He elbows me playfully and we both laugh. I know Carter was with someone else last night, just like I was, but I don't care. I don't have any emotional attachments to Carter. I don't hate him. I don't *anything* him. He's just pretty to look at sometimes.

"So." Tatum rolls onto her stomach as I grab another cup and fill him up. "I heard you hooked up with Jenny Prescott last night?" She wiggles her eyebrows for added effect. "I heard she can do this little trick with her—"

"Stop," Carter laughs, almost choking on his drink. "But yeah, she does a trick."

"Oh, gross," I mutter, looking to Tillie.

"Jealous?" Carter grins at me. *Oh, dear.*

"Definitely not."

His smile falls slightly.

"I can back her answer, because she was with—"

I hit Tatum with my leg.

"Oh?" Carter quirks. "With who?"

"No one. With myself." I smile at him.

"Oh, I see. No kiss and tell?"

I zip my lips and throw away the key. "Never."

He leans back on his elbow, taking a sip of his drink. Bishop and I never had the conversation about how open we are about sleeping with other people, even though that's not how I am at all. And even though I did make him say it just before sex, I don't think that counts. Carter looks up at me. "Whoever it is, be careful, yeah?"

I look down at him, very aware of how close he is to me. I nod. "Of course."

He smiles sadly then takes another drink, just as the tent entrance pulls over and in walks Bishop, Nate, and Hunter.

Bishop looks to Carter, his jaw slightly clenched, and suddenly, I feel guilty. Why the hell do I feel guilty? There were no promises made between us. But even so, I can say without a shadow of doubt that I don't like being near any other guy but Bishop. Having Carter so close to me doesn't feel right, but having Bishop sucking on my flesh does.

Bishop's eyes narrow on me, taking in Carter and me. He instantly has the wrong idea. Surprise, surprise. Instead of throwing a hissy fit, though, Bishop takes a seat beside Tatum as she pours them all a drink.

"Party in our tent then?" She looks to Bishop, Nate, and Hunter. Bishop's eyes haven't moved from me, so I look to Tatum, handing her my cup. "Another?" She raises her eyebrows. "If I didn't know better, Montgomery, I'd say you want to get wasted."

I shrug. "Well, since I didn't get to have any last night…" I look at Bishop with a fake smile. "Yes, I want more."

Nate shuffles over to the other side of me, his arm wrapping around my waist. I close my eyes, calming my breathing. "Sis," he whispers into my ear, his hair tickling my earlobe. "I'm sorry."

I open my eyes and look at him wide-eyed. "For what?"

"Everything, but most importantly, what's still to come." His eyes search mine desperately. Every sharp angle of his jaw and his straight nose pisses me off.

"I'm sick of the riddles," I whisper.

He grins and then leans into me, running his lips over my cheek. "I know." Then he pulls me closer to him and noticeably away from Carter. I take my drink from Tatum, bringing it to my lips.

"Music!" Tillie says, looking between me and Nate uncomfortably. I look back at Bishop, who is leaning into Tatum, and she is looking at me in silent question.

Jesus. What sort of fucked up group are we?

I shake my head at Tillie, hoping she knows Nate and I are not like that. Tillie pulls out her sound dock and hits Play on Escape the Fate's "One For The Money." I smirk at her. I love her taste in music; it's so different from Tatum and Nate's hip-hop obsession. Not that I dislike hip-hop, I just have an eccentric taste in music and like to listen to different genres all at once, not the same over and over again.

Nate pulls out what looks like a brown cigarette, and then pulls out a Zippo, sparking it up. He takes a big toke and then passes it to me. I fight internally with myself before thinking, *Fuck it*, and taking the cigarette off him. The sweet, woodsy smell of marijuana smoke fills the tent and engulfs my senses.

Nate points to the tent entrance. "Bumboy, close the tent!" Carter looks at him with narrowed eyes before getting up and shutting the entrance.

I bring it to my mouth and inhale like I've seen in movies. *Thanks, Redman and Methodman.* The smoke hits me right in my throat and then in my chest. I cough spastically, my lungs feeling like they're closing up, before handing it to Carter. A second later, my eyes are heavy and the thick smoke that's starting to fog up the tent all starts to swim around everyone's frames, slowly getting thicker and thicker.

I lean into Nate and laugh. "Are we hot-boxing the tent?"

He kisses me on the head. "Yeah, kitty, we are."

My eyes find Bishop's. He's leaning on his elbow, but slightly into Tatum. His legs are sprawled out in front of him, but again, it looks like he's open to her. He grins at me, and then leans into her, whispering something into her ear. Anger, jealousy, and hate fills me to the brink as I look to Tillie, trying to find something to take my mind off whatever the fuck Bishop is doing.

"Tillie! Come here." I wave her over as she takes a long hit on the joint. "Whoa," I laugh, as she takes a seat between Nate and me. "You're hitting that like a pro."

She shrugs. "I mean, it isn't my first time."

Nate grabs onto her and places her on top of his lap. "You're so fucking sexy right now. I could eat you."

"Please don't," I murmur, taking the joint from Tatum and bringing it to my mouth before taking another hit. This time, it goes down my airways a little smoother. I let the taste sit on my tongue, closing my eyes and feeling every inch of myself relax and loosen. All the stresses and worries I had thirty minutes ago mean nothing. Bishop across from me whispering sweet nothings into Tatum's ear? Means nothing. I lay on my back with the joint between my fingers.

Carter bends over on his elbow, taking the joint from me. "The thing is for sharing, Madi. Puff, puff, pass!" He laughs, moving in closer to me once again.

I laugh. "Oh, Carter," I announce loudly. "I don't share anything, and if something of mine thinks I do share, I can show them in more ways than one on how I don't."

The tent falls silent, everyone understanding the meaning in my words. Everyone but Carter. *Stupid Carter.* I bring my hand up to my face, an inch away, but the smoke is so thick I can barely make out the outline of my fingers.

"But!" I add. "Good thing I'm a free agent, huh?"

A hand glides up my leg, and I know it's not Bishop's slightly rough hand. This hand is too soft. "Yeah, lucky for me."

I turn my head toward where I know Carter is.

Nate laughs, but it sounds like it's muffled. "Maybe we should get Hunter someone to play with. Then this can be one big orgy."

Filled with anger, betrayal, and jealousy—jealousy, because Tatum probably has Bishop's hands on her—my thoughts pause. My core clenches and sweat beads on my head. The thought fills me with excitement, hate, jealousy, and... lust? Why? Why does that thought turn me on? Annoyed at myself for being such a mess, I turn onto my stomach.

"Naw." I giggle, my eyes lazy and my movements slow. I rest my head down on my arm. "Hunter can play with me. I can take two... just ask Bishop. He knows just how much I can take in bed."

Hands wrap around my ankles, and I'm suddenly tugged roughly, flipping onto my back. Yeah, those hands... those are Bishop's. The weight of a body falls over me, lips coming down to my ear. He pulls my lobe into his mouth. "Careful, kitty. I don't share either."

"You be careful." I shove at his chest and he laughs. "Go back to doing what you were doing."

Bishop pulls out his phone and flashes it into the corner, where two people are making out. Hunter and Tatum. They must have connected after the smoke got too thick.

"Hmm," I murmur, tilting my head.

He looks back to me, pressing his lips against mine. "But the questions is, why did that bother you so much, kitty? Do we need to have the talk?"

Carter murmurs from behind me, "I'm just going to go." Then he slips out of the tent quickly, letting some of the smoke out, but not all. At least now I can see the profile of Bishop's face, just as Breaking Benjamin's "The Diary of Jane" starts playing out of the dock.

"I don't know. I'm not very good at this," I reply.

"At what?" he whispers across my lips, pushing me down onto my back with his body. He stretches my legs wide with his, resting in between until his bulge is digging into me—right there. "At this!" I gesture between us. "I... I don't think I can do it and not *feel*, Bishop. I'm not you."

"Feel this." He takes my hand and brings it down, pressing it against his thick-headed cock. "That's all you need to feel."

"I warned you."

He ignores me, grinding his hips into me. "I might know what I'm doing." He brings his lips back to mine and kisses me, his tongue entering my mouth, and I massage it with my own.

"I have no doubt that you do. It's me I'm worried about."

"As you should be," Nate warns from somewhere in the thick smoke. "Just for the record, if you cause one teardrop from her eyes, B, I get one swing."

Bishop chuckles against my lips. "She understands the guidelines of the game. *No. Feelings*," he murmurs, planting a kiss on my lips after each word.

"Yeah, except she's a girl—shocking, I know—and they always feel. How you feeling right now, Tillie?" he murmurs seductively.

"Oh stop!" I shuffle up. "We are not all going to have sex in the same room."

Tatum groans from the back. "Speak for yourself."

"Nope!" I launch off the floor, walking toward the tent entrance and pulling it open, the crisp, fresh mountain air awakening me somewhat. Bishop comes after me, taking my hand. "What's wrong?"

I turn to look at him, searching his eyes. "Nothing. Just... my friends are sort of skanks."

He laughs, tucking me under his arm. "Yeah, that I can agree with."

Later that night, I'm sitting on one of the logs surrounding the bonfire, with Bishop next to me talking with Cash, his arm around my waist.

Tatum comes bouncing up to me, handing me a drink. "Sorry about before."

I laugh, shaking my head and patting the spot beside me. "Don't worry about it."

She leans on my shoulder. "One more night here."

"Yup." I pop the P. One more night, and all I want to do is read my book. I don't want to pull it out here, because someone might recognize it, and then Miss Winters might land her ass in trouble. So instead, I've had to let it burn in the back of my brain. But Bishop has been keeping my brain *and* body occupied, so it hasn't been that hard. But alas, I'm still struggling with the urge to read what else is going on. The train of thoughts she was feeling has evoked something deep inside of me that I can't let go of.

"So you and Bishop? All out in the open?" Tate whispers into my ear.

I bite down on my lower lip and shrug. "I don't know, but I think so?"

She laughs, shoving me playfully. "Well, just be careful. Don't show him all your cards."

"Is this you giving me advice?" I whisper back loudly into her face.

"Yes!" she hisses with a grin. "I'm too pretty for prison, and I *will* kill him if he hurts you."

I laugh, shaking my head while taking a sip of my drink. "Thanks, Tate."

I look toward Bishop to find him staring at me. He swallows the rest of his drink and then tugs on my hand. "Come on."

Cash is staring at me with a hint of a smug grin on his face.

The music changes to Red Jumpsuit Apparatus's "Your Guardian Angel," as we slowly dodge people and make our way deeper into the forest.

"Is this the part where you kill me?" I joke, our fingers lacing together. My heart skips a beat with how right it feels to have him so close.

He looks at me over his shoulder. "You laugh now…," he teases.

My smile falls. "I swear to God, Bishop, if this is ano—"

"Shut up!" He spins around, pressing his finger to my lips. "Stop talking." His eyes slice through every single restraint I thought I had. I nod and he drops his hand. "Good." He keeps walking deeper into the forest, dodging fallen limbs as I follow his lead.

"Where are we going?" I ask.

"It's not far." We keep walking for another twenty minutes, and then he stops, facing a thick area of shrubs. "What's this?" I ask, tilting my head.

He pushes through a thick bush and steps ahead.

"Bishop?" The bush flies back into the same position it was in.

"Step through, kitty. Stop bitching out."

I push my hands through and separate the little sharp branches, and then step one foot in until I'm on the other side. Letting it go, it flings back into place and I wipe my hands on my legs. "Jesus, what—" All thoughts skyrocket out of my head. "Oh my gosh," I whisper, stepping forward and taking in the surroundings. The bright moonlight is reflecting off the silky still water of the lake, and there're thousands upon thousands of fireflies that have lit up the dark, murky forest around us. It looks stunning, something out of a storybook. I step forward again, and Bishop's hand finds mine. Slipping off my shoes, I let my toes sink into what looks like silicon sand. "How'd you know about this place?" I ask, looking back at Bishop.

He shrugs, stepping up to me and taking a seat in the sand. "We sort of had to do a once-over of the perimeter—you know, to scare this chick…."

I shove him. "Dick."

He laughs, his pearly teeth gleaming against his tan skin, reflecting off the moonlight. He tugs on my hand. "Sit."

I follow his command, shuffling into his warmth. "This weekend hasn't been something I expected."

He nods in agreement. "Yeah, tell me about it."

"Pretty sure you knew your intentions." I roll my eyes.

"Maybe—" He grins, looking out over the water. "—but you're not like most girls." He looks back at me. "You've never made shit easy for me."

"I don't know," I murmur. "I seem to be an easy slut when it comes to you."

He laughs, leaning back on his elbow. "You're not a slut, Madison. You're just a chick who loves to explore her sexuality. In whose eyes does that make you a slut?" he questions. I pause. He continues, "It doesn't matter. What they think of you isn't your business. But you're not a slut. I know sluts, and trust me, if you were one…" He stops, grinning at me again. Smug bastard. "There would be no way in hell you'd be caught bouncing on my dick."

"Charming." I roll my eyes. He wraps his arm around my waist and pulls me into him more. "Why would I need to be charming?" he mocks. "You're a slut, remember?"

I shove him, trying to contain my laughter. "Can I ask you a question?"

"No."

"Well I'm asking you anyway," I mutter, lying flat on my back and gazing up at the twinkling of the stars. "What happened to your ex?" Silence. Maybe I overstepped the line? No, I know I overstepped the line. I knew I was before I even opened my mouth.

"Who told you about her?" he asks, relaxing his grip around my body.

"A few people."

"Tatum." He shakes his head, then whispers, "That girl has the biggest mouth in the history of Riverside."

"Hey!" I shove him again. "That's my best friend."

"Well then I take back my earlier statement," he declares, though I know there's a hint of humor in his tone. "You definitely have shitty judgment."

"Well, I slept with you, so…."

He looks at me, his lip twitching at the corner, hinting at a smirk.

"Stop changing the subject." I look at him, watching for anything. He shakes his head, no emotion pulling over his face.

"She wasn't what you think, if that's what you want to know. We weren't what you think."

"Okay, smartass, and what do I think?"

"I don't know." He looks down at me, and I snuggle into him more. "She was a means to an end. That's all you need to know for now."

"So many secrets."

"You have no idea." He squeezes into me more and kisses the top of my head.

"So I take it The Elite Kings Club is very much real?"

He laughs this time, squinting out at the lake. "True, but Madison?" He looks back to me, pulling me on top of him until I'm straddling his waist. I fight the urge to kiss him or grind on him, because apparently, I have zero self-control. He tilts his head. "This is not a joke."

"I know," I whisper softly, though I actually don't know, because he won't tell me much. I appreciate what he has already told me though, knowing that alone was a brave move for him.

"God, there's so much you should know," he whispers, his hands falling on my hips.

I inch forward and run my lips over his ever so softly, fighting to suck on his plumper lower lip. "Just tell me, Bishop. Tell me what it is."

"I can't, baby. Even though I want too, both Nate and I want to, we can't. It's not safe for you to know, and will only leave you with more questions."

I sag against him, curling into the crook of his neck. "Fine, but one more question?"

"Yeah, go for it, kitty."

"Is this real, what's happening between me and you? Or is it all part of one of your games?"

He pauses for a second and then looks at me. His eyes fall soft, a softness I have never seen the whole time I've known Bishop. "Yeah." He clears his throat. "Yeah, fuck, I think it is."

CHAPTER 25

I walk back into the house with Nate next to me, dropping my bags onto the ground. "Dad?" I call out, throwing the keys to his Aston Martin on the table in the kitchen.

Nate opens the fridge and pulls out the OJ, twisting the cap off and taking a long swig. "Mom!"

Elena comes into the kitchen in her gym gear. "Hey, you two. Have fun?" she asks with a smile, before scowling and walking toward Nate, swatting his hand off the orange juice and placing it back into the fridge. "You!" She points to his chest. "Need some more etiquette training."

"Old dogs and all that," I mutter, taking a seat on the stool.

Elena grins. "Very true, Madison." She walks to the sink and fills up a glass of water. "Your father is out at the moment but will be home a little later. Are you okay?" She turns to face me, taking a sip of her water. She truly is beautiful. She has dark auburn hair, blue eyes, and soft milky skin. She doesn't look forty-one, that's for sure. She had Nate young, and I've never really asked about Nate's dad, but I gather it's a dark story since no one has bought it up. Elena Riverside—her name alone holds more substance than Nate's lack of ability to turn down a lay.

"It's okay." I shake my head. "We had a great time, thank you." I stand up from the stool. "But I'm dying for a shower."

Nate grins at me, taking a bite out of a leftover roasted chicken leg. "Yah, I just bet you are."

I narrow my eyes. Elena rolls hers. "Nate, leave her alone. You could do with a shower too."

I laugh, poking my tongue out at him. His lip curls and I walk out the kitchen, picking up my duffle bag and walking up the stairs. I slip into my bedroom, dash into the bathroom—locking Nate's side—shower, and then quickly shuffle into some loose gray track pants that hang off my waist and a relaxed white shirt. I loved being out in the forest, but damn it's nice to be home.

I've never wanted to get attached to any of our houses before, but I don't know. Something feels like this is it for us. I hope I'm right, because I will seriously be thinking about letting Tatum's parents adopt me if my father thinks he can pack us up again and leave. I lotion up my hands and feet before slipping on some socks. Picking up my duffle bag, I rip through all my clothes until the tips of my fingers skim over the familiar brown leather book. My phone vibrates on my bedside table, but it's too late. I'm already flipping the cover and skipping to the chapter I'm up to.

4.

The tomorrow

What happens when everything you possibly thought you knew, everything you were educated on, was suddenly nothing at all?

Choosing a husband to bear my children wasn't easy for me; my parents chose him, and at the time, he seemed like an appropriate fit. He was hardworking, charming, and well-spoken. I thought he was everything I ever wanted in a companion, everything a girl ever needed in one, but it's only lately I've started to realize just how distant and out of touch my judgment may have been.

Lying Damien back into his woven crib, I hummed to him softly while continuing to rock the little crib in hopes of not waking him.

"Katsia, there seems to be an awful racket going on out there tonight."

I nodded, stepping away from the crib. "I hear that, too. Fear not, it shouldn't go on much longer."

Maree looks at me as if she was waiting for some sort of confirmation. I bobbed my head in understanding. She wouldn't let this go unless I spoke to my husband, and rightly so. Maree has a new-born baby just like I. And where Humphrey holds his gatherings, it so happens to be right beside her home.

"I won't be long." Giving her a curt nod, I walked past her and out the door, the soles of my flats pitter-pattering across the dusty forest floor. The moon was setting behind the overgrown forest trees, while the ash from Humphrey's fire hovered through the night like fireflies lighting my way. His words caught me as I opened my mouth, halting any coherent words from passing my lips. Suddenly, I knew I wasn't wanted here during this gathering, and if he found out I was, my safety would be in question.

"We kill him!" my husband's righthand man salutes proudly.

"No, we should not rush this," my husband replied. "This needs to be done carefully. I want people to know it was me but can't prove it. I want to be feared. I want to rule this fucking village, and you're going to help me do it." He paused. "Tomorrow," my husband continues. "Tomorrow I will put my ax through his skull."

He was going to kill one of our leaders? For power? Why? What must he need to do so badly that he needed full power and control? Things were spiraling out of control. Every passing day it seemed things were getting worse, and worse.

They were.

"What?" I whisper to thin air, trying to wrap my head around the latest events in this story. Why? Why did Humphrey want to kill one of their leaders? To rule? Sounds like mighty big actions for something that is still, realistically speaking, not really up to him. He would have to win the people over as well. My phone dings again in the background, this time ringing, and I blindly reach for it, my eyes still on the book.

"Hello?"

"Are they still home?"

Bishop.

"Who? Are who still home?"

"Your dad and Elena."

I huff, standing from my bed, and walk toward my sliding door that leads onto my little balcony, pushing the elegant white curtain out of the way. Peeking out the slit, I shake my head. "No, they're gone. Why?"

"Pack a bag, and tell Nate to pack one too."

"What?"

"Pack a fucking bag and be ready in five minutes. We're almost there."

The urgency in his tone doesn't go unnoticed. "Why?" I straighten my shoulders, my eyes darting around the room.

"Ask questions later. For now, for once, just do as you're fucking told." Then he hangs up the phone. I look down at the now blank screen, my eyebrows drawing in.

"Nate!" I yell, dropping my phone onto the bed and walking toward our conjoined bathroom. Pulling open his door, I instantly slam my hand over my eyes at the sight of Nate riding some girl. "Nate! Oh my god! For fuck's sake!"

"Join in or get out!" He laughs, though if I take in the sounds correctly, I'd say he's not stopping his penetrating.

I keep my hand over my eyes. "Bishop just called and said we both have to pack a bag and be ready in five minutes."

"What?" He stops. *He stops?*

"Yes. So can you hurry up?" I roll my eyes, dropping my hand to my side when I realize I don't care, until my eyes fall on Tillie. Oh no. Once? Fine. Twice? Not fine. My smile falls. "Tillie?" Her cheeks turn red as she pulls the covers up to her face. Nate rolls his eyes, tugs the bedding down, and then crawls off her, pulling his jeans on. "Don't hide from her."

"Jesus," I whisper, my hand now coming to my forehead. "You and I will talk about this," I hiss toward Nate.

"Jealous?" He wiggles his eyebrows.

I'll punch him. I swear to God, I'll punch him.

"No!" I scrunch up my face. "Get ready." Then I leave them both, walking back into my room and straight to my closet. Pulling out my duffle bag, I yank down random clothes and shoes, shoving them inside before darting into the bathroom for my toothbrush, shampoo, and all the essentials I'll need—including my birth control pill. Nate walks in, his door swinging open to show Tillie shuffling her jeans back on. He walks toward the sink and snatches his toothbrush, watching me closely in the mirror.

"Hurt her, Nate, and I'll kill you."

"Threats are cheap, kitty!" he hollers, as I walk back to my bed and shove all my toiletries into the side pocket before kneeling and scooping up the leather-bound book from under my bed, slipping it into my bag. "That wasn't a threat." My voice is calm, stoic. My bedroom door crashes open, hitting the wall to show a fuming Bishop.

"Holy fuck!" I yell. "What the hell is your problem?"

"Get downstairs, now! Where's Nate?"

"In his room. Hey!" I walk toward Bishop, taking in his disheveled hair, and the sheen of sweat on his tanned skin, and his eyes. His eyes are furious, dilated to almost black. Can this man ever look ugly?

"Don't." He shakes his head. "Just get the fuck downstairs."

Nate chooses now to walk in. "What's going on?"

Bishop looks at Nate, Nate looks back at Bishop, and then the smug little smile that was on Nate's mouth falls instantly. "Oh fuck."

Bishop snatches my hand and pulls me into his body, just about to drag me out the door, when he catches Tillie in Nate's bedroom. "Really?"

Nate looks over his shoulder briefly. "You are in no place to judge anyone's choice of bed partner."

Bishop's jaw tenses. "Except you and I both know I didn't exactly *pick*."

Ouch.

Nate rolls his eyes, scooping up his bag from the floor. "She can come."

"To the Galleys?" Bishop scoffs. "Definitely fucking not."

"B, you don't get a say in this, this time around. She's coming." Nate tugs Tillie's hand.

Bishop steps toward Nate. "I *always* get the last say. Remember that."

"Bishop, let her come. Stop being an ass," I whisper.

He looks at me over his shoulder briefly, seeming to struggle with something, before looking back to Nate. "What? You think because she says, I'll do it? Are you forgetting who I am?"

"We're wasting time!" I yell. I don't know for what reason, but it probably has something to do with how tense Bishop is.

He steps back, his eyes still locked on Nate. "Interesting, pup. You actually give a shit about his girl," Bishop taunts him, snatching my hand and pulling me out my bedroom door. I glance over my shoulder toward Tillie and Nate. When her eyes find mine, I mouth "I'm sorry" to her, and she shakes her head with a small smile. Nate pulls her under his arm and kisses her forehead as we all walk out the front door.

Bishop opens the passenger door to his Maserati before walking around to the driver side. Nate and Tillie get into the back seat, and just as I'm about to slip into the driver seat, I notice the line of cars parked behind us. The driver in the Lamborghini behind us I recognize as Ace, and I guess the rest of the expensive cars have the rest of The Kings in them.

"Get in, kitty!" Bishop yells from behind the wheel.

I slip inside and pull my seatbelt on. "What's going on?" I ask, clicking it in just as Bishop skids out of my driveway. I look into the side-view mirror to see the rest of the cars pulling out behind us. "Bishop!" I snap, looking toward him. "What's going on and why am I in here?"

"You gonna explain, or should I?" Nate murmurs smugly from the back seat.

Bishop gives him a death stare into the rearview mirror. "That night you were with me."

"Which night?" I add.

"The race."

"I'm following."

"You remember how I said something vague like 'he won't recognize you'?"

"Yes."

"Well, he recognized you." He drops the gear into second and floors it onto the main highway, away from the city.

"And who is *he*?"

Bishop looks into the rearview mirror at Nate before bringing his eyes back to the main road. "My dad."

CHAPTER 26

"Wait." I turn in my seat to face him. "That was your dad? And why does it matter?" Bishop looks to Nate again, his jaw tensing. "He thinks you're someone else."

"Well, that's easy then." I fling my hand around. "We'll just tell him he has it wrong."

"Yeah, that's not how stuff works with him."

"Well, explain," I squeak. Bishop takes a turn, and I look behind us to see the rest of the boys following close behind. "And your mom's famous! It can't be that bad."

"See, that's the thing, though," Nate says from behind me. "These people, every single one of them is in a powerful position."

"Nothing makes sense," I whisper, watching the blur of trees pass as we head deeper out of town.

Bishop growls, his fingers tensing around his steering wheel. "They think you're someone else, and it's hard to explain without letting something I can't slip, slip, but they just…" He pauses, searching for the right words. "They think you're someone else."

My body jolts from the bumpy road and I peel my eyes open, a yawn slipping past my lips. It's dark out, the high beams the only light we have as we head deeper down a narrow dirt road that is lined with nature. Thick nature. I turn in my seat to see Nate and Tillie both asleep, Tillie cradled into the crook of Nate's arm, and Nate with his hoodie up and his cap shading his eyes.

I look back to Bishop. "How long have we been driving?"

He adjusts in his seat. "Five hours."

Five hours? Holy crap. "Where are we going?" I question, watching as the forest gets darker and darker and the road starts to look less like a road.

"To a cabin." He stretches his neck out.

"Why can't you just tell him he's wrong?"

"Because I can't, Madi." He looks at me from the corner of his eyes. "If it were that simple, I would have done it by now."

"Well, I need something else. Because nothing is making a lot of sense to me right now."

He grins for the first time since I saw him yesterday, his trademark smirk coming across his lips. "Aren't you used to it by now, though?"

Pulling up to a wide stretch of land, he drives the car up closer to the log cabin that overlooks the rest of the secluded forest.

"Who owns this place?" I ask, looking at how it's a little on the richer scale to be classed as a cabin in the woods—which admittedly is what I was thinking. You know, the kind the serial killer drags you back to. But it's not that at all. Even though it seems up-scale, I can see how the gardens are overgrown, the vines snaking up the pillars that sit on each side of the front porch. Someone hasn't been taking care of it.

"Me." Bishop pushes open his door and gets out.

"What?" I gasp, slipping out of the passenger seat. I'm just about to ask him more, when multiple headlights light up the dark, misty night, waking Nate and Tillie in the back. I shut my door, rounding the car toward Bishop. His arm slips out, wrapping around my waist as he pulls me into him more. I cave, melt, or whatever you want to call it. It feels good after being in a car for hours on end, that's for sure.

His hard chest is flush up against my back when I run my hand over his muscled forearm, as the rest of the boys pile out of their cars, carrying a variation of bags.

Bishop nudges his head. "I'll unlock," he calls out, stepping backward and taking his body heat with him. He takes my hand. "Come on." Leading me up the front steps and unlocking the door, instantly, soft musk hits my senses, mixed with old pine and something sweet and... masculine? Bishop flicks on the lights, dropping the keys on the table beside the coat hanger.

Pinching my eyes closed briefly, I then take in the now bright area. "Wow. This is all yours?"

Bishop nods. "Yeah."

"But is this smart?" I ask, just as Hunter, Ace, Abel, Brantley, and Cash walk through.

"Yeah, Bishop, is it smart?" Brantley seethes, evil eyeing me as he passes through.

I ignore him.

"It's the last place they would think to look," Bishop reassures. He walks into the sitting room, which takes up most of the ground level, overlooking the forest through floor-to-ceiling windows that are shaped like a triangle, pulling in from the middle.

"How so?" I ask, following him in farther.

"Because the first place they'll look is your place, and then the rest of the boys'. By the time they've finally figured it out, we will have sorted our next plan of action.

I walk to where he's leaning against the kitchen counter. "And exactly how long is this supposed to be?"

He pauses, looking directly into my eyes. "I don't know."

"Come on." He pushes off the sink, taking my hand in his. "We'll go up to the room."

I think about arguing with him, but figure I can still do that in the room, so I let him lead me up the stained wooden stairs.

Walking in, he puts our bags onto the bed, taking a seat beside them.

"Here's the thing," Bishop starts, removing his shirt. My mouth waters and my eyes skate over him slowly. He catches my perving, pauses what he was saying, and quirks his lip a little before continuing. "My dad is a part of this... firm. These people, they all work for my dad." He tosses his shirt into the corner and then takes another seat on the bed. "They follow my dad's lead. In everything. You can think of him as sort of a

CEO, I guess." His eyes look into mine. "Madi, my dad isn't a good man. Not that any of us are, but he's definitely not a good man."

I take a seat beside Bishop on the bed, my eyes locked on the wall opposite us. "What does he want from me?"

Bishop curses, tugs on his hair in frustration, and then braces his elbows on his knees, leaning forward. "He's—I can't. We can't even talk about it."

He goes to continue, but I cut him off. I know what he's implying, and I don't want to make him feel like he has to tell me and then feel guilty or whatever for sharing something so big. But if I guess, then it wouldn't be his fault. "CIA?" I whisper, finishing his previous sentence.

"What?" His head tilts in confusion.

"You know...." I insinuate.

Recognition sparks in his eyes and he smiles, almost in relief. "Yeah," he whispers. "Yeah."

"Okay, but what do they want with me?" Now that I know his father works for the CIA, I feel more at ease. The Elite Kings, they're just a bunch of rich boys out spending Mommy and Daddy's money. They're exactly the kind of boys I suspected they were. I'm mentally rolling my eyes at Tatum and her overdramatic rumors about them all. Typical Tatum.

Bishop leans back onto his elbows, every muscle tensing in his movement. "They think your dad is laundering money for one of the major trading companies in Las Vegas."

Recognition slips in. My dad is always in Vegas, more often than not lately. Maybe that's why we always moved? Maybe we weren't moving because he couldn't settle. Maybe we were moving, because he was running from something—or someone. It makes sense in my head, the puzzle pieces slipping together slowly.

"So now what?" I ask, looking at him over my shoulder. "Is this what you guys couldn't tell me?"

Bishop nods reluctantly. "Yeah, babe."

"Huh." I look forward. "Why didn't you just come right out and hint to me earlier?"

"Because I didn't trust you. They—aside from Nate—still don't trust you."

Before I can ask him what they have to do with anything, there's a light knock on the door.

"Fuck off," Bishop snaps.

"Come in," I say sweetly, both of us in unison. Way too cheesy. The door creaks open, and Tillie pops her head around it. She's wearing one of Nate's hoodies and is looking at me like she has thousands of things she wants to say, so I pat Bishop's hand and look at him. "Give us a second."

He watches Tillie closely, too closely, and she looks back, her mouth slightly open. Something passes between the two of them before Tillie swallows nervously. Bishop shoves past her. *Always the asshole.*

Tillie smiles sadly at him with a nod and then takes a seat where he was on the bed.

The door closes before I turn to her. "What was that about?"

"What did he tell you?" she asks, her eyes searching mine.

"About what?"

"About this... what did he tell you?"

"I can't say. Sorry, Tillie."

A fake smile sprawls over her face. "It's okay. Anyway, I wanted to talk to you about—"

"Tillie, it's totally fine. Was a shock initially, but it's totally fine. Just one thing..." I hold one finger up. "Please be careful. He's not capable of the things you might be expecting out of him."

Her shoulders slack in defeat. "Thank you, but I'm sure I'll be fine, Madi." She looks around the master bedroom. "I thought the room we were in was nice, but this is something else."

I look around absently. "Yeah, it's nice."

Tillie turns to look at me. "So, um, did he say how he got this house?"

I shake my head, standing from the bed and picking up my duffle bag off the floor. "No, but I do have to say that a lot of shit makes sense now. And I need to have a talk with Tatum and her crazy imagination over these rumors." I'm shaking my head and unzipping my bag when Tillie interrupts me.

"How so?"

"Let's just say that they aren't as bad as they seem." I wink at her easily. Her face goes pale, her muscles tense, and her smile drops instantly. "Tillie?" I walk toward her. "Are you okay?" Goose bumps spring up all over my flesh from the look she is giving me, but in a flash, her smile is back.

"Yeah, sorry," she tries to reassure me, but I don't buy it.

"You sure?" I question, touching her arm. "Looked like you saw a ghost."

She laughs me off easily. "Don't be silly."

I turn back to my bag and pull out my black leather jacket, slipping it on and doing up the buttons before tugging on my Ugg boots. "Shall we go downstairs?" I go to walk past her, and just as I'm about to reach the bedroom door, her hand comes to my arm, stopping me.

"Your turn to promise me that you will be careful, Madi."

I search her eyes with a smile, but when I see how serious she is, her eyes glassing over with unshed tears and fear rippling over her features, I pat her hand and give her a sincere nod. "Of course I will, Tillie."

CHAPTER 27

The flames from the log fire Bishop and the guys set up outside in the large front yard of the cottage flickers into the starry night, licking over my skin with each flash. I wrap my jacket around my body tightly again just as Bishop takes a seat on the log beside me, handing me what I assume to be a glass of whiskey. I take it happily, the ice cubes clinking and breaking our silence. A few of the guys are still awake, spread out over the logs that are outside, as well as Nate and Tillie, who are snuggled up on the ground and sitting against one. Nate kicks a stone into the fire. His other knee's pulled up with his elbow resting on it, and Tillie's tucked between his legs.

"Nate?" I call out to him softly. He pauses, his jaw tensing.

"What?"

"What's wrong?" There's never been any beating around the bush with Nate. I think, from day one, he's just always been that person I feel like I can trust, despite his shitty decisions. So they play games. When you have as much money as we all do—except Tillie—you find pleasure in shallow tricks.

He looks to Bishop, his lip curling slightly. "No, nothing. Everything is peachy, sis," he almost hisses, before looking directly at me. His eyes soften a smidge when they lock with mine, and he stands from the ground, making Tillie shuffle up quickly. Walking toward me, he stops directly in front and gently brings the back of his fingers to my cheek, running it down softly. I close my eyes. "Look at me, Madi."

My eyes open to Nate looking down at me, ignoring Bishop. I could cut the tension.

"I'm sorry," he says. Then he leaves, tugging Tillie behind him, who watches me from over her shoulder as she gets led back inside. Why is it that even though Bishop just told me what everyone was hiding, I still feel like I'm the only one out of the loop?

Sighing, I hand Bishop my drink and stand from the log. "I'm going to bed."

He takes my glass, his fingers grazing over mine. "I'm just going to talk with Saint for a bit. I'll be up soon."

I smile down at him. "Okay." Walking back inside the quiet cottage—despite the number of rowdy guys under this one roof—I trudge upstairs, with nothing but my thoughts. Pushing open our door, I pull out some panties and a loose tank before walking into the en suite. Flicking on the light, I place my clothes on the adjoining sinks and turn the faucet on. As the steam fills the large bathroom, I strip out of my clothes and pull a clean towel out of the cupboard, wrapping it around my body.

Why do I feel like there's a major part I'm missing? I trust Bishop, though. I believe he's sincere, and that might make me stupid, but why else would he feel like he has to hide something from me? His father being a part of the CIA makes a lot of sense. It aligns every single thing that has happened. That damn missing piece, though. It's staring at me, flashing itself at me.

Chalking it up to me being overtired, hungry, and just exhausted, I drop my towel and slip into the shower, scrubbing up quickly but relishing in the hot droplets of water that cascade off my drained muscles. It feels so damn good. Remembering I want to get a quick read in tonight before Bishop comes to bed, I flick the faucets off and step out of the shower, wrapping the towel around me to dry quickly before stepping into my clothes—or lack thereof.

Hanging up my towel, I pull the door open, welcomed by uncongested air, and peek out the blinds next to the bed, checking to see if Bishop is still out there. He's there, chatting with Saint and Hunter. I quickly shut the blinds, pulling *The Book* out from my duffel bag and slipping under the blanket. Lying down, I open to where I was and lose myself back in the story.

5.

Lost innocence

After that night I heard my husband plan the deaths of our leaders, I decided to bury this book until I could decide whether it would be safe or not to continue with writing it. My son turned fourteen today, and tonight, it's his ritual. At fourteen, my son will lose his virginity to a woman who has far too many years on him than any mother would care to acknowledge. The years I had no say in. I used to fight Humphrey at every turn. Every decision he made that I didn't like, I would fight him. It started with him yelling at me and then beating me, but he soon realized I took everything he gave me. Once he realized that, he would punish me by beating my son. That worked effectively, because the one day he threatened that, was the day I started obeying his every word. That was the day my shoulders dropped in defeat, and I swore to myself, as God as my witness, that I hope he dies one day soon. Dies a quick death, but dies nonetheless.

"Ma, I'll be okay. No need to fuss."

I pressed the crinkles out of his linen shirt, a smile on my lips. A fake smile, a smile he knew so well. My precious son, the one person I wanted nothing but happiness for, but I knew he wouldn't get it.

"I know, my son. I know."

He smiled. "This is for the best, Mother. Father knows what he's doing. The people trust him. I trust him. You should trust him too." My heart broke a little, but I was grateful he didn't know what the kind of monster his father was. It was better this way. Nothing good can come for him if he knew. I didn't want to ruin how much he looked up to his father—even though his intentions were not noble.

I rubbed Damien's chest. "You're all ready."

He smiled. Damien's white teeth gleamed across his face, the scar he got on top of his lip from when he fell off one of our horses still there. He was four at the time, and now he was fourteen. About to make love to someone who didn't deserve it, all because his father said so. Because it was his coming of age. Because the younger he found someone, the longer they had to reproduce. The thought had my stomach churning with disgust, but I kept my smile on my face for my son.

"I love you, Mom."

"I love you, too, Damien. Now—go ahead."

He smiled at me again and then left our hut. It was much larger than our old one—and my husband always made a note to remind me of that. Of how I owed him for getting me out of poverty, as he would say.

Damien escaped through the curtain. "I love you so very much." I could feel him slipping through my fingertips already, and no matter how hard I tried to grasp onto anything I could at keeping him near me, I couldn't. It was out of my hands.

Humphrey was succeeding in manipulating the most powerful men of our time. He had other men—leaders, but not in charge like him—who stood behind him. All had money, all earned power and respect, and together? They were untouchable. Nothing went through their intelligence. No one dared disrespect or cross them. They were feared amongst our people—amongst other people. We had money now. We didn't know suffering, but I'd rather have no money and a family at peace, than him with all his riches.

I wasn't prepared for what I was about to discover today—amongst Damien's initiation. My worst fear. The worst possible thing that could ever happen, happened.

I fell pregnant.

My phone beeping with a text pulls me out of my story. "Fuck." Frustrated at how it interrupted me just as I'm getting to something juicy, I close the book. I slip it back into my bag, deciding it's probably a good idea to turn it in for the night, considering. Flicking off the bedside lamp, I snuggle into the blanket and unlock my phone to a text from Tatum.

Tatum – *Are you okay?*
Me – *I'm fine. How are you?*
Tatum – *Bored. Why couldn't I come?*
Me – *'Cause you weren't banging Nate while it happened.*
Tatum – *No way!*
Me – *Yes way.*
Tatum – *Tell me more, and where are you?*
Me – *No! Ew. And I can't tell you, sorry.*
Tatum – *Well you're no fun.*
Me – *I won't argue with that.*
Tatum – *Can I ask you a question?*
Me – *Always.*
Tatum – *Do you think you're falling in love with Bishop?*

What? I read over her message again, my eyebrows drawing together. Why would she want to know that? Bishop and I are not even in a solid enough relationship to start talking about love—that, I am sure of. Before I can reply to her spastic message, my bedroom door swings open and Bishop walks in.

"Oh," he mutters. "You're awake."

"Disappointed?" I ask, locking my phone, thus shutting out any light. The bed dips on his side, and I hear his shoes drop to the ground and a shirt fall before a belt buckle clangs, and then the bed sinks again.

"Why would I be disappointed?" he grumbles, his voice right near my ear and sending vibrations through my bloodstream. I close my eyes and count to ten. I must contain myself with this man or he will ruin me. His hand wraps around my left cheek. "Madison."

"I'm confused," I blurt urgently. He pauses, his hand moving. Must be the dark that has my confidence shining rather brightly. No doubt I'll get my ass burned. "I'm confused, because one minute you hate me, and then the next you're touching me. I'm confused about this whole"—I flick my fingers through the air, even though I'm well aware he can't see me—"thing."

"I don't hate you." He breaks through. My heart swells in my chest at his words.

"What?"

He brings one leg between mine and sinks on top of me, his elbows resting on either side of my head. Running the tip of his nose down the bridge of mine, his lips gently stroke over mine. "I. Don't. Hate. You," he whisper-yells each word, laying little kisses on my lips, and then suddenly his tongue slips out and drags over my bottom lip. "I just really need you to spread those legs for me and let me get lost in you for a few hours." The cushion of his thumb caresses little circles over the side of my jugular.

"Okay," I whisper through my parched throat.

He chuckles, his hips grinding into me so his erection presses against my leg. "That wasn't a question, baby. Now, open up." Then his head disappears under the blanket, and I'm getting a taste of ecstasy-spiked heaven.

CHAPTER 28

W hen I open my eyes, the first thing I notice is how numb my thighs and legs are, and then the next thing I notice is the bright sun glaring into our room through the... open fucking blinds!

"No!" I moan, covering my eyes with my arm. "Shut them."

"Get up, baby. Come have breakfast."

"I don't wanna."

Bishop grabs my arm gently and tugs it down, away from my face. "Come on."

I peek my eyes open when I notice he's blocking the sun with his massive body. *And* he's clutching a loose white towel around his waist with droplets of water cascading down the ripple of his V before dipping under his—

"Madi!" he snaps.

"Hmm?" I look up at him innocently.

"Looking at me like that will get you fucked. Hard. And judging by the bruises on your neck, wrists, and..." He peeks under the blanket. "...thighs, I'm going to go with you don't really want that right now."

I shake my head. As much as I love sex with Bishop—*love*—I'm nowhere near ready for another round. The man is rough, no, *lethal* in the sack. The first time he left bruises on me, I thought it would bother him when it was over. You know, seeing how much he hurt me when he was so lost in his lust, but nope. He merely laughed it off like it was the most normal thing in the world, so now I just go with it and hope that one day, I won't be on the news with the headline: *Madison Montgomery, death by penetration.*

It'd be just my luck.

"So get up." Then he walks to his gym bag and pulls out some loose jeans and a plain white tee. Dropping his towel, he grins at me when my eyes go straight to his thick cock. Thick, hard cock. Grasping it, he slowly pumps himself, pulling his bottom lip into his mouth. *Oh, God.* "Like what you see, baby?" A little bead of precum wets around his head.

I nod slowly, rubbing my thighs together in an attempt to stop the sudden ache that has started. He sees the movement under the blanket and his eyebrows tug in. "Pull the blanket off."

"What?" I mumble through a croaky throat.

"Don't answer back, kitty. Just follow instructions. Kick the blanket off."

I do as I'm told, swinging the blanket off my legs but keeping them closed, aware I didn't put my clothes back on last night. Neither of us did, because Bishop fell asleep while still pumping inside me. This was after my fourth orgasm. I actually second-guessed if it was possible to die from having too many orgasms.

The cool morning air whisks through the open window and glides over my sensitive clit. My eyes close as I try to contain the moan that threatens to pass my lips.

"Open your eyes," Bishop demands, so I do. I open them to him as he continues to pleasure himself. His rough hand glides up and down his thick shaft, squeezing as he gets to the rim of his head before sliding back down.

"Touch yourself, baby." Slowly, I run my hand up my thigh before spreading my legs wide, well aware of how direct his view is of me, but one thing I know is that no one knows my body like Bishop does. He knows how to work it and what to do with it. He knows ways to make me come that I didn't even know were possible. "Spread yourself open for me, let me see all of you."

I do as he says, my breath coming in harder as my index finger and my pointer finger slowly spread my lips open, giving him a perfect view. I grind against my finger as it rests beside my clit, watching Bishop's hand work himself up.

"Slide a finger inside. Just one. Do what you do when you're all alone."

Again, I follow his command, slipping in my index finger and thinking about what I do when I'm alone. What I've done while alone and thinking about Bishop. Running my eyes up to his, I pinch one of my nipples between my fingers and let my hips roll, grinding against my hands. Then I bring the hand that was pinching my nipple down to my clit and rub vigorously, all while pumping myself in and out, my eyes locked on Bishop's and his on me. His movements become faster until he lets go. "Fuck this." Then he walks toward me, wrapping his hands around my ankles and pulling me down the bed. Taking a seat on the edge, he picks me up until I'm straddling his hips and then smacks my ass before lying on his back. "Turn around and sit on my face."

Doing as I'm told, I spin around, sit on his face, and suck his dick into my mouth.

After breakfast, Saint walks into the living room where Bishop, Nate, Tillie, Ace, Hunter, Abel, and Cash are. The rest of the guys have gone to get supplies for tonight. Apparently drinking and laser tag is a thing they do. Who knew we could make fun out of the weird situation we're in?

Saint takes a seat on the sofa opposite me, and I shuffle uncomfortably. I know he's Cash's older brother, but I've only met him maybe one or two times before this, and both times were awkward—to say the least.

"Do you have any questions about what's going on, Madison?"

I look at Saint. "Yes, when can I go home? Where is my dad? And I'm sure there has to be a misunderstanding. My father may be a lot of things, but he's not a thief."

Saint chuckles, his hand rubbing over his five o'clock shadow, his brown hair styled messily on his head. Bishop picks up the pack of cigarettes on the table and lights one before tossing the packet to Saint, who follows. I don't see him smoke often—but he makes it look hot, as does Saint.

Saint takes a long pull off his cigarette before blowing out the thick cloud and lean-ing back in his seat. "When we say so. He's in Vegas. And I'm sure that's what every little girl says." He leans forward, flicking his ash into the ashtray on the coffee table. Bishop props his leg up against it, caging my body in. If I didn't know any better, I would think that was an almost protective gesture. Saint's eyes lock with mine, his dark ones daring me to question him. "But let me be very clear, kitty. Your father is no innocent in this."

"Maybe he didn't know?"

Saint laughs, looks to Bishop, and then takes another pull of his smoke. "She's cute."

"Up until last night," I hiss toward Saint, "my father was my hero. So forgive me if I don't trust any of your words over someone who has never given me reason to not trust him—ever." I look to Bishop. "Unlike some." Then I stand from the sofa and walk toward the doors that lead out to where we had the bonfire last night. Flopping down in the swing on the porch, I look out to the thick forest. We're in the middle of nowhere. Actually, I don't even know where we are. I'm surprised we get cell phone coverage. Who knows, maybe Bishop owns the cell phone towers, too.

"I know you have every reason to not trust me," Bishop states, looking out toward nature's playground, with his hands pressed into his pockets. "But trust me when I say that anything I do—we do, Nate and me—is for your own good." He looks at me now, his eyebrows tugging together, making his features turn serious and hard. "Promise me you'll remember this. No matter what."

I search his eyes, trying to find something. Anything. "But you've told me everything—right?"

He stops, smiles, and then nods. "Right. That I have."

"You've told me everything?" I repeat.

He nods again, looking away, and then walking up to me. "Yes. What are you look-ing at?" He takes a seat beside me on the swing.

"Out there." I point. "I'd love to go hunt some deer."

"No." Bishop shakes his head with a small smile. "Maybe save that for another trip."

I shrug. "It's not like I have my guns here anyway, but I just wish I could."

Bishop stops and then smiles. "Yours aren't, but mine are." Pulling me up from my seat, he gets me to my feet and leads me back into the house. Fishing the keys out of his pocket, he unlocks a door and then flicks on a light that shows stairs leading down to a basement.

"Come on." He holds his hand out to me, looking up at me from a couple steps down. "I don't bite."

"Yes, Bishop. Yes, you do bite."

He laughs this time, pulling me into him as we venture deeper and deeper into the dimly lit basement. "True that, but I can't help it. You're just so damn tasty."

Bishop unlocks a cabinet that hangs on the wall on the far side of the basement. The collected dust particles that are sprinkled over the fine woodwork illustrates just how long ago it had been opened.

"If you tell me there's a musket in here, I will shoot you."

Bishop laughs, pulling open the cabinet. "Nah, babe, no musket." It opens out onto a couple AKs, Glocks, semis, and shotguns. I run my hand over the cool black metal of the M4, and Bishop watches me in amazement. "It's sort of getting my dick hard watching how much this turns you on."

I roll my eyes and unhook the gun from its spot. "Trust you to find something pervy out of something so dangerous."

"Hmm...." Bishop grins, unhooking the M16 and some shells. "I can think of a few things we could do with these." He gestures to his gun, tilting it sideways with a cocky smile on his face.

"Most definitely not!" I turn around and walk back the way we came, passing all the old boxes piled up, and desks, decorations, and tables with white sheets draped over them. I grip onto the stairway's railing. "That is never happening. Do you even know how dangerous that could be?" I ask, walking back up the stairs. But then I consider how he doesn't seem to be bothered when I'm hurt during sex, so maybe the same goes if he accidently fucking kills me.

We walk out the front door, passing Nate and Tillie on the way.

"Wow, wow, wow, is this a good idea?" Nate looks to Bishop, eyes wide. Tillie chuckles beside me, toast in midair.

"It's fine, Nate," I say, patting his arm. "You can come."

He looks to Bishop and then shakes his head. "Next time."

I nod, then hook my arm with Bishop's. "So, how long will this go on?" I ask, as we step off the last stair and walk toward the clearing of the forest.

"Hopefully not long. The school and your dad have been taken care of. They think we're visiting colleges. Made up some bullshit about wanting to get in extra early to see our options and that it would be better if we all go at the same time."

"Right." Colleges. I never thought of that. We all leave at the end of this year. Where is everyone going? I haven't even decided yet, and it's much too far away to figure it out.

"Once we work out how to approach my dad, everything can go back to normal. Hopefully." We step through the clearing and Bishop takes my hand, pulling me closer to him.

"Have you been hunting before?" I ask with a smile.

He pauses and seems to mull over what my question is, and then smiles mischievously. "Probably not the same kind of hunting."

Rolling my eyes at—what I assume is—his playfulness, I draw up my gun and look through the scope. I could get used to this real quick.

A couple of hours later, we walk back up to the house, and Bishop takes me hand, grinning from ear to ear and pulling my body in to him. "You got my dick hard. Now—"

He's cut off by Nate. "B, your dad is calling my phone."

"Fuck." Bishop walks toward him with me tucked protectively behind him. He snatches Nate's phone and looks to him, something passing between the two of them.

"Answer, man, I don't want it to spread out."

"It already would have. They'd all already know."

"Know what?" I ask, tugging on Bishop's hand.

Tillie walks out the front door, watching me with a worried look. "Come on. We can put those away before someone gets shot." She smiles weakly, gesturing me to come inside. I let go of Bishop's hand and walk around Nate, toward her. We both walk into the house in silence, passing the guys who are all in the sitting room.

Walking down to the basement, she breaks the silence. "Are you okay? You and Bishop looked cozy."

I laugh, opening the cabinet with the keys I got from him. "Yeah, I don't know what we are."

"Do you trust him?" she asks, as I hang the guns back, placing the shells on their shelf.

"Yes, I do." She pauses, so I look at her over my shoulder. "Why?"

Shutting the cabinet, I lock it again and put the keys into my pocket. She turns around, leaning against one of the old shelves. "I don't know. It's just... I knew his ex."

"Khales? Yeah, he has sort of mentioned her."

"What did he say?" Tillie asks, her eyes watching mine.

"Just that it wasn't as people thought it was—whatever that means."

Tillie shakes her head, hiding a scoff. "Games, always games with these boys."

"Tillie? I trust him."

She looks like she wants to say something else, but changes her mind. "Okay."

Nate lights up the fire pit and then walks toward me, handing me my drink. "You know..." He grins, flicking the Zippo between his fingers. "...Bishop inherited this house."

"Really?" I perk up, wanting to know more. The sun is setting, letting off a beautiful orange hue in the sky, and the drinks are going down smoothly, and despite the circumstances of me being here, I feel great. "Do tell me more."

Nate takes a seat on the log beside me, casting a small glance toward Tillie, who's chatting with Saint opposite us. His eyes stay there for a beat longer, watching her and Saint.

I nudge him with my arm. "Hey."

He looks back toward me with a smile, just as Cash takes a seat beside me on the other side. I look at him and smile; he smiles back. I haven't spoken to Cash much, if at all, and I don't really know his story, but I know he's Saint's younger brother. "Hey." His blond hair drops to his collar. He has sort of a surfer look to him, with bright blue eyes and golden skin. So different from Saint, who has dark hair, a dark five o'clock shadow on his strong jaw, and dark eyes that could pin you with one stare. They must be half-brothers.

I look back to Nate. "Keep going."

"Is it story time already, Nate dawg?" Cash teases with a smirk but then takes a long pull off his beer.

Nate shrugs easily. "Why not?" Then he takes a sip of his own beer. I don't miss the silent communication that passes between the two of them. Nate brings his beer to his lap and wipes his mouth with the back of his hand. "As I was saying, Bishop inherited this cottage."

"His grandparents or something?" I ask, looking back to the beautiful, large structure. You can see it has some age to it, but not old enough to go back any further.

Nate chuckles sarcastically. "Something like that."

"Carry on," I probe him.

"Well..." He leans forward, the rim of his bottle dangling between his fingers. "This house is sort of like a family heirloom."

"Some heirloom," I mutter, taking another drink of my whiskey sour.

"Okay!" Bishop grins, dropping a whole bunch of black bags at his feet.

I smirk at him. "Why do you have no top on?" His beautiful body is on full display, and he's put a baseball cap on backward, covering his hair. I fight the urge to lick my lips, because the way the ripped denim jeans hang off his narrow waist, showing the edge of his Calvin's, makes me want to melt into a puddle on the ground.

"This is how we play, baby."

"Play what?" I ask, inching forward as Nate stands, drinking the rest of his beer in one go and then tossing his bottle to the ground. He grips the back of his collar and tears his shirt off, all his muscles tensing at the action, and his tattoos—a little more than Bishop has—coming into view.

Nate smirks down at me. "Paintball shooting."

"Really?" I stand instantly. "I'm in!"

All the boys remove their shirts, and my eyes find Tillie's instantly. We share a look that's something like "Well gawd dayum," then both laugh. I feel the tension ease off my shoulders in our laughing, and then I look back to Bishop, who is giving me the sexiest evil grin I have ever seen in my entire life.

"Nawww," I tease him, walking past Nate and coming to the front of Bishop. Circling my index finger over his left pec, I grin back at him. "Jealous?"

He snatches my hand and then sucks my finger into his mouth before biting down on it roughly. "You're mine, and I don't share."

"Since when did the no sharing rule come in?" I taunt him.

He hooks his arm around my waist and pulls me into him. "Since a couple days ago."

"Rule change?" I tilt my head up at him.

He points to his chest. "Rule maker."

I smile and then look down to the bags at his feet just as Nate comes up to us and takes one of them, handing me a vest. "Put this on."

"You guys aren't wearing vests."

"We never have," Nate replies, and then shoves the vest into my chest harder. "Put it on."

I take it from him and slip my jacket off before pulling the vest over my tank top. "How long have you guys been playing?"

They all pause, and an awkward silence hangs between us all. I look to Tillie, who looks to Nate and then Saint awkwardly.

Bishop grins, his eyes gleaming like dark orbs. "It's a sort of tradition, baby. Put the vest on. Only I'm allowed to mark you."

"You need help." Cash shakes his head at Bishop.

"Naw, don't think that's only you, kitty," Brantley snarls from across the fire pit. "Khales used to come over with all sorts of marks and bruises on her. If you ask me, yours are pretty tame." He looks to Bishop, who is frothing at the mouth. "What? This one just not hitting the spot like Khales did?"

I zip up my vest. "I don—" I look up to Bishop, only he's not there.

"You say so much as another fucking thing toward her, and I'll break your fucking jaw." I walk toward Bishop, about to calm him down, when Cash takes my hand and pulls me backward. I look down to where his hand is then look up to his face. He shakes his head at me. Bishop continues, chest to chest with Brantley. "Are you forgetting who runs this show, pup? Or do I need to remind you who the fuck I am?"

Brantley searches Bishop's eyes before he cuts them over his shoulder to me. "Nah, I'm good." He bends down, picking up his gun and slinging it over his shoulder. What the fuck is his deal with me? It's been no secret how much he has hated me, but I thought he'd got over it. We had a good patch, but since we've been here, he's gone back to being a grade-A jerk. I already know he blames me for why he's here, but Bishop said it's no big deal, that they're only here to keep his dad guessing. To keep him chasing us. I don't—

"Madi!" Bishop growls, his eyes still on Brantley.

"Yes?"

"Got your vest on?"

"Yes."

Bishop grins. "Good." He points his gun at me, and before I can ask what the fuck he's doing, he pulls the trigger and a heavy thud smashes against my chest.

"Ouch! Bishop!" I scold him.

"You're out. Sit the fuck down."

"But I—"

"I said sit the fuck down." He points toward the log.

I huff and take a seat. Nate walks toward Tillie and points at me, and then she starts walking over, her bottom lip slightly puckered.

Plopping down beside me, she sighs. "I wonder what the big deal is?"

I shrug. "Who the hell knows with these boys? I mean seriously, right?"

Bishop Walks off, loading up his gun, with Nate and a few others following behind him. I look to Tillie and grin. "Who says we can't join in?"

Smirking, she gets up from the log and reaches her hand out to mine. "Exactly." Once all the boys have disappeared deep into the dark, gloomy forest, Tillie pulls out a gun from the bag she would have had. I walk toward her, bending down and picking up mine from the bag Bishop left behind too.

"Shit, shall we do this?" she asks, shuffling into her vest and looking from left to right, taking in her surroundings.

"What?" I mutter, loading up my paintballs into the gun. "Of course!"

Tillie laughs, shaking her head but following through with me. "Madi, you're such a rebel. Won't Bishop get mad?"

"That's why I'm doing it." I grin at her.

She shakes her head again as I swing my gun over my shoulder. "You're so bad."

We start tiptoeing into the forest, the thick branches instantly giving us coverage from the sun. "I'll follow you," Tillie whispers out.

I roll my eyes. "Yes. Follow me, but these bullets can't kill anything that might try to kill us, so if like, a mountain lion or anything comes after us, I can't help us."

Tillie pauses just as we make our way through the clearing. "But you don't actually hunt mountain lions and stuff, do you?"

I stop and turn to face her. "Of course not! But I would shoot to kill any human who does."

Her mouth slams shut and then she laughs me off. "Oh, you're not being serious."

I laugh with her, though I'm very serious. My dad had to physically restrain me after some stupid bimbo slut and her bimbo-ass family uploaded a picture of them on Facebook with a dead lion that they had killed, holding its lifeless body proudly. One day, I'm going to reenact that very photo, only holding their first-born child.

Okay, so that was too far.

Yeah, that was a little far, but alas, whatever people think about hunters, I love animals. More than I love people. I—me and my family—have only ever hunted deer, unless it was duck shooting.

"Madi!" Tillie whispers into the back of my neck, her breath misting across my neck.

"What!" I hiss back, drawing my gun up. Tillie is following closely behind me, her chest rubbing against my back every two seconds. If we were in a horror movie right now, she would be the death of us.

"It's getting dark."

"Well, that's what happens when it's almost 8:00 p.m. Chill out." I go to step over a fallen log, when I slip and fall to the ground, just as a bright green splatter of paint shoots over the trunk that's near us. Tillie snaps out of her questionnaire, looks to the green paint, and then screams out in shock just as another splatter of paint hits her square in the jaw. I slam my hand over my mouth in shock. That could have easily knocked out some teeth. Rolling onto my stomach, I prop my gun up against my shoulder and peek through the scope, the diameter giving me zoom view. A bush rustles opposite us, but I know that's too easy and was obviously set up. Noticing the bush moved from the right first, I whip the end of my gun toward the right where, sure enough, Brantley and Ace's faces come into view, where they're laughing at Tillie's—and possibly my—stupidity.

I grin. "Boo-yah motherfuckers." And then I squeeze the trigger, my gun pointing toward Brantley's smug-ass face first. When I see the bright pastel pink splatter all over his shocked mug, I quickly point it toward Ace and squeeze again, this time getting him exactly where they got Tillie, on the corner of her jaw.

They both scream aloud. *"Fuck!"*

I laugh and turn back to Tillie, who's weeping up against the trunk of the tree, tears pouring down her cheeks, smudging the green color on her face.

"Hey." I shuffle closer to her. "It hurts, huh? Don't worry. I got them."

She shakes her head, the tears not threatening to leave. "It's not that, Madi."

"What's wrong?" I ask, shuffling closer to her, but my finger still trigger ready.

"My dad. Well, um...."

"Your bruises?" I whisper, more to myself than to her, putting two and two together, her being upset, and then the first thing she says is her dad.

She nods. "He's a drunk. My mom left when I was two, and he has always reminded me about how I owe him because he stuck around when she didn't." She swipes the tears off her cheeks again. "He gets rough most nights."

"You don't need to talk about it if you don't want to, Tillie. It's okay."

She smiles, pushing her long mousy brown hair away from her face. "Anyway, I just wanted to explain why I overreacted about that."

Footsteps get closer, the crunching of their closeness vibrating out, and I quickly stand, shielding Tillie and raising my gun to whoever is coming.

"Whoa!" Bishop grins, his hands raised. "Just me, baby."

I narrow my eyes. "Oh yeah? Last I checked, you said I wasn't allowed to come and play. So, um…" I look down to Tillie, and she smiles at me with a knowing twinkle in her eye. I wink at her and then look back to Bishop. "That makes it *us* against *you*." His smirk drops, and then just as he's about to pull the trigger, I squeeze mine, and bright pink paint splatters all over the front of his hard chest before I turn the tip to Nate, giving him two solid shots to his chest. Grinning, I drop my gun. "See—"

Black paint hits me across my chest just as a sharp sting plows into me. "Oh my God!"

Bishop keeps grinning and then lowers his gun. "For a trigger-happy chick, you sure bitch like a girl."

I go to whack him with the back of my gun, when he pushes it out of the way, his hand coming to my throat. He drops me to the ground with a thud, his grip still around my neck like a collar. He runs the tip of his nose over the bridge of mine, his waist pinning me to the ground and a smile tickling the corner of his lips. "See, baby? Don't get fucking cocky."

Nate rolls his eyes just as Brantley and Ace come around one of the tree trunks. "Fucking bitch," Brantley grumbles, wiping the pink paint off his jaw.

Bishop grins devilishly before correcting it. He gives me a slight kiss on the lips, ever so softly, before he jackknifes up and turns to face Brantley. "Strike two, pup. Don't let it get to three, 'cause I'll enjoy ruining your pretty little face way too much."

I get up from the ground, swiping the dirt off the back of my pants. Taking Bishop's hand in mine, I pull him closer to me. "It's okay." Whatever problem Brantley has with me, he obviously thinks it's valid.

Slinging the gun over my shoulder, Nate bends down to pick up Tillie, cradling her into his chest. I watch them closely, slightly confused, until Bishop catches me. "Yeah, I think it's safe to say the playboy has found his chick."

"You think?" I ask, head tilted.

Bishop scoffs. "Yeah, pretty much."

Bishop is talking on the phone when I come out of the shower, clutching my towel. He eyes me walking in, but continues to answer questions on his phone, watching me closely.

"Yeah," he says. "No, she's fine."

I pause, grabbing my clothes out of my bag. "Yeah, I'm fucking sure, Dad. Call it off."

Hope flares up in my chest, but I bend down and slip my underwear on under my towel, trying to be as quiet as possible. "Okay," he murmurs. "Yeah, deal."

Deal? What deal?

He hangs up his phone and then stands, walking toward me. The late afternoon sun setting shines through the windows, glowing against his tanned skin. "It's done. He knows. I have to talk with him when I get home, but I think I convinced him enough to not chase you."

I drop the towel. "Shall we celebrate, then?"

He smirks, walking toward me and pulling off his shirt. "Abso-fucking-lutely."

CHAPTER 29

I'm drunk, and as much as I've tried to give myself a pep talk, there's no denying that.
No, Madison, the ground is not supposed to spin like that. And, no, Madison, there are not two Bishops. But I'm happy and in good company. Since Bishop got off the phone with his dad, everything has calmed down significantly. The tension Brantley has been throwing my way has died off immensely, so much so I'm pretty sure I've caught him smiling at me a couple of times.

We all decided to spend one more night here and head back to The Hamptons tomorrow, and then back to school the next day. If I'm honest, I have a lot of bookwork to catch up on when I get back, so to say I can't wait to be home, in my bed, is an understatement. Not that I haven't enjoyed being here with Bishop and, admittedly, the other guys, but home is home, and my bed is far too amazing to swap for something in the forest.

"Hey." Tillie nudges me, taking a seat on the log beside me.

"Hey back." I smile at her, moving my hair out of my face and letting out a long breath. The flame from the bonfire heats my flesh, and I close my eyes, a smile spreading across my face. I open my eyes, bringing my drink to my lips.

"So you and Bishop are a thing?" she asks with a quirked eyebrow, taking a small sip of her drink.

"Well, I mean… you and Nate?" I retort.

She smiles. "Touché."

"Just be careful," I whisper to her. "I know. He's Nate, and he's very charming… and he has that damn tongue ring."

She bursts out laughing and then covers her mouth with her hand to keep from spitting out her drink. "Sorry, but word! It's the tongue ring," she teases. Though we both know that's not true. She looks across from us, and I follow her line of sight, my eyes falling on Bishop, who is staring at me so intently it has me shuffling in my seat—or log. "Seriously?" Tillie shakes her head in disbelief. "It should be illegal for any man to be that good-looking."

"Who, Nate?" I ask, because yes, Nate is very pretty.

"No." She shakes her head, swallowing her drink. "Bishop. I see the appeal and why everyone—and I mean everyone—wants him. I mean", she rolls her eyes, "look at him

"I'm hoping you." I laugh sarcastically before turning serious. "Seriously, I have enough girls to worry about chasing after him. I don't want to have to worry about my friends too."

She laughs, her head tilting back. "No, you don't have to worry about me." I look back at Bishop again to catch him still staring at me. The orange hues of the flame ignite his cheeks, adding a blush to his tan complexion. Tillie leans into me. "And I wouldn't worry about him, either. I mean, he's never been a whore anyway, always selective and secretive. He's always had the unattainable reputation. But with you, though?" she murmurs, almost to herself. "I don't know. It's different. You're different to him."

"Well, I hope so!" I laugh her off, averting my eyes from Bishop and his intense gaze. "All things considered."

She smiles. "So have you heard from Tatum?"

"Yeah." I lean forward. "She texted me the other night. She's fine... just same old Tatum. I'll text her and tell her we'll be back tomorrow." She takes a stand from the log and my hand goes out to her. "Seriously, Tillie, just be careful, okay? I love him; don't get me wrong. He and I... we grew close quite quickly, and although he has done some questionable things to me, I know he wouldn't intentionally hurt me."

"I know, Madi. I'll be fine. I promise."

An arm wraps around my waist and I grin, knowing who it belongs to. Tillie smirks too and then winks at me. "Seems we're both going to be a little busy tonight." Then she walks back to Nate, who is waiting for her with open arms. They're so cute, yet different. Nate, though... I don't know. He's never had a relationship before, according to everyone I've talked to, so that worries me. It worries me that I can feel he's going to do something bad to fuck things up with this girl one day, but I know for a fact I will be there for both of them.

"Come on." Bishop nudges his head, a bottle of Macallan in his hand. I stand, wiping the dirt off the back of my pants just as Pretty Ricky's "Get You Right" starts playing on the sound dock, floating through the dark forest and hidden behind the laughs and drunken slurs of my friends. Yeah, friends. Some weird friendship we all have going on. "I wanna show you something."

"Oh?" I prompt, settling into his step and snuggling into the warmth under his arm. "Another firefly night?"

He smirks. "Not quite." We head farther and farther away from the group and toward the back of the cottage, until darkness floats all around me. He pulls out a mini flashlight from his pocket and turns it on, shining it toward an overgrown bush area. "Come on."

"What?" I ask in disbelief. "In there?"

Shining the light under his chin, he nods. "Yeah, in there," he whispers scarily.

I shove him. "Can you try to not be like, the boogie man?"

That earns me a throaty laugh. "Baby, I'm much worse than the boogie man."

"How so?" I follow him anyway.

"Easy, the boogie man isn't real." He runs his rough fingertips over the inside of my thighs, dragging them over the zipper of my short shorts, and rubbing my clit through the denim material. "Feel that, baby?" he whispers into my ear. "That's real, and that's how I'm much, much worse than the fucking boogie man."

My breath catches in my throat, but I swallow through it. "You're such a fucking dick."

"Yes, but I have a fucking monster one." He yanks me, so I quicken my steps. "Come on."

"Where're we going?" I ask, following him through the overgrown shrubs.

He pulls me and I fall forward, the bush I stepped through swinging back into place. "It's not far." I swipe away the broken little twigs that cling to my shorts and follow him. "I inherited this house from my parents. When my dad was fifteen, it was his, and then when I turned fifteen, it came to me."

"Hmm." I grin. "That's some family heirloom, though, right?"

He chuckles as we keep walking. "Yeah, that's one thing you'll come to realize. Nothing is done in halves."

He stops, and I almost crash into his back. Stepping around his body, I walk forward and follow his sight. "Holy crap, what is it?" I whisper.

Bishop looks down at me, bringing the rim of his bottle to his lips and taking a swig. "Hmm, I'm not really sure how to answer that."

I step around him, walking toward the cave that looks to be made of stone. There's a dark door entrance with no windows, and the cave is surrounded by loose, overgrowing vines and shrubs.

"Have you been in it?" I ask, looking back up toward him.

"Never." He shakes his head. "It's just some old shit my dad used to talk about when I was a kid."

"Kinda like the boogie man?" I tease him.

He takes my hand in his, and I ignore how my chest contracts and my core tingles at our contact. "Something like that," he murmurs so lightly I almost miss it.

"So why did you bring me here, then?"

He grins. "'Cause we're going in."

I shake my head. "I don't wanna."

"Baby?" He smirks—at least I think he's smirking. The small light coming off his flashlight is hinting at a smirk from the crisp, sharp shadows over his cheekbones and jawline. "You're coming."

"Fuck." I snatch the bottle out of his hands and bring it to my lips, swallowing the harsh amber liquid. Letting out a hiss, I wave toward the entrance of the stone. "Lead the way!"

I follow as he walks toward the dark, gloomy rock. Goose bumps break out over my flesh just as we near it. It feels haunted, as dark shadows are dancing around in the silence.

"Did you hear that?" I whisper to him harshly.

"What?" He grins over his shoulder. "Naw, babe. Come on." Pulling me into his warmth, he throws his arm over my shoulders as we walk into the entrance. I hold my breath, ignoring how the damp, congested smell of lake water engulfs my senses.

"Won't there be like, bats in here or something?" I whisper.

"Probably."

"You've been here before, haven't you?" I call him on it because he's way too calm.

"Meh." He shrugs. "Once or twice."

The dusted rocks and loose gravel crunch under my feet as we get deeper and deeper into the cave. The oxygen thickens, making it harder for me to breathe the farther we go in. "Bishop, it's fucking with my breathing."

He pulls me under his arm. "Woulda never pegged you as a chicken shit, Montgomery."

I shove him playfully and then we stop, looking toward a large opening. There's a massive hole above us where the moonlight shines directly in and onto a stage-like plat-form. "Creepy," I whisper, rubbing my hands over my arms. Tilting my head, I look at all the dark stains that spill over the rock. "Really fucking creepy." He steps up onto it, the light from the full moon lighting up his body, shadowing his face. "Is this the part where you tell me to ask you what you eat?"

He chuckles. "No. This is the part where I tell you my dad is a dangerous man. My family are dangerous people, regardless of what you hear or see in the media. All of that is just shadowed by my mom because of who she is. It's why my dad married her proba-bly, to keep the spotlight off what he does." Bishop pauses and tilts his head at me.

"Sounds like you've thought long and hard about this."

Bishop laughs, jumping off the stage and stepping toward me. "I know a lot of things that would shock you, kitty." His hand comes up as he runs the back of his knuck-les over my cheek. "I do a lot of things that would undoubtedly repulse you." He takes a short breath. I hold mine, trying not to think too much into what he's saying or what he's implying, because truthfully, a big part of me wants to know more about Bishop. Why he does what he does, why he's so mysterious, why he and Khales broke up. Where is she, and why do people think she just went missing off the face of the earth?

But I know Bishop enough to know he doesn't just give straight answers. He's too smart for that, too many steps ahead of everyone to make an amateur move like say something he shouldn't. Sometimes I wonder just how old he is, because he's so smart. Not book smart, but street smart, and that's not something you see in people our age.

He continues, breaking my train of thought. "I can't let you know." His fingers wrap around the back of my neck possessively. "I can't take the risk." His thumb spreads over my bottom lip. "I can't lose you to this."

"You won't lose me, Bishop." I take his hand in mine and search his eyes. Eyes that have seared through mine with so much hate it could light up the gates of hell. But right now? Right now, they're mixed with something else. Confusion, lust, want?

He shakes his head, the corner of his mouth hinting at a smirk. "Yeah, I will, kitty. When all is said and done? I will."

CHAPTER 30

Scrubbing the loose dirt off my skin, I let the hot congestion of the shower engulf me, embracing just how amazing it is to be back in my room. In my shower, about to get back into *my* bed. Smiling, I turn the faucet off and step out of the shower, moving the glass door out of my way.

"Oh my fucking God!" I scream out, reaching for my towel and wrapping it around my body quickly. "Nate!" I hiss. "You cannot just come up in here and scare me like that. Fuck!"

His hand is rubbing over his sharp, pretty jaw, his perfect eyebrows pulled in. He's thinking—hard, and not the least bit concerned over the fact I just gave him a full frontal view of my lady fucking bits.

Lady bits? FML.

"Question," he starts, bringing his eyes to mine slowly, still serious, and again, not one bit bothered about what I'm wearing—or not wearing.

"Always, Nate, but for fuck's sake, stop coming in here when I'm taking a shower." I shove him out of the way, squeezing the towel around me more and reaching for my toothbrush.

"Do you love me?"

"What?" My hand hovers over the end of my toothbrush, shocked by his question. "What do you mean?" I squirt paste onto it anyway and then slip it under the cool tap water, bringing it to my mouth.

"Simple question, kitty." He smiles sadly, turning toward me.

I pause my brushing when I see the sincerity in his eyes. *They say women are confusing? Nuh uh. Men take the cake for this shit.*

I drop my hand to the sink. "I mean, I've never had a sibling before, but I can honestly say that if I ever had one, I'd want him to be you."

Nate smiles sorrowfully, the dimples in his cheeks sinking in slightly. "Thanks, sis."

"Why do you ask this, though? Are you okay?"

He exhales slowly. "Me and Tillie, what are your thoughts?"

Well, I wasn't expecting that. If I asked him what his thoughts were on Bishop and me, I have no idea what he would say.

"Um." I spit out my toothpaste, rinse my toothbrush, and then put it back into its slot. "I mean, I don't know. I just don't want you to hurt her, Nate."

"What if I can't fucking help it?" He looks to me pleadingly. "What if I'm just one epic failure of giant proportions? What if I get so scared anytime I think I come close to me giving a fuck about a chick... I fuck it all up?"

"What have you done?" I ask blandly.

"I... I... fuck." He pulls on his hair. "Why do I give a fuck about her, Madi?" he whisper-yells at me. "Why the fuck do I care? I've had little fuck buddies before, but I don't tap more than once, and if I do, they're with chicks who know the rules. And even if they do get attached? I have no problem breaking their itty bitty, little tender fucking hearts. I laugh at them, Madi!" He pauses, his chest rising and falling, his eyes furious and his jaw tense. He pulls at his hair frantically again.

I reach up and grab it, bringing his hand down. "What. Have. You. Done?" I murmur again, searching his eyes for any clues.

His shoulders go slack. He reaches out to his door handle, twists it, and shoves it open. "I fucked up."

I let out a long, annoyed breath, my eyes staying on the naked body of some slut that's spread-eagle on Nate's satin red sheets. Without turning to face him, I launch my elbow back and clock him square in the jaw.

"Ouch!" He steps back, rubbing his jaw and quickly shutting the door.

"No!" I scream, a little crazily if I think deeply about it. "Why the fuck do you care if that slut hears?"

"Madi!" Nate shakes me, his hands wrapping around my upper arms. "Shh!"

"Fuck you!" I hiss, reaching for the door again, ready to pull the bitch's hair straight out. I'm acting a little on the insane side, but he had one thing to do—not break my best friend's heart—and he did it. This would undoubtedly shatter her. They may not be exclusive, but sometimes you don't need to say the words "we're together." Sometimes, you know deep down what the fuck you're doing is wrong, and by the way Nate is acting and how he came in here, asking stupid fucking questions... that tells me he felt like shit while he was doing it. Hence, cheating. He cheated on her. He knew what he was doing was wrong, label or no label, so fuck him.

"Madi, we weren't together, but I can't do this with her!"

"Do what?" I yell again, my hands going in the air like a crazy person.

"I can't do commitment! I've never been able to!"

"Why?"

"Shit!" He pulls at his hair again, his muscles tensing with the action. "I can't do this with you right now."

"Well...," I murmur. "You have until I wake up in the morning to tell Tillie, or I will, and I'm not playing around. Nate, I may care about you like I do a brother, but blood or no blood, I would still act the same. Tillie is my best fucking friend, and she *likes* you— only God knows why—so fix this shit."

Then I turn toward my door and storm back into my room, a little on edge and a lot annoyed. Flopping down onto my bed, I stretch wide and count the squares on my ceiling. I can't fucking believe it. We've been home for approximately three hours, and he has managed to sink himself into someone else. What the hell is his problem? Are all men like this? Should I be checking on Bishop?

With that thought, my stomach churns with unspoken emotions. Nope, not going there. Bending over my bed, I pull out the leather book and sit back against my headboard, flipping open the page and looking over the double infinity sign again.

"Who are you, Katsia?" I whisper. I need last names or something. Who is this person and her mysterious husband? With so many questions hanging in my balance, I flick to the next page and start reading.

6.

Plot holes

Pregnancy went very slowly. Almost like a train that was about to crash, but in slow motion and you were the only passenger on board—with your pregnant belly. You knew it was coming, but you just hoped it was a different outcome. My husband always said how excited he was about us having another son. He said it was another soldier for his plan and that his right-hand man, Mathew, was also expecting a child. Around the same time as me too, they said. I was feeling very unnerved, not because I was pregnant at a later age, but because he was adamant it was a boy. Like he already knew I was bearing his son, the next boy in line.

What made him so sure I was carrying a boy? And why did that scare me? Why did I feel like there was always something missing when it came to what I knew, like something was always being held back from me? Stepping into the little nursery I had designed, I folded the little rug and placed it into the wicker drawer.

"Ma'am, I don't mean to interrupt, but the meeting is about to begin and I need to escort you to the Landing."

Nodding, I straightened my dress out, my hand running over my swollen belly. "I'm ready." I was not ready, and I had no idea what was in store for me, but I knew I had four months before I gave birth to my baby. I had to find out as much as I could before those four months were up, because I knew, deep down, that just like the calm before the storm, something was going to blow up, and I was adamant that I, or my child, would be in the vicinity when it happened.

I jolt from my sleep, attempting to keep my eyes peeled open but failing miserably. Closing the book, I push it under my bed and shut my eyes, promising myself that I will continue it tomorrow. Though the book is thick, I'm so engrossed in the story that I know it won't take me too long to finish.

"Madi come on! We're going to be late!" Nate yells from his Porsche.

"Well, you can wait!" I hiss to myself under my breath, reaching for an apple in the fridge and flicking my long hair over my shoulder. I've been wearing a lot of scandalous clothes lately—probably Tatum's influence—so I decide on ripped boyfriend jeans, a tight white tank top that shows just a smidge of my flat, toned belly and a lot of my boobs— not hard considering the size—and my Chucks. Leaving my hair in natural loose curls that flow down to my tailbone, I pinch my cheeks, trying to get a pink blush to spread across my skin, my leather bangles rubbing across my jaw in the movement, and then walk out the front door, closing it behind myself.

"Calm down!" I scold him, clutching my books in my hand.

He tips his aviators down his nose and checks me out from the driver seat just as I pull open the passenger door. "Well, damn, sis. Do you ever look bad?"

"Yes," I reply curtly. "Usually after I kill cheating men."

Nate rolls his eyes and pushes his glasses back up his nose, putting it into first gear and skidding out of the driveway. "Stop being dramatic. She didn't even care."

"I call bullshit. She would care."

"And how do you know this? Maybe she's just different."

I grin, a thought popping up in my head. "Well"—I shrug, checking my nails with a slight smirk on my lips—"I mean, if she didn't care, maybe it's because she has this super sexy—and when I say sexy, I mean fucking *gushing* sexy, Nate. Like, one look and I was ready to tear my own panties off and shove them in my mouth just to have his hot body under—"

He slams on the brakes, my head jolting forward.

"Nate!" I scream at his impulsiveness.

"Yo! You hear that, dawg?" Nate hollers into his phone. His phone that is connected to his stereo. His phone that has the Bluetooth light flashing. His phone that—

"Yeah, I fucking heard that," Bishop growls. So low it sends chills down my spine. Double shit. Fucking me and my unquestionable loyalty to my friends, always getting me into trouble one way or another.

"So who is this friend?" Nate asks, eyebrow quirked.

I laugh. "I'm not telling you shit."

"Madi!" Bishop snaps. "Who is he?"

"I don't know! We met him a few days ago when we went to pick her up from school." Nate pulls back onto the road and continues to drive us toward school. "Anyway, Tatum and a little bit of me were saying how hot he was, and Tillie said how they sleep together. But they've been doing it since they were young and it's just something comfortable between them. Zero awkwardness." I look toward Nate. "You can't get mad, Nate the Snake."

"Did you just call me Nate the Snake?" He narrows his eyes at me.

I shrug. "Well, you know, since you boys like riddles so much."

"Your mouth... it's going to land your ass in hot water one day," Nate replies, pulling into the school parking lot.

Walking into my first class, I instantly know something is wrong. The classroom falls silent as I open the door.

"Madison, you're late again. Why am I not surprised?" Mr. Barron says, not lifting his eyes off his chalkboard.

"Sorry, sir."

"Take a seat, Madison," he replies blandly.

I shuffle to the back of the room, ignoring the hissing whispers that start bouncing off the walls. It's almost like my first day all over again. I drop my books down onto an empty desk and slide into my seat. I don't even have Tatum in this class to ask what all the stares are about.

Sinking into my chair, Felicia—I think her name is Felicia—who has black hair, black clothes, and black smudged eyeliner under her lashes, leans toward me, her eyes staying on the teacher, careful not to gain his attention. "Psst."

I lean toward her slightly, just as my phone vibrates in my pocket. "What?"

"So is it true? You're like, sleeping with all of them?"

I snap my eyes to her, my heart pitter-pattering in my chest. "What do you mean?"

She reaches into her pocket and then pushes a couple of buttons before turning the phone to face me, hitting Play on a video. The first part shows me and Nate and our embarrassing kiss in our living room, and then skips amateurishly to me and Bishop kissing and hugging at the campsite, before jumping to me and Brantley. And then it goes to Bishop and me having sex in the tent, showing my silhouette dropping my clothes, and the video doesn't stop. You can hear me murmuring and whispering out my pleasures for everyone to see and hear, my body rocking over his through the shadow. At the end of the tape, a little black box comes up with pink writing:

"You're next, bitch. Your days are numbered—just like mine were!"

"Oh my God!" I whisper, tears threatening to surface. Shoving my chair back, I catch Ally smirking from the front of the classroom.

"Madison!" Mr. Barron scowls at me. "Sit down, or I will have to refer you to the principal's office." Everyone looks at me, their laughs circling around me, echoing in a swirl, pounding through me.

"I... I'm—"

"A whore?" Ally sneers.

The whole classroom erupts into laughter, and I quickly gather my books, my hair falling over my face as I dash out the door and down the corridor.

"Hey!" Tatum comes crashing into me, her phone plastered to her ear and her eyes watering, looking around frantically. "Oh, thank God!"

"Tate?" I break, my tears pouring over my cheeks.

"Come on, let's get you home."

I let her pull me under her arm as she takes me to the elevator. Slamming on the button vigorously until I'm sure she's about to break it, the doors ding open and she pulls me in forcefully. Once the doors close, she swipes the tears off my face and kisses my lips. "It's okay, Madi. It's going to be okay," she tries to reassure me, looking me in the eyes. "Goddammit, I'm going to kill that bitch!"

"Who?" I ask, swiping the tears off my face, as the door dings open again onto the underground parking.

"It was Ally, Madison. It may not have been her who recorded it, but she uploaded it onto her account on YouTube. She wanted people to think she did it."

"Why?" I yell, following her to her car. "Why would she do this to me? Why?"

"Bishop, babe, it's all for Bishop."

"But the note at the end? About my days being numbered...?"

"Who knows?" Tatum unlocks her car, and I slip into the passenger seat as she slides into the driver seat. "But it was her, Madi."

"I'm so embarrassed, Tate. I've never felt so humiliated in my life."

"I know, babe. I know. Well, I don't—but I can imagine."

"Not helping."

"Okay, totally not helping. I'll take us back to my house if you're not ready to face the Kings."

I nod, swiping the tears again. "Sounds good, thank you, but can we quickly stop there and pick something up? I feel like I could do with the distraction."

"No questions asked." She pats my leg, driving out from the garage. "We will figure it out, okay?"

I nod again, trying to work out how exactly she thinks we're going to figure it out. "Yeah, sure."

Walking into Tatum's high-class, modern home, I shut the door behind us, carrying a box of Krispy Kreme donuts and enough Carl's Jr. to feed half a state.

"Feel a bit better?" she asks, smiling at me and flinging the keys onto a table.

"A little, but I haven't had food yet. Ask me again after I've had enough carbs to impregnate me."

Tatum giggles. "Come on. We can go into the theater room and stuff our faces in there, with a bottle of tequila and some trashy romance movies."

I follow her down the dark hallway, through her sitting room, and then through another door that leads down to the theater. "Your parents aren't home?"

"Huh?" she asks, opening the door. "Oh, no, they left last night. I'm sure they'll be home either tomorrow or on the weekend." We walk into the room, Tatum hitting the lights until a dim hue settles over the triple row of large sofas. Each sofa is enough to sit two adults comfortably, and there are around ten of them in the theater. There's a tiny bar tucked away in the corner with a popcorn machine and candy display, and then beside that is a large—no, scratch that—*massive* projector screen. Tatum walks to the bar, and I drop our food on a sofa, my bag onto the ground.

"Okay! Now I'm not good at cocktails, but we can just drink it straight. The end result is just the same."

"Thanks for this, Tate. You're a great friend."

She pauses, handing me a glass and twisting the lid off, pouring some clear liquid into it. "You would do the same, Madison. It's nothing."

And I would. God knows I'd move heaven and hell for her if I had to. We sit down and my phone vibrates again. Peeling my burger cover off, I look down at the screen to see Bishop's name flash across the phone. Exhaling, I take a large bite out of my burger, to the point where Tatum is looking at me with raised eyebrows.

"Hungry, or stressed?"

I shake my head. "He stresses me out," I murmur around my burger.

"It's not his fault, Madi."

"No, I know it's not, but I can't talk to any of them right now."

She nods, popping a chip into her mouth. "Totally understandable." Shuffling back to the ginormous sofa, I kick my shoes off and finish the rest of my burger in silence.

"I found this book," I say, starting on a donut.

"Oh? Kinky kind?"

I roll my eyes. "No, though I wish, because this one is kind of making me a little depressed." I lean forward to grab it, when my phone lights up again, this time showing a text message.

Bishop – *I'm sorry.*

Ignoring him, I reach for the book and flash it at her. "See!" Then I flip it open. "It's title-less, and Miss Winter wasn't actually supposed to allow people to check it out of the library, because it's some link in history. But after my third visit to the library, she must have felt sorry for me and let me take it."

"Miss Winter is weird as fuck. I don't understand that woman."

"She's not weird."

"Give me a look." Tatum waves for me to pass the book over.

"Tatum, wipe your hands!"

"Are you serious?" She pauses and then rolls her eyes, wiping her hands with a napkin. "Next thing I know you'll be calling it your precious."

I smile at her wit and then hand her the book. "So it's about this woman, right? I'm only up to chapter 7—at least I think they're chapters. It's a very different book... but it's intriguing. I'm still not sure what it's about. I went into it blind, because it has no title, no blurb, none of that."

Tatum takes a swig of her drink. "There's no sex?"

"No."

She hands it back. "Sounds boring."

I snatch it back from her. "It is not boring. It's fascinating."

"So what is it? Like a memoir or something?"

I shake my head. "Apparently, it's her suicide note."

"In the form of a book?" Tatum squeals, taking a chocolate cream donut out of the bag. "How poetic."

I flip the page open to where I was up to before falling asleep last night, and start reading out loud.

8.
Why?

"No, no, no, no, no..." I shook my head from left to right as another contraction rippled through my insides. "I don't... I'm not ready. It's too early."

"It's not too early, ma'am. You're only two weeks early. That's enough time for the baby to survive on its own."

Leaning my head back on the cold, hard ground, I looked up to the stars. "It's not time—"

"Enough, Katsia. It's time. Do as you're told and do it with class."

I looked toward my husband. "Don't you dare use that tone with me!"

"Woman! You are to do as you're told, or so help me God, I will slap some sense into you!" he roared, launching at me. I didn't flinch. My insides were tearing open, my stomach rippling with such pain it could put the fear of death into any man. I was ready for war. I didn't know it at the time, but there was a reason why so many people were surrounding me. My husband's right-hand man sat in the corner with his wife, who was cradling their newborn son, as well as the rest of the soldiers—as he called them—surrounded him.

"Ma'am, you're ready to push."

"Why here?" I whispered out to no one in particular. "Why here?" I scream, just as a contraction hits. I pushed roughly, until my stomach rolled over in pain and my pelvic bone felt like it was shattering under the heavy pressure that was being lumped on it.

"One more push, ma'am. That's it. I can see its little head."

Breathing in jaggedly, I gave one last scream and push. With a pop, a bright, burning ring of fire around my crotch, and a wet river flowing between my thighs, I pushed until all the pressure I was feeling was no more. A soft cry sounded out and my maid smiled, wrapping the baby in a throw. "Ma'am, you have yourself a daughter."

"What?" I smiled, love filling my being. I would have loved my child regardless, but knowing it was a daughter filled me with a different kind of love. The same amount, just different feelings.

The room cut silent. "Repeat what you just said," Humphrey demanded, moving up the stone step. "Did you just say daughter?" he questioned her, his head tilted. I saw the look pass in his eyes, and I knew instantly right then and there that something was wrong. So very wrong. Husband was livid, absolutely spewing. A girl? A girl had no place for him in his world.

The maid nodded, fear flashing over her face. She looked toward me frantically. "Yes—yes, um...."

He snatched the baby from her hands, and I rose from the stone bed. "Humphrey! Give me my baby right now."

He took her down, one step at a time. "No. No girls."

"What do you mean?" I screamed at him, blood dripping down my thighs and my body swaying from side to side.

"Girls that are born from the first nine," he seethed, turning to face me, "are to be taken care of. Sit down, wife, and do as you're told."

"No!" I screamed, stumbling down the step. "Humphrey!" Everything blurred and spun, the cold walls going in circles in my brain.

"Ma'am," my maid said, her face coming into view in threes. "Ma'am, sit down so I can tidy you up." Her voice echoed and repeated. My eyes closed and my head tilted back as everything under me fell. I dropped onto my back, smacking the back of my head. Tilting my head up at the dark sky, I watched as the full moon blared down at me.

"How odd," I whispered to my maid in a daze. "How odd that in this old cave, there's a hole in the roof."

I gasp, slamming the book closed. "Oh my God!" I hiss.

"What?" Tatum's shoving popcorn in her mouth, totally engrossed in the story.

"I know this place that she was talking about, Tatum!" I yell. "We need to go—now!"

"Why?" She stands from the sofa, shoving some Ugg boots on.

"Because I think this place, this cave that Katsia was talking about... I think it's at Bishop's cabin, and how cool is it that we could go see it? Maybe I could study it a bit more."

Tatum stops. "That's just weird. Maybe it's a coincidence. That would be so trippy if it was."

"Maybe." I shrug. "But I still want to show him this book and read the rest, see if maybe it is, and then we can all go and have a look!" I can barely contain my excitement.

"History really gets you going, huh?" Tatum teases, throwing her hair into a high ponytail.

"Yes, and more importantly, it's taking my mind off Ally."

She nods. "All right then, my history goddess, let's go!" She smiles sadly.

"Hey, are you okay?"

"Yeah," she murmurs. "My dad used to read me old stories when I was a kid. That's all."

"Oh, well that's really nice. Why does that make you sad?"

She stops, seeming to think of her memories, and then exhales. "I trust you, and I know you care about me."

"I do."

"My parents haven't been home in months. They're fine, though, because I've opened bank statements and seen they're still spending money. I called the penthouse that kept showing up on these statements and got them to put me through to them. Sure enough, my mom answered. My trust account is still large and I still have access to it. The mortgage and bills still get paid. But they just don't care, Madi."

I'm shocked. My mouth hangs open in utter shock, but most importantly, I'm hurt. Hurt for Tatum. "I'm sorry, Tate. Do they usually do this?"

She shakes her head. "I mean, they were always out, but they wouldn't leave for longer than a week."

"How long's it been?" I run my hand up and down her arm as a tear slips out the corner of her eye.

"Two hundred and eleven days."

"Oh my God!" I whisper, disgusted, and it's right here when I decide I hate her parents.

"Anyway," she shakes me off, "let's go see if Bishop's cabin has some creepy history on its land!"

We get into Tatum's car and I turn to face her. "Do you know where his house is?"

"Everyone knows where Bishop's house is."

I laugh, shaking my head. "I guess that was a stupid question."

"So tell me more about this Katsia person."

I start talking about what I've read so far in the book, and then I turn to face Tatum. "It probably sounds stupid, but I feel a bond with Katsia. Like she's lived through all this... dark stuff, and I've been able to watch it through her words."

"It's not silly." Tatum shakes her head, turning down Bishop's road. "It's not un-heard of. It's why I read."

"You read?" I ask, shocked.

Tatum giggles. "Don't act surprised, Madi. Yes, I read. Religiously. It's what takes me out of my life." Up until a few minutes ago, I always thought Tatum had a perfect life. Two parents at home, no messed up shit in her background. And now I feel terrible I made that assumption.

"I wish you had told me earlier, Tate. We could have had so many more sleepovers."

She smiles. "I know," she murmurs, turning into Bishop's gated driveway.

"It'll be locked."

She pulls the car up the curb. "Well then, we're jumping!"

I laugh, pushing open the door with the book hidden under my arm. "Looks like we are."

I walk toward a tree that's close to the walkway, a branch dangling over the top of the fence that surrounds Bishop's house. "There! Hold the book. When I get over, toss it and I'll catch it, and then you follow."

"Okay." Tatum nods. "Jesus, I can't believe we're doing this. His dad is scary as fuck."

"His dad isn't home. He's away until this weekend. I heard them talking about it while we were at the cabin. Come on." I hitch my foot on a smaller stub and grip onto the rough bark of the tree, propping myself up. Swinging my leg over the final limb that hangs to the fence, I look down to Tatum.

"Are you sure about this?" she murmurs. "I mean, I know you're not heavy, but that branch doesn't look very thick."

"It'll be fine, and if I fall, it's not like it's a very long drop."

"Ha ha." Tatum laughs dryly.

"You'll be fine. You're a twig."

"Yeah, but you—"

"Tate? Shut up."

"Okay, okay." With shaky limbs, I slowly stand on the branch, ignoring the creaking my body weight is drawing from it. "Shit," I whisper. "This is fine. I can totally do it." I look forward, my eyes staying on the thick trunk, and take the first step. "Shit, shit, shit." I hurry my steps, and just as I get to the end, I jump and land on the top of the gate. "See?" I grin down at Tatum.

"Yeah, okay, hurry up, show off."

I jump down off the fence. "Okay! Toss it over."

The leather book comes flying in the air and I jump to the side, landing on my stomach to catch it. "Shit!"

Tatum jumps down off the fence, landing on her feet. "That wasn't so bad. Damn Bishop and him not answering his fucking phone. Seriously? Since when does he stop answering the fucking phone when you call?"

I shake my head, dusting myself off. "I don't know."

We start walking toward his house. "Hey, have you heard from Tillie?" Tatum asks.

I shake my head. "No, I tried to call her last night, though, but I know Nate has spoken with her."

"What's up with those two anyway?"

"No one knows. They're weird. Nate slept with someone else last night and I lost my shit, told him I'd tell her if he didn't."

"I'm not even surprised."

"Right? But they were so cute at the cabin, Tate. Like, they were like a real couple. But apparently Tillie is fine with Nate sleeping with someone else. I haven't heard from her, though, and she's not answering my calls."

"Like you and Bishop cute?" She smirks, and the sound of his name and me in the same sentence has my stomach fluttering.

"Sort of." I smile.

Reaching his house, I follow the path to his bedroom at the back of the main house and near the pool.

"Jesus, it's like The Adams Family house, only newer."

I laugh. "Yeah, I know, right?" Walking toward his bedroom, I stop when I hear voices coming from what sounds like the ground.

"Did you hear that?" Tatum confirms my theory.

"Yeah, it sounds like Bishop's voice. They must be in the main house." I walk to the back, opening glass doors that open out onto the pool and Bishop's room opposite.

"You sure about this?" Tatum whispers, grabbing my arm.

"Yes! It's Bishop and Nate. We'll be fine."

"I'm not buying it," she mutters, looking around the house.

"It's open!" I whisper, pointing to the sliding wall.

"Oh, fuck's sake," Tatum grumbles. "I'm scared."

"Yeah, I guess I would be too had it not been for the cabin weekend."

"Bishop is a nice guy now?" she asks, trying to reassure herself.

"Definitely not."

"You could have lied!" she scolds, as we step into the sitting room.

"I'm not a liar," I whisper calmly.

"Nah, dawg, nah...."

"Nate!" I whisper to Tatum. We turn and follow a door that's cranked open under the double stairwell.

"Madi, I don't know about this."

"Okay, you stay here."

"I can't let you go down there on your own!"

"Well then, come. Either way, I'm going." I walk to the door, pulling it open to voices that are louder.

"Don't fucking care," Bishop replies, his tone dark, tormented, and almost unrecognizable.

"You stepped out of the rules. She's a civilian!" Brantley roars.

I flinch at his tone and sounds of a scuffle from all the glass smashing and someone shoving someone else.

"You and I both know she ain't no civilian, Brantley." I clutch the book close to my chest and take the final step down. My eyes find Brantley's instantly, and he grins. "Well, looks like you got some explaining to do, B." He smirks at me with a snarl. I can see the rest of the Kings in the room in my peripheral vision, but everything blurs when my eyes land on Ally, who is lying in a pool of her own blood, her neck sliced open, with a dark red gash splitting her throat, blood still pulsing out of it. My hand flies up to my mouth as an earth-shattering scream ripples out of me. In a flash, Bishop is flying toward me.

"Madi!"

I shove him away and turn, running up the stairs.

"Fuck!" Nate barks, and I can hear Bishop's footsteps chasing me up the stairs. My heart pounds in my chest vigorously. *He killed someone. He killed someone. He killed Ally.* Tears stream down my face as prickles of fear ripple all over my body. *He's a killer. Bishop is killer. He killed someone.* I push open the door just as vomit threatens to surface on the back of my throat. My eyes blur from the river of tears that are pouring out of my eyes, and when they land on Tatum, who is standing there waiting for me, my face pales. I run toward her, only to end up colliding with another body. Falling on my ass with a thud, the book flies through the air and lands on the floor. I can feel all the Kings behind me, watching me, all coming up from the basement.

I rub my hand over my forehead and slowly bring my eyes up to who I just collided with, guessing Bishop's dad is home. Swallowing through the bile of everything I've just witnessed, my vision reaches the owner of the body, and I gasp, shock spreading over every inch of me.

"Dad?"

"Madison!" my dad snaps at me in surprise. "What are you doing here?"

"No." I shake my head. "What are *you* doing here?"

Dad looks down to the book that's spread open as Bishop steps up beside me, look-ing down to it too. There's an audible gasp that sounds through the air, and I turn to Bishop, my eyes heavy and weak from all the tears. His hand covers his mouth in shock, his eyes wide as he gazes at the book. He tugs at his hair, and I look down to the book, confusion clouding me everywhere. Shuffling over the floor on my hands and knees, I reach it, the next chapter open and ready.

9.

The Silver Swan

The truth is I don't know what my husband did to my daughter. He said girls are tainted. There is no room for girls in his master plan, and that's how it always will be. He said they would sell the girls, but something dark and doubtful always tickled the back of my mind. My husband was a liar, a cheat, and a manipulator. There's absolutely not one part of his body that is truthful or redeemable.

Later that night, after my maid had cleaned me up, Humphrey came back into the cave, sat down beside me, and said, "Girls cannot be born into our covenant, wife. They're weak by human nature. They must be taken care of at their birth."

"You're not God, Humphrey. You cannot deem who bears what when pregnant."

"No," he replied simply. "But I can take care of it."

I shook my head, my heart in tatters, and my life turning bleak, dark, finished. "There will be no Silver Swans born into this family or any of the first nine. They will be demolished."

"Silver Swans?" I asked, clipped and annoyed.

"The Silver Swan is, in old times, what they would call a tarnished being. Every girl that would be born into the first nine is a tarnished being. It's no place for a her."

"Humphrey Hay—"

I swipe the tears from my eyes, not wanting to read anymore. "Dad?" I tilt my head at my father. "Why are you here?"

He swallows roughly. "I was just sorting out a business deal." His eyes pinch, wor-ried. "Just some business I had with Mr.—"

Flashbacks come in at full force.

"Your dad has shady business dealings."

"She's a civilian!"

"She's no civilian and you know it."

"Do you know anything about us?"

"Have you been to The Hamptons before? And be honest with me!"

"Fuck your dad!"

"Trust me, Madison. Your father is no innocent in this!"

"He recognized her! Fuck!"

And then finally, Bishop's words from the cabin. *"Just promise me that you will always know we've done everything for your safety."*

All the secrets. The questions, the empty answers and promises. The lies!

My mouth drops open and my chest freezes as realization becomes clear. "Oh my God," I whisper, my hand coming to my mouth. I look up at all the Kings and then look to my father, whose shoulders are slack in defeat. I look over his shoulder to see a strapping man in a tailored suit. His jaw is square and tense, his eyes dead and emotion-less. He flicks the cufflinks on his wrist and glares right through me.

"I'm the Silver Swan," I murmur to myself, searching the floor for some sort of clue that I'm overreacting. Everyone pauses, no one correcting me. "You all lied to me!" I launch off the floor and point to them all. Hate builds up in force. Tears stream down my face as I turn to face Bishop. "You *lied* to me. Oh my God!" I step backward, Tatum, being Tatum, following my back. *"Who the fuck are you?"* I whisper to Bishop, then turn to Dad. "And who the fuck are you, too?" I shake my head.

"Madi, wait!' Bishop yells as I run through the door, clutching the book in my hand.

"Leave her, son."

"Don't talk about my daught—"

They all cut out as I pick up my pace, Tatum chasing me down the driveway. We reach the fence, and it slides open instantly as we get there.

"Madi!" Bishop yells, running down the steps of his house.

"Hurry, Tatum!" We run through the gates, and she beeps open her car. The gates slowly close behind us, and I quickly slide into the passenger seat, with her getting into the driver's.

"Drive," I hiss, my heart breaking when I catch Bishop's eye, his hands curled around the bars of the fence.

"Where to?"

"Anywhere but here."

"Okay. Are we running, Madi? 'Cause I'm with you all the way."

"Yeah, Tate, we're running, and we're not coming back."

They are not the boys I suspected they were. They're the kind of monsters you warn people about. Not naïve children, but adults. The kind who lie, cheat, manipulate, seduce, and kill, just to get what they want. They're the kind you *run* from.

I'm Madison Montgomery, and I thought I knew who I was. But I was wrong. I'm not just some average girl whose mom killed herself after killing the woman my father was having an affair with.

I'm the Silver Swan.

And now? Now I'm just the remnants of the broken puppet they all used me as. Everything human inside of me has been taken out and replaced with nothing but cotton and fake love. There's no coming back now—not ever.

The End
(For Now)

ACKNOWLEDGEMENTS

I'm always terrified that I'm leaving someone out when I write my acknowledgements, because there are just so many incredible people who have contributed to my writing career one way or another, whether it be their friendship, their advice, or their eyes. This doesn't go in order. I'm totally winging it (surprise, surprise). I want to start with a huge thank you to these girls: Caro Richard, Andrea Florkowski, Franci Neil, Michel Prosser, and Amy Halter: my beta team! Thank you for caring about my stories enough to tell me when something is shit.

Isis Te Tuhi & Anne Malcom: my girls. I adore each of you, thank you for being there for me every day—no joke, I hit them up every single day. Nina Levine, for being your sweet self and being there for me for anything, I adore you! My Wolf Pack, I can't shout out how much I love these girls. They're my tribe, at times my rock, and above all—my girls. Jay Aheer for the beautiful cover, you talented little human. Kayla Robichaux for being my top bish, my soul sister, and my editor! Barbara Hoover for polishing my words at the very end and always doing it in such a respectful way. The girls from Give Me Books, for all the hard work they put into promoting authors like me! You girls are the real MVP. To the bloggers, I can't express how much I admire and love you all. Thank you for all that you do! My loyal, amazing, sassy readers: I love you HARD. None of this would be possible without all of your undying support, thank you! Last but not least, my little family. There have been times where you've all had to live on Weetbix (hey, kiwi kids and all that…), toast, and leftovers. There have been times when I've had to lock myself away and ignore you, because I had either found my flow or I was on a deadline (they never come at the same time. Oh no, that would be too easy). Love you, munchkins! For us! Think this is long enough? I think so.

THE
BROKEN
PUPPET

THE ELITE KINGS CLUB BOOK TWO

PLAYLIST

Jason Derulo "Stupid Love"

The Weeknd "Or Nah"

Dead Prez "Hip Hop"

Avenged Sevenfold "Hail to the King"

Machine Gun Kelly "Bad Things"

The Game "It's Okay"

David Guetta "Where the Girls At"

Cheat Codes "No Promises"

Redman "Cisco Kid"

Cypress Hill "Tequila Sunrise"

Kendrick Lamar "Humble"

Tash Sultana "Jungle"

Tsar B "Escalate"

Tsar B "Myth"

DEDICATION

To the girls who have been through hell but come out with its fire burning through their soul, its crimson bleeding from their heart, and the devil as their side bitch.
This one's for you.
For us.
Straighten that crown.
Deuces.

PROLOGUE

Mommy? I ducked behind my closed bedroom door.

As I peeked around the corner, my mom started raising her voice, stabbing her finger into the man standing in front of her. *"No, this wasn't part of the plan!"*

The man smiled in a way that made me clutch my teddy, Puppie, tighter. *"You don't call the shots. She's a Venari. You will have to run, and run fast if you don't want this catching up with you."*

My mom clutched the locket on her chest. *"She...,"* my mother whispered, tears slipping down her cheeks. *"She's just a kid, Lucan. She... she—"*

"Is the Silver Swan, Elizabeth. You must run. Now, before Hector finds out."

My mom sucked in a breath just as I stepped backward, quietly running to my bed. Slipping under the covers, I wiggled into the warmth and clutched Puppie closer. It was my birth present from a close family friend, and I'd slept with her since. She had ballerina slippers, a loose dress, and her hands stuck up in the air when the puppet strings were attached. When my door finally cracked open, my eyes slammed shut as I began to scratch one of the button eyes on my teddy. The material was worn, and the puppet strings were now broken. I was seven though, so I should've been too old for Puppie to be sleeping in bed with me. But I know why the man was here.

He comes here every Friday.

I know what he does next.

Bleeding echoes reverberate around Madison's bedroom as sobs wrack through her body. Clutching her knees up to her chest, she scrunches her eyes closed, attempting to block out the familiar memories that assault her every night. Like a murky walk down a cold, damp road, alone, unable to break free from the confinement of which she's constricted to.

"This is part of who you are, Silver."

Goose bumps break out over her flesh at the slithering invasion of that voice. And then everything changes, as if she's watching herself from the outside as a different person.

"No!" Madison tossed and turned in his arms, attempting to break her wrists free from the tight grip strapped around her.

"Shhh, Silver, you're not your own."

"What?" Madison gasped, tears streaming down her cheeks. "What do you mean I'm not my own?" The hand that was around her wrists went to her loose ponytail, and he tugged it down

slightly. *"Please don't. Not tonight,"* Madison pleaded, her throat constricting through the pain, and the betrayal.

"You best get used to this, Silver. This is only the beginning of your life."

"But I'm little."

"This is better than being dead." Then he gripped onto Madison's pajama bottoms and tore them off, flicking them across the room. She closed her eyes and dreamed of a day, a better day, where her family secrets and ties weren't coming into her bedroom every Friday night. Black Friday was what Madison called it. She feared it, despised it, and one day, she hoped to put a bullet between its eyes. The first time, he stole her virginity. And Madison knew the blood that trickled down her innocent thighs wouldn't bleed without retribution.

CHAPTER I

"Madison? Are you sure you want to leave?" Tatum asks, looking at me from over her arm, her hands resting on the steering wheel.

"Yes," I answer, gazing out the window. "I can't be around them right now, Tatum."

She looks at me, pulling onto the highway. "Do you want to talk about what happened back there?"

I hit the radio, hoping to drown out her questions. Jason Derulo's "Stupid Love" starts playing.

"So yup, that's a no then," Tatum mutters, taking her attention back to the road. I close my eyes and lose myself in the lyrics of the song. Fuck love. Fuck any feelings that resemble love, or show it. The one person who was supposed to love me unconditionally betrayed me too. What does that say? What, am I that unlovable? Or do so many people think I don't deserve their truth? Both of which are shit, if I'm being honest. Which I am.

The song finishes and I turn the radio down, realizing it's not Tatum's fault.

"You don't have to do this with me, Tate, but I can't be here, with them, around all the lies."

She sighs. "Madi, I'm not leaving you. I know our friendship moved fast, but... I've never had any friends before, and I'm a little..." Her face turns red before she looks back to me. "Lonely. So I'm not leaving you out here—alone."

"But you do realize that you'll have to ditch your credit cards?" I point out, watching her reaction.

Realization slips over briefly before a smile snaps back onto her face. "Yes, Madi. Consider them gone."

"Really?" I ask, my eyebrow quirked.

"Yes." She nods, and I almost buy it. Then she casually adds, "Right after I withdraw a few thousand."

Laughing, I shake my head, turning the music back up. What the fuck are we going to do?

"Okay," Tatum inserts, running her hand through her hair as she continues to drive us wherever the fuck we are going. "So we need to go back to your house quickly and gather whatever we might need."

"Like what?" I ask, horrified that we need to go back home. "No, Tate, I don't want to go there."

She looks to me. "Well, what then, Madi? We don't have many options, and we need passports and all that!"

"Okay," I whisper, resting into my seat and trying to think of a solution. "Okay, this is just a real blind shot, but I promise if this fails, we can break into my house and take whatever I need."

Tatum relaxes. "So where are we going?"

I swallow. "To Riverside. To the library."

Pulling up to the school, Tatum parks the car out front and turns in her seat to face me. "Are you sure about this?"

"Um." I search for the word I'm looking for, but fail. "No." I push open the door and get out just as Tatum's door closes.

"Well, lucky I have my running shoes on." She rounds the car and comes to stand next to me.

I look down at her feet. "Those aren't running shoes, Tatum."

Heading toward the school with Tatum in tow, we sneak down the side of the girls' classrooms, ducking under any windows where people might see us, and make our way past the pool, straight toward the library that's tucked behind the gym. As we reach the student-only entrance, I slide my student card over the little box until the green light flashes and beeps. Pulling open the door, we step inside. It's fairly quiet, a few students hanging about here and there, but no one who would take notice of Tatum and me. The door slips shut, breaking the kind of silence that can only come from a library.

Miss Winters's head snaps up to the entrance, pulling her out of the book she was engrossed in. Her eyes widen when she sees me, so I give her a pleading look. She gets to her feet, shoving her glasses up her nose. Walking toward Tatum and me, she watches her surroundings closely, her paranoia obvious.

"Girls, how can I help you?" She plasters on a fake smile.

"I know" is all I manage to say. All the times I've wanted to ask, *What the fuck is going on?* is replaced now with those two simple words.

Miss Winters pauses, her head tilting to the side as her eyes drift over my shoulder briefly before coming back to me. "You know?"

I maintain eye contact, my shoulders squaring. "I. Know." In a blink of an eye, she forcefully grabs onto Tatum's and my arms and directs us back toward the entrance we just walked through. Pushing the doors open, she shoves us back into the late afternoon sun, closing the doors behind herself.

She exhales, her hand coming up to her forehead where she rubs across it softly, in an almost meditating gesture. "Shit." She cranes her neck, closes her eyes, and then breathes out, "You know you're the Silver Swan?"

"The Silver what now?" Tatum asks sassily, looking toward me with a crinkled eyebrow.

"Yes," I hiss. "But I don't know what the fuck that means or how you know about it or why everyone has been lying to me."

"I can't...." Miss Winters shakes her head. "I'm sorry, Madison, but I can't get involved with all of it. It's too dangerous."

"Well then, can you help me disappear?"

Miss Winters snaps her head toward me. "You can't run from the Kings, Madison. They'll kill you." She ends her sentence in a whisper.

"They'll kill me anyway. Assuming I read the book correctly."

"Where is that book?" Miss Winters asks, looking around nervously.

"It's in my bag. Are you going to help me or not?"

She pauses, searches my eyes, and then pulls out her phone. "Look, I know a guy. Tell him Tinker sent you."

"Tinker?" I ask as she scrolls through her cell.

She looks up at me. "Yes, Tinker." She pauses, dropping her arms to her side.

"What?"

"It's just.... Listen, you need to do this right if you're going to do it. Get all the documents he needs from you, but withdrawal all the cash you need for now. He's not cheap. You can't carry over ten grand in cash if you fly internationally, so withdrawal ten thousand, and then another eight to get everything you need from Benny." She pauses, giving me his number, and I quickly add it to my phone. "He will charge you four thousand each." She pauses and looks at me. "Run, Madi. Run and don't ever come back, because regardless of what Bishop feels about you?" She searches my eyes. "It means nothing. It meant nothing when it came to Khales, either."

"What do you mean? What do you know about Khales?"

Her face turns hard. "I know he put a bullet right between her eyes."

CHAPTER 2

After running back to Tatum's car, we both slip inside before she skids out and takes us toward the bank. "What the fuck does she mean? Bishop killed someone?" Tatum's eyes are wide as she looks between me and the road ahead.

"I don't think that was the first person he ever killed either," I murmur, looking outside my window.

"You never did tell me what you saw in that basement, Madi."

I want to tell her, but a strange part of me doesn't want her to know something that could be used against Bishop. *Stupid girl*, I scold myself. Also, it's safer for Tatum to not know anything.

"I don't really want to talk about it, Tate."

She smiles and pats my hand. "We're getting the fuck out of here." Pulling up to the curb, we both jump out.

I close my door. "You go to your bank and I'll go to mine. We can carry ten each. That should get us through."

Tatum nods, but something flashes through her eyes and I pause. "Are you okay?"

"We're really doing this?" she quickly asks.

"You can back out now. I don't want to drag you into my mess anyway."

"No." She shakes her head. "I'm coming with you. I have nothing here."

I smile sadly. "Okay, then it's settled. Meet back here in ten minutes." Tatum nods and then quickly dashes into her bank as I cross the busy road to mine. Pushing open the doors with my head ducked, I collide into someone. "Sorry," I mutter, stepping around them.

"Madison?"

I look up to see Ridge staring back at me. "Oh, hi," I murmur, eyeing over his shoulder. I don't want to take long here; I need to get in and out as fast as possible, no stopping.

"Hey, I was going to come look for you. Have you heard from Tillie?" he asks, tilting his head. I look at him, properly this time, and notice the tired bags under his red-rimmed eyes and his disheveled hair.

"No, not since we came back from the cabin. Why? Is everything okay?" Now that he said that, it is odd I haven't noticed Tillie not contacting me. I've been so caught up in my shit that I haven't stopped to think.

He shakes his head. "No, no one has heard from her."

"I'll call her. I'm sure she's fine." She could be anywhere, but then again, she could really be okay. From what she told me about her dad, I'm not entirely surprised she hasn't gone home.

"Okay." He pulls out his phone. "Can I give you my number so you can call me if you hear from her? Please, I just want to make sure she's okay."

I nod, surveying inside toward the bank teller. I really need to leave. "Sure." He tells me his number, and I push it into my phone…. My phone! Shit! "Actually," I start, going for relaxed tone, "could you write it down?" He looks at me, pauses, but then nods, drawing out a pen and taking my hand, scribbling it down.

"Thanks, I'll call you." I sidestep away from him and walk the rest of the way into the bank. There's a fucking line. Of course there's a fucking line.

Fifteen minutes later, I'm walking out of the bank, tossing my ATM card into a trash can nearby, and heading back to the car.

Pulling open the passenger door, Tatum is smiling at me from the driver seat. "I actually feel really fucking excited about this."

"Makes one of us," I mutter, taking out my phone. "Drive." I pop open the glove compartment and pull out a pen and paper, transferring Ridge's number then scrubbing it off my hand. "I'll call Benny now."

Tatum nods as she continues to drive.

The phone rings until a deep voice picks up. "Who sent you?"

"Uh… uh…." I look around, confused. What a weird way to answer the phone. "Tinker?" God, I feel ridiculous saying that name out loud.

A pause.

Silence.

"The corner, on the last stretch of Highway 4."

"Uh, okay?"

He hangs up. I look down at my phone and then at Tatum.

"What'd he say?" she asks, looking between me and the road.

"We have to go to the corner on the last stretch of Highway 4."

Tate nods. "I know where that is."

"Give me your phone." I put my hand out to her. "Do you need any numbers from it?"

She pauses, eyes glassing over slightly before she squares her shoulders. "No. No one will even know I'm gone."

I smile sadly at her before winding my window down, tossing the cell out. Searching through my contacts, I take down a couple of numbers that might come in handy. Through my scrolling, my finger pauses over Bishop's name, and my heart sinks slightly.

Fuck him.

Not only did he kill Ally, but apparently he killed Khales too. I pass his name and keep searching until I get to my dad. My heart sinks further, but I keep scrolling up.

Nate.

I close my eyes, squeezing my phone in… frustration? Sadness? A combination of both? Winding down my window with my eyes still closed, I toss it out. "I don't need anyone either."

Pulling up to the almost abandoned crossroad off the highway, I notice it's empty—and it's getting late, the afternoon sun casting shadows through the large branches of trees that reside on the edge of the cul-de-sac.

"No one's here. It's quiet."

"Too quiet," I add. We pull to a stop and I get out of the car, slamming my door.

Tatum winds my window down. "Madi! Fuck's sake, can you not be a badass today, please? I don't want to die right now. Or ever."

I roll my eyes. "Miss Winters gave us this dude's number. She wouldn't fuck us over."

"You put an awful lot of confidence in Miss Winters," a voice says, a figure walking toward me out of the shadows. I spin around and see an older man making his way to me. He's wearing a hoodie and ripped dark jeans, and he must be in his midforties.

"Well, it's all I've got."

He nods in understanding. At first glance, no warning bells go off. "I've been in touch with Tinker. I have all your documents ready to go."

"That was quick."

"We have them at my beck and call. It's why I charge so much."

I shrug, not needing the details. "Let me see." He hands me two manila folders. One says Amira and the other says Atalia. Both last names. "We're sisters?" I look up at Benny. "Amira and Atalia Maddox? Could you not go with something simple?"

Benny looks at me deadpan. "Hand the money over."

I pull out the thick envelope and pass it to him. He takes out the cash and flicks through it. "I take it it's all here?"

"Of course. You know we're good for it."

He pauses, watching us for a split second before appearing satisfied with my answer. "This didn't happen. Have a nice life, Amira."

I'm Amira? Of course I am. Stupid fancy name, it doesn't suit me at all.

I walk back to the car, swinging the door open, and hand Tatum the folder that says her new name on it. "Here you go, Atalia."

She scoffs, and then her smile drops. "Seriously?"

"Seriously."

"Well damn. Let's get this started." She puts the car in first gear and we drive to the closest airport.

Not long after, we're parking the car in the garage. We both get out and walk toward the building, me with my duffle bag and her with her own small bag.

"Where are we going?" Tatum asks, looking at me.

I squint my eyes at all the flights. Smiling, I nudge her with my elbow. "How long does it take to get a visa?"

CHAPTER 3

The visas were rather easy to obtain. There's a kiosk counter set up toward the back of the airport, and since the country we're flying to has a direct agreement with the United States, all it took was a quick questionnaire online and done; we were accepted directly through the visa waiver system.

"I can't believe this," Tatum whispers. "We're going to New Zealand? Couldn't you choose a different country, like, I don't know… Dubai?"

I turn to face her. "And where do you think they'll look first, Tate?"

She sighs. "I guess so."

"And besides," I add, "I haven't even heard of New Zealand. I doubt Bishop has. And also…" I look toward her ungrateful ass, "it was either this or some small town in Indonesia or Thailand."

"Could have got cheap new tits in Thailand."

Rolling my eyes, the voice overhead calls our flight name, and I look to Tatum, my heart beating in my chest. "Are you ready?"

She looks back at me and takes my hand. "Yeah… yeah, I am."

Two Months Later

"I don't know, Ta—Atalia."

Tatum grins at me, walking around the back of the bar in her skimpy shorts and lace push-up bra that hangs out of her ripped crop top. "Well, you know you can work here." She nods toward the stripper pole. We've been here for a couple of months now, and plan to stay for a couple more hopefully, but I need to find a job to keep my mind busy.

I turn back around and grin. "You know, I may not care anymore, but I won't be sucking on any poles." I take a sip of my drink and lean back in my chair, scanning the paper in front of me and flinging my pencil through my fingers. It's 12:00 p.m. here, which means it's around 8:00 p.m. the previous day back home.

Since coming here, Tatum and I have been staying in a little apartment right on the beach. We landed in Auckland thirteen hours after we boarded the plane and immediately purchased a little booklet of the country. We both agreed we wanted to be near the beach, grasping something that resembles home and keeping it close to us. So we found this small town in the middle of the north island called Mount Maunganui. I can't pronounce it and have noticed a lot of the locals just call it The Mount.

It's beautiful here. Sandy beaches, big waves, little shops lining the main beach where houses and coastal homes are set up opposite. The entire strip of the shoreline goes on for around ten minutes by car and eventually takes you to another small suburb called Papamoa. New Zealanders are friendly—sometimes a little too friendly—the food is fresh, and the air is like walking into a sauna for the first time. It's lovely. But I haven't been able to find a job since we got here. The flat we live in is a small studio apartment—nothing over the top—but it costs a fortune. It turns out this town isn't exactly cheap to live in. Of course, trust Tatum and me to choose one of the more expensive towns in the whole of New Zealand. She found a job right away, working for cash in hand as a bartender-slash-stripper—I shit you not. I love Tatum, but I can see her slowly losing herself.

Is it happening to me too?

Whenever I try to dig inside, in search of my true feelings, I come up blank. I have none. I've thought once or twice about taking Tatum up on her offer and joining her as a stripper, but then I remembered I can't dance for shit and my ass jiggles a little more than it should.

"Nice drawing," the guy next to me interrupts my thoughts, pointing down to my piece of paper.

"Thanks," I murmur, leaning forward and taking my drink.

"How long did it take for you to draw that?"

"Hmmm." I swallow some of my drink and then look back at him. "About twenty minutes."

His eyebrows pull together. "Can I take a look?"

I nod. "Yeah, sure." I hand it to him, watching his expressions change. He has messy but well-styled light-brown hair, a five o'clock shadow, a straight pointy nose, and olive skin. His shoulders are square, much like his jaw, and he's wearing a dark leather jacket with a plain white shirt underneath, dark jeans, leather bangles on his wrists, and heavy black biker boots. Oh, God, please don't be a biker.

"These are fucking mint." He grins, studying my latest drawing. I don't know what the term "mint" means, but I take it it's some kind of New Zealand lingo. The drawing is a pink lotus flower that's half blossomed. There's a bullet sitting in the middle, the petals of the flower guarding it protectively. The shading isn't quite finished, but yeah, it's not bad.

"Thank you," I reply shyly.

He looks up at me. "I heard you tell your—" He looks toward Tatum on the pole. "—friend you're looking for a job?"

"Yeah." I nod. "We're from America."

"Backpacking?"

"Something like that," I answer through a tight smile.

"Jesse." He puts his heavily tattooed hand out.

I take it, surprised his palm is a little soft considering what he looks like. "Amira."

"Amira?" He grins. "Sort of sexy."

"Ha!" I laugh nervously. "Good one." Is he flirting? I can't tell.

His grin relaxes to a sly smirk. "Here." He slides his card across the bar. "I own

Inked, the tattoo parlor two shops down." He points to my drawing. "I got you a job if you want it."

"What?" I gasp in disbelief. "I haven't tattooed anyone—ever!"

He shakes his head. "No, but I have, and do, and you draw fucking amazing. I can teach you. Or, you can just draw for me. I only do custom designs. So if you come in and sit down as I go over each client, you can draw what they say. Catch my drift?"

I swallow. "Shit."

"Scared?" He grins at me again, a dark eyebrow quirked.

"Sort of."

"Hey!" Tatum comes bouncing with bills stuffed under her bra. Jesus fucking Christ, this girl. She looks to Jesse and smiles, her eyes lighting up like the Fourth of July. She puts her hand out. "I'm Atalia!"

Jesse looks between us. "Similar names, or...?"

"Sisters," Tatum chirps, gripping onto the bar, jumping up, and planting her ass on top. Jesse walks over to her, picks her up from under her arms, and shakes his head.

"Don't go sitting your little ass on tabletops in this country, girl."

I laugh at Tate's pouted lip.

"Okay," I say to Jesse, and his eyes come directly back to me. "I mean," I correct, "I don't know if I'm what you're really looking for, but I'm willing to give it a try. Since, you know... I was rather close to going up"—I point toward the stage—"there."

He grins. "Yeah, come now." He nudges his head toward the front door, and I look between it and him and then back again.

"You're not a murderer, are you?"

"Guess you won't know until you follow me."

Pausing, my eyes lock onto his before I down my drink and get off the stool.

Turning to Tatum, I smile. "I'll be back soon."

She shrugs and then bounces back onto the stage. I follow Jesse out the door, the cool summer air hitting me across the face. He nudges his head toward the sidewalk.

"This isn't the part where you kill me, is it?" I chuckle, shoving my hands into my jean pockets.

He laughs, throwing his head back. "This is New Zealand, babe. You're safe." From what I've seen so far, it is safe here.

We walk down the sidewalk until we come to a shop that has black paint licked over the front with red stripes going diagonally down the brick structure. Jesse pulls out his keys, unlocks the door, and then ushers me inside.

Flicking the lights on, he gestures out in front of himself.

"It's clean!" is the first thing that comes into my brain, and me being me, of course I say it out loud.

Jesse laughs, closing the door behind himself to shut out the line of boy racers that are flooring it down the main street. "Yeah, I guess it sort of has to be." He tilts his head and then walks forward to the dark concrete counter. It's all rustic with a dose of modern. The floors are glass mirror tiles, and the seats are black leather with intricate designs carved into the armrests. All the booths are wide open but have the option to pull a curtain across for privacy. There's also a private booth at the back.

"Piercings and such," Jesse mutters, handing me a beer when he sees me looking at the booth.

"Thanks." I take it. "So what exactly do you want from me?"

He takes a swig and then looks at me. "When clients come in, you can sit in during their consultation, get a vision of what they want, and draw it for them. Just roughly sketch it."

"Okay, and when you don't have clients?" I ask, watching him carefully. He has a couple of beauty marks on his face that instantly draw my attention, so I look away quickly, not wanting to get caught ogling. He's a little more than hot. He has a rough sexiness about him. I wonder how old he is.

"You can stay at the front desk? I can pay you hourly plus give you a percentage out of the drawings you do—all cash in hand."

I think over his question and then look toward some of the artwork that's hanging on the walls. "I guess I'm in."

He steps forward, pushing his hands into the front pockets of his jeans, and tilts his head. "What's your story?"

Casually sucking in a breath, I bring the bottle to my mouth and swallow. "I don't really have one."

"Okay, and how long are you in NZ for?"

"Only for a couple of months. If that. So please don't think this is a permanent thing for me. I'd hate to give you the wrong impression."

The corner of his mouth tilts up slightly. "I'm not really into permanent."

I run my eyes up and down his body, once again failing to hide my attraction to him, but anytime I think, *Okay, I can do this. I can find a man just to have something casual with,* Bishop possesses my body and my thoughts. It's not entirely fair, considering he has probably moved on already, but it's just not in me to do it yet. It's too soon.

I halt him with my hand, sensing he was going to go into the dating territory. "Please don't. Not yet."

He grins. "I can do not yet."

Handing him my barely touched beer, I smile at him. "I better go, but I'll see you tomorrow?"

"Yup, 9:00 a.m.," he agrees.

I nod, turn on my heel, and walk out the door. Figuring I'll walk the rest of the way back to our apartment instead of calling a taxi, I eventually make my way to the main beach. Stepping down the sandy steps, I inhale the thick, salty ocean air and close my eyes, shutting out any noise but the crashing of waves and the crickets chirping within the trees. New Zealand is beautiful; there's no doubt about that. But I miss being home in the US. I don't know what's happening back home. No one has found me, or no one has looked—not sure which of the two is correct.

"You okay?" Tatum comes down the steps and walks to where I'm standing. I take a seat on the sand and draw my knees up, my hair falling over my shoulders.

"Not really."

Tate plops down beside me, her long coat wrapped tightly around her body.

"Are you wearing clothes under that?"

"What?" She bats her eyelashes innocently. "Of course I am! And also…." She pulls out a bottle of whiskey and what I'm pretty sure is a joint. "Tada!"

I shake my head and laugh. "You're a hot mess, you know that?"

"I know," she sighs, resting her head on my shoulder. "Be a hot mess with me?"

I swallow, looking out to the dark ocean, wondering what lies are on the other side of what seems to be an endless bank of water. "Yeah, I think I'm ready to be just that."

The thoughts of Bishop and my dad have been eating away at me ever since I left the US. Maybe the reason why it's not affecting Tatum so much is because she's always high or drunk—or having sex. Although I'm not ready for the sex part—and I don't even know why, because it's not like Bishop and I were together—I still feel like I'm betraying him. Why the fuck should I care if I'm betraying him though? He betrayed me! He lied, cheated, manipulated, and killed someone. He's exactly—

"Make it stop, Tate," I whisper through fresh tears as my throat clogs. A single tear trickles over my cheek and Tatum catches it with her index finger. She then grips my chin, turning me to face her. She searches my eyes, and for a second, she seems stone-cold sober. "We will make it stop together, Mads."

Swallowing, I nod and take the joint from her. Lighting it up, I put it between my lips and inhale deeply until my lungs catch on fire and my throat turns to stone. Blowing out the smoke, a sputter of coughs come out of me, so I snatch the whiskey from her hand while passing her the joint. After twisting the cap, I bang on my chest and then put the tip to my lips and swallow, allowing the burning of the cheap whiskey to coat my already parched throat.

Tatum falls onto her back with the joint tucked between her lips and I lay back with her, the stars swimming in the dark abyss of the sphere, a bottle of whiskey between my fingers, and my hair sprawled out over the sand.

"Do you think he ever cared, Tate?" I whisper, tilting my head and lining up the southern cross that hangs brightly in the sky.

"Bishop? No. Nate? Yes." She coughs loudly, banging on her chest. I sit up, taking a drink until the burning turns my throat numb and my head throbs with intoxication. Tatum passes me the joint. "Sorry, Mads. I just don't think he did. But I wouldn't take it personally. He doesn't give a fuck about anyone or anything." I toke on the ganja, this time holding it in longer to intensify my buzz, and then blow it out slowly.

"Why the fuck can't I bring myself to get laid."

"That will come, babe. I said he didn't care. I'm well aware that you did."

"I'm stupid."

"No." Tatum shakes her head, handing me the whiskey. "No, you're not. You're Madison Montgomery, and you're a fucking boss-ass bitch who feels, Mads. That's a big deal. More people should feel."

"Felt," I whisper, my tears now dry. "They used me as their puppet. Now I'm broken."

"Broken but hot, and who, by the way, has found a hot tattoo artist!"

I laugh, pulling my bottom lip into my mouth. "He is a bit hot, huh?"

"A bit?" Tatum looks offended. "Honey, he will do you fine until our next stop."

"Have you decided where we're going next?" I slur, my eyes narrowing on her to try to focus.

"Mmmm, Milan?"

"Spain?" I ask, shocked. "What about London? Can we do Bristol?"

"Why?"

"I don't know. Just really want to find a hot British guy."

"To bang, or to complain to me about how you can't bang?"

I laugh, shoving her shoulder. "Shut up. Come on." I get up off the sand and pull Tatum with me. Only we both spin out and... I'm falling. I land on the sand with a plonk, the hard surface sure to bruise my ass.

"Fuck!" Tatum curses behind a chuckle.

I can't help it. Undiluted laughter erupts out of me, and I clutch my belly. "Holy shit." I shake my head, my cheeks now aching from all the smiling.

"Well that's a laugh I haven't heard in a while." Tatum clutches her stomach, wiping the tears from her eyes.

"Yeah, I promise I'll try to do it more."

CHAPTER 4

"Morning, hot stuff." Tatum walks into my room, a joint between her fingers.
"Morning," I answer, pulling on some cutoff shorts and a tight tank. "Is this too much?"

"Nonsense!" Tatum hushes my insecurities, stepping forward and handing me the joint. She pushes my tits up and ruffles my hair. "This is a tattoo parlor!"

I bring the smoke to my lips and take a hit. "True!" I agree, before handing it back to her and walking out to the living room. Our apartment—or flat, as they call it here—is small. It has two bedrooms, a small living room, and a kitchenette that overlooks the main beach strip. We pay a small fortune to live here too, but it's what Tatum wanted, and since she was the only one working at the time, I let her do it. Our savings are still healthy, thanks to Tatum working pretty much right away, but that's the money we have to live on when we skip countries. The kitchenette is a mustard yellow, and the living room is neutral beige. It's a beach house, and the family we rent it from also own the bar Tatum works at. It worked in our favor, and we were really lucky.

After pouring my coffee, I bring it to my lips. "Work tonight?"

Tatum nods. "Yep. What time do you finish?"

I shake my head. "I don't know. We didn't really talk about that."

"Jesse?" Tatum asks. "He's interesting-looking, right? What's the NZ nationality?"

"I don't know, and I'm not asking."

"He looks Cuban or something."

"You finished?" I ask as she gazes off into the sky, resting her feet on the wooden coffee table. The flat came furnished with just the necessities. Sofas, fridge, beds. There's no television, but we don't really need it.

"Okay, see you after work." I wave to Tatum, who is still smoking her joint. Figuring it's probably a ten-minute stroll down to the main town strip, I decide to walk instead of catching the bus. Saving money and all that too. I get there five minutes later, and sucking in a deep breath, I push open the doors and step inside. Some rock song is playing that I haven't heard before, but I kinda dig it, and I step toward the front desk where a girl with pitch-black hair and a whole lot of ink is sitting.

"Hi," I say to her.

She looks up at me from the computer. "Hey! What can I help you with?"

"This one's mine," Jesse announces, stepping out from behind one of the closed booths. I know he didn't mean it as in *I'm his*, but I squirm anyway. I hate that I squirm. I'm an idiot for squirming. Yet I want to swoon.

"New girl?" the dark-haired girl asks Jesse.

Jesse nods. "Yeah, this is Amira. She's the artist I told you about last night."

"Oh, right!" she says, clicking her fingers in recognition. "Hi! I'm Kiriana!"

"Ki-what-what?" I ask, shocked, my eyes fluttering. "Sorry, I'm... can you break it down for me?"

Kiri something laughs and pats the seat beside her. "Kiri, like kitty only you roll the R, and -ana, which is... yeah, -ana!"

"Kiriana?" I say, sounding ridiculous because my accent just won't let me roll anything, so I end up pronouncing it like ki-ree-ana.

She waves me off. "That'll do. Come, sit. Show me what you got."

Jesse winks at me and then walks back to his booth. After drawing for two different clients, I get off at 5:00 p.m. Picking up my bag, I nudge my head at Jesse. "Thanks for today. I needed it."

"No problem." He winks again. I smile and then walk out the door, heading straight to the bar Tatum works at.

Pushing open the doors, it's pretty empty because of the time. A few people are scattered around the place, but it's nothing like when it's in full swing.

"Hey!" Tatum smiles, waving me over to the bar. I grin and start walking toward her. I need to get Bishop out of my head one way or another so I might take the way that has an endless supply of alcohol. Taking a seat, Tatum pours a shot and slides it over to me. "Bottoms up, bitch!" I clink her glass and then toss it back.

"Yeah." I smirk. "Bottoms up," I say and slam the shot glass down onto the bar. The Weeknd's "Or Nah" starts pulsating through the room and I bang on the bar. "Another!"

"That's the spirit," Tatum squeals, pouring me another shot. She twirls the bottle between her fingers like a pro, and I narrow my eyes, knocking my shot back. "How'd you learn to do that, *Coyote Ugly*?"

"What? Not bad, huh?" She does it again and I roll my eyes.

"Show off," I tease, throwing back another shot.

Hours and many shots later, I get up off the bar stool, my head spinning. "Wooo." I reach for the edge of my stool, looking around the now fully decked-out club.

I lean over the bar and into Tatum. "I need to pee. Be right back!"

She nods, shooing me off. Dead Prez's "Hip Hop" starts playing, and I push through the crowd, making a beeline for the toilet. Walking into one of the stalls, I shove my pants down and let it all go. Sighing, I reach for my burner phone and pull it out of my pocket as it rings. Who even knows this number?

"Hello?" I slur, smiling at how drunk I am.

"You think you can fucking run from me, kitty? Nah-uh."

I scream and drop the cell, quickly standing from the toilet and shoving my pants back on. Reaching for my phone, I toss it into the toilet bowl, flushing it furiously, and then run out of the stall, my heart beating in my chest. Holy fuck! How did Bishop get my number?

That voice.

Pushing back through the crowd, I look directly at Tatum until I come face-to-face with her.

"We need to leave."

"What?" she asks over the deep bass.

"We. Need. To leave. Now!" I borderline scream at her, though it's slurred because of all the alcohol.

She searches my eyes until understanding sets in. "Oh, fuck."

"Yes, fuck is right."

She nods, tugging off her apron and throwing it on the bar. Running around to me, she snatches a bottle, and we hurry out of the bar.

Jesse.

Shit. I don't even have time to tell him I won't be coming back. Maybe I could leave a note under the parlor door. No, I can't risk it.

We catch a taxi to the flat, and as soon as we get inside, we start pulling out our bags. I rush into the bathroom, scooping up all my toiletries, and then walk into the closet, pulling down the little safe I keep my money in, throwing it into my bag. After I'm sure all my shit is gathered, I go out to meet Tatum.

"Ready?" I ask.

She nods, wheeling her suitcase. "Yes, yup, shit."

I glance down at my suitcase and then back to Tatum. "It was Bishop. How did he find my number?"

"Mads, I've already told you. "They own the school and their level of pull that they have on people is mysterious, to say the least."

"I guess they still want to kill me."

"Kill you?" she asks, shocked.

Shaking my head, I wipe my frown with a smile, nudging my head toward the door. "I guess it's time for Bristol."

CHAPTER 5

The glass sliding doors open out onto a chillier atmosphere than what was in New Zealand. It's almost December, so I guess we chose a cooler time to come to this side of the country, as opposed to New Zealand, where it's summer in December. Not that we had a choice or anything. Tatum comes up beside me, her teeth jittering. "Jesus, let's choose a warmer place next time."

I smile at her, waving down the taxi that's pulling up beside the curb. It stops in front and I run to the passenger window. "Are you free?"

He nods. "Yep!" Then he pops the trunk for both of us to put our bags into.

"Where are we staying, exactly?" Tatum whispers.

I shrug, putting my bags into the trunk. "I don't know. I guess we'll ask him to take us to a cheap motel or whatever it is they call it here."

"Good idea." Tatum nods, getting into the back seat.

A few days later, after finding a good little place to stay in, "Hail to the King" by Avenged Sevenfold is pumping through the massive speakers, shaking the floor. I tip my drink back and Tatum winks at me.

"I think I'm going to like it here." She looks around until her eyes land on two guys who are so obviously checking us out.

"Come." She grins, gripping onto my hand.

"Tate—"

"Mads, please, when are you going to get over this shit with Bishop? He's a liar and doesn't deserve you!" Her hands come up to my cheeks. "Repeat after me."

I suck my bottom lip into my mouth to stifle my laugh.

"Bishop Vincent Hayes is a cocksucker," she says calmly, waiting for me to repeat.

A giggle erupts out of me from all the alcohol. "Bishop Vincent Hayes is a cocksucker."

"Atta girl, now…" She tips her head back, swallowing her shot in one go. "Speaking of sucking cock." Then she pulls me through the crowd of people until we're in front of the two guys who were eye fucking us.

"Hi, boys." Tatum grins. "Which one of you is buying us a drink?"

They both launch off their chairs. "Subtle," I snicker under my breath.

Not my type at all.

The ground starts swimming, or it's swimming in my mind when one of the guys pulls me into him.

"Wanna dance, pretty girl?"

Pretty girl? I shrug, because what can a dance do? He pulls me onto the floor just as "Bad Things" by Machine Gun Kelly starts playing. It's more of an understated beat and a little personal, but whatever. It's not like we're at a nightclub or anything; this place is just a bar. It's actually under the room we're staying in, and we thought we'd check it out. Homeboy pulls me into his chest again—a chest that is the complete opposite of Bishop's. A little squishier than I'd like, and when I look down, I see his beer belly.

Oh gross. Nope, I can't do this.

"Sorry," I push at his chest, "I can't do this."

"Nonsense." He grins, saliva covering his mouth.

"Yeah," I answer again, pushing at his chest. "Just not really feeling it." He grips my wrist and pulls me into him again. "Hey!" I yell, though it's still a slur. Where's Tatum? I spin around, trying to find her, but I can't see her anywhere. He starts to drag me toward a back door that has an exit light flashing over the top.

"No." I try to pull my hand out of his grip, only it doesn't move. He tugs me roughly, and I look around to see if anyone knows what he's doing, but the music is too loud, and there are too many people to know what's happening. Reaching the door, he pushes it open and my eyes shut, consciousness coming in and out. Oh no.

"Stop," Tatum moans in the distance.

"Tatum!" I look down the dark alley and see the other guy with her, tugging her dress up.

"Little American slags," the guy who is pulling me mutters. "We'll show you."

"No!" I scream, shoving at his chest. Oh my God, why do my limbs feel like Jell-O, and why am I in heat? I rub my thighs together in an attempt to calm the throbbing need that has started, but nothing happens. If anything, the feeling intensifies. I launch toward the fat shit, scratching him across his face until I can feel his flesh peel away and clog under my fingernails.

"You bitch!" He slams me up against the brick wall, my head smashing against it with a crack.

"Tatum, wake up. Stay with me." The guy who has her has pulled off her panties. The guy who has me up against the wall starts to make a beeline for my own. "Get the fuck off me, you fat slob!" I won't cry. No way in fucking hell will I cry. I look at him square in the eye. "If you so much as come near me with that stubby thing you call a cock, I will rip it off."

He laughs. "I doubt that, honey." Then he tears off my panties, clutches me around my upper thighs roughly until his fingertips are digging into my flesh, and hikes me up the wall. "Open up like the good little snatch you are."

I roll my tongue and spit in his face, just as a gun blasts off in the distance, blood and brain matter spraying all over my face. His eyes pop in shock for a split second before he drops to the ground in a shallow thud. A blood-curdling scream ripples out of me, and then Tatum screams as another pop sounds off and the guy who is clutching her falls to the ground, the flesh on his scalp turning to dust, spraying all over Tatum.

She screams, and I drop to the ground, blackness coming in and out. Just as hands scoop under me, I hear a "Fucking stupid bitch" before sleep takes hold.

CHAPTER 6

Something jolting underneath my body wakes me. Looking to the side, confused about where I am, memories start to take hold. I gasp, sucking in a breath. There, sitting on the seat beside me, is Bishop.

Fuck.

"Surprised?" he asks, his eyebrow quirked.

I clear my throat. "Well, no, actually."

He clenches his jaw, so obviously frustrated. "That's it." He shakes his head, whispering under his breath, "I'm locking you in the basement until this shit is sorted."

"What?" I shriek, and that's when the sting and the taste of metal touch the tip of my tongue. I touch my lip, memories flooding through my brain. "Oh, fuck!" I lean over, holding in my gag.

"Jesus, Kitty, out the fucking window!"

I hit the button blindly until the window cranks down. "You, you killed them."

"I did."

"You kill people?"

"I do."

"Why?" I yell, just as my stomach heaves again and I lean out the window, spilling all of whatever I last ate out into the dry night air. Leaning back in, wiping my mouth, I look back to him through blurry eyes. "Why, Bishop?"

"For reasons you will never understand, Madison." He looks toward Tatum, who is lying flat on the seat in front of us. I don't know whose limo we're in. Everything seems dreamlike.

"She's asleep. I didn't kill her." He interrupts my thoughts with a bored tone.

"Well, I appreciate it." I roll my eyes, failing at my attempt to not be snarky.

"Watch your fucking mouth, Madison. This is your fault. All of this!" His arms stretch wide. "You started a fucking war when you left that day."

"Me?" I burst out. "How the fuck is that possible?" The tangy aftertaste of my being sick simmers at the back of my throat. "You did this. All of you! I still don't understand anything!"

"How much of the book did you read?" he asks, leaning forward and bracing his arms over his knees.

"The book?" I question, tilting my head back on the headrest. My mind still swims in a daze.

"The book, Madison, the book!"

"Oh." I clear my throat. "Um, only quarter of the way through. Why?"

"Do you have it on you?"

"It's in my bag back at our place."

Bishop leans forward and taps on the glass that separates us from the front seat. The window cranks down. He orders the driver to take us back to our place, the exact address.

"Wow!" I shake my head, my hands going up.

Bishop leans back into his seat. "What?" he snaps.

"How'd you know where I live?"

He laughs, pulling his hoodie over his head. "It's cute you think I'd let you get out of this alive, Kitty, and I've always known where you lived. This little detour in the limo right now is just so you calm down enough to pack your shit."

Pulling up to our low-class flat and the bar, I get out of the car, slamming the door behind me, which wakes Tatum from her deep slumber.

"Wait!" Bishop gets out, shutting the door. Ignoring his intrusive behavior, I start walking toward the side stairs in the back alley. "Madison!" he yells, his heavy footsteps getting louder and louder. "Would you fucking wait?" He grips onto my arm, tugging me backward.

I let out a frustrated scream, yanking my arm out of his grip. "Can you fucking not? God! You—"

His hand flies up to my throat, leaving me gasping for air. Pushing me backward until my back slams against the bricks, he steps between my thighs and grazes me higher up the wall. "First of all," he squeezes until I'm sure my face is going to burst, "don't fucking forget who the fuck you're talking to." He tilts his head, glancing over my face. "Second of all, you don't get to throw your fucking weight around, Madison. I'll lock you in a cage as soon as we get you back to the Hamptons if you don't watch your fucking mouth." He releases me, my feet hitting the ground.

"Fuck you." Spinning around, I run up the metal stairs, push open the door, and head straight to my bedroom, fighting back the tears that are threatening to surface. Where the hell is my dad? Why is it that Bishop is the one who was sent to "collect" me? Did I really think I could run from them? Well yes, yes I did. Pulling open my closet, I start tearing my clothes off the hangers and throwing them onto my bed just as Bishop walks in.

"You have five minutes to get everything that means anything to you and get back downstairs. You try to run," Bishop says, his voice dipping, "and I'll kill you myself. I'm done playing games." Then he walks out and leaves me in my room, clutching the dark sequined dress I wore last weekend—back when things weren't so complicated. I mean, as complicated as us being on the run from my psychopathic whatever he is. Ex? No. That doesn't sound right.

"Jesus," Tatum murmurs, walking in, her hair all over her face. She rubs the palm of her hand over her forehead. "What the hell happened?"

"You passed out," I mutter, still annoyed at Bishop and shoving clothes into my suitcase. "And you have five minutes to pack before Bishop carries us both out."

"I saw that." Her eyes widen. "So he found us, huh?"

I chuckle, walking into the bathroom to grab my toothbrush. "No, we were never lost from him."

CHAPTER 7

L anding back in The Hamptons wasn't as bad as I thought it would be. Despite the fact that Bishop refused to even glance my way for the entire flight, I guess a sense of calm has come over me. Running is tiring. Keeping up with your aliases and fake appearances... I was tired of it to a degree. Did I want to get caught? No. But at the same time, it's like it's finally over.

Or just begun.

Stepping down off the steps and onto the tarmac, I grip onto Tatum's arm and tug her forward.

"Ouch!" she protests. "Geez, Mads, I'm fragile right now."

"What are we going to do, Tate?" I whisper as we head toward the awaiting black stretch limo. "I mean, seriously, what if they kill us?"

She rolls her eyes, pulling her arm out of my grip. "Madison, they're not going to kill you. You're being dramatic." She looks at me and I narrow my eyes. "Fuck," she exhales. "Fine, okay. Well, if they do, I won't go down without a fight. All right?"

"Tatum." I shake my head.

"Move." Bishop shoves me toward the limo. I snarl at him, gripping the door handle just as a black Audi Q7 flies down the strip, skidding to a halt in a cloud of smoke. I wave the smoke away from my face and squint my eyes.

"Jesus fucking Christ," Bishop curses, shoving me behind himself.

"Nah-uh!" a voice barks behind the cloud.

I know that voice.

"Nate!" I yell, running toward the smoke and straight into his arms. He's wearing his trademark red baseball cap flipped backward. I've never been so fucking happy to see that stupid cap. Pulling me into his chest, he lifts me off the ground, and I wrap my legs around him.

"Hey, Kitty, how you been?" He squeezes me into him.

"Not good," I answer truthfully. I didn't realize just how much I missed Nate until I heard his voice. I don't know if it's fair that I forgive him and not Bishop, but at the same time, Nate hasn't threatened my life a hundred times within the space twenty-four hours.

Nate steps backward, his hands dropping down to mine. "It had to be done, sis. You know that." He searches my eyes. "Right?" I pull my bottom lip into my mouth.

"Listen, things have changed. If Bishop didn't come get you, someone else would have, only you wouldn't be coming home in a seat on that plane. You'd be coming home in a box."

I exhale. "I just... I... I guess we have a lot to talk about."

"Yeah." Nate smiles, but it doesn't reach his eyes. "I guess we sort of do." He looks directly over my shoulder and grins. "Oh, come on." I throw a glance over my shoulder to see Bishop flipping Nate off. He tugs on my arm and points to his car. "Get in." Then he looks to Tatum. "You too!"

Tatum huffs and then stomps toward the car. Slipping my seat forward, I let her slide into the back before pushing it back into place and getting into the front. As I close the door, she whispers from behind me, "What do you think this is all about?"

"I don't know," I answer, watching Nate and Bishop talk. "I mean, I know some, but not a lot. At least not right now." I close my mouth, thinking about *the* book. They know I still have it. Will the boys let me read it? Are they still going to hide information from me?

Yes. I don't trust them at all. Though I'm probably dreaming, I've never gone down without a fight, so it's my turn to start playing the dealer, and these boys are about to become my pawns.

Nate pulls open the driver-side door and slides in. "So where are we going?"

I shrug, watching as Bishop gets into the limo and it slowly pulls away. "Take me somewhere."

Nate winks at me then puts the car in reverse until we're skidding out in a cloud of smoke. "I know just the place."

CHAPTER 8

"Why can't I come?" Tatum moans, stomping her foot just as she gets out of Nate's car. Nate points toward her front door. "Get your ass inside, woman! I'll deal with you on Monday. At school!"

I whip my head toward him just as Tatum trots off in defeat. "School?" I squeak. "No. No. No. No!" I shake my head, leaning into my door. "No, fuck no, Nate!"

"Hey!" He grins, putting the car into first gear and driving forward. "Not my orders, sis."

"Oh, okay!" I snap. "And whose orders are they? Because I swear to God, Nate, if you say Bishop, I will kill you. And don't play with me, because I've seen enough death to not flinch if I need to put a bullet between your pretty little eyes."

"I see you're still a badass."

"I see you're still not very smart!" I quip, shuffling in my seat to face forward. There's a long pause of awkward silence.

"Look, here's the thing. I get that you're all fucked up and broken and messed up in the head over all this shit that's going on, sis, but this goes a lot deeper than you could even wrap your mind around."

"Are you going to tell me what this is?" I ask, looking back at him.

He gives an instant "No."

"Then fuck you. We're done here." I lean forward and hit the radio until The Game's "It's Okay" fills the silence. What does he mean orders? What—Bishop? Or has something else happened since I've been gone? My dad hasn't reached out to me. Did he know Bishop would be after me? If what Bishop said is true, and if he really did know where I was all along, why did they never take the opportunity and get me? Nothing makes sense, as usual. Leaning my head on the cool window, I close my eyes and try to think of happier times.

"Madison! Don't touch that!" my mother scolded me, hitting my hand away from the pretty blue frosting.

"Why? I'm hungry!" I demanded, reaching for the cake again.

"Because it's not for you and you have to learn how to be patient."

"But whose cake is it?" I asked, tilting my head. I always thought my mom was beautiful. She had long brown hair and kind hazel eyes. Dad said I got his eyes because mine are green, but I think I have some of my mom's eyes too, because they twinkle in the sun.

"Madison." My mom smiled, looking over my shoulder. "Honey." Her hands came to my shoulder. "I want you to meet someone."

"Okay, but who?" I wasn't really a small girl. I mean, I was turning five soon. That wasn't small anymore; that was old enough to start school.

"Madison!" Nate snaps me out of my haze. I turn to face him, swiping the tears off my cheeks.

"Yeah?"

"You okay?" he asks, looking between me and the road ahead of him.

"I'll be fine."

I won't be fine.

Pulling up to our house, I turn in my seat to face Nate. Gazing into his eyes, I smile. "You know... I don't like you boys much."

His hand comes over his chest in mock insult. "Really?" he gasps, his eyes wide. "Who would have known?"

"Shut up." I shove him. "You coming in?"

"I've just got to go handle something. I'll be home a little later."

"Letting me face the 'rents on my own, huh?" I ask, inspecting the modern-style brick house. The house I've come to call home.

"Sorry, sis, but hey!" he calls out, just as I get out of the car. "If you need like an alibi or anything, I'm your guy." I roll my eyes and slam the door behind me. If there's anyone I will need an alibi for, it'll be against him and his pack, not our parents. Exhaling, I step toward the house and push open the front door. The scent of disinfectant, flowers blossoming, and tarnished wood floats around the familiar surroundings.

"Hello?" I call out, shutting the door behind me and dropping my bag.

"Madison?" Elena calls out, stepping out of the kitchen and wiping her hands. "Oh my God!" She runs toward me and squeezes me into her chest. Tears wet the side of my neck and I inch back, slightly confused.

"Are you okay? Where have you been? What happened?" She panics, her hands running up and down my arms. "Jesus, Madison, your father and I have been worried sick!" Confusion wiggles itself under my skin. No one told her anything? Not even Nate?

"S-sorry," I mutter, unknowing what story I should be going with. Fucking Nate, couldn't even give me a heads up before I got out of the car.

"Sorry?" she squeals, her hands running over my cheeks. "I was worried, Madison. So was your father. Come on, let's get you something to eat." I follow her into the kitchen, tugging out one of the stools and taking a seat. She pulls open the fridge and takes out some deli meats.

"Do you want to talk about it?"

Shaking my head, I answer, "No. Sorry. Not right now. Where's Dad?"

Putting the sandwich together, she cuts it and then slides my plate toward me. "He'll be home soon. I'll call him to let him know you're home."

"Okay, thank you." Picking up the sandwich, I take a small bite and chew slowly. The dry bread and lettuce isn't helping my parched throat, so I slide off the stool and go to the fridge, taking out the carton of OJ. Closing the fridge, I see a note dangles on the door, but it's written in some foreign, weird-ass language. Latin, I think. I vaguely remember a friend talking about Latin back at one of my old schools, and the words look similar. Why would there be a note written in Latin on our fridge? It's a dead language; no one uses it anymore, which makes it even more absurd. It would make more sense if the note was written in Japanese.

Tugging it off the magnet, I read over the fancy wording.

Saltare cum morte solutio ligatorum inventae sunt in verbis conectuntur et sculptilia contrivisset in sanguine et medullis.

Pulling out my phone from my back pocket, I punch the wording into Google Translate.

Riddles dance with death when the words are inked in blood and carved with marrow.

The words hit me like a train of destruction. Why would this be on our fridge? Why today of all days? I flip the note over and scan the back. The paper is fresh, the ink clean. It doesn't look old at all, and—

"Madison, your father is on his way home." Elena walks in, and I quickly push the note into my back pocket.

"Okay." I smile.

She points to my sandwich. "Eat up."

After eating, I climb the stairs and head to my room. I push open my bedroom door and pause at the threshold. Everything is exactly as I left it. My four-poster bed is rooted in the same spot, my net curtains still shade my patio door, and my TV is still sitting nicely on my dresser at the foot of my bed. Walking into my closet, I pull off some hangers and toss them onto the bed. I know I need to unpack and get settled back into my life here, but I have a plan to carry out, and following through will take a lot of time and preparation. Emptying my duffle bag into my clothes basket, I swipe my hair out of my face just as a thump hits the top of my laundry. Bending down, my fingers skim over the worn leather, curving over the emblem embossed into the cover. Tilting my head, I suck in my bottom lip and pick it up, flipping the pages as I make my way back to my bed. Whatever my plan is, I need to continue this book—or diary, or suicide note. It's the key to everything; I just know it.

Flicking through, I land on the chapter I was up to, after finding out about the Silver Swans.

9.
The Silver Swan

The truth is I don't know what my husband did to my daughter. He said girls are tainted. There's no room for girls in his master plan, and that's how it always will be. He said they would sell the girls, but something dark and doubtful always tickles the back of my mind. My husband is a liar, a cheat, and a manipulator. There's absolutely no part of him that is truthful or redeemable. Later that night, after my maid had cleaned me up, Humphrey came back into the cave, sat down beside me, and said, "Girls cannot be born into our covenant, wife. They're weak by human nature. They must be taken care of at their birth."

"You're not God, Humphrey. You cannot deem who bears what when pregnant."

"No," he replied simply. "But I can take care of it."

I shook my head, my heart in tatters, and my life turning bleak, dark, finished. "There will be no Silver Swans born into this family or any of the first nine. They will be demolished."

"Silver Swans?" I asked, clipped and annoyed.

"The Silver Swan is, in old times, what they would call a tarnished being. Every girl born into the first nine is a tarnished being. It's no place for a her."

"Humphrey Haynes!" I exasperated, trying to calm my frantic beating heart. I leaned toward

him, inching closer until my lips were a mere whisper away from his cheek. "Did you have our daughter killed?"

He brought his cold, dead eyes up to mine and grinned a devilish grin that churned my stomach. "I did. And every girl after her will also be taken care of. Girls have no place in our lineage."

I inched backward, my heart sinking in my chest and my eyes watering with grief. "I—I...," I whispered, speechless in the heartless way Humphrey spoke about our child. My heart snapped in two. "I have to leave." I ran out of the room and into the forest, the leaves and branches shielding me from the full moon. Kneeling down, I let my tears overflow and my grief overpower me. Crying, yearning for my daughter that I will never know.

I suck in a breath, slamming the book closed. He killed her? And all other Silver Swans? Why? Why am I still alive, and how am I still alive? Are there any more like me?

There's a knock on the door that pulls me out of my frantic thoughts.

"Come in." My door opens, and my dad stands in the threshold, his hands pushed into the pockets of his slacks.

"Thinking of running away again?" he asks, his head tilting.

"Are you going to be honest with me?" I retort.

He steps into the room and closes the door behind himself. Dad still looks the same, young, fit, with a sprinkle of gray hair on the sides of his head. "Madison, I can't answer all the questions you're going to ask."

I inch up onto my knees. "What does that mean exactly? You, Dad, I trusted you."

"Madi," he whispers, shaking his head. "This world... it's complicated."

"I'm the Silver Swan?"

His eyebrows tug together in worry. "Yes." He takes a seat on my bed and looks toward *The Book.* "Have you read much more?"

I follow his eye line and nod. "A little bit. They kill the girls? So why am I still alive?"

He looks at me out of the corner of his eye. "Because I was supposed to keep you safe, Madison. Your mother and I, we love you very much."

"Mom's death," I whisper, "was it what I was told?"

Dad looks at me. "No. It's more complicated than what you know."

"What?" I screech, shooting off the bed. "Explain."

"Madison!" Dad's voice booms with an authoritative tone. "I will tell you what I think you need to know right now. Any other questions will have to wait. Do you understand?" His eyes narrow as he pushes up off my bed. He brushes my cheek. "I love you, Madison, but this is not something you can pry into. I need you to just leave it to me and the Kings." He leans down so his eyes are square with mine. "Do you understand what I'm saying?" I understand what he's saying, but there's no way I'm going to sit on my hands and be left guessing. Not like last time. But I nod, because that's not something Dad needs to know or worry about—right now.

"Yes. I understand." I swallow past the lump in my throat. He nods, a small smile spreading across his face. "Now get some rest so you're ready for school in the morning." He walks back toward my door and yanks it open. "Oh, and Madison?" he adds, looking at me over his shoulder. "Elena doesn't know anything. She thinks you ran off for a couple months to be rebellious. I'd like to keep it that way."

"Sure," I whisper. "Night, Dad." He leaves, shutting the door behind him. I walk into my closet and pull out some pajamas before slipping into my bathroom, flicking the lock on Nate's side. Stepping into the hot cascading water, I scrub the last two months off my skin.

CHAPTER 9

"So what did your dad say?" Tatum asks, sucking the juice of her orange off her fingertips. Being back in the atrium isn't as weird as I thought it would be. It's like Ally didn't exist, though. Like everyone just forgot that she had gone, or died, or whatever they thought. What did they know? I understand we'd been gone for a couple of months, but you would think a death in such a small school would impact it a lot longer than that.

"Uh, he didn't say much. Just gave me the rundown about how I need to keep things away from Nate's mom."

Tate pauses. "Why? Hey." She leans in closer, checking to make sure no one can hear her. "What the hell is going on? You know you can trust me, Mads."

I know I can; that's not my issue with Tatum, never has been. I trust her with my life, but it's the people you trust with your life who you want to protect the most. Telling Tatum every single thing about this... life would only put her in danger.

"I know, Tate," I whisper back to her. "You know that if I could, I would tell you everything, but I can't."

"Can't or won't?" she snaps at me.

"Won't!" I reply, leaning back into my seat. "Now ca—"

"Mads?"

I turn in my seat. "Carter? Hey!" I smile, standing.

He pulls me into his chest. "Where you been, girl?" I don't miss the deep inhale he takes into my hair.

"Oh, being a rebel." I smile, pulling away from him slightly.

"Ah." He grins. "That's not surprising at all."

"No," I answer, ignoring the way everyone in the atrium has silenced. "I guess it's not."

Carter's eyes flick over my shoulder, his smile falling slightly. "Hey, I'll text you."

I inch my head around slightly, not bringing my eyes to the group before looking back at Carter. "Okay, I have the same number." He nods and then yanks me back into his chest again. I exhale. "Hey," I whisper into his chest. He stills, so I take that as he heard me. "Are you all right?"

He releases his breath, so much so that his chest relaxes. He lets go, drawing me back. "I'll text you." His smile stays, but his eyes drop slightly before he turns and walks back out the door.

I stay still, not wanting to turn around and sit back on my seat, because I know that when I do, I'm going to be faced with the Kings. The whispering starts again as all eyes remain glued on me. It's like the first day all over again, only Ally isn't here to fuel the fire. Exhaling, and with a slight eye roll, I turn around, my gaze instantly locking on Bishop. I suck in a deep breath at the way his eyes command mine immediately. Everything ceases to exist whenever he's in the vicinity, which ultimately pisses me off. I hate that I can never control my body whenever he's in the room. Walking toward the boys, I swallow any and all feelings that I have.

Reaching for Nate, I tap his shoulder. "Can I talk to you?"

He turns to face me. "Yeah, you okay?"

I pull in my bottom lip and tilt my head, ignoring the glare I'm receiving from Bishop. "Yeah, I think."

"What's wrong?" Nate asks, pushing his hands into his pockets.

I look over his shoulder at the rest of the Kings, and Nate tilts his head over his shoulder and grins. "Sis, these guys know more than you could ever imagine. Anything you have to say to me is fine to say in front of them."

"Yeah," I mutter, looking back to Nate. "For some reason, I have trust issues."

He grins at me slowly. "Well, hell, I wonder why that is. I told Bishop scaring you in the forest was a bad—"

"Nate," Bishop grunts from behind him. "I'll handle it."

I clench my jaw. "No, it's fine. I'm sure Nate has me handled. Thanks."

Bishop wastes no time, stepping toward me, taking hold of my arm, and dragging me out of the atrium. The whispers and chatting stops, and when we reach the entryway, I tug my arm out of his grip.

"What the fuck is your problem, Bishop?" I yell at him, my voice echoing throughout the empty hall. He pushes open the supply closet door and shoves me into the dark room.

"Bishop!" I yell, just as his hand slams over my mouth, pushing me up against the wall.

"Shut up, Madi. What did you want to ask?"

I whack his hand off my mouth. "Can you turn a light on?"

"No."

Exhaling, I lean my head against the wall. "I want to know why no one is asking about Ally."

A long silence drags between us until he finally says, "It's simple. Ally moved away. Anything else?"

So he says Ally moved away and no one questions it? No one questions the Kings? It's like Khales all over again.

"Yes," I scoff, suddenly annoyed at his arrogance. "I wan—"

His chest presses against mine and I slam back against the wall again. Opening my mouth, he cuts me off when his soft lips press against my neck, setting off goose bumps all over my body. Fuck. I really need to find a grip on my feelings when it comes to Bishop, or my plan will turn to shit. I'm taking him down, but I won't complain if he goes down with his face buried between my thighs. May as well enjoy it while it's happening.

"Bishop," I warn, and his mouth kicks up in a grin against my hot flesh. "Bishop," I repeat in the same tone. My eyes close, my breath falling heavily.

"First of all," he growls against my skin, "you don't ask any other questions. You follow ours." His hand skims over my bare thigh and squeezes—enough to leave a bruise. "Second of all, if you want to ask anyone questions," his minty breath now falls over my lips, "you come to me." He pulls my bottom lip into his mouth and bites down on it. He goes to step backward, but I grip the back of his neck and pull him into my lips. He stills, his lips not opening, so I jump up and wrap my legs around his waist.

Stepping forward, he slams me against the wall, his mouth opening to let me in. He groans, tangling his fingers in my hair before yanking it back roughly.

He looks down into my eyes, the faint creak from the door being slightly open lighting the dark room just enough to see him. "What was that about?" I ask.

"What was what about?" he counters, and I tilt my head, studying how his dark jade eyes now look almost black. How his eyebrows pull in, displaying his concentration.

"I don't know," I murmur, looking away. He lets me go, my feet dropping to the floor. Just as he's about to hit the door, I bite my lip. "Bishop!"

"Yeah?" he mutters, turning and looking over his shoulder.

"Why do you like breaking me?"

He smirks slightly, just enough that I see his dimple on the side of his cheek. "Because it gets my dick hard to put you back together."

His response doesn't surprise me, not in the slightest.

"But," I add, stepping forward, "you never put me back together properly. You steal parts of me, so when you do put me back, I'm all crooked, cracked, and still visibly broken."

His smile pauses briefly, not enough for me to really catch any meaning behind it. He turns to face me, his eyes locking onto mine. "Because being broken is how you're going to survive this life, Madison." Then he turns and leaves, the door closing behind him. I remain in the darkness, his words playing on repeat in my brain. What the hell did he actually mean by that?

CHAPTER 10

Shutting the front door after a long day at school, I drop my bag on the floor. "Sammy?" Sammy walks in, wiping her wet hands on the dishtowel she has hanging off her belt. "Ah, Madison!" She whacks me with the back of her hand. "Where the hell have you been?" Shrugging, I go on with the lie my dad has me saying. "I disappeared." Walking into the kitchen, I tug open the fridge and start unloading all the ingredients for grilled cheese. Sammy comes in behind me, leaning against the doorframe.

"Why?" she asks, crossing her arms in front of herself like a worried mother.

"I don't know." Pulling out four slices of bread, I place them on a plate and reach for the butter, swiping it on both sides before slamming some cheese in the middle.

"Who were you with?" she questions in the same tone, eyeing me skeptically.

"Uhh, Tatum. We just traveled a bit. I was mad at Dad for something and didn't feel like coming home. Seriously, Sammy, I'm okay." I put on a completely fake smile for added effect.

Sammy pushes off the doorframe, waving her hands in the air. "*Estúpido jodido adolescente!*"

Flipping my sandwiches, I raise my eyebrows at her retreating back. "Huh? You swearing at me, Sam I am?" I tease, grinning, knowing damn well she can't see me. She's still muttering off in Spanish when Nate walks in, with Bishop following closely behind him. Great, appetite will no doubt be ruined.

"'Sup?" Nate pulls me into him, kissing me softly on the head. "Oh yum." He reaches down and steals a sandwich straight out of the pan. I slap the spatula on the back of his hand, a second too slow because he's already retreating and stuffing his mouth with my delicious creation of carb goodness.

"Screw you, Riverside." I look over my shoulder and sarcastically smile sweetly at Bishop. "Do you want the other one, since I will have to make more anyway." I flip the grilled cheese out and place it on a plate. Walking back toward the middle island, I look up at Bishop when I notice he hasn't answered me. "Hellooo? You want it or not?"

He doesn't answer, just stares.

"You're doing that stare thing again. I thought we were past that phase?" Placing the plate on the counter, I slide it toward him. Ignoring his weird Bishop behavior, I pull

I look up at him, sucking the cheese off my thumb. "Yes?"

"Don't fucking do that."

"Do what?" I smile around my thumb.

His jaw clenches. "Unless you want to get fucking ruined right here with Nate in the next room, I wouldn't do that again."

"Need a better threat than that." I roll my eyes, walking back toward the stovetop and placing my sandwich on the pan. "What was your question?" I turn a little over my shoulder and look at him.

He picks up the grilled cheese and takes a bite. "What do you know about your mom?"

I pause, shuffling around the kitchen to find some paper towels.

"Ahhh, she was my mom?" I answer sarcastically. "I knew all there was to know about her—well, what she would share with me. Why?"

He shakes his head. "Doesn't matter right now."

Rolling my eyes, I finish up my meal and then flip them onto a new plate. Walking toward the bar stool, I slide on top and pick up my food. "So why ask then?"

He shrugs, and just as I'm about to ask another question, Nate walks in with his top off, the shirt tucked into his jeans. "What are we talking about in here?" He grins, sliding onto the stool beside mine.

"Oh, you know, random shit." I take a loud and large bite out of my sandwich. "Oh!" I tap Nate, covering my mouth until I've swallowed my food. "I forgot to ask. Have you heard from Tillie?"

Nate looks around the kitchen. "No? Not since the cabin deal." Nate hasn't heard from her either? That's weird. I mean, it was weird enough that Ridge hadn't heard from her, but the fact that Nate hasn't got her stashed away somewhere for him to play with whenever he pleases cuts out my idea.

"That's weird." I place my sandwich on my plate.

"Why?" Nate and Bishop both ask at the same time. I reach into my pocket and pull out my phone, tapping on Ridge's number.

"Because Ridge hasn't heard from her either, and she never came home from the cabin."

"That was two months ago," Nate mutters, his eyebrows pulling in.

"Exactly."

"I dropped her off at her house, and yeah, she never texted me back, so I left it," Nate adds, lost in thought.

I hit dial on Ridge's number and bring my phone to my ear.

"Yo!"

"Ridge?"

"Yeah, who's this?"

"Sorry," I murmur, realizing that I never texted him my number. "It's Madison."

"Oh!" He sounds surprised. "Hey."

"Did you ever hear anything back from Tillie?"

"You didn't hear?" he asks in muffled tones. Beeping cars and light chatting fade off in the distance.

"Hear what?" I answer as my heart pounds in my chest.

Please, God, no.

"She's been a missing person case since. No one has heard from her and no one knows where she is."

"What?" I look up at Nate, who is watching me intently. He looks worried; I can see it in his eyes. "No one told me anything because I've been out of the country for the past couple of months." I put my phone down and put it on speaker. "You're on speaker phone, and Nate and Bishop are here with me, okay?"

"Yeah, okay," he snickers, though his tone doesn't seem too impressed.

"So can you tell us everything, please?" I urge him, pushing my plate out of the way with my now suddenly lost appetite.

"Well, Nate dropped her off at home after your guys' trip. She stayed for the next couple of weeks but was sick. I went to see her a couple of times, and she was throwing up, pale, and just... sick. Anyway, the last time I saw her, she was acting weird as fuck. She always loved our kick-back sessions."

I look up at Nate, not being able to pass the opportunity. Grinning, I say, "You mean your sex sessions?"

Nate evil-eyes me, flipping me off. I grin deeper.

"Uhh...," Ridge mutters. "Yeah... she told you?" he asks into the phone.

"Yeah, anyway, so what happened?"

Bishop pulls out the bar stool next to me, his thigh brushing mine. I flinch slightly, annoyed at myself once again how much my body sparks to life at his mere proximity, let alone his freaking touch.

"So she rushed me out of the house and then I never heard from her again. Her dad said she left with a suitcase and took his car. They found his car off the interstate a couple of days later, but it was empty with the keys left inside of it. The trail has gone cold and, yeah, again, no one knows where she is. Her cards haven't been used or anything either. She's just gone."

A ball forms in my throat. "Why would she leave?" I whisper, confused. Why would she leave and not even leave a note for anyone? I wouldn't know if she sent me a text because I haven't had my phone, but what is her reasoning?

"Ridge," I start, my brain ticking through ideas. "Who else did she hang with?"

"No one. When it wasn't me, it was you."

"Okay," I murmur. "What do I do?"

"There's not much we can do. I've tried everything. Now all we can do is hope she just comes home."

"Okay. Thanks, Ridge. If I hear of anything, I'll call you. And you do the same?"

"Yeah."

Hanging up, I turn to face Bishop. "What do I do?"

Bishop looks to Nate, and I watch as they both exchange a look. Realization dawns at just who is sitting in front of me.

My face straightens. "I swear to God, if you two have anything to do with this, I will kill you."

"We have nothing to do with this," Nate says, walking toward the sink and filling up a glass with water. He turns to face us, leaning on the counter. "But it's weird as fuck."

"Weird as fuck?" I scoff, getting to my feet. Bishop's hand brushes over my thigh, and I look down at it before looking up at him and then looking back to Nate. "That's an understatement."

"Just leave it for now," Nate tells me, shaking his head. "She obviously doesn't want to be found."

My shoulders slack in defeat. "I guess. But why didn't she come to me if she needed help?"

"Who knows why anyone does anything, Kitty?" Nate walks up to me, kissing me on the head. "I gotta bounce."

I turn around and watch Nate leave the kitchen before looking to Bishop. "You're not leaving?"

He shakes his head. "No."

"Why?" Honestly, I could do with some time alone.

"I just want to ask you something."

"You always seem to want to ask me something."

He gets to his feet and walks toward me. His chest brushes against mine before his finger comes up and tucks a loose strand of hair behind my ear. "Do you have any memories from when you were young?"

One.

Two.

Three.

Four.

Four.

Four.

"No," I answer, keeping my face straight and my posture stern.

Bishop searches my eyes, his dark green ones daring my secrets to come out. "No."

He leans down, tilts his head, and narrows his eyes. "Are you lying to me, Kitty?"

Lie.

"No."

He pauses, leaving a beat of silence to stretch between us before inching back. "Fine." He steps away and turns to walk out the door. "If you lied to me, I will punish you." Then he's gone, like a fucking tornado whisking up a whole bunch of untouched old emotions. Emotions I have fought hard for years on end to bury. A ten-worded question brought back ten thousand feelings that I have worked so hard to forget. Slamming my eyes shut, I breathe in and out slowly.

In.

Out.

In.

Ou—

"Fuck this." I walk to the liquor cabinet and pull down a bottle of Johnny Walker. Twisting off the cap, I bring the tip to my mouth and swallow. The harsh whiskey hits the back of my throat before slipping down, cloaking all the feelings Bishop raised. Looking down at the bench, an idea pops into my head. I know Elena and Dad have gone away for the week. I grin, taking out my phone. I haven't thrown a party yet, and since Nate has thrown plenty, I think it's time for me to play catch-up. Unlocking my phone, I look at the time quickly. 7:45 p.m. Perfect. I hit dial on Tatum, and she picks up on the second ring.

"Yaaas?"

"Tate?"

"Yes, bitch. What's up?"

"Party at my place."

That perks up her attention. "Oh? When?"

"You come now. The rest can come any time after 10:00 p.m. Spread the word."

"You know I will," she says.

I can just picture her from here, wiggling in her chair with excitement. I take a swig of the whiskey and smirk. "See you soon." Hanging up, I flick my phone between my fingers and listen as the clock ticks loudly in the background. My breathing starts to come in thick, so I take deep intakes of breath and close my eyes.

It's not real. You're here, older, at your house. Home. Safe, warm. It's not real.

One.

Two.

Three.

Four.

Four.

Four.

"Why don't you like me? It's your birthday today. You're supposed to be happy," I whispered toward the mean boy in the sandpit.

"Because you're disgusting. Because you're a life ruiner. Because I fucking hate you."

"That's a bad word," I replied softly, even though I wanted nothing more than to burst into tears. I swallowed past the rejection and handed the boy my shovel anyway.

"I don't fucking want that. Why the fuck do you think I want that now that you've touched it? You're disgusting." He got to his feet, kicking at the sand until the sharp stings cut through my eyes.

"Ouch!" I cried, no longer able to fight the tears as they poured down my cheeks. "What did you do that for?"

"Because I fucking hate you!" the mean boy roared, and then he stormed off back toward his mom.

Why did he hate me? I'd done nothing wrong as far as I knew. The first time I met him was today.

"Brantley!" a woman yelled toward him. "Get here now."

"Hey!" I called out, dusting off the sand from my sundress. "Your name is Brantley?"

"Shut up, freak."

"Madison!" my mom yelled out from the porch. She was holding a tray of little pirate-shaped cupcakes and wearing a yellow and white sundress. She looked beautiful. I wanted to be as beautiful as her one day. I skipped toward my mom, wiping the tears out of my face. Mommy wouldn't be happy if she saw me crying, and I didn't want to get the boy into trouble. I didn't know why; he was not a very nice boy. I should've wanted to get him into trouble.

"Brantley," my mom said once we both reached her, bending down to my level while still balancing the tray with one hand. "This is Madison." Brantley must've been at least two years older than me. He wore a baseball cap and had an angry scowl on his face. I didn't know why, but I instantly liked him.

"Hi!" I smiled, holding my hand out to him. Maybe if I introduced myself properly, he would like me better. Mommy always said people liked good manners. "I'm Madison. Are these your cupcakes?" I looked up to my mom. "Are these his cupcakes? Is that why they're blue and why I'm not allowed to eat them?" My mom looked at Brantley and me nervously.

"Mom?" I asked again. She was starting to fidget, which she only did when she's nervous.

"Yes, dear. Why don't you and Brantley go play while me and Lucan have a quick word."
I must've been confused. Lucan? Bringing my eyes to the new body that stood beside my mom, I
looked up the black suit pants, until I finally found ice-cold blue eyes, tanned skin, and blond hair.
The man was looking down at me with a dirty stare that made me cuddle into my mom's legs. He
kneeled in front of me.
"Well hello. You must be Madison."
I nodded, wrapping my hand in my mom's frilly dress and using it to cover my mouth. "Yes."
"I'm Lucan."
"Hi, Lucan."
He leaned forward, his eyes squinting. "I think I'll call you Silver."

I suck in a breath. Brantley? What the fuck? I remember part of that day now. I recall it so vividly it scares me a little that I didn't remember it until this point. Brantley and I had met? I was at his birthday party? The rest of that day is a little blurry, but there was so much more, because I remember driving home with my mom and dad later that night. So there's still a whole day unaccounted for.

Maybe I could ask my dad.

I frown, grasping the glass bottle. There's no way I can trust my dad with anything now. Can I trust anyone? I know I can trust Tatum, I think, but then again, at one point, I completely trusted my dad. I would have trusted him with my life—and I did on multiple occasions, but yet, he still let me down.

Can I trust anyone?

Can I trust myself?

My brain fuzzes as white noise rings through my ears.

Something has happened. Something has switched inside of me since Bishop asked that question. It has triggered a dark part of my soul I never wanted to acknowledge again.

Have I ever really been safe? Even as a little girl, it seems the adults I trusted and the people I was supposed to be safe with let me down. Feeling more than overwhelmed with my thoughts, I bring the rim of my bottle to my lips, pounding down another couple of mouthfuls until I can't feel the burning sensation in my throat and everything turns numb.

"Trust no one. Fear no one. Fuck everyone," I whisper to myself, pushing my long hair away from my face. grinning, I walk toward the stairwell and climb up two at a time. I hope Tatum doesn't take too long to get here, but then again—can I really trust her?

Pushing open my bedroom door, a sense of power rushes over me. I trust no one, and that means no one can hurt me. No one can touch me. I'm untouchable because of this revelation. I can't be hurt again. I will fight for my control and my freedom for that little girl. For that broken part of me that yearns for it. Slamming my bedroom door, I take another pull of JW and look toward my closet.

Smirking, I place the bottle on my dresser and make my way to my closet. Flicking on the light, my eyes find my black skinny jeans. They're ripped at the knees and stick to me like a second skin. Grabbing them, I run my fingers over all my crop tops, opting for the most revealing one I can find. A straight across strapless crop top that shows all of my toned stomach. Looking at both items, an idea clicks in my head. Taking the clothes back to my room, I toss them onto my bed and pull open my underwear drawer, taking out my fishnet stockings. Yes, so much yes, this is perfect. Taking everything to my bathroom—and the bottle of my old pal Johnny Walker—I lock Nate's side and my side and turn on the shower. Slipping under the hot cascading water, I take my bottle in with me and sit on the bathtub floor. Hugging the whiskey, I squeeze my eyes closed as the first teardrops. The beading water trickling over my flesh, down my arms like an assault, reminds me of Black Friday's touch.

His rough, aged hands squeezing my nipples tightly.

His rough bearded face scrapping down my delicate chest.

A sob escapes me before I can stop it and I scrub my face angrily. Angry that he's getting tears and hurt so many years later. Bringing the bottle back to my lips, I take a few long pulls of the liquid until I no longer feel like crying. Then I get to my feet and turn off the faucet, the condensation a reminder of my surroundings, bringing me back to the now.

I'm here.

Now.

At home.

Safe.

Safe? Am I? My sanity is because I trust no one. No one will have the power to let me down. I'll expect the worst in people to save disappointment. Wrapping my towel around my body, I quickly dry myself and slip into my little Calvin Klein G-string and then into the fishnet stockings and black jeans. I pull the fishnet waistband up to my ribs so you can see it ripple over my flat stomach and everywhere my jeans are ripped, before sliding on the little crop top boob tube. Smiling down at my outfit, I run the towel through my hair. I look hot and I feel reckless, a toxic combination for me.

I blow out my hair and throw on makeup. Going heavy on the eyes and bright red on the lips. Well, Dad would be proud of the look I have going on right now.

After battling over how to do my hair, I settle on a high messy bun that sits like a bundle of brown curls on the top of my head and grab my bottle. I'm slipping my original Adidas sneakers on when my bedroom door swings open, and Tatum walks in fully dressed in a tight little skirt and heels, clutching a plastic bag in her hand.

"Now, I got Absinth and a couple of kegs," she murmurs, rushing into my room without looking at me. She places the drinks on my bed and finally turns toward me. Her face changes, a small smile creeping onto her mouth. "Well holy shit who fucked on a stick. Where is my friend? And please, don't bring her back."

I roll my eyes and take another drink. "She's gone."

Tate looks impressed. "Well, I like it. Totally digging this look. Carter is downstairs with Ridge starting the music. I hope that's okay, by the way. I saw both of them in town while I was getting alcohol and sort of dragged them with me. But I kind of got the impression you wanted a full house tonight so you wouldn't mind." She adds a cheesy smile.

"Of course I don't mind. A thick bass line starts thumping against the walls as the alcohol warms my blood even more. "I want to dance. Let's go." I pull her toward the door and she pulls back.

"Wait!" She reaches for the plastic bag again and smiles. "Okay, now I'm ready!"

We pound down the stairs, me with my bottle of whiskey clutched between my fingers and Tatum swinging the plastic bag. Hitting the bottom of the stairwell, Carter whistles at us, a mischievous grin on his face.

"Damn, mami...."

"Hey!" I smile. He pulls me in for a hug, and I slouch into him, my muscles slightly relaxing for the first time since this afternoon. Inching back, he pushes a couple of loose strands away from my face and smiles his boyish grin.

Pressing back softly, I look over his shoulder at Ridge, who looks like he has almost finished setting up the little makeshift DJ booth area in the sitting room. I point to the floor-to-ceiling doors and nudge my head at Tatum. "Open up the doors and turn on the Jacuzzi and pool lights. Tonight is going to be a long night."

"Long night, huh?" Tatum wiggles her ass, sliding open the doors. "Well, as long as I get fucked, I don't care."

"All class, Sinclaire," Carter murmurs.

Tatum flips him off. "Never claimed to be classy, Mathers."

I roll my eyes, leaving the two to banter between each other and making my way toward Ridge. "Hey!"

He looks over his shoulder, putting all the wires and cords back into the little black boxes.

"Hey, Madi. Hope it's okay. Your friend," he looks over at Tatum, "is a little persistent. Anyway, she somehow knew I DJ'd at one of the underage clubs in town, so here I am."

I laugh, not surprised that Tatum knew that information about Ridge. She probably knows his address, birthplace, birthdate, and blood type too. "No, please, you're doing us a favor. It was sort of an impulse idea."

Ridge chuckles, walking behind the DJ setup and putting on his headphones. "The best nights start with that line right there."

"I hope so." I smile at him and tilt my head. He's cute, in a boy-raised-on-the-wrong-side-of-the-tracks kind of way. He has a sort of swagger to him that makes him even more appealing.

"Sorry about her." I laugh, looking toward Tatum, who has opened out the ranch slider doors. "She's a little—"

"Intrusive?" Ridge interrupts, smirking at me.

I laugh, my eyes locking with his. "Yeah, I guess you could say that. But she means well."

"Yeah." Ridge winks, his arm wrapping around my waist as he pulls me into him. "So tell me—"

"No," I cut him off, looking up at him. "I don't want to answer any questions tonight." I bring my hands up to his chest and press lightly. "I just want to forget everything." He steps back and searches my eyes.

"Everything okay?"

Smiling, I nod. "Yeah, everything's fine." He turns back to the DJ deck and flicks on some sort of remixed, hard, house song, and I turn around, finding Tatum straight away. She wiggles her eyebrows at me suggestively, and I roll my eyes. I swear, only Tatum would take me talking to a guy the completely wrong way. Walking up to her, I squint my eyes. "What?"

"Oh, nothing." She grins, dancing around in a circle just as the doorbell rings. "Oh look, the party is here!"

I smile, shaking my head and taking a long pull of the whiskey again, relishing how it numbs everything inside of me, physically and mentally. The more I drink, the more I forget. With that thought, I take another sip just as the song changes to "Where the Girls At" by David Guetta. Tatum lifts her drink in the air, and with a whole bunch of people walking in behind her, she screams, "Let's get fucked up!" at the top of her lungs.

I raise my bottle in the air in salute, grinning at her. Spinning around, I start dancing in the middle of the floor, grinding and pressing against the sea of bodies. The song changes to "No Promises" by Cheat Codes and I spin around, lost in the numb feeling the whiskey has given me.

Until my eyes lock onto Bishop, who is standing in the entryway of the sitting room with Nate and the rest of the Kings in formation behind him.

Bishop's scowl deepens when he sees someone rubbing up behind me. Rolling my eyes, I walk toward them, an innocent smile on my face. "Hi, boys!"

"Madison!" Nate snaps at me. "What the fuck?"

"What?" I slur, my head swimming in a deep pool of whiskey. "Like I can't throw a party, what?" I laugh sarcastically. "I'm not Nate Riverside." Nate grabs my arm, but I yank it away from him. "Screw you, all of you. Leave me the fuck alone." Then I push through them and make my way toward the kitchen. Leaning down into the cabinet, I pull out a glass and fill it up with water. Turning around, I find Bishop leaning against the doorframe, arms crossed in front of him.

"Why throw the party, Madison?"

"Why not, Bishop?" I retort, matching his tone. I tip my water out and go to walk out the door, only his hand catches my arm.

"Why you acting out?"

I pull my arm out of his grip. "Why don't you mind your fucking business?" Then I walk back onto the dance floor, snatching a bottle of whatever the fuck it is out of someone's hands. Cisco Kid from Redman starts pumping through the speakers, and I let go. Dancing and riding the beat, I grind up on the closest person near me. Turning around and wrapping my arms around his neck, I bring my eyes to—

"Brantley?" I go to pull away, but he grips onto my arms, locking me there.

"Nah-uh, you ain't going anywhere. You don't grind up on a man's dick like that and expect to walk away."

I narrow my eyes, the room spinning. "I can do what the fuck I want."

He laughs, a menacing chuckle that vibrates against my chest—a tone I know I should run from, because this is freaking Brantley. Though Bishop is just as terrifying as Brantley—if not worse—I know Bishop on a level I don't know Brantley. I know how far I can push Bishop for him to not hurt me. Do I think he could still hurt me and probably would if I push him far enough? Abso-fucking-lutely.

I search Brantley's eyes, lost in the music and intoxicated by whiskey. I lean my body into his a bit more and bring my hands down his sharp jawline, running my index finger over the bottom of his plump lip. He catches my index finger between his teeth, and I give him a menacing grin. Wrapping his lips around my finger, he unlatches his teeth and sucks on my finger; it comes out of his mouth with a pop. Closing my eyes, I ignore the way my nipples are pushing against the cups of my bra, or the way my flesh has come alive.

Before I know what I'm doing, I come up on my tippy toes and kiss him. He opens his mouth, letting my tongue in as his arm hooks around my bare waist and his finger dips into the band of my fishnet tights, flicking at it. I lick his tongue, pulling on it slightly before he bites down on my lower lip. Pulling back, I bring my nose to his and search his eyes. His eyes that are lit with lust—dark, domineering, and powerful lust. Do I dance on this line? This dangerous line of something I know I could never come back from?

Yes.

"Go upstairs?" I whisper against his lips.

He smirks, the curve of his mouth pressing against mine. His dimple pops out and I groan like an unhinged horny teenager.

"Naw, babe. That's too mainstream for me." He takes my hand and tugs me toward the open doors. "Come." I take another drink and go to place it on the countertop, only for him to pick it back up. "We're gonna need this."

We pass Tatum briefly near the stairwell, and she looks at me, eyes wide. "What the fuck?" she mouths, shock evident on her face.

I shrug and follow Brantley anyway. Stepping outside, he pulls me again, tucking me under his arm and leading me toward his RT Dodge Charger. I pull open the passenger side and slip into the dark leather seats. The car is nice, sort of looks like the one Vin Diesel drives in *The Fast and the Furious*. Brantley gets into the driver seat and roars her to life, the deep V8 engine vibrating underneath me.

"Where we going?" I ask, turning to face him.

He smirks. "You have no idea." Then he floors it out of the driveway. As we pass all the streetlights and overgrown trees, I begin to sober a little. "Brantley?" I whisper as he drops it down to second gear and accelerates. I look toward him. "Brantley, where are we going?" His face straightens, all playfulness that I saw earlier gone. That's when realization sinks in. I just got into a car with Brantley—thinking I was going to fuck the shit out of him, only now I'm fearing for my life. I've made a lot of mistakes in my life, but I have a feeling this one is going to take the cake. My phone vibrates in my back pocket, and I sit up, pulling it out and opening the message from an unknown number.

Riddle me this...

CHAPTER 11

Fuck!

   I look toward Brantley. "What the fuck is this?"

   Brantley laughs and floors it forward. "As I said—you have no idea."

   Slamming my eyes shut, I squeeze my phone in my hand, ignoring the text and not wanting to read on. Brantley must sense this because he decides to take over.

   "Riddle me this, Kitty. What happens when you drink from poison, thinking it's love, but when you get hit with the buzz, things start to fuzz, until you can't breathe, and your suffocating becomes the release?"

   Fear prickles over my skin and I shake my head. "Nate said he was done fucking with me. Bishop wouldn't do this to m—"

   "Oh, but he would. You see..." Brantley grins, dropping gears and driving us onto the highway. "Human emotions are a fickle thing. They can blind even the smartest of people and make them think that someone won't do bad, but people will always do bad. There's no stopping that. So tell me, Madison." He looks at me now as he applies more pressure on the accelerator.

   "Brantley, your speed."

   His eyes stay on mine, the darkness of them sucking me in like sinking sand. "Don't care. But tell me," his smirk deepens as he puts his attention back to the road ahead of him, "what makes you think Bishop really gives a fuck about you?"

   "He does, a little bit," I murmur, realizing how deluded I must sound. This is Bishop Vincent Hayes—king of no emotions and zero fucks given. Why am I cocky enough to declare he gives more than a fuck about me?

   Brantley laughs. "Oh, Madison. There's so much you don't know, and won't know. But one thing you should know is that Bishop has no feelings for anyone. He plays the game right, draws them in enough to think he gives a fuck, but ultimately, he doesn't. There's a reason why he's the king of the Kings, Kitty, and it's not because of his over-whelming river of feels he pours upon girls. It's because he ends lives without flinching."

   I swallow past the ball of fear that has developed in my throat. "You won't win this round, Brantley." I look at him, really regretting the alcohol consumption and inwardly declaring I will never drink like this again.

   "Naw, Kitty." Brantley grins again, pulling down a long dark road. "We've already won." Then he slides into the driveway and floors it until we reach the cabin we all stay at months ago. Memories come flooding back, and I realize how naïve I've been when it comes to Bishop and Nate. I was deluded with the idea of loyalty, when in fact that didn't mean anything to them. Never did. They warned me that I was just a pawn in their game—I move when they want me to move, speak when they want me to speak. I just didn't realize it until now.

"What do you want?" I ask, my tone flat. "You guys give me whiplash with these games."

Brantley smirks and then gets out of the car, walking around to my side, and then yanks it open. "Get the fuck out."

"No!" I snap back at him, and he reaches inside, pulling me out by the arm. "Let me go!" I scream at him, only it falls on deaf ears, because he grabs me by the back of my neck and starts tugging me toward the front door. The bright headlights from the car beam on the modern log cabin I had been to what feels like not that long ago. Bringing my hand up to my forehead to shade from the bright light, just as we hit the bottom step, the car revs behind us and I spin around, catching Brantley grinning. His other hand lets go of my arm as he puts a cigarette between his lips, sparking it to life. Looking back to the car in confusion, a light shines from inside of the car, displaying long black hair. Who the hell is that? She looks right at me and smirks, but even from here I can tell she's beautiful. Exotic-looking, but beautiful. She turns to look over her shoulder and floors it backward before spinning and driving down the long driveway.

"What is this?" I ask out loud, my eyes and focus remaining on the fading headlights. When Brantley doesn't answer back, I turn to ask him, "Brant—" Only he's gone. I spin around a full 360, trying to find where he disappeared to. "Brantley!" I growl. "This is not funny!" The temperature suddenly drops, thick fog slipping out of my mouth between each word. Figuring he's definitely not coming back, I run my hands up and down my arms, rubbing the goose bumps off my flesh. Taking the front steps carefully because I can't see shit, I feel around for the railing. Opening and closing my eyes, they slowly begin to adapt to the surroundings, but not enough for me to really see what I'm doing.

"Shit!" I mutter under my breath, grabbing my phone from my back pocket. I quickly slide it open and go to press Call on Tatum when I see the service bars keep dropping in and out. "Motherfucker." Using the light from my phone, I aim it toward the front door and grab onto the handle, wiggling it but it doesn't unlock. Giving up, I start walking along the wraparound porch when my phone goes off. Swiping my phone open, I read the message.

Run.

An overwhelming sense of terror rushes over me. I spin around suddenly, finding no one there. Nothing but my damn imagination. I know these boys play games—this isn't my first rodeo with them—but the thing I don't know is how far they'll push it. I've seen Bishop kill three people now. I'm not about to play Russian roulette with my life and in the hands of a psychopathic billionaire, or whatever the fuck he is.

"I'm not playing your games!" I yell into the dark night. Waiting for a reply, or even a laugh, I hear… nothing. The mere whisks of wind brushing through the dry almost-autumn leaves is all that replies. Swallowing past my fear, I walk along the porch more, remembering the back door. Maybe Brantley just left me here as a sick joke. It wouldn't surprise me if that was his stupid plan. Rolling my eyes, I walk farther until I get to the side door that's tucked behind the kitchen. Wiggling the door handle, but it's locked too.

I turn around, banging the back of my head against the door. "Fuck," I murmur. Rustling leaves catch my attention, and I whip my head toward it. "Brantley!" I snap. "This isn't funny. We can leave now! You've made your point."

"A little cocky for a chick who hasn't been on the scene for too long, don't ya think?"

I know that voice all too well.

"Well, how not surprising it is to see you come out of the shadows, Bishop. Take me home. It's cold." I push off the door and go to walk past him, only his hand flies up to my arm and he pushes me backward. The back of my head smashes against the door. "Fuck! You—"

His hand slams over my mouth while his free one clenches over my throat. He squeezes tight, enough to have my head pulsing with the lack of oxygen. I tap on his arm, looking deep into his eyes. I'm barely able to make out his sharp eyes and jaw in the dark. His lip curls in a devious grin that makes me both weak in the knees and in the head, because that grin should really put the fear of God into me—and it does. But it also has my stupid lady bits tingling.

"Cut the fucking shit, Madison. What the fuck is with you tonight, and only answer me honestly." He tilts his head, dragging his eyes up and down my clothing. "Remember that game we played in the forest?" He unlatches his grip from my throat and releases my mouth, stepping back slightly. Pulling out an army knife from his back pocket, he flicks it open and then in a flash the blade is pressing into my neck, and his hand is back, covering my mouth. He runs his nose over mine, searching my eyes. "Mmmm." He smirks, his deep growl vibrating over my chest. "You're distracting."

"Nothing is wrong," I snap when he releases my mouth slightly. I keep my head up, staring at his eyes as he glares back at mine in challenge. "Let me go."

He slams me up against the wall again, the knife still pressed against my neck and his knee coming between my legs. He presses his leg against my clit, and my eyes close, but the knife running down my collarbone sets off electrical currents that have my senses working on overtime. I'm so fucked with Bishop. How can we be so attracted to each other—unwillingly—but hate each other all the same? My eyes pop open when he slices the middle of my strapless crop top, my nipples aching as the cool night air licks over them, igniting them to life. *Focus, Madison. Focus.*

"Stop fucking lying to me, Madison!" Bishop yells, getting more up in my face. Bringing both arms to either side of my head, he cages me in. "Why. The fuck. Did me questioning your past today trigger something with you? Hmm?" he asks, grinding his thickness against my tummy.

Fight it.

"It didn't."

"Tell me the truth, Madison."

Lie.

"It triggered nothing."

Bishop brings the knife back down and runs the blunt side of it over my nipple. I suck in a breath and hold. *One second. Two seconds. Three seconds.* My body's will to breathe wins and I exhale just as the blade comes down to my jeans. He cuts the waistband to my fishnets, and it springs loose, hanging over the top of my jeans.

"One more time, Madison, or I'm going to fuck you with this knife and lick your blood clean off as you watch."

I close my eyes. "Not—"

He launches his fist into the wall beside my face. I've never seen Bishop so out of control, and I don't know why it's my reaction to my past that has set him off—but it has. Set. Him. Off. "Stop fucking lying!"

Clenching my eyes closed, I take in a few deep breaths. Don't walk down that aisle. Don't do it... don—

Walking down the blood-red hall, Madison squeezed the man's hand. "Where are you taking me?"

"You'll see, Silver. You'll see."

"Will there be any other kids there to play with?"

The man looked down to Madison and grinned. "You'll see."

"No!" I rock back and forth on the concrete in front of the door, cradling my knees up to my chest. Tears pour down my cheeks and sweat beads my skin regardless of the fact I'm sitting in the brisk cool night with absolutely no shirt on. "No, no, no..." Shaking my head, I can still hear his voice in the back of my consciousness. "It's just a dream. It's just a bad dream. He won't come back," I repeat, rocking back and forth and fisting my hair.

"Madison, Madison! Fuck!"

Whose voice is that?

"No!" I shake my head again, lost in my dark abyss of bleeding memories. "He always comes back."

"Madison!" another voice roars in the background. A different voice.

"Come back, baby."

I know *that* voice.

My eyes spring open, a blood-curdling scream ripping out of my chest. "Don't fucking touch me!" Consciousness starts to seep in, and I look up to see Bishop, Nate, Hunter, Brantley, Cash, Eli, and Chase circling me. I cover my front right away, and Bishop rips off his hoodie, pushing it over my head before tucking his arms under my legs and lifting me off the ground. I snuggle into his chest, inhaling his spicy, sweet scent.

"What, what did I say?" I murmur through sobs.

"You said enough for us to know enough." Bishop's jaw tenses as he looks directly at Nate, who still hasn't looked at me.

"Nate?" I whisper, but he doesn't acknowledge me. His eyes stay locked on Bishop's. A wave of humiliation washes over me. Is he ashamed of me? That this happened to me? Does he look at me differently now? All my worst fears come crashing into my chest like a freight train. I'm dirty. No one can love something or someone who has been through what I have. His knowing what I've been through has now tainted what he thought of me; I just know it. My heart snaps in my chest and my throat swells as tears start to pour down my cheeks again.

"Take her home," Nate replies emotionlessly.

"Nate?" I try again through a broken throat. "Talk to me."

He doesn't move, keeping his eyes on Bishop. "Take her home."

Bishop's grip tightens around me. "We'll talk about this later," he warns Nate.

I don't see Nate's reaction, because I've buried my head into the crook of Bishop's neck, his pulse pounding against my nose. Putting me in the passenger seat, Bishop shuts the door and then comes to his side, sliding in and firing up his Maserati.

"Madi, we don't have to talk about anything right now, but eventually, I want to know 100 percent of what happened and everything in between—okay?"

I don't say anything, watching how the dark night dances between the tree branches and leaves.

"Answer me."

"Yes," I reply. "I'll tell you everything I remember."

He floors it forward as we leave the cabin in the distance.

"Why?" I croak out once we hit the highway.

"Why, what?" He looks to me every couple of seconds while still keeping his eyes ahead on the road.

"Why did you have to do it this way. Why scare me?"

He pauses briefly until the silence stretches out. "Fear is your patch, babe. We all have our patches. Those little spaces that could bring us to our knees if dabbled with."

The answer surprises me. "Oh, and what's yours?"

He pauses again, long enough for me to guess he's not going to answer, so I lean my forehead on the cool window and close my eyes, suddenly feeling tired and drained.

"You."

My eyes snap open. Not wanting to be overly obvious about how surprised I am, I keep my eyes locked on the dark road ahead. "What?"

"I didn't have one," Bishop confesses. "It's how my father raised me, why I am who I am. Our blood, I mean, who we are, we can't afford to have a patch. My dad doesn't have one either. He married my mom for a cover, not for love—not that I'm talking about love." He looks toward me to enhance his point then focuses back on the road. "But I'm just saying, I can't have one. The fucking feelings I get when I think someone is fucking with you, though?" He breathes out a gush of air. "I'd kill them in an instant and not think twice about doing it. That may not be because I caught feelings for you or anything like that. It could just be because we're sort of... friends. In a fucked way."

"Friends?" I mimic, trying that word on my tongue. So he's overprotective of me and has some sort of feelings for me. If not, then why would he kill someone over me? He sounds confused, about as confused as I am about him. I get where he's coming from, Bishop has always been different for me too, regardless of whatever fucked shit he put me through. Is that really dangerous for him though? To feel that strongly about a "friend?"

"Why is that a bad thing?" I quickly ask before I can stop myself. "I mean, why is having a patch a bad thing?"

"It's a weakness. I had nothing to lose until I met you. I can't afford to have a weakness, not in this lifetime."

"Well maybe we'll meet each other in another lifetime, and I can be more than a patch to you." I glance at him, and his eyes lock onto mine. The dark depths sink into mine, clinging like a flame does to embers.

"And what would that be?" he asks, his brows pulling in as he looks from my mouth to my eyes.

"Yours."

Pulling up to my house, Bishop gets out of the driver side and opens my door.

"I can walk, Bishop."

"Yeah," he murmurs, scooping his arms under my legs and lifting me from my seat. "But you don't have to." After our brief talk on the way home, I've realized I need to let him go. I can't keep holding on to whatever it is I think we could have together, because it's not going to happen. He's Bishop Vincent Hayes, and I'm me. A fucking mess.

I turn my face to him just as we reach the front door. The front door that is showing no display of the house party that was raging earlier. I guess someone—or some King— shut it down. "Can I ask you something?"

He opens the door wide. "Yeah."

"If I ask you something... will you tell me the truth?"

"That depends," he answers, walking inside and closing the door behind us. "If it's about me, then yes, but if it's about the club, then no."

"Loyalty?" He puts me down and I make my way upstairs with him following behind.

"Something like that," he mutters under his breath. It's so quiet I almost miss it. Walking into my room, I stretch out on my bed, blowing my hair out of my face. The mattress dips where Bishop takes a seat. "I need to ask you something, and I need you to be honest with me," he begins.

I swallow down any nerves those words raised, and nod. I know what he's going to ask, and I've been mentally preparing myself for it the whole way home, but it's still unsettling me. I've never said the words out loud. I've never told anyone my darkest secret, let alone a guy I have feelings for.

"Did someone do something to you when you were little?"

Turning toward him, I prop my head up onto the palm of my hand. The shadows from the dim lamp cast sharp lines over his jaw and perfect nose. He has the profile of a GQ model, but the twisted mind of Michael Myers. Ahh, charming. Exhaling, I close my eyes. "Yes."

He grits his teeth, and I open my eyes and watch as his hands ball into fists on top of his knees. His nostrils flare. "Who?"

I know his name. I don't know where he is or what happened to him, but I know his name.

"I don't know who he is. I don't remember much of it. All I know is it started when I was young." I lie on my back and bring my hands under my head.

"Give me any details you can," Bishop urges, turning to face me. "I mean it, Madison."

Oh, I know he means it, and I know if I give him the name, he will have no problem finding this guy. It doesn't matter if Lucan is in China or if he's six feet under already. I know Bishop will find him, and he will kill him if he's still alive, but that's *my* kill. I promised myself long ago that one day I will get my retribution, and I'm not about to cheat my younger self out of that promise, so I lie. "I don't know his name."

Bishop studies my face closely, and I start to panic. I know he can read people; he reads people so accurately, but he has always said how he struggles to read me. Even though I know this, paranoia kicks into overtime, and I clear my throat, knowing I have to give him something so he can back off a little. Bishop opens his mouth, probably about to call me out on my obvious lie, but I interject. "He would call me Silver."

"Silver?" Bishop asks, thinking over those words. "What, like as in he knew you were the Silver Swan?"

I shrug. "I honestly don't know."

Bishop gets up and walks toward the door. Pausing, he inches his head over his shoulder. "Get some sleep." Then he walks out and leaves me there brewing. Shit. Did I give too much? Has he worked out who that is? Surely not. No one knew that was what Lucan called me except me and Lucan... and....

Forget.

But Bishop is smart—too smart. He picks up things that slip past normal ears and eyes.

Swinging my legs off the bed, I reach underneath until my hand skims over the worn leather I've become so accustomed to touching. Pulling it out, I shuffle up my bed until I'm leaning against the headboard. Flipping open the first few pages, I jump to where I was up to.

10.

Revelation

Et delicatis praetulissem, sicut truncum arboris fluitantem olor et quasi argentum bullet sicut mortiferum.

- As alluring as a floating swan, but as deadly as a silver bullet.

"I want to know why," I probed, trying to get Humphrey to confess. Why is it so important that a woman is not to be born into this cult?

"I told you, woman. You only know what I want you to know. None of this has to make sense to you, because you're a woman." Biting down every reaction I had, I took a seat on one of the chairs. Gazing into the scalding hot flame that flicked up to the stone fireplace, I whipped my head toward him.

"Tell me." Deciding I was going to fight him on this, I got up off my chair and walked toward him. "I want to know. I have a right to know—my..." I stopped, the swelling of my throat halting any and every movement.

One.

Two.

Three.

I began counting internally, ordering the tears to sink back into their sockets.

Humphrey rose up off his chair and headed toward me. His expression changed, all the lines and wrinkles that carved through his face deepened, and that's when I knew I had struck a nerve. I always did. He reared his hand back and slapped me across the cheek, the sting causing a rush of heat to flame up my face. I fell to the ground in a heap, holding the throbbing ache and looking up at him.

He kneeled down beside me. "Now, I'm going to tell you a little something, not because you asked, or rather, demanded, but because I want to. Understand me?"

I nodded, because I had no other choice if I wanted to see the sunrise tomorrow or my son again.

He inched toward me, his breath heating my earlobe. I shivered in disgust, but hid it, knowing rightly that him becoming aware of the fact he disgusts me would warrant me another beating. "Because women can't be trusted. Because women are easily distracted by fame and money. Because the amount of power the Silver Swan could gain would be immense, because that thing between your legs is a weakness. A patch. It's alluring, and it's distracting."

"So you do this because she would have too much power?"

"Ahhh," Humphrey grinned, "she gets it. Yes, she would also be too appealing to the other Kings. Far, far too appealing. There's no way, and that is why we can never have a Silver Swan. As alluring as a peaceful swan floating on water, but as lethal as a silver bullet."

"What if, in generations of times from now, one slips through the cracks?" I asked, genuinely concerned for the future Swan, as there was a high chance there will be plenty. But whether any survive will be a different story. I do hope someone in this cult shows compassion at one point and saves her.

"Then she will grow to wish she was never born."

"Well, you got that right, fucker," I murmur, closing the book and sliding it back under my bed. I sure do fucking wish I was never born sometimes, but what did he mean by that? Why was he so sure that if any of them made it out alive, they would wish they were never born? I could say it was just Humphrey and his cocky character, but something about his certainty throws me off. My head pounds, reminding me of my long night, and I slide off the bed, dragging my overly tired ass to the bathroom.

Turning on the faucet, I wait for the water to warm up to a scalding heat and slide in. Squeezing some shampoo into the palm of my hand, I throw it into my hair and scrub, letting the soapsuds rain over my skin. I'm lost in thoughts of the latest finding in *The Book* when the bathroom door swings open, and the curtain gets ripped away, revealing Nate standing there, no shirt on with gray sweat pants.

"Nate!" I scream, covering my private bits. "Get the fuck out!"

He doesn't say anything, his pupils are dilated, and his chest is heaving as he takes in deep breaths.

"Have you been running?" I ask, totally off subject but finally noticing the glistening of sweat covering his skin. Reaching for my towel, I still keep my eyes locked on his to make sure he doesn't cop a look, but he doesn't. He just stares at me, his eyes looking between each of mine intently, like he's searching for something important. Answers, maybe, answers I can't give him.

"Nate!" I repeat when the awkward silence gets too much. Grasping the towel, I quickly wrap it around myself. Feeling more secure now that I'm not butt-naked, I reach up and touch the side of his cheek. "What's wrong?" I care about Nate, I do. More than I like to admit it, but I do. I've always had an inkling of feelings for him deep down, and though I squash them and bring it down to him being my brother, I can't help it. My heart aches when his does and beats when he's happy. Whether that's what usually happens when you have a brother, I don't know—I wouldn't know. The feelings are new to me, so I'm still trying to work them out.

His eyes close once my palm touches his cheek, a small breath hissing between his teeth. His abs tense, every muscle in his body looking overworked. "Nate?" I whisper again, getting out of the shower so my body is flush up against his. He's almost a good foot taller than me, so I look up to him. "Talk to me."

He wraps his arm around my back and pulls me into his chest. Reaching down, he brushes off a few strands of hair that were stuck to my face. "I… can't—fuck!" He lashes out at the end. "Who?"

"Who what?" I answer, even though I know I'm playing with fire. I've not seen Nate quite this dark before, and though it's terrifying, I know with more certainty than I do about Bishop that he would never hurt me.

"Don't." His voice is sharp, full of dominance. That simple word twisting my heart into two.

"I told Bishop I don't know his name. All I know is that he called me Silver."

Nate tilts his head, his eyebrows pulling in as the wheels start to turn in his head. "Silver?" His other arm comes behind me so he has me locked in both now. "As in the Silver Swan? As in he's a motherfucking King?"

"I don't know what he is or who he is, Nate. I don't want to talk about this anymore."

That sobers him a little, his features relaxing for the first time since he stormed in here. "You know," I murmur, wrapping my hands around the back of his neck, "one of these days you're going to need to stop storming into the bathroom while I'm showering."

The corner of his mouth kicks up in a small smirk, showing one of his dimples. "Yeah, I guess one of these days I will. But not today, or tomorrow, or even next month." The cushion of his thumb traces along the bottom of my lip. His eyes zone in on the motion, and in the back of my brain, I know what's about to happen.

My breathing shallows, my chest constricting. I want to make him feel better. I hate that he's so worked up over something that has to do with me. Something he shouldn't feel worked up over because I buried it long ago. Closing my eyes, I inch up on my tippy toes and press my lips to his. He stills at first. A couple of seconds pass, and he still hasn't relaxed, so I go to pull away, only his hand comes to the back of my neck, stopping me. He pushes my lips into his more and opens slightly, his tongue licking across my bottom lip. My stomach flips, my flesh sparking to life from the connection, and I pull him in more. Our kissing turns hot and needy, and in a second, he's whipped the towel from my body, his hands gripping around the back of my thighs and lifting me off my feet.

"Fuck!" He pauses, catching his breath. I count to five in my head, attempting to slow my erratic breathing—and hormones. Closing my eyes, he leans his forehead against the wall beside my head, my sex pressing against his stomach and my legs still wrapped around his waist.

"We can't do this—and I can't fucking believe I just said that, because God fucking knows I want this with you, Mads." He places soft kisses on my collarbone.

"How long?" I whisper out.

"How long what?" he replies, his lips brushing over my shoulder and his lip ring leaving a cool sensation in its wake.

"How long have you been in love with me?"

He pauses and squeezes me tightly. "Longer than you know."

I pull in a breath. "Nate," I warn. "I know I feel something for you too. I mean, I always have. And I've always fought it—but love? I mean I love you. I love you so very much, but in love? That's not something I know."

He steps back, placing me back down to my feet slowly and picking up my towel again, wrapping it around my body. He tightens the front and smiles a sweet smile that doesn't reach his eyes. Placing a small kiss on my forehead, he whispers, "I know." Then he walks out the bathroom and into his bedroom, and just like that, everything is back to normal.

Did I just imagine that? He came into my bathroom like a tornado, leaving a massacre of feelings behind. Fucking Nate Riverside. Fucker. But I love that fucker, very much, but if I were to compare the two feelings—Nate and Bishop—they're oh so different. Both intense, but incredibly different. Now I've just got to figure out what means what. Like a love puzzle of mass destruction, only we don't know who will pull the trigger. I slide under my sheets, and then twist and turn for hours until I finally get some sleep.

I got shit for sleep last night, and I haven't been able to stomach any food all morning. The hangover of doom awaited me with the sun this morning, and now I don't want to live, let alone adult. Throwing on some sweatpants and a loose white tee, I walk downstairs, twisting my hair up into a messy bun.

"Morning, sweetheart," Elena greets. She's chopping up all sorts of fruit and putting them into the blender to make one of her godawful smoothies.

"Morning." I, on the other hand, head straight for the pot of coffee, praising the gods when I see it's full.

"Sleep well?" she asks, putting the lid on the blender and unleashing hell upon my ears.

"Actually," I yell over her intrusion that comes compacted in green slime. "I slept like shit!" I yell, only she cut off the blender just in time that I didn't just yell; I sort of screamed.

"Wow." Nate grins, walking into the kitchen with dark sweatpants and no shirt on. I quickly avert my eyes, guilt washing over me as I think back to what happened between us last night. "I would have thought you slept like a baby, sis." Instantly, I cut my eyes to his and growl under my breath. He did not just "sis" me after we were seconds away from doing the deed not long ago.

"Well, I didn't," I snap at him, sipping on my coffee and making my way to one of the barstools.

"Oh, well that's unfortunate." Elena bounces around the kitchen in her running gear, slurping on her green juice. "I have some flaxseed oil that might help you with sleeping, Madison. It has a good history, and—"

"Thanks," I interrupt. Usually I'm not so rude, but I have a pounding headache from Hades, and horns are starting to grow out of my head. "I'll keep that in mind." I offer her a little smile, leaning on my elbows and massaging my temples. Elena walks out, leaving Nate and me together in the kitchen alone.

"You all right?" He grins at me, leaning against the counter and sipping on a mug of coffee. Something so natural but looks way too smoking coming from Nate. I need to get out of here.

"Fine!" I clear my throat, standing to my feet.

"Where you going?" he yells from behind me as I take the first step upstairs.

"Going to shoot shit."

CHAPTER 12

After I've packed up my guns, I load them into the back of the Range Rover and slip into the driver seat before making my way to the area my dad and I used to shoot when I was a kid. I remember it vaguely, and it's a bit of a drive away, but I need some time away from my house and everyone in my life. I'm starting to get cabin fever, or people fever, so I think hiding out where I have good memories as a kid is the best way to ground myself again.

I get into NYC later that evening and my phone has been ringing nonstop. None from my dad, just from Nate and Tatum, and even a few from Bishop. They won't understand my need to get away—no one ever does. I love my friends—and whatever the hell the Kings are—but I'm not about to pour my life story to them and drop all the walls I spent years upon years building. I like to think I'm smarter than that.

Pulling into the old ranch, I make my way down the gravel drive, the trees and gardens all immaculately groomed and trimmed. I don't remember it being this impeccable, but then again, I was all of ten the last time I was here.

I pull up to the front entrance and the valet comes to my door.

"Name?" he asks, the brim of his hat hiding his young features.

"Oh, um, I haven't made a reservation. Do I need to?" I look around, taking in the rich scale and vast size of the place. It screams elite; of course I need a reservation.

"Yes, I apologize, ma'am." He speaks English, but he doesn't sound American.

"Oh!" I act surprised. "That's okay."

I'm just about to close the door when a woman's voice stops me. "Excuse me!" she interrupts from the main entrance. "Madison? Montgomery?" I look her up and down, not sure whether I should respond or drive off. How could she know my name?

The young boy stills, his jaw tensing.

"Uhh." I internally battle with how to answer. Looking at her again, I notice how she's dressed immaculately. Tight black pencil skirt, blood-red silk blouse, dark hair pinned up in a tight high ponytail, sharp stilettos. Oh yeah, this woman oozes power and money.

"Yeah?" My brain-to-mouth filter malfunctions, because I sure as fuck did not authorize that answer.

"She doesn't need a reservation." The woman floats down the marble steps and

"I don't?" I reply, confusion no doubt evident on my face.

"No, honey." She smiles, taking my hand. "Come on in. I'll get the keys to your room." She must know my father; that's the only explanation I have. Because how else would she know my name and who I am?

Looking over my shoulder at the young valet, his face is tilted toward the ground, his expressions not visible from where I'm walking. When he looks back to me, his eyes catch mine like a magnet, and I instantly feel a strange sense of familiarity with him. His eyes are milk chocolate, his skin pale, his cheekbones are high and defined, and his jaw is angular. From what I can tell, he can't be older than sixteen, maybe seventeen—he's young. His body isn't very large either; it's more of a lean stature.

Bringing my attention back to where I'm going, the woman walks through the main glass doors and pauses at the threshold, gesturing for me to enter. Taking this moment to case out the place, I grip onto my shoulder strap and look around uneasily. The place looks the same from my memory, maybe a few things being upgraded, but the concept of the ranch remains the same. Rich, old, and classy. It's situated on the outskirts of New York, deep in the woods. My father would tell me this was a safe place where we could go shooting in the woods and not be disturbed. I'm beginning to think his idea of disturbed was a little warped. There are red and white drapes that hang over the floor-to-ceiling glass walls in the waiting area to the left, which overlooks the woods. The reception is directly in front of the main entrance, and to the right is where the round stairwell leads you to the bedrooms upstairs.

"Come on, Madison," the woman says, and it's then I realize I didn't catch her name. She must see the look that goes across my face, because she smiles, waving her hand in the air. "How rude of me."

I step inside, taking her outstretched hand. "I'm Katsia. Nice to meet you."

And that's when everything stops.

CHAPTER 13

S he's still smiling when I tilt my head, looking over to her. She doesn't catch my surprise, or I hide it well because her smile doesn't drop.

What.

The.

Fuck?

Shaking my head, I figured I must have misheard. "Sorry," I answer shyly. "Hi, I'm
Madison. Sorry, I didn't quite catch your name?"

"Katsia!" she repeats, none the wiser. I shake her hand and mentally slap myself. I
knew I shouldn't have driven off, but if I leave now, will she know that I *know*? Whatever
it is that I think I know. It would be too obvious if I did, though. And then she might kill
me with her sharp-as-fuck stilettos, and I've had enough near-death experiences to last
me a lifetime, so I play dumb.

"Nice to meet you, Katsia."

"Come on." She waves me over, and I follow as she heads toward the front reception desk where two more young men are working. All are wearing the same uniform as
the valet, only when these boys look at me—I feel nothing. Nothing like I felt with the
boy outside. One is of darker complexion, a stoic look on his face, and the other looks
Hispanic. They both straighten their shoulders when they see us walking toward them.

"Miss K." They both do a small bow, and I look toward Katsia again before looking
back to the boys who haven't glanced at her but rather kept their eyes straight ahead.

"Thank you. Please, give me Montgomery's key."

I watch as their eyes widen in shock but don't move from their position, locked on
the wall ahead.

"Now," Katsia urges, and they jump, spinning around and disappearing behind a
small door.

"Excuse me." I clear my throat, figuring this might be a good time to ask. "But can
I ask how you know who I am?"

Katsia turns to face me, her eyes staring into mine with an unreadable expression.
It's a mix between awe and something else I can't quite peg. "Well, I guess we can chat
about that once you're all settled in. I'd like to show you the grounds, if you don't mind. I
know you haven't been here since you were a little girl." Deciding I don't want to appear
as if I'm onto her or know anything about *The Book*, I nod before going back to wait

for the boys to return with the key. Because, really, I shouldn't be that surprised. My dad could have told me about this place. I can't show an inkling of my knowledge of the Kings, because I don't know this woman or what she's capable of.

The boys return, the darker one handing Katsia the key. "Here you go, ma'am."

She takes it and gestures toward the stairwell. "I'll show you to your room, Madison." We walk up the stairs and down the long, dimly lit hallway, passing red doors with gold numbers attached to them. The hallway is a lot longer than I remembered it to be.

Forget.

Reaching the end, Katsia pushes a button and elevator doors ping open. Stepping inside the small enclosure, the doors close, classical music dancing between the silence. I'm not a fan of this particular genre, but anything beats complete silence when in an enclosed space with someone you're not sure is a good or a shitty person.

The doors slide open and we walk out then down another long hallway, only now the walls are glistening in gold paint, and the doors are all licked in white. It's interesting how vivid the two colors are, but maybe that's part of their deco and what they were aiming for. One would hope. If Tatum sees it, she'll flip out, what with her deco-loving brain. Thinking of Tatum, I need to text her just in case I don't make it through the weekend.

We reach a door, but where there were numbers marking the red doors, on these there seems to be some sort of foreign writing on them. I can't make out the name because the cursive font is hard to read, let alone it being in a completely different language, so I brush it off for now.

Katsia pushes the key into the hole and opens the door. "I can meet you back downstairs when you're all settled and ready."

I nod, taking the key from her and stepping inside. Shutting the door behind me, I walk in, dropping my bag on the floor. The room, if it's the same one I was in as a child, looks unrecognizable. Skimming my hands over the old oak wood that lines the deep gold walls, I check out the rest of the room. A large California king bed is tucked away to the left, on a platform that overlooks the woods from the floor-to-ceiling windows. There's an en suite, walk-in closet, a fully functioning and stocked bar, but no TV.

Walking to the other side of the room, I open up a cabinet, thinking a TV might be hidden in there, only it opens up to a fully loaded cabinet full of guns. Semi-automatics, shotguns, the works. This is not surprising. There was a reason why dad liked bringing me here; it's obviously a free-for-all ranch that supported the second amendment. Closing the cabinet, I pick my bag up and take it to the bed, pulling out all of my clothes. Deciding there's no way I'm going to make an effort with my attire, I shove everything back inside and take out some skinny jeans and a long-sleeve shirt.

Slipping into the shower, I scrub up in double-time—even though I want to sit there forever. I seriously need to talk to Dad about getting a showerhead that fills the entire shower stall, because that shit's amazing. Shuffling into my clothes, I let my hair down and fluff it up to fall in my natural curls, skip the makeup, and shove on my Chucks. I came here to shoot, not to play Clue with Mrs. Robinson, but color me intrigued. Although not much surprises me anymore since meeting the Kings and discovering the history, this has me enthralled enough to sit down and chat.

When I walk into the main lobby, the young valet from earlier is talking to Katsia.

From where I'm standing, I can't make out what they're saying, but judging by the movements of his hands and the expressions on his face, they're not talking about anything light.

The boy—who I should probably stop calling "boy"—stops his talking, his mouth slamming shut before he inches his head toward me slightly, like he felt me enter the room. Well, the connection is mutual, and I have no idea what to make of it at all. His eyes lock onto mine and something pangs in my chest. Recognition, guilt, confusion. They all swim inside me, and I have no idea what to do with it. He storms away from Katsia and into the back of the reception area. Katsia continues watching him with careful eyes. She looks back to me, plastering on a, what seems like, a fake smile before waving me over.

I walk toward her. "Sorry, didn't mean to interrupt."

She brushes my words off casually. "Don't you worry about Damon. You hungry?" she asks, leading me into the large restaurant on the other side of the stairwell. I remember this place a little, but walking into it, it's like I've never been here before. Everything has changed and been upgraded. Chandeliers hang from the high ceilings, and all-glass walls line the entire room so you have a vast view of the woods anywhere you sit. We take a table on the other side of the room, tucked away enough for privacy.

She picks up the menu and smiles. "The fish is good. If you still like fish, that is."

Smiling, but not sure of the angle she's aiming for, I nod. "Love fish."

The waiter comes and takes our menus, and as she suspected, I ordered the salmon and steamed veggies. Pouring us both a glass of water, she looks at me. "So, how'd I know who you were?" she asks my unspoken question with a smile.

Nodding, I take a sip of water.

"Well, I've known your father for a while now."

"I sort of figured that. I remember this place a little," I answer, placing my glass down.

"How much do you remember?" She aims for casual, but I pick up the hitch in her tone, and though the question could be interpreted as one that has a double meaning, she says it with such etiquette that it doesn't have me second-guessing her intention. In fact, if I hadn't read some of The Book, and if I didn't know what I knew about my father and the Kings, her question and the way she said it would've slipped right past me.

"Not that much. I just remember him bringing me here as a kid. He would say it was his freedom. I just needed to get grounded a bit more."

"Oh?" That perks her attention. I once again caught her tone. As if she realizes she may have seemed a little too interested, she drops her smile a notch. "Well, I hope we can give that to you." The waiter comes, placing breadsticks and garlic bread on the center of the table, and I reach for one immediately, wanting something to occupy myself with that doesn't include being interrogated.

"Yeah." I shrug like any other teenager would. "I mean, just school and my friends. It's all a little much. My love for shooting only intensified as I got older, and I don't know," I mutter. "I guess I wanted a change of scenery and to get away for a bit."

She nods as if in understanding, but I can see a thousand questions hidden behind that calm and collected posture she's holding so well. "How long do you plan on staying?"

"Just the night. I have school on Monday, so I should get back tomorrow afternoon sometime."

She smiles in acknowledgment. "Well, I hope you enjoy your stay." The waiter comes back, placing both our dishes on the table and leaving. Picking up a fork, I slice into the salmon and place some in my mouth, it melting in an instant. Fighting the urge to moan in approval, I chew slowly while picking up my water.

"So you and my dad are good friends still?"

She pauses her chewing and swallows. "Well of course. I assume he told you to come here?"

"Actually, he doesn't know where I am right now. I just packed my car and left. I remembered this place and drove." She places her knife and fork down, dabbing the napkin over her mouth.

"So he doesn't know you're here?" she clarifies, though I already said that.

"He doesn't, no. Is that a problem?" Tilting my head, I watch her reaction.

Her face relaxes before she smiles. "No. No problem."

The bitch is good. Whatever she's playing at, she's good at it. Getting to her feet, she smiles, but not enough for it to reach her eyes. "Make yourself at home, Madison," she murmurs in a way that has chills breaking out down my spine. "I'm sure there's enough here to keep you occupied with your time." Then she leaves in a hurry.

Turning back to my food, I toss the salmon around on my plate, thinking over what the fuck just happened. Who is this woman and why is her name Katsia? Deciding the salmon is way too good to go to waste, I finish it all before washing it down with my water. Leaning into my chair, I think over my options—which, admittedly, isn't much. I could text Nate, or Bishop, and ask them about this new finding. But that would defeat my purpose of getting away, because I know they'll both be here in a flash to get me. Then again, they might be able to give me answers, ones I so desperately need because of this new discovery.

Exhaling, I pick up my glass and take a sip. No, I can't do that. For one, I have too much pride, and two... I have too much pride. I'll just have to figure this shit out on my own and hope I don't get killed in the process. Swallowing the cool water, movement catches my eye from the outside patio, and I look toward it. Noticing the outline of the valet's hat, I get to my feet, drop a couple of bills, and head toward the doors, which are open, displaying the cool woodsy night. There are tea lights outlining the wooden rails that frame the porch and a couple of rocking chairs that sit looking out toward the forest. Looking from left to right, I catch the boy's back as he turns and disappears around a corner. Gaining a bit of speed in my walk, I follow him. Just as I turn the corner, a hand comes to my mouth.

"Shhh," a voice whispers into my ear before I have a chance to scream bloody murder. "I—I not hurt you. Nod if I let go and you no scream."

I nod, feeling like I've dodged being killed enough times to be able to write a book about not getting killed. He releases and I spin around, my breath catching as I attempt to slow my erratic heartbeat.

"What the fuck?" I whisper-yell toward him. "Was that necessary?"

His response is instant. "Yes."

My mouth snaps closed as I study him closer. Close up, he looks a little older than me, now that I can see some imperfections on his face, but still young. His eyes are a warm chocolate brown, circled with long eyelashes.

"Who are you?" I ask, not fully comprehending what I should be asking, but I figured asking who he is was a good start, and it gives me a few seconds to gain my wits after his surprise.

"Damon. You're Madison Montgomery?"

"Damon?" I whisper, searching his face for clues.

"Yes," he responds through his broken English, "It's Latin. You are Madison?"

"No, I just like to pretend to be her, you know, because the perks are *awesome*." I can't help the sarcasm. His face remains poised, still, and unimpressed with my sense of humor. He's a little serious and a lot dry. "It's a joke," I deadpan after the silence gets awkward.

"A joke?" He tests out the word on his tongue. "What is joke mean?"

Tilting my head, I narrow my eyes. "What do you mean?" Something seems off about this kid, and it has fear creeping into my throat.

"*Non fueris locutus sum valde bonum…,*" he begins, and I suck in a breath in confusion. He notices my puzzlement and then corrects himself. "Sorry, I mean, I don't fluent English." Well, that makes a whole lot of sense, and makes this thing a lot more complicated.

"Okay," I answer slowly. "What is your language?" Maybe it's Spanish. My God, I hope it's Spanish, because I know a lot of that.

"Latin."

Fuck.

Rubbing my forehead, I shake my head. "I know jack shit about Latin. Okay." I look up to him, his face still the same, like a lost puppy bursting at the seams to speak but only knowing how to bark. I can almost feel the frustration radiating off of him.

"You," I point to him, "meet me in my room in fifteen minutes. It's not safe here."

He nods. "Number?"

"No, I'm on the Gold Level. I don't know what the name says on my door, but I'll put this…" I pull out a piece of paper from my pocket. "…on my door. Okay? Understand?"

He seems to think over my words and then nods. "Yes, I understand."

Jesus fucking Christ. Of course my only way of finding something out here only speaks fucking Latin.

There's that language again.

Nodding, I set off on my quest back to my room, slowly coming to the realization I may not be getting as much shooting done as I had initially hoped.

Pacing back and forth in my room, I wait as the time passes. It's been forty minutes since I told him to meet me back here, and I'm starting to get impatient. My phone ringing has merely settled into background music until I finally give up.

"Oh for fuck's sake!" Walking to the bedside table, I pick up my phone, sliding it open and bringing it to my ear. "What?"

"Don't fucking *what* me, Madison. Where the fuck are you?" Bishop growls down the phone.

"I'm away. I'll be back tomorrow night."

"That didn't answer my question."

"Well good thing I don't have to answer to any of your questions!" There's a knock on the door, a slight tap I could have missed had it been two seconds earlier with Bishop growling in my ear. Changing hands, I walk toward the door and pull it open, seeing Damon on the other side.

"I gotta go," I mumble into the phone.

"Sorry I'm late," Damon mutters, walking past me and into my room.

"Who the fuck is that?" Bishop shoots off in my ear.

"That is... I can't explain right now, so just wait until I get home."

"I swear to fucking—"

I hang up my phone and switch it off, having about enough of his bullshit. Turning around, I smile at Damon. "Sorry about that."

He sits on the chair across from my bed, his back straight and his hands placed rigidly on his thighs. His face stays the same, his eyes remaining on me as I slowly make my way to sit on the end of my bed. "So," I test out, not knowing what else to start with. "How are we going to do this if your language is Latin?" I ask myself the question more than him.

"You are in danger here. You must leave."

Well, that's a pretty good way to start. "I figured," I whisper, bringing my eyes back to his. "But why? And why are you helping me?"

He shakes his head, his eyes glassing over. "Knowledge not power. Knowledge in this world can be a weapon, or a reason." He stands from his chair and walks toward me, stopping just at the foot of the bed. A little close, but I don't feel uncomfortable about it. He takes my hand and I freeze slightly, unfamiliar with his presence, but again, not uncomfortable with it.

Pressing my hand to his chest, I look up at him, my heart pounding in my chest. "What is this?" I ask, shaking my head.

"You feel too?" he replies, so softly it almost takes my breath away. Being with emotionless assholes for way too long has me appreciating a man who has no problem with displaying his feelings. If that's what he's doing.

"Yes." Unable to lie, or deny it, and not wanting to, I stand to all my five foot three inches and crank my neck so I can see him more clearly. "Who are you?"

"I'm not good man."

I laugh. I don't mean to, but I do. "I know bad men, Damon. You are not one of them."

"Only you see light where others see dark, Madison."

Shaking my head, I pull my hand away. "Maybe. But I see dark too, Damon. And I don't see it on you."

"Because it's caged in my soul," he replies, taking a step back.

"Who are you?" I whisper again, searching his beautiful features. The angelic way he carries himself and the way he looks straight into me tells me he's deluded. He's not a bad man; there's no way this person standing in front of me right now is bad.

He sits back down, burying his face in his hands and shaking his head. "You..." he begins. "The Silver Swan."

I gulp, my blood turning slightly cold. "Yes."

He whips his head up to me and narrows his eyes slightly. Probably the most display of emotion I've seen on him as far as features go. "You… know? About yourself?" he asks again, his English choppy but enough for me to understand what he's trying to say or imply.

I nod. "Yes. I've known for some time now."

His face changes. "You must leave, Madison."

"No." I shake my head. "I'm stubborn. I have to know what this all means. I came here for clarity, to get my feet back on the ground, but I have a feeling that isn't happening now." I look at him as he watches me. I realize he probably has no idea what I just said, but I appreciate him listening anyway.

He gets up from his chair and walks toward the door. As he pulls it open, I think he's about to walk out when he widens it, checking down the hallway, but he looks back to me. "See?" He points to the cursive name on the door.

I look to it and nod. "Yeah? I don't know what that says."

He runs his index finger over the embossed lettering, every flick and curve that is inscribed into the door. He says one word. One word that sucks all the good out of my thoughts and replaces it with murky memories. "Venari."

CHAPTER 14

I shoot up off the bed and walk toward him, pulling him back inside the room before slamming the door, resting my head against it. "How the fuck do you know that name?"

He shakes his head. "I know"—his arms widen—"everything, Madison."

Locking my eyes on his, I nod. "Okay, it's settled." Pushing off the door, I go straight to my bag and start shoving all my belongings back inside. "You're coming home with me."

"No!" he answers, walking toward me and halting my arm. Not roughly, but enough for me to realize this boy is a lot stronger than what he looks.

Interesting.

"I can't leave," he continues, releasing my arm.

"Why not?" I zip up my bag anyway.

"Katsia... she...."

"Who the fuck is she?" I drop my tone an inch. "Seriously, Damon, I've read the title-less book. Her diary or suicide note or whatever!"

Damon's eyes turn hard and cold. *"Tacet a Mortuis."*

"Pardon?" I ask, confused with his Latin again.

"Tacet a Mortuis is the name of the book. In English is *Whispers from the Dead."*

"Oh." My eyebrows pull together in confusion. *The Book* is still easier to say than *Tacet a Mortuis*, but okay.

A look flashes over his face. "Where is that book?"

"Um, it's at my house. Why?" Dammit. I shouldn't be so quick with trusting people.

"You must take care of it. People—" He stops. "I must leave now."

"No!" I yell to his retreating back. "Please, you're my only hope in figuring out what the fuck this world all means!"

"I've said too much. I will be punished. I'm sorry, Madison." Then he walks out the door, the silence of his departure deafening.

Huffing out a breath, I sit on my bed.

What did he mean he would be punished? None of this makes fucking sense. Everything that should be simple is a fucking vortex of mind-fuckery, and the only person I can really rely on is myself. Deciding I won't be getting any sleep tonight, I pick up my packed bag and walk toward the door. If I need to escape quickly, I don't want to have to leave anything behind. Running down the hallway, I reach the elevator and press the down arrow a few hundred times before it dings open. Thanking my lucky stars it's empty, I walk in and press on the Ground key. Once I reach the lobby, I step out and look around, scanning the area to make sure Katsia isn't walking around before dashing out the front sliding doors, narrowly dodging the two reception boys at the desk. Why are they working throughout the night? I doubt anyone else would be checking in at this time.

The cold air hits me like a breath of fresh air when I see Damon. Quickly, I walk toward him. "Hey." I look over my shoulder out of paranoia.

"Madison, what are you doing?" He looks around, making sure no one is behind me.

"Look, I just need to put these into my car in case I need to get out of here fast."

Damon watches me closely before nodding and pulling my arm so I follow him to his valet desk. He unhooks my keys and hands them to me. "Parking spot fifteen. Madison, you must leave now."

I shake my head. "No. I need answers. I'm sick of waiting for people to tell me when they're ready. I need to know now."

"I can't." He shakes his head. "Madison. I have person very close to me who will be in danger if I tell anything."

I smile. "It's okay, Damon. I can figure it all out on my own."

"No." He shakes his head. "You not understand."

"I do," I reply softly, touching his arm. "I understand. I have people who I'd protect too."

He shakes his head again. "Person is you, Madison."

Wait.

I squeeze the keys in my hand. "Me?"

He nods. "Etiam."

"But you only just met me."

His eyes glare into mine, the stare so strong I almost flinch at the electricity that passes between us. "You think this first time we've met?"

A long stretch of silence passes through us as I look from one eye to the other. "I... I—" But even as I'm about to say it, I know I do remember. "I—yes? I don't know, Damon!" Feeling myself getting frustrated at all the mystery, I blow out a whoosh of air. "Tell me."

He grips my arm again and starts tugging me toward the parking lot. "Come."

I follow, noticing how his grip loosens as we get closer to my car, like he knows I'm safer the closer I get. "Open." He gestures toward the SUV, and I obey, beeping it unlocked as we both slip inside. I toss my bag to the back and shut my door, the enclosed space feeling safer to talk now.

"You gotta give me something here, Damon. What is Venari? What does that mean? I haven't heard that word since—"

"Lucan," he finishes for me, and I flinch, my heart crushing in my chest at someone else saying that name.

"How?" I ask, fighting the tears, fighting the memories. I feel the dark murky fog rising inside of me, slowly seeping into my inner peace, and threatening to shatter every single thing I worked hard for over the years.

Damon looks at me. "I'm Lost Boy."

"A what?" That had nothing to do with what I asked, but I know his English isn't very good, so I go with it.

"Lost Boy. How much book have you seen?" he asks, the words jumbled, but again, I understand what he's trying to ask.

"I'm up to 11 I think."

His jaw tenses. "You have far to go."

"Like, how far?" I know how thick the book is, but I was sort of hoping it wasn't that long.

"Final page 66/6."

"Well, that's poetic. The mark of the beast, just great."

Damon looks to me, his features frozen. "Sixty-six chapters, six pages in final."

"Did she mean to do that?" I ask.

"No," he shakes his head, "she not. You learn about Lost Boys soon. I am them."

"Okay." I look around the car. "But how do you know so much about me?"

"I just do. We all do. But I know the most."

"Why?" I ask, needing to know more information. "Why do you know the most? Why do I feel a connection to you I've never felt before? Why is it that I trust you even though I trust barely anyone?"

He looks at me. "You are my sister. I'm your twin."

CHAPTER 15

"What the fuck?" I shoot up in my chair, hitting my head on the top of the ceiling. "No... no, that makes no sense at all, because my mom and dad would have told me. And that makes no sense because that would mean you would be a King, but you're not. You're a lost boy, and you're here, living this..." I look outside. "...weird-as-fuck life, and my mom and dad are actually good people. I mean, I'd like to think they're good people and they would never leave you to be living this life and—*what the fuck*?" I repeat after my freak out. "Okay."

Breath in and out. Slow intakes of breath.

One.

Two.

Three.

I look at him, but his face is still the same. He's watching me in fascination, like I'm a foreign object he wants to learn about. "Don't do that," I murmur, suddenly realizing how uncomfortable it's making me now, because it's as though he can read my thoughts.

"I can." He nods.

"What?" I snap. I swear to God, if this turns all supernatural-y, I will demand that Dean Winchester roar into my life in his fucking muscle car and sweep me off my feet, or I'm done.

"I read what you think, but not because I read mind. Because I read your expressions. You need to control them."

"My expressions are fine the way they are."

"Fine?" he asks, confused with the word.

Oh, sweet mother of God. I came here to relax, and instead, I've been thrown into a pool of more questions. Finally calming my breathing enough to ponder his revelation, I turn in my seat. "If that's true, and you are my brother, my twin brother—"

"It's true. I do not lie, Madison."

"Let me finish." The way he cuts into my conversation has me thinking he's obviously my brother.

"Why? Why are you here? Why did Mom and Dad not tell me about you?"

"Those are questions I not answer. Not me. Not now. Another time. You must go."

"No!" I yell, just as his hand touches the door handle. "You can't drop a bomb like that and leave! What is this place?" I look up to the ranch and then back to him. His eyes are sad as he looks back to me.

"Hell."

"Who else lives here?" I ask, pressing with more questions and wanting him to bleed out more answers.

"Katsia and Lost Boys."

"Katsia is your boss?"

He shakes his head. "Katsia owns Lost Boys."

He goes to open the door again, and I stop him. "What? This is obviously not the same Katsia as the one in the book." Again, I remind myself about my earlier statement of Dean Winchester.

He looks back at me, confused. "Never mind. But is she good or is she bad?" Though I already know the answer to this, I just need clarification. I've been wrong in the past.

"*Malus*," he whispers, finally getting out of the car. I inch up off my seat, reaching for my phone in my back pocket, and switch it on. *Malus*? This fucking language is going to kill me one day. Typing *Malus* into google translate, the word *Bad* comes up in the little white box. Great, as suspected, she's bad. Are there any good people left in this world?

Leaning back in my chair, I think over what my options are right now. I could leave, tell the boys, and then come back and get Damon. But what if they already know I have a brother? What if they already know about this place? About Katsia? No, I've only got myself. Tilting my head, I look toward the ranch again, watching as Damon stands outside the main entrance, his hands behind his back and his eyes remaining forward. Such posture, poise, and discipline.

Starting the car, I put it into Drive and head toward the front entrance, where Damon is standing. He looks at my truck and then quickly looks behind him, checking to make sure no one is coming. Pulling open the passenger door, his jaw tenses. "What are you doing, Madison?"

"Get in."

"I can't—"

"Get the fuck in this car now, Damon. I'm dead serious. Nothing will happen to you." He looks over his shoulder and then looks back to me. Removing his hat, he tosses it across the sidewalk and gets into the passenger seat, slamming the door behind him. Skidding out of the ranch, I make my way down the long driveway, the darkness of the night soaking through all the trees. During the day, this driveway looks incredible, all bright colors and positive energy, but at night, it looks like it could be the driveway to Hades. The trees reach over the long road, casting shadows in the night. I look toward Damon, the dash lights illuminating his features a smidge.

"Are you okay?"

He shakes his head. "This is not good. Katsia—"

"Will do nothing," I snap, then relax a little. "Look, I don't know if you can understand fully what I'm saying, but I'm going to go with it anyway. I don't know who I can trust in this world or who I can't. I've trusted the wrong people before, and it won't be the last time, but I trust you."

He looks to me now, his eyes softening. "You trust me?"

"Yes," I respond, taking my eyes back to the road ahead and making a right turn onto the main highway. "I can't explain how or why, but I do. But know this," I murmur. "I won't let anything happen to you, Damon."

"I don't need your protection, Madison."

"I know. But Katsia won't do anything."

"You not understand," he whispers. "I'm the alpha Lost Boy." Even the word alpha sounds weird coming out of his mouth because he doesn't seem like that kind of guy to me. I haven't seen him in an alpha form, so I giggle a little.

"Madison," he shakes his head in disdain, "so much you don't know."

"Well, we have a forty-minute drive back."

"You never should come back, Madison."

I look at him then the road and then back to him. "What? Why?"

"He knew no take you there but did anyway."

"Who?"

He looks at me dead in the eye. "*Your* father."

The drive back was done in silence after Damon's little outburst of how I shouldn't be back in the Hamptons. I wanted to press to learn why, but I can't. Not yet. I can see how Damon will only share what he wants to share, and he's not the type of person that can be swayed.

We pull into our underground garage, and I look at the clock in the dash. Just past midnight, so everyone should be asleep, if my dad and Elena are even home. I don't see Nate's car anywhere, so I know he's not in for the night. Probably out terrorizing some poor girl. Pushing the button to close the garage door, I get out of the car and round to the passenger side. Damon follows, shutting the door behind him.

"Come on. You can sleep in my room until I figure some stuff out."

"I can't stay." He shakes his head.

"The fuck you can't." I take his arm, and he tenses at my touch, yanking away from me.

"Sorry," he mutters when he sees the shock on my face.

"It's okay. So you don't like being touched. That's probably the least of the weird thing I've come across as far as phobias go." Beeping the car, I make my way toward the door with Damon following closely behind me.

"It's not a phobia," he confesses, just as we make our way up the stairs to the main living area.

I turn over my shoulder a little. "It's okay. You don't have to talk about it."

He pauses, his eyes searching my face before he nods. "Thank you."

I smile softly, and then round the stairs, taking the first step. "I'll get some of Nate's clothes for you. He won't mind, and even if he did, he could eat a fat...." I notice he's not following me anymore and turn around, finding him still on the first step and looking to the ground like he's trying to add something up in his head. "Damon?"

"Nate?" he whispers. "Nate?" he repeats, searching the ground once more.

"Yes?" I take a tentative step back down. "Nate Riverside?"

Damon stills. "Not Riverside."

Huh? I swear this is too much. "We can finish all these conversations tomorrow. Come on, let's get some sleep." I reach my hand out to him and he takes it, letting me lead him up the stairs and into my room. As soon as he's inside, he pauses, looking around.

"No pink?"

I shake my head. "Not a pink girl."

Damon looks like he wants to giggle, but doesn't. In fact, I don't recall ever seeing him smile, much less giggle. "Not surprising."

I tilt my head. "I'll set you up on the floor. I'll just go and get something for you to wear from Nate's room." Though Nate is noticeably larger than Damon, I'm pretty sure he can make it work until I take him to get new clothes.

Slipping into my bathroom, I open Nate's door, the dark room a little creepy. Hitting the light, I walk straight to Nate's closet.

"The fuck are you doing, sis?"

"Shit!" I scream, spinning around and coming face-to-face with Nate. Damon comes barging through the door, his eyes feral and his stance stiff. "It's okay!" I tell Damon, noticing how he looks about ready to rip someone's head off.

He isn't looking like the Damon I've just met and spent a bit of time with.

"And who the fuck are you?" Nate quips, getting out of bed with his Calvin Klein briefs on.

"Nate, get back into bed."

"No," he says, narrowing his eyes on Damon. "I *know* you."

"No, you don't," I brush him off while praying he doesn't so I can leave this conversation until tomorrow. I'm hungry, tired, and I didn't get the rest I wanted and needed, so I'm about ready to jump off the cliff of "calm and collected" and dive straight into the ocean of "lost my shit" with five-foot swells of "I'll kill you all."

"Yes," Nate continues, slowly stepping closer and closer to Damon. "You..." Something clicks in his head, and he suddenly launches toward Damon, his fist flying toward his face.

"Nate!" I scream, throwing myself toward the two of them, but latching onto Nate's back, my arms connecting around his throat. Damon swerves, dodging his punch calmly, his face not showing any distress. He looks almost disinterested—bored.

Nate falls to the ground with me on top of him.

"What the fuck?" I slap Nate on the back. "Dick!"

Nate flips me on my ass and gets to his feet, pointing down at me. "Stay the fuck there." Then he turns to Damon. "*I fucking know you.*"

I get to my feet. "Leave him alone."

Damon looks to Nate. "I know you do."

"Shut up, Damon!" I snap. He needs to shut his mouth before he says something stupid. Hopefully, he'll say it in Latin.

Nate tilts his head. "*Et tu puer vetustus amissus....*"

Well, there goes that theory.

"You speak fucking Latin?" I yell toward Nate, but he throws his hand up, halting me. Getting my phone out of my pocket, I quickly pull up the translate app, so I can type at least one word I catch into the program. I snap my mouth closed, sensing the tense energy in the room. It's almost like two devils have come head-to-head, and one of them is going down. It's eerie, creepy, and goose bumps break out over my spine at just how seriously terrifying this is.

Damon's stance changes. The air shifts as his shoulders square, his eyes break into black marbles, and his lip curls.

I step back, realizing how little I know about him. His entire being just morphed in front of my very eyes. No longer is he the quiet valet boy who speaks hardly any English. Now, I'm seeing him—as he put it—the Alpha Lost boy.

"Pueri et im amissa."

Lost Boy.

Okay, so Nate knows about them. Or something was said about the Lost Boys. Of fucking course he does.

"Well this is all great and everything, but I'm tired—"

"Madison! Shut up!" Nate snaps at me.

He turns back toward Damon, stepping closer. My fingers twitch, wanting to get between them to stop any other altercation from happening. *"Non potes habere eam,"* Nate seethes, his lip curled and his steps calculated. Like a hungry tiger, waiting to take its kill on his prey.

Can't have her.

Okay, what the fuck?

"Have me?" I ask, looking up from my phone. "What are you two actually fuckin—"

The door bangs open, revealing Bishop standing there, his dark hoodie over his head, in his loose, torn jeans, and with his combat boots on his feet. His eyes scan over me first before going to Nate and Damon.

"Are you kidding me?" I yell, quickly making my way toward Damon.

Nate is lethal; he could snap someone's neck with his bare hands and not blink, but Bishop? Bishop is a different level entirely. He'd not only snap your neck; he'd dissect your body piece-by-piece and send each of your organs to a member of your family.

"Madison," Bishop growls. It's so low, it catches my breath. I look toward him, but press my back against Damon. Bishop's eyes are dark, almost black, his head down slightly, his jaw tense, and his lip curled in disgust. He doesn't flinch. All his focus is solely on Damon. "Get the fuck out of my way."

"No!" I snap. "Damon isn't like the others, whatever they're like. I wouldn't know, because I don't speak motherfucking Latin!" I'm losing my shit a bit, but I'm sick of being the quiet voice in the house.

"Madison. Get the fuck out of the way before I fucking move you myself."

"Madison," Damon says gently from behind me, and I shiver at the cool calmness of his voice. It's petrifying, but peaceful. I know he won't hurt me, so I trust him.

"Shh," I hush him over my shoulder before looking back to both Nate and Bishop.

"Now both of you are going to let me finish speaking." I look between the two of them. "Damon left Katsia—and yes, I know about Katsia, and before you both fly off the handle, I drove to the ranch, not knowing what it was, only remembering what is was like there as a kid."

Forget.

I take a big gulp of air. "I needed a fucking break from you guys, so I drove to the only place I remember my dad taking me as a kid—that ranch. It wasn't until I got there and met Damon and then Katsia..." I shake my head, still in shock from that revelation. "...that I realized the place was something else entirely. I look toward Bishop, his eyes still on Damon like he's ready to feast on him for dessert.

"Bishop?" I narrow my eyes. "Did you guys know he's my brother? My twin?"

Bishop's focus snaps straight to me before going back to Damon. "*Et nuntiatum est illi?*"

"Stop fucking talking in Latin!" I yell, annoyed with everyone even though the way the syllables roll off Bishop's tongue has my lady bits tingling. "Did you both know?" I repeat, looking toward Bishop and Nate.

"Yes," Bishop answers, dropping his hoodie to sit around his neck. He cranks his shoulders, rolling them out before looking back to Damon. "But that doesn't mean shit. You shouldn't trust him."

"Why?" I scoff. "Like I shouldn't have trusted you?"

His mouth snaps closed. "That's different."

I roll my eyes and look back to Damon. "Go into my room. I'm okay. I'll handle it."

Damon pauses then nods. "Okay." He turns and walks back to my room, and I shut Nate's door, spinning around to look at both boys. "The fuck is your problem?"

"Madison," Nate says, his tone empty of any humor. This is Nate's serious voice, and usually I take it seriously, but they need to trust *me* now.

"No, Nate. I trust him. He's not going to hurt me."

Nate steps toward me, but Bishop's hand comes up to his shoulder, stopping him. He looks toward Bishop, and Bishop shakes his head. "I'll handle this."

I swallow.

Bishop walks toward me, his finger hooking under my chin to nudge my head up. He looks down, towering over me. "First thing I'm going to say is that when I say you don't trust someone, Madison, I usually mean you don't *fucking* trust someone. Second thing? Do you know what the Lost Boys' job is, Madison? What their *main* job is? What Katsia is? Who she is?" His fingers spread over my cheeks as he pushes me backward until I hit the wall behind me. He drops his tone, his hand squeezing my cheeks so tightly my lips pucker. "I'm so fucking angry at you, Kitty. I don't know whether I should *fuck* you or *kill* you or *both*," he whispers angrily, his lip curled and his breath falling over mine. My heart pounds in my chest.

Oh, God. I've really pissed him off. Usually, I enjoy this, but not when I see the anger lingering in his eyes. That anger is a caged beast, seconds away from breaking free.

"Of course I don't know, Bishop." I nudge my head, trying to get my face out of his grip, but he doesn't budge. Instead, he steps in between my legs and pins my waist to the wall with his, feeling his cock push into my stomach.

Narrowing my eyes, I look down to his perfect lips. "You don't tell me shit."

His jaw tenses, and then a smirk licks the corner of his mouth. But it's not a nice smirk. This is Bishop's other smirk. The one I saw when he slit Ally's throat. Fear whistles through my bones, just lightly. Enough to make me brace myself for what's to come.

He brings his mouth to my ear. "When I fucking say don't trust someone, Madison. You don't trust them."

"What do they do?" I ask, closing my eyes.

Please don't say what I think you're going to say.

"Lost Boys?" Nate grins, walking up behind Bishop. "Who do you think takes care of the little Swans, Madison?"

"Take care?" My eyebrows furrow. I look to Nate, his grin not changing. My stomach curls in disgust as realization sinks into my thought process. "Oh my God."

Bishop's hand moves from my face to my throat, and he squeezes slowly. "Gotta say, this is getting my dick hard like nothing. It's a dangerous thing you have me feeling, Kitty.

The angrier you make me, the more I want to fuck you until you're so fucking bruised that you feel the wrath of my anger for weeks after."

"But... but he won't hurt me." I ignore his sick innuendo.

"Oh?" Nate scoffs, walking to the little bar fridge he has in the corner of his room, pulling out a bottled water. He looks to me in disbelief. "What? Because you're fucking blood? That doesn't mean shit, Madison. He's not a good person. He is probably here to obtain you—ever think of that?" Nate tosses the bottle onto his bed and walks back toward Bishop—who hasn't released my throat—and me.

"What about Katsia?" I ask. "Who the fuck is she and what does she play in this game? She's obviously the descendant of the Katsia in *The Book*—sorry," I correct myself, "*Tacet de Mortues*." In a flash, Bishop squeezes tight and slams me up against the wall again. "Who the fuck told you that?"

"What?" I wheeze out. "Let go, Bishop!"

He loosens his grip, but when I look into his eyes, I see it. That same caged beast. This is the other side to Bishop I'm talking with right now, and I'm not sure I like it anymore.

"Bro." Nate notices Bishop's shift. "Step back."

"Fuck off, Nate."

Nate looks to me and then to Bishop, knowing he can't say anything. Bishop loosens his grip and I nod at Nate, signaling he's released it.

I stretch my neck. "Do that again, and I'll knee you in the nuts, grab my .45, and shoot your fucking hand clean off."

Bishop smirks, his tongue running over his bottom lip. "You do that..." His eyes dance in mischief—black magic kind of mischief. "...and I'll wash your hair with my blood while you choke on my dick."

"More like I'll bite it off," I mutter, challenging the devil himself.

"Naw, baby. You and I both know you love it too much."

"Fuck you. I'll cut it off and make you watch as I fuck—"

"As excited as I am about this very disturbing and very sick dirty talk—" Nate looks between Bishop and me. "—seriously, y'all need help—we have a *very* serious matter that is currently sitting in the next room."

I shove Bishop, and he steps up to me again in challenge, his chest brushing against mine, bringing my nipples to life. Fuck. Why do both our hormones have to feed on hate? I'm fucked.

I bring my palm to Bishop's chest, narrowing my eyes at him. "Anyway." I look toward Nate. "Okay, so what does Katsia play in this? In the book, she was good."

"*She,* being the original, yes," Nate murmurs, taking a seat on the end of his bed. "But this one... no."

"Who is she? This one, I mean."

"In short," Bishop says, finally getting out of my bubble and grabbing the water bottle Nate tossed onto the bed. "She's—realistically speaking—on our side. She's not a part of The Kings, but Katsia's family have played this role for generations. The one in the book, she started the original Lost Boys."

"The original Lost Boys? But wouldn't that mean she agreed to get rid of the Silver Swans?" I ask, confused. "That makes no sense, because she was always... not like that."

"No," Nate interferes. "That wasn't the original purpose for the Lost Boys."

"What was?" I ask them both.

"How far are you into the book?" Nate asks, looking up at me from under hooded eyes.

"11. Why can't you guys just tell me? Fuck."

"No," Bishop shakes his head, "it's important you read it. We all had to."

"What?" I scoff, sliding down the wall and taking a seat on the hard floor. "You guys all read it?"

They both nod. "After initiation, that was what we had to do."

"That's fucked up," I whisper, looking off into the distance. "When did my life get so messed up? It's always been messed up, but the more I discover about it, the more questions I have." I look back to both of them. "Will this ever be over?"

They look back at me. "No."

"Well, thanks," I mutter dryly. "Can we just… give Damon a chance? What if he really is on my side, huh? And you guys knock him off when he really could have been helpful!"

"Not taking the chance," Bishop says instantly.

"I wasn't asking you, so sh—"

"Watch your fucking mouth. Everything that has to do with the Kings, Madison, goes through me. Everything to do with you also happens to go through me. So whether you like it or not, *you* go through me. So you may as well do it on your hands and knees with your ass in the air like a good little kitty," he hisses through a smug grin.

"The kitty has claws, so I'd watch it," Nate warns.

Having about enough of Bishop's smartass mouth, I tilt my head. "I don't remember her scratching last night." I smirk at Nate, and he looks back to me, his eyes wide, slowly shaking his head. He brings his hand up to his throat, making a cutting motion for me to stop. Too late, I've committed. Swinging my eyes back to Bishop, his jaw now clenched. "Oh no,"—it's my turn to smirk now—"if I remember correctly…" I pretend to look up to the ceiling, thinking about what I'm going to say next. "…there was a shower… a towel…. Wait!" I throw my hand up and chuckle. "No," I laugh forcefully, looking back to Bishop, my grin wide and my mouth slightly open. "That's right. There was no towel. Just a whole lot of… grinding… kissing… and—"

"Now, bruh, I can explain." Nate quickly gets to his feet, stepping backward with his hands up. "That was not how…." Nate looks to me, his stare evil. "Why you have to open your fucking mouth?" he grounds through gritted teeth.

I smirk.

Nate looks back to Bishop, who is looking directly at Nate with so much hate it makes what he was giving Damon seem like child's play.

Rolling my eyes, because I actually love Nate and don't want to plan his funeral—just yet—I interrupt. "Calm down, Bishop. It was a hard night, and you can't say shit."

"Oh really?" Bishop looks to me. "Because I don't remember the last time I was sucking face with another girl since you, Mads, so fill me in here. Is that what I need to do? Start fucking around so you fucking get where I'm coming from?"

"Bishop," I stand to my feet, "you're being ridiculous. We're not together. Never have been! You're the one who said all that 'no labels' bullshit at the lake."

"Didn't know I had to outline 'don't be a slut,' Madison."

"I'm not a fucking slut!" I yell. "I haven't slept with anyone but you, so fuck you!"

Bishop shakes his head. "Nah, you just like making guys think they can fuck you."

"Fuck—"

"Enough." Damon walks in, shoving his hands into his pockets, still wearing the pants he wore earlier, which reminds me why I'm actually in this room. I turn back to the closet and flick the light on, pulling Nate's clothes out and tossing them over my shoulder.

"What are you doing?" Nate asks, coming toward me. I fight down the tears that threaten to surface. Truthfully, I had no idea Bishop thought of me in that way. I knew he cared, but not so much that he's willing to use it as a weapon during an argument. My heart feels like it's been shanked with a blunt steak knife and then ripped up to my throat.

Swallowing my emotions, I swipe the stray tears that fell off my cheeks. Fucker made me cry, but I probably asked for it. When you fall for the devil, make sure you don't land face-down with his horns stabbed through your heart. "I'm getting something for Damon to wear."

I feel Nate crouch down beside me, leaning over my shoulder. "Hey—"

"Leave me alone," I whisper, grabbing some sweatpants and a plain white shirt. Admittedly, Nate doesn't have much else aside from assorted ripped jeans and tees.

"No, fuck that. What's wrong? Bishop?" he whispers.

"Everything, Nate. None of this shit makes any sense to me. I feel like I'm slowly losing my mind."

Nate chuckles, and I don't know how, but it takes a little dark smoke out of my feels. "We've all lost our mind, baby, but that's how we all found each other. We're all lost, but we're all lost on the same road."

I look to him; Nate actually making sense. I giggle, sniffling. "There are not a lot of times you've made a hell of a lot of sense, Riverside. But you did just then."

"We're pirates, baby. It's what we do. Now get your bad self up, take whatever you want, but make sure that fucker doesn't ruin any of my clo—For the record," he interrupts himself, "I still don't trust him. But I'm going to trust you, on one condition."

I nod, gripping onto the clothing and internally thanking whoever is listening that he has agreed. I mean, I would have done it anyway, but having Nate agree just means I get to go make something to eat before the sun comes up.

"Our doors are to stay open. He sleeps on the floor, and later today, he is to sit down and tell us all he can."

I look over Nate's shoulder at Damon, who is watching Bishop closely. Bishop, who hasn't taken his eyes off me. I ignore him, looking back to Nate, and nod. "Deal."

Nate gets to his feet, holding his hand out to me and helping me up. "Grilled cheese? I can hear your stomach from here."

I exhale, leaning my head on his shoulder, feeling every muscle loosen. "Yes. Fucking God, yes."

Walking out of the closet, I toss Damon the clothes. "Go and get changed. I'll bring you something to eat."

He smiles, taking the clothes and disappearing back into my room. I look at the alarm clock Nate keeps beside his bed, noting the time is 2:00 a.m. Damn, we were really talking that long? When my eyes connect with Bishop's, I mutter, "I've lost my appetite."

Nate pulls me into him. "Naw, don't mind him." He sends Bishop a wink. "He just doesn't like others playing with his toys."

"I'm not his toy."

"I'm right here," Bishop grunts.

"Really?" I say sarcastically. "Because I don't see you."

"Okay, Kitty," Nate chuckles, tucking me under his arm. "You're not you when you're hungry. Let's go."

CHAPTER 16

"Okay, that's it," Tatum announces, trying to tear into her packet of crackers. "I want to know 100 percent of what is going on. It's not fair!" she whines.

"Don't do that." I rub my temples, still tired after the shit for sleep I got on Saturday night. "I seriously have so much going on right now."

"I know," Tatum whispers, giving up on trying to tear open her pack of carbs. "Remember? I was there."

"There's more. God." I sit back. "There's so much more, but I don't even know where to start and what to tell you because I already know you're going to have more questions. Questions I don't know the answers to." I exhale and open my mouth, just about to continue, when I see the Kings walk into the cafeteria out the corner of my eye. Tatum picks up her unopened crackers again when she sees them all walk in. "Now I *need* carbs."

Bishop takes a seat beside me, and Nate goes on the other side as the rest of the boys squeeze in next to Tatum and Bishop.

"I don't remember calling you over," I snark.

"No need." Nate grins, biting into his apple.

Rolling my eyes, I look back at Tatum to see her staring at something over my shoulder. Her mouth is agape, cracker in the midair.

I inch my head over my shoulder to see what she's looking at when my mouth slams closed. "Excuse me," I murmur, getting off my seat and making my way toward Damon. He's standing there in some of Nate's clothes—loose jeans, black tee, and white high-top sneakers. It's all Nate, since I still haven't found time to get Damon his own.

"What are you doing here?" I ask, watching as everyone stares at him.

What on earth are they staring at? I know he's funny-looking, but now people are just being rude. Or maybe I just think he's funny-looking because he's my brother. I wouldn't know.

"I need to talk to you."

"Talk."

He takes my arm and pulls me back through the girls hallway. Waiting for a couple of people to walk past, his voice drops. "Katsia wants to meet with me."

"What? How do you know?" I whisper back, smiling to a girl who is in my English class as she passes by, looking at us suspiciously.

"Obviously because I've left. Have you read any more of the book?" he asks urgently.

"No, I haven't found time, and why does she want to meet with you?"

"Find time to read. Because she need me." He pushes off the wall and walks back down the hallway then out the front doors.

"Well goodbye to you too!" I yell toward him as the doors slam shut.

Walking back into the cafeteria, I head to my chair, pulling it out and taking a seat.

"What'd he want?" Bishop inquires beside me.

I ignore him.

"Who is he?" Tatum asks, her eyes searching him out.

"My brother and he's gone."

Her attention snaps to me. "What? How?" She lowers her voice. "Madison...?"

"As I said earlier," I reply, tossing my salad around with my fork, "I have a lot to tell you."

"You're not telling her shit," Bishop snaps, looking at me.

I finally acknowledge him. He's so close—too close to me—that I can almost feel his breath fall over my lips. "And I said you can't tell me what the fuck to do, Bishop."

He chuckles, tossing a carrot in his mouth—*my* carrot. "Oh, Madison. You have no idea the kind of things that tone does to me."

I'm just about to open my mouth to say something else, when Nate interrupts, "Anyway!" He looks between both of us, his eyes wide like he's scolding a couple of toddlers. "Tatum is fine, B. She knows almost everything else that has happened."

"Not everything," I mutter under my breath.

Tatum cuts her glare to me. "Oh? What else don't I know? Hmm?"

Pushing my chair back, I get to my feet, picking up my tray. "I'm done. I'll see you later." Walking out the atrium doors, I make my way toward PE. I'm halfway down the corridor when I decide I don't want to even be at school right now. Turning around, I start heading to the elevator that leads down to the student parking lot when a thought pops into my head. I haven't seen Miss Winters since I've been back.

Turning back around again, I jog toward the library, pushing open the large wooden doors. The smell of dusty old books hits me, and I inhale, relishing in the familiar scent. It has to be my favorite aroma, aside from whatever Bishop wears. Usually. Not right now, because right now I hate him. Bypassing the two quiet students who are studying, I make my way to the front desk.

"Hey!" I smile down at the blonde.

The girl raises her face, and my smile falls. "You're not Miss Winters." I look around. "Where is she?"

"She left about two months ago."

"Left?" I scoff. "Left where?" She can't leave.

"Left, as in doesn't work here anymore, as in I don't know where she is."

I step backward and dash for the doors. I don't know why, but that doesn't sit right with me. Why would Miss Winters leave? Two months ago? That was around when I left. No. She wouldn't leave, and if she did, where has she gone? Pushing my hair out of my face, I jog back to the elevator, pressing the Down button more than what is necessary. The doors finally ding open, and I step inside, pounding on the SP button. The doors close and the elevator takes me down to my car as I think over all the possibilities of where she could be.

Truthfully, I know nothing about her really, but if she was going to leave, I feel like she would have told me the day I got the number from her. Or at the very least hinted. Something's wrong. The doors ding open and I rush to my truck, beeping it unlocked. Opening the door, I'm just about to slide in when something goes over my head, cutting out my vision, and a hand slams over my mouth before picking me up. I scream muffled cries, kicking and turning as he tosses me into what I'm guessing is a van. I go to rip off the... whatever the fuck it is that's over my head, when another pair of hands grab me from behind, wrapping cable ties around my wrists and binding them together.

"Who the fuck are you?" I yell out. I smell her before she speaks though. That rich, unique lemon, rosey-ish scent of Chanel No. 5.

"I just want to talk, Madison."

"Talk?" I laugh. "You fucking kidnap me to talk?" I end my sentence with a screech.

"Take the mask off her please." In an instant, I'm met with Katsia sitting opposite me and looking extremely out of place in her two-piece suit, with two armed men beside her, both wearing ski masks, as well as the guy sitting next to me.

"What do you want to talk about?" I seethe, pissed off. "For the record, I'm usually a pretty easy girl. You can just be like 'Oh, hey, girl! Can we chat?' and I'd be like 'Yeah, for sure, girl! Let's do coffee!'" I act the scene out with bound hand signals and high-pitched tones. My face turns flat when I finish. "You don't need to fucking kidnap me."

She smiles, but it doesn't reach her eyes. I don't think it ever probably has. Unless she's like, having dinner with the devil. Bet the bitch smiles then. "You're funny."

"Thanks," I say sarcastically. "My friends wouldn't agree with you."

"Maybe you need new friends," she retorts, one eyebrow cocked.

"No." I shake my head, seeing where she's going with this conversation. "It's hard enough to find one person who likes me, much less a gang."

She tilts her head, studying me closely. I cringe inwardly at how she regards me with her stare. "What makes you think they do?"

"They do—what?" I ask, matching her stare, scanning over her attire the exact way as she does mine.

She snorts, as if she knows exactly why I did that. "The apple doesn't fall there," she mutters under her breath. I only just catch it.

"What?"

"Another time," she replies.

"No, you were—"

"Another time," she cuts me off, but her smile remains.

This bitch is chilly.

"But tell me," she continues, reaching forward to take a glass of wine from a little table that's set up between the two seats that are facing each other. "What makes you think they actually like you?"

"Well, I don't know. They put up with me."

"That's a terrible answer, Madison." She giggles from behind the rim of her glass. "People put up with a lot of things. Wives, husbands, headaches. Under all that though, is that a way to live? To just put up with someone? No," she shakes her head, taking a sip, "and for the record, you're wrong."

"Wrong about what?"

"Well, that's the kicker." She smirks, her eyes lighting up like a Christmas tree. Oh, this bitch is crazy. "All of it."

"Are you going to fill me in or am I going to be left guessing?" I don't trust her. At all. But am I open to hearing what she has to say? Yes.

"Well, let's start with your brother."

"Let's," I reply, overly excited and a little sarcastic.

She looks at me for a second too long before her eye twitches. "How much do you know about him?"

"Only parts. What he's told me, and what Bishop and Nate have sort of told me."

She laughs. "Mmmm, those boys. I swear, every generation, it happens."

"What?" The confusion must show on my face, because she giggles again. "Oh, Madison. Tell me," she leans forward, "why do you think your father brought you back to The Hamptons?"

That's the question I haven't been able to figure out yet. Why would he bring me back here if he knew it was dangerous for me? "I don't know," I answer honestly. I look directly into her eyes. "Do you?"

She leans back, taking a sip of her wine, all while keeping her eyes locked on mine. "Yes."

"Then will you enlighten me?" I ask her, and she pauses again, looking over my features like she's studying every inch of my face. As if she's fascinated by me.

She leans back. "No. Too soon."

"Too soon?" I scoff. "Are you kidding me? Do you know how much shit I've been through?"

"Oh," she laughs. "I know."

"Oh, right." I snort sarcastically. "Because you own the Lost Boys and have for generations. I get it." I roll my eyes for added effect. "Why did you kidnap me anyway?"

"Because I want Damon back."

"Well, by all means, ask him yourself."

She looks at me like I'm stupid. "He won't."

"I wonder why that is."

"Listen to me very carefully, Madison. Damon is a tricky soul. He may be your brother, your twin brother, but he was born..." She looks around, searching for the correct word. "...different."

"Different—how?" I ask, narrowing my eyes. "And why do you say it like you care?"

She smirks. "I care because Damon is very good at what he does. I care because what Damon does is needed. And I care because Damon needs it too, and if Damon doesn't get what he needs, there will be a massacre."

"Damon wouldn't hurt a soul."

She chokes on her drink, gripping her throat. "You sweet, deluded child." She leans forward, placing her wine back on the small table. "Damon wouldn't willingly hurt you— no. But, honey, what do you think his name means?"

"I don't know. It's a common boys name."

She shakes her head. "No, the correct spelling of his name is D-A-E-M-O-N, Latin for Son of Satan." I clench my jaw, attempting to fight back any words that are egging to spill out of my gob.

"But I saw how his name was spelled on his shirt. It was spelled D-A-M-O-N."

She rolls her eyes. "His name is bad for business. We had to… citizenize it."

His name was bad for business? Who even says shit like that? "I still don't understand. Daemon is the sweetest guy I know. I was draw—"

She waves her hands around. "Honey, he's not only your brother, but he's your twin. You both felt that—" She connects her hands together. "—pull. But he should never have left. He's been trained by the best of the best. He was supposed to walk away."

"But he didn't," I whisper.

"No," she replies, an eye twitching again. "He didn't. He defied the natural order. He will be punished, but the longer he stays, the worse his punishment will be."

"Well, fuck you then. I would never hand him to you willingly, but even more so now."

She does that smile thing again. "Look, I don't expect you to understand." The van stops and I look out my window to see we're back at the school. My truck door is still open. "Just remember this one thing, Madison." She searches my eyes and I meet hers. "He's not a good man. He's the worst of the worst. You wanna know why?" she asks, tilting her head.

"Why?"

"Because he feels nothing. No remorse, no love, no nothing. Daemon is void of natural human emotions. He does not feel physical pain, nor emotional pain. He was born this way. Then he was trained on top of that. He's a very rare human, but he also suffers from the shadows."

"Like congenital insensitivity to pain?" I ask, still stuck on her first revelation.

She nods, leaning back. "Yes. One in a million get it. It's genetic, you know?" She smirks. "But I know it hasn't run through you."

"His emotional lack of feeling though, is there a condition for that?"

"There are lots of conditions that could trigger it, and truthfully speaking, Daemon probably has all of them." She pauses as if to think over how much she should actually disclose. "Ask him about the shadows, Madison, and then call me. I'm sure you will want to talk." She hands me a card. I look down and read over the gold cardboard with the name Katsia embossed in white and a simple phone number underneath.

The man who is sitting beside me, leans forward, cutting the cable ties off from around my wrist. He slides open the door, and I get out, turning to face her one last time. "Why do you think he can't feel emotions?"

"Because I've seen it, and you will too."

The door closes, and the van takes off in a whoosh, like it wasn't there trying to tear into my life a second ago. Picking my bag up from the ground, I throw it into the truck and get into the driver seat, pushing Start. I spin around in my seat quickly when an eerie chill, a chill as if someone is watching me, creeps up my spine, but I'm met with empty seats.

"I'm losing my mind." I put the car in reverse and drive the fuck out of there.

Mondays.

CHAPTER 17

I'm making a sandwich in the kitchen when "Tequila Sunrise" by Cypress Hill comes blaring through the sound dock. I roll my eyes and pull out my phone, scrolling through my Spotify playlist. Fucking Nate, adding his music to my song list. I shove my phone back into my pocket, giving up and going back to my sandwich. Slamming ham onto my bread, I squirt on some mayonnaise and then add tomatoes, relish, and cheese. The catchy beat catches me off guard, and I start bobbing my head to the beat. I judged a little too soon; this song is actually pretty good.

Taking a massive bite out of my sandwich, my eyes come up to the entry to the kitchen when I see Nate, Bishop, Cash, Brantley, and Hunter standing there watching me. It used to be intimidating, having them in my personal space almost all the time—although this isn't all of the Kings. But now it hardly itches on my skin.

"What?" I ask, chewing my sandwich.

Bishop shakes his head. "Nothing. Where's your brother?"

"Upstairs." I swallow. I haven't had a chance to talk to Daemon about the shadows. Truthfully, I'm a little scared. Because once I ask him, there's no going back. What if his answer changes my view on him? I don't want that. There're many things I want answers to in my life, many things I would sacrifice to get those answers, but Daemon isn't one of them. I feel a strong sense of overprotectiveness when it comes to him, which makes me think… "Am I the younger twin or is he?" Thinking out loud always helps.

Brantley and Cash walk into the kitchen, taking a seat on the bar stools. "You're the older one," Cash answers when he sees no one else is.

"Knew it." I grin, taking another bite.

"Why?" Bishop asks, leaning against the wall.

"Just wondering."

"You're wondering why you feel so protective of him." Bishop takes the words out of my thoughts, pushing off the wall and coming into the kitchen. He pulls open the fridge and takes out a water, twisting the cap off. "He's dangerous, Madison."

I roll my eyes. "If you truly believe that, then why would you let him around me?"

"Well we tried to stop that," Nate interjects. "But good fucking job we did."

"And I said he's dangerous," Bishop finishes. "I didn't say he was dangerous to *you*."

"But the first night you were here, you didn't like him. You almost wanted to kill him."

Bishop laughs, placing the water on the counter. "Almost? There's no such thing as almost when it comes to me, Madison. I don't make mistakes; I make moves. If I do something, you bet your ass I thought about every single thing that had to do with it. I'm not unhinged. I'm calculated. I know exactly what I'm doing when I'm doing it, and you wanna know why that makes me the worst kind of monster?" he asks, though he really doesn't want me to answer, so I stay silent—for once. "Because I've thought about the act over and over again in my head, and every time I asked myself if it was the right thing to do?" He inches closer to me, shoving his hands into his pockets. "It's always a yes. So no, Madison." He leans against the counter. "I don't 'almost' kill anyone. If I want them dead, they will be dead. No matter what."

The word *dead* coming out so close to Daemon's name makes my stomach churn. I place my sandwich down, suddenly losing my appetite.

"Prince Charming obviously." I brush Bishop off.

Brantley laughs. "That's cute. But no, more like a dark knight."

My stomach growls, and I pick up my sandwich again, biting into it. "If you could refrain from hurting my brother, that'd be great."

Bishop looks at me, his eyes sinking into mine. "If he doesn't hurt you—which I don't *think* he will—then deal."

Chewing softly, the front door opens and Elena and my dad walk down the hallway, both pausing when they see the gathering in the kitchen.

"Madison, Nate," my dad greets.

My back straightens as I use the back of my hand to swipe at my mouth. "Dad! Hey!" I make my way toward him. When I pull him in for a hug, he tenses. "Everything okay?" My dad never tenses with me. Ever. He has always been my rock and always told me what was going on, except when it came to the Kings.

He forces a smile. "Everything is fine."

I look to Elena and she gazes back at me, totally oblivious to what just passed between my dad and me. "Hi, Madi. How was your weekend?" She looks up to Nate. "Come and greet your mother, please." Nate pushes off the wall.

"Of course, Ma." He pulls her in for a bear hug, wrapping one arm around her waist and lifting her off the floor effortlessly. He kisses her on the cheek. "Missed you."

She pulls back, pinching his cheeks. "You're doing just fine, boy. Taking good care of your sister I see." She looks back to me.

"Speaking of," I say to Dad. "Can we talk?"

"What have you done?" he asks Nate, and I quickly interfere. "No, it's nothing like that. Just… something. Can we talk?"

He nods, placing his suitcase down just as Sammy comes through the front door dressed in casual jeans and a knitted sweater.

"Sorry, I wasn't expecting you home until tomorrow." She picks up the bag and winks at me. Huh, Sammy is ultra-happy today, but those questions will have to wait.

Dad gestures toward the hallway. "My office."

Following him down, I step into his space, suddenly engulfed with rich pine, red leather, and ancient books.

He takes a seat on his chair, unbuttoning his suit and removing his tie. It's the first time I've really gotten to look at Dad in a long time. The skin around his eyes sags more than ever, his stubble is a couple days old, and his eyelids look heavy and tired. Just when

I'm about to tell him to forget it, not wanting to add to his obviously already stressful life, he opens his mouth. "I realize you have a lot to ask after what happened at Hector's house."

I swallow. "Well, actually, yes and no."

"How much do you know already, Madison?" he whispers hoarsely.

My anger picks up a little. "Why the hell do people keep asking me that? Like they're trying to find a barrier to which they won't cross. Fearing they might say too much, but it's okay for them to say too little. It's deceiving and dishonest."

"Madison," he exhales. "No one is honest in this world. I'm sorry that you're a part of it. I never... we—your mother and I—never wanted you to be a part of this world. It's why we were on the run for so long." He leans back in his chair.

"So why bring me back here then, Dad, if you knew I was in trouble?"

He pauses, running his index finger over his upper lip while he watches me. Probably thinking about whether or not he should be honest with me. Fucking people and their honesty.

"Because...." He leans forward, resting his elbows on the desk. "God, Madison. There is a natural order to how things operate in the Kings. A way that no one has tampered with for generations and generations. Roles that each of us have that we always have had." He pauses, looking up at me from beneath his lids. He exhales again, but I think I've already worked it out.

"You're wanting to change the order."

He looks at me and narrows his eyes. "Yes. But Hector can't know."

I look at him, taking a seat on the chair in front of me. "What do you mean? So why does he think you brought me back?"

He pauses, leans back, and rests his elbow on the armrest. Realization comes in. "Wait. Does he think you brought me back to... kill me?"

"What?" my dad exasperates. "Of course fucking not."

Information is swimming around in my head. Information that may as well be in Japanese, because I have no idea what all this means. "Well, can you enlighten me? Because I can't see why else Hector would let me walk free, considering the Kings hid me away to try to make sure he didn't find out I was back here."

Dad's eyes turn to stone, along with his jaw. "That wasn't the whole reason why those boys took you away, Madison. You must never forget who they are, who their loyalty belongs to, because it's not you. It never is to anyone else but to the Hayes men. Must remember that."

I swallow, trying to find the words I want to say. Even though I've been brewing on all my questions for months, now that I can ask my dad anything and he'll probably tell me, I'm coming up dry.

"What does Hector think?" I whisper, glancing out the old wooden window that overlooks our yard.

"He thinks I've come back to send you away with someone."

"Someone?" I ask, whipping my attention back to him. "To who? And why?"

"The Lost Boys, and to be lost."

That brings my attention back into the circle. Into why I'm here. "Well, that's not going to happen."

"What do you mean?" he asks, looking at me sideways.

"Daemon is upstairs and has been here for a few nights now. And before you flip out—he's not dangerous toward me, but I do have questions."

Dad's face falls. He pauses, and then he shoots off his chair like his ass just caught on fire. "What the fuck do you mean he's here?" he roars, his hands flying out. The office door bursts open and Bishop strides in, checking me over quickly before giving my dad a death glare. "She knows he's her brother, her twin," Bishop starts.

"Thanks," I mutter under my breath, turning back in my chair. "I was just getting to that part."

"And that's all she knows."

Hold up. "Wait." I put my hand up. "What does that mean? And why did you just storm into this office like you were afraid my dad was going to say something?" I look back at Dad to see his face soften slightly before eventually falling completely. He looks to me. "Baby girl, go upstairs. I need to talk to Bishop."

"No." I shake my head. "You can talk in front of me."

"The fuck we can. Get your ass upstairs—now." Bishop glares at me.

I wince, but square my shoulders. "Why? Why can't you stop fucking hiding shit from me?"

Bishop takes one step. "Because..." Another step. "You are Madison *fucking* Montgomery..." Step. "The Silver *motherfucking* Swan." Double step. "So get your *fucking* ass upstairs." The tip of his shoe hits mine. "*Now,*" he growls.

I run my eyes up his dark jeans, past his clean black shirt, over his thick neck and plump lips, until I'm finally staring into eyes that are like the gates of hell. Only, I would let the fucker push me in and lock them behind him. "One day—" I tilt my head. "—I will know everything, and you won't be able to control shit." I stand, almost nose-to-nose with him.

He looks down at me, his dark glare turning into a grin. "Maybe. Not today though, so get the fuck out."

I turn in my step and walk out of the office before he can yell at me some more. Only he's not yelling at me. Only Bishop has a way about him where it feels like he's yelling at you without actually raising his voice. Must be an intimidation tactic of some sort. He's stella in those.

Taking the stairs one at a time, I walk into my room, slamming the door behind me. Flopping down onto my bed, the fluffy blankets puffing out beneath me, I tilt my head to face the ceiling as I replay over all the new information. I know I'm not going to get anything solid out of anyone around here.

"Madison...," Daemon whispers softly.

I keep my vision locked on the ceiling. "Yes, Daemon?"

"The book."

Pushing myself up, I reach under the bed and search for the book. Something has happened with Miss Winters too. How has she disappeared? And Tillie. Where the fuck is Tillie? There's so much I still have to figure out, but for some reason, I feel like my answers will lie between the words in this book, not by trying to decipher the Latin language from my long lost twin brother.

Fuck this book.

Flicking open the page, I sink into my bed and continue where I left off.

12.

The birth of the Lost Boys

One…Two…Three…Four…Five…Six…

I counted each head. "Why are you here?" I asked, tilting my head at Joshua. Joshua was the first person to put his hand up when Humphrey decided to cook up this idea. Why? I don't know. Humphrey comes from a good home. I thought he was a good kid too.

"Because I want to do something useful with my life. Make my family proud."

"Proud?" I asked. "Proud of killing innocent babies? Because that's what you will be doing."

He swallowed, and I saw his jaw flinch. "I—I don't. I will do what I need to do, ma'am."

"What if I gave you another job? Something that will still make your family proud but won't have you doing such disturbing jobs." I pushed off the counter and walked toward him. "I'm offering you an ultimatum, Joshua. Will you accept it?"

He looked deep into my eyes, and I saw it. I saw his silent cries for help. The way the corner of his eyes crinkled when I offered him a different job. "I will do anything, Miss Katsia. I think that much is obvious."

I nodded then come-hithered the other five boys who were waiting patiently for me at the back of the empty cave. "Who knows about fireflies?"

They all stepped forward, shaking their head. "Not much," one of them replied. This one was strong. I could see it in how his shoulders squared with self-assurance and the way he didn't flinch.

"Well," I began. "What do you know about beetles?"

They all shook their heads.

"Okay, so what's more appealing? The firefly or the beetle?"

"Firefly," they all murmured, looking at each other for approval.

I smiled. "But did you know that the firefly is still only a beetle? They're just nocturnal members of the family."

"What's your point, Miss Katsia?" the cocky boy asked, and I admire his no beating around the bush attitude. He's going to need it.

"My point is, how they see us…" I pointed out toward the outside of the cave. "Has to be the beetle. We have to remain within the same family. They have to think we're of the same family. Fighting for the same cause."

"But we're not going to be—are we?" Joshua whispered, looking to me in awe.

I shook my head slowly, a small smile tickling my lips. "No."

"So what would you be having us do, Katsia?" the cocky boy asked.

Looking back to him, I tilted my head. "What's your name?"

"Benjamin."

"Benjiman… who?"

"Benjiman Vitiosus."

"Ahhh," I mumbled. It made sense. He was a Vitiosis. I didn't recognize him earlier because the order of the Lost Boys worked like this: If you're a sibling who doesn't have what they call Elite Blood, then you get thrown in to be a Lost Boy, who—what Humphrey wants to do—are cleaners of the world. Humphrey has lined out the world very thoroughly. We have breeding time, which is the only time that we can try for babies. If you don't fall pregnant, then you will have to wait four years before you can try again, and you only get to try twice. You see, Humphrey has made a natural order in the most unnatural way. You get the first two tries, and then you cannot try *again. It's about breeding them, but we need them in fours. Humphrey was too smart for his own good, for all of us. He had everything mapped out, and no one was stopping him. Not now—not ever.*

If you had a child or a nephew who didn't have Elite Blood, meaning they didn't have what it took to be a King, then they got thrown in to be a Lost Boy. Trained. Well, that was what I was supposed to be doing, but instead, I have another plan for these boys. I want to fight Humphrey. Fight his cause and fight it to the death. He took my baby girl and killed her. Now... now I start a very detailed plan to kill him.

Slamming the book closed, I think over what I just read. I'm beginning to see the shift in Katsia from what she was in the beginning. She's stronger. There's vengeance in her blood, and we all know that once vengeance seeps into your blood, there's no extracting that from your system. The only way that gets siphoned out is by getting your revenge. So all Lost Boys are somehow intertwined into the family of one of the Kings. This world is, once again, messed up. Flipping over, I hit my light and slide under my covers, snuggling into my warm sheets and drifting into a deep sleep.

Fog from the empty night expels from my lungs, and I stop running, leaning over to catch my breath. "Riddle me this, Kitty."

"NO!" I scream, shielding my ears with my hands. "Fuck you!" Slamming my eyes closed, I shoot forward, the damp leaves sliding under the soles of my shoes. My heart pounds in my chest and my blood tears through my veins like bullets full of adrenalin. I keep running blindly as sweat trickles down my cool flesh, goose bumps breaking out over my spine, so I open my eyes and stop. Looking out to the still lake in the middle of the forest, I whisper in confusion, "What?"

I spin around to try to figure out where I just came from, but nothing is there. Only the bushes that hide the lake—the same lake Bishop and I fooled around in. A single bright firefly flutters in the air, swimming around in front of my face. I smile, letting the little bug light something inside of my gut. Reaching out, I go to touch it, but just as my fingertip connects with the little body, it turns to blood, dripping down over my finger.

"Ew!" I pull my finger back then look around the empty lake again. "Why am I here?" Wind whisks through my hair, igniting my skin and senses, and that's when I smell it—the sweet, soapy scent of man. Inching my head over my shoulder, I smile softly.

"Took you long enough."

Bishop steps forward so he's standing directly beside me and looks out to the lake. "You run faster now."

I grin, turning to face him. "Or you've gotten slower." Looking him up and down, I take in what he's wearing and my eyebrows pull together in confusion. He has no shirt on, his delicious body on full display, and his ripped jeans cover his long, lean legs. Barefoot, standing there like that in the middle of almost winter seems ridiculously strange. Actually, this entire setting feels strange. I look out toward the rock Bishop and I played around on what feels like years ago now, and smile. "There's that rock." When he doesn't answer, I turn to face him, but he's gone.

"Bishop?" I call out, looking around for him. Something doesn't feel right. Actually, everything feels extremely wrong.

"Kitty," Nate murmurs, and I spin around, seeing Nate leaning on his elbows in the sand, with no shirt on either.

"Aren't you cold?" I ask him, finally having enough of all the lack of clothes.

"I don't know." Nate runs his eyes up and down my body then grins. "Aren't you?"

"No, I...." I look down to see I'm wearing nothing but a little black G-string and a black bra. "Oh my God!" But he's right. I'm not cold.

"Nice. Can see why you're both hitting that." Brantley's dark voice comes in from the shadows behind Nate.

"Bishop, yes. Nate, no," I correct, my hands on my hips.

"Nate, almost—twice." Nate smirks.

I open my mouth, just about to correct him again, when Hunter, Jase, Ace, Saint, Eli, Cash, and Chase slowly come in behind Brantley, all similarly dressed.

"The gang's all here?" I ask, shaking my head.

Nate glares over my shoulder, his eyes going dark. "Now they are."

A hand runs up my thigh while another grips onto my hip, holding me into place. I close my eyes. "Bishop...."

His lips skim over my shoulder, his breath falling on my cool skin. "Who owns you?" Then he licks me from shoulder blade to shoulder blade while his hand on my thigh travels up to my apex. "Who owns you, Madison?"

I moan out slightly, biting down on my bottom lip.

He squeezes. "I'm not a patient man."

"Why?" I ask. Even in the midst of my lust, my stubborn ass still can't let some shit go.

His fingertips dig into the flesh of my thigh. "Say it. Tell me what I want to hear," he growls, his lips pressing against the rim of my earlobe.

"You."

Shit.

He chuckles into my ear. "Good." His hand sprawls over my stomach. "Because you're about to get fucked like I don't."

Wait, what?

I turn to face him, confused. When he sees my puzzlement, he grins and looks over my shoulder. Another hand comes to the front of my throat and squeezes down.

Shit. Double shit.

Why does everything feel so good? Bishop drops to his knees in front of me as whoever it is behind me grips onto my throat, tilting my head to the side as his teeth latch onto my neck.

"You want this and you know it."

Brantley.

Fuck.

Bishop tears my G-string off, and I look down at him as he brings it up to his face and inhales deeply. "Mine."

I want to kick him and say, *If I'm yours, then why are you sharing me?* but everything feels too good. Like I'm floating on a cloud of ecstasy.

I feel no shame.

Then Bishop draws his tongue out and runs it over my panty line, a devilish smirk coming to his mouth as his eyes light up like fire. Then he hooks my G-string over his neck and wears it like a damn necklace.

Jesus Christ, is he kidding?

Brantley's hand comes up to my bra and cups my boob, squeezing roughly just as the cool air that was whisking past my clit is replaced with Bishop's warm mouth. "Oh my God!" I groan, my head tilting back and hitting Brantley's chest. Brantley tears off my bra and pinches my nipples as Bishop's tongue circles my clit, switching between rough and gentle.

"Lay down," Brantley murmurs into my ear.

"What?" I'm still coming out of my daze when he wraps my hair around his fist and yanks me down to the sand. "Lay the fuck down." I fall onto my ass, and both him and Bishop look down at me sprawled out on the ground.

"Well, damn," a third voice says, coming into view.

Saint. Cash's older brother.

He unbuttons his jeans and I gulp. Holy shit. He has six years on all of us.

"Scared?" he asks, rubbing his hand over his dick. I watch as the muscles in his chest flex. His angular jaw tenses and I look at him with fresh eyes. Or horny eyes—either one. He has a sprinkling of hair over his jaw, groomed perfectly. His nose is a little wider, but his skin is golden and his hair blond. He sort of looks like that actor Cam Gigandet, I've decided. He nudges his head. "You good with this?"

I want to say no. I should say no. Shit. I don't want to say no. Nodding, I slowly pull my bottom lip into my mouth. *What a fucking whore.* He gets down to his knees and Bishop and Brantley both step aside, parting like the Red Sea to let him in.

"You gon' purr tonight."

He pushes his jeans down, tugging on his cock a few times, and then lays over me. I drop to my back, my arms going out, giving him access. His bulky body weighs on me as the tip of his thick cock presses at my entrance before slipping in, thanks to Bishop's foreplay. My eyes pop open and I arch my back, letting out a moan loud enough to shake the trees.

He grins against my cheek. "That's not even half, baby. I'm going to break you." Then he pulls out and flips me onto my stomach, grabbing one leg and hitching it onto his hip as he dives inside me again. The way the tip of his cock collides with my cervix says I'm taking it all. Hands wrap around my hair and I look up the best I can to see Bishop. He unzips his jeans, pulling them down enough until his cock springs free, and then he lies back on the sand, leaning back on his elbows. Biting down on his bottom lip, his hair slightly ruffled and his eyes weak with lust, he nods down at his cock. "You know what to do, baby." Putting my weight on one hand, I grip his dick with my other hand, sliding my lips over his head, and swallow him deeply. Bobbing up and down, I swirl my tongue around him and take him deeper until he's hitting the back of my tonsils. He looks directly at me as Saint dives into me over and over again, hitting some sweet spot hidden deep inside me. I pause my sucking, swinging my hair over one shoulder, and look up to Bishop. He moves some of my hair out of my face sweetly, smirks, and then wraps it around his fist, tugging my face up to look at him more.

"Nate!" he calls out, his eyes not moving from me. Saint withdrawals from me, taking all my pleasure and buildup with him.

"Yo!" Nate answers. I can't see where he is, but I'm guessing he's right behind me—with a great view.

"Tell me how good she tastes."

I narrow my eyes at Bishop and open my mouth to protest, but his grip tightens and I flinch, my eyes slamming closed. "Who owns you?" he growls.

"But—"

"Shut the fuck up. Who owns you?" I open my eyes, tears creeping out of the corners. Tears from my hair almost getting ripped out, or tears from the feelings of abandonment I've started to sense deep in my chest. He doesn't care. I really am just a trick to him. A game. If he cared, I wouldn't be getting tossed around like public property. Before I can blink, I'm angry. Angry at him, but turned on by that anger.

"You own me, Bishop." I give him what he wants while ignoring the stabbing feeling I feel in my throat.

"Now, spread them open and let him in."

I look up at Nate and he smirks at me. "Promise to be gentle."

I roll my eyes, because as far as I know, Nate isn't nearly as ruthless as Brantley and Bishop, so that's the least of my issues. Nate leans down, placing a kiss on my lips. I lean into him, his mouth meshing with mine.

"Kitty," he whispers against my lips.

Something pokes into my chest, and I turn from left to right, not wanting this kiss to stop. Nate does kissing well.

"Kitty...."

There's that prodding again. What the fuck? In an instant, the front of my belly has been doused in water and ice prickles over my nipples.

I shoot off the bed, reality slowly seeping its ugly fucking claws deep inside of me. "Fuck!" Rubbing my eyes, I look down at the front of my shirt, seeing my pajama top is soaked through. "Double fuck!" Then I look up, seeing Nate standing next to my bed with a water bottle in his hand and a grin on his face.

"You!" I narrow my eyes and slowly start to crawl down the bed, like a tiger about to eat its prey. I'm about to eat my prey—that prey being Nate.

"No," he retreats, his hands coming up in surrender. "That's not what.... I was waking you up because...." He looks around my room, trying to find a valid excuse. Squaring his shoulders, his face turns serious. "Imagine if the house was on fire, Mads!"

"But it's not. Is it?" I challenge, standing to my feet. I watch him, and he looks over to my bedroom door briefly before looking back to me. "Madi, I can explain. It's...." Then he makes a dash for it, launching toward my bedroom door and slamming it behind him. I fly toward it, twisting on my door handle and banging on the wood. "Open this fucking door, Nate!" I scream.

"No! Say you won't, like, hurt my balls or something."

"I won't fucking hurt you!"

"Lies!" he yells back. "I know when you're lying, because you add a 'fucking' in the middle. Tell me the truth!"

Exhaling in defeat, I open my mouth, just about to surrender, when I see my bathroom door open. Grinning, I slowly step backward. "Okay, I'm sorry. Do you forgive me?" Silently, I step into the bathroom, slide over to his door, and twist the handle open. It's unlocked. Grinning from my cleverness, I pull the door open, but my face falls instantly.

"Going somewhere?" Bishop is standing in front of me, shirtless with those ripped jeans on. He basically just walked right out of my dream. Life is not fair and the universe obviously fucking hates me.

"I-uh…" I look around the room, hitching my thumb over my shoulder. "…am just going to go." I spin around and start to run back toward my room, but Bishop hooks his arm around my waist, lifting me off the ground and throwing me over his shoulder like I weigh nothing.

"Bishop!" I yell. "Put me the fuck down!"

"Ah, see… you put a 'fuck' in there. You must be mad." He slaps my ass cheek, the sting vibrating over my skin. "Calm yourself, woman!"

"I hate you!" I shriek, just as he throws me onto my bed. The morning sun glaring through my porch windows catches his messy bed hair. The chestnut brown color sets off the contrast of his tanned skin.

His eyes turn almost black. "Yeah? Well, I don't give a fuck. You've hated me for so long now."

"This is different!" I shout back, suddenly angry at him.

"What?" He matches my level of loud. Spreading his arms out, he smirks. "How? How is this different?"

"You let Saint fuck me and Nate go down on me!" I scream, tears suddenly slipping down my cheeks. Jesus. When did I become such a girl? I make a mental note to check the dates, because I must be due for Mother Nature's visit. There's no way I'm this much of a pussy-ass bitch.

Bishop stops. His eyes look straight into mine, commanding the entire room while summoning my fucking soul. Because that's what he does. When his stance changes to this one—one I've only seen twice now—he stares into my eyes and summons my soul. But with my soul come my demons, and I think that's the part he's only just figuring out.

"Come again," he growls softly. Too softly.

I shiver in fear, because I should be fucking scared. Every survival instinct the human body has is on high alert within me right now. Run. I should run. But I can't, because he's fucking summoned me. Because—

"Madison," he repeats in the same tone, cocks his head a little, and slowly walks toward the foot of my bed. "Repeat what you just said, and think very carefully about your next words, because my fingers are twitching to snap some necks…" He pauses, breaking our eye contact and glaring right at my throat. "…and yours is looking rather snapable too."

Oh shit.

"Okay, hang on." I stand up from the bed, feeling more confident on my feet. "I meant that—" He pushes me back down onto the bed. "Bishop!" I yell, propping myself up on my elbows and looking up at him.

"Did any of them touch you?"

"Bishop—"

He grips onto my leg and pushes me up my bed, stepping between my thighs. "Don't, Madison. Don't fuck with this."

"I meant it was—"

He presses his lips to the crook of my neck and bites down on it roughly.

"Was what?" he asks, his voice vibrating against my skin as his other hand comes up to my throat. His thumb caresses my jawline gently as he kisses and licks all over my neck. Biting down on my bottom lip to fight a moan, I close my eyes, but then he presses his dick into me, and I lose it.

"Was a fucking dream!" I yell, still slightly angry at him.

He stops, pauses, and settles his face into my neck. Seconds pass when I feel his body jerking on top of me.

Narrowing my eyes, I slap him in the ribs. "Are you fucking laughing?"

Then he bursts into fits of laughter, rolling onto his back while clutching his stomach. "Fuck."

I'm staring at him, confused and annoyed, and just when I'm about to hit him again, I realize this is the first time I've ever seen Bishop laugh. Or even smile this big. Or just smile without there being an ulterior motive behind it.

Before I can stop myself, I giggle. "Stop laughing. It's not funny."

He slams his mouth closed as he tries to contain his fit, and then he looks to me, his eyes dancing with humor. "Sorry, babe. But that's fucking hilarious. You getting mad at me over a dream."

"Stop. It was more than that, and it felt like…."

He hooks his arm around my waist, lifts me up, and puts me on top of him so I'm straddling his waist. Placing his arms behind his head, he stares at me, so I look away, scared he'll summon some more of my soul and never give it back. "Hey," he whispers. "Look at me."

I shake my head. "I sort of don't want to."

"Why?" he whispers again, and I know in his tone that he's being honest.

"Because."

"Because why, Madison?"

"Because you steal some of my soul every time you do that thing with your eyes."

He slams his mouth closed again, his stomach jerking beneath me.

Oh no he is—

"Are you laughing at me again?" My eyes snap to his and he bursts out laughing once more. I go to get off him when he grabs me around the waist again and pulls me down so my lips are within an inch of his. "Hey," he repeats, his warm breath falling over my lips. "Look at me."

Knowing he will never let up, I look at him. I mean, eyes a little crossed, front row seating, soul clenching, really look at him, and my heart launches in my chest. *That's* what needs to get summoned… right the fuck out of my body.

"What?" I meant for my tone to be harsher than what it is when it comes out.

"I'd never fucking share you. Period. Yes, we fuck around a bit, but the boys know there's a line when it comes to you, and if any of them cross it, I have no problem being a King short."

I laugh, shaking my head. He can't mean that. We fight so much; he's never told me how he's felt—only maybe once before, outside my house—but I never know when he's being truly sincere, because everything is always a game. And I usually always lose. This, though, the way he's looking at me and how he's talking to me, it's putting dents in my solid plan to get revenge.

"I know what you're doing." His fingers dig into my hips.

"Oh?" I ask, pushing off his chest so I'm sitting on him properly. "And what exactly is that?"

He smirks. "You wanted to get revenge on me. On all of us. Hell, I knew that a long time ago. Why do you think I never came to get you back from overseas when I could have?"

"What do you mean?"

"I mean, you think I didn't know you were in New Zealand? That you used to sit at that little black table and draw for the tattoo artist, Jesse? That you started having a little thing for him? I knew everything, Madison. There wasn't a second when you weren't under my protection."

I blink, and try to gather enough coherent thoughts to ask some questions.

"How? But why didn't you get me then?"

"There was stuff going on here that needed to be cleaned up, and you needed to calm down. I would've rather had you out of the US while everything was getting sorted."

"Did it get sorted?" I ask, wiggling up his body so I'm away from his dick.

"No." He pushes me back down so now I'm directly on top of it.

Shit.

"So why did you bring me back?" I try to shuffle off, annoyed at how horny it makes me with him pressed against me like that. And aside from the fact I am angry about that dream, it turned me on the same.

He pulls down on me, hard enough for me to hiss. Narrowing his eyes, his other hand comes up, and he hooks his finger under my chin, tilting my head up. "Someone touched what is mine. That's what the fuck happened."

"You say that, yet you don't tell me what 'we' are, or anything."

"A label? You want a label?"

"No!" I shake my head. Exhaling, I get off his lap, and he lets me. "I don't know what I want, but I know I want you."

"Well fuck the rest of it. That's all that matters."

"But what does this mean?" I ask, gesturing between the two of us, my girl brain ticking at a hundred miles an hour.

"It means you're mine. That's all that means."

"And... what about you?" I laugh sarcastically. "If you think I'm going to watch as you go around—"

"Have you ever seen me be a slut?"

"I've seen you touch one," I mutter under my breath, remembering him and Ally. My tone is 100 percent salty and not a single fuck is given.

He doesn't reply, so I look up at him. He's standing in front of me, his knees leaning against the mattress of my bed. Bending down, he spreads my legs open and steps between them. Leaning down, he runs his lips over mine. "And she's dead. So I'll ask you again, have you seen me be a slut?"

The way he talks about Ally being dead—and the fact he's the one who killed her—should upset me, but it doesn't. I don't know why he did it. Hell, I don't even understand what Ally could have done to deserve being knocked off. But for some crazy reason, I don't care.

"No." I shake my head slowly, and he leans down again, pressing a kiss against my lips. My bedroom door swings open. "So, that was—" Nate stops, and Bishop smiles against my lips before stepping backward. "Did I interrupt something?"

"Go away. Please go away," I laugh at Nate.

"Well now, you've just made it more exciting for me to stay." He walks in and sits beside me on my bed, a Cheshire grin on his face.

"Motherfucker."

His grin deepens.

"I've got shit to sort anyway. I'll see you at school," Bishop announces, looking at me briefly before walking out the door, back into Nate's room.

"Put a shirt on!" I yell toward his retreating back, and he chuckles slightly, closing the door behind him.

"So!" Nate turns to me, putting his hands together like a little girl excited that she just got invited to a sleepover. "Tell me all the goss'!"

"Fuck you." I roll my eyes and get off the bed.

His shoulders sag. "You're no fun."

I walk into my closet and flick the light on. "Let's just say," I murmur, scanning through my skinny jeans, "he's finally claimed me." I settle for the black ones with rips in the knees. Pulling down a tight, V-neck, long-sleeved shirt, I turn to face Nate when he's silent.

He's smiling. Like I knew he would be. "He claimed you that first day you walked into Riverside, Kitty. You're gonna have to give me more than that."

Removing my clothes, I tug on my jeans... then tug some more, because apparently I've put on weight, and then button them up. "No, but it's... I don't know... different now. There's so many layers to Bishop. I never know when he's actually being truthful." Throwing on my shirt, I pull my hair out of the back and fluff it up.

"Well..." Nate begins, standing from the bed and walking toward me. "When it comes to real shit, I mean shit he cares about—which is pretty much nothing, aside from you—you're safe. I can vouch for that, Kitty." He pulls some loose strands out from under my shirt. "He won't hurt you."

"Promise?" I ask, looking into his eyes.

Nate nods. "I promise."

CHAPTER 18

Unlocking my truck, I slide into the driver seat, as Nate gets into the passenger, deciding he doesn't want to drive today. "How's Daemon?" he asks, pushing buttons on the radio.

"He's okay. Katsia wants him back and is demanding a meeting with him, but I want to be there."

Nate looks straight at me. "You're not going anywhere without the Kings, and you damn well know that."

"No, look, I need to handle this on my own. I read a bit about the Lost Boys last night, and I just…. I have questions I need answered, and I know if you guys are there, she's less inclined to give me those answers. So please." I look to him, putting the car in drive. "Just let me handle this on my own."

He doesn't fight, just shrugs and hits Play on Kendrick Lamar's "Humble."

I laugh, shaking my head as I pull out of our driveway. "I swear you were living in the hood in your past life."

"Tsk tsk." Nate shakes his head. "Don't stereotype." He starts bobbing his head to the beat and raps out the chorus. Laughing, he waves his hand. "Come on… rap it with me…."

Shaking my head, I turn onto the main highway that leads to school. "No thanks."

School is boring, and I truly feel like I'm over it. "At least this is our last year," I mutter to Tatum.

"True!" she agrees, shoving books into her locker. I pause, thinking about the order Katsia spoke about in the book. So if we're all leaving for college, then that means there's a new group of Kings that are going to be starting next year. I need to call Daemon. Pulling my phone out of my pocket, I shut my locker and press Call on his name. He picks up almost instantly, his voice soothing like hot chocolate on a cool winter day.

"Are you okay?" he asks, curt, straightforward, and blunt, but it's Daemon, and from how short I've known him, you don't usually get any other tone.

"Yes, but hey, I need to talk to you about something. Are you home?"

"I am."

"Okay, be ready and I'll pick you up."

"See you then," he replies with the same tenor, hanging up.

"Jeez," Tatum murmurs beside me. "His tone? Does he hate the world?"

Her assumption annoys me. Daemon is a lot of things, some things not even I completely know yet. "No," I snap. "He's just... different."

She shrugs, and we both start walking toward the elevator. "Different, as in Ted Bundy and Jack the Ripper different, or different, as in 'I draw naked in the moonlight' different?"

I roll my eyes, pushing the button to take us down. "Probably more on the Jack the Ripper side, I'm guessing," I murmur, and she looks at me.

"No way."

"I said probably, not definitely. Anyway, keep your paws off him."

"Hey!" She throws her hands up, and we step into the car. "I don't want to be another victim. I'll stay away."

She won't stay away.

We get into the truck and I put it into reverse. "I'll drop you off. I just need to have this conversation with Daemon alone."

"Are you going to tell me what is going on?" she asks. She didn't ask in an entitled tone. It was more in a way as if she's worried and wants to know everything is okay. Which is Tatum. She's outgoing, blunt, a little flirty, and a lot sassy, but she's real. She's always kept it real with me, and she will forever be my best friend.

I exhale. "I am. Just... give me some time?" I look at her briefly as I pull out onto the main road.

"Okay," she nods, "I can do time."

Driving up to my house, I beep the horn, deciding to wait in the car for Daemon. He comes walking out in a dark suit, buttoned up at the front.

"Huh!" I look at him as he slides into the passenger seat. "You go shopping?"

He looks down at his clothes and then back to me, his eyes expressionless. "Yes."

Pulling out of the driveway, I turn to him slightly. "This talk, can we do it in English?"

He nods. "Yes. I might be little slow, but yes."

I smile and turn the radio on. "Jungle" by Tash Sultana starts playing, and I hit it up a notch. I love this artist. She's from Australia and completely underground, but her voice is soulful and her music touches you deeply.

"Are you okay?" I ask Daemon when he doesn't say anything.

He nods, unbuttoning his jacket. "Yes. What do you want to talk about?"

I shuffle around in my seat. "Katsia, mainly, and the Lost Boys. And also, the next generation of Kings. Is that going to be okay for you?"

He nods again. "That's fine. The next generation of Kings isn't so easy to..." He pauses, looking for the word he wants to use. "...explain. They are..." He looks to me again. "...hidden. Unknown as to what the next move is or if they are starting."

Well, that makes entirely no sense, but we continue driving until I come to the turn off to the forest we went through on Halloween. Pulling down the long stretch of road—the road that is so much less scary than it is at night—and follow it right to the end.

"I know this place," Daemon announces, a little sketchy.

"You do?" I answer, turning into the little parking lot.

"Yes." He looks at me, confused. "How do you know this place?"

"Well, long story short, a friend threw a party here."

"A party?" he asks again.

I pause with my hand on the door handle. "Yes, you know…." I gesture up to my mouth as in drinking, and then boogie in my seat as in dancing.

He looks at me, bored, not catching any of my hints.

"Well this is going to be a long chat then," I mutter, getting out of the car. He follows, shutting the door, and I lock it.

I'm just about to walk toward the clearing, when he grabs onto my arm, tugging me back. I look down at his grip and then back to his face. "What's wrong?"

Shaking his head, he whispers, "You should not have been here, Madison. This isn't your place."

"My place?" I step toward him. "What do you mean? It's beautiful here."

"Something is wrong." He searches the forest and then looks back to me. "Get back in the car and do it slowly."

"What?" I look around the area but don't move my head—making it less obvious. "What do you mean?"

"Don't ask questions. Just do it."

Searching his eyes, I can see him pleading with me. "Okay." Slowly, I sidestep and walk toward the driver door, beeping the alarm system and sliding in. Daemon stays in the same spot, his shoulders square and his stance in fighting mode. It sends chills down my spine, and my fear kicks up to inhumane levels. Pulling the door open, I'm about to slide in when it hits. A sharp sting stabs me right in the head, and I'm falling.

Looking up, the tips of the trees are coming in and out in a distant view. Ringing starts piercing my ears, and I tilt my head as the sun blares right down on my face. Daemon is there, but his face is blurry, and he's yelling at me. Why's he yelling? Why am I on the ground? *Am* I on the ground? Daemon's eyes are furious, almost black. There's spit flying out of his mouth as he screams at me, but I can't hear anything because I'm deafened by the ringing in my ear.

I laugh because this is the first time I've ever seen Daemon out of control. Why is he so intractable? He wouldn't be like this unless something was extremely wrong. Metallic liquid floods my throat, and I start to panic. My heart launches in my throat as my airways start to slowly clench, making breathing damn near impossible.

Daemon is like this because something *is* wrong. So terribly wrong. I look back at him, bringing my hands to my throat, wanting to rip off my skin to give myself air to breathe, but it's no use. Daemon looks down at me, his eyes pained and his face strained.

Why's he got blood all over him?

Is that my blood?

That's when it hits me.

I'm dying.

CHAPTER 19

Daemon

The voices.
        One.
    Two.
    Three.
    Four.
    Five.
    Six...
    Six...
    Six....
    "She belongs to us. To the dark. Don't put her in the light. She'll burn there, Demon. Don't put her in the light. It's bad for her. Bad, bad, bad. She needs to be where we are, in the dark. Hidden, where it's quiet. Where no one can hurt her."
    "Kill her!"
    "No, don't kill her! She's special... so special. Look at her. She's beautiful."
    "Shut up!" I roar, banging my fists against my head. "They... they won't stop!" I look down at Madison. Sweet Madison. My sister. My twin. The only person I've ever felt for. The only human I've ever felt a connection with.
    "Connection?" The voice snickers. *"The only connection is you know you're supposed to kill her. You know it, so do it. Kill her. She's already dying. Hell, she might even be dead."*
    Sucking in a breath, I look down at Madison's body. Her tiny frame unmoving and still. What have I done?
    I did this.
    She shouldn't have been here.
    Grabbing the mobile device Madison gave me, I dial 911. I'm not completely clueless, it's a part of my job as a civilian to know emergency services number. I do not care about the Kings right now. She needs medical help, and I don't know who they use. I trust no one. "Trust no one. Trust no one...."
    "Nine-one-one, what is your emergency?"
    "Trust no one."
    "Sir?"

I clutch my phone tightly, pressing it against my ear. Biting down on my fist, the metallic tinge of blood hits my taste buds, and I recoil. I've done bad things. Very bad things in my lifetime. Unspeakable things. But they're all I know. I've swum in the blood of innocents and drank from their soul without flinching. But this is Madison. My sister. My twin. I care about her.

"You don't care about her," the voice laughs. *"You care because you want to kill her. Imagine what it would be like slicing into that delicate skin."*

"Shut up!" I scream, slamming my eyes closed.

"Sir?"

"I need help," I speak, though my English is not very good. "My sister. She's hurt."

"Okay, where are you?"

I look around. "I'm at the clearing on State Highway 50."

"Okay, sir, I have someone on the way. Tell me what's wrong with your sister."

I look down at her and freeze. Her skin is pale, the blood still oozing.

"She's hurt so very bad."

"Okay, I get that, but is she breathing? How is she hurt?"

"She...." I lean down, pressing my two fingers to the side of her neck. A faint pulse taps against the pads of my fingers. Distant, but there—only just. "Her pulse is slow... so very slow."

"Finish her," one of the voices snarks.

"Tace!" I order. My shoulders square, the dark spell coats my flesh, and my lip curls. He's here. It's here. *"Ego sum magister vester!"*

The voices, all five of them, run, slithering in fear. *"Yes, yes you are our master."*

Reality gets sucked back into view, and I'm standing there, clutching my phone while the paramedics are working on Madison. Everything goes in slow motion, and I drop my phone, falling to my knees and clutching my head. What happened?

What happened?

Why do I feel like this is my fault?

Stretching my arms wide, an earth-shattering scream erupts out of me as tears pour out of my eyes. I've never lost control. Never. I'm always in control. Nothing touches me. I don't feel. I don't feel anything. But seeing Madison motionless on the ground, it's like I suddenly feel everything.

"Sir!" A paramedic comes rushing over, blood on his hands. "What happened?"

My chest heaves as I take in deep breaths, my head hanging between my shoulders in defeat. I slowly look up at him and snarl, "She shot in the head."

CHAPTER 20

Madison

Beep. *Beep.*

Beep.

Pain.

Beep.

Feels like a thousand bricks are weighing down on my head.

Beep.

I try to wiggle my toes, only they don't move. I don't think they move. Where am I?

Beep.

I strain to open my eyes, but not sure whether they're opening.

"No."

A voice! Whose voice is that?

Beep.

I'm so tired. Like sinking sand, I feel my consciousness slowly detach itself from wherever I am. The beeping sounds distant now.

Beep.

"Did you try to kill her?" is the last distant thing I hear before the depths of nothingness envelop me completely.

My throat throbs, like I've swallowed gallons of sand. Moving my head slightly, I groan. My head pounds like a bass line is vibrating directly through my brainwaves. It's almost too painful to bear. Wiggling my fingers, this time I feel them respond and someone grabs my hand beside me.

"Madison?"

Who is that? Slowly, I open my eyes. Heavy and tired, like glue has set on my eyelashes, but I stubbornly fight it.

"Water," I urge, still not knowing who that is. There's a straw pressing against my lips, hitting the cracks. I open my mouth a little, enough to fit the tiny straw in and suck. The water is warm, but it slides down my parched throat perfectly. Moving my head back after drinking all of it, I wince.

"Hurts."

"I know, babe."

"Who is this? I can't see."

"Open your eyes, babe."

I fight for it, God knows I do, and when my eyes finally open, my eyebrows pull in. "Tillie?" She looks the same from what I remember, only I'm seeing three of her, and her voice is echoing in and out.

"It's me, but I can't stay long." Her words reverberate, and I can slowly feel the familiar sinking sand slide out from under me.

No!

"Tillie...." I want it to come out excitedly, happy that she's here, but it comes out more like pain.

"I'm sorry, Madison." She kisses me somewhere on my head. "I had to make sure you were okay, but I have to go now."

"Go?" I mutter. "No! You just got here." I peel my eyes open a little wider, but she's still blurry. "Please don't leave."

"I have to. It's not safe for me here."

"Tell me, Tillie," I croak out. "I can keep secrets. Please."

"I know you can, Mads. But I can't. I just can't. I have to go. I love you."

"Tillie!" I groan, and as she snatches up her hoodie and heads to the door, she turns over her shoulder to face me. "I'm sorry." Then she leaves. I rest my head back, ignoring the excruciating pain.

"Madison?" Bishop murmurs, but I can't see him.

"Bishop?" I gasp, looking around the room for him. I look to the corner and see the outline of his body, the tip of his white sneakers glowing from the moonlight peering in. He's leaning forward, his elbows resting on his knees. "Did you see that?"

He chuckles. "It's amusing you think I'd let any motherfucker near you. Of course I saw that. I allowed it."

"Oh," I murmur, wincing at the pain. I want to ask why he allowed Tillie in, but I sense he won't tell me anything right now.

"You okay?" He gets up from his chair and walks toward me. He's in his usual clothes, looking like he always does—perfect. But when he leans down and places a kiss on my head, I see him closer. He has bags under his eyes like he hasn't slept in days.

"What happened?" I whisper, confused by my choppy memories. "All I remember is... pain."

I wince again, and he pushes the button on the side of my bed. "Stupid fucking Daemon called the paramedics," he mutters, almost to himself.

"Daemon?" I go to sit up, but it feels as though someone just launched a knife through my head. "Ahh." I reach up to rub it, and Bishop shoots toward me.

"Lie down. Don't try to act like a warrior. We all know you're tough; now just lie down."

The nurse walks in, putting her hands into her front pockets. "Hi, Madison, you're awake." She pulls out a little flashlight, hooking a stethoscope around her neck. Leaning forward, she smiles at both Bishop and me. "I'm just going to run a quick check before I give you more pain meds."

"No," Bishop interrupts. "Give her the meds now. The general practice bullshit you usually do will not fly in this room."

She goes to argue with Bishop, but then runs her eyes up and down his body, squaring her shoulders. "Very well."

She moves one of the drips around and turns the nozzle. "This is morphine. You will feel better soon. Can you tell me any other pain you are feeling aside from your head?"

"No," I murmur. "Just my head. It hurts really bad, almost unbearable, and I like to think I have a high pain threshold."

She smiles sweetly, but it doesn't reach her eyes. "Understandable. Your injury is severe."

"What is it, by the way?"

She looks to Bishop before looking back to me. "You were shot. Please, try to get some rest."

I was *shot?* Holy shit! How ironic is it that the one thing I love doing is the one thing that almost ended me... that ended my mom? Feeling tired, I close my eyes.

"Bishop?" she continues quietly.

My sleep can wait. Why does she know Bishop's name? I act like I'm unfazed anyway, keeping my eyes closed but kicking my hearing up a notch.

"These people have to leave."

"I know. But they're not going to."

People? What is she talking about?

"Well, it doesn't matter. They can't be sleeping on mattresses on the floor. Not only is it not sterile, but they're getting in the way."

"Jessica, leave."

"Bishop," she whispers, and I can almost feel the sadness in her tone.

"Leave!" he snaps at her.

Okay, I sense history there. I put that in the box of "will ask him one day." Once I hear the door close, I let my tiredness take over and drift into a deep sleep.

The next morning, I wake up almost instantly, and though I feel no better pain-wise, I feel a lot more alert than I did last night. I guess the Tillie thing is going to get ignored until I bring it up—and I will bring it up. I want to know why Bishop let her in. He must trust her to a certain extent. Usually, I would think maybe she has something to blackmail him with in some way, but this is Bishop. No one has anything on him, and if they did, he would just kill them. Problem solved.

"Sis," Nate murmurs, getting off the mattress on the floor. Now I know what the little nurse was talking about last night. Nate and Tatum had obviously been sleeping out on the floor. Or more, wrapped around each other.

"Hi," I mutter, sitting up in my bed slightly. Bishop walks through the door, coffees and a bag of donuts in hand, just as Nate stands.

"Sorry, baby, you can't eat."

"What do you mean I can't eat?" I snap, my stomach growling on cue at the donuts he's holding.

"If they need to do emergency surgery, you have to be prepared, so you can't eat solids."

"Oh?" My eyebrow quirks. "Well guess who else isn't eating."

"What?" he growls.

"Drop them, Bishop."

"Fuck no! I'm hungry."

"Then you should have eaten them before you came back."

"I'm not dumping them."

I look at him.

"Fine, fuck. I'll leave them over here."

I look back to Nate. "Hi." He smiles, but his eyes are crinkled around the edges just like Bishop's. "Have you slept?" I look to Bishop. "Have any of you slept?"

They both shake their heads. Then Nate takes a seat on the bed. "We.... I need to tell you something."

"Okay?"

He grips my hand, his thumb caressing my palm slightly. "Daemon is currently locked up for questioning."

"What?" I go to shoot off the bed, but then wince when my head takes the beating. As I lean back, Nate scolds me. "Do that shit again and I'll fucking kill you myself."

I roll my eyes, because only Nate can get away with threatening to kill me right after I almost got killed.

"But he didn't do anything!"

Nate searches my eyes. "You don't know that."

"Fuck you, I know that."

I see Bishop take a seat on one of the hospital chairs out the corner of my eye. Even from here, I can see how much he wants the donuts.

"Madison, you don't know Daemon. Yes, I know you guys are twins and I know you have that bond... but he's a very, very dangerous guy."

"Not to me." I look back at Nate. "I'm serious, Nate. He didn't do shit that day. He told me.... I remember, he told me to get back into the car and that something didn't feel right."

Nate doesn't flinch. Like he already knew I was going to say that. "Exactly, Madison. *He* knew something was going to happen."

"What does that mean?" I scoff, my anger reaching the boiling point. "You're not making sense."

"Fuck." Nate clutches his hair.

"Madi!" Tatum screams, launching off the mattress on the floor and diving onto my bed.

"Jesus fucking Christ, Tate!" Bishop jumps off his chair. "Get the fuck off her!" She climbs up my bed.

"I'm sorry! I'm sorry! It's just—" She bursts into tears, digging her head into my chest and curling up into a ball on top of me.

I pat her softly. "I know."

She swipes her tears angrily and slaps my arm. "Don't ever fucking do that again!"

"All right." Bishop wraps his arm around her waist and picks her up with one arm, removing her from my bed and putting her back down at the end. "Enough of that shit. I'm feeling unstable."

Tatum evil-eyes Bishop, brushing off her clothes snobbishly. "Don't you caveman me, Hayes!" Her eyes dart over his shoulder and her face lights up. "Oh!" She claps her hands and dives for the bag of donuts, pulling one out and biting into it. "Yum, donuts."

I can't help it; I laugh. Bishop gives me a dirty stare. "What? So she can eat a donut, but I can't?"

"Exactly."

He rolls his eyes and comes back up to my bed, sitting on the other side of me. I open my mouth, about to tell Nate to go on about Daemon, when the doors swing open and my dad and Elena walk in.

"Madison!" Elena wipes tears from her cheeks. "Oh, good Lord." She rushes near my bed and pulls me into a hug. I can hear Bishop growling beside me, the over-the-top male that he is.

"Hi," I whisper into her hair softly, looking up to my dad. His eyes are bloodshot red, wrinkles more prominent, and his suit looks a few days worn. "Hey, Dad."

Nate pulls his mother's arms off me. "All right, let her dad have a turn now. Ya stage five."

My dad leans down and kisses me on the head, leaving his kiss there for a beat longer. "I'm sorry, baby girl."

Closing my eyes, I exhale. All the stress and pain, somehow he takes it all away. "It's not your fault, Dad."

He steps backward, his eyes searching mine. "You say that, Madison. But—"

I shake my head, and by God, it hurts to do so. "No. It is no one's fault."

His face changes, morphing into anger. "Madison," his voice turns into the firm one he uses whenever I'm in trouble, "you do not know anything about Daemon."

"How can you say that? He's your son!"

He opens his mouth and then closes it again. Looking over my shoulder to Bishop, he then looks back to me. "What do you want me to do?"

I smile. "Thank you. Get him the best lawyer. He will need it."

"I don't think this is—" Nate starts, but I cut him off.

"Shut up, Nate!" I look at Bishop. "Are you going to fight me on this too?"

He looks at me and then looks at my dad. "No. I got you, babe."

Those words. So simple, but meaning so much to me. My shoulders drop, and my heart slows for the first time since I've been here. "Thank you."

"I'll call around. I know one in New York. He's the best defense attorney in the state."

"Okay." I smile at my dad. "Thank you for doing this."

"For the record"—he looks at me, his eyebrows pulling in—"I'm not happy about it. There's a lot you have to learn. But I will respect your wishes enough to grant this for you. But if I find out that Daemon and his...." Dad pauses, then looks back at Bishop. "Never mind. Just—I'm doing this for you. No one else."

I nod. "Thanks, Dad."

"We better go. When can she come home?" he asks Bishop, and I don't miss the fact that Bishop takes charge of every situation. Even with my dad, who is decades older than him, it's still Bishop who runs shit. It's just Bishop. You don't get more... alpha? I don't know whether that's the right word to use, but he just commands everything. Like he's the alpha of a wolf pack, but the wolf pack is the human race in general. His tattoo is right; he pretty much is a god, and he doesn't even try. I don't know whether I want to kiss him or smack him. His ego doesn't need more feeding, so I'll go with a smack, and then kiss. Or a combination of both.

"She can leave today. She's been here for seven days because her heart skipped a couple beats after the incident. They said it was because of the trauma, her drifting in and out of consciousness was her body's way of dealing with it. The police want to ask her routine questions, too, and they have to because it's protocol. I'll be there the entire time, so no need to worry about that."

My dad straightens his tie that looks like it hasn't been knotted for at least a couple of days. "Thank you. I'll start on this phone call for Daemon, see if we can get the ball rolling faster."

Backpeddling, I just remember Bishop saying seven days, so when my dad and Elena leave, I turn to face him. "Seven days? I've been out for seven days?"

Bishop nods, walking toward Tatum and snatching the bag of donuts out of her hands before tossing them into the bin. "Yeah, but your injury is straight forward. You were grazed by the bullet, not actually shot." I guess that explains how I'm still alive and my throbbing headache.

Tatum snarls at him, leaning back in her chair. "Okay, so anyway." She looks to Bishop with her eyes large before smiling back to me. "Do you remember anything from that day, Mads?"

They all stop, Bishop and Nate both focusing in on me. I bite down on my lip, thinking over that afternoon. I remember it all. But do I tell them that? Or should I give them parts? I trust them, I do, but like Bishop and Nate have both said in the past, knowledge is power and secrets are weapons. Especially in this fucked up world.

I shrug her question off, picking at the old hospital blanket on my bed. "I mean, I remember some, not all. There's like, blank spots." I instantly feel awful for lying, but when I look at both her and Nate, I see they buy it. Until my eyes connect with Bishop, and instead of buying my lies, he sees straight through them. The slant in his evil glare gives that away.

Fuck.

Fuck Bishop and his ability to read people. Is there anything this fucker isn't good at? Because I've got nothing. I think I need to find what it is Bishop sucks at so I can attack it. Just for shits and giggles, and also because I know it'll drive him crazy. And I sort of like him when he's mad. That's a dangerous thing.

"Okay, well that's okay, right, Nate?" Tate looks to Nate, but he brushes her off, not giving her a second glance. She looks to the floor briefly, gathering her wits again after being shot down so easily. I see it. Right there, I see she's caught feelings for him.

"Agh," I moan lightly, annoyed at everything and everyone. "I just want to go home, to my bed, to my shower, to eat food, and watch Netflix in bed all night." I was meant to say that in my head, but I then realize I said it out loud.

Bishop chuckles. "Done. I'll go hurry the nurse. You will need to eat something solid before they let you leave though."

"Yeah, but I'm pretty sure Bishop runs the shots in this hospital too, so he will probably get you discharged anyway, what with all the pull he has. Must be nice being a king," Tatum adds sassily, one eyebrow raised to the high heavens. Ah, I see. That's why she's being extra salty toward Bishop; she knows, or has picked up on, or is just being Tatum—about something. Bishop is still glaring at her with his lip curled when he walks out the door. Silence doesn't last long once he's gone, because Tatum is instantly at my side.

"I saw Bishop with that nurse lady!" she whispers into my ear. Well, it was supposed to be a whisper, only Nate heard her from the other side of the room as he gathers up all his belongings.

"I heard that, and Tate? Leave it the fuck alone." Nate doesn't look at her or acknowledge her presence—at all. This would bother Tate, because as much as she keeps to herself at school, and as much as she's a loner, she's a loner by choice. Tatum is beautiful—drop-dead stunning. What with her lush blonde hair and rosy cheeks. She looks like a Victoria's Secret model. It's her attitude that needs fixing. But who am I to judge? That's probably why we get along so well.

"Why?" she snaps back at Nate.

He exhales, folding up the blanket and tossing it onto the chair. "Let's start with, it's none of your fucking business, and finish with, you'll just end up pissing off both our best friends." Nate stops, raising his eyebrows at her in challenge.

She squares up. "How about... your best friend is a piece of shit, because while my best friend, AKA his...." She looks to me, and then looks to Nate, and then looks back to me again. "What are you two anyway?" she whispers.

I shrug. "Not something, but not nothing either."

Tatum's face drops. She's not impressed. "Madi, no, that's not a good place to be with a guy, because they have no rules and no boundaries. Men are simple creatures. They need lines. Simple lines."

"Well it works for us right now," I answer, pushing myself up off my bed. When she doesn't reply, I look at her. "Honestly, it really works for us right now. Whatever we have, it needs to be built slowly. We're too explosive. We wouldn't just blow each other up if this goes wrong; we'd take you all down with us."

Tatum mulls over what I've said and then walks back toward Nate. She spins around. "Okay, fine!"

"But...," I add.

Nate tosses the pillow on the other side of the room. "I knew it. I fucking knew this was coming."

"Fuck you," I snicker at him before looking back to Tatum. "What was it you saw?"

She searches my eyes then looks to Nate, and I brace myself. Brace myself for what everyone does when Nate, Bishop, or Brantley are in the room. It would probably happen if any of the other Kings were in the room too, but I just haven't been in the position. Tatum tilts her back as laughter erupts from her. Sarcastic laughter, but still laughter. She clutches her stomach, bringing her glare right back to Nate. "Naaw, Natey, I don't owe you or your pack of wolves shit. My loyalty is to Madison." She pauses and looks to me. "If I go missing, check their houses first." Then she slices to Nate. "She is my best friend, so fuck you and fuck Bishop."

"Fuck me?" Nate grins, and I fight the urge to massage my temples. "Well, you sure did, baby girl. Last night, in fact."

"Oh, gross, with me in the same room? Really?" I look at Tatum, because I expect more from her, though I really shouldn't.

She giggles. "My bad."

Rolling my eyes, I tilt my head up to the ceiling. "You were saying, Tate?" Bracing myself for the worst, while having an internal argument that whatever Bishop does is none of my business, Tatum opens her mouth.

"He had her up against the wall. He was... he...."

I don't need her to finish. I already know what she's going to say, and though I hate it, my heart sinks a little, and it's like sand has been siphoned down my airways every time I swallow. "He fucked her," I whisper through a clenched throat, swiping at the stray tear that has fallen down my cheek. Why do I care? I have no right to care. We're not together; we've never been official. This is probably why he didn't want us to go official, because he wanted to be a slut, and sluts don't like relationships.

But he's also told me things, things you shouldn't tell people unless you want them to grow feelings for you. My blood starts to boil a little before I start imagining what they were doing while I was in the hospital bed, what they—

"Madison!" Tatum snaps at me, clicking her fingers. "Jesus, Mary, and Joseph, girl! You really know how to zone out and get lost in that brain of yours." She has no idea. "As I was saying before you so rudely interrupted me"—she looks at me pointedly—"he had her up against the wall... by her throat."

I pause, blinking and catching what she's saying. So what? Bishop chokes me out during sex to the point of blacking out. What's her point?

She laughs, shaking her head. "No, you stupid cow. As in he was about to kill her."

Nate stills. "For the record, this is why we don't tell you anything. Remember this moment when you're throwing a tantrum about how you don't know anything." He tugs on his hoodie, zipping it up. Walking toward me, he presses a kiss to my head, hooking his finger under my chin to tilt my face up to his. "I'll go get the house ready for you, okay?"

I nod. "Thanks, Nate."

"Anytime." He smiles at me softly before glaring at Tatum. "Shut your mouth, Tate. Watch what you say if you like breathing."

She rolls her eyes and sits on the bed. Once Nate is out of the room, I look toward Tatum. I can see she's a little upset about the way Nate has been acting all morning. "For the record," I note, "I totally said you and Nate sleeping together would be a bad idea."

She opens her mouth, ready to defend herself, when she exhales in defeat. "Girl, you have no idea."

Actually, I do.

The door opens again, and Bishop walks in with the nurse from earlier scurrying not far behind him. "Usually the doctor would need to discharge you, but he's left it to me. You will need to eat something and sign paperwork at reception on your way out." She smiles, but it's strained, not reaching her eyes. She's just about to say something when another nurse walks in, pushing a cart full of food.

"Thanks," I murmur. I hate hospital food, but I can stomach a sandwich. Especially if it gets me out of here.

I take a bite, finishing it in record time before looking back to the nurse. "Thank you." I nod then gaze to Bishop, who's staring at me with his jaw clenched. Great. What the hell have I done now?

"Where'd Nate go?" Bishop finally breaks the awkward silence as the nurse starts removing my IV drips.

I wince slightly. "Home to get my room ready or something."

Bishop smiles and then looks to Tatum. "You didn't want to go with him?"

Tatum narrows her eyes on him. "Why would I want to do that?"

"Because you're you."

The drive home was painful. Between Bishop and Tatum both making a fuss over everything, I was almost ready to jump out of a moving vehicle on the freeway and walk home. And if I did, I would have survived, because for the first time ever, Bishop was going 10 mph, not wanting to go over potholes and bumps in the road.

Walking up the stairs, I push open my bedroom door, annoyed at both of them and wanting some space, but when I walk in, I gasp. "What the...?"

Nate sits on a mattress at the foot of my bed and has spread out the entire surface with cheesecakes, gummy bears, and my favorite chocolate, Debauve & Gallais's Le Livre.

There are sushi rolls lined in a circle platter with soy dipping sauce in the middle. Next to it is a round of tacos, and all the dipping sauces for fries and potato skins.

"Nate!" I smile. If I wasn't so sore, I'd jump his bones.

"Hey, Kitty." He grins, and because he's Nate, he looks all seductive. Or maybe I'm turned on by the food. "You hungry?" He wiggles his eyebrows and flexes his pecs.

I roll my eyes. "Yes, my God."

"Wow, Riverside, you sure know how to put on a show," Tatum mutters, walking into the room and grabbing her bag. She looks at me. "I'm going to go home, sleep for a hundred days in my own bed, and not talk to anyone for at least a month. She smiles, walking up to me and pulling me in for a hug. "I'll text you, okay?"

Nodding, I smile. "You better." Then she turns and exits, leaving me to deal with both Nate and Bishop.

"Actually," Nate smiles, getting off the mattress and dusting off his pants, "I didn't do any of this. Bishop did." He leans down, stealing a taco and shoving it into his mouth.

"So you just took it? No correcting me or Tatum?" I arch my eyebrow.

He shakes his head, swallowing his food. "She's fun to play with. That's all."

I unzip my hoodie and toss it onto my bed. "Don't hurt her, Nate."

"Hey!" He throws his empty hands up. "She knows where I stand. It's not my fault if she catches feelings. She's good in bed. That's all I want."

"What? And fuck around on her in the meantime?" I ask, reaching up and touching the gauze that's wrapped around my head.

He watches me and then cusses under his breath. "None of that matters. We aren't a thing. There's only one—or maybe two girls who had the power to change that, and one of them was you. Anyway, you feeling okay? You need anything?" He looks to Bishop, who is sprawled out on my bed, shirtless with gray sweatpants on and the rim of his Calvin Klein briefs poking out the top.

I'm screwed.

"I'm sure B will take care of you, right?"

Bishop reaches forward on my bed and grabs the remote, flicking the TV on. "Go to bed, Nate."

Nate winks at both of us before walking back through to his room. Bishop must push Play on a movie because it cuts through our silence. But it's not an awkward silence or the kind of silence you feel when you're in a room with someone you're uncomfortable with.

"I'm just going to take a shower," I say to him, walking to my closet to get a pair of sweatpants and a tank top.

He nods, watching as I pass him. Once I've gathered everything I need, I flick the light off and start walking back toward the bathroom, only Bishop catches my hand as I pass him, his fingers caressing my palm.

I turn to look at him over my shoulder. "You okay?" He's not usually touchy-feely, so this is new territory we're both walking through, but it feels right. He makes my heart race and my blood rush, but it feels right.

Tilting his head, he looks into my eyes then runs his thumb over my knuckles. "Yeah, yeah, I am now. Want me to run you a bath? You don't want to get that wet." He points up to my head, and I touch it, remembering the bandage and remembering I got shot—or grazed.

But still, I got shot.

Oh my God.

"What's wrong?" he asks, obviously noticing my facial expressions. Tilting his head to the other side, his fingers stay laced with mine.

I grin a little. "I'm a bit of a badass. I've been shot!"

He chuckles, letting go of my hand and slapping my ass. "Get in the shower."

I bite down on my lip and quickly rush into the bathroom.

"And lock that fucking door!" Bishop yells, his voice vibrating through the thin walls.

I laugh, shaking my head and unbuttoning my jeans before slipping them off. Scrubbing myself in the shower, I want to stay in for longer than I do but I also really want to be near Bishop right now, so I flick off the faucet and grab the towel, wrapping it around myself. Drying my body, I already feel much better than I did five minutes ago. Slipping on my boy-shorts and my loose gray sweatpants, I toss on my tight black tank and put my towel in the hamper before pulling open my bedroom door. Leaning on the doorframe, I smile at Bishop, who's biting into one of the sushi rolls.

"Good?"

"Not bad, but I guess it will taste even better to you because you haven't eaten in so long." I push off the wall and make my way toward him, taking a seat beside him on the mattress. Grabbing a taco, I dip it into the guacamole and bite into the crispy shell.

"Mmmmm," I groan, unable to help the pleasure that takes over my body as my taste buds get their first taste of the taco.

Bishop pauses, sushi roll midway to his mouth. "Don't do that."

"Do what?" I ask innocently, licking the sauce off my fingers.

He drops the sushi roll back onto the platter. "Madison...."

I roll my eyes. "I won't do that, but! Only because I'm starving and I actually feel like I'm about to eat every single thing on this platter."

"Good." He grins, picking up the sushi roll and popping it back into his mouth.

I chow down my taco, not making a single sound. Reaching for my water bottle, I twist it open, swallowing the cool liquid.

"So tell me, how'd you know all of this was my favorite food?" I ask Bishop, stretching out on the mattress because my stomach feels like it's about to explode. Looking up at the ceiling, I eventually look toward him when he doesn't say anything.

"I know all there is to know about you, Madison." He moves the platter to the other side of the mattress and slides beside me. "Ask me anything."

"Hmmm." I bring my finger to my lip, pretending to mull over some questions. "Okay, how about this?"

Bishop raises his eyebrows cockily.

"Where was I born?"

"New York, try harder than that."

He's right; that was too easy. "My first pet's name?"

"Billy and he was a goldfish. You were seven and demanded your mom buy it for you so you'd have a friend, because you were an only child. Furthermore, you used that same excuse for Jasper the Persian cat, Slash—by the way, nice choice of name—the Pomeranian—not a fan of giving such a powerful name to such a tiny dog either—and Jupiter, your parrot." He tilts his head, egging me to challenge him.

I don't. I just stare, because what else could I do? Nothing surprises me much in this world now since finding out about the Kings, but it's still a lot to take in.

"Wow," I whisper out, rolling onto my stomach. I lean my head on the palm of my head and look up at him. He's sitting up with his back leaning against the bedframe, but his legs are spread out in front of him.

"You have me at a disadvantage then," I whisper, locking eyes with him. "I don't know much about you."

He snorts, leaning back, his ab muscles tensing as he does it. "Don't take it to heart. No one knows anything about me." He closes his eyes and reaches out. "Come here." Two simple words but so commanding. I don't fight it. I scoot up the mattress and snuggle into his warm, hard arms. His familiar scent starts to smell more like home and less like Bishop. Running the tip of my nose against his chest, I draw lines across his pec, over the tattoo that is inked into his skin. It's an eagle, soaring freely. "This is cool." I yawn.

He grunts. "Yeah, but I bet you could draw something better."

That makes me smile. "I could."

My eyes drop heavily, and I can slowly feel myself slipping into sleep.

"Will you draw one for me one day?" he asks in a tired voice. The sexiest sleepy voice I've ever heard. I sound like a man when I'm tired, so I clear my throat.

"Yes."

He squeezes me into him softly, and just like that, I slip into a deep sleep.

Cool air drifts over my legs, goose bumps breaking out over my skin. I reach over blindly to grab the blanket when Bishop tosses and turns. "No!" he yells. I shoot up and look at him. Sweat is dripping over his skin, his arm thrown over his eyes. He starts punching his head. "No! Leave him alone. Leave her alone!"

"Bishop!" I grab onto his arm, wanting to stop his assault on himself. "Bishop? Shhhh...." Lava builds in my throat as tears threaten to surface. What's he dreaming about?

"Bishop?"

"No! Leave him alone, leave him alone, leave her alone...!"

Rolling over, I straddle his waist, clearing the sweat from his chest. "Hey," I whisper, leaning into his ear. "It's me."

His jaw clenches before he finally opens his eyes and looks straight at me.

"Hey," I repeat, running my fingers down his cheeks and swiping away the sweat. "You okay?"

He stares at me, unmoving. It starts to get awkward, so I swing my leg off him but he clenches down on my thigh. I look back at him. "Bi—"

His fist comes to my hair and he wraps it around, pulling my face down to meet his.

"Well," I mutter under my breath. "Good thing my graze in on my temple."

I don't say another word. I go with it. Something has happened, something inside his head, so I'll do what I can to help. Kissing me, his tongue slips between my lips. I open my mouth wider, giving him more access. Gripping onto my thighs, he flips me onto my back and spreads my legs wide with his, pinning my arms above my head.

His eyes skim over the side of my head. "Are you good to go?" I know what he's asking. He's asking if I'm ready to fuck—fuck Bishop style.

"Yes," I answer truthfully, because I am. Aside from a little headache, nothing else hurts, and if it does, whatever, I'll pay for it in the morning, and I'm sure it'll be worth it.

"Fuck," he growls, his voice unrecognizable.

Looking over his face, his eyes slam closed as he pulls his bottom lip into his mouth. "Yes, Bishop," I repeat softly. "I promise—no limits. I can take it. I can handle it." I'll probably regret that,

I reach out to swipe the bead of sweat that's about to drip off his chin, but he hits my hand away. "Don't."

"What?" I murmur.

"Not now."

He pins my hands above my head, his palms gliding up my thighs until he gets to the waistband of my sweatpants then tugs them off. His fingertips glide over the lining of my underwear before slipping underneath to press inside me.

"Get up."

"What?" I whisper, confused. He gets to his knees just as "Escalate" by Tsar B starts blasting from Nate's room. The song has a heavy bass line, and it sounds so clear that it's as if it's playing in here.

Bishop pulls down his jeans, getting to his feet at the side of the bed and tossing off his boxer briefs. I stare down at his cock and watch as he slowly pumps it, his eyes locked on mine. Grinning, he nudges his head. "Get up, baby."

Crawling, I tilt my head. "But why?"

"Because you're going to do what I say."

"Bu—"

His hand flies up to my neck, and he instantly squeezes, tugging my head up to look at him. His shoulders are square, his stance stiff, strong, and thick like always. This is Bishop, and always will be Bishop. He's alpha out there; he has to be because of who he is. But in the bedroom, his alpha tendencies have no bounds. The song must be on repeat because it plays again.

I close my eyes, nodding. "What do you want me to do?"

His grip loosens and he steps backward, grabbing his pack of cigarettes off the chest of drawers, the moonlight sneaking through the cracks of my patio door, outlining him perfectly. His face, his profile, that body, that… dick. He's perfection wrapped in a case of C4. He puts a cigarette between his lips, flicks his Zippo, and looks at me after lighting it, a grin on his face. Sucking on his cigarette, he tilts his head back to blow out the smoke, his neck straining at the movement. I look down at his hand, still holding his dick, slowly pumping it, and my mouth waters. Holy shit. I've never seen something so erotic in my life. Sweat beads on my flesh as my clit throbs between my thighs. I want him.

Fuck. I want him. The way my nipples feel, as though they're getting whisked with the breeze, and the way my hips start rolling to the rhythm of his pumping, tells him how badly. He chuckles, leaving the cigarette between his lips, and walks toward me. His legs hit the side of the bed, and he takes the smoke out of his mouth.

I look up at him, my hands running up his muscular thighs. Pulling in my bottom lip, I run my tongue over it and reach for his cock.

Blowing out a cloud of smoke, he looks down at me, our eyes entranced in each other. Locked in a cell that's sealed with lust. "Suck." His lip curls slightly, the grin still on his face and his smoke between his thumb and pointer finger.

I look down to the tip of him, licking my lips again, and lean forward, wrapping my mouth around him securely. His precum hits the back of my throat, and I moan slightly, my tongue dancing up his long length. He grips onto my hair, piling it all on the top of my head then tugs on it, yanking my head backward. Again, I'm thanking whoever it was that saved me that day for the bullet skimming the side of my temple, and not anywhere near where any hair pulling happens.

I look up at him, my lips wrapped around him while my head bobs. He sucks on the last bit of his smoke, then turns toward the porch door and flicks it out before turning back to me and shoving me onto the bed. "Lay down."

"Like I have a choice." I roll my eyes.

He pins my hands above my head, spreading my legs wide open with his, and runs his nose down the side of my neck. "Mmm," he groans, and it vibrates over my flesh before sinking into my bones. I quiver, goose bumps rolling over my skin. His grin presses against my flesh before I feel his tongue slide down my collarbone then down over my nipple. Pulling it into his mouth, he bites down roughly, and I wince.

"Bishop," I warn, remembering how rough he can get.

"Not your place to say, Kitty. Remember that."

"Safe word."

"And I said fuck your safe word." As he circles my nipple with his tongue, my eyes close and my hips rise to grind against his, needing more. More friction. Needing him inside of me, filling me until I can barely take the pain of his size.

"How will you know if it's too far for me?" I ask, circling my pelvis into him. He raises slightly, not letting me gain any more friction or pleasure, and I have to fight just putting my hand down there and taking care of the ache myself.

He continues his travels, leaving a warm trail of goose bumps in his wake. "Guess if you die, that's a sign."

My eyes snap open and I lean up on my elbows. "Bishop!"

He peers up at me, hovering just over my pelvic bone, his arms rippling from holding himself up. He grins, his eyes darkening. "I'm just joking." His tongue comes out and licks over my clit. "I think." Letting go, I drop onto my back, my hair sprawling out everywhere. He grips onto my thigh and pushes me open wider, while his other arm hooks my thigh over his shoulder. He licks me at a perfect rhythm, never stopping, never changing. Never too fast and never too slow. Just as my stomach clenches and sweat trickles over my abs, I'm grasping onto the edge of sanity, about to fall off into my orgasm, when he stops. Everything turns cold, my entire body dropping to an icy temperature instantly.

"Agh!" I scream, getting onto my elbows. He crawls up my body, licking his lips while his eyes fuck every inch of me.

"Mine." His hand comes to mine and he flings them over my head again, pinning me down. "Don't fuck with me, Madison. You're mine." He squeezes roughly, rough enough to leave marks on my wrists, and I flinch. He smirks and then releases, flinging me onto my stomach, he rubs my ass cheek softly before whacking it hard, the loud slap breaking through the song I can still hear. Moving my hair to one side, he grabs onto my thigh and hooks it onto his hip before I feel his weight fall over my back and his cock press at my entrance.

I moan at the sudden intrusion, and his other hand comes up to the back of my neck, pressing me into place as he sinks farther and farther into me, pushing every single limit I have. Gripping onto my thigh, the tips of his fingers dig into my flesh as he pulls out of me, thrusting over my G-spot every single time and then launching into me again, my body almost flying forward. His grip on the back of my neck tightens and then loosens as he brings his body back over mine while still gripping my thigh up against his hip. He thrusts into me, circling and rubbing me deep. My pussy clenches around him, clinging on and not letting go. Every extraction, I clench harder. Lost in the way his cock presses against every single inch of my core. Owning me from the inside out.

"Yes," I moan. "Bishop, fuck me."

He lets go of my leg, pulls out, flips me over, and picks me up, rolling onto his back. I climb on top of him, slowly dropping my weight over his hard dick. Leaning on his chest, I roll my hips, his cock thrusting inside me as his pelvic bone collides with my clit. I swing my head back, and his hips buckle as he clenches onto mine.

"Come."

As if on cue, I let go, sweat dripping off both our bodies. I clench around him, throbbing as the orgasm smashes through me and I jerk through the ecstasy.

"Fuck!" His hips slam up, pushing my body up faster and harder, plowing through my orgasm to reach his. He sets me off again, and wave after a wave, another orgasm collides into me, my clit swelling, my nipples cool. Bishop leans up, catches one of my nipples in between his teeth, and bites down on it. It stings, but the sting with the pleasure is too much. His hand comes up to my throat while his other stays on my hip and he lies back down, a touch of blood on the corner of his lip. I don't have to look to know where that's from; the stinging of my nipple says enough.

His fingers dig into my hips, his grip around my throat tightening to the point where air is coming in and out slowly, like I'm breathing through a thick cloud of smoke. He pounds into me, his balls slapping against my ass as I try to regain control being on top of him, but there's no point. He is always in control no matter what, so I let go. Dots dance in my eyes from being choked, my thighs throb from his grip, and now my hips are stinging too. He slams into me harder, and I feel it again, the build-up. My head swings back. I'm exhausted, but I'm not able to stop the pleasure. He's fucking the life out of me, quite literally, because I can feel myself losing consciousness every now and then, but I notice how he loosens his grip every few seconds too, as if to give me little cracks of air.

I'm just about to hit the tip of my orgasm when he comes, his dick throbbing and pulsing inside of me. He lets go of me instantly, and I ride it out with him slowly. I wanted another, but I know I'm being greedy, and I can already feel how sore I am, not only everywhere where he's physically hurt me, but down there too. Wincing, I swing my leg and get off, feeling his cum drip down my thigh.

"I get the depo shot," I say sleepily, dragging my sore and severely fucked self to the bathroom and pulling down a towel to clean myself up. He still hasn't said anything, so I look at him. "Are you okay?"

"Yeah," he answers through a dry throat. Getting up, he tugs on his boxers and walks toward the little bar fridge I have in the room. Surprisingly, even though I just had rough sex, my head doesn't feel bad. Or I'm just that sore everywhere else on my body that my pain threshold has sort of tilted this way.

Bishop gets a bottle of water and twists off the cap, taking a drink while looking at me.

"Wanna talk about it?" I ask, throwing the towel into a hamper and going back to bed. Fuck the rumpled blankets; I can't even be bothered remaking my bed, so I just slip under, sliding onto the side I sleep on. When Bishop doesn't answer, I look over to the little alarm clock that sits on my bedside table. Fucking 5:00 a.m.? Mother fuck.

"It's 5:00 a.m.!" I yell, honest to God shocked at the time.

"Then we fucked for three hours."

"How do you know that?" I ask, watching as he slips back into bed with me.

He stretches his arms out, pulling me into him. I don't know why, but I smile, my heart calming at his touch, his smell, his flesh pressing against mine. All those things are why Bishop is home to me.

He kisses me on my head. "Because the terrors happen at the same time every night."

"Why?" I whisper, yawning and beginning to feel more and more pain all over my body. I'll hate to see what I'm going to look like later in the morning.

"Because I've done bad things. And those bad things like to remind me every night that I did them."

I swallow, my eyes heavy even though my interest in this convo is piquing. My body and mind can't keep up. "Did what?"

"Killed and fucked."

CHAPTER 21

I can't move. That's not a figure of speech. I literally cannot move a muscle in my body, and I'm not sure if I should be genuinely concerned about this or not.

"Bishop?" I croak. Gross, I hate my morning voice. I sound like a man that's been lost in the desert for years.

His arm is clenched around my waist, pulling me into him while his leg is over mine. So not only am I in pain and can't move, but his heavy-ass weight is holding me down too. Surprise, surprise, he's even possessive in his sleep.

"Bishop!" I get a little louder, trying to pry his limbs off mine.

"What?" he groans, letting me go and rubbing his eyes.

I go to move my leg and... nope, that's not happening. "Nothing. I just... I can't move," I laugh, shaking my head.

He stops rubbing his eyes and looks at me, and fuck him. His ruffled hair is messy everywhere, his dark green eyes fresh, his skin pure, and his lips kissable and plump.

"I think," I murmur, tilting my head at him. "Nope, not think—I definitely want to punch you."

He bursts out laughing. "Well—" Lifting the blanket, he scans over my naked body. "I don't think that's a good idea, babe. I mean... you're in a state right now."

He drops the blanket, and I pick it back up and peer down at myself.

"Oh my God!" I gasp in shock and then narrow my eyes at Bishop. "Are you kidding me? I look like I've been beaten."

"Hey!" He throws his hands up. "You know how I get, and I'm pretty sure I went a little easy on you."

"Oh really?" I scold him, flicking the blanket off my body and walking toward the bathroom. "'Cause I'm pretty sure that's my blood on your fucking lip!" I slam the door closed and then bite down on my fist, holding in my scream. My whole body throbs. My hips, my thighs.... My neck feels like there's a massive ring still clenched around it, and my freaking nipple feels like it's been torn off, and to make everything worse, my vagina feels fucking swollen, because oh no, he can't just mark me in one place; he has to absolutely destroy me. Flicking on the faucet, I slowly step into the hot, steamy water, and I scream before I can stop myself. "Motherfucker!"

Nate bangs on his door, because I locked it. "Mads! What's wrong?"

"Leave me alone," I yell out. "Pretty sure you knew what was happening too, motherfucker," I mutter under my breath, grabbing the soap and sliding it through my hands. Now that the initial sting is gone from stepping in, the water pounding on my bruised flesh is actually comforting.

Bang.

Bang.

"Madison!" Nate calls again through the door. I roll my eyes and flip him the bird, grabbing my towel and wrapping it around myself. "What?"

"Are you okay?"

"I'm hungry. I'm going to get something to eat."

"I'll do it. Go back to bed!"

"Don't—"

"Madison," he growls.

"I want to see Daemon. Shut up and stop telling me what to do!" I go to grab my clothes when I realize I didn't bring any in with me. Fuck.

I walk out, but Bishop is gone. Looking around my room suspiciously, I check the closet, coming up short. Staying in the closet, I wiggle into some white skinny jeans, a black top, and some sneakers before grabbing a sweater. I remember the nurse saying I can remove the Band-Aid today, so I unwrap that from my head, feeling the coolness whipping over my newly exposed skin. There's still a couple of butterfly stitches where my wound is, so I leave it there. The wound itself doesn't hurt anymore; it's just the light headache that throbs in the back of brain that does. Then again, that could be from Bishop's hair pulling the night before. Though I know that he could have been a lot rougher with the pulling than he was.

I toss the Band-Aid into the trash and grab my keys. I don't care what either of them say; I want to see my brother. He didn't do anything wrong. I just know he didn't.

I was wrong about one thing, though. I definitely regret nothing about last night.

Walking into the local police station, I go straight to the front reception desk. "Hi." The receptionist looks up at me from her typing, pushing her glasses down. She's old, and by the looks of the scowl she's giving me, she's not having a good day. "I was wondering how I go about seeing my brother? He was brought in a few days ago after an incident."

She stops me with a simple whip of her hand. "Daemon—"

"Madison?" My dad's voice breaks through from behind me. "What are you doing here?"

I turn to face him, plastering a fake smile on my face. "Oh! Hey, Dad!"

I look back to the receptionist, where she looks at me with an eyebrow quirked, eyeing me up and down. Looking back to my dad, I walk up to him. "I was just wondering if I could see Daemon."

Dad looks at me suspiciously. "He's out on bail. Happened just this morning. I take it he will be at home now."

I can't help the smile that comes onto my mouth, my chest warming. "At our home? Okay, I'll go up there now."

"Madison." My dad puts his hands into his pockets. "We need to talk about Daemon though, so I'll get Sammy to meet us back at home."

"Okay," I whisper, relaxing so much more, now that I know he's on bail and at home. I can't imagine Daemon in a prison cell, and he doesn't deserve to be in a one. I know what people say about him, but he would never hurt me—regardless of what he does or has done to other people. I don't know why I have such certainty about Daemon, but I do. My ease with him is effortless. Maybe it's a twin thing, I don't know.

I follow Dad back out of the station and wait as he tells Sammy that she can meet us back at home.

"So," I begin, unlocking the truck and getting into the driver side. Dad gets into the passenger seat and clips in his belt. "What is it you want to talk about?"

"Daemon."

"Yes, we can start with him," I murmur, pulling out into the oncoming traffic. "Why?"

Dad looks at me. I can see him from the corner of my eye. "Why what?"

"Why didn't you and Mom want him?" I ask, risking a quick glance toward him. "I mean, it just doesn't seem fair that I got this life and he got his."

"Whose life do you think is worst?"

Interesting question, but that's Dad for you. He has always had a way of expressing his knowledge—a way I hated growing up.

"I don't know," I scoff. "Don't make me answer that. I got a luxurious life, though it hasn't been easy at times, and I've...." I clear my throat, not wanting to get too touchy with this subject. "But Daemon's life seems messed up, Dad. So why? Why'd you and Mom decide he wasn't worthy of your love?"

"It's not that, Madison. He wasn't fit to be a King, so he had to be a Lost Boy."

I laugh. I can't help it, but "he's not fit to be a King" just grinds me the wrong way. "That makes no sense."

"You will never make sense of this world. You need to understand that." He looks at me, and I glance back at him. "Trying to figure out this world will never happen, Madison, and it will kill you like it has killed many others who tried."

Taking my eyes off him, I look back to the road. "There are so many questions."

Dad nods. "Yes," he looks ahead of himself, "and just when you think you know everything, something else gets thrown into the mix," he mutters under his breath, almost like he didn't mean for me to hear.

"Like what, Dad?"

He looks back to me and smiles, the wrinkles around his eyes deepening. "That's not for you to worry about. Just be careful with Daemon. I know he wouldn't... intentionally hurt you. But he's a dangerous sort, Madison. He's so very dangerous."

"Why do people keep saying that?" I don't mean to, but it comes out as if I'm annoyed. I guess I am. I've seen a glimpse into the dark side of Daemon. I say glimpse because of the way people are talking about him makes it seem like he has a very, very dark part about him. But even in that mode, he wouldn't hurt me.

"Because it's the truth." Dad exhales. "Just be careful. If I tried to explain Daemon to you, it still wouldn't scratch the surface, but I have rules."

"Rules?" I inch my head back. "Since when do you give me rules?"

"Since a bullet grazed your temple, Madison!" He raises his voice a little toward the end but then breathes out, exhaling all his anger. "Look, stick to these rules or I will father you, and I don't care how old you are."

"Fine." I slump into my chair, pulling down our street. "What are your rules?"

"You are not to be alone with Daemon under any circumstances. The Kings know, so if you want to spend time with him, one of them needs to be there with you."

"That's bullshit!"

"No, that's the rule. They don't have to be right beside you, but they need to be there." I pull into our gated driveway. "Elena and I are flying to Dubai tomorrow morning. Stick to that one rule or I will be on the first flight home, understood?" He looks at me just as I pull up the emergency brake.

"Fine."

"Good." Dad smiles. "Oh, I've moved Daemon to the bedroom on the other side of Nate's room."

"Why?" I ask, getting out of the truck and rounding to the front. "Why not beside my room?"

Dad stops, tilting his head at me. "Does it matter?"

I open my mouth, ready to answer, but close it again. "I guess not." Because it doesn't. At least he's here, and Dad is allowing him to stay. I have to be grateful for that, though Katsia will want that meeting ASAP. I can't stand her and I don't trust her. She's apparently a descendant of Bishop's family line, and though I've only met Bishop's dad a couple of times, I don't like him. He's the king of the Kings, and there's no way in hell I'd ever cross him. Same as Katsia.

Taking the stairs one at a time, I go straight to Daemon's room and knock.

"Come in."

Pushing the door open, I lean on the frame. "Hey, you."

He smiles, a genuine, big smile, and his eyes light up. He gets up off the bed where he was sitting oddly, staring at…. There's no TV there, so he was staring at the wall. As he pulls me in for a hug, I wrap my arms around his waist and sink into his embrace. "I'm so sorry about all of this, Daemon."

"Hush," he murmurs into my hair. "They just like you safe. Like me. I like that too."

"Yeah, but they should trust that I trust you."

Daemon inches back slightly, his eyebrows pulling in as he seems to mull over what I just said. "Trust," he whispers, and then looks down at me.

"Yes, trust. It's the feeling you get when you know someone won't hurt you. It's loving someone and knowing they wouldn't betray you."

Daemon shakes his head, and lets go, stepping backward. "No, Madison. If that is trust, I do not deserve yours. You should not trust me."

I step forward. "Daemon, I do though."

He shakes his head, stepping back again until the backs of his legs hit the rocking chair that is in the corner. He takes a seat. "No. You cannot."

"Daemon—"

"Madison," Bishop speaks up from the door, and I turn to face him, searching his eyes.

"What?"

"Leave. Now."

"What?" I snap, then look back to Daemon. "Do you want me to leave?"

Daemon looks up at me from leaning on his elbows, his eyes pained and his face strained. It's the first time I've seen him in any other light aside from my brother, and he's beautiful. Beautifully ruined. "*Ita.*"

I look back to Bishop, not knowing what that means. He simply nods, so I look back at Daemon. "Okay."

I push past Bishop and walk toward my bedroom, flopping down on my bed. Seconds and then minutes pass before Bishop walks back in, shutting the door behind him.

I shoot to my feet. "Is he okay?"

He walks farther into my room, taking a seat on the bed beside me. "Yeah. When he's like that though, Madison, you need to let him have space. Nothing good will come from pushing Daemon to a point where...." He stops, seeming to think over what he's about to say.

"Bishop," I warn, looking toward him. "You need to not lie to me." He lies down on his back, and I follow, rolling onto my stomach. "Please. Just don't lie to me. I can handle everyone else lying to me, but not you."

Turning his head, he looks between my eyes. It's intense. His stare is always intense; it makes me want to look away, but I'm afraid I won't feel it again. I want to feel it for as long as I can. Soak it up, bathe in it, swim in it. Now I sound crazy, but maybe I am. Maybe when it comes to him, he brings out the dark, crazy side of me that I've always suppressed by being the quiet girl. Because he gives me confidence, all the confidence I need to tackle or do anything, and that's lethal.

Reaching out, he tucks some of my loose hair behind my ear and smiles softly. "I promise I won't lie to you."

I inhale, unable to contain the warm feeling that overflows my insides at his promise. Not once has anyone—not my father, not Nate, no one—promised me those words since I've found out about this world. Leaning down, I kiss him, running my lips softly against his. I'm just about to pull away when his hand comes to the back of my neck and he grips onto me, pulling me back down to his mouth. His tongue darts inside and everything in me instantly comes to life. Picking me up, he puts me on his lap, and I straddle him, raking my hair out of my face.

"I'm not used to this," he murmurs, his hands coming to rest on my thighs.

"Used to what?" I ask, running my pointer finger down his hard chest, over each ab muscle, and eventually down to the lines that disappear under his jeans.

"This, what this is. I'll fuck it up one way or another. You're prepared for that—right?" he asks, his tone sincere.

I shrug, looking back into his eyes. "I guess we can cross that bridge when we get there." I open my mouth, wondering whether or not I should ask the question that is itching at the back of my brain. "Khales?" I must have decided I was going to go there, because before I can stop myself, I say it.

His jaw tenses. "It's not as you or everyone thinks." He taps me, and I swing my leg off him, scooting up the bed and leaning on the headboard.

"So tell me then. What was she?"

"A close friend. We were always together, because she was a friend. You know your Tatum? The girl you met before you knew about the Kings?"

I nod, slightly nervous at where this conversation could go. It's the first time Bishop has ever opened up about Khales, and I don't want to say something dumb and have him clam up again. "Yeah, but haven't you boys always known about the Kings?"

He laughs, running his hands through his hair and leaning on his elbows, his back turned toward me. "No. It's not until you're of age when you're given the book. I had known Khales since we were in preschool."

"Who was she?" I ask, tilting my head. "I know she went to Tillie's school and all that."

"Yeah." He clears his throat. "She had a shitty life, and then eventually started playing with drugs. I always tried to help her where I could, but sometimes you can't help those who don't want to be helped. Anyway, she kicked the drugs, and after I was initiated, she and I got close again. That is until my father decided otherwise."

"Initiated? You mean after you...?"

He looks at me over his shoulder then turns to face me fully, leaning back on one of the posts at the end of my bed. "I'm sure you know about the initiation process."

I blush. "Yes... how old?"

"Thirteen." He looks at me carefully. "I'm sure you know what happens after...."

"Your first kill?" I ask lightly. I already know the answer, so I pull my eyes away from his and look at the wall.

"Truth?" he replies gently.

My eyes snap back to him. "Always."

"Then, no, it wasn't my first kill."

I breathe in deeply. "Well, okay."

"Okay?" He chuckles, shaking his head and pulling his bottom lip between his teeth. "I tell you that I killed someone when I was younger than thirteen, and you say 'okay?' Like it's the most natural thing in the world?" He looks back at me, a mixture of awe and anger in his stare.

"Well," I reply, "in our world, it is natural."

"True," he agrees.

"So your dad? He made you kill her?" I want to tread carefully around her, and I probably should have found a better word than kill, but I need straightforward answers, and to get straight answers, you need to ask straightforward questions. Leave them no gap to dance around their answer.

His jaw clenches. "Something like that." I can see it's a touchy subject, and aside from the fact that Bishop isn't someone who opens up, I don't want to push it. I don't want to use the fact he just promised me he wouldn't lie to bleed answers out of him.

Smiling, I shake my head. "Hungry?"

He snaps up at me in shock, "What? You're not going to push for more answers?"

I shrug, getting off the bed. "No, I figure if I go in too hard, you might clam up, and I really am hungry." My phone dings in my pocket and I pull it out, opening the text from Tatum.

Tate - You home?
Me - Yep.
Tate - I'll come up soon.

Tossing my phone back on the bed, Bishop looks at it then back to me. "It was Tate," I answer his unspoken question. "She'll come up soon."

He laughs, getting off the bed and stretching his arms high. "I figured."

The following few days have gone better than I expected. Aside from Daemon's lawyer building his case, Bishop and I have fallen into a smooth... relationship? I'm actually not sure what we are, and I don't want to interrupt the flow of things by asking for a label. Daemon hasn't left his room though, and that worries me. Everyone I have expressed my angst to about him not leaving his room has told me to leave it alone and that he's dealing with things the way he knows how. So out of respect for Daemon, I do just that. I've left it.

"I need to ask you something," Tate says, peeling off the lid of her yogurt. "Please don't get mad at me for bringing it up, but it's been itching at me for some time."

Biting into my apple, I roll my hand for her to continue—at least until the boys get here, and then I'm sure she will tense up like she always does. I'm not sure what is going on with her and Nate, but I've decided to leave that too, not wanting to go near their drama.

"Okay, so the tape…," she starts, and I pause my chewing, looking around the cafeteria in panic mode.

"Tatum!" I snap at her through a whisper. "Why would you bring that up?" I sit straight, biting into my apple again.

"Well, I don't know. Maybe because you haven't mentioned it."

"Well I just want to forget." I give her a pointed stare.

"I just have this thing. So who sent it? Ally?" She won't stop. Someone needs to gag her.

"Apparently so—yes."

"But here's the thing." She spoons her yogurt into her mouth. "Ally was apparently at a retreat the day that video got leaked. As in, she couldn't have done it, because you're not allowed phones."

I pause again, thinking over what she said. There's no way that it couldn't have been Ally. All signs pointed to her, and she admitted it was her. "It was her, Tate. She confessed."

Tatum shrugs. "Ehhh, I just think that's Ally. She's going to take credit for any pain that has been inflicted on you, just because it's you. But I don't think she sent it."

"Well, maybe not." I drop my apple, appetite gone. "But she definitely had a part to play in it."

"Mmm," Tatum murmurs. "Which is my next thing. There's someone who was working with her if that's the case."

I look around the cafeteria, watching all the students, in small cliques, some laughing, some drawing, some playing the guitar, and some just alone. "I haven't had any trouble from it since, so I don't want to look into it. Let's just drop it?"

Tatum nods. "Consider it dropped."

If she's right and someone was working with Ally, then there's someone here who is working against me. Could it be Lauren? But since Ally disappeared, she's been hanging around the nerd group.

Just as I'm about to open my mouth, Bishop walks into the cafeteria with the rest of the boys following closely behind. He takes a seat beside me, Nate sitting next to Tatum. I should really ask what's going on between the two of them, but I won't. I'm scared he's just using Tatum as a rebound from Tillie, because I saw how he was with Tillie. Without sounding completely bigheaded, I didn't even exist when Tillie was around, and since she's been gone, I can see, just slightly, not in an obvious way, what her absence has done to him. I know I was told not to look for her, but once all this shit is sorted with the Kings, and Daemon, and Katsia, and all the other things I've left out, if she's still not home, I will look for her.

Bishop wraps his arm around me, pulling me in and kissing me on the head. "Hey, baby."

Swoon.

I smile shyly. "Hey."

Tatum kicks me from under the table, so I look at her, widening my eyes to ask what the hell she wants. Her eyes shoot over her shoulder, so I follow, looking where she's pointedly staring, and that's when I see it. The whole school has pretty much stopped what they were doing to watch Bishop's and my exchange. It's unsettling and it's weird, but I've gotten used to it over the years. Not just because Bishop is who he is, but from always being the new girl. But attaining Bishop has made people's heads spin. He's the standoffish asshole. No one was good enough for him—until me.

"So, just a quick little question while I have everyone here. Carter is throwing a party this weekend to mark...." Tatum thinks over something and then shakes her head. "Never mind. I forgot what it was for, but anyway! I'm going. Mads?" She looks at me, her eyes wide like innocent little saucers. The innocence is a lie.

I stick my straw into my mouth. "Think I'll pass. I have a few things to do this weekend."

"Bishop being one of them?" she quips back, fluttering her eyelashes.

"Bishop being all of them," Bishop answers for me, picking me up from my seat and placing me onto his lap. I feel bad. I know I shouldn't, but I do. I know Tatum feels like she's losing her best friend since Bishop and I have been spending so much time together, and I don't want her to feel like that at all. Tatum's eyes drop to her food, and she picks at her orange.

Rolling my eyes, I turn to face Bishop. "Shall we go? Just for a little while. We don't have to stay late."

Bishop tosses one of my carrot sticks into his mouth and winks. "Yeah, babe." He looks over Tatum's shoulder, directly at Carter. "We should go." His eyes do that dark thing, and I spin back around, his hand gripping possessively on my thigh.

"We will come."

Tatum claps excitedly. "Yay, okay, so outfits—"

"Oh no." I cut her off. "Nope. You're on your own with that. I'll wear whatever I have."

Nate sits beside her, chatting to Eli and Brantley about something, ignoring our entire conversation.

"Nate?" I question, waiting for him to answer.

"Yo?" He stops midconversation.

"Party at Carter's this weekend. You in?"

He looks to Bishop then slowly smirks. "Yeah, sounds good." Why do I feel like I've missed something? Why are they suddenly so interested to go to one of Carter's parties? Spinning back around to face Bishop, I see he's already staring at me when my eyes lock with his. I open my mouth, but he shakes his head, eating another carrot stick. "Later."

Giving him a small smile as a reply, I settle for it and turn back around. "So, outfits?" I grin at Tatum.

She wiggles her eyebrows. "Outfits."

"Jeans and a t—"

"More like skirts and G."

Bursting out laughing, I shake my head. "Oh, Tate."

CHAPTER 22

"I hate you," I mutter to Tatum. "I can't believe you're making me wear this."

She laughs, walking out of the bathroom, spraying her Coco Chanel perfume all over herself. "Well, you know I know what's best for you. Like that dress—that dress is what's good for you."

I pick at the skirt. It's a tight, knee-length, black leather pencil skirt with a split that goes almost all the way up to my hip. She paired it with a thigh chain that dangles over my very exposed leg, and a little bralette crop top. Yes, the outfit is almost no outfit, and because the split is so high, I decided it was either a G-string or commando kind of night. Commando won. I slide on the nude lipstick and ruffle my hair into a nest of tousled mess. "Well," I mutter, slipping on some red pointy heels. Totally don't know how this is going to end, what with me in heels and everything, but again, that was Tatum being Tatum.

She snatches her bottle of vodka off the dresser. "Let's go. Is Sammy driving us?"

I nod. "Yeah, she's already waiting."

"And Bishop and Nate?" she asks, going for casual, but I see what she's doing.

"They'll meet us there, had something to take care of beforehand." I don't know what it was they had to take care of; I didn't care to ask. I respect there will be some things that Bishop can't tell me, especially when it comes to the Kings, so I won't pry for information unless it directly impacts me. Daemon still hasn't come out of his room, but I try every day. I knock, but he doesn't answer. I'm not sure what's going on with him, but all I know is I want to be there for him. Whatever it is he's going through.

Piling into the limo, Sammy gets into the driver seat and looks at me in the rear-view mirror. "You be safe now."

"I'm always safe, Sammy."

She rolls her eyes. "Dressing like that is only asking for trouble."

"Just drive," Tatum says sassily to Sammy.

"Tate!" I growl her. "Shut up and drink."

She takes a sip and then passes it to me. "I don't want to get white girl wasted, but I'll have a little bit."

"Myth" by Tsar B starts playing, and I take a sip of the vodka, ignoring the way it stabs my throat when I swallow. "Sammy! Turn it up!" She does as she's told, winding up the window separator while she's at it. I give the bottle back to Tatum, and she scoots over beside me. "Oh! Selfie! Right now." I move next to her and she snaps a hundred different selfies. All ranging from serious to duck face, to smiles, laughing, to funny faces. I laugh, leaning back in my seat, and look to Tatum. "I enjoy our friendship. You know that, right?"

She waves me off. "Don't go soppy."

"I'm not!" I reply defensively. "Okay, maybe just a little, but I just don't want you to feel left out now that Bishop and I are...."

"Are...?" she prompts, an eyebrow raised. She must realize she's being a brat, because she rolls her eyes, her shoulders dropping. "Look, okay, I'm just worried he's going to hurt you." After drinking some vodka, she hands me the bottle.

"With good reason, but I don't think he will." I stare in front of me, watching the tinted back window and the headlights of the car following us.

"What? So you're in love?" she asks.

I take a long pull of the vodka. Longer than I intended. I really wasn't planning on getting drunk tonight, but with the way this conversation is going, I'm going to be legless before we even reach the party, and that will probably do all sorts to piss off Bishop. Only because he's not there right now—I don't think.

"I don't know. Love is a weird word."

"It's not a word, Mads." Tate looks at me, taking the vodka from me and bringing it to her lips. "It's a feeling."

"Well, I don't know what I'm feeling."

"Then it's love."

Turning my head, I look at her. "What do you mean?"

"It is what it is, Mads. You're in love with him, and for that reason alone"—she shoves the vodka into me—"you're going to need this a lot more than me."

I take it from her, taking another swig. "So you and Nate?"

She freezes then taps on the divider window. "Yo! Sammy! When are we there, homie?"

I laugh, fits of giggles erupting from my belly. She looks at me, pauses, and then starts laughing too. We're both swiping the tears from our eyes when the car stops outside of Carter's house, music blaring out and people already standing outside on his front porch drinking.

"Gah, I don't feel like going in now."

She laughs. "Just because you have a man to go home to, bitch. Come help me find my next victim."

"What?" I smirk as she opens her door. "You're not going to be in the room next to mine?"

She pauses then pushes open the door. "Okay, no, I won't be. I wanted something more, and he couldn't give it to me because apparently, he's into someone else. I can have him for sex only."

I step out of the car, thanking Sammy briefly and telling her I'd text her if we need a ride home. "You don't want that?"

She swallows, a sad look passing through her eyes. "With him? Unfortunately, not. I caught fucking feelings."

Hooking my arm with hers, I nudge my head toward the house. "Well, let's go get you a bed bud then!"

She grins, tilting the vodka up to her lips and swallowing. "Sounds brilliant."

Passing all the drunken people on the porch, I push open the front door just as my phone starts ringing in my little bag. I pull it out, blocking one ear to cut out the music, and search for a quiet corner to talk to Bishop.

"Bishop?" I yell into the phone, trying to drown out the music.

"Madison? Go home. Now!"

"What?" I can't hear his words properly; every time he says something, someone does something loud.

"Bishop?"

"Fuck!" he roars down the phone. I heard that.

"What did you say before?" Finally finding a bathroom, I close the door, the deep bass shaking through the walls.

"I can hear you now."

"Good. You need to leave right now. I'm on my way."

"What? Why?"

"Just fucking do it, Madison. For fuck's sake, I will kill you myself—"

Banging on the door interrupts. "Hang on. Wait there. Someone is knocking like they're the fucking five-oh."

"Madison!" he screams, just as I pull open the door.

"What the fu—" I pause, tilting my head. "Brantley?"

"Is that Bishop?"

I look down to my phone. "What? Yeah?"

"You can hang up. Come on, I'll get you out of here."

Swallowing past my distrust, I put the phone back into my bag, not hanging up. I've got scattered memories as a kid of Brantley and me, but I don't trust him. Every memory I have of him, which there is only one or two, it's clear he hates me. Even now, I see that he still hates me. Why though? I don't understand why he hates me.

"Madison?" Brantley pulls me into his side, his mouth coming to my ear. "There are some people here who are going to take you. I know you don't trust me, but you trust Bishop, who trusts me."

Wait!

"Wow! What?" I pause, just as we're about to get to the door. I look over my shoulder briefly, watching Tatum bump and grind up against some hottie to a techno song. How different our lives are going, like two different lanes. "I don't want...." I shake my head.

Brantley pulls open the front door and grips me around my arm, squeezing roughly. I look down at his grip and then look back to his face. "That's too hard."

"Shut the fuck up." We reach the end of the path just as a black limo pulls up, one much like ours. The back door swings open and Brantley grabs my hair, shoving me into the dark interior.

"Agh!" I scream, crawling to the corner of my chair.

Brantley gets in after, sitting beside me and unbuttoning his suit. "What the fuck?" I scream at him, but his eyes haven't moved. They're stationary, stuck on someone in front of him. When I follow his sight, I suck in a shocked breath. Not someone, someones.

Bishop's dad, Hector, sits directly in front of me, and though I cannot see the man who is next to him due to the shadows cast over his spot, I see he's wearing a suit to match Hector's. "Um?" I clear my throat.

Hector just stares at me, fascinated. He's more than intimidating; he's downright lethal. He sucks the oxygen out of everyone sitting in the space. Now I see the apple doesn't fall far from the tree for Bishop.

He clears his throat. "You're quite the nuisance, Madison."

I look to Brantley, hate brewing in my gut. I trusted him; Bishop trusted him. That must be why Bishop told me to leave. I look back at Hector. "Wish I could say I was sorry."

Hector pauses, tilts his head, and then chuckles, pulling a cigar out from his suit jacket. "Well, I guess you have been reaping all the benefits."

"Why am I here?" I ask, sounding way more confident than I really am.

He rests his ankle on his knee, taking a puff of his cigar. "I thought it was about time you were filled in on something. A few things, actually."

"Oh?" I whisper out hoarsely. Secrets revealed just gives him more of a reason to kill me if he wants, but I'll take it.

"Does the name Venari mean anything to you, Madison?" His eye squints as the smoke puffs past.

Swallowing, I close my eyes, shutting out my early distant memories.

Don't remember.

Let it go.

Build the wall and stay over it.

"No." I open my eyes and plaster a fake smile. "It doesn't." Wall back up.

He narrows his eyes at me, as if to try to read my mind. He won't find anything by trying, just darkness and pain I've suppressed from childhood memories. Memories I used to fight every day to forget. But I'm curious how he knows that name. "Why?"

The limo stops and he looks to Brantley, gesturing toward the door. "Let's take a walk down memory lane."

He gets out of the car and I follow, shutting the door behind me. Walking around to the front of the car, the bright headlights beam up toward the log cabin.

Brantley steps up beside me as we both watch the front door. "Bishop may be the king of the Kings, but he forgets there's a higher power than him. His dad."

I know this already, as I'm sure Bishop knows this too. Hector smiles at Brantley and pats him on the shoulder. "Good boy." Then I watch as he walks into the cabin.

"Brantley," I whisper. "What the fuck is going on here?"

He doesn't answer. He simply gestures toward the door, but it's not in an insolent way. His jaw is clenched, and there's fire in his eyes. He's not happy; actually, fuck that—he's pissed.

"I believe you already know who this is." Brantley puts a cigarette into his mouth and lights it, just as Hector steps down the cabin steps with—

I gasp, my legs turn to jelly, and my stomach recoils, breakfast threatening to come up.

Brantley's lip curls. "Daddy dearest, AKA—Lucan Vitiosus." Voices come in and out, my head pounding as memories start flooding back. All the hard work over the years I put into blocking them out doesn't mean shit now, because the wall hasn't just dropped.

I look up, my eyes connecting with my childhood abuser, and that wall shatters to a million pieces. There's no rebuilding that.

Sucking in a shaky breath, I turn around and go to run, only someone steps in front of me, blocking me from going further, and I fall flat on my ass. That person isn't Brantley, because I see Black Converse shoes and tight yoga pants. I bring my eyes up to the small torso and frame until I'm met with one of the most exotic-looking girls I have ever seen in my entire life. Her black hair floats effortlessly and naturally down over her chest, her eyes curve in almonds, and her skin holds a natural golden tint. She's stunning in an obvious way. The kind of way that she'd gain attention anywhere she goes no matter what she's wearing. All that beauty gets washed out when she opens her mouth.

"You're so much prettier in photos." She tilts her head, and I stand to my feet, brushing off the dirt from my butt.

"Who the fuck are you?" I whisper out, I meant it to be harsher than it came out, but with tears pouring down my cheeks, I'm not in a very badass state right now.

Hector appears beside me and tsks. "Madison, play nice with Khales. She's a good little puppet."

I freeze. All thought processes mute, and my skin prickles to life. Khales?

I say the first thing that comes up in my head. "I thought you were dead."

She laughs, flicking her hair over her shoulder. "Naw, honey, there's so much"—she steps toward me and presses her finger to the tip of my nose—"you just don't know."

I step backward, squaring my shoulders. Is she intimating? Yes. But I've grown accustomed to being around a pack of wolves, so instead of running from them, I learned how to play with them. If she thinks I'm going to roll over and submit to her ways, she's deluded. Even if I'm feeling emotional about coming face-to-face with Lucan, I won't bow to her. "I don't doubt that at all, but why am I here?" I look to Hector. "Where is your son?"

Hector puts a cigar in his mouth. "He's not here." He lights the tip of the cigar and rolls it around in his mouth. The silence between all of us borders on awkward, so I turn around to focus all of my attention on Hector.

"And what exactly do you want with me? And why is she alive? Does Bishop know? Does anyone know? Why bring him out?" I point toward Lucan, the mere sight of him making my head spin and my hand itch. I think I've passed the shocked phase. I can feel myself slowly brewing, my anger like a swimming pool of lava at the bottom of a volcano, ready to erupt.

I look back to Khales. "And who *are* you, by the way?"

Hector shakes his head. "That's not important right now. What's important is this—"

"No." The word is instant and automatic.

"Oh?" Hector's eyebrows shoot up in surprise. "I see you've grown a little backbone now that you're not hiding behind my son."

I tilt my head and watch as the gray cloud of smoke floats into the dark night. "I never hid behind your son. He shielded me. There's a difference."

Hector leans back onto the car, and I step back a little so I can see both him, Khales, Brantley, and Lucan in my peripheral vision. "And anyway," I add, shooting a glare at Brantley, who is standing on the other side of the car. "Loyalty and all that—right, Brantley?"

"You don't know shit about loyalty," Khales murmurs, stepping up to me, chest-to-chest. I can feel her breathing labor as she looks down her nose at me.

I stand up straighter and match her stare. I don't know who I'm kidding; I've never been in a fight before, but I won't let someone hit me and get away with it. "You don't know shit about the shit I know, Khales, so step the fuck back."

"Okay, girls." Brantley grins, stepping between the two of us. "As much as this is getting my dick hard, we need to stay focused."

"You're disgusting," I mutter to Brantley, eyeing him up and down. I don't know what he's playing at or why he's here. I'm not even 100 percent sure if he's on our side anymore.

"One question," I state, looking directly at Brantley. "Your birthday party, when we were little...."

Brantley's face drops. Hector remains quiet, watching me carefully.

"What of it?" Brantley asks, folding his arms in front of himself.

"What happened that day?" I whisper, leaning against the car. "I mean, I remember vague parts, but not all of it."

"So, what?" Brantley snarls. "You suddenly having memories and shit now?"

"No!" I snap back. "I just want to know why no one told me about this earlier."

Brantley looks to Hector, then to Lucan, who then looks to me.

Hector then looks to Lucan. "What birthday?"

My eyebrows pinch. "Wait!"

Brantley freezes.

Closing my eyes, I think back, digging for more from that day, but I was so young... so young.

"Where are we going?" I asked the man. He was the same man who hurt me at night. I didn't know why he hurt me, but he'd tell me not to tell any adults. I had to respect my elders, so I didn't tell a soul, afraid I'd get into trouble.

"You'll see, Silver," he murmured, his rough hand clutching onto mine as he pulled me down a long, dark hallway. We passed so many doors. All of them the color red. Not a nice red, a blood red. He stopped at a door, a door that had Vitiosus on a gold plate hanging on the door. I looked up at the man, tilting my head. Over the time he hurt me, it would only ever be in my bedroom. I didn't know why he had brought me here. To this place.

He pushed open the door and gestured toward the room. "Go and get on the bed, Silver."

"No!" I scream, dropping to the ground. Shaking my head, I clutch my hair and pull at it, wanting to scratch the memories out of my head.

"Madison!" Who is that? It sounds like Bishop. "Brantley—"

Looking toward the bed, I swallowed, slowly stepping into the room. It was a big room. Gigantic. It was dim, almost dark in the room, and there was a big bed sitting to the side. I looked closer, stepping toward the bed, my heart beating in my chest and my throat clogged. All the lights were dim, but there was one shining on the bed, only when I got closer, I saw it was a camera sitting on a stand with a light pointing toward the mattress.

My eyebrows pulled together. "Wha—"

"Go to the bed, Silver." That voice. I hated that voice. I felt sick, my tummy not feeling good.

Something was wrong, like it was always wrong when he was around. I hated him, but I obeyed because that was what I'd been told to do. I had to listen to adults; they always knew best. But why did he make me feel dirty? No other adult made me feel dirty. He made me sad, hurt, and angry all at once. I was confused, I think.

Walking toward the bed, I stopped at the foot of it. There was a small boy curled up on top of the covers, but he was wearing no clothes. Why was he wearing no clothes? He must've been cold.

"Silver, on the bed!" Lucan raised his voice at me, and I flinched, quickly crawling onto the soft mattress.

"Hi," I whispered out to the boy who was crying. "What's wrong?" I asked, wanting to know why he was so sad. Did he feel like I did? Did Lucan make him feel the same way I felt?

The boy sobbed then buried his head into the blanket. "Go away!" he yelled as he continued to cry. He was angry and sad, so maybe he did feel the same way as I did.

I stopped, sitting on the mattress as Lucan loosened his tie and pointed the camera at us. "Silver, take your clothes off."

"No!" I scream, sweat oozing out of my flesh. "Leave me alone. My name isn't Silver! It's Madison! Madison Montgomery! I'm not Silver!" I rock back and forth on the gravel road, trying to pull myself out of the memory.

"I—what about the boy?"
Lucan looked toward the boy on the bed, his lip curled. "Brantley, make room for Silver."

My eyes pop open and I shoot off the road, ignoring the tiny stones that are embedded into my flesh. "Brantley!" I scream.

Brantley turns to face me, a blank look pulling over his features.

I turn pale, all blood leaving my body. The pain, the anger, the sadness, it's all been cracked open again, and suddenly I'm that scared little girl again.

"What the fuck are they talking about?" Hector booms, losing his cool slightly. "And what the fuck just happened there, Madison?"

Headlights flash up the cabin, but I ignore them. I ignore everything.

And suddenly, rage. Pure rage electrifies me like a rush of adrenaline. Squaring my shoulders, I finally look directly at Lucan, the man who abused me as a child. The man my parents trusted. The man I thought I could trust. The man who made me keep secrets by using his "I'm an adult" card on me.

The man I want to kill.

"You!" I seethe.

His eyes join with mine, and he still looks the same, only older. So much older. His head is bald now, his face free of hair, but his eyes. His eyes will forever be the trigger to that feeling. That same feeling I felt when I was a little girl starts slowly slipping into me, but I fight it. I'm not her anymore. I'm older. More experienced. And though I may feel this pain for the coming months after being face-to-face with him, I know whatever I do it will be worth it. Car doors close in the distance behind me, but again, I ignore it. I ignore everything because my focus is solely on Lucan. Everything in my peripheral is closed.

I can hear people, or someone, walking toward us behind me, their feet crunching against the gravel, but I ignore it.

He chuckles. "Ain't no one gonna believe you, Silver."

The footsteps stop.

Ice cold wind whips my hair across my face, and that's when I know. I know those footsteps belong to Bishop and the Kings.

Lucan lunges at me, gripping my hair and pulling my back up against his front. It happens so fast I barely blink, but when I do, I see them. With my back pressed against Lucan's front, his gun pressing against my temple, I look pleadingly right at Bishop, but he's not looking at me. His shoulders are rising and falling in anger, his eyes zoned directly in on Lucan.

"What the fuck is going on here, son?" Hector asks calmly, not fazed I'm about to get my brains blown out everywhere. My heart pounds in my chest, and goose bumps prickle all over my flesh as fear ripples through me. No. There's no way. I didn't survive through all the memories, all the suppressed bullshit, only to go out by his hands. His hands already took so much from me; I won't let them take my life too.

Bishop steps forward, his lip curled and his eyes black. So black. I've not seen this look before; this is feral. Casting a look over his shoulder, Nate is there, the same position, his knuckles cracking. He starts jumping in his spot, craning his neck as if he's ready to fight. Which I have no doubt he is. The rest of the boys are there too, ready to throw down if they need to. Whether they know the story or not, I see it right there. Their loyalty to Bishop. It's unquestionable. This is The Elite Kings in full form.

"Ah!" Lucan presses the gun into my temple more. "Don't fucking move. Now, since people will be dying tonight, I want to get a few things out there for Silver so she knows the deal."

"Don't call me that," I hiss, my lip slightly curling.

"Hey, I'm doing you a favor."

"Fuck you."

He laughs, his breath falling over my neck. I can't hide the disgust; I dry heave, ready to spill my guts all over the road.

"What the fuck is going on?" Hector asks again.

Where is Brantley? This was all a setup. He and Khales are nowhere to be seen. I look around again, as much as I can from the position I'm in, and sure enough, they're both not where they were a few minutes ago.

Hate.

"First, let me start with this. Silver, do you know much about the last names of these boys here?"

What?

"The hell has that got to do with you and what you did to me all those years ago?"

"I'll get to that part." He grins. I can hear it in his sick voice how much he's getting out of this, and that's the thing about age. The tone of your voice is one of the last things to change. Therefore, Lucan still has the same voice.

"What are you doing, Lucan?" Hector warns. His tone should be enough to put the fear of God into Lucan, but it doesn't, because he continues.

"Hector and Bishop Hayes... Hayes meaning 'The Devil,'" he starts, and just as I open my mouth to ask another question, his hand slams over it, pausing me. "Everyone shut the fuck up and let me finish, or I swear to God I will shoot her."

He clears his throat, before smugly murmuring, "Now, where was I? Oh yes, the names. Lucan and Brantley Vitiosus. I'll get to the meanings of the names and the English translations when I've finished." He laughs. Then his lips skim over my earlobe before he whispers, "and you know how theatrical I can get, don't ya, Silver?"

The first teardrops, followed by anger. Rage.

He continues. "Max, Saint, and Cash Ditio. Phoenix and Chase Divitae. Raguel, Ace, and Eli Rebellis." He laughs at these last two. My eyes shoot toward Nate, who is now being held back by Chase and Cash. He looks absolutely feral. The lack of light and smudged tears in my eyes make for hard looking, but even if I couldn't see it, I could sure as fuck feel it.

Lucan carries on. "Nate *Malum*-Riverside." Then he laughs, bringing his lips to my ear again.

I shut my eyes, fighting the bile that's about to spew out of my mouth from not just his proximity, but his touch. "Johan, Hunter, Jase, and Madison *Venari*."

I freeze. All life drains from my face.

"You hear that, Silver? You're adopted... you and that skitzo brother of yours."

What? More tears spill out of my eyes. This can't be true. There's no way. He's fucking with me. My dad is my dad and my mom was my mom. Lucan is being what he is.

I look at Bishop, who is finally looking directly at me, and I see it. The look. It's the look he gives me when it's just us together. His eyebrows are furrowed and his eyes are zeroed into mine.

Not only is it true, but he knew.

Sobs wrack through my body, and my knees buckle, but Lucan yanks me back up. "Careful, careful... maybe you can talk with your man here about the meanings of those last names and what they mean in regards to each family's duty in The Kings, but let me tell you this, Silver," he whispers so harshly into my ear. "When you know all there is to know about this—they will kill you."

I don't care.

I'm adopted. My whole life was a lie. I was wrong. I can't trust anyone. I can only trust Daemon. *Daemon.* His face lights up inside my head, but instead of it soothing me, it brings on another set of tears.

"So I'll make this easier for you and tell you the big firework kicker!" he yells, laughing hysterically. Leaning down, I pause, my heavy breathing the only thing breaking the silence.

"You—"

A gun fires and Lucan screams, his hand loosening from around my mouth as he falls to the ground.

I freeze, static buzzing in my ears from the gunshot.

Pain.

Anger.

Rage.

Rage.

Rage.

Heat rises inside of me as I think over everything. His touch when I was a kid. What he made me do to Brantley. And what he made Brantley do to me as a kid.

"Stop!" I scream, my eyes unblinking and fixed on the car in front of me.

Silence.

I slowly turn around, noticing Bishop is beside me, kneeling down next to Lucan, who is bleeding out on the road.

I look at Lucan, tilting my head. Smiling, I whisper out, "Seeing you in pain soothes my anger."

Lucan looks at me square in the eye. "I will live in your memories, Silver. Forever."

Squaring my jaw, I bend down to Bishop's level, bringing my hand to his boot. I feel up toward where I know he keeps a knife. I feel him freeze, realizing what I'm about to do, but before he can stop me—if he was going to stop me—I unclip the holster and pull out the large hunting knife then slowly raise it into the air. Lucan's eyes follow it slowly.

"You see this?" I run my pointer finger down the blunt side of the knife. "It's a Fallkniven A1Pro Survival Knife." I smirk, admiring how the boys—except for Bishop, he's still crouching beside me—watch me with awe, or fear, or a combination of both, and are all standing behind me. They have my back—but I won't need it. I launch the knife into Lucan's pelvis area until I feel his bones crunching against the blade. He screams out, a loud, curdling scream, his back arching and tears pouring down his face.

I bend down to his ear, running my lips over the lobe like he did to me not long ago. Feeling his blood spilling over my hand, I grin and whisper, "You know, since you love to be theatrical... this knife is a survival knife." I circle the blade, my hand sticky from his blood. It blankets my anger, soothing it like an ice pack on a burn. Putting out the pain.

Pulling the knife out from him, I inch backward, both hands wrapped around the blade, ready to stab it into his head. Needing it to finally put out the burn I have inside me. The burn has only been temporarily eased, when Brantley appears, snatches the knife out of my hand, and stabs it right between Lucan's eyes. Blood sprays out all over me, the tang of blood overpowering every taste bud in my mouth.

Brantley screams, veins popping out from his neck, his eyeballs almost bulging from their sockets. He has anger; I was right. He has anger just like I did, if not more, because Lucan was his father.

My breathing slows, and when Lucan's head drops to the side, his death stinking up the air, I collapse into Bishop, my head resting on his shoulder.

He wraps his arm around me, kissing me on the head, as Brantley pulls the knife out of his dad and launches it back into him again. And again. And again. I flinch, digging my face into Bishop. His smell, his just—Bishop. The only sound I can hear is Brantley slicing into Lucan. Again and again.

"Come on, baby," Bishop says into my hair when he sees Brantley isn't stopping anytime soon.

"Well," Hector says, and I turn in Bishop's grip to face him but away from Brantley making dues with his abusive dad. "This is all lovely, but do any of you fuckers want to tell me what the fuck is going on and why my right-hand man is dead? Brantley, hear that? He's dead so you can stop that now." Hector pauses, looking at the mess Brantley has created, and then shrugs like he sees that type of shit daily. He probably does. Actually, all of them seem unbothered by it.

Bishop squeezes me into him. "Lucan would rape Madison when she was a little girl."

Hector sucks from his cigar, but just there, below the surface, I can see it enrages him somewhat, and that surprises me because he's Hector Hayes. I wouldn't think something like that would bother him. He must catch my notice in him, because he laughs.

"Don't take it to heart, sugar. I personally don't like you, for a lot of reasons." He looks at his son and then back to me. "But I don't condone rape."

"And…" Bishop pauses but then continues. "…and Brantley."

The stabbing sound has stopped; now it's sobbing. Not the quiet sobbing, it's the ugly kind, and I turn in Bishop's embrace, finally bracing myself to look toward Brantley.

He has his arms wrapped around his knees and is rocking beside what is left of Lucan. Blood drips from his hair, face, and hands, but he just rocks, sobbing loudly. "I didn't want to. Why? Why did you have to make me do it? All those times…." He shakes his head. My heart snaps. I slowly start to walk toward him, when Bishop grabs onto my arm.

I turn to face him, and he shakes his head. "Don't."

"What do you mean, don't? No wonder he hates me, Bishop," I whisper, searching Bishop's eyes. "He needed someone to blame, so he blamed me for what his father made us do that day. He blamed me, because if I didn't exist, that wouldn't have happened."

Bishop shakes his head. "No, babe." But then his eyes go over my shoulder.

"Thirty-seven," Brantley whispers from behind me, and I quickly spin around to face him. "Thirty-seven young girls."

What? I want to ask, but I don't in fear that he might snap at me. Instead, I remain silent, hoping he will say more, which he does.

He looks at me, the headlights from the car shining on his face now that he's level with it. Blood paints his face and clothing, the knife gripped in his hand. He tosses the knife over and it lands near Bishop's feet. "You're right though," he starts, sidestepping around the mangled corpse on the ground. "I hated you. I never understood why you came back. When we were kids, at my birthday party, I hated all kids, not just you, but my father had already started talking about what he was going to get us to do together." He pauses. "When you started Riverside, I didn't know at first whether you remembered me or not. At first, I thought you did remember and you were—I don't know—fucking with us after some revenge for what Lucan did." Shit, that makes a whole lot of sense. "But also…" He pulls out a pack of smokes and puts one into his mouth, lighting it. "…you were my first. So there was hate for you from that as well. I didn't make the Silver connection to The Silver Swan, which I should have. I'm an idiot for not making that connection. I just figured it was because of your eyes. They're murky green now, but when you were a kid, they were silver."

I nod, because they were. It was always strange.

He steps up to me, leaving the smoke in his mouth. "Do you feel that?" he asks, tilting his head.

I look deep into his eyes, a sense of peace washing over me. The fire I had burning for so many years from undying hate toward Lucan had gone out. Smiling, I nod. "Yeah."

He blows out a cloud of smoke. "At least that's one of us." He narrows his eyes at me.

I frown. "You still hate me?"

His eyebrows shoot up in surprise. "No, fuck." His eyes dart around the place. "It's just—never mind. But I don't hate you. I feel peace with *you* now." Then he smiles. The first time I have ever seen Brantley smile, and it's at me. I want to jump on him and hug him, but that's probably going too fast for him. Baby steps.

Turning back around, wrapping my arms around Bishop, I look over his shoulder, directly at Hunter and Jase. My brothers. Biological brothers with Daemon.

Hunter steps backward, shaking his head and walking straight toward the parked car, slamming the door behind him. I frown, my shoulders dropping. I don't know what I expected, but it wasn't for Hunter to act like that. He's always been warm toward me.

Jase just stares at me, his dark eyes glued to mine. The last string in my heart is about to snap when he smiles at me. Giving me a wink. For the older brother, that surprises me. I haven't spent much time with Jase, if any, but I know in that moment that will change.

Bishop tucks me under his arm as the rest of the boys walk back to the cars. He looks at his dad. "Want me to call Katsia about this mess, or do you want to?" he asks his dad, nudging his head toward the destruction on the road.

Hector looks at me and then looks at Bishop. "I'll call her." Then he looks to me. "There was a reason for my bringing you here tonight, and it wasn't that."

I sink into Bishop, and his grip tightens around me. "Though, I did plan to tell you that you're adopted." He looks to Bishop. "But you see, as much as I love my son, he did something bad tonight. Something that is against our rules. And we only have one rule, Madison." Hector looks right at me, and chills break out over my flesh. "So now that your adoption is exposed, I guess it's only fair I find something else to tell you since my son is so trigger happy tonight."

I look up at Bishop. Trigger happy?

Hector steps forward, pushing his hands into his pockets. "I'm sure you're familiar with the initiation process of a King?" he questions, looking at me. I nod. "Very good. So you know..." He gestures behind him, and Khales reemerges from the shadows. Bishop freezes, his grip turning to steel. "...that Khales was Bishop's..." My head spins and my stomach recoils. Someone else steps out of the shadows. "...as was your adopted 'mother.'"

The End

ACKNOWLEDGEMENTS

I just want to thank everyone who has helped contribute to not only my stories, but to my sanity. Don't all laugh at once!

First of all, my children and partner. They're my rock, my home, my loves, and my most favorite people walking this earth. Everything I do, I do for them.

I want to thank my family who continues to support me.

Isis! My best bitch. Somewhere between a sister and a soul mate. You've been my #1 supporter, counselor, therapist, just basically my all-around PERSON. You're *my* person.

My Wolf Pack! You girls keep me going even on my darkest of days. You make me smile when I want to frown—this is getting soppy… oh look! The D…

My betas, thank you for reading my unedited words. Truly, you probably deserve a medal or something.

Kayla for editing my words! The girls from Give Me Books for handling all my promo, Jay Aheer for always getting my covers on point. And Champagne Formatting for making the words all laid out nicely.

Thank you to my author buds who always keep it real! Nina Levine, River Savage, Chantal Fernando for the epic sprint sessions and our meme shares, Leigh Shen, Anne Malcom, Addison Jane. You girls are rad, got mad love for all of you.

tacet a mortuis

whispers from

the dead

PLAYLIST

Desperado—Rihanna

Adore—Amy Shark

Hail to the King—Avenged Sevenfold

B.Y.O.B.—System Of A Down

Toxicity—System Of A Down

Talking Body—Tove Lo

Hey Baby (Drop It To the Floor)—Pitbull, T-Pain

Bad At Love—Halsey

My Life—50 Cent, Eminem, Adam Levine

Everything, Everyday, Everywhere—Fabolous, Keri Hilson

F**kin' Problems—A$AP Rocky, Drake, 2 Chainz, Kendrick Lamar

Familiar Taste Of Poison—Halestorm

Tourniquet—Evanescence

Touch It—Monifah

#icanteven—The Neighbourhood, French Montana

Nice & Slow—Usher

Last Night—Keyshia Cole, Diddy

Slow Jamz (feat. Kanye West & Jamie Foxx)—Twista, Jamie Foxx, Kanye West

I'm Sprung - Trick Daddy & YoungBloodz Remix—T-Pain

Wonderful—Ja Rule, R. Kelly, Ashanti

My Boo—Usher, Alicia Keys

Everyone Nose (All The Girls Standing In The Line For The Bathroom)—N.E.R.D

Climax—Usher

Crawl—Breaking Benjamin

Hate That I Love You—Rihanna, Ne-Yo

Bonnie and Clyde—DJ Hit-Man

Right Now (Na Na Na)—Akon

A Place For My Head—Linkin Park

Look In My Eyes—Rains

I Fucking Hate You—Godsmack

Pray For Me (with Kendrick Lamar)—The Weeknd, Kendrick Lamar

Behind Blue Eyes—Limp Bizkit

Kiss Me Thru The Phone—Soulja Boy, Sammie

Light Up Light Up—Baby Bash, Z-Ro, Berner, Baby E

Move to L.A.—Tyga, Ty Dolla $ign

Sex With Me—Rihanna

It's A Vibe—2 Chainz, Ty Dolla $ign, Trey Songz, Jhene Aiko

Bad Mother F*cker—Machine Gun Kelly, Kid Rock

Water—Jack Garratt

Get Dough—Dead Obies

Something I Don't Know—Miras

wRoNg—ZAYN, Kehlani

Bad Intentions—Niykee Heaton, Migos, OG Parker

Lullaby—Niykee Heaton

I'm Ready—Niykee Heaton

Zombie—Bad Wolves

Hero—Skillet

Torn to Pieces—Pop Evil

Your Betrayal—Bullet For My Valentine

Stupid Love—Jason Derulo

Addicted—Saving Abel

I'm Not An Angel—Halestorm

Infinity—Niykee Heaton

Ghetto Flower—J.Williams

I Was Never There—The Weeknd, Gesaffelstein

Hurt You—The Weeknd, Gesaffelstein

The Other—Lauv

Believer - Live/Acoustic—Imagine Dragons

Believer—Imagine Dragons

Call Out My Name—The Weeknd

Innocence—Halestorm

Whoring Streets—Scars On Broadway

RECAP

The Broken Puppet

"No!" I scream, dropping to the ground. Shaking my head, I clutch my hair and pull at it, wanting to scratch the memories out of my head.

"Madison!" *Who is that?* It sounds like Bishop. "Brantley—"

Looking toward the bed, I swallowed, slowly stepping into the room. It was a big room. Gigantic. It was dim, almost dark in the room, and there was a big bed sitting to the side. I looked closer, stepping toward the bed, my heart beating in my chest and my throat clogged. All the lights were dim, but there was one shining on the bed. Only when I got closer, I saw it was a camera sitting on a stand with a light pointing toward the mattress.

My eyebrows pulled together. "Wha—"

"Go to the bed, Silver." That voice. I hated that voice. I felt sick, my tummy not feeling good. Something was wrong, like it was always wrong when he was around. I hated him, but I obeyed because that was what I'd been told to do. I had to listen to adults; they always knew best. But why did he make me feel dirty? No other adult made me feel dirty. He made me sad, hurt, and angry all at once. I was confused, I think.

Walking toward the bed, I stopped at the foot of it. There was a small boy curled up on top of the covers, but he was wearing no clothes. Why was he wearing no clothes? He must've been cold.

"Silver, on the bed!" Lucan raised his voice at me, and I flinched, quickly crawling onto the soft mattress.

"Hi," I whispered to the boy who was crying. "What's wrong?" I asked, wanting to know why he was so sad. Did he feel like I did? Did Lucan make him feel the same way I felt?

The boy sobbed then buried his head into the blanket. "Go away!" he yelled as he continued to cry. He was angry and sad, so maybe he did feel the same way as I did.

I stopped, sitting on the mattress as Lucan loosened his tie and pointed the camera at us. "Silver, take your clothes off."

"No!" I scream, sweat oozing out of my flesh. "Leave me alone. My name isn't Silver! It's Madison! Madison Montgomery! I'm not Silver!" I rock back and forth on the gravel road, trying to pull myself out of the memory.

"I—what about the boy?"

Lucan looked toward the boy on the bed, his lip curled. "Brantley, make room for Silver."

My eyes pop open and I shoot off the road, ignoring the tiny stones that are embedded into my flesh. "Brantley!" I scream.

Brantley turns to face me, a blank look pulling over his features.

I turn pale, all blood leaving my body. The pain, the anger, the sadness, it's all been cracked open again, and suddenly I'm that scared little girl again.

"What the fuck are they talking about?" Hector booms, losing his cool slightly. "And what the fuck just happened there, Madison?"

Headlights light up the cabin, but I ignore them. I ignore everything.

And suddenly, rage. Pure rage electrifies me like a rush of adrenaline. Squaring my shoulders, I finally look directly at Lucan, the man who abused me as a child. The man my parents trusted. The man I thought I could trust. The man who made me keep secrets by using his "I'm an adult" card on me.

The man I want to kill.

"You!" I seethe.

His eyes join with mine, and he still looks the same, only older. So much older. His head is bald now, his face free of hair, but his eyes. His eyes will forever be the trigger to that feeling. That same feeling I felt when I was a little girl starts slowly slipping into me, but I fight it. I'm not her anymore. I'm older. More experienced. And though I may feel this pain for the coming months after being face-to-face with him, I know whatever I do it will be worth it. Car doors close in the distance behind me, but again, I ignore it. I ignore everything because my focus is solely on Lucan. Everything in my peripheral is closed.

I can hear people, or someone, walking toward us behind me, their feet crunching against the gravel, but I ignore it.

He chuckles. "Ain't no one gonna believe you, Silver."

The footsteps stop.

Ice cold wind whips my hair across my face, and that's when I know. I know those footsteps belong to Bishop and the Kings.

Lucan lunges at me, gripping my hair and pulling my back up against his front. It happens so fast I barely blink, but when I do, I see them. With my back pressed against Lucan's front, his gun pressing against my temple, I look pleadingly right at Bishop, but he's not looking at me. His shoulders are rising and falling in anger, his eyes zoned directly in on Lucan.

"What the fuck is going on here, son?" Hector asks calmly, not fazed I'm about to get my brains blown out everywhere. My heart pounds in my chest, and goose bumps prickle all over my flesh as fear ripples through me. No. There's no way. I didn't survive through all the memories, all the suppressed bullshit, only to go out by his hands. His hands already took so much from me; I won't let them take my life too.

Bishop steps forward, his lip curled and his eyes black. So black. I've not seen this look before; this is feral. Casting a look over his shoulder, Nate is there, the same position, his knuckles cracking. He starts jumping in his spot, cracking his neck as if he's ready to fight. Which I have no doubt he is. The rest of the boys are there too, ready to throw down if they need to. Whether they know the story or not, I see it right there. Their loyalty to Bishop. It's unquestionable. This is The Elite Kings in full form.

"Ah!" Lucan presses the gun into my temple more. "Don't fucking move. Now, since people will be dying tonight, I want to get a few things out there for Silver so she knows the deal."

"Don't call me that," I hiss, my lip slightly curling.

"Hey, I'm doing you a favor."

"Fuck you."

He laughs, his breath falling over my neck. I can't hide the disgust; I dry heave, ready to spill my guts all over the road.

"What the fuck is going on?" Hector asks again.

Where is Brantley? This was all a setup. He and Khales are nowhere to be seen. I look around again, as much as I can from the position I'm in, and sure enough, they're both not where they were a few minutes ago.

Hate.

"First, let me start with this. Silver, do you know much about the last names of these boys here?"

What?

"The hell has that got to do with you and what you did to me all those years ago?"

"I'll get to that part." He grins. I can hear it in his sick voice how much he's getting out of this, and that's the thing about age. The tone of your voice is one of the last things to change. Therefore, Lucan still has the same voice.

"What are you doing, Lucan?" Hector warns. His tone should be enough to put the fear of God into Lucan, but it doesn't, because he continues.

"Hector and Bishop Hayes... Hayes meaning 'The Devil,'" he starts, and just as I open my mouth to ask another question, his hand slams over it, pausing me. "Everyone shut the fuck up and let me finish, or I swear to God I will shoot her."

He clears his throat, before smugly murmuring, "Now, where was I? Oh yes, the names. Lucan and Brantley Vitiosus. I'll get to the meanings of the names and the English translations when I've finished." He laughs. Then his lips skim over my earlobe before he whispers, "And you know how theatrical I can get, don't ya, Silver?"

The first teardrops, followed by anger. Rage.

He continues, "Max, Saint, and Cash Ditio. Phoenix and Chase Divitae. Raguel, Ace, and Eli Rebellis." He laughs at these last two. My eyes shoot toward Nate, who is now being held back by Chase and Cash. He looks absolutely feral. The lack of light and smudged tears in my eyes make it hard to view, but even if I couldn't see it, I could sure as fuck feel it.

Lucan carries on. "Nate *Malum*-Riverside." Then he laughs, bringing his lips to my ear again.

I shut my eyes, fighting the bile that's about to spew out of my mouth from not just his proximity, but his touch. "Johan, Hunter, Jase, and Madison *Venari*."

I freeze. All life drains from my face.

"You hear that, Silver? You're adopted... you and that schizo brother of yours."

What? More tears spill out of my eyes. This can't be true. There's no way. He's fucking with me. My dad is my dad and my mom was my mom. Lucan is being what he is.

I look at Bishop, who is finally looking directly at me, and I see it. The look. It's the look he gives me when it's just us together. His eyebrows are furrowed and his eyes are zeroed into mine.

Not only is it true, but he knew.

Sobs wrack through my body, and my knees buckle, but Lucan yanks me back up. "Careful, careful... maybe you can talk with your man here about the meanings of those last names and what they mean in regards to each family's duty in the Kings, but let me tell you this, Silver," he whispers so harshly into my ear. "When you know all there is to know about this—they will kill you."

I don't care.

I'm adopted. My whole life was a lie. I was wrong. I can't trust anyone. I can only trust Daemon. *Daemon.* His face lights up inside my head, but instead of it soothing me, it brings on another set of tears.

"So I'll make this easier for you and tell you the big firework kicker!" he yells, laughing hysterically. Leaning down, I pause, my heavy breathing the only thing breaking the silence.

"You—"

A gun fires and Lucan screams, his hand loosening from around my mouth as he falls to the ground.

I freeze, static buzzing in my ears from the gunshot.

Pain.

Anger.

Rage.

Rage.

Rage.

Heat rises inside of me as I think over everything. His touch when I was a kid. What he made me do to Brantley. And what he made Brantley do to me as a kid.

"Stop!" I scream, my eyes unblinking and fixed on the car in front of me.

Silence.

I slowly turn around, noticing Bishop is beside me, kneeling down next to Lucan, who is bleeding out on the road.

I look at Lucan, tilting my head. Smiling, I whisper, "Seeing you in pain soothes my anger."

Lucan looks at me square in the eye. "I will live in your memories, Silver. Forever."

Squaring my jaw, I bend down to Bishop's level, bringing my hand to his boot. I feel up toward where I know he keeps a knife. I feel him freeze, realizing what I'm about to do, but before he can stop me—if he was going to stop me—I unclip the holster and pull out the large hunting knife and slowly raise it into the air. Lucan's eyes follow it slowly.

"You see this?" I run my pointer finger down the blunt side of the knife. "It's a Fallkniven A1Pro Survival Knife." I smirk, admiring how the boys—except for Bishop, he's still crouching beside me—watch me with awe, or fear, or a combination of both, and are all standing behind me. They have my back—but I won't need it. I launch the knife into Lucan's pelvis area until I feel his bones crunching against the blade. He screams out, a loud, curdling scream, his back arching and tears pouring down his face.

I bend down to his ear, running my lips over the lobe like he did to me not long ago. Feeling his blood spilling over my hand, I grin and whisper, "You know, since you love to be theatrical... this knife is a survival knife." I circle the blade, my hand sticky with his blood. It blankets my anger, soothing it like an ice pack on a burn. Putting out the pain.

Pulling the knife out of him, I inch backward, both hands wrapped around the blade, ready to stab it into his head. Needing it to finally put out the burn I have inside me. The burn has only been temporarily eased when Brantley appears, snatches the knife out of my hand, and stabs it right between Lucan's eyes. Blood sprays all over me, the tang of blood overpowering every taste bud in my mouth.

Brantley screams, veins popping out from his neck, his eyeballs almost bulging from their sockets. He has anger; I was right. He has anger just like I did, if not more, because Lucan was his father.

My breathing slows, and when Lucan's head drops to the side, his death stinking up the air, I collapse into Bishop, my head resting on his shoulder.

He wraps his arm around me, kissing me on the head as Brantley pulls the knife out of his dad and launches it back into him again. And again. And again. I flinch, burying my face into Bishop. His smell, his just—Bishop. The only sound I can hear is Brantley slicing into Lucan. Again and again.

"Come on, baby," Bishop says into my hair when he sees Brantley isn't stopping anytime soon.

"Well," Hector says, and I turn in Bishop's grip to face him but away from Brantley making dues with his abusive dad. "This is all lovely, but do any of you fuckers want to tell me what the fuck is going on and why my right-hand man is dead? Brantley, hear that? He's dead so you can stop that now." Hector pauses, looking at the mess Brantley has created and then shrugs like he sees that type of shit daily. He probably does. Actually, all of them seem unbothered by it.

Bishop squeezes me into him. "Lucan would rape Madison when she was a little girl."

Hector sucks from his cigar, but just there, below the surface, I can see it enrages him somewhat, and that surprises me because he's Hector Hayes. I wouldn't think something like that would bother him. He must catch my notice in him, because he laughs.

"Don't take it to heart, sugar. I personally don't like you, for a lot of reasons." He looks at his son and then back to me. "But I don't condone rape."

"And..." Bishop pauses but then continues, "...and Brantley."

The stabbing sound has stopped; now it's sobbing. Not the quiet sobbing, it's the ugly kind, and I turn in Bishop's embrace, finally bracing myself to look toward Brantley.

He has his arms wrapped around his knees and is rocking beside what is left of Lucan. Blood drips from his hair, face, and hands, but he just rocks, sobbing loudly. "I didn't want to. Why? Why did you have to make me do it? All those times..." He shakes his head. My heart snaps. I slowly start to walk toward him, when Bishop grabs onto my arm.

I turn to face him, and he shakes his head. "Don't."

"What do you mean, don't? No wonder he hates me, Bishop," I whisper, searching Bishop's eyes. "He needed someone to blame, so he blamed me for what his father made us do that day. He blamed me, because if I didn't exist, that wouldn't have happened."

Bishop shakes his head. "No, babe." But then his eyes look over my shoulder.

"Thirty-seven," Brantley whispers from behind me, and I quickly spin around to face him. "Thirty-seven young girls."

What? I want to ask, but I don't in fear that he might snap at me. Instead, I remain silent, hoping he will say more, which he does.

He looks at me, the headlights from the car shining on his face now that he's level with it. Blood paints his face and clothing, the knife gripped in his hand. He tosses the knife over and it lands near Bishop's feet.

"You're right though," he starts, sidestepping around the mangled corpse on the ground. "I hated you. I never understood why you came back. When we were kids, at my birthday party, I hated all kids, not just you, but my father had already started talking about what he was going to get us to do together." He pauses. "When you started Riverside, I didn't know at first whether you remembered me or not. At first, I thought you did remember and you were—I don't know—fucking with us after some revenge for what Lucan did." Shit, that makes a whole lot of sense. "But also..." He pulls out a pack of smokes and puts one into his mouth, lighting it. "...You were my first. So there was hate for you from that as well. I didn't make the Silver connection to The Silver Swan, which I should have. I'm an idiot for not making that connection. I just figured it was because of your eyes. They're murky green now, but when you were a kid, they were silver."

I nod because they were. It was always strange.

He steps up to me, leaving the smoke in his mouth. "Do you feel that?" he asks, tilting his head.

I look deep into his eyes, a sense of peace washing over me. The fire I had burning for so many years from undying hate toward Lucan had gone out. Smiling, I nod. "Yeah."

He blows out a cloud of smoke. "At least that's one of us." He narrows his eyes at me.

I frown. "You still hate me?"

His eyebrows shoot up in surprise. "No, fuck." His eyes dart around the place. "It's just—never mind. But I don't hate you. I feel peace with *you* now." Then he smiles. The first time I have ever seen Brantley smile, and it's at me. I want to jump on him and hug him, but that's probably going too fast for him. Baby steps.

Turning back around, wrapping my arms around Bishop, I look over his shoulder, directly at Hunter and Jase. My brothers. Biological brothers with Daemon.

Hunter steps backward, shaking his head and walking straight toward the parked car, slamming the door behind him. I frown, my shoulders dropping. I don't know what I expected, but it wasn't for Hunter to act like that. He's always been warm toward me.

Jase just stares at me, his dark eyes glued to mine. The last string in my heart is about to snap when he smiles at me. Giving me a wink. For the older brother, that surprises me. I haven't spent much time with Jase, if any, but I know in that moment that will change.

Bishop tucks me under his arm as the rest of the boys walk back to the cars. He looks at his dad. "Want me to call Katsia about this mess, or do you want to?" he asks his dad, nudging his head toward the destruction on the road.

Hector looks at me and then looks at Bishop. "I'll call her." Then he looks to me. "There was a reason for my bringing you here tonight, and it wasn't that."

I sink into Bishop, and his grip tightens around me. "Though, I did plan to tell you that you're adopted." He looks to Bishop. "But you see, as much as I love my son, he did something bad tonight. Something that is against our rules. And we only have one rule, Madison." Hector looks right at me, and chills break out over my flesh. "So now that your adoption is exposed, I guess it's only fair I find something else to tell you since my son is so trigger happy tonight."

I look up at Bishop. Trigger happy?

Hector steps forward, putting his hands into his pockets. "I'm sure you're familiar with the initiation process of a King?" he questions, looking at me. I nod. "Very good. So you know..." He gestures behind him, and Khales reemerges from the shadows. Bishop freezes, his grip turning to steel. "...That Khales was Bishop's..." My head spins and my stomach recoils. Someone else steps out of the shadows. "...As was your adopted 'mother.'"

TACET A MORTUIS

"Lost is not a place. It's a soul in paralysis…
Waiting to feel moved."
-Atticus

Bishop
Ten-Years-Old

"I want you to think of a wall, a bulletproof one that no matter how hard any weapon hounds on it, it could never break." Rob had said, pacing up and down in front of the seven of us. We had been close all our lives, whether by family or by choice, they were my brothers. I chose to care for them, no amount of family influence could have forced the kind of brotherhood we shared—which made us the most lethal Kings created. The generations before us, my father had said they always fought or struggled to get along sometimes. Whether it be by girl or just by personalities not being compatible, it never happened. They never had a generation that flowed fluidly like we did, so they had big plans for us.

"A wall?" Nate snickered. "You brought us here to teach us about a wall?"

Rob waved him off diffusely and continued his army march backward and forward in front of us. "I want you to start building this wall inside of your brain, but before you do so, I want you to make sure there are six seats there beside you. Not eight, not two, not any other number but seven total," he paused, looking down at me. I wasn't a short kid. For a ten-year-old, I was pretty tall, but staring up at Rob in this moment, I felt two-feet. "I want you to start building this wall today. Work on it, I mean really train your brain to build it, because by the time you initiate in, I need that wall to be solid. To be unfuckwithable. This"—Rob gestured around—"was who you trusted. No one else."

"What about my dad?" I argued, looking at the guys who all glared at me like "shut the fuck up." Rob was scary, but I didn't scare easily.

"Even your dad. He went through the same when he was your age, and so will the next ones who come after you."

"What, as in we have to have kids?" Hunter scrunched up his face.

"Yes." Dad interrupted, walking around the back of the cabin dressed in one of his fine suits. "You will have kids one day."

"No, I'm good. I don't want kids." I knew at a very young age that children didn't appeal to me, and I doubted that would change in the future. Call it the only-child curse.

"Oh I bet you will, I bet you and Khales will have kids by the time you're sixteen," Eli snorted, only no one joined him.

"No. I don't want them."

My dad kneeled down in front of me, searching my eyes. "You will, son, and lucky for you, I have someone lined up."

My eyebrows pinched together. "What? Who?" I was still not having kids, but I'd ask him who he thought I could be matched with anyway.

He reached into his front jacket pocket and pulled out a small photograph, flipping it around to show me. It was a little girl, had to be around the same age as me or younger—unless she was just really small. She had brown wavy hair, chubby cheeks, a bright smile and blue eyes. A couple of freckles were scattered over her cheeks and she was holding a hunting rifle. "This girl."

"That girl?" I questioned, obviously my dad was off his meds. That girl wasn't anything great, I had seen better at my school, but she had something contrastive about her, an imbalance if you will, but her eyes. Her eyes ate up the distance between us, even if it was a photo that she was staring at me from. "Who is she?"

Dad looked sideways at me, noticing the other guys trying to get a look. He folded it and pushed it back into his pocket, shooting them all a warning glare. "Someone who is going to arrive in your life at the exact moment you need her to."

"Like fate?" I asked. I didn't really know what that word meant, but I had heard it be thrown around a lot with the adults.

He laughed. "Not fate—karma. Your wake-up call."

CHAPTER I

"What the fuck!" I gasped, stepping backward until I'm colliding against a hard body. Spinning around, my eyes shot straight to Bishop. I searched him for more answers, but as per usual, he guarded his emotions with a wall that was probably built from all the people who died at his hands. His eyes were always evasively beckoning, and could summon me within seconds, but he had kept too much from me for too long. Now I was internally battling with myself on whether I trusted him or not. I tilted my head, scanning his features for something. A simple flick of light to pass over his face— but I got nothing. My shoulders slacked in defeat. I didn't trust him anymore. I could no longer trust any of them. My mother, who was actually my adoptive mother, was alive. She didn't shoot herself, and all my brain could manage to think was: well, shit, I got bullied all those years for fucking nothing! That could have something to do with the fact that she had fucked Bishop, though. And then I remembered who else just arrived back from the dead along with her. Khales. Nothing was making sense to me—as per usual. My body hummed with a numbness so bleak that the only thing I could feel was the trembling of my fingers and the sweating of my palms. You will not look weak right now. Through all the revelations that had been laid out tonight, and between the bloodshed, I could feel myself slowly slipping again. Losing touch with what was happening in front of me. Was it possible to have a mental break from the people around you driving you so fucking crazy? If not, I was probably going to be the first one to have it happen to.

Hector raised a cigar to his lip, lit it up and then blew out a cloud of fog. "Madison, my son never killed Khales, or, so I've just found out tonight."

I turned back to face Bishop. "I thought you told *me* you did?" I fought to add to that sentence *just like you told me a lot of fucking things*. I hissed the 'me' to accentuate how livid I was by yet another one of his lies.

"Well, this is all grand, but that's not why I'm here." Khales stepped forward and my eyes cut to her.

"Don't you fucking come closer." Then I glanced at my mom. The person I mourned for years after her apparent death. I realized, there was a lot that went on between her and my father that I probably didn't know. But even though my gut churned with distrust when I looked at her, I trusted my dad. Amongst all the chaos that he had put me through, I believed he had a good heart, well, at least when it came to me, anyway. I'd been wrong about this type of shit in the past, so at the same time, I wasn't entirely sure. I was overwhelmed, so overwhelmed that my hand started to convulse, and my legs quivered. A sharp zap started shooting through my bones, leading to my knees, and then suddenly, I was on the gravel road with stones imprinting into the flesh of my knees and palms. Silent tears began to trickle down my face, and in my peripheral, I caught Bishop sinking down beside me, his arm curling around my back. I froze as every sound, every ounce of talking that was going on, started to slip into white noise. The revelations, this world, it had been slowly breaking me since I first stepped foot into the Riverside Prep marble hall. The finery that screamed elusive, now roared at me in caution. I could feel my thoughts tremble as they slowly started to lose the fight. I thought I had my mom, I thought I'd always have her, even when she was dead, I still thought I had her. But it turned out, I had nothing but plastic promises that were delivered by a cheap imitation of what a mother should be.

The hands that were clamped around my upper arms tightened and began to shake me. I stared at Bishop instantly, but I had nothing else to give. *Nothing.* My mouth opened, and in my mind, I was ready to tell him to take me away from all this. To whisk me away from the imposters, and the fakes, but...*I didn't trust him.* One thing was clear through all of this mess. "You loved her."

His eyes searched mine cautiously. "What?"

"You loved her." This time it came out as though I was more confirming it within myself and less like I was asking him a question, because deep down, I knew. He must have felt something for her to not have ended her life all those years ago.

"Madison." A voice so familiar, it lit up my memory bank like a matchbox full of explosives and drifted through the frosted midnight air, lashing over old wounds that have now opened again.

My eyes closed in reply. "Don't."

"Madison, there's—"

My eyes slammed open and I narrowed them at her, finally, having enough courage to face the monster head-on. I slowly, and on shaky legs, stood from the asphalt, dusting off my pants and squaring my shoulders. I faintly heard a car pull up behind me, but ignored it. All of my focus was on *her.* I stepped forward and watched as her eyes darted around the place in panic, probably unsure of how I was going to react. I considered lunging at her but figured enough blood had been shed tonight. As much as they were all so used to witnessing scenes so graphic, I was not. She looked the same, too, well, somewhat the same—which angered me further. I guessed I would have liked to think that while I was mourning her fake death, she wasn't out living a lavish life. My eyes found her wrist, where a white gold watch was fastened around it. It had enough bling sparkling around the face of it to make Flavor Flav jealous. Yeah, she was definitely living a pretentious life.

Laughter cracked out of my throat before I could stop it. I was so incredibly angry at everyone, but I was going to start with her. "You know I've just spent the last few seconds hoping that the reason why you faked your own death, the reason why I had spent months mourning your *death*, crying for *you*, was because you were held captive somewhere against your will. Because what kind of mother would do that to her own daughter, right? But it turns out..." My eyes fluttered back down to her watch, and then lazily dragged up and down her body, examining the way her silk top hung off her lean arms, and the pearl beads that fell around her neck were clearly visible, and let's not forget the way her face appeared freshly made up of the finest—probably Chanel— makeup. Nope, no smudged eyeliner here. No sunken black eyes, bruises or scarred flesh. Just another housewife pissing away too much money and pretending like they give a shit. "—You're a fraud all on your own."

"—Madison…" She strode forward, but I yanked my hand away from her as she reached for it.

"Don't. I don't want to see you—or talk to you."

"Madison." A voice thundered out from behind me and I stilled. All thoughts, all movements, paralyzed by that imperious tone.

Turning around, my eyes landed on my dad. "Did you know?"

He observed me, and all though I couldn't make out his expression very well, the headlights from multiple cars that were parked up had somewhat given me a sneak into it.

He exhaled after a beat. "Come home. I will explain there."

"Madison…" Bishop decided to add in his two cents, his hand coming to mine.

I recoiled. "Don't fucking touch me, and everyone shut the fuck up and stop saying my goddamn name!"

His jaw clenched, then he dropped his hands to his sides. Taking one step at a time, I headed straight to my dad's car and slid into the passenger's seat.

"Kitty, wanna talk?" Nate must've hopped in behind me a second later.

"No." Was all I could manage. Sometimes, I wished I was just a normal hormonal teenager. Battling acne prone skin the night before formal instead of living through this hell.

Slamming the front door closed, I ignored the constant glaring from my dad and Nate and headed straight for the stairs. Taking them two at a time, I wanted to quickly reach the safe confinement of my bedroom. My bubble. It never failed me. Even if at this moment, I disliked some of the people living under the same roof.

I felt as though my mind was spinning on a never-ending Ferris wheel powered by NOS, and all I could think about was how before this night, everything was starting to make sense. Things were slipping into place a little better. But now, my whole life and what I thought I knew had again, been shredded into itty-bitty pieces—actually, the pieces were looking rather irreconcilable at this point. But like in true me life fashion, just when I thought I had gathered up all the pieces, ready to connect them back together, they get smacked out of my hand and scattered over the fricking Pacific Ocean. *Someone is taking the piss out of my life.*

Hitting the faucet on the shower, my eyes came to my hands. The dark red blood now crusted over my skin. My chest rose and fell heavily, panic slowly starting to ooze in. Without another thought, and through a shaky breath, I got into the shower and stood under the scorching hot water. Clothes and all. Running the palm of my hands over my face and pushing my hair back, I watched as the water that was pooled at my feet began to slowly run red. Tears pricked the corners of my eyes, descending down my face. Swiping at my cheeks, irritated, I slowly undressed, throwing my clothes into a pile near the sink. *I helped kill someone tonight.* I dry retched, my hand flying up to cover my mouth as my throat clogged with vomit. I quickly dashed out of the shower, leaning over the toilet just in time to unload the contents into the bowl.

"Kitty…" Nate walked into the bathroom just as I was wiping the residue off of my mouth. He shut the door behind himself and leaned against the door, putting one leg up to rest against it. We were so far gone past the awkward-naked phase, that I didn't even bat an eyelash when he entered. He had seen me naked more than any brother should. Step or not.

"Nate, please," I pleaded, snatching the mouthwash and taking a swig before spitting it out in the sink. I closed the toilet lid and took a seat. "I helped kill someone tonight, my boyfriend is a liar, and owns his very own fucking wardrobe of Narnia, only instead of walking through and seeing lions and shit, I'm walking into a dark smoky past filled with secrets—all of which he is obviously hiding from me—Then there's my mom, who isn't really my mom, but I have thought she was my mom all my life—who I thought shot herself, but is actually still alive—and had also slept with my somewhat boyfriend. Did I miss anything? Oh yeah, I'm a freaking Venari, not a Montgomery, so my whole life is a fucking lie."

Nate came closer until his hand was wrapping around my arm, and then before I could protest, he scooped his other under my upper thigh, lifting me up off the floor. "Get in the shower, Kitty." I couldn't control it anymore, sobs broke out and tears spilled down my cheeks. It wasn't a pretty cry either, it was an ugly cry. The kind people make memes out of.

Nate growled, and then squeezed me into his chest harder before stepping in, under the water with me still wrapped up in his arms.

"Why are you like this?" I asked through hiccups, lifting my head off his shoulder to look into his eyes. Water was pelting down against mine, but I ignored it, I ignored the sting from the water hitting my eyes, because looking into his felt like home. Nate felt more like home to me than this damn house did. I knew right then and there that I would be okay in life. I'd make it. As long as he and I were always on good terms. I could never lose Nate and survive it.

He paused, seeming to ponder over how he should reply. "I'm not like this with… everyone."

"Just me?" I asked, even though I knew the answer. Everyone sort of knew the answer to that question. Nate was… picky about who he allowed into his life. It was all part of the charm. In saying that, all of the Kings were like that, and I was beginning to think it had something to do with their heritage.

"And…" I knew that he was about to say Tillie, but I offered him a small smile instead, so he didn't have to say her name out loud. I knew he loved me. He once said he was in love with me, and I'm unsure if he still felt that way, but I knew without a shadow of a doubt that if it ever came down to it, it would always be Tillie. They had something, shared something, something that I recognized, only because I was the exact same with Bishop. When Tillie disappeared, it pained him. So agonizingly so that he never spoke of it. We shared that common bond, in a way.

"I know," I broke off in a whisper, patting his big bicep. "and you can let me down now." He complied, slowly placing me on my feet. I stepped under the water as soon as I was grounded, grabbing the soap and squeezing some into my hand. "Take these off."

I pinched at the elastic band of his basketball shorts, but his hand flew out to stop me. My eyes snapped to his and a chill shuddered over my spine. His eyes darkened, but remained weak and lazy, yet totally on fire, and that's when I realized we needed to draw the line—again.

"Sorry," I muttered, turning and rinsing out my hair, my back now facing him.

"You know how much I want you, Madison, but it's never going to happen. It's best we don't tease each other with what-ifs."

"I know," I whispered my answer, turning back around and twisting my long hair in one big knot. I reached for his cheek and then gently pressed my lips to his. It was supposed to be the kind of kiss you give your first love before saying goodbye, harmless, tentative, warm, soft, comfortable, *familiar*, hot, sensual, sexual... *oh oh...*

I jerked back to search his eyes, my body slightly caught up in the moment.

He groaned painfully, his hand clutching his crotch. "Get out, Kitty, before I fuck you so hard, you'll be calling me Bishop." That was effective, it was like an ice bucket getting doused over my head. I stepped out of the shower, wrapping my silk robe around myself and then brushing my teeth. My slightly bloodied clothes caught my attention just as I was reaching for the door handle. "What will happen to the body?"

The shower cut off and then Nate strutted out, in all his naked glory out of the corner of my eye. He followed my line of sight, down to the clothes, and his eyes connected with mine again. "That will get handled, as will those. I'll bag 'em, you'll never have to look at that shit again." His tone was light as if he was talking about football, or who he had slept with the last weekend.

"You speak like you do it every night."

"I do it enough," was all he said. I pulled open my side of the bathroom, heading straight for my bed. Yanking back the sheets and cover, I slipped into the cool, clean sheets. Inhaling through the smell of fresh lemon and lavender, I turned to face my patio door and kept my eyes glued on the stars that speckled through the dark sphere. I had witnessed too many things tonight. Things that I could not explain, and things I'm not entirely sure that I wanted to explain, but I couldn't hide or run from the fact that it was all there, in front of me. As bright as the glittering stars in the sky.

I helped kill someone tonight, and although my soul may be too far gone to save now, tomorrow was a new day, and I wouldn't shed another tear about this night again.

CHAPTER 2

"Bishop..." Dad started, just as I watched Madison and Joseph drive off with Nate. I tried to ignore him, like usual, but it never worked, like usual.

"What?" I snapped, pulling out my phone and dialing the cleaning crew.

"Son, I could have done that," he gestured to my phone, but I raised my eyes up to his, unbothered. "This is what you have been training me for, don't act surprised when I use my initiative."

"Yo! Bro? We're gonna take Brantley home, dawg. He needs to rest and shit," Ace called out, throwing open his car door. Hunter and Jase had long since left, what with Hunter in a shit about Madison being his sister. So from what I saw here, the rest of the guys were jumping in with Ace and Eli.

I nudged my head. "Yeah." I'd deal with Brantley tomorrow, see where his head was at. I'd been worried about him for a while now because he was always trigger happy. I never really understood why, but because our training covered how to conceal our opaque pasts, I figured that was what he was doing. I never knew the depth of his scars until tonight.

"B?" My eyes closed at that voice and my jaw transmuted to stone. "B, please—"

"Shut the fuck up!" I yelled, cutting her off and finally allowing my eyes to go to her. "Both of you!" I gestured to her and Elizabeth. "Do you both have any idea the shit you've caused just now?"

"Actually, me." My dad stepped closer, slicking his hair back and popping the collar on his suit. "They've both been back for weeks now, waiting for you to make a mistake. Tonight, you decided to go on a rampage and shoot up *my* club. You can't get away with it that easy. Son or not." He came closer to me and leaned into my ear. "You may be a monster, son, but remember the beast you learned from." Then he leaned back. "Now, your mother is away filming in Costa Rica, so Khales will be staying with us."

"The fuck she is!" I roared, fighting the rage that threatened to be unleashed. "No way in hell."

"Actually, yes, she is," he answered matter-of-factly. I watched as he slowly made his way towards the Range Rover. "Get in the car, son." Something wasn't right. There was something he wasn't telling me.

We all got into the SUV, and once the clean-up crew had arrived, we pulled out onto the road. I found myself struggling to bite my tongue the whole way to Madison's house.

I wanted to know what the fuck had gotten into my dad, but I knew that there was one person walking this earth who I couldn't read—and that was him.

Elizabeth got out, shutting the door, and I pressed my middle finger against the glass window. "I'll talk with you soon, Hector."

He looked toward her out of the corner of his eyes, and then slowly nodded. "Sure. You have my number." Anyone that doesn't know dad would miss what happened there, the silent exchange charged by lack of eye contact.

We pulled out of the driveway and I cranked my head slightly to face him. "So when did you and Elizabeth start fucking?"

CHAPTER 3

13.
Retribution

It had been many months since I had last written a paragraph in this book. I hoped that one day, it fell in the right hands. In the hands of a silver swan. I pray it does not become the crux of all things to do with the Kings. For days, I'd been conducting a plan to bring retribution to Humphrey, but I'd been struggling with my anger toward him, which had me making not very good decisions when it came to the plan.

"Katsia..." My maid, Maree, entered the room, carrying my recent bundle of joy. "Ma'am, Humphrey is back from hunting."

My face fell, as with my gut. "Oh."

I wasn't ready to see him. I headed to Maree and put my hands underneath my son.

"Hello, my dear. Are you ready to meet your father?" I just hoped he liked the name Hector.

WHAT? I SLAMMED THE BOOK closed so hard the dust particles from the previous century skyrocket to the ceiling. But, it did make a lot of sense. So Hector was related to Humphrey and Elizabeth—we already knew that. Hector was a far too strange name to bring it down to pure coincidence if you didn't already know.

A sharp knock on my door pulled me out of my thoughts. "Come in!"

It opened, and Nate popped his head around the corner. I relaxed, all my muscles loosening. "Since when do you knock?" Flopping back down, I wriggled under the fluffy feather down cover, pulling it up to my mouth. He sauntered in shirtless with nothing but his Calvin briefs on, his glorious muscles tensing with each step, and then he did exactly the kind of thing only Nate could get away with doing—he slipped right under my blanket.

"Nate!" I whacked him with the back of my hand. "I didn't invite you into my bed."

He sunk in deeper and tugged the blanket up farther. "Since when do I need an invite."

"Why are you here?" I'm still reeling from the events of last night. Nothing made sense but I could slowly feel myself growing stronger, mentally. Slowly, being the key word there.

His arms came out and tucked under his head, just as his eyes connected with mine. "Oh come on, there's a thunderstorm happening outside."

"So?" I argued, casting a quick look at the alarm clock beside my bed. "It's eight a.m, haven't you got some sort of King business to do?"

His eyes narrowed, and then a smirk slowly touched the corner of his mouth. "No, Kitty. I'm all yours. All day." He pressed each word with the syllables rolling off his tongue.

I groaned, reaching for the remote on my bedside table. "I'll make you watch The Notebook."

He laughed, staggering up farther on the bed, his arm hooking around my body. He pulled me closer to him. "You hate The Notebook." He knew me too well.

I pressed play on Banshee, snuggling into his warm hard chest. Circling the skull tattoo over his rib cage, I whispered, "Why couldn't it have been you."

His arm clenched around me and I gazed up at him, his eyes searching mine. "You don't think I ask myself that same question every day? Fuck, Kitty..." He fixed his focus ahead of himself briefly, and my eyes greedily took in his sharp jaw and soft lips. *Why am I looking at his lips?* Because I knew how they felt pressed against mine? Because I want to feel them against mine again? It was then that I realized he was back to glaring down at me.

"Kiss me."

"Mads, I—"

"—Nate?" I breathed out heavily. "Kiss me."

He let out a throaty groan, then hooked his finger under my chin, tilting my head up to his lips. They softly pressed against mine, and my heart thudded in my chest, butterflies roaring deep in my belly. My hand went to the back of his neck as I opened my mouth, allowing his tongue to slip inside. I tilted my head to give him a little more access, then he groaned again, his arm tightening around my neck. That feral sound shot straight down to my lower regions. I inched my leg toward his until it was pressing against his thigh, testing how far he'd let me go before ordering me to stop. Only he grabbed onto it and pulled me on top so I was straddling his waist. Without thinking twice, I quickly searched his eyes and he mine. It was a fleeting moment of pause. A quick second guess. But before either of us could protest, our lips were colliding, my fingers were tangled in his hair and my shirt was coming off. He threw it onto the floor and halted, leaning back to take in my naked chest. "Damn, Kitty." My cheeks heated briefly. For some reason, it was different between Nate and I this time. We sort of always knew it was sexual, there was always something there, but we hid behind our family and Bishop to simmer the tension down. Thinking of Bishop had me squirming, so before I could explore that any further, my lips went to his neck. I sucked on his skin, biting down on his flesh in my retreat. He moaned, his hand tugging at my hair to bring my face back down to his.

"We doing this? And choose your next words very carefully because I'm about to tear into that forbidden territory with no fucking shame."

I pulled my bottom lip into my mouth and nodded. "He hurt me. Too much, Nate. He's done... *too much.*"

"This a revenge fuck?"

"What?" His question was valid, but I asked 'what' just to give myself a few beats to decide how to answer, but I didn't have to think hard. "Of course not!"

He grinned. "You sure? I wouldn't give a fuck. You can ride on my dick for any reason you need."

I chuckled, my head tilting back. "Nate!" I hit his chest just as he came up and sucked one of my nipples into his mouth, his tongue swirling around it. I felt him harden under me and I moaned, tilting my head back while my hand found his neck again. Slowly I started to rub myself over his length before dropping my mouth back to his, sucking his tongue into my mouth and biting down on the bar of his tongue ring. Reaching to the waistband of his shorts, my fingers slipped under, sweat dripping off my skin from the pleasure the friction was giving me. I saw nothing but Nate's eyes, rimmed with fire and burning with need. I heard nothing but the deep intakes of our breaths with the occasional moan, and I felt nothing but his hands gripping my ass, hips, and then slowly, he slid beneath my underwear. I went to yank his shorts down as his thumb pressed against my clit, putting everything into first gear and hitting straight into sixth - fuck second, third, fourth and fifth.

Something caught the corner of my eyes. I screamed, grabbing for the blanket to cover my body.

"Oh, don't stop on my account..." Brantley stepped forward, pushing his hands into his pockets. His head tilted and his eyes turned hungry as they ran down my body, taking in the scene that was playing out in front of him.

"Brantley!" I snapped, clicking my fingers to pull him out of his pervy state. I could feel Nate's body jiggling underneath me from laughing, his hand covering his mouth.

"Brantley!" I repeated in the same tone.

"Hmm?" He casually brought his eyes to mine, and they darkened even more. His eyebrows pinched together and his mouth kicked up in a grin. It was the kind of dark grin Brantley usually gives me. You know, the one that sets chills off over my spine? Yeah, that one. My focus was still on him when Nate thrust his hips up to mine, his thick cock grinding against my clit. My eyes closed and my lips parted, my cheeks flashing with heat. Another moan slipped from me involuntarily, and I bit down on my bottom lip. Reality hit me and my eyes slammed open, back onto Brantley. Slowly, like a lion would approach its unknowing prey, he strode backward, his eyes staying on mine and then in one click, he pushed the door closed. My eyes dropped down to Nate. I felt safe with these guys—*mostly.* Okay, not ever with Brantley, but I do with Nate, so when he nodded his head, I tugged my lips in, looked to Brantley, and gave him a slow approving smile. Brantley waltzed toward the bed, his eyes clouding over in lust. He hooked his fingers under his shirt and tossed it across the room to the pile where my shirt was. His chest glistened in a golden glaze, and both his freaking nipples were pierced. His abs and chest were so defined you could probably stencil every single line and vein with a pencil and paper. He had the Elite King tattoo over his chest, with the skull and the crown and his last name *"Vitiosis"* in cursive writing underneath it. I noticed all of the boys who I've seen with no shirt on, all had the same king tattoo, but what I thought were scribbles underneath, I now know was their Latin last names. These boys dripped and oozed sex appeal, way too much for little old me. *But…*

My eyes closed again as I felt the bed dip beside me.

"C'mere, girl." Nate's fingers wrapped around my chin as he pulled my mouth down to his. He slowly ran his warm soft lips over mine and whispered, "You good?" I swallowed past my fleeting nerves, just as Brantley pressed a kiss to the back of my neck, igniting a whole new wave—no—tsunami of waves to come crashing over me. I shuddered, my legs going weak and my sex throbbing.

"Yes," I moaned out my answer as Brantley came behind me, his chest brushing against my back every so often as his mouth and tongue ran circles over the nape of my neck. His hand massaged my breast, his fingers twisting and twisting my nipples between his fingers. A pool of heat slicked between my legs as my thrusting became more urg—the door swung open.

"Hey, Mads, I wanna tal—" Jase cut out and I, once again, reached for the sheet. I drew the line at blood brothers. "Holy fuck!" Jase's hands flew up to his eyes, but he didn't leave.

"Unless you wanna add incest into your river of sins, brother, I suggest you back up and forget what you saw."

Jase's jaw clenched. "I ain't going anywhere. Mads, put some fucking clothes on and meet me downstairs." Then he turned and left anyway, slamming the door behind himself.

"Fuck! What's a girl gotta do to get laid around here." I huffed, pushing off Nate and getting to my feet, making a beeline for my shirt. "Seriously," I muttered under my breath, talking to myself. "I'm surrounded by ten of the hottest guys known to mankind—well, eight now because two are my brothers—some of them already have a connection with me—"

"—all of them…have a connection with you," Brantley interrupted, but I cut him with a glare, shoving my top over my head.

"I can't even get laid. My ex-boyfriend is a lying piece of shit, my family are deranged maniacs, my brother—"

"—step, if you're about to start on me," Nate interjected, climbing out of my bed. I sliced him with a glare too and finally walked out of my room, down the long hallway and then double stepped down the swivel stairs, still muttering cuss words under my breath. I hadn't even decided to tidy myself up before I came down, so I'm wearing a shirt that weirdly falls to just above my knees, and my hair was a freaking bird's nest all over the place. I needed a trim. And a change of color. I'm sick of being brunette, but I'll never go blonde, so maybe I could think of something else.

"Morning, Sam!" I chirped, just like old times, bouncing into the kitchen.

"Morning," she smiled at me, and then went to the fridge. "What do you want for breakfast, Trigger."

"Hmmm." I put my index finger to the side of my cheek. "Can you make waffles?"

Her eyebrow quirked in judgment, but before I could say anything else, Jase was blocking my view into the sitting room. I paused and then gestured out toward the backyard patio. "It's sheltered. We can talk out there."

He nodded, and then I followed him out the floor to ceiling doors, shutting them behind myself. Pulling out a chair, I pulled my knees to my chest. Shit. I stared down at my chest and realized I was wearing Brantley's shirt. I discreetly bring my nose to the collar and inhale. Sand, leather, and cigarettes. Interesting combination of smell.

Jase cleared his throat, sitting down on the chair. "That..." he hitched his thumb over his shoulder. "Should not be talked about."

"I'm single."

"Hardly..." he began, his eyes slanting.

"Did you come here to scold me like a real big brother?"

He sighed, running his hand over his shaved head. It was actually shaved really short, and it's the first time that I see his King tattoo is on the side of his scalp. "No. I'm just saying, be careful. Yes, you have an effect on all of the Kings—which is why I'm here—but you need to tread carefully with how you allow it to play out. If you want more than one, talk with Bishop about it first."

"Want more than one?" I cut him off, slightly shocked by his choice of words.

He shrugged as if it was the simplest thing in the world. "It wouldn't be the first time a girl has had to be shared around."

"What!" I was truly interested to know who this other girl was, not at all slightly jealous that there was someone before me.

He must see my reaction—it would be hard not to—and corrected himself. "Not their generation. Ours."

"Like yours and Saint's?"

He offered a small smile. "Yeah, that's a whole lot of shit you ain't ready for, but anyway, all I'm saying is don't hide things from Bishop. You're playing with fire and it *will* start a war."

Now it was my turn to sigh. "You're right."

"I don't even have to ask you to know who it is and who it will always be when it comes to a King, so keep it to him. As much as Bishop is dark and broody, he does have strong feelings for you, Madison, so don't take that shit lightly."

"But he lied," I whispered, looking out to the clearing in the backyard. Behind the pool house, there was a forest. Filled with old log trees and probably more trees. My mind was waiving, trying to run away with the issue at front.

"He did, and he has hidden a lot from you, as he was *trained* to do, Madison. Remember that before you start any more of that shit."

"I won't forgive him. He's slept with the woman I thought was my *mother* and he had kept his *ex* alive all this time. He may have strong feelings for me, Jase." I braved my eyes to his. "But I wasn't the first, or the only one."

He offered me a small smile and then leaned back in his chair, just as Sam walked out with trays of waffles, maple syrup, and whipped cream. She placed it all on the table with plates, knives, and forks, as well as a large jug of iced orange juice and some crystal glasses. I gestured to the food and Jase dug in.

"Actually, you're wrong," he added in. "You are the *only* one."

"So why did you come?" I asked, deflecting this conversation and pouring syrup on my waffles with huge chunks of butter and cream. He watched me every now and then, loading his own waffle.

"Ah—seriously?" He glared down at my third squirt of maple.

"What?" I questioned innocently, sucking the residue off of my thumb.

"God, I walked in at the wrong time," Nate muttered from the doorway with Brantley behind him. I popped my finger out of my mouth and smiled softly at them both. "Come eat. Sam makes mean waffles."

"Want some waffles with that syrup?" Jase continued to judge me, folding his and eating it with his hands. The caveman.

I glared as Brantley and Nate both got comfortable on either side of me, getting started on their waffles.

"Don't judge my waffle skill. Anyway..."

"I will if you continue that bullshit. One word for you: diabetes."

He tossed the waffle onto his plate, licking his finger clean. "It's Hunter."

My chewing slowed, but Nate and Brantley continued to eat like it was nothing. "Okay," I edged him to carry on.

He poured some OJ and took a swig. "He's not happy about you being our sister."

I paused my chewing and I put my waffle back on my plate. "I gathered." Then I poured some juice. Maybe he just hated me all along and the smooth exterior he held was a fake. Funny that I used to think he was the nicest King and Brantley was the worst. How things can change in one night.

"I've come to shed some light on that."

I waved for him to carry on. "Okay."

"Hunter, like the others—" he shot a piercing glare and Nate, who, with a mouth full of waffle and syrup dripping down his chin, paused and looked around dumbfounded. "What?" Then he eyed Brantley.

Brantley shrugged. "I know."

"I don't!" Yet again, I'm left out of the loop.

"You're not out of the loop, Madison. From now on, you will know everything we know."

"Okay well, can you start with Hunter?"

"He, like the other kings, had feelings for you. Strong feelings for you. So when he found out—"

"—I was his sister he got grossed out."

Jase's face softened.

"Well, he should have come to me, because I too, have had thoughts about him."

"Yeah?" Nate queried, an eyebrow perched.

"Yes... it was, well, all of you, in this dream."

Nate grinned, leaning back. "Do go on, Kitty, I'm quite enjoying this."

I flipped him off as Brantley chuckled beside me. Since last night, I had a newfound peace with being around Brantley. Like I had a deeper connection with him now that I knew our history. A history we still hadn't spoken about.

"He won't. He's too ashamed and he has way too much pride."

"Well, now I know where she gets it from," Nate muttered from behind his glass. I kicked him under the table and his eyes cut to me. "Ow!" he continued to glare at me while taking a massive bite out of his waffle.

Ignoring Nate and his typical childish shenanigans, I looked back at Jase. "Will he talk with me?"

Jase shrugged. "We can tie him up in the basement and make him listen."

I chuckled, picking up my waffle again. He shot me a small wink before continuing to eat his. We all fell into an easy breakfast chat, the talk ranging from Nate wanting to throw a party this weekend, to college next year. It's then I realized we will all be going separate ways—maybe. It made me ask, because terror slowly seeped into my bones about not having these boys with me.

"Um, college? Where—"

"Madison?" That voice made my attention snap straight to the entryway.

"*Mother*," I snarled, throwing my waffle back to my plate.

There goes my appetite.

CHAPTER 4

ASAP ROCKY WAS RAPPING ABOUT how he loved bad bitches, and with every pull-up, sweat spilled over my flesh. My fingers squeezed the slippery bar. *Thirty-four, thirty-five.* I started rapping the words, unlatching and dropping to the ground. The door to my gym swung open, but I ignored it. Part of me knew who it was, and the other part hoped it wasn't. The song continued to drown out the silence as I moved to the bench, laying down and wrapping my fingers around the barbell. Madison was angry with me, for the fucking hundredth time since I've known her. The essence of her anger was probably her mom's shit, and then there's me not telling her about it all this time, but I've been with her long enough to know that she'd be more hurt than angry. Angry Madison I could deal with, hurt Madison was territory I was unsure of. The fact that I kept Khales alive would have only intensified her anger even more too, no doubt.

"B?"

My jaw clenched, anger bubbling inside, so I started pumping the heavy iron.

"I know you're mad at me."

I hooked the barbell back onto the latches and sat up. "That's where you're wrong, I'm not fucking angry. I'm confused as to why the fuck you let him find you."

She sighed, taking a seat beside me on the bench. "I had heard you moved on, and then he—"

I turned to face her, my eyes hardening. "You outed yourself out of jealousy?"

"What? No, well, I don't—"

"—you better be careful with your next words…"

She stood, running her fingers through her hair. "Well, shit, I don't know, B! You've never had anyone else but me, what the hell was I supposed to do about finding out the one guy I loved, my first love, had moved on with some new girl. Why didn't you tell me about her?"

My eye twitched.

I sucked in a breath, stood and walked toward her. She stepped back, but I countered it. "You did this out of jealousy?"

Her eyes darted around the room. You could almost hear her brain trying to reach out and snatch whatever excuse she could find from thin air. "Do you not care about me at all, B?"

Her back collided with the wall and my hands came up to either side of her head, caging her in. "Listen very carefully—" my phone vibrated in my pocket and I reached inside, seeing it was Nate before sliding it unlocked. "What?"

"Yo, so I'm thinking I want to throw a party this weekend since everything has been so fucking depressing."

"Why?" My eyes remained on Khales'. Hers dropped to my mouth, and then came back to my eyes. I knew what she was doing, and if she tried any shady shit, I'd rip her lips off.

"Well, our girl isn't doing so good..."

"My girl," I corrected through a growl.

Khales' eyes slanted, so I brought my hand to her throat. Shock flashed across her face.

I grinned. "Continue."

"Yeah, you might need to get used to sharing her."

My grip around Khales' throat instinctively tightened. "What the fuck do you mean?"

She started tapping at my hand, so I released her a little.

"She's mad, I get it."

"Nah, she's not mad. She's... numb."

"What? You feel what she's feeling now?" I grilled, letting Khales go and stepping backward. There was something he was hiding, and whatever it was, better not have any-thing to do with them both fucking around with each other again. My patience was thin. One more misstep with her, and I was throwing in the towel. No point fighting for some-one that doesn't wanna be fought for.

"There was an incident..." Nate cleared his throat.

"What kind? She kill someone incident, or she trip and fall on something incident?"

He cleared his throat again. "Ah, well, a Peyton problem...."

My hands squeezed around the phone. Peyton was Tillie's older sister who in short, was messing around with Jase's generation of the Kings. She had four of them wrapped around her finger, and when they were over fighting about it, they all decided they'd just share her.

"You and who."

"Ah, Brantley."

"How far did you get?" My eyes narrowed on Khales', then dropped down her body.

"Pretty far, but then Jase walked in."

"I'm done," I murmured. "I'm done with her, dawg. I've not fucked up once since she's been here, aside from secrets and shit. This is the third time she's run off into some-one else's arms. She's your issue now." My eyes connected with Khales', who was smirk-ing in triumph. "Oh and bro? I'll throw the party." I threw my phone against the wall until it smashed into a thousand pieces. Khales jumped in shock but quickly collected herself. I stepped backward, reaching for the door.

"You're too good for her, B. You gave her too much."

"Shut the fuck up and don't touch me." I shoved past her and walked out the door. She was right in a sense. I did give Madison too much leash. I got too soft on her, cared too much, let her get away with too much shit. If she thought I was an asshole when she first met me, she ain't seen nothing yet. I took the stairs two at a time, and just as my feet landed at the top, my dad walked out of his office.

"You gonna tell me your plan with Khales?"

He grinned, pushing his hair back. "Have I ever?"

Leaning on the stairwell, I crossed my legs at the ankles. "Well, give me something to go on before I kill her."

His grin deepened. He knew I wouldn't, but that's not to say I couldn't. "You won't do that, son." Sidestepping around me, he made his way down the glass stairs, just as my mom entered the lobby.

"Oh good, I've finally got you both in the same room. Come and sit down, please." A bit rich, considering she spends most of her nights jet-setting all over the world working on new movies, but whatever. I headed down and went straight to the living room, resting in the corner and kicking one leg up to rest on the couch while the other remained spread. I stretched my neck, running my hands through my hair. What the fuck was Madison playing at. I understood her anger. Finding out I had slept with her—who she had always assumed was her—mother, as my initiation process would be a hard pill to swallow, and then Khales. But she didn't even fucking ask me why I did it. In her defense, she probably assumed I'd just keep it a secret like I had with everything else, but it wasn't that at all. Khales was under my protection. I always had her under my protection, as kids, we were inseparable. Through me sleeping with Victoria Secret models to A-list actresses, she was still there. I fucked around on her a lot, fucked with her head even more, but I had never fucked up on Madison, yet, she still did me dirty. It wasn't cheating, because we technically weren't together, but fucked if it felt like it. If what Nate told me was true, they'd just trampled on my stomping ground, and there will be repercussions for that—as they will know it. This was a no trespassing zone, and you know what they say about trespassers...

My dad sat in his chair, which was the same as my mom's throne—as she and I called it—but only where Mom's was white, Dad's was black. Both of them had high back pieces that wrapped around their shoulders and arms.

Mom started pacing up and down, one hand on her hip and the other over her chin. My mom was beautiful really. She had short brown hair that cut around her jaw and sharp, prominent features. I didn't have much of a relationship with her because she was always on the road. "I don't like this."

"Like, what?" Dad rested his ankle on his kneecap, grabbing his cigar and clipping it. My eyes darted between the two of them.

My mom stilled, her eyes narrowing on Dad. Oh, this was about to get interesting, so I wiggled into the sofa more, resting my head back against the top of the couch, my eyes now directly on the ceiling above.

"You knew I didn't like that woman, yet, you saved her? She was" —my mom faltered, and God, was that emotion in her voice?— "what she did, I will not agree with, Hector!"

"—you don't agree because you have never understood this life, Scarlet."

Their bickering died off in the distance until my mom's voice snapped me out of my slumber. "Bishop!"

I sat up. "What?"

"Get that girl out of my house, too. I don't like her."

"Who, Khales?"

My mom just stared at me, or should I say glared. I rolled my eyes. "Yeah, I'd love that, but Dad was the one who invited her in."

Mom snapped her attention back to Dad. "Get rid of her, Hector. I mean it." Then she reached into her handbag, pulling out a set of keys. "I guess now's a good time to do this, then…"

Dad stood to all his six-foot-three-inches. "Not now, Scarlet."

She threw her hand up to stop him from talking. "Shut it. Since you like to go ahead and make decisions without me, I'm making this one." She looked back at me and her angry features softened. She smiled a little, and then tossed a set of keys onto my lap.

"Congratulations, son. Happy birthday."

I picked up the keys, looking at them in confusion. "Wait, what's the date?"

Mom walked toward me and took a seat on the sofa beside me. "It's not until this weekend, I know, but I figured I'd give you the keys now."

I searched her eyes, and noticed for the first time how they looked tired. She had fine lines almost surfacing at the edges of them and her deep dimples looked more like smile lines. "Mom, I don't think I need another car…"

"It's not a car…"

My face lit up. "Wait, you got me my own jet?"

My dad turned his back on us. "Jesus fucking Christ."

Mom giggled, her hand resting over mine. "Not today, honey. It's your own condo in New York City. Penthouse, because only the best for my boy." Her hand came up to my cheek. My throat swelled, information floating inside my head.

"You bought me an apartment?"

She nodded. "Yep! The best one I could find that was close to NYU."

"—If he attends college," Dad's interruption went unnoticed.

She pulled me in for a hug before I had a chance to thank her. "When am I going to meet this Swan girl? Color me intrigued…"

I let out a pent-up breath, relaxing back into the sofa with the keys balled in my fist. "Probably never."

"What'd you do?" Her tone was accusatory, with good reason. She knew me and my father well.

"That's the thing, aside from keeping secrets from her, I did everything right. Never cheated, never did any shady shit."

"Keeping secrets is a big thing, son. And I'm guessing she has found out about Elizabeth and you, and also, the walking slut in the next room." A laugh exploded out from me. Hearing a crass word come out of my mom's mouth was humorous.

She stood, squeezed my hand again and looked to Dad quickly. "Whatever it is, give her time. But don't let her make a joke of you." She straightened her shoulders and carefully straightened her blouse. "Now, hate to love and leave my poster family, but I have to go back to LA where we're filming." Yeah, I bet. Just before she exited the room, I called out, "Hey, Mom?"

She turned to me. "Yeah?"

"Thanks for the apartment."

CHAPTER 5

"Bishop just texted me," Nate announced, going for another plate. My mom wasn't here for long before I said if she didn't leave, I would.

Leaning back in my chair, I took a sip of orange juice. "Saying what?" I already started to feel confused about how I was beginning to be forgiving, even a little guilty about how irrational I had been with Nate. He wasn't mine. Neither was Brantley, and Bishop had always said time and time again that if anything happened between me and another King, he'd take care of it and make sure consequences were filled. I lashed out. *He slept with my fucking mom.* This was beginning to get more twisted than even I cared to admit.

"He's throwing the party since it'll be his birthday this weekend."

"Oh," was all I could answer with, now that it was just Nate and I, I felt like I didn't need to hide behind a mask. "What day?"

"June 20th, he's having it at his new condo in the city."

"Wait, what?" He got a new condo?" I sunk into my seat, now deeply regretting ever going near Nate and Brantley. I was being a brat, and it wasn't fair. So what if I was angry with Bishop, I should have handled it another way, not this way, because in all honesty, I didn't want anyone else's hands on me. Now learning that it was his birthday soon, I needed to find something to get him.

"Don't get him anything," Nate murmured, reading my brain.

"Why?" I asked.

He shook his head. "He's not with it. Hates it."

"Too bad." I swallowed my guilt. "But what do I get the boy who has everything?"

"Easy," Nate answered. "You get him nothing like I said."

I sighed. My thoughts were strangling me with the help of my buddy guilt.

"Kitty…" Nate whispered, sliding his seat beside mine. "I know. And it's okay."

I shook my head, wiping a stray tear from my cheek. "It's not okay, Nate. I fucked up—again. Royally."

"Hey!" His finger hooked under my chin, tilting my face up to his. "We mess around a lot, it was a given because we had chemistry. Bishop knew it, everyone knew it…"

"But I shouldn't have with you, Nate." My eyes met his. "You and I both know who

His face sobered, and he leaned back in his chair, silence now stretching out. Nate didn't silence easily, but one mention of Tillie and he would clam up like a shell.

"Nate..." I urged.

His elbows came to rest on his knees. "There's something wrong with her disappearing act, Mads."

Mads, not Kitty. He was being serious.

I leaned closer toward him, my hair falling over my shoulder. "I know..."

He shook his head and then leaned into his chair. "I haven't seen her since we were all out at the cabin. Feels like fucking years ago now."

Wait. So he hadn't seen her in that long, which means that when I saw her while I was in the hospital, he didn't know. My eyebrows furrowed, and I pushed up from my chair.

"I need to, um, go for a second, I just need to see Daemon."

"Kitty, you know he won't see you."

"I have to try, Nate. He's my brother."

I walked back into the house, ignoring whatever Nate was about to say and climbed the stairs, taking them two at a time. Heading down the long hallway, I stopped outside his door, resting my forehead against the cool wood.

"Daemon?" I whispered, banging my head softly against it. "I could really do with you right now." Daemon hadn't spoken to me since the incident out in the woods, and the handful of times I had seen him, he seemed distant, reserved, and confused. Even more than usual. I grasped onto the metal door handle, and just when I thought about twisting it and opening the door—basically invading his privacy, I exhaled, turned and rested my back against it.

"Well, if you're not going to open for me," I started anyway, sliding to the floor, still in Brantley's shirt and booty shorts that I slept in. "I guess I'm just going to talk and tough if you don't want to hear it." I really shouldn't be testing him. "It's Bishop, Daemon. I don't know what to do. I can't talk to anyone else about him because they all have bias views on him." I paused, hoping that would have worked. It didn't. I carried on anyway. "I messed up, he messed up, we're both sort of just messed up, and I don't know how to get through our bullshit. It seems whenever we finally start to get things back on track, something else interferes us, and we're back to square one."

A ball of emotion rose in my throat, threatening to surface. "I feel too much for him, but he doesn't feel enough for me." Before I knew it, a tear had dropped down my cheek. I swiped it away angrily, then chuckled. "So I found out last night that he had slept with my mo—Elizabeth"—I stopped, then corrected myself—"who I thought was my mom, as part of his initiation process, and if that wasn't bad enough, I also found out that he had been keeping Khales alive all these years, for god knows what reason. I don't even want to ask him because I already know what he's going to say." I sucked in a breath. "Secrets are weapons, and in this world—" Suddenly I was falling backward, my back hitting the floor and my eyes now in view of—"Daemon?" He was standing over my body, the door handle still grasped in his hand. I leaned up onto my elbows and pushed myself up.

"I—I..." Now I was the one rendered speechless. He looked more on edge than normal. His messy fine dark hair was scruffy on his head, his face showed a couple day's stubble, the lines around his mouth were more indented than normal, and his eyes, so dark, so haunting, like the peak of midnight on a calm bleak night, looked—tormented. He wore a dark hoodie and jeans.

"Madison," he slurred in his half accent.

"Daemon, I—" I launched toward him, my arms squeezing around his torso. "God, I missed you so much!" I didn't even realize that tears were pouring out of my eyes, wetting his hoodie. His body was stiff, his arms refusing to reciprocate my hug.

"*Adfui etiam…*"

I didn't have my app to translate, and I didn't care what he had said, just that he had said anything at all meant a lot to me. Finally, an arm hooked around my waist and he buried his face in my hair.

"Sorry. So sorry, Madison."

"Shhh." I squeezed him tighter. Daemon hadn't been a part of my life for very long, but as soon as I saw him, I knew. He knew. We had an instant bond and now I could never imagine my life without him. Probably had something to do with the fact that we were twins. "Nothing matters. It doesn't matter. Dad is getting your charges lifted, and hell, I'll lie on oath and say it was someone else that I didn't see—just to get you out."

I took this chance to look up at him. God he was beautiful.

"Madison, *amore perit.*" His thumb softly pushed away my tears, then he leaned toward my ear and whispered, "Love dies." I really needed to take some Latin Classes If I was ever going to keep up with these boys and the language they all speak so fluently.

I sobered. "I'm starting to realize that." I walked in farther and he closed the door behind me. Taking a seat on his bed, I drew my knees up to my chest.

"Have you…" he paused, searching for the word he was looking for. His lack of knowledge of English has warmed to me, and I usually just end his sentences now.

"Told him that I loved him?"

He nodded, his brows furrowing in worry.

"No," I shook my head. "And I guess, he wouldn't want to hear it now."

"Why?" he inquired, walking toward the bed and taking a seat beside me. I lay back, my hands coming to rest behind my head. "I guess I messed up. I sort of kissed Nate—again, and Brantley, when I shouldn't have wanted them all, all this time, and I haven't wanted them, but there were times when I did want them all. But I love Bishop, and he's irreplaceable in all sense of the word, but I also have so much anger toward him with this life, the secrets he has held from me, and for the love of God." I sat up, resting on my elbows. "He knows something about Tillie!" I'm well aware my imbalanced brother probably didn't give a flying fuck about my teen drama, but I also knew that he probably didn't know what the fuck I was talking about.

He visibly stilled beside me, and I turned to face him. "Daemon?"

He shook his head and sighed. "She safe. For now."

"What!" I shoot off the bed. "What do you mean? What do you know?"

"Too much," was all he said, absently looking over my shoulder. He laid backward and curled into a ball, and my chest tightened. He was suffering so much, and I couldn't do anything to help him.

Leaving him to get through what he was battling with, I left his bedroom and walked into mine. He knew something about Tillie too. I needed to see her. She needed to come home and keep Nate on a leash. Flopping down onto my unmade bed, I cringed at how it felt. The sheets felt like betrayal and the pillows smelled of deceit. I quickly flew to my feet and stripped my bed clean. I carried the sheets out my door and dropped them in the hallway, walking to the linen cupboard and taking out fresh pillowcases, sheets and then search for a blanket cover.

"Come on," I groaned, flipping through the masses of linen but coming out with nothing. I sunk onto the floor, fighting tears again. I majorly fucked up.

"You ok?" Nate asked, coming toward me. "No offense, but you don't look too good."

I snorted, wiping my nose and swallowing through the swollen boulder in my throat. "I—I'll be fine." Then I move my eyes to his. "I need to go see Bishop."

"Ah, I don't think that's a very good idea right now, just saying…"

Standing to my feet, I shove everything back into the closet and close it. "I'm going to see him, Nate. Whether he wants to see me or not."

"Er, ok, well, I'll take you."

"Fine," I huffed, scurrying to my room to change quickly. I slipped into some hipster white skinny jeans and a little black strap top that showed a slit of my belly. Obviously, Tatum had been rubbing off on me a lot lately. Speaking of—I swiped my phone from the bedside table and quickly typed out a text to her.

R u ok?

I hadn't actually replied to her since the party before all this shit exploded. I didn't even check on her to see if she got home ok. Panic started to set in my gut and my eyes darted around the room.

"She's ok."

I turned around to see Nate leaning up against my door frame.

"Jesus. I'm a terrible friend, Nate."

He shook his head, pushing off the door frame and coming into my room. "No, you're not. It's only been one day, and you've seen a lot of shit in that one day. Cut yourself some slack." He flipped his cap backward and his eyes glittered with mischief. "Let's ride."

CHAPTER 6

I really freaking wish I had spent more time on my hair and makeup instead of being rushed out the door by my own anxiety. I only managed to splash on some tinted moisturizer and mascara. I leaned up from the plush leather seat, grabbing my cherry lip balm out of my pocket and smothering some on, just enough to make my lips feel kissable. Stupid.

Nate's matte black 2018 Audi-something pulled to a stop, just outside the front doors to Bishop's home. I swallowed the memories that this house raised and reached for the door handle. Nate cut off the loud car, halting me with his hand on my other arm.

"Seriously," I gritted. "How much did this car cost you?"

He shrugged. "Was a present, it'd be rude to not accept."

"Trust fund brat," I muttered, just as his door closed. I pushed mine open and got out, noticing Bishop's matte black Maserati GranTurismo. "Did you make it this low and supped up? Like what is with all of you boys, you all ride in damn near half a million dollar cars and SUV's, then you guys all modify them to look like something fresh out of Fast and Furious."

I eyed Nate's new car. It really was beautiful, even though it was extremely low to the ground. The wheels were splattered with gloss black and the windows were also black.

"Well, dear sister, first of all, have you forgotten we all race?" He quirked his eyebrow, closing my door. "Well, for shits and giggles mostly, and to run shit around town for Hector daddy boss."

"No, I hadn't forgotten, I'm just waiting for the time to bombard you all with my millions of questions. I figure if I ask you separately, you're more inclined to answer me. Whereas if I push all these questions on you all at once, there's a chance you guys will let a few answers slip and I may not catch them. I'm being thorough." We were walking through the side gate now, heading straight for Bishop's pool house. The architecture continued to render me speechless. His pool house was an exact replica of the main house, only smaller, and it was more like a two-bedroom loft, fitted with an open fireplace, a small bar, lush red marble counters, and the stairs that lead to his bedroom were built with glass. Nerves began to eat at me, and I stopped walking, silently freaking out. What if he was in bed with Khales? I couldn't be mad at him, but I knew it would shatter me. Besides the fact that yes, I had handled things erratically in the past, I didn't think I'd ever allow another man to physically put his dick in me—no matter how dizzy I may be at the time. Bishop, on the other hand, was a male. And he was—Bishop. *Shit.*

"Kitty, it'll be ok. Whatever happens from here, just swallow what you see."

My eyebrows pulled in together, then I let myself get lost in Nate's eyes. The comfort of knowing I could trust him eloped me, and I quickly nodded my head. I could do this—regardless, and I needed to do this. I needed to tell him everything and fuck the consequences. We continued toward the pool house and then climbed the little wrap around porch. Adrenaline spiked through me, and just as Nate went to knock (even though I damn well know he never knocked with Bishop or any of the other guys before), I twisted the door handle and pushed open the door. Fuck it. I was Madison fucking Montgomery, and Bishop Vincent mother-fucking Hayes was *mine.*

There was laughing in the kitchen, then it went silent. Bishop stalked around, my lady parts humming. He looked *pissed,* and pissed Bishop was always a glorious sight. He was shirtless, the ripples of his tight body on display for me to wander, then my eyes dropped down to his jeans. Slightly loose, with tears and rips in all the right places, bare feet, and then my eyes slowly traveled their way back up again. He had a cap flipped backward, his hair sticking out the edges slightly, a bottle of Jack dangled from between his fingers, and then I zeroed in on his eyes. They hardened on me, and he bared his teeth with a slight hiss, eyeing me up and down in disgust.

Oh shit.

He was way past pissed.

He sauntered into the little room even more, his swagger mixed between a relaxed soldier getting ready to go to war, and a loose teenage boy who gives no fucks.

He was... *was he drunk?*

"Bishop?" Stupid first thing to say, but it was all I could manage.

"Oh, shieeetttt," Nate shuddered, quickly opening the door again. "Yo, Kitty, we should come back..."

Suddenly, I felt an overwhelming rush to run. It was as though Nate and I just walked straight into the lion's den, and I'm almost certain we were about to be ripped to pieces. Dumbest decision ever. Why the hell did I think it would be a great idea to come and poke the monster that I created? Well, because like the stupid girl I was, I thought the monster would forgive me. Monsters don't forgive, especially ones who have tattoos and drive Maseratis.

I sucked down my nerves when his chest brushed against my breasts. I stepped backward quickly, my back smashing against the wall, knocking down a painted canvas.

His nose came to mine, and I slammed my eyes closed. I couldn't open them. I couldn't face him.

"Open your fucking eyes, Kitty," he whispered devilishly, his lips brushing against mine ever so softly. So faintly, I fell for it and my eyes opened. Terror seized my muscles when I saw his pupils were dilated, his eyes almost pure black. They looked erratic, deranged and unhinged. This was Bishop *not* in control. He would always say how he hated getting drunk, and it really just wasn't in his nature to do so. He was always in charge of his surroundings. It was unchartered territory him being drunk, and I was going in completely blind.

"Leave, dawg," was all he said, his eyes staying on mine, but his words directed at Nate. His hips slowly pressed into my pelvic area, pinning me to the wall. He raised the bottle to his lips, took a swig, his eyes still on mine, and then dropped his arm, the other coming up to the side of my head, half caging me in. He smelled like Bishop. Minty, leathery, with a slight dose of cologne and soap, but now that was also mixed with whiskey. *Shit.* He tilted his head toward Nate when he saw he wasn't moving. "I'll deal with you this weekend. The way *we* deal with things. For now? Get the fuck outta my face, *bruh.*"

"What's going on in here!" an unfamiliar voice interrupted jokingly. I tried to peek around Bishop to see who it was, but he blocked my view.

"Nah uh, kitty. Don't want you getting ideas with this one."

"Nate?" I whispered, my eyes on Bishop's. There was no way I was going to be able to escape this. So I would stick it out and with him. Anyway, I'd rather I be here with him while he's in this state so I can look after him. "I'll be ok."

Nate's eyes flew between the two of us, but I witnessed right then and there the power difference between Bishop and Nate. If you didn't know it yet, you would definitely know right then that Bishop was the alpha.

Bishop laughed, his head going back as he pushed off the wall, his dick pressing into my stomach roughly before standing straight with his shoulders back. "She definitely won't be ok, but you can't do shit about it." Now he was going toward Nate. "I'd leave right now. We all know what happened last time I was this drunk, huh?"

Nate took a deep breath, and then looked back at me. "Text me if it gets bad. I don't believe he'd hurt you—regardless."

"That's why you aren't very smart, pup," Bishop grinned at him, and then headed for the sofa in the lounge.

My head bobbed. This wasn't the first time I had been terrified at the hands of Bishop, but no matter how scared I had been in my life, there was always a firefly sitting underneath that fear. That firefly held the light of hope.

Nate left, closing the door, and then I finally let my eyes go to the other guy who was in the room. He was shirtless too and was a little older than Bishop. He was bulky in the muscle department, veins popping out everywhere and had a long, thick dark beard. He didn't look *that* old, because his body was beautiful, and his face looked young, I would say he had to be around thirty-one, or something. He was eyeing me as if trying to make a decision on me, and then he scoffed and shook his head, leaning forward on his elbows. Bishop lit up a—what I'm guessing—was a J, brought it to his mouth and inhaled before passing it to the big guy.

He hit play on his phone which was linked to the massive sound system set up he had around the entire room. He grinned, leaning back on the sofa, his leg perched up on the coffee table where there was a little mirror sitting on with lines of cocaine laid out and a rolled-up dollar bill. Fucking hell. The song started playing, and it was "#icanteven" from The Neighbourhood. Great. I have a whole night of this shit.

"You might wanna get into something more revealing than that, Kitty. Go in my room," he paused, his eyes boring into mine with intensity. His lip curled into an evil grin. "I'm sure Khales left some of her shit in there from today."

Big guy started coughing and laughing, banging on his chest with smoke escaping out of his mouth and nostrils.

"I'm good. Thanks," I bit out, ignoring the fire of jealousy that ignited deep in my gut.

His eyes raked down my body. "You really ain't."

Ouch.

Ignore him. I took a seat on the floor in front of the fireplace. I forgot all about Khales for the brief second I was here, and I really hoped she didn't come in.

"Kitty, c'mere." Bishop looked over his shoulder and patted the spot next to him. I stood and followed his orders, sinking down onto the sofa. "Nice and Slow" by Usher started playing next. *Cringe.* A little intense.

Big guy nodded at me. "I'm Justin. This little shit's older cousin."

My eyes ran over his body, and up close, I could see the silver scars marring into his skin. In old English writing, the word "Lost, don't find" was across his chest. He was a Lost Boy? I didn't want to ask any questions, so I just smiled. "I'm Madison."

Bishop's arm casually snaked around the back of me as his head tilted back with the joint in his mouth.

Justin chuckled, picking up the rolled-up bill. "I know who you are, *Swan.*"

"I guess you would." The slow song was really throwing me off with the setting, and my fingers itched to change it to something more upbeat. I could see Bishop's head tilt toward me out of the corner of my eye.

"What's the matter, Kitty, don't wanna play games anymore?" He curled a few of my strands around his finger, and then stood, dropping the roach into the ashtray. "Too bad." Then he climbed the stairs. "Get changed, cos."

Justin's eyes found mine again. "If I wasn't so pissed at you for putting him through this, I would say it was nice to meet you, but, I'd be surprised if you make it through to-night without getting killed."

He stood up and stretched like he hadn't just threatened my freaking life, and then went to the small bedroom behind the kitchen. With both of them out of sight, I finally let out a huge sigh of relief and reached for my phone. I saw Nate had texted me a few times and quickly opened them.

He won't hurt you, but I can't do jack shit, mads.

Text back, you all good?

Fuck.

I quickly texted out a reply.

I'm fine. We're going out somewhere though.

Then I opened Tatum's texts.

Dude, I think I'm still drunk.

I hit reply.

Wish I was, but unfortunately, I'm on babysitting duties.

I hit send and then opened to send her another.

BTW, if I go missing, Bishop totally killed me.

CHAPTER 7

I tucked my phone back into my pocket and stood to my feet. I started tidying up the glasses and empty bottles, taking them to the kitchen and dumping them in the garbage bin. I knew where everything was, so I pulled down a glass and opened the fridge, trying to find something non-alcoholic to take the edge off, but I'm shit out of luck when I only find Redbulls. I grabbed one anyway and cracked it open.

"Guys! I think I'm finally ready, I know, I know, but perfection takes time," I heard coming from the lounge. I rounded the kitchen cupboards, can pressed to my mouth and eyebrows quirked. I didn't really give a shit if she had fucked Bishop. He was still mine and there was no way I was going down without a fight. Her eyes flew to mine. "What the fuck!"

I waved, and then lowered the can so she could see my grin. "Nice to see you again, too, and I totally disagree, that's not perfection. That's…" I tilted my head. "Fake."

"Fuck you," she spat, her hands coming to rest on her hips. "And who the fuck invited you?"

"Down, girl," Bishop chuckled, walking down the stairs throwing a shirt over his head. He had changed his faded jeans to darker ones and had military boots on his feet now. He had also lost the cap, his hair now in its normal style, scruffily clean on the top of his head. His eyes came to me. "You really coming in that?" He was still drunk, I could see it in the way his eyes beamed with crazy. "Some of your shit is still upstairs."

Khales was wearing a short leather skirt that made it almost painful to witness, and an equally leather crop top. Her hair was straight, coming down to her hip bones and her makeup was heavy everywhere. I internally shriveled a little, feeling way too underdressed. And considering Bishop had raised this subject twice now, I figured I better go up and see what he's got. He sat on the sofa, picked up a rolled dollar bill, snorted a line, and then cleared his nose and handed the bill to Khales, who took it with a grin while sitting beside him.

Fuck. I really, *really*, wish Tatum was with me right now. Walking upstairs to his bedroom, there were three things that I noticed instantly.

1—His bed was ruffled with pillows and blankets were thrown around everywhere.

2—There were two sets of towels on the floor, with a pile of girl's clothes beside it.

And 3—The makeup that was scattered all over his dresser.

The floor started to sink below my weight as my vision faded in and out. *You can do this. You were kissing, rubbing up on two guys earlier. It's fine.* My guilt subsided a little. Now I was sort of glad I had something on him because he obviously had something on me. I looked at the leather headboard to his bed, noticing scratch marks indented in the leather and lipstick smeared on the sheets.

Fuck this.

I felt the last string I had snap inside my head and I went straight for the walk-in closet but found nothing. I wanted sexy. Just as I was diving through the last of my clothes in there, a little red lace bra crop top caught my attention. It was Tatum's "skanky" top. The breasts were covered by lace, and the thin spaghetti straps trailed over my back, criss-crossed and then connected to a thin strap that had lace slightly dripping off it. It was sexy, hot, and totally something I would *never* wear, but fuck it. I threw my innocent top off, tossing it in Khales' pile of clothes and squeezed into the little bra. My jeans were tight enough, I knew I didn't them, so I fluffed up my long dark hair and went for the makeup. I caked it on, full on contouring (because I watched Tatum), and dark eyeliner. I lined my lips and then filled them in with dark burgundy that made my green eyes pop. "Shit!" I backtracked as I was on my way out, grabbing a pair of silver spaghetti heels and slipping them on. Thankfully, the heel wasn't high, so I should be safe, and hopefully, I didn't start drinking.

I headed back downstairs, checking my phone with my hair falling in waves over my shoulders when I started bobbing my head to the song that was playing. It was "Devil's Night" from D12, and it reminded me of Halloween night in the woods...

I hit the bottom of the stairs and tucked my phone back into my pocket. "Ok, I'm ready to go," I announced, looking up because aside from the song, everyone was silent.

Bishop's eyes were on my chest and then came to my face. "I think I regret that."

Khales flicked her hair over her shoulder, and Justin grinned from behind his glass.

They started walking out except Bishop, he was still staring at me. He took a swig out of that fucking bottle again.

"Bishop, can we talk?"

He snorted. "Now you wanna talk?"

I winced.

He shook his head, snatching the baggy from the table and shoving it into his pocket. "Get in the car, Madison." I followed him out into the cool night, goosebumps instantly assaulted my flesh.

I grumbled. "I need a drink."

His arm went back, handing me the bottle. "Trust me, Kitty, you will need it for tonight."

I thought about it for a few seconds and then took it, wrapping my lips around the rim and my mind briefly drifted off to how Bishop's mouth was in this very spot not so long ago. I could still feel the wetness from his lips. Creep, much?

I handed it back to him. "Thanks." There was a stretch limo waiting for us, and I watched as Khales disappeared inside, but just as we reached the door, he stopped in front of me and turned to face me.

"Why?"

Shit. "I was hurt."

"So you wanted to hurt me?" he urged, his head tilting. Then he stepped closer to me, wrapped his hands in my hair and yanked my head back so my face was there for the taking. We probably looked like a messed up couple bordering on domestic violence, but whatever. His lips smashed down onto mine and his tongue invaded my mouth. His lips worked over mine harshly, and then he pulled back, his teeth catching on my bottom lip, biting down. The metallic tang of blood hit my throat. "I don't get *hurt*, Kitty, and I don't get *even*. I get *cold*." Then he grinned, and let go of my hair, my scalp now throbbing from the pain. "And you mean shit to me now. Get in the fucking car."

Tears prickled the corner of my eyes, but I shoved past him and got inside the limo. He chuckled as he slid in beside me. "Get mad, Kitty, you know how that gets my dick hard. Only you won't be the one soothing it tonight." Then he shoved the bottle into my chest. "So as I said, drink. You'll need it." I took it, ignoring whatever bullshit Khales and Justin were talking with Bishop about, and drank. I didn't take too much, because I didn't want to get too messy too fast, but at the same time, I wanted to forget him. This was us, though. It had always been messy. It used to be beautiful, but now it's more chaotic. It's a storm that won't stop and a tsunami that keeps rolling, but I'm addicted. I'm chasing the storm, regardless of the danger.

Bishop leaned back in the seat and looked at me. "Why you acting hurt? Now you can have any of the Kings you want."

I ignored him because he's drunk.

He laughed. "Good thing, since they're all meeting up with us soon, and your friend Tatum will be there, so don't worry."

"I wasn't worried, Bishop." I was talking shit right now, but I wouldn't let Khales have the satisfaction of witnessing how Bishop and I could be. I took another sip, and then Justin leaned forward and handed me the rolled-up bill. I looked at it and then looked at the little table in between us. Reaching for it, Bishop pushed my hand away. "No."

I gritted my teeth. Okay, I wasn't really going to snort a line, I was actually going to throw it out the window, but whatever. I huffed and waited it out until the car finally came to a stop outside a club. There was a massive line out the front that ranged from young college people to middle-aged people, to even older moms who obviously needed the break. Just saying, they should always get let into clubs before anyone else. Putting up with little kids has to like, I don't know, offer some sort of advantage. Free wine and first priority into clubs.

Bishop opened the door and climbed out. I followed, and then saw he was already making his way to the bouncers. He started talking to them and then pointed toward us before walking through the front doors. I walked toward them, thinking he had probably locked me out, but they unhooked the little gate and let me through. I pushed through the doors and loud music instantly blared. The familiar smell of sweat and alcohol staining the air. There were dancers up in cages above us and the bar was one huge circle in the middle. I headed straight to the circle, deciding he could look after himself, and right now, I just wanted to forget about tonight. I'd talk with him tomorrow—hopefully—or not—Jesus, I was so confused. I banged on the bar. "Hey!"

The bartender came to me. He was quirkily dressed with leather bangles, blue hair, and two hoops in his ear. "What can I get ya, sweetheart?"

He wasn't going to ID me? Score.

"Something strong, please."

He smirked. "I know just the poison." I shot it back and ordered another as well as a vodka lime and soda and opened my phone. Tatum had texted me.

I'm here at this club. U here yet?

I got a little giddy.

I'm near the bar. Come alone.

"Boo!" Tatum grabbed my back and I turned to her, smiling. "Hey!" I pulled her into a hug and almost lost it right then and there.

"Are you okay?" she asked into my ear, and I shook my head.

"I don't think so." She leaned back and threw up her fingers after pointing to my drinks, gesturing how she wanted what I was having.

"I saw Bishop!" she yelled into my ear.

I just smiled.

She leaned into my ear again. "He was with a chick! Shall I kick her ass?"

I laughed. "It's Khales! Don't worry about her, and she's mine…"

"I thought Khales was a brunette?" I thought over what she said, but then shrugged. Oh well. She leaned into me again. "Don't look, but they're all up in the VIP area above us, that you have access to as well."

I shrugged again, sucking down my drink. This put a whole new meaning to fuck my life. I started to sway on my feet now, and I grabbed Tatum's arm, dragging her onto the dance floor. "Closer" by Chainsmokers started playing and we started bumping and grinding on the dance floor. Whatever this night brought, I just hoped that something would come from Bishop and I. A few songs later, we headed back to the bar and got more drinks. My phone vibrated in my back pocket, so I pulled it out, and my heart fluttered when I saw Bishop's name.

Come here.

I read it, ignoring the way my cheeks heated. God. How can I hate someone and love them, and want to kill them, and need to fuck them, all at the same time? It's Bishop voodoo.

No

Ha! That showed him. Oh no, I was really drunk. I giggled. Suddenly, the severity of the entire situation meant nothing.

Laughing, I turned to face Tatum. "Dude! We nee—" I was upside down, swung over a set of thick shoulders as my hair fell down and I was face first with a glorious ass.

"Bishop!" I growled, but he continued to take me upstairs to the VIP area. He threw me onto the sofa and then sat next to me, a cigarette sticking out the side of his mouth and picked up his drink, blowing out the smoke. "What were you saying?" he casually asked the blonde, who was looking between the two of us nervously.

I brushed my hair out of my face and shoved him. "Fuck you!"

"Ignore her, she loves it." He winked at the blonde and sat back, perching his foot on the table in the middle. I dragged my eyes around the boys and saw all the Kings, except Nate and Brantley.

"Where are Brantley and Nate?" I drilled Bishop, trying hard not to make eye contact with Hunter and Jase. In fact, everything was rather tense. Everyone was watching Bishop like he was Tony Montana and about to shoot up this club. Maybe I need to try a new tactic. He was obviously a lot more angry about this whole thing than I imagined. He hadn't completely lost his cool with me, but he was *off.*

"Bishop," I whispered, just as Tatum came to us. Her eyes found Khales and Justin, and her eyebrow went up.

"What the fuck are you doing here, bitch?"

My girl was feisty as fuck.

I laughed. "Sic 'em, girl…" Then went back to more pressing issues, leaving Tatum and Khales to argue, but silently praying Khales threw a punch so I could smack her one. Just once. Maybe twice. I needed water.

Bishop ignored me, smiling at the blonde girl, but his jaw tensed and the vein on the side of his neck pulsed. He was mad as shit, so mad that he was masking it with all of this bullshit. I looked up at Jase who was already staring at me. He shook his head, gazing at Bishop worried.

I did this.

Closing my eyes, I opened them and then lowered my voice. "Bishop?" My hands went to his thigh and he stiffened. That was like swallowing a harsh pill. "Can we go for a walk?"

It was as though all the Kings were watching our exchange. This was my fault, so I had to somehow fix it. Bishop's smile dropped. "Leave," he said to the blonde, who was so quick out of her seat I barely saw it happen. He turned his head toward me. "Pretty sure we talked about this."

"Pretty sure we fucking didn't," I snapped back, my eyes piercing his in a challenge. He stood up, grabbed my hand, and then started dragging me out of the club.

CHAPTER 8

His grip was tight around my wrist as he dragged me out of the club, tight enough to leave a bruise. We hit the back exit, out onto an alleyway.

"Talk!" he said, too calmly. I looked around the dark alley, empty and cold. At least we were alone. For once.

"I'm sorry."

He sneered. "You're sorry?" Maybe I shouldn't have said that. Shit.

"Yes!" I quipped, coming closer to him. "I—I lashed out. I didn't, I don't, God, Bishop! I make shitty decisions."

He backed me up against the wall, the cool concrete freezing my back, then wrapped his hands around my thighs and hooked them around his waist. "I'm not done with your punishment."

"Punishment?" I implored, tilting my head. His eyes started getting distracted by my clothes, his head moving all over the place.

"Yeah. And don't get me started on Brantley and Nate, which you will watch, by the way." His hand came to my nipple and I sucked in a breath as his thumb swiped over it. He pulled my breast out, the cold night air whisking around it boldly, and sucked it into his mouth. Biting on it harshly, he pulled back and lowered me back to my feet.

"We're going to a bar."

"What?" I tucked my tit back into my bra. Damn caveman. Then trailed after him.

"There's a reason why I don't drink, Kitty, and you're about to witness why."

"Witness? I think I've seen enough. Can we go home."

His laughter echoed off the brick walls and set up shop in my bones. "No."

I followed him down the main street as we passed clubs and late night restaurants. He tore his shirt off and tucked it into the back of his jeans pocket before stopping abruptly. I slammed into his bare back, trying to ignore the massive tattoo that stretched out wide against his flesh. The skull just below his wings on the back of his neck had a crown sitting on its head and the words "King" was tattooed over his nape. The man was sex on legs. I really needed to take him home. "Now what?" He was a man on a mission.

I watched as the bright red neon lights blazed over his smirking face.

I followed his line of sight. "Oh no..."

"Oh yes..." he mimicked, crossing the road—fuck the cars that are zipping past.

"Bishop!" I yelled, running into the road while dodging beeping cars and following him across. He pushed open the front doors that led into the tattoo studio and I quickly slipped in behind him. A tall man with a long beard and a motorcycle patch on walked out, stopping in his tracks when he caught both of us. His eyes ran over Bishop. "Is this a coincidence, B, or what?"

Of course he knew this scary man. Why wouldn't he.

Bishop's head cranked over his shoulder, a grin tickling the corner of his lips. "She wants something."

"I do?" I quirked my eyebrow.

Big scary biker dude's eyes flew to mine, then he grinned. "What you want, pretty girl."

"Hey, eyes off."

Biker dude chortled, then nudged his head towards the hallway he just walked out from. Bishop led the way, his bare muscled back taunting me. We passed a couple of smaller stalls, all set up differently. There must be around four artists who work here. I admire the work hanging on the walls as we continue down. Biker dude walked straight ahead, his stall obviously at the head of the hallway.

"Wow," I took in all the art. "This is amazing." Stealing my gaze away from the beautiful colors and grey shading, I looked down at the red seat that reclined into a bed in the middle, and biker dude sat down on his chair, picking up his gun. I gulped.

"You know, I used to work for a studio in New Zealand."

"Yeah?" Bishop interfered, sitting in the chair beside the bed. "What? Do I need to fly over there to add him to the list?"

I hopped up onto the red leather, grasping the edge. "Don't be stupid. It never got that far."

Bishop laughed, his head tilting back and his glorious abs tightening from the motion. "Right, because he isn't a King. I forgot, you only do royal cock."

"Bishop!" I snapped, then looked back to biker dude who was putting gloves on. "Sorry, he's a little…"

"I'm fine." Then he took his attention to Biker dude. "Lemme do this one. I'll owe you."

Biker dude's eyebrow rose, and then he looked between the two of us. "You don't owe me shit, and sure."

"Ah!" I threw my finger up. "Hello, but I've never seen your artwork and I don't know what I want. How about I sketch something up right now and let biker guy stencil it up and *then* you can tattoo me." Jesus Christ, I was losing my mind. He wasn't a hundred percent sober, but I was going to let him tattoo me anyway. Usually, when couples go in to do this sort of thing, it's romantic. Not us though, oh no. I'll be getting inked out of hate.

"No deal, Kitty," Bishop pointed to the bed. "Lay down."

"Jesus," I whispered, laying back.

His hand came to my bare rib, and his thumb glided over it softly, the tenderness of his touch sending tingles down to my toes. I looked at him, catching his stare right at me. A moment passed between us, my heart thundering in my chest. Then the gun sounded, breaking our eye contact and the silence, and Bishop dipped the tip into the little pot, then stretched my skin out over my rib cage just below my bra line. A sharp sting sliced through my flesh and I flinched. "Jesus."

"Yeah," Biker added, finally jumping in. He stood and tilted his head at the spot. "That'll be tender, sweetheart. So you're an artist?" he asked, and I appreciated the attempt at taking my mind off whatever I just allowed Bishop to indent into my skin—for life.

"Yeah," I cleared my throat, trying to take my mind out of the pinching pain. The gun stopped and then started again. "I drew for him, his custom pieces. I loved it."

"Why'd you leave?" I didn't look at him, because I was too afraid to move.

"Well," I let out an exhausted breath. "I was running away from this psycho." Biker crackled out a laugh.

"Ah, I see. I'll have to check out your work some time." It turned out, I made a mis-judgment. Big scary biker dude is actually a nice human and not scary at all.

"I'd like that." Flinching, twenty minutes passed before the gun stopped and Bishop threw off the gloves.

"Oh God, I'm scared."

"It's done." He stood from the chair, looked down at his work, and then a dark smirk crept onto his mouth.

Biker's lips pinched together, holding in his laughter and I swung my legs off the bed, walking to the full-length mirror that was on the other side of the room.

"Bishop!" I squeaked. His laugh reverberated in the background. Just below my bra line was the letters **B V H**. Deep breaths. In and out. I twisted my torso, actually liking the placement, and it's not like he splashed **B I S H O P** over me in big letters. It was subtle, yet faintly possessive. He came up behind me and my eyes flew to his in the mirror. His strong, tanned muscles against my tiny frame.

His laughing died out when he saw my face. "You like it."

"I sort of love it."

He seemed to sober a little, his eyes looking less frantic.

I clapped my hands together. "My turn!"

He froze. "Oh no, nope, fuck off."

Biker was laughing in the background, and I turned to take the chair Bishop was sitting on. "Behind Blue Eyes" by Limp Bizkit started playing in the close distance, and I nudged my head, a cheesy smile spread on my face. I already knew what I was going to do and I couldn't wait to see it in person instead of the intricate design being splashed inside my head. Slowly, Bishop started walking to the table, and I leaned into Biker. "He's had a lot to drink so we might need extra wipes."

Biker dude's eyes shot up in shock that I had known that, and then he reached over, grabbing the wipes and handing them to me.

"Guess you're about to see my work," I teased, giddy that I was about to leave my mark on Bishop.

Bishop laid back and his eyes came to mine. "Go on then, baby, give me your worst." Yeah, he was probably hoping I'd do something reckless, but Bishop's body was a perfectly carved canvas, and I respected art too much to scribble nonsense on him in the name of revenge. Dipping into the ink, I fired up the gun and stretched the skin on the side of his neck. The gun vibrated in my hand, it definitely looked easier than what it was. I totally underestimated artists. Pencils don't shake. But as soon as the needle struck his neck, it flowed smoothly. My vision became zoned onto the task at hand, and an hour later, I was done.

I sat back, cracking my neck. "Done."

"Fuck," Bishop smirked at me.

Biker came in from making himself a coffee and paused when he saw the new ink. "Holy shit."

"I'm not even surprised, you know I'll get you back for this, right?" Bishop grunted, getting to his feet and looking a lot more sober than he was a couple hours ago. The time must be pushing close to midnight by now and my weeping muscles would agree with me.

Bishop went to the mirror and I watched as his face changed when he took in what I had done. I came up behind him and scanned the crisp new piece. It was a smudged Swan, shaded in a way that made her look silver. She had a crown pressed slightly on top of her head, and shards of broken pieces spraying out everywhere, with a bullet embedded into the metal. It looked peaceful, yet compelling. I was totally taking a photo of this.

"That's fucking amazing." His eyes came to mine in the mirror.

I smiled. "Thanks."

"Hey! Just saying," Biker called out from behind, breaking our contact. "If you ever need a job, I'm here."

"Thanks," I grinned smugly, but I probably wouldn't take him up on it.

"Or, if you both just wanna come use my shit, I'm cool with that too."

My grin turned evil on Bishop, and he chuckled. "Bro, don't give her any ideas."

We left not long after that, with Bishop handing him a decent stack of cash. I waited outside for him, after learning that biker dude's name was Malcolm. My phone started ringing in my pocket, so I reached for it, swiping it unlocked.

"You okay?" Tatum called through the phone.

"Yep! We're good! Hopefully I can drag his ass home now."

She chuckled. "Dude, he looked so pissed. Nate is taking me home."

"He's there?" I straightened. "Put him on."

There was muffled silence and then Nate's voice came through. "Hey, Kitty." He sounded tired, defeated.

"Hey! Are you okay? What's going on?"

Silence.

"Nate?"

"Yeah, not much, everything is all good. Do you need a ride or anything, since I'm apparently an Uber service." I could just picture him glaring at Tatum. Poor Tatum. I knew how strong her feelings were for Nate, but unfortunately, his feelings were rooted elsewhere.

"I'm good."

"You sure?" His tone was suspicious.

"Yeah, I'll be home later. Maybe."

"Alright then. Holla if you need me." Then he hung up. Actually hung up on me.

"Rude," I muttered, shoving it into my pocket just as Bishop came walking out the door, pulling his shirt over his head. Thank God.

"Home?" I asked, hoping he'd say yes.

"Yeah," he grunted, suddenly looking tired. He pulled out his phone and sent a text, then looked back to me. "They'll be here in five."

"Okay," I added, my eyes staying on his. I needed to say something. There was so much tension between us, intangible and undiluted tension that I knew the minute we were alone back at his house, hell was going to erupt. He shook his head in disbelief and yanked his eyes away from me, gazing out in front of him.

I went to open my mouth to say something else when the limo pulled up beside us and the back door swung open. Bishop's smile returned and he slid into the back. I stopped for a second, thinking what the actual fuck I was doing.

"Get in the fucking car, Kitty!"

Guess I was getting in the car.

CHAPTER 9

I squeezed into the limo, because now all the Kings, plus the slut was in the back. Slut being right beside Bishop and me on the other side. Remembering it was close to midnight, I yawned. My body was aching and my eyes were heavy.

"Bishop, can you take me home?" I needed sleep, stat.

"Gladly," Khales snickered, her hand going to Bishop's thigh. I turned rigid, then my eyes went to Jase.

"What were you two lovebirds doing? You're both still alive, which is a good thing…" Jase chuckled.

"Getting tattoos," I admitted as if it was no big deal. Their eyes scanned me up and down, and then went to Bishop, finally seeing the swan on his neck. That became the topic of conversation and I took this time to gaze out the window, wallowing in the empty feeling that had settled in my gut. I hated feeling like this, I hated feeling like I didn't matter to him. I still didn't have any answers, and like usual, everything was moving at Bishop's pace—not mine.

"Mal is a fucking dope artist," Cash nodded, gesturing to the swan.

"Thanks," I muttered, my eyes closing. "I don't think I'm too bad either, but last I checked, I owned a vag."

"Wait, you did that?" Jase exclaimed, Hunter was still silent beside him. Probably still glaring at me.

"Yes." I opened my eyes onto Bishop. "But that was after he stamped his initials over my ribs."

They all started laughing, all except Khales. He still hadn't moved her hand from his thigh. His eyes searched mine briefly and then his arm went behind my neck as he pulled my face into his, his lips now pressed against my ear. "I should make you pay, Kitty. Fucking badly, and I will, because you don't get away with that shit easy, but for now…" His lips dropped to my neck and my eyes closed again as his tongue slipped over the most sensitive parts of my throat. "I'll play with you a bit." Then he sat up straighter, moved his thigh out of Khales' grip and called out to the driver. "To mine, man!"

We pulled into Bishop's driveway, and when the car came to a stop he got out with Khales, but I stayed in my seat. I needed sleep and food asap.

"Kitty…" he growled.

"I'm tired! Can we do this cat-mouse thing tomorrow? I don't feel like fighting."

"Get out. Now."

I grumbled. "Bye, guys," then stopped, just as I got out of the car and leaned back in to look directly at Hunter. "You and I are going to have words!" Then I shut the door and left Bishop behind, heading straight for the side gate. I spun around and looked directly at Khales, fuck my aching feet and drowsy eyes. "You can fuck off."

"What?" She looked at Bishop, who was still looking at me.

"She's right. Leave."

"But—"

Bishop turned his eyes to her. "Leave. This is between her and I."

I grinned, an eyebrow quirked and ran my eyes over her body. "You won't wanna get blood on that pretty little outfit."

Bishop snorted and shook his head, then I turned back around and sauntered to the pool house, opening the door and slamming it behind me when I noticed he wasn't following me straight away. What the fuck was his deal with her. There had to be something else other than the fact that they were friends or whatever when they were young. She had to be of value to Bishop, or she wouldn't be alive right now—that much I'm certain of. I rummaged through the kitchen pantry and pulled out a bag of potato chips, popping them open and then hopping onto the little kitchen island. I had mad food munchies going on right now.

"Bishop! I'm heading back to LA, can you please—" the voice cut off when it hit the kitchen, probably seeing me on the counter.

"Sorry," I sucked the salt off my fingers. "Not Bishop." I swung my eyes to where it came from, to see who it was when I paused. The woman was beautiful. She had razor sharp short hair that hung to her angular jawline, dark honey eyes, and a sun-kissed tan that actually looked natural. *Oh holy shit.* This was Scarlet Blanc, as in Bishop's mom, as in A-lister star of all time. And I was sitting here, still slightly drunk, chomping down on potato chips and sucking salt off my fingers.

A smile curled her lips. "Well, considering my son doesn't bring girls home, I'm gathering you're Madison?"

I beamed embarrassingly, but my damn mouth. "Well, there is one other exception," I finished with an eye roll. "I'm sorry, I'm still a little drunk and it's been a long night, which is far from over, and I'm rambling. Yes, I'm Madison, so nice to meet you. I would give you my hand to shake, but it's covered with salt and saliva, so I guess…" she hated me. I could tell.

She erupted in laughter, displaying her straight teeth. "It's alright. I don't need to. I've been wanting to meet you for some time."

"Really?" I squeaked, slightly scared about why she would be wanting to meet me for 'some time.'

She nodded. "Yes, of course. The girl who pushed my son into a frenzy, my very unattainable son and stable son, may I add…" The words seemed harsh, but the tone in which she said them was harmless. I heard the door open and then close.

Bishop strolled in and paused, taking in the scene. His mom winked at me and then eyeballed Bishop. "Bring her to Thanksgiving. I'm sure the family would love to meet her." She paused at the threshold where the kitchen meets the living room. "Oh, and that's no girl. I believe the correct term for her is... slut?" Then she left. I was speechless, but uncontrollable laughter escaped.

Bishop snatched the potato chips out of my hand.

"Hey!" I scolded him, but he dived in, grabbing out a handful.

I flopped forward, my shoulders hunching from fatigue. "I'm so hungry, and your mom is awesome."

His eyes remained on me, shoving potato chips into his mouth. May as well get this war over with, Mr. & Mrs. Smith style.

I pulled my bottom lip into my mouth and dropped the smile. "Bishop, I'm sorry, okay, I messed up majorly and I know that."

"How far did you get?" He went to the fridge and pulled out a bottled water and then back to where he was standing.

"Um, not *that* far. Kissing, touching." His jaw ticked. *Abort, abort.* "Ah, it lasted like three minutes before Jase walked in."

"And if he hadn't?"

Okay, there was his issue. "I wouldn't have let it get that far, Bishop."

"And I'm supposed to trust you?" He set the water beside my thigh, the cool moisture melting against my warm skin. I grabbed it, suddenly parched.

"I guess you have every reason not to," I explained, my head starting to thud from the lack of sleep. "But I'm new to all this, Bishop. I've just found out all this new shit about my life, I made a fucking mistake, okay?"

His eyes searched mine. "Yeah, you keep saying that."

"What the fuck am I supposed to do!" I didn't even feel the tears leaking out of my eyes. "I find out that my mom wasn't really my mom and oh yeah, the guy I loved *fucked* her, and then he had been hiding his first love—whatever the fuck that slut is to you—all these years and didn't actually *kill* her like he was supposed to!" I sagged, my eyes feeling heavy. I jumped off the kitchen counter. "I'm going to bed." I went to brush past, but his hand caught mine and he tugged me into him.

His fingers hooked around my chin and he tilted my head up to look at him, his eyes searching mine. "You love me?"

My eyes started darting around the room. *I said that?* Shit. I did.

Defeated, I shrugged. "Yes, Bishop, thought that much was obvious. I'm tired."

He pulled me under his arm and I followed his lead up the stairs to his bedroom. Everything was throbbing so bad that as soon as I belly flopped onto his puffy blankets, my eyes closed and sleep took hold.

CHAPTER 10

A buzzing sound alerted me from somewhere in the distance, but my eyes refused to open. There was no way I was waking up yet. It was still dark, or maybe my eyes were still closed. Deep vibrating motion started shaking over my ass and I exhaled, groaning while reaching for the annoying device.

"You better be dead."

"Madison," Daemon? I shot up instantly. "Are you okay?"

Silence.

"Daemon!" I called into the phone.

"Yes, yes, I'm fine. I need a—I need to go. Are you with Bishop?"

I switched the phone to my other ear and shoved Bishop awake. I'd been around my twin brother enough to decipher what he's usually trying to say.

Bishop's eyes opened and he gazed at me. Not fair. At all. He looked far too beautiful to be hungover. His light brown hair hit the early morning sun front on, as if it was burning from the heat and turning to the soft ash that settled through his strands. His soft lips were plump and smooth, and his skin glistened with not one single flaw. He licked his lips and his dimples sunk into each cheek.

"Mmm, what?" His arm wrapped around my stomach as his eyes slowly drifted closed again.

"It's Daemon, he needs a ride somewhere and asked if I was with you."

Bishops eyes opened again and he snatched the phone from me, instantly speaking in Latin. My lady parts weren't going to survive him. It would be even hotter if I knew what they were all talking about though.

He hung up the phone and slid out of bed, going straight into the bathroom. Tossing the covers off my body, I started stripping and slipped into the shower. Steam eloped me everywhere and I sighed, closing my eyes as the hot water slipped all over my flesh, washing last night's shenanigans off me. I stilled when the palm of his hand opened on my belly and he pressed down, his lips coming to the back of my neck.

I shivered, a cool sweat breaking out over my skin, but cranked my neck, giving him more access. His hand traveled down lower until he was cupping my sex, his thumb pressing against my clit.

I bit down on my lip to try to contain my groan and the fireworks that were erupting inside my belly. Only Bishop could do this, only he had the power to completely disarm me while putting me on high alert all at the same time. He licked me across the back of my neck as his fingers continued to play with my clit. One finger slipped inside and circled, hitting something deep that had my toes curling and my back arching. His other hand traveled up my stomach, over my breast as he pinched roughly, biting the back of my neck at the same time. Both sensations unleashed waves of toxic euphoria flushing through my veins. I could feel I was on the edge of combustion, so I went to turn to face him, but his hand flew straight to my throat and his lips came to the back of my ear.

"No, Kitty. You won't move unless instructed to and you won't fucking speak unless I ask you to." Bishop had always been dominant in bed, but something about his rough tone had me thinking this had to do with a lot of other reasons; not just his overbearing alpha male, domineering attitude. He clenched my throat. "Do we understand each other?"

I nodded, but my eyes were still closed and I continued grinding myself into his fingers. "Yes." Then he let go, pushing me out of the way. All the tightened pleasure I was feeling, snatched from me instantly. It was as though his touch was a distant memory, and like a fool, I instantly missed it.

"Good. Get changed, we're taking Daemon to the airport."

"Err..." I went to answer, but he was already getting out of the shower. I grabbed the soap and scrubbed up super fast, and angrily, considering he had worked me up that much only to leave me hanging. I had a feeling this had a lot to do with my *punishment*. And If I knew Bishop, which I did, this had only just begun and it was only going to get worse, but the joke will also be on him because he's not getting any sex either.

Unless he does...

I hit the faucet off and grabbed a towel, wrapping it around myself. Walking out to the bedroom, I headed straight into his closet and rummaged through what clothes I still had here—or Tatum's clothes. Pulling out some cut-offs and a loose off-white shirt, I threw it on and slipped on my Vans before letting my hair back down my back.

I hit the bottom of the stairs and stilled when I saw Khales was on the sofa eating granola.

"Seriously," I muttered, rolling my eyes. Stomping into the kitchen, having about enough of her presence, I stopped when I saw Bishop. "Why is she still here?"

He barged past me, walking to the front door. I followed, flipping the slut off on my way. Bishop let me through the door. "She stayed in the house."

Wait, what?

"Why?"

Bishop's jaw ticked as we rounded his Maserati. "Because she doesn't have anywhere else to go, and because of my fucking dad." Pulling open the passenger door, I slid in and clipped my belt on. Great, so Hector was keeping her around for some reason.

"I need food."

He fired the car up and pulled out. "After we drop Daemon off at the airport."

"Airport?" I asked, an eyebrow perched. "Why is my brother going to an airport?"

"Why do you still ask so many questions?" He retorted.

"Why do you still keep secrets?" I snapped back.

He grinned, seemingly pleased with my wit, then he sobered. "There's something I'm going to tell you, but it cannot be known that you know about this place yet." He dropped it into third, looking at me and then looking back to the road. "Am I clear?"

"I get it," I deadpanned. I was used to secrets now, and regardless of the poor decisions I had made where Bishop and I were concerned, I had never spilled one of the many golden secrets I knew from this world.

"Daemon is from an island called Perdita, it's Latin for—"

"—lost," I interrupted, remembering that word from one of the many translation games I played with my phone.

His head dipped, as he turned down my street. For once, I was annoyed about how close we lived to one another. Obviously, Bishop was in the sharing mood, and that was something so rare, so unheard of, that I wanted to take it for complete granted.

He stopped at the entry to our high wired gates, waiting for them to open.

"This island is on the outskirts of the Bermuda Triangle, but remains completely off the radar, because of my dad."

"Your dad?" I questioned, and then internally smacked myself. That wasn't important right now. The gates opened and I turned to face him, needing more answers. "Tell me more before Daemon gets in."

"This island is run by The Lost Boys but owned and orchestrated by Katsia. This island, Madison"—his eyes collided with mine as we came to a stop outside the front door— "is where things you can't even comprehend happen. This is the crux of The Elite Kings."

"Wait!" I paused, trying to gather my thoughts. I was so confused but excited by how he was being open with me. "I thought the cave was on your property? The cave in the book?"

"Oh, that cave is." His eyes hardened. "But after the war, they all moved to Perdita which was where our families settled until they took back what was theirs, here, in New York and The Hamptons."

My mouth hung open, still in shock, then the front door opened and Daemon came walking down. He wore worn jeans, a white polo shirt, and a red bowtie. An interesting combination, but it was Daemon. He closed the back door and I turned to face him. "Bishop sort of filled me in, sort of didn't, but, are you sure you want to do this?"

He tilted his head, his eyes going to my mouth and then coming back to my eyes. Fucking language barrier. I pulled out my phone and typed up google translate—untrusty fucker that it was—but it would at least give me something.

Bishop rolled his eyes and floored it out of our driveway, my head slamming into the seat. *"Vos certus vos volo facere?"*

My tummy tightened and my legs clenched together. It was my secret that Bishop speaking Latin was a major turn-on—*goddayum*.

Daemon nodded and shot me a tight smile. Daemon always smiled in a way that—either by twin instinct or not—I knew something was below the surface, threatening to spill over. I just hoped he would let me take some of the load. "I'm sure, *Soror mea.*"

I went to type in that word in google translate, but Bishop did me a solid. "It means my sister." We traveled in silence, and it wasn't long until we were pulling up to the airstrip. Bishop handed the security officer his ID, and then the gates opened and he drove in. Pulling to a stop, I gulped.

"Let me guess," rolling my eyes, I pushed open my door. "The black jet with the gold crown on it is yours."

Bishop slipped on his aviators, getting out of the car with the sun hitting his tan skin.

He flashed me a grin, his dimples sinking into his cheeks. "Dad's, yeah."

I turned around and jumped into Daemon's arms. "I promise I will get you out of this shit, mmkay? But in the meantime, I think it's the best to have you out for a while, but I'll see you soon."

His eyebrows pulled in, obviously confused, but I yanked him in for another hug. "I love you."

He froze, and then his arm hooked around me, tightening around my waist. He kissed my head. *"Te amo."*

My heart soared in my chest, my knees weakening. I knew what "amo" meant in most languages, so I already knew what he had said. He let me go, and I watched as he boarded the plane. Bishop was already waiting in the car for me, so I ducked back in.

"Are you sure this is a good thing?" I clipped my belt back on.

Bishop drove us out of the airstrip. "Yeah, it is. Now that the charges have been dropped, he has the chance to settle with Katsia."

Hold up. "What!" I snapped. "I thought the reason why he was leaving was because of the charges!"

Bishop shook his head, calmly driving us onto the main highway that would lead us back to our neighborhood. "What? No. Of course the charges were dropped." When I don't answer, he glanced at me, and then back to the road, letting out an exasperated breath. "Madison, he's not just a Lost Boy, he's *the* Lost Boy. He's Princeps of the Lost Boys. He has a commitment, and this life is all he knows—you can't take that away from him. I get that this world is new to you, but there's some shit that you're just going to have to understand, while still understanding that you're never going to know *everything*. It just is what it is. You're a Silver Swan, Madison, you're lucky you're alive, let alone allowed to roam free amongst us." I sunk back in my seat, suddenly feeling like a child getting scolded.

"Harsh, but I get it. Which by the way, how *am* I still alive?"

He smirked before chuckling. "How do you think?"

"You?" Excitement jumped inside of me like a naïve little girl.

He rolled his eyes. "You give me way too much credit. But, yes and no. A lot of it you have to thank your dad for, and the rest is me, and, well—"

"—well, what?" I snapped, getting frustrated with his snail pace explanation.

"My dad."

CHAPTER II

After swinging by In & Out, we're getting out of the car back at my house when Madison started with her questions again. As long as she didn't ask why I was keeping her away from her house—I didn't care.

"What did you mean by your dad?" She shoved a few fries into her mouth and I snatched the bag from her before she ate them all.

I took out my burger. "Exactly what it is."

"Oh, ok, Mr. Cryptic."

"It's not the fucking Davinci code, Madison," I scolded her, walking to the side of the house that led to the pool house. "It's just fucking wait and I'll tell you."

I took my burger out of its wrapper and bit into it, then handed the bag back to Madison.

"Fine!" She huffed. "But I want to talk about Tillie."

My chewing paused briefly. I knew it was coming, I just dreaded when she was going to mention it. Just as we came out the side, I saw my dad talking with Justin near the pool. I stopped in my tracks which had Madison slamming into my back.

I pointed to the pool house. "I'll meet you inside." Even though Dad had a lot to do with why Madison and her father were still alive, I wasn't too keen on testing the strength of his patience with her.

Her eyes darted from Dad to me and then back again.

"Now," I growled, pointedly looking to my room.

She rolled her eyes so hard it made me want to smack her, and then stormed off into the pool house. She made me fucking violent. Once the door closed, I made my way to Dad and Justin. "What?" Biting into my burger, I watched them both carefully.

Dad took out a cigar and lit it, inhaling. "I now understand the Khales' bullshit."

"What?" I paid him no attention because Dad liked to beat around the bush a lot. He was powerful—probably one of the most influential and powerful men in this country, but he liked to fuck around before getting to his point. He wasn't only known by the underworld either—nicknamed *Patronus*, which is Latin for Godfather, but he also had his influence over the legal system in everyday life. He was more powerful and lethal than any man walking this fucking planet—more than the goddamn president. Madison underestimates his power, which was why I'd always have to shield her, for the mos

He handed me a photo, and I took it with my free hand. My eyes fell on it and then went back to the both of them, sucking the grease off my finger.

Keeping my poker face in check, I shrugged. "So?"

"So?" my dad exclaimed. Fuck. "The reason you hid Khales was because she was pregnant with your kid?"

Pausing, I looked between the two of them, then once I realized they weren't fucking kidding, I started laughing. Yeah, the image showed Khales pregnant, but— "That was not my fucking kid." My eyes bored into Dad's. "And you *know* it."

His eyes slanted at me, and then he shot Justin a look. "Leave." Justin, who looked confused as fuck, left and went straight into the pool house. He got thrown into the world of Lost Boys when he was born—but he's a soldier. One of their best. Built for war.

Dad rubbed his jaw. "When the fuck did this happen?"

"Well, about six months after you put your dick in her."

"Now's not the time for your smart mouth, son."

"Hey, I ain't judging." I took another bite. "I mean, it's a little sick considering her age and all…"

"She was sixteen, not twelve."

I deadpanned, "My point exactly." I mean, he wasn't an ugly guy. He had salt and pepper hair, scattered through golden strands. He always kept it short on the sides and long on the top, slicking it back. He had a good dose of ink tattooed on his flesh—including his wings on the back of his neck—identical to mine. Only *The King* had those wings, and the only ones who could obtain them was of our bloodline, meaning, either me or my cousin Spyder needed to have a kid one day.

Nope.

He sighed, rubbing his hand over his hair. "Shit. How long had you known?"

I chuckled, my head tilting back. "What? All along. You were chasing young pussy and she was looking for a way to get back at me, only I never gave a fuck. Once she figured out that the game she was playing with you had no effect on me, she was pregnant and it was too late."

"What happened to the baby?" he asked, ignoring my admitting that she only did it to get back at me. Which was true, but I also knew that she had grown feelings for him— and maybe he had too, I wasn't sure, and I sure as fuck wasn't about to get into that pool of bullshit. My mom would kill her, but then again, maybe she knew all along too, which was why she had never really liked Khales. My mom may be a hard ass bitch, but she had a heart under the cold demeanor. Probably something we shared.

"It's dead." I wasn't lying, she had a miscarriage far along in the pregnancy.

He stiffened, his eyes flying to me. "You're sure?"

I didn't flinch. "Positive." Then I bit into my burger again. "Are we done? I got shit to do."

"With Madison?" Her name coming out of his mouth had all sorts of feral venom rising to the surface. I was completely aware with how protective I was of her, so much so that even my dad saying her name had me wanting to sink a blade into his neck, but that was the exact reason why I needed to be careful with how I proceeded with her.

She was the only person walking this earth who had the power to fuck my head up. I didn't like that—at all. I was Bishop fucking Hayes, always in control of my shit. Except her.

"Yeah," I grunted, then my eyes came to his. "She's not a threat."

His lip curled into a smug grin. "I wasn't saying anything, son."

Yeah, sure.

I turned and headed back toward the pool house, pushing open the front door. I paused when I saw Madison and Justin on the sofa, laughing and watching some bullshit on the TV.

Justin caught my glare. "Chill, neph, we're just talking."

Slamming the door, I strolled into the kitchen and yanked open the fridge door, grabbing a drink. "I didn't say anything." I wasn't surprised that Justin had warmed to Madison. It wasn't hard to do, and at first, I thought it was because she was hot, and not in an obvious way. It was in the way that she didn't need to push her beauty onto you. She was just that, beautiful. But she was edgy, sexy, weird and quirky, and she shot guns, and had a smart mouth, and it was confusing as fuck. She sent my mind into a spiral the first time I *saw* her because I wasn't expecting her to look like she did....

CHAPTER 12

I was heading out of the house when my dad's voice stopped me in my tracks. "He won't know, and we will keep it that way." His tone, which was usually smooth and controlled, was now a little shaky toward the end of every syllable. I backtracked a little, hoping to hear more of the conversation when his voice snapped through again. "Bishop?"

Fuck.

I grinned, even though he couldn't see me. "Yeah?"

"Stop snooping and get your ass in here now." Like I usually did, I followed his instructions, pushing through his office doors. He and Rob Rodrigues were near the large window that overlooked the entrance to our house and the long driveway. Dad's office was always a little outdated compared to the rest of our house. It was all mahogany wood, high ceilings and a bookshelf that was rooted to the tarnished flooring, reaching right to the beams in the ceiling.

"Yeah?" I shut the door behind myself and entered, taking the chair beside Rob. Dad leaned back in his red leather chair, a cigar in his mouth. "I need to talk to you about something important. A new girl. Call a meet." Even though I didn't understand why the fuck he was telling me about some new girl, I reached into my back pocket and pulled out my phone, opening a group message to the Kings.

Dad is calling a meeting. My place - now.

I let it rest on my lap, ignoring the vibrating notifications and took my attention back to Dad. "Why does this matter?" I was raised with secrets, and it somehow managed to morph me into who I was today. But all this time, without even knowing it, I was being engineered to take the gavel when my dad passed. There was a knock on the door and Eli, Nate, Brantley, Hunter, Cash, and Chase slowly walked through the doors, searching between Dad and me.

"Come on in, boys." I still wasn't sure what the fuck Dad was playing at, but whatever it was, I'm sure someone was about to die. None of us, though, because it was against the law to do so. Yeah, we had our own laws.

"There's something I hadn't told any of you before, not even Bishop. Well, I had hinted at it once before... but, there's a chance that a Silver Swan has slipped through the system. We know what lineage she has come through, and we know everything there is to know, except what she looks like. Seems there are no photos of this girl. But I wanted to make you boys aware because she is in your generation."

"How do you know?" I asked, leaning back in my chair and running my index finger over

the edge of my upper lip. He was most likely being paranoid—like usual, but I guessed in his life, paranoia came with the job description. Only when he got paranoid, blood was always spilled.

My dad's eyes shot to Rob and then came back to mine. "A valuable source. In the meantime, we are hunting down this error so we can take care of it once and for all, but just so you boys know, this will be in your jurisdiction to take care of."

"What? That's not what we do…" I began to state, obviously a little annoyed that I'd need to add to my kill count. "I'm not a Lost Boy."

Dad leaned forward, his eyes hardening. "You will do as I say, son." Then he leaned back, his cool demeanor coming over his face—yet again. Pretty sure the old man was a psychopath. "Consider it a test."

"Fine." I stood from my chair. "Is that all?" He nodded, and then dismissed us all with a simple flick of his wrist. We were walking out to our respective cars when Nate, being Nate, was the first one to say something.

"Yo, I can't be all up in this drama. My mom has this new fucking man, and apparently his daughter is moving in today. I can't be coming home with blood on my shit. Might freak her out a little."

"—She hot?" Eli interfered, getting into the back of Nate's pick up. Nate flipped him off. "I don't know—dick." Rolling my eyes at their bullshit, I beeped my car unlocked and got in. My phone dinged and I opened a message from Adriana.

Miss me?

I shot her back a reply. **My dick does.** Then I floored it forward, shooting past all the boys as we raced our way to school.

The next day, classes went annoyingly slow, I swore every single year it went slower. We were sitting around in the atrium when Nate started. "Dude, I'm not playing, my new stepsister is fucking hot with a capital H. Think Madison Beer—only she doesn't know how hot she is. But she plays with guns and shit, so I ain't with it. I don't think. But fuck me, that's a fine piece of ass living under my roof. Her mom…" His words drifted off when I noticed a girl walking into the atrium, alone, holding a lunch tray. She was new here, obviously, because not only did I know every single person who attended Riverside Prep, and their social security numbers, but the way her features withdrew and her fingers clamped around the tray nervously was a dead giveaway, too. She had long dark brown hair, fair skin that held a tint of something exotic, long fuck—fucking long legs that I could latch around my waist easily and then, in slow motion, her wandering eyes looked right at me from across the room as though she could feel my gaze on her, like a lion being caught hunting its prey. I didn't break eye contact, I relished in how her eyes stared back at me with a storm so chaotic it could put a category 5 cyclone to bed. I watched as her cheeks flushed, right before she quickly sat at a table with Tatum. Fucking Tatum. That annoying bitch needed to be put in line. I shook my head, seemingly irked that a fucking high school girl could steal my attention so effortlessly. Pulling out my phone, I sent another text to Adriana.

My house at nine.

"Oh! There she is!" Nate pointed to the table where hot girl had just walked to.

Nah, no way.

"That's her, dawg, that's the new stepsister. I wanna play with her for a bit."

"Play with her, how?" Just the mention of playing and her in the same sentence had my dick swelling in my jeans.

Nate looked at me knowingly. "You know how."

"Yeah, no offense, but the last time we all shared, we almost killed the girl, so unless you want to kill your new stepsister, I'd say no."

Nate chuckled. "I don't know, there's something different about her."

I rolled my eyes because gaining Nate's attention wasn't hard to do—keeping it was impossible, but gaining it was easy. I went back to my phone. Recognition slowly frosted over my bones, and my eyes leisurely drew back up as I watched her laugh at something Tatum had said.

That smile.

So familiar, so...

"Fuck."

"What?" Brantley barked, his eyes still on the new girl, but his frown etched so deep into his face that you would think this girl for real insulted his existence.

"She's the Silver Swan."

Brantley didn't jump in shock, but his eyes hauntingly remained on her. Nate sucked in a breath, Eli jumped from his seated position, Hunter, Chase, and Cash both let out a mixture of noises, and then it hit me.

I knew this girl.

My mom knew this girl.

My dad knew this girl.

Why the fuck did I know her?

A French fry hit my face, yanking me out of my memory lapse, which was a fucking good thing, considering what happened next. "Earth to Bishop."

"We're throwing a party. I was going to book the ring at Backyard Bucks, but I have a better idea."

Justin's eyes came to mine, worry etched into them. "Dawg, I just—"

"—You know how it is." Was all I had to say.

"How what is?" Madison asked absently, kicking off her shoes and tucking her legs under her ass. I knew, if I didn't already know, I knew right then and there, that it didn't matter what this girl had done. It didn't matter what she was about to do, and even though my thoughts and feelings were always conflicted where she was concerned, make no mistake, I'd end any motherfucker who dared come near her. With her, it always felt right, and that's cliché as fuck, but she had a habit of doing that. Bringing shit out of me that I didn't know was ever there. I just needed her to remain oblivious for now, and I needed to put a wall where my feelings were until I knew I could trust her. I'd never given my heart to anyone, not only because I struggled to give enough of a fuck to pull it from my chest and hand it out, but because I knew no one wanted a washed up, lifeless, damaged mess of what whatever the fuck was left of it.

"The consequences to fucking with what's mine, that's what."

Madison's body stilled beside me. She looked between Justin and me, and then she opened her mouth. "What? What do you mean?"

Justin chose that time to interfere. "Are you having the party here?"

I shook my head, propping my foot on the coffee table. "Nah, at the condo."

"Mommy dearest doing you a solid, huh?" Justin grinned.

"You have a condo?" Madison yelped. "Oh wait, yes, Nate said something about that."

"Yeah, Mom got one in the city, close to campus."

Her eyes dropped to her hands as she fiddled with her fingers. "You're going to NYU?"

I shrugged. "Possibly. My mom went there, and her dad and so on."

Madison's phone dinged in her pocket. She read something on the screen and then shot off the sofa. "I need to go home." My eyes darted to Justin, who knew exactly why I was holding Madison here. To keep Nate from telling her what was about to happen at this party.

"I'll take you." If Nate bitched out and spilled everything to her, it'll only make his punishment worse.

I jogged up the steps to my house and slammed the door open. "Dad!" I called out, heading straight for his office. He had his phone pressed to his ear, but his eyes flew to the entrance when he saw me appear. "I'll call you back."

My chest rose and fell. "That girl."

"Yes?" He seemed interested.

"She's the girl you showed me all those years ago, isn't she?"

My dad's grin deepened. "You met her? She's at your school?"

I nodded. "Yes."

"Then you know what you have to do."

"You've never seen what she looks like?"

Dad shook his head. "Only when she was around ten. Why? Is she ugly? Not your type?"

"Something like that," I lied. "I'll do what I need to do."

CHAPTER 13

I stopped over at a store on my way home to pick up Bishop's present. It's honestly nothing great, and he probably won't even like it, but it was all I could think of. "Nate!" I hated being back here. Over the past couple of days, I had loved being away. Or I loved being with Bishop, not sure which was more true. Maybe a bit of both.

"Hey, Kitty," Nate called out, coming down the stairs.

I turned to face him. "Hey!" Then I pulled out my phone. "Dad texted me and said he was calling a meeting?"

Nate gave me a strained smile—actually, his whole face was strained. "Yeah. It has to do with your mom coming back and shit."

"Where is she?" I walked into the kitchen, needing a drink. Milk, not alcohol. Finding chocolate flavored, I took it out and then a glass before pouring.

Nate pulled out a bar stool. "She's coming too."

"What!" I snapped. "Nate, I don't want to see her—ever again. As far as I'm concerned, the bitch can stay dead."

"Lovely, thanks for that, Madison. Great to see your father has done such a stellar job at controlling that mouth." I didn't flinch, my eyes remained on Nate as I swallowed the cool, creamy milk.

I put my glass down. "Did someone speak?" I asked Nate, ignoring her. He stifled a laugh, cranking his head over his shoulder, tensing.

"Madison, come on sweetheart." My dad gestured to the sitting room. The layout of our home was more traditional than Bishop's. The sitting room hung off the kitchen which was joined by three big white pillars. Our house sort of reminded me of a modern Greek establishment.

"Are you okay, sweetie?" Elena asked me, her arm snaking around my shoulders. Since I first met her almost a year ago, I instantly warmed to her. She was much like Nate in that aspect. Warm and inviting. Something about their aura just had you craving to be around them.

"I'll be fine once she's gone."

Elena's lips pinched together. "I understand that, Madison, and I'm sorry."

I offered her a small smile, appreciating how well she was taking my dad's ex coming back from the dead. A lot better than I took it, that was for sure. I sat down on the sofa as Nate stretched out beside me, his arm coming to the back of my neck, cradling my body into his more. He was relaxed by the naked eye, but I could tell the stance he had smoothly shifted into he was ready to jump on my mom at any given moment, and I loved him for it even more.

"Can we hurry this along because I had a big night last night."

Nate stiffened slightly, but I ignored it, hurrying my parents to get this bullshit over with.

"Madison, first of all, your father and I never wanted you to hate us. We—"

"—Wait!" I corrected her with a raise of my hand. "Correction, I hate *you*, I don't hate Dad—never will. He did his best, still does his best, and even though he's..." The words frizzled out in my throat, threatening to choke me. I hadn't spoken them out loud since finding out. Before I could stop it, a single tear leaked out, slipping down my cheek. Nate caught it with his finger, and my gaze locked with his. Slowly, he brought his finger to his lips and sucked the tear off, while his arm tightened its grip around me.

I looked back to Dad and Elizabeth. "Not my biological father," I cleared my throat. "He is more of a parent than you will *ever* be."

She flinched, then sat back in her chair. Running the palms of her hands down her hair again, I noticed her eyes darting around the room faster as if she was trying to pull something from thin air. She let out a breath of air. "I get that you're angry about Bishop."

"Don't say his fucking name," I seethed, my eyes narrowing on her.

"What about Bishop?" my dad inquired, looking at her sideways.

I leaned into Nate, a grin on my face. I was smug as fuck—with good reason. She looked at my dad, and then back at me. "It's not important. Listen, there's something you don't know about him—"

I snorted. "Oh, I'm sure there's a *lot* that I don't know about him. I gave up trying to work that shit out months ago."

My dad interrupted again, just as Elena sat beside Nate. Her hands rested on her knees delicately.

Elizabeth looked between my dad and me again. "I was his initiation."

Dad turned rigid.

Elena visibly paused. It never crossed my mind to wonder exactly how much she knew.

I leaned toward her and whispered, "Did you know about all this crazy shit?" I didn't know why, but I just had never thought she did, but then again, her son was a King.

She gave me a somber smile. "Yes, sweetheart." She didn't elaborate, and I could understand why. Time and place and all that, but I did really want to know who Nate's dad was. He never spoke about him, actually, no one spoke about him, and I think that made me more curious, but I respected his privacy, and hers. If they wanted me to know, I'd know.

"Get out." My dad's eyes were focused in the distance, then his head snapped back to her. Elizabeth swallowed. "I need to talk to you about something."

"Well, hurry up before I put a bullet between your eyes for real this time, woman."

"Or me. My aim is a lot better now. Must be from all the anger I've caged in," I deadpanned.

She winced again, before stumbling around with her words. "Listen, what Lucan was going to tell you right before your lot killed him, was that Bishop and Madison were destined to be together."

"That's a bit dramatic, even for you." I rolled my eyes.

Nate growled, "Who told you."

Her eyes went to Nate, and they softened, but I tilted my head to block her view. "Touch him, so much as flutter those fake eyelashes in his direction, and I'll kill you myself."

Nate's thumb started doing circles on my bare arm, sending shivers over my flesh. She diverted her gaze. "I've known since she was born. It was part of the reason why we took her. Johan and Jimima couldn't keep her, but before Hector allowed her to come to us, he made us swear on a blood oath that she and Bishop would unite one day and continue the legacy."

My eyebrows pinched together, then I slowly collected myself again. Well, appeared to collect myself. When she noticed no one was about to interrupt her outburst of honesty, she continued, "So we all took the blood oath. Your father who you trust so purely included."

"And if she didn't end up with Bishop? Hmm? What if she ended up with me? 'Cause I'm telling you now, she was fair game for a bit there, and there have been a couple times—no offense, Pops." He gave my dad an apologetic smile, and it was the first time I had noticed their easy banter. *Had they become friends?* My dad smiled weakly at him before cutting his glare back to Elizabeth.

She shook her head. "No, it wouldn't have worked. He had to be with her in order for her to live a normal life."

"What the hell do you mean a 'normal' life. This is the twenty-first century, not the fucking stone ages. These people have no power to do such things." But even as the words left my mouth, I knew that that wasn't entirely true. They had far more power than what was visible to the naked eye.

Elizabeth let out another breath, and I fought the urge to ask her if she needed a nebulizer. "Madison," she said sadly, and I looked to my dad for reassurance. Nate's grip tightened around my thigh. Reassuringly, or warningly, I wasn't sure which.

My dad's eyes dropped low, and that was when everything started shutting down. First, my eyes zoned to the glass tiled floor, and then my knees buckled. Had I not been sitting, I would have stumbled to the ground. "I'm sorry, Madison, but he was *ordered* to be with you. At first, he didn't care. He swore that he'd kill you himself if you didn't comply. Then something changed, he must have realized you were pretty, or interesting, and he tried to hide you from Hector—they all did. They were under the assumption that Hector only knew what you looked like by a photo of you at age ten, so they thought they could get away with it. Only, he..." She paused, and everything zoned out.

My memories started crashing into me like a bad movie on repeat. I heard Nate's voice faintly in the background, attempting to bring me back to the now, but it was too late, everything she was saying was already making sense in my head.

"You goin' explain or should I?" Nate murmured smugly from the backseat. Bishop gave Nate a death stare into the rearview mirror. "That night you were with me."

"Which night?" I added.

"The race."

"I'm following."

"You remember how I said something vague like, 'he won't recognize you'?"

"Yes..."

"Well, he recognized you." He dropped the gear into second and floored it onto the main highway, away from the city.

"And who is he?"

Bishop looked into the rearview mirror at Nate before bringing his eyes back to the main road. "My dad."

CHAPTER 14

I sucked in a breath and shot from the sofa. Nate's arm snatched out to me, his fingers grabbing mine. "Madison, it's not exactly as she—"

I shook my head, my eyes going to my mom. "I don't even care anymore. Regardless of whatever this bullshit life is." I swiped the tears away from my eyes, my heart aching in my chest. *I was a fucking pity bitch.* "It doesn't matter because I'm used to it." I glanced at my dad. "Why did you bring me back here? You knew the risk."

"I love you Madison." His hands dove into his pockets. "But I have an obligation to this life. I hated it, hated it so bad that I couldn't be here to watch it unfold." He sighed, massaging his head. "I quickly recognized the look in Bishop's eyes. It was obvious his feelings were real, and then I witnessed the way you were with Nate and the rest of the Kings. I knew that something was about to change."

I was speechless. The words I wanted to scream were caged in my mouth, leaving me parched and pleading for air.

My dad stood and pointed to the door. "Get the fuck out of my house, Elizabeth, and don't ever come home." I didn't entirely understand why he was upset with her because he must've played a part in her faking her death, but whatever, I no longer cared.

I marched up to my room, dialed Tatum and sunk into my bed.

"I hate my life."

"What?" she asked groggily. I must've woken her. "I'll be there in a few."

"You don't have to," I choked out, struggling to contain my pain.

"Fuck," she cussed, then the line cut out. Dropping my arm to the side of my bed, I let the tears silently run down my face. My life was so messed up. Just when I thought I had something good going, something else was thrown from the left field. My chest tightened every time I thought of how stuck with me Bishop had been, and how he said his dad was one of the main reasons why I wasn't killed. It all made stupid sense now and I hated it. I wished I was back to not knowing anything. There's a light knock on my door.

"Mads, it's me."

I slid off my bed and opened the door for Tate, then shut, locked, and sunk back to my bed, wiping my tears angrily.

Once the blurs had disappeared, I pointed to the bags in her hands. "Whatcha got there?"

She held up the bags, and it was when I realized she was wearing her cotton pajama pants with little unicorns on them. Fluffy slippers covered her feet, and her blonde hair was piled on top of her head in a messy bun. I smiled, grateful, once again, for my best friend. She jumped onto my bed, took my phone from me and turned it off, and then snuggled into the covers.

"This is everything we need for at least a couple days. Thank fuck for summer break, or else imagine having to go to school. It's Monday tomorrow, by the way." She gestured at my clothes. "In case you've forgotten the day just like you obviously have the shower."

"Tate!" I scolded her through a laugh.

She shrugged. "What?"

I dug into the bag and took out a bag of potato chips. "I found out some shit tonight." She didn't say a word, just sat with a tub of ice cream resting on her thighs as I yapped away. At the end of my rant, she handed me the ice cream and went back to digging into the bag.

"Thoughts?" I was worried. Usually, Tatum had a lot to say. Had I broken my best friend? That was it, she finally had had enough of my crazy life. She pulled out a spliff, and put it into her mouth, lighting it up.

"Tate!" I looked at the door. Usually, I would care, but we were on the other side of the house, and anyway, my dad probably wouldn't care. I mean, you can't not bat your eyelashes at murder but scold me for smoking weed.

I took it from her and inhaled. I hadn't smoked since we were out in the forest.

Tate lay back on the bed. "And you and Bishop?"

I shrugged, handing it back to her. "I don't know. I got him a present for his birthday, though."

"Lemme see it! When's his party?" she asked, sucking on the smoke.

"Tonight."

"Then we go and fuck shit up."

I nodded. "We go and fuck shit up."

I stretched my arms wide, feeling a little better than last night.

Tatum's ass pressed into me. "Quit it, you know how I get morning horny."

I chuckled, swinging my legs off the bed. "I don't forget. What do you feel like doing today?"

"Mmmm." She pressed her index finger to her cheek. "Avoiding the guys is one, but other than that, whatever you want to do."

Her mentioning the guys had me slowly drifting back to reality. I was... hell, I wasn't entirely sure how I felt. I guessed I felt betrayed. None of them thought to mention this to me earlier, which is what hurt. If it never played a big part in Bishop being with me all those times, and us being, well, us, then why didn't he tell me? I slipped into the closet and pulled down my bikini.

"I really want to go shooting. Maybe go back to the place where I met Katsia."

"Nope," Tate muttered, getting out of bed. "That's way too heavy for today. We can do that next week. Today?" She pulled out a little red bikini from her bag. "We lounge by the pool and day drink."

"We can't get day drunk, Tate, we have a party to crash tonight."

"Shit." She massaged her temples as though she had just remembered. "Okay fine.

She stripped naked and slipped on the tiny little... bikini? Looked more like a hoochie outfit for a Mardi Gras. "We start drinking at a more appropriate time, and we go slow, start with cider, and *then* we hit it hard before we roll up."

I laughed, shaking my head. "I like this plan." Then I took out my white bikini. We were heading downstairs just as Nate was coming out of his room.

"Hey!" he snapped, but I rolled my eyes, ignoring him. "Madison!" he repeated. "You can't ignore me forever." I flipped him off over my shoulder, going into the kitchen.

"We can skip food," Tatum says, pulling her oversized glasses down over her eyes.

"Speak for yourself," I muttered, reaching for the bowls and pouring some of Jimmy's famous homemade granola in. Best. Ever. I headed out the kitchen doors, the sun kissing my skin instantly.

I inhaled the fresh morning air. "Today is going to be great."

"It better," Tate whisked. "I need to get laid, stat!"

I chuckled, wiping my mouth and taking a seat on one of the lounge chairs. "What's happening with you and Nate?" I was sort of rooting for them in the beginning, but I had witnessed how Nate was with Tillie to how he was with Tatum. There was no denying he was only using Tate, but Tate was starting to catch feelings. With Tillie disappearing for the past months, Tate and Nate managed to come to an agreement, but nothing else has happened between them after their little "talk." Nate probably got cold feet.

"Don't make me laugh. I'm not working out my abs today."

I snorted, my head tilting back. "We will get you laid tonight. Have you seen Bishop's cousin, Justin? He's not bad at all."

"We have different types." She gestured to me with her free hand as her other rubbed oil over her leg.

I shook my head. "I don't know, I think you'll like him." I placed my empty bowl on the ground and hit play on the sound dock. "Everybody's fool" by Evanescence starts playing, and I lay on my back, letting the sun seep into my pores.

***

"Mads!" Someone was shoving me in the arm, my eyes slowly peeled opening to the bright sun. I raised my head up to see Tatum passing me a J. "It's two P.M, you slept most of the day away. I thought about waking you but thought better of it. What'd you do this weekend to warrant such lengthy sleepy time?" She stood up and dived into the pool.

"Jesus, I don't know, get absolutely wrecked by trying to save Bishop, and then ended up getting this." I pointed to the tattoo that was over my ribs.

Tatum swiped the water off her face and started laughing. "Girl, you are owned."

I shrugged. "His is bigger, and he has two."

"He has two?" She quirked her eyebrow, pushing herself up and out of the pool.

I nodded and then chuckled. I thought I was wide awake before, but that has nothing on how I'm feeling right now. Tatum dipped behind the little Bahama hut bar we had tucked away at the side of the pool and grabbed out some bottles. "Your dad and Elena are gone, Nate is gone, it's just us and these poor, innocent bottles of wine."

I bit my lip. "Hand it over."

She gasped. "No way, we're at least going to be classy about this."

"When are we *ever* classy?"

She paused, pondered over it for a few beats, and then nodded. "Good point, but, I do want to try my hand at some of these cocktails I saw on Pinterest." Oh no, Tate and her Pinterest addiction.

"Fine." I walked to the edge of the pool and dove into the cool water, pushing off the hard floor and coming out the surface. "Just make sure mine is strong!" She started dancing, and shaking, and then dancing more, and changing songs. Tatum moved at speeds that made my head spin. I dried off, straightening my tits in my bikini and headed back to her.

Sinking the first cocktail she had made, I moaned at the taste of silk sliding down my throat. "Damn, that was so delicious. What was it?"

"It was a milky way, be careful, that shit has enough liquor in it to put you on your ass." She made another one, and then we went back to the lounge chairs, cranking the music higher.

"You know" —she waggled her eyebrows at me— "I think you should talk with him, maybe a little later."

I shrugged. "I will, just not right now. Right now, I want to be a little angry at them."

She lifted her glass. "I'll drink to that." Tate pulled out her phone, and she shuffled closer to me for a selfie. I pulled my tongue out and crossed my eyes, pulling a silly face as she pouted her lips. She uploaded with a grin on her face.

"What was your caption?"

Tate was famous for her captions. They were either extremely dry or over the top. There was no in between, but either way, they always managed to make people laugh. I wasn't that active on Facebook or any social media. I had only just started using Snapchat, and even then, I almost always forgot to upload photos and videos.

"Beauty and the Beast have all the treats, with a little cocktail emoji."

I cracked up, clutching my tummy. "You're a dork."

She shrugged. "Maybs, but you love me anyway."

She was right, I did.

Around four cocktails later, we both began climbing up the stairs. We weren't wasted, but you could definitely notice that we were under the influence. I think. No, I felt fabulous. Laughing about something Tatum had said, we stumbled into my bedroom. "I need something to wear. Something I know will drive Bishop crazy."

"Girl, do you like seeing him mad? The man is lethal, I wouldn't be poking the tiger."

"Actually, I sort of do, but I am mad at him. I need... answers. I just need answers."

She sighed. "I don't blame you." Pulling out some clothes she brought with her. After getting frustrated with my average closet, I turned in a huff, my eyes falling on the see-through mesh long sleeve dress she was holding.

"What is that?" I pointed to it. It was probably one of the most scandalous things I had ever seen, which meant I had found my outfit.

She threw it at me. "You're to wear like, a tank or something underneath," she mumbled, but I was diving into my closet, pulling out a little black lace bra. It had straps that lined over my breast skin and was all held together by lace and scandal. I wiggled on the spot with glee. Oh, this was perfect. Then I paused. What the actual fuck was I going to wear as pants. I couldn't go in underwear, I didn't want to get killed, so I took out tight little leather boy shorts from my top drawer.

"Are these yours?" I dangled them in front of her face.

"There they are!" She went to launch for them, but I snatched them into my chest.

"I'm wearing them tonight."

"Fine," she grumbled, taking out a white dress. "I'll wear this."

"Good idea," I nodded, heading to the bathroom. "You look good in white." I'm setting everything on the counter when Nate's side opens. Ignoring him because I'm used to doing so, I unclasped my bikini while holding my breasts from his view.

"What?" I snapped.

"Are you coming to the party?"

"Yes," I hissed, reaching for the faucet and turning it on.

"You can both come with me, and have you heard from Bishop?"

I shook my head. "No. I haven't checked my phone, though."

Nate glared at me, and I quickly slipped under the pelting hot water. "Anything else?" I called out, annoyed at his presence.

The door slamming was all I got as a reply.

Daemon

One two three four five six…six…six…

"Shush!" I roared to the internal battles inside of my head. Creeping down the dark and gloomy corridors, I pressed the palm of my hand against the damp concrete wall, my head tilting at the sounds.

Deep breathing was coming from one of the rooms. One of the many rooms in this quarter. The island was separated by quarters, each functioned by your importance to the Elites and your lineage. This was the royal quarter, also known as the Regiis quarter. Then there was the Secundus quarter, Tertium quarter, and finally, the Nihil quarter. Each faction was eloquently designed for their cause. The royal quarter was exactly as it was. I inched farther, closer to the white door where the sounds were coming out from and pressed my ear to the frosted wood.

Deep breathing was coming again, and then a faint scream.

"That's it, keep going. You can do it. Push." The door swung open and Jaysena, one of the nurses on the island was staring back at me.

"Sir." She bowed. "Are you ok?" Her head remained dipped, her eyes searching the floor. So timid. So docile. So "Kill her, I'm sick of seeing her face."

'Shut up,' I shouted in my head, my strength at keeping the voices under control getting better.

"Fine. What is happening?" She got what I was trying to say, and gestured wide, allowing me to see inside the room.

"A Swan, my lord."

I tilted my head, and a girl with pink hair that hung down to the dip in her waist was crouched, hugging a baby wrapped in a blanket. Her eyes came to mine, and she whispered, "Please, don't say anything yet. I'm best friends with your sister, my name is Tillie."

CHAPTER 15

"I'm done." I smoothed my hair down. I decided on flat and straight for tonight, sharp enough to slice some Kings. Obviously, the liquor was hitting me at full force, but I swiped my phone off the drawers and tucked it into my bra. The little see-through outfit I was wearing was to die for, but I totally wouldn't wear this if I were sober.

"I'm ready too," Tate slurred, standing on her wobbly legs.

"Impressions, we were going to make some impressions." I was chanting to myself as my door swung open and Nate's eyes fell on mine.

"What the..." he paused, his mouth hanging open as he slowly took in my outfit. His eyes flew from my face to my breasts, to my feet, and then back again. "You can't rock up like that, sis."

I shoved past him. "I can do what I please." We all headed out of the house and I got into the front of his Audi.

He fired it up, shaking his head. "You're in fucking trouble, girl." I didn't care. At that very moment, I was drunk and pleased with myself. I hadn't heard from Bishop—at all, since I left his house yesterday, so I was feeling... irrational. But I still had his gift in my pocket. We turned the music loud and started dancing. I hit play on "Sex with Me" by Rihanna and Tatum started singing the lyrics in the back like a twit, accentuating every word. Nate picked up what she was doing and laughed. We all fell into a breezy trip and it wasn't long until Tate pulled out her phone.

"Yo! Smile."

I turned my head over my shoulder with a smirk, my hair tricking over my other shoulder, throwing up deuces, and Nate flipped the camera off, his eyes staying on the road.

"What was the caption?" I asked, just as we pulled hit the city.

"When incest looks hot."

"Tate!" I snapped, and Nate broke out in tears, his laughter not looking to subside.

"Jase 'liked' it."

"Of course he did," I muttered just as we pulled underneath an underground parking lot.

"And of course Bishop owns a five-star penthouse, I mean, totally logical."

Nate chuckled, shifting the car into park. "Yeah, understatement of the century, wait until you see this set up."

We rode the way up the elevator, Nate punching in a code that took us straight to Bishop's penthouse. The doors spread out and opened onto a sea of young people and rock music blaring through all the bodies. I couldn't even admire the house as much as I would have liked because there were people everywhere, but from what I could see, it was set up like a three-story loft. I walked to the edge of the little balcony that the elevator opened out on and peeked at the place.

Nate gestured to the back of himself. "Basketball court, too." He shot us a wink before disappearing. He was acting weird lately, weirder than usual.

After taking the two steps down onto the main lobby, I snatched a drink from a waiter passing by and took a long swig. I felt people's eyes on me, but I ignored them all, focused on my search for Bishop. The song moved to "It's a Vibe" from Ty Dollar sign and I couldn't fight the eye roll. Obviously, Nate had found the sound system.

I started slightly pushing through the bodies and taking the two steps down from the lobby and kitchen area, down to the open sitting room when my eyes fell on Bishop who was stretched out on the sofa. His bare chest rippled under every movement, his tattoos flexing along with them. He had a red bandana tied to the front of his head, jeans that looked to have been out in the sun for a beat too long, and since he hadn't actually texted me since a couple days ago, I was trying hard not to make it obvious how much I was checking him out. And—yep, he was drinking again. His eyes collided with mine and I felt as though the air was sucked out from my lungs. Machine Gun Kelly started rapping about being a "bad mother fucker," just as the rim of his bottle touched his lip. His eyes stayed on mine, as the corner of his mouth slowly kicked up in a grin. I was hoping for a reaction. A caveman Bishop—if you will, but all I got was a brush off. Jesus. Was he still holding a grudge about Nate, Brantley, and I? I guessed it would be valid since he had let me off on it lightly, but I knew Bishop. He was calculated. He did everything for a reason and he performed it with expertise. Or maybe I had broken him a little, but even as I thought those words, I knew that that wasn't possible. You just couldn't break someone like Bishop. He was too... unbreakable.

So I did what any sane girl my age would do while under the influence. I yanked my eyes from his and went in search of my partner in crime. Bypassing the sea of people, I found myself again, annoyed that I couldn't truly appreciate Bishop's new condo, with the influx of women and—few men. Huh. There were more women than there were men. Surprise, surprise. Yet again, I didn't know what game he was playing at, and before I could allow my brain to begin sifting through the possibilities, my toes started to tingle and my legs wobbled like jelly. Maybe I shouldn't have started drinking so fucking early. Searching for a room—any room—away from all the people, I shoved through a pair of black doors and came into what I was guessing was the master bedroom. There was a bed that looked as though it was floating in the center, a large television hanging on the wall opposite, and directly in front of me was a wall of glass overlooking the city. The sheets and blankets were all silken black and red, and even the little seat that was in the corner was more like a throne in blood red leather. There wasn't much else to the room—the penthouse itself felt more like an art studio. It wasn't warm and inviting, and on that thought, I started backing up, ready to get the fuck out of here while deeply regretting even attending. Tate and her stupid decisions. Slowly stepping backward, I collided with a hard wall of muscle and a small squeal leaped out from my mouth. Jumping around to see who I backed into, Hunter's piercingly dark eyes were glaring down at me.

I calmed my erratic heart down. "Hey." My newfound brother and I weren't really on great terms, so I was still unsure of how I should step around him.

"Figure we may as well get this talk over with." He tilted a large bottle of bourbon up to me, and then brushed past, heading straight toward the window. For a brief second, I considered running, but I'd been wanting to see Hunter for a while now. Since he found out about us being biological siblings, he had gone more than cold on me, so, I followed him to the window, looking him up and down. He looked good, like they all did. Wearing jeans and a tight fitting black shirt, you could almost make out the lines of muscle in his arms.

"I'm sorry." Because I was obviously shit at this—being an only child all my life and all, 'I'm sorry' was the first thing that came out of my mouth.

He snorted and then raised the bottle to his mouth. "What exactly are you sorry for, Madison?" He didn't look at me, he merely kept his eyes forward, watching as the busy streets of the Upper East Side remained awake.

"I don't know." I followed his line of sight. The tension between us was loud. "Existing?" A chuckle slipped out before I could stop it and his eyes slammed into mine.

"This is funny to you?" he accused, his eyes narrowing on me. They dropped to my lips and then to my eyes. "I wanted to fuck you, and then I find out that the girl I used to pull off on is my *sister*..." he smirked. "I guess that makes me a little sicker than Brantley, and that's saying something." His eyes went back to the window.

"You're not sick, Hunter," I muttered, swallowing past the emotion that was threatening to surface in my throat. "And you weren't the only one who had thoughts..."

His movements stilled. I took this moment to reach over and snatch the drink from him, wrapping my lips around the rim and tilting back, letting the warm liquid slide down my throat. "There was this one time," I laughed, suddenly realizing how bad this was about to sound. I swiped the residue from my lips and handed the bottle back to him. I could feel his eyes watching me as he absently took the bottle from me, waiting for my confession. "I had this very *intense* dream that involved all of you. In my head, I had already fucked you, so there, I trump yours."

There was a long pause and I couldn't bring myself to look him in the eye. "And if you tell anyone, I'll kill you."

Suddenly, his laughter cracked through the cold room and my eyes snapped to his, catching him rubbing the tears from his cheeks. "Well, yeah, that makes me feel a little better, but I can assure you, I fucked you in my head too." After that, I felt a sense of calm come between us. A lot easier than what it was a second ago.

"Tell me about Daemon and I'll tell you about your biological parents."

That was unexpected. I hadn't thought much about my biological parents, mainly because I didn't have time to. My life was an information dictionary and I was constantly being fed the unedited version that had to continue to be revised and changed.

"Well," I started. "I don't know much about him because he's new in my life, but what I do know about him I go off instinct. Probably some sick twisted twin thing, but it's hard to explain. I don't *know* him, but I *know* him. It doesn't even make sense, it's like a bond of natural instinct. He doesn't speak much English, but he's fluent in Latin—like all of you, only better at it—no offense—"

He chuckled, throwing his hands up. "Hey, none taken. He's a Princeps Lost Boy. Latin was his first language."

"So weird," I added absently. "Anyway, he's... different. It didn't take me long to figure that out." Hunter stepped backward, falling onto the bed. I turned to face him, my back pressing against the brisk glass. I slid down until I was seated on the floor. "I don't really know what's wrong with him, but Bishop and everyone keep saying he's different."

Hunter searched my features. "I'm not going to lie to you, or hide anything from you because I feel like you're in this shit way too deep to not know, so I'm going to do you a solid and tell you that yeah, Daemon is *different,* I guess you could say." My jaw felt as though it had hit the floor. For once, someone was being straight up with me. Hunter continued, his eyes carefully watching mine as if he was waiting for a reaction. "He has a—I guess you could say—a form of schizophrenia, only, a lot darker."

I faltered. "Schizophrenia?"

Hunter dipped his head. "Only it's worse for him. He has six 'voices,' only they're not voices."

"Okay." I was totally not handling this very well, but I wasn't about to disappoint my new brother by being a little bitch, and besides, I didn't want to make him regret opening up to me. "What are they?"

Hunter gave me a somber look. "Demons."

"Say what now?" I cocked my head, floored by his response. "Demons aren't real."

"To you and I and everyone else who walks this earth, sure, but in Damon's head, they're so very real, Madison. His head is a *very,* very dark place. That's why we couldn't trust him with you, and that's why we know he was the one who shot you."

My eyes closed from the pain those words caused. I had always questioned it deep down. I mean, the evidence was there, but my denial was stronger than any evidence. I couldn't believe that he would hurt me, and in essence, he didn't. The sharp stab to my heart, though, proved that I was still hurt by it.

"I know," I whispered out hoarsely, wiping away the tears that had come out. "I knew it was him. I guess I was just in denial, and I still to this day don't think he would hurt me."

"I believe you're right," Hunter agreed. "About him not *wanting* to hurt you, but Madison, he's not always Daemon."

That hit home for me. Was it going to be possible for me to have a relationship with my twin brother? Or was he just too sick to even know? My heart snapped a little in my chest.

"Anyway, tell me about your parents."

Hunter snorted. "Well, I wish I could tell you that they were amazing parents and would welcome you with open arms, but, Dad is always away for business and my mom is sick."

"Sick?" I asked, my head tilting.

Hunter nodded. "Yeah, she only has a few years to live."

"I'm sorry," I muttered, realizing that me and these guys have so much more in common than any of us would ever care to admit.

He shrugged. "It's life. Jase and I have been doing this shit since we were little. Well, Jase was the one who raised me—mostly. My dad just provided the funds."

"So these Kings, they all grow old and just—stop giving a shit? I see a pattern here."

He chuckled. "Probably. Not sure where the disconnect is, but yeah, I'd say you were mostly right. Except for Hector."

"Hector?" I quirked an eyebrow. "He's a good dad?"

"The best. He may be a scary fucker, but there's nothing he wouldn't do for his son. It's something we could all do with." Once again, I'm wanting to ask about Nate's dad, but that would make me a shitty person if I took Hunter's good deed for granted by using this. Nate would tell me when he was ready. Or until I fought it out of him eventually.

"Which brings me to my next thing," Hunter announced, standing from the bed and reaching for my hand. "There's something you probably want to see right now. But, I'm going to say that you won't like it, but, I'm sorry. Bishop does want you there and as much as I've loved our little bonding chat, he's my loyalty." These damn boys and their loyalty.

CHAPTER 16

I followed him out of the room and down the long hallway. The crowds of people had died down a little to what they were earlier, so it was a lot easier to surf through. Hunter took a hard left turn, pushing open another set of doors, these ones tarnished wood, and when they opened, the smell of rubber mixed with sweat shot up my nostrils. My eyes went straight to the crowd of people who were bunched in the middle, cheering, yelling, and screaming with their hands flying over their head with cups grasped in their hands.

"What's going on?" I asked skeptically, my eyes staying on the crowd.

"This is Bishop's basketball court room, but tonight, it's also a fighting ring."

"Oh no," I muttered, barely above a whisper.

"Oh, yes," Hunter announced, taking my hand.

"Who?" I asked as we made our way to the crowd, who were now spreading out. It was making it a lot easier for us to step through the bodies.

"Brantley and Nate against Bishop."

"What!" I screeched, my feet picking up speed.

"Chill, baby sis, they had to be held accountable for their actions."

"But Nate fights as a sport! And there's two of them." Just as I was babbling off, the crowd parted more, and the scene played out in front of me. Bishop reared his fist back and slammed it right into Nate's, a loud crush vibrating through the air, and then he roundhouse kicked Brantley in the stomach. I swore I heard the crunching of his ribs from here. I wanted to interrupt, I wanted to scream and stop it, but another part of me knew that this wasn't my place. These boys had rules and rituals. Even if I may not understand them, it didn't mean that they didn't exist. And besides, I had a feeling this had everything to do with me.

"They'll kill each other," I whispered to Hunter, but I couldn't take my eyes off the fight, even when Nate's blood sprayed through the air. Right before he tried to attack Bishop with a left hook, it got blocked by a massive hand, and then Bishop laid into him one more time. A loud, yet silent, "oh…" sounded out through the crowd, and I froze, the blood pulsing through my veins turning to frost.

"Nawww," Hunter grinned. "They'll just play around for a bit." Then his eyes came to mine. "Hope you weren't hoping for your stepbrother to be all jiffy with you again." Then he returned his attention back to the died down brawl. "Because he just got a huge

I couldn't watch anymore, so I sunk into the crowd and backed toward the way I came, spinning around and pressing through the doors. The silence that broke through from being in that loud room made my ears bleed. There was no one out here now, I guessed everyone was in that room watching Bishop as if he was a lion in a circus. This was his circus and those were his monkeys, and Bishop Vincent Hayes was most definitely the ringleader. This place was far more extravagant than I would have ever thought. I knew Bishop had money, and his family had money, but this was extreme—even for him. Making a beeline for the elevator, I press the button anxiously and then press it a few more times. If it could not decide to come slow today, that would be great. Where the hell was Tate, too? She just disappeared.

"Leaving so soon?" My finger stopped an inch away from hammering at that little circle button again.

Without turning to face him, I shrugged. "You have enough company here to keep you occupied, Bishop." I realized how sober I was at this point, which was very unfortunate considering the drinks I consumed were for the sole purpose of once again, coming face to face with my high school nemesis-slash-first love. Bishop was my kryptonite, but I was no Lois Lane, and he was no Superman. What he was? Was an addiction I couldn't break. No amount of time spent at a rehab clinic could help me, because I didn't want to help myself. I was addicted to the burn that crusted over my vulnerable heart every time he broke it, because sometimes, the very few times that I have seen another side to Bishop, made all those pieces worth breaking for. Made him worth it. I was a junkie chasing my next high, and just hoping, that this wasn't the time I overdosed on a love so toxic, and so far out of my reach, that I would damn near kill myself just to know how it feels one last time. I wasn't afraid to die, I was afraid I'd never feel the heat from his hand wrapped around my heart, right before he'd shatter it into millions of pieces. I was, in short, a lost cause.

So, even though I heard the doors to the elevator ping open, I turned to finally face him, pinching my lips together when I saw the cut below his right eyebrow and the blood slightly seeping out from his bottom lip. He still had no shirt on, and his tank, I could see, was tucked into his back pockets. He only wore his military boots on his feet, and sweat glistened off each and every tight muscle he had. I didn't think I'd ever get used to seeing Bishop in all his glory. He was just too magnificent for the average eye. Finally, my eyes collided with his, and I was waiting for a cocky comeback. Maybe something funny. But I got nothing. I got a blank stare that gave away nothing. I hadn't received this impassive look since I first met Bishop.

The doors closed, and the longer our eyes remained connected, the more it felt as though all of the oxygen was being sucked out of the room. The walls were closing in, everything in my peripheral fading black, and all that I could see was him. His frighteningly vacant eyes. The kind that holds your interest and has your thighs clenching together, all while sending chills down your spine. His lips. The curve of his upper rim and how it dipped in the middle, while his bottom one seemed plumper. The sharpness of his jaw, that was as though Greek gods had sharpened it with a magical fucking sword of beauty. With that, you had Bishop, who had you second guessing all biblical and scientific history lesson you ever got as a kid, because there was no way someone this perfect was created out of sheer genetics.

I cleared my throat out of my daze when everything came back into real time. Stepping closer toward him, I reached for his cheek, and his eyes dropped to my mouth.

"I'll clean you up before I leave."

He didn't answer, and I searched his features for a clue or any kind of reaction, but again, was met with the same vacant, hazy look. So I hooked my index finger around his, testing the waters to see if he was going to allow it since he hadn't said anything before then. I felt him still, and then his eyebrows pulled together, and just when I thought he was about to tell me to fuck off, his finger tightened around mine and he pulled me into his chest. I ignored the spraying of blood that was strewn over his flesh as his other hand came to my face. His fingers grasped my chin as he tilted my head up toward him.

"I. Don't. Share. Madison. *Ever.*"

I swallowed past the massive lump in my throat. So it was still about that. "I—"

He shook his head, his finger squeezing my chin. His eyes pierced into mine, as his lips lightly brushed over my mouth. "Ever."

I gulped and then nodded. "Okay."

Then his lips crashed down onto mine and all senses inside of me exploded everywhere, unlocking the latch that kept my legs up. His arm hooked around my back as his tongue dipped into my mouth, sliding against my own before he pulled away slightly, taking my breath away but leaving the soft tang of metallic slipping down my throat.

"I'll get these fucking people out of my house." He pressed his lips to mine, so softly, so gently, giving one peck of a kiss. That, against all of the other kisses I had been owned by from him, this was the one that seized my heart. I was putty in his hands. He took me out the kitchen, catching Jase's eye. "Tell everyone to fuck off."

Jase stared between the two of us and then grinned. "How long is this little cute act going to last this time?" Bishop's arm, that was wrapped around the back of my neck, tensed. I thought it was from Jase's remark, but then he tucked me under his arm farther and kissed the top of my head.

"Has it ever really *never* been her?"

Jase's grin deepened, his eyes continuously going between the two of us. "I guess not."

My heart felt swollen in my chest, but my legs and muscles ached from fatigue, so I was thankful when Bishop led me to the stairs that were in the sitting room. I thought the room I went into earlier was the master bedroom, I guess not.

"Hey!" Jase yelled out, just as my hand landed on the railing. We both turned to look over our shoulders to find Hunter, Nate, and Brantley, all now smiling with eyes sparkling with adrenaline, grinning at us. It was the first time since before Bishop had found out about my *shenanigans* that there had been any sort of air of peace surrounding us all. I understood now. Why Bishop had to do what he did tonight. It was not only to make a point but to restore the peace within the group. The trust. They were like brothers, and unlike girls, they weren't catty. They took their shit into a ring, punched it out, and then got over it. I guessed in their world, it was the only way they could live to survive amongst each other. It made sense.

"She's still my little sister!"

"—Our..." Hunter added, whacking Jase.

"—Our plus me, fuckers," Nate added, giving them a dirty look as he pulled open the fridge, taking out a drink. People were slowly pouring back into the main living areas now, the silent space slowly being filled with soft chitchat.

Bishop scoffed. "Don't give a fuck. She's Bishop's, her eyes say so, her body says so, her" —he lifted my shirt so they could see his initials on my ribs— "skin says so—"

I interrupted, sending them all a wink. "Her heart sort of says so, too…" It was no secret to Bishop how I felt about him, I knew that, and I'm pretty sure everyone else knew that too, so it didn't bother me with how forward I was with my wording. His grip tightened around me anyway, and then he led me upstairs.

"We've decided we're too young to be uncles!" Nate called out from down below. Bishop flipped him off over the railing and I laughed, shaking my head. That would be a nightmare. Then it started to sink in…*did I ever want kids?* Right now wasn't the time.

"Wow." I took in the bedroom and all its glory. Where his room back home was all black and disturbed young teenager, his room here was an off-white. White enough to know it's white, but a tint of cream stirred in to accentuate the pearl trimmings. It was an attractive and clean contrast that was warm and inviting, regardless of the bareness of it all. His bed was to the far left side of the room, so whoever was on one side got a full view of the city while the other could see downstairs. I loved it. I watched as flames from the gas fire licked up the wall opposite the bed, sending out hues of burnt orange to fill the dimly lit room. I let out a soft sigh.

"This place is truly beautiful, Bishop."

When I didn't get a response, I looked directly at him, only to find he was already watching me. An interesting look pulled over his features. It wasn't something I had seen him display before, and made me a little nervous and jumpy. He still managed to make me feel fear, and I think he always would because that was just who he was, and who he was to his core. It wasn't a front, it was just Bishop. He was real and would never put on a front to make someone more comfortable. You either took him as he was, or you didn't. Either way, it would never bother him. No one bothered him—and that was half of the charm and half of the fear.

"What is it?" My fingers laced with my hands nervously.

He shook his head, running his fingers through his hair. He took a seat on the edge of the bed, slightly leaning over and resting his elbows on his knees.

I followed, sitting beside him on the mattress, silently waiting for him to say something. Anything. For so long, I'd been wanting, praying, for him to open up to me a little. But every time he did open up, it seemed like all It would do is crack open more dark corners of his soul. It was an endless game of hide and seek where the counting was limitless.

"Goddammit, Madison," he whimpered with so much emotion, it damn near almost knocked me flat on my face.

"What'd I do now?" I mentally began sifting through my memories with the help of my good pal anxiety, flicking through those pages to make sure I hadn't done anything else wrong.

"Stop."

There was that one morning that I had said some bad things abou—

"Madison." His hand came to my cheek and he turned my face toward him. His eyes pierced into mine. "I said, stop." Then his thumb brushed softly over my bottom lip, his eyes watching the movement. "Stop overanalyzing and overthinking my move, for once." He paused and then continued. "Usually, this would be the part where I'd say 'you can't figure me out, so give it up,' but I've come to the realization that…" he grinned. "I'm a fucking liar."

"A what?"

"A liar." His thumb stopped moving and instantly, I missed the caress of his rough touch. "It's fucking you, Madison. You're the only person walking this earth that could ever figure me out. You're the only fucking person walking this earth that I truly know I'd kill a motherfucker for, and you're the only fucking girl walking this earth that *has* me."

"Has you?" I whispered, tears threatening to surface. I wasn't sure how to fully take in this side of Bishop. I had seen snippets of it in the past, but as quickly as I had seen it, it had been ripped away from me again before I could fully comprehend, or even enjoy, what I was feeling. "I have you?"

A small smile tickled his lips. It wasn't a cocky smile or a smug smile. It was genuine. "You've always had me, Madison. You know that."

Do I?

Pulling my bottom lip into my mouth, I take my gaze off him and look to the floor to ceiling window in front of me, this would be my side when I was staying. I didn't want to risk the chance of breaking whatever moment we were having right now, but I needed to know before I took another step in the direction of what was Bishop and Madison.

"Can I ask you something without you flipping your switch on me?"

"Anything," he expressed, his voice low and soft.

I took a deep breath. "I know about your deal with your father."

Pause.

I continued, "So I need to know one thing, and I will only ask you once." Then I finally let my attention go back to him. He was watching me, and I him. "Is this real, or is this a game?"

He searched my face. "Madison, does this—what we have, the connection and everything that we've experienced since we met—does that all seem fake to you?"

There was no second-guessing that answer. "No. But I never second-guessed my feelings, it was yours I was unsure about."

His arm snaked around my waist as he lifted me up, placing me down on his lap so I was facing him with my legs straddled around his hips. His hands fell to my ass and he squeezed. "I may not fully understand my own feelings when it comes to you, and I never have, but when I do, you'll be the first person to know about it."

I smiled, my hand coming to his face. If that was as close to a 'I love you,' that I was going to get for now, I was happy. I wrapped my arm around the back of his neck.

"Now, can you ride on my dick for a few hours so we can sleep." My head tipped back as I laughed, just as he pulled me down onto the bed and tore off my little dress. "This is sexy as fuck, Mads." His fingers traced the mesh material.

"You like?"

His eyes flew to mine. "It's a favorite for sure, but right now, it needs to be on the floor." Then he threw it across the room before his hands came to my back, and he pushed my chest down onto his face.

"Wait!" My hands came to his chest. "I almost forgot." I arched my back so I could access my back pocket and took out the 10kt heavy white gold curb chain. The shotgun bullet shell that dangled off of it was lightly engraved. BVH + MMV. It was cheesy, and I was scared.

He took it, his eyes searching mine and then going back to the chain. "Baby…"

"Happy birthday."

He kissed me hard, wrapping the chain around his fist. He leaned back. "Put it on?"

I nodded and got up, taking the chain from him. When it was securely around his neck, he turned around quickly, shoving me back onto the bed. My laughter was cut short by his teeth catching my nipple. He bit down, and I moaned, my head tilting back. I could feel his hardness pressing against my clit and I slowly rubbed myself over him. His hands fell to my hips and he squeezed tightly, his eyes rolling to the back of his head as his tongue slid out and wet his bottom lip. Sexy. As. Fuck. He caught my smile, narrowed his eyes, and then flipped me onto my back. I screamed out in shock, then his head dove into my neck while his knee hitched my leg up, pressing himself into me while his tongue licked over my collarbone.

I guessed he liked his present.

CHAPTER 17

"I want you to think of a wall, a bulletproof one that no matter how hard any weapon hounds on it, it could never break." Rob had said, pacing up and down in front of the seven of us. We had been close all our lives, whether by family or by choice, they were my brothers. I chose to care for them, no amount of family influence could have forced the kind of brotherhood we shared—which made us the most lethal Kings created. The generations before us, my father had said they always fought or struggled to get along sometimes. Whether it be by girl or just by personalities not being compatible, it never happened. They never had a generation that flowed fluidly like we did, so they had big plans for us.

"A wall?" Nate snickered. "You brought us here to teach us about a wall?"

Rob waved him off diffusely and continued his army march backward and forward in front of us. "I want you to start building this wall inside of your brain, but before you do so, I want you to make sure there are six seats there beside you. Not eight, not two, not any other number but seven total," he paused, looking down at me. I wasn't a short kid. For a ten-year-old, I was pretty tall, but staring up at Rob in this moment, I felt two-feet. "I want you to start building this wall today. Work on it, I mean really train your brain to build it, because by the time you initiate in, I need that wall to be solid. To be unfuckwithable. This"—Rob gestured around—"was who you trusted. No one else."

"What about my dad?" I argued, looking at the guys who all glared at me like "shut the fuck up." Rob was scary, but I didn't scare easily.

"Even your dad. He went through the same when he was your age, and so will the next ones who come after you."

"What, as in we have to have kids?" Hunter scrunched up his face.

"Yes." Dad interrupted, walking around the back of the cabin dressed in one of his fine suits. "You will have kids one day."

"No, I'm good. I don't want kids." I knew at a very young age that children didn't appeal to me, and I doubted that would change in the future. Call it the only-child curse.

"Oh I bet you will, I bet you and Khales will have kids by the time you're sixteen," Eli snorted, only no one joined him.

"No. I don't want them."

My dad kneeled down in front of me, searching my eyes. "You will, son, and lucky for you, I have someone lined up."

My eyebrows pinched together. "What? Who?" I was still not having kids, but I'd ask him who he thought I could be matched with anyway.

He reached into his front jacket pocket and pulled out a small photograph, flipping it around to show me. It was a little girl, had to be around the same age as me or younger—unless she was just really small. She had brown wavy hair, chubby cheeks, a bright smile and blue eyes. A couple of freckles were scattered over her cheeks and she was holding a hunting rifle. "This girl."

"That girl?" I questioned, obviously my dad was off his meds. That girl wasn't anything great, I had seen better at my school, but she had something contrastive about her, an imbalance if you will, but her eyes. Her eyes ate up the distance between us, even if it was a photo that she was staring at me from. "Who is she?"

Dad looked sideways at me, noticing the other guys trying to get a look. He folded it and pushed it back into his pocket, shooting them all a warning glare. "Someone who is going to arrive in your life at the exact moment you need her to."

"Like fate?" I asked. I didn't really know what that word meant, but I had heard it be thrown around a lot with the adults.

He laughed. "Not fate—karma. Your wake-up call."

My phone vibrated on the kitchen counter, pulling me out of the task at hand. Cooking. I wasn't bad, because neither of my parents were around much, which meant I learned how to make the simple things, like toast, and eggs, and bacon, and that's all that I really needed to live on, so I stopped my skill level right there. Reaching for my phone, I slid it unlocked and pushed it onto speaker when I saw it was Mom.

"Yeah?" I picked up the spatula and pushed the creamy eggs around.

"I'm just making sure you haven't scared that girl off?"

I snorted. "Not likely."

She paused, and I leaned over to check to see if the call was still connected. "Bishop, how much does she know?"

I checked on the bacon in the oven and licked the juice off my fingertips. "Enough but not all."

"And how much are you planning on telling her?"

"All."

"Bishop..." she warned. "I would say some, but all could be too much for her to take in too soon."

"Mom, I thought you would have been all for this since Dad left you in the dark for so long and you were all 'don't keep too many secrets, son.'"

"For her safety, Bishop. You know your father, need I say more?"

I slammed the oven door and sighed. "You don't need to, but if it came down to it, I'd handle him."

"My son the knight..." She was playing with me because I could hear the slight humor in her tone, but I could also hear the apprehension. She was afraid. With good reason. No one goes up against my dad, but if there was anyone who ever would—it would be me. As much as I respected him, and obviously searched for his approval in most things I did, when it came to Madison, no one else mattered and I think he knew that.

"Where are you, anyway?" I flipped the oven off and took the pan off the stove top.

"I'm actually on my way home. I'll explain once I get there, are you in your new place?"

"Yep. I gotta go. Talk soon."

"Ok. Love you, son."

"Yeah, you too, Mom." I flicked it off and pushed my phone into my pocket. I was aware I never had outwardly told my mom that I loved her, but she was one of those women who just knew.

"Cooking? Have you been holding out on me all this time?" Madison was leaning against the entryway to the kitchen.

I grinned. "Nah, probably saved your life." She ran her fingers through her hair, brushing it away from her face. It fell loosely around her shoulders anyway, and that's when I noticed she was wearing one of my shirts.

My eyes narrowed. "You wearing anything underneath that?" I asked, gesturing to her legs with the spatula.

She looked down, gripping the bottom of the shirt and shrugging. "Um, no?"

I dropped the spatula into the pan and made my way towards her. She smiled when she saw I was coming for her, a look of shock passing over her eyes. Good. She should feel strange. Gripping her from the backs of her thighs, I lifted her off the ground until her legs wrapped around my waist and tightened. Pressing my lips to hers, I slipped my tongue into her mouth and sucked her bottom lip into my mine. "Fuck you taste good this early."

"Yeah," she rolled her eyes. "That's because I brushed my teeth."

A rumble of laughter escaped me. I always admired her flare for honesty. It was refreshing that she didn't truly care what anyone thought of her. The sound dock turned on and Marilyn Manson "Killing Strangers" started playing, and I grinned, walking her towards the kitchen island and dropping her onto it. The back of her head smashed onto the marble and she groaned, her eyes rolling to the back of her head.

"That hurt?" I asked, an eyebrow quirked.

She bit down on her bottom lip and shook her head. "Not really." With her stretched out on the counter, I stood between her legs, gripped her thighs and pulled her toward me so her crotch was pressed against my cock. Then the palms of my hands slid up her thighs, pushing the shirt above her head until she was bare naked in front of me. I stepped backward, taking in every curve and slim line that marbled her tanned skin. "So fucking beautiful."

Her cheeks reddened, and I fucking loved it. I loved that I could have that kind of effect on her with my words alone.

"Wait, I'm hungry." She went to get up, but I shoved her back down.

"So am I." Then a dipped my lips to her inner thigh and slid my tongue over her skin. Defeated, she dropped backward and arched her back. I took my tongue out and circled her clit, her taste invading my mouth. I lost it, and wrapped my lips around her, sinking a finger deep inside of her. She moaned out, pinched her nipple with her finger and arched her back farther.

I stood up, my thumb still pressing to her clit, circling it softly. "Wait." Letting her go, I sucked my finger and went to the freezer, taking out a tray of ice. Her eyes lit up brightly, her cheeks flashing red. "I've not... is that dangerous?"

I chuckled. "No. It's not." I banged the ice cubes on the counter until they scattered out everywhere, then picked one up and slid it up her inner thigh. "Close your eyes, Kitty."

I pressed my tongue to her clit and pushed the ice cube inside of her. A gasp left her instantly, her back arching off the counter in shock. I continued pushing it up, feeling the contraction of her insides and the melted ice dripping down my finger. Her body confused as my tongue ran circles on her. "I'm—I'm—"

"Come, baby. All over me."

She moaned and I felt her walls pull my finger in deeper as she rippled through her orgasm. Standing, I yanked her closer to me, spread her legs wide and sunk my cock deep inside. Sweat fell off her smooth flesh and her lips parted, her eyes rolling to the back of her head.

"There's something weird about Mrs. Winters," Madison threw out absently around a bite of her bagel. "Like I haven't seen her since Tate and I got her to get our passports." Then she stilled, her eyes coming to mine where they narrowed.

"Woah!" I threw my hands up in defense. "I haven't got shit to do with her disappearing act, so point those eyes elsewhere." She went back to eating, as did I. I wasn't lying, I didn't have anything to do with Tinker doing a runner. She would have done that all on her own as soon as she found out I knew where Madison was. She was a fucking idiot for thinking I wouldn't know it was her that helped Madison though. We finished up eating and got dressed. I snatched my car keys off the counter as Madison was coming down the stairs, tying her hair into a high ponytail.

"Where we going?"

"We are going to teach you how to fight."

Her hand stilled, still clutching her hair. "What? Why?"

"Because, all though you have me and the Kings, we may not always be around if you fall into trouble. And now that everyone who is anyone knows your affiliations with us, you're pretty much a walking target, and I'm not about to take chances. Not when it comes to you."

She seemed to think over what I had just said, and then shrugged, feigning nonchalance. "But I have my Glock."

I forced myself from not rolling my eyes. "That's good and all, but here's the thing about relying on a Glock. That metal bullshit may not always be easily accessible to you when you need it, but do you wanna know what will *always* be accessible to you?"

"I get your point. But I don't know if combat is my thing."

"Well, we're about to make it your thing." I shoved the car keys into my back pocket and headed for the front door. "Come on, princess."

She flipped me off.

CHAPTER 18

"I don't wanna…" I whined like an annoyed toddler. "Seriously, this isn't fair!" We were back at the cabin and the sun was blaring down on my skin. I had yoga pants and a loose tank on. Too loose. So I wrapped the front into a bun and tied it tightly under my sports bra.

"Oh come on, this will be fun!" That was Nate, grinning from his seat. All of them were here. Nate, Jase, Hunter, and Chase were sitting on the logs that surround the bonfire. Their sunglasses covering their eyes while they sat there, shoving potato chips into their annoying gobs, drinking beer, and basically, looking like they were ready to watch an hour long movie. Bishop, Brantley, Eli, Cash, and Saint were semi surrounding me in a circle. All dressed accordingly. You know, with no shirts and various colors of jeans. Some worn, some not so worn, som—

"Madison!" Bishop snapped.

I brought my eyes to him where they were squinted. "What!"

"Watch those eyes."

I turned red. I didn't even realize I was obviously checking them out—without checking them out. "I was looking at all of your jeans, actually," I mumbled under my breath grumpily. Then I cranked my neck. "I'm really not sure about this." Saint had laid down some combat mats. Which proved my earlier statement. He was the brains of the group. I heard a car speeding down the long private gravel road and everyone revived to alert. The guys shot up from their seats while Bishop slowly stepped in front of me. Then they all relaxed and mumbled annoyances. I couldn't see around Bishop's block of a body but when I heard the voice, I laughed.

"If you think you boys get to beat her ass without me watching, you're mistaken."

I giggled. "Tate, tell me you brought vodka or something." I had a feeling our holiday was going to be fueled by alcohol and poor decisions. Oh, and I have a new boyfriend who isn't really new, and I guess we haven't really made it official. Crap. Is he my boyfriend?

"Kitty!" Bishop growled, pointing to my arms that were not so defensively to the sides of my body.

"Oh, I really don't want to do this," I whined.

I could hear mumbled arguing to the side of me, so I turned to see what was going

"Seriously!" I deadpanned at the both of them. "I mean I expected it from Nate, but not you." I pointedly glared at Tate.

She looked around the group innocently, licking the salt off her fingers. "Oh come on." She rolled her eyes. "You've totally got them all. And besides, I haven't been laid in what feels like, weeks. This will be like live porn."

"That's not pervy at all," I retorted, then turned back to a grinning Bishop.

"Oh it's totally pervy, and I'm not ashamed to admit it."

"Wait, you haven't had dick since mine?" Nate asked, staring at her.

She turned Ferrari red and I relished in the fact that her mouth had once again, landed her ass in hot water.

She shrugged. "I'm fussy, so what."

Jase was staring her up and down. "I mean, I can rectify that if you want. Can't guarantee you'd survive a real man, though…"

Nate flipped him off.

I rubbed my forehead with the palm of my hand. "Fuck me. I have idiots as friends and family."

Music started playing through the big boom speaker that was huddled near Nate, and I recognized the song from one of their parties. "Get Dough" by Dead Obies.

An hour later, sweat was dripping from my skin and Bishop's body was pressing into my back with my face squished into the mat. "Okay! Alright! Fuck!" He circled his crotch into my ass. I flushed. "Stop it…"

The entire time we've been doing this training-fighting thing, Bishop was going hard on me. And I don't mean his dick. I will most likely have bruises all over my arms and butt for weeks after this. Brantley was no exception either. He almost knocked me out, waiting for me to get out of the sleeper hold. They weren't playing around at all, but now I was tired, sweaty, and thirsty. Not for water.

"Can we continue this next week?"

"No," Bishop answered, jackknifing off me and getting to his feet. "We all have to stay out here…"

I looked around at them. "Why are we staying out here?" I couldn't believe I didn't ask anyone earlier about why we were all out here. Bishop's phone went off in his pocket and he stepped backward, answering it. I turned to Nate and Jase. "Seriously, what's going on?"

His eyes drifted over my shoulder. "What?"

I followed his line of sight, facing Bishop.

"We'll leave tomorrow."

"Leave?" I asked, my eyes darting around the place. "Leave to where?"

"Come here…" He gestured with his fingers, and I followed, hooking my fingers with his. He sat on a log and pulled me onto his lap. "We have to go to Perdita."

I sat for a beat, thinking over what he had just said.

"Three questions," Tate yapped off in the background. "What's Perdita, do they have margaritas, and should I pack my bikini?"

"I'll answer all those three for you," Nate snapped back. "One, you're not coming, two, you're not coming, and three, you're not fucking coming."

"Really?" She shot back with a roll of her eyes. "Because I specifically recall you 'coming' all over my tits last week."

"Jesus Christ," Jase muttered, getting to his feet. A few guys chuckled, but I was so used to Tate and Nate's banter, I brushed them off. Even if their banter had intensified over the past week. Must be Tate not getting any sex.

"Ok, why?" I quizzed through more of a whisper, searching Bishop's eyes, which were on mine, studying my reaction.

"We're not sure yet, but we know we have to get there."

My confusion turned to excitement when I realized I'd get to see Daemon. "I'll need to grab some clothes."

"Babe, I'd rather you not come."

"Too bad, I'm coming."

"Mads..."

"Bishop..." I countered his tone. "I'm. Coming."

He pulled his bottom lip into his mouth, his eyebrows pulling in softly as if he was searching for what to say, or internally fighting with what he should do. Too bad, I wasn't giving this up. I'd sneak myself onto that plane if I had to.

"Fine," Bishop agreed. I wiggled in his lap in excitement and his hands flew to my hips where he stilled my movements. His eyes narrowed. "Watch it."

"Wait, she can't come. We can't have a liability on Perdita."

I flipped Hunter off. "I'm not a liability!"

"Nah, she's right. She needs to be near us. She's not safe here on her own and we can't afford to leave anyone here to watch her because we need all the manpower we have over there."

I gave Hunter a Cheshire Cat grin.

His face deadpanned. "I don't like having a baby sister."

"You'll warm up to her." Nate winked at me. I smiled.

"To her or *on* her?" Hunter snapped back.

"Okay!" I stood from Bishop's lap. "So I want Tate to come with me."

"You do?" Tate's face lit up.

Nate's sunk.

"Yes, I do."

"Ah... I don't thin—" Bishop started to say, but I cut him off.

"—she's coming."

"Now do you still think it's a good idea her coming?" Hunter flicked his wrist in my direction, but his eyes were on Bishop.

"Mmm," Bishop mumbled and then stood.

"Please tell me were not throwing a party..."

Bishop shook his head. "Nah, just us out here. If you two need to go home to get some clothes, I'll take you now since I have to stop at my parents' and see Dad quickly."

"Ok," I nodded, and then hitched my thumb over my shoulder, toward the cabin. "Is there still no food up in there?"

Bishop gave me a look that said "correct."

"We'll stop and get food. I'm starving and I need a shower."

Bishop's hand sprawled out over my belly and he pushed my body into his, his lips falling to my shoulder. "Shower later. Come on." He slapped my ass and then made his way to his car. Tatum brushed off her pants and shot Nate a scolding look before following Bishop.

"Just out of curiosity," I muttered, slowly walking toward where Nate was sitting. "What did you do to piss her off so bad?"

"What?" He threw his hands in the air innocently. "Why do I have to be the one who had done something wrong?"

I quirked an eyebrow at him. "Because you're you?"

He pretended to think over my reply. "Valid."

I rolled my eyes and started following Bishop and Tate. "You." Was all Nate had said, just as I passed him.

I turned back to face him, my hands on my hips. "What?"

He shrugged and leaned back in his chair. "She's mad about what we did with Brantley, only she wasn't sleeping with Brantley."

"Wait, so she's mad at me too?"

Nate shook his head. "No. She was mad because I got in between you and Bishop. She's team Madship."

My eye twitched. "Team, what, what?"

He snorted. "Go do your thang, girl." I looked at Jase and Hunter, who were watching me carefully, then turned to make my way to Bishop's car. Was she mad at me for hooking up with Nate? I didn't even think of her feelings while I was doing what I was doing. Damn. I was such a bad friend.

"You alright?" Bishop asked, dropping to third and flooring it out of the driveway.

"Yeah, I think." Truth was, I wasn't sure. I knew that how I had acted in the past was shit, but for the first time ever, I'd made it impact Tatum too. She's an innocent in all this.

CHAPTER 19

We pulled into Tate's driveway first and I slid my seat forward to let her out.
"I'll be in in a sec!" I called out to her as she jogged up her front steps.

I turned to face Bishop. "I upset her, I think, with all that Nate stuff."

Bishop's eyes followed Tate. "Nah, I don't think she's mad at you. Him probably."

"I won't be a second." I climbed out of the car and followed her up the steps. Closing the door behind myself, I headed straight for her bedroom which was on the first floor. She converted the media room to her bedroom because she hated the sunlight so much. My best friend was a vampire, but it worked for us. Netflix and chill dates were like business class luxury at Tate's. Not that her parents would give a shit. They checked in on her once every three or so months but always kept the trust fund full. I wasn't entirely sure what the crux of their issues was with Tate, but apparently, according to Tate, it had always been like this. There was a cleaner and a cook that lives here full time, sort of like my Sammy and Jimmy, but other than that, her parents never came home. To some, it may sound amazing. A twelve-bedroom mansion all to yourself with a bank balance that could match CEO executives. But to Tate, I knew she craved something more, it was why she always had so much to give. Which was why I was such a terrible friend.

I walked into her bedroom and giggled at the bed. "You actually converted the seats to a bed?"

She halted her packing and looked over her shoulder. "Why of course. Jump on it, it's so comfortable." I took a step closer and sunk into the bed. She was right. It felt like my ass was being caressed by a marshmallow. "Hey, I wanted to talk to you about something."

She continued her packing, throwing in bikinis and short skirts. I was too focused on my apology to stop her. "You're mad at Nate about what happened?"

She paused, then continued. Standing to her feet, she headed out the door and turned toward her bathroom. "Sort of!" she yelled out from the hallway before entering with her toothbrush in hand. "I mean, I'm not mad at him for hooking up with you because I'm jealous. I was mad because he knew what he was doing and knew his loyalty to Bishop, but continued to pursue you anyway."

She zipped up her duffle bag. "Tate, it was me as much as him."

She slung her bag over her shoulder and glared at me. "Oh, I know. And I'm still mad at you about that—hence the reason I wanted to come watch you get your ass beat today." She chuckled, but when she noticed I wasn't amused, her face fell. "Mads, you know I love you. I just didn't entirely agree with your actions, but I'd never judge you."

"It sort of feels like you're judging me, Tate."

She walked toward me and placed her hands on my shoulders. "I am not judging you. I love you and you're my best friend, but I don't agree with what you did—that's all, and that's going to happen, Mads." I didn't know why this shocked me, but I think it had to do with the fact that Tate was the easygoing friend. The free spirit and well... sexually active. Very active. Tillie was the free spirit, wild friend, but not over opinionated and snappy like Tate. More submissive and easygoing.

She repeated, "I'm not mad at you now. I'm over it." Then her hands dropped to either side of herself. "I guess if you looked at it like that, I am sort of upset about Nate. God!" She exhaled and dropped back onto the bed, her hands covering her face. "I'm such a fucking idiot, Mads. I knew what I was getting myself into when I jumped into bed with him. I knew he was a slut, yet I did it anyway." Her fingers spread apart and her eye peeked through. "This is the part where you tell me I'm not an idiot and that he is good at what he does and that my Bishop will come along one day."

I snorted, and then pulled her up by her arm. "Bishop is complicated, and it would truly terrify me if there were more like him out there, have you forgotten all the shit." When I saw her face not registering, I rolled my eyes. "Never mind. Get up!" I yanked her up to her feet and wrapped my arm around her waist as we headed back toward the front door.

"I love you too, Tate."

She squeezed me. "Are you going to tell me what happened to Tillie?"

I smiled sadly. "I will when I know."

We put Tate's shit into the trunk then got back into our seats. Bishop gave us both a cautious stare. "You both good?"

"We're good!" I said, gesturing to the front of us. "Let's get my stuff quickly, go to your house, and then get food. I don't feel like cooking, so maybe we should order some pizzas on the way back to the cabin."

Bishop laughed. "You got this all figured out, huh?"

"Oh for fuck's sake, lovebirds. As much as you're making my heart weep with feelings, I'd really love to listen to music right now."

Bishop hit the music and a soft song came on with a woman singing a catchy hook. "What's this song?"

Tate answered for me. "'Something I Don't Know' by Miraz." She turned her head to look out the small back window, a sad look pulling across her face. I felt for her because her feelings for Nate were obvious, but I knew he wasn't on the same page as her—and never would be, because he was lost and stuck on the first chapter of Tillie. Maybe if she wasn't in the picture, he could draw one with Tatum, but she was in the picture, so it wasn't looking good for Tate.

"Hey, when are you going to tell me about Tillie?" I asked Bishop, turning to face him a bit more.

His jaw clenched as his eyes flew to the rearview mirror briefly, checking on Tate. He took his attention back to the road and dropped down gears. "Soon."

I guessed that was code for 'don't ask me right now,' so I left it alone. We drove up my driveway. I sighed, hating that I was back here.

"I'm starting to really not like this place."

"Want me to come in with you?" Bishop asked, his index finger running on his upper lip.

I nodded. "Okay." Then I turned to face Tate. "Can we leave you unattended for a few minutes?"

She clutched her chest, mock shocked. "Oh, well, I'd never…"

Bishop and I both laughed, getting out of the car. The sweat from the fighting had long since dried over my skin, but the smell was still there.

"I really need a shower. I might have one quickly before we leave."

Bishop pulled his sunglasses over his eyes, his arm hooking around my waist as he led me to the front door. "Suits me."

"Oh, hi sweetie!" Elena was coming down the stairs when we entered. Her eyes went to Bishop and her smile softened even more. She rested her palm on his cheek. "Honey, you should have said something about Elizabeth."

He shrugged. "It wouldn't have made a difference."

She squared her shoulders, her brown hair falling over her shoulder. "Oh I can assure you, it would have. I'm having lunch with your mom tomorrow. Does she know?"

Bishop shook his head. "No, she doesn't, mainly because, well…"

Elena smirked. "Because your momma is one woman who you do not want to be on the bad end with."

Bishop chuckled. "Exactly."

"Well, I can't lie to her if it comes up. It was her who asked to have lunch with me, so we all know that in this world, that means either a favor is about to be asked, or some information needs bleeding. Or both." She dropped her oversized glasses over her eyes and gave him one last pat on his shoulder. "Take care of our girl." Then she left like a hurricane of summer, warm milk and cookies. I swear, she had to be one of the most interesting women I had ever met. She smelled like fresh daisies on a hot summer day and cold ice tea, but to be so deeply involved in this life, she had to be built from the strong stuff too. And I had witnessed on more than one occasion how she could flip from cute housewife to scary mob boss wife.

I walked up the stairs with Bishop hot on my heels and then headed straight into my bedroom. "I'm grabbing a quick shower."

He went to my closet. "I'll pack your bag."

"Thanks," I gave him a smile and he walked up to me, pressing his lips to mine. It took everything inside of me not to melt into a puddle on the floor if it was physically possible.

He pulled back, his eyes searching mine. "Some information has come to light about exactly what might be going on over there. Something we didn't know about until this morning."

I brushed away my nerves. "Dangerous things?"

Bishop clenched his jaw a couple of times. "Yes."

"And who did you hear this from?"

Another clench. "Daemon."

"Is he ok?" Panic set in as it usually does whenever my brother was mentioned. I had a bond with him that was unimaginable and just the thought of harm coming his way was crippling.

"He's fine, babe, but we need to check on a few things."

"Why?" I whispered before I could stop myself. "I mean, obviously he has ties to The Elite Kings, but why are you guys all helping him all of a sudden when it wasn't too long ago that you all sort of couldn't stand him? Well, aside from the fact that he is my brother."

Bishop waited, and then sighed. "Because it's not that we couldn't stand him, Madison, it's what he's capable of and who he is. But he's your brother, which means he means something to me now."

"Thank you." I exhaled, rubbing the palm of my hand over my forehead. "Thank you for understanding when it comes to Daemon. Why didn't you want Tate coming?"

Bishop's smile faltered. "I like her, and that says a lot because I don't like anyone, but..." He searched my eyes, seeming to swim above the surface on something, then just as his mouth twitched, he shook his head. "It's nothing. I just didn't want to hear her and Nate arguing all the way."

"Word," I mumbled, pulling my eyes from his.

"Hey." His thumb and index finger curled around my chin, tilting my head up to face his. "She's loyal as shit to you, so that makes her a friend of mine. Everything I do, I do for you. Remember that, okay?"

I raised my hand up to his face. My finger curving over his sharp jaw, and then down to his chin. I watched as his lips slightly parted as he sucked in a breath. It was discreet and subtle, but I didn't miss it.

"I love you," I whispered, my eyes staying on his lips. When his jaw tightened, I quickly dropped my hand, snapping myself out of my trance. "Sorry." I knew he wouldn't say it back, and I'd never expected him to, but the longer he goes without saying it, hurts a little more. At first, I was okay. Like, so he needed time to feel his feelings. I could give him that, right? But that was the second time I had told him I loved him and he didn't reply. I quickly dove for the bathroom door.

"—Mad—" I slammed the door on his face, right before he could jump up to stop me and flipped it locked.

Tears threatened to surface and my chest tightened from the rejection. Before I could stop it, one spilled from my eye and I quickly scrubbed it away. Angry that I was getting so worked up over something so sparse and stupid. I hit the faucet and turned the water onto scolding hot then stepped inside. I needed it hot enough to take my mind off what just happened. To remind me that emotional pain isn't real, it was a figment of our imagination. We didn't bleed. We didn't die from the injuries that emotional pain gave us. But even as I replayed that mantra in my head, my heart was screaming at me and calling me a liar. A sob came out and I reached for the soap, lathering it between the palm of my hand—a loud smash shocked me out of my slum and I quickly pulled the curtain away to see what the fuck had just fallen in my bathroom, only to find Bishop heaving and my door split in two. My eyes dropped down to his combat boots to see the residue from him kicking my door dusted over the leather.

"Bishop!" I swiped my cheeks and sniffed my nose. "You could have walked through Nate's entrance!"

He didn't say anything, he simply stepped toward the shower, his shoulders rising and falling and his teeth clenched together so tightly I was sure his jaw was about to snap.

"You didn't even give me a chance..." he started as he slowly continued to come closer. I went to answer but his hand flew up to shut me up. His eyes were dilated, his cheeks flushed red. God. He was mad as fuck at me, which slightly pissed me off because the person who should be mad—for once—should be me. He ripped the curtain out of my hand, his eyes staying on mine. He didn't drop them down my body seductively, they remained solely on mine. They'd darkened to a feral state. I flinched slightly. "Bishop—"

His hand flew to my chin, his fingers spread out over my cheeks. He stepped into the shower, clothes and boots on and backed me up against the wall. His lips came down to mine and softly brushed over them, sending tingles shooting down to my core. "Am I supposed to tell you those three little words in order for you to feel more secure? Mads? Fuck no!" His fists came up to either side of my head, caging me in. His head tilted, his eyes searching my face. "Do you know how many pieces of shit people tell their partner that they love them but go and do some shady shit behind their back? Do you wanna know what I think of the word love, Kitty? I think it's bullshit. The word is bullshit, the meaning behind why people say it is bullshit." His hips pressed forward, his jean-covered cock grinding against my bare pussy. My eyes drifted closed. I felt the tip of his nose near my earlobe. "It's all a fucking fantasy. Putting words to that feeling doesn't mean shit. I don't need words to tell me what the fuck!" he paused, then bit down on my neck. His hands clamped around my upper thighs, hiking me up. I wrapped them around his waist and he slammed me against the wall again, the shower pelting down on us. "I feel."

His lips went back to hovering over mine. "Open your eyes," he growled over my lips. Shit. My stomach was doing somersaults and everything south was clenching in angst. "Now, Kitty," he ordered, his chest rumbling against my nipples. I opened my eyes, ignoring the droplets of water that were slipping through my lashes. His eyes were on mine, his hair soaked from the water and his dark t-shirt clinging to his flesh, curving around every muscle. "I *feel* something for you, Madison. Something I've never felt for anyone—ever. But love isn't a strong enough word to even come close to what the fuck I feel for you. The word love is the most overused fucking word in the dictionary, and I can say right now that I've never told anyone those words *ever*. Not even my mother." He paused, and took a breath, his finger brushing over my lips. "But fuck me, Mads. If this is love, then I've loved you since the day I first saw you in the cafeteria." My chest swelled so thick it felt as though my heart was going to pound out of my chest. My eyes were going cross-eyed from looking at his lips. Then his mouth came to mine. I opened up for him slightly, his tongue slipping into my mouth and then he pulled back and searched my eyes. "I love you, too."

My knees buckled and all feeling below my knees went numb. His grip on my thighs tightened and my head sunk into the crook of his neck. Sobs came slowly.

"You better not be fucking crying, Madison, I swear to God."

I laughed, bringing my head up to face him. My hands came to his cheeks, and even though it felt as though my throat was raw and swollen from everything that had just happened, I shook my head. "Kiss me." I had nothing else to say to what he had just said. He hitched me up with one hand and used the other to tug off his shirt from the back of the collar. He threw his shirt out of the shower and his lips smashed into mine. My arms wrapped around the back of his neck as I squeezed him into me more, grinding myself over his belt. His hand reached down as he unbuckled it and tugged them down. His hand brushed over my sex and I moaned, biting down on my lip from his touch. He chuckled and slowly put me back on my feet.

"What're you doing?" I asked absently, already missing his touch. He dropped down in front of me, his belt unbuckled, his abs tensing from the motion, and hiked my leg over his shoulder. He smirked up at me from below. I moaned again from the view. I was taking a mental photo of this picture, for later use... then his eyes went straight to my core and his tongue came out to lick his lips. He enclosed his mouth over me. I groaned, my head pressing into the hard wall. "Oh my God..." His tongue swirled around my clit and his finger came to my entrance where he sunk it in and curled it, hitting my spot effortlessly. I rode against him shamelessly, my orgasm building at fast speeds. He switched up, his tongue diving inside, and I lost all of my control as my muscles tightened, then released as my orgasm rippled through me. He stood back up, licking his fingers like you would food.

"Come here." Then he grabbed my legs again and wrapped them around my waist. His lips crashed into mine as he sunk himself inside of me. I tightened around him, still pulsing from the aftershocks of my orgasm, but his intrusion was enough to set me off again.

"Look at me, baby," he growled, slowly pulling out and then sinking back in. "This is mine. Do you understand?" His motion picked up to a faster pace. "Kitty..." he warned, his hand coming to my throat. "I may love you, but I'll still fuck you until you're black and blue. Don't test my shit, Madison." His grip tightened around my throat and I choked from the lack of air.

"I'm all yours, Bishop. Forever."

"No one will touch this. Ever." He pounded into me relentlessly. I was sure there would be bruising inside from his brutality. Our skin slapped together and sweat leaked out of my pores. His other hand went back to my thigh and he clenched down roughly as his pace picked up again to a feral penetrating motion. My inner thighs were stretched and aching from the roughness of his slamming.

His lips came to my collarbone, and it was enough to unleash my second orgasm. My body jerked painfully yet throbbed blissfully as I came down. His teeth sunk into my flesh and he growled out a low groan, just as his cock jerked inside of me. We stood there for a few more beats, collecting our breaths, then he laughed and stepped backward, pressing a light kiss on my lips. "I'm goin' need to go get some clothes from Nate's room."

"Okay," I smiled, my cheeks red and my body aching from being fucked to the brink of insanity.

His eyes twinkled, and his lip kinked in a grin. "You ok?"

I rolled my eyes—totally bluffing—"Of course. This isn't my first rodeo with you."

He laughed, then got out of the shower, disappearing into Nate's room. I shut the curtain and bit down on my bottom lip. I couldn't stop the smile that was spread over my mouth. He loved me. Bishop Vincent Hayes said he loved me. My chest tingled with excitement and it took everything inside of me not to scream in happiness. I felt like a part of me had finally slipped into a puzzle of what was him and I. For almost a year our relationship had done circles, but we had never been here, and it gave me hope for our future. I quickly re-soaped my hands and scrubbed myself down again, even though I really didn't want to because Bishop's cologne had left a faint smell lingering over my flesh, then I turned the faucet off and got out, slipping the towel around my body.

"Oh, what the hell did I miss?" Tate said from my bedroom, probably noticing the door. I peeked my head around the broken door to see her entering my bedroom.

Her worried eyes came to mine, and then they softened. "Giiirrllll… I need to know everything." I guess I was actually smiling from ear to ear.

"You will, but first I need to quickly pack and get changed."

"And where's our GQ brooding caveman?"

I hiked my thumb over my shoulder. "Grabbing some clothes from Nate's room."

She shook her head and laughed. "This ought to be good."

She had no idea.

CHAPTER 20

"Ok, so we've got enough food for the morning and for the guys if they get hungry later. Now we just need to order pizza's!" I figured my chat with the old man could wait. The girls looked tired, and I didn't have the energy for him right now.

Coming to a red light, I thought over where we could grab pizzas that were on the way and were also decent. I smirked. "I have an idea." Then I slid out my phone and typed out a group text:

Meet us at CK's

I put my phone on my lap and floored it to the pizza parlor. The girls were a lot quieter this time around than they were earlier in the day. Madison had every reason to be tired, considering, but Tate, I didn't know. I was getting tired by just watching her brain tick over with all her overthinking. I gave a bit of a shit about Tate because I knew how much she meant to Madison. So in short, I didn't want to see her get hurt.

I hooked into the parallel park outside Gengy's Pizza. The "G" was hanging off an old electrical wire and flicked on and off, so sometimes, it looked more like "Engy's Pizzas", but Gengy, the owner, he was a good friend from when I was a kid. My mom would bring me here all the time to get his pizzas. It was probably one of the only real memories I had as a kid with my mom.

"I won't be a second." I could feel my phone vibrating in my pocket, and just as I was about to grab it out, Gengy's cussing in his heavy Puerto Rican accented voice caught my attention.

"No, fuck you, man, that's not how it's going to go down. I'm telling you, McGregor is about to beat some ass!"

I chuckled, shaking my head as I entered the shop. "Good to see you're still talking shit!" I yelled out, pulling my phone out from my back pocket.

Gengy's shit talking stopped and his attention came to me. He gave me a shit-eating grin. "Oh! B, my man!" Then he leaned over the counter and pulled me in for a hug. "Where you been, broki? I could slap you upside your head not coming to visit me more!"

"I know, homie, that's my bad. You still haven't gotten that sign fixed though…"

"Hey!" He shook his finger in front of himself. "Don't come up here in your rich pretty boy sports car and your clothes and throw money at me like I'm some stripper and about to give you a lap dance, I told you, I can handle my own."

"You've been telling me that since I was ten, and how much would that lap dance cost me? I got a couple dollars in here..."

"Smart shit!" He laughed, tossing a dishcloth over his shoulder. Gengy was a sixty-year-old, beer belly, pot smoking, foul-mouthed, stubborn son of a bitch. But he and I bonded from day one and the rest was history.

"Whatchu want, B?"

I yapped off the pizza's I wanted to order and he went about making them. I looked down at my phone, catching up the texts from these idiots.

Nate: Why?
Jase: We haven't been there in a while, B.
Eli: Got blunts?
Cash: Can I bring Cindy?
Hunter: Who the fuck is Cindy?
Cash: She's the chick I'm fucking
Eli: What like right now?
Cash: Someone take this kid to school...
Eli: Who the fuck you calling a kid? I had your mom under me last week.
Brantley: I'll gather the children and be there.

I shook my head. Fucking idiots. The lot of them. Sliding my phone into my pocket, I caught Gengy up on all my bullshit from the past year, paid for the pizzas, and then went back to the car.

"Just saying," Tate mumbled through a yawn. "If I catch salmonella poisoning—I'm totally blaming you, B."

I snorted. "Don't let the outside fool you. He's cleaner on the inside than most of those pretty thousand dollar strips we go to."

"Huh, uncanny," Tatum snickered, more to herself but I caught it. I was on edge about how this was all going to pan out come tomorrow. I've kept big fucking things from every-one, and eventually, those big fucking things turn into mountains. You water shit for long enough and it will help plants grow. I had a feeling Nate was about to lose his shit. I don't know what game Nate was playing with Tatum, but I could see it fucking with her head. Aside from her, he always tried to brush off his feelings for Tillie, but we never bought it.

It was easy to say you don't love someone when your feelings weren't being shoved in your face every day by that person breathing the same air as you. It was why long distance relationships never worked. You don't see that person for long enough, the illusion that your feelings slowly start to dissipate into thin air begins, then suddenly you wonder if you ever really felt anything at all and how could you fall so hard so fast and then just *poof*, feel like it's nothing. You move on with your life, put it down to making memories, and live happily. Until you see her again. The air electrifies between you, eyes collide like comets shooting through the sky, and in those moments, your world has flipped fucking upside. Gravity un-leashes you and once again, you're falling. I don't know about soul mates and all that bullshit that people like to bring it down to, but I know a bit about connection, and that shit never lies. The space between the next time you see each other can be as long as you want, and yeah, maybe you do subconsciously build a shield that gives you false security, making you think you never really had feelings for them to begin with, but that's easy to do when you're not seeing them day and day out. Feeling the magnetic pull that brought you together to begin with. It takes a second for two souls to connect. Connections never lie, and that's why when their eyes attach again after so long, I know for damn sure that Tate will be fucked.

I pulled out of the parking lot and drove us towards CK's. When we got there, I watched Madison's face morph into horror.

"Bishop. I swear to God, if I get a riddle text, I'll kill you. I'm not playing around anymore."

I chuckled because her paranoia was valid. "Get out of the car." I opened my door and stretched out. The old parking lot had hay barrels drifting in the wind and old dirt was kicked up in the air from us driving in.

Madison got out of the car, holding the pizzas. "Wow. How did I not know about this place?"

I walked around to her side and took them from her. "This place used to be the spot to hang out when we were kids. They shut down years and years ago, no one really knows why because business was always good. Tate climbed out, straightening her skirt.

"I haven't been here in years." Then she opened a pizza box and took a bite.

Madison was still staring at the old amusement park. I followed her line of sight. The entryway to the park was a rainbow-colored sign that read "Cranksy Klanksy's Fun Park" in circus font. There was a single chain that linked one side of the entry to the other that had a panel with the words: "Trespassers will be prosecuted" on it.

"Come on." I took Madison's hand in mine and walked toward the entry, just as a few cars pulled up behind us. Doors shut and then Hunter and Eli ran up to us, taking a box of pizza as the rest of them laughed, heading deeper into the amusement park. I rolled my eyes.

Madison cranked her head over her shoulder to check on Tatum but she was already under Nate's arm. I shook my head and sighed. He was walking on dangerous ground unless he was serious when he said he was over Tillie

"Is it safe here?" Madison asked me as I led her deeper into the gloomy park. It was a full moon, so it wasn't too dark and the boys had torches and were running around like a pack of hyenas in heat.

"Yeah." I pulled her under my arm and kissed her head. Dropping the rest of the pizzas onto a small table, I grabbed one box and jerked my head toward the old Ferris wheel.

"Nope." She shook her head. "No, Bishop. I don't do heights."

I grinned. "Do you trust me?"

"No. Yes. No and yes."

I stepped closer to her until I could smell her sweet perfume covering the old musk smell of the park. "What is it, Kitty, do you, or don't you trust me?" I tilted my head. My eyes fell to her lips when she licked her lower one and tugged it into her mouth. My dick swelled in my pants. "Fuck," I cursed under my breath, stepped forward and yanked her in the direction of the Ferris wheel.

"Promise me we will stay low."

"I promise." This time. The next time I brought her here, we were going to the top. She finally relaxed and stopped fighting against my hold. I ducked under the chains and she followed.

"Bishop..." she warned as we got closer to the floating chairs.

"Get in, Kitty."

I stepped in first and sat down. It swung from my weight, but I was forty percent certain it was safe. Madison slowly stepped onto the thick plastic. When it moved, she squealed and then pounced on my lap.

"You're cute as fuck." I swiped her hair out of the way from her face and she blushed before sliding off my lap and sitting beside me. After a few seconds, I felt her body visibly relax from under my arm.

"Not so bad, huh?" I asked her, my eyebrow quirked.

She looked behind us, her eyes running over all the metal and hinges—that were no doubt rusted. "I guess not."

"Next time, we'll go to the top."

She faltered. "Sure."

I laughed again, then my laughter died out. "Shit might get ugly tomorrow, Mads." I turned to face her. The beam from the moonlight hitting every angle of her features. Her swollen lips, sunken in cheekbones, slightly pointed chin and thick eyelashes. I always noticed that she had two prominent points on her forehead too. She was by far the most beautiful girl I had ever laid eyes on. There wasn't a speck of imperfection on her, but the thing that I loved most about her, was that she was oblivious to how beautiful she was. She never flaunted it like Tate did, and never tried to hide it like Tillie did. She was just... Madison. Herself, constantly. It was intimidating and inspiring how secure she was in her own skin.

She looked straight ahead, grabbing the strands of hair off her face that had swept up with the wind. "Doesn't it always?" She smiled briefly, then turned serious, her eyes coming to mine. "I can't have anything bad happen to you or Daemon, or Tate, or Nate, or—" she laughed, shaking her head. "Or any of the Kings. God, Bishop." She brought her attention back to me. "My list of people who I give a shit about has extended extremely."

That brought a smile to my face because these boys were my brothers, so to hear that she cared about them took a load off my shoulders. I never doubted her anyway, that's just who she was, but we had done fucked up shit to her in the past. I wasn't sure whether that had done some permanent psychological damage to her. Guess time would tell how deep the scars were, especially the ones that were signed with my initials.

I squeezed her to me. "I know."

She rested her head on my chest and snuggled into me more. She wasn't short, but she was tiny up against me. "Tell me your favorite color." She yawned, lacing her fingers with mine.

"Black. Yours?"

She giggled. "Mine's blue. Well, more like a teal color. A mix of green and blue, but more of a green. It's like that pastel color."

"You couldn't just say red or something simple," I snorted. That was part of her charm.

She shook her head against my chest. "No, I'm not simple, so you should probably run away now."

"Sorry, baby, running shoes don't go with my outfit."

She giggled, the high pitch notes of it hitting the lifeless rides. Her laugh itself could breathe life back into the dead, let alone this abandoned amusement park.

Her laughter died out, then she tilted her head up to look at me from under my arm. Our eyes stayed locked together until my chest fucking tightened. "What?" I whispered, my eyes falling to her lips.

"Is this real?"

"If it's not, I'll kill the mother fucker who created it."

"I can't live without you, Bishop."

"Shhh." I pulled her head back under my arm. I wasn't going to tell her that she wouldn't have to worry about that. At least not until we had come back from Perdita.

We were driving back out to the cabin. The rest of the cars following behind me. Tate had jumped in with Nate, and Hunter tried to jump in with us, but I kicked everyone out. The more time I spent with Madison, where it was just her and I, I started craving more of it. The pups will have to learn to give us some space.

"I love this song." Madison bobbed her head, turning the music up.

"What's it called?" I asked. Usually, this kind of music wasn't really my thing, but the voice, lyrics, and beat was catchy.

"It's Nikyee Heaton 'I'm Ready'…" she smiled at me looking out of the corner of her eye. "Most of her songs are about love and sex, mostly sex."

"Fitting lyrics."

"Yup!" She popped the P. "Which is mainly why I love this song."

She turned it up louder and then hit repeat when it ended. By the time we were pulling down the private driveway to the cabin, I was pretty sure I knew every lyric to the song.

We both got out and shut the doors as the rest of the cars pulled up. It was hitting close to midnight, so I threw up deuces to the guys and led Madison inside and up to the master bedroom. The cabin had been in our family for generations. The main level had a full wrap porch, the whole house built from tarnished logs. Then there was the second level that had around five bedrooms, and then the master bedroom took up the entire third level with a wraparound glass wall so you have a full view of the grounds. My dad created this extension, him and his paranoia, but the cabin itself had been in our family for generations. I swore the ghosts of my ancestors still walked these halls, and proof would have it that that wasn't a very reassuring thing to feel.

"Wow." Madison ran her hand down the old four-post wooden bed. The engravings in the wood filled with intricate designs and patterns. "I swear nothing should surprise me anymore." She yawned and stretched her arms above but flinched.

I removed Nate's clothes and tossed them into the corner before pulling the covers back. "You alright?"

She flushed. "Fine." Then tossed her clothes off and onto the floor. I stilled when I saw the blue and black bruising around her thighs, arms, and even slightly around her neck.

"Fuck." I shot off the bed toward her.

"What?" She panicked, then her eyes dropped down to her thighs. She relaxed. "Oh," she pulled the covers back and slid into the sheets.

"No, Mads, not 'oh.'"

"What's the big deal?" She yawned again. She was tired, so I didn't want to annoy her. I sunk into the bed and pulled her into me. "I'll try to go softer, but I can't guarantee it."

She shot off the bed as if she wasn't just yawning like someone who hadn't slept in weeks. "No. Don't. I love it."

I paused, trying to pick up any dishonesty, then sighed. "Thank fuck, because I honestly can't help myself. Now get back here. I won't fuck you tonight, but in the morning, your ass is mine."

CHAPTER 21

"This sort of feels like our last feast…" Tate mumbled around her pancake.

I rolled my eyes.

Nate sneered at her with his lip curled—as if he didn't have his tongue down her throat last night.

Bishop laughed. "It could be…" Eyes fell on him, but he brushed them off. I so desperately wanted to ask what was about to happen, but the other side of me would rather not know until I got there.

"Girl can cook!" Hunter was onto his fourth pancake. I must've made over one hundred pancakes this morning, and match that with pounds of greasy bacon, about twenty-four eggs (scrambled), and an ungodly amount of bread, and you have a casual breakfast for the Kings. It took Tate and I hours this morning, but I was adamant to do it. These guys had turned into family, closer than some of my blood family. When I looked around the table at all their faces, I now understood the saying *blood means nothing, loyalty means everything*. Because time and time again, it had been these boys who had shown their loyalty to me. Yeah, so they've also put me in harm's way, almost run me over, chased me through a forest in the dark night, fucked with my head, and I'm probably missing a few other things, but above all, they're my family.

"You ok?" Bishop's arm snaked around the back of my neck, pulling me into his chest. He was wearing a dark hoodie, relaxed jeans, white high-top sneakers and I knew for a fact that he had his white Armani briefs on underneath. Images flashed through my head of our four a.m. sexfest and suddenly, my thighs were clenching, my cheeks were flushed, and my bottom lip was being pulled between my teeth. His fingers tightened on my shoulder. "Kitty…" he warned through a growl, but it was too late, I was already back there…

Warmth covered my nipple, and I groaned, slowly coming back into consciousness. Sweat already licked my flesh and my pussy throbbed from being woken.

"Mmmm, what's the time?" I asked through my sleepy slumber. He didn't answer, and slowly I cracked my eyes open but was met with nothing but opal darkness with the shadow of Bishop hovering above me. His mouth dropped to mine and I parted my lips, stretching my legs wide. He settled between them, his naked skin rubbing on me. His dick slowly sunk inside of me. Heavy breathing fell over my mouth as he slowly pulled out and then dipped back in. My arms came around the back of his neck. His tongue licked the edge of my lips, then traced down my

neck, sucking on my collarbone. He continued his slow thrusting, Beads of sweat dripped from his forehead and fell onto my face, creating a whirl mixing with my own. His arm snaked around the back of my neck. It was humanly impossible to get closer to anyone than what we were right now. He filled me everywhere and engulfed me completely. He slowly rode my body, not saying a word. His mouth came back to mine, kissing me, eating me, relishing me. His kisses turned slow, sensual and tentative as his thirst deepened. The pace was slow, but the depth was brutal. Lights flickered in my head from the pleasure. My core was extracting and my pussy was tightening. He was making love to me and I never wanted it to end. Our bodies slapped together like mush, the perfect melody of sexual perfection. His mouth never moved from mine, his tongue never stopping the deep caressing. My body locked up, my muscles holding on to every single feeling it was receiving until I combusted, my orgasm drowning me with the anchor wrapped around my ankle. Bishop groaned into my mouth as his cock throbbed against my saturated walls, and then his sweaty body fell to mine in deep breaths, pulling me into the spooning position and kissing my head. "Sleep."

My palms tickled with sweat and my body temperature kicked up to an unnatural level.

"Sorry," I answered, bringing my eyes to his but hiding my chin behind my shoulder. I gave him a small teasing smile before clearing my throat and getting back to more pressing issues. Like Nate and Tate already arguing.

"Guys," I snapped at them both. "Please shut the fuck up. I don't want to have to listen to this shit through a two-hour flight."

"Word," Cash muttered, getting to his feet while pulling out a smoke. He put it into his mouth and went to light up.

"Um, and you can smoke that outside."

Bishop's body was shaking beside me and I whipped my head around to look at him. He was hiding his laughing behind his hand. "Why are you laughing?"

Bishop coughed, shook his head and cleared his throat. "Nothing, baby. You're just a little moody today."

My face relaxed a little, realization sinking. "Oh." A wave of guilt washed over me and my cheeks heated. "I'm sorry."

"She's either hungry or needs a nap." Nate pointed to me with a floppy pancake.

My eyes shot down to the cooked flour and then went back to his eyes. "Well, Nate," I seethed, getting to my feet. "I had a great sleep last night and I've eaten enough this morning."

"Baby girl, you aren't fooling no one. We heard your moans through the fucking walls early this morning."

I rolled my eyes and headed for the front door. Stupid boys. Cash was sucking on his cancer stick, his eyes squinting from the smoke. It was a habit I noticed they all shared, except Nate and Jase. I had seen Nate smoke cigarettes maybe once, and that was the night he found out about my past. Other than that, he mainly sticks to pot.

The door closed behind me and Cash grinned, blowing smoke out in front of him.

"Sorry," I mumbled, crossing my arms in front of myself. "For snapping at you back there."

He shrugged, flicking the ash off the tip of his smoke. "Not bothered, babe." I ran my eyes over Cash. I hadn't really had much bonding time with Cash as I have had with the others. Same with Eli, Ace, and Saint, but all though we may not have a huge relationship like I did with Nate, Bishop, Brantley, Hunter and Jase—I still cared for them. The invisible bond between us all remained tight around my neck, like a noose. Cash had on dark jeans, combat boots, and a dark shirt. He always had a five o'clock shadow that scattered his fine jaw, and his eyes were as dark as Brantley's, only not as tortured. He had dark floppy hair that he kept shaved close to the scalp on the sides and a beauty spot was below his right eye. He reminded me of one of the One Direction guys, I couldn't tell you which one. The hot one. He flashed his long eyelashes and gazed out straight ahead. "Why are you looking at me like I'm something to eat?"

I snorted and took a seat on the step in front of us. He stayed standing, his legs crossing at his ankles and his shoulder leaning on the beam. "I'm not. I just, I guess…"

"Scared?" he answered for me, and then sat down beside me. His knee brushed against mine.

"Yeah, I guess." I tucked my long hair behind my ear, wishing I had tied it up now. I chose black tights, my white Converse with the red stripes, and a light loose t-shirt that hung around my ass. It was me, comfortable enough to run if needed.

"You have every reason to be scared, Mads. Perdita is no joke, in fact, we were all surprised Bishop agreed to letting you ride."

I looked at him, my eyebrows tugging in. "Really? I mean, that wasn't why I was afraid."

His eyes searched mine. "Daemon?"

I nodded. "Yeah. I just…" I looked out straight ahead. "I can't live without him and it's terrifying to have the fate of your happiness in the hands of someone else, you know?"

Cash kept a straight face. "Nah, babe. I can't say I do know, but, I can hear what you're saying."

I snorted, shaking my head. "Have none of you boys ever fallen in love?" I quirk an eyebrow at him, dropping my Ray Bans over my eyes.

"I didn't say that…"

"Ohhh…" I lean back on my elbows and stretch my legs out in front of myself, raking my hair out of my face. "You have to tell me the gossip."

He didn't look at me, his focus remained solely in front of himself, but I could see the grin that stretched his cheeks. He took another puff of his smoke. "Who would be the King you would least expect to show love?"

I didn't need to think long. "Brantley."

His grin deepened and he turned to face me. "There's your answer."

Confusion pulled at me. Brantley had loved someone before? No way. He must see the shock—I made no effort to hide it. "Baby girl, you really need to stop making assumptions."

"Wow, I'm not, I'm just, I guess shocked."

Cash flicked the smoke out to the dirt at the bottom of the steps. "It was a long time ago and didn't end well, so we don't talk about it, but she still haunts him in his sleep."

"…His nightmares," I whispered out in realization. It was more for myself than for Cash. That was what Brantley had nightmares about? I always assumed it had something to do with his fucked up dad.

"And that…" Cash answered my unspoken thoughts.

"That's deep…"

"The depth of Brantley Vitiosis is an endless pit of lava. Don't go down that road, baby girl. Only one person could've saved him, and she's not here."

I didn't want to press the subject any more than I already had, so I opted to change topics. "I really hope Nate and Tate don't fight the whole way."

"Oh, I have no doubt they will," Cash laughed, getting to his feet. He reached for my hand to help me up and I took it, dusting off my pants.

"Thanks for the chat." He winked and then walked back inside, just as Bishop was exiting.

"You bonding now?" He grinned, carrying our duffle bags.

I smiled at him. "You know, it's amazing the things you learn when one is alone with a King."

"Easy, Kitty..."

He dived for me, his arm wrapping around my waist to pull me into him. He snapped at my lip, his teeth sinking into my flesh and pulled back. His eyes fell to my mouth and then came back to my eyes. "You don't wanna be the next missing person case over the Bermuda Triangle, do you?" He said it with such seriousness that my laughter quickly died out as I turned and watched him carry our bags to his Maserati.

"Not funny!" I hollered out.

His head tipped back in laughter.

Asshole.

I smiled. He was an asshole, and I loved it. I wouldn't ever want Bishop any other way. Even though we're an item now, and even though he's mine and I'm his officially, he was still the same Bishop. He wasn't some watered down version of himself just because of me. A loud slap sounded out just as my ass cheek stung in pain. I yelped and grabbed onto my cheek, turning to see who the fuck wanted a knuckle sandwich.

"Come on, bitch. I'm ready!"

"Tate!" I scolded her as she brushed past me and made her way to the Maserati instead of Nate's Audi. "Um, why don't you ride with Nate so you can both have a chat about how you're *not* going to argue on the plane ride!" I yelled out, just as she dropped her bag into the trunk of Bishop's car.

"How about no! Because you might be down a brother if I do."

Jesus. Nate came up next to me, shoving an apple into his mouth. "What did you do?" I didn't look at him, my eyes stayed on Tate.

"What did *I* do?" he asked, turning to me. I finally looked at him as he crunched down on his apple. "What I did was be honest with her. It's not my fault she can't handle it."

"But were you nice, though?" I quirked an eyebrow at him.

His eyes darted over my shoulder absently. "I'm always nice."

"Nate!" I punched his shoulder.

"Ouch!" He rubbed his wound. "That wasn't very nice, sis."

"Pot meet kettle."

He rolled his eyes and walked down the steps. "I've always told her from day one that I ain't with relationships. It's her that couldn't handle it." Somehow, I feel like there's something he isn't telling me, and if that's the case, I'll be disappointed. I thought we were all beyond that stage. I headed down and climbed into the front seat, shutting the door behind myself. Bishop was still talking with Saint and Chase, so I turned in my seat to face Tate who was looking absently out the window.

"What is going on? And don't lie to me, T."

She sighed. "He pulls me in, makes me feel things, gives me incredible sex and tells me everything I want to hear, and then after all the excitement is done, he goes back to telling me that I'm just a bit of fun and that we can't go anywhere."

"Congratulations, you're sleeping with a male."

She laughed a little at that, which made my heart a little happier, then her eyes came to mine. "I'm serious, Mads. It's seriously fucking with my head, and I'm such an idiot because I keep going back to him like a fucking twat. I've turned into one of those girls I make fun of."

"Well, yes, you were a dick for making fun of those girls, but Tate, give yourself a break. Not only is Nate, well, —"

"—Hot, dangerous, sexy wrapped in tattoo's, piercings, and muscles?" she ended for me.

"Well, yes, that, but what I was going to say is that you're a girl, Tate. We do this. You're not alone. My advice, if you want it, is to stay away from him until you can grasp your feelings, or else you're making this too easy for him and also, every time this happens you sink deeper and deeper into feelings. It's a pointless dive."

"Because he loves Tillie." Her face fell and she went back to looking out the window. "You know," her tone turned angry. Hopefully Bishop waited until I had cooled her down before jumping into the car. "I don't fucking get it! She is *not* even here. She ran away and left all of us! He had been with her once! Like they haven't even shared the same memories as he and I have." I wanted to bite my tongue, but she was beginning to get silly over it.

"Tate, all that shit doesn't matter when it comes to that *one* person, and I know that will be hard for you to hear, but when you get that person, you'll understand. You could have a million memories and good times with someone, but if that someone is in love with someone else, that single memory doesn't mean anything up against even *one* memory of the person they truly love." I turned back to face the front of the car because my neck felt as though it was cramping up. "I love you, you know this, and I do think Nate has feelings for you, but I had seen him with Tillie too, babe, and I'm not saying this to hurt you. I'm saying this so you can prepare yourself for that day she may turn back up, okay?" I looked in the side mirror and she swept a tear from her cheek, not knowing I could see her.

She cleared her throat. "Yeah, you're right. I won't go there again. But I hope she comes back in one piece too. I'm starting to get worried." Something about her tone told me that this time, she was serious about not sleeping with him.

"Me too."

CHAPTER 22

"Did we bring snacks?" Tate asked, buckling into her seat belt in front of Bishop and I. She was beside Cash now, with Nate at the very back of the jet—alone. Where he should be. I couldn't be angry at him. He had been nothing but honest with Tate, but if he had been stringing her along too, I'd be having words with him when we get home. Fucker.

"You don't need snacks. We just had breakfast. It's not like we're flying to Europe."

"There's a thought," she muttered, so quiet I almost missed it. "Oh!" She bent around her seat to look at me. "We should do Europe for your birthday, Mads! Oh my God!"

I shook my head at her, giving her the universal glare that silently screamed 'shut the fuck up.'

She returned my unspoken words with her own dirty stare. "Oh please. He already knows your fucking birthday is in a couple of weeks. Twat."

"Is twat your new favorite word?" I asked politely once she had turned back in her seat.

"Apparently. But seriously, we should hit Greece."

"I just want to get through all this bullshit first." I looked up at Bishop, who was already watching me.

"It's cute that you thought I wouldn't know about your birthday."

"I guess, but I don't know. I've never made a big deal about my birthday before, so I didn't see the point in telling you."

"What? You've never had a party?"

I shook my head and squirmed. "Oh, no. Contrary to what you may think, I don't really like the attention on me."

His arm came around my shoulders as the seat belt light flickered on. The pilot yapped off about preparing for take-off, just as Bishop's lips came to my ear. "Actually, Kitty, I know exactly what you're like." Then he bit on my earlobe and I had to squeeze the armrest to stop from straddling his lap. My eyes darted down to his destroyed denim jeans and how they hung casually off his slim waist. His other hand came to his crotch. He squeezed his junk. My eyes shut and I sucked in a breath of air.

"Like what you see, Kitty?" His voice vibrated over my flesh.

"Bishop…" I warned through a shaky breath.

He chuckled and pulled away from me, leaning back in his chair. "Because I need you focused, I won't fuck you up against the wall in the back cabin, but on the way home…"

Needing to take my mind out of Bishop and his sexcapades, I pulled my phone out and opened Spotify. Grabbing my ear pods out of my pocket, I untangled them and put them into my ear. The plane began speeding down the runway and I watched as the asphalt slowly started to disappear, and all that was in view was the thick clouds and the sinking city. One of my ear pods getting pulled out of my ear snapped me out of my daydream and Bishop took my phone from me.

"Listen to this song…" Out of any other guy's mouth, that would be cheesy, but this was Bishop. He wasn't cheesy. He wasn't a broken ass loved-up fool. He was just *Bishop*. Once you knew him, his name alone was like warm, rich hot chocolate sliding down your throat on a snowy winter's day. With added whiskey…

"Sure." I smiled at him. He started flicking through my music, and then he pushed play on a song that had an electric guitar opening it. A guy's smooth voice filled my ears. By the time the hook came in, I had goosebumps breaking out over my skin. The lyrics, the electric sound, the fact that this song meant something to Bishop. I was about to choke on the rock of emotion that had appeared in my throat.

"What's the song called?" I managed to choke out.

His eyes searched mine. "'Torn to Pieces' by Pop Evil."

"I love it." A small smile slid over my mouth, and I took the phone from him, opening a new playlist on Spotify. I thought about it quickly and then smiled while typing out *"Madship's Playlist"* I began adding all the songs that we had listened to previously into the playlist. One of them caught my attention.

"This song is one of my favorites." I pushed play on "I'm Ready" by Nikye Heaton.

He chuckled. "Yeah, you do love this song, huh." He took my phone back and flicked through.

"I do," I nodded. "It resonates with me on a deep level when it comes to us, I guess."

His finger paused for a second, his eyes flicking to me briefly before he continued to scroll through.

The song finished and then Bullet for my Valentine "Your Betrayal" started playing. I giggle-snorted—straight ugly snorted—when I heard it.

"That day at the lake?" I smirked, my eyes coming to his.

"You remembered?"

"Your face was buried between my thighs while our friends were doing backflips off rocks in the water fifty meters away from us—yes, I remember. I remember this song was playing from Nate's sound dock." My eyes glassed over from the memories. "God, it feels like so long ago. Put that in our playlist." He does something on my phone, and then pulled out his. He started fiddling around with both phones and then tucked his away.

"I joined our playlist to both our accounts. Now we can both add songs to it for the other to listen to."

The gesture may have sounded normal to most people, but again, this was Bishop, and I'm still warming up to this side of him. The caring side. Receiving love from someone who spent so much time hating you gives you a euphoric high that no drug could ever give you. It was intoxicating, deadly, and completely addictive. I took my phone since he could now use his, then pushed play on "Stupid Love" from Jason Derulo.

"Really?" he deadpanned.

I shrugged, sliding the song to our playlist. "It came on when we were on our way to the airport to fly to New Zealand. It connected with me around that time so it's going in."

His eyes narrowed.

I narrowed mine back.

"You wanna play? Okay, let's play."

"What are you, Tony Montana," I teased, and watched as his thumb shuffled through the songs on his phone. "Killpop" from Slipknot started playing.

I tried listening to the lyrics, even though I was acquainted with the song.

"Isn't this about a drug dealer who falls in love with his junkie?" I raised my eyebrow at him.

A beat passed, and then he slowly raised his eyebrows. Realization sunk in pretty quickly once I had just choked on my own words. "Oh, well, then, it's perfect."

"Hey." He tilted my head to face him. "This shit with you and I, it's always been messy, fucking chaotic, but that's just us. Don't resent that, baby."

"I'd never." I shook my head. Halestorm "I'm no Angel" started playing next, and I leaned my head on Bishop's shoulder. His arm came up again, pulling me into his side so my face smashed into him. I loved his scent. I wished I could bottle it up and carry it around with me. Leather, soap, man, and mint. "I've been through a lot of traumatic things in my life, as you know, and up until the point I met you, I would have given anything and everything to change my past. But, if I had to go through all those things to meet you, then I wouldn't change a thing. You're well worth it, Bishop."

He was silent, so I figured he may not have heard me, and before I knew it, my eyes closed and I fell into a deep sleep.

CHAPTER 23

"Baby, wake up."

My eyes popped open and I stretched my arms wide. "Are we there?"

"Yeah." He stood, tugging me to my feet. Nate had Tate huddled in his arms, her head in his neck. What the actual fuck. Those two confuse me like no other. Bishop must see my puzzlement.

"She was asleep. Don't think into it." As they disappeared out the door, I stepped aside to let Jase and Saint pass.

"Are you trying to convince me that he doesn't care?"

Bishop took my hand and led me down the walkway. "I didn't say that he didn't care—just not enough…"

I rubbed the palm of my hand into my eye, feeling almost defeated by his words. "You boys."

"Not me. They, and I, always knew with *you*. Nate, and us, and you, know that's not the case with Tatum."

I sighed, then started shuffling out of the plane. "I guess. I just wish she didn't need to get hurt." Once we come to the door, I sucked in a breath. "What is this place?" The airstrip was lined with dark bushes and tall accent stone statues, carved with thick patterns shaping weird faces and moss spilling out from the cracks. The air smelled of tropical leaves with a slight spritz of saltwater. I cranked my head to find any sign of life.

"Where's the airport?"

Bishop snorted, taking my hand and leading me down the stairs. "You won't find an airport here, Kitty." I stayed quiet, unsure what to say. I didn't know what I was expecting, but it wasn't this. I expected more life. There were three white Mercedes trucks waiting for us that were square in shape and resembled military tanks. I faltered, and just as Tatum was about to slide into one of them with Nate's hand on her lower back, she sent me a playful wink. I smiled at her reassuringly, but I wasn't so sure. I felt like a fraud giving her that smile, but there was only so much people could do to help someone before it became too exhausting. Bishop started to lead us toward the truck at the front of the other two and pointed to the passenger door.

"Get in and put your belt on."

I followed orders, opening the door and quickly clicking my belt on. I felt a sense of urgency rush through me. Like we were on borrowed time. The back doors swung open as Nate, Hunter, and Jase slid into the back. Bishop got into the driver's seat beside me.

"This feels a little tense." I glanced out the window, unease slowly seeping in.

"Because it is," Nate mumbled in the back. Bishop's eyes shot to him in the rearview mirror before putting the truck into first and flooring us out of there. The silence that fell was comfortable, and actually, I preferred it. This way I could take in my surroundings without having to maintain small talk. I watched as the thick shrubs started to morph and melt into the fat green wild forest, and the asphalt road transformed to dirt. The closeness of the overgrown trees, long grass and wilderness made it feel like our trip was more of the off-road trip. I turned in my seat to see the other two trucks still behind us, my panicking semi-subsided. My eyes dropped down to Jase's lap, and then to Hunter's and Nate's, all to catch them loading up AK's.

"Why do I feel like we're walking into a war zone?" I turned back in my seat, my hands skimming over the metal door. I bet if I googled this make of Mercedes, it would tell me it was bulletproof.

"Because we are," Bishop replied casually, flooring it. We shot forward faster, so fast that I could no longer enjoy the scenery outside because everything looked like an oil paint mixture gone wrong.

"Nate, what are you doing with Tatum?" I asked.

"Mads, I don't think this is the right time to ask me that."

"Well, why did you put her in with Eli and Saint?"

"Because we all wanted to be near you, and you're my priority."

I sighed, resting my head on the cool window. "Why are you stringing her along then?"

He sneered. "I'm not, and sis, this really isn't the time, but know that she knows exactly where I stand and where I've always stood. I've been nothing but honest with her, it's not my fault if she allows her feelings to control her."

"Nate? Just stay away from her, please."

Silence.

"I need to tell you something, but I didn't want to until we got here, because I didn't want you to have to be stressing all the way"—Bishop's eyes came to mine—"Ok?"

"Ok?" I answered.

"The reason we're here is because Daemon called me yesterday. He sounded…off."

I froze. My heartbeat slowed to a thunderous pace. "Wha—what?" Then just like that, everything zipped back into real time. "What!" I screamed, frantically looking around. "What do you mean *off*?"

"See" Bishop rolled his eyes. "I made the right decision," he shot a stare at someone in the back through the rearview mirror.

"Someone better start talking…" I warned.

Bishop shuffled in his seat, cutting a hard left turn and onto a track that barely looked like a track. Branches slapped the windshield like thunder and the wheels of the truck dipped us low and high through the bumpy puddles. "He called me yesterday and the call cut out. I couldn't get through to him after that, but from what he told me, it's not looking good here right now."

I massaged my temples. "Bishop, please cut the shit."

"Through the broken speech, I made out Silver Swan and Madison, and that's it.

Then the call was cut. Hearing that, put us all on high alert. I called Dad and he dispatched us here to check things out. If we need, we can have more back up, but we've never needed it before. This island, it's separated by four fractions, but all within a vast gated community. *Nihil* (Nil), *Regiis* (Royal), *Secundus* (Second), *and Tertuim* (third). Each faction is chosen by your family lineage and how important you are. Everyone is fluent in Latin, hardly any speak English. I need you to stay directly beside me."

"I'm sure we'll be fine," Nate mumbled off more to himself, I was guessing by the volume of his answer.

"People, Nate. They're just people."

"So that's why we're here? Because it's a threat to me? Daemon mentioning me and then something about a Silver Swan?"

Bishop nodded reluctantly. "I think so, and because I wanted to check on Daemon."

My heart warmed a little by his confession. Whether it was entirely true or not, I couldn't care right now.

"Okay." I shook off all of my other feelings and straightened my head. "So what's the worst that could be happening right now?"

Bishop cleared his throat. "The worst would be that Daemon is dead, Katsia has gone rogue, and the Lost Boys have finally taken ownership of the island. There would be riots and havoc, so we do not want this one."

My eyes closed as my chest tightened. "No. That can't be an option."

"The other one is that my instincts have gone to shit and I'm wrong."

"Shit," I exhaled, my chest squeezing again. "That's obviously not an option either, but there's no way about Daemon."

Bishop nodded. "Agreed. He will most likely be safe because he's smart and strong, but I really fucking hope I'm wrong about everything." The bumps started dipping harder. My head almost smashing against the roof of the truck.

CHAPTER 24

"Bishop! This place is fucking creepy!" Khales ran up behind me, tossing her hair into a high ponytail. "Do you come here often? Is this your secret playground? Is there cake here?"

I chuckled. "Shut up. No, I don't come here often. I have to run an errand for my dad."

She looked around the little township in skepticism. "This is an errand?"

I shrugged and pointed to one of the little shops. "There's cake here."

Khales eyes lit up, then she grabbed onto my hands and pulled me toward the cake shop. The bell dinged up ahead as we entered. I shook my head. "You'd be too easy to kidnap you know. Just wave some cake and they've got you."

"Ah, but will they keep me, that's the question…" She winked and skipped the rest of the way to the counter where a glass cabinet displayed all sorts of different cakes cut into delicate slices and sitting on tiny plates. I turned to look outside, a shiver of terror running through my veins, but I was met with people wandering down the dark street, the only light coming from the fairy lights dangling ahead of them. Some were dressed in gym gear, some were in suits and armor. Perdita was an odd place, but it was all these people knew. It looked pretty on the surface, but most of these people weren't aware what laid below their feet. They lived, thinking that this was the only life available. Generations back, there was a crock of shit cooked up to make them believe there was an apocalypse that wiped out the rest of humanity. They were caged in the town, without a clue. It was really just a well made-up story that started generations ago, all for what? Power. Power, money, respect, and order.

"Here!" Khales handed me a piece of vanilla cake, but I shook my head.

"I'm good."

"Oh, come on, B. You need to loosen up a little. You're too tense all the time, but I get it, I mean, what…" Her voice died out in the distance as we walked out of the cake shop. People moved and parted like the red sea whenever I was here. They knew who I was, but they didn't know where I came from. Their knowledge was very limited when it came to Perdita, and they all spoke fluent Latin. No one knew English. As far as they were concerned, English was a dead language. I continued to walk down the main strip with Khales still venting beside me. I snarled at a passerby and bit at her with a grin on my face. She screamed and ran off, ushering her child away from me. I was the monster that lived under her bed.

"B! That was mean," Khales giggle-snorted, grabbing my hand.

I pulled away from her grip.

She rolled her eyes. "Oh, what, so we can fuck, but I can't hold your hand?"

"We fuck, Khales. We're friends who fuck, we're not friends who hold hands."

She grumbled something under her breath that sounded like "asshole" just as we reached the
entry to hell aka Regiis.

That was the last time I took her anywhere. Fuck she was annoying. Yanking open
Madison's door, I gestured for her to get out, but she remained frozen in her seat, her
eyes going up to the building in front of us. I couldn't blame her, the first time I saw
Perdita I was all of five years old and it looked the same scary now as it did through the
eyes of a five-year-old boy.

"Babe, come on."

She slowly gathered her wits and slid out of the truck. I wasn't sure exactly what we
were walking into, but I knew whatever it was, unless the island had really turned to shit,
we were safe. The Kings were royalty, and the Lost Boys were the shit on the bottom of
our shoe. The reason for our safety was the same reason for my apprehension, though.
They had a lot of reasons to hate us, under all their loyalty. There was one other thing
that was floating around in my head. *Tillie.*

Pulling Madison under my arm, we met the rest of the boys in the center, and then
I let my eyes come up to the main building on Perdita. The island itself was natural. With
bushlands and wildflowers growing through the soil, and animals that were only found
on this island, it was exotic, foreign and protected. It simmered behind the fog and mist
of whatever you thought you knew about not only our world but our country. Right at
the center of Perdita was where the township resided. Where we stood, there was the
entry building which was armed with guards and led you into the township. The reason
why the island remained for the most part untouched was because The Lost Boys and
Katsia's army remained behind the one-hundred-foot brick wall which circled around
their entire township. The entry, which was where we were standing in front of, was built
by the same stone. Milky white marble with streaks of black slicked through in intricate
patterns. The stone was called *de regno diabolic,* which in English translated to *The Devil's*
Kingdom.

"What the hell is this place?" Tatum whispered, walking to the other side of
Madison.

"Hell, that's what," Nate muttered, flipping his cap backward and putting a J into
his mouth.

I walked up the thick, long stairs that lead to two heavy metal doors. Reaching
for the white button that was strangely put in the center of the door, I pressed it, then
waited.

And waited.

I don't like waiting.

I turned back around to see Madison walking up the steps with the rest following
her. Exhaling, I rested my head on the door, waiting. A loud lock slid across from the
other side of the door, vibrating my head. I shot up and spun around. The door cranked
open wider.

"Boys."

Madison gasped. "Mrs. Winters?"

She grinned, then her eyes came directly to me. "I heard my niece is back from the
dead?" Her eyebrow rose. Fucking Khales.

"Your niece is a whore." I shoved the door open and walked closer to her, only her guard who was dressed in steel armor (like he had just walked off the set of a Game of Thrones episode) put himself between both of us.

"Aw." I tilted my head at the man in armor. I could see the bead of sweat coming down the center of his forehead between his eyebrows. "Tinker, why don't you tell your Peter to move his shit before I snap his neck." I ended my threat with a small smile and a wink.

She rolled her eyes, pushing him away. "He's not *my* Peter, you and I both know who that is." She gestured, the door opened farther. "Well, come on then. We were expecting you to come, just weren't sure when."

I walked farther in without looking back, my hand flew out behind myself and caught Madison's. I pulled her behind my back protectively. Tinker gave me a look. "B, you kn—"

"—Shut the fuck up, Tinker," Jase sneered at her. Instantly her mouth slammed shut. She pushed her glasses up her nose, straightening her shoulders. Good to know Jase still owns that shit.

I chuckled, shaking my head. "Some shit will just never change."

"That's a bit rich…" she started, and I swung around, eyebrows raised.

"What's that?"

She shut the door in a huff and then gestured out with her hand. "Well, come on then." We walked through the old building and out onto the township.

Madison's eyes were flying around everywhere. "Wow. It's really, beautiful in here."

"Don't let this shit fool you," Hunter grunted, walking past us and taking the lead behind Tinker.

"He's right." We began following Tinker down the steps and into the small township. There were small stores lined on every side of the main street which was lined with lilac daisies and black roses. Each store had their own signage out the front. *Weapons.* One read, with the next, *Food,* and the next, *medical supplies, hospital, gym,* as we walked past each one, Madison noticed how there were no people wandering around.

I watched as her head turned to me out of the corner of my eye.

"It's daylight. Everything is backward here. They're nocturnal. Sleep during the day, and work, shop, everyday shit we do during the night."

"So strange." Her interest grew the farther we went in. Slowly, the purple flowers began to sink into the dark roses until there was no more color. We reached the end of the main street and the stone had come back, leading upstairs that once again, brought you to two heavy metal doors.

Madison turned around with Tatum copying her. "What? Is that it?"

Tinker pressed the button on the door. "No. And girls, if you want to live, I would watch your words beyond this door."

My eyes cut to Tinker. "Threaten them again and I'll slice your fucking neck like I did your mother. Open the fucking door. I'm done playing games, Tinker."

Madison stilled beside me, her hand squeezing mine instantly. The gesture in itself was cute, but I wasn't mad or raging. I hardly ever lost my cool, which was exactly why I was where I was.

Tinker's face flushed. "Sorry." She opened the door out onto the stone floor and lobby to what looked like a normal mansion home entry. Only it wasn't a normal home.

Soft piano music was whispering through the air, and I pushed Madison back, walking in first. Nate was behind me, and then Jase, Hunter, Saint, and whoever else followed. Madison was second to last, sandwiched between Eli and Cash.

"Well, well, well, to what do I owe the pleasure of having the elite in my home?" Katsia came walking down the spiral stairs in nothing but a white silk robe, displaying her black lace panties and bra. Her hair was messed up and falling over her shoulders. She had a glass of scotch dangling from her hand. Running her fingers through her hair to push it out of her face, her eyes raked down my body.

"You're growing well, B." She licked her lips and then curled her finger. "Come on, we can talk in the sitting room. You woke me."

"We woke you?" I rose an eyebrow.

She bit her lip, flashing me a grin over her shoulder. "Well, sort of." The story of Katsia was a complicated one. *Katsia Stuprum.* In English, she was Seduction. She oozed sex, even when she wasn't trying. There were rumors that said she would do things to the Lost Boys, and I wasn't sure how much of that was true, but Katsia being Katsia, I was sure the boys would be fighting to get into her bed.

She had fucked all of the Kings in our generation and everyone in Jase and Saints generation - bar one, too, but not me. Not from lack of trying on her part, because she had, but she wasn't my type, and I don't mean the age. I mean just the her.

She pushed open doors that were at the end of the corridor and they spread out onto a sitting room that looked the size of a basketball court. There was a large gas fire lit and sitting in the middle of the vast space with lazy boys scattered out of order. There was a large U-shaped sofa that faced one cosmic floor to ceiling window. It gave you a direct view to the ocean. The white silica-like sand was immediately right there, and the pearl crystal ocean was crashing against the untouched rocks.

"Jesus," Tate exhaled, nudging Madison.

I took a seat on the sofa and pulled Madison down beside me. There was a large white leather hand-shaped chair which was opposite us, where Katsia took a seat, with two armored guards standing on either side of her. She crossed her legs, smirked, and then took a sip of her drink. "Good to see you again, Madison. Not surprised but slightly disappointed that you're still alive."

Madison didn't reply, she remained impassive as her arm brushed against mine. I leaned back on the couch, allowing my arm to go over the edge of it, pulling her into me more.

"What's going on, Katsia? Why the fuck am I getting phone calls?"

She cleared her throat, resting her glass on her knee. "Who do I have to fuck to get out of this?"

"You can't fuck your way out of this one. You have someone who is one of our own."

Her eyes came to mine, and behind the seductive glare, I saw a stroke of annoyance. Good. I want her angry because that's the only way to get truth out of Katsia.

"He is not *yours*, he is *mine*." Her eyes finally rested on Madison where she dropped her stare to icy levels. "Blood or no blood, make no mistake, he is mine."

Madison shuffled in her seat. "Um, so I'm confused, are you talking about my brother? Because if you are, trust me, he's all yours, but I just want to make sure he's safe."

Katsia's eyes slowly rolled, her smile coming back to her face. "As safe as he'll ever be." Then she looked at me. "But that's not speaking for all."

Fuck.

CHAPTER 25

I could feel the slight twitch in Bishop's arm as soon as Katsia said 'but that's not speaking for all.' I turned my attention to her. "What does that mean?"

Her smug smirk deepened. "Oh, he didn't tell you…"

"Tell her what?" Nate interjected, leaning forward on his elbows.

Katsia burst out laughing, her head tilting back while she swirled the whiskey around in her glass. "Oh this is great." Her eyes cut to Bishop. "You're quite the secret keeper, King."

"What the fuck is she talking about?" I whispered, my eyes fluttering closed.

Nate tilted his head, his eyes flying to Bishop briefly.

"I didn't tell either of them because it's a distraction."

"And you gave her your word…" Katsia's eyebrow quirked.

"My word doesn't mean shit with anyone else but a King or Madison. I would break it in a heartbeat if I needed to, but I didn't need to," he challenged Katsia.

I shuffled uncomfortably. "Well, as much as I've gotten really easy with letting you keep your secrets, I feel like I need to know this one."

"Word," Nate mumbled, leaning back. Tate's eyes were going between the three of us.

"Well," Katsia giggled, leaning forward and setting her glass on the small table in front of her. "As much as I'm loving this little thing that's going on, I'm on borrowed time, so…" She cranked her head at one of her guards, gave him a direct look and then nodded her head. The guard turned and walked out of the room. The silence that stretched out between all of us was deafening and only made me more uncomfortable. Katsia's grin was firmly fixed on her face the entire time.

The heavy footsteps broke the silence and my head swung to the opening. The guard stepped away, and— "Tillie!" I shot off the couch, my breathing sinking in shallow heaves. I couldn't believe it was really her! It was her, wasn't it? I reached out to touch her.

Katsia giggled, standing from her chair. "She's been here the whole time."

Nate stood up behind me, and I chanced a quick stare at him. His eyes were fixed on Tillie, and hers on him. "Did you know this whole time?" was all he said.

"Me?" My hand came to my chest. "No!"

"Not you." He cut his eyes down to Bishop. "You."

Bishop's jaw was ticking under the pressure; his lip was slightly curled at Katsia. "Yes."

I exhaled, my fingers coming to my temples. "What the fuck is going on?" I started walking toward Tillie, but the guard stood in front of her again, blocking me. "Get the fuck out of my way."

"Kitty," Bishop growled.

"You can shut up," I replied softly without looking at him. I was angry that her being here wasn't new information to him and that he had known for a long time—probably all of the time. "Tillie?" I tilted my head to try and get a clearer view of her behind the big man of steel in front of me. He slowly stepped aside, and it was the first time I got a real look at what she looked like now. She was in a white gown that cut off at her knees. The straps were thick and rolled over her shoulder, displaying her arms. Her face was bare of any makeup and her eyes looked like ripples of lightening laced in a blue sky. She looked broken. Her hair had been brushed down, falling over her shoulders, with the pink now washed out to a faded pastel color and her re-growth evident.

"Tillie?" I stepped toward her again. Her face fell. "Are you ok?"

She raised her head and her eyes came to mine, a single tear sneaking out. "I—I'm, I mean, I was…"

"That's enough!" Katsia snapped, and then quickly composed herself. "Take a seat with Nate, Tillie." Katsia rolled her eyes. "Before he kills me."

Tillie came toward us and as soon as she was within reach, Nate's arm snaked out and pulled her into him. He sunk her down next to him and I dropped down on the other side of her. She smelled like bleach and antiseptic. Something was going on, something that I couldn't understand—again, and until I found out exactly what it was that Bishop was hiding from me this time, I wasn't sure how I felt with him. Again. Yes, I loved him, but love should never be used as a doormat. When will this shit end. Right now, Nate needed me more than anyone else, so when his hand went over the edge of the couch, I brought my right hand up to where his curled around my shoulder and laced my fingers with his. At the connection, I felt a jolt of power and anger. Anger amongst all that Nate was a King, yet something was held from him about Tillie—*why?*

"Why?" I snapped, suddenly having enough of the song and dance and ready to put her on a plane with Daemon and fly the fuck out of this place.

"Why, what?" Katsia quirked an eyebrow at me. She was an expert at making you feel inferior, but this time, my anger wasn't going to allow me to cower to her like I had in the past.

"You know what, Katsia, cut the bullshit. Why was Tillie here?"

"Oh," Katsia waved her hand casually. "Well, she was pregnant, of course."

I sucked in a breath. My head pounded and colorful little dots danced in my bleak vision. I felt Nate's hand still in my grip. He let me go and leaned forward, resting his elbows on his knees. "*What?*" The depth of his tone was enough to put the fear of the Lord into the devil.

Tate stood from the corner of my eye and walk to the window. Bishop's leg pressed against mine roughly and I could hear the shuffling of a couple of the Kings who were standing behind me.

"Suddenly, shit makes sense," Jase mumbled, rubbing the scruff on his jaw.

Tillie swiped away the tears that were streaming down her face. "*Was* being the correct word there."

I stilled.

Bishop's leg stopped flat, and Nate shot up off the couch. An armored guard stepped forward, grabbing Nate's arm. "What do you mean *was*."

Katsia's eyes flashed to Tillie, and then to Nate. For once, I saw fear flash through them briefly. "You know the rules, Nathan."

"Fuck you, tell me right now what the fuck is going on or I'll snap all your guards' necks and then feed them to you through a fucking straw!"

Katsia swallowed, shot the rest of her drink back and stood. "She couldn't exist."

I buried my face in my hands as realization snuck in. "What?" I whispered to myself, and then my hand came to Tillie's. I was going to be strong for her. I didn't know what she had been through and I don't know why, but I didn't care. She was my best friend and no matter what, I would stand by her. She sniffed, looked at me, and then squeezed her fingers with mine.

"I'm not walking out of this place without answers," I whispered to her, squeezing her fingers.

"Did you kill my kid, Katsia?" Nate asked, stepping closer to her.

Katsia laughed. "Oh, wait, what made you think it was *your* kid?"

"And the plot thickens," Hunter grumbled, standing from the couch to check on Tatum.

"Because I fucking know, Katsia, quit the fucking games. I'll give you ten seconds."

Katsia snickered. "You give her too much credit."

"Nine."

Bishop stood, walking beside Nate. Bishop tilted his head, pulled a smoke out of his pocket and lit it up. "Eight." He blew out a cloud of smoke.

"Jesus Christ," I whispered. "There's going to be a war." I could smell the heavy scent of spilled blood already.

Tillie's hand squeezed mine. I looked at her. She shook her head.

"What? What's wrong?"

"Nate! The girl had to be taken care of. You know the rules! We can't have another"—Katsia paused just as I caught her glaring at me—"mistake out in the open."

"Fuck you." I flipped her off.

Bishop took another drag of his smoke, biting down on it. "Six."

"What?" Katsia's eyes flew between him and Nate. "I answered!"

"Yeah, but you see, we had a deal." That was Bishop.

"The deal went out the window when she was born a *swan*," Katsia retorted.

Bishop shook his head, taking the smoke out of his mouth. "The deal was that when the baby was born, I would say what happens—not you. You think you can run around and act boss bitch, Katsia? You forgot one thing." Bishop threw the smoke onto the beautiful marble floor and squashed it with his dirty boot. "I'm the fucking boss around here." Then Bishop's elbow flew out to the guard beside him, knocking him onto the floor. Nate squeezed the other guard's head and slammed it into his knees. Suddenly there was a swim of violent chaos lurking at my feet.

"We need to go!" Tillie pulled me up, but I yanked at her hand.

"No! I can't leave them!"

"They'll be fine, Mads, *we need to go*. Now." Her eyes searched mine pleadingly like a silent conversation was being passed. *Now, Madison.*

Tatum came up behind Tillie. "Let's go with her and let the boys finish the job here."

My eyes went to Bishop just as his fingers dived into one of the guard's eye sockets and he ripped out the balls of mush. Jesus. I watched in fascination as he then slid his blackout from his back pocket and slit it across his throat. Blood sprayed every, dancing in the thick breath of the Reaper.

I scrunched my eyes closed and nodded.

"Madison! Go with Tillie!" Bishop ordered. "Now!"

"Okay!" I snapped back at him, a jolt of shock rippling through me. My legs began following her out of the sitting room of carnage with Tate close behind me.

Tillie looked from left to right, checking the corridor, and then grabbed my arm. "Quick, we don't have long."

"Don't have long for what, Tillie?"

I was answered with silence as she continued to jog down the hallway. We passed artwork knotted in serpentine strokes brushed onto blank canvases. We were all born as a blank canvas, perfectly untouched. Then life happens, and the more you age, the more paint you need. In the end, some of us would escape with our morals, leaving beautiful paint strokes from a tractable life behind on our canvas. But others, like me, will be ending with brushstrokes far too acrimonious to warrant us a ticket through the golden gates of whatever the fuck was waiting on the other side. No matter how unpleasant our canvas may be at the end, all that mattered was who was willing to gape appreciatively at us. My eyes caught a cabinet nailed to the wall. Quickly, I pulled it open and smiled when I saw it was lined with shotguns. Snagging the AR15, I checked the rounds and then quickly caught up to Tatum. Tillie pushed open a door at the end of the hallway and disappeared inside. I followed behind her and then Tatum, who I was hoping wouldn't be too affected by not only Tillie being here but the fact that she had a kid with Nate. My head was spinning from the overload of information that it had collected over the past few minutes. I couldn't dwell on it too much right now—couldn't decipher my feelings in the middle of a war, but I wasn't sure how I felt about it. About everything. All I knew was that I needed to follow Tillie. There was obviously something important that she needed to tell me or show me. She flicked the light on and I squinted from the influx of the brightness. Shading my eyes with my hand, I gazed around the room. It was small. No bed, a pile of boxes to the side. It smelled of dust mite corpses that had suffocated horrific deaths by the contained space and lack of oxygen. That's when I saw hands clenched around the opening of a window.

"Daemon!" I whisper-screamed, just as he climbed up. He lifted the rest of himself through the window, and then gave me a small smile before turning back.

"What's going on?" I asked, confused with the movements.

Tillie rushed towards him, her hand going around his waist as she peeked over the windowsill. I slowly started walking towards them, my eyes going around the room. They eventually landed on Tatum, who looked as confused as I felt.

"Dae—" a baby crying broke through. I paused, leaning outside.

Tillie took the baby that was wrapped in a soft pink blanket and cradled it to her. When I looked back out the window to see who it was that passed the baby through, all I could see was the back of a retreating Tinker.

"Figures," I muttered, snickering at her retreat.

"She's the good in this, Mads. I promise."

I brushed her off, which I guess I didn't have much evidence to do that. She did help

Tate and I escape, and she's been nothing but helpful, but there was always a nudge in my gut when it came to her. Confusion, or something else, I wasn't quite sure yet.

"Okay," I breathed out, leaning against the windowsill. "Okay," I repeated.

"She's not okay," Tate mumbled under her breath.

My chest tightened and the grip I had around the wooden edge compressed. A cold sweat broke out over my brow, my breathing coming in shallow heaves, then a cool, yet familiar hand brushed against my arm. I slowly whistled out the pent-up breath, my eyes going to Daemon. "What do I make of this, D?"

His Adam's apple bobbed as he swallowed. His eyebrows crossed. "I don't..." then he paused, before continuing. "All good things, Madison."

"We're going to work on your English when we get back," I mumbled my reply grumpily under my breath.

There was another cry. Turning around, my eyes fell on the little bundle that was wrapped up tightly in Tillie's arms. I couldn't see her face, and I wasn't sure whether I was capable yet. Something told me I should wait—until Nate at least gets to see his daughter first. I felt as though I was trespassing on his turf by just looking at his baby before him.

"I'm sorry, Mads. The whole thing is so complicated, and I—"

"—don't have to explain right now." I offered her a small smile. "We have a two-hour flight you can fill me in on. For now, we need to go look for the boys." Just as the words left my mouth, the door smashed open and Bishop stood on the threshold, shirt-less with blood splattered all over his abs and his chest drawing in and out. His shoulders lifted and dropped as he sucked in each breath. I jolted to him, going on instinct to see if he was okay, but his eyes cut to mine and I flinched. His eyes were black orbs of hell and in that moment, he was barely recognizable. I stilled, my fists clenching together.

"Bishop..."

He shook his head at me, and then kicked the door open wider to let Nate, Jase, Hunter, and Saint walk in behind him. They looked like they had just stepped out of World War III.

"Fuck," Nate coughed out, stepping backward to stabilize himself.

There was a long pause until Tillie finally broke the silence. "Do you want to hold her?"

Nate's eyes closed, a hiss escaping between his teeth. He dropped to his knees, the silence was enough to haunt me.

I began slowly drifting to Nate, ignoring the pull I was feeling between Bishop and I. "Nate?" I whispered, although my voice came out shaky. "You can hold her..."

"Can't." He shook his head, choking on his words and standing back to his feet. "Not like this. We need to leave. Now."

"He's right," Bishop agreed. "We only got rid of who was there, and amongst all the bullshit, Katsia slipped away."

"Well, of course she did." I rolled my eyes. I hated her.

"She doesn't know Micaela is alive. We just have to make sure we can sneak out before then."

"And what the fuck makes you think you should be alive?" Nate seethed, his eyes cutting to Tillie. The energy in the room immediately shifted. Unease oozed through me.

"Nate!" I snapped. "She's the mother of your child and my fucking best friend!"

"She was nothing more than a walking sack of amniotic fluid. She doesn't *need* to be alive anymore. Her job here is done, oh" —he cut his eyes to me— "and I don't fucking trust her."

"Trust her?" I yelled, a little too loudly because Bishop came closer to me. "You fucking loved her!"

Nate barked out a laugh. "Watch the way you use that word, sis. You and I both know that if I loved her, I wouldn't have been sinking my dick into Tatum every day of the fucking week." His eyes narrowed at me, and I shot daggers back at him. He wasn't only being rude, but he was lashing out. I expected something to happen with him in the brief moments we were standing here waiting to decide to find the guys, but I didn't expect him to lash out quite like this—I especially didn't expect him to take his anger out on Tillie. I could see it now, though. The change in his demeanor. The monster that always lurked beneath the surface, cloaked under his cool swagger, was now prowling back and forth with fire seething between its lips. The rage that was pelting off him was igniting smoldering flickers of anger inside of me.

"That was a shit dig, Nate," I mumbled in disapproval, shaking my head. Bishop threw a shirt on, and it was then that I realized why he didn't wear one. So he didn't get blood on it. He was way too good at this, obviously.

"We need to leave, now," Tillie said, not giving Nate a reply. "There is underground access that can take us straight to the airstrip, but we have to leave out this window."

"Done," Bishop started to the window, grabbing my hand on his way.

"Nah uh." Eli shook his head. "I'm with Nate. I don't trust this bitch."

"Trust me or not," Tillie finally said, giving the baby to Daemon. "But I'm all you have right now."

Eli looked to Nate, who then looked to Saint and Jase. I shot Jase a glare who then nodded. Hunter joined him.

"You ambush us, woman, and I'll show exactly why you should be afraid of me—you hear?" Nate answered, slowly making his way to the window.

Tillie nodded, her eyes going to her feet before she's leaping out the window. Daemon handed the baby out to her and then followed. Nate went to jump out, but my hand flew to his chest. "Hey! I get that you're angry and confused but try to simmer the anger down. We don't know what she has just endured, Nate. Try not to be an arse."

He winked at me, gripping onto the edge. "I'm always an arse, sis." Then he leaped out the window.

"That's it. I'm calling it. He has schizophrenia."

"Your turn." Bishop pointed out the window.

"Bishop..." I whispered. "Look at me."

He wouldn't, his eyes remained on the window. "Get out of the fucking window, Madison."

"What have I done now!"

"Jesus Christ, girl! For once, just once, can you do as you're fucking told!" Hunter gripped my arm and shoved me toward the window. "Get out. Now!" I shrugged my arm out of his grip and jumped out. My feet hit the dusty ground with a thud and vibrations shot up my leg from the impact. Nate took my hand and pulled me into him.

"What'd I do now?" I asked, looking up at him. Daemon was on the other side. He took my other hand.

"He's had real life hit him in the balls over the last thirty minutes."

"What does that mean!" It wasn't my intention for my question to come out as a whine, but it did.

"It means don't fucking ask until we're back on our soil."

Then Nate pushed me into Daemon and scrubbed his eyes with the palm of his hand. Nate had never handled me in any threatening way, but again, the energy felt different tonight. There was an obvious change in the dynamic and I was dreading coming to terms with whatever was about to go down. Bishop was the last one to exit the window and as soon as the soles of his feet touched the ground, we all shot off, following Tillie and Daemon, who still had the baby in his arms. It was strange, but I sensed a story there. The Lost Boys had a job to do when it came down to it, and that was to end all of the Swans—or get rid of, as they would say—and I knew for a fact that Daemon had done it before, so why was he hesitant with this one? My legs continued to carry me forward in the silence with nothing but the heavy pity patting from our shoes hitting the road.

Tillie stopped, and that's when my eyes flew around the place, taking in everything. We were outside, running through a meadow, which was odd, considering. But if I had to guess, I would say we were in the backyard, only the backyard looked to be the size of a damn football field. Tillie pointed toward a barn that was hidden discretely at the back of the house. "In there. There's a manhole in the floor that leads underground. It's where they transport stuff that they don't want documented—ever."

"Are you saying that some shit has been going on here behind the Kings' back, or are you saying my dad knew about it and they're hiding it from The Circle?" Bishop asked from behind me, where he had been the entire time. He had barely touched me since coming back from his slaughtering, and if it wasn't for the dire situation we were all in, I'd overthink the fuck out of it.

"The latter and then some," Tillie admitted. She started jogging toward the metal barn. We all followed and waited as Daemon opened the heavy tin door. There was a loud creaking sound that filled the deserted meadow, but once it was open, we all ran inside. Tillie kicked off the manhole cover. It was large enough for us all to jump down and walk through. She went first, and then Daemon handed her the baby before jumping in himself. The order went much like the window, and before I knew it, we were all walking down hidden tunnels. The walls were made of dirt and there were rail tracks that lined the clay ridden rode. Smaller than what you would find for a train, but definitely big enough to hold a small cart.

"These tunnels have areas that curve off to not only all four factions of Perdita but every section too."

"Every section of this *area* of Perdita?" Bishop wanted to clarify.

Tillie shook her head, hiking the baby higher. "No. I mean, everywhere on the island."

"That's messed up. What the fuck is going on here."

We continued our trek deeper into the tunnels. Twenty minutes later, the air was tight and sweat was falling off my flesh with every step.

"Tillie," I called out, wiping away some fallen dirt that had dropped onto my face. It smudged into my sweat and turned it to soft clay. "Is the baby ok?"

Tillie gave me a small smile over her shoulder. "She will be fine once this is over." Then her legs picked up. "There it is!" We all jogged to an opening archway to the left of the trail. I looked up above, seeing a small metal plate that had "Airport" engraved into it. I let out a sigh of relief just as Tillie pushed open a door and walked through. The space was small, so small that we couldn't all fit inside at once. Tillie banged on the manhole above her head, and then banged another three times. A lock slid open and daylight slammed into the small enclosure.

"You're all ok?" Tinker asked, worry evident on her face. "Come on, you're running low on time." She reached down and pulled Tillie out, and then Daemon, again, they both switched who was holding the baby—who hadn't made a sound through the whole way. I was impressed, she obviously got that side from her mother. I grabbed Tillie's hand and she pulled me up until I was out of the hold and sucking in crisp air again. My chest loosened and relaxed. I turned back to pull Tatum out and then we both grabbed Nate. While the guys were coming out, I took this moment to turn to Tinker.

"What's your deal?"

"My deal?" Tinker smiled. "Not all of us get to choose our path, Madison, so" —her eyes went over my shoulder before coming back to me— "choose yours wisely."

I turned my head over my shoulder to see who was there. Bishop.

"Thank you for the advice, but it seems, I can't choose mine either."

"You can't." Bishop shoulder barged past me. "But I can."

I swallowed past the hurt that crept up from my chest and into my throat. Sadness gripped to my bones. He cannot be serious.

CHAPTER 26

I hung toward the back on the way home. My hands sunk into the pockets of my hoodie and my eyes squeezed shut. I think over the day. I was stuck between two fucking walls in my life. One was the path I knew I should take, and the other was the selfish part of me. I couldn't say I was battling with either side, because the truth was I wasn't. I loved Madison, which meant I wanted to be with her at all costs, but when the equation was made up of eighty percent being the risk her life, I wasn't with it. My mouth felt dry and my palms were sweaty. My shirt clung to my flesh, the residue of blood acting as glue.

Fuck. I hit my playlist. I was being unsociable, considering I really should be asking Tillie how she was holding up. I needed a moment to gather my thoughts. The Weeknd "I Was Never There" started playing and my fingers tapped to the beat. My hoodie remained low, above my eyebrows. I continued to chew my gum as thoughts flashed through my head with the song. *Madison.* Without her, none of this would fucking matter. I shuffled in my seat. *Gripping her ankles, I tugged her body down the bed, flipped her onto her stomach and grasped her hips. Her ass perched in the air, her legs spread wide. "This sweet little cunt is mine, Madison." She rubbed her bare ass into my dick and I grunted, biting down on my bottom lip before dropping to my knees and turning. I began slowly running my nose up the back of her thigh and felt as her muscles twitched with uncertainty. I would too. She was getting used to being blindfolded under my command, but there was always a small part of her that would never fully let go. Was probably her survival instincts. They were, after all, always right. I smirked at that thought. I rode her ass so hard about her instincts being shit with me when all along, I was just throwing her off. The tip of my nose came to the curve of her ass and I inhaled, the sweet scent of her pussy igniting every dominant strand I had hanging inside of my body. My eyes flew open and I drew my tongue out, licking the split of her pussy from her clit, all the way to the skin that separated her ass. I growled out when the tang of her arousal assaulted my taste buds, licked my lips and then dove back in. I stretched her legs wide, laying onto my back and then wrapped her thighs with my arms. My hands came to her ass cheeks as I pushed her weight down onto my face.*

My chewing was harder, my knee jiggling at Olympic speeds, and my finger still tapped at the song that was now playing. "It's a Vibe" by Ty Dolla Sign. Fuck. I shifted in my seat again, stretching my neck up but keeping my eyes closed and pulling my hoodie lower to cover my eyes. I let my head rest back, so I was facing the ceiling. My other hand came to my jean covered cock and I squeezed the bulge that was fighting to rip through my zipper.

"Ride my face, baby." Madison started rubbing herself against my lips, her hands still bound to her back and her eyes still covered in the red silk blindfold. Her hair was up in a high messy bun with loose tresses falling around her face. Sweat covered every inch of her lean body, and her abs tensed as her thighs clenched around my face. She was close, I could feel it in the way her legs trembled and her pussy squeezed my tongue. I flicked it inside higher. My hand came to the back of her ass as I rubbed the nub of her from behind. I sucked and licked her like she was my favorite fucking dessert. And she was.

"Bishop!" she exhaled, her slow ride now turned harsh. Her pussy lips rubbed over my mouth and I pushed my finger inside of her ass. She tensed but carried on. "I'm goin'—I'm—" I pulled away and stopped.

"You're what?" I growled from underneath her.

"Bishop! she screamed out in utter frustration.

"That's right, you're Bishop's. You're mine, Madison. Play any kind of shit like you did with Nate, and all these punishments will look like child's play, are we clear, baby? 'Cause make no mistake, I will fuck your shit up if you ever so much as bat those pretty little eyes in the direction of anyone that has a cock." I slapped her ass loudly and she squealed out in shock. "Do we understand each other?"

She paused, her hips slowly grinding against air.

"Mad—"

"—yes! Fuck. We understand each other."

"Now tell me what you want." I slowly ran my hands up her thighs, my eyes burning with need as I watched her cum slide down the inside of her thigh.

"I want you to make me come."

"Come where?" I grinned, even though she couldn't see me.

"In your mouth," she semi-snapped. There was my sassy little bitch. I squeezed her ass cheeks until it felt like jelly in my hands and pressed her pussy down onto my mouth. I feasted on her like a starved man, licking every inch, my mouth salivating as I took in more. She was made for me. Only not in a romantic way, in a way poison was made to kill a specific person. She was my goddamn anti-venom and I was the serpent that hunted. She was everything pure and I was everything bad.

A groan escaped from my lips slightly, my cock pulsed in my jeans. I need to get fucked, but since the only girl who I'd want to do the fucking with is not on board right now, I'd have to make do. Ripping the ear pods out of my ears, I shot out of my seat. Not looking at anyone else, I turned straight into the small confinement of the bathroom, flicked the lock down and looked down at my crotch. My cock was swollen and pressed against my jeans, throbbing to be sucked, fucked, or touched. Yanking down the zipper, I pulled out and slowly tugged. My eyes rolled to the back of my head as memories flashed through my brain. *Madison.*

The sheen of sweat that soaked her skin and dripped onto mine as she rode my dick. The head of my cock massaging her entry before slamming against her cervix. *The little cry she would make as I hit the border.* My pulling sped up and my breathing was heavy. Sweat tickled my temple. *"I'm yours, Bishop. I always will be."* My balls tightened and my cock jerked as hot cum shot out of me and toward the toilet. My racing heart slowed to a deep throb and I quickly cleaned up, washed my hands and went back to my seat, feeling a lot less tense than I did a few minutes ago.

"B, you ok?" Hunter asked over his seat. They were all scattered everywhere, but I could see Nate was on the other side of Madison who was near Tillie, looking at the baby and chatting with her. So much had happened over the day that I couldn't process it all with everyone near me. First thing's first, I needed to text Madison's dad.

"Yeah," I answered Hunter, picking up my phone and putting the ear pods back in. I slipped that Weeknd song into "Madship's" playlist, and then clicked on his new album. Opening up a new text, I quickly shot one to Joseph.

You're right. I'll try to let her go.

Then I opened up Spotify again, ignoring the notification that pinged almost instantly after. Thanks or no thanks to Wi-Fi in the air. I pressed play on "Hurt you" by The Weeknd and let it play, closing my eyes again.

"I don't know what to do, bro," Nate exhaled, burying his face in the palms of his hands. We had dropped everyone else off. Me without saying shit to Madison, but managing to sneak a look at Micaela—as did Nate. I could see it, even if he couldn't, I saw what happened when he laid eyes on his daughter. It was love at first sight, which was why I knew what his issue was right now.

"What do you mean? About Tillie or about Micaela? Which by the way, I need to talk to you about that."

He shook his head, bringing one foot up to rest on the dash. He ran his index finger over his upper lip. "No need to explain, B. I know that there's always reasoning to your chaos." He said it as if he would explain the weather—with ease.

"Alright, but just so you know, what happened tonight was always the plan. Daemon had been helping Tillie since she gave birth. Apparently, he, Tinker, and another nurse were the ones who helped her through the birth. He called me up and let me know what was happening," I paused, my eyes flying out to the side window before I took the onramp to a new highway. I needed to get the fuck out of here for a while, and going home right now wasn't an option. Out of all the Kings, it was no mistake who my numero uno was, and he earned that on more than one occasion. If there was anyone whose company I didn't mind when I was feeling this fucked up in the head, it was Nate's.

Nate let me continue as I drove. "I didn't know she was pregnant before that point, dawg. On my life. When Daemon told me, I cut a deal with Katsia. Only the bitch tried to get Micaela killed." I shot him a quick look to see his eyes zoned out.

"I believe you." His jaw turned rigid.

I focused on the road again. "Anyway, I should have picked it up. A few months ago, after that shit went down with Madison and Daemon and she was in the hospital, I caught Tillie trying to sneak into the room."

I could see Nate look at me out of the corner of my eye. "I asked her what the fuck she was doing and she said she couldn't talk but that someone had told her that there was an incident and that Madison was hurt. I didn't even think to look at her stomach because she was so fucking small, but the was wearing an oversized hoodie, which now that I think back, was fucked up, but her, in general, was fucked up. She was off, different. More than usual. I knew she cared about Madison, so I let her see her, but before I did she told me that Katsia had captured her after that night at the cabin." I chanced a glance at him now. "Katsia couldn't have known that she was pregnant at this point." I looked back to the road. "Anyway, I said I'd get in touch with her when I need to and I let her see Madison."

"This shit doesn't make sense anymore. Lines are getting blurred and I don't know, bro, I just feel like there's a war brewing."

I nodded. "Agreed which is why I've come to this conclusion." I sucked in a breath. "The girls need the fuck away from us."

CHAPTER 27

"Madison, this is bad. Just having her here with that baby is putting all of us at risk."

"Dad!" I snapped, putting my hands on my hips. "I need to do this."

His eyes glassed over. His brows were furrowed. He was worried and my heart sunk more. I was being selfish.

"I have a solution, but you're not going to like it."

"What?" I asked, defeated. "At this point, I'll take anything."

"Actually, *we* have a solution."

Bishop's voice launched butterflies in my chest. I turned to the door. "What is it?" He and Nate walked inside and then came into the kitchen. They both took a seat on a bar stool.

"Bishop?" I urged him, leaning against the kitchen island.

"You need to run. All three of you, and the kid."

"No."

"Madison…" Bishop sounded exhausted, rubbing his hands over his head in frustration. "Look, not for long, just until we sort out this war. We have never had to worry about casualties until you three came into the game. Now? Now we have you and Tillie and Tatum and for fuck's sake a newborn baby who has a damn hit on her head, Madison. Think, be smart. You know it, we all know that this has to happen."

Tears spilled from my eyes and rolled down my cheeks. I didn't even bother to wipe them away, because I couldn't bring myself to move. My arms felt like they were weighted down on either side of my body and my legs felt like Jell-O.

"Why, what's happening? I'm going to need to know one hundred percent of what's going on if you want this to happen."

Bishop nodded, his palm cupping his mouth and his eyes boring into mine. My eyes stayed locked on his, as though he and I were the only ones in the room. "Katsia is rebelling against the Kings and has gone rogue. We have reason to believe she's trying to build her own army and plans to either expose us, or fight us, or both." He leaned forward, his eyes darkening. "You see, I can't have you here when all this shit blows up, because she will come for you *first*, and then? She'll find out about Micaela."

The realism of everything hit me like a ton of bricks. My legs finally gave way as I curled up on the cool kitchen floor, drawing them to my chest.

"Madison," my father started, since he had been quiet. "This has to happen. You're too important."

Bishop's boots came into view, but I didn't look up at him. He knelt beside me and his finger hooked under my chin, tilting my head up to face him. He searched my eyes. "Do you see the importance of this, baby? I could have gone another route to drilling things into your brain, so I really hope you listen to the orders I give you."

"You were going to break up with me?" I whispered, searching his eyes as more tears overflowed.

He gave me a small smile. "Almost."

"I'd kill you," I stated matter-of-factly.

He laughed, his straight teeth flashing, lighting up the room. I didn't laugh. I didn't even smile because I wasn't kidding. "You laugh, but I'm not joking. I can't—" I shook my head as terror crippled through my veins at the mere thought of Bishop not being mine.

"Hey!" he snapped me out of the spiral that had started to spin inside my head. His thumb pressed over my bottom lip. "Yes, I was going to do that."

"What changed?" I asked, wiping the tears from my cheeks with the back of my hand.

His lip kicked up in a grin. "I remembered that I love you and I promised you that I would change the things I *could* change—that's what."

My heart warmed, and the hiccups that had formed slowly started to subside. "Ok." I nodded, standing to my feet. "We will go, but where? I'm not leaving the US."

Bishop shook his head. "No, but I need you way the fuck out of here, somewhere no one would guess... so I have a plan..."

I narrowed my eyes. Nate couldn't contain his laughter anymore, his chuckles practically vibrating off the walls.

"Good to see your taste in décor is still as shit as ever, Joseph."

I spun around to see Bishop's mom standing there, pushing her sunglasses over her short dark hair. Then her eyes came to me. "Hi, sweetie."

"Oh," I purred, and then when I registered what she was doing here, my eyebrows shot up. "*Oh!*"

"Yes! Oh!" She smiled, and then walked to Nate, leaned down, pecking him on his head. "Lucky your taste in women has improved, Joseph."

My dad rolled his eyes. "Always a pleasure to see you, Scarlet."

She smirked. "I know."

Sometimes, I forget that my dad and their generation probably had stories on stories of the drama they lived through being Kings and associates.

Tillie chose this time to enter the kitchen. My eyes automatically flew to Nate.

"Oh, who is this!" Scarlet started toward Tillie with a smile on her face.

"Mom..." Bishop warned. She pulled back, a pout on her lip.

Nate slowly went to Tillie, his eyes remaining on her. I didn't realize I was holding my breath until Bishop said, "Breathe, you're turning purple."

I let out my breath.

Nate started. "I hate you. I will always hate you. You didn't once try to contact me and tell me what the fuck was going on." Tillie went to open her mouth but his hand flew up to silence her, just then I noticed Tate and Daemon sink into the background.

"I'm not finished. I fucking *hate* you, Tillie. More than I've ever hated anyone, and for as long as you live I am going to make your life a living fucking hell, and hey..." His eyes dropped down to Micaela before coming back to Tillie with a sadistic smirk on his face. "Looks like you're stuck with me for at least eighteen years." Then he took the baby from Tillie who was visibly shaking as tears rushed out of her. As soon as Micaela was in Nate's arms, he coos sweetly at her. As if he didn't just verbally annihilate the woman who gave him his daughter. I get his anger, I understand why, but I'm still fuming for my best friend.

"Nate!" I snapped at him.

He was mouthing "shhh" with a smile on his face as Micaela curled her little hand around his finger. "What, sis?"

I stared at him in disappointment, and when I opened my mouth to cuss him out, I came out flat. Exhaling, I shook my head. "I'm disappointed."

"And I don't care," Nate responded, taking Micaela out of the room.

My eyes flew to Bishop who was watching me carefully. "Give him time, baby. It's a lot to take in, and with all the circumstances around it."

I rested my head on his shoulder and he pressed a kiss to the top of my head. "Mom's going to take you all somewhere safe. She's shooting her movie right now and I think it's the safest place you could be because Katsia wouldn't expect it."

"Why would she not expect it?" I mumbled into his shirt.

"Because I hate all of Bishop's girls," she shrugged, putting a grape into her mouth. She's such a fucking queen.

I giggled.

Then I pushed off Bishop's shoulder. "Promise me a couple of things?"

Bishop moved my hair out of my face.

"First one, is don't die."

He threw his head back in a laugh. I punched him in the shoulder. "I'm serious."

"Ow." His laughter died out, rubbing the spot I just assaulted. "Okay, next thing?"

"Look after Daemon, please..." My heart ached as the words left my mouth. The thought of Daemon being in the line of any danger was enough to not only make me sick but have my head spinning and bile rising in my throat.

Bishop sobered. "Done. Anything else?"

"Kick Nate's ass and drill some sense into him."

He laughed again. "Can't promise that, but I'll try."

"Hunter and Jase..."

"Baby, no one is dying under my time. I promise you this..."

I relaxed, my shoulders falling. "Ok. I feel better."

"Good, because the car's here to pick you up. Don't miss my texts or my phone calls, and I want a song a day added to the playlist while you're gone. Deal?" he asked, an eyebrow quirked.

I smiled, my arms flying around his neck. I leaped up onto him, my legs latching around his waist. "Promise." I kissed him, and then I kissed him another hundred times.

"Madison, honey, I love you, but I don't want to see this..." Scarlet said, hustling out the door. I was still pressing kisses to Bishop's lips when he started walking us toward the front door.

"Kitty, maybe we should start calling you Koala."

I flipped Nate off while squeezing Bishop. When we reached the door, I dropped down and Bishop hitched his thumb over his shoulder. "I need to show you your present before you leave, so I'll be back in five."

I nodded, watching Bishop's retreating back. Daemon came into view and my smile dropped. I walked to him, my hands lacing with his. "Daemon?"

"Yes?"

"Please look after yourself."

A sad smile pulled over his mouth as he took me into a hard hug. "Always."

Tears threatened to surface. I hate that we haven't had a smooth run of getting to really know each other, but it has always just been easy instinct when it came to him and I. "I love you."

"I love you too, Madison." My throat throbbed and my eyes welled with tears again. For Daemon to say that meant everything to me because not only was he void of emotions, but he—apparently—had a demonic case of schizophrenia.

"Alright, baby, come here." Bishop walked back into the foyer. My eyes shot up to him. "You didn't need to get me anything."

He chuckled. "That's cute." Then pulled me under his arm. "I'll see you on the day, no doubt, but I wanted to give you your present now."

"How come?" I asked, snuggling under his arm as he led us outside.

"Because it's fucking over the top," Nate muttered, following behind us to go to Tillie. We headed toward the garage where all our cars were. It looked more like a show-car garage because the entire front—including the door—was glass. The cars were always parked neatly in their homes. It was my dad's thing. He loved cars. Bishop opened the garage door as if this was his house. I shivered.

"Bishop, why—" the door opened and in front of me flashed a pastel teal colored Lamborghini. I gasped. "Holy shit!" My hand flew to cover my mouth as my legs slowly carried me toward it. "Is this mine?" I squealed in excitement. "Bishop! I love it, and I love you, but this is too much! Most people just get roses or something…"

He walked toward me and wrapped me in his arms. Kissing me softly on the top of my head, he whispered, "You're not a *most people* kinda girl. You're my people."

I looked up at him, wrapping my arms around his waist. "Thank you, I love it so much."

He handed me the keys. "Go take a look before you have to leave. I got everything custom. The paint job and the interior is all custom." I walked around the side, it was so beautiful I was at a loss for words. It had black tinted windows and black mag wheels. It also sat so low to the ground. The teal color was a splash of sass on a car you would take seriously—my favorite color. I slid up the doors and took in the inside. Black leather encased the seats with bits of teal in little nooks and crannies. The steering wheel was teal too. The rich smell of leather and fresh rubber told me this was new.

"No words." I shook my head, shutting the door and turning to face him again.

"Your mother-in-law is cracking the whip, Mads—" Tate rounded the garage and paused when she saw the car.

"Oh yaaaasss!" She clicked her fingers. "Oh my fuck! This is perfect! Girls trips…" She jumped in the spot.

Bishop rolled his eyes, leading us out the garage and back to the limo that was awaiting us.

"Mom…" he warned, leaning into the window. I climbed in behind him. Nate closed the trunk and tapped it.

"Packed some good panties in there, sis."

Bishop glared at him, and then came back to me. "Behave yourself, baby."

I offered him a smile. "I will."

"She won't." Scarlet was fast becoming one of my most favorite people.

"Mom…" Bishop warned again, his eyes staying on me.

"Oh calm down, Bishop. I'll take good care of her."

He leaned in and pressed his lips to mine. "See you soon." Then shut the door, stepping backward as the limo pulled away.

"Yeah," I cleared my throat. "See you soon."

"Everything is going to be fine, sweetheart." Scarlet patted my leg.

I smiled, looking out the window. I wasn't sold on if this was going to be fine. I had just left a whole bunch of guys that I love to fight a battle, while I went off and hid. It felt wrong and went against everything I stood for. Every fiber of my being was screaming to jump from this car and run back to them. I didn't want to run. I understood why Tillie and Tatum did, but not me. What if something happened to Bishop. My heart cracked in my chest and sweat broke out over my flesh. I needed to squash all thoughts that involved Bishop in harm's way. Or any of them, for that matter.

"So," I exhaled, hushing my thoughts. "Where are we going?"

She looked up at me from her phone. "Just to LA. Trust me, if the baby had a passport, we would be flying out of here." She went back to tapping on her phone as the limo continued to drive us toward the airstrip. With every mile that we took, it felt like my heart was being ripped from my chest.

Resting my head against the headrest in the chair, I looked over at Tillie who was with the baby opposite me. We still hadn't had a chance to talk, I guessed I was just waiting for the right time. Hopefully I'd get that time in LA. The jet engines fired up and I pulled my ear pods out, putting them in my ear and opening up a text.

Just about to fly out. I miss you

Seconds pass and I don't get a reply, so I turn my phone into airplane mode and open Spotify. Pressing play on Luav "The Other," I sink into the tune and engulf myself in the lyrics. The smooth sound of heartbreak. Looking down, I quickly add it to our playlist. That's song one in my song a day. Hitting repeat, I let it put me to sleep like a soft lullaby.

CHAPTER 28

With Nate riding shotgun and Daemon in the back of my Maserati, I drove us back to my house. I'd been running away from this place because I knew Khales was there, but I needed to call a meeting with Dad to get to the bottom of whatever the fuck was happening within the Kings.

"A Lambo? Like, really?" Nate hadn't stopped going on about my present to Madison since we left the house.

"Yes, really," I deadpanned.

"Why do you have to show us up like that? Now it's going to make my one look shit not to mention Hunter and Jase, and I heard Saint, Eli, Chase, Brantley, and Cash all got her something too."

"Nate, it's not a competition."

"Oh but it is, though! You know I'm an overachiever."

I sighed, hitting the indicator to my street. I looked in the rearview mirror. *"Bonum est tibi?"* Asking if the kid was okay seemed like the least I could do—since he was stuck with us for however long. I still wasn't sure how to characterize him yet, and if it wasn't for his relationship with Madison, I'd kill him myself for shooting her—but I couldn't. When it came down to my rage, there was only one other feeling that trumped it. *Her.* I didn't trust him, I couldn't. I trusted no one outside of my circle.

He nodded, then took his glare back out the window. *"Ne putes illa erunt discedite?"* Asking me if Madison would stay away was a given. You didn't have to be a Madspert to know the girl goes down with her own. I open my mouth to answer, but Nate cuts me off with a scoff.

"Ney!"

He was fluent in Latin as we all were, he was just being a smart ass—per usual.

I shrugged, pulling into my driveway. *"Nos autem non scire nisi runs."* Because I would know if she did. I'd have my mother grilling me. I jumped out of the car and my feet hadn't even hit the asphalt when I heard Khales' voice.

"B?"

"Oh for fuck's sake!" Nate slammed the passenger door after letting Daemon out. I turned to face her and watched as her eyes widened on Daemon.

"Holy shit, is that?" Her attention followed them as they passed her and headed to the side of the house.

I shut my door. "Daemon? Yes."

"I've heard so much about him. They call him Six."

"Who are *they*?" I narrowed my eyes.

She crossed her arms in front of herself, finally looking back at me. "Everyone in The Circle."

"The Circle is full of shit, and what the fuck do you want?"

"I was coming to say hi and to see if you were ok. You haven't been home—"

"When do you leave?" My eyebrows rose.

"Um, well—"

"She's not," Dad interrupted, walking down the steps with his hands in his pockets.

"What the fuck do you mean she's not?" I threw my head back.

His arm rested on her shoulders as he pulled her into him. "She's *staying*, son."

"Oh, you've got to be fucking shitting me," I deadpanned, and then grinned. "You're getting more senile with old age. You don't buy her shit, do you? And what about Mom?"

"Son, you know deep down that your mother and I haven't exactly been *together* for some time, and you're grown. Swallow the fucking pill so we can move on."

My eyes flew to Khales before they went back to my dad. "Huh." I stared off into the distance, and then smirked, looking back to Khales. "And how do I taste? Since she's licked my balls more than once..."

Dad chuckled, pulling out a cigar and lighting it up. "About the same as I do, apparently."

I shook my head in disgust.

He blew out a cloud of smoke. "Now back to business, get in the office so we can talk."

I looked at Khales one last time, and she watched me in worry, but her shoulders were relaxed under Dad's handle. She wasn't faking it. I knew this girl inside and out, and she seemed to genuinely love my dad. My eyes slid to him, but there was no use in me trying to analyze him. He hid his emotions better than me. I can decipher and read any human walking this earth, but not him. He trained me to be like that. I think the only person who could read him was my mom.

I shot Khales an evil glare and shoulder barged past her. I didn't give a fuck that she had moved on with my dad, but I gave a fuck that she was now going to be around a lot more than I ever wanted her to. I saved her all those years ago because she was a friend. As much as I hated her now, I wouldn't pretend that I hated her back then, because I didn't. I didn't love her, but I didn't hate her. She was just there, and I cared about her, so I saved her. Now I wish I hadn't. Now that I see what's going on between her and Dad, though, I'm thinking there's a lot more that he isn't telling me either.

I sunk into one of the leather chairs in Dad's office as he watched me from behind his heavy mahogany desk. "What happened?"

I leaned back. "Well, a fucking lot, but first I need to ask you if you knew about the underground tunnels on Perdita?"

"Yes." He nodded, leaning forward to flick off his ash in the ashtray. "Of course I knew."

"And you used them?" I shot back, watching his reaction.

His eyes squinted from the smoke. "Yes."

"What for?"

"Why all the questions?" His eyebrow quirked.

"Why all the secrets?" I shot back.

He sighed and ran the palm of his hand over his slicked-back salt and pepper hair. "There are no secrets." He flicked his ash again, and I watched as his suit jacket rode up to display the edge of his sleeve tattoo. He had swagger for his age, I'd give him that, and girls—of all ages, *apparently*, gravitated toward him. The smart ones ran after sex, the dumb ones like Khales stayed and thought they could tame him. He could never be tamed. Before him, was my pops. He rode a Harley until the day he died and ruled the underworld just as my dad does and as I will when he passes. Some days I miss my pops though. He was the only one who really understood the shit that I felt. He was still hard like Dad but wasn't cold like him. He had a heart when it came to family, but was ruthless with everyone else—my dad wasn't like that. He was just flat out ruthless to everyone, fuck family.

"That underground pathway is used for a lot of things. Weapons, bodies, and anything else there may be."

"Drugs?" I asked flat out because I needed a straight answer from him. I'd never known the Kings to be in drugs, and Pops would turn in his grave, but the way my dad was, one could never be too sure.

"No. You know that." So money, trafficking woman, and other "things," I thought to myself. I wasn't going to press the issue anymore, so I continued with the conversation at hand. "Katsia got away."

"I see that, but why was she running?" he asked, tilting his head. "She's sacred, son, you can't go around killing everyone who threatens Madison."

"It had more to do with Nate."

Dad sucked in more smoke. "What of Nathaniel?"

"He has a kid."

He faltered, only slightly. "And?"

"And it's a girl."

His eyes closed, his nostrils flaring. "Jesus. Who's the mother?"

"Tillie."

Dad sighed and leaned forward. "I can't be hiding any more Swans, son. It's going to make me look weak. Something has to give. Right now? We have a war brewing because Katsia wants retaliation on you lot, and she wants to expose the Kings and The Circle. Generations of hard work is about to crumble."

I leaned in my chair and tilted my head. "Then we kill her before she can."

"She's sacred, son. We can't."

"Sacred to who? She's the shit on the bottom of my shoe as far as I'm concerned."

Dad massaged his temples then put out his cigar. "Bishop, not everything is black and white. We can't touch her because of her lineage. If we end her, we would end her family line, and we can't be held responsible for that."

"But she's fucking testing both the Kings and The Circle."

"The Circle isn't our business, son. They will handle her accordingly, as we will."

"Alright." I pulled out a smoke and lit up. Dad narrowed his eyes at it and I smirked, edging him to tell me to throw it away, but he didn't. His features relaxed. I blew out a thick cloud of smoke. "So what are you thinking, then. Because I know you have a plan."

"I do." He nodded. "But first, where is Madison and Tillie?"

I chuckled, flicking off the ash. "Guess."

He shrugged, his attention drifting to the side like he didn't give a shit. "I don't know, holed up in a hotel somewhere?"

My grin deepened. "Wrong. Try again."

"Bishop, riddles are your thing, not mine. Cut the shit."

"One more guess. Come on, entertain me…"

"How about I'll buy you some strippers to entertain you and you hurry up with whatever you're getting to."

A laugh shot out of me, my head tilting back. "Alright, old man." Then I pressed my lips around the end of my smoke with a smirk. "With Mom."

"What!" he snapped, his eyes shooting directly to me. "What do you mean with mom?"

"They're with her, Tatum too and the kid."

Dad seemed to mull over what I had just told him, then realization set over his features as they softened. "Well, shit, I would never guess that. It's no secret how much your mother hates all your girls. She takes every chance she gets to mention it in every magazine interview she does."

I snickered. "Exactly why they're with her, and it never scared girls off."

He snorted. "You're my kid, that's why."

Dad and I hadn't thrown around banter in a while, and it felt good to pull out the verbal boxing gloves with him. "Khales…" I went on. His face fell. "I'm just saying… she's young."

"Don't get into it with her."

I shrugged. "As long as you know what you're doing. Just means I'll be in the city full time come this war being over."

"You can be wherever you need to be. For now, back to the plan." I noticed he didn't say college. It was because he didn't want me to go. He had plans to have me under him full-time and learning the depth of the family businesses and how they're run. My mom, on the other hand, was all for college. She never wanted this life for me. She didn't realize how much she didn't want it for me until I was much older. Little do they know, I'd already decided what I wanted to do. This was my life, I'd take over after my old man. I don't know what the dynamic is between my mom and dad, but I'm almost certain she wouldn't be cool with Khales banging her husband in her house.

"What's the plan?"

"Katsia is still in Perdita, which is good. We don't need this drama spilling out on our turf, which means we can fly there with *all* of the Kings who are willing, and settle this as it is."

"Or?" I asked, skipping past the part where he said he'd have all the Kings on the same island.

"We will cross that when we get there." He stood from his chair. "We can plan to leave for Friday, that way we have a couple of days to organize everyone." The Kings before our generation were my cousin Spyder, Jase, and Saint's crew. A few of the others who rolled with them scattered all over the place. All though I know Jase kept in contact with them, they had pretty much moved on to live their life, having fulfilled their duty.

"You can talk with Jase and make sure he can gather his Kings, and I'll get to the rest."

I stood up. "Dad…" I called out, just as he was about to leave. "Does Mom know about you and Khales?"

"Son, she's known for a long time, now." Then he left. As quickly as he comes, he goes.

I stretched out my neck, annoyed at both my parents now, but sympathizing with my mom. It must've hurt her to some extent, surely. Aside from Dad's words, he loved her once. She was his entire world, I knew this because I'd seen the photos and heard the stories. They were their era's modern-day Bonnie and Clyde—mafia style. So whatever the hell was going on between him and Khales, there had to be something in it for him. I headed toward the pool-house, ready to fill in Nate and Daemon. Thank fuck this house was so large, it ran the risk of running into Khales less. I headed inside and shut the door. Both Daemon and Nate were on the sofa, speaking in Latin.

"We need to talk." Then my eyes fell to Daemon before realizing I needed to switch to Latin.

CHAPTER 29

Women. Some read that word and think beauty, assholes read it and think sandwiches, but those who bathe in intellect read that word and feel power. Our bodies, built in all different shapes and forms, all bared one thing in common; power. Without us, humanity would not exist. We bear our flesh and our bodies to create new humans, and then continue to nurture and care for them, that's why when I'd see the word "women," I thought of power. Despite my rocky relationship with my mother, and not knowing my birth mother, I was beginning to explore more of this mindset each and every day, and I think Bishop's mom had a lot to do with that.

"Hi, honey." Scarlet walked into the room, leaving the door slightly ajar. She wrapped her light mesh throw around her slender waist. "Can I come in?"

"Of course!" I tucked some of my hair behind my ear and shut my nail polish. Sliding off the side, I tucked my hands under my thighs, slightly nervous about what our conversation could lead to.

She took a seat at the end of the bed and turned to face me front on. "I know we haven't spoken much, but I want to always be completely transparent with you." She cleared her throat and tied her short hair to a small bun at the nape of her neck. "I met Hector when I was around your age. I was new to town, and he was the born and bred rock star of The Hamptons," she paused and sent me a small wink. "Like father like son. Anyway, I caught his attention pretty much instantly, which, like Bishop, was always hard to do. He, again like Bishop, only dabbled in slightly older women who were either models, actresses or singers. Just to clarify, the reason why they choose A-listers is because those people understood the dynamic of privacy. The Hayes men are taught at a very young age to keep their business out of drama and to eliminate that, they never messed with high school girls or college girls." She paused, pulling her lip into her mouth. "I thought he loved me. He made me feel wanted and chased. I mean" —her face lit up like the Fourth of July— "obtaining the unattainable, sets off endorphins similar to running ten miles. So we fell in love. My parents struggled to like him. They knew there was something he was hiding, but I ignored all the warnings. I met his family and bonded greatly with his dad. He was everything Hector wasn't."

My eyebrows shot up. She shook her head, a horrified expression falling over her face.

"Oh! No! God no. I just respected him so much. If he were still here, he would have loved you." Her eyes fell to her hands before coming back to me. "Anyway, I got my first acting gig on a small TV show, and Hector was supportive. There through it all. We have great memories together." Her smile fell, and suddenly, the room felt smaller than what it was a moment ago. "Two years later was the first time he cheated on me, and I'm not telling you this because I think my son is the same, I'm telling you this because Bishop is a lot more like his grandfather than he can see. I thank the Lord every day that Bishop got twelve good years from his pops, because he planted the seed of good in his heart. Yes, Bishop is cold and calculated like his father, but I see the way he looks at you, and it's not the way Hector used to look at me. It was how his pops looked at his gran." She swiped away a stray tear and reached for my hand. I didn't know what to say, I was rendered speechless.

"His pops may have planted the seed of good in Bishop's heart, but you water it every single second that you're in his life, and for that, I will always be on your side, Madison."

Emotion caught in my throat and my tummy flipped inside. "Thank you," I whispered harshly.

"No need to thank me!" She swatted at me playfully.

"No, I do," I answered, fighting the tears. "Just before you walked in here, I was having an internal battle with myself. I loved my mom, and when I thought she died, I mourned her death every single day. I couldn't imagine my life without her, but I dragged my feet through it every day, waiting for the ache to subside. Anyway." I pulled myself away from the downer I was headed to. "When I found out I was adopted, she was alive, and that she had slept with Bishop, I lost it. I lost all and every single feeling I had for her. Now I can't even stomach to be in the same room as her, let alone look at her. So just before you came in here, I was thinking about the word 'Women' and what that might mean to some people. I think of power every time I see it, and I don't know why because the only mother I had ever known was a fraud and a skank, but I knew it when I looked at you."

She smiled at me sweetly. "Well, thank you, but I'm not that strong."

I snorted. "You're married to Hector…"

"True!" She nodded. "About your mom, your adoptive one, when and if you want to learn about your birth mom, I'll be here, but your adoptive mom… she's a piece of work."

I tucked my feet under my butt. "Tell me more."

She laughed and got more comfortable. "Nothing too juicy. She was the mean girl at school. Everyone was scared of her—except me. I was her sworn enemy. She hated Elena too, and Elena is my best friend. She was the wild, crazy…" she paused and thought for a second. "Elena was my Tate."

I chuckled, my hand coming to my mouth. "Did you have a Tillie?"

Her smile dropped. "I did."

"Did?"

Her eyes flicked to the door. "Let's just say that it didn't end well, and it's still not going well."

"Sounds like a Tillie," I smiled. "I don't know what to do about her."

Scarlet stood from my bed and patted my leg. "Everything will be revealed soon, I promise, but know this. Tillie *loves* you, Madison. She's a good friend. She's not like my Tillie. Maybe while we're here you could spend some time with her? Hear what happened?"

"I'm that obvious, huh?"

She inched her fingers close. "Little bit."

I sighed. "Ok. I'll make the effort tomorrow." She leaned down and kissed my head like a mom would kiss her child goodnight.

"Sweet dreams." Then she walked out of the bedroom and left me to my thoughts. I didn't think I was being that obvious about my reservations with Tillie. It wasn't that I was even upset with her, well, maybe I was. I wasn't sure why, but I felt hurt that she didn't come to me, I guess. She should've known I would have done everything for her, but at the same time, she would do the same, I guess. If I was in her shoes and I knew telling her something would put her in danger, would I do it? No. Not at all. And with that thought bouncing around in my head, I tucked myself under the blankets and flicked off my light.

I opened my messages to see (0). Bishop still hadn't replied to my text from earlier, but I sent him another one anyway.

Goodnight x

Then I tucked my phone under my pillow and let my mind sink into unconsciousness.

CHAPTER 30

"This air BNB is nice. Why did I think those things were old and run down?" she asked around a spoonful of granola.

Tillie bounced Micaela on her lap softly, tossing her fruit around in her bowl.

"You ok?" I asked her, taking a small bite out of my pancake. Scarlet had to go to work early this morning so we ordered breakfast online. Buttermilk pancakes, fresh fruit, crème fraiche, and warm chocolate milk. Spiked with whiskey. I was starting to worry about Tate's alcohol intake.

Tillie looked at me. "Not really. We haven't talked much—"

"—I know, I'm sorry. There's just so much going on." I got to my feet and rounded the table. "God, she looks so much like Nate."

Tillie chuckled, a small smile coming to her face making her deep dimple pop. "She does, right?"

"Can I hold her?"

"Of course!" Tillie turned and handed her to me.

"Wow! She's heavier than she looks!"

"That, is like her mama," Tillie chuckled back.

"Lies," I whispered against her small head that smelled of milky soap suds.

I went back to my seat and continued to slowly rock her with one hand and pick my food with the other. "So when you want to tell me anything, you can, Tillie. We're your friends. Ok?"

Tate agreed beside me. "Yes, we're your friends, but while we're on the friend thing, um, about Nate…"

Tillie shook her head, cutting Tate off. "Don't. It's okay, Tate, and he's all yours. I just hope he won't hate me all of her life, if you know what I mean."

"He'll come around." I looked up at her. "I know him, and he'll come around." I don't bother to brush off her giving Tate the green flag on Nate, because I didn't want to hurt Tate.

"No, nope. I won't go there again," Tate said.

"So anyway." Tillie shuffled in her seat. "I'm ready to spill everything. So the night at the cabin, after Nate and I had, you know, he went downstairs to make us something to eat. I got up to wander around the room to burn time and ended up finding myself in the closet, where I found a small lock box. I opened it and all these photos were in there—that I still have. So I came across this one, and it was a woman. Young, tender, beautiful. She had long blonde hair and gentle but mischievous eyes. She was extremely young. There was a man standing beside her, double her size with his arm draped around her shoulder. There was something about the woman that drew me to her. She felt—familiar. In the photo, she was visibly pregnant, and I turned it over to see if there were any names on the back, and there was." She took a deep breath. "It said *Katsia Steprum—pregnant with expected due date: November 18th*. I remember just... being rooted to the ground. I couldn't move and I couldn't think, and I didn't know why. So her expected due date was my birthday? I mean, how many times do babies come on their due date..."

"Jesus..." I whispered, chills breaking out over my skin. "Keep going."

"So I put the rest of the photos into my back pocket and waited on the bed for Nate to get back to ask him about the photo I found. When he came back in, carrying two plates filled with food, his eyes dropped to the photo that was in my hand and then he cussed, his head tilting up to the ceiling...

"Fuck." Nate walked farther into the bedroom and kicked the door closed so hard a photo fell from the wall and smashed.

"Is this? Has this got something to do with me?" I asked him, lifting my hand that held the image.

He put the plates on the bedside table and took a seat beside me on the edge of the bed. The blankets were still ruffled from our two-hour binge fest, and I wore nothing but his shirt with my hair wild all over the top of my head, but in this moment—none of the feelings I was feeling earlier mattered. I needed to know about this image and why I was so drawn to it.

He looked back at me and licked his bottom lip. "Yes."

"Yes—what?"

"Yes, that is you, and yes, that bitch is your mom."

"What!" I shot off the bed and threw the photo away like it had caught on fire. "Nope. No way!"

Nate stood up and readjusted himself through his grey sweats. His skin still glistened. "Yes way, can we do this tomorrow?"

"So yeah. We didn't do it tomorrow, I urged him for answers until we had a huge fight—"

"—I remembered that fight. I could hear you both from upstairs."

Tillie nodded. "Yep. Then I texted Peyton to see if she knew—which she did, of course." Tillie wiped the tears from her face. "Turns out, Katsia had both of us and gave both of us to the same family. Why? I don't know. My adoptive mom was a junkie and my dad used to beat me—and Peyton. I don't know the depths of why, and the story which centers around her, but—"

"Holy fuck, Katsia is your mom. How old was she when she had you and Peyton?"

Tillie laughed. "Huh, very fucking young. Must have been thirteen with Peyton and around seventeen or sixteen with me. I don't know what the age gap with Peyton and Jase is, but I know they're not born in the same year."

"What about the man in the photo? Do you know who that was?" I asked, pushing my plate away. I had suddenly lost my appetite.

Tillie shook her head. "Something else I haven't gotten to the bottom of yet, either!"

"Well, this is a little messed up. So what happened and how did you get to Perdita?"

Tillie leaned into her chair and tucked a loose strand of faded pink hair behind her ear.

"She came for me, and I don't know why. I still don't. I was almost home and a white van pulled up and threw me inside and then I woke up in Perdita. She didn't know I was pregnant at the time, but when she found out, it only made her more interested," Tillie paused. "Just for the record, worst mother ever."

"Bet mine could give her a run for her money."

"And mine," Tate mumbled, taking a sip of her orange juice.

"So where is Peyton?" I pondered aloud.

"She's with The Circle," Tillie let out bitterly.

"I've heard that name be tossed around a lot, but still don't know who they are?"

"So there's the Kings, and you know what they do and why they do it, but obviously there has to be someone sitting in the Pentagon and White House who foresee everything. I mean, they run a damn island. Anyway, The Circle is just that. They're a clang of people, who only very few people know about, that are scattered all over the world and sit in high power positions that make sure everything King related flies under the radar. They're sort of like the CIA, I guess, but far dirtier." Interesting to see how deep the Kings' circle ran, and terrifying at the same time. I wonder why Bishop never thought to tell me about them, probably the same reason why he has always hidden everything from me.

"Why the hell is she with them?" Tatum asked, shock evident in her tone.

Tillie shrugged. "She was always going to go the political way, she only stuck around for Jase."

I cleared my throat. "About that, I'm not sure if anyone has told you, but since you've been gone a few things have happened on this side, too." I exhaled. "Hunter and Jase are my brothers, as is Daemon who is my twin, but I'm sure you already knew that part."

She gasped. "Wait, Hunter and Jase? Blood brothers?"

I nodded. "Yeah, turns out I was adopted into Dad's—or Joseph and Elizabeth's family. I'm actually a Venari. Daemon got the shit side of the stick and was tossed into The Lost Boys with Katsia."

"I swear, sometimes I wonder what the fuck I was thinking bringing her into this world." Her eyes fell to Micaela.

"Well, she's in it now, and not going anywhere."

My phone vibrated on the table and I snatched it, seeing it was Bishop.

"Hi, are you ok?"

"Yeah, everything's fine. Sorry I didn't text you yesterday, we've been getting some shit in line."

My eyes went to Tillie, who got up from her chair and came to take Micaela. "What sort of shit?"

"I'm gathering all of the previous Kings that I can find, and bringing them in, because on Friday we're all flying back to Perdita to settle this."

"I want to come."

"No."

"Bishop…" I whined, even though I knew that it would never work on him.

"No, Madison. No fucking way. You stay there and stay alive."

"And what about you?" I whispered, anxiety taking a hold of my airways and trying to suffocate me. I never thought I'd end up being one of those girls who put all her feelings into one guy, but Bishop crushed those assumptions. The thought of anything happening to him would almost put my heart into cardiac arrest.

"I'll be fine, baby," he answered smoothly. "I gotta go. Listen, I need to talk with my mom about something…"

"Oh?" I shuffled up in my chair. "She's at work right now."

"It's my dad. Him and Khales, they're…"

"Oh ew!" My face scrunched in disgust. "He would never!"

"Nope, he had, and is…"

"That's disgusting." I shook my head.

"Yeah, but don't tell her yet. I'll tell her when I see her. I just wanted you to have a heads up. Looks like she might be hanging around longer than I would have hoped."

"That sucks." Another phone call beeped through and I looked down at my screen. "Carter is calling me…"

"Mathers?" Bishop asked, shocked. "What the fuck for?"

"I don't know. Call me later?"

"Yeah alright."

After hanging up on Bishop, I answered my phone, giving Tate a confused look. "Hello?"

"Madison?" He sounded desperate.

"Carter? Are you ok?"

"Are you in town?"

"What? No. I'm out of town right now, why?"

He sighed. "Can you text me when you get back? I need to talk with you." And he hung up.

"That was weird." I put my phone back on the table and pushed it to the middle. "I haven't heard from him in months and then he calls me out of the blue."

Tillie shook the baby bottle, her eyes going between Tate and me. "What ever happened to him?"

"Nothing," I answered, picking up my plate and carrying it to the sink. I rinsed it quickly before turning and leaning on the counter.

"I don't know what to do," Tillie whispered under her breath, feeding Micaela.

"How so?" Tate asked, her head tilted.

Tillie shrugged. "I think I need to leave."

"Leave—where?" I tried hard not to sound critical, but it came off as that instantly. "Elena doesn't know that Micaela is her granddaughter, and then there's Nate…" I added.

"Exactly!" Tillie shrugged. "I just think that he would prefer I not be in his hometown, if you know what I mean."

"No, I don't, and please don't tell me you're thinking of running because honestly, Tillie, he would kill you if you took his daughter away."

"He's going to kill me anyway, Mads!"

"Why!" I threw my hands up, suddenly annoyed at the whole situation. I loved Tillie, but sometimes we didn't exactly see eye to eye.

"Because I—I may have met someone else, and I don't know, I think that he would hate that some other male would be a big part of her life, ya know?"

"I need a holiday." I rubbed my temples with my fingertips. "Ok, here's what we are going to do." I pushed off the counter and made my way back to my seat. "We are going to all sit the fuck down when all of this is over, and have a flat-out chat about what we are going to do with little princess. Tillie." I brought my eyes to hers, drilling them into her. "I do not, under any circumstances, think you should run from Nate. He will find you, and the erratic way his behavior has been since finding out he is a dad, I wouldn't trust his intentions with you once he does find you, so I *honestly* think you should take my route, and ju—"

"—Ok!" she snapped at me with a smile on her lips. "You're still persistent."

"That shit will never change," Tate muttered, standing and going to the sink to rinse her plate.

"Now," I grinned. "Who is this man you've met?"

Her face fell.

"What?"

She shook her head. "Honestly, it would never work out. We had a moment, and I don't know... I just, I don't think it's a good idea."

"Well, who is it? Do I know him? Please don't tell me it's one of those weird guards at Perdita."

She shook her head. "No. I'm wasting my time because it could never happen. He's too involved with Katsia to look at me again, and we had a moment or two, but then he went cold and I honestly think it's a waste of time me even mentioning it. It just made me realize that if something ever did happen between me and someone, Nate wouldn't allow it."

"I do have a plan, though," I said.

"Oh goodie!" Tate bit into an apple. "Let me guess, you want to gatecrash this war?"

I smirked.

"And how are we supposed to get past the wicked witch of the west?" Tatum asked, crunching on her apple loudly.

I skipped toward her. "Well, the wicked witch isn't as wicked as she seems."

We finished up breakfast and washed the dishes. The house we were staying in was a two-story loft air BNB. There were two bedrooms upstairs and one downstairs. Tillie and the baby stayed downstairs while Tate and I crashed in here. Flopping onto the bed, I bring my phone up to my face and send Bishop a text.

Weird conversation with Carter.

What did he want

I flipped onto my tummy. **I don't know. He said he wanted to talk with me when I got home.**

I waited for the three little circles to pop up, but they didn't. Two minutes pass before I decided to send him another. The thirst was real. **How are your plans going?**

Fast. We have a good lot of people coming in today and tonight. We will be all flying out tomorrow night. You? How's Mom?

Okay, so they were going to be leaving Friday night, not morning, which put a slight dent in my plans. I was hoping that they would leave in the morning so we could get there later that day.

Mom is awesome. I want a swap. Mine for yours.

I realized my bad joke as soon as I hit send and cringed. My face was scrunched and my cheeks were on fire when Tillie walked in.

"Hey! Do you—" she stopped when she saw my face. "Are you ok?"

"No. I just sent a really stupid text to Bishop. Anyway! What's up?"

She walked in farther, stopping near the end of the bed. "Did you ever hear from Ridge?"

I leaned up on my elbows. "I did. I sort of bumped into him at a bank a few months ago before Tate and I ran away to New Zealand, why?"

She paused, her face falling blank. "Okay, I need to know one hundred percent what happened while you were there, but it's just that, I don't know, I thought maybe he would have looked harder for me?"

"He probably did, like I did, but always came out with dead ends. It makes sense now that I know now, though. Katsia hiding you and all that…"

Her finger came to her lip. "Can I ask you something?"

"Of course?" I scooted up the bed, tucking my legs underneath me.

"What was Nate like after I left?" Out of all the things I was expecting her to ask me, that was not one of them.

"Honestly, he was off."

"Off?"

I nodded and pulled my bottom lip into my mouth. "There were a few times when he would say something about you, and, okay, I'm not good at this. He had feelings for you, Tillie, real feelings. I hadn't seen him with any other girl like he was with you, and I witnessed my fair share amount of Nate-hos in the months you were absent."

A sad smile came to her mouth. "Thank you. When I was away, I became obsessive with the memories I had of him, of us. I'd replay every little thing in my head."

"I know." I leaned forward and patted her hand. "We do that, replay the memories we have of someone because it makes us feel closer to them. We try to grasp onto every piece we have of them because were afraid that they'll disappear."

She sighed heavily, getting to her feet. "Is it weird that the fact that Tate and he have history doesn't affect me?"

"Yes…" I teased. "Because I know you're lying. You may not feel it right now, but if you saw them together it would hurt, Tils. And that's not because you're a girl, that's because you're a fucking human."

"I don't deserve you." She wiped away a stray tear.

"Say that again and I'll use your ass as target practice."

She laughed, and walked out of my room, just as my phone started ringing on my bed. I blindly reached for it, swiping it unlocked and bringing it to my ear.

"Hello?"

"Hi, sweetie! So I finished early today, are you girls home?" Scarlet asked. I could hear the echo in my ear, signaling she was in a car.

"Yes! We're home, and perfect! There's actually something I want to talk to you about."

"I'm almost there!" Then she hung up, and I slipped off the bed and jogged downstairs.

"Scarlet is almost here. We need a plan!"

The door swung open. "I have an idea!" Scarlet closed the door behind herself, removing her glasses. She stepped toward me. "I don't feel right about Bishop going into this alone, and like I told you last night—Hector and I have…"

I smirked. "You want to gatecrash their war?"

Her eyes shot to mine. "How'd you know?"

I snorted. "I was about to pitch you the same idea." Would Khales be there? I hope so. Maybe I could accidentally push her in front of a stray bullet. I hate how this is going to go with Scarlet.

"See, this is why the Hayes men are dangerous because look at the women they choose?" Tate mocked, gesturing to both Scarlet and I.

"She's not wrong," I muttered under my breath.

"Ok, so here's the deal. You," Scarlet pointed to Tillie. "Obviously will be staying behind with the princess, but us three will be flying there around four hours after everyone has left."

"How?" I asked, my legs tingling in adrenalin at this sneaky plan.

Bishop was going to kill me.

"I have a friend," Scarlet announced, sitting on the edge of the chaise. "He owns an airline and has a private jet we could use."

"Oh," I chimed. "Of course you do."

She gave me a dismissive smile, and then looked to Tate. "You don't have to come if you're not willing."

"Are you crazy? Someone has to make sure Batman over here doesn't upset the Joker…" She hiked her thumb toward me.

I chortled. "This is actually true. So, when do we leave?"

CHAPTER 31

"That was probably the longest flight ever!" I exclaimed, sliding out of the back of the limo. It wasn't good to be home, because this place hardly felt like home anymore.

"That's because you couldn't stop jiggling with excitement." Tate got out of the car and helped Tillie. "Seriously, your love for danger has me second guessing our entire friendship."

"Like you're one to talk!" I shot back. It wasn't until the silent engine of the car behind us cut off when I realized someone had pulled up behind. Crap. We got caught.

I turned around slowly, biting down on my lip and hoping I could sweet talk my way out of this— my face instantly fell into disgust. "What the fuck do you want?" I snapped, just as Elizabeth shut the passenger door. She was in a pearl white Lexus with chrome wheels and her driver looked half her age.

"Got yourself a new boytoy, I see."

She winced but straightened her shoulders. "I understand why you're mad at me, Madison. I guess I wanted to come see you before I left, to see if there was anything salvageable with our relationship."

"Well, there's not." I flicked my hand toward the car she arrived in. "You may leave."

My eyes went to Scarlet, who was shooting daggers at Elizabeth. She glided closer to her like a butterfly would if it had fangs, and her voice dropped to deathly tones. "I would listen to Madison, Liza, because if I so much as get within an arm's reach of you, I'll strangle you myself and bury you in an unmarked grave at the back of my home" —Scarlet grinned, whispering— "and you and I both know who your neighbors will be."

Pain flashed over her face, then she looked back at me. "I do love you, Madison. I always have. When you're ready to forgive me, I'll be waiting for you." Then her head bowed and she retreated back to the car. A twinge of guilt pulled inside of my chest, showing my humanity. I spent most of my life loving her, and now I'll probably spend the rest hating her.

"Okay, so if we could get organized that'd be great as we are supposed to be at the airstrip in two hours," Tate ordered, going straight for the front doors. Just as she was about to open the door, it flung open and Elena stood there with an apron wrapped around her waist and flour embedded through her hair, smudged on her face.

My lips widened, but before I could start spewing a whole bunch of excuses, she interjected, "Come on, you're on borrowed time!" My eyebrows shot up in surprise. *She knew?* Then I remember the conversation Scarlet and I had last night. The Tate to her Madison.

"Come on, Swan," Scarlet tapped my butt while walking past, and just as I was about to take the steps up to the front door, I noticed Tillie wasn't following. Turning around, I looked at her. "Coming?" Then realization washed over me, and I spun back around to look at Elena, who was watching Tillie with interest. Her eyes flew between Tillie and the baby and then back again, and just when I thought the level of awkwardness couldn't get much worse, Elena gestured into the house.

"I'd love to meet my grandchild."

I exhaled a loud breath of air, shaking my head and walking into my house. "I'm not cut out for this lifestyle." Dropping my bags near the front door because I knew I'd need them again, I headed straight into the sitting room where Tate was hunched in the corner suite and Scarlet was helping herself to my dad's scotch.

"Cheers, Joseph, you fuck." She lifted her glass in the air and shot the amber liquid back. I could almost taste the hard liquor hit the back of my throat just by watching.

"You don't like Madison's dad?" Tillie asked, slowly handing Micaela to Elena.

Elena smiled adoringly down at Micaela. "Aw, she has never liked Joseph." Then winked at me and took her attention to the baby. "I've baked pie."

"You did?" Scarlet snorted, one eyebrow lifted. "Judging by the amount of flour on you, I would have to debate."

"Don't listen to her, she's just scratchy!" Elena said in a baby voice to Micaela, then brought her eyes up to mine. "Before you do this, honey, you need to realize that your birth mom and dad will both be there. Are you prepared to face them?"

The room fell silent. I mulled over her words. I thought I was. They gave me up, which was probably the only thing I would struggle to come to terms with. *I miss my guys and my guy.* I feel unwanted from people who were planted in my life through blood. Jesus was obviously on crack. I'd struggle with it, though. I'd come from being quite secure in my family home, single child, with both parents being married and in love, to finding out they weren't in love, I was adopted, had three brothers, and one was a schizophrenic who had demons whispering in his head.

I gulped. "I have no choice."

Elena looked at Scarlet, a silent conversation quickly passing through them before Scarlet got to her feet and came to sit beside me on the sofa. Her hand grasped around mine. She tucked her short jawline hair around one ear. "Honey, when you are ready, I will be here to talk with you about anything."

"We both will be," Elena added, and that's when I realized that it didn't matter if Jesus was on crack and put me in the wrong family, because what made these people special was they didn't have obligations to me. Their loyalty didn't come from some false sense of need because we were blood—it came from the purest form. Friendship and love.

I gave them both an appreciative smile. "Thank you both so much."

"Power." Scarlet winked at me and then shot to her feet. "Right, so..." she glared down at her watch. "We're meeting Miller in an hour. Tillie? You'll be okay here with Elena, okay?"

Tillie looked between all of us. "Okay."

"You can both stay in my room and keep using my clothes and whatever else you need. When we get home, we will all sit down and talk about what we spoke about, *mmkay?*" I was really hoping that Elena would work some grandmother magic and make Tillie see that she wasn't alone. She had me and Elena, and Nate—even though he hadn't realized it yet—but she had him as Micaela's father, and that was what was important for right now.

Tillie pulled her lip into her mouth. "Ok." And just when I went to leave to get some last minute things organized, Tillie quickly jumped to her feet. "I'm really sorry!"

I paused, tilting my head in confusion. "Sorry for what?"

Tillie shoved her hands into her front pockets, her eyes falling to the ground. She patted down some of her hair that had fallen over her shoulder, her silver bangles jiggling in the movement. I noticed she still had her silver dream catcher diamond necklace on through it all. "For messing up your guy's dynamic, I guess."

"Tillie," I started, but Elena stepped in for me.

"You, sweet girl, are not a nuisance." Elena wrapped her fingers around her chin, lifting her face. "You and Micaela are family now, just like Madison, and Tate, and the rest of the Kings. Just like Scarlet and I. You will find that no matter how much we may hate each other at times, we *always* take care of our own." She pulled in a breath. "I believe my son loves you."

I gasped. Even though I knew it was true.

Scarlet grinned.

Tate shuffled in her spot.

I began to think Scarlet was more of Tate and I was more Elena.

Elena continued. "But right now, he's so clouded in hate and confusion that he won't allow any other emotion in. Time, please just give him time."

Tillie's shoulders relaxed slightly before she nodded. "Ok. I can give him time."

Wrapping my belt on, I leaned to the side, catching Scarlet staring at me. "Hey, so how many people affiliated with the Kings are actually going to be there?"

I was getting comfortable, scanning around the plane. It was a lot different to the Hayes' jet. Theirs seeming more superior.

"All of them."

I froze. "Shit."

CHAPTER 32

"When we get in there, I need all of you to pay attention to my body language. You don't move unless I fucking say, or fucking incline that you are going to move, do we understand?" I called out, facing all of them. The trip was fast because we had two jets flying here with around forty or so men.

"Yes, boss," Spyder teased, cocking his head. Fucker.

"Son, it'll be fine." Dad came up beside me.

"I know." I inched my head over my shoulder. "But I don't want any mistakes. I don't want to lose anyone."

"And you won't. Hey, I'm proud of you, kid."

I gave him a small smile. For my dad to say that, it meant a lot, but right now wasn't the time to relish in it.

"Remember," I added, looking around at all the faces that were here, ready. Some I hadn't seen since I was a young pup, and some I had never met, but we all had one thing in common: loyalty. "The Lost Boys are not standing with Katsia, mainly because they're smart, but also because they're very black and white, and they know who is in charge and who merely acts in charge. Katsia has her guards, but not that many. I'm not worried about what's going to happen when we enter these gates, but I am stressing that you don't make any irrational moves. We don't want to kill her. Yet."

Everyone mumbled in agreement, so I turned to face the high gates, pulled out the card that my dad gave me earlier which gives us access to wherever we need to get to on here, and swiped it over the laser panel.

Daemon

One, two, three, four, five, six...six...six....

Quiet! I ordered in an attempt to hush them all. *Trickery, War, Rage, Deceit, Evil...* The six demons were running wild in my thoughts. They had names, because they had their own voices. I became aware of this very young. There was no love, I had no love in me, but when Madison was around, I felt the closest thing I could ever feel that came close to love. She engulfed me, completed me and brought joy to my life. I knew not of joy, or happiness, until I met her. The bond between us both was unshakeable, unbreakable and as strong as a rip current in the middle of an ocean. I would die for her and then come back to life to kill whoever tried hurt her and then die for her again. The day in the forest was still a blur for me, but I figured out quickly that *Deceit* had taken over. His presence was still on the tip of my tongue hours after his retreat. I hated myself, still hate myself, and I will never forgive myself for that day. How do you kill the very things that haunt you in your head? How do you strangle something that morphs into smoke the second you try to mentally grasp around its neck? How do you kill someone that essentially is you? I was sick. So very sick. I didn't deserve to share the same blood as Madison, let alone the same womb for nine months.

"Daemon, don't you think?" Bishop asked, leaning against one of the panels that were outside the shops on the only street of Perdita. The war was no longer brewing; it was ready to be served.

I shoved my hands into my pockets and walked toward where Bishop was, beside Hector but front-on to Katsia and her small army of men. We weren't outnumbered, but it would be a good fight should the war erupt. "Of what?"

"That Katsia would look better with her blood spilled over the ground." I felt the energy shift before I saw her. The room fell silent as I turned to see who it was, and my gut clenched. Scarlet, Tatum, and Madison were walking toward us, breaking through the thick gathering of Kings and others. *Oh yes, she's here, let's kill her. Get it right this time.* I ignored *Deceit*.

"Madison!" Bishop shouted, enough to cut the silence. Madison winced. My fists clenched at her discomfort. "What the fuck are you all doing here?"

"Oh!" Katsia taunted. "This is perfect. The Elite ladies, all in one place..." Katsia stepped forward. I leaped in front of Madison, shielding her.

Katsia snorted. "The stray Lost Boy, move, Daemon." As much as she tried to sound strong and demanding, the edge of each syllable fell off her tongue with a small shake. She knew what I was capable of—truly capable of. She sat with the therapists when they diagnosed me, then turned me into her own weapon. I was always loyal to her, right up until the point where Madison came back into my life. She was the game changer.

"No."

Madison's hand came to my arm. "It's ok, Daemon."

Bishop pulled Madison behind him, his eyes slanting on her. "I will beat your ass for this."

Madison smiled. "I count on it."

Turning back to face Katsia, Scarlet stopped beside me, her arms crossed. "I have a bone to pick with you, oh sacred one." She tilted her head. "Turns out, you're not the final line of your blood. Congratulations, you've just made yourself disposable."

Katsia stilled.

I smiled.

Hector pulled Scarlet into him, but she shoved him away. "Don't touch me." Then her eyes went to Khales. "Ever again."

"As much as we all love this song and dance," Spyder announced, walking between us all. "I have a party to get back to, well the fuck away from all you fuckers!" Bishop's wild older cousin who led the Kings in the previous generation with Jase, Saint, Ace, and Ollie, announced. There were only five that year, where there were seven this generation.

"Your pussy fest can wait," Bishop snapped, his head turning over his shoulder.

"'Cause, they really can't..."

"I don't know what you're talking about, Scarlet." Katsia played dumb, stepping forward.

This is getting boring. Let's kill someone. Start with her. Start with Katsia. Always hated her. It will start bloodshed! Yes, let's do it.

Quiet! I roared inside my head, but they continued to push.

Yes, now. Let's do it now. Now, Daemon, enforce it, let it happen. Feel the power seep into your fingertips and embrace it. My eyes slammed shut, my lips pursing. Shut up! A loud round of hyena-like giggles erupted in my head, bouncing off the empty walls of my scarred soul. *Mine.*

"As much as I'd love to continue this cute little chitchat" —darkness cloaked my vision, and my lip curled— "I'm feeling like I'd prefer to see the color red." I slowly slipped my knife down from under my sleeve, grasping the heavy metal handle, then launched forward to Katsia, slicing it across her neck until her blood sprayed across my clothes and her death danced on the tip of my tongue to a metallic melody. My eyes rolled back in euphoria. It was like my first hit of heroin, the feeling of clouds seeping into my bones. A charge erupted through me at the same time as relaxation drifted through the air.

"Oh my God!" Madison screeched, and then hell broke loose. I smirked as one of Katsia's guards hit Nate square in the face with his fist, and a loud crack sounding out. Nate fell to the floor. The guard jumped on him, pulling out his own knife and sinking it into Nate's stomach. Madison started screaming again in the background. Scarlet jumped in front of a stray bullet that was heading straight for Madison. It hit her in the throat with a loud *clap* and she fell to the ground, Hector's arm shooting out to catch her. "Scarlet!"

I pounced forward, grabbing hold of the guard's throat that stabbed Nate and twisted effortlessly until the snap vibrated through my bones. My head whipped to where Bishop was fighting with two of Katsia's men. One had a knife and the other had nothing but his hands. I was about to walk towards him when a sharp pain ripped through my leg. I paused, slowly turning around. My attention went down to the long machete that was sticking out of my leg, and then I smirked, bringing my eyes to Katsia's man. I pulled it out, flicked it around on my fingers, and then launched it into his neck, where it sliced it right off. A puddle of blood bubbled where his head was once attached before he finally slid to the ground. I could see Tate lying on the floor heaving, blood was coming out of her mouth and she had a knife sticking out of her upper thigh.

"I'm fine!" she snapped at me. "Go help Madison!"

Spyder pulled Tate into his arms and flicked his wrist to Bishop. "Fucking go, demon boy!" I spun around, just in time to see Madison weeping near Scarlet, holding her hand.

Bishop roared, "Mom!" shoving one of the men off him. More Kings flew in behind Bishop, after fighting off more of Katsia's men and taking out the two that he was fighting.

A gunshot fired.

Silence.

Bishop stopped, his face falling, his expression unreadable. Madison instantly stopped crying, wiping the tears from her cheeks with her blood-ridden fingers. *Red.*

"Bishop?" she asked softly, before carefully standing to her feet. Bishop's head tilted downward. I followed his movement, and my eyes caught the red stain of blood slowly seeping through his white shirt. His hand came to his stomach before he fell to the ground.

"Bishop!" Madison screamed with such high pitch tones that it shook the street.

Whoever was still fighting instantly stopped mid-air, the last of Katsia's men took the distraction as a time to escape, all scattering off quickly into the wild bushes. Madison flew to where Bishop laid and dropped to the ground. Hector ran, following Madison. Nate used his arms to drag his body along the pavement in an attempt to make it to him.

Bishop's chest was heaving up and down. Nothing was heard but the crackling of his own blood caught in his throat. The curdling desperate attempts of breathing. The hopeless endeavors at staying alive.

Madison's screaming grew more frantic. "Don't you die on me!" *Red.*

I started walking toward him.

Madison's cry slowed to a desperate plea, and when Hector pulled Bishop's shirt up to inspect the wound, I knew instantly it wasn't good. Blood was gushing out of his wound, trickles leaking out between his lips. He struggled to string any words together, but his hand flew to Madison's and he pulled her down to his chest, burying his face in her long hair.

"Bishop! Don't you fucking die on me," she continued to howl into his neck. I tilted my head.

"Son, I need you to hang on tight, you hear, we have a medic team here. Don't you fucking go anywhere, son! I just lost your mother, I can't lose you too!" Hector roared, his palm tightening around Bishop's other hand.

Blackness slowly started to fade with the electrifying color of vibrancy coming into view.

The smug smirk I had so proudly worn slid off my face instantly. "This is my fault." Guilt slammed into me as Madison's grief shook my bones.

"No!" she screamed. "No, no, no!" She banged on Bishop's chest. *So much red.*

Nate tried to pull her away as Tate sat down beside her. "Madison, honey, come here."

"No! Leave me alone! No, he's not dead. He's—he's, Bishop!" She howled again, her screams sending birds to dart from the trees. Her weeping pulled so much emotion that tears fell from the grown men who were huddled around Bishop.

My heart broke into two. *Te amo, soror mea.*

"This is my fault." I slowly lifted my hand that held the thick heavy knife and launched it into my throat. Pain shot through as my own blood started to slip over my hands like slime.

"Daemon!" Tate yelled from somewhere as I fell to the ground.

"Daemon?" Madison screamed again, her voice coming in and out.

"I'm—I'm sorry," I gurgled, blood filling my throat as my vision blurred. The clouds in the sky swirled with the soft blue endless sphere, and my eyelashes fluttered. I tried to suck in more air, but I was drowning. Drowning in my own blood. I deserved it. *Red.*

"Daemon!" Madison's voice was coming in quick, her face hovering over mine. My vision was now completely vivid in color, no more stygian.

A hyena laugh ricocheted off the lifeless walls inside of my brain.

My eyebrows pulled in, confusion seeping into every nerve.

We. Win.

"*Trickery!*" I roared, my back arching off the ground just as death's grip took hold of me.

CHAPTER 33

"What the fuck!" Nate pulled at his hair, stepping backward.

"Daemon?" I wiped the tears that were pouring down my cheeks. I cradled his head under my arm and kissed his forehead. "No, no," I wept, slowly rocking him. Something snapped in my chest, opening up and seeping its pain through my veins. My heart was lifeless, my fingertips numb and my legs aching. *"No!"* I screamed when his eyes lifelessly fell to the back of his head.

I squeezed at the wound on his neck, not wanting to take the knife out. "No. You're going to be ok. It's ok. I'll fix you. I'll always fix you," I mumbled to myself, pawing at his wound like a cat would.

"Madison…" A hand came to my arm.

I reared back. "No. He's not dead."

Heavy combat boots came into view. "Baby…"

My eyes flew to Bishop. "No! He's not dead!"

Bishop watched me carefully. "I'm going to tell you about a demon called Trickery, one of his six…"

I shook my head, wiping the tears off my cheek with my blood-soaked hand. "No. I don't want to hear any more. I don't" —my eyes cut straight to Katsia— "You…" then I slowly put Daemon's head back to the ground. When he was safe on the pavement, I gripped the knife that was in his neck and pulled it out. Flicking it around in my fingers, I flew toward her. "Bitch!" I pounced on her like a tiger would on a gazelle, wrapping my legs around her waist.

Her eyes popped open in shock. "Mad—" I reared my hand back that held the knife and stabbed it deep into her jugular.

Her guards knew they were outnumbered, and they knew she had done wrong. There was no way they could have fought us and lived, and they knew that. It was then that I realized they were mere peacekeepers—as such.

Blood sprayed over my face and retribution sunk into my pores as the sweet taste of revenge slid down my throat. Thick choking sounds vibrated from her throat, her hand coming up to the wound. Arms wrapped around my torso from behind, pulling me off her.

"Shhh, baby, it's going to be ok."

I hiccupped and pushed away from Bishop.

Spinning back around as Hector started chatting with Katsia's men, I ran back to Daemon and cradled his head again, swatting away the flies that started buzzing around.

"It's okay. I got her. She's gone, you can wake up now. I took care of her, I—I—" I wheezed through my breaths, my chest tightening again. When my throat dried from my rushed breathing and adrenaline shot through me, a guttural scream erupted from my chest. I dropped my head into Daemon, weeping the loss of my brother. My other half, my constant. "I love you. I love you, I love you, I love you, goddamnit, Daemon! Why!" I continued to sob into his chest. "I just got you back," I whispered. "*Te amo, frater.*" My swollen eyes scrubbed against his shirt.

"Baby?" Bishop sat beside me and I could hear Tate sobbing somewhere. She loved Daemon, too, even though she didn't display it that much.

I didn't answer Bishop. I couldn't form words. I didn't want to move, I didn't want my mouth to move, I didn't want to talk. I wanted to stay here forever and rewind what had happened. I wouldn't let go of him. Ever. *Te amo, frater*

"I'm going to tell you about Trickery and circa 2014. Daemon's biggest slaughter," Bishop's voice beamed with something. If you mixed fear and pride into a bowl, your finished product would be his tone. "Trickery was one of Daemon's demons that he lived with. In April 2014, he was sent to one of the biggest jobs for The Circle. He was told to do one task, bring in the men, and leave. Shake them up a bit, but not to harm anyone. There were twelve grown men, and *none* of them lived. Up until he came back into your life, we all believed that he had snapped and just gone full schizo, but he hadn't. That night when he and I had that talk, he told me the truth on what happened the night he brutally dismembered twelve men three times his size, sending the pieces back to The Circle in circular shaped suitcases..." He took a breath, and even though I knew there was no way he was about to get a response out of me, I wanted to hear his story. "Poetic, got to give him that. So we had the talk, because I wasn't completely comfortable with him being around you, like you could probably remember. He told me about his de-mons. *Trickery, Deceit, War, Evil, Rage, and Death.* They were numbered, and Deceit was the strongest voice of all, he had said. It was probably the one that took over him the day he shot you..."

I didn't wince. I didn't move. I'd trade places with Daemon in a heartbeat, and a part of me wished I did die that day, then maybe he wouldn't have been here today. It was my fault.

"Trickery took over him in 2014. Daemon saw the man who raped him as a small boy when he looked at all their faces and annihilated each and every one of them. It wasn't until they were dead that Trickery finally released him, but by then, it was too late."

I didn't answer.

"That's what happened today. His greatest war was within himself, baby. He will be at peace now."

His words were like rubbing salt into a wound. The tears started pouring out again.

"Mads?" Tate came closer to me. My eyes went to hers. She was rubbing the tears off her cheeks, but I noticed a guy with a big spider-shaped scar on his neck standing closely behind her. It was so big that it was one of the first things I noticed. Then it was all the tattoos. Then it was his blatant resemblance to Bishop, only with dark hair and bright blue eyes. "Please stand up. We need to take him home."

I shook my head, my fingers gripping around him. Her attention went to someone beside her, who I was guessing was Bishop. She nodded, and then someone was pulling me off Daemon. Inhumane screams exploded out of me as tears soaked through my shirt. "Come here." Bishop's arms wrapped around me tightly.

"Bishop, take her to Miller. The jet is ready. All of you, go with her." I stopped fighting when I realized it was no use. My muscles throbbed and every inch of myself ached. My arms swung around the back of Bishop's neck where I clung on tightly. Silent sobs broke through again, and unable to contain them anymore, I let them flow. *Te amo, frater.*

CHAPTER 34

"I don't think she's going to be ok," Nate said, just as the seatbelt light turned off. She had fallen asleep long before take-off. We had waited for Spyder and Ollie to board the plane, both of them fucking around.

"What the fuck took you so long?" I asked Spyder, my eyes drifting to both him and a guilty looking Ollie. "If you tell me you were hitting on a chick, I swear to God, I will punch you."

"Aw," Spyder grinned, winking at me. "You and I both know I hit harder, little cos."

"Our last fight was when I was five…"

He nodded. "Exactly."

"You make no sense."

He pretended to think over what I had just said, then slowly smirked. "Exactly."

I hated him.

I looked back to a nervous Nate. "She'll be fine. It will take her a while, but she'll pull through. If anyone can, it's her."

Nate squeezed his eyes closed. "I can't ever see her in that kind of pain ever again, so you're not allowed to die."

"Ditto," I muttered before Spyder's voice stole my attention.

"We were helping your old man." He tilted his head up to the ceiling, his eyes looking at me. "He has a lot to clean up after your girl there went firecracker and killed the only *Steprum* walking this earth."

"She's not the only one." Nate shook his head, his finger running across his upper lip. "Scarlet was right, Katsia was lying. Tillie is her daughter, who is a *Steprum*, which means my kid is half *Steprum*." His eyes closed again, I could see he was battling within himself to come to terms with everything he had just learned over the past few days.

"Well, shit," Spyder grunted, closing his eyes. "I should have stayed around here, seems like more drama happens."

"You can stay in New Orleans," I corrected. My cousin and I were actually close, the banter was just what we always did since we were kids.

"I don't know." A slow smirk crept onto his mouth but his eyes stayed closed. "I might have just met a reason to stick around." Ollie's attention flew to where Tate was sitting, a smug, knowing look passing over his features.

"Of fucking course," I snorted.

Brantley sat on the seat in front of us. "She'll be ok, man. No one is as strong as that girl there."

"That's what I'm worried about, though," Nate said, gesturing to where she was curled up under a blanket toward the back of the plane. "She shouldn't *have* to deal with this bullshit. She fucking loved Daemon, man. Like full on fucking loved him. They shared a sibling bond that I had never seen before, and now he's dead? I don't know." Nate shook his head. "I don't know if she'll come back from this. She barely came back from her little trip around the world stunt. She's about to feel real loss, fucking crippling loss. Not the superficial kind, the fucking life shattering, earth moving kind. Not many people can survive it."

Brantley looked at me. "She survived the shit that went on with my dad. She survived being fucking raped as a young girl, Nate. You're wrong. That girl wasn't born capable of dealing with that kind of loss, because she built the wall around herself to handle it, and do you know how she did that?" he asked, his eyes finally settling on Nate, who was watching him back eagerly. "By collecting every fucking brick that was thrown at her from this shitty life."

Nate gulped. I swallowed, and Spyder's eyes cracked open. "That's some rough shit."

Brantley's eyes glassed over. "You have no idea."

We all watched him, and it was like watching someone relive their most horrifying memories in full HD. Brantley was haunted every day by what his dad put them both through, and none of us truly knew the extent of it, but I did know that it was worse than what we knew. He refused to tell us anything else and lived with the shadows of it all every single day.

Ollie cleared his throat. "It was good to be back, I gotta admit, even though the circumstances were fucking shitty."

"Ollie?" Nate muttered under his breath. "Stop fucking talking." Those two cousins, on the other hand, flat out hated each other. Wasn't sure why, Ollie seemed like a down to earth guy. As down to earth as you can get within us all. He lived to surf and had the jaw length blonde locks to go with it. He had the blue eyes and tattoos all over his skin to go with that, too. He looked like he had just fallen out of the set of The OC.

I pushed off the seat and made my way back to Madison, pulling up her blanket and resting her head on my lap. I moved hair off her face, my thumb circling her hard cheekbone. I wanted to know what was happening with my dad and mom, and why they both stayed behind. Actually, all of the elders stayed behind. My thumb halted its movements as I looked around the plane. All of our generation and Spyder's generation were here, while the rest were back at Perdita. *Odd.* But whatever their reasoning, I'd hear about it when they came home.

"B? Can we talk?"

My jaw clenched.

"Please?"

I looked down to Madison before slowly getting back to my feet and placing her head on the seat. I led Khales toward the back of the plane, away from any ears just in case no one knew about her and my dad. "What?" I snapped, unable to stop my jaw from clenching.

"I'm sorry about what happened back there. I misjudged Madison, and you, and

I guess—" She stopped, her eyes falling to her fingers. "I'm sorry, Bishop. When I first came back, I was so angry and enraged by how you had moved on. I hated her so much." She took in a deep breath, and I took this time to study her face. I knew Khales inside and out. I knew when she was lying, when she was happy, sad, or both. I knew if she was hiding any emotion from me. She was transparent to me, unlike Madison who was like a closed fucking book.

"I lost my shit for a bit, B, but you know me, you know I'm not vindictive, and I see it now."

"See—what?" I tilted my head at her.

"I see how you are with her."

I leaned on the wall. "She doesn't like you."

"I know."

"Which means our friendship will never go back to how it was."

Her face fell. "I know."

"Then I wish you and my dad well." I pushed off the wall and headed back to Madison. Just as I slipped back into my seat, I chuckled. "Oh, and good luck with Mom."

Khales flinched but slowly went back into her seat. I did care about her once upon a time...

I liked riding my bike. I liked riding it even more when it was heading in the opposite direction of my house. I couldn't stand it. So there I was, on my silk black BMX, equipped with handlebars that had been dipped in chrome, riding toward the other side of town. With my hoodie thrown up over my head, and my jeans hanging off of my hips and my skater chain dangling off my belt loop, I was riding to where I always went when it became too much at home. When the air became tight and the tension would be close to snapping. Most parents loved each other, whereas mine barely tolerated each other. A car honked from the other side of the road and I kicked my feet back to hit the brakes, skidding to a halt. Turning toward the car, my eyes narrowed. I knew that I shouldn't have stopped. I was young—pretty much still a child. Eight, to be exact. I'm not exactly legally allowed to be riding across town on my own, so without a second glance, I peddled forward and made my way to Newtown Beach. It always took around twenty minutes to get there, and today was no exception. I came to a halt, kicking my bike stand out and looking out to the trailer park.

In a clean layout, there were roughly around twenty metal moveable homes all parked. All with different designs, and obviously, you could see who had the most pride. It ranged from old OCD grandma with florals and cats, to old bins strewn over front yards and rusted swing sets that had seen one too many days in the sun and rain, and not enough being ridden on. My attention went straight to the metal grey trailer I was familiar with. The dents and scratches were clearly visible, even with a brief glance. This trailer was a neglected as the child who resided in it. Not to stereotype trailer parks, because some of them here had blossoming flowers lining their walls and gardens, along with a couple of lazy chairs and tables set up nicely, this one didn't. There wasn't a spec of pride that whistled off of this trailer, and like always, I headed straight for it. I was just about to tread across the fake grass that had long faded from its unnatural plastic of green to a dingy shade of yellow, when the metal door swung open, smashing against the side of the beat-up oversized shit-hole as Khales stormed out, her long brown hair sticking to her heart-shaped face.

Her eyes connected with mine. Her frown turned soft. "Bishop?" She scrubbed the tears off of her cheek, sniffed, and then put her nose up. That pride was going to kill her one day. "You shouldn't have come, Bishop. He's angry today. Like, extra angry."

My heart pinched a little for her. I hated my parents, but they'd never do the things Khales' dad did to her, and I despised the expensive architecture I called home, but it wasn't a run down, beat up, dingy metal on wheels shit-box that on a good day, stinks like beer, sweat, and stale cigarette smoke. Where on a bad day, it smelled of whiskey, sweat, stale cigarette, and Khales' tears mixed with her dried blood. I felt my anger drop to its knees inside of me and beg to travel through my veins and rest on the slight tingle at my fingertips.

"What'd he do?" I asked her, pushing my hands into my hoodie pocket to hide the way my nails sunk into the palm of my hands. I wanted to protect her. She was the first friend I had outside of the Kings, and I'd known her since pre-school. I'd had a front row ticket to this same shit-show since we were kids, and I was about ready to punch our ticket and end it once and for all.

"He's just drunk, Bishop." A smile, so weak, so placid, came onto her face. "Can we go to your place? Or have you taken the pegs off your bike?"

My anger simmered out a little, and my shoulders slightly rested. "I haven't. I won't, not until you don't need them anymore." She pulled her hair into a high ponytail and then snapped a fluorescent pink band around it before she gestured to the bike. "Let's go then."

"And your dad?" I questioned, watching as she bounced over to my bike and turned to wait for me. "Screw him."

"He will hurt you, Lees, and you know it. I don't want him to hurt you ever again." I headed toward her, taking the handle bars into the palm of my hands and sitting on the chair. She stood on the pegs, her hands coming to my shoulders. "I can't stop him, B."

Maybe she couldn't stop him, but I could.

And I did a couple years later. He was my first kill. I remember calling my dad, panicking with the gun hanging on the tips of my fingers. Dad, my uncle, and Johan came. I thought I would have been in trouble. I just committed murder at age thirteen, you would think that was a big deal. It wasn't. It was a part of my initiation process, and I was the only one to ever begin at that age. My dad was proud. The Kings were proud.

I pulled my phone out when Madison's head was rested back on my lap, and pulled out my ear pods. I pushed play on "Whoring Streets" by Scars on Broadway, and slipped it into our playlist, closing my eyes and reliving, soaking every inch of what I remember of her.

"What are you doing here?" Madison asked, stepping outside cautiously and shutting the door. She was somewhat smart to be cautious around me, that was for sure. I took a seat on one of the marble steps, and looked directly at her, only hers were on my car.

"I told you," I answered matter-of-factly. "We need to talk." I didn't even hide the fact that my eyes were undressing her. She wore cute little shorts and a tight tank that rose up to display her belly. When my eyes fell to her socks, my eyebrow rose in shock. "Is that Banksy's work?"

"I'm shocked," she snorted sarcastically, and I had to fight the urge to rip her fucking clothes off and eat her on her parents' doorstep. My fingers twitched, and just when I was about to throw my 'talk' out the fucking window, she fucking insulted me. "You know Banksy?"

"I know his artwork," I retorted.

I could see her trying her hardest to not meet my gaze, so she flipped the box of chocolates open and gestured them to me. "I can share."

Her eyes finally came to mine, and I leaned into my shoulder, using it to shield my mouth. My attention stayed on her, studying, trying to crack open every single cage she kept hidden. What the fuck was it with her. I fucking wanted her. "What?"

I shook my head, breaking our eye contact and looking straight ahead. "You're different."

"I've been told that all my life." My jaw tensed. I knew that she meant that as an insult, but I didn't say it as an insult, it was a good thing. A fucking dangerous thing, but a good thing nonetheless.

"Is that what you wanted to talk about?"

"You and Carter?" I threw her off track.

"Are none of your business."

"Really?" My lip curled. "Pretty sure you made it my business the second you were screaming my name and clawing up my back."

I fought the smirk that was possessing my mouth and leaned back farther into my chair. Just thinking about that night was making my dick hard all over again.

My karma may be a bitch, but damn the bitch is beautiful.

CHAPTER 35

"I've felt loss. I've suffered and lived through what felt like my heart being ripped from my chest. Death was a brutal thing. Its behavior could be unrestrainedly ferocious, and at times, radiated toward the people who didn't deserve to be at the receiving end of its wrath. It tore your heart into two by taking your loved one and replacing them with nothing but the sweet whispers of their memories. Those memories will become the shoulders you cry on."

– Amo Jones

(on losing the most important father in her life)

The trip back to my house felt long, and the hours felt as though they stretched into days. By the time we reached my driveway, I was tired again, my eyes struggling to stay awake through all the trauma. Bishop's arm never left me, and I snuggled into him deeper, burying my face into his chest. He leaned down and kissed me as the car came to a stop.

"Come on."

Finally, my mouth opened and words left me. "I love you."

"I love you too." He searched my eyes. "You're going to get through this."

I nodded, even though I didn't believe a damn thing he said.

"Oh, um." My eyes flew to Nate, who was taking off his seatbelt. "We're having a meeting today, with Tillie."

Nate softened, his hard features instantly changing. "Why?" he whispered.

"She wants to leave."

"Like fuck!" he roared. I winced from the sudden lash out.

"Nate!" Bishop scolded him.

"Sorry, sis, but she can't leave. I'll k—" He paused, his eyes going to Bishop and then changed his tactic. "Too soon. She just can't leave with my kid."

"She won't, but that's what we need this meeting for." I waited for Bishop to get out of the car then slipped out behind him. "And then, I'm going to plan my brother's funeral."

A second car pulled up behind us with Jase, Hunter, Eli, Chase, and Brantley inside, and then another behind theirs with Spyder, Ollie, Tate, and someone else I didn't care to recognize. Tate tried to come with us, but Nate kicked her out.

I left everyone behind and went to the front door, pushing it open. "Tillie?" I called out, but my voice was weak. It physically hurt to speak, and the sooner this day was over, the better. Bishop, Nate, and Jase walked in behind with the rest of the gang. I headed to the sitting room.

I looked at Elena. "Where's Tillie?"

I didn't want a shower. I wanted to stay as I was, with the last bit of Daemon left on my skin, so when Elena's eyes went to my hands, she flinched.

"Daemon," I whispered, my throat swollen.

"And Katsia," Nate added, climbing onto the couch with his mom.

That's when I heard Nate ask, "What's wrong?"

My eyes swung back to Elena, who met mine. "I'm sorry about your loss, sweet-heart. I know how much Daemon meant to you," she paused. I winced, tears pooling again. She stood, wiped her pants and squared her shoulders, putting on a fake smile, even though tears were threatening the corner of her eyes.

Her eyes went to Nate. "She's gone."

"What!" Nate flew off his chair. My throat swelled, my eyes closing. "When?"

I shook my head. "She wouldn't leave, Elena. She was happy that Micaela had her dad."

"Stop defending her, sis, not everyone has the same thought process as you."

Elena's eyes came to mine. "No, she's right. Something doesn't feel right, Nate. I took her and the baby to register Micaela. I dropped them at the front and told them I'd be right back after finding a parking spot. Tillie wasn't erratic. She left the diaper bag in the car and asked me to bring it in with me because her hands were full with the papers and documents she needed." She paused. "I just got home. I spent hours there trying to find them. I demanded to look at CCTV footage but without a warrant, they can't show me anything." Her eyes came to me. "Something is not right, Madison."

"And if she has run?" Hunter asked, coming closer to me. Jase followed him when suddenly, I had my two brothers behind me, Bishop beside me, Tate coming up closely, and Nate sitting directly in front of me. I exhaled a shaky breath. "First, I want to bury my brother" —I paused, my head tilting over my shoulder to Jase and Hunter— "our brother." Then I looked at Nate. "Then we can get her back."

His knee jiggled. "We better bury him tomorrow, then, sis, because if she's missing, that means my kid could be in danger."

He was right.

I pulled my phone out of my pocket and dialed my dad, who was still on Perdita.

He answered. "Madison? Are you ok?"

I cleared my throat. "Yes. How long until Daemon can be here? I'd like to bury him tomorrow, and we have a situation here where Tillie may be missing with the baby."

Dad paused. "Jesus. Ok. Yes, I'll have everything sorted for a burial tomorrow. Do you have any requests on caskets?"

"Black, and Dad?"

"Yeah, baby?"

"I love you."

There was a long pause. "I love you too."

Hanging up, I sighed, massaging my temples. "Dad will have everything sorted for a burial tomorrow. I assume he will be buried in our family plot here." Bishop pulled me under his arm.

"We will find her, Nate, I promise."

Later that night, I'm climbing the stairs after a long hot bath when I hit the top of the stairs and head into my bedroom. Bishop and I wanted alone time but didn't get it, because now my bedroom was filled with not just the ten Kings I was familiar with, but the other three who were from the previous generation, too.

And Tate, of course.

They all paused watching their tv show and their attention came to me as I opened my door. "Thanks for all being here, but honestly, it's not necessary."

Tate perched up on her elbow. "It's okay, Mads. Let us."

I internally battled with myself, but when my eyes went to Bishop, who was freshly showered with grey sweatpants on and no shirt, my brain seized. His gaze assaulted my body, and I flushed before going to the bed. It felt empty not having Daemon here with us. I slid under the cover and Bishop pulled me under his arm. Kissing my head.

The next morning, my muscles felt tight, unmovable. My eyes slowly cracked open, and I sat up slowly, looking down at the mass of bodies that were still snoring on the floor. The patio door was open all night, allowing a soft breeze to maintain its calmness through my bedroom.

"You ok?" Bishop asked, leaning up on his elbows. I turned to face him over my shoulder, my eyes falling on his soft lips.

"I will be. I think." I got up from bed and strategically made my way to the door that led into my bathroom. I slowly teased at sliding my shorts down and nudged my head toward the tub. "I could do with a bath though?"

He bit his lip to try to hide his grin and then followed behind me, shutting the door behind us. His hand sprawled out over my tummy, his arousal pressing into my back. "Stay there."

I closed my eyes, and soaked up every touch, every whispering movement that he cascaded over my flesh. Tilting my head, his lips came to where my neck met my shoulders. He sucked on it softly, his hand slowly moving under my panties. His thumb pressed against my clit in slow circles. My mouth opened as a gasp left me. My chest rose and fell as his kisses on my neck became more desperate and his index finger slid inside of me as his thumb continued to rub my clit. His other hand came to the bottom of my tank and dipped underneath, his thumb and finger finding my nipple. He twisted it—hard, the pain and the pleasure both intertwining together in an intimate embrace. My orgasm ripped through me and stars exploded inside my head as my breathing came down slowly. He pulled out from inside of me, dipping his finger into my mouth. The sweetness coating the tip of my tongue. Turning around, I wrapped my arms around his neck, and his hands came to the backs of my thighs, lifting me off the ground. He stepped farther into the bathroom, my legs still wrapped around him like a vise. He leaned over, flicking the tap of the bath on. Our silence was broken by the loud splashing of water as it filled the tub.

"Am I going to be ok?" I asked him, searching his eyes as he busied himself pouring all sorts of oils and bath salts into the bath.

He didn't answer, he put me on my feet and continued to undress me. I stepped into the hot scolding water, wincing from the temperature before slowly dipping myself into it. The pinching slowly started to dissipate and the steam rose, swimming around my face in a mix of sweet lavenders and fresh cut green grass. Bishop slid in behind me, opening his legs and pulling me against his bare chest.

"I don't know, baby, no one knows." He cleared his throat, kissing my head. "If you are, then I'll be here, and if you're not, then I'll be here. I'll always be here, Madison. Through the good times, but most importantly through the ugly times. I'm not going anywhere, and I can't promise you that I'm not going to fuck this up somewhere along the way and piss you off epically, but I'll always be loyal to you. There was no one before you and there sure as fuck won't be anyone after you. I begin and end with you, baby." He kissed my temple. "So I don't know if you're going to be ok, but I do know that I'll be here regardless."

Tears fell down my cheeks. I sniffed, clearing my throat. "That's all I need." Then I turned to face him, and his arms fell to the side. I climbed on top of him and watched his features soften as I lowered myself onto his cock. His eyes rolled to the back of his head, his bottom lip pulling into his mouth and a soft groan vibrated from him. I slowly lifted, and then circled my hips, my walls clenching around his thick length. It felt natural, like a piece of my puzzle was now in place every time he was inside of me. I was addicted to the feeling of him being inside, filling me. His hands came to my hips, his fingertips gripping my hip bones, then he tapped my thigh. "Get up." I stood, following his orders, and he leaned my body in half, propping one leg on the edge of the bath. I hung onto the bathroom sink for support and he gripped onto my hips again, pulling me into his cock. He pulled out and sunk back in, then one of his hands came to my hair, wrapping it around his fist as he pounded into me. Water splashed around our ankles and sprayed all over the floor. Moans were leaving my mouth, and his hand flew to my throat, where he clenched down roughly, using it as a handle. He continued to lay into me relentlessly.

He pulled out, and I stood to my height when he sunk back into the bath and I sat down on top of him again, reverse cowgirl. Using his legs to lift myself up, I slowly rode his cock until sweat beaded off of my flesh and the water turned cold. His thighs clenched under my palms and my body vibrated from the lead up of my orgasm. When his cock stroked my pussy once again, I let go, my core exploding inside of me. His cock throbbed, emptying himself with every thud. I dropped into his chest and he pulled me into him, kissing my head.

"You're going to be fine, baby."

I remember the day I bought this dress. I saw it in a storefront window. The way the black lace weaved over my chest and the tight material curved over every bone, and muscle on my body. It was held together by lace, with the middle strip missing, displaying the edge of your abs—if you had them, which I didn't. My lack of food intake was beginning to show, and it was the first time I realized my collarbone was sharp enough to cut through rock. I stared back at myself in the free-standing oval mirror, really looking deep into my own eyes.

"Te amo, frater." Tears formed at the surface again, on the brink of spilling over, but there was a knock on the door and my head tilted towards the entryway.

"Hey, Mads, I have a couple people who want to meet you," Jase said, hinting to who it could be. "Is that ok?"

I stomped down my feelings, cleared my throat, and then ran my hands down my dress. Black. The color was symbolic to death, which was why I chose to wear white. I refused to believe my brother was dead. He deserved more than what the color black could give.

I nodded, wiping my eyes. He opened the door wider, and a man and woman stood there. The woman was dressed in a black long dress and was holding a large hat that had lace hanging off the front. She was beautiful, had honey brown eyes, skin that held a tint that no amount of sun could give you which told me she had something else in her blood. Her eyes met mine and her eyebrows pulled together. My own went to the man standing next to her. He wore a dark suit and a dark tie. He was tall, towering over her small frame, had grey hair and aged skin. He had to be pushing his early fifties. He looked somber and held a different softness on his shoulders than most of the other Kings.

"Madison," she started. "I'm Jamima, your—" she paused, her fingers twisting around her hat. "Birth mom." She stepped forward, and that's when I caught Scarlet leaning against the wall behind them. She sent me a sneaky wink, and I knew what it meant. She had my back if I needed. Jase stayed, opening the door wider. I appreciated it because it didn't feel like I was closed off in this room with nothing but the parents I didn't know who, essentially, gave me and Daemon away.

"Why?" I asked quickly.

The man cleared his throat. "I'm Johan, Madison, I'm sorry we had to meet like this. Jamima and I understand that you will have questions, and we don't want to hold back on answering those for you. You deserve honesty," he paused, and his eyes went over his shoulder, straight to Scarlet, who gave him a look I wasn't sure how to decipher. It was like a mother bear protecting her cubs. My heart warmed instantly, and with that small notion, I knew I could handle whatever they dished me, because they didn't matter to me right now. What mattered was the strength I felt radiating off of Scarlet. She was the only mother I *needed*, anyone else didn't matter. I nodded. "Thank you. I'd appreciate that."

He looked back at me. "I'm sure you're familiar with how our world spins by now. When your m—Jamima found out she was pregnant, she was ecstatic, when we found out that we were having twins, we were even more pleased. Twins were rare in any case, but there had never been twins born into our world. When we found out that one of you was a girl, we kept it quiet, though we were shattered. We knew we couldn't share it with anyone because the risk was too high. You were a Silver Swan; you were sure to die." His hands dove into his pockets, and Jamima finished it off.

"We were close to Elizabeth and Joseph. They were cousins, so they agreed to take you and run. Run for the rest of your lives. But when your brother was born, Elizabeth didn't bond with him, so she sent him to Katsia's mother where he was raised on Perdita, speaking only Latin. They tried to teach him English as well, like they did with Katsia, but he refused." She cleared her throat. "I understand that you have a lot of love around you, and we don't deserve a nick of your time, but we wanted you to know."

My eyes went to Scarlet. "What will happen now? Now that Katsia is dead? What happens to little girls now?"

Scarlet smiled at me. "Now they will be welcomed." She pushed off the wall and came to me. "That's why we stayed behind, to have a conference with The Circle. Your father pushed for it, as did I. Hector on the other hand." She rolled her eyes, but her hand found mine. "He came around, though, and now? Because of you, sweet girl." Scarlet's hand came to my face. "No King needs to worry about having a little girl. Nothing else would change, only that the girls would be accepted into the family alliances now."

"Jesus take the wheel," Nate muttered from somewhere in the background.

I snorted, my hand coming up to cover my mouth. "Thank you, Scarlet. For being everything I ever wanted in a mom."

She wrapped her arm around mine. "You can call me Mom."

Scarlet's eyes went to Jamima and Johan. "Are you done? We have a funeral to attend."

They both nodded and exited the room.

"You don't like them?" I asked, not looking at her.

"No. I never have. I don't agree with what they did and how they went about it. You suffered greatly as a child and even as a young adult. They failed you as a daughter, and failed as humans."

I swallowed. "I don't care now. I can't or it will consume me."

She patted my hand just as Bishop entered my room. My mouth watered and my jaw almost hit the floor. He wore black slacks and a white shirt with the sleeves rolled up, displaying his tattoos. His hair was styled perfectly on the top of his head, and his skin had a light sheen over it, glistening against the light.

"Are you ok?" he asked, tilting his head. His eyes flew between his mom and I. "Do I need to be worried about this little bond you two have together? Like are you going to team up on me a lot?"

Scarlet and I both looked at each other, then back at him. "Every chance we get," we both answered in unison, then laughed.

Once everyone left my room, and only Bishop and I remained, he leaned into me. "I know you don't want to talk about this right now, but it's your birthday next weekend."

I shook my head. "I don't want to celebrate anything this year. Please. I really don't. Maybe next year."

He nodded. "Okay, baby. I respect that." Then he leaned forward, his hand going under my bed and pulled out the book. "You need to finish this."

I took it from him.

His eyes searched mine. "You've made history, baby. You're a damn hero. Now because of you? This Katsia gets her final wish."

I opened up to the final chapter.

16.

Legacy

Today is the final time I write in this diary. I can no longer live through this crippling pain Humphrey inflicted on me and my family on a daily basis. My thoughts had turned dark, like an infectious disease he implanted into my cranium, it slowly spread like cancer, consuming my thoughts with dark depression. Days were harder to come by, I could no longer live with the guilt of knowing what was happening amongst our world. I could no longer live with what my husband was doing to baby girls or their families. No one would ever confront him, this would continue for years to come and I could no longer live a second more in this hideous place we call life. The Lost Boys have turned evil.

No one stands with me.

To Maree, my maid, my friend, my confidante, I plead you live a life full of happiness and freedom. Please leave Phillip, becoming a Venari would seal your fate of living behind an aging cage. You will never grasp true happiness by being confined to the palms of his hands.

My son's:

I wish that you both always rule with more love than power. Use the light to see you through, as darkness could never lead you through darkness, only light could do that.

I wished for a better world. Where the Silver Swans could be unleashed to bathe in the crystal water of purity and not be crucified.

Signed, Katsia Hayes

Katsia put her pen down on top of her desk for the final time, stood on the chair she had sat at numerously throughout the years, wrapped the noose around her neck, and took her final leap.

I sucked in a breath, my hand coming to the front of my throat.

Bishop came to me, pulling me into his arms. "You gave Katsia her final wish, baby."

I wiped the tears from my cheeks and sunk into him as he slowly rocked me. "You're my little hero."

We made our way downstairs, and then outside. Bishop beeped his Maserati, but I froze. "Wait!" My hand dug into my handbag and gripped around a set of keys. I dangled them in front of my face.

Bishop grinned.

"I think Daemon would have loved to see this."

We both slipped into my Lamborghini, and Bishop gestured to the pedals. "I trust your driving, but just saying, you need to go easy—" I floored it forward and flew out of the driveway, passing everyone who were on their way to Daemon's funeral. "Or not."

Adrenaline spiked through my veins as my fingers clenched around the leather steering wheel. I turned to face Bishop. "We're going to be ok."

He grinned back at me. "Always, Kitty."

My phone vibrated, and I opened it, slowing to a safer speed.

Bishop: Riddle me this, Kitty, what's round, smooth, and is home for a sparkling stone?

My eyebrows pinched together.

I looked at him. "What?"

His lip kicked up in a grin. "Don't worry about it, baby. Don't worry your pretty little head about it, I'm sure you'll figure it out someday...."

I put my phone back down and floored it to the funeral.

If you had told me that I'd be where I was when I first started Riverside Prep, I would have laughed at you. I struggled to make friends, let alone turning a whole bunch of friends into family. I smiled, even though today was one of the saddest and hardest days I would have to face, I recognized the amount of support I had around me. If it weren't for these people, I may not have survived losing Daemon. I now understood the name "Silver Swan." I was built to handle any and everything life threw at me.

As graceful as a floating swan, but as deadly as a silver bullet.

People gathered around the burial ground like I'd seen in so many movies before. The parts that they don't show in the movie though, is the feeling of your world stopping as its happening. Micaela twisted in my arms and tears streamed down my face. My heart snapped in my chest. I struggled to keep my emotions at bay.

"You see, sister." Peyton leaned forward as we watched my friends and family mourn the loss of Daemon. "You don't belong with them. You belong with *us.*"

She sat back in her seat. She was so wrong. I deserved to be there, with them. They were my family. *Daemon was my family.*

I glared at her from across the dark black limo.

"It's for the best, Tillie, those people aren't good people," Carter added, his eyes coming to mine.

"Why are you here, Carter? You were Madi's friend. How could you?"

His laughter was smug. Mocking. "I never was her friend. She killed Ally."

"You and Ally?" I asked, confused.

He leaned back in his chair. "That's right. Ally didn't send the video—I did."

"Let me go," I deadpanned.

Peyton shook her head and laughed. "Never. They will get what's coming to them, and then some. You see" —she leaned forward again— "The Circle doesn't even know that I've been working with Katsia all along, our *mother.* You need to learn your loyalties, *sister.*"

Carter's eyes came to mine again. "They'll get what's coming to them."

I wanted to scream, to demand they let me and my daughter leave, but then an excruciating pain thudded on the side of my head and everything went black.

"I think I love you, Daemon."

His head tilted, but his eyes studied my lips. He always watched me with importance. He made me feel like I mattered. Cherished, loved.

"Te amo?" Then his eyes glassed over as he slowly rocked Micaela. "I—I'm not—not good."

I shook my head, my hand falling to his thigh. "We can make this work. I know we can."

His eyes connected with mine, and I saw something flash over the surface. Since Daemon walked into the room the day I was in labor, he hadn't left my side. He refused to leave us here to go home, even for Madison. I could never tell her. I would never want to steal that away from her because I knew how overprotective she was of him. I had heard stories about their bond. But our bond was unique, too. It was instant, and easy. He moved, I moved. Even though we lacked communication for the most part with the language barrier, his eyes gave me what his words could not.

His touch.

He placed Micaela into the little crib Tinker stole for us, pulling her blanket up to her chin. I wrapped my arms around his stomach. His body, so still and stoic, relaxed in my embrace.

"I love you, Daemon." My heart beat for him. I knew his did for me too.

His hand came to mine and he turned in my embrace. His eyes searched mine, his finger coming to my lip. He slowly kissed me, his warm lips caressing mine so softly it stole my breath. "Te amo, amans."

DELETED SCENE

Do NOT read past this unless… you know… those dirty fantasies were on the Reverse Harem side…

Two Feet "Go Fuck Yourself" was thumping through the boom speaker. The smell of charcoal BBQ drifted through the air and my sunglasses dropped, covering my eyes.

Nate staring up at me caught me off guard. He had his cap flipped on backward and wore shorts that cut off at the knee. Bishop, Cash, Brantley, Chase, and Nate were all here at our favorite waterhole. Eli decided to stay with my brothers.

"Why are you staring at me like that?" I asked.

"Like what?" Nate teased, his eyes going from my lips to my eyes.

"Like you want to eat me."

His tongue caught his bottom lip and he grinned. "And if I do?" His hand slowly trailed up my inner thigh. I bit my lip, ignoring the tingle that followed his touch.

"I'd say how hungry are you?" I should stop teasing.

Bishop came over, dropping to his knees in front of me and shaking out the water in his hair until it was sticking up above his head. He pushed past Nate, resting in the middle of my thighs. I laid back, ripping my sunglasses off. "What are you doing?"

"Oh come on, Kitty. Don't act like you haven't played out this fantasy before…"

"This is my dream, isn't it? I'm dreaming again…" My eyes narrowed.

Bishop smirked, tilting his head. I couldn't read his expression because the sun beamed behind him, shading out his features. "Is it? Or isn't it? Does it really matter?"

Cash sat down on my other side with Brantley. "Go with it, Kitty."

I swallowed.

Bishop's lips came to mine, the soft cushions opening my mouth. His tongue slipped inside. I moaned a little, and his teeth caught my tongue.

He stood, stepping backward and putting a smoke into his mouth. "Brantley, show me how you've always wanted to fuck her."

"What!" I snapped, looking at Bishop.

Brantley came into my view just as Bishop blew out a cloud of smoke.

His hands came to my thighs, spreading them wide. His face dropped down to my middle and he inhaled roughly, the tip of his nose sliding up my slit. "You smell the same. Only dirtier."

My cheeks flushed bright red. "Brantley…"

His finger hooked under my bikini bottoms, yanking them off. The warm summer day breezed over my swollen clit. Brantley's face dove between my thighs, his tongue licking me, and then circling.

I moaned, lying back down, my back arching off the sand.

Nate's hand came to my breast and he yanked my tit out of my bikini. The coolness of the air was soon replaced by his hot mouth. His tongue circled my nipple roughly as his hand came up to my other and twisted. His teeth scraped over my nipple as Brantley's tongue assaulted my pussy.

Cash came into view, his blonde hair shimmering from the sun. He grinned his million-dollar smile, dropped beside me and took my mouth. A soft moan left me, my hand flying to the back of his neck, pulling him closer. My pussy throbbed as Brantley continued sucking and licking, and Nate's bites got more aggressive.

Cash let up just as Brantley stopped. I propped up on my elbows and saw Bishop standing near Brantley, watching me with his heavy cock in the palm of his hand, stroking himself. My mouth watered, and my hips circled the air.

"Easy, tiger," Brantley whispered, gripping my thighs roughly and yanking me down. He rubbed his cock from the outside of his shorts. "Want my dick, Madison?"

My eyes shot to his, my eyelashes flittering. "Wha—what?" I looked at Bishop.

"Don't look at him. Right now, you belong to all of us. So I'll ask you again..." he paused, his head tilting. He wore my arousal like lip balm, glistening in the sun. "Do you want my dick, Kitty?"

My hips circled the air again as my eyes dropped to his hand. He squeezed and rubbed the thick bulge from outside his shorts. Nate continued to suck on my nipple, and Cash's hand came over my stomach, down to my pussy, rubbing my clit and then he slid a finger inside of me.

"Oh my God," I moaned, tilting my head back.

"You do?" Brantley asked again. My eyes were closed and my hips were grating against Cash's fingers. He pulled out and then raised his finger to my mouth.

"Suck if you want this, Madison," Cash said, his lips coming to my ear. "I'll pretend like you have a choice."

"And if I don't?" I quirked an eyebrow at Brantley, the sweet scent of my pussy on Nate's finger.

"Then I'll rape you," Brantley said, his eyes coming to mine.

Fear slid into my bones, but all it did was feed my desire. I wanted them all, and the thought of them being rough with me only spiked my need.

I kept my eyes on Brantley, then slowly turned my head and sucked myself off Nate's finger. I circled it with my tongue, my eyes still watching Brantley.

His eyes darkened, his hands falling. "Fuck." He stopped his groping and crawled back over my body. "I'm going to break you, little girl."

"Again?" I teased. "Break me, and then fuck me, and then break me, and then fuck me..."

His hands came to my thighs. He ripped me off the ground, turning me onto my stomach.

I arched my back, my hair falling over my shoulder and my eyes catching Nate's. "Come here."

He bit his bottom lip, pulling his shorts down until his cock sprung free. Thick, long and heavy, like him. A bead of cum surfaced at the end of his dick and my mouth watered. I turned my head, relishing in Brantley massaging my ass. He slapped it loudly and I screamed out from the impact. Nate came to the front of me, his eyes watching me. I bent down and took him in my mouth, salt and soap hitting the back of my throat.

His hand came to my hair and he tugged on it roughly, pinching my flesh. "Fuck."

Brantley's mouth fell to the back of my pussy, his tongue diving inside and circling. "I need to eat this forever."

"You can't. Just for today," I heard from somewhere.

Brantley's cock circled my entrance, just before he rammed himself into me.

"*Oh my God!*" I bellowed out in pleasure, veins ripping out of my neck and Nate's cock resting on my lower lip. I spat on it, circling it with my hand. Dropping my lips to his balls, I sucked him into my mouth. Marilyn Manson's "Sweet Dreams" started playing from the speaker. I sunk him deeper into my mouth, as Brantley's cock continued to fuck my pussy. I throbbed, and pushed, and throbbed against him. His fingers gripped around my hip bones as he smashed me back and forth.

Brantley sat me up, hiking up my leg. Cash came closer, my eyes connecting with his. He slid under me, sucking my nipple into his mouth as Brantley continued to fuck me from behind. I sucked Nate deeper into my mouth, and then a hot mouth covered my clit.

"*Shit, shit, shit, shit!*" I screamed out in pleasure again, sweat dripping off of my flesh. Brantley pounded into me as Cash's tongue circled my clit again. Brantley's grip on my thigh tightened. I moaned again, my muscles clenching, tightening. I could feel myself get closer to my peak. Cash wrapped his lips around my clit and I lost it. My pussy throbbed and cum trickled down my thighs. I looked up just in time to see Bishop's hands wrap around my hair, yanking my head back. He stood to the side, just as Nate's cum shot on my face, soaking my lips. I licked him off.

"You like that, huh. Because you're my little slut," Bishop grunted, he replaced Nate's position. Now in front of me. He rubbed Nate's cum off my face with the tip of his cock and then shoved it into my mouth. "You like the taste of him, Madison? Hmm? You like being a little slut." His hand gripped around my hair roughly and he shoved his cock deeper into my mouth. I gagged on the intrusion, tears pouring down my face. Wrapping him in my hand, I sucked him roughly while trying to suck air in every few seconds.

Brantley's cock pulse inside of me on his release, and then he slapped my ass, pulling out, but he was only replaced with Cash.

Cash's cock circled my entrance, wetting his tip. Then he slipped into the opening of my ass. "Open wide, princess. This might hurt a little."

My eyes flew to Bishop, who was grinning down at me. "Nah, I've been there, dawg." Cash pushed inside deeper.

"*Ouch! Fuck! Fuck!*" I screamed, my eyes slamming shut from the tightness and pain. It felt like knives skinning me from the inside.

"Suck my dick, Kitty." I sucked Bishop into my mouth, circling his delicious cock with my tongue, groaning against him. I was full from Cash, but it was delectable. My ass pulsed but my pussy wept from want. Cash pounded, shoving me into Bishop's cock so that with every movement, Bishop's dick was sinking deeper and deeper into my throat.

Cash slapped my ass so hard I yelped out. That was sure to bruise. Bishop's hand came to the back of my neck and he yanked harder. "Take it like a slut, Madison. This was what you wanted, now take it." Cash pulled out of my ass and shot cum all over my back. He swatted my ass again. "Good girl, Kitty."

Bishop yanked me to my feet and then gripped the backs of my thighs. I wrapped my legs around him and then felt Nate behind me. Nate's lips pressed against the small of my neck. "Ready to get fucked?"

I gulped.

Bishop lowered my body onto his cock, his mouth coming to my breast where he sucked on my nipple. Then Nate's cock pressed against the entrance of my ass again, his arm snaking around my stomach. I could still feel Cash's cum sliding out and down my crack. I moaned, licking my lips.

Nate's dick filled my ass, with Bishop owning my pussy. Being loaded by both of them was a fulfillment like no other. "You're going to break me."

"Then you better fucking hold on," Bishop whispered in my ear. He thrust into me as Nate pounded from behind. We stayed like that for minutes. I moaned, and then bit down on Bishop's lip as another orgasm exploded inside of me. Bishop slowly began laying down, and Nate unlatched. They all hovered with perfect fluid-like movements, like they had done this before. I was straddling Bishop now, riding him. Nate came up from behind me again, bent me at my waist until my hands flew to Bishop's chest, keeping me upright. Nate's cock sunk into my ass again. His hand came to my hair where he tugged on it roughly. He continued to pound into me. Brantley smashed my pussy, his mouth sucking on my tit until it pinched with pain.

"I'm—I'm..." Another orgasm ruptured through me. My muscles were severed. My eyes were shutting. Bishop's hands came to my hips and Nate's gripped my ass. They both hammered into me like a ragdoll until I felt them both empty inside of me. Filling me to the brink. I dropped onto Bishop's chest, my breathing heavy. Nate withdrew from me, and I sucked in heavy breaths.

"Holy shit."

ACKNOWLEDGEMENTS

I have so many people to thank, but I don't want to drag this on.

My children who inspire me daily.

My partner who puts up with my crazy, and my mummy who always has my back.

My brothers who are my everything, and my sisters who, even though we don't always see eye-to-eye, I will always be here for.

To my favorite sister-in-law, Chacha! I miss you, girl.

To my best bitch, best friend, Isis. For the everything. For tolerating me, for never judging me, and for accepting me warts and all…even though you have beautiful skin. Bitch.

My readers who continue to support me and have my back!

My bloggers for taking the time out of their busy days to read, review and share me, and my three best friends, who read my words raw and give me the best feedback.

My agent, Flavia! Thank you for exceeding all my expectations and loving my books like they're your own.

Ellie! For editing my words. Girl, draaaannks on me in Vegas. I just said dranks. Bet you hate me now, if you didn't already. Tough, I have screenshots of you telling me you love me. Screenshots don't lie.

My PA Caro! She needs a pay raise. Like a massive one.

My PR unicorn and the girls from Social Butterfly! (lifts wine glass).

The authors who inspire, support, and encourage one another—my tribe!

Chantal! You're stuck with me.

Ofa & Priscilla my OG bitches!

To Jaci—for keeping me sane most of the time.

My Wolf Pack—(howls).

Jay Aheer—I love you. Thank you for my beautiful covers. For learning my vision and nailing them every single time.

And lastly, to all the readers who may be about to read me for the first time ever: thank you for giving a girl a shot.

THE ELITE KING'S CLUB BOOK FOUR

MALUM

PART ONE

Nuncupatura
To the girls who don't just walk through fire. They dance in it.

INTRODUCTION

This is the first time that I have ever put a trigger warning at the beginning of my book. I usually say that my name itself is your trigger warning. You know how I write, the stories that come pouring out of my imagination and bleed over my keyboard, but this time, I need to give a warning. There is a scene in this book that is not just dark, it's disturbing, but it's real. It happens, and it has impacted me in my lifetime. It was very hard for me to write this scene, and throughout the writing process of this book, I tried to avoid it. I bitched and whined to Chantal about how much I didn't want to do it. I tried to take this story down different routes, but it didn't matter, because we always ended back at this point. I promise I softened the scene as much as possible, and usually that's not my style, but in this case, I felt it was imperative to do so. At the end of this book, there will be help links for anyone that may be dealing with similar circumstances. I have also put warning signs leading up to the scene, so you will probably know where I'm about to go with it and have the choice to skip forward.

I have always stayed true to my characters and how they unravel their stories in my head. I didn't want to deny them that, and for that, I am sorry.

PROLOGUE

How many times in one lifetime do they say you find a soulmate? Is it once? Twice? Three times? Ice cream slipped down my throat as I thought of this. The quote scribbled on a rusty piece of paper read: *You find three types of love in your lifetime. The first will show you all that you did wrong. The second will show you how you should be loved, but the third will show you what it feels like to die while still being alive.* I didn't know why my small, six-year-old brain had taken those words and twisted them inside of her head, but that didn't sound right to me. *Why would I want to love three times?* That sounded too exhausting.

I'd rather lick this ice cream.

"Tillie!" my sister, Peyton, called out to me, robbing my attention away from the storefront window.

"What!"

My sister was the opposite of me. I was blonde, she had red hair. Fire hydrant red, too, and the freckles to match. She was the popular girl at school, mainly because she cared entirely too much what people thought of her, and I was the nerd.

"Hurry up, dipshit. If we're late, Dad will get mad and you know what happens when he's mad."

My ice cream cone smashed to the filthy ground as realization sunk in from the onslaught of her verbal throw down.

I wiped my hands on my shorts and nodded. "Okay, let's go."

Metallic slapped my mouth as I fell to the ground. Everything in the room spinning in a carousel that I'm all too familiar with.

"You were late. Why were you late?" A thick boot slammed into my rib cage and a loud crack vibrated through the air.

"I was eating my ic—ic—ice cream."

He chuckled so loud that I winced. *I hate your laugh.* The smell of stale cheap whiskey danced with musky cigarette smoke and exploded around me to form the distinguishing smell of Darren Lovett, aka, my dad.

I focus on a single dent in the floor of our trailer. The place my eyes always found when I was beaten into this position. I used to flick my marbles into it for fun, now I use it as sustenance to know that I'm still alive.

The beatings carry on for around an hour. An hour of pure terror. The back and forth toss up inside of my head on whether I'm going to live through it. *Will I want to be alive by the end of it?*

"It's my fault, Dad. I let her get the stupid ice cream," Peyton protested.

Dad didn't pay her any attention.

Like usual.

I close my eyes and let my thoughts carry me to a wondrous world where pain doesn't exist.

Pain exists everywhere though. It always has. At six-years-old, I knew that my life would be filled with nothing but pain.

They say that losing your lover can be an agony that's so unbearable the mere thought of it can cripple you.

I take a tentative step toward the gravesite, placing a bouquet of flowers over the gravestone while ignoring the people that are gathered here today.

They lied. The most crippling pain that comes isn't from losing your lover, it's from losing something that was so precious that you didn't deserve it to begin with.

Nate

14 years-old

"I fucking hate this place," I murmured to Bishop around my chicken drumstick. I tried hard to ignore all of the stores that lined the main street of Perdita and watched as people moved away from us. I felt like Moses parting The Red Sea. People were afraid of us here, with good reason. Our reputation never failed us. Of all the times I have been here, there has always been one place that I can't ignore—Caesar's Chicken. The man grills his chicken to perfection, so every time we're in Perdita, you can bet your ass I'll be in Caesar's first. Fuck our mission, or whatever else I have to do here. First stop is always Caesar's. I make all The Kings wait too.

"We don't have to be here long, chill."

I take a big bite and tear the meat from the bone while eyeing a woman walking with her kid. Not a fan of kids. Annoying little fuckers. She quickly tucks her son's head under her arm and pulls him along.

I bare my teeth and bite down, snapping at her. She lets out a small scream and runs off like a panicked little rat.

Bishop shakes his head. "Stop scaring the locals."

"Fuck em'." I look forward to the endless path ahead of me, the path that I know leads straight to Katsia's dungeon. You know, if a dungeon was a mansion that was built from the rarest marble and stone and then hammered together with carved diamonds.

"What does she want?" I ask, tossing the bone into a passing bin.

"Don't know yet. Probably your dick."

I flip him off as we reach the entry gates, the gold metal stretching out in high stakes, enough for you to not get so much as a glimpse into the fortress that lies ahead. A guard steps forward and hits the button to unlock the latches, then steps backward, letting us through.

Once we're inside her house, bypassing the rock gardens that lead to her front door, Katsia greets us by coming down the stairs in a long gown, the blood red silk falling off her ivory skin in waves of slaughter. Her eyes light up on me. "Nathanial. You're growing up to be handsome..."

"I've always been hot. What are you talking about." I don't like Katsia, never really have. She looks at men like they're pawns, and they are. As in, she actually has a group captive to use at her disposal. That's her role as a Stuprum, though, always has been for generations before and Lord have mercy, the generations after her.

The goddess of seduction.

I almost choke on my own thoughts and words. I mean, it's not that she's not attractive, because she is—for her age, but it's that she radiates desperation. I like my girls with a bit of bite because once they've mastered how to veil their fangs, they suck dick better.

She rolls her eyes and gestures to the large sitting room that is tucked behind the twin glass stairs she just descended from. "Ever the cocky Malum..."

My body stills at the mention of my dad's last name, but I ignore her proverbial jabs and follow Bishop into the room. She takes a seat on a large single sofa that resembles a throne straight out of a posh medieval set.

She smirks, then looks over my shoulder. "Ah, here he is. Boys, I want you to meet someone very important."

I turn around to see who she is looking at and I'm met with a dude that has to be at least a year younger than me. He's skinny looking with sharp features, murky shaded hair, and the darkest colored eyes I have ever seen. They almost look black, and it's not even the color that makes them look dark, it's the manner in how he stares at you. Like you're an object, not human. I've seen that stare before, my brother and King Brantley shares that same look.

Only I know Brantley, and I don't know this fucker, so the way he's staring at me and Bishop right now has me sitting on the edge of my seat, a little twitchy.

"Daemon, meet Bishop and Nate. They're the head of The Kings in this generation."

Daemon walks toward us, and I go to put my hand out to shake it, but he strolls right past it, pushing my very generous hand out of the way. He leans into Katsia, kissing her on the lips.

"Homeboy must have major mommy issues," I mutter, shaking my head.

Katsia licks her lips and watches as he dips behind her chair to stand guard like a good puppy. Her eyes stay on his. "Oh, you have no idea..."

I kick my leg up to rest my foot on the coffee table. "Why are we here?"

Her hand comes to Daemon's, who has his resting on her shoulder. It's creepy. The dude is Norman Bates creepy. "I need to tell you something, and I need your word that you will keep this secret for years to come."

Bishop doesn't flinch.

I laugh. "You have the audacity to ask for our word on a secret like you're a King."

Her eyes come to mine. "I have a daughter. I would like to not have a daughter. I need your word that after I'm gone, you will see to it that she no longer exists. In return, I will give you all that you want."

I lick my lips, tilting my head to try and get a read on her. She's not lying. I can see it in the way her eyes meet ours after every word. "Go on."

"If, and when I leave, you will make sure that my progeny will not take this throne, and in turn, I will let my people know that you are to take charge of Perdita. I know how long The Kings have wanted this." Her eyes go between both of us.

"Good plan. Let us know when you've done that, and I'll be sure to kill you myself," I answer smoothly, blowing her a kiss for added sugar.

"Oh, Nathanial. Ever the charmer." Then she lets her attention settle on Bishop. "If my death is by the hands of any King, the deal is off."

I open my mouth to tease her a bit, maybe tickle her in thight places and make her all wet, right before slapping her across the face with my cock and telling her to go fuck herself.

But Bishop beats me to it. "Deal."

CHAPTER 1

Tillie
Pregame

"Love is savage, love is blind, love is something they may not find..."

Droplets of water slide down the glass, reminding me of that one time my sister and I stayed up late, waiting for my mom to come back from grocery shopping. We sat near that window for two hours. I may have only been four-years-old, but I remember the memory so vividly that I could replay it in full HD inside my head for the rest of my life. On repeat. Constantly. With every detail, every scent, every gentle tick of the old clock ringing inside my head.

Tick.

Tock.

Tick.

Tock.

When she walked out on us, she didn't just take herself, she also yanked away diminutive parts of my sister and me, and more viciously, my father.

That's when the beatings began.

That's when he morphed from a deferential father to impertinent evil.

I don't remember much of him prior to that day, only the good things, but every single day after that day is imprinted in my head like a boulder cemented into the ground after a volcanic eruption.

"Are you okay, Puella?"

Releasing a thick inhale of breath, my shoulders relax and my muscles release tension at the mere sound of his voice.

Licking my lips, I turn to face him, my hand resting on top of his. "I'm okay, Daemon."

His eyes drop to the baby in his arms, my baby, and then come back to me. His beautiful eyes light up when they rest on me, like they've been dead all his life until this moment.

"We're not too far away from being done, Tillie. You've done really well," Tinker assures me softly from somewhere between my legs. I've managed to numb out the pain, or maybe it's because I've just pushed out a monstrous-sized baby girl, but whichever is correct, I know that I wouldn't have the strength to do this if it wasn't for him.

Daemon looks back at me, his eyes glimmering in a way that I pictured her father's eyes would twinkle. "She's beautiful, Puella."

I chew on my lip nervously as he places her small body onto my chest. She lets out a small crackle of a cry, her fist going to her mouth as her little head shakes from side to side.

Tinker comes up beside me, removing her surgical gloves. "Oh, sweet girl. She is hungry."

"I don't know how to do that?" Because I don't. I actually didn't think I had one maternal bone in my body until this very moment. This moment that sheer panic set into my bones from the thought of not being able to effectively feed my spawn. I know without a shadow of a doubt that I will protect this child until the day I die.

"It's okay," Tinker says, propping the baby up so she's closer to me. Her little face looks squashed against my boob. "She will know what to do. It may feel uncomfortable at first, but it should not be painful. If it's painful, hook your pinkie finger into her mouth gently and unlatch your nipple from her, and then start again. Her mouth should cover all of this part." She gestures over my areola.

I do it again, this time following closely to Tinker's instructions, and her little mouth latches on. My nipples turn hot, like water is rushing to the tips of them, and then her loud drinking breaks the silence.

Tinker giggles. "She's hungry!"

The other nurse who was helping stitch me up downstairs packs up and leaves. It's not until she's out of earshot when Tinker says, "They're coming, Tillie. They're all coming." Her tone remains balanced and even, she could have been talking about the weather that's how calm she was.

I freeze. "What?" For months now, my brain and my heart have been in a tug-a-war of feelings where Nate Riverside-Malum is concerned. Some days, the bad ones when I'm locked in my room in Katsia's mansion in Perdita, I have nothing but the memories of Nate and I playing on repeat. I've used our time together, the feelings I had for him, as comfort. I undoubtedly fell in love with Nate, my heart and brain know this, right down to the very veins that run through me. It has and always will be him, but I'm not naïve. I knew what I was getting myself into the day I allowed myself to open the gates that contained my feelings toward him.

Nate is a player.

I have no doubt at all, that he would absolutely despise me. Not because he probably thought I ran from him, but because I have now, in his mind, hid his own daughter from him.

"Tinker," I whisper-yell, my grip tightening around my daughter. "What do you mean they are coming? The Kings?"

Tinker runs her finger down my daughter's face and smiles lovingly while answering, "Yes. You don't understand, Tillie. Katsia wants to hurt this baby."

"Hurt?" I almost screech. The mere thought of anyone coming near this baby with ill intent has my claws rearing to the surface.

Tinker shoots a look at Daemon.

Daemon grabs my hand. "I have a plan, Puella."

My eyes zap around the room, unconsciously looking for any exit. One door that leads to the main hallway that is most likely heavily guarded as is every sector in this shitty big house.

"There's no other option, Tillie. Hear Daemon out, okay?" The door opens and the nurse from earlier comes back in, clutching a phone. I tense, but Daemon rests his hand on my shoulder.

"Trust me, Puella?" he asks, his eyes searching mine. His endless black pits that I have no doubt hide some of the most disturbing secrets known to man.

I swallow and then nod. "Yes. I trust you."

He presses a kiss to my forehead and reaches for the phone the nurse is handing to him. She clears her throat. "You have roughly around five minutes before they ask why I'm back in here. Please hurry, Daemon."

I tilt my head, examining her. Was she a good one too? Seems there was only Tinker and Daemon, but maybe I was wrong. My attention falls to her name badge. J E S S I C A is sprawled out in black block letters.

Jessica.

"He's not answering his phone." Daemon hangs up, his eyes going to Tinker nervously.

"We have to buy time." Tinker's attention goes to the nurse. "Can you buy us some time?"

The nurse looks reluctantly at us all, so I take this moment to get her attention. "Jessica? Please. If there is anything that I can ever do for you, I will be forever in your favor."

"Okay," she exhales. "I'll say that you haven't had the baby yet and there are complications, but you should know, that I do have to deliver the baby to one of the Lost Boys after birth. Me not taking her already has put me and my family in grave danger, Tinker."

"I promise you, Jessica. You and your family will be protected through this," Tinker reminds her confidently. I know we have her when the corners of Jessica's eyes relax.

"Okay." I look around my room again. The room I've been hidden and kept in for the past months. I didn't really care before when it was just me. Even though I was pregnant, the reality of having a child wasn't real—now it is, and I will undoubtedly do what I have to do to get us out of this situation.

"Okay, what are we going to do. She has to take her to a Lost Boy. Then what?"

Daemon looks up at Tinker, then back to me. "You don't have to worry about that part, Puella. It will be me that she will come to. I will make sure no harm comes to her and that she is returned to you safely, but we need to keep her quiet and still until The Kings arrive. Do you understand?" He runs his fingers through his hair, his eyebrows pulling together in stress.

I reach for his hand, stopping his movement. "I understand, Daemon. I will do anything you need me to do, okay?"

He nods and then drops his hand. The phone he's holding lights up and he quickly answers it, speaking in Latin.

Tinker comes closer to me. "Nate is going to be angry, Tillie, but only because he doesn't know how to harness his feelings. There's so much that you don't know about yourself and your lineage of family. So much you have to learn, even train in, things that if you allow it, Nate could train you in. You can't fight this lifestyle, Tillie. Don't do what Madison did and ignore the signs, or not ask the questions. You, your family, you hold power in this world. Take that power by the balls and own it."

"What are you talking about, Tinker?" Maybe she has finally lost the screws that were loose inside of her head.

She offers me an apologetic smile, though I'm not sure what she's apologizing for. "It's not my place, but truth is coming and when you reign, it's going to cripple the system."

Before I can ask what she is talking about, Daemon cuts in. "It's done. They will gear up." Daemon's eyes come to mine, and my grip around my baby intensifies. He notices. "I promise, Tillie. I won't let harm come to her."

My throat swells as a single tear falls from my eye and rolls down my cheek, falling to my chest. "Promise?"

Daemon nods. "I promise."

Daemon leans down, kissing my head. "Have you named her?"

I shake my head, swiping the tear. His hand comes to her cheek as he whispers. "Micaela."

When the syllables fall from his mouth, I knew instantly that it was done. "Micaela," I repeat, smiling. I look up to Daemon out of the corner of my eye, my heart thundering in my chest. Daemon and I have had a strange relationship since I've been on Perdita. Not sexual, just connected. On a deep level, a level I haven't felt since—for a very long time. Where Nate and I had an intense deep connection, it was also sexual, fire, explosions and a mixture of hate. Don't let Nate's pretty face fool you, though. The devil furnishes his darkest souls with the prettiest smiles. Daemon and I, it's pure, tame, calm. It was something more than friendship, but less than lovers, though I loved him dearly.

"Do you trust me, Puella?"

"On one condition," I whisper, slipping Micaela into his awaiting arms. "Don't die."

Daemon gives me a small smile, running his lips over my head. "I won't. I'll never die, Tillie." He glares at me. "Do you trust that?"

I clear my throat. "Get her back to me safe, and then I'll answer you."

CHAPTER 2

Tillie

Emotions. Human emotions, to be exact, can be rather annoying to come to terms with. For instance, having a sister. Mine has always been deranged, crazy, and a little bit over the top. In the (very far) back part of my brain, I've always wondered if we were actually related.

"You're doing that thing again…" Peyton says, flicking her fork in the air to accentuate her point. At least, that's what I think she's doing. "Do you not like your dinner, Tills? I mean, you should be thankful. God knows Nate would have killed you by now if you were on your own."

I grind my teeth in an attempt to ignore the verbal jab on a subject that she realistically knows nothing about. "No, Peyton, it's not the dinner."

She shrugs her plump shoulders, the tips of her red hair bouncing from the movement. She has gained weight over the years, but it looks good on her. Of course it does. See what I mean—not related. "Suit yourself." I watch as she continues to shovel spoon after spoon of food into her mouth when Carter clears his throat.

"Tillie, are you aware of what we are telling you? Do you know how important this is?"

"Important what is, Carter? The fact that you want me to go back to my life with my best friends and carry on like nothing has happened in hopes of gaining dirt for The Circle?" I choke on my words, unable to say them aloud.

He grins. I have to squeeze my fist underneath the table to stop it from flying across the table and clipping him in the jaw.

I hate Carter with enough fire to burn the world down.

I recollect myself, picking up my glass and taking a sip of water. I allow it to slide down my throat before I gather my next words. "I'm not going to do it. I'm not a snitch, Peyton, and I will not draw my friends out to get hurt."

"Oh but you will," Carter counters, slowly lifting his drink into the air and grinning at me. "Where is Micaela, Tillie?"

Something sharp caresses my heart at his tone, but I swallow down the fear and answer, "She's in her crib."

Realization sinks into my bones at the thought of what he and Peyton are capable of. They wouldn't hurt her, Tillie. Chill. I shoot up from the table.

Carter's eyes only darken, a devious smirk towing across his mouth. I run out of the room instantly, the adrenalin seizing my limbs. Long, dark walls of the hallway melt to a puddle under my feet as my heart thunders in my chest. One step. Two steps. You're almost there.

She wouldn't touch her. She wouldn't. Micaela, in Peyton's sick mind, is the leverage that she has over me. As long as she has my daughter, she knows that I am the puppeteer and she's pulling the strings. If she so much as touches a hair on Micaela's head, that snaps all the ropes and releases the monster she abetted to craft. I was beaten as a child. Continuously. I am not only on a first name basis with abuse, but he and I go way back.

Entering my bedroom, silence falls around me with nothing but the pitter-patter of my light footsteps.

I suck in a breath as I reach the crib. My eyes close. I open them— "Peyton!" I scream, spinning around and running the exact way I came from. Only this time the blood spilling from the walls is my rage. I'm going to kill her and anyone that gets in my way.

Peyton is sitting at the head of the table, a fork with potato hanging an inch away from her mouth.

I attentively step closer. "I swear to God, Peyton, you have roughly five seconds to tell me where the fuck she is before I rip your goddam throat out."

Her eyes flick over my shoulder where guards stand, strapped with automatic weapons. "See, I think you won't, because you can't, Tills. Because I own you. I always have, and truthfully, I probably always will." She pats her mouth dry. "Now. If you take a seat, I can explain exactly what is going to happen from here on out, and you will nod and agree like a good little girl, or I will" —her eyes pierce mine, pinning me— "destroy the only thing you care about. Capiche?"

She went there.

I collapse onto a chair, my throat swelling. "God, Peyton, when did you turn so dark." I'm disappointed in myself for not taking her evil seriously. I never would have thought she would lower herself to harming me, let alone threatening her twelve-week-old niece. I see it now, though. I see whoever it is that's working behind the scenes has taken control of her. There's no saving her now. I know this. The realization slaps me across the face like a heavy backhand. She's my enemy, and I am hers.

Peyton giggles, swiping her hair out of her face. "Probably around the same time you tried to steal my boyfriend, Tillie. Now, I am truly sorry that I have to do this to you. Or I'm not, I can't really decide, but maybe." She leans forward, her eyes slicing through me. "It is your fault for the life that you live, did you ever think of that?"

"Fuck you!"

Rage bubbles beneath my skin. "You so much as breathe near her, Peyton, I'll burn you in your sleep and dance around your corpse. The only reason I haven't done something drastically insane is because of Micaela." I lean forward, resting my elbows on the hard wood table. "So give your niece a kiss. She's the only reason you're still breathing right now." I know that if I kill Peyton, there's a chance someone will harm Micaela. I'm not open to gambling on her future. I don't care for the idealism of perfect parenting. The perfect mother is one who is the best version that she can be, not something the media and society state they should be. I mean, look at who Micaela's father is... *who I am.*

My thoughts go back to Peyton and her stupid comment about her—whatever he was to her. Boyfriend? Hardly.

"What boyfriend?"

She's had many over the years, and yeah, they've all mostly enjoyed my company more than hers. That's mainly because she tries too hard to please people. When she would be dressing up in short skirts with a face full of makeup for movie nights, I'd be in the living area of our trailer with my Ren and Stimpy pajamas on.

Her face morphs into hatred, her eyebrows pulling in tight enough for wrinkles to form on her head. "Jase always preferred you." She exhales. Jase as in the older Jase Venari. He was *hardly* her boyfriend and she was shared amongst him and a couple others. "Fuck Jase and fuck you. I'll bring you all down now. I'll do it for our mom, for our name as a Stuprum, for it all," she whispers, standing from her chair to glare at me. "You will get your daughter back when you've done as I've said. Comprende?"

I grit my teeth. "How do I know you are taking care of her, Peyton?" Peyton clicks her fingers, and I turn in my chair when I hear the door open behind me.

The nurse who helped deliver Micaela, Jessica appears, holding Micaela in her arms. Micaela smiles up at Jessica, her small little hand coming to her neck.

My mouth opens slightly, as I battle with the biggest war that lives inside of me. Trust. Trust is the hardest to deliver, but the easiest emotion to receive. When my eyes clash with Jessica's, I can see her silent reassurance. She will take care of it. I know this. At least until I've satisfied this sadistic bitch that is my sister. A guard yanks Jessica back through the door, and I twist back around to look at Peyton.

"What the hell do you want," I seethe, gritting my teeth.

She smiles, relaxing back into her chair to continue eating. "I'm glad I have your loyalty, sis. Sit."

I do, squeezing the armrests of the old oak wood as I slowly plant my ass back down. "What is it?"

She cuts into her sirloin. "I need you to be my eyes and ears. Do you understand?" Peyton snaps, and I flinch from the tone of her voice.

My eyes come to hers. "Yes, I understand."

I hate her and I hate this dining room. It's everything that Peyton would want, only in a damn office in the tallest building in New York City.

"Good," she mutters, leaning back in her chair. "Because you're going back out there tomorrow, so be packed and ready."

"Peyton," I deadpan, trying my hardest not to upset her while trying to coax my utter anger and deceit underneath a cool demeanor. "I can't just walk back into their lives and not expect questions. What about Micaela, Peyton? Huh? You think Nate is going to not ask fucking questions?"

Peyton watches me and then smirks. "That's why you're going to turn up on Madison's doorstep, crying that I took your baby. Realistically, you don't have to pretend." She shrugs like it's nothing too much to stress about. Her eyes come back to me.

"Then they will feel sorry for you while also wanting to come after me. They'll invite you back into the exclusive pack and then?" She takes a sip of her drink. "Then you wait for my call for the next move."

"You're crazy." I shake my head. "What makes you think I won't tell them everything?"

She pins me with a glare. "Because under all those pretty features and hot little body, Tillie, you're smart. You are the smarter one out of the two of us, and you know what will happen if you do so."

I lean back in my chair, my brain spinning with all the possible ways I can take this scenario. Right now, I know I don't have many options. She holds all the cards in her hand right now, so for right now, I have to play the hand she has dealt me.

I exhale. "Fine. I'll do it."

CHAPTER 3

Tillie

I knocked three times with no answer, so I sink onto the cool steps in front of my best friend's plantation-style mansion. There have been so many times that I've been on these steps, and not one time did they ever feel empty like they did now. Wind whisks through the trees that line her long circle driveway, causing the spray from the water fountain to splash against my face in light misty waves.

Madison was raised with money, but make no mistake, her life was not privileged. I think that's why she and I clicked so hard and so fast. Her other best friend, Tate, on the other hand...

I don't have anything against Tate, but she is everything you would expect from a rich bitch who was raised with a gold (that's right, not silver, gold), spoon in her mouth, but even when Tate and I don't see eye-to-eye, we still have a common ground to form a bond on—Madison.

I sink my face into the palms of my hands, for the first time, reality starts really sinking in. She took my daughter. My sister is undeniably fucking crazy, and there's a very real possibility that she could harm her if I don't do exactly as I'm told.

I lost Daemon.

I lost my sister—somewhat.

I lost my daughter.

I have no one. I am no one. Nate is going to hate me for thinking I ran with his daughter, and if he doesn't already, he sure will when all of the truth comes out. Either way, I can't win and the walls inside my head feel as though they're closing in on me.

I hear a car pull up, headlights sneaking through the cracks of my fingers. I swipe the tears off my cheeks and zero in on the car. A matte black Audi comes into view with the license plate "KINGII." My heart thunders in my chest. There's only one person who would have that license plate.

Nate.

I shoot up from the step, swiping the fresh tears from my eyes. A car door slams shut, and then another with heels clicking against the stone driveway. I know instantly that that wouldn't be Madison because she doesn't wear heels. It could be Tate. I choose to ignore all theories and remain focused.

"Tillie?" His steps are slow, calculated. I can't see anything else but the outline of him. He's wearing dark jeans, heavy boots, and a leather jacket with a hoodie underneath.

I clear my throat, thankful that I can't see his face, or his eyes. "She took her, Nate, and she's not giving her back."

He pauses and then cranks his head over his shoulder. "Get the fuck back in the car."

I wince at the tone, only to realize for once, it's not aimed at me. He turns back to me. "What do you mean she took her?"

I can't stop the tears now, they're free-falling all over the place. I try to swipe them away, angry at the fact that my body might be doing it robotically from Peyton ordering me to show up all damsel in distress. "Peyton took Micaela and she's not g—" I choke on my words, a hiccup interfering my speech. "Giving her back."

Nate flies forward, his hand coming to mine instantly. He pulls me into his chest. I didn't expect it. My body turns rigid.

His hand comes to my chin, and he squeezes so roughly that I flinch. This, I expected. He yanks my head up to face him. I see his eyes now, at least the curve of them. "If I find out that you're lying to me, Tillie, regardless whether we have a child together, I'll fucking kill you, do you understand? Don't fuck with me when it comes to Micaela, Tillie. I swear to God..."

"Nate!" Madison's voice claps through the air like a bolt of lightning.

I pull my face out of his grip just as Madison pushes him to the side where he falls beside me lazily. "Oh my god!" she screams, her hands coming to my face. "I tried to tell them that you wouldn't run. I told them..."

I exhale my held reprieve, pulling her in for a hug. "I wouldn't run, Madison, but Peyton has Micaela and she's not giving her back. I can't do anything, I'm powerless." It's not a lie.

Madison turns to face Bishop and then turns her head toward the house. "Come on. We can talk more inside. Nate!" she snaps at Nate as he's walking toward the house. "Get rid of your ho."

He flips her off, and then pushes a couple of fingers into his mouth, whistling out. I watch as a blonde girl crawls out of the passenger side of his car. "Yeah?"

Oh glorious, she actually responds to his dog antics. Gross.

"Find a ride home." He turns, dismissing her.

"Good to see he hasn't changed much," I mutter under my breath.

Madison scoffs, hooking her arm in mine. "Oh, he *has* changed. He has gotten worse."

Pulling out one of the bar stools that are tucked under the oversized granite kitchen counter, I slide on top, picking up the glass of whiskey Madison has poured.

"Just saying, aren't you both too young to be starting this..." Bishop points to the glasses.

Madison shoots him a glare.

His hands come up in defense. "Alright, alright."

"Talk, Tillie. Quit fucking stalling." That's Nate.

I take a long shot of the amber liquid, letting it rest on my tongue before throwing it back and relishing in its scorching travels down my throat before it blisters in my belly. "She took our daughter and she will not give her back. After Daemon's funeral, she had us locked up in a place in New York City. I'm not sure where it is or what it is, because when they'd transport me, I'd be blindfolded." Not a lie. This isn't so bad. Daemon's death impacted all of us. He was Madison's long-lost twin brother who was the leader of The Lost Boys and held on an island called Perdita. An island my deranged mother ran and operated for The Kings. Something about a birthright to do so and family lineage, I'm not completely sure. I only not long ago found out about Katsia *being* my mother. Daemon spoke fluent Latin and hardly any English. He was silently disturbed. The kind you don't speak about because you can never get close enough to him to have an opinion.

Only, I did.

My eyes finally go to Nate's, and I regret it immediately. His pupils are dilated and He's seething, absolutely livid, and all that anger is aimed at me.

"If you hadn't run in the fucking first place, then I could have fucking protected you!"

I narrow my eyes. "I didn't run, Nate! I was fucking taken! There's a difference."

He steps closer to me and I instantly freeze, every single warning bell inside of me ringing, signaling me to shut the fuck up or this boy will kill me. "Yeah? There's a difference is there? Care to test that theory?"

"Nate!" Madison snaps, but he doesn't retreat. His eyes are solely on me, and mine on his. I won't back down, I refuse to. He can be angry, but I'm over being made out to be the bad person just because my options are tied and have been tied since I damn well came into this world. Not all of us have the freedom that money and power provide. Some of us have to actually unlock ourselves from what keeps us shackled, not pay our way out.

"Maybe you should..." I counter, challenging him.

His eyes weaken, and a lazy smirk pulls up the corner of his mouth. "Now, now, princess, don't go asking for things you know you can't handle."

"Last I checked, I handled it just fine, thank you," I mutter, finally taking my eyes away from him and concentrating on my drink.

"Okay! Sorry I'm late, but I had—" Tate cuts off from behind me. I don't turn around to see her, because somewhere inside my brain, I know that she hates what Nate and I have.

Madison leans closer to me, her elbows resting against the counter. "Stay here for as long as you need, okay? We will get her back. I promise."

I smile. "Thanks, Mads. I appreciate it."

She stands again, rounding the counter to take my hand. "Come on. I'll show you into Daemon's old room. You can stay there while you're here."

Pain slices me in the chest, but I swallow it down, aware of all the eyes I have on me.

I don't make eye contact with any of them. I keep my head bowed low and let Madison guide me to Daemon's room.

We stop outside the door, and Madison's grip tightens in mine. "I know about you and Daemon, Tills."

My head snaps up to hers. "What do you mean?"

She swallows, and then her eyes slowly open onto mine. "I know about you both, and what happened between the two of you."

"Okay," I answer because I don't really know what else to say to her and I really, really hate lying to her. Out of everyone on this earth, she is the one person I really don't want to lie to. I need to find a way out of this mess I've found myself in.

"I just want you to know that it's okay to mourn him in here. I haven't come into his room since it happened, mainly because I haven't been able to stomach it." She pauses and swallows. "But also because I felt like it wasn't my place to touch."

"That's insane, Madz. He was your twin brother..."

She shakes her head, cutting me off without actually cutting me off. "I know that it seems that way, but I've always felt deep down that it wasn't my place to touch. I know that it is yours. So please, take your time. Sleep in here, and when you're ready, maybe you can help me box up his items?"

I let out a loud gush of breath. "I don't know if I can do it. Sleep in here that is."

She smiles, her hand finding the door handle. "You will. But if you don't, you know you can jump in with Bishop and me."

"Hard pass," I mumble, smiling at her from the corner of my eye.

She chuckles, then twists the handle and pushes it open. "You know where I am if you need me."

CHAPTER 4

Tillie

There should be a color that is darker than black. The word "black" just doesn't seem enough to be able to express a color as dark as the ones that are licked on Daemon's bedroom walls. The trimmings and windowsills are white, but the walls display a color so dark and bleak, that they somewhat almost matched the pits of his eyes.

I squeeze the door, trying to find a balance before I lose my footing. Closing my eyes, I try to ignore the soft scent of cologne that he always wore. Clean soap mixed with sugar and spice. I take another step inside, the floor creaking under my weight. Shutting the door, I lean against it and swipe at the tears that are flowing down my cheeks. I hate that he is gone. I hate that I wasn't there to say goodbye, and I hate that he lied to me.

"You promised you wouldn't die," I whisper, it comes out hoarse. I clear my throat and push off the door, making my way to his bed. Silk black sheets are unmade on his bed, and it stops me for a moment. Before I can think of anything else, my phone vibrates in my pocket. I fish it out, answering without checking to see who it is.

"Hello?"

"Go to the window."

"Who is this?" I answer, looking around the room.

The muffled voice has been filtered through a voice box to hide the owner. "Follow my instructions very carefully, Tillie. Now, go to the window."

Slowly, I switch sides and push my phone to the other side of my head as I tenderly make my way to the window, pinching the net curtain between my fingers to crack it open. There's a dark tree right outside the window cutting off most of the view of the driveway, but when I look to the right, I see a dark SUV parked with its lights on.

Confused, I crank my head to try to get a better look, when the driver's side opens up and a man in a dark suit steps out.

"Now open the window and climb down. Be careful not to disturb anything too much."

"Who are you? I'm not coming down there until you tell me who you are."

"I'm someone who has a lot more pull than your sister. I can help you, Tillie Stuprum, but you have to follow my orders and move now."

"I can't. She has my daughter and she is watching my every move."

He seems to pause and then retreat back to his SUV. "I'll be back, and when I do, you're mine."

He hangs up and I watch as the lights sink into the darkness before disappearing toward the street.

I don't know who that was, and I don't think I want to know.

There's a sort of bliss that comes with ignorance, like the saying goes. Because if you ignore all the signs that are being flashed in front of you, you can pretend that your world isn't burning to a crisp.

I slowly make my way back to Daemon's bed, flopping down onto it and pulling his sheets into a tangled mess around my ankles. I wish he was here, just to remind me that everything is going to be okay. To put pressure on the wound that Nate always seems to inflict, to just be here to mend my broken mind. My eyelids feel heavy, my mind slowly sinks into oblivion.

"You're a Stuprum. Power comes with that name, but you have to learn to harness it, Tillie, or it will destroy you like it did Katsia."

"No!" I shake my head, running through the dark corridors of some random abandoned building. Old graffiti is splashed over the aged concrete, and every single door is hanging off its hinges.

"You can't run from this life, Tillie!" The voice laughs, echoing from the walls and sinking into the bones in my body. *"You will never be able to run from this life. You think you know, but you don't. You've just begun to know."*

I crash through the first closed door I see, one that isn't open and grungy, one that needed to be open. I lean forward on my knees, sucking in each breath with deep inhales and exhales. An arm latches around my stomach, and I still before turning in the embrace. I recognize the ink that's displayed so professionally onto the golden skin and turn to face him.

"Nate?" I whisper, confused. His touch is like fire and ice, it both burns to the touch and freezes to be healed.

He clenches his jaw in the way that makes it pop out slightly, his eyes on mine. This isn't playful Nate, this is angry Nate. "You're my enemy, Tillie. By blood, and now by choice."

I launch from the bed, rubbing my drenched skin viciously to get rid of the residue of sweat. The dream was vivid, a little too vivid because minutes later I'm still trying to get the images out of my head. After tossing and turning, I give up on sleep and crawl out from the sticky sheets. One of the drawers is slightly open in the bedside table. I don't remember it being open when I went to sleep, but then again I don't remember actually looking at it to know for sure. I quickly check the door is closed before kneeling down to open it farther.

I feel like maybe I'm intruding on Daemon's privacy, and for a second, I pull my hand back, shame washing over me. "Actually," I whisper as if he can hear me. "Maybe if you didn't want me snooping through your shit you should have stayed alive." Fleeting anger possesses me, so I yank open the drawer, and a medium-sized wooden box catches my eye. The words *Puer Natus* are engraved into the ancient style wood box with burnt crusted markings on the edges. It looks mystical, otherworldly. I pop it open, and a black book with the same words are scribbled sharply over the top. My fingers run over the markings, the flap of leather catching the cushion of my thumbs. Whoever did this carved the wording with some sort of blade.

There's a voice inside of me that says to put it back. To not open things that I find in this house. That I shouldn't open boxes that I have no intention of closing. But there's another voice, one that lives in the particles that float in the air I breathe. One that has urgency rippling through my veins. Quickly pushing the box and drawer closed and slipping back under the sheet, I wriggle into the mattress and squash every thought that is echoing inside of me and let the one outside have its way. The soft lampshade gives me just enough sight to read, but I run the palm of my hand over the words anyway and my heart catches in my chest. My throat swells with a strange stir of emotions and I know instantly that this is Daemon's writing.

I open the cover and the first page shows a drawing of a young boy standing in front of a small cabin style home. It's all shaded in pencil, smudged with black and grey, no color. Madison can draw, and I guess Daemon could too. The art makes me sad and I'm not sure why. There's something empty about the image that shows little while feeling like it's displaying just enough. The window in the building is cracked, there's no grass or any detail of the landscape, just a small boy facing a diminutive style cabin. There's an old chair that's facing the doorway and a fireplace behind it.

On top of the image, are the words CAPITULUM I. I grab my phone off the bedside table and type the words into Google translate. *Chapter One.*

I suck in a breath, chapter one? As in a novel? I know that Daemon wasn't very good with English, but he was fluent in Latin, why didn't he choose to write it in Latin, instead of using images? I ask myself this, but realistically I know the answer. He's Daemon, his brain worked inversely to others. Almost like where we saw numbers and words, he saw pictures and evil.

I let it go for now, running my hand over the first page. *Was this him as a child?* Is he showing me his first memory?

"Goddammit, Daemon." I flip the page over to find another drawing, this time the boy is inside the house, the door slightly open with his shadow sprawled out over the busted porch. There's a dark rocking chair that's opposite him in front of a fireplace, again, with very little detail. I feel like he didn't add anything extra to the drawings that he didn't feel necessary, therefore, what is in here is very important. Squinting my eyes, I look closer at the rocking chair. It's all smudged in with grey pencil, but if—I freeze. Eyes peer back at me in almond blue orbits. They're not obvious, only there.

Licking my lips, my eyes feel heavy again, but I want to go through the book more and see what else is in it. Another part of me also knows that I can't rush through. Every page is a chapter to a story, a story I have no idea what it is about. A story that needs to be whispered like a gentle lullaby to be sure you don't miss any important lyrics rather than speed rapped and everything goes over your head.

CHAPTER 5

Tillie

My phone vibrating on the bedside table alerts me as I viciously rub the sleep from my eyes. Reaching for it visionless, I hit answer. "What?"

"I need an update, sister."

"Listen, I'm doing what you told me to do, Peyton. They know you have Micaela, you've successfully awoken Nate's feral side, what is the next step?"

She stays silent for a beat, and I swing my legs off the bed, pulling my hair out of my face. "This time next week, I need them all, and Tillie when I say all, I mean all, at a location I will send to you the night prior. Understand?"

"Yes," I grumble, and then notice the door open. Nate leans against the frame in nothing but grey Nike sweatpant shorts. He looks sweaty, ripped, and did he get his nipples pierced? The tattoos over his body have multiplied since I last saw them too, including two large angel wings that fan out over his chest. They're beautiful. I'm drawn to them right away.

He clears his throat and my eyes go up to his, only I flinch. It's hard coming face-to-face with someone you once loved. It's like a big fuck you from the god of love. My stomach sinks.

"Who's that?" he asks, pointing to my phone.

"Ah, I need to go…" I mumble into the phone before hanging up quickly. "What do you want, Nate?"

He licks his bottom lip. "Answer the question, Tillie, who was that?"

Oh well, nothing has changed where his possessiveness is concerned, though I've heard through Madison that he usually doesn't get into the whole caveman antics and that he's more into sharing.

I've yet to see that side of him.

I stand, ignoring his jab and head straight for the bathroom. My travels don't get far because, in a flash, Nate is right in front of me, one arm hooking around my back and his other hand coming to my hair. He tilts my head up until he's glaring down at me. "Who the fuck was that?"

I clench my jaw. "I don't remember the part where I have to answer to you, so fuck you."

His lip curls, the grip he has in my hair intensifying. "While you're invading my fucking life, there are to be no fuckboys sniffing around you. In fact, you can grab the shit Madison left on the bed for you and move your ass into my room."

"Nate!" I yell, fighting the anger that's simmering to the surface. This is going to be a lot more difficult than I imagined. "I'm not staying in your damn room, and though there are no fuckboys, unless you count yourself, I do not have to freaking answer to you!"

He unlatches his hold and shoves me onto Daemon's bed. My hair flies out around me, and just as I inch up on my elbows, he pushes me back down with his body, crawling up like a predator. His arms cage me in on either side of my head. I keep my legs closed, my head tilted sideways to stop from vanishing into his gaze. *You can't get lost there again, Tillie. Remember? He doesn't give every part of you back.*

"Listen to me, princess, you will do as you're told whether you like it or not, in fact, keep not liking it, you know that bravado gets my dick hard." His chest presses into mine as his mouth comes to my ear. "Did you think you could just walk into my fucking house and not live with a set of rules? I mean, come on, baby, I know it's been a while since I've been balls deep in this." He shoves one of his legs between my thighs, forcing my legs open.

I hiss, slamming my eyes shut. Out of sight, out of mind.

He chuckles, his chest vibrating against mine. "But you know how I play."

"Actually," they pop open and I turn to face him square on until he's leaning up on one elbow to look down at me again.

His eyes come to mine, his face so close I can feel his deep breath fall against my lips.

Agh, this feels like too much. Too much Nate.

"Actually, what?" He challenges me with a grin, his voice cracking with a tone that my insides are all too familiar with. *He's too much and you're too weak right now.*

Fuck. "Actually," I continue, gripping onto some false sense of security my subconscious has created out of the undiluted fear this man sets off inside of me. "I've heard you don't play like that usually, so I don't actually know how you 'play.'"

He pauses, his eyes searching mine. "You're right, Tillie, I don't. The same set of rules that apply to every other female walking this earth have never applied to you. You feel me?"

I do. I feel you everywhere which is precisely the problem. Asshole.

"No, I don't. You said that I know how you play, when in fact—"

He cuts me off. "You have about three seconds to stop talking before I fuck you on Daemon's bed, and you and I both know how fast that act alone will conjure his spirit back to us. I'm not really keen on being haunted, so…"

I freeze.

He jackknifes up, the weight of his body instantly gone. I ignore how my stomach throbs with emptiness from this fact, and slowly make my way off the bed—again—

Nate stops when he reaches the door, his back turned to me. "…Regardless of what kind of monster you think I am, Tillie, and make no mistake, I can be a fucking monster, I never let that side of me touch you. Ever. However, if I find out that you're hiding something from me, that side won't just touch you, it will annihilate you."

Then he leaves, shutting the door behind himself.

I exhale a deep breath, overwhelmed by him. Everything that is Nate Riverside is just too much. He's too much everything for me, but I won't let that feeling be a weakness for me. I choose to use it as a weapon instead.

After showering and throwing on some of Madison's clothes that mainly consist of skinny jeans and Harley Davidson t-shirts (that show way too much of my stomach). A stomach that isn't exactly flat after Micaela, I make my way downstairs to find her.

I can hear whispering coming from the side lounge that sits off the kitchen and turn toward it, leaning against the entryway when I get there.

All of The Kings are here now, not just Bishop and Nate.

Brantley, Cash, Chase, Ace, Hunter, Jase, Saint, and Eli.

"Am I interrupting?" I ask, looking directly at Madison. I can't stomach looking at any of The Kings. They're not just intimidating, they're downright terrifying. Madison always handled them with excellence, me, not so much.

Madison smiles, pointing at the sofa that's empty. Some of The Kings are standing, spread out on the U-shaped couch, and some are apprehensively pacing.

I can see Brantley glaring at me out of the corner of my eye, he's the one spread out on the sofa, one leg kicked up on the coffee table.

"Tillie," Brantley says my name with just enough warning to let me know that if I don't answer him, I probably won't like the consequences. Out of all of The Kings, Brantley has been the one that scares me the most. More so than Bishop and Nate.

I turn to face him. "Yes?"

"Is there anything that you're not telling us? Anything that we need to know as far as the kid goes? Because I'm giving you your chance now to speak up and trust us. Any time after this, you'll be dealt with as an outsider if you've betrayed this trust."

She has your daughter, Tillie. Right now, I have no other option but to lie. Who knows what Peyton has hidden. Who knows if she has cameras set up in this very house that we don't know about.

Lie.

"You know everything. She took me the day before Daemon's funeral and wouldn't let me go. She kept Micaela and I holed up somewhere in the city," I pause, clicking my fingers together. "Oh, wait, and also, Carter is with Peyton and The Circle…"

"The Circle is being dealt with as far as I know," Bishop interferes. "And Carter we already knew about."

"Anything else?" That's Nate, and my eyes find him instantly. He's against the wall on the other side of the room, one leg propped up and his finger running across the top of his lip.

"Not that I can think of right now. Before I got here, she took Micaela and wouldn't give her back. I don't know what she's playing at, but I sort of have a feeling that she has this sick side of her brain that thinks she's taking over for our—" I pause, hating the next words that are about to come out of my mouth. "Mom."

"Wait, but she can't, right?" Madison turns to face Bishop, and when he doesn't answer her, she turns around to face Nate.

Nate shrugs. "Yes and no. Yes, because Perdita still needs to be run, and the only person who can run it is a Stuprum. Khales has been spending some time over there though.

The Lost Boys are funky little fuckers. They're far more warped than you can imagine, and they don't take any orders from anyone but a Stuprum. It's all cult-like, but it's the world they, and we, live in. No, because we don't fucking allow it."

I rub my temples. "That can't happen. Surely, and what has that got to do with The Circle, and also!" My eyes snap to Nate. "You're not exactly freaking out about our daughter..."

He straightens, his shoulders pulling back in defense. "Are you fucking kidding me, woman! You come in here—"

"—Alright!" Madison snaps at both of us, then her face softens when she looks at me. "He's not freaking out because they won't harm that child, Tillie. She means too much to too many people. They're bluffing, but we're going to get her back before this night is up."

I hear the front door slam closed and then heels clicking across the tile floor. Oh god, if this is Tate, I cannot deal with her distracting Nate right in front of me right now.

"Where the fuck is my granddaughter!"

Nate smirks at me.

Crap.

I clear my throat. "We're trying to figure that out."

Elena's blue eyes cut to mine with sharp precision. Just when I think she's going to start yelling at me, her face softens. She yanks me up from my seat and pulls me into her arms.

"Whose fucking side are you on, mother?" Nate scolds her in the background.

She ignores him.

Pulling back, Elena's hands come to my face. "We will get her back, honey." She pauses, her attention going around the room. "And then she will not be easily accessible to being kidnapped and you and my son have to sort through your differences and come up with a somewhat healthy routine for her."

I squash down my initial thought to call her out on her overactive brain. All I can think about is not having her in my arms right now. Any discussion about Nate and I will have to wait.

Elena's eyes lock onto her son. "Do you know everything you need to know about the whereabouts?"

He nods. "Yeah. We're ready to go."

"Already? I answer, nerves wreaking through me. How can they already know where she is? How can he be so confident? Something doesn't add up.

Joseph enters the room, going straight for Madison and kissing the top of her head. It was a shock to find out that he wasn't Madison's biological father, but that fact hasn't come between their bond. "The Circle is not your issue. We can handle them."

"The Circle are a pack of old Kings who have gone rogue by choice." Brantley must see the confusion on my face, and again, he frightens me. He's always watching everything that is going on around him without actually *watching*.

"Right," I answer. "Well, at least that's something I didn't know yesterday."

Joseph nods. "We're handling it. The Circle are not our enemies, but they're not our allies either. In the meantime, another thing that you all need to know is that the new generation is starting Riverside prep after the new year. There will obviously be the ceremony that will start them off that will be happening after Christmas in a few months. Though I shouldn't have to remind you..."

A new generation of Kings. That doesn't sound fun at all. Are they all scary brats like these fuckers?

I keep my thoughts to myself.

Nate chuckles. "Good times…"

My mind wanders back to Daemon, like it usually does. The book I found last night, I almost completely forgot about. Obviously, Madison doesn't know about it, and I know that I might not be able to decipher it on my own, but a selfish part of me doesn't want to share it with anyone yet. Maybe after we get Micaela back, I can show it to her and we can look more in-depth to find out what it means.

I ignore everything going on around me until my phone vibrates in my pocket.

"Hello?"

I can't hear the voice on the other end, so I excuse myself, blocking my other ear with my finger and quickly dash out through the glass slider that opens onto the backyard and pool. Once I've shut out the noise, I repeat myself. "Hello?"

"Tillie!"

"Oh my god!" My hand goes over my mouth. "Ridge?"

"Yeah, babe, it's me. You're a hard girl to get hold of these days."

I exhale, flopping down onto one of the sunbeds beside the pool. "You have no idea. Seriously."

"Are you okay? I know we haven't spoken in a long time and we have so much to catch up on."

"Actually, I don't think I am okay, but I'm trying to adapt to it."

"Well listen." He clears his throat. "I'll send you an address in town, so we can catch up."

I smile, the mid-morning sun hitting my cheeks. "Sounds like a good idea. Text me."

"Will do. Stay safe, Tills."

"I'll try," I whisper, hanging up and clutching my phone in my hand.

Growing up, Ridge and I were inseparable. He was my first kiss, my first—everything, really. When we were fourteen, we decided we may as well be each other's first "time" too, you know, get the deed over with so we could move on. Only he was like a bad habit and I was addicted. We sort of continued to sleep together right up until I met Nate, actually. When he was with a girl, or I was with a guy, we wouldn't. It wasn't something we agreed on or anything, it was just natural. If we were single, we were probably having sex.

"Hey!" Madison shuts the door behind herself and skips over to me, her long dark hair flying all over the place. My eyes go over her shoulder and land on Bishop, who is standing behind the glass, watching her closely from the sitting room.

They went through some crazy and survived, maybe I can too. I mean, it's not like I can get it worse than she did, *right?*

"Hey!" I pile my hair on the top of my head, twisting it into a knot.

She hands me a mug of coffee. "Are you hungry? When was the last time you ate?"

I shake my head, blowing inside the mug until steam hits the tip of my nose. "I can't."

She sinks down beside me, tucking her feet under her butt. There's a long stretch of silence that lies between us before she says something. "I know Nate is struggling a lot with whatever goes on inside that messed up head of his, but you didn't see him when you weren't here."

I nod. "And I'm glad I didn't. Can't imagine enjoying him and Tate parading their relationshit around for me."

Madison's eyes go to my hair. "It wasn't like it was with you, though," she snorts. "It was actually hard to watch because I wanted to kill him most of the time for the things he did to her and how he treated her."

I shake my head. "I don't really want to hear about it, Madz."

"Okay," she sighs and then stands back to her feet. "But we need to refresh that hair, so let's do a girl's day while these guys prepare for tonight." If I really thought Micaela was in trouble, would I really be off getting my hair done? The answer is no. But maybe it will take my mind away from the fact that people are about to die tonight, and anyway, everyone knows what Madison is like when she gets her heart set on doing something. Like Nate, for example. *Don't go there, Tillie.*

"Deal. But if Ridge texts me, you're coming for lunch."

We make our way back into the house just in time for Nate to be walking down the stairs, a joint hanging out of his mouth. He looks freshly showered with more clothes on than he did this morning.

"You move your shit?"

"What? No. I said I wasn't going to sleep in your room."

He looks at Madison, ignoring me point blank. "She needs to be in there before I get back tonight."

Then he stomps down the stairs, leaving.

"He's fucking impossible." I shake my head, annoyed with Peyton for planting me here. Which reminds me...

"I'll be back in a second, I just have to grab something." I shoot up the stairs and leave Madison waiting for me near the front door.

Pulling out my phone, I dial Peyton's number. She picks up on the fourth ring.

"Talk."

"Remind me again why I'm doing this, without using Micaela..."

She pauses. "Because Micaela."

I close my eyes, sinking down onto Daemon's bed. "I don't trust you, Peyton. I don't trust anyone right now and it's making my brain somersault in my head because I don't know what way is right."

"Well how about this. My way is right so if you have something to say, say it..."

I swallow past the large boulder stuck in my throat. If I do this, there's no going back. I have two roads to choose from right now. I can hang up the phone and tell Madison, or I can tell Peyton, the woman who actually has my daughter in her care and keep her alive. "They're getting ready to come for you tonight, Peyton. To get Micaela. So, here's the deal, if you give her to me right now, they won't end you..."

There's a long stretch of silence, and then she laughs. "Honey, they can't end me. I have The Circle—"

"—Peyton! The Circle are just old Kings who have gone rogue. Underneath their rebellion, they're still Kings and your ignorance might not allow you to see how very important that is, but trust me when I say, this is a war you don't want your hand in..."

She ignores me. "Tillie, The Circle are not just old Kings..."

I hang up the phone because Madison opens the door. "You okay?"

I smile, trying to hide my reaction. "Yeah, it was just Ridge. I can meet with him another time."

"Okay, well come on then! We need some more pink in that hair."

CHAPTER 6

Nate

"**I** don't trust her." I turn my car off and lean back in my seat, watching as Tillie walks into the salon with Madison.

"I get why you wouldn't, because I ain't fucking with it either. She's hiding something..." Brantley says. He's almost always riding shotgun with me now that Bishop is all loved up with Madison and beside that, what with Madison killing his dad, Brantley has been left with too much money, houses, and cars, and he's found himself, for the most part—bored. "But what are you going to do if you find out she is hiding something, bro? She's not just Tillie to you. She's that chick to you, and then you had to go and be a dumb fuck and knock her up. Now she's your baby mama, and you're stuck with those bitches for life."

My lip curls. "For a smart fucker, you sure say some dumb shit."

He pulls out a pack of smokes and lights up. I crank our windows down and blaze a joint to counter the smell of nicotine.

"So we just gonna stay here until they're done?"

I blow out a cloud of smoke. "Yup. Then I'm going to fuck with her for a bit until we leave. She's hiding something and I ain't about to walk into a fucking trap."

Brantley grins around the cancer stick between his lips. "Got any ideas?"

I lick my lips and smirk. "Yeah, Tillie is the opposite of Madison when it comes to fear. Madison cowers, gets scared and does a bunch of dumb shit that would have gotten any other girl murdered on the spot."

Brantley turns his attention to me. "And what does Tillie do?"

CHAPTER 7

Tillie

"You know, for a brunette, your hair is pretty high maintenance," I tsk Madison as we're leaving the salon. The sun is setting in the background, igniting burnt hues in the sky. It's beautiful the way it kisses over your skin.

"Because it's not brunette, you heard her, it has tints of red in it too..."

I roll my eyes. "This is why I have pink hair. When it runs out, it has a faded punk look that is totally okay to rock."

Madison clears her throat. "For you!" She beeps her pretty turquoise Ferrari and I slide into the passenger seat. I want to ask why she's not asking me about Micaela, but deep down I already know why. It's because she has complete faith in Bishop.

"I'm naturally blonde so I guess it's fine. Have you heard from Tatum?"

We've been dancing around the T-word all day and I've noticed how any time I even steer the conversation toward her, Madison clams up.

"She'll be coming over tonight, actually, and she's okay. I just don't want it to be weird between the two of you, you know?" Madison drives us out of the parking lot outside the salon.

"It won't be. Honestly, Madz, Nate is not my property. If they could just not rub it in my face, though, that would be great."

Madison doesn't answer, turning the stereo on. I get it. I know that it must be hard for her to be in the middle of this cluster fuck, and deep down I know I'm the outsider out of the three. They say three's a crowd, and even though Madison does her best to not let it fall that way, it doesn't stop how I feel when her and Tate are together. They just...exist with each other. And although Madison and I have a bond and so do Tate and I, I haven't really felt like I fit into the puzzle when we're all together at once. Or maybe that's just my own insecurities getting the best of me.

Madison growls and then hits the stereo before pulling onto the shoulder of a gravel road. I look out the window, the angry sky now dark enough to awaken nocturnal creatures.

I shiver. "What are you doing?"

"Here's the thing," Madison declares. "I love you, and you know this. I also love Tate, and I hate lying to either of you. She loves you too, just saying, but—"

"—But what?" I urge, wishing she would just spit it out.

"I can't breathe." She flings her seatbelt off and launches out the car door. I follow, unclipping my belt and stepping outside. The temperature this time of year in New York isn't cold but isn't warm, though tonight it feels a little chillier with the strong gusts of wind smashing through my hair. "Madison!" She's pacing back and forth in front of the car, the headlights the only way to see.

A big semi-truck flies passed us, flicking my freshly washed and salon dried hair up around my face. "Seriously, Madz, can we do this in the car? We just spent that money at the salon, or rather, you did..."

"She's in love with him!" Madison spins around, her hands flailing around the place. "God, I'm so sorry, Tillie, but she's in love with him. Like she cannot let it go in love with him."

Okay, so they were obviously more serious than I thought.

I lean back on her car, blowing out a gust of breath and folding my arms in front of myself. "Well, that's fine."

"No," Madison shakes her head. "You see because h—"

A large black SUV pulls up behind our car and I turn toward it, shading the head-lights with my hand.

"Tillie, get in the car," she murmurs softly, and I watch as her face morphs from anger to complete and utter fear.

"What?" I turn toward the SUV before coming back to her. "Why?"

Her face pales and she springs forward, but it's too late, a hand is covering my mouth and a black sack is being shoved over my head. I scream, kicking and punching thin air.

"I swear to god!" Madison screams, but then she goes silent and I'm being thrown into the backseat of the SUV as if I weigh nothing.

"What the fuck!" I yell, but a rope is being tied around my neck and then—shit! It tightens and my breathing shallows. I start panicking, trying to suck in more air but I find the more I panic, the thicker my breathing. Sweat starts trickling down my temple. We're driving away quickly and handcuffs are being clasped around my wrists. "Who the fuck are you?"

I'm met with silence again.

The drive carries on for another ten or so minutes before the SUV takes a hard left and the engine cuts out. Hands grip around my upper thighs and yank me down the seat.

A door opens behind me and I'm tossed out, rolling through loose branches and stones.

"You have about a ten-second head start..." The voice is filtered with a recorder.

"I don't know where I'm going!" I yell, frustrated.

"Nine."

I bolt forward, ignoring my fear of accidentally running straight off a cliff. Wind zaps past me.

Seven.

Six.

I start to count down as my legs pick up speed. The skies open up and thunder claps angrily just as the first droplets of rain begin trickling down my cheek.

I scream a little, taking a hard right. Blinded, I have no idea where I'm going, but I need to at least try to run. Something deep inside of my brain, though, is telling me that I shouldn't have run. That maybe whoever it is, wanted me to run. Images of the man who called me that night and tried to get me into his SUV flash through my brain and fear ripples through me again as my legs gain speed.

One.

They're coming. I'm battling with myself right now on what I should do. Hide, even if I don't know if I'm really hiding, or keep running even though the fear of someone chasing me is enough to figuratively chop my legs off. Before I can take another step, a body crashes down behind me and then I'm falling, mud sloshing against my chest.

My voice challenges the rain hitting curved leaves and rocks as I scream, "What do you want!"

The rope that's tied around the sack over my head loosens, the handcuffs unlatching from my wrists. I tear the sack from my head and let the darkness of the forest fall over me. Holy crap. Rain pours over my face and leaks into my eyes, my hair matted down against my cheeks.

"What aren't you telling me, princess..."

"Nate!" I yelp, but he shoves my face into the ground again, turning me around onto my back. Pressing his forearm into my throat, my eyes search his frantically. "What do you mean!"

"I know you're walking us into a trap, Tillie. You showing up out of nowhere, calm and collected about your psycho sister stealing Micaela, it doesn't fucking piece up right."

"I don't know what you're talking about!"

He shoves me again, his mouth coming down to the side of my neck. "Don't lie to me, Tillie."

"I'm not!" I yell, rearing up to his face until our nose tips touching. "I fucking said I'm not lying to you, Nate. She took her, and then dumped me back at Madison's. What more do you want from me?"

"Is that a serious question?" He growls, and my heart thunders in my chest at the soft caress of his fingertip sliding over my collarbone. "Because right now." He grinds himself against me. I slam my eyes closed in an attempt to mentally remove myself from the onslaught of sensations that he's thrashing into me. "There's a whole fucking lot that I want from you that what you've had a taste of wouldn't even classify as a snack."

I yank my face away from him. "Your games aren't going to work on me, Nate. I'm not one of your preppy princesses. You can't break what you didn't build."

He chuckles, and then he wraps his fingers around my chin, yanking my face up so that I'm glaring right at him. "You saying I haven't contributed to the fucked-up shit that goes on in that pretty little head, princess, huh?"

I narrow my eyes. "I didn't say that, but you didn't break me, Nate. I was damaged when you found me, you just inflicted more scars." I'm frustrated with his weight pressing down on me. Not frustrated because I want him to get off but frustrated because I don't want him to get off.

He pauses, his jaw clenching. Water drips down from his hair and falls onto my lip. I lick it off until the taste of his conditioner or whatever it is that he has in his hair slips down my throat. "You. Ran." The words leave his mouth through pained lips, and it momentarily stops all of my thought processes.

"I didn't run, Nate," I answer softly. My chest feels heavy and my throat feels clogged. "You should have, Tillie."

"I, wait— what? Now you're saying I should have run?"

His mouth comes to mine, but not enough to kiss me, only enough for his lips to lightly tease mine. He growls out so softly that I almost miss it "Yeah. To *me*."

Pain flashes through me and threatens to take hold when his hand gently comes to my neck and his fingers wrap around my throat. "But you didn't." *Abort, abort.* His soft tone is now replaced with anger, venom dripping off every syllable. "Now you've caused a whole lot of shit that could have been avoided. So I'm going to ask you again, as me. As fucking Tillie and Nate." he kisses me this time. His soft lips brushing over mine. I don't open at first, afraid that letting his tongue slip inside of me will also grant him access to my soul. He pulls back slightly, and I have to hammer down my breathing. His eyes search mine. "Are you hiding something?"

I shake my head, the lie falling effortlessly from my mouth. "No."

He growls, and I barely hear it over the pounding of the rain crashing against the leaves, then one of his knees presses between mine, spreading my leg wide.

I swallow. "Nate…"

His other leg joins, pressing my other wide until I'm open season for him.

"Nate…" I repeat myself, hoping it'll snap him out of it.

"Shut up, Tillie. Me having my dick exactly where it wants to be right now is balancing out the fact that I want to kill you. I'm seeing fucking red right now, baby, and you have the flag hanging off of your sweet little ass."

We're doing this. Right here and right now.

His hand grazes up my outer thigh, hiking it up his hip. His head tilts back, his eyes searching mine. Water dropping off his long eyelashes. "Want me to fuck you right here in front of Brantley, maybe show him exactly how loud you can scream?"

I clench my teeth, narrowing my eyes. "Why stop there." I grin, my eyes flicking to where Brantley is leaning up against a tree trunk, a toothpick flicking around in his mouth. "Why not let him join? I mean, I've heard that you're not against sharing, in fact, you all share your girls around pretty—"

His hand flies to my throat and he clenches down until I struggle to take in any air. "I'm not Bishop." This is the side of Nate that is hidden in the shadows of the cheesy smile he parades. His demons dance behind his mischievous eyes, not at the front like Bishop and Brantley. Boys like Nate are lethal, because you fall for their charm, their jokes, and their beautiful faces. By the time you find yourself lost in their darkness with their demons lurking around you, it's too late. They suck you in with charisma and spit you out with sin.

"Bishop didn't allow it to happen, Nate, you just did it anyway." I grate my teeth together. For the first time since I've been back, I'm annoyed at the hypocrisy of Nate. He's been with Tatum for months, seeing each other—in fact—and he has feelings for Madison too. Regardless whether Madison is now with Bishop, Nate still has feelings for her and before I can stop myself, I'm raging with undiluted jealousy.

He's watching me, but I suddenly don't care. My eyes go back to Brantley. "Wanna fuck me, Brantley?"

Brantley doesn't flinch, not the slightest bit of surprise flashes over his face. The toothpick slows down, his eyes falling down my body, stopping, and then coming back to meet mine. Brantley is everything your parents told you to run from—if you had parents, which I didn't. He's not just bad, he's evil. You can see it in his eyes, how they look through people. He's cold and irrecoverable, but I bet he'd be a good lay. Bonus points too because it'll piss Nate off.

"Don't call my bluff, Tillie. I'll let him fuck you so hard you won't be able to walk straight for a week just to show you how much I don't give a fuck about you anymore."

"Then do it," I bite down in an attempt to simmer the rage that is threatening to spill out of me. "Maybe you can show him how you fucked Tate."

Brantley must have pushed off the tree because suddenly he's looking down at me, his boots near my face.

"You weren't kidding. She's fucked in the head. It's hot."

Nate leans down and bites my lip between his teeth. "You have no idea."

My arm goes around Nate, and I grind into him. He stills, searches my eyes and then groans. "You really want to do this?"

My eyes flick up to Brantley and then come back to Nate. "In the time that you've had me pinned to this dirty ground, getting drenched in rain after running from you for fifteen seconds, and again, after you kidnapped me, I've come to the conclusion that I'm mad at you, so yes, I do want him."

Nate's eyes narrow.

I continue. "And you."

"I'm not touching you, Tillie." Then in a flash, he's up from the ground and the warmness of his body is instantly gone.

Wait. What? My face doesn't hide the shock I'm feeling. He doesn't want me.

Tatum.

"Right," I snicker, getting up from the ground. Fuck Nate. Aside from everything else, fuck him for this the most.

My eyes go to Brantley, who steps forward, grabbing me by the wrist and pulling me into his body. I lick my bottom lip, my eyes staying on his. Dark orbits peer back at me. I've always thought Brantley had dark brown eyes, but up close, it's almost like there are also blue flecks through them. Or maybe I'm hallucinating. Or maybe it's the moon playing tricks on me.

He backs me up until I crash against a tree trunk, then his hands come to the backs of my thighs.

"Will he fight you after this?" I whisper, my eyes going from between his lips to his eyes.

"It's cute you still think he gives a fuck."

"He doesn't?" I already know that he doesn't, but I guess there is still a very small part of my brain that needs to be reminded.

Brantley pins me with a glare so cold and distant, it almost has me running to hide behind another tree. The fact that he's pressing against me is what is stopping me. "Use me to fuck with him, Tillie. He won't and can't do anything about it. The shots are yours to make, it's part of the rules..." He doesn't elaborate, and I shoot a quick look at Nate. He's leaning against the same tree Brantley was at, grinning at me while running his index finger over his upper lip.

He thinks I won't do it. He's made a mistake. He's gone into this thinking I'm like

Madison and will go cold right before things kick off. He's made a mistake because I'm not his property. Sex is something I can't live without—I use it as a way to mask a lot of my issues. And I'm not Madison. I wasn't raised with a silver spoon, I was raised by blood sodden knives, and girls like me, we learn to use them as weapons. Love shouldn't be offered up as a gift to just anybody, it should be preserved and used as a weapon to protect our heart.

Keeping my eyes on Nate, I draw my tongue out and lick Brantley's neck all the way up to his earlobe, and then whisper with enough lip movement for Nate to know what I've said.

"Fuck me."

Brantley growls, pressing into me and grabs my hands, yanking them up above my head. He rolls his hips into me. Nate is lost in the back of my head.

Brantley's hands come to the waist of my jeans and he pops open the button, yanking them down. His hand cups me and I moan, biting down on my bottom lip while tossing my head back. He glides my panties to the side—Nate's phone lights up and starts ringing, breaking the moment.

Brantley lets go, turning back to face Nate like we weren't just about to fuck in the name of revenge in the middle of a forest in the pouring rain.

The atmosphere and realization of the situation starts to seep into me more and more as the minutes pass.

I guess fear does weird things to different people. To me, I fight where some flight. If Nate wants a challenge, I'll give him a war. I don't owe him loyalty, and I'm not going to offer it up as a peace offering either.

Nate doesn't look at me, his eyes go to Brantley. "We gotta bounce."

Then they both start walking away.

"Pull your pants up, princess."

We're driving back to Nate and Madison's when Nate hits the stereo on. He's driving and I'm in the backseat, which means his eyes in the rearview mirror are in direct line to me, not that he has actually looked at me yet.

Lauv's "There's No Way" starts playing.

Something feels off about this whole night, like someone isn't saying something. My teeth are chattering, and my lips have probably bruised to a deep purple. Nate and Brantley had long since ditched their shirts, now both of them are sitting in damp jeans and—I should stop.

My eyes flick to the rearview mirror and my heart stops in my chest when I catch Nate watching me. His eyes are flat, like the ocean, but just like the ocean, you know that beneath the surface there's a whole lot going on that you don't see. It's unnerving. He looks back to the road and I sink back against the door, rubbing my arms.

For a brief moment, I can feel him pushing contrition into me. If I was a better girl, I would feel guilty. But I do regret getting worked up over it. I was caught up in proving I was different than Madison and angry at him for having feelings toward other girls that it weaved me into a web of fury. From the chattering teeth to the frost sprinkling over my brain, I've decided that you can't change the way people feel about others. I can't stop how he feels about Tate and Madison. I just have to remove myself from the equation.

Easier said than done.

CHAPTER 8

Nate

"Burbons and Lacs" by Master P is playing in the background, sweat dripping off my body. I crank the treadmill up to level thirteen, picking up my stride. We got back twenty minutes ago, and I have roughly thirty minutes before we leave and get my damn daughter back, but the shit with Tillie and Brantley has left a fucking sour taste in my mouth, which is precisely why I'm trying to exude some pent-up energy in here. It was either the treadmill or a full-on fight between Brantley and me, but that would only prove the fact that Tillie still owns a small part of me. A very irrational, deranged and wild part, but a part, nonetheless.

And then there's the rest…

I hit the treadmill off and grab my water bottle, bringing the tip to my mouth just as the glass sliding door slides open and Tatum walks through. The gym's wall is made up of glass with a direct view of the pool, the pool house opposite and the main kitchen with living area connecting off it to the right.

"What do you want?" I wrap my lips around the water bottle without taking my eyes off her.

She stumbles in closer, raking her long blonde hair out of her face. Tate has the whole girl next door look going on, but she fucks like the mom. "I—I—" she slurs, and it's then that the smell of alcohol fills the gym, mixing with my sweat.

"Are you drunk?" I catch her as she falls into me. Her head comes up, her eyes catching mine.

"Nate. Why don't you love me?"

Oh Jesus. I've always treaded carefully around Tate, because Madison will have my balls if I don't, and if she's not sucking on them, I'd rather she stays the fuck away from them, but as of late, keeping Tate at arm's length has become more difficult. She's gone from a cool chick who was down with fucking on the go, to a clingy stage five.

"Because I don't do love, I told you that…" My arm wraps around her back to stabilize her.

She searches my eyes as they glass over. Fuck. She better not fucking cry, I can already feel Madison's wrath. "You're a liar, Nate Riverside," she whispers through a broken voice.

"How am I a liar?" I reply. *Gentle, gentle if I want to protect my genitals...*

"Because I've seen the way you look at Tillie."

The door to the gym opens. "—okay fine. We can—" Tillie stops, her eyes going from me to Tate who's slumped in my arms, and then back to me again. "Never mind." She walks out, slamming the door so hard that she basically bounces her jealousy between the bolts and hinges holding it together.

I growl, clenching my teeth, and then look back down to Tate.

She shrugs. "Oops."

I let her go and she falls to the ground.

"Tate, don't get me wrong, I don't want to hurt you, but if you don't stop this bullshit, I'll stop caring about Madison's little feelings where you're concerned and treat you like the rest of the bitches who cling to my dick by their teeth..." I step forward, internally trying to calm myself down while fighting the urge not to run after the most stubborn chick I've ever known. "I'll fucking tear them out."

Her face falls, and I watch as emotions pass through her features, ending on sadness. "Just leave it alone, Tate. Tillie is your friend, too, or are you that blinded by my nine-inch cock that you can't see that anymore?"

I leave, throwing my shirt over one shoulder and make my way out to find Tillie.

CHAPTER 9

Tillie

I'm being irrational. I know this, really, I do. Ridge and I shared beds for years while I watched him bounce around others, and then come back to me and vice versa. It never bothered me—ever. I never experienced a throbbing pain pound against my belly to the beat of Eminem "Love the Way You Lie." But right now, I feel like I'm about to light that match and burn every single inch of the walls inside my head that hold a memory of Nate.

Holy hell.

I run my fingers through my hair, grinding my teeth while pacing back and forth.

"It's fine, Tillie. Cool your shit."

My eyes go to the ground where Daemon's book is. I dash for it, shoving it into a small overnight bag that I found in his closet. I don't know why I feel a little fragile right now, but I don't like it. I don't like not being in control of my feelings, and that probably stems back to not being in control of my father and his temper when I was a small child.

I'm not touching that right now.

I toss in the clothes that Madison gave me and zip up. Did I really expect to stay here, living out of Madison's shadow and not have a life? I have a daughter. I should be thinking about our life and what I'm going to do, but I can't. My life is a fucking mess because of—I look around the room. This. I miss my baby more than I can say, but at the same time, I'm disappointed in myself for bringing her into this world. I don't regret her existence, not one bit. There is nothing in this world that can spark every single emotion in my body but my daughter. And maybe the father… but I wish. I wish I had a better life to offer her.

I fall to the ground, exhausted by the marathon my head is running around me and lean back against the mattress on the bed, my eyes zoning in on the pattern that is imprinted into Daemon's ceiling.

The door opens and then closes, but I don't pay it any attention. As much as I wish it was Madison, it knew it wasn't.

"I'll get her back," Nate says softly, but I still don't look at him.

"And then what, Nate? I have nothing to offer our daughter, who deserves the world. I'm lucky I'm smart so I have enough grades to graduate high school, but college isn't in the picture for me." I finally turn my attention to him. "What have I got to offer her? I've failed her before I've had a chance to enjoy her."

He sinks down onto the floor opposite me, and I fight with myself not to let my eyes drop to his naked chest. Nate naked in any sense is a damn vortex for girls. He sucks you in and laughs as you lose yourself in a never-ending spin of pretty colors and ecstasy.

He props one arm up on one knee, leaning his head back against the door while his eyes stay on mine. "You haven't failed her, Tillie. We will figure it out when she gets here."

I shake my head, swiping the tears away from my eyes. "You don't get it."

"Yeah, I do, and fuck, if you want to go to college, then you can go to fucking college. You know damn well I'd pay—"

"—Nate!" I snap, my eyes going to him. "I'm not a fucking charity case."

"No." His eyes narrow on me. "You're the fucking mother to my kid, so if I want to put your ass through college, I fucking will, so shut the fuck up and calm your stubborn ass down for once in your goddamn life."

I exhale, turning my head to face the ceiling again, losing the urge to fight with him. "I hate you so much."

"Yeah, ditto, baby, but we have a kid. So when she gets back, we're seriously going to talk about what you want in the long term and how we can make that happen. But we're also going to sit down with Mom and Joseph and toss around ideas to keep Micaela safe until this shit with your sister is taken care of. Can we agree on that?"

"Right now." I stand from the floor. "I just want her back. We can talk about the rest once she's back in my arms."

"Deal."

CHAPTER 10

Nate

I never thought much about the day that I die. I think I assumed that I'd acquire some sort of superpower by that time and figure out how to become immortal. But as I flick my military blade around my fingers and think more on it, leaning back in my seat as Bishop drives us toward New York City, it's not the way in which someone dies that matters. It's what they died for that it comes down to, and I'd lay my life on the line in a heartbeat to save my daughter. I may not have had much time with her since she has been born, but your kid should always be the exception when it comes to time.

"Did you get anything out of her?" Eli asks from the backseat.

I don't answer.

"Either way," Bishop exhales, leaning to the side of his seat while taking us onto the highway. "We're prepared enough." In this ride, there's Bishop, me, Eli, Cash, and Spyder, Bishop's cousin. In the Range Rover behind us is Brantley, Ace, Hunter, Chase, and Jase. Then in the SUV behind them is Joseph, Hector, Max, Raguel, and Johan. Basically, all of the olds are in that vehicle.

"Mmmm," I answer, looking out the window.

"Will you be able to handle it if you find out that she has lied to you?" Eli further asks and I have to stop myself from snapping at him.

"I already fucking know she has lied to me."

Bishop doesn't answer, because he knows too.

"What?" Eli pushes forward to lean on the center console. "How?"

"We've known all along," Bishop cuts in for me.

We continue driving and Eli eventually drops the subject once he figures out that neither Bishop or I were going to go further into it. It's another five minutes before we're entering the bright lights of New York City.

I push the buttons on the GPS system that's sitting on the dash, programming the address into it. She starts yapping off and I close my eyes to count to ten.

I inhale on eight, a smirk riding on my lips. "You smell that? Smells like murder."

"Okay, but I thought we weren't supposed to make a mess..." Cash adds, looking around at all of us. Cash is the only one out of all of us, apart from Eli, I think, that doesn't "like" to commit first-degree murder, or murder on any ground and they especially aren't really fond of the sight of blood.

Spyder tsks from the back seat. "There are ninety-seven ways you can kill someone without drawing any blood."

"I'm not going to ask how you know that, but okay," Cash replies. The complete opposite of his brother Saint, who runs in the same circle as me and Bishop when it comes to becoming the reaper when needed. We're just below Brantley, who is a product of someone who has walked through the gates of hell and lived to talk about it.

We pull into an underground parking of a skyscraper building. As soon as Bishop parks, we all jump out, shutting our doors loudly.

Hector Hayes, Bishop's old man and the godfather of all of The Kings, flicks his suit while grinning at us all. "Ready for playtime?"

CHAPTER 11

Tillie

"Stop pacing and sit down. You're making me dizzy." Madison massages her temples, leaning forward. We're all in the sitting room. Elena and Bishop's mom, Scarlet, has joined us.

"Seriously." Oh, and Tate.

I flop down onto the single sofa, flicking my rings around my finger. "Sorry."

"Don't be sorry," Elena coos, offering me a gentle smile. One that doesn't quite reach the corners of her eyes. "But don't worry. She's coming back."

"That's sort of not really what I'm worried about. I mean, I know she's coming back. I know they'll get her back."

"What then?" Madison asks. She doesn't snap at me, her tone is warm enough to almost melt the truth right out of my mouth, but I slam my lips closed.

I freeze. "Nothing."

Tate curls up in a ball on the sofa and it's not long before she's snoring softly. She was drunk, very drunk, and an irrational side of me wants to hate her for everything that she's making me feel, but I don't. My beef isn't with her, it's more with Nate. He's the one who is a whore and has made me feel like I'm just another girl he cares about in his life. Or maybe it is an underlying insecurity from my daddy issues. Who knows. Either way, I sigh as I get up from my seat and grab the throw blanket that is perched over the top of the sofa, spreading it out over her little body.

"She doesn't mean to be the way she is," Madison says through a whisper.

"I know," I agree, and it's as though neither of the moms are in this room right now. "Love changed her."

Madison sighs. "When she figures out that it's not love that she's feeling, she will come back."

"I hope so," I answer softly, going back to my spot on the sofa. Unable to sit still, my fingers start twisting on my lap. "Do you think they'll be okay?"

Scarlet looks at me over her martini glass. "Yes."

All of the cars pull up at once. The Range Rovers, the Bentley, and finally, the one I knew Nate was in. I chew on my bottom lip as the backdoor swings open. Madison grabs my hand beside me and squeezes. "It's going to be okay."

My breathing stops, my legs wobble like jelly and when I see Nate finally step out of the car, I let out a small exhale as he turns, and Micaela is cradled in his arms. I jolt toward them, reaching out to her, but Nate turns her away from me.

"Inside. Now."

"What?" I snap, my eyes leaving my daughter and going back to Nate. "You can't do this." I barely noticed the blood stains on Nate's hands or everyone else that was there because they're blurred into the back of my brain.

Finally, I turn and leave, going back inside and into the sitting room. The gas fire flicks angry flames against the wall which is a direct display of my own rage.

Nate walks in alone with Micaela in his arms. He slowly brings her toward me, and I fly off the sofa, taking her in my arms.

"It feels longer than one day that she has been gone."

Nate doesn't say anything, he simply lowers himself onto the sofa. "Sit down, Tillie. I need to talk with you about something."

I inhale Micaela's scent, closing my eyes. "If it has to do with whatever you had to do to get her back, I don't care."

"Really?" he asks, leaning back in the sofa. Micaela starts stirring so I bounce her around. Nate's eyes land on her. "She's been looked after by that nurse."

I nod, running my finger down her cheek. "I know. It's why—" I stop. Biting down on my tongue. It's too late, though, because he caught it.

"Oh?" He pikes up, leaning forward to rest his arms on his thighs. "You knew?"

Shit. Shit. Shit. shit. "I knew that Peyton would us—"

"—cut the fucking lies, Tillie. You can't fucking be honest even when it comes to our daughter."

My eyes snap to his. "So you've never lied?"

He pins me with a glare, staring straight through me. "Never about her." Then he stands to all his six-foot-whatever inches, his shoulders squaring in defiance. It's at this very moment that I realize just how pissed he is.

"So this is what is going to happen, babe." Only Nate could call me babe through lips that are seething with rancor. "I didn't kill your stupid fucking sister, because it turns out that I didn't need to."

I step backward. "What do you mean?" My grip around Micaela tightens.

"I mean," he says, countering my step. "She's not a Stuprum, Tillie, she's not Katsia's daughter."

I freeze. "What? That's not right. She's always been there. She's my sister."

Nate tilts his head. "You have the same dad but different mom. She's been kicked onto the street by The Operation. They want nothing to do with her and in fact, she will probably be dead by the end of the week."

"I don't understand."

Nate shakes his head slowly, his eyes darkening on me. "You're going to give my mom Micaela until we sort this out."

"Fuck you," I spit, squeezing her into my arms again.

"Pass, thanks, and Tillie, shut the fuck up and let me finish." His hands reach out to her. "This is the only way we're going to keep her safe for now. Stop being so fucking selfish."

I falter, his words penetrating my brain like a broken record. Is he right? Am I being selfish for keeping her in my arms even if it means sacrificing all that she could be.

No. She's my daughter. Mine. The best thing a daughter can have is her mother, not money or opportunity.

Nate must've been able to read my expression, because his eyes darken on me. His shoulders pull back and his legs spread, his stance switching. It's as though I'm watching a dark cloud sneak into a warm summer's day, sucking in all of the sunshine and replacing it with gloom.

"You don't have a choice, Tillie, she's my daughter just as much as she's yours, and now shit has changed."

"What? What has changed?"

"Give her to me." I'm too busy trying to figure out what he had just said that I aimlessly hand her to him.

"What do you mean, Nate?"

The doors open behind him and all of The Kings stand in a line.

I gulp, my eyes going back to Nate. "What are you going to do with me?"

He steps forward, kissing Micaela's head. "Get upstairs and go to my room."

I rush past him, annoyed with not just him but myself for allowing myself to get into this position to begin with. The control I craved for my daughter starts to slip between the cracks because he's right. She's just as much his as she is mine. I have no right to be the only person calling the shots when it comes to her livelihood. I have to learn how to share her time between us.

I shove his door open and freeze, the sight in front of me falters not just my footsteps but all thoughts of cussing Nate out too. There, in the midst of Nate's bachelor-slash-skanky ass room of red paint, black silk sheets—hopefully freaking washed—is a matte black crib. It has black blankets and bright pink sheets and the curve of it is more of an oval than a rectangle.

A pang of guilt crashes into me. I haven't given Nate a chance to be a father, sure, but I've barely myself been a mother. I'm constantly failing at it. I could bring it down to my age, or circumstance, but not every situation is ideal. I just have to find a way to cope with what fits my current predicament.

"Shhhh." Nate rocks Micaela, shooting me daggers as he enters. Her small little face is tilted backward, her cherub lips parted as she snores softly in the safety of his arms.

Nate yanks his eyes away from me, taking the disdain with him and I watch as his features soften when he looks back at his daughter. There has never been a delusional part of me that thought just because Nate and I have a baby together that we would just miraculously get on and would be a happy family. This family is not like others, and our world, the one we live in, plays a big part in this. Luckily, Micaela is still a baby, so she's not old enough to see how toxic her parents are. Hopefully we can sort something out before she starts talking and her first word is "fuck."

When he places her into her crib, he reaches for the TV remote and turns it on.

My eyes shoot to where Michaela sleeps peacefully. He turns the volume to a medium level, enough for us to talk and not wake her.

"I'm not sleeping in here, Nate," I finally say as he removes his heavy boots and tosses them into the corner.

He reaches for the collar of his shirt, pulling it over his head. I notice there's no blood on his clothes, but I see droplets of it behind his neck and on his hands. I know they fight shirtless for this reason, but something pangs in my chest and I need to know. "What happened tonight?"

He stands, turning to face me full on. His chest is wide and tanned, the ink etched into his skin beautifully. Nate isn't bulky, he's lean, cut to perfection for his height. He has large angel wings tattooed over his chest and one arm covered with a sleeve, including old English font that goes over his ribcage. "I got our daughter back, that's what. And from now on, she's not leaving this fucking house, you hear me?"

I open my mouth and then slam it closed. "I get that you're her dad, Nate, but she's mine too—"

"—yeah?" He yanks open his belt and flicks his button until his jeans are hanging off his lean hips. I divert my eyes, nervous that he would pick up on my gawking. "Good fucking entry she has gotten from you so far, Tillie. Top job."

"Fuck you." I'm raging, hanging dangerously close to the line of not giving a flying shit and saying what I want. "I did what I could for her—always!"

His eyes stay on mine. "Like lie to me?"

I still, running my palms down my pants. "I—"

"—Save it. Get in the shower, put one of my shirts on, and get your ass into bed. I need to sleep, and then tomorrow, we will talk about the next steps we take from here."

I exhale, exhausted from today but relieved I have my daughter back and admittedly, it is thanks to Nate, but it makes me nervous that I don't know what one of my lies he knows up to this point. Going straight for his dresser, I yank open his shirt drawer and dive into the bathroom, locking the door behind me. I hit the faucet and place Nate's shirt on the bathroom counter, squeezing the curve of the sink and slowly counting to ten.

I'm at seven when Madison's entry to the bathroom opens and she freezes. "Shit, sorry!"

I shake my head, smiling at her. "It's okay."

She walks into the bathroom. Really need to remember that I need to lock her side too. This bathroom and the secrets that are contained between the walls is enough to make a priest burst into flames.

I flip down the toilet cover and take a seat.

Madison's eyes go to Nate's door and she leans closer to me. "Are you okay? He can't hear anything in here. These walls are actually pretty soundproof."

I chuckle, tucking my hair behind my ear. A tear drops from my eye, but I quickly swipe it away.

"Tillie," Madison sighs, her hand coming to my knee. "He will come around. Maybe just give him time?"

"Nate?" I ask, confused. "Oh, yeah no that's not what I'm upset about. As much as I know it looks most of the time because we're always fighting, I can handle him."

Her face softens and her eyes crinkle around the edges. "I know." Then she sinks down onto the floor. "You're actually one of the few people who can."

I lick my lips, the salt hitting the tip of my tongue.

"What's wrong then, babe? You know we're practically sisters, so..." she jokes, shoving my legs.

If only that were true.

"It's just, I don't know, Mads. It seems I can't do anything right. I'm a failure. What am I going to do from here? Nate holds all the cards as far as Micaela is concerned. And that's not even mentioning my crazy stupid life. I'm broke, I'm not starting college with you guys after the holidays. I'm a mess." I shake my head, my thoughts swimming dangerously close to the dark side of the ocean. I think they're all starting NYU. Even Tatum, and Nate, I think. Nate and Tatum... shit.

"Well, Bishop isn't, if that makes you feel better."

I roll my eyes. "That's because he's a legacy or whatever and now he has to play Papa King."

Madison bursts out laughing and it's not long before I'm joining her. My tears soon dry and my stomach throbs. "God, I missed this."

Madison's hand comes to my knee. "Me too. Well, don't get mad, but you can live here. I heard Elena and my dad talking and they want to offer you the pool house. Just... act surprised when they ask you."

I freeze, my eyes stretching wide. "I could never—"

"Tillie," Madison starts. The twinkling in her eye has started. It happens every time she's about to get real. "You are family now. You have my niece, Elena's grandchild, Nate's child. Every decision you make is going to impact her. So please, just—think of her when you make the decision. The pool house is well away from Nate yet not so far that he gets anxiety with being away from Micaela, because that's what's going to happen. He won't be letting her out of his sight—forever, probably."

I sigh, standing from the toilet. "I guess I have a lot to think about."

She nods, getting to her feet and pulling me in for a hug. "Please make the right decision." Then she leaves me, alone with my thoughts. I undress and step into the shower, relishing in the hot water.

Could I live here? I mean really. If it's the pool house, that's practically not in the same house. I will need to start job hunting first thing Monday. At least, I can go from there. I use Madison's shampoo and conditioner and then soap up before getting out, drying off and slipping into Nate's shirt and his briefs. I have to roll the waistband a few times until they're not falling down, but they work. I really need to go shopping and get some clothes. Being back in civilization again after being on Perdita and locked up with Peyton has made me realize how much time I've lost.

I'm met with complete darkness and Eminem rapping in the background to "Stronger Than I Was" when I enter the bedroom. He has our daughter sleeping to Eminem. I don't know whether to punch him or swoon. Nate must have turned off the TV while I was in the shower. I drop my clothes in the hamper near the bathroom door, hitting off the bathroom light and making my way back to the bed. Thank god Micaela is a good sleeper. She's an incredible child. So settled for a baby that has had a sketchy start to life.

I tug the sheet back and slide into the other side of Nate, aware that he has Micaela's crib on his side. I lay back, trying to not breathe loudly, or even move too much, afraid he'll swear at me or something. Moody Nate isn't fun. I miss how we used to be before.

"Nate?" I whisper, pulling the covers up to my chin. Colored dots dance around in the room as my eyes adjust.

"Go to sleep, Tillie."

"Did you kill anyone tonight?"

Silence, and then just when I think he isn't going to say anything, he murmurs, "More than one."

"Do I need to get rid of your clothes?"

More silence. "Go to sleep, Tillie."

I do as I'm told and drift off to sleep.

CHAPTER 12

Daemon

S tones indented into the cushion of my feet with each step. The sun burned into my flesh and the sweat dripped down my face like it had so many times before. I'm being punished. Punished for being something I should not. I was raised with a set of rules being hammered into me from a young age, but one was feelings. It was basic human nature to feel, or so I'd been told. We sweat when it's hot, we shiver when we're cold. But emotional feelings, feelings of attachment—that is something that is optional.

"You will not draw that again, Daemon!" Katsia said in fluent Latin.

"Draw what?" I asked in Latin, the only language we speak, so simply that it shook the surprise off Katsia's face.

She pointed down to my latest image. Chapter Six. "That!"

I stared down at the green eyes. Like mine in shape, but green in color. The almond tilt and the long fang of lashes. Just two eyeballs glassed over. "Why?"

Katsia couldn't answer or wouldn't. She merely watched me with a careful eye. "Throw it away. I don't want you drawing anymore!" The car door slammed, and the tires skidded in her departure. What did I do wrong? I don't know what I did wrong…

Human nature is to feel, so they turned me into a machine.

I blocked the sun out of my eye, watching the trailer that was parked right at the entryway to a park. It rocked back and forth as yelling and screaming spilled from the beat-up windows. I ran toward it, using the old potted plants with withered flowers as a step stool. I peeked through the window, but it was hard to see. The edges had mold spurting out of the seams, but I could see a small girl curled on the ground. She had to be maybe a little younger than me. Her hair is matted in blood, sticking her blonde curls to her face. Her clothes had dark smeared blood on them and her lip quivered as her arms covered her eyes to shield her head.

The girl's eyes meet mine. Turquoise blue, the same color as the tropical ocean that wraps around Perdita. Everything slows as she blinks, her thick eyelashes damp with tears fanning over her swollen cheeks.

"Daemon!" Katsia mutters from behind me.

I turn to face her, the woman I was to trust. But how could I trust her if this is what she did to her own daughter. "Why don't you help her?"

Katsia's eyes darken. "She is not my issue."

"You're her mother."

"That means nothing. I am a Stuprum first."

"But, maybe you can be both?" I tried to bargain with her, unable to get the girl's eyes out of my head.

"Impossible," she snapped, and then yanked me by my arm and toward the waiting dark SUV.

I will save that girl one day. I will save the girl with a soul so battered blood is seeping out of her haunted eyes.

One day, I think to myself. Yes. One day.

CHAPTER 13

Tillie

I wake the next morning with ease. Nate isn't in the bed, having probably left early for something atrocious like working out. I can hear Micaela tossing and turning in her crib and I fly off the bed, making my way to her.

"Hey, baby girl," I coo, and her eyes come up to meet mine. She's growing so much bigger every day. I can't believe it has been almost four months since I gave birth to her, but now that I look at her. Really look at her, I can see how she has lost the newborn features. Her skin is tighter, giving her features more definition. Her eyes. *My god her eyes*. It's like looking into Nate's. The admittance of that grips at my chest with an iron fist. Not because I dislike it, but because—well.

"She awake?" Nate asks, walking through the door, with yup, his shirt tucked into the back of his gym shorts. Sweat pelts off his chest as he tosses his water bottle across the room, onto the small two-seat sofa that's in the corner.

I clear my throat. "Yeah."

He ignores me, going straight for her. I have to fight myself not to snap at him and tell him to fuck off because I still want cuddles with her, but he nudges his head toward the door. "Mom made breakfast. Kings are here."

I don't move, mainly because I don't know what to do. What does he--

"Tillie, that means go downstairs and I'll be right behind you with her."

"Oh," I whisper, running my fingers through my hair and tying it into a ponytail on the top of my head. With another rubber band, I tie a knot in the front of Nate's shirt that I'm wearing so it doesn't look all that ridiculous. This makes it ride above my belly button now, his boxer briefs remain rolled up to sit below my hips. I wait for him near the door while he changes Micaela's diaper. Yes. Nate Riverside-Malum is changing his daughter's diaper. Again, I have to keep my swoon in check. This man hates—no, despises me. I cannot and will not swoon over that. Why should a woman swoon over a man doing his fatherly duty anyway?

When he finally turns, dirty diaper crumpled in his hand and ready to take downstairs, the smile he was giving Micaela falls.

"What!" I snap, my hands on my hips.

His eyes rake over my body. "When the fuck did that just happen?"

"What?" I repeat because I'm flat out confused.

"Never mind," he grumbles, walking straight past me and heading down the hallway.

I'm behind him taking the stairs, confused again when Elena greets us from the bottom. Her face lights up in glee when she sees Micaela.

"Nate, give me her."

"No," he says, hugging her away from his overbearing mother.

Elena huffs. "Nate, now. Please. Oh my gosh, I never thought I could love someone more than I do you, Nate, but she has changed that…"

I chuckle, pulling my bottom lip into my mouth to hide the smile that wants to take over.

"I ain't even mad," Nate grins, finally putting his mother out of her misery and gently handing her Micaela.

Elena's eyes light up and then she looks to me, sharing that same smile. "Morning, Tillie. I made pancakes and waffles. You might want to dig in before the army of hungry wolves scarf it all down."

I flash her a small smile. "Thank you. You really didn't have to do that." My stomach grumbles, as if to say yeah, *yeah she really did, bitch now go eat*. I can't remember when the last time I ate was, so I slowly make my way into the kitchen as Elena takes Micaela into the sitting room to cuddle with Joseph. I'm still watching them when I enter the kitchen, ignoring the very crowded dining table on the right side of me.

Joseph grins down at Micaela, and I'm almost certain she just smiled back. My heart sinks. Seeing the three of them together hurts me and I can't fathom why.

"Tillie," Nate bites, and I finally turn to face him, but freeze when I take in all the bodies. Yes. They're all here. Not only The Kings, but Madison too (of course), and… Tate.

"What?" I act as if it's no big deal, but it is a lot to take in. Just one of them exudes enough power to make a girl uncomfortable. Imagine having all ten of them plus a girl who is, generally speaking, one of my best friends who just so happens to be in love with my ex—whatever he is-slash-baby-daddy.

I really hate drama. Did I mention that? Yet, this world is like a soap opera gone wrong, you know, if Quentin Tarantino directed said soap opera.

"Eat," Nate orders, gesturing down to the table. The size of the dining table is obviously fit to cater around thirty people because there are still a few empty seats scattered around, yet, Nate yanks out the one directly beside him, his eyes pointedly staring at me.

Everyone is silent.

I clench my jaw, keeping eye contact with him while thinking whether or not I should purposely sit somewhere else. Maybe beside Brantley.

I decide I can't be bothered fighting this early in the morning and take the seat beside him. I swear I hear a few exhales of breath as I do so.

I start piling waffles onto my plate and then spoon fresh fruit on top.

"So!" Cash interrupts, clapping his hands together hard enough for the heavy Rolex to hit the Cuban gold chain around his wrist. It's not as thick as the one Nate wears around his neck, but I'm almost certain it has diamonds encrusted into the design.

I take a big bite out of my waffle, yanking it between my teeth. These people have too much money.

"What are we doing today? I need to get laid, it's been a while, so I was thinking we could go out tonight."

"Yeah," Brantley says, and my eyes go to him. Surprise shoots through me briefly when I find him already watching me. "Ditto. You know how murder makes me horny." He says all of that while not moving his eyes from mine. I cough, choking on my waffle.

"You okay, babe?" Madison coos, rubbing my back.

I look up at her as I take a sip of Nate's juice. Her eyes twinkle with knowledge. I should have known she would catch the little moment between Brantley and I. Nothing gets past her. Unless you're Bishop. Oh no. I know that look. I swear this girl is turning into one of them with the games she plays.

"Fine." I smile, running my tongue over my bottom lip. I find Brantley again. "Think something got stuck in my throat." Okay so she's not the only one who likes to tease them every now and then, but the banter with Brantley momentarily pauses my thoughts of Nate and his moody, unattainable bullshit playboy ways.

Madison leans back, smirking into her— "Is that a mimosa?"

She grins, and my eyes find Bishop who is glaring at her from across the table.

"Sure is," she mutters, pointedly ignoring B. "Want one?"

"She's good," Nate answers for me, ever his moody self lately.

"Yeah, I do," we both ignore Nate, and Madison giggles, grabbing my hand. "Come. Tate, you too."

I snatch my plate from the table, not ready to give up this glorious food right now. Madison is still laughing when we enter the kitchen, her eyes swinging between both of us.

"Okay. So, sit. We need to talk about tonight. The boys are going out, but I feel like we need a girl's night, you know, have some bonding time."

This doesn't sound good. I bite into my strawberry, my lips wrapping around it. Juice slips down my thumb and I slowly bring it up to my mouth, sucking it off. Something is obviously going on with Madison, and I know she's trying to help Tate and I bu—

"Tillie!" Nate barks from the table in the dining room and my attention snaps to him instantly. *Damn open plan dining.*

"What!" Now what have I done wrong? He's scowling at me, his eyes on my fingers. I look around the table to all of them—bar—Bishop, and their eyes are all watching me.

Bishop's back is jiggling like he's laughing.

"Oh shut it, Nate! If you can't handle how hot she is maybe you should—" Madison stops herself, exhaling. "Never mind."

I turn to face Madison, ignoring what just happened. There's no way that's what that was about. "As much as I'd love to, I can't. I have Micaela now."

Elena comes into the kitchen. "Tillie, can I talk to you for a second?"

I drop my strawberry and swipe my hands on a dishcloth. "Sure."

Madison squeezes my arm as I slide passed her.

I walk into the lounge room, my eyes going to Madison's dad. "Hi, Mr. Montgomery."

He flashes me a convivial smile. "Please, call me Joseph."

I know he's not Madison's biological dad, but I swear they look similar.

I take a seat on the sofa opposite him, and Elena sits beside me with Micaela in her arms. She hands my daughter back to me, and I take her, bringing her to sit up against my belly.

"Tillie, I, don't really know how to say this so I'm just going to go right out with it."
She exhales. "We want to help you any way that we can, and I mean that in the sincerest
way possible."

Micaela's fingers wrap around my index finger and I jiggle my legs softly. "Okay."

Elena looks to Joseph and then back to me. "We want to offer you the pool house.
It doesn't have to be permanent, but it is yours for as long as you need it. I don't want to
sound pushy," she says, and something clogs in my throat. I watch both of them, the love
they share exploding around me. I wish I had a family like this. Nate is a lucky bastard.
"But we want you to know that we are your family now. Regardless of your relationship
with Nathanial, this is as much your home as it is his and Madison's." I fight the tears that
are threatening to fall from my eyes. Living with Nate is probably not the best idea, but
Madison's words echo inside my head. *You have to think of her now too.*

Elena carries on. "I would also like to say that, um. I will be here at all times. Joseph
will be traveling for business, but he will be home a lot more now too. Tillie, we want to
help every way that we can, which is why…" She chews on her bottom lip. I've never seen
her nervous before, but it fills my heart to know she's trying to help. She exhales. "I want
you to know that college can be an option for you. I want Micaela to have the best life, and
that means that I want you to have the best life." Joseph shuffles in his seat, his smile is a
little lopsided now. Maybe he doesn't agree with Elena, either way, there's no way I could
accept the college offer. I gave up on that dream a long time ago. She continues on, "We
know you will be graduating with an above average GPA and we have enough strings we
can pull at NYU that we can get you into the classes that you would like to take…"

I lick my lips. "I—I am not sure what to say. Thank you for the college offer, I do
appreciate it so much, but there is no way that I could ever accept that and be okay with it.
I gave up on college a long time ago." Elena's face falls, her eyes going to her hands on her
lap. Joseph reaches over to rub her back. It's a warm and loving gesture, one that I couldn't
relate to. "However, I would love to ah, take you up on the pool house?"

Her eyes snap up to mine, a smile stretched wide. "Really?"

I nod, pulling my lips between my teeth. "Yes. I will figure out work and pay rent—"

Elena shakes her head. "No. No rent is needed. Can I ask you one more thing?"

Why not. I nod, nervous about what she's going to ask me next. Her eyes shift to
Joseph, who looks almost statue-like. "You know my active life in The Kings. So, I just—"

"—Honey, don't bore her with all of that."

I sense she's not telling me something, but it's probably got to do with Nate and his
asshole ways.

Elena's eyes cut to him, but come back to me and Micaela, who has started wriggling
in my arms. She must be hungry.

"I—please use me, with her. I know that Nate has told you that we are happy to have
her if anything happens or comes up, you know that we would guard her with our life…"
the way she says that raises warning flags, but I nod slowly.

"I know."

"Also, I want you to go out as much as possible, Tillie. You're eighteen, you should
be going out and having fun. Please, please let me do as much as I can. As I said, I am
here now and—" Her eyes go to Micaela and glass over. "God I love that girl. She's like an
apology for Nate," she jokes and I laugh.

"Hey!" Nate snaps from the archway. He's leaning against it, his eyes on me and Micaela.

Tate comes up beside Nate, leaning up on her tippy toes to whisper in his ear. He grins, throwing his arm around her.

My heart shakes in my chest. Jealousy and rage bubbles to the surface. *You will not look weak. You will not look weak.*

Nate and Tate disappear together.

"I'm sorry," Elena murmurs, and my eyes snap to her.

"About what?" I clear my throat, afraid I'm going to explode. I think I'm acquiring an anger problem.

"About Nate."

I shake my head. "Oh, don't be sorry. He and I will never be in a relationship, and we will probably kill each other one of these days. So I should probably write my will, right?" I laugh, but they're not joining. I sigh. "Anyway, thank you for offering the pool house. I think if it was a room in here, I wouldn't have accepted. You know..." My voice drifts off and Elena's hand comes to my knee.

"I'm sorry," she repeats, and I hate it. I hate how everyone feels sorry for me because of how Nate is.

I ignore her this time. I will just have to show them how his actions do not affect me. He's becoming an amazing father, and that is all I care about. "So, um, I think Madison wants us to—"

"—Yes!" Elena claps her hands and shoots up from the sofa.

"Wait, how did you even know what I was going to ask?" She's adorable.

Elena smiles a full tooth grin at me. One that somewhat resembles her son's. "I want to babysit every day. Yes. I mean it, Tillie. Live your life, you're young. You have me and Joseph to support you. Use us."

I lick my lips, exhaling. "Thank you."

Then she steps forward. "Want me to feed her?"

"It's okay." I smile, needing some Micaela cuddles while silently cursing myself for bitching out on breastfeeding. "I can do it and then I guess you could take her?"

She nods in glee, her lips curled under her teeth to stop a big smile.

Jesus. I'm not sure if it's normal for grandparents to act this way or not, but Elena is adorably intense with Micaela.

"Oh, Tillie?" She calls just before I enter the kitchen.

I turn back around.

"We will go shopping tomorrow to grab some things for the pool house?"

"Oh, there's no need. I don't mind—"

She shakes her head. "—Please."

Jesus.

"Okay."

I excuse myself quickly before she asks me anything else and make my way into the kitchen.

"Her bottle is in the warmer. Nate made it up before leaving," Madison says, taking Micaela off me.

I remove the lid off the warmer and shake it vigorously. "Well. I guess I should be thankful."

We make our way back to the dining table. The guys have all disappeared, nothing but the faint mist of their cologne hangs in the air. Madison watches me.

"They all left for Brantley's. We all decided that the party house can no longer be this house because of the princess of the *princess*," Madison teases the Princess nickname. "And since you know, Brantley is all alone in that big freaky house…"

I nod, taking Micaela out of Madison's arms and pushing the teet to her mouth. "Tills. Are you okay with this whole Nate and Tate thing? I'm sorry. Like seriously, they stopped for a while and I don't know what they were playing at this morning or why they took off together just then, but—" Her words die out. God. I'm sick of it.

I shake my head. "Madison, I really don't want to talk about those two right now. Tate can do what she wants. If she likes being treated like a piece of ass, then by all means, be his piece of ass." I ignore the way my stomach sinks at my own words. "I really wish people would stop feeling sorry for me."

I hate that my options are limited and Nate acts like the puppeteer. I really need a plan. I can stay in the pool house, at least I don't have to watch all of the girls he brings home, but I do need a long-term plan.

My phone dings. **We were supposed to meet up!**

"Shit." I start typing out a reply with one hand.

Madison nudges her head. "Who is it?"

"Ridge," I murmur, hitting send on my message.

T: **So sorry. Life has been crazy.**

"Invite him tonight!" Madison's eyes beam in mischief.

"What?" I snort, ignoring the next text that comes through. "I thought it was a girl's night?" Micaela finishes up with her bottle and Madison puts her hands out, eager to burp her. I place her in Madison's arms, sitting back down on my seat.

"Well it is, but he is your friend. He can come here and pre-drink with us in the pool house while we get ready, then he can meet this adorable little soul." Madison squeezes Micaela's cheeks.

"True," I agree. "Hey, I was wondering," I look around the room, and then my eyes come to hers. "If you would want to be Micaela's godmother?"

Madison's eyes glisten a little, and then her face breaks out into the cheesiest smile. "I don't know what that means but yes!"

"It—well I don't know what it means, but I'm gathering it means that you will pretty much always look out for her. Like a real-life angel. I was going to ask Ridge to be her godfather, but pretty sure Nate will want to choose that role and pretty sure it will be Bishop."

Madison chuckles, putting the bottle onto the table and lifting Micaela up to pat her back. "You're really good at this." I gesture to Micaela.

Madison laughs, her face falling. "I guess it's just something that comes naturally."

Hmmm. We will need to talk about that face drop, but I know Madz. She needs to be drunk before the truth starts spilling out all over the place. I open Ridge's text.

R: **I get it. But I miss you.**

T: **Wanna come over and meet Micaela? We're going out tonight too, so you can tag along?**

The text reply is almost instant. R: **Done. Send me the address.**

I send the address and then take Micaela. "I'll go change her upstairs and then we can start moving what little things I have into the pool house. But I need to go shopping. I have some money left in my account from a while ago, so you up for it?"

Madison grins. "Absolutely."

CHAPTER 14

Tillie

"I'm exhausted. I still hate shopping." Madison growls, pushing her hair out of her face.

I chuckle. "I think we're good though."

Madison moves her head from where it was leaning against the back of the chair and looks at me, her eyelids weak. "Yes, I think so."

We order some lunch and dig in. Shopping should count as cardio. "I can't decide on the red one or the black one."

"Red," Madison says around her bite of sushi. "Red is your color, which is strange because of your pink hair, but it works."

After lunch, we make our way back out to Madison's teal blue Ferrari. I still can't get over Bishop buying her this car. We slide inside and as soon as she turns it on, the radio starts playing Juvenile "Slow Motion," and I crank it up.

Madison chuckles. "Snapchat, now!"

I laugh, tying my hair up into a high ponytail and sliding my Ray-Bans over my eyes. I pucker my lips and start dancing, moving the camera to Madison. She drops it down into third and floors it. The video is cut off by us laughing our asses off. I add it to my story, captioning it "Girl's night out tonight" with the celebration emoji and champagne glasses.

"God, can we make a rule for tonight?" she asks, turning the music down a little.

"Sure." I gaze out the window.

"No talking about The Kings."

"Mads…" I warn, worry taking hold of me. "Are you and B okay?" I love Bishop, and it has absolutely nothing to do with the fact that he has never dogged around on Madison. Maybe it does.

"What?" Madison turns to face me, and then sighs, going back to the road. "We might be fighting."

"Want to talk about it?"

She shakes her head. "Not really."

I turn the music up. "Then let's just drink."

We empty all our shopping bags out of the car and quickly run across the backyard to the pool house. It's a small apartment style with a glass wall that looks directly out to the pool. I've only been here maybe once or twice, and when I flick the light on, I see not much has changed. The décor is all white and red. The glass wall that looks out to the pool is tinted for privacy. There's a small L-shaped leather couch that somewhat separates the main living room and the small kitchen. There's a square marble coffee table that sits smack bang in the middle and a white rug tucked underneath it. To the right is the large king-sized bed with enough pillows to fill two beds and white sheets spread over. Elena had obviously been in here to freshen it up because there's a candle burning on the coffee table, igniting a sweet cedar tree smell through the air. It's warm and inviting. There's also a small crib beside my bed, but not the same as the one that's in Nate's room. I wonder when she found the time to buy it and set it up. To the right of the bed is a door that leads into a bathroom. I take a step toward it and peek in. It's all white marble and has a small counter with delicate soaps. I know that they had this as a guest house, but it's really nice.

"Well!" Madison says, flopping down onto the couch. "I'm ready to get drunk." I want to ask what's wrong with her, but I know she won't tell me until she's ready.

I decide to shift the subject to one that's a little more uncomfortable for me. "Is Tate coming?"

Madison doesn't say anything, her eyes stay on the ceiling, her head tilted back against the edge of the couch. "She will probably meet us there." Then she turns to look directly at me. "She's not been herself lately. Nate and her, they, I don't know. Is it okay for me to talk to you about this?" She leans forward, her eyes coming to mine. I feel like I might be too sober for this conversation, but I nod my head anyway because I don't want to seem, I don't know, vulnerable. Besides, everyone already tiptoes around me where Nate is concerned. I don't need any more pity.

"Sure."

Madison exhales. "Okay, so she slept with Bishop's cousin Spyder the other night, and then all of a sudden, she's back into Nate, only more forceful this time. It's fucking strange. *She* is fucking strange right now." I don't know what to say, the fact that Tate has slept with Bishop's cousin doesn't surprise me, the girl is the female version of Nate.

I shrug, engaging my poker face. "Well, I'm sure she's not the only one Nate has been with either so..." God, I fucking hate him.

Madison sighs, standing from the sofa and making her way to the kitchen. "True that." Then her eyes come to me. "I'm sorry if any of this talk hurts you at all..."

I shake my head. "I don't care." *Lies.* "He's a good dad to Micaela, for that I'm thankful. I knew he was going to hate me, Madison. It just is what it is with him and I. It's fire and ice and when it collides, it explodes and those closest to us get hit with the shrapnel. The way he is with you isn't the way he's with me. Well," I pause, my thoughts flicking back to the first time we met. "At least it hasn't been for a while." *You will not think about those memories.* I snap my attention back to Madison who is staring at me with a strange expression.

She clears her throat and puts her cup onto the counter. "That's enough talk of them, huh?"

I smile. "That would be ah-mazing."

Looking down at my watch, I point to the shower. "I'll go in first. You mix those cocktails you were going on about."

She grins, getting busy in the kitchen. After my shower, I wrap the towel around my body and grab my new makeup. I happen to love makeup—a lot. I don't wear it that much, but when I do, I think I'm pretty good at putting it on. I start with a moisturizer, and then a good pore refining primer, and then the foundation before putting the setting powder on. Madison walks into the bathroom and pauses, spitting her drink out.

"What the hell is that on your face?"

I roll my eyes. "It's banana powder to cook my makeup so it doesn't melt off in an hour." I start on my eyes, deciding on smoke as dark as my mood.

"Oh, you are so doing my makeup. I forgot how amazing you are at this. You totally need to do a makeup tutorial on YouTube."

I snort. "No thanks, but yes, I will do yours. Give me forty minutes to finish up. Go take a shower."

Two hours later, we're both ready. My makeup is heavy on the eyes with a nude lip, and Madison is light on the eyes with dark burgundy lips. Her hair is in soft curls that trail down her back, and mine is dead straight, my ends hitting just above my tailbone. I don't have the heart to cut it just yet.

"God, I fucking love that dress on you!" Madison says for the hundredth time, tipping her head back as she drinks her frozen slushy-type thing. It does look good. It's a strapless silk mini dress that hangs just below my ass. There's a small slit on the left side too and the material clings to my body everywhere. I managed to score a good deal on a pushup bra too, so the girls are pushed up to the high heavens. For shoes, I'm wearing plain black strap heels. Nothing too fancy since the dress is on its own level.

I grab my clutch, pulling out my phone. "Ridge is almost here."

Madison claps her hands together. She's got about two drinks on me since she has been sipping them like they're water and she's starving in the Sahara Desert. I really need to pine about what's going on with her and B later.

I pick up my glass and sink the rest of mine, taking me up to drink three. Just as I'm pouring another from the jug, a jug that is filled with some sort of slushy that tastes of every single alcohol you could think of, there's a knock on the door. I walk over to it, opening wide to Ridge.

"Holy fuck," is the first thing he says, his eyes going up and down my body. "Jesus, Tip." Ridge steps inside and I flush at his nickname for me.

"You look amazing, Pidge."

He rolls his eyes at my nickname. He hates it. But he does look great. Wearing nice jeans and a dress shirt, he looks so much different than the guy I grew up with. He looks—older. Grown. No backward caps or basketball shorts. His tattoos are obviously still there, but his style has changed. His hair has grown a little since too, now flopping over his forehead. This is probably a good thing, now his style won't remind me of a certain asshole.

"Damn, Gina, you look hot too. I'm going to need to call backup. There's no way I can fight them all off you both."

Madison laughs, flicking her leg over her other, her eyes raking up and down Ridge.

I don't have to worry about her though, as much as her and Bishop fight, they are always okay. She would never.

She licks her lips.

Right?

"So!" I yell, shutting the door. "You wanna come see Micaela? I'm not sure if she's still awake, but we can sneak in." It's nine p.m, I know she won't be awake. Ridge nods his head, a smile beaming from him.

"Yeah, I'd love to."

Madison stands, running her hands over her black slinky dress and gestures to the door. "You ready to see the most beautiful girl in the world?"

Ridge winks. "If she's anything like Tillie…"

"Well, she's more like Nate, but we don't tell him that," Madison mutters.

I laugh and we all stumble over to the main house. The door opens just as we reach it and Elena is on the sofa, her cheeks dipped in soft pink rose, her skin glowing. How is it my child is making her glow.

"Hey, sorry to interrupt. This is Ridge, he and I grew up together. He hasn't met Micaela yet."

Elena smiles from the sofa, waving upstairs. "She's in our bedroom. I have a crib in there too, you know, for when she's here, and I didn't want to put her in Nate's room tonight without you there too."

I exhale, my shoulders relaxing. She gets me. "Thank you." There's a silent conversation that goes between Elena and I. I'm so glad she thought of that. Would Nate bring someone back here though? Now, with Micaela here? I don't want to be naïve in saying no, but I really don't think he will. Tate is different, she's in our group, but even still, I can't see him taking her into his room now that that's basically Micaela's room too.

We head upstairs and into Elena and Joseph's room. Ridge shakes his head, exhaling while running his finger down her face. She's sleeping peacefully, wrapped up in a muslin wrap. Her small little face pops out the top and her hair is brushed backward.

"She's going to have lots of hair," I say to Ridge, my heart clenching in my chest. God, I love her so much it cripples me. I don't know how I feel about loving something so much and having her live in this cruel world.

"She looks so much like you, Tip."

We leave after another five minutes, then we are back in the pool house and the music is playing. Madison puts on "Bad Bitch" by Bebe Rexha and I end up dancing on the coffee table, sipping on my drink. I twist my body around to the beat while bringing my eyes straight to Madison's phone that she's got on me from the kitchen. I've always loved dancing, and I'm not half bad. It's one of the first things that got Nate's attention.

I will not think of him…

Ridge comes up behind me, pulling stupid shit into the phone. Madison laughs as the song changes.

She lowers her phone and sinks the rest of her drink. I think we're up to six each. "Right! Let's head out."

"Where are we going first?" I ask, picking up my clutch.

"We have to pick Tate up from Brantley's." Madison rolls her eyes. "I hope that's okay?"

"Of course!" I say, brushing her off while ignoring the way my stomach flips from knowing I'm about to see Nate. God, what if they're all over each other?

Fuck it. Liquid courage has my back. We all shuffle out of the pool house, sloppily making our way to the front of the mansion where there's a limo waiting for us, because of course there is.

Madison wiggles, sliding into the back seat.

"Wow, Tip," Ridge jokes as he gets in behind her. "This is a step up from the Skyline's back in the day…"

I laugh, shoving him as he dives into the back seat. I scoot next to Madison when my phone vibrates in my clutch. It's a Snapchat from Tate.

My face falls.

"What is it?" Madison asks, leaning over to look at my phone. "Oh."

Ridge is watching us, taking the bottle of champagne from the ice cooler and popping it open.

"Open it," Madison rushes.

"What if it's her and Nate?"

"I thought you didn't care?" Her eyebrow is raised, but it's not in a malicious way.

I open it and a video starts playing. "Welcome to Detroit" by Trick Trick and Eminem is playing loudly in the background, and then she drops the phone to a coffee table where white powder is lined up beside a one-hundred-dollar bill. The phone then drops down, where a hand is wrapped around her tanned thigh. A hand I know is Nate's because of the skull tattooed over it and the letters "E L I T E" inked into each finger.

"Motherfucker." I exit, not watching the whole video because I can't fucking stand it. I hate Nate so much I could spew. Snatching the champagne off Ridge, I take a huge drink. I'm going to need it for what I'm about to walk into.

"If Bishop is playing in the snow tonight then I really need to stay away from him. He'll start groping me and then well, I'll end up in bed with him," Madison adds, talking about cocaine.

I exhale, looking out the window. "I hate that I give a shit."

Madison's hand comes to my leg. "I love that you do. He does too, you know…"

I choke on my wine. "You are kidding."

She gives me a sad smile but looks away without continuing. We're pulling down Brantley's driveway when Ridge says, "Ah, Tip, I need to tell you something."

My eyes go to his. He licks his lip. "I'm getting married."

I freeze. "What?"

He smiles so wide that I almost feel guilty for snapping in shock. "To who!"

"Her name is Ashley. You don't know her, she's from Australia. We can talk about this later since…" he gestures over his shoulder and my eyes go to the large stone mansion. It resembles The Addam's Family home. It's all dark stone with Victorian style window panes. There are trails of vines growing up some of the cracks, and the four stone pillars at the entranceway have flowers wrapped around them too. The actual gardens and grounds are always kept tidy, so I know that the style of the home is just that. The style, not by neglect.

We all start climbing out and Madison leans forward to the driver. "We will try not to be long. Slong? Wait, I'm drunk." While she's doing that, I grab Ridge by the arm, my initial shock over.

"Does she make you happy?"

His eyes twinkle, and he nods. "Yeah, Tip. I wouldn't be marrying her if she didn't."

I sigh. "Well alright then, I supposed I will be your best man. Does she know we used to…"

He chuckles, pulling me under his arm as we make our way up the stairs. My heart begins hammering in my chest when I hear the loud music shaking the house, spilling out the windows. People laughing and bottles crashing comes from the backyard and I momentarily have to talk myself into what it is I'm about to see. "Love that you knew I was going to ask you, and no, she doesn't."

I give him a small squeeze with my arm. "Secret is safe."

Madison shoves the door open, glaring around the place like she's the queen of fucking everything. There are crowds scattered around everywhere, but it's funny to watch as every single girl (and guy) eyes us. They know who Madison is, and no one would dare approach her.

I laugh, letting go of Ridge. My brain is muffled somewhat from all the alcohol, but I find myself not being uncomfortable from the unfortunate situation we have found ourselves in. Well, more I have found myself in. Must have been that pep talk a few minutes earlier, and the confidence Madison exudes helps. "Adrenaline Rush" by Twista is playing as we enter the main living room. The walls are all deep reds, with varnished wood lining the middle. There's a large door that leads out to the pool area where more people are. The music is playing from in this room so the deep base shakes me to my core with Twista's fast rapping taking over.

"Are you ready!" Madison screams toward somewhere to the left of me. Somewhere I don't look because I know Nate is there, probably under Tate.

I lick my lips and my eyes start wandering.

Do not look.

I look. My eyes go to Nate, who already has his on me. He's wearing a cap flipped backward and has no shirt on, displaying his lean muscles and muscles and muscles...and. His black jeans have tears by the knees and his white Chucks are loosely tied on his feet.

Goddammit.

My eyes go back to his, bored. Then he licks his lip and the corner of his mouth kicks up in a sly grin. Fucker. Of course, they don't disappoint because Tate is on his lap. My eyes fall to his hand that's on her thigh and I watch as he clenches it tightly.

Madison breaks my attention when she leans into me. "She's not ready yet so we will wait a few."

I nod. "Sure thing." Turning around, I set off to find a drink when I bump into Brantley who is walking down the stairs in the foyer.

"Whattup." He nudges his head. "Damn, girl."

I can't help the small giggle that leaves my mouth. Brantley is quiet, reserved and before that little drama in the forest, never spoke a word to me. Rather, acted as though I was invisible, like he does with everyone.

"I need a drink, and like, something stronger than cocaine to get through this night."

He doesn't laugh, because his eyes are still going up and down my body. He hands me his drink and I take it. "You've always been hot, don't get me wrong, but I straight up want to eat you right now."

Before I can laugh, he yanks me into his chest and starts walking us toward the room Nate and everyone else are in.

Brantley leans into my ear. "Play along."

As soon as we're back in the room, Brantley's arm hooks over my shoulder and he pulls me under. Bishop's eyes go between both of us and Madison leans back up from taking a line of coke. Great. Now she's going to be extra wild tonight. I'm not a hater, but I was raised in a neighborhood where drugs actually ruined families, and I don't mean it in a way that the kids get left with millions of dollars in a trust fund, I mean it as in the kids are left homeless because of the parent's addiction. It's just never been my thing.

Madison clears her nose, handing me the rolled-up bill. I shake my head.

Nate shoves Tate off his lap when he sees us, his eyes dropping to icy levels. He brings his drink up to his mouth, his eyes on me.

"What do you say we cockblock the girl's night out?" Brantley says it to everyone, but I know he's looking at Nate.

Wait.

"No!" I shake my head, stepping out from under Brantley.

"Good idea." Nate stands from the couch, grabbing a joint off the table and putting it behind his ear. He snatches his shirt that's swung behind the sofa, taking his cap off to put it on.

"No!" Madison's hand comes to Brantley's chest, but it's too late, Bishop is yanking her down onto his lap, laying small kisses onto the back of her neck. Jesus, I swear this lot are crazy. Then Bishop stands and takes Madison's hand. "Let's go."

I don't know what the fuck Brantley is playing it, but I go along with it.

CHAPTER 15

Tillie

I shouldn't have gone along with it. We all pile into the back of the limo, me sitting opposite Nate, and Brantley sitting on one side of me with Ridge on the other. Tate is on the floor between Nate's legs and Bishop and Madison are beside him.

Jase leans in through the door, glaring at Madison. "Sort your shit out, Madz. We'll follow you." Then he slams it closed.

Great. They're all coming because of course they are.

I turn to face Brantley, ignoring everyone else. "What about your house?"

He shrugs, lifting the bottle to his lips. I watch as he wraps them around the rim and takes a pull. Liquid leaks from the side of his mouth and drips down his neck. Is it possible for a neck to be sexy? I'm going to go with yes because that's exactly what Brantley's is. Then again, he just is that, but he's dangerous. It's a lethal combination what he has. Whoever he settles with would have to be just as fucked up as he is because there's no way any sane and normal—somewhat normal—girl could ever be okay with him. He would scare the shit out of them.

Brantley's staring down at me, his lips glistening from his drink. "You should probably stop staring at me like that if you don't wanna get fucked, *Princess*."

I shrug, looking away from him when my eyes connect with Nate. He's glaring at me, like always. "Or Nah" by Ty Dolla $ign starts playing through the loudspeakers, but it's a different version. It has an electric guitar in the background and sounds live. Better than the real version.

Nate keeps his eyes on me as his hand goes to Tate's head, then he licks his lip and grins at me as his hand wraps around the front of her throat.

I don't know what Tate does because I can't break the eye contact with Nate. He tilts her head backward so it's resting between his legs, and then he leans over, his eyes still on mine, and licks her across her lips. It feels as though someone has punched me straight in the chest. I struggle to breath. The dress is suddenly too tight, and I'm suddenly not drunk enough.

Fuck him and fuck her. I decide I hate Tate now and there's no way I'm going to make an effort with her, not unless she stops this shit with Nate. It goes against girl code, King or not. I don't give a fuck.

I lean into Brantley, and his arm goes over my shoulders. When Nate sits back, his eyes go to Brantley. This isn't fun because it's not hurting Tate, and by the looks of it, Nate isn't bothered.

Nate's jaw muscles clench. Or maybe it does.

I turn to face Brantley and smirk. "I don't know. It's been a while since I've been fucked—" Then I look to Nate. "Right."

Madison spits out her drink. Nate glares and Bishop barks out a loud laugh.

Once Bishop has stopped laughing, he shoves Nate. "Oh, this is hilarious. Looks like your karma has pink hair."

Nate still hasn't taken his eyes off me, his lip curled. "Fuck you."

I shrug. "You can't, but Brantley can."

Nate works his jaw, dragging his eyes away from me. The rest of the trip is filled with everyone talking amongst themselves and Madison trying to plan a big Christmas. Typical of her.

We pull up outside a club with a massive line of people out the front and two big bodyguards holding a clipboard standing at the front entrance. It's not until I get out of the limo when I realize how drunk I am. It takes a few moments for everything to start spinning, but I'm on a roll. I'm ready to grind up against some random person in the middle of the dance floor.

With Madison glued to Bishop and Tate with Nate, (not that I would drag her with me), I hang back behind them all until the guards let us through. I turn around to see the rest of The Kings following with a couple of other guys that I haven't met before.

Jase throws his hand over my shoulder. "Tillz, this is Spyder and Ollie, and you know Saint."

I nod, my eyes falling on the one who looks so much like Bishop it's weird. The only difference is this guy has like, blue-black hair and strange eyes.

"That one is Spyder," Jase whispers in my ear. "And if you wanna play, he and Tate have a thing going on."

"Really." My eyebrows shoot up, and I see the exact moment Spyder puts two and two together. He's wearing blue jeans and a white shirt.

Spyder grins at me. "You're the baby mama, aren't you..."

I lick my lips. "I am."

He pulls out a pack of smokes, biting one between his teeth. He lights it. "Yeah, this will be fun." He steps forward and grabs my hand, pulling me into him where I go happily. Jase is laughing behind me and I'm thankful that even with the weird history between him and Peyton, we can still have a good friendship.

We enter through the doors where "New York" from Ja Rule is playing. This club is closer to Brooklyn, so a fair bit away from where they usually party.

I can feel eyes on me, and I look to the VIP area that's tucked to the left of the club, away from the dance floor and opposite the bar, but with enough view to see the whole club. Everyone is watching us. Well, Spyder and I. We slowly start making our way over with Jase and Saint when I stop him, my hand grabbing at his arm. I lean up and whisper in his ear. "Let's dance."

I shoot a shocked Tate, and an uncomfortable looking Nate one final glare, and slowly grin at them both. I have to fight the urge to flip them off. I'll save that for another time. Spyder and I make our way to the dance floor, swiping some drinks on the way.

"You and Tate?" I ask Spyder, my hand still on his arm. He's lean, but not as big as Nate and Bishop. More on the skinny, lean side.

"Yeah," he growls into my ear. "But since your baby daddy is always around, she's been using him to ride on my shit."

I chuckle. "Likewise." We stop in the middle of the dance floor and his arm wraps around my waist. His eyes drop to mine, a smirk on his face. I don't know why, but I feel completely comfortable with him. I know we're using each other, and it feels amazing. I never claimed to be mature, or even sensible. My soul is deep, and the deeper you are, the darker it gets. I'm reckless, impulsive, and I think I'm acquiring an anger problem. So...

I fling my arm around his neck as we dance against each other.

When he drops his forehead to rest against mine, I lick my lips with a grin, but just as I reach for his to press them against mine, he's being yanked backward, and I'm left with a seething Nate directly in front of me. I tear my eyes away from him as they go back to the VIP section.

Bishop is laughing so hard I almost think he's going to die, and the rest of them are joining in on it too. Even Brantley looks amused.

I look back to Nate. "What the fuck are you doing?"

His hand comes to my throat and I'm well aware we look like a domestic violence case. He leans into the side of my ear. "What the fuck did I tell you earlier?"

I whack his hand away and he lets me, releasing his grip. "You don't get a say in who I fuck!" I know I'm yelling, but I'm drunk, frustrated, and fucking hurt. Yes, I'm fucking hurt because aside from not telling him about Micaela, I feel like I have done nothing to warrant this much wrath.

Nate steps up to me, his body pressing into mine. "Get your fucking ass into that section and stay there, Tillie."

I'm so frustrated by him that I'm left speechless. I turn around, ready to listen and go and sit down because I'm fucking tired, but instead I take a sharp left turn and run straight for the door.

"Tillie!" I hear Nate yell, but I ignore him.

Kicking off my heels, I pick them up and start running down the partially empty street, passing the long line of awaiting party-goers. I keep running, annoyed, drunk and feeling a little fucking lost with my life.

What the fuck is wrong with me? Why is everything such a mess and why did I have to have sex with him, like way way back? *God, I'm fucking drunk.* My running slows as I reach the main street that leads deeper into town. There're crowds of people now, with the flashing lights and the bright billboards. I swipe the tears off my cheeks. I hate feeling like this. I can't offer my daughter anything, and I know that in the back of my head, I need to sort out my shit. But while I'm around Nate, I can't think straight. *So. Drunk.* He's constantly playing games with me, games that I don't mind playing and games that they all play, but right now, I need a nap. *Yes, yes I need a nap. And water. And to never drink again. Goddamn Madison.* I dip into a small pizza place that looks like it could probably do with a health check, and order spinach and chicken. I'm sitting waiting for my order when my phone starts vibrating against the mustard yellow tabletop for the one-hundredth time since I bolted from the club. It hasn't stopped ringing, with multiple texts coming through. I don't want to check the messages just in case I decide to reply.

"Tip?" the pizza boy calls out my name, holding my receipt. I take the box and thank him, tossing an actual tip into the jar before making my way back onto the busy street. I see a taxi at the curb and quickly pull open the door, sliding into the backseat. The pizza box is hot against my thighs, but I don't care. It reminds me that I can feel, I'm awake and in the now. I am not dead in a gutter. *Alcohol is bad. Ba-aa-ad.*

I blurt off my—well, Nate's address and the taxi pulls away. My phone starts in my hands again and I see Pidge flash across the screen.

I answer instantly, completely forgetting that I left him behind. "I'm so sorry, Pidge, I just can't be there right now."

"It's okay, I totally get it. I'm heading home now, I think Ash is angry with me for being out for so long and Nate rushed out straight after you. The dude has a major chip on his shoulder."

Not sure I like this girl already, but I keep my *very* drunk thoughts to myself. "Well, I will eat that chip as a snack." He laughs. I continue around a bite of pizza. "Thanks for coming. Don't be a stranger and come see Micaela when she's awake."

"Oh, I plan to. Hey, Tillie?"

Tillie, not Tip. "Yeah?"

"Don't forgive him. Don't take him back. Ever."

I sigh, massaging my temples and somewhat confused as to why he feels so passionately about Nate. "Sure, Pidge. Sure thing." I hang up, a little miffed at Ridge's comment. It was always Tip and Pidge. Our names swapped around just for us to use, but now I'm angry at him. I know Nate is fucked in the head, deranged, a smart ass, hot-headed, and a little possessive at times, but I—I stop my thoughts. I will not go there right now. Pidge is right, not that I'd ever have to make that decision, but he's right. I could never take him back.

CHAPTER 16

Tillie

After paying for the cab, I take out another slice of pizza, moaning around each bite. Somehow, I manage to balance the box with one hand and my heels and clutch in the other. I'm walking to the side of the main house toward the pool house when my phone starts vibrating again.

"Fuck off," I mumble, without looking at it.

I'm looking down at my slice while climbing the steps when I freeze.

Nate is sitting in front of my door with no shirt on and blood on his knuckles. He's got one leg perched up with his arm hanging off it and the other resting beside his leg with his phone in his hand.

He glares at me, and God his eyes are the kind you could never erase from your brain. They penetrate every thought process and take every logical side of you and replace it with everything that is him.

"What are you doing here, Nate, and what happened to your knuckles?"

"This is my house, Tillie, and the knuckles are nothing compared to Spyder's face."

"What did you do?" I swallow my thick bite whole. *Incoming heartburn in 3-1—no. 3-2-1.*

He glares at me. "How the fuck do you do it, Tillie? How the fuck is it you that conjures all so—". He stops, shakes his head and bites his lip. Drunk or not, that lip bite was sexy.

I ignore him, and the sexy lip bite, taking a seat on the cool step. "I'm tired, so if you've come for round—whatever we're up to—can it wait until tomorrow?" I keep chewing my pizza, throwing my shoes onto the ground.

He doesn't say anything, so I look up at him again. He's still watching me, his head tilted back against the door, his face blank. I hate that I get this part of Nate and everyone else—Madison and Tate included—get the fun side. "Why'd you run?"

I suck the sauce off my finger and his eyes narrow on it. I stop instantly. "I told you, Nate, I didn't have a choice."

"But you did. You knew I would have—" He stops himself, running his hand through his hair until it's ruffled and standing all over the place. "Fuck, you know what?" He stands up, throwing his shirt on the ground and putting his phone in his pocket. "It doesn't fucking matter. Do what the fuck you want, Tillie. You're going to anyway." He goes to walk past me and I'm so fucking confused that my hand flies out to his arm.

He stills as goosebumps travel over my flesh from the connection, his head leaning to look down at my hand. I ignore the pang of electricity that zips through from him to me, I'm used to it now. This is a Nate thing. He probably has it with other people too.

He laughs, but it's not a friendly laugh. It's a sarcastic chuckle that tears at my chest with its sharp claws. He turns full-on to face me and suddenly, I shrink in my spot at his mere size and proximity. He steps forward, and I step back, pizza in hand. "You come back into my life with my daughter, and then run with her, and then come back without her because of your crazy sister, so I get her back, and now, now, you have the audacity to fucking touch me like you own me?" he yells, and something snaps inside of me.

My back hits the stair rail and now I'm trapped. I narrow my eyes. Fight or flight, and I will always fight. "I didn't have a fucking choice, Nate! Have you forgotten who my mother is? Have you forgotten everything that happens in this world?" My hands are flinging everywhere, and I drop my pizza in the process. That only irks me even more.

His hand comes to my face, his shoulders slightly pulling back and his legs separating. I notice the stance, I see the shift of his eyes. He's mad. He brings his mouth down to mine, but not enough for our lips to touch, just enough to be able to feel his breath tickle over my flesh.

"You don't get to come back into my life and fuck with my head again, baby." He squeezes harder, so much so that my lips pop. I clench my jaw tight, my eyes searching his in defiance.

"You left. You don't get to run circles around and around in my head. I'll trip you the fuck over and watch you fall on your face."

"Why do you hate me!" I yell, ignoring the pang in my chest from his verbal stab. My throat clogs with unshed emotion and I have to physically stop myself from crying. God this night has been the worst girl's night in the history of girl's nights.

He narrows his eyes, something flashes over them momentarily, and just when I think maybe I had struck a nerve, it's gone and a snarl curls in the corner of his mouth.

"Because you're a fucking trailer park slut. You don't belong in this world." Then he pushes me forward. "Leave, Tillie. You aren't welcome here and you don't fit into this world. Leave my fucking daughter here, though, and if you come for her, I'll take you to court, and who do you think has the most money to splurge on a lawyer? Oh, that's right—me, and even if I didn't, who has most of this damn city in their pocket, oh, that's right—us," he hisses, his eyes piercing mine. He gives me one more up and down stare before he turns his back on me and makes his way across to the main house.

I drop to my knees and exhale the pent-up breath I've been holding. *Strength is a muscle. You exercise it enough, you become a big motherfucker.*

But I am still human, and a girl, so pain rips through my flesh, cutting me open and exposing all of my impurities and insecurities. He's never been so cruel to me—ever. Yeah, he's Nate Riverside, the school playboy, but he has never been cruel. I feel like my world has stopped spinning, gravity threatening to release.

Picking up the pizza box and my shoes, I make my way into the pool house, leaving Nate's stupid shirt on the porch.

I flop onto the bed, dropping the pizza box on the coffee table and close my eyes. *So. Fucking. Drunk.*

The next morning, I wake at seven with a pounding headache. Slipping in and out of the shower quickly, I throw on some skinny jeans that I bought yesterday and a slightly loose shirt. As soon as I'm inside the main house, I can hear Micaela and I quickly round the corner that leads from the sitting room into the kitchen, but my smile falls when Nate has her on the dining table.

His eyes come to mine, but he looks right through me before going back to Micaela.

"Oh, morning, Tillie!" Elena says, walking into the kitchen with a coffee mug between her palms. It feels awkward, and the words Nate said to me are ringing in the back of my head.

"Morning. Thank you for watching her last night." But it won't be happening again.

"Oh." She brushes my comment away. "Don't even mention it. We had lots of fun. How was your night?"

I pause, swallow and then shuffle uncomfortably. "It was, fun," I lie, because I don't have the energy to get into anything right now.

Nate is still ignoring me when Elena tells me to again, help myself to the kitchen. I don't like it, so I shake my head. I'll have to go shopping today after looking for a job. This blows.

I make my way into the dining room, taking the seat far away from Nate.

He licks his lips and stands, handing her to me. I ignore the ache that sets over me when his arm brushes against mine as he lays her in my arms.

"I won't be back tonight. Text me if you need me." Then he looks up to his mom. "Did you write up the contract?"

What? I look between both of them, confused. Elena's pained face flinches. "Not yet, and you're not leaving yet. Sit down, we all need to talk."

Nate shakes his head. "Nah, fuck that. You know where I stand."

"Nathanial! Sit!" His mother points back to his chair. Shit.

God, I'm so not ready for this. I can't leave because I couldn't take Micaela with me. He'd have me arrested for kidnapping if I do, so again, fuck my life.

Nate glares at me, dropping down to his chair. "Mom, I got shit to do today and tonight. I'm sorry, but can you rush this along? Fuck."

Joseph enters, takes one look around the table and then looks at me. "Tillie, might be a good idea if I take Micaela, yeah?"

I chew my lip and then nod, knowing he's right. Once Joseph has bounced a happy Micaela out of the room, I look directly at Nate. "What's happening?"

He searches my eyes, and then says, "We're going to have shifts between both of us on who gets her. Just like joint custody if you weren't living here."

I clear my throat. "Why? I haven't tried to stop you from seeing her?"

I'm confused why he would feel the need to do this. We live together, for fuck's sake.

He leans forward, his eyes flat. I already know that he's about to say something hurtful. "I don't want to see you, Tillie."

"We run in the same circles, Nate," I shoot back using his own tone.

He looks to his mom. "She's right. But I still want guaranteed nights that I get her alone."

Elena seems to be watching both of us. I shrug. "I can agree to that, Nate." Then I flinch. "All you had to do was ask. You know, communication."

His hate for me is real. He's been so up and down and right to left that I don't know how to take him anymore.

"Okay, then it's settled." Elena reaches for my hand.

Nate's eyes follow her gesture, but he doesn't display how it makes him feel.

"What days do you want?" I ask him, my head pounding slightly.

"Every Tuesday night, Thursday night and the whole day on Sunday. I've already spoken with Hector, and he's cool with it."

I forget he's a King. I nod. "Sure." Because I don't want to be difficult. Then mainly because I'm tired of fighting with him and generally feeling reckless as fuck anyway lately. I stand from the table, ready to leave.

Elena's hand comes out to stop me. "Can I speak with you for a second?"

I smile down at her. "Sure."

Nate keeps his eyes on me as he stands. "I take it you'll be with Madison tonight?"

I shake my head. "No. I'll stay in with Micaela."

He grins. "Good." Then he storms out, leaving me confused as fuck and still without answers about his broken knuckles.

I exhale, taking a seat back on the chair. Elena clears her throat. "We know you don't have a car right now so since we have too many to count..." She grabs a set of keys off the table and hands them to me. "Use one of ours to get around in, you know, if you ever need a break from my son or just to take Micaela out in general."

I shake my head. "I can't accept that, thank you, though."

"Tillie," Elena says, her eyes coming to mine. They're so much like Nate's, only gentler. "Please. I would hate for you to think you're ever stuck here and unable to get away for a bit."

I sigh, slowly reaching for the keys and taking them from her. "I have no way that I can ever repay you..."

"Oh." Elena looks over her shoulder but sighs when Nate has already left. "About that..."

Oh no.

She must read the expression on my face because she laughs. "No, no, I'm not about to offer you an absurd amount of money" —she clears her throat— "but Nate is, I mean has. I'm sure if you check your account you'll see. It's the first month's child support and you'll get your payments on the first of every month. Another thing is we have a trust account for Micaela set up already. She is included in the same accounts Nate has, but she also has her own for college and anything else she will need for as she gets older. They get more demanding the older they get."

I'm stumped. Speechless. Child support didn't even cross my brain—at all, and the fact that Nate did it without me telling him—"Wait!" I freeze. "How did he get my bank details?"

Elena stands from her chair and makes her way to the coffee pot. "There is nothing that boy doesn't and can't know, honey."

Joseph comes back in, bouncing Micaela. He hands her to me, and I thank both of them for the car and again for allowing me to live here. I take Micaela back to the pool house, my thoughts so confuddled and murky from all of the revelations.

After changing her diaper and putting her in her day clothes, a cute little denim tracksuit with a few tears here and there—realizing it's one of the things Nate bought her—I turn the TV on and put Netflix on as background. Turning Micaela onto her tummy time, I open my bank app to check my account and shoot off the bed when I see the amount.

"Holy fuck!" I look down to a shocked Micaela. "Sorry, baby," I whisper and wink at her. She smiles and brings her hand back to her mouth to suck on it. God, she's so cute, and of course she has her father's dimples. My eyes go back to my phone.

Available balance: $20,468.

The $468 was mine, but he paid me goddamn twenty thousand dollars! I start pacing around the place and then flip Micaela onto her back before continuing to walk around the small apartment.

I need to call him.

I hit dial before I know what I'm doing. I don't know why I'm doing it, he has made it clear that he hates me, but what's there to lose now. More of his love? Sure.

"Micaela okay?" he answers straight away. The fact that he's a great father is making it harder and harder to hate him.

"Yes, no, she's fine, but we need to talk about the twenty large you dropped into my account."

"Why do we need to talk about it? It's child support, Tillie. Chill."

I shake my head. "That's too much." Shoving on some fuzzy socks, I let the phone rest between my shoulder and ear.

"The fuck it is. I'll put as much as I want in there, now are you done?" I can hear girls in the background.

"Yeah," I murmur. "Sorry I called..." I flop back onto the sofa.

He curses. "Fuck. Wait." Then he tells everyone to shut the fuck up in the background. "You there?"

"Yes..."

He exhales. "Don't fucking apologize for calling me, Tillie. You can call me when it's about Micaela."

"But it wasn't about Micaela... it was about child support."

"You're awfully testy for someone who complains about my moods..."

I rub my temple with my other hand, walking back to the bed. "Forget it, go back to your girls."

I hang up before he can answer, and I instantly know I've fucked up because he hates being hung up on. He doesn't call back, which surprises me because he usually would.

My eyes go to Micaela. "Well, baby girl, what shall we do today?"

You know, since your father is as rich as he is an asshole.

Just as I'm gathering up some extra diapers and a bottle to take with us, my phone dings.

Madz: **Upto today?**

I type out a reply. **Going to take Micaela out somewhere. Dunno where.**

Madz: **I want to come! Be there in 5.**

I put my phone down and pick Micaela up. "Your aunty Madz is a little pushy, but she loves the shit out of you."

Micaela looks between my eyes and my mouth, a gummy smile beams up her beautiful face. "No." I shake my head. "Please no." Tilting my head sideways. Micaela's smile turns into a half smirk, one dimple sinking in completely, her eyes still on mine in fascination. "Fuck!" I exhale and then flinch. "Sorry, baby, but fuck," I whisper out, annoyed.

"What's up?" Madison says, walking through the front door.

"She has his grin."

Madison cracks up laughing, pushing her glasses out of her eyes and onto the top of her head. She looks me up and down. "I can't believe you've had a kid. Like everything shrunk, but your ass and that is a very, very good thing…"

I roll my eyes, handing her Micaela as I gather up the last of our things. "I have stretch marks, Madz. Stretch marks!"

Madison looks me up and down. "I didn't see any on your stomach."

"My thighs!"

Madison rolls her eyes. "So, some people have them without getting an adorable little girl. Be grateful."

"I am!" I snap, putting my Ray-Bans on my head. "I was just saying, I'm not perfect and I'm not one of those moms who get like, nothing and get all nice and skinny straight away. I had to get abducted by my crazy sister to not eat and lose the weight."

We make our way outside when Madison stops, looking at me. "Wait, what car do you have?"

I bring the keys up to her, and her eyes go wide. "Oh wow, they're giving you the G-Wagon?"

"They're not giving it to me, I'm just borrowing it."

Madison smiles at me like I'm crazy before we go toward the door that leads to their glass show garage.

Madison taps the light switch and after a few flickers, they flash on and— "Oh my God."

Madison laughs. "Yeah, our family is a little over the top. Well, Dad is. He's always been a car guy, but this is nothing. You should see Bishop's dad's garage. It's insane, I mean, cars on platforms."

I shake my head, looking over the line of roughly around twelve cars. The G-Wagon, there's a Porsche, a Range Rover, another big SUV, Cadillac, I think, and a few other small sports cars.

"Insane."

I beep the white G-Wagon and cup the window to try and see inside through the tint. I can see the outline of a baby car seat. Everything is so full on. I feel like I don't deserve all of this shit and I don't know why, but it makes me feel dirty. Like I planned to have Nate's baby for this reason.

Sighing, I open the door and Madison clips her in. I jump into the driver's seat, afraid to touch anything. "It smells new."

Madison slips in, pointing to the dash. "Because it is. They only got it a couple of weeks ago."

It feels like a set-up.

"Where should we go?" I ask Madison as we reverse out of the garage. I slam on my brakes when I see Tate standing there, tears down her face. "Oh for fuck's sake. Can we have one day."

I get out of the car, Madison right behind me. "What are you doing, Tate?" I swear, if she has come around to cry about Nate being Nate to her, I'm going to hit her.

Hard.

She swipes her eyes. "I'm sorry. I'm sorry, okay, I shouldn't have been messing around with Nate since you got back—" Her eyes go to the car, and then come back to me and Madison.

"He told you to fuck off, didn't he?" Madison says, crossing her arms. I never noticed the distance between the two of them until now. Was Madison taking my side over this? That would surprise me. I love Madison, always have, but her and Tate are tight. Like the real deal tight. I was the third wheel in our little triangle, I always felt out of place. For the exact reasons Nate mentioned last night. Thinking of that only annoys me so I bring my attention to the problem at hand. Another product of Nate's stellar decision making.

"Yes," Tate admits. "But that's not why I'm here. I mean, he always tells me to fuck off, and he did punch Spyder last night for legit touching Tillie. Listen." She clears her throat, and I can't help but think Nate's lips have been all over her. Everywhere. Down her neck, over her lips. *I feel sick.*

I need to simmer down. "Why are you here?"

Tate comes up to me, her hands reaching for mine, but I pull them away. "Don't touch me."

She flinches. "I'm sorry. I swear I didn't. I just, I really liked him and when you were gone, we were seeing each other, for so long and I'm human, okay? I'm human. I fell in love with him with the full knowledge that I'm not fucking you, but I did anyway and when you came back it messed with me. I—"

I exhale. "First of all, it's a good thing you're not me because you wouldn't want to be me right now, not when it comes to Nate so don't say that and second of all—" I pause, looking her up and down. Her long blonde hair is whiter than it used to be, her bright blue eyes peering at me with sincerity. "Get in the car." I can't hold a grudge against her, I know this. He was fair game when I left, but I can be angry about her decisions after I got back, which we will work on, I guess.

Finally, when we're all inside, I start to pull out again. Tate is cooing to Micaela in the back and my eyes find her in the rearview mirror. Just like that, Micaela melts another person.

Rihanna's "Lost in Paradise" starts playing and Madison turns it up, opening her camera and taking a selfie video. She starts talking into it. "Girl's day out since girl's night out failed last night..." Then she puts the phone around the car and I stick my tongue out. She goes to the back. "And of course, with the baby princessa herself!" Madison's Latin is getting pretty good.

"Where should we take her?" I say, lost.

"Oh, we can take her to the park! There's a good one. I'll put it into the GPS." Madison continues doing that, and then we're on our way to this mysterious playground.

Pulling up around fifteen minutes later, I park us right out front. "This isn't a park, Madison, it's a carnival!"

Madison shrugs. "I know, but nothing short of brilliant for my niece."

"You're so extra," I mumble, jumping out of the high truck.

I'm rounding the car when Tate already has Micaela in her arms. She smiles up at me. "I hope it's okay, I just couldn't help myself. She's so adorable, Tillie. You've done well."

I bite the snarky comment I want to make about how of course she would find her adorable, she looks just like Nate, but I don't.

I smile. "Thanks." We all start walking toward the large wooden archway that's sprinkled with colorful LED lights.

"Stop!" Madison's hands fly out, and then she annoys an innocent passerby who is with his daughter. "Excuse me? Could you take a photo of us?"

"Madison," I whine.

Her head snaps toward me.

"She's getting worse," I complain.

"I know," Tate mumbles.

Madison runs back and pulls us together with her arms wrapped around our necks. Tate turns Micaela against her tummy so she's facing forward, and we all smile. Then I look to Madison and Madison looks to me as Tate looks down at a smiling Micaela. Madison runs back and grabs her phone before coming back to us. She shows us the images and the man actually took a whole bunch and they're decent, some even candid. Madison opens Instagram and her fingers hover over the caption.

"Don't you dare," I chuckle, knowing what she and Nate are like with their stupid captions. It's like a constant competition between the two of them.

She grins and then types. "One he loves, one he adores, one he tolerates, and one he hates..."

"Madison!" I scold her. "That's so not cool!"

"What!" She shrugs. "You don't even know which is which."

I roll my eyes, shaking my head. Tate shrugs like she doesn't really care, and maybe she doesn't. God, I hope she doesn't, it would make the whole forgiving her that much easier.

Throughout the day, we move from place to place. Madison won a teddy bear, and Tate gave Micaela her first taste of cotton candy. I hit her for that, not hard, just across the arm. Then we all took her on the small teacup ride. It went really slow and we all got bored, Micaela included, but we got some good photos, so it was worth it.

The sun is setting and we're all hungry, so we start making our way across the road to a dimly lit Chinese restaurant.

"You cheated to get that." Tate points at the bear.

Madison tightens her grip around it. "I don't know what you're talking about."

I roll my eyes, smiling. Today has been amazing, and for the first time in a long time, I'm really thankful for them both being a part of my life. Even if we bicker, and fight, and don't see eye to eye at times, they're the real deal.

The sun kisses my skin, setting off a warm hue radiant enough to make me miss summer as we quickly run across the road. When we enter the Chinese restaurant, the young girl escorts us to a table, handing us menus and asking if I wanted a high chair. She scurries back with it as we look over the drinks menu. The girls order wine, but I stick to soda since I'm driving home.

"Come on," Madison whines. "Just come, it's going to be fun!"

I shake my head. "Even if I didn't have her, I still wouldn't. I just need a rest day. Next weekend, I'm all in. I've just got a lot to sort out."

"Suit ya self," Madison says, taking a sip of her wine.

"I'll probably be there with Spyder…"

I choke on my drink, my hand flying up to stop it from spilling. "Oh, okay?"

Tate sighs, throwing her napkin on the table. I cradle Micaela in my arms and shake her bottle before giving it back to her.

"Spill."

We all eat and laugh as Tate goes through what's been happening with Spyder. He seems really into her, and she him. Not sure why Tate is being all shy. The girl is never shy.

After dinner, we drive home, buggered from the day. I park the wagon thing out front and say goodbye to the girls as they head off to get ready for their night. They tried to get me to agree to let them pre-game in the pool house, but there was no way. I could probably sleep into tomorrow and I'm exhausted from today.

I carry Micaela inside and shut the door, heading straight for the bathroom to give her a quick bath. There's a large tub in here, bulky enough for probably three people. I hit the tap on, and then take my phone out of my handbag, seeing the message from Madison with the photos from today.

I go to Facebook and change my profile photo to the selfie of all of us on the tea-cup ride. We're all laughing, hair flying everywhere while Micaela looks unbothered. Typical. I put my phone down just as I get a text.

Nate: **Whts up with these photos.**

What do you mean?

He doesn't reply, so I carry Micaela to the bath, but then step backward. I need one too. I quickly strip once we're in the bathroom and sink into the warm water with her in my arms. I put some bubbles into the water and lit a couple of relaxation candles, silently thanking Elena for putting them there. Music is playing from the small dock out in the lounge. My phone is going crazy, but I ignore it. I can't be bothered and there's no way I'm getting out. I wash her hair, massaging the sweet lavender shampoo into her hair. Once we're both done, I climb out, taking her with me and quickly wrap a towel around both of us. I dress her first, my hair in a messy top knot. I puff talcum powder on her and then do up her diaper. She's smiling up at me again, but her eyelids are heavy. She must be so tired.

The door swings open and I jump. "Shit!" Nate is standing there, his eyes going to her and then coming back to me.

"Goddammit, Tillie. Don't ignore me when I text you."

"I was taking a bath with her!" I snap back, forgetting that I'm standing here in a towel.

His eyes drop to my body and then go to Micaela again.

I wave my hand. "Can you close the door? It's cold out." I pick up my phone and read the text he had sent after.

Nate: **I want a motherfucking family day.**

He kicks it closed and then comes closer, taking off his leather jacket and cap. Instantly he eats up every single space with his presence. All he has to do is yank the towel off me and I'd be naked. I wouldn't put it past him either.

"Ah, what do you think you're doing? Don't get comfortable, Nate."

He glares at me and then picks Micaela up. "I've missed her."

I don't have the heart to tell him to leave, so I take this time to grab a long t-shirt that cuts off around my upper thighs and some panties. I get changed quickly in the bathroom, letting my hair out to brush it.

"Are you going now?" I don't mean to be hostile, but I got the feeling today that he didn't want to be seeing me as much.

"Yeah," Nate says, giving her back to me. I place her down in her crib, switching the main lights off and leaving the light from the TV as a night light. "Come outside so we can talk."

"Again," I whine. "I don't have the energy, Nate."

His jaw clenches. "Now."

For fuck's sake. I patter behind him, closing the door once we're outside. It's fucking cold, so I'm hoping he knows what he wants to say and spits it out in fast time.

I run my hands over my arms and take a seat on the step. He drops down beside me, putting his cap on backward and slipping back into his leather jacket.

I lick my lips. I need to stop watching him with fascination. "What is it, Nate?"

"There's some shit that we need to discuss, shit that you might not want to talk about right now. But have you had any strange calls?"

Should I tell him about that first night and the call I got telling me to go outside before all of this Peyton stuff blew up. I decide no. "No, why?"

His jaw ticks in that same way that makes his already prominently square jaw enlarge slightly. "Nothing, it's just dangerous right now and there's shit happening behind the scenes that I can't tell you about just yet. When I can, I will."

I chuckle, shaking my head. "I'm not Madison, Nate, I don't sit well with secrets. You either tell me or shut up."

His eyes cut to me. "You will fucking do as you're told because it's not just you anymore, Tillie. You—we—have to think of her!"

I know he's right, so I don't answer. He stands, coming directly in front of me. The zipper of his jeans is now directly opposite my eyes. *Shit.* His hand comes to my chin and he tilts my head up to face him. I feel miniscule down here. I tug my lip into my mouth and his thumb follows the movement.

"Fuck." He exhales and turns to leave. I watch as he slowly disappears into the dark night. I stay seated until I hear his loud car start and drive off.

What the hell was that about?

Leaving it all alone, I go back into the pool house, flopping onto my bed. I flick through Netflix, trying to find a show to watch when eventually, my eyelids feel heavy and sleep takes me under.

CHAPTER 17

Tillie

Pandas are dancing to an annoying tune. A tune I know, wait, I know this song. I aimlessly fling my arm around, trying to find my phone on the bedside table. Without opening my eyes, I sink into the bed more, sliding it to answer.

"Someone better be dead," I grumble, annoyed.

"Someone will be if you don't get down here—now, Tillie," Madison rushes, her tone has me on edge, but not enough to leave the comfort of my bed.

"What time is it? And I told you, I'm not coming."

"Tillie! Nate is drunk as fuck and he's fighting. I need you to get down here now."

"What the hell makes you think I can stop him?"

She pauses, seeming to think of what to say. Or what to lie about. I rub the sleep from my eyes. "Because I know!"

I fling my blankets off my body. Annoyed that he's interrupted my sleep. "Fine! Where are you guys?"

"At Brantley's, and Tillie, I'm serious, hurry."

I get a Snapchat notification from Tate. I open it and see Nate with no shirt on and blood smeared over his chest, his jeans hanging off his waist. When she zooms in, he's laughing, but his eyes are wild. He's absolutely drunk. Drunk and crazy. I don't know if it's a good idea I go… then the phone drops and there's a guy not moving on the ground with people crowding around him. The guy finally gets up, but he's in a bad way.

"Who's next?" Nate grins, his arms stretched wide.

I shoot off the bed and bolt out the door to the main house. God, I really don't want to do this, but I have no other choice, thanks to her crazy ass son.

Knocking on Elena and Joseph's door, I yell, "Elena?"

The door opens after a few seconds and she wipes the sleep from her eyes.

"I'm so sorry," I whisper, careful not to wake Joseph. "But Madison just called me, and Nate is drunk and fighting people and for some reason, she thinks I can help. Can y—"

Her eyes pop open. "—Shit. Yes, go." She pauses just before I go back to the room to get changed. "Tillie? Be careful when he's like this…"

I try to push down the fear that comes to the surface at her warning, and then nod and run back to my room.

I throw on my black yoga pants and my Harley t-shirt, tucking it in slightly on the side. Tying up my Chucks, I pile my hair into a high ponytail and grab the keys.

God. I have a really bad feeling about this.

I get to Brantley's in record time. Jumping out of the truck, I quickly run into the house, shoving past the bodies of teenagers. People start moving for me when they recognize who I am. Walking past a group of girls, one with sleek black hair snickers to her friend. "That's his baby mama. Tragic, really, that she tried to lock him down…"

I bite my tongue, moving to outside. The cool air is welcome after the humidity of ass and sweat in the house. "Crank That" by Travis Barker is roaring through the speakers and my head snaps to the circle of people behind the pool. I can't see anything clearly, so I quickly start to make my way when Madison's face appears.

"Thank fuck!" She yanks me toward the crowd.

"Why the fuck hasn't Bishop or any of The Kings stopped him?"

"Are you kidding?" Madison snorts, shoving through people to get to the middle. "They're putting bets down." She shoves a group of girls who are in the front. "Fucking move!" They slide away and I gasp. Nate is on top of a guy triple his size, Nate's fist plowing into his face. Blood splatters everywhere and my eyes go to his chest and back where there is dry blood crusted over.

I'm at a loss for words, because what the fuck…

Something kicks up inside of me. "Nate!" I bark. He falters but then carries on.

I go forward. "Nate get the fuck off him before you kill him."

He stops now, turning to face me over his shoulder. "Forgot About Dre" starts playing now.

Nate turns his head slightly and then climbs off the boy. He's— "What the fuck are you doing here?"

I knew this was a bad idea, but fuck it. "Madison called—you know what? That's not the problem here!"

His eyes are on fire, furious as they go up and down my body. Then he licks his lip and grins. "Actually, yeah, sure thing, baby, you stay here." Then he turns to face the crowd, snatching his drink off Eli who is standing beside Bishop who is also filming this whole thing.

"Nate…" I warn, my jaw clenching.

"What the fuck do you want, Tillie? I fucking told you, I don't want you near me. Stop acting like my fucking girl just because we have a kid!"

I freeze, my eyes flying to Madison, who looks at me apologetically. I scoff, shaking my head. "You know what, Nate? Sure thing, you're right. Kill him for all I care." Then I turn to leave, annoyed that most of Riverside Prep just witnessed Nate and I screaming at each other.

"Oh no you don't!" His hand comes to my arm, yanking me back.

I turn around, seething. "Get your fucking hands off me."

He smirks, his other arm snaking around my waist to yank me into him. Then his mouth drops to my ear and I try to block out his scent. Sugar, spice, and leather only now mixed with a pang of liquid metal and sweat. "You just caused a scene, baby. I don't know why you're here, but now, you're going to do exactly as you're told."

Then he bites my ear and stands back, his hand coming to mine and turning me around. He starts dragging me toward Bishop and The Kings. and I turn just in time to see a smug looking Madison. She's such a little shit.

Nate points to a seat around the pool. "Stay there."

I roll my eyes, annoyed that I came. But when my eyes look around the party, I count five guys with busted faces, maybe I'm not that annoyed for stopping his fighting.

Nate stands opposite me, talking to Jase and Saint. "Numb" from Rihanna starts playing in the background. His eyes come to mine, a smirk evident on his face.

I fucking hate him and his sexy stupid body, and his cocky grin. Even with blood all over him, he's by far the hottest guy I have ever seen in my entire life. He brings the bottle to his lips, his eyes still on mine, They're not frantic or angry anymore though, they're weak and heavy. These are the exact eyes that got me into bed with him in the first place. And Madison and Tate too—probably.

Goddammit. Tipping his head back, he downs the rest of the whiskey, liquid dripping down the side of his face and falling onto his chest over the two large angel wings. Those are my favorite, I decide. I don't know why he got them, but they're my favorite. He's still talking with the guys, but his eyes never stray far from me.

Madison and Tate both drop down beside me, and when Nate sees Madison, he licks his lip but moves straight for me. "Take me home?" he slurs, heavily intoxicated.

I give him a bored expression. "Sure." Seriously over his shit.

His fingers wrap around mine and he pulls me up, his other arm hooking around my waist. He buries his head into the crook of my neck. "Mmm, you smell good."

I shove him.

His tongue glides across my collarbone. "Fuck, Tillie," he groans, exhaling against my flesh. "Why do you fuck me up?"

My body freezes as I try to calm my racing and erratic heart. *He doesn't mean anything he says, he's just drunk.* "You're being an idiot," I answer, shaking my head.

"Am I?" He snarls as his lips brush over my skin. I have to mentally talk myself out of his games as his hips slowly press into me, planting me to the spot.

"You ready?" I ask, taking a step backward. When I look at him, he's smirking down at me, his lips glistening from the drink.

His eyes go over my shoulder, landing on someone behind me. He grabs my hand. "Yeah, let's go."

Once we're out by the car, I have to shove him into the passenger seat, tucking his arm inside. I shut the door with a little more force than what is necessary.

"Tillie!" Madison comes running out of the house just as I'm about to open the door.

"Thanks for calling me." I roll my eyes. "Not."

Madison shuffles uncomfortably. "Listen, I really nee—"

"—Madison!" Bishop snaps at her from the front door.

Madison stills, and then looks at me pleadingly.

"What is it?" I probe, crossing my arms in front of myself.

She chews on her lips nervously and then plasters a fake smile on her face.

"Nothing. I'll talk to you tomorrow." She turns, shoulder barging past Bishop, who is still watching me.

"Bye, Tillz."

"Bye, B." A flash of something falling over his face before it's gone.

My door swings open. "Hurry up!"

I roll my eyes again, getting into the car. I crank the heat up and start driving us out of Brantley's driveway.

"You mad?" Nate asks lazily, and I can hear the humor in his tone. Nate's drunk voice is even more sexy than his normal voice.

"No, I'm not. Why were you fighting?"

I see his head turn away from me out of the corner of my eye. "Because I fucking hate what your eyes do to me." He turns the radio on. *I am Tillie Stuprum and I am confused as fuck with this guy's mood swings. But slightly turned on.*

Pulling into our driveway, we both get out and Nate starts doing the Connor McGregor walk as we head toward the pool house, laughing loudly when I shove him.

"You're an idiot."

He turns around in a flash, his face and chest pressing against mine. I stop, my flushed cheeks cloaked by the dark night. "That's the second time you've called me an idiot, Tillie."

I shove past him, annoyed with his up and down. "Probably won't be the last, either."

"Where's Micaela?" he asks just as we tread up the stairs.

"Your mom texted me and told me she put her in her room."

I yank the door open, seemingly pissed that I was dragged out of bed over him, but as soon as I swing it open, both of his hands slam it shut on either side of my head, caging me in. I can feel the heat radiating off of him from behind me.

"You act like I don't affect you," he whispers against the nape of my neck, the strong smell of whiskey whiffing through. "Like you don't remember what it's like..." His hand comes to my stomach, his fingers sprawling out. "To get fucked." He tugs my body into him, and my ass hits between his legs.

Oh, he's really doing this.

"Nate, you're drunk. Go to your room." I try to open the door again, but he won't budge. "Nate."

His arm snakes around my belly, and I turn in his grasp. Too close. We're too close. His nose touches mine and his breath falls over my lips.

I look up at him. "Go to your room."

"You don't mean that." He grins, his eyes crossing when they drop to my lips. The fact that he looks adorable right now is irrelevant, but it's fact.

"I do, because you'll wake up in the morning—"

His lips touch mine softly, not hard. There's no eagerness to his movements, because he doesn't need to. This is all Nate. He's never desperate or needy, he hangs himself out as bait and dumb girls like me take it, unbeknownst about the poison that comes with that first taste. He is every girl's wet dream, and he damn well knows it.

His lips glide over mine, and every single nerve that holds me together starts to slowly tremble.

"Stop talking, baby," he whispers, and then softly pulls my bottom lip into his mouth.

Shit. Shit. Double fucking shit.

I can feel my resolve slowly slip away with every second that passes, and his mouth is on mine.

"Kiss me," he whispers, the deep rumble of his chest shaking mine.

"I—" His tongue slips over mine and my legs give away.

He pulls me back up with one arm, using the other to reach around and yank the door open. He lifts me with the arm that's around my waist and my legs instinctively fly around him.

Fuck it.

I kiss him back, my heart thrashing against my chest and my stomach flipping around like it's been thrown in a blender. Our kiss doesn't stop, and once we're inside, he kicks the door closed with his foot, carrying me to the bed. He pushes me down, falling on top of me. In the back of my brain, I know this is a bad idea, when that part comes rearing to the surface, I push at his chest.

He growls at me.

"Don't growl! I'm just saying, this isn't a good idea. You wouldn't want to do this if you were sober."

He settles between my legs, bringing my other up to rest on his hip. "You sure about that?" he teases, grinding into me.

"Positive, since every other time that you've been sober up until this point you've been cold and very vocal with how you feel about me."

His hand goes up my shirt and under my bra. He squeezes my nipple and rests his weight on his other arm. He's looking directly down at me and I try hard not to bring my eyes to his but fail.

He licks his lips, grinning. "I'm sober enough to put my dick in you, Tillie. Stop thinking too much into this."

He starts rotating his hips into me and I bite down on my bottom lip to stop the moan from leaving my mouth. Then he leans up, grabs the band of my yoga pants and yanks them off.

"Nate..." I warn, but fail because his other hand covers my mouth.

"Shut up, Tillie. Stop fucking talking. I need you right now."

Shit. He continues, his knuckles grazing over me.

"Nod if you want this."

I do, I nod my head, arching my back. His fingers dip under my panties and he tears them off. I fist the sheets between my fingers, my back arching farther, and then his tongue presses against my clit and I lose it. He throws my leg over his shoulder and slips a finger inside of me.

"Nate, I—"

"Let go, baby. You taste so fucking good." He growls against me and my hand comes to his head. I tear his cap off and toss it across the room, my fingers diving into his hair.

"Look at me, Tillie," he murmurs from below. I forgot what he gets like in bed. "Now, baby."

I inch up on my elbows, looking down at his face buried between my thighs. The shadows cut his jaw perfectly as he presses his whole tongue against me. I'm climbing, so close. "Ride my tongue, Tillie. Ride it like you ride on my dick." I fall to the bed, my head tilting back as my orgasm rips through me in violent waves.

"Too easy, as usual," he mocks, crawling up my body. "Can I trust the pill you're on?"

I nod, heat flashing over my cheeks.

"Good." He grips onto my hips and flips me onto my stomach. He slaps my ass hard and then wraps my hair around his fist, yanking my head back. Hovering over my body, he tilts my head to the side, sucking where my neck connects with my shoulder. I arch my back, pressing my ass into him, desperate to feel him. His finger slides inside of me from behind and I moan, my breathing coming in heavy.

He pulls out, bringing his finger to my mouth. "Suck."

I wrap my lips around his finger, the sweet taste hitting me instantly, then he takes his finger away and grips onto my hips again. I feel him slide over my entrance and I'm basically panting for him now, my chest tight with need. I need to feel him everywhere—he sinks inside of me and I clench around his length instantly.

He smashes into me relentlessly, spewing dirty words. Sweat drops off my forehead as he pulls out and flips me over onto my back. He spreads my thighs wide and slides inside of me again. I have the perfect view from here, every muscle tensing as he pulls in and out slowly.

He licks his lips, looking down at me. He drops down onto his elbows and presses his pelvic bone into my clit, thrusting his cock inside of me relentlessly. "I'm—"

"Come, baby." He sucks on my neck, biting down on it roughly. I let go, just as he stills and spills into me.

He rolls over, swiping the sweat from his forehead. "Well, shit, I'm sober now."

I freeze, turning onto my side to watch him. "Was that a mistake."

"Tillie." He shakes his head and then glares at me. "The fuck would you say that for?"

My eyes drop to his chest. "Get up!"

"What?" He leans up on his elbows. "It's fucking near three a.m. I'm not going anywhere."

I sneer at him. "Get in the shower, Nate."

He stumbles into the bathroom, obviously not as sober as he thought he was. As the minutes pass while he's in there, it occurs to me that I will need one too now since...

When he's out, the towel wrapped around his waist, I scoot into the bathroom and jump in the shower, quickly scrubbing my body. I watch as the water turns a murky burgundy color and try not to gag. He just fucked me with other people's blood smeared on his chest.

Gross.

I get out, drying my hair. My eyes shoot around the small bathroom. Fuck. I forgot to bring extra clothes in here. I open the door and slip into the dark room, quickly grabbing a pair of panties from my top drawer and the first t-shirt I find.

"Come here," he mumbles from my bed, his voice low.

I wince, and then make my way to my bed, slipping under the covers. He wraps his arm around my waist and yanks me into him. After a few minutes, we both fall asleep.

CHAPTER 18

Tillie

"Wait!" Madison says, raising her hand to stop me from talking. She and Tate came over early this morning. "So you're telling me that you guys slept together last night and then he left this morning?"

"Wow." Tate rolls her eyes. "I'm so shocked...."

I don't know why, but it annoys me that she said that. Like I didn't know what I was getting myself into when it came to Nate, but it's... well, it's Nate.

I spoon some granola into my mouth and watch as Micaela grabs Madison's mouth. "Yes, but like I said, this won't change anything. I'm not naïve," I glare at Tate.

She flips me off. "I love you too." Chuckling and going back to her breakfast. She starts whining to Madison that she wants Micaela for cuddles.

"This is your fault!" I say around a mouthful, stabbing my spoon toward Madison.

Her eyes shoot to me in fear.

I clear my throat. "I was kidding..."

She relaxes and then laughs me off. "Oh."

Why did she just act like that right now?

"Why did you just freeze up like that?" I ask, cutting straight to the point.

Madison gives me a soft smile. "Nothing. It's just Bishop and I—nothing. Don't worry. We can talk about it another time."

I want to push her. I do. But I'm not a pusher, and she's someone who is used to being pressed about everything, so in my head, the equation doesn't seem justified.

"Well, at least school is done." I roll my eyes. I can't imagine having to tackle school right now. I mean, I left around the time I got pregnant and abducted, but for Madison and Tate at least they're done.

"True!" Madison says, switching back on her charm. She looks to Tate before clearing her throat. "Ah, we're going to check out NYU this week. I mean, I'll be living with Bishop, but, did you want to come?"

I shake my head, already knowing my answer. "No. I won't be doing the college thing."

Madison chews on her bottom lip and I've come to notice this may be a nervous trait. *The hell is going on with her?*

"Hey." I nod my head. "What were you going to tell me last night before Bishop came out?"

I watch as her attention slowly drifts off into unknown territory. "I don't remember," she mutters from behind her mug, giving me another smile. "Sorry, Tillz. I must have been so drunk. What are your plans today?"

Well, I don't know, hopefully read a picture book that you know nothing about.

I put Micaela down for a nap and start cleaning up around the pool house. Nate made a mess last night, including smudging blood all over the sheets. I hate that I gave into him so easily last night, but at the same time, I know not to think too much into what happens with him and I. It just is what it is with him.

I toss the sheets into the wash in the main house and tell the maid to bring them back when they're finished, which she agrees to do. It still feels weird bossing someone around to do something I could do since I was four years old, but whatever.

Sighing, I flop down onto the bed and take out Daemon's book from under the mattress. I flip past the first two pages that I've already seen and go straight for CAPITULUM III. This image is strange. A simple drain with its lid slightly pushed off. Everything is smudged around it to make the grey blend with the lid. There are white words that are engraved into the lid. *Perdita.* I flip back to page one with the boy at the house and then to page two with the ice eyes.

Were these drawn on Perdita? Daemon was raised there, it would make sense. I flip the page again to CAPITULUM IV and see the numbers 446 shaded in the same grey pencil. The numbers take up the whole page in block font. "That's odd," I murmur to myself, shuffling off my bed to grab my water bottle out of the fridge. The number 446 was our trailer park number. Total coincidence, I know, but it is still peculiar.

I flick the lid off my bottle, flipping back to the first page. There's something about this book that has the gears inside my head turning. Why would Daemon do this? There has to be a reason. Daemon was eons ahead of his age. I sip my water, looking closely at the second page. Everything drifts to the back of my mind as my eyes connect with the blue ones peering back at me on the page. "Who are you..." My phone rings, scaring me out of my trance. I quickly shuffle back to the bed, tossing the book underneath and answering before it goes to voicemail.

"Hello?"

Silence.

I look down at my phone, seeing it's an unknown caller. I bring it back to my ear. "Who is this?"

They hang up with a click and I squeeze the phone in my hand, my thoughts drifting back to what Nate said last night about strange callers.

The door opens, bringing me out of my frantic thoughts. I freeze when I see it's Nate, because of course it is. Only he would barge in like he owns the place—which he actually does.

"Hey," I say, my eyes going to his.

I can already see the malice all over his face, so when he comes straight up to me, picking me up from the ground and hooking my legs around his waist, I'm not all that surprised. Part of me is, though, because it's starting to feel so much like it did when we first got together. Rekindled loves don't have much of a success rate. The only kind that last a second round are the ones whose spark was volatile enough to burn and simmer perpetually. Did we have that? I'm not so sure.

He whispers into the crook of my neck. "I need you." the simplicity of his words knock the doubt out of me. *Yes, we did.*

I whack him, my head tilting back as I contain my laugh. "You can't just come in here and say *I need you* and expect me to just open my legs for you!"

He tilts his head in the adorable way he does and bites down on his bottom lip, his dimples sinking into both cheeks. "Really? Because I mean," he squeezes my thighs—that are open. Chuckling, he puts me back down onto the ground. "Just kidding, Tillz, chill, fuck. You think too much into everything. I'm not fucking asking you to be my girl or anything." *Okay so maybe not.*

My mouth pops open, and then slams shut, but then pops open again when I realize what he has just said. Luckily Micaela is asleep, or I'd be throwing shit right now. He goes over to her crib. "I just fucking miss her. Drives me crazy."

I'm still trying to decide whether or not I'm going to bite. "I never said anything about me being your girlfriend, Nate," I whisper. I aim for neutral, but the nip at the end of each syllable would prove otherwise. Nate picks that up, because he's smart. He's leaning over the crib, his arms tensing as he grips the edge. His head is hanging low, watching Micaela sleep, but as soon as those words leave my mouth, his hooded eyes come up to mine, a smirk on his stupid mouth. "Good. Don't want any confusion here."

"None at all," I declare. Maybe I answered that a little too fast.

"You answered too fast."

"Fuck you. Are you done?" I hate how he gets to me, but we've always been different. This is why I always thought he and Tate would've made a better couple. They made more sense because they both had no issues with sleeping around.

His eyes don't move from mine. "You're coming with me tonight."

"What?" I cross my arms in front of myself. "To where?"

He stands straight. I can't read his expression. What the hell is with everyone and their unreadable faces? This world sucks. "Be ready at nine. Mom already knows she has Micaela." He turns to leave, but just before he steps outside and closes the door, he cranks his head over his shoulder, smirking. "And wear something short and tight."

He steps out and shuts the door before I can swear at him. Daemon's book is now squashed to the back of my brain, although it's ties are still latched onto me by a thread.

I reach for my phone, dialing Madison. She answers after a few rings. "Hola."

"What's happening tonight and why is Nate picking me up at nine?"

If I can't get any answers out of Nate, I'm cashing in on girl code.

"What? He's bringing you?"

I pause. "Bringing me where?"

Just when I think she's not going to say anything, she exhales loudly. "Wow. Okay, um, on a run. It starts at a meeting point and—you'll see. Bishop is here now, but hey, can we talk tonight?"

"Of course?" I say, confused why she would need to ask if we could talk. We hang up and I go around cleaning everything quickly while Micaela is asleep. It's just after six when I'm finally nestled in bed with Micaela, gazing at my phone.

I know that I shouldn't.

I mean, I really know that I shouldn't.

I pick up my phone and hit dial.

"Well, this is unsuspected," Peyton purrs down the phone.

I briefly choke on my words, and then clear my throat. "Ah, yeah..." there's a reason why I was calling her, and I need to get to that reason now. "Where are you?"

She scoffs, and I'm reminded why I really don't like her, regardless whether she is my sister by blood. "Like I'd tell you."

"Listen," I turn over to the other side when I catch Micaela watching me. "I need to know something."

"Hmmm, and what makes you think I'd tell you anything that you need to know?"

"I don't really care, Peyton. I know when you're lying and when you're telling the truth, so I'm going to go with that."

She pauses, and then exhales. "Fine. What?"

"Daemon..."

The sound of a high-pitched hyena cackles through my phone, and the image of what her face would look like right now has my fists bunching. "Aw, honey. I can't tell you anything about Daemon. But here's something I can tell you..." She stops again, and I roll back over the bed, swinging my legs off. I hang onto the silence by the tips of my finger nails. "Nate is playing you, this much I know. He is playing you big time."

"Why would you think I'd care if he was playing me? Him and I are nothing."

She lets out another cackle. I really fucking hate her laugh. Have I always hated it, or is it a new thing for me? "You and he will always be a something." Then she hangs up, leaving me annoyed with her cryptic message. I go to call back but get a recorded voice message saying that this number is no longer in service.

Typical Peyton. Flips everything upside down and walks away.

A knock on my door yanks me away from my deciphering. I quickly get up and open it.

"Hey!" I say to Elena, who is standing there with a huge smile on her face. "You're early?"

She wiggles, looking around the room for Micaela. "I know, I just miss her because I haven't seen her all day, and als—"

"—let me through! Her cool aunt is here," Scarlet, Bishop's mom, pushes past both of us.

Elena sighs. "—also her."

I snort, waving Elena inside to follow Scarlet. Kicking the door closed, I exhale. "Well, you guys are early, but I guess I can find something to do to burn time."

I make them tea, but Scarlet wanted coffee, so I change hers to coffee. The silence is awkward, but having Scarlet here is a good thing. It stops Elena from giving me half a million-dollar cars or money.

"She's so beautiful," Scarlet coo's, cradling Micaela in her arms.

"Thank you," I smile at Scarlet before Elena steals my attention.

"Are you excited for tonight?"

Not really.

CHAPTER 19

Tillie

"Where are we going?" I ask as Nate drives us onto the main highway.

He smirks, dropping it down into third gear and flooring it forward. "On a run. You'll see Madison and everyone there."

"Ah, okay, but why are you taking me?" My fingers clench around the door handle. I can't think of any reason as to why he would be taking me with him, and it makes me nauseous what with the brief conversation I had with Peyton, and with Nate's track record.

"Did you have something better to do?" He clips back, and my attention snaps to him instantly. His jaw is slightly taunt and his fingers are flexing around the steering wheel.

"What? No. I'm just wondering why you would bring me with you."

He doesn't answer, so I hit the radio and let the music waft between us.

The drive is around twenty minutes, and it's not long before we're pulling into a long gravel driveway. Trees shade over the road with fresh cut grass spread behind as a backdrop. I can see a glass octagon shaped house right at the end with fairy lights hanging around the edges, beaming it bright.

"What's this place?" I ask, leaning forward to get a closer look.

Nate hits the volume down slightly, but the base is still shaking the metal. "This is the meet. Stay close to me and don't take drinks from anyone."

"What?" I ask, horrified. "What is this place?"

"It's called the meet. This is where the night starts and ends." He pulls to the front of the entryway where a large man stands wearing all black and a clipboard in his hand. "Nate!" I whisper as he climbs out of the car. I grab the handle, opening the door wide. Swiping down my white short-shorts, I chew on my lip, second guessing my clothing. Its casual, but it's sort of—tight.

Nate looks me up and down, and slowly comes closer to me, backing me up against the car. I can hear people in the background, but I'm so caught up in his eyes that I don't break the cerebral contact. His hand comes to my upper thigh, squeezing me. "The Artist" by Jay Sean is spilling out loudly from the octagon shaped house thingy. Nate lifts me up by my thighs, his hand coming to my throat. He licks me across my bottom lip and then bites on it roughly. "No wandering off tonight, *principissa mea*. You know where this belongs." He grins, his hand coming around to cup my ass as if to accentuate his point. He kisses me before looking back. "At least, while I'm around."

He puts me back down to my feet, his eyes going over my shoulder, and I turn to follow his line of sight. Madison, Bishop and Brantley are there.

"Where's everyone else?" I ask, nudging my head.

Brantley grins. "It's our turn this week." His eyes fly to Nate. "You're a greedy bastard. Some shit *does* change."

Nate flips him off. "Just with her."

Brantley returns his bird flip. "Yeah? I'll remember that next time you have the Raven jumping around on both of our dicks."

I suck in a breath, hopefully not obviously. *Who the fuck is The Raven.*

Nate doesn't seem bothered, and why would he be. I knew who he was when I decided to, as Brantley well put it, bounce around on his dick. I can't deny the sting though.

Madison grinds her teeth. "Not sure I like her yet."

"Who?" I ask, annoyed with being out of the loop.

Bishop chuckles, pulling Madison into him. "Chill, baby. She has nothing on you."

"He's lying," Brantley rolls his eyes, walking past us. "She's by far the hottest chick I've ever fucking seen. Isn't that right, Nate?" I can almost hear Brantley grinning.

And I'm over this shit, but at the same time, I can't show that it's affecting me. I just have to stop Nate from being too hands on. Of course he's been messing around with girls, but what annoys me is that this girl has obviously been a regular, and apparently he's shared her with Brantley—*no surprise there*—and she's nicknamed Raven and—*big and*—she has Madison pushing on the insecure side. No one, and I mean no one can make Madison insecure. Consider me intrigued.

Madison yanks on my hand. "Let's get a drink, shall we? Also, ignore Brantley. He hasn't gone there because—*gross*—and neither has Nate. They're fucking with you. This time." She whispers into my ear. I want to ask her what she means by "gross", but she is already dragging me forward.

"Yeah." I look right at Nate as I let Madison drag me toward the glass house. "Good idea."

His eyes stay on me until I drag them away. *No deal, buddy.* No way am I letting him run playboy on me.

The big guy waves us through and as soon as we get inside "What's Happenin'!" by Ying Yang Twins is thudding loudly.

"Is this a club?" I lean into Madison.

She shakes her head, dragging me toward a table where around four other guys are seated. A couple are young, really young. I'd have to say around sixteen. Too young to be here. The entire area is circled with tables and small bars, and then you take a few steps down, and—I lean over the railing.

"Holy shit!"

There's a massive UFC shaped octagon downstairs with a fight happening and people screaming, throwing money around. The rowdy people don't surprise me. It's the tables of immaculately dressed men surrounding those people, hidden in the shadows. Smoke drifts up through the air as they all watch the fight in unperturbed ease. One man in the corner with a fedora hat looks up at me and I stop. Immediately looking away.

Madison follows my sight, handing me a bottle of some pre-made drink. I take a sip, the vodka hitting my throat instantly.

"Are you okay?" Madison asks after downing half of her drink.

I turn to face the railing and watch as two guys fight in the middle of the ring. Both shirtless, both ripped, and both—"ouch!" someone got a kick to the face. The smell of sweat mixed with cologne, cigar smoke, and weed lingers around the place.

"Tillie?"

"Hmm?" I turn to face her, my mouth around the rim of the bottle. I drink the rest and gesture to her. "I need another."

"Okay so that's a no," Madison murmurs, and then hooks her arm around mine and drags me back toward the table where the guys are seated. I haven't seen any of them in my life.

Their eyes all come up to us, and I take a second to draw in their appearance, because I'm in the mood to be shallow. There are four of them, two are young, around sixteen, I'd say, and the other two would have to be older. Like around Spyder's age, so twenty-four-*ish*. I can feel the distinct sound of blood pulsing through my ears as the alcohol begins to seize my thoughts, relaxing my muscles slightly.

"What you girls up to?" One of the young guys grins at us, his eyes raking over my body. He has a square jaw and cheeky eyes. His nose is slightly crooked, giving his otherwise pretty appearance a rough edge. The other young guy has long hair that hangs around his neck and has muscles for days. The other older guys have buzz cuts and if I'm being honest, seem to slightly resemble each other.

"Nothing." Madison smiles. "Looking for drinks!"

The bold one with the crooked nose gestures down to the glass fridge beside him. "By all means, Swan, help yourselves, but tell me..." He leans forward, his eyes pointedly on me. "Who the fuck is this beauty?"

A few of them snort but carry on with their game of poker.

"This is Tillie, and she's—"

I cut Madison off, "—really good at poker."

He flicks his tongue out and then gestures to the seat beside him, but I take the one closest to the older guy. Madison slips beside the bold one after handing me my drink. She glares at me but with a smile and I shrug. I'm done playing nice girl with Nate while he's off being a ho and I'm home playing baby mama. Just because a girl is a mom, it does not mean that she can't have a life. You know, outside of mom-hood. I'm going with that anyway.

"He's a little straight forward," the one beside me leans into my ear after dealing us up.

I shrug, taking another sip of my drink. "I don't mind. Is it Texas Hold 'Em?"

They nod and I pick up my cards. We keep playing as more music blasts through and more drinks disappear.

"Alright, girls," bold one, whose name is actually Lennox, says. "You riding with me?" He looks at me, and in my fuzzy brain, I shrug, standing from the table. Not sure where we're riding to, but right now, I don't care. I haven't seen Nate all night, and there's a dark part of me that thinks he has probably found the blackbird chick. Whoever she is.

Madison's hand comes out to mine. "Don't be reckless..."

I yank it out of her grip. "I'm not you, Madz. I don't deal well with games unless I'm playing."

She chews on her lip nervously then stands up, leaning close to my ear. "Listen, there's something I need to tell you, but I don't want you—"

"—Come on, pretty girl, let's go have some fun..." Lennox says, hooking his arm around my neck. I drop the shot that's on the table and let him drag me out of this glass house of doom or whatever it is. I probably should drink some water soon if I want to wake up in the morning with some memories.

A couple of the other guys are following us out when Lennox beeps a Maserati. "Ride shotgun, baby."

"Hold up." My hand comes to his chest. I'm experiencing a wave of honesty and I feel bad if I'm dragging some poor kid into mine and Nate's rip of drama. "Do you know who I am?"

He seems to search my eyes, and it's the first time I notice the flecks of blue in them. He really is gorgeous, as are the other guys, but I've come to learn over the year that the only people associated with The Kings are beautiful one way or another. On the outside. They're rather shitty human beings on the inside.

He smirks, leaning into my ear until his lip touches my lobe. "Yeah, baby mama, I do. You wanna play or what?"

I lick my lips, my eyes going to the other three guys who are watching me. "You do realize Nate will kill you, right?" I'm bluffing. Nate doesn't care.

Lennox grins again. "You do realize, he's probably fucking Laken right now, right?"

"Wait!" I shake my head, trying to clear the fog. "Who is your sister and how old are you?"

"Get in the car, baby." He points to the car.

I lick my lips. "No. Who is Laken?" Raven, Laken. I'm not leaving without answers.

He pauses, searches my eyes and then smirks. "Laken Sloan. You don't know her—yet. And I'm sixteen."

Reality comes crashing back into me. He's sixteen, I'm not a fucking cradle snatcher. "You know what? Pass." I start walking toward the gravel road. Everything is spinning in my head and I'm not sharp enough to catch onto a word that has been said. I pull my phone out and see a text from Nate.

Nate: **Where the fuck r u?**

I flip my phone off because that's mature. This was all his stupid idea anyway. Headlights stream from behind me, but I hear the car before I see it. Stepping to the side of the road, I signal to let the car pass, only it doesn't. It hangs behind me, engine idling loud enough to wake the devil himself. Definitely a V8. I turn, shading the headlights from my eyes. Black with circle headlights, looks like an old-style car. Something you see on *Fast and Furious*. It rumbles up closer, pulling right beside me. The windows are tinted so I can't see inside, but even if they weren't, I wouldn't be able to make out much of anything. The back-window slides down as the deep growl of the engine reverberates around me. I almost have to block my ears it's that loud.

Three guys are in the back, and—I squint my eyes. "Okay, I didn't realize it was Halloween in April?"

The back door opens, hitting me in the leg.

"Ouch!"

My eyes go over them again, each of their faces are painted in the Dia los Muertos face paint. Black and white with translucent eye contacts in. I wouldn't recognize them from a damn line up.

"Get in the fucking car, Tillie."

Well, I recognize that voice.

"Nate?"

His hand comes out, pulling me into the backseat.

"What are you doing!" I yelp, falling across not just Nate's lap, but the rest of whoever is in the back.

Nate slams the door closed, grabs me by the back of my neck and slaps my ass cheek. Hard. A loud clap breaks out along with my scream.

"Nate!"

My short white shorts have probably ridden up high enough to flash the curves of my massive ass.

"I fucking told you to stay the fuck away from anyone while I'm around, and what do you do?"

I lean up on my elbow, trying to get up but the guy I'm over tenses when my elbows dig into his hard thigh muscles.

"Let me up..." I moan.

He flips my legs off his lap and brings each of his legs over mine. His lips touch the back of my neck. "What. Do. You. Do?"

I gulp, licking my lips. "Let me up." He pushes my legs away and they drop to the ground as he takes his seat again. I inch up, my eyes going straight to the guy whose lap I'm sitting on. "Who are you?"

I turn to look at the rearview mirror, and my eyes drop to the driver's neck where I see the familiar demon inked. Just as recognition zaps through me, I catch the smile that tickles Brantley's mouth in the rearview mirror.

"This is your car?" I should have known Brantley would own something like this.

He chuckles, dropping it into second as he shoots us forward on the highway.

Spinning back around, I glare at the guy whose lap I'm on. "Who are you."

"Fucking chill. It's Bishop. I'm not going to slip one in you..." There's a pause. "In this lifetime."

I relax slightly because he's right. He wouldn't do that. I look to Nate, who is watching the passing trees out the window, his fist clenched on his lap.

"Where are we going?"

Nate doesn't answer, just continues to ignore me. I try hard not to take in the strength of his jaw and neck.

"You're on a run, boo, and sucks to be you because these never end well," the guy in the passenger seat says, and I recognize his voice instantly. It's Hunter, Madison's brother. Well, this is all new news, so I don't know if I'm actually allowed to refer to him as her brother, but whatever, and also, I'm still drunk.

"I feel funny." I sway in Bishop's lap.

His arm snakes around my waist. "Wow! You alright?"

"Umm..." I click my lips together to end the 'um.' "Not sure, don't think so. Is it hot in here?" I start fanning my face in an attempt to cool down my suddenly hot flesh. My cheeks flash in the humidity.

My eyes go to Bishop's. "You look hot in this mask. I don't know, it calls to something inside of me." Sweat drips down between my boobs, and my hands come to the bottom of my shirt. I yank it up and throw it to the front of the car onto Brantley's lap.

"Woah!" Brantley grabs it, his eyes coming to me in the rearview mirror. "Nate, check her. Now."

Leaning forward, I arch my back so my ass is the only view for the backseat trio and hit the stereo. D12's "Devil's Night" starts booming through the subwoofers. I close my eyes and wriggle back onto Bishop's lap. Nate yanks me off, putting me directly on his. I hear chuckling somewhere, but Nate curls his fingers around my chin, tilting my head down to face him.

"Did you take anything?"

I yank myself out of his grip. "What do you mean?"

"Did you snort anything, pop anything?"

My brows cross in confusion. "What? No. I just drank. You know I don't like drugs that much."

His eyes go to Bishop and he shakes his head, rolling his eyes. "Yeah, babe. Sure." Then he turns to Bishop. "With her like this, it's going to make this whole thing a little more difficult."

Bishop laughs. "God I'm loving karma right now."

"Fuck you." Nate flips him off.

The music continues to take me over. "Where are we going?"

Nate's eyes come to mine—finally, but now that I have his attention, I'm not sure I want it. He's mad. "You'll see."

With the blanket of the music, I know the guys can't hear anything that is said between him and I. I don't break the eye contact, ignoring the way my stomach clenches the longer I'm in his trance. Like a captured butterfly, my time is limited.

"Are you mad at me?" I don't know why that's the first thing that I say, but it is.

His jaw flexes in a way that makes it expand a little at the edges. When I figure he's not going to answer me, I rest my head on his shoulder. I don't care if he doesn't want it there, it's staying there anyway. Now I just have to stop myself from falling asleep.

About twenty minutes later, we're pulling up to a high gated house. There's old brick lining the perfectly manicured grass. Brantley winds his window down, leaning out the window slightly and looking directly into a camera. Nate's hand is on my thigh and in my attempt to ignore that, I wriggle in his lap. He clenches his grip and his lips come to the back of my neck.

"You're making me testy, Tillie. I've been fucking light on you when it comes to this world, but that's all about to change. When tonight is over? You'll be running from me."

Unable to entertain his idea, I ignore him. Brantley throws my shirt at me. "You might need this."

Two minutes later, shirt now back on, we're still driving down the long gravel driveway. The road begins to narrow, the trees caving in on us. Goosebumps break over my flesh. Getting driven into the unknown is sobering. Brantley's car finally comes to a stop, the heavy rumbling of his engine beneath us and the headlights illuminating the masses of trees in front. In my clouded thoughts, I internally question what tonight is actually about, but before I can think too much into it, Nate's lips touch the back of my neck again, his smile pressing against my flesh.

"Remember how Madison used to bitch about the games we played?"

I chew on my bottom lip. "Yeah." My eyes fly to Bishop, who is watching me carefully.

Nate chuckles, his hand sprawling out over my tummy as he swings the door open with his other. "Well, now you're the object. Run." He shoves me out the door, and I swing around to glare at him.

"You brought me out here, wearing that, to play a game? No, Nate. I'm not Madison!"

Nate gets out of the car, and I hear the rest of the doors shut in the background. "Nah, that's not why. But since you're here, let's play, baby. Ten."

"Fuck you."

He smirks. "Always so feisty. Eight."

"You missed nine." I roll my eyes. I'm feeling bold from all the alcohol I definitely should *not* have consumed.

"Two."

My eyes snap to his.

His darken. "Run, princess."

In my daze, I find myself looking over the artistic skull painted onto his face with perfect sharp precision, totally forgetting what he had just said. Only for a second, because a blood-curdling scream ripples out from somewhere behind me, and it shocks my feet into moving. Before I know it, I'm jogging through an unfamiliar forest with sweat dripping down my temple. My legs ache in protest, my feet throb from being inside my thigh-high boots, and my head spins from moving so fast, but realization slams into me like an unexpected wave of truth, threatening to pull me down and drag me out to sea. There is always a reason to their madness. *Why am I here?*

"No! No! NO!" That same scream reverberates through the air and every single hair on my skin stands to life.

What the fuck is going on.

I stop, swiping the sweat from my forehead. How did I get from drinking, to here, running through a damn forest, away from the most dangerous guys ever, with the screams of someone playing in the background. Is it playing?

Spinning around, I try to take a second to take in my surroundings. Everything is silent, with nothing but the heavy inhales of me sucking in air. Did they even chase me? Or was that a game to them too? Madison said that they liked to play games and actually compared them to The Riddler, but I'm feeling a little more like I'm in the middle of a *Saw* movie. All that's missing is Billy the Puppet to roll up in here on his little trike.

"Help! Please!"

That voice isn't going anywhere, so I decide to follow it. Running in the direction of where it was coming from. My white shorts will be ruined by the end of the night. Gripping onto the bark of a tree, my movements slow as I catch flickers of burnt orange raging in the air. A bonfire. My gaze shifts to the side where there's a girl locked in a cage, her arms wrapped around her knees as she rocks back and forth like a caged animal. She has a dirty rag tied around her eyes and her hands and feet are tied together with rope. I can see from here that where the rope has rubbed against her skin has blistered as if she's been like that for some time. My eyes drop to the floor of the cage where urine stains leak over the edges. I take a step forward but stop. I was too busy looking at her that I missed what was going on around her. My eyes go to the men standing around the fire. They're all dressed in hooded robes, thrown over their faces. I count them. I get to nine when my stomach feels like it's going to roll over. One of the guys that is directly opposite me, standing on the other side of the fire slowly lifts his head, not enough that I can see, but enough that I can make out the Dia los Muertos face paint. He smirks, his eyes coming to mine but his head remaining hunched over. My hand flies to my mouth in shock. Am I really shocked, though?

"Aww, come here, *mea principessa*." Nate curls his finger at me.

I shake my head, stepping backward. My eyes drop to his naked chest where the robe ties at his collar.

He tilts his head, amused. "You can't run from us, Tillie. You know that."

The girl yells again. "Please help me! Please!"

I step back again but slam into a rock-hard chest. I scream, spinning around just as a hand comes to my mouth and squeezes. I see the tattoos on his neck and know it's Brantley. Madison is crazy, these guys are not scary. The word scary does not even touch the level of darkness that they exude. They're villainous degenerates. They dig their claws into you without using their touch and suck the life from your soul.

"Shut the fuck up, Tillie, and do as you're told." He spins me around to face everyone, thrusting his cock into my ass to push me forward. He brings his lips to my ear. "You wanted to play with the big boys, baby, so let's play." His grip tightens around my mouth. "Do you know who that girl is in there?"

"Shhhh," Hunter chuckles from beside Nate. "Don't spoil it."

My eyes go straight to the girl, the flames from the fire now licking its heat over my skin. I don't recognize her. Should I?

Nate still hasn't said anything, he's just watching me carefully. My eyes fly around the area. Behind the cage is a large pickup truck, Ford Raptor, I think, with its tailgate down. There are giant logs lined around the fire to offer as seating.

"What is going on?" I ask, clearing my throat.

"Tillie," a soft whisper comes from the cage. "She's here, isn't she?" the girl yells. "Let me out! Please let me out!"

I crank my head toward the girl, anxiety splitting me open. "How do you know who I am?"

Nate stands in the way, forcing me to stop my analysis of the young girl.

"I know you, I know you! I know you. *Fuuuuccckkkk!*" The girl's screams are raucously desperate.

Nate's hand comes to my face, just when I think it's going to be a gentle gesture, he squeezes my cheeks. His shoulders straighten, and I watch as his lip curls and his teeth are bared. I know this pose, I've seen it many times. It's like a whole other side of Nate comes to the surface. It terrifies me in all the ways it should terrify me. This is the side of him that makes him second in command as a King. This is why he's Bishop's right-hand man.

"Sit. Down," he orders through a growl that's soft enough to squeeze. "Your final warning, Tillie."

I take a step back and drop onto a log. My eyes keep going back to the caged girl, but before I can ask anything else, laughing starts to emerge through the forest. There's another group of young people. All in the same face paint. Their laughs stop when they see me. Their eyes go to The Kings. My kings.

"Wow," one chuckles, shaking his head. "You actually brought a Stuprum to a meet?" His eyes go to who I'm guessing is Bishop. "Your pops know about this?" I feel outnumbered. There are two girls, and one is locked in a cage. The rest are guys, some I don't even know. Not that it matters, because the ones I do know are scarier than any man I've ever met. I want to ask Bishop where Madison is, but I find my mouth glued shut, sealed by fear. Possibly.

"You can't do this to me," the girl shouts through her weeping. "I'm—you can't!"

"What is going on?" I glare at Nate.

One of the new guys laughs, taking a seat beside me. "She's a swan. Obviously."

"So?" I snap, my annoyance growing balls. "Madison broke all of that bullshit."

"Except…" The guy leans in, his lips coming to my ear.

Nate growls. "Watch your proximity, young pup, or I'll tear your lips from your face."

The boy backs away slightly, but still close enough to be able to whisper. "Some parents are fucked up, Tillie, and hers, are the worst."

"How?" My eyes search his. Since I'm getting answers from him, I'm going to milk it. "How are hers the worst?"

He pulls back slightly, his eyes dropping to my lips. It's then that I realize who this boy is. It's the guy from earlier. Lenny? Lennox? I've already forgotten. "She's a Vitiosis."

"And?" I wait for the ball to drop, but instead, Nate steps in and intercepts it.

Yanking me up by my hand, he turns me around to face the girl, his hand traveling around my stomach. He uses his other to wrap my hair in his fist and tilts my head to the side. "Look at her, baby," he whispers softly against the side of my neck. "Look at her. She's all hopeless and at our disposal. She's the next known swan but only two years younger than Madison, so do you know what that means? Hmmm?"

I don't answer. I'm borderline ready to knee him in the balls and save that poor girl.

"Answer me, Tillie." His grip tightens in my hair.

"No!" I gasp. "I don't know what that means."

He chuckles, and then I feel his teeth sink into the flesh of my neck. He swats my ass forward, dismissing me. "It means that her parents have decided they don't *want* her, so unless someone else of her line accepts her." Nate's eyes flick up to Brantley and then come back down to mine. "Then she's gotta bounce."

"Bounce?" I snort. "But why did you bring me here? Why, Nate?"

He chuckles, and the sound grips on my fear and squeezes tightly. "Because I want you to see why it's important for you to *listen* to me. Take in this scene, Tillie. Remember it."

Turning around to face Brantley. His eyes are already on the girl, his finger running lines over his upper lip.

"Brantley!"

He doesn't look at me.

"Brantley!" I repeat, my voice a little higher.

He finally turns to face me, his eyes narrowing. "What?"

"You're a Vitiosis. Take her."

There's a pause, and at first, I think nothing of it. I don't even question why everyone has suddenly silenced. The new guys who came in have stopped their chatting. Like never mind the fact that this girl is caged here, ready to—whatever was about to happen to her.

Brantley continues to glare at me, his face expressionless. "I don't want to."

Nate rips off his robe and stretches his neck, his eyes going up and down my body. It's the first time I've noticed the blood on his chest. He swipes his mouth with the back of his hand, his eyes still on mine. "Stop trying to interfere, Tillie."

"You brought me here, Nate," I snap, going back to Brantley who is still watching me.

"You want me to save her?" Brantley asks the question with discernable hesitancy as if he's wondering why I would *want* to save a human being. "Tillie, the reason why she has fallen on our lap is because of your mother. If she was here, doing her job, then we wouldn't have come face-to-face with who this girl is." I ignore his comment about Katsia.

"Please," I plead, watching him. Brantley has no other immediate family. His father died when Madison killed him for what he did to her and Brantley as children, and his mother died when he was young. Him having someone, anyone, would have to be better than having no one. "You're alone, Brantley. Bring someone in."

His eyes narrow, but his lip kicks up in a devious smirk. He leans over, running his index finger down the side of my face. Chills break out over my skin. "Tsk, tsk..." His fingers grip around my chin as he tilts my face to his. "What makes you think I'm alone." *Why does that statement chill me to the bone?*

Our eye contact is broken by a voice I haven't heard in some time.

"Time's up. Do it."

I spin around, my eyes clashing with her figure. Tall, long dark hair, enough makeup on to be classed as a Sephora shop, and heels as high as the shoe that's shoved up her ass.

Khales.

I clench my jaw, raising to my feet and leaping straight for her. She sees me and for a second, fear flashes through her eyes before she quickly composes herself. "Well, well, well, if it isn't the little pink haired hobbit."

"That's real cute," I laugh, snarling and coming face-to-face, nose-tip-to-nose-tip with her. "But you and I have unfinished business."

She grits her teeth. "We are done. I'm with Hector now, or did you forget?" Then she smirks, and I have to physically clench my fists together to stop them from flying straight into her face. "You can't touch me." She swings her bored eyes over my shoulder toward Nate and Bishop. "End her. I'll send the crew after, and boys, you still have a job to do tonight." She looks around all of them. "And we need it done rather quickly." She winks at Bishop. "See you all later." She leaves as quickly as she appeared. I let out a frustrated scream and then swing around to Bishop, who is watching her exit with venom seeping through his eyes.

"How has no one killed that bitch yet?" I scream, my arms flying up around me.

Bishop's eyes come to mine. "Good question."

I stomp toward the girl in the cage, gripping the metal and slowly dropping to my knees. "I'm going to get you out, okay?"

She doesn't answer, her lip trembles.

"What's your name?" I ask while mentally trying to think of a plan that doesn't get us both locked inside.

"Bailey. Bailey Rose Vitiosis."

"Okay, Bailey, well I'm going to get you out." I stand, swiping the dirt from my knees. Brantley is already watching me. His jaw clenches, and then he rolls his eyes, his strides eating up the distance between us. Oh shit.

"Fine, but I swear to fuck, Tillie, she is your responsibility." He looks to the new boys who entered, the younger ones. Brantley grins, and it's the kind of smirk that would disarm the devil.

A couple of the guys share a worried looks between each other, and and I could have sworn I saw an Adam's apple bob every now and then.

"Guess what, boys?" They all look at Brantley. "Looks like you'll have the honor of having the first Elite King girl in your year group once you actually drop your nuts and get initiated in December."

"How old is she? How old are they?" If those little shits lied to me...

Brantley laughs, pulling the keys to the padlock out of his pocket. "Sixteen. They have done the first initiation, but they don't take the second ceremony until December thirty-first, which is when they become official Kings. Since Madison broke history, family had come out to say that they had a daughter and are moving her to Riverside."

I shake my head, information spilling at the seams, but I drink it up like a thirsty hooker greedy for those tips. "This world is mental."

"Her name is Bailey, but she's also called The Raven..."

Interesting. Madison's *'gross'* comment makes sense now. "I mean, they look older..."

Brantley rolls his eyes. "You almost fucked a sixteen-year-old. So what." I'm going to ignore that because it's Brantley.

"What's with this Raven chick? Is she going to be a King with them? Or queen, or whatever."

Brantley turns to face me, his fingers wrapping around my chin. "How have you not figured all this shit out yet, Tillie. You're fucking smart. Smarter than any girl I've ever met."

"That's not exactly a compliment, Brantley. You don't fuck very smart girls."

"Oh really?" His eyebrow raises, but his half grin is visible.

I ignore it. He continues. "There's only *one* queen in *this* world."

"Madison." I nod, already knowing the answer.

Brantley growls in frustration and then presses his index finger to my forehead. "No, not Madison. She's Bishop's queen, but that's all. You are the queen in this world. By right, and by blood."

What the fuck is he talking about?

He opens the cage door, but the girl is quiet, subdued. He turns to me and gestures to her. "Well, take her back to my house. We've still got to do the meet."

"How? I didn't drive here. I came with you."

He shrugs his shoulders, throwing his keys to me. "We've got other rides." I instinctively seek out Nate. Craving his comfort. My insides yearn for him like a bad habit, one that's worth overdosing on. "He's gone, Tillie. Stop with the thirsty face."

I growl, turning around to the girl before spinning back around to Brantley. "Wait!"

He stops, just before he's about to disappear into the forest. "What?"

"How do I get back?"

He points to the clearing that I came out of. "Just walk straight. It's not far, obviously."

I wave him off and then drop down onto my knees to help the girl.

"Sorry. This might hurt."

I take off the blindfold from her eyes, slowly unraveling it. I toss it across the ground, ignoring the smell of old urine and feces, my attention comes back to her. "Let's get—" I pause, *her eyes*. Her eyes are captivating but familiar. "Do I know you?"

She watches me carefully, her bright turquoise eyes searching mine. She sighs and then shakes her head. "No."

She is downright perfection. I can see why Madison was insecure about her now. Even in this cage, muddy and stinking of piss, she looks like she's walked straight off a Victoria Secret runway.

"But before, you said my name?"

She seems to be looking for something on my face. Or tossing up whether she should be honest with me right now or lie. "I heard The Kings talk about you, that's all…"

I get the feeling that she's lying, but right now isn't the time to press for truths. I take her hand after untying the binds around her ankles. "Let's get you home."

"Oh, I can't. My mom and dad, they…"

I shake my head. "Your—whoever Brantley is to you— is taking you."

"Brantley is my first cousin, and why would he do that? He gives me the creeps."

I hook my arm around hers and start leading us in the direction of where Brantley said. "You and me both, sister. You and me both."

We're trekking through the fallen branches when I hear something rustle to the side.

"Shh," I say, stopping Bailey's movements. She wasn't talking, but at least she's smart enough not to make more noise by pointing that out. "Huh." I shrug as we start moving through the trees again. The wind picks up, kicking my hair all over my face and chills spit through me. "If we could hurry up, that'd be great."

A loud banging claps through the air, causing me to jump. I swear, my head is so dramatic. Bailey doesn't move as if nothing frightens her. The loud bang sounds out again, and I look to the right in the direction it's coming from.

"Let's just go…" Bailey says, urging me toward the opposite direction.

Bang! It's like a door slamming open and shut relentlessly.

"Seriously," Bailey brushes me off. "It's probably just a barn or something."

Before I can contest what she's saying, my feet are carrying me toward the sound.

Bang!

Bang!

I speed up, breaking out into a jog with Bailey being dragged behind me.

The sound gets closer, my heart beating faster as sweat oozes down my head. There's a small clearing, so I shove the branches away, reaching for my phone and turning the light on.

I point it toward the noise and then freeze. The rusted wooden door, the steps leading up to it. The aluminum roof that provides it little shelter.

This was the small shack Daemon drew in his book.

"What?" I gasp, my head tilting to get a better look.

"Tillie, we should leave this place," Bailey says, her eyes flying around the area. I understand her fear. I don't blame her. What with being locked up in a cage for however long, awaiting her fate.

"It's okay. I've seen this place before…" I take a step forward, the damp leaves rustling under the sole of my shoe. The wind whistles a sweet lullaby that sings through the strands of my hair, but like an interrupted record, it suddenly stops at the touch of Bailey's hand on my arm.

I turn to face her. "What?"

She's looking at me with fear, but her eyes frantically go over my shoulder and to the cabin. "We need to leave, Tillie."

My eyes narrow, my suspicions about just how much this girl knows growing a little stronger the longer that I'm in her presence. I rip my arm out of her grasp and turn back to face the cabin. It's not livable, it's barely still standing against the wind. I start taking more tentative steps forward, looking around the yard. There's a small tin roof that leads off to an old garage, but that wasn't in the book. There's a well in the front with an aged splintered bucket dangling from damp rope. My attention snaps to the front door when a dark shadow zips past in a flash.

"Tillie!" Bailey yells, but it's too late.

I zip forward and run straight for the steps, taking them two at a time with my heart thundering in my chest. Ignoring the protesting stairs and old porch wood, I kick open the door that has been slamming open and shut and stand at the threshold, every single inch of myself is saying to run and that I do not belong in this place, but my rebellious side is disputing my logical side. I slide my finger into the small hole where the door handle used to be. Lightning starts flashing above me from the skies, thunder clapping angrily, as if it's remonstrating my being here.

"Hello?" I say, pushing the door open even more.

I feel like a fucking idiot—you know, the kind that asks hello after walking into a place they shouldn't be walking into. It's usually a couple of minutes before they get murdered, too. I shine the spotlight of my phone into the sitting room and gasp, my knees shaking, threatening to give way. A torn up single lounge chair is seated in front of an old fireplace. There's foam spilling out of the split seams, illustrating the lack of usage. It's the exact same chair in Daemon's book. My eyes catch the fireplace since there seems to be nothing else in here where furnishing is concerned. It's dark, like a cemented block of blackboard plastered against the frame of a fireplace, but I find myself squinting in an attempt to get a better look. Something flickers inside of it, too small to have me think maybe I imagined it, but big enough to catch my attention. It floats up, and it's then that I realize it's a firefly. How peculiar, to have a firefly here, in this weather. It flutters again, enough for its light to hit the right angle. The curve of something penetrates the light of the bug, and when I take a small step closer, I almost think—

"Who is there?"

I take another step forward, but a hand slams over my mouth, yanking me back out of the cabin and up against the outside wall. Nate is glaring at me, his hard body up against mine. My eyes go around to look for Bailey, but I can't see her anywhere.

"Why do I always find you getting into trouble?"

I try to yank my face out of his grip, but he doesn't budge, only loosens enough for me to answer. "Maybe because you have a bad habit of leaving me alone."

His eyes flick to the crack of the door. "I don't fucking want you wandering the fuck around without me—especially when you had orders to go straight to Brantley's!"

I shove him away. "Well, maybe I don't fucking take orders from you!"

His body presses into mine farther, his face so close that the tip of his nose touches mine. He growls, "Well maybe you should."

I straighten my shoulders in defiance. "I will never take orders from you."

He thrusts into me harder this time, so hard that I can feel the outline of his jean-clad cock pressing itself against me. "Is that a challenge?" I hate that even when I'm angry with him, completely fucking furious, I still want to tear his clothes off. Nate is pure sex and defiance. He's the feeling of adrenalin roaring through your veins.

"If it was, it wouldn't be yours for the taking." Everything in the air shifts as he grips onto my thighs, lifts me up and wraps my legs around his waist. Even though his face is still painted with the mask, I can make out his expressions in the dim darkness. All that's giving us light is the flashing of dry lightning and the shade of my phone spotlight that is still switched on. It's going to rain down and I'd rather be in the car when it does.

He moves over me, enough to cause friction over my core. I bite down on my lip to stop from moaning, but it's a shit attempt because a breathy moan sneaks out.

"Don't ever get this twisted, Tillie," he mutters as he swipes my shorts to the side, his finger slipping under my panties and circling inside of me. He puts me back down to my feet before yanking my shorts and panties down—leaving me feeling *very* exposed and *very* cold. "I am the only taker when it comes to this." He picks me back up, my head falling backward and smacking against the cabin wall. I don't know what's wrong with me, but everything is heightened and all I want to do is run, fuck, and fuck some more. Maybe they were right, and I did take something. Maybe I can blame my feelings on some random drug that I took.

I grab the back of Nate's neck and smash his lips against mine.

Yeah, I'll go with that.

His mouth opens as his tongue separates mine, licking my own. I suck his bottom lip into mine and then run my tongue across the rim. His own dives back into my mouth and I feel the silver ball skate over my teeth. Nate tugs on the top of my shirt and yanks it down, exposing my nipples to the cold air. He sucks them into his mouth and then comes back up, the bitter air slashing against them violently at his departure. Unzipping his pants, I bite at his neck, and grip his heavy cock in my hand, rubbing him roughly. I'm angry. I'm needing to be fucked.

"Nate, I need you to fuck yourself out of my system," I say, as he slams himself inside of me. I scream as his fist grips my hair.

"No can do. I'm here to fucking stay. Who owns you?"

I don't answer, wrapping my arm around his neck as he slows his pace and vigorously thrusts his cock inside of me with gentle force, my head smashing against the wall to a silent rhythm.

Slam. "Who fucking owns you, Tillie? Whose cock does this sweet little pussy weep for?"

He flicks my nipple so hard that I scream in pleasure but cry out in pain.

"Answer me."

He circles his hips, his arm hooking around my back as he pulls out. He spins me around and snaps my back until I'm touching my toes. He enters me from behind and I have to stay on tippy toes to reach his height. His fingers dig into my hips and he pulls me back a little, more obviously so that we're directly in front of the doorway.

"Who do you think of when you fuck yourself, baby? Who? Who fucking owns this ass and always will?" He thrusts into me slowly now. I feel every inch of him rubbing against me, working me higher and higher. Closer and closer. "Who do you come back to like a good little girl?"

He picks up his pace until he's relentlessly thrashing me. His fingers dig deeper. *I need to let go. I can let go.* My core tightens as I hit the very tip of my pleasure. "You're mine."

I scream out through my orgasm just as thunder claps through and rain starts to pelt down on the tin roof. "I'm fucking yours!"

He loses it, pulls out and empties himself over my ass. I'm still trying to catch my breath when I feel his hand rubbing his warm cum into my ass cheek. "Mmm, fucking missed this view." Then he tugs my head backward by my hair roughly with his other hand and brings the same fingers that were rubbing his cum into me to my mouth. "This is what you think about when you fuck yourself, Tillie, and this is why no matter what happens, you will always..." His eyes flick to the inside of the cabin as I suck his cum off his finger. He smirks. "Be mine."

There's no awkward silence between us as we drive back home. I think that's one of the things that I can appreciate about Nate and I is the fact that it's never "awkward." "Something's Gotta Give" by Camilla is playing softly through the speakers. I try to block out the lyrics that are pungently drilling into my ears when he cranks it down a bit.

"Hungry?"

I chuckle, my eyes feeling heavy. Fatigue has settled into my bones. I drop my head to the cool window. "Starving actually." My thoughts race through all the events that happened tonight, or—I look at the time on the dashboard—last night, since it's a little after one a.m. I miss Micaela. I'm excited to get home to her, but at the same time, I know that I can't exactly see her until tomorrow.

Nate pulls into a drive-through joint, one I don't recognize. "No way!" I look up at the building. The bright red lights flashing up reading *Chinese Takeout*. My head whips to him. "Since when do they have an all-night Chinese takeout?"

Nate just watches me with fascination. After searching my eyes a few times, he shakes his head and smiles. It's a genuine smile, one that doesn't grace the likes of Nate's lips too often. It almost rattles the gates that contain all of my feelings for him.

Almost. Because then I remember who he is and what he's like and like an ice bucket of cold water against a hard erection, I shrivel.

"You like Chinese?"

I wriggle up on my seat and turn off the warmer, since my ass is starting to literally feel like it's on fire and I'm not sure whether it's a mixture of the sex and the semen, but it doesn't feel too great. "Love. It's my favorite food. I want to go to China just to eat the food."

He rolls his eyes and drives us through. "Stop being dramatic, we have this food everywhere."

"Honey chicken!" I say to him before he has even opened his mouth. "And chicken fried rice and deep-fried prawns—oh and Mongolo—"

"—Tillie?" He glares at me over his arm. My eyes flick over him to the bored—and severely tired—looking teen who is staring at me like I'm a reel of some sappy romance movie.

"Hmmm?"

"Shut up and let me order."

I sit back, ignoring how my tummy rumbles at the mere thought of food. "Okay."

We're sprawled out on my bed in the pool house and I've just finished tying my hair into a messy bun and kicked my muddy shoes off when I grab a fork and dig in. "Can I ask you something?" I start, shoving a big bit of deep fried honey chicken into my mouth.

Nate shrugs, sucking the juice off his thumb while still chewing. How can something so normal look stupidly sexy. Oh yeah, because it's Nate fucking Riverside.

"Did I take something tonight?"

He pauses, picking up some chicken with his fingers and putting it into his mouth. He has no manners. At all. He refuses to even use a fork to eat, and that shouldn't be sexy, but it is. "I don't know. I'll find out."

My brows pull in. "Where'd you disappear to while I was with Madison? Did you do the meet?"

His eyes don't meet mine as he continues to eat. "Had business to handle." His eyes darken, a smirk evidently sprawled out on his face. "And *this* meet happened. T'was fucking perfect." He glares at me. "Why? What were *you* doing when you were with Madison?"

For a second, a very short second, I think that maybe he's jealous.

Then he laughs, shaking his head. "Whatever, Tillie. You do what you feel like you need to do, as per usual, and I'll make sure I kill the motherfucker that touches you without my permission, as per usual."

I want to ask him a hundred questions, and then clarify that we are not a couple, but we're actually not screaming at each other right now, we have Chinese food to enjoy, and I'm exhausted from the night, so I put that on the list of things to ask about tomorrow.

I push my bowl away and slip under the covers. "I'm so tired."

"Mmmm," I hear him say as he keeps eating.

"Can you turn the light off when you're done?"

"Yeah."

"Nate?" I murmur through a yawn.

"What, babe?"

"I'm too tired to wash your cum off my ass."

Sleep takes me under before I hear his reply.

CHAPTER 20

Nate

There are times in your life where you battle with yourself. You're equipped with your thoughts as your weapons and your wrath as your armor. This battle is different because you don't have a dominating army. All you have are the remnants of what's left of you after you've ripped yourself apart. So you're probably thinking 'fuck that, that's not a battle worth fighting.' But sometimes, very rare times, someone comes along and shows you that they're worth losing yourself for.

"Nate, son, I need to know where your head is with this?" Hector demands from his leather chair. He leans back, rolling a cigar between his teeth.

My head is between Tillie's legs. "I'm in."

Hector leans forward and Bishop shuffles beside me. The Kings are sprawled out everywhere in his office. "Are you sure? This is a touchy scene with you, what with the involvement of your old man…"

I shrug. "I don't give a fuck about him. I'm in."

Hector watches me, his eyes darting between mine. "Alright, son. I trust that you're ready for this."

Am I? I haven't seen my father since I was probably around three years old. The memory is brief but vivid.

"You shouldn't be here. I told you not to come!" I heard my mom whisper out harshly, closing the door slightly and standing between the crack. I didn't know who she was talking with, but I sat on the top of the stairs and peeked through the barrier. There was a man dressed in a dark suit. He had a funny hat on his head, one that looked like Freddy Krueger. He mumbled something and my mother's body visibly froze. She stepped backward to slam the door in his face, but his eyes shoot up to mine just in time.

"Out of curiosity, why him?" I ask, running my finger over my upper lip. "Don't get me wrong, I don't care, but I just want to know why him."

Hector seems to ponder my words. He's good at that, making you think you have him worked out, or at the very least, working him out.

"Because there's only one man walking this earth that holds about as much power as I do, and that's your dad. But the difference between him and I is that I have morals. I care for the legacy in our world—he doesn't."

I let his words fly over my shoulder.

"So you want me to kill my old man?" I ask, my eyebrow cocked.

Hector shakes his head. "You can't kill someone who lives incognito. No one knows where he is, all we know is that he has his own people. Different from our people."

"So he has The Circle?" Bishop asks, throwing out the question that we all want the answer to.

Hector nods, flicking the ash off of his cigar. "Yes, but more than that, he has the Rebels." The Rebels are old Kings who have done something to break one of the Elite Commandments and have been exiled from their position, whereas The Circle are Kings who have left by choice. It's not ideal to leave The Kings, and is actually fucking frowned upon, but the men who occupy The Circle have warranted reasons as to why they have left.

Hector continues. "The only way that this will work in our favor is if we had Perdita, but we don't completely because of how Katsia was killed. We're lucky they're somewhat taking orders from Khales, but that won't last long. I think the majority of the reason as to why they are, is in an attempt to keep the island contained and their people safe. Right now, no one is working against The Kings, and they won't—mainly because they're smart but a little because they don't have the numbers." He looks directly at me. "Gabriel Malum is on a different spectrum. He can't be killed, and we don't want him killed. He'd be much better as an ally until we get Perdita under control. There are a whole lot of Lost Boys and no one to run them. The island itself is being held up by Khales, as you all know, but like I said, that can't be a permanent thing—as much as she would love to have that power—it's not hers to take."

I kick out my leg, mulling over his words. "So put Peyton on there. Only we know that she's not Katsia's real daughter. They don't need to know that and she's still under our control."

Hector eyes me. "She has run. We're in the middle of finding her, but it seems she has a very good hacker in her pocket that deletes every single CCTV footage of her when it comes up."

I let out a soft growl, fucking annoyed that I let him talk me into keeping her alive. The only reason she has the legs she ran away on is because I didn't fucking snap them. Now I'm irked. Ignoring that, I turn to look at Hector.

"Where do you want me to meet Gabriel?"

CHAPTER 21

Tillie

"Ah...ah..." I blow soft raspberries on Micaela's bare stomach. She's almost five months now and is getting more and more beautiful as the days go on. She reminds me so much of Nate, without the annoying parts.

My phone vibrates in my back pocket. I grab it out, still talking to Micaela. The number is strange.

Do you have it?

What? I click on the number but all it says is **446**

I text back anyway because curiosity gets the best of me.

Have what? Who is this?

I wait. And then wait some more. After twenty minutes of pacing around my room, it dawns on me that they're probably not going to text back. I toss my phone onto the couch and make my way back to the bed, picking Micaela up to put her down for a nap. Once she's all tucked in, I grab Daemon's book and open to the page I was up to. I flick through the pages I've already seen but find myself back to CAPITULUM I and II - the cabin. This time, I run my fingers over every detail, trying to find a clue. So Daemon has been here before, but why did he draw this? Why has he even created this book? Daemon never does anything without a reason. I have started feeling bad for not sharing this with Madison too, but the selfish side of me doesn't want to just yet. Not picking up anything different with the drawings, I flip to the next part. CAPITULUM V. Hands clenching a jail cell, with one pole broken and bent. The ground is shaded to look like 3D. I bring the book closer to my face in an attempt to make out what it is that's laying on the ground.

A short shaped stick connects to an oval-like ball. There are squares and circles colored into it. This is the first item I have come across that has color and so much detail. My stomach curls when I realize it's a baby rattle. I slam the book closed and rush for the bathroom, pulling my hair back as everything I ate over the last twenty-four hours comes spewing out of my mouth. Swiping my lips with the back of my hand, I flush and then go to the sink, washing my hands. I know this. I know what happens. I know the duty of The Lost Boys, and of course I knew Daemon was the Princeps. That should bother me. I peer at myself in the mirror. My ivory skin has been invaded by a flush of pink spread over my cheeks. Cupping water in my hand, I scoop up some water and rinse out my mouth. Why doesn't the fact that I know what Daemon has done impact the feelings I have toward him? If Nate had done something like that, it would bother me so much so that I'd probably accidentally drive his car off a cliff. With him inside. So why not with Daemon? I can see that there aren't many more pages left, thank God, because I don't know how much more I can take.

Making my way back into the sitting room, I check on a sleeping Micaela, my eyes finding its way back to *Puer Natus*.

Nope. Not today.

I pick it up and slide it under my bed, annoyed with my curiosity.

Lying on my bed, I count the lines on the ceiling until I slowly drift off to sleep again, tired from last night.

When I was twelve, I experienced my first crush. I think it was the first time that I ever really crushed on someone. The stomach clenching, heart aching, palm sweating, need to have him. His name was Jordan Samuel. I thought he liked me too until he made an ass out of me in front of the whole school by playing a prank. *"No, Tillie, ew, I don't want to date you... leave me alone. Nerd."* I can still feel the burn on my cheeks and the knife turn in my gut. I quickly learned why they call it a crush. Because the feelings you develop for that person are heavy enough to fucking *crush* you. Love is something else entirely, and although I'm not sure I've found out exactly why I think it's something else entirely, I think the reason why I know is sitting on my bed, playing with our daughter.

"What's up?" he asks when he catches me staring. He woke us from our nap to have cuddles with her.

I shake my head, my eyes falling to Micaela. "Nothing. It's just that I love seeing you with her."

He doesn't answer, so I swing my attention back to him. His go lazy, his lip kicking up in a grin. "Are you swooning?"

I freeze. "What? No..."

He licks his lip and chuckles, picking Micaela up and hugging her into his chest. "Mommy is swooning over Daddy," he coos into Micaela's head, but his eyes are still on mine. There's something different about the way he's staring at me this time. I almost see the Nate I fell for last year. He's something made from witchcraft. Everything alluring and evil, his magic and charisma like a stubborn magnetism that ultimately brings you to your death.

"No, I'm not..." I shake my head, sucking in a copious amount of air.

I back up.

He counters my step and wraps one arm around my back, pulling me into him. "Admit it." He grins. "You think I'm adorable."

I roll my eyes. "I wouldn't say ado—"

His lips gently touch mine, his fingers burrowing into my hair, caressing the back of my head. I part my lips a little and his tongue slips into my mouth. We're interrupted by Micaela's little hand coming up to my face.

We both laugh, pulling back and looking down at her. "She really is fucking perfect," Nate says softly.

"I know," I agree, running my index finger down her cheeks. "We did one thing right, at least."

"Yeah." He smiles and then gestures outside. "Tonight, Hector is organizing a poolside dinner. It'll be all of us, Bishop's cousin Spyder, and a few old generation Kings. I want you to come."

My eyebrows shoot up in surprise. "Really? Why?"

"Because I want all of us there. Micaela is in this world now, too. It's a part of her whether we like it or not. It'll be safe, baby, you don't have to worry about anything happening to her again. She's with me now."

I chew on my bottom lip. I know I trust Nate when it comes to that, and I somewhat trust Bishop, but as far as the rest go—that would be a solid no. I catch Nate smiling down at Micaela, the proud look on his face is all for her. I can't take that away from him. We can talk more in-depth of future "dinners" after tonight, though, because I'm not interested in making this a reoccurring thing.

"Okay," I whisper just as he's placing her down onto the playmat.

"Yeah?" He smirks up at me.

I nod. "Sure. How bad could it be?"

After rushing around the room, packing Micaela's bag, getting ready, choosing a dress, and then blowing out my hair, we are officially late. I tried to wear a black dress, but Nate said the women are to wear red and the men wear black. We dressed Micaela in a little red gown that puffed out around her legs, and then we were ready.

Nate drops down gears and zips onto the road. He watches his speedometer every two seconds though, making sure he isn't driving too fast over the speed limit. Micaela is strapped in the backseat of his car. A few minutes later we pull into Bishop's driveway and Nate reaches forward, handing me a small red velvet box. I run my fingers over it, turning to face him.

"What is it?"

He shrugs. "Open it and put it on." Flipping open the glove compartment, he takes out a box around the same size, maybe a bit bigger. I open mine and my eyes land on a black lace masquerade mask. Only it's not the usual masquerade mask where the lace is pretty with twirls. This one looks a little different. I tie it around the back of my head and flip the mirror down to take a look. I was right, it's very idiosyncratic. Each strap of lace is apportioned specifically on a patterned line to reveal a skull. It's beautiful, but a little frightening. I love it. Nate is tying his at the back of his head.

"Let me see yours."

I can see the side of his cheek smirk. "If you show me yours?"

I roll my eyes, about to say how stupid he is when he turns his face full to mine and my breath catches in my throat. "*Holy shit.*"

Thick white—what looks like bone—is carved into a half skull on his face. There are three holes, two for his eyes and one for his nose. The top of his lip is where teeth are carved into it, with the fangs stabbing downward, pressing against his lower lip. You can still see the sharp edges of his angular jaw and his plump lower lip. It's disturbingly sexy. That mask mixed with his Armani suit that is tailored to perfection, with his sleeves rolled up to his elbows and the bow tie hanging loosely around his collar. My ovaries may not survive this night. I need to calm down.

I lick my lips. "You look great."

He rolls his eyes. "I look better than great, *mea principessa*, quit playin'." He climbs out and I slip out after him.

"Seriously. What is it made of?"

He's in the back, unhooking Micaela from her seat. When he comes back out, his eyes slam into mine. I can make out the curve in his cheek that he's grinning at me.

"If I told you, you wouldn't believe me." Then he shuts the door.

"Actually, I would," I mumble under my breath. Nate tosses the keys to a valet who is standing near a long line of cars. I swear the keys fly in slow motion until my eyes come directly to the boy, who is watching me eagerly.

He's young, maybe sixteen. Very good looking with boy-ish features. His shoulders slack submissively. He bends one leg and bows his head.

Nate snaps at him. "Don't even start, bumboy. Just park the car."

Confused, I look to Nate for answers, but he just shakes his head, hiking Micaela up farther into his chest. "Why did I get the impression that he was about to curtsy me or something?"

Nate rolls his eyes. "You're a fucking Stuprum, Tillie. Get used to it."

"Yeah," I answer, chasing his steps. "But why would *he* curtsy me?"

Nate brushes me off. "Just leave it."

I decide to leave it. For now. I can jump on that subject after the night is over.

Soft music is spilling out from the foyer and the door is opened slightly. I've been to Bishop's parents' house a few times, but it's never looked like this before. There are twisted rope lights illuminating the front door and the foyer inside the house. I can hear the chatter of people mixing with the soft classical music playing. Nate takes my hand, pulling me farther inside the house. To the left of the foyer is a single twist staircase that's all glass with clear railings, leading up to the second level.

"Come on."

I clear my throat, my eyes catching the soft red lights that are melting against the walls in the main living area.

Before Nate can drag me in there, I tug on his hand. "Is this party going to be suitable for Micaela?"

He nods. "Yeah, for now. If not, Mom and Joseph are here."

I chew on my lip and then follow him into the sitting room. There are a few people here, mainly men and a couple of older women. The fireplace is on and I can see now that where the back of the living room meets the foyer, there's a man playing on a piano, dressed in a suit and a metal masquerade mask with a long nose.

"Ah, the prodigy son is here..." A voice pulls me out of my nosey thoughts and I take a second to quickly look over all who are here. The man who spoke is sitting in the main chair of the room with a cigar tucked between his fingers. He's in a suit and again, in a mask similar to Nate's, only his is blood red. I know instantly that it's Hector.

"The boys are outside, but come, I want you to meet a few people."

Nate seems to tense beside me, his eyes watching the man sitting beside Hector. They don't move, and I reach for his hand, but he doesn't allow me to take it. Circling my finger against his palm, he lets out a slow exhale and I feel his fingers slowly stretch, and then intertwine with mine. My heart jolts in my chest and protectiveness seizes me. Right now isn't the time for me to evaluate where the lioness instincts have come from, but they feel good. Powerful. It's then that I realize the depth of my feelings for this impossibly frustrating, painfully sexy, asshole of a man. I'd jump in front of a bullet for him, I'd lay my life down for him, and it's in this moment, that I realize I'm still in love with him. If I ever climbed out of that hole to begin with.

"Shall we go out and see the crew?" I try to coax Nate, what with my newfound senses, I'm feeling a little brave.

Nate grunts, and then pulls me out of the room, toward the kitchen where there is one glass wall that bows out and opens to the backyard and pool area. We see everyone instantly.

I take a seat beside Madison who is next to Bishop. On the other side of Bishop is Brantley, who is wearing a thick black mask that does look really *really* good on him.

Brantley snorts the final line of coke from the table at our appearance. "Something doesn't feel right about tonight."

"What do you mean?" I cut in, mainly because my daughter is here and I don't want any trouble around her. Again, Nate and I have a lot to talk about when it comes to this world.

Brantley's eyes go to Micaela. "She shouldn't be here tonight."

Nate shuffles in the chair beside me, and I look directly at him, ignoring Madison asking Brantley and Bishop something. Nate looks at me, pinning me with a glare, and then goes back to Brantley. "I didn't know he was going to be here."

"Who?" Madison asks, obviously annoyed with Bishop again. Probably because he's still keeping secrets from her. Cue major eye roll.

Nate licks his lip and looks directly at me. "My dad."

"Shit." I sink back against the chair. "That was your dad?"

Nate's jaw flexes from obvious frustration. Brantley is right. We shouldn't have brought Micaela here tonight. I don't know anything about Nate's dad, but that's because Nate and I have never spoken about him. I figured he was just non-existent. It would have explained why Nate seemed to have so many issues.

"Yeah, it's complicated, so Madison, before you hound me for answers, know that I'm not Bishop and I'm not telling you shit."

Madison sucks in a breath. "Nate! I wouldn't!"

"Hey!" I grab Nate's hand again, and I half expect him to shove me away, but he doesn't. His eyes come to mine, and for a second, I see a flash of vulnerability wash over him, but then it's gone, and the cold wall of ice he keeps is back up again. "Don't snap at her."

He leans his head back against the chair, his eyes going to the sky. Micaela starts twisting in his arms and I take her, rocking her softly in my arms.

"So what does this mean?" I ask. "I'm not asking to be nosey or because I feel like I'm owed an explanation. I'm asking because I would like no one to die tonight." I know well and truly how The Kings operate, but I've not seen Hector and his generation—aka—top dogs and how they work, and that somewhat frightens the shit out of me.

Nate shakes his head. "It means after dinner, Micaela is going home with Mom and Joe."

"Agreed." I nod, catching Brantley who is watching Nate and me.

"Are you two finally together?"

Nate rolls his eyes. "Does it matter, motherfucker?"

Brantley grins, his eyes darkening. "Not really."

"—Anyway!" Madison interferes. "What does this mean? How come no one told me about your dad? Why is no one telling me anything."

"Madz?" I squeeze her hand. "That isn't your place to know."

"Thank you!" Bishop yells, and then stands from his chair, storming back inside.

"Thanks, Tillie..."

I sigh. "You know I don't mean it like that, but it's just you know. You can see that he's trying here, but he's about to take Hector's crown, Madison. There are some things that you can't know."

Her eyes fall to her hands. "I know. It's what I'm scared of."

I mentally add a note to have a girl talk to see what's going on between the two of them.

"Dinner's ready!" Scarlet says from the doorway, and I freeze when I see her. God, she's so stunning. Wearing a bright red gown that sticks to her where it should and falls where it can't. Her deep red face mask outlines and hides her features. She's beautiful.

We all make our way into the kitchen where a table big enough to feed over fifty people sits. It's lined with candles and plates filled with the finest food. Actually, the whole room has candles. Some against the walls, on mantles and hanging from a chandelier above our heads.

Nate pulls out my chair and brings a highchair out for Micaela, leaning it back so she can be more relaxed. At least one of us will be. I take a seat. Madison is beside me with Bishop on the other side of her and Hector is at the head of the table beside Bishop. Scarlet is on the other side of the table, with Elena beside her and Joseph next to Elena. On the other side of Hector is Nate's dad, who I have been purposely avoiding, and then there's a couple of people I have not met yet on that side with their wives. On our side is our generation of Kings, with Brantley right beside Nate and then Cash and so on.

"Tillie," Hector says, catching me off guard.

"Yes?" I answer, looking directly at him as two maids come out to line the table with more food.

"I do hope you'll stay after dinner, for the ball."

"We will," Nate answers for me, and then adds, "But Mom and Joe will be taking Micaela home."

"Of course," Hector says, and then gestures to the food. "Dig in."

Dinner goes off without a hiccup, but you can feel the awkwardness throughout the night. I'm on my third glass of champagne when my eyes finally go to Nate's dad.

He's already watching me. I almost drop my fork. Something about him seems familiar, but not enough to catch a clear recollection.

His mask is the same as Nate's almost, and it's eerie how similar they already seem.

I quickly divert my gaze by drinking a large gulp of champagne. Placing it back on the table, Nate slides it away from me. I almost want to smack him, until he leans across and his lips brush my ear in a way that has my core clenching.

"I need you snappy tonight, baby. No more champagne."

He's right. I was being reckless. I pat my mouth dry with a napkin, slightly pushing my plate away. Micaela starts tossing and turning in her chair, so I turn to take her out, pulling the hem of my short strapless dress down.

"She's beautiful, son." I freeze at the unfamiliar voice, knowing there's only one person that can be. Squeezing Micaela's high chair, I think over my options. If I have her in my arms, I can't contain Nate. Not that I think I can, but I have slowly come to realize the effect I have on him at times.

Turning my head to look over my shoulder slightly, my eyes go straight to Elena who is already watching me. She stands from her chair and saunters fashionably toward me.

"Can you take her home?" I ask through a whisper to Elena.

She nods. "Of course, sweetheart. I was hoping you would ask."

I can hear Nate's voice behind me, and warning bells start ringing.

"Would you like her to sleep with me tonight or in your room?"

"Yours might be better because I'm not sure about tonight."

Elena nods, and then her fingers wrap around my chin and she tilts my face to hers. "Be very careful tonight, Tillie. Something isn't right in the air."

I gulp, already heeding the warnings my own gut is sending off. "I will."

She takes Micaela and I press my lips to her soft little head, inhaling her scent. I would do anything to be able to smell her forever. To be able to take her away from this world and give her a normal life.

Nate stands too and gives Micaela a kiss, and then thanks his mom for taking her before taking his place back at the table. I'm still watching Elena leave, longing in my heart. I wish Nate and I could go home with her and cuddle. Just us three. I make time for that in my head, maybe tomorrow we can have our first family day.

Nate's fingers come to mine and he gently brings me back down onto my chair. "This is Tillie."

I slowly take a seat, my heart somewhat calm now that Micaela isn't here. I feel my vulnerability leave with Micaela's departure and invisible war paint smear over my cheeks.

"I know," Nate's father says, his eyes remaining on mine.

"And how do you know this?" Nate asks, shooting back his drink.

Hector interrupts when he clears his throat. "Let's head to the next room."

We all collect our belongings and I watch as Madison glares at Bishop again, storming off outside. I get that she's always angry at him over things that he can't change, but honestly, even I'm getting annoyed with it.

We head into a boudoir tent that has been set up behind the pool.

"What is tonight about?" I ask Nate, leaning into him more as we make our way toward the exotic looking set-up. The tips are stretched high, reaching for the dark sky. There are lights that dangle around the edges and as we get closer, the music becomes more profound and the guards standing out front become larger.

Nate clears his throat, his arm draping over my shoulder. "We don't know. This is new."

"What is new?" I mumble, worried about where tonight may take us.

"This whole fucking thing," he grinds out through a whisper, his hand touching my lower back to lead me into the tent. Waiters are walking around balancing trays on their hands, some with champagne flutes with pink cotton candy sitting inside, and some with small inimitable appetizers. I snatch a glass and take a sip.

Nate glares at me. "What'd I say before."

I wave him off. "I feel like I might need this, and I'm not a light-weight so chill."

He's still glaring at me when Bishop appears with Brantley and Eli.

"Where's Madison?" Nate asks Bishop, and you don't have to be a Nate whisperer to know he's not impressed with whatever is going on between the two love birds.

"Gone," is all Bishop says, and then his eyes come to mine. It's the first time I notice his mask. Black with silver fangs where Nate's are bone. "She won't be back."

I shrug. I'll talk with her tomorrow to see what's really going on between the two of them. If it's still just the secrets thing, I think I'll be more pissed than before. And I'm not even sure with who.

"Where'd all these people come from?" I ask Bishop since this is his parents' house.

He looks around the room. "They're associates of The Kings. Senators, even the fucking President's people are here somewhere. I've seen one or two people from The Circle too." His jaw clenches, his attention going solely to Nate. "Which is what's confusing the fuck out of me. Why would he invite them all here if he was going to kill Gabriel?"

I choke on my drink, my hand clenching around my throat. "I'm sorry, but what and who?"

"Gabrielle is my dad," Nate says to me and then answers Bishop. "Because he doesn't want to kill him. He has already made that clear. But why all of this... tonight?"

Brantley's phone rings. He looks down at the screen and then curses, sliding it unlocked. "Fuck, what?"

Silence.

"No. Leave it alone, Bailey."

I almost forgot about the troubled little teen. I'll need to make some time to visit her.

I perk my eyebrow at Brantley and he flips me off. Because after all, this is my fault. I snort, drinking the rest of my champagne. The lights dim and people quiet down as Hector takes the center of the makeshift stage. A single spotlight beams on him as he flips up the collar of his suit, a smirk on his mouth.

"Thank you all for attending this very last-minute event tonight." He pauses, and I feel Nate's fingers tighten around my hip. We're all watching and waiting for the ball to drop. Hector Hayes doesn't do things in halves. There's a reason why we're all standing here right now. Someone is either going to die or fall. "I bet you're all wondering why I called this meet." Then his eyes come to me. "I want you all to meet Tillie. She's accompanied here by Nate Riverside-Malum..." He pauses, and then his grin deepens farther. "She is a Stuprum. The only *living* Stuprum left—aside from her very own daughter."

"Motherfucker." Nate pulls me closer into him.

The crowd gasps and my eyes catch a figure near the side of the stage. Khales stands in her full black gown, a scowl on her face as she glares at me. I thought everyone knew who I was, but why is Hector making such a scene about it.

Hector lifts his drink. "No pressure. I just wanted to throw this party for her, so everyone knew who she was."

Nate grabs my hand and starts hauling me toward the exit with a few boys following closely behind us.

"What the hell, Nate!" I yell once the cool outside air crashes over my face. "Why are you dragging me out?" He doesn't stop until we're outside the front of the house and the young valet boy scatters off to retrieve his car.

"I can't believe he fucking did that. I don't know about him. That's not the *fuck…*" Bishop yanks the mask off his face, throwing it across the ground. I take that as my cue to finally be able to remove mine, so I do.

"Why? What's wrong with him saying something?"

Brantley is quiet beside Bishop. Nate is pacing back and forth like a caged lion. I look to Brantley. "Why?"

He seems to think over what he's going to say, that same blank look on his face. "Because now that it's common knowledge of you being alive as a Stuprum, remember that no one knew about Peyton, even before we found out she wasn't a biological daughter, you will be hunted, chased, and caged until you are able to claim your given birthright."

I fling my hands in the air. "I don't want to run this fucking island!"

CHAPTER 22

Tillie

"No," I shake my head. Now my heart is slamming against my chest and sweat is trickling down my face. "This is the twenty-first century! You guys cannot walk around in your own little community and think that what you do is okay!"

Nate snatches the keys off the young boy, and it's then that my eyes come to his. I recognize the empty pits that summon me with a simple glare. I exhale, just as Nate opens the passenger door. "You're a Lost Boy."

Nate shoves me in the car, slamming the door and then getting into the driver's seat. He skids out of the driveway, the burned rubber flying up with the smoke.

"Nate! Slow down."

He doesn't answer, his jaw is working on overtime as his eyes stay on the road.

"Nate!"

He drops down to third and floors it forward until we're pulling into our house. He gets out of the car, runs up the stairs to the front door and points to the pool house. "Get in the room, lock the door, and don't open it unless it's me, my mom, or Joseph."

"Okay," I nod, and then quickly jog to the pool house. I know when to question him and when not to. Right now is not the time.

Five minutes pass and I've already changed out of my dress and into some loose grey sweatpants and a white tank when there's a knock on the door. I peek through the blinds and see it's Nate carrying Micaela before quickly unlocking the door and letting him in.

She's asleep, cradled in his arms. He goes straight for the crib and gently places her inside. Hitting on the main light switch, I wait for him to say something. Anything.

He takes his mask off and removes his bow tie. "Tomorrow. We're leaving."

"Leaving to where?" I ask, afraid of the next thing he's going to say.

"Leaving this shit. I can't keep you and her safe if we stay in New York. Shit has changed."

I sigh, taking a seat on the bed. "Nate, I'll just say no..."

He laughs sardonically. "You can't say no, Tillie. You don't have an option."

"Well, we can't run!" I shout, exhausted. "I refuse to give her that life."

His eyes go to the crib. "You have no idea the type of shit that this world does, Tillie. Bishop has always pussyfooted around Madison when it comes down to it, giving her half-truths." His eyes come to mine, and it's the first time I have ever seen fear. It's there, roaring to the surface in the rawest form known to mankind. It hurts that it's Nate emanating it. "I won't lie to you. I won't hide shit from you, mainly because I know you can handle it and also because that's just not me. So I'll tell you now, Tillie, they would hurt Micaela. They would drown her like they have all the others."

Unable to have enough time to wrap my head around the cruel words he just spoke, I say the first thing that pops into my head. "But she's not a swan, why would they hurt her?"

He shakes his head. "You don't get it. They would do that to get to you, and I can't have that."

I exhale, standing to peek down at her sleeping with the angels. Her chest rises and falls, her beautiful long lashes fanning out against her cheeks. "I don't think we should run. I think we should sleep and think about it tomorrow. Your mom, Hector even, I feel like there's more to why he did this tonight. Not just to 'out' me. There's another reason. A reason why your dad was there too, Nate. You're being irrational."

I make my way toward where he's sitting on the bed, stepping between his legs. My hands come to his face, tilting it up to look at me. He looks so vulnerable like this, with me here and him there. It gives me a sense of power. The same reaction I felt earlier tonight washes back over me in a second wave, only this time I'm swimming in lust.

"I want to make you feel better," I whisper, tracing my finger over his lip. Leaning down, I kiss him softly. I stand back up, removing my shirt and throwing it across the room. "Let me make you feel better." I watch as his gaze fades from worried, to feral, they drop down from my face to my breasts.

He doesn't touch me, he stays where he is and growls. "Remove the pants."

I abide, my thumbs hooking inside the waistband of my panties to wriggle them down. I stand naked in front of him, waiting, wanting, needing him to touch me. Touch me in ways he has never touched me before. I reach for the button of his shirt and flick them off, his bare chest sprawling out in front of me. Tracing my fingers over the two large wings across his chest, I want to ask him what they mean, but I'm too afraid it will break the mood, so my hands come up to his shoulders where I push his shirt down his taut arms.

His eyes come up to mine, his hands ruffling through his hair. "Nothing can happen to you or Micaela, Tillie."

"Shhhh." I press my index finger against his lip. "Nothing is going to happen." I go to straddle his hips, but his lips come to my apex. He blows air against my clit and then presses kisses. My fingers dig into his hair, my head tilting back as a moan leaves me. He flicks his tongue inside of me and then licks up again, his hands coming to my ass cheeks. Finally, unable to contain it, I straddle his waist and crawl up his body.

He chuckles darkly, his eyes rolling to the back of his head as he licks his bottom lip, the ball of his tongue ring catching the soft glint of the bathroom light. "You think you're fucking slick sitting on my dick like that, huh?"

I smirk, and then rock myself over him, his cock bulging through his slacks. He flips me over and I scream as he dives on top of me. I use my feet in attempt to push the waist of his slacks down as he flicks open his button. The sound of his zipper dropping singing through the silence.

He sucks my nipple into his mouth and I groan, grinding against him.

Hopefully tomorrow will be a better day.

The next morning, I roll over to Nate who is sleeping with his arm slung over his eyes. I peek under the sheet, getting a better look at his tattoos when Micaela starts stirring in her crib. I stand, throwing on my tank and some panties before tossing my hair into a messy bun.

"Good morning, baby girl!" I beam at her. Her little face lights up like I'm her very own angel. Her small lips stretch wide over her gums giving me the most beautiful smile ever. That looks like her father's. Picking her up, I bring her back to the bed, laying her on the covers.

Nate rolls over sleepily and grins. "Is that my girl?"

His arm hooks around Micaela, and he squeezes her into his chest. My heart explodes with emotion, so I quickly reach for my phone, snapping a range of photos. These memories might fade one day, and I don't want to forget them if they do.

"You feeling better today?" I ask when Nate has rubbed his eyes and is clearly awake.

"Yeah." He clears his throat. "I'll go see Hector today and see what last night was about. Sorry about flipping out on you, it's just when it comes to you and her, I won't take any chances."

"Nate," I sigh, shaking my head. "I love that you would do that for her—"

"—and you…"

I smile, trying to ignore how that makes me feel. When you've wanted someone and something for so long, when it finally happens, the feeling is surreal. "And me. But this is your world. Your family."

He shakes his head. "Baby, if they come for you or her, they will no longer be any of those things. In fact, they'll be my enemies."

That scares me. Not because I know Nate can't hold his own, because God knows he can, but this is The Kings. There's no way.

"Okay," I answer instead, keeping my frantic thoughts to myself. "Well, maybe call Hector, and you can see him later tonight? I sort of want us to have a family day today. You know, since we haven't had one of those yet."

A lazy smile spreads over his face. "Yeah, I'd like that. Give me a second." Reaching for his phone, I pick Micaela up and take her into the bathroom to change her. He's still on the phone when I enter the bedroom, but he's not being hostile, so I take it as a good sign.

"Yeah, good," he murmurs, and then hangs up the phone.

The truth is, I don't know what he and I are, or where this is going, but over the last twenty-four hours, there has been progress. So I'm going to go with it and see where that takes us.

"What's the plan, do you have one or had you not thought that far ahead?" Nate asks, taking Micaela from me and heading into the kitchen to feed her.

"I hadn't, but I'm sure we can think of something." Normal. I want one normal day.

The day goes rather quickly. Nate decided to take her to a small beach that his mom used to take him to as a young boy. He just couldn't resist himself when we walked past a Tiffany & Co store and purchased a little silver charm bangle for Michaela. Her first of many, was his exact words. We snapped a whole bunch of photos and even went as far as to burying Nate in the sand with Micaela next to him sprawled out on a towel, laughing. Her eyes are always on her daddy, and his on her. Their bond is something indescribable. Unmovable. After the beach, we went to get ice cream and Nate fed her up on a whole bunch of sugar and food that no child her age should be having. It's sundown and Micaela is yawning when we finally head home. Taking the steps two at a time, Nate's hand touches mine just as I'm entering the pool house.

"Hey."

"Hey," I answer back, searching his eyes. I saw Nate today. Really saw him, in his element with our daughter, and it was a beautiful thing.

His fingers graze my cheek. "I might be out late, but I'll come in in the morning."

I smile, knowing that this is probably the closest I've ever felt to him. I want to wrap this feeling around me and keep it forever. "Okay."

He leaves, after kissing me and Micaela on the lips and I get busy with her bath. I put some random playlist through the sound dock and wash her up, dressing her in nice warm pajamas. When it's time for her to go to bed, I pull out a children's book that I found in the closet. The worn crinkled edges exhibit the age. I'm guessing over one-hundred years.

"Dorothy lived in the midst of the great Kansas prairies…"

Minutes later, I'm lost in the story when I hear Micaela snoring softly, her body limp. I take this time to twirl one of her curls around my finger, smiling down at her. She may have come unexpectedly, and her father and I may battle like War and Peace, but if everything I have lived through would bring me to this very moment, I would go through it over and over again just to have her in my arms, like this, snoring her sweet little head off. With my heart full and my legs throbbing from our long day, I gently tuck her into bed and press a few too many kisses on her warm forehead, closing my eyes as her soft inhale and exhale of breaths mist against my cheek. I gave life, and I would take one if it meant saving her.

"I love you, my angel. For always and forever."

With a smile on my face, I slip under the covers, turn the lamp off and drift to sleep. In the back of my mind, I argue with myself on whether or not I locked the door, and just as I get up, I remember pushing the lock in after Micaela's bath. Sleep sucks me deep.

When I was thirteen, I had a crush. This one was different from my last. Jordan Samuel was innocent. As innocent as butterflies fluttering in your belly. This one was electricity, zapping through my guts.

"What's your name?" I asked the boy.

He had been following me since my twelfth birthday. I noticed him one day, standing at the gate of my school. He looked odd, out of the ordinary, standing stagnant in black overalls and a suit like shirt underneath. He must have been a little younger than I was. I wasn't afraid of him. The first day at school, he watched me as I walked out of the gate and headed back to our trailer. He followed me all the way there, and I don't know why, but I never asked him what he wanted. This went on for weeks. We didn't speak, he would just watch me walk home, every day. Following a close distance behind me. On the sixth week, I decided to walk beside him.

Again, we didn't say anything, I just walked beside him right until we got to the trailer, and then he would leave. To where, I wasn't sure. Today was the first day that I had spoken to him. A stranger I had become so comfortable with, a stranger I had developed a crush on. I never noticed until today how his long lashes curled around his dark beady eyes. Or how his ivory skin was blended to perfection, or how his cherub bow lips managed to always stay in a flat line. I crushed on him, and I crushed on him hard. For six months. Now, it was time I asked him what his name was.

He stopped, just short of the trailer park gate. He opened his mouth, his eyes attempting to say the words that his mouth could not. I waited for him to speak. I had dreamed of what he might sound like. Would he have a cute voice? But he just turned and left. Clouds caved into the sky and rain started pouring down from the heavens.

That was the last time I ever saw him.

And I never got his name.

I wake the next morning, stretching my arms wide. My sleep last night was quite broken, and I don't know why, but I found myself tossing and turning all night. Waking up at 3:05 a.m., I even went so far as to check my messages and then curl back to sleep. I never wake through the night. Once I'm out, I'm out, but something about last night had me sitting uncomfortably, even if I wasn't completely aware of it. It either has to do with the dinner party at Hector's, or me remembering my crush.

Noticing Micaela not doing her daily wriggle routine from her crib, I smile, whisking the blanket off my legs.

"Well at least one of us slept like an angel."

I tiptoe toward her crib, and my smile instantly drops. Terror seizes every inch of me when I see that she's not only not moving, but her skin has turned purple.

"Micaela?" I whisper, shock capturing my hands. In a rush, I tear off her blanket and pick her small body up, noticing how heavy she is. *No, no, no. She doesn't feel right. She doesn't feel right.* "Micaela!" I scream, cradling her to my chest. "No. No. No." I shake my head, rocking her back and forth on the ground. "I'm dreaming. I'm just dreaming. I will wake up, this will be a nightmare." I squeeze my eyes closed, and then open them. I'm still here, in the pool house, with Micaela in my arms. I look down at her sweet face, her lips are parted slightly, with lines circled around her mouth. Her eyes are closed peacefully, and her cheeks are swollen purple. I graze my finger over them, the old hard sensation so unfamiliar. "No." Tears pour over my face. "It's a dream."

I stand from the floor, gently placing Micaela on my bed. I tuck her small blanket into the sides of her body and rush into the bathroom. Yanking open the drawers and cabinet, I search for the one thing that will be able to pull me out of this dream. This nightmare. My eyes land on the silver razor and I grab it, rushing back to the bedroom. Even in my dream, I don't want her to be alone. It's okay. I will wake up and my beautiful baby will be here again. The angels can't have her. She's mine. I press the tip of the razor into my wrist and watch as blood spills over the incision, and then I yank the blade downward, toward my elbow.

CHAPTER 23

Nate

Have you had your world ripped apart so fiercely that it leaves you with nothing but the shell of the man you used to be?

Because I have.

CHAPTER 24

Tillie

A beeping clock echoing off of empty walls. The sound of haunting church bells on a Sunday night mass. *Pain*. Empty thoughts from a vocal mouth. My eyes open, and I don't move. The throbbing sting from my arm is enough proof that last night happened. *It happened*. I shoot up from the bed, tearing the lines out of my arm. Madison and Tate are curled together on a small sofa, sleeping.

"Where's my daughter. Where is she." I rip the sheet off me and swing my legs over.

"Tillie!" Madison rushes over, her arm coming around my back.

"Where is she. I need to see her. I need. We, I, we read *The Wizard of Oz* last night. She needs to know how it ends. She needs to know the end of the story. I need to tell he—"

"—Tillie." Madison's cheeks are wet with tears, but I don't care. I need her. I need Micaela.

"We can see her soon. Not right now, okay?" Her coaxing me only makes me angry.

My eyes go to Tate who is now sitting up, sniffing back her tears. "I'm—I'm sorry, Tillie." Tate bolts out the door, bursting into tears.

I have nowhere inside of my head that I want to retreat to. Everywhere is a memory of Micaela. I find myself looking directly into Madison's eyes. Smoked Macha powder stirred with honey. "Where is she?"

"I'm sorry, Tillie…"

"Stop fucking saying sorry and tell me where she is!" I grab my chest and squeeze. Waiting. Waiting for simple words to extensively split me open.

"She passed away in her sleep—"

My legs give out, dropping to the ground. Reality blurs in and out. She was right here. She was mine, and I was hers. I was supposed to take her for her first day of school, be the tooth fairy when she lost her first tooth. I was supposed to watch her

grow and mature into the girl she was going to be. I will never know what she was going to grow to look like. Whether she would be sassy and smart, what her voice would
sound like when she'd ask me for another cookie.

Another pang of pain slices through my chest, and my breathing becomes slow and
labored. I can hear the gushing of blood pound behind my eardrums.

"The angels can't have her," I whisper, rocking back and forth on the ground.

I can see Madison out of the corner of my eye, crying hysterically while trying to
get me up, but her movements are in slow motion. My once colorful world has now fallen
to a dull sepia.

I lost my angel, now I want to sin.

I stand from the ground, straightening my shoulders. Madison swipes the tears from
her cheeks.

"Tillie. We can leave. Come on."

I shake my head, trying to build a wall where my broken heart lays beating to a strum
that orchestrates the sound of death. "I can't leave without her."

"Okay," Madison says, and then walks toward the same doors Tate departed out of.
"Give me a second."

"Madison." I stop her movements. She pauses, her hand on the door. Like she knows
what I'm about to say and she's dreading it. "Where is Nate."

She sucks in a breath, and I watch as her shoulders tremble.

"I'm sorry, Tillie."

Then she leaves, the swing of the doors the only thing left inside this room. My eyes
close and I lean over the bed, my hand coming to my stomach. After everything she went
through. My head throbs and my fingers itch for something. Anything to take this pain
away. To take away the hollow pit that's now leaking residue out of my chest. Madison
returns with a man dressed in a long white coat and a woman attired in a blue plaid dress
that hangs down to her shins.

"Hello, Tillie, I'm Doctor McIntyre and this is one of the nurses, Jenny. I'm very sorry
for your loss. Are you prepared to have a talk, or it can wait for another time?"

I take a seat on the bed, shaking my head and swiping away my tears angrily. "I want
to know everything right now."

I zone out but hang off of every word that he spews. "There are no known causes
for SIDS, just that recent studies have shown it may be connected to a defect in the portion
of the baby's brain that controls breathing…" I hear the word "healthy" said every two
seconds, and that it is very "common" in children under the age of one.

Something feels wrong. Blinking back the tears, my eyes come to his. They feel heavy
and lazy, tired from being awake. Tired from being alive. Tired of breathing air that I do
not deserve to breathe. It should be her breathing, not me.

"When can I see her?"

His hands come to the front of his body, and I watch as his thumbs twirl together
like small tornados. Maybe it's a nervous trait. Who knows.

"We can release her into family care as early as tonight."

I look to Madison. "Her funeral."

Madison hasn't stopped crying and I have to fight the urge to scream at her. I know she
loved Mi—my daughter. But I need her, someone, to be strong for me right now because
I'm not feeling very resilient. I feel like Icarus, flying too close to the sun, only my wings

don't melt off because I fly straight into the core and burn myself to ash. I need to be able to break down. I suck in a breath.

"I will go back to her father's house and start making plans."

"One more thing," the doctor says, his eyes dropping to my arm. I follow his line of sight, pressing down on the thick bandage.

"I wasn't trying to kill myself. I thought I was dreaming. I tried to wake myself up," I admit truthfully.

His eyes crinkle around the edges. "Very well."

Madison signs me out after I've changed into some clothes Tate had brought to the hospital. I'm guessing The Kings have some sort of play into how fast I was discharged, but I don't question it.

Tate brings her car around the front of the hospital. The silence is haunting, and every single mile we drive away from the hospital I feel like I'm letting her down. She will be all alone. Alone without me. What happens on the other side when people die? Will she be sitting in purgatory wondering where her mommy is? Will she be playing with the angels? Will they know that she likes her milk a little warmer than average and that I didn't get to finish *The Wizard of Oz*? Will they read it to her for me?

I swipe the tears that fall down my face.

"She's all alone," I whisper, tucking my head between my knees. "Why did this happen to me. Why her. Why. Why would God do this, take my daughter. Who would be so cruel." I have never considered myself a religious person, but I've always thrown the word "god" around the place when I'd need to accentuate a point of safety or serenity. Now the only place I'll be throwing his name is in the trash. I'm a fucking atheist, a heathen, a goddamn vixen with no soul.

CHAPTER 25

Tillie

Seven. That's how many people have asked me where Nate is. The next person who says his name, I'm going to punch straight in the face. We arrived back to Nate's house a little over two hours ago, and since being here, Elena and Joseph have started arranging the house for visitors. I want to bring her home so all those close to her can say our final goodbye. Elena and Joseph agreed. Elena hasn't stopped crying, and Joseph has a constant painful look in his eyes. I've been curled in the corner of the sitting room that overlooks the backyard and pool for the past hour, a bottle of Jack Daniels in hand. Alcohol has never been my go-to, in fact, I don't drink much at all compared to other girls my age—friends included. I just need something. Anything to numb the everlasting pain that's throbbing in my chest. But every sip I take, the more my feelings become heightened and the reality of everything comes crashing into me. I haven't been into the pool house, and I won't. So instead, I rummaged through Daemon's clothes in his room to put on one of his hoodies, but Daemon owned suits, not hoodies. I grabbed a black velvet suit jacket and rolled up the sleeves slightly, treading back down to my spot. I can't go into Nate's room, that would mean seeing M—my daughter's bed and items she had in there. I could go into Madison's room, but she has locked herself in there since we got back. I don't want to disturb her. I've never felt grief like this before. Daemon was the only person I lost who meant something to me, but even his death seems like the shallow end of the pool when it's matched with this. My chest is hollow with nothing but a gaping hole where my heart used to be.

"Tillie?" Elena says, coming to sit beside me. She rubs my arm in an attempt to soothe the pain, and the very hurt side of me, which is every side, wants to laugh in her face and swear at her. But I don't. I take another long pull of the whiskey instead. "She will be here soon. Would you like to come and wait at the entrance for her with us?"

I swallow the burning amber liquid that ignites my internal organs. *If I swallowed a lit match, would I burst into flames?*

I don't answer. I stand. Because of course I will. I will do anything and everything I can until she is—I take another drink, brushing past Elena and heading for the front door. Their house resembles The White House, a modern-day plantation style home. There are around six large pillars that line the front of the wrap-around porch. It's large enough to fit a small army.

When I step outside, I see Madison sitting on a swing seat, her legs pressed to her chest and her forehead resting on her knees, her shoulders shaking. My eyes flick up to Tate who is on the other side of the porch, her arms crossed around her stomach. Joseph takes Elena's hand and tugs her under his arm where she loses herself and cries uncontrollably. A white Cadillac pulls up with a funeral home sticker on the side. It's now that I realize Joseph had probably already organized everything for me. I take note to thank him later when I don't feel like any sudden movement is going to rip the flesh off my bones. My eyes flick over the funeral car when I see Nate's Audi R8 roll up behind, and then Brantley's V8 behind that, and Bishop's Maserati behind Brantley. There are also two black Range Rovers behind Bishop. It's hard for me to be happy to see Nate, because I don't feel happy. I don't feel anything but pain, but I know I'm grateful that he's here. Me second guessing him on it was unreasonable of me. They all climb out of their cars, but my eyes can't move from Nate.

I can only make out the sharp edges of his sharp jaw because he's wearing a black Nike hoodie and cap on his head, covering his face. He's wearing dark ripped jeans and combat boots. His jaw is set in stone, and even though I can't see his eyes, I know that I don't want to. I don't want to because the one thing, person, that Nate cherished and loved more than anyone in this world is now gone. I fear for what is going to be left of him now.

The boys go to the back of the hearse and the director steps away, sensing the sudden hostility. I step backward, my back crashing against the house. *Inhale. Exhale. Inhale.* I watch as the boys surround the back of the car like a pack of loyal wolves, and then Nate pulls at something softly, and the small pink casket comes slightly into view. I burst into tears, my hand coming to my chest to rip my heart out so it can stop hurting. I can't do this, I can't survive this. I squeeze my eyes shut, and practice my breathing again, only when I open them, my eyes come straight to the sight in front of me. Nate at the front of the coffin, holding the top right, Bishop behind him holding the bottom right, Brantley at the top left, and then Cash behind him, holding the back. I'm too busy zoned in on the coffin, that when I look up to Nate, I freeze. He's already glaring at me, the rim of his hoodie draped over the better part of his eyes.

His lip curls.

There's my answer.

I shiver, straighten my shoulders and wait for them as they pass me and head into the house. I follow behind them until I reach the kitchen. I know that Elena said that they'll keep her casket closed, because I pushed it. I don't want everyone to have the last memory of her being what she is now. I want them to remember her bright smiles.

Heading straight for the sitting room, the boys have already placed her small casket onto the stand, for a moment, I test my control, my eyelashes fluttering closed. I can't contain the pain anymore. I can't do anything. I know that this is a time to be strong, but I feel like I'm walking around soulless. A mask of absolute tragedy. Everyone is watching me, waiting for my reaction. I hate it. Despise it. She was the one person I had in my life who was a constant. She was my forever. I step backward, shaking my head as my heart seizes in my chest. I back into something hard and arms come around my stomach.

AMO JONES

"Come sit down." Brantley's voice utters into my ear. He takes my hand with his and drags me toward the over-sized U-shaped lounge that has been moved to face the casket. Brantley takes a seat and then yanks me down beside him. My eyes go to Nate, who is sitting beside the coffin, his elbows resting on it and his hands buried over his face. He doesn't move. He stays in that position. Stationary.

"I don't want to feel like this anymore."

When Brantley doesn't answer, I look directly at him. His face is an inch away from mine, his warm breath cascading over my swollen lips.

He licks his and then bites down. "You won't. It will always be there, but it won't always hurt this bad."

"Bullshit, Brantley." I take my eyes away from his, back to Nate. He's laying his head on the casket now, his head facing the opposite way to us. "I'm scared for him."

Brantley leans back on the sofa, his arm coming behind me. "You should be."

Madison and Bishop walk in and come sit beside me. Madison's hand rests on my knee. "I don't know what to say."

"Nothing will be nice," I answer, sick of talking and answering questions.

"Okay," she whispers, leaning her head on my shoulder. "Are you sure you want to do the burial tomorrow?"

I nod, my face blank. "Yes."

I shoot up from the couch and make my way into the kitchen. I start rustling through the cupboards in search of an old friend.

"Jack. Hello." I twist and flip the cap off, taking down a tumbler glass and pouring to the rim. Leaving the bottle there, I head back into the sitting room and flop down beside Brantley again, who is eyeing the glass skeptically.

"Now is not the time to be looking like that," I snap without looking at him. "You know better."

He snorts. "I'm not judging. Hell no."

I lick the hot liquid off my lips and look at him. I mean, really look at him. His brazen prominent jaw and swollen lips. His ink dark eyelashes and eyebrows, and the way his skin looks as though he's been baking in the sun for a couple of days. That's just Brantley though. Then his eyes come directly to mine.

"I thought that we already had this discussion about you looking at me like that, Tillie. Trust me, I'm sorry for your loss, but don't test my restraint, because I have none."

The rest of the night goes slow. Painfully slow. Everyone moves around me while I stay still, in my very own haunted tranquility. Drinking. When midnight hits, and everyone is either asleep in the sitting room or have left, I let out a soft cry. My glass slips from my fingertips, dropping to the ground. Madison and Bishop are asleep on the sofa and Brantley is right beside me, one arm over his eyes as he sleeps. Eli and Hunter are sprawled out on the floor and Tate is curled in Jase's arms beside them.

Nate hasn't moved. He's still beside her coffin, his head turned the other way. Guarding her like a prowling lion. Now that it's quiet, and the room isn't busy, I let the tears run down my face uncontrollably. My shoulders shake, my stomach twists and pulls my organs in the palm of grief's hands. My chest is numb. Either from the alcohol or from my pain threshold being completely razed. Everything is anesthetized by my anguish. My eyes sting from being so swollen and my cheeks burn like sandpaper has

598

been scrubbed over them harshly all day. Brantley's leg is pressed against mine, setting off warm ripples shooting through my leg. The only sensation I can feel right now. A lifeline, maybe. I'm not sure.

Nate's movement catches my eyes. The only light coming from the outdoor pool lights breezing in through the high floor to ceiling glass windows and door. He turns his head to face me, his eyes connecting directly with mine.

Fear slams into me at one-hundred miles an hour. My mouth opens and then closes. Fuck it. I already know that he absolutely despises me, so I may as well ask him right now, while it's just us two.

"Do you blame me?"

He doesn't answer, but his eyes don't move off me either.

"It's not about you, Tillie." The venom that drips off every syllable is evident. I don't need him to say anything else to know that he does. "But you have until the day after tomorrow to move the fuck out of my house and out of my life."

I wince, even though part of me knew that was coming. "I will." *He's hurting too, Tillie. He's hurting too.*

Then he sits up, shoving his hands into the pockets of his hoodie. "You are the worst thing that ever happened to me." I don't answer, because I know he's not done. "You gave me life." He looks at the coffin and then comes back to me. "And then ripped it away from me like you're the goddamn Grim Reaper."

"Nate..."

"Save it," he exhales calmly, his head tilting back to rest on the chair. "I don't want to hear shit."

"I lost her too," I whisper, the first time I've ever said it out loud. I choke on my next words. "I didn't even get to finish *The Wizard of Oz*. We started it the night before, and—" My words are mumbled, unable to speak.

Nate stands, and storms out of the room. I've pissed him off. I spoke when I shouldn't have. I squeeze my eyes closed and stand, making my way to his now vacant chair. My hands tremble as I reach out to touch the smooth glossy casket.

I clench my fist when I realize I can't touch it. Fear rips through me. How do you survive a war that has one enemy—you.

I jump when I see the edge of the book I was reading her last night come into view. I see Nate's tattooed hand, the words E L I T E stamped into each finger sprawled out over the cover. I lick my lips, swiping away the tears.

"Finish it."

When I reach for the book, he takes a seat on the chair and yanks me down onto his lap. His arms feel like home, but the feeling that's crashing into me is something more distant. Like this is the beginning of the end between him and I. For good.

I stare at the book for—I don't know how long. The last time I held this, we were sitting together on my bed. I zone in on a small speckle of scratch near the Lion's orange mane. That imperfection was there last night. Before all of this happened. It sounds silly, but it's as though everything is rolling into me in brutal waves and I'm for sure about to drown.

"Finish it, Tillie," Nate says, snatching the bottle of Jack that was on the small table beside his chair.

I clear my throat, only for it to swell again and tears to pour down my eyes. I flip to the page I was up to and begin reading. We read Micaela her final story, even though hers ended far too early. Like an unfinished project.

"*Then that accounts for it. In the civilized countries, I believe there are no witches left; nor wizards, nor sorceresses, nor magicians. But, you see, The Land of Oz has never been civilized, for we are cut off from all the rest of the world...*"

I think to myself about the irony of that line. For I too, know of a place similar to Oz...

CHAPTER 26

Tillie

I wake the next morning to the scent of cedar, leather, and soap surrounding me, with familiar tattooed arms and a hand possessively wrapped around my upper thigh. Nate has me curled into his chest like a baby. I slowly inch up until I see his face tilted back, asleep with his hoodie completely covering his eyes and nose. I slowly wrench myself out of his grip, before my eyes come to everyone who *was* asleep in here last night awake and watching us.

I divert my gaze and slip off his lap quickly, no longer scared to wake him.

Madison is crying again.

I rake my fingers through my hair and grab the almost empty bottle of Jack that's on the floor, taking a sip.

"Leave it alone."

They all stay silent. I slowly stumble my way into the kitchen. I know that I should tidy myself up, but why. What's the point of putting makeup on if my grief is just going to wash it off. There is one thing I want to tackle before the burial. I need to box up her belongings and I'd rather do it sooner than later. Like ripping off a band-aid, only so I can spill my blood all over the floor for everyone else to see.

Elena comes into the kitchen. "Hi, honey. Would you like some coffee?"

I shake my head, my fingers clenching around the bottle.

Her eyes find the movement, but she offers me a small smile instead of judgment. "Very well."

"I was hoping to box up her belongings today if that's okay. If I'm going to be out of here by tomorrow, I'd like to get this part out of the way now. While I'm feeling brave enough to do it, at least. I know after today I won't be feeling very brave."

Elena pauses, her eyes are rimmed bright red and the dark circles that are indented under them have intensified. "You don't have to leave, Tillie. You will always be family."

"I appreciate all that you have done for M—us. I do. Thank you. But there's no need for me to be here anymore." I know I have no family. Nowhere to live. I leave that out though because despite it all, I know what I have to do. I also know that what I'm about to do is going to change the course of the way things go from here on out.

Elena doesn't fight it. She nods and carries on, off to find the boxes I need. Once she's gone, I shove my phone into my back pocket, push my hair into a high messy ponytail and tread my way over to the pool house.

I stop at the bottom of the steps. My heart pounding in my chest. Good to know it's still there.

Slowly, I take the steps up until I'm face-to-face with the front door. My hand comes to the handle and I twist it open, stepping inside and flicking on the lights.

I suck in a breath and hold it in.

One.

My eyes fly around the room. The room that still has the innocent smell of baby powder swimming in the particles in the air. *Two.* My eyes go to her crib. Images flash through my brain of how I found her. Then they drop to the blood on the floor from when I cut myself open. *Three.* My hand comes to the bandage instantly. I look to the small clothes, the baby bag, the toys. *Four.*

Five. I let out my breath at five, taking a step backward. It is interfered with when I crash into a hard body.

Spinning around with tears pouring down my face, I find Nate, searching my face.

"I hate you. I fucking hate you, Tillie. But I'm going to be here for you until she's gone because I know that this is about her right now." He side-steps around me, entering the bedroom. "I'm not doing this alone."

I don't want him to. Even though I don't understand why he hates me so much right now—even more than before—I enter the room and slam the door shut behind myself. He hits the sound dock on and scrolls through his phone until a random song starts playing. He turns it up. Loud. The walls shaking from the music, then he takes his hoodie off and starts picking up all of her stuff in the room.

I understand why he put the music on so loud. It's to drown out our emotions so we can do what we need to do. I appreciate it. I exhale a shaky breath and get started on cleaning up the blood. Once that's done, I start folding her blankets from her crib, the tears falling down my face now a constant waterfall. They don't stop. "Lost in Paradise" by Evanescence starts playing and I have to fight the urge to change the song. I quickly fold the blankets up and put them in a box and then start taking the crib down while Nate rummages around the room in speeds so fast I barely catch what he's doing.

Two hours later, everything that meant something to me is packed away in insignificant boxes. That's all I have left of my daughter.

"Have a shower. We're leaving here in forty minutes."

I go to say that I don't want one—that I don't care. Instead, I walk straight for the bathroom, slipping in and out of the shower when a silver bracelet on the floor catches my eye. It's the one Nate bought for her on our family day. *It was supposed to be the first of many.* I take the bracelet and squeeze it in my fist, my eyes coming to the mirror. I'll keep this forever. It will be the anchor I use to remember who I used to be.

The drive to the cemetery was long because the Malum plot of land is on the other side of New York. I didn't ask why she was going to Malum and not Riverside. I figured Nate is doing what he thinks he needs to do and if it was Riverside, then it would be

Riverside. The line of cars is a little excessive. I'm pretty sure I had never met these people before, but again, Nate probably had. Who knew, The Elite Kings Club have hearts.

I climb out of the back of the car, Nate, his mom, Madison's dad, and Madison were in and start walking straight for the pit.

I need this day over with. I cannot take it for much longer. I need to put her to rest. The closer I get to putting her to rest, the more my blood pumping through my veins feels like poison.

I stand the closest to the empty pit and wait.

And wait.

People eventually crowd around, and the casket is finally sitting on the top of silver poles. I watch, zoning everyone else out as it slowly lowers into the ground while the minister sputters off lines from the fucking Bible. Since she has gone, I feel like I've died one-thousand deaths, only every time I die, I wake up and she's still not here. I pick up a tulip and press my lips to the smooth petals before throwing it down.

"Mama loves you, baby girl. Forever and for always."

I turn and walk away. I'll wait for them in the car.

I wait for an hour before Nate and his family start coming back. He's wearing a suit fit for a king. I giggle to myself at my thoughts. *King.* Tailored to fit every single inch of him perfectly, and a pink tie.

Pink. Her favorite color. Well, at least I assumed it was. Nate joked once about it because she would always grab my hair.

I take another sip of whiskey as the doors to the limo all open.

Everyone slides in, but it's a blur. I'm hot, sweaty and bothered. Everything aches. I'm sick of being in pain. I want my daughter back in my arms. The thoughts are crippling. I slam my eyes closed and bring the rim of the bottle to my mouth, taking large gulps.

Elena sits beside me on one side and Nate sits beside Madison opposite us. I don't look at him because I can't. The drive home is far longer than the drive there and every single mile feels like the air is being extracted out of the car.

I feel reckless.

I feel lost.

But most of all, I feel nothing like me.

CHAPTER 27

Tillie

We're all in the pool house later that night, most of us blinded from top-shelf alcohol.

"I'm leaving tomorrow," I slur, standing on the middle of the coffee table. Nate and Brantley are behind me stretched out on the sofa and Bishop and Madison are in front of me on the lazy boy. Hunter, Jase, and Eli were here but disappeared, probably when they saw how dark we all were feeling. People mourn in different ways, yes, but I also feel like it depends on the ferocity of the hole that person leaves in your life. The bigger the hole, the bigger the mess.

I lift my arm high, tears slide silently down my cheeks. Not an obvious tsunami like earlier.

"Shut up, Tillie," I hear from behind me, and I don't have to turn to know who it was.

I ignore Nate and continue dancing to "Deuces" from Chris Brown. The slow song possessing every limb of my body. If only music could seize every thought too, turning them into simple music notes instead of the ghosts that meet me behind my closed eyes. I will never recover from losing her. Not ever. There's no point in me living the rest of life within boundaries. It's time to shove those to the side. I just want to feel good. Sweat slides down between my boobs as I continue to dance until I trip and fall, subsequently landing on Brantley's lap. "Talk that Talk" by Rihanna starts playing next. I lick my lip, my eyes dropping to Brantley's mouth.

Brantley smirks, his arm tightening around my back. He leans in closer, his lips touching my ear. "Careful, *princessa*. You're fair game now."

My eyes flick to Nate, who is watching us carefully, a grin on his face. He has no shirt on and loose faded blue jeans. His muscles clench with every movement. I know how ripped he is, but that's not what I'm looking at right now. Right now, I'm lost in a trance that is his stupid fucking eyes.

"Fair game?" I ask, my voice coming out way too soft. I don't even feel hurt. There's so much of myself that is in pain right now, that nothing, and I mean *nothing*, can touch the pile of shit that's already inside of me. Nate included. Seems he's almost willing to test that theory though.

The song switches to "Blueberry Yum Yum" by Ludacris, just as Nate blows out a cloud of smoke from inhaling his joint.

"Yeah, B. You're fair game." Nate flicks his hand out, gesturing to my body but looking at Brantley. "Have at it. You two have been dripping all over each other from the beginning. Go on." He leans back on the sofa, his legs spread wide with a joint hanging between his fingers. I snort, turning around to face Madison and Bishop but staying on Brantley's lap. Brantley doesn't touch me. Merely leaves me there, allowing me to grace his lap with my presence. Trust me, any girl who Brantley doesn't want on his lap will not be there. He's particular with who he allows to bounce around on him, even more so than Bishop. I swear these guys are the biggest motherfuckers to ever walk this shitty, fucked up world.

I watch as Madison takes a line of cocaine and then clears her nostril, grinning at me. "Care to pop that cherry?"

I want to.

No I don't.

Yes, I do.

Wait. "Will it fix me?"

Madison cranks her head. "No. Drugs don't fix people. They just numb the broken ones."

I could do with some numbing. I gesture for the rolled up hundred-dollar bill and reach for it. Last time I did this Nate whacked it out of my hand—even though I wasn't going to try it that time. This time, he's ignoring me. Not caring. Cold and distant. I don't blame him.

I lean down and snort the line, the taste of harsh chemicals hitting the back of my throat on the first suction. I clear my nose and lean up, handing it back to Madison. Everything feels semi-better. Like I can handle being alive for a little longer. Maybe this isn't too bad. I could do this. For now. Turning around to face Brantley, he's grinning at me in the way Brantley does. Sometimes, which admittedly isn't often because he's so serious. When his legs widen, and he looks to his dick before looking back up at me under hooded eyes, I almost jump on him. "Gods and Monsters" by Lana Del Ray starts playing and I slowly start dancing on Brantley, my ass digging into his crotch. I feel him expand under my butt and a shock of power surges through me. The thing with power, though, is it cuts out. His hand comes to my throat and he pulls my body down against his chest, his other hand coming up my inner thigh. "Wanna fuck me, *regina meis?*" my queen.

I gulp, my eyes drifting open and closed. When they open, Bishop and Madison are making out on the lazy boy in front of me. Madison stands and slowly removes her shirt, leaving her standing there in nothing but her little white panties and lace bra. She winks at me, her head swinging from left to right. Bishop's eyes are lazy, heavy and on her.

I lick my lips. "Yes."

Nate chuckles beside me, and then moves to the center of the room. He goes to the table with the coke on it as Brantley's hand comes up my inner thigh, his pinky slipping beneath my panties. Nate's eyes are still on mine as he leans down, pressing the rolled-up bill up one nostril. On mine as he leans down and positions the tip to the start of the dusted trail. And still on mine as he takes his hit. Just as he sucks it all in, Brantley's finger slips inside of me and I moan, biting my lower lip. My eyes flick to Madison who is straddling Bishop's lap, his hands on her ass as he directs her grind over his crotch. Her head tilts, the ends of her hair touching her lower back, and just as Brantley's thumb presses against my clit, Bishop flicks off her bra.

"I was never there" from The Weeknd starts straying through the room, my head pounding and lost in the moment. When my eyes open again, Nate is standing directly in front of me and my heart thunders in my chest. His fingers wrap around my chin as he tilts my head up to him. Brantley's fingers are working hard inside of me, his thumb pressing against my clit. My breathing is rough and hard, but my eyes are on Nate.

My eyes drop to his crotch and I bite on my lip. Nate chuckles, then lowers himself to my level. "You like that?" He asks, tilting his head, his eyes going straight to Brantley's hand that's under my skirt. Nate's hand touches my other thigh, his eyes staying on mine.

"Play with her tits. She likes that, but you gotta be rough."

I know that without the mask of my pain, what's happening right now would hurt me. It would hurt me to see his disinterest in me and treating me like one of the EK hoes that they always have hanging off them. I can't find that hurt because the pain of losing the most important person to me is a darkness so bleak that it hides everything else.

I close my legs and wriggle, grabbing the ends of my dress. When Brantley realizes what I'm trying to do, he pulls his fingers out and I removed my dress, now I'm standing there in nothing but my Victoria Secret panties that have the word SECRET stamped over my lower belly.

"Take them off..." Brantley orders, and I spin around to face him, knowing damn well Nate is right behind me, my ass directly in his face. It's about to get closer, because I hook my thumbs under the bands and wriggle my panties down, making sure to bend over, my eyes staying on Brantley. I rest my hands on either side of him, and open my mouth, my tongue poking out slightly. Brantley grins, his eyebrows lifting in surprise. He presses his finger that is still slick with my wetness inside my mouth and groans. "Damn. She's fucking *bad*."

My lips wrap around his finger as I suck myself off him. "Numb. The word you're looking for isn't bad, it's numb."

Nate's fingers grip around my hips and his mere touch goes straight to my chest. I know he's using me right now, and this scene right here isn't something that would be happening on a day that he thinks he cares about me. At least cares enough to not share me. But maybe I'm using him too. And Brantley. I can hear Madison moaning in the background and the sound of flesh slapping together. It smells like rich cologne, perfume, weed, cigarettes and candy. Sex. It smells like sex. I feel the tip of Nate's cock press against me from behind and I moan, my head tilting back.

Brantley takes a swig of whiskey, his eyes going over my head. His jaw flexes a few times, and then he mutters, "Can she fucking touch it at least?"

What? I missed something.

Brantley starts unzipping his jeans, and my eyes fall to his crotch. Nate slams inside of me and I let out a slight scream, my back arching. I feel myself clench around his thickness and my eyes roll to the back of my head, my thoughts lost in pleasure taking ownership of my dark thoughts. In Nate. Lost in Nate, but slightly distracted by Brantley's cock. Two small silver balls are on either side of his tip, and then there's a ladder going down his shaft. *Holy fuck.* I didn't expect him to have his cock pierced. I somewhat expected Nate to have it, since he has other piercings. Nose, tongue, and nipples. Brantley has none—just his cock.

Butterflies roar inside of me, excitement lashing through my blood like a lethal injection of heroin. I reach for it, my hand clenching around his hardness. I feel Nate's grip on my hips squeeze tighter and I flinch from the pain. *That was fucking sore.* Angry at him, I start tugging on Brantley and watch as one of the scariest guys I have ever met starts to come undone under my hand. He sucks in a breath, his eyebrows crossing as his eyes come to mine. My mouth waters and I want nothing more than to take him between my lips and suck him deep into my throat. Nate hits me hard from the back and I moan again, riding the wind of pleasure that tears through me like a category five tsunami. *Fuck it.* I lower my face closer to his dick, but Nate's hand slams against my throat and clenches.

He yanks my head backward, his lips coming to my ear. "If you want to be able to walk after I'm done fucking you, I'd advise you not to wrap those pretty little lips around his cock."

Brantley rolls his eyes, his head tilting back to rest on the sofa. "Pussy."

I continue rubbing Brantley's cock, his thighs clenching under my touch. A bead of cum spills over the tip and I use the cushion of my thumb to massage it over him. *I'm so close.* Nate's hand comes to my tit as his cock fills me relentlessly, his balls slapping against my clit. I can feel a slight sting ring out around me down there from the slaughter, but I ignore it, dancing on the line that crosses pain and pleasure. Hot cum shoots out of Brantley's dick and I slow my tugging to a soft massage, pointing his cock onto my tits. Brantley grins and winks at me. A small "fuck you" to Nate. But then I'm screaming in my own pleasure because my orgasm slams into me at lightning speed and I feel Nate's cock pulsing inside of me. We're all panting, our breaths slowing as Nate pulls out, his hot cum dripping down my thighs on his extraction. His finger comes to my inner thigh and he swipes up his cum, then I feel his finger come to my mouth. I keep my eyes on Brantley and suck, twirling my tongue around him.

Brantley groans, snatching the pack of smokes from the sofa and putting one in his mouth. "Fuck me. Lucky bastard."

Nate disappears, taking his presence with him and I instantly miss his touch.

"Was. Was a lucky bastard," he corrects as he comes back in. He shoves on his jeans, leaving them unbuttoned to hang around his hips and putting a smoke in his mouth, even though I know he hates cigarettes. He lights it and blows out the smoke, dropping onto the ground to lay on his back, watching the ceiling. I want to climb onto his lap. I want him. His touch. I want him to tell me we will get through this together. But I'm deluded. He plays with his phone, and then "American Psycho" from D12 starts playing. When the chorus comes on with Eminem, he raps it perfectly.

Madison laughs, and it shocks me because I almost forgot about her and Bishop having sex right opposite me. Any other person would be embarrassed, maybe even a little awkward, but it's not like that with us. It doesn't feel that way. Madison comes over to me, wasted off her head and naked up top—panties on bottom. She takes my hand and tugs me to my feet. Bishop hits the light, leaving nothing but the outside illumination of the pool spilling into the room. It's enough to give more of a laid-back vibe, without being completely dark. I love it, it feels secluded. I've got to admit, the coke is lame. I don't know why Madison has been doing it lately. I mean the guys have always done it as a party "upper," but Madison? I need to talk to her about that one day. When I can be bothered. I yank my panties on since I was still fully naked and dance with Madison to the song until it changes.

Madison's hands come to my cheeks. "I'm sorry."

"Shut up, Madz," I whisper, shaking my head.

She kisses me on the lips, her breasts pressing against mine. She pulls back, searching my eyes. "Okay. I'll shut up. Let's just dance."

We dance for hours until sweat drips off us and a soft burnt orange touches the sky.

"Baby," I hear Nate's soft voice from the bed. I look toward him, tilting my head. I lived through last night, and now I'm sober. "Come here."

Like a good puppy dog, I go to him. One last time, because after this, there will be no alcohol to cloud my thoughts. There will definitely be no drugs, and finally, there will be no Nate and Tillie.

CHAPTER 28

Nate

I can't seem to think straight. I don't want to think straight. I want to tear apart every single fucking straight thing in this piece of shit world and rip it to fucking shreds.

I'm angry.

I have a rage burning in the pit of my stomach that is untamable.

Turning to my side, I clench my jaw, hate seething to the surface. *Is it hate if it makes your fucking heart beat faster?* My eyes fall to her perfect soft lips, how they curve and dip in all the right places. Her thick eyelashes that are naturally fluffy but tamed and arched in a way I know most bitches would pay money for. The natural glow of her flawless skin with a complexion that could be painted on. Her thick dark eyelashes that fan out over her high cheekbones, and the fact that I know when she opens those perfect almond eyes, the brightest aqua ocean is going to fucking drown me. Her hair is still pink, though a little faded now, but when it's not pink, you could see that it was blonde. Same as Micaela. Every fucking thing about Tillie is Micaela.

My heart seizes in my chest and I fly off the bed, tears threatening to prick the corners of my eyes again. I hate that I can't stand to be around her. She's a constant reminder of how I was given the most beautiful girl in the world, and I ruined it. My hands are not made to carry pretty things, they were made to destroy them. I couldn't even take care of my daughter, and that was the one thing every father has to do. Hell, even junkies and deadbeats manage to not lose their kids the way I have.

I pick up my phone and walk out of the room, dodging Brantley's body that's sprawled out on the floor. "Motherfucker." I shake my head but chuckle. I don't know if last night was a good idea. I know that his cock is hard for her, and I think I just made it worse, contributing to their foreplay. I'm shaking my head when the edge of something brown catches my eye under the bed. I reach forward, pulling it out while checking that Tillie is still asleep. Her mouth opens slightly, a small snore leaving her mouth. *Yeah, no one is touching you for as long as you live.* I'll make sure of it. At the very least, he would need to not be a piece of shit like me.

Back to the box, I pull it out and see the words *Puer Natus* carved into the wood. I freeze. I know what the fuck this is and why it's here. But how the fuck did Tillie come about it and why the fuck hasn't she said anything. My eyes flick up to her body and then I stammer through the pages. Sketch after sketch flipping past me.

I put the book back under the bed and stand, making my way out of the house. Yeah, this is not fucking good. We had a fucking deal.

I climb the stairs, making my way up to my room while hitting dial on the foreign number.

"Hello?" Peyton says.

My jaw clenches. "We need to fucking talk."

"You know where I am…"

I hang up on her and have a quick shower, scrubbing away the cigarettes I decided to smoke last night and the coke I hardly ever snort. Once I'm done, I dial Hector on my way out. I'm beeping my car unlocked when he answers.

"We need to talk. Now."

I short shift all the way into the city, frustrated with ghosts whispering from their grave, sharing secrets they shouldn't be sharing. If Tillie finds out what's at the end of that book, and if she takes her place as it should be and as it is written, then we're all fucked. Her included.

I pull into the underground parking to one of the properties Hector is developing for us in the city. It's going to be The Kings new HQ, because Bishop didn't want to bring business back to his home. Typical Bishop, still bleeding secrets into his and Madison's relationship over a year in. Don't know how he does it. I'd rather cut myself open and let my secrets spill. Then I'll be able to see if my girl will let them drown her or learn to swim through them. If she drowns, she drowns, but if she swims, I'll be waiting on the other side ready to play with her tits.

I already know where Tillie would fall on this scale. She has proved time and time again that she can handle any and everything. But she won't be able to handle the end of that book—and neither will I.

I slam my door closed and head straight for the elevator. There are three levels, and although they're not done yet, the third level is almost finished, which will be where we will be conducting most of our business. With Hector stepping down next year, Brantley and I have already decided we will be stepping up as Bishop's right- and left-hand men. The rest of the boys are going off to college, but they're still Kings, nonetheless. They just have the option to go off and have a life. A family. Jobs. But when the bell is calling, they always have to come running. Unless they want to be ridiculed and thrown into The Rebels. Our gen is good. It's solid. I know Hunter wants in with us too, but Jase won't let him because he wants him to try out a "normal" life.

The elevator dings as I reach the floor and I step out, seeing Hector and Peyton instantly. "She has Puer Natus."

They both freeze.

Peyton's hand comes to her forehead. "Fuck!" She starts pacing, and Hector's eyes come to mine. "How did she get it?"

I shrug, running my hands through my hair. "Don't know. Found it under her bed this morning."

"Son." Hector looks at me, the wrinkles around his eyes softening. "You don't have to do this right now. You just lost your daughter."

I shake my head, clenching my jaw. "Keep me busy."

Hector tosses a file toward me, landing on the construction table beside a saw. "I need you to check on The Rebels. They're making noise, rustling the leaves with some very powerful people that ride on the straight and narrow. Can't have their noses in our business."

I nod. "I'll handle it." I flick through the folder, images of young people in dirty rooms, girls dressed in old clothes with heroin needles stabbed into their arms. Some of the images are old, dating back to when we were all kids. I pause on one image. A little girl with the whitest hair I have ever seen falling over her little face. Mud smudges her porcelain-like skin, and she has to be around four-years-old, wearing a soiled white dress. Her eyes catch me, stall me even. Not so much the color, because I can't make them out, but the shape. The way they look at you through a photograph. It's haunting. A deep cut on the side of her neck catches my attention next, it's so deep it would leave a nasty scar. I shake my head, disgusted in The Rebels and what they're still dabbling in.

"They're still trafficking?" I ask, my eyebrow quirked as I look up at Hector.

The Rebels live in the shadows, the cracks between broken mountains and sand dunes, always creeping around, watching. It has been a law for us not to take out one of our own, and that law was something we took very seriously, which is how the Rebels were created. But by the looks of it, Hector wants to take them all out. They've always lived a fairly low-key life, but for the past year, they've been kicking up dust. You would think that they're all dirty and lost, living in the slums, but they're not. They look like everyday people with everyday jobs, doing less than everyday shit. They live in a small community on the edges of Syracuse.

He bites on a cigar. "Seems so. They're getting reckless. I want them all gone."

"By gone, you mean 86'd?"

"You always have to go gangster, Malum. Yes, I want them all dead."

I chuckle. "Yeah, sure. What about the Ghost? Want me to send out a warning first?"

Hector smirks in a way that resembles his son. "Do we do warnings?" His face straightens. "It needs to be rectified. Put in its place. See if *it* knows anything about it."

I leave the meet with a clear head. Peyton is still with Hector when I tread down to my car. She's been a fucking nuisance through all of this, and I still don't quite know why Hector is keeping her alive. The man rules with a twitchy trigger finger. Any other person would have been dead the day we found her with Micaela.

"Nate!" Peyton calls out, pausing my movements.

I squeeze the door handle, not bothering to turn and face her. "What?"

"I'm sorry about Micaela…"

I snort, yanking the door open. "Fuck off, Peyton."

I climb into my car and head home to prepare for the trip.

CHAPTER 29

Tillie

After everyone has left my room and I've showered and dressed, I take out the book from under my bed, desperate for a distraction. I've decided I'm going to finish this book, but not just finish it, I'm going to try to see the places he has sketched in hopes to find anything to connect the transparent dots that seem to be disappearing before my eyes. Shoving the book into a duffel bag I found in the closet, I swing it over my shoulder, tying my hair in a long ponytail. I'm making my way toward the front of the house to catch a cab when Elena comes out dressed in yoga pants and a loose sweater.

"Hi," I say, unsure of what we talk about now.

"Morning, Tillie, can I speak with you for a second?"

I lick my lips. "Okay." Then follow her into the house, taking a seat at the dining table. "Is everything okay?" God, I really hope she's not wanting me to leave today. I know Nate has said so, but I haven't managed to find a home or even a car. I know I still have Nate's money in my account, maybe I can use some of that to go get a car since Elena wouldn't let me pay for her funeral.

She places a black coffee in front of me. I adjust myself on my chair, getting ready to brace myself for whatever she's about to say.

"I want you to stay for as long as you need."

I exhale, my shoulders slacking from the pent-up nerves I had worked myself up on. "I appreciate that, but I think you and I both know your son. He wants me out, and I don't blame him."

"My son is hurt, Tillie, broken beyond repair, as are you, but make no mistake, he loves you and will never really want you to be homeless or out on your own."

I appreciate her telling me this, but Nate and I have never said the "L word," and it grinds on my gears that she threw it out there so carelessly. She doesn't know what her son feels, because I'm almost certain he feels nothing at all.

"Wooo." I blow out my breath. I need to calm down, remember that she is not the enemy here and all she's ever done is help me. I take a small sip of my coffee in an attempt to do that. Once I place the mug back onto the table, my fingers wrapping around the warm ceramic, I smile at her. "Thank you. I will stay for a couple more days until I find something else. I might be out and about for the next couple of days, though, don't be alarmed. I'm just trying to find a car."

She pushes the keys toward me. "The SUV is yours, Tillie. Please take it."

I toss and turn.

"Please."

I grab the keys and look up at her. "Thank you for all that you've done to help me, Elena. I didn't know my mother."

"—It's a good thing," she murmurs.

I chuckle, the first real smile to touch my mouth since losing her. "Yeah, but you're amazing. Nate is very lucky to have you."

She swipes her cheeks. "Please come to me if you ever need to talk about Micaela."

My blood turns cold, my jaw turning to cement. "Thanks." I stand abruptly, making my way to the front door. My heart is pounding against my rib cage and when I step outside and slam the door closed, I slide down until my ass drops to the cold tiles on the porch. *Micaela.* It's the first time I have heard her name be said aloud since losing her. I've even refused to say her name in my head because it is just too painful. That one word can dismember me in the blink of an eye.

The tears start again as I'm reminded, *yet again*, how much I have lost. Time stands still when you're numb. You lose track of it, of meaning. Like why do flowers bloom if they're just going to wither? That space between that first blossom and that first wilt is meaningless. It all reaches the same fate. Like me. Like human life.

I push from the ground, swiping the tears from my cheeks and unlock the Mercedes. Climbing in, I tug my phone out of my back pocket and call Brantley. He picks up after the sixth ring. *Sixth.*

"*Principessa...*"

I ignore that annoying pet name. Think I'll take Madison's "kitty" over princess any day of the week. "That cabin..."

Brantley silences. "Yes..."

"Where is it?" I ask candidly, flooring it out of the house of doom. I can't stay here for much longer. I know that. Everything reminds me of Micaela, it hurts too much.

"Off the I-5—why?"

I hang up, knowing I can find it myself if I really search my thoughts deep enough.

It takes me a little over two hours, but eventually, I'm pulling into that same driveway that we all went down before I got chased into the forest. The building where the fights were doesn't look nearly as intimidating as it did that night. That night that feels so long ago.

Tragic.

I cut the gas, putting the keys in my pocket. The time catches my eye as I look around the place. Just past four p.m. That gives me enough time to gather what I need. I swing the duffel bag over my shoulder and trek into the forest. The wind whisks through my hair, setting goosebumps over my flesh. It seems darker in here, where the trees keep you secluded and caved away from the sun. Ten minutes later, I'm separating a large shrub of brush and I'm face-to-face with that same cabin again. I begin walking toward it, the same withered boards holding it together by the rattling metal roof. I open the door, finding it exactly how it was the last time I was here. Only thing missing is the fireflies in the fire-place. I walk inside, ignoring the heebie-jeebies that have worked themselves inside of me. Taking a seat on the rocking chair, I swing back and forth, the tight squeak of the old wood rocking against the floorboards the only sound filling the room. I flick open the pages.

The number. I run my finger over it, the curve of every angle. I'd say it's identical to my trailer when I was growing up, but why? Why would it be my trailer. This is the cabin from two drawings, but the one that perks my interest the most is the drain cover that says Perdita on it. I flick through to another page that I haven't seen yet, and it's a sketch of the gates of Perdita. The ones that lead into the township. The soft gray smudges are flicked high, the edges as sharp as the gates in real life. I flip the page to the next chapter, and it's a dungeon. I notice a small signature on the bottom. It's a scribble, and I have to squint my eyes just to make out the words. *Perdita*. I stand from the old lounge chair, pushing the book back into my duffel bag.

I know where I need to go, but I need someone to take me there.

I know what I need to do to make that happen.

I floor it onto the highway and dial Madison's number through the Bluetooth. She picks up.

"Hey, I was about to call you…"

"Where are you? There's something I need to show you."

Pause. "At Bishop's."

"Okay, I'll be there soon."

I hang up and make the trip into the city, my nerves wracking around inside of me. It's a good distraction from the pain.

My eyes flick to the rearview mirror and I notice a dark SUV following. It's been on my tail since I got on the highway. I chew on my lip, trying to figure out what to do. I see a shoulder coming up ahead and pull in, the tires skidding against the asphalt.

The SUV follows, and I take a second to sit there, my eyes on the rearview mirror. I can't make out the driver through the small rearview mirror and the tints. I open up my phone and send a message to Madison.

If you don't hear from me, there was a dark SUV following so I pulled over. I think it's the same car that came to Nate's the first night I was there and told me to come outside to meet him. Sorry I didn't tell you about it. I kept so much to myself. I guess I like secrets just as much as the guys… Anyway, I was coming to show you something. When I slept in Daemon's room, I found his sketchbook. I wanted us to go to Perdita because a lot of the sketches are drawn there, but a couple are done of a broken cabin in the woods, and my trailer number—weird, huh? I'm jumping out of my car now to see who these motherfuckers are that have been following me. Love you. Please take care of Nate, Brantley, and Bailey. I forgot to tell you about Bailey, Bishop will fill you in. X

I climb out of the car, slamming the door closed behind me while clutching the strap to my duffle bag. The back door opens, and I see a polished Oxford shoe peek out, landing on the dusty road.

I tuck my hair behind my ear, just as the door closes. My eyes travel up his body, and then land on—Nate's dad?

Confused, I step forward, licking my lips. He comes directly to me, popping his collar.

"Tillie, nice to formally meet you…"

"I wouldn't call this formally, but okay. Why are you following me?"

"If I say to come with me, will you listen? I don't want to hurt you. We won't hurt you."

I think over his words, my eyes searching his. "Why?"

He turns his gaze over his shoulder to look back into the Cadillac and then back to me. "Because I have information that you will want. I promise I will bring you back to your car when we're done. If that is what you want…"

Why would it be something that I *wouldn't* want?

If he wanted me dead, he's had plenty of chances to do so.

I tilt my head. "Why did you want me to come outside when you came to Nate's?"

He gestures toward the waiting SUV, just as a large truck zooms past, my hair flying up everywhere and the wind almost knocking me to the ground.

"Alright," I mutter, making my way to the SUV. "I appreciate you not trying to kidnap me."

"Oh, trust me, I almost went there…"

I roll my eyes, gripping the door handle and slipping inside the warm enclosure. I assess my surroundings. Two suited men are in the front, both wearing dark glasses, shading their eyes. Gabriel climbs in beside me and the truck pulls away, back onto the highway.

I can feel my phone vibrate in my bag, but I ignore it. My point was made. Madison knows.

"So, talk."

Gabriel stretches his neck, his eyes coming to mine. He looks so much like Nate in this lighting. They have the same square jaw, only Gabriel has a grey shadow of a beard scattered over his. Handsome for an old dude. "To start off, your mother, Katsia." He places a leather satchel on his lap and pops it open, taking out a piece of paper and handing it to me. "She has left you with this account."

My eyes fall to the paper. It's a trust account with enough money to survive for three lifetimes. "What?" I freeze. I've never seen that many digits in my entire life.

"It's true. She wanted you to have this, but only when you were ready, Tillie."

"Ready for what?" I ask, looking back to him.

He offers me a small smile. "Ready to do what it was written for you to do. The one thing that The Kings have been trying to stop you from obtaining."

"And what is that?" I question, my tone hanging off a bite.

A slow merciless smile comes onto his mouth. "Take the throne, of course."

"The what? Speak American, not Elite King."

Gabriel flexes his fingers. *Nervous trait maybe?* "You need to take over Perdita, Tillie. Only you. There is no one else that is born for this duty."

"Nope." I shake my head. "I don't want that job. Give it to someone else."

He chuckles, pulling out a cigar from his jacket and clipping it, pressing the end into his mouth. "You don't have a choice."

"I don't want the money."

"With or without the money, you still have to do this."

I think over everything that has happened the past few days. How my world has crumbled, and my insides feel as though they have been poisoned with cyanide.

"Tillie. Right now, The Kings have Khales running it into the ground. She has locked up most of the Lost Boys into cages, not feeding them while keeping her favorites near. She has time and time again proved to be a nuisance. She's running around playing queen while destroying everything that Perdita was built for."

"And what is that, exactly?" I bite out, my anger reaching a new level. "A place to kill newborn baby girls? A community that keeps people sheltered and away from the real world? Those people don't even know that this world exists!"

"It's the way the movie plays in this world, Tillie."

I exhale, licking my lips. "I know. I just wish I understood it more."

"You will," he says, his hand coming to my knee. My eyes go up to his, the blue depths reminding me so much of his son. "You're smarter than everyone else. More street smart than your mother, resilient from your upbringing. Now that the power is offered to you, are you going to take it?"

I think over his words, the same throbbing pain in my chest from missing Micaela thumping inside of me. Everything reminds me of her. "Take me to Perdita. I'll make a decision then."

I already know what my choice is.

His lip kicks up in a smile. "Deal." Then he hands me a small leather pouch. I pop it open and peer inside. Three credit cards are inside as well as a few other pieces of papers. "The account is yours anyway, Tillie. Whether you choose to take on your rightful duty or not. I wouldn't hold it over you."

"And why not?"

He looks outside his window. "Because I am no longer a King."

CHAPTER 30

Nate

"What the fuck do you mean she sent you a text?" I grit my teeth, making my way into my house. I called the hit on The Rebels. Kings don't do the dirty work unless it's personal. The Rebels aren't personal. They're not worth us getting our hands dirty over, so I sent Rob in. Rob resembles Bullet Tooth Tony from the movie *Snatch*. Accent and all. He's ruthless, expensive, and about as lethal as a virgin on a stripper pole.

"I mean she sent this text saying someone was following her."

My body stiffens, my foot landing on the third step. "I gotta go."

I hit dial for Hector as soon as I've hung up on Madison. He picks up. "Yes?"

"We have a problem." I begin telling him everything Madison just told me, including her little attempt to go onto Perdita to follow Daemon and his stupid fucking sketchbook.

"Call a meet!" Hector barks down the phone, hanging up. He's not happy. With good reason. Hector has been wanting to shut down Perdita for a while now, buying time until he figures out how to do that by putting his cock warmer in charge over there. If Tillie takes over—as she was supposed to—that means that we no longer have control over Perdita or the soldiers and people on there. I mean, under it all, we have power and pull, but they only ever answer to a Stuprum. Handing someone like Tillie that much power can be catastrophic. Not to mention...

I send out a group text. **H has called a meet at his house. Be there asap.**

I'm walking passed Daemon's room when I stop, slamming his door open. I let it swing open and hit the wall, my eyes flying all over the place. "Motherfucker."

Hector is one of those people who exude power, like most of us. Wherever he is, whoever he is with. He could be sitting right beside the President and he'd still pour out more dominance than him and his crew.

"This has to be Gabriel's doing..." I mutter once we're all in Hector's office.

Brantley clears his throat. "Why? Why does this have anything to do with Gabriel?"

My jaw remains as hard as rock.

"Because." Hector's eyes come to mine. "Let me tell you a story about Gabriel and Katsia..."

What? "What?" That has my attention. "If you tell me that Tillie is my long-lost sister, I swear to fucking Judah I will slice every motherfucker in this room and then myself before I wait for you in Valhalla."

Hector rolls his eyes. "Malum, sit down. She is not your sister, but her mother and Gabriel did have a brief fling. As you all know, the girls that are accepted into our way of life are often shared amongst us."

Brantley kicks my chair.

I flip him off without looking.

Bishop laughs, so I flip him off too. "Oh don't get me started on Madison." I grin at Bishop and his eyes narrow.

Hector exhales. "Point made..." Then he lights his cigar. "But Katsia and Gabriel were different. She wanted exclusivity. Which is fine, most women do, but the ones who patter into our world don't last long if they don't at least have an open mind. Katsia never did to begin with until she found her right on the throne. Her story is not mine to tell, and I'm sure Tillie will learn about it one day, but their love is what pushed Katsia onto the throne. As I am sure" —his eyes come to mine— "Tillie's will too. We have to stop it from happening."

Fuck.

CHAPTER 31

Tillie

I follow the three guards and Gabriel as they lead me to the gates that open onto the township of Perdita. My nerves pick up again. I don't know what I'm doing here, but there's only one reason why I would willingly fly miles out to the middle of the ocean back to this small island.

I pull out Daemon's sketchbook and flip through the pages as Gabriel's guards ramble off to the ones at the front of the gate.

"….where'd you find that?" Gabriel points down to the book.

I look up at him briefly before going back, finding the chapter I want. "In Daemon's bedroom."

There's commotion going on in front of us, so I slam the book closed and shove through our guards, only to come face-to-face with the burly, hairy men who are known as the gatekeepers of hell. Not really of hell, I just like to call this place that.

I square my shoulders. "Let us in."

They glare down at me, lip curled. "We don't answer to you."

"Really?" I say, eyebrows quirked. "So who do you answer to? Because last I checked, the woman who ran this place died. Is that right?"

The big blonde Viking looking one narrows his eyes at me. "I can't confirm nor deny."

I smile sweetly. "I can. Because that woman was my mother, and my best friend is the one who killed her. Now…" I cock my head. Their eyes fall to the side of it, and they straighten, noticing something of importance. "Let us the fuck in."

The big brunette one fumbles with the locks, unlatching them quickly. They're both dressed in black slacks and black wife beaters. He pulls the gate open and we all step through. Turning to face the two gatekeepers again, both of their heads are down.

The Viking one is the first to cut the silence. "Please forgive us, *mea principessa*. We did not mean any harm."

My eyes flick to Gabriel, who is grinning at me. His eyes twinkle and gleam. "Bringing you here was the best thing I have ever done."

I lick my lips. "Don't worry about it." Facing the long-marbled road that leads to what used to be Katsia's home. Perdita is a township. A very odd, small township where the people sleep during the day and live through the night. It's daytime right now, so the street is empty. The small little shops that are built on either side of the glossy marble pavement all have "Closed" signs hanging over their doors.

We begin our long walk to the end of the road, passing every store. I take this time to get a good look around. There are convenience stores, knife-wielding stores, weapon stores, bakeries, clothing shops, and even an alcohol shop.

Huh. Well, at least they get to enjoy something of our world.

Once we reach halfway, Gabriel opens his mouth. "You know Khales has been here?"

My jaw clenches. "I've heard." I also despise her.

"How do you suppose we are going to deal with that, *mea principessa,*"

I roll my eyes. "Gabriel, please don't start with the *mea principessa* shit. I have The Kings pet naming me variations of 'my princess' and 'queen,' now the gatekeepers too." As soon as I've finished my sentence, I stiffen.

Everything stops.

I turn to face Gabriel. "What is going on?"

Gabriel searches my eyes, a knowing glint speckled over his irises. "Ah, she's intelligent too, not just street smart."

"Don't fuck with me right now. I'm feeling a little on edge."

Gabriel exhales, cracking his neck. "Yes. They have all known about you needing to be here. They have all fought it within every inch of themselves to stop this from happening. To stop you from coming back here."

My eyes narrow. "Why?"

Gabriel gestures to the gates of Katsia's mansion. The tips, jagged glass as sharp as blades. The gate resembles ice. Clear, but you can't see from the outside in. I'm adamant that Perdita is made up of wizardry. These witches are my ancestors, the ones who couldn't be burned.

"Because with you here, they no longer have control. Perdita is a world of its own, Tillie. The Kings have been wanting to take the reigns over it for generations but have always failed."

"So why didn't they just kill me?"

Gabriel's eyes come directly to mine. "Because of your relationship with the swan. But make no mistake, Tillie, Hector is a man *not* to be taken lightly. He rules with a heavy fist and he has no problem *smashing* things and *people* to get what he wants."

"Seems an awful lot to risk just to not piss off a girl who I irk on a daily basis, and what do you mean? I know Hector is cruel, but what has that got to do with me?"

"Well, until you went AWOL, you have been living on a very slippery slope, Tillie. People have wanted your head for some time, some more than others and some hiding it better than the rest. When you came back with Nate's daughter, that was your lifeline. But..."

"—now she's not here," I finish for him, and then look up to the gates.

"Yes, and I do not know where my son and their generation sits when it comes to their loyalty to you, but I can tell you right now—" Gabriel pauses, and I suck in a breath, awaiting him to continue. "There's a whole lot more to what is going on here.

You are in the middle of a world that you barely know. A foreigner, if you will. But I can help you."

"We can finish this conversation later," I murmur, my eyes going back to the mansion. "When we aren't sitting ducks."

He nods.

I shove past our guards again and hit the speaker box with the palm of my hand.

"Well, well, well, look what the cat dragged in," Khales purrs through the voice box.

I grit my teeth. "Let me in, Khales. We have unfinished business…"

CHAPTER 32

Tillie
Past

"Do you trust me, Puella?"

"On one condition," I whispered, slipping Micaela into his awaiting arms. "Don't die."

Daemon gave me a small smile, skimming his lips over my forehead. "I won't, I'll never die, Tillie." He glares at me. "Do you trust that?"

No. "Yes."

I watched as his back retreated through the doors. I had been pacing for a solid hour, waiting for the next thing that was about to happen, when my door swung open and Khales waltzed through, a smirk on her mouth.

"What are you doing here?" I asked, confused. Shit. This meant The Kings were here.

Khales stepped forward until her chest brushed against mine. "When this is all over, and when I have gotten rid of the people I need to be rid of, I will be the one running this island. Remember that!"

I flinched, confused at what the hell she was talking about. "Whatever, Khales. Whatever."

She shoved me backward until I fell on my ass and glared down at me. "You're disgusting. You and your friends think you know everything there is to know about this world, but you're wrong. I'm the only girl in this group and it will always be me." She spat on my face.

I swiped it away as she disappeared back through the door.

Bitch.

I hadn't known her well, only saw her around the island a few times with Katsia. Aside from the fact that she went to my high school, I knew she was also with Bishop for a while. I always figured she would be on their side, but maybe I was wrong. She must be a great actress because Bishop isn't someone who would keep someone like her around.

There's a tapping at the window and I rushed over, yanking it open. Peering down, Tinker was standing there looking up at me. Funny how the Riverside Prep librarian turned out to actually be a badass bitch who is on our side. "They're here. We've got Micaela. Just follow the cues, and Tillie," she paused, searching my eyes. "Stay safe."

I closed the window and sucked in a breath. "Sure." I let the cool window caress my back, leaning my head against it. Cramps ripped through my lower abdomen and I winced, leaning forward. Liquid began dripping down my thigh, so I reached down, swiping some of it with my index finger and bringing it to my face.

Blood.

I waddled back to the bed and took a seat. The door burst open but this time Jessica stepped in, slamming it closed behind her. I knew instantly that something was about to happen today. Something big.

"We need to get you cleaned up. She will summon you soon no doubt. They're all in the sitting room."

I stilled. "Who is *they?*"

Her eyes came to mine. "The Kings."

CHAPTER 33

Tillie
Present

I sidestep past the elegantly placed rocks that lead up to the main entrance of the mansion. Gabriel lifts his hand to knock, but I pause it and reach for the handle. It's open. I shove the door farther until it slams against the wall. Just as I take a step forward, a plane roars overhead.

"I have a feeling that's a jet full of angry men..."

My jaw tightens as I enter the house, expecting something. Anything. Only I find myself surrounded by silence. When Katsia ran Perdita, everything was always busy—constantly. There was always music playing, men walking around half naked, that sort of crazy shit. I continue to trudge into the house, glimpsing up the circular staircase.

"Why is it so quiet?"

A hand falls over my face, cutting off my breathing and I kick back, throwing my fists everywhere. The body behind me is large, holding me with strength. The smell of gasoline ignites my senses and then everything slowly goes dark.

My body is heavy, my lids refusing to open. I hear something playing somewhere. It's not music, it's—a lullaby. Strong strings tinkle, the warped sound wailing the probability of a low battery. My cheek is throbbing, something cold pressing against it. Finally, I manage to open my eyes. The room is sideways. Dark concrete walls. No windows. I fly to my feet, wobbling a few steps. My hand flies out to stabilize myself, coming into connection with a cell bar. My eyes are blurry, a murky fluffy haze blinding me. Attempting to catch up to what is in front of me, I squeeze the cold pole, rubbing my eye with my other hand. Everything comes into focus at once. My eyes fly to the cell opposite the one I'm in. A baby rattle sits in the corner, worn, and broken. The intricate pattern etched into the plastic proves it's the very same from Daemon's book.

Daemon's book!

I spin around in search for my duffle bag, finding nothing but a damp puddle on concrete ground. The very ground I woke up on. *Gross.*

Muffled whispers echo off the long hallway that resembles a prison sector, with I don't know how many cells leading off.

"Who's there?" I call out, pressing my cheek to the cool bar in an attempt to get a better look.

"They won't answer," the voice that replies to my hurried question sounds robotic.

I scream, spinning around quickly to where the foreign voice came from in my cell, but no one is here. "Who is that?"

I catch movement near a dark corner on the other side of my cell, and that's when I see the outline of someone. "What do you want from me?"

There's a long silence, aside from the whispers that don't seem to stop. A dark chuckle ripples through the air like a bad frequency threatening to taint everything you thought you knew. "I don't want anything from you."

I chew on my bottom lip. "Well can you come out of the shadow, so I can at least see you better?"

"No."

I slide down the cell door until my ass hits the cold ground. "Are you a prisoner?"

"Yes." There's a roughness to the way he talks.

I'm intrigued. Aside from the robotic tone.

"God I fucking hate that bitch." I decide to change the subject, massaging my temples. "I'm going to kill her."

"Yeah?" the voice says, and I don't miss the bite in his tone. "Make sure you save me her tits so I can tear them off and feed them to my dog."

I don't bother to look toward him. I know I can't see. "Your dog likes silicon?"

He doesn't answer.

"What's your name?"

I turn my head to look over my shoulder, my eyes going back to the baby rattle that's sitting in the middle of the cell. It's a haunting reminder of what I've lost and what I also need to find.

"Don't have a name."

I turn back to face the shadow. "Well, that's just sad…"

That was a dumb thing to say. I blame it on stress and confusion.

Silence. Nothing more than silence fills the cold space between us.

This is getting weird, talking to someone who I can't see and who has a strange voice. "This is ridiculous. I can't believe I'm locked in this shit cell." *Shut up, Tillie. Stop talking. Find a way to get out.* My head hurts. I slam my eyes closed and pull my legs up to rest my face on my knees.

"Do you know why you're here?" the voice asks. I should call him Shadow. Since he is nothing but one.

I turn to face the shadow. "Yes and no. Do you?" Where the fuck is Gabriel?

"…Yes." His voice. There's something about it that sparks something inside of me.

The sound of a door opening and heavy heels click across the concrete hallway. I stand, stepping backward until I bump into shadow man. I didn't realize I had ventured into his space. "Sorry."

His chest is to my back. I can feel every intake of breath that he takes. I can also feel how rock hard his chest is pressing against my back. He's tall, and…built.

His lips come to my ear. "Are you the *mea principessa*?"

My body stills. I step away, but the man's hand presses against my flat tummy, holding me against his chest. "You wanna kill her, *principessa*? Then do it." His voice falls over us like a cage of darkness. I feel safe within his grip. "Show me what you've got..." I feel cold metal slide over my lower belly and tuck into the front of my panties, gliding over my flesh. I know instantly that it's a knife.

Shit.

His smirk pressess against the back of my neck, right as the cell unlocks and Khales comes into view. Dressed in a short crop top and a leather miniskirt, her black hair is tied in a high ponytail. She's looking right at the shadow.

She smirks. "Ready to see your mother, Tills?"

I straighten my shoulders.

Shadow man chuckles. "*Sic 'em, girl.*"

I don't know what it is or why. I do not even know the shadow, but he gives me a direct line of confidence. One that I need right at this very moment.

I tilt my head, my eyes running over her body. "You know, you could have had something good with Hector." I glance at the guards who stand behind her, two of them. Standing staunch with their legs spread apart slightly. They waver every now and then, a little unsteady on their loyalty maybe?

Khales chuckles. "Oh, I can't even begin to tell you how wrong you are." She lunges toward me, her hand coming to my throat. Before I can register what is happening, I'm being smashed against a cold wall. "I saw you found Daemon's book." She tilts her head, looking me up and down.

"What of it?"

A small smile comes onto her mouth. "Oh nothing, just that Daemon is... complicated."

Slowly inching my hand toward the front of my jeans, I squeeze around the handle, keeping my eyes on hers. I don't care about what she's saying, just keep her occupied and her eyes away from what I'm doing.

"Oh? And why is that?" I know why and how he is complicated, but the fact that she thinks she knows what she is saying is almost comical. I say almost, but I mean all the way there.

She exhales, her fingers flexing on my neck. "Aw, because he's sick, dear."

I yank the knife out and in one movement, launch the tip of the blade into the side of her neck. I watch her eyes pop in shock as her warm blood spills over my hand. Finally, her grip lets up around my throat, going to her own in search of the stab wound.

"You don't know shit." I sink the blade in farther and she lets out a small gurgling cry. "About Daemon. And no one fucking likes you—" I shove her body away from me until it falls to the ground in a lifeless heap "—*bitch.*" Wiping the blood off the blade and onto my shirt, I look up at the two guards who are standing at the door of my cell. "Do you know who I am?"

They both look between each other and then look back at me. "Yes."

I tilt my head. "And?" I ask, narrowing my eyes.

There's a stretch of silence that seems to vibrate around us at a resonance that's silent on ears. I wait for them to say something, anything. Maybe grab me and try to drag me out of here to kill me. Or worse, just kill me on the spot. What I was not expecting, was for them both to drop to one knee, their heads bowed.

"No..." I shake my head, panic gripping at my heart.

A familiar body presses against my back. *The shadow.*

"Just go with it, *mea principessa*. Do you feel it?" his voice whispers against me and my eyes close. His fingertips run up and down my arms, igniting that same flame. He's right. This is my world, not just The Kings'. I feel the whispers of my ancestors echoing through my veins. I'll turn those whispers into roars and bring every man to his knees.

My stomach clenches, goosebumps breaking out over my skin.

His hand travels up my stomach and near my throat. "Turn around, Tillie..." I hear more footsteps. Coming closer and closer. The echoing of heavy boots now a loud pulse behind me.

Then the sound stops. I turn in the man's grip, my eyes closed.

"Open. Your. Eyes."

I do as commanded, starting with his hands. Tattoos fill his hands that sneak out from the bottom of his sleeves.

Tattoos I recognize.

The words E L I T E stamped over his fingers on his left hand, and K I N G S over his right.

Fuck.

My eyes go up. I stop breathing. "Nate!" Just as his hand curls around the rim of his hoodie. He shoves it down to rest on the back of his neck. A smirk crawls onto his face, his eyes dark and deadly. *This isn't good.*

I turn to face whoever it was that just walked in, finding Bishop, Brantley, Eli, and Hunter, standing guard. "What the fuck is going on?"

Nate's hand comes to mine and he clenches it enough to cut off the blood circulation there. He yanks me into his chest, wrapping my hair around his wrist. "Perdita is King territory, now." Then he smirks, his hand coming to my throat. "Everything that you went through to get to this point, Tillie, was planned and orchestrated. You are the last living Stuprum now—but you won't be for long." I notice he doesn't flinch when the words pass his lips. "You are now a queen without a kingdom. A fucking dog without a home." His eyes search mine, and I know he's gone. Any part of who I knew as Nate is no longer living in the depths of this man standing in front of me. He is a mere shell of who he was before, a shell constructed of stone.

He shoves me backward until I slam against a cold brick wall. "I hope you like shackles, baby, because you're our prisoner now." He steps up to me, licks his lip and grins. He spins me back around to face the cell, the one with the rattle inside. "Open your eyes, *mea principessa*..."

I do, I open them.

"Look closely," he whispers, his lips behind my earlobe. "Watch the fireflies..."

As the words leave his mouth, my eyebrows cross in confusion. Bright little fireflies float in the darkest corner of the cell.

"Show yourself!" Nate demands, his chest vibrating against my back.

The Kings part to give me more view. A figure crawls forward, out of the darkness in the cell, knocking the baby rattle out of the way.

My legs give away and I try to launch forward as a scream roars out of me.

"Daemon!"

ACKNOWLEDGMENTS

My husband. Who tolerates my bratty, princess, needy, always hungry, nap-taking, love-needy ass. You deserve so much more than I can give you, but you're shit out of luck because it's me that you get and if you stray, thanks to this book, I now know how to completely dismember the two round things that hang between your legs.

My children, who drive me so crazy that I crave the dark places inside my head just to create chaos that doesn't directly impact me. Cheers, my little monsters. You're stuck with me.

Chantal Fernando. The friend that just keeps friending. I don't know where I'd be without you. Probably saying completely inappropriate things online and pissing everyone off. Thank you for being you. You're also stuck with me. Please refer to husband's passage a couple paragraphs up…

Sarah Grim Sentz. My little Grim Reaper. The day you read your way into my life was one of the greatest days in my writing life. You're my beta, my alpha, and the girl I trust 100% with my words, my world, and my characters. Thank you for always putting my ass in place when it needs to be and for being there through not just my writing, but through everyday shit too. You have become one of my best friends and my go-to woman. Thank you for being patient with your beta notes and for loving my stories like they are your own. Also refer to husband's passage a few paragraphs up. You're stuck with me.

Ellie McLove. I don't know, man. I feel like if I explained every single thing that I loved about you, I'd be here all day. I partly want to, just to make you uncomfortable, but I won't. You're the real MVP here. You take my words and polish them respectively without meddling with my author voice. You are everything that we need. I'm annoyed it took me so long to find you, but whatever, because now, yup, you guessed it—You're stuck with me.

Petra Gleason. Thank you for proofing my words. For your friendship, and the laughs. My darkness would like to drink with your darkness. You're stuck with me.

Isis, Nichole, Lyla, Caro, Amiria, Jacq, Nikita. My little circle of home-people. My BFFs who know my crazy and tolerate me anyway. You're all stuck with me. Obviously.

Leigh Shen. For being my favorite asshole. You're as sexy as you are talented. That's just not fair. Asshole. Thank you for being you. For becoming one of my closest friends who I trust in this industry. You're stuck with me.

Anne Malcom. My best friend. You are so much more than you realize. You deserve the world, even if I have to give it to you myself, I will. But you're a queen and handle your shit, so go chase the damn thing, and guess what, I'll be right beside you, because why? Because you're stuck with me.

The bloggers who read and promote me. Your support and the time you put into reading and reviewing will never go unnoticed by me. I adore every single one of you. Thank you. Thank you so much.

My Wolf Pack and my readers! YOU'RE STUCK WITH ME! Don't test me. I love you all so much. Thank you for riding with me on my journey. For your undying support and love. I will cherish you all until the end of my days.

Jay Aheer. My designer, my everything. Thank you for meeting my demands. Your covers challenge me in ways I have never been challenged. Every time you send me a new cover, I shiver with anticipation. I hope I do your beautiful art justice with my words. You're stuck with me.

Sarah Valentino and Kayla Thomason! You girls rock my shit. Thank you for the hours you put into creating the perfect teasers and Pinterest boards. There were times when your teasers helped push me through bad cases of writer's block. I love you. You're stuck with me.

Stacey from Champagne formatting for making this manuscript all pretty!! You're stuck with me.

I think I have successfully threatened every person I love. If that doesn't say Amo Jones, then I don't know what does. Good luck.

THE ELITE KING'S CLUB BOOK FIVE

MALUM

PART TWO

This is dedicated to my Wolf Pack. For having my back when I didn't have myself and for the daily laughs, cries, and impactful messages. This is for you.

Chapter One

Tillie

Nate backs me up against the cold cell, examining me. "You like this, huh, *Princessa*…" I shake my head, refusing to show any fear. Nate is like a shark with fear. He senses it in the water, and he thinks it's feeding time. "No. I don't. What are you doing and why am I here?"

My eyes go over Nate's shoulder and land on Brantley, who watches me carefully. "Brantley?"

Just when I think he's going to say something, maybe put me in my place for questioning them, his mouth snaps shut. I watch as he disappears back through the way we came.

"He won't help you. Stay here and don't move, Tillie. If you try to escape, we will kill you."

I don't know why there's a part of my brain that doesn't believe he would do that. You don't keep someone alive through a lot of turmoil only to off them if they do something so insignificant like not listening. Nate smirks as if he hears what I'm thinking. Backing up slowly, he exits my cell, flicking the lock closed. His eyes never leave mine.

"There's always a reason why we do the things we do, Tillie—remember?"

I don't take the bait, sliding down the cold wall and landing on my butt. There's a long pull of silence before I hear the door open and close again, and then Brantley's boots come into view out of the corner of my eye.

"What is it, Brantley? You guys won. Go and celebrate by snorting more cocaine or fucking more girls…" I don't want to talk to Daemon until they've all left, and part of me is still trying to calm my erratic brain from all of the possibilities of why, and how, he's still alive.

Brantley unhooks the lock, the heavy clinking of metal jerking me out of my thoughts. He opens the cell, stepping inside. I brave myself to bring my eyes up to his as he leans down to my level, his elbows resting on his knees.

His palm comes to my face. "Kiss me."

"What?" I ask, confused. My eyes fall to his swollen lips.

He squeezes my cheeks slightly, his face coming closer to mine. "Kiss. Me."

I lean forward until our lips touch, warm velvet skimming against mine. Slinging my arm around the back of his neck, a moan slips out of me as I pull him closer. I kiss him because I'm angry. I kiss him because I'm hurt. And I kiss him for the probability of Nate watching somehow. Just as his tongue slips into my mouth, I exhale from the intrusion. His kiss is as calculated as his character. He gives enough without giving too much. He sucks on my bottom lip, licking me across the rim. His arms wrap around my waist, bringing me to my feet. Thick thighs separate my legs, stretching me wide as his body sinks against mine, shoving me up against the metal bars. He lifts me up by my thighs as I wrap my legs around him, all while his mouth continues to assault mine. My stomach flutters, my core pulsing. I want him. I have always somewhat wanted him, to an extent, and now that Nate has well and truly shattered any and all trust that I had in him, I'm feeling reckless. If you hurt someone enough, they acclimatize to pain, but just like a wound, if you don't seal it, you'll bleed out.

Brantley pulls away, placing me back on my feet while grabbing my hand. "Now, you owe me twice for getting him mad, and princess, I will be collecting." He continues to drag me out of my cell, unlocking the one beside Daemon and shoving me inside. I turn, just in time to see him shutting the door.

"Brantley..." I want to apologize. I want to say so many things.

He shakes his head. "Don't, Tillie."

I know I owe him for saving me from Nate more than once or twice, but before I can address my gratitude, he leaves, and it's not until I hear the heavy steel door slam closed that I slide down to my ass, drawing my legs up and turning my head to face Daemon.

"I'm sorry you had to see that."

Daemon scrapes closer, grasping onto the bars that separate our cages. "I have seen much worse, Puella."

My heart squeezes in my chest from the use of my nickname. I thought I'd never hear it again. "I thought you were dead, Daemon. We all thought you were dead. We all mourned you." Madison pops up inside my head and I wince. "Did everyone know but me?"

Daemon shakes his head. He's wearing tattered jeans and a shirt that looks like it's seen better days. "No."

I massage my temples. "My god. Madison doesn't know you're still alive?" I screech, shaking my head.

Selfishly, it does make me feel better knowing that my best friend didn't betray me, but a bigger part of me is now terrified about what's going to happen when she does find out. Her and Bishop are already on struggle street, I'd hate to know what's going to happen when she finds out that he's been hiding the biggest secret of all from her. Her fucking twin brother being alive. My eyes fly up to the little camera that's sitting in the corner of my dark cell, the bright red dot signaling they're watching. I flip the camera off.

There's a light chuckle from the corner and I freeze. "Who's that?"

Daemon clambers backward, and though I can't see much in this lighting, I catch a glimpse of the scar on the back of his neck, reaching to the front. *How the fuck is he still alive?*

I narrow my eyes in an attempt to get a better look at the silhouette hidden in the darkest corner of my cell. "I swear if that's you again, Nate, I'll cut your dick off this time."

Another chuckle, and then the figure steps forward, the slight light from the small window forcing itself through the bars on the window.

He's wearing a dark hoodie, shading most of his face but I can see the fine edge of his sharp jawline. His jeans are destroyed from wear, not for vanity. A heavy black belt hangs low around his waist. My eyes travel up both of his arms that are covered with long sleeves, but I can see tattoos sneaking out on his hands. I continue up his large chest, past the Nike emblem on his hoodie, up to his neck. His neck. I freeze, licking my lips. His neck is completely covered in dark ink, skulls and roses and some kind of scripture. Tanned skin lays underneath. I suck in a breath, coming to his lips. Perfect bow lips that curl in all the right places, his bottom one slightly plump. His jaw is cut sharp and perfectly symmetrical. Both points of his jaw are tipped at the same place on either side. Sunken cheekbones, and then I finally drag my eyes up to meet his.

Holy. Shit.

"Do I know you?" I whisper, all thoughts flying out of my head. He is beautiful. But he looks familiar. He looks. So. Familiar.

He brings his hand up to his hoodie and flicks it off to rest around the back of his neck. "No."

"But..."

His jaw ticks, his eyes flying to the body lying in the cell opposite me. I can't stop staring at him, though. I probably should stop staring. Next to Nate, he would be the second hottest guy that I had ever seen. That used to be Bishop, but—I freeze, my wits now one-hundred percent working because I step forward, grabbing his chin with my hand, forcing his face back to look down at me.

His emerald eyes search mine, not giving anything else away.

I stop breathing, my grip tightening around his chin.

The corner of his mouth kicks up in a dark smirk. The kind I know all too well, only this one is—frightening. "Yes, seems I have a relation that you know."

"Relation?" I gasp, shaking my head and finally letting the poor boy go.

He cracks his neck. "Apparently I have a brother, and apparently we look like twins."

I lick my lip. "You do. Does Bishop know that you're in here?"

He grins, and his heavy eyes find the camera in the corner. "He does now..."

He flicks his hand toward Khales. A very dead Khales. "I wanted a turn with her. Didn't think you'd finish her in one go."

Ignoring his gesture toward her corpse, I keep my eyes on him, intrigue rushing through me. "What did she do to you, and what—how are you here?"

He shakes his head. "Too much to get into right now, but she killed my mother. I was outnumbered. I didn't know about Bishop until I got here, and she dangled him above my head like fresh bait, waiting for me to snap and take my first bite."

There's so much I want to know, but I know this isn't the time. So instead, I stare at him until I form the right words that I want to say.

"So Khales brought you here?"

He nods, taking a seat on the floor. I back up and slide down near the door, sitting opposite him but giving enough space between us. I don't know him or his story, and the fact that I'm locked in a cell with him tugs on all the strings of my warning bells.

He pulls his hoodie back up over his head. "My name's Abel, I'm Bishop's younger brother, same dad, different mom. I'm still in fucking high school, and I'm a cage fighter."

"Well," I mutter. "Yeah. Definitely different upbringings."

Abel shrugs. "It helped my mom pay for shit growing up. I learned the hard way, not the privileged way."

A million thoughts are rushing through my head, but one, in particular, has hit a standstill and won't move back into gear. "Why? Why did she bring you here?"

He shrugs, drawing one leg up and resting his elbow on his knee. "Long story." His eyes pierce through me, and I have to take a moment to calm myself. "I have heard about you."

"Really..." I quirk my eyebrow and draw my knees up close. I'm fighting to look toward Daemon, the process still not fully developed in my head right now. Something is going on, something that I don't understand. "What was it that you heard?"

Abel grins. "That you had a baby to a King, and that Katsia was your mom."

Chapter Two

Nate

The way some people can manipulate you with their personality and decide what you want to see in them is bullshit. Unfortunately, most of us are those people, and I'm a fucking expert.

I slam the door closed, shaking my head and pacing back and forth in the room like a caged lion. Brantley keeps watching me from across the table, a smug smirk on his face.

"What the fuck was that?" I ask, challenging him with my shoulders back.

He doesn't falter. "That was an angry Tillie, and you know what she gets like when she's angry…"

I clench my jaw, chuckling. "Oh, brother, you have no idea…"

The door slams shut behind me and I turn, clenching the chair with my fists and watch as Bishop strolls in with a pale face. His eyes are blank. All emotion and color has drained from his face. I instantly go on alert, the thought of Madison flashing through my head. "What's wrong?"

Bishop drags his eyes up to meet mine. "It seems I have a fucking brother."

There's a long pause for a few seconds as we all process his words.

"What do you mean a brother?" Eli asks, leaning forward on the table. Cash is sitting beside him, flicking a toothpick around in his mouth.

Bishop pulls at his hair and starts my pattern of pacing back and forth. It's not like him. He's usually calm and collected, but everything has had him on edge for a while now. I have thought up some theories on why he's being like this, but truthfully, I've been so occupied with all that's been going on in my life, I wouldn't be able to pinpoint exactly when Bishop and Madison lost their shit. I could say it was around when Micaela was still

"Playtime, boys," Hector grinned, cranking his head and biting down on a thick cigar that was hanging out of his mouth. "Before you get excited, keep in mind that I have granted this girl a clear path out of here with her life, and we don't break our word."

"Why!" I snapped, just as we made our way into the elevator. "Why would you promise her that?"

"Because if we need her to control that island, son, she can do that. They still think she's a Stuprum. We need her alive to be able to do that. And there's another issue that I've been handling behind the scenes. I've been told that she's been attempting a takeover..." His voice died out, a deep melody thundering through my ears.

All I want is my daughter. I don't give a fuck about anything else right now. The soft melody blaring from the speakers was a poor attempt at calming the pheromones that were seeping off each of us. There were twelve of us all in total, with a couple standing guard downstairs and a sniper on the building over. You know, precautionary. We didn't like to take someone out that way, but if one of The Kings were in danger and none of us were able to help, it was better to have an easy shot than no shot. Everyone is in position, and I can't fucking wait to hold my daughter.

Every level that the elevator climbs, my heart thunders in my chest in sync to hers. Will she remember this when she's older? Fuck, I hoped not. The elevator dings and the doors separate. Hector's head raises, coming to the front of himself as a smirk touches his mouth. We're instantly inside of a penthouse apartment with marble floors and white counters. I take one step inside and I fucking swear I can smell her. The innocence of a baby mixed with death is a heady combination, something that I wouldn't give a fuck about had it not been my daughter. Peyton walks out into the sitting room with six other men, slowing her footsteps. She cradles my daughter in her arms, rocking her softly.

"Look, baby, there's Daddy..."

I snarl at her, about to pounce when Bishop's hand comes to my arm. "Give me my fucking daughter."

Peyton rolls her eyes. "Always so dramatic, Nate. Tell me, how much did it hurt that Tillie kept her from you?"

My jaw clenches, my fist balled at my side.

Bishop brings his hand to my arm, stalling my movements. "Give me Micaela, Peyton, and we might just have our deal left on the table..."

I chuckle, leaning back and licking my lips. Like fuck am I letting this bitch walk out after taking my kid.

Her eyes come to me as if reading my thoughts. "For some reason, I don't believe that I'll walk out of here with my life."

I don't give her the reassurance that she so desperately wants. I'm no fucking liar. I remove my leather jacket, and then my shirt, tucking it into the back of my jeans. I smirk at Peyton, and she gulps, glaring at Bishop as they make a silent exchange. Something I'll touch on later. She shifts closer to Bishop, putting Micaela into his arms.

As soon as she was safe, I flew forward, shoving Peyton out of my way, my hand coming straight to Carter's throat. Peyton screamed in the background, but everyone else fell to silence. I squeezed roughly until I felt his throat cripple under my palm. "You have no idea how long I've waited to do this..."

"—Can we not be theatrical right now? There's a baby in the room. I don't know, but I feel like that would be wrong..." Eli muttered in the background.

"B?" I murmured, my eyes never leaving Carter.

I waited a few seconds until I knew Bishop would have turned Micaela away. It momentarily snapped me out of my rage, but not enough to not kill Carter. Just enough to realize I have my blade strapped to my belt. I snatch it out and in one movement, slice him across his neck until blood splatters all over my chest.

Brantley chuckles behind me, his hand coming to my shoulder as Carter's body drops with a loud thud to the floor.

Hector tsks from behind me. "I can't leave any of you unattended."

"I hate him," *I answer honestly.*

Turning in my spot, I catch Bishop grinning at me while covering Micaela's eyes and ears. "For being a part of this, or for having a hard dick for Tillie?"

"...You gonna off me, too? Because I gotta say..." *Brantley squeezes his jean covered cock.* "Somethin' about her..."

I shove him, swiping the blood off my face. "Fuck you."

Hector shakes his head like a father scolding his young before looking back to the other three men Peyton had behind her. "We have a problem here?"

They shake their heads.

"Good. Because if I see any of you again, you'll meet the end of my cane. You included, Peyton."

Peyton pauses, her eyes frantically searching Hector's. "I can go?"

"I'm many things, young girl, but we gave you our word. You gave him back his daughter, we give you your life."

Chapter Three

Tillie

Rubble is embedded into my flesh, my throat dry from thirst.

"Daemon?" I whisper hoarsely, tilting my head to face his cell.

He comes closer until he's leaning into me, my back touching his. Warm comfort flushes through me, and I sigh, exhaling instantly.

"What, Puella?"

"How are you alive? I heard your death was brutal. You died."

When he doesn't answer right away, I turn to face him, bringing my hand to the back of his neck. I crank his face toward me. "How?"

His eyes search mine, empty black pits of obscurity. Daemon breaks my heart. He was doomed from the start, never given a fair go. Even less than me, or—I look toward Abel, watching as he tilts his head back to rest on the cold wall, his hoodie dropping over his eyes. Maybe even Abel.

I go back to Daemon. "Then what happened?"

Daemon, in his broken language, starts to slowly explain. "They fixed the parts they could and the others…"

"The others?" I whisper, my hand coming to his arm.

"Are still broken."

"You've been here this whole time?" I ask, anger simmering.

He shakes his head. "No, Mic—"

I shake my head. "No, Daemon. I won't talk about her."

His face falls. "Okay, Puella."

"I will get us out," I say, rubbing my palm up and down Daemon's arm. I look to Abel who has already got his eyes on me. "All of us."

Abel gives me a strange look but doesn't say anything else.

A door cracks open and slams shut. Footsteps thud down the cold corridor matching the beat of my heart.

I know who it is without looking.

"Let me out," I retort, my tone flat.

I see his shadow shift out of the corner of my eye, kneeling down to my level.

"I thought you didn't mind playing games?" Nate's voice takes hold of my heart and squeezes.

I bring my eyes to his, dead and expressionless. "I do when I'm the coach."

I try to squash what he does to me, but it's no use. I will always be powerless when it comes to Nate, but I control how I exude it. Conceal, don't feel, and all of that.

He stands, swiping his hands on his pants and unlocking my cell door. "The two of you need to come with me."

I crank my head over my shoulder to look at Abel. "I take it Bishop knows about him now?"

Nate's hand comes to mine and the electricity that zaps through has me rearing away from him.

We start walking down the corridor, following Nate's broad back. He unlocks a heavy metal door and pushes it open as he leads us up large rectangular concrete steps. Candles line every step, like something out of a medieval castle. The walls are elegantly decorated with expensive looking art, framed in thick gold metal.

"Nate?" I whisper, but he doesn't answer.

We get to the top to find another door. He opens that and instantly, the aged medieval feeling is replaced with modern furnishings and marble floors. We're in the foyer of the mansion. Flushed with crystal furnishings, white-washed walls. I follow Nate down the hallway until he stops at the opening of a room at the very end that has no door.

He turns to face me, his eyes hardening on mine.

"Why?" I ask the one thing I've wanted to know since I woke up in the dungeon. "Was nothing real for you? Was she not real for you?"

His hand flies to my throat and he squeezes roughly. "Don't fucking speak of her ever again."

I slap his arm and my knee flies between his thighs, hitting him straight in the dick. "I lost her too, asshole."

He lets go of me like I stung him and backs up, his face going pale. It annoys me that he doesn't falter at my violence. I at least wanted him to fall to his knees in pain.

I shrug him off and step forward into a room large enough to hold a business conference. There's one stretched rectangular table that's displayed in the middle of the room with about twelve chairs all placed with precision around it. And every chair that's around it has a King sitting in it. Bishop is at the head, and when Abel and I enter, Bishop's eyes go straight to him.

"Sit." Bishop points to the chairs and I move over to them with Abel right behind me.

We both take a seat, Nate pulling out the empty one beside me. His presence instantly makes me queasy.

"Tell me why Khales had you locked in a cell and why the fuck do you look like me?"

Abel flicks his hoodie off his head.

Nate chuckles. "Twins?"

Abel shakes his head. "Nah. Different moms."

Bishop works his jaw so hard I think it might pop. "Carry on."

"Khales had been using my mom as bait since I met her last year at a party. We fucked, and then fucked some more. Obviously now I know why…" Abel runs his fingers through his hair. "She told me about you. She came clean with the parts she wanted me to know, but not everything I should know. She told me that I had a brother and that he didn't know about me. A few days ago, she caught me in bed with someone else. Lost her shit and killed my fucking mom before bringing me here."

"Sounds like her," I mumble. Nate's thick thigh presses against mine under the table and my chest tightens from the connection, but my fury simmers above the surface.

Bishop pauses, tilting his head. "Why did she keep you, that's the question. I'm not at all surprised about your existence, but Khales never made impulsive decisions. Everything was always calculated with her."

Abel shrugs. "Don't fucking know. But she kept me for something."

Bishop nods, his finger working over his upper lip. "We'll find out."

My eyes catch Brantley, who is already watching me. "Aw, what's the matter, Bran Bran. Why are you looking at me like that?"

Perdita isn't good for my soul. I can feel it digging its claws into me. I need to get out if I'm not going to stay. I need to escape and take Abel and Daemon with me.

Brantley doesn't falter, his lip kicking up in a snarl. "Bran Bran? Pretty bold nickname coming from someone who I can fuck without permission, don't you think?"

I tilt my head and give him back his smile. "Who's to say permission wouldn't be granted, Bran Bran."

"Tillie!" Bishop snaps at me and I divert my attention back to the head of the table. "Yes?"

Bishop stills, his eyes piercing into me like I had seen him do to Madison so many times before. Being on the receiving end of it, though, not so funny. I won't show him that. If you cower in the presence of a King, he'll have you kissing his feet for life.

"Let me go—"

"No," Nate interrupts, and I snap my attention straight to him. This table is full of Kings and Abel is sitting right beside me, but all I see is Nate. All I care about is Nate and why he thinks he can hold me here.

"Why!" I throw up my arms to add to my dramatics.

My chest tightens when he looks at me. His eyes are enough to grip onto every single human emotion that's inside of me and flip it upside down. I feel for Nate. I do. I'm in love with him, but I will never expose my feelings to him. You can't. Once you expose your love for someone, you've surrendered your power, and in this case, my forgiveness. I won't let him win. Not this time, and not any time soon.

Nate leans forward, his elbows resting on the table. "Because I don't want to."

I pause, allowing his words to sink into my brain. I blink a few times, count to ten, and then open my mouth. "Because you don't want to?" Then I look around the table, my eyes falling on Bishop. "You mean to tell me that the reason you're keeping me here is because he wants me here and that's it?"

Bishop grins. "That, and the fact that I can't have you running back to Madison and spilling all of our secrets."

I freeze this time, balling my fists under the table. "She doesn't know about Daemon, does she?"

Bishop runs his index finger over his upper lip, shaking his head with a smirk. "Nope."

"Why are you doing this to her, Bishop? You guys are solid. Set in stone. Fucking Madshop. Why?"

He seems to ponder over my words and then leans back in his seat. "You wanna know why we're fighting so much lately?"

"Yes. I do." Even though I know he's not going to tell me. Bishop always answers a question with a question, or words his answers in a way that you don't understand.

Bishop opens his mouth, and then just when he's about to say something, fucking Nate steps in and interferes. "—Don't."

Bishop instantly looks to Nate, and I watch as Bishop's hard exterior slowly melts away and for a second, he looks vulnerable. Hurt. Deceived. *God, Madison. What did you do?*

Bishop shakes himself off and then shrugs. "Fine. But she's going to find out sooner or later. You can't protect her from everything, Nate."

I scoff, because Bishop must be on some A-class shit to say that. *Only I know that he is.*

Abel, who has been quiet, finally speaks. "Where does this leave me?"

Bishop looks back at him and licks his lips. "How do you feel about the sight of blood?"

Chapter Four

Nate

I run my fingers through my hair, watching the sun set over the trees behind the mansion. I fucking hate staying on Perdita for longer than a day, but we're in day two and I'm getting fucking cabin fever. I mean, I'm about to slaughter some fucks if they say the wrong thing. Bishop let them out of the cells. Keeping Abel locked in a cell wasn't our play, it was Khales. We don't see either of them as a threat, and there's no way they can get out of this house, let alone off this fucking island.

I hear the bedroom door open and close behind me, and then a tumbler glass of whiskey on ice coming into view. "Think she will work out what we're doing?"

I take the glass from Brantley and bring it to my lips, shooting it back. "Yup. She's fucking smart. Way smarter than anyone we've ever had around."

"Agreed…" Brantley nods.

"But she can't know what we know. She will get reckless in her revenge and we can't have that."

Brantley leans forward, resting his arms on the barrier. "Also agreed."

"You care about her…." I try the unspoken words on the tip of my tongue. Don't much like how they taste.

Brantley chuckles, shaking his head and hanging it between his arms. "No. I don't think I care about her, but I also feel a little bit protective over her. If that makes sense."

"It doesn't." I sigh. "But I get it, man. Who would have thought, though. Out of everyone…"

"That she'd be the one who would pull on my rusted strings?"

We both laugh. "Yeah. Exactly. Was beginning to think you were built without

Brantley's jaw clenches. "Yeah, unfortunately, I am."

"So we agree?" I add, watching him carefully. "She isn't going to know?"

Brantley nods. "Yeah. We all agree. Right now isn't the time. It might make her worse."

Her being worse than she is now isn't something anyone wants.

Chapter Five

Tillie

I run my finger down his skull, over the lumps where the stitches were. "I'm sorry, Daemon."

He cranks his head, and I watch as his slim neck glistens under the candlelight in the room Nate put me in. Technically, Daemon should be in his room, but he and I have too much to talk about. I've yet to tell him about Micaela, which I'm dreading.

I climb off the bed and kneel down in front of him, where he's sitting on the floor at the foot of the bed. I search his eyes, black orbs that any other person would be afraid to look into. They're someone's nightmare, but my fantasy.

"I found your book, Daemon…"

He searches my eyes, and it's the first time I've noticed his hair. They must have had to shave it all off for surgery. It's not as short as it probably was, now it looks more like a military cut. It hardens his handsome features.

"I know, Puella."

"Do you need to tell me something?"

He opens his mouth and then closes it. "Yes, but—"

I lean forward, running my finger over his bottom lip. "I need to tell you something too, Daemon." My throat swells before I've even so much as flicked my tongue over the first syllable. He doesn't speak. He merely watches me with fascination. God, he's so beautiful. Too beautiful for earth, but too haunted for hell. "She passed away." It's the first time that the words have been on my tongue, threatening to slice me across the heart.

Daemon doesn't flinch. His eyelashes flutter closed and a flash of pain passes his face. "How?"

I curl my legs out from under my butt, massaging my temples. "Sudden Infant Death." I stand abruptly, my mind shutting down from the conversation I so openly started.

I don't want to talk about it anymore.

Why did I tell him? I wasn't ready. I thought I was ready. I start banging around the room in search of something to numb the ache that has started in my chest.

Daemon's hand comes to my arm.

I freeze, turning in his grip slowly.

His fingers come to my face, his thumb on my lip. I know what he's trying to say, I see it in the way his eyes peer into mine, like they're trying to speak a foreign language.

I smile, laying my face into the palm of his hand. "Go to bed. I will see you in the morning. I have a plan."

"A plan?" Daemon asks just as I reach for the door handle.

I smirk, not bothering to give him another look. "Yes. A plan."

I'm making my way down the twin staircase after Daemon heads to bed when Nate appears at the bottom. He's wearing grey sweats and nothing else. He's been working out, judging by the sweat that is dripping off his finely chiseled torso.

I cross my arms in front of my chest.

He smirks, his eyes eating up my body. "You look good in that..."

I roll my eyes, taking the final steps down and shoving past him. "Let me guess, you fucked my mom too."

A strong palm collides with my arm at the very place that Daemon just touched. Only where his was gentle, this was dominating.

"Don't do that."

"Do what?" I snap, spinning to face him. "The no-talking-to-you thing? Get used to it, Nate, because I hate you. You kidnapped me, brought me here, told me that everything was a plan from the beginning, told me you wanted to kill me—all for what?"

Nate doesn't say anything, his jaw set taut and his eyes glaring at me like a demon. A beautiful, unhinged, total bad boy demon. *What the fuck.* I need a drink.

I turn to go find some alcohol when his voice stops me. "I wasn't lying, Tillie."

"Yeah, well neither was I when I said that I hated you, so leave me the fuck alone."

Finding a bottle of Proper Twelve in the cupboard, I take down a tumbler and fill it with the amber liquid, shooting the first one back and inhaling the cloak of numbness that comes with the first swallow. The pain begins to dissipate into the back of my mind, so I pour another and put the bottle back tidily near the—fully stocked pantry.

I growl softly, piecing things together. They obviously had been planning this for some time to have all this food. There's shit in here from our world, not from Perdita. Swirling the liquid in my glass, I take a closer look around the kitchen. It's splashed in white marble and black trimmings, with one glass window that overlooks the backyard. There's an adjacent dining room on the other side and I quickly step in, noting the twelve-piece dining suite. To the right is floor to ceiling glass that opens out onto the backyard. No pool. Interesting. I push on the door, stepping out into the cold soft wind, closing it behind myself. There may be no pool, but there are beautifully kept flowers that are blossoming against what lighting there is.

"Can't sleep?" a deep, familiar voice interrupts my downtime.

I don't bother to look toward it. I know that it's Brantley. "Well, that amongst other things."

"What do you think of flowers?" he asks, and that question was random enough to conjure me to look at him. He's sitting on a small iron set chair near a stone fountain that's decorated by small hedges and vines of roses.

I take a couple of steps down, sinking deeper into the dark night. "Hmmm, I've never thought much about it. Why?"

Brantley chuckles and then stands. When he comes opposite me, his presence is intimidating, but I don't falter.

"Why did you all bring me here?" I try him.

"Because this is where you should be."

I pause, contemplating whether I should or should not cuss him out for pulling a Bishop on me and lying straight to my face. "Every time you're vague to me, I'm calling you Bran Bran."

His head snaps in the general direction of yours truly. "I think the fuck not!"

I chuckle, swirling my whiskey around inside my glass. "Your reaction has just so-lidified the fact that I indeed, will be calling you Bran Bran every time you are vague, or I think you're lying to me."

He kicks my chair, so I look at him. Which I do, over the tumbler glass as I bring it to my smug lips. "Don't like that name, *Princessa*."

"Then don't lie to me."

He seems to ponder my words until we've sat for another fifteen minutes in pure silence. The only sound is coming from the rustling trees, and very faintly, the soft crashing of waves in the near distance.

He lights a smoke. "Have you spoken much to Daemon?" He tosses the pack onto the table in front of us.

"No?" I reach for the pack, suddenly itching for something a little extra to take the edge off. "Well, not as much as I would have liked. Not yet. I will. He seems more distant and stranger than usual."

Brantley snatches the packet from me, glaring and tossing it back onto the table. "That's expected. After everything he's been through. I'm surprised there's anything left of him at all upstairs...." He bites out the end of his sentence, which again catches my attention.

"What do you mean?"

He doesn't answer, and I catch the way he licks his lower lip with his tongue against the moonlight. Brantley has surprised me most when it comes to The Kings. He's the one I thought I'd least have a connection with. I thought maybe Eli, the jokester, or Hunter, the up-and-coming dark and moody rock star. Or even Bishop, or Cash, or Ace. Any of them but Brantley. The connection we have is something that I will feel until the day I die. It's easy without being boring. Like a shadow, I always know he's there.

"He's not the same as he used to be, Tillie. Just be wary of the way you are around him. He's not the same boy you knew."

I figured as much, from what I've seen so far but the fact that Brantley has confirmed it only intensifies my feelings.

"Okay. I will. Thank you. One more question... is Nate going to let me go?"

Brantley's eyes go over my shoulder. "Maybe you should ask him." He starts to stand, moving closer to me and wraps his fingers around my chin, tilting my face up to his. "One day, when this asshole isn't lurking around you like a hungry lion protecting his prey, I'm going to play some games with you."

I bite my lower lip, my cheeks igniting in flames at his words. My thighs clench together as his grip tightens around my chin, his thumb pressing against my lower lip.

"The kind where there are only two players until it's Game Over."

He leans down and presses his lips to my head. "Night, *Princessa...*"

I'm still shocked by what just happened, but when he's walking away, I quickly compose myself and yell back, "Night Bran Bran!"

The whiskey isn't helping much, so I look down at the table and see Brantley's left his pack of smokes. I snatch up the packet and take one out, inhaling deeply. The thick nicotine sets in my lungs before I exhale. It's been a long day, and when I step back to evaluate everything that's going on in my life right now, it still doesn't make much sense.

"Bad habit," Nate interrupts from behind me. I forgot he was there.

I don't look back. "So it seems. Just add it to my list of the others." I bring my eyes to his as he rounds the table. I suck in the smoke and curl my lips in an O to puff out perfect smoke rings. "Bad habits."

He pins me with a stare, not answering. He looks good, but then, he always does. No one has said anything about Nate Riverside-Malum's appearance. Because they can't. It's what he hides beneath the pretty smile that people should talk about.

"When are you taking me back to civilization?" I ask, flicking the ash off my smoke and picking up my glass of whiskey. The liquid is doing what is intended, my head spinning in a Ferris wheel of confusion.

"Do you want to go back to go back? Or do you want to go back to be away from me?" he asks, and I don't have to be able to see his face to know that one eyebrow would be cocked and a slight smirk would be on his lips.

I ignore him, not ready to admit how it feels to be here. Away from reminders of—my life before. Not ready to admit that his danger dances around me, teasing me to come play. Until I get lost in the maze that constructs their world. Their beautiful, fucked up world.

His shadow moves closer to me and the chair scrapes against the concrete as he takes a seat.

He's so close. Close enough I can almost hear his thoughts.

"Tillie."

I ignore him.

"Look at me."

"Fuck you."

Silence. He brings his hands to both sides of my chair and pulls me closer to him. I still don't look. He wraps his fingers around my chin and forces my attention on him. I clench my jaw.

He's wearing a dark hoodie and jeans. I can see his eyes peering at me from underneath, and even more so, the gloss of his high cheekbones.

"I meant after Micaela died. Not before. Everything *after* was planned."

I bring my smoke to my mouth and suck, inhaling. I blow out in his face, because I know how much he hates cigarette smoke. "Is that supposed to make me feel better?"

He snatches the smoke from between my fingers and squashes it with his bare hand. "It's supposed to make you fucking realize that I'm not a goddam monster, Tillie. My shit has purpose. Real fucking purpose."

"You're not a monster?" I ask, tilting my head while softening my voice.

"No, I'm not. I can be, yes, but like I've always said, I've never shown that fucking side of me to you."

"That's funny…" I mutter, bringing my face close to his. Close enough for the tips of our noses to touch. "Because your demons whispered all your secrets into my ear the day you dragged me through your hell, and let me tell you something, you are a monster, Nate. And a liar."

His mouth slams shut.

I stand, shoving his hands off me. "And your words mean nothing to me, Nate. In the morning, I'm going to find your father, and I'm getting to the bottom of whatever the fuck is going on here."

I start walking back toward the house when his words stop me. "You'll trust him before you'd trust me?"

My body stills as my feet mount the cement steps and guilt threatens to take hold of all my self-restraint. I can't let him win. I can't. He has to pay for his actions, even if it means I risk losing him forever.

"Yes," I lie, walking back up the stairs.

"Then you're not as smart as we all thought."

Chapter Six

Tillie

I woke this morning with a whiskey hangover from Hades. Whole head throbbing, mouth frothing, hunger panging type shit, but after quickly washing in the shower and dressing into Khales', or Katsia's clothes, I feel a little more like a human and less like the asshole of one. Who knew they both had similar taste. I settled for Khales' because fuck her. So I found myself in tight little leather shorts that covered just enough of my ass cheeks and a skate shirt that was torn in odd places. I matched the shorts with black thigh high-boots and a leather jacket, and I was good to go. Not really, because this style was not me by any sense, but it wasn't like I had many options.

"Tell me about yourself…" I mutter as Abel and I walk down the main street of Perdita. I couldn't find Daemon this morning and couldn't risk bumping into any of The Kings and having them stop me from my plan today, so I snatched Abel on his way out of the shower and we left. I let him put some clothes on, although after seeing him half-naked, I sort of wished I didn't.

"Not much to tell."

"For some reason," I start, looking down each alleyway of the main street of Perdita. "I think you're lying."

He chuckles. "I'm a lot of fucked up things, but a liar isn't one of them."

"Yeah, sure, that's what they all say."

"I'm not them."

His words are simple, yet his tone tells me he's implying The Kings.

I stop, turning to face him. I don't know why, but it doesn't feel right. I don't like judgment in any case, but even more so from a boy who doesn't understand how this world works. "And what do you mean by that?"

He searches my eyes, and I actually feel myself start to burn up, his beauty is that toxic. Like Medusa, you don't want to look directly into his eyes. He doesn't flinch, and it's scary.

"I kill for less."

I believe him. "I want to know your story one day."

He snorts. "I'm not here to give you what you want, *Princessa*."

"Well, you're like your brother in that sense."

"In what sense?"

"You're both assholes."

He chortles. "I'm nothing like him."

I point to the chocolate store. "That's why we're here."

"We're here because of chocolate?" Abel asks, stopping in his tracks as I start heading toward the storefront.

"I've heard about their Ruby chocolate. We will make a quick dash, and then go and find daddy Gabe."

We're making our way back to the mansion when Abel asks around a mouth full of chocolate, "Why don't you trust them?"

"Because they're bad people," I answer instantly, not having to think too much about my answer because it's truth.

"Are they bad people, or are they just always given bad choices?" Abel asks, and his annoyingly intelligent brain irks me.

"You're too hot to be that smart."

The guard lets me in, his head bowed. A small sense of power comes with that, but it's power that I'm not interested in dabbling in. I didn't earn it. I don't want it.

We enter the main lobby, shutting the heavy wooden doors behind me.

"Tillie!" I hear Nate yell out from the kitchen.

I roll my eyes.

Abel smirks.

We make our way toward the annoying voice, entering the kitchen, I see all of The Kings seated at the table, including Nate's dad, Gabriel.

I take a step forward, but he shakes his head. I see the worry etched into his features. The way his eyebrows furrow over his dark eyes.

I pause, straightening. "What's going on?"

Chapter Seven

Nate

I can count on one hand how many times I have been shackled by a woman. Rendered fucking speechless and brought to my damn knees by a simple blink of her eye. Three times. Twice was Tillie, and the other was Micaela.

Even with her standing there, at my disposal, glaring at me like she hates sharing the same air as me, my dick is rock hard, swollen against the zipper in my pants.

"Are you talking?" she asks, placing her hands on her hips.

I smirk. Because it's fucking cute that she does shit to try to make herself appear stronger than she feels. Not saying she's not, she's definitely the most glued together girl we've ever had around. She's level-headed, smart, fucking sassy, and she can hold her own. She doesn't do drugs, (usually), and doesn't give a fuck if anyone else is doing it. She hardly drinks and doesn't sleep around. How'd I manage to fuck all of that up epically in the span of a few months? Right. Because I'm me.

"Yeah, babe, take a seat." The smirk stays, biting down on the toothpick in my mouth.

She glares with force this time.

I laugh. "Easy tiger, take a seat so we can talk."

She crosses her arms. A step up from them being on her hips. My eyes drop, my smile deepening when they land on her arms, but then they go lower, and I'm smack bang face to face with her sexy as sin legs. My smile instantly drops, and I shuffle in my seat to readjust myself.

"Are you going to be honest with me?"

"Yes," I answer instantly, because I'll always be honest with her, with the exception of what I *think* she needs to know.

She slowly lowers herself onto the chair. "Talk. Why the fuck did you kidnap me and bring me here?"

"First of all." I lean forward, blazing my joint. "We didn't bring you here. You walked your little ass right up to this house all on your own. Second of all." I blow out a thick cloud of smoke, her beautiful fucking face still glaring at me through the smoke. "I wasn't lying when I told you that it was planned to get you here."

She waves the smoke away. "And why is that?"

Bishop's phone goes off and he quickly leaves the room, answering it as he slides the glass door closed. I falter a little, wanting to ask him what the fuck is going on with his phone and who he has been talking with for the past day. Task at hand.

"Because we needed to take you away from civilization for a while."

"Why? What's happening? And you couldn't just tell me? You had to be dramatic and lock me in a fucking cell!"

She's angry now. Good. She's always cute, but when she's angry, there's something inside of me that recognizes her fire and wants to build an inferno with her. The only problem is that those closest to us get burned. She holds all of the cards when it comes to me. But my poker face is too good, so she just doesn't know it yet. Connection is rare, I fucking know this. As much as there's still so much that she doesn't know yet, I have every intention to keep her safe. How I go about that, though, is completely up to me. Those are the cards that I'm dealing and that's the hand I'll be playing.

I stare at her, lick my lip and smirk. "Because I was bored."

She doesn't bite, and just as her mouth opens, Bishop is back inside, slamming the door closed with force.

"Bitch."

I narrow my eyes at him. "Who you calling bitch?"

He yanks out his chair and rakes his hands through his hair. "Don't fucking start with me, Nate."

I find Brantley, who is already watching me carefully. Something deeper is going on between the two of them, and we all know it's only going to get worse when Madison finds out about the Daemon shit. Did I know about it? No. For generations now, the Hayes name has been feared amongst the Elite, the mundane, and anyone and everyone who even knew a smidge about our life, but that's about to change, because Bishop has let some humanity sneak through. He's not as vicious or cold-hearted as his father, and trust me, that's a very fucking good thing, but more than that, we come first with him, not the throne. Which is why he battles with a lot of his decisions. I can see him struggling. I haven't seen him in such a bad place since before Madison walked into his life.

"Carry on." Tillie pulls my attention away from my inner thoughts.

"Until we tie up a loose end with something, your ass needs to stay here, and that's all there is to it."

Her eyes whip to my dad, who is sitting on the other side of the table. "So you were in on getting me here too?"

"No," I interrupt, grinning from ear to ear. "Gabriel is something else entirely."

"But this doesn't make sense to me. You bring me here—" She pauses, her eyes glazing over as they go over my shoulder.

My blood turns cold, my jaw tensing. Having this fucker hanging around isn't ideal, considering he and Tillie's connection. I'm not a fucking idiot. I saw what they had. It makes me want to rip the flesh from his face and feed it to her. Instantly, hate and anger bubbles to the surface, threatening to spill over the edges.

Tillie turns, and I watch as her shoulders visibly relax. "Oh, hey."

Bishop's eyes come straight to me. He's trying to reassure me. Settle me down. It isn't working.

My lip curls into a snarl and I open my mouth to tell him to fuck off, but Brantley's foot connects with my leg under the table, breaking the trance that had me seeing red with the *Kill Bill* theme song playing on loud.

I look at Brantley, who shakes his head at me.

Exhaling, I clench my fist a few times, cutting out whatever the fuck it is everyone is talking about, now lost in my rage. I need to calm down. I've never felt such fucking anger until I met Tillie. She's the only one who can reach the string and tug on every single fucking emotion that is inside of me.

I hate it.

She's a fucking weakness.

Push her away.

"I need you back on land," I find myself blurting out, and Bishop kicks me now. I don't give a shit. She's my game, not his. He ruined his game and now his key player is damaged beyond repair, for reasons I still don't fucking know.

I bring my eyes to Tillie. "I need you back at the house. Until I say otherwise."

She laughs, her little face tilting back as a sarcastic chuckle spills from those sexy fucking lips. "I don't take orders from you, *Nate*."

I push up from my chair, the scraping breaking through the silence. I start walking toward her slowly, not moving my attention from her. "Really?"

She doesn't call my bluff. Any other chick would be afraid, maybe even cower. Madison always did. But not Tillie, and it fucking turns me on.

She smirks, leaning back in her chair and licking her lips. "*Really.*"

"Ah, not to be the asshole in the room," Cash interferes. "But I'll be the asshole in the room. You're both insane."

I lean down, both my hands landing on either side of her chair. "It's cute." I run the tip of my nose over hers, smirking while ignoring her scent.

"What's cute?" Her eyes cross in briefly, her chest rising and falling slowly.

Click! I clasp a handcuff around her wrist, the other side around mine.

She gasps and then yanks on the handcuff.

I smirk, nipping her lower lip between my teeth before standing straight. "The fact that you think you have any power when it comes to me. Because just to be clear, princess, you don't. Get up." I yank her until she's standing.

"I hate you."

I roll my eyes, dragging her behind me until I'm back in my seat. She stands beside my chair awkwardly, the sight making me laugh a little.

"Shut up, Nate. I hate you."

"Don't have to like me to sit on my dick, princess." Then I yank her down until her ass is pressing into my cock.

I groan, biting my lip while readjusting her position so she's not right there.

She flicks her legs over so she's sitting across my lap now, instead of directly on my cock. She moves again, smirking down at me. "You think you have the power, but last I checked, I'm the one with the pussy."

I chuckle, my hand coming to her upper thigh, squeezing hard enough for her to cringe beneath that fake confidence. With my other hand, I grab her chin and tilt her face down to mine. "I'm well acquainted with your pussy, *Princessa*, but if you pull that shit again, I'll tear off your clothes and fuck you until you're black and blue and bleeding out on this table. Don't fucking test me, baby, because your pussy will not be so testy once I'm done with it."

Her eyes narrow on mine, and I wait for her to answer. "What?" I tease. "You know I can do this all day..."

"—I think we've been distracted enough. Nate, tell me what you mean by you wanting Tillie back on main soil. I thought we agreed she was to stay here until we figure out—" Bishop stops, with good reason.

Tillie can't know what we know. Not because I'm being a cunt by not telling her, no offense to Bishop, but because I don't think she can handle it right now. And that's saying something because she can handle a fucking lot, but this? No.

I lick my lip, relaxing into my chair. "Changed my mind. We can't be here. We need to be back and I'd rather her be with me all the way through."

Bishop's eyes fly between the two of us. He sinks back in his chair. "This is King business, Nate. You know the rules."

I shrug. "Fuck the rules. This is her world too, B. She has every right to the information as we do. Hell, she'll be here, running this shit once we're done with her."

"Ah—excuse me bu—"

I ignore her. "So it's best for her to be with us until we've solved the first thing we're trying to figure out—"

"—yeah, but I don—"

I cut her off again, "—Does anyone contest this?" I ask, my eyes going around the table to a shake of heads.

"—yes! I fucking d—"

My hand slams over her mouth.

"Good. It's settled. Pack up the Lost Boy and Abel. The same goes for the two of you."

Tillie slaps my hand away from her mouth. "Agh!" she screams. "I fucking hate you! Handcuff me to Bran Bran instead!"

"Woah!" Brantley glares at her. "I didn't fucking lie to you! That nickname is only allowed if I fucking lie to you!"

She smiles at him, and I watch as his eyes narrow to slits. "*I changed my mind.*"

Brantley's face morphs into a cold, neutral expression. I have to hide my laughter. "You're a pain in not just his ass, but mine too, but I don't get to eat that ass, so this shit isn't fair."

I push Tillie off my lap, and she fumbles to her feet like a new baby fawn.

I laugh, standing. "I might let you taste it if she doesn't behave herself."

Tillie swipes her hair out of her face. "Well, in that case, I'll misbehave all I can."

The teasing with Brantley doesn't bother me. I've seen them do some pretty fucking questionable things, and it didn't bother me to a degree, because I know what they have. The twisted little bond that they share isn't something that I'm worried about, nor do I give a fuck about. He's just her...me.

Besides all of that, he's my brother. But Daemon? He so much as breathes near her and I turn into fucking Lucifer. Do I want to wife her? Fuck no. Do I even want a relationship with her? Also fuck no. I'm not ready to have my cock on a leash, but do I have feelings for her? Yeah. I'm man enough to admit that. To myself, not anyone else. Tillie plays with my emotions like a fucking fiddle. I've seen what happens when I give her half of me. I lose myself in her, lost in a fucking daze that I never want to wake from. Give her all of me? I'd never survive. So for now, she'll just have to eat my words. Or choke on them. Whichever will work for me.

"Where?" Bishop interrupts. "Where are we going to be keeping these three?"

I tilt my head. "The parents are away from tomorrow onward, but with Madison walking in and out, it's not the ideal place."

"True. Also, that rules out my house, and my parents' house," Bishop says, his eyes going to Brantley.

"—I can just buy a fucking house," I interrupt before he calls out Brantley.

Brantley looks at me, his jaw tensing. "Nah it's good. We can put them at mine. Lots of rooms we can lock her up in if she doesn't do as she's fucking told." He's glaring at Tillie now.

"You sure?" I ask, ignoring his statement about Tillie obeying orders. The girl will never obey fucking orders, only when her lips are wrapped around my cock. My eyes bore into his. I'm probably the only one who knows Brantley through and through, but even I know there are secrets that he's hiding, all of which are confined in that creepy fucking house.

"Yeah, I'm sure."

Lies.

Chapter Eight

Tillie

"Why am I still handcuffed to you? You know I'm not going to run!" I yank my hand up to illustrate my point. The flight was long, like it always is, and we're pulling up to Nate's house now in a large stretch limo. Bishop sits beside Nate who is beside Brantley. Next to me is Abel and Daemon, who hasn't spoken much at all. I take this time to glare at Bishop.

"You keeping him from Madison is going to brew a storm that none of us are prepared for, B."

His eyes stay on mine. "Maybe she should have thought about that a long time ago, Tills."

"What's that supposed to mean?" I question him, my eyes narrowing. I'm a girl's girl. Yeah, so I might be spending more time than I want around all The Kings, but that means jack shit when it comes to Madison.

He chuckles, shaking his head. "Maybe you need to talk to your friend when her nose isn't lost in snow."

My mouth snaps shut. "You did not—Bishop! You know damn well she doesn't usually do drugs. She's, she's—"

"—changed," Bishop snaps at me. "She has fucking changed, Tillie. She's not the same fucking girl that I fell in love with. It fucking happens. It fucking happened," he sighs, just as the limo pulls to a stop. Bishop buries his face in his hands, shaking his head. His hurt and agony fills the small space of the limo.

"B, do you want to talk to me about it?" I ignore everyone else in the car, because right now, none of these fuckers matter. All that matters is that the most epic love story to ever grace our world is on the edge of complete annihilation. An apocalypse of love

"Just get out."

We all pile out one by one and Nate leans back inside the car for a few minutes. When he finishes talking with Bishop, he shuts the door, his eyes going to Bran Bran.

"He'll be back tomorrow," Nate murmurs, yanking me with his arm until I have no choice but to follow as he leads us up the stone stairs to Brantley's home.

It's freaky, but I've been here a couple times now, so the air of surprise is gone. Nate pushes open the door and we're met with complete silence.

"Bran Bran, where are your lights?"

He groans in pain. "I swear to god, Tillie, I'm going to start giving you warnings. You get three a day." The light flicks on and we're met with this beautifully dark and haunted mansion. "You get to three and I'm taking you over my knee and beating your ass blue. Deal?"

I raise an eyebrow in defiance. He doesn't even look at me through all of that, it was a simple matter of fact. When he notices I'm not answering and everyone around us has fallen quiet, his eyes come to mine. "Deal?"

I shrug. "Deal."

Nate yanks on the handcuff. "She's just going to play up on purpose now. Stop feeding the monster."

Brantley turns to look over his shoulder, his eyes darkening. "I happen to like my little terror." He winks and then goes back to leading us through the house. The walls are blood red and black with old tarnished wood lining the framework. The windows are all stained glass with cross wood through them. The living room resembles a damn church and the fire is flickering slowly, burning to embers.

"Who lit the fire?" I ask, yanking on Nate's arm in an attempt to drag him toward the sofa.

With my hundred thirty-five pounds against his what, one-eighty? That doesn't do anything.

I pause, turning to face Nate who is trying his hardest to hide his laugh.

"Move!" I groan, getting angry at him and his stupid Nate antics. He finally follows and drags me onto the sofa beside him.

Brantley doesn't answer my question. "So here's the deal," he says instead. "You all will stay here, but you will stay on the first level since there's only one way in and one way out down there. You will be allowed up during the week, but know that I have guards all around this joint. They shoot to kill, so I wouldn't try anything. I'm sure you've heard of the Vitiosis graveyard that sits in our backyard? Yeah, well, not all of the blood that has seeped into that soil is Vitiosis blood—if you know what I mean."

Abel clears his throat. "What am I doing here?"

Brantley's eyes come to his, and he leans forward, his face blank. "You, young pup, are going to be our little prodigy."

I massage my temple with my free hand. "Oh no. Oh!" I answer, finally remembering. "Oh my god! Where is Bailey?"

Brantley stills.

"Bran Bran…" I swear if he has killed her or given her away, I'll never speak to him again and the next body in the Vitiosis graveyard will most definitely be a Vitiosis.

"That's your second warning, and she's in the right wing. Never see her much. Thank fuck."

I exhale, exhausted from the day.

I feel the heavy clip around my wrist loosen, so I stretch out my hand, turning to face Nate. "Thanks."

His eyes stay on mine, and for a flash, I think I see something. Something familiar but broken. We haven't spoken about her, or anything since he locked me in the cell, and I'm not sure whether I'd want to.

"How do I trust you?" I ask him, wanting to know the answer to the golden question. "You're all always playing games."

Nate's lip slowly kicks up in a smirk. "Simple really, you don't." Then he grips onto my arm and yanks me to my feet. When Daemon stands, Nate comes face-to-face with him. "Do I need to warn you about your hands, young one?"

I tap at Nate's arm, anger simmering to the surface at how he's being with Daemon. "Nate, leave him alone."

Daemon's eyes come to me, and then back to Nate. "No. You do not, though I am not sure she likes your hands either."

"I'm tired. Just, let's go to bed."

"Abel stays up here," Brantley murmurs, pointing to the sofa. "You'll be sitting in during our meet tonight. Better you start learning now."

Abel drops back onto the sofa.

"Here, I'll take them down. You sit with Abel and talk him through shit," Brantley orders Nate, who is watching him with careful eyes. Something passes between the two of them and I'm not sure we catch it.

Nate switches with Brantley. I have a feeling that whatever it is that passes between the two of them, it has nothing to do with me.

Brantley pushes past me, and my eyes find Nate once more, but he's already talking with Abel. We make our way down the dark hallway. It's furnished with old portrait paintings that cling to the ancient walls. Nate has been even more complicated since being in Perdita and leaving. He's like a stitch, trying to seal all the splits that have happened with him, but his evil is too dark and strong, spilling between the seams. I want to help him, but I also want to punish him. Punishing him only encourages him and turns him on, so I need to go the opposite way of both love and hate.

I need to go numb with him.

Brantley was right, there are a few bedrooms downstairs. It's a weird level, giving me creepy vibes. The walls are all dark burgundy, and there's just one stretch of hallway that's so small it has my fear of small spaces acting up. There are three doors, all of which open up into a bedroom. In those rooms is one single bed and a small bathroom.

Brantley is leaning on the door frame when I lower myself onto the mattress.

"Are you locking my door?"

"No," Brantley says. "But I will be locking the main door up the hallway."

I sigh, leaning forward. "Why do I still feel like a prisoner?"

"Because you are." He turns to leave, tilting his head over his shoulder slightly. "I've left both yours and *Daemon's* doors unlocked. Try talking with him, Tillie. See where his head is at."

"Brantley?" I call out just as he's about to leave. "Where's Nate's dad?"

Brantley chuckles. "All in good time."

"B?" I whisper and I see from the corner of my eye his footsteps falter. My focus remains on a rough patch on the wall, isolated. So *fucking isolated*. "Tell me he will be okay. That this up and down bipolar thing isn't going to be forever."

Brantley turns around, and I finally bring my eyes up to his. My throat swells with emotion, but I choke down any tears. They cannot see any of my weaknesses, and Nate is my biggest.

"You'll come to learn, or are already learning, that there are two sides to Nate. This is just him. This is how he is. How he reacts to different circumstances is always erratic, we can never be sure which side we're going to land on. There's the jokester side, then there's his Malum side. He battles with the two personalities a lot, I know this, but one thing you should always remember is that both of those sides have one thing in common."

I tilt my head, snuffling my nose. "And what's that?"

He stares at me blankly. "You."

Chapter Nine

Tillie

You can't explain why people do the things they do or why they can be so vastly different. I've tried. Being surrounded by somewhat off-balance individuals for the better part of my life has been the biggest teacher of all when it comes to this.

So why is it that when it comes to Daemon, I can feel so strongly for him while really knowing nothing much about him. Connection? Sure. Love? A little bit. But mystery? Danger? Definitely. Daemon is the calm before the storm. You know it could be deadly, but it's also controlled. I used to think the same about Nate and Bishop, but lately, their decisions have been driven by something far more powerful.

Love and Hate.

"How's your head?" I ask, taking a seat on his bed beside him. This room is much like mine. They're identical. "This place gives me the creeps."

Daemon shuffles closer to me, his feet dangling off the bed. I turn to face him, for the first time with it just being him and I and a long stretch of silence.

"I've missed you."

I lick my lips and turn to face him, my hands coming to his. He looks so different with short hair. It gives his very pretty face a rougher edge. I miss his hair. My hand comes up to his head and I stretch my fingers out over his scalp, feeling the spikes brush against the palm of my hand.

His eyes close, peace falling over his features. "I missed you too."

His eyes slowly open onto my mouth. I freeze. With the language barrier, we've always gone by what feels right in the moment. He comforted me when I needed it and I lit him on fire when he craved it, but kissing him right now would feel wrong. I can't lead him into thinking that we can pick up where we left off all those months ago. Too much has changed, so much has hardened. I'm not the same girl I was when he left me, and he's not the same boy who I knew when I left.

I run my finger down the side of his face, dragging it over his bottom lip. "You need to be free, Daemon."

"Free," he mimics, his lips curving with each letter.

I nod. "Free."

He leans away from me slightly. "I'll never be free, Puella. Nothing can free me. Not even you." His eyes bore into mine.

I stifle a laugh. "How could I free you?"

He doesn't answer me, his eyes staying on mine. I fight the urge to crawl onto his lap. "Did you—" He pauses, searching around the place. "Finish my book?"

Everything fast-forwards and I'm instantly thrown back into the pages of Puer Natus. I shake my head. "Not yet."

"Finish it," he orders and then turns to face the wall.

I don't have the heart to tell him that I don't know where it is right now, so I settle on, "Can't you just tell me how it ends?"

He doesn't answer. He's shut off. I slowly stand from his bed and tiptoe to where he lays. Leaning down, I press my lips to his head, holding it there for a second while inhaling the smell of dirt, blood, and something sweet.

"I'm sorry, Daemon."

I leave, sinking into my bed once I get back into my room.

Why can't I save him? I want to save him. I can't save him. No one can save him but himself, and even then, I don't even think he could save himself.

Wind whisks through my hair, flicking it up into the air as I run down the concrete path. The city is empty, and when I stop and look up, I see I'm directly outside Madison and Bishop's apartment. There's no doorman. No cars. No lights. No power. The sun is setting, and the burnt orange hue is slowly dropping into a deep brown. My toes curl against the rusted leaves that have fallen. Why was I running? I turn around to see ten men standing in a line, black hoodies covering their faces. Their heads slowly come up and the Día de Los Muertos face paint comes into view, but then the paint starts to slowly melt from their faces. I scream as the song "Pop Goes the Weasel" starts playing. Slamming my hands over my ears, I fall to the ground and begin rocking back and forth.

"Stop!" I scream so loud my throat throbs from the pain.

Silence finally cuts through the torturous sound. I slowly peel my eyes open, only now I'm in the middle of a cemetery. I recognize it. The stone in front of me catches my eye and I see D A E M O N spelled in Celtic font over it. Nothing else. Just Daemon.

"What?"

"Pop Goes the Weasel" starts again as the grass melts away from beneath my feet and I'm falling.

"No!" I shake my head, darkness enveloping me in the small grave. "No!" I scream, reaching for the walls but dirt fills my hands and the darkness gets more opaque. The ten Kings all circle the grave above, peering down at me.

"Let me out!"

Dirt flies into the grave, hitting my face—

I fly off the bed, but someone is sitting at the foot. Sweat is dripping down my face.

"Daemon?" I clutch the blankets up to my chin, the nightmare still fresh on my mind. *It wasn't real.*

"Nightmare?" he asks without looking at me.

I lick my lips. "Yes." I wonder what the time is, but if I'm guessing by my body clock, I would say pushing close to early morning.

"Are you okay?"

Daemon turns to face me. "No. Finish the book, Puella. For me."

I gulp. "Okay."

He stands and makes his way back out the door. He came in here to tell me that? Why does he scare me more than usual since he's been back?

I rub my temples, closing my eyes while trying to form the right words or thoughts. Exhaling, I flick the blankets off of my body and step all the way down the hallway until I reach the door. I pull on the handle, but it's locked. Just as I'm about to bang on it, it flies open and Nate is standing opposite me.

He dips his head. "Come on."

"What about Daemon?"

Nate's jaw clenches and he shuts the door. "He's staying down here. By choice. Let's go."

I follow him as he leads me up the stairs and back to the main floor. When we reach the kitchen, Bailey is sitting on a bar stool, eating granola.

"Hey!" Her face lights up and she swings her little body off the chair, making her way to me. "Brantley said you were here, so I thought I'd come say hi."

I pull her in for a hug, the familiarity strong. "Are you okay?" I ask, my hands coming to her arms as I search over her. "He hasn't hurt you?"

"Stop being so dramatic, little terror."

My cheeks hurt from the smile that's stretching over my face. "Can I say that I prefer little terror over princess?"

Brantley pours some coffee into a mug and that's when my eyes come to him. He's wearing loose grey sweats and no shirt. Did I say no shirt, because I meant no *fucking* shirt. His floppy dark hair falls over his forehead slightly, his dark eyes zeroing in on me. The dick print is strong, and I have to fight with myself not to do something girly like bite my lip or moan.

When my eyes finally come back to Brantley's, he's smirking at me over the rim of his mug. "You're drooling like you haven't seen what's under these pants."

I roll my eyes, taking my attention back to something safe, like Bailey.

"How are you?"

She shrugs. "I'll be okay. I have orders that I'll be starting Riverside Prep next year, so I guess I'm just winging it until then."

My eyes shoot to Brantley. "Is that right? Awful school…"

Nate kicks the backs of my legs. "That's my school you're talking about…literally. I own it."

I flop down onto a bar stool as Brantley slides over a cup of coffee. I take it, sipping on the hot drink. "So what have you been doing while you've been here? Are you attending your old school until RPA?"

"No, I've taken the rest of the year off until I start."

"Oh, that's awful. Being stuck in this house with this bossy bastard?"

She shrugs. "It's not all that bad. Brantley throws platinum cards at me and bought me a shiny new car."

I smirk at Brantley. "I would call that love in their language."

Brantley flips me off. "Shut up."

I giggle, looking back at Bailey. "Have you heard from your parents?"

Her body visibly halts, her face falling. "Yeah once. When I told them that Brantley had taken me in, they apologized for everything and tried to cover what they had done to make me come home. I told them no. I think they were scared, to be honest."

I snort. "With good reason. Has Brantley told you about the Vitiosis graveyard in the back? Because let me tell you…"

Bailey starts laughing, her little face tipping back. She's so beautiful. She's going to own that school, not just with her beauty, but with the Vitiosis name attached to it too.

"Yeah," she chuckles. "He has. That was the first threat he gave me." She stands from her seat, just as Bishop and Eli walk into the kitchen. "Oh! I got you a gift."

I sit up straight. "Me? Why?"

She flushes. "I don't know. You saved me. I'll always owe you, but for now…"

She leans over the kitchen island, her perky, young ass in the air for all the boys to see. My eyes go straight to Nate. Bet the fucker is eating it up, but when my eyes land on his, he's smirking at me. My stomach clenches at the stare he's giving me.

"Surprised?" His smirk darkens.

Damnit.

Bishop isn't taking notice, but Eli is. He tilts his head, his lips forming an O.

Brantley shakes his head, laughing.

Bailey stands back up, thank god, and hands me a small Tiffany & Co. box. "Here you go. It's just something that reminded me of you, because of your tattoo on your thigh."

My hand comes to my thigh before I flip open the box.

"Holy shit," I whisper. It's a rose gold crown with flush white diamonds glistening over every single piece of it. The chain glistens as it hits the sunlight.

I slam it shut. "I can't accept this, Bailey. It's too much. I like—"

"—She likes Chinese food," Nate interrupts, choking on a laugh.

Bailey glares. "Listen, you will put it on and love it because I will be offended if you don't. It's nothing. Honestly, and if it makes you feel better, I paid for it with Brantley's money, so—"

"—That money is yours too, Bailey, it's a trust fund."

"Shhhh." I push my finger to my lips, grinning at Brantley. "It does make it a lot better." I exhale, taking it out of the box. "I love it so much. Thank you." I stand up and pull her in for a hug. "I mean it. And saving you was no problem. I wish I went with these ass-holes more often. Maybe I could save a few more girls," I joke, but she stiffens in my grip.

"Yeah. If only," she whispers, her face falling.

"Jeez, little cuz, looks like we need to work on your poker face. It's shit." Brantley tugs on Bailey and starts to walk her out of the room.

What? What?

"What was that about?" I ask Nate, who is still smirking at me. "Stop fucking smirking at me."

His smile drops, and his face goes blank. Why. Why does this infuriating, frustratingly beautiful man have to be the bane of my damn existence? His lip kicks up in a smooth grin. "That is none of your business."

Bishop tosses me a small box. "You need to get in contact with Madison and Elena. They're both freaking out that you're dead or gone missing. I told them that you're fine, but I think it'll be best if you call her yourself."

I grip the box that contains a phone. "Really? And what *am* I supposed to tell her?"

Bishop's eyes flick to Nate before coming back to me. "Not about Daemon. Just say you're with us until we've sorted something."

"What's the thing? And you want me to lie to her about Daemon?"

Bishop glares at Nate.

"Bishop!" I snap at him, sidestepping the view of Nate. "You want me to lie to my best friend about something that will potentially push her over the edge?"

I see Bishop's eyes harden. "She's already over the fucking edge, Tillie." Then he looks to Nate. "You both need to talk with her once this is over. Because there's a whole lot that she's not telling you." He storms off as quickly as he stormed in. My chest tightens. I'm so sick of the dramatics.

Turning around, I find Nate. "Why is this all so difficult?"

I don't even manage to ask where Abel has gone.

Once I'm back in my bedroom, I turn my phone on, my legs curling under my butt as I dial Madison's number. I know her number by heart.

"Hello?" Madison answers after the fifth ring.

"Mads?"

"Tillie!" she screams through the line. "Where are you? I'm coming to get you."

I shake my head. "I can't. I'm sorry. I can't."

"Tillie," Madison purrs. "They've gotten into your head. Let me come and get you. You need some clarity."

Well, if Daemon wants to stay down here, I guess I can tell him that she's coming, and he needs to stay away. I hated telling him about her. It broke him just like I thought it would. Now I need to find Gabe because I need that book.

"I'm at—"

The door swings open with Nate glaring at me from the other side.

"I'll call you back."

"What the fuck do you think you're doing?" he asks, his eyes narrowing on my phone.

"I was going to tell her to come over and just tell Daemon to wait down here."

Nate tugs on his hair in frustration, making the ends stick up, which in short, only accentuates his sex appeal. "Tillie, she cannot come here right now."

"Nate, I'm going out of my fucking mind sitting here, waiting for God knows what! I'm bored."

Nate cocks his head, his eyes dilating.

"Nope." I shake my head. "You stay there. I'm not doing this."

He saunters in, gripping my arm and pulling me up to my feet.

"I'm getting rather sick of being thrown around like a damn ragdoll."

"It could be worse," he murmurs, leading me out of my room.

"How could things possibly be any worse than being dragged around like a ragdoll?"

"You could get fucked like one too. Move. Brantley is throwing a party tonight and I need you to wipe the sad out of your eyes."

"Hard to do—" I pause, squeezing my eyes shut to blink out the memories. *Dorothy lived in the midst of the great Kansas prairies...*

My breathing harbors my screams of when I woke and found her threatening to choke me.

"Hey!" Nate's hands come to my arms.

I rear back. "Don't fucking touch me." I shove past him. "Good thing Brantley is having a party tonight. I could do with some distractions." I stop outside Daemon's room, pushing the door open slightly. I need something to pacify my rage that brutally rose to the surface.

His bed is empty.

I turn to face Nate, panic seizing my bones. "Where is he?"

Nate stops outside his door, staring between me and the bed.

"Goddammit, Nate!" I shove his chest. "What did you do!"

He falls backward, letting me shove at him. His eyes glass over and his jaw tenses. "He's gone out. Will be back later." Then he storms off and leaves me there, with an empty room and untamed thoughts.

Chapter Ten

Tillie

I tug on the hem of the dress that I borrowed from Bailey. It's a long sleeve, see-through black garment that cuts off at my upper thigh. I paired it with a lace black bra underneath and—black cheeky boyshorts. I'm not proud of this dress choice, but I'm feeling hasty tonight. I don't want to think about my past. I want it to disappear. *I want to feel numb.* I'm tired of hurting. As much as I think to myself that I need to turn dead inside against certain things or people, I don't work like that. I can act like situations don't affect me, but I'm only lying to myself. I'm good with lying to myself, and to others around me. If this is the only way that I'm going to be able to swim to the shoreline of peace, then I'll make sure I float and not sink.

The music is blasting, spilling inside from the outside garden. At night, it's even more spooky out there. I'm not sold on it. The back of Brantley's house shows the design of the actual house. The left and right wing is cut into a U-shape, the whole inside of that U-shape is a mass garden. Flowers of all sorts springing up, displaying the only sign of life. It's interesting, and not something I would have expected out here. Behind the gardens is where a large bonfire is blazing through the dark night, right before the backyard morphs into the forest and, yes, the Vitiosis graveyard which is obviously hidden between the trees in the forest somewhere.

I shiver, goosebumps breaking out over my skin. Everything Bran Bran is so creepy.

A glass is handed to me from behind, so I turn to face the owner. Cash is staring down at me with an eyebrow raised. "Thought you might need this."

"Thanks." I take it from him, bringing the rim to my lips.

"I take it boyfriends one and two haven't seen you yet?" He raises a perfect eyebrow

"Bran Bran and Nate? No." I shake my head, chuckling to myself. I didn't plan to drink tonight. I still don't like drinking, but one glass won't hurt. I let the burn soothe my erratic heart and thoughts.

"Come, there are a whole bunch of people here that would love to see you..."

"Really?" I smirk, assessing him. "You're an awful friend, Cash."

"Aw." He presses his hand to his chest. "I'm hurt, princess. Truly hurt."

I shove him playfully as we make our way to the bonfire. There are people scattered around, sitting on old logs and drinking out of plastic cups. People I haven't even seen before. When we get close enough, they all pause, everything falling silent, except for the song that's playing through the loudspeakers that are set up outside.

My eyes drop, the silence annoying me. I quirk one eyebrow before they all go back to talking.

I turn to face Cash. "Are they all in our world?"

Cash laughs. "Hell naw. They just know who you are."

"Huh." I swallow a large gulp of my drink. "Interesting."

"How is that interesting?" Cash asks, studying me carefully.

"That they know who I am, yet I don't." It's true. I don't. I used to know who I was. Why I was here and my purpose. I had a vision for what my life was going to be like, but I had a life worth living because I had someone to live for. Now I don't. Giving birth to a baby is only a small part of becoming a mother. I had become a mother when I saw those two pink lines telling me that I was pregnant. That was when my thoughts started to shift into mother mode. Now? I can't.

I take another sip of my drink, refilling it with the bottle of whiskey that's sitting beside Eli. *So much for just one glass and I don't drink.* It's just Eli, Cash, Jase, and Hunter sitting with me. I notice how they all surround me like loyal wolves. They may be savage, they may be heartless, ruthless, and completely unattainable to most people, but with me, they're different. I know that and respect it. It is subtle, but it's there.

"*Princessa*, I think you've had enough..." Hunter says, judging me while passing the bottle of whiskey.

"Last I checked." I snatch the bottle from him and pour more into my glass. That's right. Glass. I get a motherfucking whiskey glass while everyone else here is drinking out of red Solo cups. "I'm my own woman, and also, no one owns me—"

"—You sure about that?" Nate's voice interrupts us. I stiffen, refusing to turn and face him. "break up with your girlfriend, i'm bored" by Ariana Grande starts playing.

"Positive!" I roll my eyes, ignoring the fact that he looks more beautiful than ever.

His hair is a deadly combination of *I don't give a fuck* and *I stepped off the cover of a GQ magazine.* His tattoos sneak out of his collar, wrapping around his neck, as well as all of his arm tattoos that peek out from beneath his sharp white tee. All of that matched with black ripped jeans and Timberlands is a pot of witchcraft, threatening to spill over the edges and curse us all.

"You gonna be mad at me forever or what?" he jokes. His jokes are never funny when his lips are curved in that satanic smile. I shoot back the rest of my drink.

"Yes."

I stand up, realizing I want to switch my poison. I'm not really a whiskey girl. In fact, I hate the stuff. If I'm going to drink, I'd like to get a sugar hit as well.

Nate stills, his eyes falling down my body. *I fucking love this song.*

"Well, well, well, my little terror clearly looks like she's out to play tonight," Brantley mutters, sidestepping Nate and making his way to me.

I feel his hands on my waist, but Nate's eyes are what I feel the most. He's not touching me, but he doesn't need to. That's just Nate. That's me, and that's him, but whatever we have, it's not enough for me to forgive him. I still don't understand his wrath when he locked me in the cell, and until someone tells me why, I'll continue to not understand it. He turned feral, and I saw the worst of him, but lately, he has also been showing me more of the side that made me fall in love with him to begin with. I hate it. It's so much easier to hate him when he's being mean.

"Play, she will," I whisper, swallowing the remainder of my drink anyway. Nate's eyes are still on mine. I hate that I'm a slave to the way he makes me feel. I don't like not being in control, and that's exactly what he does to me—he takes my control. When he watches me, he doesn't just look at me. He studies me, examines me, strips the flesh from my bones with a simple squint of an eye.

I quickly shove past everyone and make my way into the kitchen in search for something with an actual taste instead of drinking lighter fluid.

My phone vibrates in my back pocket and I answer it without checking to see who it is.

"You're at Brantley's, aren't you?" Madison says through the phone. I go to open my mouth to tell her that I was going to actually mention that to her, but she cuts me off. "Don't. I understand, Tillie. I just wish—I wish I could talk to you."

"You can, Madison. Whatever is going on with the two of you, you know that I'm always here and I understand—"

My response is cut short because the front door opens, and Madison and Tate walk through, dressed to the fucking nines.

Chapter Eleven

Tillie

I rush forward tripping on my two left feet and tipping over glasses on my way.
Madison smiles before throwing her arms around my neck.

"Madison…"

"Is he here with someone?" she asks.

"What? Who?" I ask, confused. My face falls when I realize that she's talking about Bishop. "Mads, no. What the fuck? *No!*"

"Are you defending him?" Tate adds her two cents.

I still, my eyes going straight to her. "How about you step the fuck off, Tate."

"Both of you shut up, please?" Madison exhales.

I shake my head, my eyes going back to Madison. I'm angry. I don't know why, but I'm angry at her. I know it's unreasonable, but a big part of me understands this life on a whole level that these two girls will never understand—and that makes me protective. Protective over not just Nate and Brantley, but Bishop too. I love Madison, she will always have my loyalty, but she needs to stop with the drama.

"Madison, I won't shut up. You can tell Tate to leave if she's not willing to shut her trap." I glare at Tate. "Shut your mouth about shit you don't understand, or leave."

Tate rolls her eyes. "This isn't your house, Tillie. They aren't your friends!"

"Actually, she's right, Tate. What she says goes. You can get the fuck out if she doesn't want you here," Brantley interjects with tranquility, his presence falling heavy on my back.

Tate eyeballs Madison, who is now standing silent. "Are you going to let them talk to me like this?"

"Like what, Tate? You came in here from hearing just one story, and trust me, I get it. We both love Madison, but I don't think you're good for her right now."

"Oh, and you are?" Tate sasses, glaring at me.

I'm about to punch this bitch. Maybe it's because Nate and I are in a vulnerable position and I don't feel like dealing with Tate dropping to his *unholy* feet, or maybe my patience with this girl has snapped and I no longer care, but whatever it is, I can't deal with her right now.

"Madison kne—"

Madison turns to Tate, snapping at her. "Shut up, Tate! Just meet me in the car or go and get a drink."

I watch as Tate huffs and storms into the house, going straight for the kitchen, but she sidesteps when she finds herself in the living room instead. She's never been here before—not surprised.

"Sorry," Madison exhales, rubbing her hands over her face. I look over my shoulder to face Brantley, whose focus is solely on me. He pins me with a stare, bringing his bottle to his mouth.

I nod, a silent conversation passing between the two of us. He nods his head and leaves, stumbling slightly. Is he drunk?

I fight the urge to chase him and see what's going on. What is with the people—myself included—in my life. We're all a fucking mess, but maybe that's why we all found each other, because we were all lost on the same path.

"Can we go somewhere to talk? I don't want to see Bishop right now."

"Yeah." I clear my throat, gesturing to the long hallway. "We can find somewhere in this creepy fucking house."

She laughs, but tears are falling down her cheeks. Shit.

We continue down the hallway in silence. My legs feel like jelly from the alcohol, and now that she's here, I regret being reckless even more. I had a weak moment.

I turn into the first room I see and flick the light on after searching aimlessly on the wall for the switch.

The light turns on in a blaze and suddenly we're met with a large office. Floor to ceiling bookshelves line the back of the desk and a large leather seat tucked behind it tidily. I can almost smell the dust particles in the air.

"I wonder if this place ever gets used?" I think out loud.

Madison's eyes fly around the room, panic setting in. "This is Luce's office." She backs up, but then her eyes slam closed as she shuts the door behind herself.

"I need to talk to you," she murmurs instead.

"Finally," I answer, treading deeper into a room I most definitely should not be in.

Madison's eyes fall to the corner behind me, and I turn to see what she's looking at, finding the alcohol cabinet. "I'll need something strong first."

I don't fight her, and I don't fight her again when she pours the amber liquid into two glasses instead of just her one.

She passes one to me and takes a seat beside me on the brown leather two-seat sofa that's on the opposite side of the room.

She takes a swig. "Bishop and I—we're not together."

I choke on my drink. "What?!"

She takes another drink. "Yep." Then she stands, making her way toward the alcohol cabinet, taking the whole glass bottle this time before coming back to join me.

"Why?"

She pours more into her glass. "Number of reasons, but mainly..." She sinks more of the booze. "I fucked up."

I shake my head, shooting back my drink in one go and reaching for the bottle. "That's not allowed. You two are it. You've always been perfect for each other!"

"—Really?" Her eyes come to mine, and it's the first time that I see how deep her pain really is. How have I missed this before? I've been a terrible friend. I feel guilty instantly.

She laughs quietly. "I don't know. I'd take what you and Nate have in a heartbeat."

I choke on my drink again—only for different reasons this time. "Why would you— what the fuck, Mads. No. We are—*no*."

"You are what, Tillie? You are his world. Everything begins and ends with you. He doesn't hold secrets from you. You are a big part of this world, they all fucking love you—I damn well envy you." She sighs, burying her face in her hands. "I know that's pathetic. I know that I love Bishop and he loves me, but sometimes love isn't enough to get through, you know?"

"Yes, I do know, but not when it comes to you. Jesus, Madison, what happened? Also, don't be ridiculous about Nate. He *hates* me. He has been cruel to me for months since I came back, and it got worse when—" I stop, snatching the glass bottle and pouring more into my glass. *I'm not done having my weak moment.* "Anyway, no. We're nothing to be envied." Nothing to be envied at all. Maybe we had a chance before, but since we both lost someone we loved so much, love isn't what we're feeling right now. All love does is remind us of what we've lost.

"I mean it when I say you will both work. The only thing that's stopping you from being together is both of you being so stubborn—"

"—That's not all, Mads. We will never work. We're too toxic. Anyway, this isn't about Nate and me, it's about you and Bishop."

"Right!" Madison sighs, massaging her head. "I cheated on him."

"—What!" I rear off the sofa, dropping the glass to the carpet. I'm about to swear at her when she shakes her head.

"Stop, let me finish."

"Madison..."

I've always been very envious of how Bishop has been loyal to her all along. He's not a ho like Nate and I've always envied that.

"How could you!" I whisper, shaking my head.

Bishop.

"It's not that simple to explain, Tillie. I didn't—he didn't—I tried to—" She pauses, her eyes coming to mine, rimmed bright red. "He raped me."

I freeze. Anger crashing over me in violent waves. My fingertips zap with rage. "*What?*"

She's a sobbing mess now, swiping the tears from her eyes angrily. "I'm so mad that I'm letting this affect me still—to this day. I can't help it..."

I haven't moved. My limbs are rock solid. I don't want to move. I want to smash things. I want to rage. The first thing that comes out of my mouth, though, is, "Does Bishop know?" Because if he does and is blaming this on her, I don't know and won't be responsible for my actions.

She shakes her head, her eyes going wide in pain. "No, Tillie. Please don't tell him."

"Don't tell him?" I whisper-yell. A little too harshly, I know, but what the fuck?

She pins me with a glare. "You have to promise not to tell anyone…"

"Why?" I ask, searching her eyes for clues. *Any clue.*

"Because if he finds out, we will all die."

"What the—"

The door swings open and a seething Bishop is standing in the doorway.

"What the fuck are you doing here, Kitty?"

I feel her leg shake against mine, and I launch off the sofa, standing directly in front of her.

"Bishop. Leave."

His eyes cut to me. "What? Did she tell you what she did? See…" Bishop steps into the space and I'm thinking of one-hundred different ways that I can knee him in the nuts. I mean sure, he will definitely kill me, but at least it will give Madison time to run away. *Madison.* "I don't like being cheated on. I let the first couple of bullshit antics with Nate slide because he's a King, and we play games, and they never went all the way, and I didn't call *fucking* red. At least we're gentlemen, though. We make your heart beat before your pussy—"

"—Bishop!"

He steps into my space. "Move, Tillie."

Chapter Twelve

Nate

Brantley paces back and forth in front of a bedroom door, a bottle of scotch dangling from his fingertips.

I tip my head. "The fuck are you doing?" I had a feeling the whole Tillie thing would get to him, but this is taking the cake. Maybe he cares more for her than I thought...

"Shut the fuck up with your thoughts, Nate. It's not about Tillie."

My brain is buzzing with alcohol, turning my limbs numb, but I don't give a fuck. I'd rather feel the cool buzz of nothingness than the molten lava of Tillie fucking Stuprum blazing through my veins. I slide down the wall opposite and watch as he continues to pace back and forth like a caged lion protecting his prey.

"So what has gotten into you. Never seen you like this before. Should I be worried? Has our dark prince fallen in love?"

He pauses, snarls at me and then takes a long swig of the amber liquid. Then he continues pacing in front of the door. Figuring he's not going to answer me, I kick my leg out and hang my arm on my knee. "You think Tillie will forgive me one day?"

Instant. "No."

I snort, licking my lips. "Yeah, you're probably right."

He continues pacing. He's deranged and unhinged. Like a wild animal threatening to break out of its cage. My eyes catch the door handle. Its gold pattern lingers in my attention for longer than it should. It's not that the door handle is odd, because this whole fucking house is creepy and peculiar. It's the Dark Mansion, and it well and truly holds its title with pride. With its sharp concrete rooftops and the cement hidden gardens that take you from one wing of the house to the other; It's all fucking Addams family and gothic, but the house has been in the Vitiosis family since way the fuck back then. My eyes fly to the other door handle beside this one. It's silver, plain, and smooth. Nothing to it and it's certainly not gold. I examine another and then swing my head to the other side to check the rest of them. My skin is itching with curiosity when my attention lands back on the door handle in front of me. Gold that sparkles so bright it reminds me of an angel's halo, and a single pattern of what looks like a lotus flower on the base.

I fly to my feet, adrenaline coursing through me. "What is behind that door?"

Brantley freezes momentarily before flying toward me, wrapping his fingers around my throat and shoving me against the back wall. He tilts his head, examining me closely. His pupils are dilated. Yeah, he's fucked up right now.

He leans in closer, his mouth touching my ear. "You can't have her," he whispers, kissing my cheek before pushing away from me to continue his pacing.

"Well, now I'm really fucking curious. You hiding her behind that door, Bran Bran?" I throw Tillie's nickname at him.

He flips me off.

I smirk, pushing off the wall before walking directly up to him. I don't want to test him. No one tests a fucking wolf unless they want to get eaten, or unless you're fucking Tillie.

"Let me see her."

He can't possibly have a girl in there. I mean—really? That would be fucked up... *which would be totally something Brantley would do.*

He snarls at me, his jaw clenching. He opens his mouth to say something just as Eli's voice breaks out from behind us. "Yo! Madison and Bishop have just had a massive fight and Tillie was in the middle of it!"

"What the fuck!" I slam my fist against the wall and kick up from my seat. I don't know what the fuck is going on between the two of them, but whatever it is, they need to sort it out before I lock them both in a cell on Perdita and throw away the key.

Actually, that's not a bad idea.

Brantley and I both fly down the hallway and jog down the stairs from the third level, down to the second, and then down to the first. My feet hit the foyer when I hear Madison screaming from down the main hallway—coming from Luce's office.

Brantley stills when he realizes that they're in there, but then Tillie's voice comes through and we both rush forward.

"What the fuck, Bishop! You selfish fucking—"

"Enough!" I snap, entering the room, my heart erratic and my eyes checking over Tillie quickly to make sure she's not hurt. Be awfully unfortunate to have to turn on a brother...

Madison runs toward me, her arms wrapping around my waist.

"Shut the door," I order Brantley, even though this is his fucking house and Bishop is the leader. But the leader is damaged right now, so naturally, I'm going to have to step up.

I press my lips to Madison's head, my fingers curling under her chin to lift her face to mine. "Who do I need to kill?"

Tears pour freely over her swollen cheeks. She's always so painfully beautiful, but it's hard to notice that when Tillie is in the same room.

"It's nothing."

"Madison..." Tillie urges.

Madison swipes at her tears. "It's nothing. I cheated on Bishop, so he hates me and we're over and that's why we're fighting. I'm going home now."

"Hold up!" I pull her back by her arm when she tries to take off. Because that's what she's good at—running. Except now she's running on my patience and if it's true, that she really did cheat on Bishop, then she and I will really have a problem. Because I'm a hypocrite like that—she can only cheat with my cock. *Could.* I'd never touch her now or ever.

"Nate!" Madison screams. I flinch, letting her go. She quickly bolts out the door, disappearing into the dark and I honest to God have no fucking idea what to say, so I bring my eyes to Tillie.

"Tell me everything, now."

Tillie glares at me in defiance. "I'm not telling you shit." Then she barges out of the room, leaving Bishop, Brantley, and Eli in here with me, standing around like *what the fuck just happened.*

"Bravo, boys. Way to choose your women..."

"Shut the fuck up, Eli," I snap.

"Crazy girls fuck better." Bishop chuckles, swiping his mouth. "But they don't know shit about love."

"Is it true?" I ask Bishop, wanting to hear his side.

He flings his arms out wide. "Yep. Saw it with my own eyes."

I drop down onto the sofa, my hand running through my hair. "I swear to fuck, these girls are aging me every day. Between Tillie and—all of that—" My eyes go around to them all, and for a second they all sober. "—and Madison and this. What happened?"

Bishop drops to the floor, bringing his knees up to his chest. "Don't know. She fucked him in our house. On my bed. It was recorded and sent to me. It was there in black and white, but I still asked her. She admitted it. That's that. It was the day before—" Bishop pauses. "When it happened. That stunt at your house after, was the final time I fucked her. Put my cum inside her pussy to remind her who owns it." He pauses, his eyes glassing over. "Or owned it."

I snicker at the pussy comment. "Nice."

"Jesus Christ," Eli mutters, just as Hunter, Jase, and Ace pad in, all drunk as fuck.

I make sure to fill them in until we're all sitting around on the floor.

"Did you know him?" I question Bishop, my hand covering my mouth.

Bishop shakes his head. "Never seen him before in my life, but when I do—"

I nod in agreement. He doesn't need to say the words that he's thinking, because it's already done. If Bishop doesn't find him, I sure as fuck will. In fact, it just bumped up on my list of things to feed on.

"What are we going to do about Tillie?" Brantley asks, breaking through the tension.

I exhale, leaning back on the sofa. "I don't know, but I think it's time to tell her why we snatched her ass and placed her in Perdita."

"Really?" Bishop asks, his eyes coming to mine. "You think she could handle that right now, considering..."

"Yeah." I clear my throat. "Fuck."

Chapter Thirteen

Tillie

Pain doesn't define us, it shapes us. We come into this world as newborns, a fresh start. New life, a crisp soul. Then life happens, and every single choice you make has an implication. Every scar has a story, or it doesn't and it's just a scar, but whether or not it has a story, it's still a scar, and that scar doesn't define us, so why should pain?

I roll onto my side, closing my eyes and willing my mind to sleep. Let the alcohol pulse out from my pores so I can start fresh again tomorrow.

But that's not how it works.

Tears slip down the sides of my eyes as I flip onto my back. Everything feels heavy. Weighted. I don't want to live within these walls anymore, living for what?

"Puella," Daemon whispers from the other side of my room and I jump up when I see him standing at my doorway. He's been quiet all night, and I feel awful that I forgot he was here.

"Are you okay?" I ask, because I always need to know that he's okay. My beautiful saving grace isn't grace at all. He's weeping with darkness and demons, but he's still mine.

Calmness takes over me as he comes closer to my bed. His hand comes to my cheek where he swipes away the fallen tears. "To cry is to feel."

I swallow. "That's the problem," I jest, chuckling softly.

"I never cried."

I swallow. I know that. Daemon is as cold as ice, but he melted parts of him to let me in, and for that, I am so grateful. He has saved me in ways that he will never know. I

I do as I'm told, lying on my back, my nerves relaxing at his touch. He pats my forehead and it feels like a light of healing every time he caresses me. He doesn't fix my broken parts, he just fills them with peace.

A small bottle of blue liquid is sitting on a table. My feet are covered in wooden shoes with red tips, pointing upward. What the fuck? I search around the room. There's nothing in here, just that small bottle. I try to take the liquid, but my hand can't grasp it. I get frustrated, sweat spilling out over my flesh. Why can't I touch the stupid bottle? I finally grab it, flicking the cork off. A tag is around the neck, on it reads "Drink me." Okay, so I'm Alice in Wonderland? Those boys are clearly fucking with me again.

I drink the liquid in one go. Sour goo clings to my tonsils, reminding me of that time when I tried to eat Play-Doh. The glass enlarges in my hand. What! It grows bigger and bigger, expanding as the seconds pass. Suddenly I'm standing beside the now monstrous-sized glass bottle.

The room has proliferated. Everything is so much fucking bigger!

The table leg catches my eye, because there's a book shape that's carved into the wood. I step closer. It's an opened book, carved with perfect precision. Weird. I step even closer and run my fingertips over it. Puer Natus.

I suck in a breath, turning to see who it is that's playing a sick joke on me, but as soon as my finger touches it, a black hole opens up and sucks me in.

I wake up in a graveyard.

DAEMON reads over the stone.

I've been here before. What is going on? The grass melts away from my feet as I sink six-feet under. I know what happens next, The Kings bury me alive.

The dirt flies over the grave, their faces not clear enough to make out. My barefoot steps on something that feels like jelly. I look down, only to see Daemon's eyes gaping up at me from beneath the dirt. He's angry, his eyebrows pulled in harshly. His fingers grip around my ankle.

"Have it your way!"

He yanks me under the dirt.

"No!" I scream, launching off the bed. That dream was scarier than the first one, and I feel like they're getting worse and more vivid as time goes on.

"Nightmare?" a dark voice asks from the corner. I instantly recognize that it's Nate.

I slither backward until my back is pressed against the headboard. "Yeah."

"Nightmares make you appreciate the good. They remind you that your life could be worse," he answers, his voice level.

I'm unsure what Nate I'm getting, and not being able to see him isn't helping that fact either.

"I guess." I don't know what else to say. He's not helping my inconsistent heart rate. I'm all over the place from last night and honestly, still feel slightly drunk. I hate drinking.

"I lied to you," he whispers hoarsely.

"I figured," I answer, lying back and pulling my covers up to my chin. If I can't see him, I may as well feel safe under some blankets. It's like when you leave your leg to dangle over your bed, but then you can't because you think a demon is going to grab you by the foot. Well, Nate is that demon and the probability of that happening is way too real.

"I hate you, Tillie. There's always going to be a part of me that hates you, and I think that's something you're going to have to come to terms with."

"Why?" I choke on my words, and I instantly hate that I've shown emotion.

"Because you remind me of everything that I lost. You remind me of her. Everything about you is a reminder of her. Your smell, your laugh, your smile."

I can't stop the tears now. They've got free rein over me. I don't answer. I'll let him finish.

"Everything that I came to love about you was buried with our daughter. The way you would make her laugh in the morning when you'd change her diaper, or when you'd put her in the bed with us and we would just fucking admire the perfection that we both created. But that's all gone, Tillie, and now all that's left is anger and hurt, and a whole lot of fucking pain that I can't afford to be feeling. It makes me distracted."

I can feel myself slowly slipping away. "Then let me go."

There's a pause. "I can't."

I stop breathing. Will he finally admit it?

"This is your world too. You deserve the crown that has been given to you, and also, you deserve the closure that I do too."

"Closure?" I ask, my attention spiked. "What do you mean closure?"

Pause.

I rip the blankets off, the dark room serving as a blanket of safety. I tiptoe to where I think he is, reaching out aimlessly to see if I can feel him.

My hand lands on his hair, and I quickly flinch away, dropping to my knees when I have found him. I don't want to touch him any more than I have to. His touch is everything good and bad for me. I can't lose myself in him again. I have to be smart. I have to make him pay. *No, you don't.* Yes, I do.

"Tell me what you mean," I whisper. I can almost feel his heavy breath falling on my lips, the smell of whiskey and cologne filling the space between us.

"When I tell you this, Tillie, I need your word that you will do as you're told and not be reckless. I think this will—" He pauses. "I think having you help us, and us getting our closure will help you."

"Help me?"

He changes the subject. "Do I have your word?"

"Yes," I answer instantly. "You do."

He exhales. "We think Micaela didn't die of SIDs."

I freeze, inching back.

His arm hooks around my waist. "I've got you. Can you handle this?"

Can I?

No.

Yes.

I have to.

"Yes…"

His arm tightens around my waist, but he doesn't pull me into him which I appreciate. It's a subtle hint that he's there. He will catch me.

"We think she was murdered, and we think Hector has everything to do with it."

Everything goes black.

Chapter Fourteen

Tillie

My skin swells with heat. An arm tightens around me. The smell of old whiskey is being breathed into my hair. My eyes pop open and the room is bright, the morning sun coming through the small window at the top of the wall.

"I'm trying really hard to be sensitive because I've just told you something dark as fuck, but your ass is pressing into me and if you wriggle it one more time, my dick is going in whether you want it or not—but let's be real, you'd want it."

I turn in his arms, ignoring the typical Nate antics. "You slept in here with me."

"I did," he agrees, his sleepy eyes searching mine, but they're guarded. I don't know if he's always been like this and I haven't noticed before, but he's more shielded than before. It's troubling.

"Why?" I ask, my voice husky and desperate. "Why did you sleep in my bed?"

"Because knowing you're okay is worth the pain that having you in my arms causes."

I wince, my heart twisting in my chest from his words. "I don't want you in pain, Nate."

"It's just the way it is. I'm used to it."

My head thuds as I turn to face the ceiling. "He really did this?"

Nate's silent, so I turn to face him, desperate for answers that I'm not sure I want.

"Yeah, we think he did. I need to ask you a few things about that night. Do you think you're up for that?"

My brain blurs like a television channel without reception. I exhale, closing my eyes. "I have to."

He inches up onto one elbow, studying me. I ignore the way the sun sets behind him from the window, highlighting his dark blond hair, or the fact that first thing in the morning Nate is always a nicer version than the afternoon Nate.

"When you went to bed that night, was there anything that felt odd? Out of place? Anything."

Pain grips onto my heart, squeezing while not letting go. I don't want to think about this. I don't want to let the memories seep into my already unstable soul. But it's too late, because images are flashing through my head a hundred miles per hour, blinding me with their speed.

I squeeze my eyes shut. "Yes, there was something." The words come out softer than I intended.

Nate remains quiet.

I shut the door that night, the cool wind brushing through my hair as I closed it. I climbed into my silk sheets. I fell asleep. I woke up in a sweat, my face drenched. *Why did I wake at this time?*

No, I didn't.

Did I?

My eyes snap open and I fly off the bed, tearing the covers from my body. "I don't think I locked the door, Nate…"

He searches my face. "That's not your fault. My house is safe enough to be able to do that. No one would set foot on King soil without given access. No one except Hector. He would have found a way in even if you did lock the door."

I start pacing back and forth, my legs tingling with speed. I need to exercise or I'm not going to make it through. "What does this mean? Is that why you kept me locked up—" The color in my face drains and my blood turns cold. "What about the masquerade party…"

"Don't know," Nate mutters, climbing out of the bed and removing his shirt, making his hair stand all over his head again. "But we're finding out tonight."

"How?" I ask, once again needing to stretch my legs. Surely Brantley has a gym in this house.

"There's another dinner party tonight. Same attire. You're coming with us, but you're sticking close to us."

I nod, rubbing my sweaty palms down my legs.

"Oh." Nate pauses at the threshold right before he disappears. "And this is a bigger dinner party than last time. Kings from all over will be there, and other girls. Girls I know." He pins me with a stare.

I pause. "Why would I care? I know your ho past."

"That's the thing, it's not really a past. I've known these people since I was little. There's someone there who I haven't seen since I was fourteen and she is the one that took my virginity." He watches for my reaction, but my poker face is too good, because he's not going to get one.

"Why are you telling me this? We're not together, Nate."

"Well aware of that, but just so you know, she's meeting me there—"

"—You're disgusting, and you can leave."

Which he does.

I want to ignore that once again, Nate has hurt me. But it's my own fault for having emotions. Feelings. I'm curious to know who this girl is, but as far as he and I are concerned, we're obviously finished. I need to remember that the only reason why he's being civil with me about this is because of Hector. Because he wants revenge, and so do I. Once that's done, he will throw me away like a bad memory—I know this.

I exhale a shaky breath. "Pull it together, Tillie. Just play the game." I flash a fake smile to myself, because you know, practice. If he wants to bring his ex—whatever she is—that's fine. I'll play, but I'm playing to win, and my first move after rolling the dice is being the hottest bitch in the room.

I'm walking past Daemon's room when I peek in, wanting to ask if he will come with me. He'll be wearing a mask and Madison most likely won't be there, so what's the harm, but his room is empty.

Again.

The space looks untouched, the bed covers are neat, like no one has so much as sat on the bed.

Maybe he's clean and he makes it tidy. He must be out again doing God knows what, or maybe The Kings have him back on Lost Boy duties.

I sigh, marching up the stairs and heading straight for the kitchen. I'm hungry and I want pancakes.

No one is in there when I arrive, so I start searching through the cupboards to find all of the ingredients I need.

Flour, eggs, butter, milk. I fucking love pancakes.

I turn the sound dock on and push play. I need something to make me feel better about Nate and his stupid confession this morning. I hit play on Halsey's "Young God," tossing all of the ingredients into the bowl and stirring it together. I start beating it fast until my hair comes out of its bun.

I stop, swing my head over by bending at the waist and rake all of it to the front before knotting it into a high bun. When I fling back to standing position, Brantley is standing directly in front of me, leaning against a cabinet.

"What are you doing?" he yells over the sound.

"Making pancakes!"

I swipe some of the batter with my fingertip, just as Halsey sings, "if you want to go to heaven then you should fuck me tonight," and I keep my eyes on Brantley, sucking the batter off my finger. This will be fun.

His eyes narrow, and mine drop down to what he's wearing. Loose sweatpant shorts and no shirt. Sweat glistens off his chest.

"Did you just workout?" I ask, pointing down his body.

He removes the blender cup, slowly dragging his eyes from mine. "Yeah. Why?" I can see the side of his cheek turning up in a smile.

I carry on. "I need to."

He nudges his head toward the stairs. "Level three."

"Isn't that where your room is?" I ask, stirring the batter again.

"Yeah, just my room and the gym. You should do it before pancakes, and anyway, the batter needs to sit in the fridge for an hour."

"What?" I glare at him. "Since when?"

Brantley stares at me, hitting the blender off after mixing his shake. "Since forever. Everyone knows that pancake batter needs to sit in the fridge for an hour before you cook it."

There are so many different layers to Brantley Vitiosis and I'm so thankful he peels a couple of them away for me. "Aw Bran Bran, you're so sweet."

"First warning of the day," he mutters nonchalantly, pouring his protein shake into a shaker.

I put the mixture in the fridge, taking out a water bottle while I'm there. "I'll listen, but you're eating these with me."

I turn around, laughing, but he's already gone. How did I manage to live in a house with a bunch of moody, hot, sexually charged men?

Oh, that's right, my fucking blood.

I made my way to the third floor after hassling Bailey for some workout clothes. We both agreed that we're going shopping today, because I really do need clothes. I almost forgot about all the money that's in my account. It's unreal.

Walking slowly down the hallway, I see one door directly at the end. It's black and has patterns carved into the wood. Brantley's room, no doubt. I wonder what his room looks like? Will it be as dark as him, or will it be all white and bland? Somehow, the latter just doesn't seem feasible.

I go for the second door and push it open. My mouth drops to the floor when I take in the space. I know that they all take their training seriously, but I could live in here. The walls are floor to ceiling glass, built to curve around the whole back of the house. You get the view of the forest and can see from here the clearing where the graveyard is. I shiver. Fucking sinister house. The gym is probably the most executive part about this whole house. The equipment is all laid out perfectly, with everything plus more that you will find in a regular gym. Including a stepper. Thank fuck.

There's a punching bag in the corner too that calls to me. I could do with a punching session. I need to exhaust all this energy before tonight, when and I'm faced with Nate and his—virginity stealer.

I push my earbuds into my ears and flick through my Spotify as I slowly pace toward the treadmill. I climb on and hit level 12 instantly. I hit Halsey's playlist, needing more of her soothing voice after this morning. "Without Me" starts playing and I pick up my pace. It always takes me a couple of minutes to find my stride, huffing and puffing like an unfit cow that hasn't worked out in months—because I haven't. Finally, my breathing becomes level and the lyrics to the song disappear. I need something angrier to match the raging sweat that's dripping down my face, not to be the counterpart of the sad beat of my heart. "Go Fuck Yourself" by Two Feet comes on instead and I leave it, because who wouldn't. This song is the best two-or so minutes in music history. That beat. I hit the ramp up to 2. My thighs burn, my heart is pounding in my chest and for the next twenty minutes, I'm thinking of nothing but the ache in my muscles.

Turning off the treadmill, I jump down but jerk in shock when I see Nate standing near the door. I rip off my earbuds. "What are you doing here?"

He doesn't answer, just watches me as I reach for my water bottle. His eyes drop down my body and I curse Bailey and her skimpy clothes—once again. I'm in nothing but a bright green sports bra and little black spandex shorts. They're so short that my ass actually falls out of them after a while.

Nate ignores me, pushing forward and going straight for the weight machines. "Working out. What do you think?"

I want to just leave after the run, but I also don't want it to be obvious that his presence disrupts me in such an obvious way.

So I go for the punching bag, pushing the gloves on while glaring at him. He removes his shirt and slings it over a bench, stretching his back muscles.

The tattoos on his back flex above his muscles. The Elite King skull sitting above New York City is over his left side. He has old English writing curving across his traps that read "MALUM" like the one that sits over his pelvic area that says "King."

I need to stop staring.

I push my earbuds back into my ears to distract me and hit play on Rihanna's "Desperado." I wrap my knuckles with the smaller gloves. *Why are there girl sized gloves here?* And stretch my neck. *Bailey, obviously…* I start with single jabs, launching them toward the hard, black sack. *Inhale, exhale.* I tense my abs with every hit, sweat continuing to pour out of my flesh. When the single jabs start to lose their effect, I start on one, two, three combos. I speed up and then slow down, all while keeping my abs tight and my core strong.

My arms burn the longer I punch, but it feels good. Ridge and I used to do this every weekend in his garage, so it's easy to pick back up on the combos. Everything that has happened up to this point in my life starts to slowly drift through my head and I find my punches getting hard. My aggression hits a new level and I swing my leg around in a roundhouse kick before going back to the jab and hook combinations. I don't want to stop. I want to beat this bag until my limbs fall off. My earbuds fall out of my ears and the loud base that Nate is obviously playing takes up every inch of the area. "Na Na" by Trey Songz is playing. I kick my earbuds out of the way so I don't step on them. One two, three. My punching gets hard, my arms burning and my abs feeling like lava.

You know when you feel eyes on you? My eyes shoot up, distracted by Nate and Brantley both standing there watching me. The bag swings and almost hits me, so I curl my arm around to steady it.

"What!" I snap at them both.

"That's supposed to make you less angry. You seem madder than before," Nate teases. "Any reason why?" He grins at me, stretching out his arms. I notice they're both in work out gear. Both no shirts and both wearing appropriate sweat shorts.

I'm so fucking fucked when it comes to these two.

"Yes, there is a reason actually," I mutter, bouncing up and swinging toward the bag again. "Pancakes."

Brantley is on the other side of the bag in a heartbeat. "Wanna spar?"

My eyes fly to his.

"I mean, I get the feeling that you've done this whole thing before. Am I right?"

"A little," I grumble, readjusting the gloves.

"There's so much we just don't know about you, little terror…" Brantley torments, picking up the sparring pads. My eyes catch Nate who has started on the skipping rope.

He's skipping doubles, his eyes slicing through me with every swing. I know that out of all of them, Nate and Brantley are the more athletic guys. Especially Nate. He does all sorts of training to keep his body in check. Including CrossFit and Parkour.

He twists his arms over all while not breaking his skip.

My eyes fly to Brantley. I smile before I start swinging, now hitting each pad.

The boys are all out back of the house, so I start on the pancakes. I'm not showering before because then I might lose my appetite. All of The Kings are here—sans Abel, who has done a complete ghost. I start on mixing another load of batter, pouring it into the one that was in the fridge. Brantley won't know that half of it wasn't in the fridge. I heat up the griddle and start pouring two at a time. The sound dock is still on and I hit play on some music. When I first got to Brantley's house, it was disturbing. But now I love it. I love the history and character that lay within the aging walls.

"It's a Vibe" from 2 Chainz starts playing and I lose myself in flipping pancakes.

I feel him before I turn around. Nate takes up every area that he occupies.

He comes closer, stealing a pancake. "Have you got something to wear tonight or are you going shopping?"

I glare at him. "They're not ready!" I gesture to the pancakes. "I'm going to get a dress and other shit I need so I don't have to keep squeezing my ass into Bailey's. I'm also taking Madison with me."

He freezes mid-chew. "Why?"

"What do you mean why?" I ask, narrowing my eyes on him.

"She fucking cheated on Bishop. I can't even—"

"—You're a fucking hypocrite if you're going to be mad at her about cheating when you've so happily done it to me."

He laughs, but it's not a nice one and I instantly know that I've just lit a match and—probably—am about to be burned. "I've never fucking cheated on you, Tillie."

"Yes, you have."

"How the fuck can I cheat on you when we've never really been together? Explain that shit to me because—"

I turn my face away from him before I smack him over the head with this spatula, but his hand grips my chin and he yanks my face up to face his, squeezing roughly. He searches my eyes, and I see by the way his pupils dilate that whatever he's about to do, it is going to hurt. "How can I fucking cheat on someone who was never mine?"

Ouch.

I yank my face out of his grip, my heart sinking to the bottom of the ocean. "You're right. That's my bad. You do you, Nate." I can't even be bothered arguing with him right now. I'm too angry at his words.

He steals another pancake. "And that's not why I'm mad at her."

I clench my jaw, my anger refusing to let go.

He carries on. "It's because—"

"—because it's not fucking you," I finish for him, piling the last of the pancakes up. This has always been an issue for me, how he cares for Madison. I'm irrational, I know, but we all want to be the only one. Not the one of two.

He doesn't answer, only making me even more angry as I flip off the switch to the griddle and snatch the plate of pancakes. I ignore him as he's clearly watching me move around the kitchen, and then I leave, going outside to where the rest of The Kings are, all of their eyes lighting up on the pancakes. I sit down beside Eli and Hunter, leaning back on my chair. Brantley is opposite me, unmoving. I zone out on the pancakes and watch as everyone digs in, only I've lost my appetite. A foot connects with mine under the table and I glance up to Brantley, who's watching me carefully.

"You okay?" He mouths, searching my eyes.

I'm not.

I'm more than not okay. I wanted to be the stronger person and reign hell on Nate, but I can't. All I can do, is move on. I need to move on and away from his toxicity. I'll never be his. If I was Madison, he wouldn't have treated me this way. I realize that now.

I shake my head, skating off the chair and storming back to my room. I need to get out of this fucking house. I fly past Daemon's room, but he's once again not there.

It makes me worse. I can feel my mind spiraling and I don't like the way it makes me feel. I kick open my door and yank out the same clothes I was wearing yesterday, slipping in and out of the shower. When I reenter, Bishop is standing at my open door, his eyes on mine.

"Hey," I whisper, reaching for my clothes while clenching the towel around my body. Can I have a few seconds away from all of these assholes? I mentally remind myself to invite Madison out this morning. I need to be around girls.

"Is there something that you're not telling me about the Madison thing?" he asks, licking his lip.

I shake my head, gripping my clothes. "Even if I did, Bishop, my loyalty will always be to her. She's my best friend and I would never do anything to mistreat that trust."

He tilts his head, his eyes going up and down my body. "Even though she and Nate are so close? That has never aggravated you. How?"

I exhale, sitting on my bed. I guess we're having that talk. "Because I'm nothing to Nate. I was something, the mother to—" I pause, my eyes closing. "But in essence, he's never loved me. He has n—"

Bishop shakes his head. "Girls and their need for love. That's part of the problem." He enters my room farther, leaning back against the wall.

"Love isn't unreasonable if you've poured everything into one person," I remind him.

"I did that," Bishop says, his eyes on mine. "And she broke my fucking heart. Now I'm feeling unhinged."

The energy in the room shifts.

He wouldn't.

His eyes drop to my mouth.

Okay so maybe he would?

"I'm not going to fuck you, Tillie. Chill out. I'm not that kind of guy. I have to admit that it would make me feel a fucking shit load better what with her and Nate."

I exhale, relaxing. "Except I mean nothing to Nate." I roll my eyes, standing up to make my way back into the bathroom.

Bishop takes one step forward. I freeze. He's so close, towering over me like a mountain.

I'd be lying if I didn't admit that I'm tempted by the idea of making myself feel better by hurting Nate, but no way in hell would that ever be with Bishop. Madison needs to talk with him before he makes a bad decision.

My door swings open, and Bishop steps back quickly.

Eli scans Bishop and me.

"What?" Bishop snaps before storming out of the room.

Okay that looked bad. It was nothing and that looked like it was something.

"Well, well, well, looks like you're finally learning the game..." Eli teases and then exits the room without even telling me what he came down here for.

I groan, going straight for the bathroom and changing before this gets worse. I need to buy a car today. And undies.

Chapter Fifteen

Tillie

With Bailey bailing on me at the last minute, I'm here waiting for Madison in Brantley's car. I could have taken Nate's, but I don't want to give him any more reason to talk to me. The deep V8 growls under my ass and I regret not taking maybe one of his new cars. Which reminds me, how the fuck am I going to park this big beast in town?

Madison jogs out of her house, down the steps and climbs into the passenger seat. I don't like this house. It holds too many bad memories. This is the exact place the hearse was parked not long ago.

I gulp, turning the radio down so we can talk.

"You stole Brantley's car?" Madison smirks as she piles her long hair onto the top of her head. "I'm impressed."

I shift it into gear and press on the accelerator. "I didn't steal it. He let me use it."

"Wow," Madison murmurs. "That's weird."

She doesn't understand and that's okay. To her, Brantley is still the big bad wolf, which he is, he just doesn't huff and puff my house down.

"I need to buy a car and clothes, including something to wear tonight," I say, driving us onto the main highway.

She clears her throat. "How has he been?"

"Well," I say, shuffling uncomfortably. "He came down to my room this morning to talk, and then Eli walked in and it didn't look good. I was in a towel because I just got out of the shower and it was right at a moment that Bishop was standing directly in front of me."

I turn toward her slightly to find her arms crossed and her eyes following the trees

She turns to face me. "I know. I know you'd never do that. But I'm worried that he's going to go to someone like Tate, who *would* do that."

"Why do we keep this bitch around?" I grumble under my breath. "You think she would do that to you?" I mean, I know that she did it to me, but I'm not as close to her as Madison.

"She did it to you," Madison gapes at me.

"Well, I think you need to come clean about what happened before he does something that he's going to regret, ya know?"

She exhales. "Yeah, I know."

"Can you tell me anything else about what happened?"

She shakes her head. "I can't. It's too dangerous."

I sigh. "Okay. Well, let's go spend my mother's money."

Madison laughs, her face changing. It's like old Madison is fighting to come through.

We end up at Porsche.

Why am I at Porsche?

"Buy it," Madison says, sucking her iced caramel macchiato. "I'm serious. I think you should."

The car salesman looks between both of us. "Are you old enough?"

I roll my eyes, pulling my card out of my wallet. "Yes."

He takes the card with his chubby fingers, greed lighting up his eyes. "And ID please, ma'am."

I hand him my ID.

He nods, reading it quickly and matching the two names on the cards. I watch as excitement takes over full force and he straightens his back. "So the 918 Spyder?"

I pinch my lips.

"Yes," Madison agrees, hooking her arm in mine. "And we should get it wrapped in pink! To match your hair!"

"No!" I snap at the salesman. "Please don't do that and ignore my friend."

"What color would you like? If you want a custom color, we can get that done and have the car shipped to you in a few business days. As well as any other modifications that you'd want."

I think over his words. "I just want it fast."

He nods. "We can add in—" He loses me with all the engine mods that he yaps on about.

I smirk, my eyes going to the car. "I want it red. Blood red."

He pauses and then gawks between me and the car. "Done."

We enter his office and I fill out the paperwork. Paying for something that is ridiculous but makes me happy. This is her money that she left me, and it's enough to last me until I die while buying one of these a day, but I still don't feel like it's mine.

We leave town, dresses, new makeup, and shoes filling up the trunk—as well as the whole backseat of Brantley's car. Mine won't be here for another three days, which is fine by me. As long as it's on the way.

"Where to now?" Madison asks, dropping her sunglasses down over her eyes.

I have a thought and smirk. "Wanna come to a masquerade party tonight as my date?"

She grins at me. "Why I would love to…"

Chapter Sixteen

Nate

I'm lounging on the sofa in Brantley's lounge, a glass of whiskey dangling between my fingers and my tie ripped loose around my neck. My mask lays on my leg, the white bone of my ancestors sitting there, staring at me and taunting me. The last time I wore it, I had Micaela in one arm and Tillie under my other.

I shoot back the whiskey, letting the burn rip through my throat.

"Did you hear?" Brantley mutters, walking in while ripping off his tie and tossing it across the room. He loosens the first few buttons of his collar and rolls the sleeves up of his shirt. "Tillie is bringing Madison tonight as her date."

I roll my eyes. "Yeah, I'm not surprised. She'll be gearing up the gang because I told her that Billie will be there."

Brantley doesn't flinch, his eyes remain on mine. "Really…"

I chuckle. "Really."

"And you've been talking to her?"

I nod my head. "Yeah."

Brantley doesn't say anything, though he wouldn't have to. I know how he feels about Billie. Hate, that's how he feels.

He opens his mouth and then shakes his head. "Tillie doesn't need backup, Nate. You know that. If she wanted to punch Billie, she wouldn't need Madison there to help her. Billie would be dead. Bringing your initiation pussy as a date is a low blow. I have to know *why*."

"Madison is coming?" Eli interrupts, entering the lounge with vodka in his hand and wearing the same suit as Nate and I, holding his mask in his hand. The bone of his ancestors on his. Bet they're not as pissed with him as mine are with me.

I lean forward and snatch the bottle of scotch off the coffee table, twisting the lid off with my teeth and spitting it across the floor. "Yeah."

"Interesting, considering how I caught Tillie and Bishop earlier today."

My eyes snap up to Eli, the same time that Brantley laughs. "What?"

Eli smirks at me, his eyebrows raised. "What? You can't be surprised, can you? I mean, considering you and Madison…"

I have two options. Feed into his shit, or ignore it. I sink my drink in one go, my eyes staying on Eli. "She can fuck who she wants."

Eli continues to stare at me, his floppy brown hair falling over his innocent eyes. He's the youngest one out of all of us by a few months, and we treat him that way, but it also means he has a smart ass mouth. Way smarter than mine.

Brantley is watching me, a dark smirk on his mouth. He knows I'm bluffing, and I hate that he reads me like a fucking open book.

"Don't get me started on you," I smirk at Brantley. "Flowers, gold, secrets…. Doors…"

He flips me off, his jaw clenching. I know he's hiding something, or someone, in this creepy fucking house. I just know it. I can feel her presence everywhere, subtly lingering in all the nooks and crannies, like she comes out at night and disappears during the day.

"So many questions for Bran Bran…"

"Are we ready?" Bishop snaps from the doorway, and I have to mentally count to ten again.

"Yup!" I stand from the sofa, swaggering straight past him.

"Nate!" Bishop calls out just as I reach the front door, but I don't want to turn around and give him any attention. We used to be tight, he and I. Bishop was my best friend, but since Madison came into the story, Brantley and I have merged closer together.

"Yeah?" I turn to face him. Shit. How am I supposed to abide by one of The Commandments if I can't even face the fact that Bishop has touched Tillie, and why the fuck does it bother me more than Brantley touching her? Because betrayal, that's why. Brantley hasn't done anything behind my back.

Not like what I did with Madison and Brantley that one time…

Fuck.

"You good?" Bishop asks, and the world stands still for a beat. Silence stretches out between us, scattering out to the rest of The Kings who are watching carefully.

"Yeah." I smirk, my fake face coming on at full force. "Always."

Never.

Chapter Seventeen

Tillie

My black lace mask is secured around my face tightly. I chose another red dress, because of course I did. It's tight around my waist, dipping like a heart between my breasts with no straps. It bands tightly down my legs until it spills out slightly around my feet. There's a long slit that goes right up past my hip, so I had to skip on wearing underwear. Madison and I both visited the salon today. My hair was so faded that I couldn't stand it anymore and wanted a change. I thought about going back to my natural blonde but bitched out. So they put another pink through and washed it out so it's back to a metallic, bright pink.

My eyes are dark and heavy with liner and smoke, and my lips are a blood cursing red.

"I think I'm going to spew," Madison murmurs from beside me as our driver takes us toward a hotel in the heart of NYC where it's being held.

"At least it's not at his house again."

"True," Madison agrees, readjusting her mask. She's wearing the same as mine, only red. Her dress is black and short. She wanted to go short, for obvious reasons. She has also been drinking since we started applying makeup.

"Will you be okay?" I ask her as she sips from a champagne flute.

"Yes," she says, throwing back the rest.

This might not end well.

The driver pulls up to the front of a hotel in the Upper East Side and we both climb out, our heels clicking across the concrete. I squeeze my clutch in my hand and grab hers

She whimpers. "I believe you."

The doorman opens the doors for us, and we step through the foyer, making our way to the ballroom I'm guessing where it's being held, judging by the signs and people filing in dressed in similar attire.

My phone vibrates in my clutch, so I pull it out, just as we reach the woman who's standing at the entrance with a clipboard.

She eyes Madison skeptically, and then her eyes come to mine and they widen. Interesting. Usually, people know who Madison is before they know who I am, but I've come to the realization that that has quickly changed, and it also depends on the people we are around. Riverside Prep kids who attended their school? Sure. But adults and grown people who are head deep in The Elite Kings world? No.

"Tillie Stuprum and Madison *Venari*." I bite out her name harshly, somewhat offended for my friend. I wish I could have said Madison Hayes and watch the judgy bitch's eyes pop from their sockets as she dropped to Madison's feet.

I chuckle to myself at my thoughts, unlocking my phone and seeing a text from Nate. My heart beats in my chest.

We need to talk.

I look up at the woman who ticks off our names, her eyes still not moving from me. "Yes, please enter. Thank you, Miss Stuprum."

I yank on Madison's arm to pull her in with me and as soon as we're inside, I'm taken over by the setting. Dim lighting, a live band playing on a makeshift stage, people talking amongst each other. They all pause slightly as Madison and I enter. I feel thousands of eyes on me and I know why.

"My god," Madison whispers, leaning into me. "I mean like people know me in their circle and at school, but this is a whole new level. Everyone is staring at you like you built the fucking kingdom."

"Not me," I grumble under my breath. "Just my ancestors."

"*Princessa*," a voice says behind me, and I turn to see a young boy that I don't recognize. "I'll escort you both to your table."

I nod my head, allowing him to take my arm and lead me to the front of the room with Madison in tow. When we get there, my eyes fly around the table to all of The Kings (my ones). Nate, Bishop, Brantley, Eli, Cash, Hunter, Ace, Chase. I know where Nate is instantly, glaring at me from across the table. I take the empty seat beside Bishop, and Madison sits on the other side of me, closest to her brother, Hunter, since Jase isn't here. The lights are low, only intensifying the already potent atmosphere.

Bishop leans into me and my hand goes to Madison's knee under the table.

"Pretty sure Eli stirred the pot this morning," Bishop purrs into my ear. Okay. Alright. I mean, one look at Bishop and he owns your ass. I think the only reason why I'm immune to him is because I'm so loyal to Madison and he has always been hers. But don't get me wrong. I totally, totally, understand where the hype comes from. Especially when he's whispering in my ear.

My eyes go to Nate. There's a girl beside him, wearing a pink lace mask. I feel bile rising up my throat. From what I can see from here, she has dark hair and tanned skin, with a skinny frame. She's staring at me, smirking, but leaning into Nate.

I could kill her. That would be okay. I know that Brantley and the rest of The Kings would help me dispose of her body, so it's fine.

"You can't kill her," Bishop chuckles in my ear, snapping me out of my plot of murder. "I mean you could, and none of us would detest it, but she's pointless. The only reason he's bringing her here is a pathetic attempt to push you away."

Madison pats my hand reassuringly as my phone vibrates. I lean back into Bishop. "I don't care."

"Really?" he answers me, but his eyes are on Nate.

"Who's that beside him?"

Bishop answers, picking up his drink. "Billie. She was adopted into an Elite family when she was two. She and Nate fucked around one summer when they were kids and she was his initiation fuck."

"So I've heard," I answer, picking up my flute glass. I lean down and reach for my phone.

Madison—Thank you for looking out. I see what Nate is doing, though, so feel free to use Bishop however you want. I know he's hurting, and I'd rather him use you than use someone else. If you know what I mean.

I reread over her words, and then another text comes through.

Obviously, you're not allowed to do anything.

I smirk. *There's my friend.*

Unless you both want to get shot.

My grin deepens, and a chuckle slips from my lips.

I love you.

I push my phone away, ignoring the next text, and then I lean into Bishop.

"Can you promise me something?" I say to him, even though he doesn't owe me shit.

"What?" He doesn't agree, but there's no surprise in that.

"Don't do anything stupid until you know the full story."

He rests his arm over the back of my seat, his grin smug as fuck. "Yeah. Sure thing." He's such an asshole.

"I'm trying not to be super weirded out about how it's so easy for us all to switch partners…" Eli murmurs, leaning into Bishop but close enough so I can hear him too.

Brantley chuckles. "I rest my case." *What fucking case.*

I ignore the rest of the banter, my eyes going around the room in search of Hector. I wonder how Bishop feels about this revelation, and I wonder what they hope to achieve by confirming this. They can't kill him, can they?

A girly laugh comes from across the table and my eyes zip to Nate and Billie. She's leaning into him, his lips on her slender neck and his hand under the table, presumably on her leg.

I clench my jaw.

"I don't mean to interrupt," a voice whispers from behind me. An unfamiliar voice.

I turn around in my seat, noticing a tall, masculine man who has to be in his mid-twenties. "Please do."

His eyes drop to me, and vivid blue hues peer back at me through a bright red bone mask. "Want to dance?"

I smile at the stranger, eager to get the fuck away from this circle, so I stand and take his hand in mine. Tattoos sneak out of his suit jacket as he leads me all the way to the dance floor, then he twists my body against his, wrapping an arm around my back.

"Can you follow my steps?" he whispers, his mouth coming to the side of my neck.

I swallow. "Yes."

He pushes me closer to his body as I fight the urge to ask what his name is.

"Listen to me very carefully, but smile and act like I'm telling you how much I want to run my tongue over your clit and make you scream my name so loud that Nate's existence in your life is questioned..." His voice is low and sexy, and his words touch me in places I've been yearning to be touched.

My thighs clench.

He chuckles. "Good girl."

I smile, though it's not fake, it's because of his dirty words and his hard body beneath the palms of my hands. *Who is he?*

"Your suspicions are not quite correct. Hector is, and is not, responsible for the death of your daughter. My condolences about that, by the way."

We dance around the dance floor as "Myth" by Tsar B starts playing. We move to the beat, like we were made to dance together. His lips move across my collarbone. "Things are moving at a speed that your Kings do not know about. We don't trust them enough to set up a meet with them. Their loyalty is and always will be with The Kings." He flings me out and then crashes me into his body again.

I lean back to get a good look at his eyes. So blue. Dark eyelashes and a shadow scattered against the edge of his perfect jaw. There're tattoos everywhere on his skin and something tells me that if he removes that mask, my panties will melt away.

"Who are you?"

He tilts his head, his lips curling with a smirk and showing perfectly straight white teeth. His hand travels down my back and rests on my ass as he presses me into his crotch. I groan, dropping into the crook of his neck. He expels sex like no one I've felt before—except for Nate. I'm well aware of how this must look to people around us. His other hand comes to my chin and he tilts my head to face him.

"I'm with the Rebels, sweetheart." His lips crash against mine and I let them, his tongue slipping across my bottom lip as I reach up to his hair to pull him back, only I end up pushing him closer. He stops and then smiles at me. "You'll get a text."

He lets me go and leaves me breathless on the dance floor with hormones raging all over the place.

Well.

Then.

Call me a rebel because I want to be fucked by one. But as soon as he's left and taken his energy with him, I start to fill with guilt. Not about kissing him, screw Nate. But about kissing a Rebel.

I make my way back to the table, Madison grinning at me with another glass in her hand.

I take it from her and shoot it back, sitting back in my chair.

I don't even bother looking at Nate, but Bishop leans into me. "Good girl, play the game. *But can I trust you?*"

I turn to face Bishop, searching his eyes. "You orchestrated that?"

Bishop doesn't answer, his eyes searching mine. "What do you think?"

I sip from my glass. "Were all of you in on that?"

Bishop smiles. "Look at Nate, he's about to rip everyone to pieces. You really think he would sign off on that? No. Just me. You wanted to play?" he asks, his eyes darkening. "Then it's time to play. Get rid of Madison."

Shit.

"Mads?" I lean into her, whispering in her ear as the music dies out and Hector takes center stage. I'm sucked away from what I'm supposed to be doing as the lights cut out and a spotlight beams down on Hector.

My breathing gets heavy, anger simmering to the surface.

He smiles, the wrinkles on his face only making him more attractive. His tattoos sneak out from beneath his suit, his hair shaved close on the sides and long on the top. There's evil, and then there's Hector Hayes. There's a reason why he is the way he is, and that's because he rules with a soulless body. He's old school and doesn't care for any other loyalties but The Kings.

"Does he know about Abel?" I ask Bishop through a whisper.

Bishop grins. "No."

My phone vibrates and I pull it out from under the table. There's nothing from Nate, but one from a random number.

I've left with your moans echoing in my ear. Wanna finish what we started?

I smirk, my lips curling in. **Is this the text I'm supposed to be waiting on?**

I wait for a text but end up putting my phone back in my clutch when someone kicks me under the table. My eyes fly to Nate, who's glaring at me.

I don't look away, I don't budge.

"I need to go to the bathroom," I mutter, not giving a shit that Hector is mid-speech.

I stand and quickly dodge through the tables and chairs, heading straight for the little hallway that has the restroom sign illuminated. Rushing through the ladies' room, the only girl who is in there quickly leaves, and I lean over the counter, my hand resting on my stomach. What am I doing? Could I sleep with someone else? Even though Nate has hurt me in ways that I have never been hurt. I need to pull my shit together.

I turn the tap on just as the door swings open and Nate is standing there, glaring at me.

"Get out," I say, flicking my eyes back to the mirror.

He's behind me in a flash, spinning me around to face him. His hand comes to my throat as he shoves me against the wall roughly. "Who the fuck do you think you're playing with, Tillie?" he asks, his fingers flexing around my throat.

"I'm not playing with you, Nate!" I yell. "I'm fucking tired of your back and forth!"

I shove him, but he doesn't budge. He spreads my legs with one knee as his other hand comes to my leg, his fingers gripping around my upper thigh. My eyes close as I internally talk myself down from the heat he's thrashing into me. His mouth touches the side of my neck as his hand goes all the way around and his fingertips brush against my pussy. He dips one finger inside and I lose my footing, but he releases my neck and catches me, wrapping my legs around his waist.

He chuckles, but it's low and dark. "You're fucking wet for him?"

I freeze, fear slipping into my bones. "No—" I start to say, but he brings the finger that was inside of me to my mouth, shoving it between my lips. I bite his finger and his eyes slant as his other fingers wrap around my cheeks forcefully.

"Bite it again and see what happens."

I bite it again.

He drops me to the floor and spins me around, pressing me into the bathroom counter.

He lifts my dress from the bottom and slaps my bare ass. Grabbing at my hair, he yanks my head up.

"Look at yourself in the mirror, Tillie."

I feel as his fingers slip into me again from behind. I blush at the invasion. Not because it's embarrassing, but because it feels so good. "Next time you think you want to get your pussy wet for someone else, I want you to remember this moment…"

I tense around his fingers, and he grins from behind his mask. He unzips himself and rubs the tip of his cock over my opening before sinking inside.

I moan, finding something to grip onto on the counter but failing and reaching for the tap. His other hand comes to the front of my throat. "Is this what you wanted? To be fucked in a bathroom like a cheap bitch looking for fresh cock?" His words sting, but I block them out. "Then I'll fuck you in a bathroom like a cheap bitch."

He thrashes into me relentlessly, his cock hitting my cervix with every movement. I feel my stomach curl, my orgasm so ashamedly close. My muscles tense briefly before my tension releases, my cum dripping all over his dick. He slows, emptying himself inside of me. He pulls back, and now that the tension has changed, I stand up straight, smoothing out my dress. Shit. What have I done? My throat throbs as I realize I've just let him have his way with me, but I don't have to be a victim to my feelings, because I'm not a fucking victim.

I run the tip of my finger over my eyebrow and turn to face him as he zips himself up. "You're right, Nate, I was wet for him." He stills, but I remain strong. "And you fucking me in a bathroom like a cheap bitch isn't going to stop the fact that I might fuck him too. Excuse me."

I shove past him, but he yanks me back by my arm and slams me back against the wall again, with his hand pressing against my throat. I don't give him anything.

"You go near anyone else and I'll kill them."

I smirk. "Fine by me. Just make sure it's after I've fucked their brains out."

Then I shove him out of the way and straighten my shoulders. Time to get back to why I'm really here, and the answer to that is—I stop once I reenter the ballroom, seeing Madison and Bishop gone from the table.

"Fuck's sake." I quickly make my way back to the table and grab my clutch. Stopping, I lean down to talk with Brantley.

"You smell like sex and I'm feeling left out." Brantley smirks behind his glass.

Hector is no longer talking shit, now it's another man dressed in a suit and looking like another rich fucker in this world.

"Where's Bishop and Madison?" I ask, ignoring his jab.

Brantley shrugs. "Madison ran out and he chased her, I think."

I see Nate take his spot back at the table, but I ignore him, standing and making my way back to the main lobby of the hotel. I dial Madison, but her phone goes to voicemail.

"What the fuck!" I bring my phone back down just as Madison's name flashes over the screen. "Thank god!" I answer. "Whe—"

"—Tillie. I need you to help me." Her tone is impassive, which is a contradiction to the words she used.

"Done. Where are you?"

"Take the elevator to the twenty-first floor. And come alone, okay?"

"Okay… are you alone?"

"…No," she answers, and I hang up quickly when I catch Nate and a few of The Kings coming my way.

I quickly run to the elevator, pressing the 'up' button one-thousand times in a second.

"Come on. Come on."

Bishop must be with her, that's why she's not alone.

The doors ding and open in the slowest time ever. I turn to the left to see Nate and Brantley glaring at me, and then jogging fast. I quickly push level twenty.

They'll know if I stop on the twenty-first floor. I'll have to take the stairs up to the next level. The soft music does nothing to calm my erratic thoughts. What the hell is going on? The elevator dings and I dash out hastily, scanning up and down the long hallway until I see the stairway exit. I rush through and yank the door open, climbing the stairs while picking up the hem of my dress. My phone starts ringing again, Nate's name flashing over the screen. I hit ignore. It starts ringing again just as I reach the door to level twenty-one.

When I see it's Madison's name flashing over the screen, I hit answer. "I'm here!"

"Room four-oh-one."

Then she hangs up.

I swear to God.

I yank open the door to the stairwell and find 401 easily, gripping the door handle.

"It's me!" I knock against the door softly.

She opens it and the first thing I notice is that she's crying.

The second thing I notice is that she's holding a knife.

And the third thing I notice is that there's blood dripping over her hands.

Chapter Eighteen

Nate

"Where the fuck!" I launch my fist into the wall, pacing back and forth down the hallway of the twentieth floor. The elevator dings and both Brantley and I turn toward it, only finding Bishop, Eli, Cash, and Hunter spilling out.

"Did you find her?" Bishop asks, his eyes flying around all of us.

"What? Tillie? No. She fuck—"

"—not Tillie, Madison." Bishop goes back and forth, anger rippling from him.

My eyes go to him, suddenly suspicious of just what the fuck these two girls could be getting themselves into.

"Wait, they're together?"

"I'm guessing so." Bishop grabs at his hair and yanks at it in frustration. "I chased Madison out, but by the time I reached the lobby, she had fucking disappeared."

"Remind me to not let my future woman anywhere near those two misfits. I ain't even playin'." Eli shakes his head, smirking.

"She fucking stopped here. At this level," Brantley murmurs.

I narrow my eyes at the stairwell, the light illuminating like a beacon of fuck knows what. I take a step forward.

"Yo! Nate!" Cash hollers from behind me, but I ignore him.

"*She took the fucking stairs*," I mutter, my feet kicking up in speeds I didn't know I had.

"Nate!" Bishop barks from behind me, but Brantley is right there beside me.

"She took the motherfucking stairs!" I yell, anger gripping at my bones.

"She's way too fucking smart for even us," Brantley grunts from beside me. "Fucking terror she is."

We climb the stairs, taking two at a time until we reach the door to level twenty-one.

I yank it open and slowly step forward.

Silence.

Pure and utter silence.

I turn to face the rest of The Kings as they all begin to file through one by one.

Bishop's eyes come to mine, his head tilting.

"This level?" he whispers as he comes closer.

I nod. "Yeah. Pretty sure."

I point to each door and set them all at a door each, and then press my ears to number 401.

Chapter Nineteen

Tillie

"Jesus Christ," I pace back and forth in the bedroom, dangling the knife in my hand. I don't know why, but I feel the need to whisper.

I stop and turn to her. "Did you kill him?"

She shakes her head. "No. I just cut him a little..."

My eyes search her blood sodden hands and then land back on hers. "Sure." I fling the knife up and down her body. "Just a little." I sigh. "Where is he?"

Madison looks up at me with doe eyes, pointing toward the master bedroom that's behind a sliding door that separates the lounge and bedroom. "In the bathroom. Bleeding out."

I wander toward the door. "Can I ask why you decided to cut this man?"

Madison's face falls. "It's him, Tillie..."

"Wait." I stop, turning to face her. "You mean him *him*?"

She nods her head. "Yeah. It's him. I still don't know who he is working for or why, but it's him."

I flip the knife between my fingertips. I've heard of the crazy shit that Madison did to Brantley's dad, so I know the actual cutting isn't what actually upset her. It's what happened to cause the cutting.

I stop flinging the knife and slide the doors open with my feet, not wanting fingerprints. Sighing, I head straight for the bathroom. I can smell the metallic tang of blood well before I reach the door, but I kick it open anyway, the loud crashing from it hitting the back of the wall echoing through the bedroom.

Oops.

I look down at the man in the bathtub. He's good looking. Young too.

When he sees me, his eyes go wide.

I kneel down to his level, running the knife up and down his chest while attempting to keep my anger in check.

He hurt my friend.

"What's your name?" I ask, kicking the door closed with the back of my foot. I lean back and hook the latch to lock it. I know what Madison is capable of, but I want to make sure she doesn't need to carry it all. What's one more sin to add to the ever growing pile of reasons why I'm so fucking mentally unstable?

"Joshua."

"Joshua." I run the pointed edge of the knife down his chest and then smirk. "Hmmm, and you like getting girls naked, Joshua? Hmm?"

I stand, placing the knife on the towel rack while stepping backward. The bottom of my dress has already been smudged in the blood that's on the floor.

He doesn't answer, but that's okay. I don't need him to answer. I slowly zip the dress down until it falls to a pile at my feet. I didn't think this through, how am I going to leave with no clothes on? Too far in to back out now.

"Do you like this, Joshua? Hmmm?" I ask, my head tilting while I gesture to my half-naked body.

When I say half-naked, I mean half-naked, wearing nothing but a bra, courtesy of my slutty dress that didn't allow me to wear panties.

Madison knocks on the door.

I ignore her.

"Am I not naked enough for you?"

My arm twists to the back and unclasps my bra. It falls to the floor. Now I'm standing here naked. Completely.

"Is this better?" I ask him, but blood is coming out of his mouth so he can't answer.

I lick my lips, stepping into the bathtub with him, letting the deep tang of metal drift over the top of my head. I can still feel Nate's cum dripping down my inner thighs.

But everything is blank.

I don't care.

I run the tip of the knife down his pretty face.

"Why do you look so familiar?"

I continue down past his jaw and to his throat. I press the blade to it.

"Why did you rape my friend?"

He doesn't answer, more blood spilling between his lips.

He's dying.

He's not going to say anything.

I lean forward, my ear to his lips. "Why?"

He whispers one word. "Cataclysm."

I lean forward just as his eyes flutter closed. I know that he's about to die, but he's not going to die on Madison's conscience. So I press the sharp edge of the blade against his throat until it sinks into his flesh like a hot knife to butter, and blood squirts all over my hands. I maintain my calm.

Breathing in and out as the blade sinks deeper.

He stops moving.

When I pull the blade out, blood squirting everywhere, that's when I register the heavy banging on the door. Suddenly it bursts open and Nate is standing at the threshold with Brantley and Bishop behind him.

Chapter Twenty

Tillie

"Oops," I sigh, dropping the knife onto the corpse.

"Oops!?" Nate whisper-yells in frustration before turning around. "Everyone but Brantley get the fuck out."

They all disappear through the two big, bossy men in my life. Nate breathes in and out, leaning against the door once it's closed. A few seconds pass before he pulls his phone out and sends a text, putting it back into his pocket.

"My little terror," Brantley smirks, coming closer to me and grabbing my hand to help me out of the tub. "I'm a little proud, and a lot fucking turned on right now." His eyes darken. "Red is definitely your color."

"Don't take her out," Nate grunts, not meeting my eyes. He ambles forward and turns the faucet to the shower on. "Rinse the blood off you."

I stand under the head, watching as water rushes over my skin and falls onto the dead body between my legs.

Once it's running clear, I turn it off and step out, just as Brantley cleans the obvious blood from the floor and tosses the towel into the tub with the dead fuckwit.

"Come here," Nate murmurs, taking my hand in his and pulling me out.

"It's cold," I shiver, grabbing for the towel he's handing me. My body shakes uncontrollably, gripping onto all of my nerves before I can take control.

Nate dries me as Brantley shuffles around the room, making sure everything is in the tub.

"Did you send out the text?" Brantley asks Nate.

"Yes," Nate says, his hand coming to the back of my neck. "Why did you do that? What happened from the time that we fucked downstairs, to here?"

I open my mouth, wanting to tell him but still shackled by my loyalty to my best friend.

"Why do you hate me?"

Why did I just say that?

"He doesn't hate you," Brantley whispers from behind me, drying my legs.

I focus back to Nate's gaze, who is staring at me with enough intensity to burn a hole into my head. "You hate me."

Nate doesn't answer.

My eyes close as Brantley's hand grazes up my inner thigh and I whimper, my head falling forward, onto Nate's chest.

Nate stiffens.

Brantley continues up, and then his lips press to my shoulder. "Breathe, my little terror, you're okay. You're fucking safe when we're around…"

I hold my breath, my fitful heart still jumping around in my chest.

I killed a man.

Someone who raped my best friend.

The smell of blood lingers with my lust, but the feeling of Brantley dropping kisses on my shoulder blades makes my head spin. I moan again, inhaling Nate's smell. He hasn't moved, his hard body still stoic.

I rub my bare ass into Brantley, who is rock hard behind me. He licks me across the back of my neck as his other hand reaches down between my legs, his thumb coming to my clit. I moan again as it circles me, my legs shaking. My eyes come up to Nate, who is watching me closely, his jaw set in stone. Just when Brantley's finger dives inside of me, Nate's hand comes around and wraps my chin, tilting my face to his.

He presses his lips to mine. "I don't hate you, baby."

I wrap my arm around the back of his neck as my other reaches behind me to grip onto Brantley's cock through his jeans.

Brantley unzips his jeans until his heavy pierced dick falls into the palm of my hand.

Nate grips onto my legs as I wrap them around his waist. His kissing slows, his tongue licking mine softly. Every flick, every caress, every thrust of his hips.

I tug on Brantley's cock as Nate grinds into me in circles.

"Fuck," Brantley groans from behind me. "I don't know how much I can take without actually putting my dick in her."

Nate stills, searching my eyes. He drops me, along with the mood, to the ground.

"Fuck!" Nate punches the wall. "Why the fuck can't I share you!" He yanks the door open and disappears, leaving me and Brantley in the bathroom alone.

"For both our sakes, we need to tuck up," Brantley laughs, shaking his head.

I swipe my cheeks. "Yeah."

We leave the bathroom, with Brantley giving me his suit jacket. I wrap it around my body closely, realizing it looks like a dress. The room is dark, but I can hear talking in the other room.

"You asked me why he hates you…" Brantley says, his hand coming to mine.

"Yeah?"

"It's because he can't hate you."

"You make it sound so simple. So relatable."

"Because I do relate to the feeling. Well."

I don't ask. "One day, I'm going to want to know what you mean by that…"

Brantley chuckles. "I bet."

I pick up my heels and slip them onto my feet, piling my wet hair onto the top of my head to fall into a long ponytail. We enter back into the main room to see everyone there, Nate included.

"Nate called it in. We need to leave so everything can get handled," Bishop murmurs, his eyes on mine. A thousand questions lay in those eyes, questions I won't answer.

Madison is sitting alone on a chair, her eyes on the floor. Nate is talking with her, but I can see everything is going in one ear and out the other.

"Do we have to talk about the fact that y'all were about to have sex in a bathroom where a dead body was, right after our little queen off-ed him?" Eli asks, his eyes going around the place. "Or are we just putting that in the bucket of things we don't talk about?"

I ignore him, heading straight for Madison.

Nate glares at me, standing back to his feet defensively. I don't care about his feelings right now. I just want to make sure my friend is okay.

My hand comes to her knee and her eyes flutter to it. "Do you want me to take you home?"

I catch something flash over her eyes. At first, I'm not fast enough to decipher it, but then I study her closely. How her eyes flick to mine, and then to Bishop, and then back to me. I know what that something is now—fear, and she's going to do the thing that Madison always does.

Run.

And no one can stop her.

"Hey," I coax, taking her hand in mine. "I'll take you home."

I stand with her behind me as Nate removes his jacket to wrap it around her body.

I grit my teeth, fighting my irrational thoughts. This is Nate. He cares. He gives a fuck about the very few people in his life. I know this, so I can't be mad.

"We'll have to take the back exit. No doubt they'll wipe footage, but just to minimize the job and keep it clean," Bishop adds, running his hands over his face.

"Then shouldn't we reduce their work by just going the way we came so they don't have to wipe two sets of cameras?" I question Bishop.

Nate shakes his head. "No, because then there are other things we have to take into consideration, like the two of you wearing jackets, and witnesses. It doesn't matter, they'll wipe the whole lot."

Nate's eyes meet mine.

I look away. New plan. Don't look him in the eye ever again.

We all make our way out as Bishop orders Cash and Eli to wait for the clean-up crew as we all slowly make our way outside via the fire exit. There are already two large black limos waiting. Bishop opens the door, gesturing for us to get in first. Madison goes straight to the far corner of the seat on the opposite side that we climbed in on and I sit right beside her.

Nate sits beside me, and Bishop, Brantley, and Hunter sit opposite us.

Hunter is watching her carefully, worry etched into his features.

Nate's thigh presses against mine, but I flinch away from him.

He laughs. "Bit late for that considering I've had my dick in you tonight."

Everyone goes about their business, well acquainted with Nate's and my toxicity on display for everyone.

I ignore him, not taking the bait. I'm tired. I want Daemon to tell me everything is going to be okay. I miss his presence and his touch. Why am I attracted to the depraved? It's like my soul attaches itself to darkness, lurking on the wicked because the disenchantment in mundane-like souls isn't enough to spark fire in mine. All the men in my life have one thing in common—evil.

Nate seems to shuffle around a lot beside me. Going from his thigh jiggling to his hand grabbing at his hair, back to his thigh jiggling.

He's frustrated, like a ticking time bomb about three seconds away from exploding.

This carries on the whole way to Brantley's house.

My eyes go to Madison when we pull up. "Are you coming in?"

She shakes her head. "No. I'm going home. Alone."

"Fuck that!" Bishop finally yells. "You're going to explain this shit once and for all!"

"I don't have to explain shit to you, Bishop! Get out!"

My eyes fly between the two of them.

"If I get out of this car, Madison, it will be forever," he growls softly.

Goddamnit, Madison! Fucking tell him. For the life of me. She's about to lose this man forever if she doesn't open her trap.

"Please do," she murmurs, her eyes looking out the window.

I watch as Bishop flies out the door, slamming it in his retreat.

"Madison..." I try.

"Don't." She shakes her head, tears spilling down her cheeks. "I don't deserve him, and there's so much."

"I'll see you tomorrow." I give her thigh one more squeeze and then climb out the door. The limo pulls away and I start thinking that Nate went with her, but then I hear his footsteps behind me.

They're heavy.

Angered.

I know our fight isn't over.

He whistles out. "Tillie!"

I don't answer, half because I'm mad at him but mainly because I'm not a fucking dog and what is with him and whistling to girls. Instead, my feet pick up their pace, the only problem with this is that my heart speeds up with it. I want to run. Not Madison run, I mean workout run. Or just run for my life run because fear ripples up my spine when I hear his footsteps thud against the pavement behind me, and suddenly, I'm flying forward, dropping my clutch to the ground and bypassing the front door, whipping to the side of the house. I drop my shoes when I pass the gardens, tears rippling down my face.

His footsteps are getting closer, heavier, but I zip forward like a bolt of lightning and head straight for the opening in the forest. Blades of damp grass whip my ankles as my hair falls from its high ponytail, flying out in the wind. The tears won't stop. *Why am I crying?*

Why is my mind a maze of scribble? *Why am I broken?* Why does he hate me so much? So many fucking questions. That's why I'm crying. I dash down the dirt path, my toes sinking into the mud. Just as I reach the entry to the Vitiosis cemetery, I stop running, wiping the stray tears from my cheeks. The high wired gates reaching for the sky in gothic spikes distract me for a second too long, because something hard crashes into my back and I'm falling forward, my hands flying out as I land face first into the dirt. Nate's hard chest is pressed against my back as he inches up slightly to flip me around, spreading my legs wide with his. He rests his weight on me, his hand slamming over my mouth.

"You're going to shut the fuck up and listen to the words that I'm about to say…"

I do as I'm told, because Nate angry is scary as shit and my self-preservation isn't on drugs.

He searches my eyes, his almost black. His lips part as he sucks in air. "You want to know why I hate you?"

I didn't want to know now.

He squeezes my cheeks which make my lips pop out. "I've already told you this, but I'm going to repeat myself one more time. *You fucking remind me of her!*"

I freeze.

Oh no. No, I don't want to do this. Not right now and not after everything that has already happened tonight, please, I don't want to do this. I squeeze my eyes shut.

"You gave me the most beautiful little fucking girl in the world, and I broke her, Tillie. My world touched her and now? Now I'm always reminded of that *because of your existence.*"

Tears stream down my face, my throat swelling from pain. Pure, undiluted pain ripples through my blood and soars through my eardrums.

He carries on. "I'm battling an internal war with myself every second of every fucking day. I hate you. I hate your smell because I remember what it smells like mixed with her innocent scent. I hate your fucking voice because I remember how you used it on her, and how it would soften every time you would say '*Micaela*'—"

Fire burns in my chest at the mention of her name. *I don't want to listen to this.*

"You're going to hear me, Tillie, because you think that my hate for you, that my feelings toward you are as shallow as Bishop had for Madison. *You know me.* I don't fuck like that. You should have known that there was more to me being like this. But you fucking didn't. You thought I hated you because fuck knows why, because you think it gets my dick hard like it did Bishop. *You're wrong.* It's far fucking deeper than that."

He exhales, his hand coming away from my mouth and resting on my throat.

"I never wanted to fucking hurt you. *Never.* But every fucking day. Every fucking day I'm reminded. I'm haunted by her through you. Yeah, that may not be your fault, but it's how *I'm dealing with it.*" His lip curls. His eyes drop to my mouth, his thumb pressing over my bottom lip. "How you used to kiss her goodnight every fucking night with these lips." Then his eyes turn ablaze, coming straight to mine. "Or how about the fact that you had more time with her than I did. I was fucking robbed."

The tears haven't stopped and my heart snaps in my chest. He's right. I thought the only reason he was throwing his hate around at me was because of some sick King game that they liked to play. Riddles, hate sex, vicious abuse. It's all their foreplay. Now he's saying that it wasn't the case with me? I'm confused. Hurt, dazed, and confused.

His hate is deeper than a flesh wound. I see it now. It's in his bones and it's there to stay.

My eyes close. "I'm sorry."

He flies off me and I slowly stand up from the ground.

"I didn't know. I didn't know it went deeper than that."

He grips at his hair and tugs on it. "You need to get your shit sorted, because I can't be around you much longer." His eyes come to mine. "I'm going to break you beyond repair if it's not done soon."

"Don't—" I shake my head, stepping forward. My fingers itch. I need to make him feel better. Just for right now. Not for tomorrow or yesterday, I need to make him feel better for right now. He stills, his eyes staying on mine.

"I'm going to break you, Tillie."

"Then don't, Nate," I answer through a whisper, my hand going up his chest and curling around the back of his neck. I stand on my toes and yank his face down to mine, my eyes searching his. "Don't break me."

He's so close I can feel his heavy breath on my lips, and then I lean forward, his soft lips brushing mine. I kiss him softly, not an open mouth kissed, but not a closed mouth kiss. It's an in-between kiss. He keeps still, not moving.

"Kiss me," I whisper against his mouth, my heart thundering in my chest.

I bury my fingers into the back of his hair and kiss him again, lighter, taking his bottom lip into my mouth softly and then kissing him again. His lip twitches and then slowly opens as his arm hooks around my back, pulling me to him. I jump up, wrapping my legs around his waist without either of us breaking apart. His tongue slides against mine, our lips meshing together. He walks me backward, laying me down onto the grass again, our lips not leaving each other. I open my legs for him as he settles between my thighs, his kissing turning gentle then hard, each stroke of his tongue a reminder of his harsh words earlier tonight, but every suck a token of his reasoning. He rips the jacket open, his hand coming to my breast as his thumb flicks over my nipple. I feel his cock press into me, and I sit up as he tears the jacket from my body and flings it to the side, our kiss finally breaking. His eyes are wild, his chest heaving as he takes in my naked body against the dirt.

"That's the last fucking time you let Brantley put something of his on you—including his fucking cock. Do you understand?"

When Nate bears his soul to you, he takes yours as collateral. I nod in agreement, because I know that I'm done with that. I love these guys, more Brantley than any of the others, but Nate is right. I can't do this either, but he was partly to blame for that, always testing just how far he could handle it like the damn masochist that he is.

He removes his shirt and throws it to the side. I inhale broadly as I take in all of the shredded hard lines of his body, just as they are hit by the moonlight. He dips and presses kisses up my thighs. I lean back, my head rolling with my eyes. His mouth comes to my pussy and I bite down on my lip, not wanting to make a sound. His tongue flicks around my clit and I whimper. Another tear slides down my face. Why am I crying? It feels good. This feels good.

I look down at him between my thighs, his shoulders flexing beneath his tattoos. He looks up at me and I lose it, my orgasm coming together as quickly as possible. He licks his lips, climbing up me while unbuckling his belt and unzipping his zipper.

I lay back down, his eyes staying on mine. They move to my lips and to my eyes again. Like he's memorizing this moment. He slowly sinks inside of me and my eyes flutter closed.

"Open," he orders, slowly grinding inside of me before extracting himself.

I obey, opening my eyes to his as my hand goes back behind his neck. My core clenches with my thighs and I grind up to meet him, eager to chase the high.

He lays back down, his mouth coming to mine. He grinds into me slowly. In and out, at a slow pace as his mouth kisses me without breaking. Sweat drips off my flesh, as nothing interrupts the sound of our bodies sliding together and the moonlight shining down on us. My orgasm builds to all new highs and I fist his hair, my kisses getting more desperate and needy. His hips thrust into me hard but remain at the same pace. He grinds into me, only every time he goes in, it's enough to push me over the edge. I moan softly as my orgasm shreds through my body, setting off explosives through my system like nothing I've felt before. He jerks suddenly, groaning into my mouth and biting down on my lip until a sweet metallic tang slips down my throat. We lay for a little bit, waiting for our bodies to calm.

That was the most intense sex I have ever had, but my heart was still broken. When he leans back, his heavy-lidded eyes searching mine, I notice every other emotion that he bared to me has vanished, and I know why.

That was goodbye.

Chapter Twenty-One

Tillie

After the cemetery drama, Nate was serious when he said that I'm not to wear anything else by any other man, so I wore his suit shirt and he walked back shirtless. We didn't speak.

He picked up my heels from the ground before we continued around to the front of the house where he grabbed my purse. He led me back downstairs to my room, and when we passed Daemon's, he stopped outside of it momentarily. Just when I thought he was going to say or do something, he carried on.

He tossed my shoes and bag onto the floor in my room and then left.

Without another word.

He stole the last part that there was of me and now I'm so drained I can't keep my eyes open.

After the longest shower in history washing away every aspect of the night, I wriggle on some underwear and slip beneath the sheets, willing myself to sleep for weeks.

Thunder crashes above me as I stand in front of Daemon's grave. Water pelts down over my face, mashing my hair to my skin. "Why am I here!" I scream through the heavy drops of rain and loud crashes of thunder. "What do you want from me!"

Daemon appears on his gravestone, his head hanging between his shoulders while his arm rests delicately on his knee. I watch as the rain soaks through his long hair, pushing it all forward.

"Daemon?" I whisper, stepping forward. "You're—you're?"

Slowly, his head comes up to meet me. "Find it, Tillie. Set me free…"

I wake, rubbing the sleep from my eyes. My phone is ringing. My phone is ringing?

I quickly dive off the bed and onto the floor where Nate left it last night.

"Hello?"

"Tillie?"

I freeze. "Gabriel."

He sighs. "It's me. I have something for you that you might want back."

"Wait," I whisper, afraid someone can hear me. "Where are you? I thought Nate took you?"

"That's not a conversation for right now. I need to meet you to give you this book. Can you meet me at a parking lot?" he yaps off, giving me directions.

"Yes," I murmur. "I'll be there at one."

I hang up my phone, massaging my temples. I'll finally get Daemon's book back and hopefully, I can navigate through it enough to solve why I found it and what it damn well means.

Chapter Twenty-Two

Nate

Tillie stands from the floor in her room, cell phone in hand. Her little body disappearing into the bathroom.

"I'm telling you, if it was anyone else, we could have put a camera in there too," Cash mutters, smirking at me.

"Put a camera in there and I'll kill you," I snap, glaring at him.

"What?" Cash mocks. "So Brantley gets to see her, but we don't?"

"He *got* to see her," I correct, my finger running over the top of my lip.

The table falls quiet.

"You two finally sort your shit out?" Brantley's mouth turns to a half-smile.

"Is she in my bed?" I pine, my eyebrow quirked.

"No, but she's on your dick, so I'm just wanting it to be a bit clearer," Brantley further teases.

"I like you better when you're angry at the world and not speaking." I go back to the camera.

Brantley chuckles. "Fucker." Then he flicks his finger to the camera. "You think that was him?"

I nod. "Yeah."

"And she's going to meet him?" Brantley asks again.

"Yeah," I repeat. "I need this shit done. She needs it done."

"You think this will *fix* her?"

Putting a joint in my mouth and blazing up, I blow out a thick cloud of smoke and shrug. "Fuck knows. Maybe she has completely lost it."

"Would that be an issue for you?" Brantley asks, and I turn to face him, giving him

"You're asking an awful lot of questions this morning, Bran Bran. You get your happy place licked last night?"

He laughs, his grin stretching wide. A few of the boys snicker.

Brantley's eyes darken on me.

"Don't fucking say it," I snap at him and his grin only deepens. "Asshole."

Bishop has been quiet through the whole thing. His eyes remaining passive on the same spot on the table.

I hand him the J and he takes it, biting it between his lips. "I don't know what the fuck to do about Madison."

Brantley shakes his head. "This is why I'm single."

"Are you though?" I ask, my eyes going to him. Your turn now. Bastard.

He narrows his. "Fuck you."

"Wait!" Cash interferes. "What does that mean?"

I chuckle, taking the J back off Bishop and putting it to my mouth. I smirk, shaking my head at Cash. "Nothing." ... *that you need to know.*

"She'll come around."

Bishop leans back, his eyes closing. He has been struggling a lot for the past couple of months, we both have.

"Halloween's coming up," I smirk around my joint. "We can play with the girls a bit."

Bishop's mouth curls. "I'm down for that."

"Party in the cemetery?"

Brantley smirks. "I'm keen for that."

Movement catches my eyes on the TV, and we all snap to it, watching as Tillie rushes around the room and then swings the door open. We hit the TV off as we hear the door open and close down the hallway.

She enters. "Hey, Bran—" Then stops. "What did I just interrupt?"

Her hair has been straightened, her face full of makeup. I know she loves that shit, but she doesn't need it.

"Nothing." Then I fish my keys out of my pocket and fling them toward her. She catches them in mid-air. "And you're taking my car..." When I said she wasn't riding on anything to do with Brantley, I wasn't just meaning his cock.

Her eyes widen. "Thanks. Mine should be here tomorrow."

"You bought a car?" Brantley asks and she drops to the floor, slipping her Chuck Taylors onto her feet.

"Yeah, when Madison and I went shopping, I bought a car."

"What kind?" Brantley and his questions.

"Let me guess," I mutter. "A Range Rover."

"Nope," she declares, standing back up with my keys in her hand. "A Porsche."

"Did you get it in black?" I ask, my eyes coming to hers. It's tradition for all of The Kings to ride in black cars. It started when we became Kings of course. It's not actually part of The Commandments.

She keeps them on mine, but they lack the typical fire that she normally has. Because she's hiding something, something she thinks I don't know. Her lack of faith in The Kings is tugging on my patience.

"Nope." She smirks, looking down at Brantley. "Blood red."

Brantley laughs and then looks toward me. "I told you—red is her color."

I roll my eyes. "Be back by three."

She waves us all off and makes her way out the front door. We all sit in silence until we hear my loud engine start up and take off down the driveway.

"Three, two, one—" We all stand and make our way out to the two Range Rovers parked at the front. I jump in the driver's seat of one, with Bishop in the other.

"Get Dough" by Dead Obies starts pulsing through the sound system and Brantley cranks it up. It's good. I need a distraction from my thoughts.

We pull out onto the main road. Brantley pushes a few buttons, lighting up the GPS on my car. We all had them installed when we got them. It's just something we do as a precaution. Every single King and close associate, like wives and such, have the same systems installed. A little green light flickers, signaling where she is. Heading into the city.

My phone rings. I switch it to speaker. "What?"

"I'm about to meet her now," my dad says into the phone. "Nate?"

I don't answer, running my hand over my jaw. "What?"

"She's in danger. You must know this."

"Yeah," I mutter. "Yeah, I do."

"And what are you all doing about the situation that holds the last living Stuprum in danger?"

I shuffle in my seat. "We've got a plan."

"Care to share?"

"Fuck no!" I scoff. "You're nomad, therefore you're even less trustworthy than a fucking Rebel and The fucking Circle."

He sighs. "I'm also your father, and the peace—"

I hang up, tossing my phone onto Brantley's lap.

"How is this cunt trying to act like daddy Malum now?" Brantley mutters. "Motherfucker."

I brush him off.

"You calling red on Tillie now?" Brantley asks, watching me out of the corner of his eye. When you call red on a girl, that's when all Kings have to back the fuck off her. You only get one girl *ever* that you can call red on. Meaning she can't be shared. Bishop never did until after Daemon died.

I think over Brantley's words. If I call red on her, that's fucking it. No one is going to touch her. Flirt? Yeah, but no more little fuck arounds between the three of us—and she's off limits to Brantley. Now, a reasonable man wouldn't call red on a chick until they've been together as in official—for a while. You know, like Bishop and Madison. However, I'm not fucking reasonable at all.

"Yeah, fucking aye I am."

Everyone bursts out laughing, Brantley included.

"Finally. How'd you get her to forgive you?" Brantley grins.

"Huh?" I look over at him innocently. "Oh, she hasn't forgiven me and we're not together. Might not ever be, might be next week—who fucking knows."

"You just called red on her!" Brantley yells around his laughter.

"Yeah." I nod my head. "Because none of you fucks are to go near her with your cocks."

"Damn," Brantley chuckles. "Never in the history of The Elite Kings Club has any-one ever splashed red over a girl without being in a relationship with her."

"Well, there is only one me." I can't help the cocky smile on my face.

Brantley shakes his head. "You like them fucking crazy."

"And you don't?" I ask, my eyes going to his. I really need to learn more about this secret he's hiding.

"No," Brantley glares. "Not anymore."

"So how do you like them?" I ask, smirking. Is he opening up a little?

"As a saint."

Chapter Twenty-Three

Tillie

I shut the driver's door after zipping up into a construction parking unit. I meet him at the top, ignoring the fact that these concrete ramps could come undone any minute.

Gabriel smiles when he sees me, but his eyes also fly around the area. He has one guard standing behind him wearing dark glasses and a suit.

"Tillie." He nods.

I smile. "Gabriel."

He hands me a suitcase. "It's in there. I hope you find closure and happiness when you finish."

I laugh. "Oh, I doubt it." Then I feel bad when I find his eyes on me. If he's pretending to be nice to me, then he's doing a good job, because every time I'm around him, I almost believe him.

"Nate let you go?" I ask, tilting my head.

"He did. He knows he can't keep me long and even he knows that I'm a better ally than an enemy."

"And could you do that?"

"Do what?" He brings his hands to his front. I watch as his thumbs twist and twirl around each other.

"Be an enemy to your son?"

"No," he answers instantly. "No, I couldn't."

I squeeze the suitcase handle. "Thanks for this." Then I turn to go back to Nate's car.

"Tillie?" Gabriel calls out. "I know you love my son, and I know that he loves you."

I clench my jaw. No one gets to say those words on behalf of him but *him*. Maybe

I'm being irrational, but I don't like when everyone else says those words to me. He doesn't even know that these people have said that to me. Do they know what goes on inside of Nate's mind? Because let me tell you, I'm almost certain not even Nate knows what goes on in his mind.

He continues. "But this world is different. Loyalties lay differently."

I swing my door open, my eyes on his. "I'm well aware of how this world works, Gabriel, and who's to say that I'm the one who is loyal to him?"

I push my Ray-Bans over my eyes and start the car up, putting it into first gear and driving out. I flick open the suitcase when he's gone and see the book. I flick through the pages, finding the one I was up to. I know that most of the drawings were done on Perdita, but I also know that the ending wasn't.

I go to the next page.

It's another drawing of the trailer park I grew up in. The light turns green and I swing around, doing a U-turn while dropping down to second. I know where I need to go, and I make it my mission to work through this damn book by the end of the day.

When I was a child, I had a crush. When I was a teenager, I had a crush. When I had... My mind aches as I pull down the long, empty road. It's worse than it was when I left. Opposite the park there's an abandoned building with graffiti splashed all over the concrete, smashed windows, and littered rubbish floating in the wind.

I roll to a stop, the familiar gate closed securely.

My eyes slam closed. "What is with this gate, Daemon. Why have you drawn me so many damn times?

Nate's car continues to idle beneath me.

I flip open Puer Natus again, drifting through every sketch. *The baby rattle.* The cell in Perdita. *Was that the cell he was in?* Yes? My head hurts and I can't remember.

I flip to the next page and I stop breathing as a bracelet drops out from between the pages. It's a knitted bracelet, plaited in a French plait. I wore this bracelet when I was little. *When I had a crush.* The drawing is two hands clasped together, pebbles and dirt scattered near their shoes. The view he drew is of that looking down. In the image, she's wearing my bracelet.

I throw the book. "Oh my god!"

I swing open the car door and start prowling back and forth, the gravel crunching beneath my shoes. "Why..." I think over my memories. Why did I not know that that was Daemon? He was my crush at thirteen. He held my hand and made my heart beat faster. *My heart.* I tore at my chest, heat melting over my skin. I need to find him. I need to ask him what the fuck this means.

I climb back into the car, slamming the door closed and reach for the book.

"Finish the book, Puella."

I scream out in frustration, flipping to the next page.

A broken heart, weeping through the pages.

I flick to the next, turning the cover around. A baby crib, dark and old, one that looks like it was the same one the biblical baby was put into. Was it Jesus? Yeah, Jesus. There's no baby inside, instead, is a sign *SOLD!* Drawn over the small mattress.

A baby was sold. Who was sold?

My heart squeezes. The baby subject is too much for me right now. Too sensitive. It touches too close to *her.*

There are only a few pages left so I flick through again, and it's Hector's house.

Hector, *her*? If I didn't see the body with my own eyes, I would think that Hector had her instead of having her—I choke.

I flick to the second to last page and it's the back of a small girl. Her hair is long—so very long, hanging down to her lower back.

I flip to the final one, and it's a drawing of Brantley's house.

There are no more pages.

Why are there no more pages? He said that I would have my answers when I reach the final page!

I throw the car into first and skid out onto the road, heading back to Brantley's.

I need to talk with Daemon, and I need to talk with him now.

Chapter Twenty-Four

Tillie

You don't judge an ocean by what you see on the surface the same way that you never, and I mean never, judge a King by his demeanor. They know more than they show and are worse than you could ever know. This can be a good thing or a bad thing. I know this, but the information that they hold from everyone, me included, is something I can only handle for so long.

I push open Brantley's front door, tossing Nate's keys onto the small table that accommodates loose items.

I press the door closed and quickly head for the door that leads to the floor level, to my room. I need to ask Daemon what this book has to do with me and why he didn't tell me that that boy was him. Is this why I have always had feelings for him? Because they've always been there, under all of the damage from my past?

I don't know, but as I move down the long hallway, I know I'm about to find out.

Lifting my fist to his door, I knock a few times, but no one answers.

"Daemon?"

I squeeze the handle and push at it, finding his bedroom exactly how it has always been. I haven't seen him for a couple of nights now, and I'm starting to get worried. He's not been the same since we found him.

I sigh, flopping onto his bed with the book in my hand. Slipping my wrist through the bracelet, I loosen it enough so it fits comfortably, and lay back, flicking through the pages again.

Maybe I've missed something between the pages. Maybe there's something in-between that I'm not catching…

Chapter Twenty-Five

Nate

Betrayal is the feeling of your stomach being yanked from your body. It's watching as someone you thought you could trust, throws it into an ocean of hungry sharks. It's feeling your trust meter completely empty. But there are a few seconds after feeling this when you go numb. You stop and think to yourself, *well fuck. Now what?*

I didn't feel this when we became aware of Hector possibly being involved in Micaela's death. I went straight to the numb feeling.

"We have to be careful with how we execute our plan," Brantley mutters, putting a smoke into his mouth.

I stay still, my eyes glued to a spot on the wall, not wanting to show any emotion.

Bishop sits with his head hanging between his shoulders. "We can't kill him."

A hiss escapes my lips. "What the fuck do you mean? If he killed my daughter, Bishop, he is fucking dead, whether I take myself down with him or not."

Bishop rubs his face viciously with the palms of his hands, the frustration evident. "He's still my fucking dad, Nate."

"And since when the fuck did that matter to you?" I shoot back, my eyes narrowing.

"Since we were plotting his fucking death!" Bishop stands from the table we've all become accustomed to at Brantley's. He leaves, the door slamming shut behind him.

Brantley's eyes come to mine. "He's a dead man if this is true."

Eli shifts uncomfortably. "Taking down Hector Hayes? The daddy of the EK? I don't know… I get that you're angry, man, but—"

"—but nothing," Jase interrupts. Jase is the older brother of Hunter and Madison, but he's always been around because of Hunter being in our generation.

Jase brings his dark eyes to mine. "If it is revealed that he was behind her death, Nate, you have my word—I got your back."

We have a divide, but I know that has to do with Bishop. If he was all in, there would be no buts about it.

Brantley stands from the table, his phone vibrating. His eyes shoot to mine. "She's got the book back. Now what?"

I think over his words, running my finger above my lip. "Now we wait."

After leaving Brantley's house, I need something to take the edge off, so I hit dial on Billie's number as I stroll back to my car. The keys are in the ignition, but everything smells of her. Her smell attaches itself to everything I fucking own, including my cock.

I groan, adjusting myself in my pants as I think of her perfect little cunt clench arouover me.

"Fuck," I groan, sending a text to Billie.

Meet me outside your hotel in 10.

The sun sets against my windshield as I drop it into second gear after picking up Billie.

"I got to say," Billie whispers from the passenger seat of my car. "I'm impressed by her royal highness," she purrs, glaring down at her phone. I look over my shoulder and see she's looking through Tillie's Instagram. "Cute kid...sorry about that..."

My jaw tenses, my fists tightening around the steering wheel.

"Where are we going?" She places her phone onto her lap.

"To a meet."

"...and why? Why am I coming to a meet?"

I run my hand over my forehead. "I need your help with something."

"With what?" Billie says, further forcing my hand.

"I need to break someone," I murmur.

Billie pauses. "I can't come to a meet, Nate. It's not allowed."

I slam on my brakes, my tires tearing up the asphalt. I breathe in and out. "You're right. Get out."

Billie reaches for me and I flinch, pulling away from her.

"Get. Out."

She spills out of the passenger seat of my car, and I slam it into first gear. She's right. Billie can't attend a meet. She's not a fucking King and she's definitely not a Stuprum.

Chapter Twenty-Six

Tillie

Sweat drips off my body as I kick the speed up to level 14 on the treadmill. My legs run at a pace that I didn't even know they were capable of, my eyes going out the front glass windows. "Love Lies" is pulsing through the speakers that are set up in the gym. I left my headphones somewhere and it took me about twenty minutes to figure out how to work his flashy speakers. My thighs burn and my legs ache as I power through, the timer reading 1:34:09. An hour and a half of solid running? Yeah, I had issues coming in here, but I won't have them going out. The moon is starting to set behind the thick trees and I take in the natural beauty of it. I understand why Brantley built the gym like this now. Not only is it therapy to train, but to train with this view is a whole new level of tranquility.

Movement catches my eyes to the right, near a bush of flowers. I narrow my eyes, but only make out a bright contrast of white between bushes.

What the fuck was that?

It almost looked like…

"A ghost?" I yell, hitting the treadmill off. My feet stop running as I squint my eyes to get a better look. The figure moves again and I freeze.

Not a ghost.

A girl.

I climb off the treadmill quickly, making my way to the glass window. *Can she see me?* She has the whitest hair I have ever seen in my life. It can't be natural. She has a round, baby face, and a very, very, petite body. She's wearing a white sundress that clings to her, while hanging off her all at the same time, and her hair looks to be in an intricate French

I tilt my head, but in an instant, her eyes snap up to me.

I still. Either entranced in her pure, innocent beauty, or in the shock of being spotted. She drags her eyes away from mine, I'm unsure whether she can see me or not, but she continues to water the flowers.

"See a ghost?" Brantley asks from the doorway.

I jerk, turning my head over my shoulder slightly. "Maybe." I shrug. "Who is that?"

He comes up beside me and I physically feel the air shift between us. When he doesn't answer, I bring my eyes to him.

"Bran?"

His jaw clenches, his thick fists burying into his pockets. "Just a girl."

"Just a girl?" I ask. "Can I ask who and why she's here?"

He turns on his heel and storms back out of the gym.

I want to stand here and watch her all night, and I could, because she's that beautiful. It's like watching an angel play the harp, you're entranced, but skeptical. Brantley storms over toward her and her face drops.

I watch the exchange from afar but feel their emotions like they're being hammered into me at speeds I cannot handle.

Her eyebrows furrow, but she yanks her elbow out of his grip. She doesn't look angry, she looks—confused.

Her eyes come up to the glass again and I shit you not, I feel her breathing down my neck. This girl is insanity. I'm instantly intrigued, yet a big part of me wants to keep this secret. I want to keep it for Brantley—even for her.

I take a swig of my water and start to step backward, realizing I look like a creeper.

My phone buzzes near the punching bag and I reluctantly make my way toward it, sliding it unlocked.

Nate—**Tell Brantley you're coming with him tonight.**

My fingers hover over the keys as I think on what to reply with.

Me—**Where to?**

Nate—**A meet. And bring that fucking book.**

Me—**Have a new girl that needs rescuing?**

Nate—**Yeah.**

Me—**Who?**
Nate—**You.**

I stand there, reading the word over and over again until my eyes close and it flashes behind my shut lids in neon white pulses. *You.*

I grab the rest of my shit and make my way downstairs, back to my room. I pass Daemon's room and see him lying on his back on top of the mattress.

I sigh, my heart resting to a light strum.

Pushing his door open, I knock on it gently. His face tilts to me.

"Hi." I enter, leaving the door open.

"*Princessa*," he whispers, his eyes closing and opening. "Are you—okay?"

I nod, pursing my lips together. "Why? Daemon, why didn't you tell me?" I take a seat on the mattress, tucking my hands under my thighs.

He exhales. "That's not the important part." His English is getting better.

"What do you mean? You knew me, Daemon. I had a crush on you."

He nods, his smile tightening. "As did I."

I lick my lips. "I haven't seen you in a long time."

He inches up from the mattress, his hand resting on my cheek. "That's a good thing, *Princessa*. Very good." His hand comes to my chest and I wince. "Heal."

I place a kiss on his head and leave him to rest. He rests a lot. I hope he's okay.

I have a shower once I'm back in my room and scrub up in triple time, running the soap suds over my body until they form foam. I wanted to ask him so many questions, but he seemed tired. It feels wrong to push him, considering all he's been through.

Shoving on some light skinny jeans and a Ramones shirt, I flick my hair down my back, toss on my leather jacket, and head upstairs to find Brantley.

He's waiting for me in the lobby, wearing a hoodie, dark jeans and a shit-eating grin.

"Why are you smiling like that and why do I get the feeling that I'm not going to like the reason?"

He chuckles. "Come on. You need to get ready for the meet." I let him take my hand as he leads me down the dark hallway, passing door after door. I need to explore this house one day. Not today, but one day. We reach the end to a second dining area, a more private one. A crystal chandelier hangs delicately from the ceiling and there's a large rectangle table with dark red chairs surrounding it.

"Hello, dear," Scarlet says, pulling out boxes of what I recognize as makeup.

"Hi!" I haven't seen her or Elena in a while, and a part of me feels guilty that I haven't made the time to see Elena. I mentally mark it in my brain to visit her.

Scarlet has always been beautiful, and you can really see the striking resemblance between her and Bishop. *Does she know about Abel?* Probably not. *Does she know about Hector?* Honestly, I'd like to say no, but I'm not naïve. I see the cracks in these people where others would see silk.

"What's going on?" I look between her and Brantley.

Brantley takes a seat. "You need to get painted to come with us, *Princessa*..."

"The meet? I wasn't painted last time..."

Scarlet pauses, her hand in the air as she continues to dip her brushes into the SFX makeup.

"That's because you weren't technically supposed to be there." Brantley's tone is smooth.

"No woman is supposed to be there." Scarlet raises an eyebrow at me. "But you're different."

So I've heard.

I take a seat and watch as she brushes strokes of black and white over Brantley's face.

"What's the meaning behind that?" I ask, gesturing to the face paint. "I know people do it for Halloween, but I never understood why The Kings do it?"

Scarlet continues on Brantley's face. "Well, the reason why The Kings have always done it is a lot simpler than why people use it during Halloween, or even why they celebrate it for All Saints Day. We use it as a way to express to our men that we all die." Scarlet's eyes come to me. "The wives of The Kings learn to apply this to their husband during meets. It's our way of telling them that they're not immortal. Their flesh is still human, and their black hearts still beat."

Interesting, I think to myself. "So now I'm wearing it?"

Scarlet chuckles. "Yes, but yours will be the Stuprum design."

Now I'm intrigued. Brantley continues getting his done and when he turns to face me, I smirk. "You look good, Bran Bran..."

He flips me off.

I take a seat on the chair Brantley was on, pushing my hair back.

Scarlet's eyes come to mine. "Yours is the same as The Kings, only you have this." She takes out a small jewel. It's red glint glistens against the light. "On your forehead."

I tilt my head. "What if it falls off?"

She laughs. "I can assure you, it will not. I will need you to look after it from now on, though. Can you do that for me?"

"Yes," I answer, offering a smile of reassurance. "I can do that."

She gets started on the mask and I ignore Brantley beside me, his phone blowing up every two seconds.

"You look good," Brantley says as I slide off the chair. "You can't wear that though," he comments, pointing to my outfit.

I raise an eyebrow, but it feels weird. Heavy, like a thousand layers of paint is on top of it. "Why?"

"Because you can't."

Scarlet clears her throat. "You're a size four, right?"

I look at her. "On a good day, yes, otherwise a six. Why?"

She pulls out a black dress that looks more like a size zero and less like a four. I take it from her, skeptical.

"Wear it. Pair it with some thigh-high boots, and Tillie?" she says as my glance drops down the small black and lace... *dress*. "Own it like the queen that you are."

Her words surge through me, power in each letter.

I smile, nodding my head. "I will." I hope. I quickly stumble out of the dining hall and dip into Luce's office that we were all in not long ago. I remove my clothes and am butt naked when the door opens.

"Woah!" Brantley spins around, covering his eyes.

"What the fuck, Bran Bran... how many times have you seen me naked?" I laugh, slipping the dress over my head.

His shoulders shake in amusement. "Yeah, but not so much anymore."

"What do you mean?" I flip my hair out from under the dress, shimmying it down.

"It doesn't matter," he mutters. "You decent?"

I roll my eyes, gathering my clothes from the floor. "Yes. I just need to go and grab my boots."

I dash in and out and I have my thigh-high boots fastened securely around my legs. Scarlet has set me up big time with this dress. It's short, tight, and where the bust dips in between my breasts, there are layers of lace sewn in. There's also a little slit on the left thigh that I'm pretty sure you can almost see my G-string through.

I stroll toward Brantley's car, rumbling angrily in the spot. I open the door and slide in, fluffing my hair up.

"Jesus fucking—" He shakes his head, dropping into first gear and zipping us out of the driveway. "Yeah, Daddy is not going to be happy about that dress."

I flip the mirror down and smear my dark burgundy lipstick across evenly. "He has never cared before."

Silence.

"What?" I snap at Brantley when he doesn't elaborate.

"Nothing, just that I say daddy, and you instantly know I'm talking about Nate..."

Shit. I slap the visor closed and shift in my seat to get comfortable. "Why am I coming? I brought the book."

Brantley is silent again and I'm getting annoyed with his evasive behavior. I don't know how Madison handled it for so long. So much as a sniff of a lie and I will pollute the air with toxic poison so when they inhale their own bullshit, they won't be able to exhale it into me.

"You'll see."

We drive for about ten minutes before I open up Instagram. I flip the camera to selfie mode and snap a photo of me leaning into Brantley's arm. He's scowling, but whatever, he's always scowling. Our face paint lights up the photo like we just rolled out of *The Walking Dead* and I smirk, proud of our first photo together.

"I hate photos."

I shrug, tagging him in it and sharing it to Instagram—and Facebook. "Tough."

Another five minutes later and we're pulling down a familiar long gravel driveway. Apparently, it was also where Madison got shot by Daemon. I didn't piece two and two together because I wasn't around during that time. I try not to lick my lips, afraid of smearing the makeup.

We pull up and there's the building that Madison and I were in watching underground fighting while I met a couple of younger Kings. I slam the door shut after I get out, looking at Brantley skeptically.

"Why are the lights off?"

He smirks at me, lighting his smoke. "Because I told you, you're at a meet."

"—and what the fuck are you wearing?" Nate barks, storming toward me, literally appearing from the forest.

"Excu—"

He grips onto my wrist, yanking me around the car.

I yank it out of his grip. "Fuck you and fuck off."

His hand flies to my throat and his eyes narrow. His white, wolf-like contacts glare at me like I'm staring into the eyes of a corpse.

"Don't fuck with me, Tillie. Now is not the time for that smart-ass mouth."

I whack his arm away, but he only intensifies his grip, slamming me against Brantley's car.

I search his eyes, his nose so close to mine. "When did you change so much?"

The corner of his mouth kicks up in a grin. "I never changed, Tillie. You just never knew me."

He shoves me back, finally unleashing his grip. His eyes go to Brantley. "It's started, but Bishop isn't here." I see a few other boys exit out of the clearing that Nate did.

"I haven't heard from Madison either..." I add, my eyes going between Nate and Brantley.

They stay quiet.

"Let's go," Nate says, nodding his head toward the forest. I run to catch up to him and fight with walking beside him or Brantley, but before I can make a decision, I find myself beside Nate, with Eli, Cash, and Hunter on the other side of me. The forest is dark, the only lighting from the moon touching the slight curves of the pathway. Orange flames lick the midnight air, and the clearing finally turns into one large circle. It's the same place we were at with Bailey, only I have obviously come in from a different entrance. There is another group of boys sitting on a log. Younger. I recognize them from that night. There are four, all slouching down and glaring at me. On another log, behind the big bonfire, is a line of three men. One, I recognize as Hector. I freeze, my jaw clenching. The reason I'm here has to be with him—*right*? My eyes catch movement on another log to the side and opposite the young Kings, and there's another line. I see Jase, Spyder, and I can't remember his name, as well as another guy.

These are the closest generations of Kings.

I see behind them there are other logs, but they're empty. Nate yanks me down onto the one that they all sit at.

Hector looks over at us. "Malum, where is my son?"

I look up at Nate to see his jaw clenched from behind the face paint. "Not sure. Was about to ask you."

Hector leans into a man who is seated beside him. I don't recognize anyone, but I don't really know because of the face paint.

"What's going on?" I look up at Nate. Nerves break through my body when I realize why he didn't want me dressed like this. I'm in the middle of a cage with some very hungry lions.

He looks down at me. "It's a meet. When all of The Kings join for one night a month to touch base." He exhales. "Look at me, Tillie."

I do, slowly bringing my eyes to his.

"This is not the place to be a brat. You will start a war if you do, but most of the men here wouldn't speak to you unless they are spoken to. Most except for Hector." He pauses, another jaw clench. "Do you remember last year when Madison came to the races? Her and Bishop had a massive fight and she ended up riding shotgun in his car to make a delivery?"

No, but I don't say that.

He carries on. "Well, that was on a meet. Every time is different. If there has been betrayal, the person who did the betraying will be there"—he points to a cage, the same cage that Bailey was in—"and we deal with it appropriately. If there's a test that needs to be done, there will be a race or a fight. The Kings run the distribution of every underground dealing in all forty-eight states across the US, although we reside in NYC and The Hamptons, we own this fucking country. We have ties to all nationalities of the mafia: Italian, Russian, Yakuza. All outfits of the five families, the MS-13, and bikers, but they don't matter. We have direct lines to The White House, the CIA, and every other fucking organized crime group you can think of, and wanna know something, *Princessa*?" he whispers. "They're all our allies. That's what makes The Elite Kings different. No one touches us because they're all our allies and we can wipe any organized crime group out with a snap of our fingers. Now, the CIA and government affiliations are a little different. We can't exactly wipe them out, but we both have an understanding."

I'm overwhelmed with the information. I've always known that The Kings were lethal, but this information wasn't something I was prepared for.

He continues. "And aside from all of that, we have our own world. We run in our circle, have our own rules."

"Sounds like too much power."

He chuckles. "It's only too much to people who don't know how to harness it. We're trained and bred for this. We not only know how to harness it, but we utilize it. Often."

I change the subject. "So these are all The Kings that are left?"

He nods. "Yeah, the ones older than Hector are either dead or have moved away, so they don't bother every month though they come when they can." He shakes his head. "Kings are rare, but they're needed in this world because without them, there's no structure."

"Why am I here?" I ask the question that has been nagging at me.

"Because this time next month." Nate's eyes go up to Hector. "It'll be Hector in that cage, and I want you there for it. I need you to recognize the setting right now. Remember who is sitting where." I look to my left, goosebumps breaking over my skin. I see the younger generation already watching me.

"When do they initiate?" I ask, nodding my head to them.

Nate chuckles. "After Christmas and New Year's. Though we have a dilemma because Abel is here, Nix isn't going to be too happy about being kicked off the throne and tossed down to second."

My head hurts. There are so many complexities to this world that my brain cannot catch up.

"But why am I *here*, Nate?"

He takes the book from me and I hesitate to give it to him. He flips through the pages and I notice how the atmosphere has fallen deathly silent.

"Have you finished it?"

I nod. "Yes, though it doesn't make much sense. I mean, I see that Daemon knew me when I was younger, and I remember him vividly. But—"

"—Why?" Nate asks, slamming the book closed and turning to me. "Do you know *why* or *how* he knew you then?"

He's searching my eyes for something. Anything. Maybe for me to finally catch on to whatever the fuck is going on, but I've got nothing because none of this makes sense to me.

I sag. "I'm still trying to figure it out."

Does he know and he's waiting for me to know or does he not know and that's why they need me to figure it out.

"Wait." My hand comes to his arm and I ignore the zap of electricity that passes between us—like usual. "You don't know, do you?"

Nate shakes his head. "No. We're trying to figure out what fucking game he's playing."

I snort out a laugh. "Daemon is playing the game and you guys don't like it. God, I love him." Jaw and fists clench. "Why don't you just ask him?"

Nate's eyes close as he shakes his head. He angrily shoots up from his spot and disappears behind the fire. I look to Brantley. "What'd I say?"

"Oh, you know, the usual. Confessing your love for another man and all that."

I roll my eyes.

Hector stands, a cigar in his hand and a fedora hat secured on the top of his head. He's everything evil, I've always known that, but to—I pause my thoughts.

"Commandment one—" he says, and The Kings all answer in unison. "Drink from the blood of your enemies and spit on the grave of your loved ones."

What? My eyes go around all of them slowly.

"Commandment two—"

"A brother in a king, open up, and share him in…"

"Commandment three—"

"Silver Swans, clipped wings, drown deep, in their sins…"

Fear grasps my heart with an iron fist, refusing to let go. I can feel myself start to hyperventilate and my eyes involuntarily seek Nate. When they land on him, I see him already watching me.

"Commandment four—"

"Betrayal is a sin, slit the throat and drain him clean…"

"Commandment number five—"

"Kill those that cross you, bury your sins with their corpse…"

Silence.

Holy shit.

My breathing is loud and thick.

"Stuprum?" Hector announces, and my eyes snap to his. I know I need to compose myself or I'll get eaten alive, but I just witnessed some creepy ritual thing that has obviously been passed down since the beginning of time. "Stand."

Oh shit. I stand, squaring my shoulders and exuding confidence that I know deep down, I do not have.

"Wear that dress and own your crown." Scarlet's words come back to me, echoing inside my head.

Hector points to me. "You're all probably wondering why Stuprum is here. She is the newest line since Katsia, and is taking her rightful place in Perdita."

No, the fuck I'm not.

I quirk an eyebrow.

Nate coughs from behind the flame, and my eyes once again fly to him. The orange flecks lick every defined feature on his beautiful face. He shakes his head.

I deflate a little, knowing I can't correct Hector.

"She needs to see how things work as her mother did not teach her the way we do things. She has a lot to learn." Hector's eyes come to mine. The fire blazes through his dark orbits. "And we need her *full* attention."

I freeze.

Nate flinches.

Brantley's head whips up to Hector.

He just confirmed it. He, without knowing it, confirmed to us that he—Tears well in my eyes, my brain fuzzing. Hector yaps on about other shit but I can't hear anything because all I hear is my blood pulsing through my veins, threatening to spill through my eyes. My ears bleed with a high-pitched screeching sound and everything cloaks in red.

Without even knowing it, I take a step forward.

And another.

And ano—

A thick arm wraps around my waist, crushing me into a hard chest.

"Don't do it, baby. Stick to plan." Nate's voice caresses my rage, soothing it like cool balm to a hot burn. "His time will come. I promise you."

He starts pulling me backward slowly, and then I'm sitting on his lap. I can't look at Hector now, and I want nothing more than to leave. I curl into Nate's chest, burying my face into his neck. I feel his pulse pump against my lips, his cologne wafting into my senses like a subtle reminder that he *has* me. Even if he hates me, he has me. His thumb circles my upper thigh, but his arms are dead bolted around me. I feel safe and warm. My eyes close as I attempt to bring myself down.

Stick to plan.

He did it.

Stick. To. Plan.

Daemon. Usually, when I think of Daemon, it's a comfort like nothing I have felt before, but being wrapped in Nate's arms, it does nothing. When I think of my go-to safety line, Daemon. It. Does. Nothing. Nothing because Nate was all I need. It's a dangerous thing to need someone who does not need you. After Hector has gone on, he cuts the meet short as he explains he needs to find his son. Something is going on between Bishop and Madison, or maybe she has told him the truth finally and he's spiraling out of control. After all, I took that kill from him.

The older Kings disappear. I inch back from Nate's chest, searching his eyes.

"Thanks. For doing that."

His fingers wrap around my chin as he forces my mouth to his. "You're the strongest fucking girl in this world, Tillie. You're smarter than most of the fuckers sitting here. Use it."

I think over his words. Then nod. He sucks my bottom lip into his mouth and slaps my ass to get up, which I do.

"Where the fuck is Bishop?" Brantley growls, and the younger generation and Jase's come toward us.

Jase's jaw clenches, but his eyes come to mine as he shakes his head. "He's probably with Madison."

"Madison, who I have not seen for almost two days?"

Jase looks around The Kings again and I step into his space. "I'm talking to you, not them. What is going on?"

He shrugs. Fucking shrugs. "Don't know." Then he leaves, and I watch as his retreating back disappears into the bushes.

We're on our way home in Brantley's car when Nate hits the music down. "Go to Bishop's."

"Why?" Brantley turns into the shoulder and hits his blinker on.

Nate runs his finger over his mouth. "Tate just texted me."

I freeze.

"Chill out, Tillie, it's not like that," Nate sneers, and I want to kick myself for giving off obvious vibes of jealousy. "She said he's throwing a party in his condo. This mother-fucker has a death wish because Madison has always said no parties."

Brantley hooks a U-turn, his tires skidding up in smoke.

Nate throws his hoodie to the back. "Put that on and don't say a fucking word. Last thing I need to be doing is fighting motherfuckers who stare at you too long."

"Um, okay but what happened to us fucking each other in the bathroom?" I gesture toward Brantley and me from the back seat.

Eli snorts beside me, Hunter chuckling too on the other side.

Nate doesn't answer, like he doesn't need to give an explanation on why he does or says things. Because he's Nate.

Cue eye roll.

I put the hoodie on, watching as it falls past my skirt and sits just above my thigh-high boots. It smells like him, and the cotton hugs me like his arms. It's reassuring and safe. He's never getting it back.

Eli pulls out his phone and shows us his new pastel green Maserati. Said he's wanted one since driving Bishop's. I try not to zone out in boredom as we continue to Bishop's. I take my phone out and snap a selfie of me pulling a sad face. It looks ridiculous because of the face paint, but I post it to my Instagram story with the caption CUFFED.

Ten minutes later, Brantley is driving us down into a bright concrete underground parking lot. One of the kinds that have concrete pillars that are holding up—literally—the entire hotel and the contents inside of it.

"How do they make sure this is safe? The structure?"

Nate chuckles. "You're in a car with us and you're worried about the structure of a building when it comes to your safety?"

We all climb out of the car and Nate takes my hand with his, leading us toward the elevator. Daemon's book is still safely tucked under my arm, the confusion of tonight still buzzing in my head.

Why did I have to bring the book to the meet?

The elevator dings and soft classical music fills the space between us all. My eyes flick around to all of them and I almost laugh at how funny it feels with the music and their big, broody bodies and personalities occupying the space.

But then I remember that I'm in a small space with them and that there's nowhere to run if I piss Nate off.

The elevator dings on the Penthouse floor after Nate punches in a code. The doors separate and we're met with darkness. I step out, looking left to right, searching for anything in Bishop's flashy apartment.

"There's no one here!" I state the obvious. "Hell—" I turn around, but they've all disappeared, the elevator door now securely closed.

I don't like fear. In fact, fear makes me violent. If someone was to sneak up on me, I am not responsible for what happens to their face. OR their dick, for that matter.

"Really?" I roll my eyes, entering the vast space farther. The moonlight is the only form of vision, beaconing through the large floor to ceiling windows that are in the lounge room. You have to take a couple of steps down to get in there. I turn to the left, to see—nothing.

Okay. I close my eyes, inhaling and exhaling. I will bite. A little.

"What do you guys want?" I keep my eyes closed, afraid that if I open them, I'm going to see my life flash before my eyes.

"Sorry it had to be like this, Tillie, but we can't do this same song and dance any longer. We've waited, fucking god we have waited..." Nate says, and I spin around to catch his voice, but I'm met with nothingness again.

"What do you mean!"

"Little terror, wake up...." Brantley's voice teases, bouncing off the walls.

"I can't, Bran Bran!" I yell, squeezing my fingers. "I'm not dreaming!"

A hood is shoved over my face, blacking out my vision completely. "What the fuck!"

Handcuffs are clamped to the back of my body and I twist and turn, trying to get out of whoever's grip is behind me.

"Move forward, baby." Nate's voice caresses the back of my neck.

I fight the urge to kick back. "I don't like games..."

He thrusts me forward as I hear the elevator ding, and then I'm shoved forward again, another hand clamped around my upper arm, the one that's holding onto Daemon's book. The lights from the elevator filters through the material of the sack over my head.

My breathing thickens. "This is a little dramatic," I deadpan, allowing my fake confidence to erupt in the middle of the small elevator.

Nate chuckles. "I'm done, Tillie."

Done? What does he mean done? We were never together. The doors ding open again and I'm being dragged back into the parking lot. There's a car idling near us and I feel them all freeze. The car sounds rich, the smooth rumble of an expensive engine.

More silence.

"You guys talking behind my back?" I tease. I really shouldn't. I'm in no position to torment them right now.

Doors slam shut before the car skids off, the tires tearing up the asphalt.

"Move, baby." Nate shoves me into the back of Brantley's car and we're off.

We're driving for twenty minutes before we slow down, the car turning around sharp little corners.

The car stops, and I'm being yanked out. If I wasn't wearing Nate's hoodie, which by the way, is doing sweet fuck all to comfort me right now, I would be freezing my ass off.

A lighter flame flicks in front of my face, sifting through the mesh. It's Nate, smirking at me. "Say her name, Tillie."

"What?" I yank my head back. "What are you talking about?"

The light disappears. "Our daughter died."

"Stop it, Nate."

The lighter flicks on again. "She died, Tillie. It broke me in half, and she took that half to the grave with her. But listen to me, Tillie. She's gone."

"Stop it..." I warn, my eyes slamming shut.

I need Daemon. Why did I do this? The first thing I'm doing when I get back is taking him and I back to Perdita. It's not bad there. At least I'll be away from monsters that lurk in the dark.

"Say it, baby."

"No!" I snap, my eyes slamming shut again.

"Why are you holding Daemon's book?" Nate asks. Is he circling me? Is it just us here? Why is no one else speaking? I feel drops of water pelt down gently on my head through the rag.

"Because you told me to bring it!"

"Did you find what you needed?" he asks.

I shake my head. "No…"

"Say her name…" Nate mutters again.

"Nate, please," I plead, my shoulders shaking. "I don't want to. Don't you understand?"

"I assure you, I do, but say her name. You never say her name out loud. Say it."

"Bro…" Brantley's voice cuts in, but he stops.

"Say it, Tillie!" Tears stream down my face, my knees weak. "She's gone. You did what you could, this wasn't your fault!"

"It was!" I snap, screaming at him. "It was my fault! I didn't lock the door, I was the last person to see her, I took her to bed, *I read her her last fucking book!*" The sobs are unleashed, now my chest is jerking. I fall to my knees, curling over my thighs. "I killed her. I did it. It's all my fault."

Nate must drop opposite me because his face is directly in front of mine. "It's not your fucking fault!"

Tears slip over my lips, their saltiness running on the tip of my tongue. "It was."

"No, baby." His hands come to my face through the rag. "It wasn't your fault. I don't blame you. No one blames you. The only person who blames you, is you—"

"—Daemon," I whisper. "I have to make sure he understands. I don't think he understands that I didn't kill her, Nate." The sobs take hold again, my throat swelling.

Nate yanks the hoodie off my head and rain falls onto my face. It's dark, but there are two cars parked behind me with their headlights shining on us. The first thing I notice is Nate is on his knees in front of me, the second thing I notice is all of The Kings, Bishop included, in a half-circle behind Nate, and the third thing I notice is that behind Nate, is a gravestone. **DAEMON**

My eyes go back to Nate. "What's going on? Why are we here?"

Nate licks his lips, his thumb pressing to mine. "Daemon understands, baby."

"No—" I shake my head. "He's different now. Lost. These nightmares—" I pause, my eyes going back to Nate. "Why are we here? This is where my nightmares are."

Nate searches my eyes and I tilt my head to study him. "Daemon was never in that cell, baby."

I rear back. "What? Yes, he was, and he's been with me since. He's in the room beside me at Brantley's!"

Nate looks at me, his eyes softening for the first time in a long time. "He was never there. You created his existence as some sort of coping mechanism to deal with Micaela being dead. To deal with the loss, and the pain, the guilt. You grabbed onto the one person who always gave you a lifeline."

"You…" I whisper, shaking my head. "This doesn't make sense because he was there, Nate! He's been there and now you're telling me I've gone crazy?!" I shake my head again. "If that's what I was doing, I would have grabbed on to *you*, Nate. Not Daemon."

Nate's jaw clenches, and then he presses his lips to mine. "No, baby. I couldn't save you with this one."

Tears pour out from me, my face falling. "I saw you both have a fight in front of me in Perdita!"

Nate licks his lips. "I've not *spoken* to him, babe. How could I?"

My shoulders slump, the tears free-falling. "I've gone crazy."

"No," Brantley murmurs from behind Nate. "You're not crazy, little terror. You're human. You reached for something that you knew would help you. Some take drugs, alcohol, sex." He grins, kicking Nate. "You reached for *love*. That doesn't make you crazy. That makes you human."

Another round of tears come, but I end up choking on my sobs, falling forward and landing in Nate's chest. "He's really not alive?"

Nate shakes his head, kissing the top of my head. "No."

I grip onto his soaked T-shirt, and we sit there for another twenty minutes in the pouring rain while I mourn my *Thirteen* crush. My crush who has been there for me more times than anyone ever has. Even dead, his spirit was an anchor for me.

I wipe my face with Nate's shirt, finally leaning back and expecting The Kings to be gone, but they're not. They're still standing where I left them twenty minutes ago, drenched from the rain.

"Say her name, baby," Nate whispers in my ear, kissing me gently.

"Micaela."

Chapter Twenty-Seven

Nate

I pick her up from under her legs and carry her back to Brantley's car, shutting the door behind her. Tillie needed someone to help her mend. Because sometimes you do need someone in order to heal. There's nothing wrong with that. It's not a weakness to need another human. It's humanity, and it's Tillie. She's fucking strong, but she's human.

"She's going to be okay?" Bishop asks, watching me carefully.

"Yeah, she is. Now I don't feel so fucked up from doing that." I unlock the handcuffs around her wrists and toss them onto the ground.

"Oh come on. It was like old times." Brantley smirks.

I glare at him. "Until the part that I had to break her open and watch her heart snap in front of my very eyes, over another man, nonetheless."

Brantley stiffens. "Yeah, I see your point."

Fucker.

"Good. Because we have another issue," Bishop mutters, shoving his hands in his pocket.

"What else could possibly go fucking wrong?" Brantley exhales, leaning on his car. "We still haven't dealt with your old man, and then there's The Rebels coming on hard with Tillie, her and Madison whacking off Madison's side piece, and then there's that book."

"—Madison has run."

I sigh, pulling open the passenger door and sliding in. I can't deal with Madison's dramatics. If she has run, then I'm not chasing her ass down. Tillie is all I give a fuck about right now. Brantley follows, rounding the car and slipping into the driver's seat. I run my fingers through my hair, squeezing the water out.

"Everything okay?" Tillie asks from the back. I'm done with lying to her about fucking everything, so I turn in my seat and look her square in the eyes.

"Madison has run."

Tillie blinks a few times, and then she sighs. "Can everyone meet at Brantley's? I have something to tell you all."

My eyebrows shoot up. "Yeah."

Not only did it not send her over the edge into a spiral, but she knows something that we don't?

Brantley throws me a side eye, and then we're boosting forward and out of the cemetery. I press my fingers to my lips and throw up deuces in the direction on the Malum plot where my baby girl lays. Brantley rips up the back tires and takes us out onto the main road. One day we will come back here together to see Micaela. But just not right now.

Chapter Twenty-Eight

Nate

I take a seat on one of the chairs that surround the main dining room of Brantley's house. I watch as all The Kings fall to their chairs, Bishop at the head of the table, me at his right and Brantley at his left. The whole drive back here, my mind has been racing about what Tillie might want to say. I spread my legs wide and lean to the side, my finger running over my upper lip. I watch her closely as she paces back and forth like a caged lion. Left, to right, to left, back to right. Once we're all seated, she exhales.

"I have something to tell you all and Bishop, please understand why I couldn't say something earlier."

I feel my brows crease as I pin her with a glare. Her eyes meet mine, glassing over in what I can only explain as apologetically.

I look to my lap.

She tilts her head in question.

My lip kicks up in a smirk as I nod to my lap again.

She gets it, and like a good little girl, she slowly makes her way around the table. Don't get it twisted, Tillie is not obedient by any means, but I know when she needs me, and right now, she needs me. I push my seat back with my legs, the sound of the stilts scraping against the hardwood floor squeaking through the tension. She sinks into my lap, resting on top of my cock. I fight a groan, my fist coming to my mouth. Brantley kicks my leg from opposite me and I wink at him, blowing a kiss.

"As you were saying, *Princessa*," Bishop murmurs, pouring another glass of whiskey and sliding it over to her. She takes it, her hair dropping low as she shoots it back. My eyes cross as I fight thoughts of wrapping her long strands around my fist and bending her over this table, fucking her little cun—

"Madison was raped," Tillie whispers from on top of me.

I freeze, now fighting the urge to do some jerk notion like pushing her off my lap and raging.

"What!" Bishop snaps, pushing the chair back and glaring at Tillie.

Tillie stands up from my lap, but my arm wraps around her waist, holding her to her spot. Her ass in my happy place is the only thing that's stopping me from losing my shit at her right now.

"Chill, I'm just grabbing the scotch…" she whispers.

I release a little as she leans over and grabs it before taking her spot back on my lap.

Where the fuck she belongs. This queen doesn't need a throne, she just needs my dick to sit on.

She unscrews the cap and flicks it off. "Yeah." She shoots back another shot. "That guy I accidentally killed?" *Accidentally.* "Well, he's the one who did it, and before any of you ask me a thousand questions, please understand that I don't give a fuck what any of you say. Madison is my best friend. I would keep her secrets for lifetimes over if I have to, and before you say anything else—" Everyone shuts their mouths like they do when Tillie speaks. "You all live in glass houses if you hold the fact that I kept her secret above my head, considering you all bathe in the shit."

I bite on my cheeks, attempting to hold in my laugh. My eyes find Brantley and he's the same, barely hiding his smile behind his hand because aside from Tillie *finally* using her status to speak, my sister got raped. I need retribution, and Bishop, well—I look up at him and watch as he flops backward, his back hitting the wall. I've never seen Bishop like this, in all the years I've known him. His face is pale, like all the blood in his system has drained and poured itself into the wrath sector. He slowly slides down the wall, dropping to the floor. Fuck.

I rub my girl's leg and then tap her, leaning into her ear. "Hop up, baby."

She does, and when I stand, she takes my seat. I slowly step toward Bishop. I have to be careful with how I approach this.

"Also, I don't know anything else, other than the fact that she said that he had manipulated her. Used something against her. Every time I would ask her about it, she would shut down. She made me swear to secrecy about it, but let's be real, she didn't really have to do that because I would have kept that secret anyway…"

I drop to the ground. "Hey…" I try to get Bishop's attention, but his eyes are glassed over, fixed on something in front of him. Totally unfocused and away with the fairies. His face is a symbol of heart-shattering regret.

Fuck.

My hand flies to his chin and I grip it roughly, tilting his face to mine. I inch in until our noses touch. "Don't let this fuck you. We will get her back, you will make it okay, and we will make them pay."

His Adam's apple bobs and he yanks his face out of my grip. "No."

I cock my head, my eyes narrowing. "No?"

His jaw clenches. "This happened because of me."

"—Bro."

He cuts his eyes to mine. "No."

"What the fuck do you mean no?" I snap at him. "We will get her back…"

Bishop laughs, his dark eyes coming up to mine. "IF she *wanted* to still be a part of this life, Nate? She would have fucking *told* me when it happened. We would have been able to deal with it correctly. Instead, she has done what Madison does and she has *run*. I'm done, dawg. I can't chase her for the rest of my life."

My heart pounds in my chest. There are all sorts of bullshit that is wrong with what he's saying. First of all, good luck to Tillie if she ever tried to run from me because I'd kill us both before I'd let her live a life that didn't have my existence around to tease her, second of all, this isn't Bishop at all.

He stands, cracking his neck. When his eyes come to mine, I see in his dark depths how the flecks are burning with rage, but there's something else.

He's fucking tired.

"If and when she wants to come back to me, I'll be here. Until then, she's not my problem." Then he shoves me away, taking a seat back on his chair like none of this happened.

He picks up his glass. "We will find out who that fuckwit was and who he was tied to. I'll deal with them accordingly for fucking with someone who was mine, but from then onward, this, her, she ends here. Until further notice."

Tillie's eyes find mine, wide as saucers. I let out a soft growl and take my place back at the table, with Tillie right back on my dick.

Tillie is loading the dishwasher when I enter the kitchen, leaning against the doorway. She turns to face me.

"Hi."

I'm tired, my damp clothes are stuck to me like a stage five clinger, and I need to sleep for a fucking lifetime, but I push off the door frame and make my way to her, my arm snaking around her waist until her back is crashing into my front.

"Come home with me."

She stills, putting another plate into the dishwasher. "Nate." She turns in my grip, her eyes coming to mine. I bring my other hand to rest behind the back of her throat, my fingers itching to pull her hair and fuck her until she's blue. "We can't do this," she whispers, shaking her head.

"Do what?" I brush her off. "I asked you to come home, I didn't drop to one knee. But if you need"—I run my fingers up her inner thigh, my index finger coming to the slit, over her damp panties—"me to drop to my knees and suck on your pussy, then done, because I'm fucking *starving*."

I shuffle back and look down on her when she doesn't answer me. Her lips are tucked between her teeth, her eyes closed.

"I can't forgive you."

I run my lips over hers. "You don't have to forgive me to fuck my face, baby. We've had this discussion." I grip the backs of her thighs and lift her up onto the black marble counter. Her legs spread as I step between them, pulling her flush up against me. I grind into her, grabbing what I can of her curvy ass.

"It'll be years before I forget what you've done..." She closes her eyes as I run my tongue over her collarbone, licking up her neck and to her mouth. I bite down on her bottom lip and watch as they part, a soft moan escaping. I want to eat her noises and swallow them.

My fingers tighten around the back of her neck as I brush my lips across hers. "Then just forget for tonight."

She wraps her arms around the back of my neck. "Just for tonight, and then you're dropping me back here in the morning."

I nod. "Deal."

Fuck no.

"Okay," she sighs, and I step away so she can jump off the counter. "Just one night."

Chapter Twenty-Nine

Tillie

Nate is driving us back to his house when we pass the Chinese restaurant we visited a couple of months ago. He pulls in without me saying anything as I continue to wipe the rest of the face paint off my face with a wet wipe.

He continues through the drive-through, ordering all of my favorite dishes. The smell distracts me from the song playing on the radio, and I turn to watch the passing trees. I can't believe all that has happened tonight, but now that I've had time to sit back and evaluate everything, I always found it strange how Daemon was here only sometimes, and those times were usually when I was fuzzy with some kind of trauma. His bed was always made neatly, and although he was Daemon, I always felt like he *wasn't* Daemon. It's why I hesitated to kiss him, why he looked different, and maybe even why my nightmare showed him killing me.

I sigh, reaching into the bag and popping open the fried coconut shrimp. My absolute favorite.

"What's going on in that head of yours?" Nate asks from over his shoulder, eyeing me skeptically.

"Just that I feel batshit crazy." I bite into my shrimp, chewing slowly.

Nate chuckles. "We're all fucking crazy, Tillie, but it's who we stay sane for that matters. You need to for you. Love is just an anchor. It can either be the reason you drown or the reason you float. You can't ride on that to keep you sane."

I take another bite and then toss the tail end back into the bag. "I see your point. So, I should stay sane for love? Or the possibility of love?" I ask, genuinely interested in his answer.

He's pulling down the gated driveway to his home, and what was once my home.

snorts, jerking up the brake. "Fuck no. You stay sane for yourself, because you can't give people that kind of power. You have to make it—for you."

"What about you?" I ask. Things between Nate and I will never be awkward. We know each other's darkest, dirtiest secrets, and power comes with trust when that person knows the dark corners of your dusty soul.

"Least of all me," he whispers, and then shoves his door open and slams it closed.

Nate is the biggest mindfuck. Dating someone like him doesn't just happen. There are many different layers that you need to peel off before you get to his core, and you can finally say, this is it. We're dating and together. I'd like to think that I'm the only one who has gotten close to that core, but I'm not sure that's something to be proud of, considering my sanity these days.

I swing my door open and step out to the cool night, chills snapping over my skin. It's freezing and my clothes are still damp. Nate beeps his car alarm and we make our way up the stairs to the front door. He kicks it closed and I instantly remove his hoodie, wanting to get rid of the heavy, wet garment that's itching against my skin.

"Oh," Elena sighs, her shoulders sagging. Her face falls as she swipes the unshed tears from her cheeks. "I'm sorry, I don't mean to be rude. It's so nice to see you, Tillie, sweetheart, it's just I thought you were Madison."

Nate slowly places his keys into his pocket, his eyes fixated on his mother.

"It's okay. I'm sorry, Elena. I will help as much as I can." I try to comfort her, but she looks distraught.

Her eyes find mine. It's the first time that I take in her appearance. She's usually glowing, (probably from all those nasty green shakes she drinks), and her body so trim and fit. But I look at her right now and it looks like she hasn't had a meal in weeks and her eyes have wrinkles around the edges that suggests she's been straining to keep them open, fighting sleep. When I notice the dark circles under her eyes, it only further solidifies my suspicion.

She tightens her cardigan around her body. "I'll go back to sleep." She has lost so much too over the last few months. It wasn't just Nate and me who lost Micaela, it was all those around her too, especially Elena, and now Madison has disappeared.

"Wait!" I say, stepping forward.

Elena turns to face me. "Yes?"

I lift the bag of hot Chinese food. "Please eat with us?"

Her face softens, a small smile on her mouth. "I wouldn't want to impose…"

"Mom," Nate growls, and I cut him a glare to soften his damn voice.

He rolls his eyes. "I mean, *Mom*," he rectifies sweetly. "Come eat with us."

She rubs her cheeks with the edge of her cardigan and nods. "Okay."

I wait for her as Nate heads into the kitchen, flicking the lights on.

"I'm sorry, Tillie, I'm such a mess right now."

"Don't be sorry," I answer, pulling out a bar stool for her. "Trust me, I am not one to judge…"

Nate snorts.

I cut him another glare.

I don't think I'm ever going to be able to live the whole *seeing someone who isn't really there* thing down. Once it dies out into the background, I have no doubt these assholes are going to make jokes about it until the day I either die or kill them all. The latter sounds more fun.

Nate pours his mother a sparkling water, and me a still, because he knows I hate sparkling water because it actually tastes like stomach acid, then he opens up the cartons and places three plates onto the counter, swinging a stool around the other side of the island so he can sit opposite us. I thought being here would be hard, but it's not. If anything, it makes me feel a little closer to her. Like I can still feel Micaela's presence in the kitchen.

We dig into our food, Elena only having a small amount, but I'm not going to push it. Any food is still food.

"How have you been, sweetheart?" Elena asks, spooning a small amount of fried rice into her mouth.

"Surviving." I smile at her a little.

Nate clears his throat. "Mom?"

Her eyes go to his.

"Where's Joseph?"

She places her fork down onto her plate. "Thank you for dinner. I'm feeling tired, I might just turn in."

Nate goes to open his mouth and I cut him *another* glare. His mouth snaps shut. Elena kisses us both on the head and disappears into the foyer.

Once she's out of view, Nate brings his full attention back to me. "Give me those eyes again and I'll shove my cock so far down your throat they'll pop out of your skull."

"Don't threaten me." I pick up another piece of shrimp, biting into it. "Do you think she will be okay?"

Nate shakes his head. "No, but she'll survive. We all do."

We sit and eat the rest of our food, and then we both move around the kitchen fluidly as we clean up. We're climbing the stairs slowly, my eyes drifting closed when he pulls me under his arm.

"You need a bath."

"Mmmm," I answer, my eyes feeling heavy from all of the theatrics of the evening.

"I'll run it." He sits me on his bed, and I watch as he moves into the bathroom. A few minutes later, he nudges his head and takes my hand. "Strip."

I roll my eyes. "Here I was thinking you had turned all cute on me."

"Never."

I wriggle out of the dress and kick my panties to the side, following him right into the bathroom.

There's no bubble bath or romantic candles, because of course there isn't, but I appreciate it so much when I sink my foot into the warm—borderline too hot—water.

I sigh, slipping my whole body under and embrace the tingles that bite over my flesh. They slowly evaporate as I adapt to the temperature. Nate tucks in behind me. I ignore how the water spills over the edge. He pulls me against his chest, his dick stabbing into my lower back.

He kisses the back of my throat.

"One night," I whisper.

His tongue traces circles around the nape. "One night," he answers.

"Promise?" I tilt my head, giving him more access.

His finger glides over my slit, small circles around my swollen clit. "I promise."

His pace slows and I slowly grind myself into him in circles, biting down on my lower lip.

"Stand up and put your pussy on my mouth." He bites on my ear lobe.

I stand, spreading my legs wide and watching as water slips over my toned thighs. Nate peers up at me, slipping between my legs with his hands grasped around my upper thighs. He keeps his eyes on mine as he edges closer, dragging his tongue up to lick the droplets of water that are surfing down my skin. He yanks me down roughly and I fall, my knees crashing violently against the bottom of the bathtub. He brings his mouth to my pussy, all while his eyes continue to remain on mine and he circles my clit gently. My head rolls back, my hands coming to his hair.

"Open your eyes and don't touch me."

I do as I'm told.

"Put them behind your back."

I do, holding my wrists together. He leans over the bathtub and picks up something, bringing it to my wrists and binding them together.

"Look at me, Tillie."

My eyes come down to his, my head tilting. My heart thrashes around in my chest. "Tell me what you want. Do you want me to suck on your pussy?"

I nod, clamping my lips closed. Why are you acting shy? I tilt my head and smirk. "Yes. I want you to lick my pussy."

A dark smirk dances on his mouth to the same tune you'd lower a casket into the ground. He leans forward and his mouth connects with my folds, his tongue flicking across. He shuffles further down and licks inside of me. I clench around his invasion, my thighs shaking. My orgasm rips through me like a category five cyclone, threatening to leave casualties in its wake, then he stands, and suddenly his slick cock is right in front of my face. The word KING inked above his pelvis, taunting me.

"You like that, baby?" he asks, his fingers tightening around my chin and yanking my face up to his. "On your knees, bound by your cum-drenched panties, and gazing up at the words that own you, because I do, Tillie. This King fucking owns you."

I lean forward, drawing my tongue out to flick against the shaft of his cock. If he owns me, then why does he groan when I use something as simple as my tongue? The smallest muscle in my body holds the most power. I gently wrap my lips around the trunk of his cock and suck, taking him in until the tip hits my tonsils. I pull back, my eyes still on his and watch as his eyebrows cross and his perfect teeth nibble on his lower lip. He piles my hair to the top of my head and yanks me back before slamming my face into his cock in jerky motions. I take it, my saliva mixing with his cum and dripping down my chin. When he pulls out again, I drag my tongue out and lick the residue off my lip, moaning.

"More."

"You're my dirty little bitch, Tillie. Nothing has changed there."

He yanks me up by my hair until I feel the follicles rip from their roots. I'm directly in front of his inked chest now, those beautiful angel wings. I lean my tongue toward his chest to trace them. My clit continues to throb with need and the taste of his cum clings to the tip of my tongue like a bittersweet reminder of, as he puts it, exactly who owns me.

"Angel wings..." I whisper, tracing my tongue over the sharp angles.

He grips my tongue between his fingers. *"Because even Lucifer was once an Angel."* Then his hand flies to the front of my throat. "Get out of the bath and bend over, facing the mirror."

I do as I'm told, stepping out and turning to face the large floor to ceiling mirror wall that is directly opposite us. Slowly, I lean over, wishing I could reach down and curl my hands around my slender ankles. I turn my head over my shoulder instead, until my long pink hair cascades to the other side.

I smirk. "Punish me."

He licks his lip, following suit. I watch as his eyes darken, and his shoulders pull back. He brings his finger to the middle curve of my pussy and presses it inside of me, circling. "You needed someone that wasn't me..." he starts, and then I feel a hard slap sting over my ass.

I wince, my eyes shutting. It was bearable, I know how much more he's capable of.

Slap! Another bite ripples over my ass, my fat jiggling under the abuse. "That was your third sin..." he mutters, his fingers cupping my pussy from behind. He rubs my clit viciously until my juices are sloshing with his movements. He lets go and I wait.

Slap! This one comes harder, a lot harder. I cry out in pain as it feels like my flesh has split open. It stings so bad.

"I touched Brantley," I whisper, wanting more. Needing to be punished more for everything I had put him through. Because after this day, he and I are done. I don't owe him anything and I don't have to feel bad with the way I went about things.

Nate chuckles sinisterly. "Another man putting his hands on you didn't bother me as much as Daemon gripping onto your fucking heart, baby."

I hear him pick something up from the ground. I gulp at the metallic sound of clinking.

Slap! The belt bites across my skin and I can't help the scream that rips out of me. The pain that zaps over my skin is in a whole new frequency that I don't think I can handle. He tosses the belt to the side and bends down behind me. I feel his tongue dive inside of my entry and flick inside my walls.

"So wet for me. So wet for the pain, and this is why you will always be mine to gain..."

Then I feel his tongue lick across my ass cheek. He stands, grabbing onto my throat and spinning me around to face him. His fingers flex around my neck and I slowly open my eyes. Shock seizes my bones when I see blood glistening over his lips.

My heart slams in my chest. My stomach hurling in pleasure.

His eyes stay on mine, hooded, dark and filled with greed. "Kiss me, baby. Kiss away your sins."

I lean forward and suck his tongue into my mouth. The taste of metal surfs over my tongue, slithering its way down my throat.

"Get on the bed and wait for me."

I lean back, my cheeks flushed red. I nod, padding my way to the bedroom. My heart is pounding from adrenaline, probably the same kind that gets girls killed. I trust Nate, though. We both need this as much as the other, it's what the unspoken pleading tonight was about. The closure we both need to end what happened tonight. What happened with Micaela.

I kneel at the foot of the bed and wait for him, a half-smile delicately touching my lips. I can't help it. I'm not submissive by any sense of the word, but I like playing games, probably as much as he does, which is why our bed tricks have always been toxic. Before we were parents. When you first become a parent, there are certain things that pound into your head. *You shouldn't say that, eat that, fuck like that...* you get the picture. Suddenly you're making every decision for how you are as a parent too...

Well, we don't have that anymore, and I can feel the toxicity seep through my pores and plant its seeds deep in my bones. The only question is, will I water them, or let them die?

Nate saunters into the bedroom, naked and broody. He tilts his head and then makes his way to the top drawer. He pulls out a silver switchblade, and I freeze. *Oh shit. That's what you get, Tillie. Playing with The Kings will get you killed.*

A cruel smirk sneaks onto his mouth. "Get up and get on the bed."

I do, fumbling to my feet and backing up onto the bed. He pushes a button and a long blade switches out. He comes close, until his stomach is clenching in front of my face. He runs the blunt edge of the knife down my chest, my breathing thick and labored. He continues to drag it over my nipple, circling.

"Do you trust me?"

I lick my lips, my eyes closing.

"Answer me Tillie, did you, and do you, trust me?"

"Yes," I whisper as he trails the knife down to my inner thigh. "Do you need a safe word?" His tone is teasing, and for a second, I see a sliver of Nate.

My eyes fire to life. "No."

"Your second sin? Was not trusting me *enough.*" The blade twists and I feel a sting slice across my upper thigh. "I always said that I loved breaking you just so I could put you back together exactly how I wanted, maybe pocket a few pieces of you that you'd never get back. Maybe we could try that literally..."

My blood turns cold as I feel it drip down my inner thigh. He leans around me as I open my eyes and I'm met with the crook of his neck. His vein stammers underneath his slick flesh and I have to fight all of the urges inside of me that want to lean over and sink my teeth into him until he screams. I feel my wrists loosen from their hold and I twist them as I bring them to the front of me.

He grins, dangling my white panties between us, as they hang on the tip of the blade he just fucking *cut* me with. *Cunt cut me.* But before I can think about that, he brings it to his nostrils and inhales deeply, a merciless grin possessing his lips.

"Mine."

He yanks them off and runs them over my body before shoving me onto my back. I fall backward, my hair spreading out beneath me. I watch as he lowers between my thighs again. But instead of sucking my pussy, he licks up the blood that he made with the knife.

"That sin was brutal. I'm sorry, baby, you know how I get jealous..."

He sucks my thighs until my hips meet air, desperate for friction. He bites down hard, and then bites on my other side, climbing to the area where my thighs meet my pussy. He nibbles, and then leans up. His thick angry cock is pulsing, cum dripping off his tip. Nate tosses the blade across the room and lowers himself on top of me, his cock filling me up to the brim.

I scream in pleasure as another orgasm wracks at my bones from his simple invasion.

I'm so fucked with him.

He pulls out and flips me onto my stomach, gripping onto my hips and pulling me up until I'm face-down-ass-up. His fingers bite into my hips when he slams into me again, just as I'm riding my second orgasm. He pounds into me, his balls slamming against my clit. Sweat drips off my forehead as he continues his assault, tearing at my insides with every thrust. He spins me back onto my back, throwing me against the headboard.

I groan as my head smashes against the hard marble. My vision blurs, dizzying in and out. He crawls over, yanking me down the bed by the backs of my thighs and sinking inside slowly.

"Your last sin, was blaming yourself."

He thrusts inside of me, his hand coming to the front of my throat. He squeezes until I wheeze for air. He presses into me again, and again, at a slow torturous pace and only giving me air when I'd tap on his arm.

His mouth comes to mine as his pace slows, his tongue slipping inside.

"Don't ever do any of that shit again or I won't release my grip next time."

He releases my throat just as he grinds against my clit and another orgasm screams out of me, my body jerking, strung-out and battered.

Finally, he pulls out and grips his cock, pumping himself until his hot cum sprays out over my chest and face. He brings his fingers to it and swirls it around, and then lifts it to my mouth.

"Open."

I do, sucking his salty liquid off the tip of his finger.

Falling back down beside me, he yanks the silk sheets up and pulls me under his arm. Once again too tired to wash his cum off me. My eyes close as he presses small kisses to my head and runs circles with his finger around my thigh.

Chapter Thirty

Tillie

The morning sun pours out from under the dark curtains, along with our prior night's sins. I go to swing my legs over his bed but flinch when they throb with pain. I lift the blanket and take a peek at the damage. Finger marks, bite marks, and dried blood cover my upper thighs where there's that lovely little cut. It wasn't enough to need stitches and the dried blood that set over the incision was enough to stop it from bleeding. How generous of him.

"Oh god." I shake my head.

We took it to another level last night, one I hadn't seen in Nate since we first slept together. I forgot how bad he can get. Picking up the first thing I find on the floor—another one of his hoodies—I slip it over my head, letting it fall to my knees. My tummy rumbles, but I promised Nate one night, and one night it was. We have to stay focused to figure out our next move. No point being battered soldiers when the battering is happening from each other, not our enemies.

"Where you goin'." He wraps his arm around my waist and drags me back into the bed.

"I need to go," I laugh.

His phone starts ringing on his nightstand. Groaning, he grabs at it aimlessly, pushing it to his ear. "What?" His eyes come to mine. "Really?"

"What?" I mouth, wondering why he's looking at me like I'm a snack. If I'm his snack, I'll make sure I'm laced with poison for that lethal sex last night.

"Be there in thirty." He hangs up and smirks at me. I fight the urge to punch his face because it's not fair he looks *this* perfect first thing in the damn morning. "Your car is here. Guess you'll be riding something else other than my dick from now on."

I throw a pillow at his face and he bursts out laughing, his straight, white teeth flashing behind his perfect lips.

"Bastard."

I don't bother changing, mainly because I don't have clothes here. Since my innocent panties were the product of how nasty we got last night, I left them there too, as a reminder for him, or if he decides to bring home any other girls, a reminder for them—to run for their lives. So all I've got is the rolled up piece of the dress—thankfully, that came off very early in the night.

We pull up to Brantley's driveway, and I turn to face Nate, noticing how absolutely wrecked we both look. Like we just came out of a war zone. He has dark hickeys all over his neck and a black eye?

"Shit. Did I punch you last night?"

He sips on his coffee, trying to find his Ray-Bans. "You kicked me when I licked your sweet little cunt for the fifth time."

"Nate!" I squirm.

I flip the mirror down and flinch. "I look like shit." Dark circles, my skin pale and my hair the next home for homeless, stray birds.

"Impossible. Get out."

We both climb out of the car and my eyes land on the new addition that's sitting in the middle of Brantley's driveway.

I smirk, walking up to it just as Brantley and Eli exit the front door.

Brantley tosses me the keys and his eyes widen as they go between Nate and I. "You both look like shit. Must have been a good night."

I catch them and unlock the car. It really is stunning. Lowered, matte black rims and blacked-out lights. The shiny blood red color gleams against the morning sun.

Nate leans into the window from the passenger side. "Good choice, baby."

I stand. "We are all going for a ride. We need to do something normal."

Brantley's eyes catch Nate's. "Yeah, because Hector has called another meet for Friday night."

"What?" Nate shouts.

I freeze. "It's not been a month—it's only been days?"

Brantley nods, his eyes staying on Nate. "Which is why it's interesting he's called it, and he has asked for Tillie to be there."

"Tillie will not be there," Nate declares matter-of-factly.

"Tillie is right here, and Tillie is fine with being there..." I add, shutting the driver's side door and making my way up the steps.

"Tillie is not fucking going!" Nate hollers from behind me.

I flip him off as I enter the house and start making my way down to the room of gloom, when Brantley stops me with his words.

"I've moved your room. You don't have to stay here if you don't want to. You're not a prisoner anymore, it was only until we sorted the Daemon thing out. We couldn't risk you telling Madison about seeing her dead brother."

I turn to face him. "I like being here."

Brantley smiles. Smiles. Not smirks, not scowls. Smiles. Rows of the straightest white teeth against his tanned skin. "I know. You're on this level opposite my dad's office. Had the maid move your shit in there."

I head down toward the door, thanking Brantley on the way. When I open the door, I'm instantly in love with the space. It has one large bay window that opens out to the back yard. The walls are white, and the bed linen one shade darker than the walls. I open one of the doors and I'm met with a bathroom. It's about the same size as the one I had downstairs—no bath. The second door is a walk-in closet. My clothes already hanging carefully on the hangers. I wonder who his maid is? I wouldn't put it past him to have that sweet innocent girl as his little slave, but even as the thought flashes through my head, I know deep down that that isn't the case. The way he moved around her, how she composed herself faced with the devil. That wasn't someone who has been on the receiving end of Brantley's wrath. That was someone, possibly the only one, who had seen a side to Brantley no one had ever seen.

Or maybe I'm deranged.

Considering the latest events, I settle for the latter, grab some clothes and slip into the shower, enjoying the warm water crashing against my battered skin.

I change quickly, after lathering oils against myself and blow-drying my hair. I don't bother to straighten it, rather letting the natural wave fall down my back. I'm slipping on my Jimmy Choos when the door opens.

Nate stands freshly showered and wearing light blue faded jeans, a Phillip Plein shirt, and his leather jacket that has a hood stitched into the collar.

I stuck to white skinny jeans, a black loose cotton T-shirt and threw on my red leather jacket—to match my car.

"I'm serious, Tillie. You can't come on Friday."

I'm tightening the final strap when I stand and reach for my phone that was charging. "I can, and I will. He asked me to attend."

"I'll cage you."

"And I'll break free." I grin at him, latching my watch around my wrist and spraying my Valentino perfume over myself.

He steps into my room, instantly making it feel smaller. "It might get ugly."

"I've seen ugly, Nate…" I murmur, bringing my hand to his cheek. "I killed ugly."

His eyes search mine and he winces, stepping out of my touch. Shit. *You idiot, Tillie. Stop touching what you can't have.*

"I hate that you took on that burden," he answers, reaching for my hand.

I let him take it. "Rather me than Madison."

"I'd rather me take it or Bishop. You two are uncontrollable."

He leads me out and I reach for my debit card, sliding both that and my phone into my back pocket. I shut my door and we round it until we're waiting for everyone at the bottom of the stairs.

There's silence, the only sound coming from the ticking of an old grandfather clock in the foyer.

"Did you hear that?" I ask Nate.

"No?" He tilts his head, then the whispering happens again and his eyes snap up the stairs. "Yeah, I heard that."

"This house is so creepy."

Nate's mouth kicks up in a smirk. "Creepy with a whole bunch of secrets. Right, Bran Bran?" Nate pushes his aviator glasses down over his eyes.

Brantley flips him off as he enters with everyone and we all slowly pile out.

Eli, Cash, and Jase are climbing into a Ford Raptor, and Hunter is sliding in with Brantley in his car.

Nate naturally goes to the passenger seat of my car and I climb in, inhaling the new car smell of freshly produced leather. The scent begins to mix with both mine and Nate's scent. I push the button to start and the car purrs to life beneath me.

"You got stick?" Nate asks, one judgy eyebrow quirked.

"Yes," I hiss, putting it into first gear.

Brantley gestures for me to wind my window down. "Follow us. We're heading out to the cabin."

I still. The same cabin Nate and I had our first fight?

"Yeah." Brantley's eyes fucking twinkle.

Oh god.

I gulp. "Yeah okay." He zips forward and before the completely blacked-out Raptor can follow behind him, I zip between the two, giggling.

Nate chuckles, shaking his head. Just as we're driving past the large garage, I watch in slow motion as the doors open and a crystal clean white Tesla peeks out from underneath. My breathing slows, my eyes and focus completely on the supped up Tesla. Then she's standing there. Like she just stepped off the set of *Game of Thrones*, with her white long hair, small petite body and soft eyes. She watches me carefully, wrapping her cardigan around her body, then just like that, I floor it into third and zip out of the driveway.

"Did you see that?" I ask Nate, but his head is turned to the other side.

"See what?" he asks, his face turning to me.

"Never mind," I grumble. I swear to God if this me seeing people thing is going to be a *thing* I'll check myself into a fucking psychiatric ward.

His hand comes to my thigh. "You're not going crazy, baby. Yeah, I saw her."

Adrenaline crashes through my body. "Who is she?" I want to know everything.

Nate shrugs. "Don't know. That was the first time I have ever seen her, but when we had that party, Brantley was acting on some next level feral shit. So I'm not very keen on raising the topic with him."

I snort, turning the radio on. "SOS" by Avicii starts playing softly in the background. The deep base shaking through the car like small thunderbolts. *These fucking lyrics.* We all merge onto the main highway and I watch behind me as the Raptor's angry front follows close behind me. I stick close behind Brantley.

"Whose Raptor is that?"

"Jase's. We would tease him about the size of his cock, but we've all seen it."

I laugh, just as a matte black Maserati flies past us and slips in front of Brantley's car.

I roll my eyes. "What about Bishop's?"

Nate laughs, leaning back in his seat. "Definitely not."

The song moves on and Nate's hand comes to my thigh. "No doubt we will be staying out here the night."

"I wore Jimmy Choos!"

He rolls his eyes, sliding his phone unlocked. He presses his phone to his ear.

"Yo, can you bring Tillie some normal shoes, and a change of clothes, and her little pink lace panties with the letters S E C R E T over them?"

I shove him.

He laughs. "Oh, and her toothbrush."

He hangs up his phone. "Done."

"Who was that?"

"Relax, like I'd let any of the boys near your fucking panties. It was Bailey. She's coming tonight too."

I smile. "Really?" Excited I'll have another girl with me—for once. I like Bailey a lot. I think she's smart for a young girl, but I can see the bitch beneath the sweet.

"Yeah," Nate murmurs and his head tilts. "And I'm pretty sure I saw two people in Bishop's car.

Madison? "No," he cuts into my thoughts. "It's Abel."

It doesn't matter that he corrected me. Now my thoughts are with Madison. "Did she run with Tate again?"

Nate shakes his head. "Nah. Tate is getting ready to start NYU. I think, for the most part, their friendship is slowly drifting apart. Tate has new friends, friends of her caliber."

Lucky Tate. Living a normal life and whatnot, but even as I think that, I feel guilty. I love my friends. "So she doesn't give a shit that Madison has run again?"

"She doesn't know. She thinks Madison is ghosting her."

"Well," I say, readjusting myself in my seat. "I'd be pissed at you guys for that."

"You wouldn't run," he adds matter-of-factly.

"True, but in any case." I can't help but feel hurt that she didn't at least try to reach out to me before she ran. I kept her secret. Through it all I kept it, but she still couldn't trust me?

Then realization sinks in. "You're acting rather blasé about the whole thing."

Nate snorts, his finger running over his upper lip. "We know where she is, Tillie. Make no mistake, we will *always* know where either of you are."

I lick my lips. "And?"

His jaw clenches. "She's in New Zealand."

We stay quiet the rest of the drive. Four hours later, we've pulled off the main highway and onto a private road. Trees burst out the soil that lines the perfectly manicured road.

"I don't remember it being this well kept out here."

Nate exhales as we all pull to the front of the cabin. The same cabin we were all at when Nate and I first got together and the same night I found out about my mother.

Heavy logs act as pillars and surround the wrap-around porch, to where I know floor to ceiling glass walls line the front of the main living room inside.

We climb out, shutting the door. I walk forward, my heels clicking across the road.

"Little terror, wearing heels to a cabin?" Brantley quirks his eyebrow at me.

"I know," I murmur, my eyes going to Abel briefly as I give him a soft smile. "Bailey is bringing me some more."

Brantley chuckles. "That cousin of mine is a royal pain in my fucking ass."

"Daddy Bran Bran. So full of secrets...."

His eyes turn to slits and I quickly run up the front steps.

"You can't run fast in those heels, *Princessa*! I would put that smart mouth on a leash if I was you!"

I giggle, pushing the front door open and step inside. The fireplace is going, candles lit around the room and the mantels all polished.

"Who came and set it all up?" I ask, looking around the large space.

The stairs that lead up to the bedrooms are directly to the right as you walk in. A large U-shaped leather sofa sits in the middle of the main living room, a massive open fireplace built into the wall behind the sofa. The trees look magnified from behind the large glass walls, and the kitchen is all varnished wood and marble. It's a clean fade between traditional and executive. I love the cabin, and start to realize none of them spend much time here. What an absolute waste.

I pick up one of the photos that are sitting on the mantle above the fireplace.

Hector and Scarlet with Bishop in Scarlet's arms. I put it back, not wanting to touch anything to do with Hector. Except Bishop.

Nate flops onto the sofa and kicks off his Adidas Original shoes. "I'm so fucked."

"Yeah, because you got fucked last night." Eli kicks his legs.

"Pretty sure I did the fucking," Nate snaps back quickly.

"Really?" Hunter chuckles. "Because I'm pretty sure that black eye speaks otherwise."

They all burst out laughing and I ignore them, making my way into the kitchen while removing my shoes. Total waste of shoes.

"Are you okay?" I ask Bishop as he pulls down a bottle of scotch and a couple of glasses. The rest of the guys bring their shit inside, making their way up to the rooms. I haven't even thought about where I'm sleeping, but I know that it won't be with Nate again. We had a promise. We have to keep that promise.

Bishop pours the liquid into my glass and slides it over to me. "Not really. But I'm giving myself the two days we're all spending out here to pull my shit together."

I swirl the scotch around in my glass. "To pull your shit together, one has to completely fall apart. Put yourself together different this time, B. Better."

He shoots the drink back and slams his glass onto the table. "Can I ask you a question and will you be honest with me?"

The TV goes on in the background, an NBA game playing.

"Yes," I answer, taking a sip of the strong liquid. I swear I hate whiskey. It is not my drink. I toss it back anyway and gag when it all slides down my throat.

Bishop laughs, shaking his head and stands from his seat, making his way to a small bar that's on the other side of the kitchen, behind the dining table. He comes back with a bottle filled with dark brown liquid.

"What's that?" I ask.

"Old Fitzgerald Bourbon. I think you might like this one more. It's still whiskey, but it's bourbon, so it's not distilled in Scotland, but in Kentucky. One's made with barley and the other, corn. It's all boring, but usually if you can drink scotch, you can drink bourbon, but if you don't like scotch, you usually like bourbon. Also, it costs four g's a bottle."

I screw off the cap and pour it into my empty glass. I take a sip and my cheeks heat. The sweet bitterness stings my mouth but soothes my taste buds. "Much better."

He smiles. "Did Madison ever tell you about the time she spent in New Zealand?"

I take a gulp of the bourbon, slowly swallowing it and bringing my knees to my chest. "A little."

I remove my jacket when I feel my blood heating. Raking my hand through my long hair. "Why?"

"Did she mention a guy named Jesse?"

I curl my lips under my teeth, placing my glass onto the granite table. "Briefly. She said they were friends. Is that who she's with?"

Bishop nods. "Yeah, and I'm struggling to stop myself from flying over there and dragging her back by her fucking hair."

I sink the rest of my drink, Nate comes into the kitchen behind Bishop. Grabbing chips and chocolate from the cupboard.

I pour more bourbon into my glass.

"Easy, tiger." Nate points to my glass with a Twinkie in his mouth. He takes it out and tears the wrapper off with his teeth. "Don't put yourself in a position where I can take your ass for granted."

I roll my eyes, another sip, and then go back to Bishop as Nate sinks back into the lounge, throwing bags of potato chips at the back of Eli's head.

"Don't," I say, and Bishop's eyes come to mine. "She'll come back when she wants. No point bringing her back. A lot has happened. She has changed the most out of all of us. If this is what she needs to do for herself right now, then let her do it. I'll make sure I'm here if and when she comes back."

Bishop swallows his drink and tilts his head, removing his T-shirt. Bishop shirtless is not a good thing. Because it's a very good thing.

"For fuck's sake," I growl, diverting my eyes.

He chuckles, tossing his shirt behind him. "My blood's running hot. Guessing yours is the same." I don't miss the dip in his tone.

It is. It's rushing around me at speeds and a temperature I can't grasp.

"Yes—"

"—Don't even go there," Brantley interrupts, yanking out the chair on the other side of Bishop while snatching my bottle of bourbon. He pours into his glass, his eyes on Bishop. Something passes between the two of them. Bishop's eyes narrow on Brantley and then come back to me.

Bishop laughs, his straight teeth flashing as his head tilts back. "You don't fucking say."

Then he turns his head over his shoulder, his eyes going to the back of Nate's head, Nate who has also ditched his shirt and has put a backward cap on.

"I've been told Tillie's color is red." Bishop teases.

Nate turns to face us, standing to all his six-foot-two-inches. His tattoos sprawling out over his tanned and shredded skin. His Calvin's peek out from under his jeans. Jeans that are unbuttoned and hanging off his hips. He cranks his neck.

"Yeah, fucking aye it is."

My eyes dart between the two of them, like I've missed something.

"Just because my car is red doesn't mean it's my favorite color," I say defiantly.

They all burst out laughing. Nate's eyes come to mine. "We know, baby. Chill."

Then he drops down onto the sofa, his eyes back on the game.

Brantley and Bishop chuckle, and Bishop stands up, ruffling my hair with his hand. "You've been a good friend to Madison, Tillz. And to us... can't imagine this life without your pink hair in it."

I clutch my chest, batting my lashes. "Aw."

His eyes roll. "Don't get used to the sweet nothings. You won't hear them again!" He disappears through the room and up the stairs, bottle of scotch between his fingers. Scotch, not bourbon.

I lick my lips, the alcohol slowly coating my fear. "You okay, little terror?" Brantley asks behind his glass.

I nod. "Hey," I lean forward. "The Tesla?"

He freezes, his eyes cutting to mine. "You saw her?"

"Yes," I hiss, whispering. *Why am I whispering?*

Brantley's eyes come to mine, darkening. "Why do I trust you?"

I tilt my head. "The feeling is mutual, Brantley."

"No." He shakes his head, tipping his head back to sink the rest of his drink. "Why do I trust you with the knowledge of the one person I don't even trust myself with?"

Because I'll protect her. I want to say.

Because I want to shield her. And you. And destroy anyone that comes near whatever it is that you both share. I also want to say.

"I don't know," I whisper instead. "Why do you?"

He pauses and then licks his lip. "I don't know. When I know, I'll tell you."

He leans over, kissing my head and I play with my glass as I watch Nate get riled up in the lounge, shoving at Eli who is making jokes about the LA Lakers beating the Golden State Warriors. Who knows. I'm bored. But within my boredom, I see these Kings as an outsider. They're the most feared individuals by anyone with half a brain in this world or the knowledge of who they are, but really, through my eyes, they're still a pack of boys, just with extracurricular activities, and who wouldn't flinch at tearing a head clean off the shoulders of anyone who dared hurt anyone they cared about.

Does that make them *bad* people? I think it only makes them *bad* to people who have ill intent. I scoop up my drink and run my fingers through my hair, swiping my hair out of my face. Padding around the space, I take in things that I maybe didn't notice the first time I was here. Like the fact that there's a sharp tower sticking up in the middle of the forest in the mess of treetops. Or that there's an array of photographs scattered all over the place, not just of Bishop's family, but of Nate, too. And Eli, and Hunter and Jase and Cash. There are old black and white photos of other families, people who I'm guessing were also a part of The Kings. I stop in front of another image. It was of Hector, alone, cradling a baby.

"Who is this?" I nod my head at the photo that's on one of the many small mantles nailed to the feature wall.

"Must be Abel," Nate states, tilting his head. The baby isn't wearing blue or pink. It's colored, but old. Nate's eyes scan it a beat longer and then he puts it back. "Definitely Abel. Way too fucking pretty to be Bishop."

Bishop flips him off, parading down the stairs as Nate takes another seat on the sofa and goes back to watching the game.

I stand, my eyes scanning them all.

Do they think I'm fucking stupid?

I want to say that Hector isn't supposed to know that Abel exists. That that is what they had told me, but I find my mouth glued shut. I'll gather my information and hit them when I need, there's no point announcing that I know this, because that gives them time to change their story, maybe throw a few lies around.

I'd rather play dumb.

I shrug, making my way back to the sofa and take a seat beside Nate.

He leans forward, resting his elbows on his knees, looking at me over his shoulder. Half his face is covered by that shoulder, but his eyes scan me up and down.

"You good?"

"Peachy!" I smile, batting my lashes. He goes back to the game and my smile falls. Asshole.

My eyes swing around to meet Abel and he's watching me closely. It's scary how much he looks like Bishop. I'd bet my ass on the fact that they're twins had they not had an age gap.

He grins at me like he knows what I'm thinking.

I wink at him.

The thing about fucking with people is that that person begins to learn the art that you fuck, and they fuck you back harder, with perfect precision and execution.

The sun has set a burnt orange hue in the sky, and I'm feeling itchy to get off this couch.

"Is there food in there to cook?"

Nate slaps my ass as I get up and I turn around, glaring at him.

He blows me a kiss. "Yeah, there should be."

I round the sofa, still glaring at Nate, who is still smirking at me. When I enter back into the kitchen, the front door swings open.

"Sorry I'm late!" Bailey hollers.

The boys don't move from their spots.

"Thank god!" I wave her into the kitchen. "I'm starting to grow a dick."

Bailey laughs, removing her large puffy jacket and placing it on the hook.

"Oh, I can assure you, I've fucked that pussy way too hard for it to turn into anything other than a drippi—"

I slap the back of his head as we head into the kitchen.

Bailey rolls her eyes, laughing.

"Okay, so I figured we can all eat outside tonight because I did say I wante—"

I turn around, and Bailey has stopped. I follow her line of sight, and hello, Abel.

I lean into her. "Oh I see…"

She flinches, turning to look at me. "What?"

I chuckle. "Nothing. Come help me before you kill yourself with all those hormones."

She blushes. Straight up blushes. Sweet, sweet girl. That boy will eat you alive. But she's a Vitiosis, so maybe not…

Bailey gets started on the salad as I pull out all the freshly cut meat. Steaks and marinated chicken.

I point to the alcohol. "Pour yourself a drink, young one…"

She laughs. "Okay, since you insist. How has everything been? Sorry I've been absent around the house." She pours some gin into a glass and then tops it with juice. "I've been studying my ass off so I'm ready when I start RPA, and when I'm not studying, I'm dancing, so it has been a little jammed in my schedule."

I raise my eyebrow at her as she sips on her Snoop juice. "Alright, Snoop Dog, not too many of those. I still feel somewhat responsible for you. Don't think that will ever change."

And it won't. I feel connected to Bailey, so it's natural. Effortless. I look at her like a little sister. She plays the part well too because I feel like she looks at me the same way. Therefore, I'd rather not get her blind drunk. Maybe I'm still a mother after all…

"It's fine," I murmur, heating up two large frying pans as she gets back to tossing grapes and pineapples into the colorful salad. "I've had a few things to deal with so I'm glad you didn't see me in that state."

She tosses everything into the bowl and then comes up beside me. We're the same height, because I'm so fucking short and she's going to be the next top fucking model. Adriana Lima looking little wench.

"Who is that?"

"Oh, so it seems you have missed that too?" I ask, laughing. "*That* is Bishop's brother."

"Bishop as in *The* Bishop Vincent Hayes?"

"The very same. The lord and the light. The fire in every young girl's heart..."

Bailey blushes. "Well, that would be Nate, no offense, but everyone is obsessed with him."

I roll my eyes. "He's overrated."

"I heard that!" Nate snaps from the couch. "And I'll remind you to check between, and on your thighs before throwing around that word again, *Princessa*..."

Bailey's eyes instinctively drop to my legs.

"Bails!"

"Sorry!" She giggles, sipping her drink.

"Go butter the garlic bread or something..."

She doesn't bother to tell me that you don't butter garlic bread, she simply slides onto a bar stool and watches me move around the kitchen.

"What else did I miss?"

We fall into easy conversation as the scent of sweet chicken and steak fills the crisp night air. Bailey tells me about some guy Nix and how him and his four friends at school think they fucking run the show. How when everyone found out she was starting Riverside Prep, everyone started adding her on social media and her online popularity has already spiked. She went from being a home-schooled nerd to the most popular girl at an exclusive private academy. I wanted to tell her to be careful, that RPA is not to be taken lightly. That school ruins kids, and almost ruined Madison, but I don't. Instead, I'll let her explore it on her own and just be here when she needs me. That I promised her.

Eli and Cash come into the kitchen and take out all the things we need to the table. Nate carries out the hot food and Bailey finishes up with the cutlery and setting the table.

I pull out the seat opposite Bailey. I'm also next to Nate, who is on the other side of the table end to Bishop. It's funny how they all fall into position. Even when they're driving.

Bishop heads to a switchboard and flicks on the fairy lights that hang above the long marble table that's tucked to the side of the kitchen outside, overlooking the rear of the house. Nature surrounds us, the crisp green leaves and heavy cedar wood cycling with the freshly cooked food. The boys all start digging in and my eyes find Bailey's, who has had a few too many to drink. When I say few, I mean three. Lightweight teens.

Music starts playing softly from little speakers that surround the wrap-around porch. I catch Bishop fiddling with his phone as I cut into my steak, forking pieces of salad.

"So what are we doing tomorrow?"

"Tomorrow?" Nate asks around a grin. "Oh no, we're playing something tonight…"

"Playing what? And I'm pretty sure I said I wanted normal." I give a pointed glare at Bailey, who doesn't know half the shit these boys do.

"She's got a lot to learn for next year. She'll be alright." Nate winks at her and I watch as Bailey blushes, slicing into her steak.

"Bails?"

"Hmm?" she asks, looking up at me.

I toss a bun onto her plate. "You might need some carbs tonight. Reserve all the energy you can."

We all fall into easy conversation, and I end up snapping a whole bunch of photos of everyone.

Bailey holds up her hands. "Wait! I have a Polaroid!"

"A fucking what what?" Eli asks, his eyes narrowing in on her. She blushes from his attention.

"Leave her alone, baby cakes." I glare at Eli before going back to Bailey. "Go grab it!"

She escapes into the house and I turn back to Eli. He's still glaring at me. His pretty features morphing into disgust.

"Did you just call me baby cakes?"

Everyone around the table bursts out laughing, bar Eli.

I giggle, bringing the glass to my mouth as Bailey reappears, a smile on her face and lifting a metallic grey square looking camera that looks like it's straight out of the 70s.

We snap multiple photos with both the Polaroid and our phones. I lean into Bailey as we grab a few selfies. Then Nate yanks me into his arms and Bailey snaps multiple photos as he's doing so, even as he bites onto my nose tip.

She shrugs, holding her phone. "Action shots."

I look up at Nate. He licks his lips.

"We promised…" I whisper.

"I've promised a lot of fucking things in my lifetime, baby. And none of them involve staying away from you."

I push off his chest, (his very naked and hot chest), needing space. And air. Because he does things to me.

"Yes, you did."

"Then for once, you can call me a fucking liar."

I'm exhausted. This isn't love. It's pure and undiluted possession. He doesn't need to throw me around to possess me, his soul attached itself to mine a long time ago, and now I can't breathe with the thought of being too far away from him.

Can you spell vulnerable? Vulnerab—I can't. Mainly because bourbon, but also because of something else. Something that tugs at my chest every time his eyes meet mine, or anytime that he's in the same room as me, or any time that he's angry at me, or sad with me, or happy with me, or playful with me—*fuck*.

I swallow the rest of my drink.

I am completely, utterly, and irrevocably in love with him.

The room spins around me. I knew I was in love with him before, but that was different. I knew I had these feelings toward him, but I didn't know what to do with them.

Now that I've accepted these feelings, what the fuck do I do? He will never want to settle down. Ever. He's Nate Riverside-Malum. His cock may had been bounced around on a lot, (high fucking traffic zone), but his heart and his soul? Completely unattainable. Now that I've found myself in this pool of feelings for him, I'm afraid I might drown in them. He can never know, because he doesn't take me seriously. He banters with me, sure, but that's all it is, and even I know that there's no way I'd ever be allowed into his heart and soul. People think that he would fall in love easily because he likes to fuck around, but that's not true at all. He gave his cock freely—to girls who he deemed worthy—for his pleasure. Putting love on the table will never be in his cards, he kept his heart in a cage.

"Tillie?" Bailey laughs, swiping the tears. "Thoughts?"

"On?" I ask, gulping past my revelations. I reach for the ridiculously expensive bourbon.

"If you had to have sex with Johnny Depp—"

I shake my head. "Stop right there..."

Bailey tilts her head and the table falls quiet.

"I will always do Johnny Depp..." I add casually.

The table laughs and Bailey giggles. "See! Okay, so if you had to choose one of his characters to have sex with, who would it be?"

"Easy, Jack Sparrow..."

Bailey's lips pinch in.

"Why?" I ask, eyebrows raised. "Who did you pick?"

"...Edward Scissorhands?"

I almost spit out my drink. "What?" Then I start laughing, my tummy hurting. "Why? I couldn't be more shocked if you had said Willy Wonka!"

She shrugs. "Well, he would be my second choice!"

Girl is weird as fuck, which is why I love her.

Love. I wrap my lips around the rim of the bourbon bottle, fake laughing as I take gulps.

"Alright..." Bishop says, grinning at us all. "Time to play a game."

"Oh no..."

Bailey's eyes light up in glee. This girl is so much like her twisted cousin she has no idea.

Bishop rolls his eyes. "It's nothing like that..."

I sag in my seat. "Okay. Shoot."

An hour later we're all strapped up with vests and helmets and little light boxes that are flashing on our chests.

"Seriously..."

"You wanted something normal, Stuprum. Laser tag is about as normal as we get."

"It's not laser tag because you're using bullets..."

"Not real bullets." Nate rolls his eyes, and I only know that he rolls his eyes because the spotlight on my helmet is faced directly at him. His sharp jaw and articulate features only accentuated under the shadows behind the light.

"They are paintballs, still bullets!" I huff, irritation palpable.

Nate leans over and licks my face. "Stop talking. It makes my dick twitchy."

I glare at him.

There are two teams. Me, Bishop, Nate, Abel, Chase, and Cash on this team, and Brantley, Bailey, Eli, Hunter, and Ace, on their team. Saint is still a touchy subject, since he disappeared a couple of months ago. Nate had said he had gone rogue, which makes me sad.

"Alright!" Chase snaps at all of us, his long blonde hair tied into a top knot. His eyes narrow on me. "Stop laughing at me Stuprum…"

"I'm sorry, you're just so pretty."

"You can braid my hair if you help us win…" He winks.

I straighten. "Let's do this shit."

We figure out a game plan and then go our separate ways. The forest blankets me in its darkness, spilling around my feet like a dead river, probably filled with the damn Loch Ness monster.

An arm wraps around my waist and pulls me against a hard chest.

I spin around, smacking Nate. "You scared the shit out of me."

"We can't fuck again."

"I know," I snap, shoving his chest. "Why did you have to scare the shit out of me just to say that?" My heart sinks.

"Just making it clear so you stop looking at me like I'm a fucking snack and you've been starved all your life."

You're a six-course meal, not a fucking snack.

"Whatever." I turn in my steps, raising my gun up and looking through the scope.

I leave him behind, confused about the arbitrariness of his words, but it only settles the fact that I can't express the way I feel about him to him. I'm not ready to say it and he's not ready to hear it.

I raise my gun at movement that shuffles through the bushes and a flash of green swipes through the blackness like a neon headlight. I shoot. *Bang Bang Bang.* Anger at Nate ripples through me. I jog to where I hit and smirk down at Ace, his black hair falling over his face.

"Fuck me, Stuprum. You trigger happy or what?"

"I'm trigger happy."

The light on his chest flips to the word **"Shot"** that flash over his small screen, and then I help him up and watch as he heads back to the house.

Something smashes against my back and I yelp, spinning around as ten more bullets fly into my chest.

"Alright!" I yell, falling to the ground.

Whoever shot me doesn't come to check on me, so I stand, rubbing off the dirt and make my way back to the cabin. There's a fire that's been started in the pit and I rip the vest off me, tossing it to the ground while snatching the familiar bottle of bourbon from Brantley.

"I hate this game."

He chuckles. "Same."

My eyes go to Ace. "Sorry about shooting you."

He shrugs, just as Bailey comes stumbling down the stairs. "Why is there three on your team here and only one from my team?"

Brantley rolls his eyes. "She accidentally shot her teammate."

I burst out laughing, swallowing my drink. "These two days are going to be great."

Once everyone is back, we all pile inside and the subject of bedrooms starts. I'm still angry at Nate, and not ready to talk to him about what he said earlier tonight, but when I find him, it's his retreating back ascending the stairs, so I guess I don't have to worry about that.

"She can sleep with me!" Bailey says, winking at me. "I stole a bed as soon as I got here. It's a double, and has another double in there, but I think Eli took it so it's fine…"

I smile. "Thanks."

Yeah, I take that back. These next couple of nights might go slow.

Chapter Thirty-One

Nate

When I say shit to Tillie, it spills out. There's no fucking filter that it goes through first to have a second thought on what I say or even how the fuck I say it.

I fall onto the bed. The queen bed that I always take whenever we're at the cabin. Bishop, Brantley, and I are the only ones who always have a bedroom when we get here. We don't have to fight over the other four rooms. It's furnished with a queen bed and a fireplace, no TV. The whole point of being out here is to get away from the world. A fucking TV just replaces your world and gives you a false one. But Hector battled for the one downstairs so that got put in.

I kick the blankets off my body, my eyes drifting out the large windows. I prefer my room to Bishop's because of these windows. They're tinted heavily so the morning sun doesn't assault you as much as if they weren't. *Should I have let her in here?* I settle on no. We have too much on the line, including going against our fucking Godfather. Bishop is still not on board and refuses to allow us to conduct a plan to kill Hector. I get it. Not only is Hector his old man, but he's the fucking Godfather. You can't kill someone like Hector without triggering the fucking apocalypse. So he has asked for time. Time to build an army against Hector, a case, but the only thing about building an army against Hector is the fact that we have to share our reservations. To our enemies, that's a fucking weakness.

I rub my hands over my face and then grip onto my cock. I should just sneak into Tillie's room and fuck her to sleep. But I won't. Instead, my hand dips under my briefs and I slip my thumb over my wet tip, squeezing roughly and thinking about blood dripping down her thighs.

The sun pounds down on me as Eminem raps through my earbuds. I pick up my pace, running through the forest like someone is fucking chasing me. *This is my legacy, legacy... yeah, yeah...* Sweat drips down my temples, my shoulders aching from doing the same back and forth swing motion. I pause, and turn around, sprinting back to the cabin. I push myself until my heart is slamming against my chest and my knees wobble from fatigue. I thrust through the clearing and ignore Bailey and Cash who are on one of the logs that surround the bonfire pit. Falling to the ground, I rip the earbuds out of my ears.

Tillie is standing over my head, blocking the sun. "Hungry?"

I look at her pussy. "Starving."

She rolls her eyes and leaves. I roll onto my side. "Hey!"

She doesn't stop, because she never fucking does. "Breakfast is ready, Nate."

I chuckle, ripping my shirt off and tossing it across the grass. I make my way inside, stacking pancakes on my plate with bacon. I love her cooking. I don't know what it is, but when Tillie cooks, it's like she creates fucking magic. I push my fork into the cakey fluff and swipe it into the maple.

"You sleep well?" I ask, winking at her.

"Fine."

She drinks a bottle of water, wrapping her arms around her body protectively. I want to ask her what's wrong, but I already know. She wants justice served and I don't have it in me to tell her that that might take a little longer than she was expecting.

Instead, I lean over, wrapping my fingers around the legs of her chair and pull her toward me. "Talk."

Her eyes come to mine, and then she smiles, flashing me every fucking fake emotion she possibly could. "I'm fine."

I laugh. "No, the fuck you ain't..."

"Nate..." Bishop growls beside me.

I wave him off, going back to my pancakes and watch as she leaves the room.

"We need to talk about what's going to happen on Friday..." he continues.

I lick my front teeth. "Why would he call a meet so soon?"

Brantley shoves his empty plate away, rubbing his mouth with the back of his hand. "It can't be good, and he specifically asked for Tillie to be present."

"Bishop," I growl, and the table falls silent.

Bishop's eyes come to mine. "I know, brother, but I can't. We can't be reckless with it, either. You will get your revenge, but give me a minute."

I swing my head back, my eyes catching the roof. *Did he give my fucking innocent baby girl a minute?* I come back to reality, my eyes landing on Brantley.

He kisses his two fingers and throws them up slightly. *Baby Kay.* It's our thing. When she passed, it was our thing to do that.

"Fine," I grumble, swallowing the entire contents inside my glass. "But we need a plan and we need one fast."

I want to say that I want my shit ended on Friday. I want to fucking hand his ass to him on a silver platter, but I know it won't happen. Not only because Bishop is being sensitive about it, but because he's right. It's going to take more than us wanting revenge to actually obtain our revenge, and we are Kings. The mother fucking Elite. The monsters people whisper about in fear because they're too afraid to say our name out loud.

He will get his retribution.

It's coming, but when it does—my eyes snap to Bishop, who is already watching me. *Is that why he's stalling too? He's not ready?* Because when we do go through with a plan, it'll be Bishop who will be taking the throne.

"And then there are The Rebels, rubbing up against Tillie…" Eli reminds us, and my eyes flash with rage.

Bishop sits silently across the table. "That's a plan that needs to go into motion. Remember, everything that we do from here is for our plan."

Bishop's phone starts ringing and he snatches it off the table, his eyebrows furrowing. He swipes it and presses it to his ear. "Yeah?"

Silence. I lick the maple syrup off my fingertips slowly as we all try to listen in.

"Why?" he asks, his eyes narrowing in on me. "Yeah. Okay. Are you going to tell me why the erratic schedule with this meet?" Must be Hector, my eye twitches. "Alright. I'll wait to hear back." Then he hangs up before announcing, "He called it off. We are to wait for further instructions."

"I'm just going to say it," Ace mutters, tossing the crust of his toast onto the middle of the table. "I'm too old for this shit and totally fucking get why Saint bounced."

We don't speak, and Brantley flinches at the mention of that name. He and Saint were cool, so I know it has nothing to do with that. Weird motherfucker.

"Saint is fine…" Bishop nudges his head. "He's happy."

"Well fuck, I want me some happy too!" Ace smirks, just as Bailey comes padding into the kitchen, groaning. She flicks the coffee pot on and leans over the sink, her mess of hair sticking up all over the place.

"You all right there, Bails?" I ask, smirking.

She flips me off.

Chapter Thirty-Two

Tillie

Later that night, we're all chilling around the bonfire, roasting marshmallows and drinking mulled wine. I have Chase sitting between my legs on the ground and I'm halfway through French braiding his hair, his broad shoulders pressed between my thighs. Tash Sultana is playing through the sound system and everyone is lost in their talks. I look up to catch Nate watching me with every tighten on the braid.

"Pretty sure he's jealous," Chase murmurs, so only I can hear. "Pretty sure he's about to kill me."

I roll my eyes, finishing off his braid and tapping his shoulder. "He will live."

They told me today that Hector had canceled the meet until further notice, and as much as that news should have settled my nerves, it didn't. It only intensified the fact that I need my revenge. I understand revenge, though, probably more than Nate. I was raised in a world where people were cruel to me. It toughened my willpower to wait for the right time to strike, instead of lashing out at every person who does me wrong. Hector will get his at the right time, because it needs to be done right. And I still want to know why. Aside from getting me to Perdita, *why* did he need me to have nothing to live for? We drink more, dance a little, and Bailey pulls out her little camera again. Later that night we all settle back into our beds, but I'm restless. Bailey is snoring softly beside me, already deep in her sleep when I fling the blankets off my body and head for the door.

Why didn't he talk to me all night?

Why is he mad?

Now I'm mad, which is why I find myself standing outside of his door, my fingers clenched around the handle. I twist and shove it open, the back side of it hitting the wall. Nate is lying on the top of the covers, leaning on one elbow with nothing but his white

Calvin's on. He's doing something on his phone and his eyes slowly come up to mine, like me barging into his room was expected.

"What, Tillie?"

"Why are you mad at me?"

He finishes what he's doing on his phone, not meeting my eyes. "I'm not mad at you."

Am I being a twat? No, no I'm not. Because I'm sick of his mood swings. "Why haven't you spoken to me?"

He exhales, tossing his phone onto the other side of the bed. "Have I not been giving you enough attention? Come sit."

"I'm not your pet, Nate. I won't sit when you tell me to sit." ... *outside of the bedroom.*

A dark smirk slides onto his mouth. "Really?"

I don't know if it's the alcohol that's coursing through my body, or just the fact that he is Nate and I am Tillie, but I narrow my eyes on him. "What did I do wrong?"

"Wrong?" he asks, his eyebrows tipping up a little. "Nothing. Why would you do something wrong?"

"Can I ask you something?" I say, leaning on the door frame.

"You're going to anyway..."

He's right.

"Where do you see yourself in five year's time?"

He pauses, seeming to think over his next words. Just when I think he's not going to reply, he opens his mouth. "Living in my house." His eyes flick to his phone. "Sitting beside Bishop as he reigns over this fucking world. Why?"

My heart stops beating for a second, or at least it feels that way, and my gut squeezes. "Doesn't matter." I turn on my heel. "Goodnight, Nate."

And that, is why we could never work.

Chapter Thirty-Three

Tillie

Pressing my earbuds into my ears, I stretch my neck out and watch as the sun peeks up behind the trees, burning the dark with its light. Fergie starts rapping about being hungry as I stretch my legs briefly. I have become dependent on exercise since being in Brantley's house. Now I crave the burn that comes with pushing your body to the absolute limit. I slip my phone into my armband and start jogging at a slow pace until I find my stride. There's nothing for at least six miles, nothing but the long driveway that leads you to the cabin, and I love it. I'll run to the end, where the high wired gates are, and back again and that would be twelve miles. The perfect distance to get me hyped. My feet hit the road faster as I find my stride, the music blaring through my ears, distracting me from that stupid conversation last night. I see the gate at the end, but I haven't had enough. Pushing it open and off the latch, I slip out and keep running. I don't know where I'm going but I know I just need to run. My chest burns, my heart thrashing in my chest so fast that my throat feels raw. A dark Range Rover pulls up beside me and I freeze, my body instantly stilling. I tear the pods out of my ears as the tinted window slides down.

I tentatively tread toward it, peeking in. I stop when I see it's the same Rebel I locked lips with. "Um…"

"Get in, baby."

He nods his head toward the door, and I reach for it, climbing in. He obviously has something to say and call me fucking stupid but there's also a part of me that knows I'm somewhat untouchable in this world. People won't cross me.

I swipe at the sweat that's dripping from my forehead. "I smell, I'm sorry."

He chuckles, his eyes coming to mine. He's wearing a perfectly tailored suit and again, I see all of his ink peeking out of places that the suit doesn't cover. Like his hands, and his neck, and even a small cross underneath his eye.

"I kidnap you, and you apologize for sweating on my leather?"

I purse my lips. "You kidnapped me?"

He smirks. "Yeah, and you made it the easiest one to date."

He turns to face me, his eyes dropping to my mouth as he takes his seatbelt off so he can turn to me completely. The car pulls away and I'm suddenly aware of what the fuck I've just done. I'll blame it on the endorphins running unleashed. *For fuck's sake, Tillie.*

He reaches for my hand. "I won't hurt you."

"How do I know that?" My body is convulsing as I come down from my runner's high. "You just stole me."

He chuckles, reaching for my hand and pulling me close to him. "You don't know *why* I stole you yet, though, do you..."

I lick my lips, being so close to him. "I smell and I'm sweaty," I say again.

His eyes drop to my neck and he draws his tongue out, licking me across my slick skin. "I don't care," he announces, coming up to look me back in the eye.

I clear my throat. "I gather that..."

"Do you know who I am?" he asks, kissing my lips softly. What is with this man and always wanting to touch me. *Why do I like it?*

I shake my head. "No."

He grins, kissing my lips. "I'm something you should have found a long time ago."

I pull back from him slightly. "You're a Rebel."

"Yes." He sits back, lighting a cigarette. "I need to talk with you about something that is of importance."

"Okay," I whisper, wiping the sweat from my head. "And then will you drop me back?"

He grins around the stick of his smoke. "Maybe." He lights up, inhaling. "Or maybe I will want to keep you." He blows out the cloud.

"I'm not a woman who can be kept..."

He chuckles, shaking his head. "I wouldn't expect anything less."

My runner's high has completely disappeared now, and fatigue is replacing it. "Please tell me what you want."

"My name's Benny Vitiosis, Tillie."

I tilt my head. "And?"

He smirks. "And I'm the one who is going to make sure you get the right options."

"Okay, I don't know what that means."

Benny taps at the driver's seat, and then brings his eyes back to me. "What are you hoping to do after Hector has been punished for his, maybe, sins?"

I laugh. "I don't know. Why?"

His eyebrows shoot up. "Because there's still the case of who is going to run Perdita."

I shake my head. "Not me. Not right now."

He leans forward, searching my eyes. "What has to happen for you to stay on that island for a couple of months?"

"Why!" I snap, throwing my arms up. "Why does everyone want to know that?"

Benny smirks, puffing on his smoke. I lean forward and snatch it from between his fingers, shocking him in the process. I wrap my lips around it and inhale.

He looks at me with new light. "Didn't think fit chicks smoked?"

"This one does," I say. "Especially when she gets kidnapped and questioned about shit she doesn't want to address right now."

"Benny shrugs. "I'll come back after you've chased your revenge, but remember this, Stuprum…"

I wait, blowing out a cloud of smoke as the SUV pulls up to the cabin. *I didn't even notice we had turned back around.*

"When it all comes crashing down, and his revenge is seeping from your fingers with nothing but your guilt there to keep you sane…. Call me."

The door flies open and Nate is standing there, seething. "What the *fuck*, Benny!"

Benny winks at Nate. "Nathanial. When will you share this fine piece of ass with me?"

Nate's lip curls. "I'll rip your fucking face off before I ever let her touch you, Benny."

I roll my eyes, patting Nate's chest as I try to get out of the car.

He doesn't move.

"Nate!" I snap, but his eyes are still heated and on Benny.

He slowly steps backward to let me out but doesn't move his attention from Benny.

"You know how I like it…" Benny smirks.

Nate launches into the car and knocks me to the side, but Bishop grabs him by the collar, setting him back. "No."

Brantley slams the door closed and the SUV slowly rolls out of the driveway.

When they're gone, Nate turns his wrath onto me. "What the fuck were you doing in his car, Tillie!"

"Well," I say, wiping the dirt from my legs, courtesy of Nate's tantrum. "I'm so glad you asked. He kidnapped me on my run, an—"

"—he what!" Nate yells, his eyes going back to the retreating truck.

"Nate!" I snap at him. "He brought me back. It doesn't matter."

Nate storms off into the house and I'm left with Brantley and Bishop staring at me carefully.

"What?"

No one answers and everything turns silent. Again.

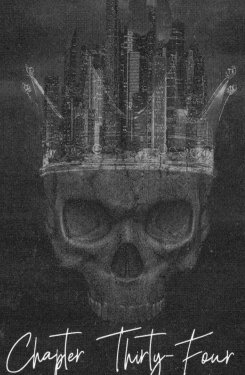

Chapter Thirty-Four

Tillie

"Pull over here…" Nate mutters, pointing to the shoulder of the road.

I obey, slowing onto the shoulder. "What's going on?"

Nate doesn't say anything. He flips his hoodie over his head, looking to the side mirror, as if he's waiting for someone. "I have a house. Did I tell you?"

"You mentioned it in passing, yes…" During the discussion of you living in it.

His fingers tap against his thigh.

"Nate, what are you doing?"

He looks anxious. Nate never looks anxious. My eyes catch an SUV pulling up behind us. I recognize it. The same one Nate's dad used.

"Turn your car off and follow my lead."

"What?" I screech. "No!"

"Tillie." Nate turns to look directly at me. "We are getting our revenge, and the motions that go into play here, are starting now."

"But Bishop sa—"

"Fuck Bishop when it comes to this."

"Wait…" My heart thunders in my chest. "You're going behind his back!?" I whisper-scream, tying my hair into a high ponytail.

"Do you trust me?" Nate asks, staring at me and waiting for my answer. "You have to be able to trust me completely from here on. Follow my cues, watch my reactions. You're smart, but you're fucking lethal when it comes to reading me, baby. I need you to put all of that skill into motion right now."

"I do." Because it's true. I trust him with every ounce of my being, which is pre-

"Then get out of this car and follow my lead."

I lick my lips and nod. "Okay."

I grasp onto the door handle, swinging it open and taking a step out. My Jimmy Choo shoes crunch the gravel beneath my feet, my skinny jeans suddenly too tight. I zip my leather jacket up and beep my car.

"What about my car?"

"Leave it. Someone will collect it."

I whisper sweet nothings at it before following behind Nate to the SUV.

Nate opens the door and the whole back seat is laid out like a limousine. He slides in and I follow.

My eyes go to the two people in front of me.

Scarlet.

Gabriel.

I wince. "What's going on?"

Nate pulls his hoodie down, his eyes going to Scarlet. "Tell me everything."

"Wait, you knew?" I snap at Scarlet.

She shakes her head, tears slipping down her face. "Of course not. I'm not a monster."

I relax slightly.

"But I believe Bishop did. I don't know what Hector gets involved in. I've always been on the outside—by choice. Not wanting to know, but I know what I heard."

I freeze. "No..." I shake my head. "Bishop wouldn't do that."

"You seem so sure, Stuprum. My son was raised by the Devil himself. What makes you think he's not exactly like his father? What makes you think there isn't more as to why Madison ran away from him?"

Everything slows, my heart thundering in my chest. My mind feels dizzy, and my fingers tingle. "No," I repeat. "He wouldn't."

I look to Nate, who is beside me.

"He wouldn't."

Nate's jaw clenches, his eyes coming to mine. His pupils are dilated, more black than blue. *"But he did."*

My mouth drops open, my eyes slowly blinking as I drag in a deep breath. My heart cracks in my chest.

Bishop had something to do with this.

Madison running away.

Madison wanting to talk to me the night we were at the party.

He fucking knew everything.

I lean over, my hands grasped around my head. "I can't believe this..."

"Tillie..." I hear Nate's voice somewhere in the far distance, trying to pull me back to the present. It's like a tug-a-war. Nate on one side, my sanity on the other.

His hand comes to my thigh.

He caresses it softly. "Baby..." Then his fingers wrap around my chin, yanking my face up to his. He runs his thumb over my bottom lip, and the darkness that was closing in around me starts to reopen, Nate's face before it all, shattering my madness to pieces.

Everything comes back to the present, my heart calming.

"Trust. Me."

I nod.

He presses the tip of his thumb into my mouth slightly, smirking, and then releases, looking back to the two in front of us.

Feeling stronger, I sit back, my eyes going to Scarlet. "And you're okay with us killing your husband?"

Scarlet stares. "No." Her glare cuts to me, and I see a glimpse of her other side. "Of course I'm not. But things work differently in this world. That is something I do understand. Do you understand that, Tillie?" she asks, tilting her head.

I feel Nate still beside me.

She continues. "Because I don't think you do. Do you know how many people have died at the hands of my husband?"

"I have an idea," I mumble.

She fiddles with her handbag and takes out a Gucci wallet. She pulls out a photo behind the one of her, Bishop, and Hector, handing it to me after smiling at it briefly.

"Hector had a daughter once too. With another woman, no less, but I still wanted her."

I bring my eyes down to the small baby in the image. It's the same image that was in the cabin.

"I tried to reason with him that I could keep her and raise her as my own, but he wouldn't allow it. Setting an example was too important. Hector is a brutal man, Tillie. He is a King before he is a husband or a father."

"I'm sorry," I say, handing the photo back to her.

She tucks it back into her wallet. "Don't be sorry. I don't want your pity. Did I kill my husband for playing a hand at her death? No. I didn't. Because I understand this world. You are weak, Tillie Stuprum. You are so guided by mundane things like revenge that it has made you weak. So you asked me if I'm okay with this? No. I'm not. Because if I didn't get to do it for my daughter, I don't think you should either."

Rage is bubbling underneath my skin, threatening to spill over. I want to smack this bitch so hard her head rolls.

"But—" she interrupts my thoughts. "I understand it. I will say this, Tillie, you have a very loyal bunch around you, I won't say anything else."

I look to Gabriel "And what have you got to do with all of this?"

Gabe smiles. "I'm here to make sure things run smoothly, Tillie."

"What?"

"—He's a Peacekeeper, Tillie," Nate mutters, running his hands over his face. I can see underneath the cool façade that Nate is filled with wrath. Someone is going to die tonight, and that someone better be Hector.

"Peacekeeper," Gabe says, unbuttoning his suit jacket. "There has to always be one Peacekeeper. When I die, or lose my mind, someone else will be assigned. I keep the peace between The Kings, The Rebels, and The Circle, as well as the civilians. I am untouchable, and anyone who dares harm me will be wiped out, as well as their entire family. So, people usually follow the law."

"Right," I mutter. "But what—Puer Natus?"

Gabriel stills. "Not now."

Nate shifts around just as the SUV comes to a stop. I look up and notice we're at Bishop's house.

"Hector is home. I suggest you get this done, thoroughly."

I glare at Gabe. "Haven't you failed your job?"

Gabriel smirks. "So quick to jump to the next conclusion."

Nate swings open the door, grabbing onto my hand and dragging me out.

"Will be here, son..." Gabriel says just as Nate slams the door closed.

Nate drags me up the stairs, through the front door.

The lights are out, and even though I'm well aware that the sun is going down outside, it seems darker in this house. Twin stairs lead up to the second floor, a crystal chandelier hanging above our head in the foyer where black and white checkered tiles lay beneath our feet. Nate pulls me behind him, leading us through a high archway where I can see flames flickering, throwing light around the dark room.

"Well, well, well..." Hector says smugly, and we both turn to find him reading a book on a single sofa. "I did wonder when I would come face to face with you both. Didn't think you'd be bold enough to confront me in my own house, though."

Nate takes a seat on the sofa opposite him, unfazed. "Really? Because I'd say that you should know exactly what I'm capable of, Hector, since you know... you've seen me in action."

Hector twists his cigar around his mouth, grinning. "True, son. Very true."

Nate hasn't taken his eyes off him, and when I don't move, his hand finds mine instantly, yanking me down beside him. "Is it true?" he asks Hector.

Hector seems to ponder over his words, like he's tossing up whether or not he's going to answer honestly or dance around in lies. "Yes and no."

"Elaborate," Nate seethes, his lip curling around his teeth. He looks feral, like he's about to pounce on his prey and rip it to shreds.

Hector leans forward, reaching for his whiskey glass. "I want to show you something, and then you can decide what that means and what you want to do with it, but let me warn you both, not because I have to, but because I look at you like a son, Nate... under any killing of a Hayes, especially me, there is a bounty out for one-hundred million dollars to whoever kills the person who killed me, and then extra for the head of their loved ones. The duty will not be done lightly. If they catch you, they will make sure that the people you love, or persons." He grins, his eyes flicking to me. "Will be tortured while you're alive, for you to watch."

Nate stills.

"So be very wise with how you continue this plan. You're not a juvenile. Tillie is smart, I trust you will both make the right choice."

Nate's jaw clenches. "Just show us what you need to."

Hector picks up a remote control beside him, as if he knew we were coming. *That bitch Scarlet.* He pushes a button and the large TV that's hanging on the feature wall ahead of us turns on.

The screen is blurry at first, like someone is wiping the lens, and then it's on my sister's face, like it's turned around.

"I hope you can see this!" Then it turns and a click sounds, and suddenly I'm facing everything that's in front of her.

"Call Hector..." a female voice says, and I recognize it instantly.

It's silent, and then my sister murmurs. "We're here. The camera is set up, we're about to proceed."

Silence, and I see the front of Khales as she stands in front of Peyton.

"That makes no sense...."

She must hang up the phone because now Khales looks confused. "What!"

I see that they're in the driveway of Nate's house, and it makes my stomach curl.

"I don't—"

"You don't have to watch it *all*," Hector interrupts, his eyes cutting to me. "But you will watch enough."

I gulp, my eyes flicking back to the screen.

"We have to kill her."

"Her as in Tillie?" Khales asks. "Done. Hate that bitch."

I snicker.

"No," Peyton mutters. "Not Tillie. Micaela."

Khales silences. "I don't know... are you sure?"

"Yes," Peyton says. "Go. I'll meet you in ten at the front of the room."

"Peyton. I'm not a baby killer. That shit is too dark, even for me."

"Tough!" Peyton snaps. "You will do as I say, or I will take back that island."

Khales submits, like the little bitch that she is and ducks away. When the crunching of stones disappears into the distance, the camera turns back around onto Peyton's ugly face.

"Sorry, Hec. Change of plans. See, your son and his friends killed my lover. They *killed* him. Does Tillie know how much it hurts to lose the only person she has ever loved? I don't think my piece of shit sister does and let me tell you." She chuckles maniacally, her eyes coming to the lens. I can see her looking right at me. "As much as she loves Nate, I know she will never love anyone as much as she does Micaela. So no can do. I won't be stealing her baby like you asked me to do. I'll be killing it instead. Peyton fucking Stuprum over and out."

Nate stands, picking up the coffee table and throwing it against the TV. "Why the fuck did you trust her!"

Hector doesn't move.

I sit in silence, tears pouring over my face. "What does this mean?"

"Where is she?" Nate's enmity is reaching new heights, and I don't want to be the person he takes down with him when he falls.

"Do we understand each other?" Hector throws back, looking at us both.

"Question." I turn to face Hector. "Why? Why were you going to steal Micaela?"

Hector watches me closely. "I don't think you're ready for that answer. Not yet."

"Enough with the fucking half-truths!" I yell, frustration pouring out of me. "Just tell me!"

Hector shakes his head, placing his glass back on the table and bringing his dead eyes back to me. "I don't answer to you, Stuprum. I'll see you on Perdita. She still defied my orders, and that's punishable, but I am a patient man." He stands, winking. "I hope you're not queasy at the sight of blood."

He exits the room, leaving me and Nate standing in a bubble of mess.

"Nate." I blink, and he drops down beside me.

"What?"

"What do we do now? Why does he have an infuriating way of not answering questions."

He chuckles. "What we do for every fucking war. We pile up the jet and fly to fucking Perdita."

I don't ask why Perdita. I agree and let him take me back outside.

Bishop is outside, leaning against his car.

Nate flies forward, his fist clenched around his collar. "You knew?"

Bishop doesn't flinch, and he doesn't fight Nate off. "Not until after. I overheard him ordering people to find Peyton and the rest of what she did. I was going to tell you. I didn't find the time to do so. Peyton went ghost and he only just found her."

"What the fuck do you mean you didn't have the fucking time?" Nate roars in his face.

"When!" Bishop yells, his hands going up. "When you were both so fucking broken that you had to bury your daughter, or when Tillie was seeing fucking dead people? I didn't want to fucking open new scars until I fucking had to, Nate!"

"Madison knew…"

Bishop flinched. "She knew when I knew, because she heard too. I kept her quiet. She started to hate me for it. She couldn't han—Listen! It's a fucking long story. What we need right now is to get the fuck to Perdita."

"Why Perdita?" I ask, sick of the fucking fighting. I trust Bishop. I know Nate does too.

"Benny will meet us there," he says, his eyes going straight to Nate.

Nate laughs, shoving Bishop away. "That's why Benny was sniffing around? Because you were utilizing him?"

Bishop shrugs. "Of fucking course. But you know Benny doesn't do anything for anyone. You know that there's no cost to what he does. He hacks, seduces, and lures in people because he fucking wants to, not for money… he fucking liked Tillie. I mean, shit, it took him the second time seeing her to realize he was going to do it, but he did it, nonetheless."

"What is going on!" I scream at the two of them. "What has Benny got to do with all of this?!"

Nate's jaw is working. "Get in the car. Both of you. We will talk on the way to the airport."

"Good," Bishop says. "Because the rest of The Kings are meeting us there."

I slip into the backseat of Bishop's Maserati and he pulls out of the driveway with Gabe following behind us.

When I can't take the silence any longer, I start. "Okay. Talk please. What does Benny do?"

"Benny is the fucking cloud in the sky. He's one of the most notorious hackers in the twenty-first century. He is part of the reason *why* The Kings are so untouchable, and before him, was his dad and so on…"

"But he's a Vitiosis?" I question as Bishop drives us toward the airport.

"Yes," Bishop murmurs. "Brantley's cousin. Bailey's brother…"

"This is so messed up," I mutter, leaning my head back. "Tell me more."

"Have you ever heard of the seductress?" Nate asks.

"Yes."

"Well, Benny is that in male form. He can make every woman fall to their knees from his charm, and men too, which he does. Often. But everything is calculated with him. He's like The Riddler and The Joker all in one. He has no heart, a big cock, and the scent of sex to lure people in. He's an assassin, but of the highest caliber. He can find anyone within seconds, kill someone without being present, and do so without batting an eye."

"Sounds deeply disturbed..."

Nate scoffs. "You have no fucking idea."

"I wanted him to get Peyton because no one could find her. He wouldn't do it at first. Said he didn't want to fuck with a Stuprum. He had a lover who was a Lost Boy and your mother killed him. Long story short? He hated Stuprums. I said you were different. You had depth and heart. He still didn't believe me, so I brought him to the ball. He was taken with you instantly, but said he recognized something within you that was similar to him..."

"What's that?" I ask, hypnotized.

"Your charm and charisma and sexual aura—his words not mine, obviously. Weird motherfucker."

I clear my throat. "So why did he come for me the second time?"

"Because he's not stupid. So far on the other side of that spectrum, you have no idea. He knew not to trust someone who was similar to him, so he wanted to meet you again. I don't know what you did that second time, but it moved him. He found Peyton instantly and had her shipped to Perdita."

I smirk. "Take me right to Perdita."

On the plane, one of two, we're almost landing on Perdita when Nate glares at me, his jaw clenched.

"What?" I whisper. "Stop looking at me like that."

My skin shivers, probably from all of the torment.

"Like what?" he asks.

When I don't answer, his hands come to my knees and he spreads my legs apart. "I need you."

"No," I snap, gazing out the window.

"No?" he questions, smirking.

"No."

"I've got too much anger for this kill. I need to let some out."

"I can't go into this broken and battered with a sore ass, so deal with it," I snap, still angry at him over what happened at the cabin.

"You're angry at me..." he announces, but his voice is like silk, brushing against my skin with tender syllables.

"I'm not."

"Hey!" His voice is soft, but I don't answer.

His hand comes to my chin and he forces my eyes to his. "We will talk after this."

"About what?" I search his eyes.

"Us."

I bark out an ugly laugh. "There's nothing to talk about and I've come to peace with that."

He squeezes my chin and I flinch, my eyes going to his. "Fuck your peace." His thumb presses over my bottom lip. "You've done good, baby."

I feel my insides warming to him again, the problem is that my thermostat is faulty when it comes to Nate. "How so?"

"We'll talk. Okay?"

I hesitate.

"Answer me, Tillie, or I will fuck you in the back room and make the pilot circle until we're done."

"Okay," I whisper, exhausted. "We will talk."

We land, and Nate takes my hand as we all move off the jet. We didn't need an army like the last time, because apparently, I do *own* this island. I'm still not comfortable with that fact, but I don't bother to fight any of them on that front anymore. I'm focused, and here for one thing. Once that's done, I can think of the others. Like why Nate wanted me here in Perdita to begin with and what the fuck is with Daemon's book. What is he trying to tell me? I can feel his thoughts inside my head sometimes, and when it happens, I feel like I'm going crazy. I'm terrified to go to sleep at night, just in case nightmares meet me there on the other side. *Where does our mind go when we're sleeping?* Pretty sure mine visits hell, judging by the people I see in them. A dark limo is waiting for us and we all pile in. Bishop, Nate, Brantley, Cash, Eli, Ace, Hunter, and Jase in ours, while there's another two SUVs behind us, waiting.

"Is Hector in that SUV?" I ask, not meeting any of their eyes.

"No," Bishop announces. "He's letting you handle this. Anything you need to know that he knows, he said will come to light through the mouth and revelations of others. Typical, people do his dirty work constantly."

I don't even bother to answer because I don't know what to say.

"You okay, little terror?" Brantley asks across from me.

My eyes find his. "I don't know. Should I be?"

This all feels too fluid, too smooth and easy. Something itches in the back of my mind that I shouldn't trust them. I've trusted them at times that I thought I could and where did that end up? In many different places in very questionable positions.

"This time?" Nate mutters, his eyes going out the side window as we make our way through the jungle of Perdita. "Yeah, you should be."

We pass through the jungle, bumping our way until we're at the high gates of the entry to the small town that I've come to know quite well. This time, when the gates open, I take in all the things I don't normally consider. Like how there are a couple of people who seem to be patrolling the area during the day, even though their kind live at night and sleep during the day. I notice the shops seem smaller than the average ones you'll find in our "world." Miniature versions without looking cramped. There are lights that line the main road we're driving down, and I know that at the very end of this road is the mansion.

I turn to face Nate. "Where are their houses?"

Nate nudges his head to the side. "Everywhere. Their homes are built randomly through the forest. There are small footpaths that lead to each house, lit by solar lights. There are no streets, no roads, just dirt paths."

"Wow," I answer, leaning forward to get a look.

"You won't see them. They're hidden."

I lean back, blowing out a breath of air. "Why did you take me here anyway?"

Nate laughs, but the rest of them remain silent.

"I'm serious, Nate!"

His jaw tenses and I have to fight the urge to either reach for him or punch him.

"You were supposed to run this island," Brantley says when Nate doesn't speak up. My eyes go to him as he carries on. "We didn't take you, but Gabe had strict orders to get you onto Perdita for us. We said that we wouldn't hurt you, and told him the plan, to which he agreed. Being a Peacekeeper, he acknowledged the reasons as to why we would do this. As your right and all of that."

"—only," Nate adds, finally speaking up. "The second you said Daemon that all changed. We knew that you weren't ready, and there was no way any of us were going to fucking force you to do it."

"Oh, okay." I roll my eyes. "Not force me but steal me and lock me in a cage?"

Nate turns to face me. "We took you with plans to teach you how to run Perdita. I didn't want to see your fucking face, you being here was the obvious choice!"

I flinch at his words but remain headstrong. "So why didn't you just tell me then and there that Daemon wasn't real?"

Nate sighs, running his hand through his hair and tugging on my heartstrings while he's at it. *"Because I didn't let that side touch you."*

Blood rushes through my ears at the soft touch of his words.

"No matter how fucking much I wanted to scream at you that he wasn't real, I fucking couldn't do that to you. Until he wasn't going away, and we figured we had to when other shit was coming up." He gazes back outside the window. "Even though I wanted to fucking kill you for it."

I don't know how to feel about what he's saying, and again, I have a hard time trusting him. It's been back and forth for so long between him and me, I don't know what to do during these times. I won't be getting any time to think too much into that because the car pulls to a stop at the high gates where guards are standing at the front. When all of The Kings pile out, I reach for Nate just as his door swings open.

"Who will take over here if I don't?"

His door slams shut and it's just us inside with nothing but our loud thoughts and silent mouths.

"Someone has to. It's how this always happens." His eyes search mine, his hand coming to my cheek. "Do you want to be here?"

I shake my head. "No. I don't, I don't know Perdita, Nate. I wouldn't know what I was doing."

He nods, reaching for my hand. "I'll introduce you to someone later, after we've dealt with your sister. Everything is your decision, you know that, right?"

"I know," I answer, though I'm not sure that's entirely true. I can't process anything because he's so close, I can practically hear his heart beating in his chest.

I want to kiss him.

I want to kiss him for our revenge. For Micaela.

I lean forward slightly, my eyes dropping to his mouth. Soft swollen lips that curve in all the right places, a hard jawline that is what models are made of.

"Don't," he interrupts my thoughts. I flinch back at his words, suddenly aware of how close I had leaned into him, with him inching the opposite way.

"What?"

I don't know why him saying that hurt so much, maybe because he has never outwardly said no to me when it came to kissing him or fucking him. It stung, and the root of that lethal sting is launched right in my heart. His sting is laced with poison, and no one is smart enough to create an antidote.

Before I can ask him to elaborate and further increase my embarrassment from the obvious rejection, he's gone, and the door is still open waiting on me to get out.

Slipping out of the car, I shuffle through The Kings until we reach the entry. Both guards bow before unlocking the gates, letting us through.

"In the dungeon," Bishop mutters, going through his phone as we continue through. Being back in this house doesn't upset me in any way, or bring any emotions to the surface, really, which I'm thankful for.

We make our way down the steps that lead to the dungeon, the flickers of the lit candles guiding the way. My heels echo against the stone steps.

"How do I know this isn't a setup?" I say loudly as we land on the final step.

"Because I'm not lying to you anymore. Come on," Nate says, gesturing down the corridor where the cells lead off.

I watch as he moves, and in the seconds between the car, or the flight, or I don't know when, I've come to the conclusion that I have forgiven him. Grief can bring out the ugly in some people. Your world shifts, and it takes a part of you with it, and sometimes, you fall between the cracks of where it used to be. I can forgive him, because my love for him is stronger than my pain. But now I think I'm too late.

We stop outside of one of the cells, and Bishop unlocks it, the heavy metal clinking. The smell brings me back to when I was down here, taunting me about my lack of sanity.

There's a dark chuckle that erupts from the darkest corner. I step forward, my shoulders stiff.

"Why?"

She waddles toward me, her plump body towering over mine. "Because you don't get everything you want."

My eyes narrow, anger bubbling to the surface. *Is she for fucking real?*

"What do you mean by that? You're saying you killed my daughter out of jealousy? No, I don't believe you. I know that it's more than that."

"How are you just so confident, little sister? Is it because you now have The Elite Kings behind you, backing your every move, or is it just because you're that cocky?"

Her hair falls from a scrunched bun at the back of her head, her cheek bleeding and her makeup smudged. Benny got rough with her. *Good.*

I slightly turn my head over my shoulder, the shadows behind me all glisten with imaginary gold crowns on their heads. I smirk. "Maybe. Or maybe it's the fact that you killed my fucking daughter!"

I can feel the rage and pain building higher and higher.

"Breathe, baby," Nate whispers from behind me, his voice softly caressing the nape of my neck. "Don't lose control or you'll rush it."

I close my eyes and count to ten. I feel his hand come to mine and that's when I realize another thing. "You were always jealous too, though, weren't you, Peyton?" I turn around, finding Jase.

Peyton snorts. "Hardly. I am so over all of that and got over it quickly."

I step backward, knowing that Jase is still directly behind me. I keep my eyes on

Peyton as my back pushes up against his front. Jase doesn't move, obviously knowing what I'm about to do.

"Lies," I whisper. "Jase was the only guy you fucked around with a lot. The one you hung off of every word, every text message. You hated that he would watch movies with me while you sulked in your bedroom. Never saw you like that with anyone else…" I tease and then watch as her eyes go over my shoulder and land on Jase. Who is completely still.

"Princessa, Nate called red on you. I can't touch you…"

My eyes don't move from Peyton. "You don't have to."

I bring my hand to the back of his and turn, running the palm of my hand up to his face.

"You loved Jase and you hated me for being a distraction for him. For being everything that you wanted to be. You started resenting me then and it played a part in the reason why you decided to do it."

I lean up on my tiptoes, pressing Jase's cheek to my tongue, licking him down to his neck. Then I bring my hand down and watch as her eyes follow, pain flashing through them within a blink. *I fucking knew it. Knew she was still in love with him.* I reach into the waistband of his jeans and grab his cock. I feel it harden and grow in the palm of my hand and he lets out a soft growl. "Fuck."

I start stroking him over his boxer briefs. Her eyes flare. She launches at me like a fucking crazed crack head. We both stumble to the ground with her on top of me, her fist connecting with my cheek. I laugh.

"Bro…" someone says.

"Leave her," Nate mutters.

She goes to hit me again, but I smack her fist out of my way while my other hand flies to her throat. I squeeze so roughly my nails sink into the flesh of her neck. I lock my grip further, until I feel blood slowly trickling down my fingertips. My laughing stops and her hitting stops, and everything fucking stops, because motherfucking terror is here.

"You kill *my* daughter and have the nerve to fucking hit me?"

Keeping my grip firmly on her throat, I shove her off me and stand to my feet as she remains on her knees, peering up at me like I'm motherfucking Mary and she's confessing all her sins.

"Nate…" I call for him softly, an unspoken question passing between the two of us.

"You got it, baby."

I grip harder until I feel the muscles and tissue beneath her skin click and her face turn puffy. Leaning down, my eyes search hers.

"Look at me, Peyton."

Her eyes fly to mine as I squeeze harder, then I slam her onto her back and climb onto her chest. I press down brutally until I know her airways are blocked off.

"You suffocated my little girl. You knew she was dying under your action."

Tears start streaming down my face as my heart once again splits open from what Peyton had done. *How could you kill a baby?*

"You showed no mercy. You were relentless. Now it's my turn. Open your eyes, so I can watch as the life slips from your worthless body and your soul gets dragged to hell."

Her face is purple now, the result of her gasping for air with desperation. Memories attempt to flash in my head of us when we were little, but at the end of every memory, all I wish for is that I had killed her back then. Her eyes start rolling back and I lean into her ear, my grip remorseless.

"I'll be here until my fucking hand cramps, Peyton. Can you feel your organs shutting down? Your heart slowing as it takes its final beats? The blood desperately crashing through your veins, chasing life it doesn't deserve?"

Her body feels limp and I lean back, her head fallen to the side, her eyes rolling to the back of her head. I thought it would be satisfying, putting an end to her, and it somewhat is. But I still have anger inside of me. She still got out of that too easy.

"I'll meet you in hell, bitch." I spit on her face just as arms wrap around my stomach, bringing me to my feet. I don't have to look back to know that it's Nate. My body responds to him whether I want it to or not.

"It's done." He kisses my nape. "But I need to leave my mark."

I step backward, gesturing to her dead corpse. "Be my guest."

Nate steps forward, removing his shirt and giving it to me. A small gesture that means so much. He's calculating, flicking an army knife between his fingers. He leans over the top of her and cuts her shirt off. I watch as he sinks the knife into her chest, over her sternum, and slices her with seamless precision, all the way down to her belly button. My stomach churns, so I look away for a second. When I hear slushing, gushing and heavy things falling to the concrete floor, I close my eyes. *Don't do it. Don't look at what he's doing.* The room is silent, with nothing but the sound of, what I'm guessing is organs falling to the ground and the strong scent of metal suffocating me. I hold my breath. But I feel him in front of me. My eyes slowly open and find their way up to him. He's watching me carefully, searching mine with something else this time. Peace? Tranquility?

"Kiss me," he whispers.

I can see the blood on his chest, but I don't care. I lean up on my tiptoes and crash my lips against his. He doesn't move into me. He simply opens his mouth wide and licks me across my lips as I devour him. Losing myself in all that is him. He consumes me more than anything in this world, the feeling is stronger than love. It's stronger than hate, or pain. He smothers me and owns every single bit of who I am. Something wet, hard, and heavy drops into my palms and I pull away out of instinct, but his hand grabs mine, forcing it back on. I squirm, my lips moving against his.

"What is it?"

He shuffles back enough to watch me. "Look at it."

"I don't really want to. Also don't really want to hold it. Whatever it is..."

He repeats. "Look at it."

I suck in a breath and then my eyes drop to my hands. Her bloody heart rests in the palms of my hands, the cardiac valves and tissue still hanging from the organ. My legs start shaking and my stomach churns.

"Nate..."

"She took ours, so we take hers." He brings the tip of his knife into the center of it and sinks it down, until blood streams between my fingers. "We done?"

I nod, dropping the heart to the ground. "Yes. We're done."

Nate looks over my shoulder. He nods at The Kings and then curls his arm around my neck, pulling me into him. "Good. I'm hungry."

We all start making our way out of the cell and just before we leave out of sight, I turn around slightly and take a mental picture of the sight inside the cell. Peyton torn open from the chest, and her bloody dead heart on the dirt-ridden floor with Nate's knife lodged into it.

"Peace out, bitch."

Chapter Thirty-Five

Tillie

After a quick shower in Katsia's bedroom—which by the way, is insane. The structure and architecture is articulate and the décor is something I have never seen before. Her bedroom is laced in soft lilac and dark greys, with large windows that overlook the front of the mansion. The bathroom is at the end of the bedroom, but open. It's odd, but freeing. The shower has six—yes, six—large shower heads that drop from the ceiling, which is one large mirror. This entire room was made for sex and screams orgasms louder than any orgasm receiving girl.

I dress in new clothes but wash my shoes carefully because I'm not leaving them here, before heading back down to the main living areas where The Kings wait. Nate hasn't said a word to me since showing me where Katsia's room was. I'm not confused anymore, I know he cares for me, maybe even loves me to a certain extent, but I'm not delusional about my future with him. It's probably not going to happen, but just because you know you might not have a future with someone, it doesn't numb the feelings you have for them. Unfortunately.

As soon as I enter the sitting room, everyone falls silent.

I roll my eyes, leaning against the door frame. "Don't worry, I'm not seeing dead people."

Eli chuckles.

Brantley watches me carefully.

Nate is glaring at me.

"What'd I do now? I always feel like I'm in trouble."

"Okay, I have to know who voted to have a girl in the group?" Ace murmurs. "I mean she is *in* our fucking clique."

I press the palm of my hand to my heart. "Aw, I'm touched. Can I call myself a King?"

Nate rolls his eyes. "I need to talk with you." He brushes past me, and out of habit, my eyes find Brantley.

Brantley nods, so I turn and follow Nate toward the foyer and out the front door. He heads straight for the gates. I run, catching up to him.

"What's going on?"

"You asked me if there was another option to who would take over the island if you don't want to."

"Yes," I say, falling into step beside him.

We make our way down the main street, passing all of the stores until Nate turns us toward a small alleyway between a weapon shop and a bakery. I follow behind him.

"Why?"

We come out the end and tree's line the back of the shops, with lights hanging in the branches. There are small cleared footpaths that lead into the forest, and he carries on forward.

I look down at my heels, and then look back up at him, praying to the fashion gods that they forgive me for the treatment I've been laying out to Jimmy Choo. The sun is setting in the sky, the day turning to night. I know that this is when the people of Perdita come out, and a big part of me is eager to see their way of life.

When I catch back up to my grumpy leader, I chew on my bottom lip. "Where are we going?"

"I'm going to introduce you to someone. I want you to have an open mind to her and not react with your fangs."

"I don't have fangs…"

As we tread deeper into the forest, I find myself looking around. The trees are all separated perfectly, giving me enough clearance to see through them. There are multiple paths that lead off in different directions, with little wooden signs that point down the dusty lanes. The names are all in Latin, so I don't understand what they say. Nate takes a turn down *Adamantem* and I follow closely beside him. I itch to reach for him, but since his attitude has been cold, I retract the urge.

"Wow," I whisper, my footing slowing as we trudge deeper.

There are small cottage style homes that line each side of the lane. Not many, maybe three or four? Nate nods his head toward a larger style cottage home with white flushed wood and glass windows.

"Come on."

I follow, because now I'm intrigued. Lights begin to flicker on along the pathway and the trees behind and in-between the homes. The darker it gets, the more lights start to turn on, around the houses, framing the windows and doors. We climb the few steps that lead to the front door and Nate knocks on it twice. And then twice again. As we wait, I admire the small gardens that decorate the front yard, with flowers I've never seen before. Mind you, I'm not a flower person so I wouldn't actually know if we have them. Pinks, and lilacs and soft beige petals flourish through the greenery, like little spurts of life springing from nature.

The door opening brings my attention back to the forefront. A girl around my age is standing still, her eyes on Nate. She *has* to be around my age, maybe younger, with long brown hair and sparkling blue eyes.

"Salve, Malum." She bows slightly, her head hanging between her shoulders as her eyes twinkle up at him.

Nate stands strong, nodding. "Salve, Adamantem. Qui scis haec?" The dead language drips off the tip of his tongue like melted chocolate. Addictive, teasing, and everything that you've ever wanted. *Also an easy way to get diabetes.*

The girl's eyes come to mine. I see fire flash through them before recognition takes hold and has her dropping to her knees.

"Etiam, domine. Stuprum…"

Nate turns to face me. "I asked her if she knew who you were. She didn't at first, but does now."

"Right. Can you tell her that she doesn't have to stay on her knees?"

"Sursum, Adamantem."

She stands instantly, running the palms of her hands over her flannel pants and coat. Their clothes are much like ours, only dated back in maybe the 90s. She moves to the side and gestures for us to enter.

Nate shakes his head as he continues to speak in Latin to her. I watch as her eyes scan over him with lust. She's hanging off of every word, her nipples hard for him.

"Have you fucked her?" I ask Nate, interrupting his rambles.

He pauses, his eye twitching as he brings his attention to me. I don't give him the same courtesy, and I'm loving the fact that she can't understand English.

I keep my eyes on hers, as she keeps hers on him. On someone who belongs to me. *At least he does inside my head. And heart.* The more I think about it, the more the rage burns.

"Yes. Frequently. Why?"

I tense, along with my jaw. I'm biting down on it so hard I'm sure my teeth will crack. "Interesting."

"What's interesting about that?"

I finally bring my eyes to his. "The fact that even in this world, you can't keep your dick in your pants."

He tilts his head. "You really want to do this right now. Right here?"

"It's your tune, baby. I'm just dancing to it…" I sass, grinning at him. He infuriates me. Just when I think I'm ready to address and claim my feelings for him, this frustrating man goes and does something dumb like this.

"Don't fucking throw metaphors at me, Tillie. Speak your fucking mind. I fucked her. Regularly. I fucking enjoyed it, and I'm pretty sure she did too. What do you want from me? You know I have a past."

Just how far back does she go, though…

I exhale. "Good thing she doesn't understand or speak English."

"Actually," she whispers softly. "I do."

I still, my eyes flying to Nate. "Who is she?"

His jaw clenches a few times. "She's an Adamantem, the English translation is Diamond. Basically, they're the only living family that has a direct blood line to the Stuprum tree. So in short—"

"—she could run Perdita…" I whisper. Nate's slut antics bumped to the back of my brain.

"Yeah," Nate murmurs. "But you would have to announce it in front of the people for them to recognize her as their new queen."

"Nate," the girl says. The fact that I don't know her name bothers me.

"What's your name?"

Her eyes meet mine. "Valentina, your majesty."

"Please don't do the 'our majesty' thing. It's creepy and makes me feel old." I look up at Nate. "What makes you think you can trust her?"

Nate's anger loosens as his hand comes to her chin, lifting her head up to face him. *Nope. Nope. I'm about to crush this bitch.*

"Because she's of pure heart, Tillie. I trust her. That should be enough."

His hand falls from her face and jealousy roars so loud in my chest that I find my feet moving in front of each other until I'm standing directly between the two of them.

I look down at her with a snarl. "You can have my kingdom, but you cannot have my King."

Her head bows acquiescently. "I understand."

Then I turn, walking away from both of them. I'm so angry with Nate, with everything. I want a normal fucking life. I want a house to come home to. I want to do nightly dinners and go clubbing with friends. I'm so sick of this fucked-up world and the fucked-up man I'm so severely in love with. Before I can think too much on the fact that it's now dark and I'm alone, because of course Nate didn't chase me because why the fuck would he, I'm back on the main street of Perdita. I push past people who don't automatically move as everything spins around me. The events of my life that have happened, all that I've lived through. I'm having a moment of self-pity when I push through the guards. It's not until I slam the front door closed and my eyes meet Brantley and Bishop's when I realize I've been crying.

"Take me home."

The door slams behind me, and I'm angry that I jump. "What the fuck is your problem, Tillie?" Nate barks out from behind. Maybe I'm being irrational, but Nate makes me ugly. He brings out my jealousy and leaves it out raw in the open, like a fatal gaping wound. I hate how much power he has over me, but that's power he doesn't need to know he possesses.

I turn to face him. "I want to go home."

His eyes narrow, and when my eyes drop to his lips, all I picture is Valentina's mouth on his. Did he kiss her when I left? Oh my god, why do I not like this girl? Is it because she reminds me of me? Because she's almost at the same level as me in this world? Or is it because I watched as Nate showed her kindness. Kindness he hasn't used on me in some time. My heart hurts and my stomach throbs from that realization.

"You can't," he answers harshly, shouldering past me and disappearing into the kitchen. Bishop follows closely behind him. Brantley rolls his eyes, tilting his head back like he's exhausted from the same shit.

He wraps his arms around me, burying his face in my hair. "Little terror. You didn't play nice with Nate's little plaything?"

I growl.

Brantley chuckles, his chest shaking. "You wouldn't be my little terror if you did."

"He has feelings for her?" I ask, but it comes out mumbled because my face is buried so deep in his clothes.

"Yes and no."

"I'm so sick of competing against other girls when it comes to his affection, Bran

Bran. Throughout our entire relationship—if that's what you can even call it—I've had to compete for a spot in his heart, only to watch him treat everyone nice, and me? Not so nice." I pause when I realize I'm about to choke on my sobs. Snot and everything dripping down my nose. I rub it against Brantley because I know he won't care. His arms squeeze me tighter.

"It's not that, Tillie. It's so much more complex than what you're thinking."

"It's not, though. I fell in love with a man who has no heart for me."

Brantley pushes me back, his hands squeezing my arms. He searches my eyes. "Baby, that man has everything for you."

"I don't believe you," I whisper, searching his eyes. "Bran Bran."

I pull away from him and make my way upstairs. I need a bath and two hundred shots of vodka. One for every time Nate has broken my heart.

Chapter Thirty-Six

Nate

Hearing her open up to Brantley like that didn't bother me as such. The tears did a little.

But hearing her say that she has had to compete for me, messed with me on a new level. I've been fucked a lot, and no pussy has fucked me as hard as Tillie's words did in that sentence. I feel hollow, and fucking shit.

I slide down the wall in the kitchen, hearing her footsteps drag upstairs. I lose myself in a daze as Brantley's boots come into view when he enters. He stops, goes straight for the cupboard, and then drops down on the floor directly opposite me.

Flicking off the top of the vodka, he takes a swig.

"I feel like we've done this more times than I've had my dick wet lately," he murmurs, handing me the bottle.

I reach for it, desperate for something. Anything to numb the ache that's roaring in my chest. The ache that I put there myself, as a product of the epic fuck up that is me.

"More than I care to admit," I answer, hissing when the poison hits my stomach.

"Two questions…" Brantley mutters, his eyes coming to mine. "One, are you going to fix this? And two, or are you going to let her go?"

I think over his words. I've done some heavy damage to her in the time that we've been together, without really being together. She deserves every fucking thing that she wants, and I don't know if it's me and this world that she really wants. Why would she want to be held by the same hands that broke her?

"I don't know," I answer honestly.

"Think of her. Not you," Brantley says before standing.

"Alright, Dr. Phil." I follow suit, handing him back the bottle. "Let's get this fucking ceremony over with so she can at least be back on world soil."

I start heading back through the kitchen and to the dining room, just as Brantley's hand comes out and stops me. "Don't tease her with Valentina. You're both past that and she's dealt with enough of that bullshit. Also, if you care for your little toy's safety, I wouldn't push Tillie too far. Your toy might end up... broken."

I chuckle. "Yeah, I know." Then I shove through and head into the dining room where Bishop is sitting, eyes distracted and lost in the distance.

"We need to talk..."

"Fuck," I mutter, pulling the seat out before I take it. "Now what."

"It's true," Bishop whispers, his Adam's apple bobbing. Brantley enters just as Bishop says the words.

"What's true?" Brantley asks, his eyes going between the two of us.

I bury my face into my hands, running my fingertips through my hair. "She can't know. Brantley, we need to tell you something..." I cover my mouth with my hand.

Brantley glares at both of us. "Fucking secrets. Really?"

"No." I shake my head, because out of everything, I can't handle Brantley being salty as fuck with me. "It was kept between the two of us until we could find proof, which Bishop has."

Brantley takes a seat, his jaw clenching.

Bishop's eyes go to Brantley. "We know about Saint."

Chapter Thirty-Seven

Tillie

We're at the front of the gates of the mansion, and I have The Kings behind me, standing firm. I turn to the left, my eyes finding Benny, who's watching me with obvious zeal. His eyes drop up and down my body, taking me in slowly. I chose the sluttiest thing I could find in Khales' wardrobe, which wasn't hard considering she owned patches as shirts. It's a small black dress that hugs all of my curves. Strapless, pushing my tits up and has a nice little slit up the left thigh that goes right up past my hip.

Hello, no panties.

I matched it with thigh-high boots and spent hours on my hair and makeup. I wanted to look unstoppable and strong. I figure if I look strong, it will hide the fact that I'm falling apart inside.

I swallow past my nerves, my eyes glassing over as I gaze back out in front of me. I don't look at the swarm of people. I keep my eyes locked on the end of the road, so far back that I can actually see. When Gabe begins talking, I start counting shops.

One.

Two.

Twenty-four.

By shop fifty, Valentina is walking up to us with a long robe on, a hoodie covering her face.

I don't look at her, because fuck her, and carry on my count.

Valentina removes the robe, and that's when I finally look at her. She's wearing a red dress that flows to the floor in lace patterns, a trail behind her.

Nothing slutty or over the top. Nothing like my mother. Maybe it will be a good thing, maybe I can trust Nate when he says that I can trust her.

Or maybe I'll continue being bitter.

I choose the latter and turn to Gabe when he takes my hand. He presses the sharp side of a silver blade into the palm of my hand. I wince as the sting resonates through all my nerves, before he does the same to Valentina. I don't flinch when he presses her hand to mine. I remain vacant, and unfazed. I never look at her once, and I ignore the heat that's radiating from the back of me. I know it's Nate glaring laser beams into the back of my skull.

I want off this fucking island.

The crowd cheers.

Gabriel turns to me, his hands coming to my face. "You're free, sweet one."

"Thank fucking god." I slice Brantley with a stare. "Home?"

He nods. "Yeah. Alright."

Nate stayed behind. Because of course he fucking did. The flight was long because of this, and it was torture because all I could fucking think about is all the dirty things he was doing to Valentina.

"I will never buy Valentino," I mutter, scrolling on my laptop as I search for houses.

Bailey chuckles. "That bad, huh?"

I nod. "That fucking bad."

"Have you heard from him since you left yesterday?" she asks, throwing fruit and all sorts of shit into the blender.

I shake my head. "Nope. All I know is that he and Bishop both stayed behind, and since Bishop is now single, and so is Nate, I'd hate to know what they were up to all night." I pause, tilting my head as I look over a house that stands away from the rest.

It's nothing too over the top. It reminds me of what I wanted when I was a little girl, cold and hungry in the middle of our trailer, with my daddy's fists flying into my face.

"You found something?" Bailey asks, rounding the table and looking over my shoulder. "Oh, I love that!"

"Me too," I whisper, picking up my phone and calling my realtor. "I want it." I smirk at Bailey.

After letting my realtor know to put an offer in on the house, I make my way to my bedroom, flicking through the contacts on my phone. I hit dial on Madison, even though I know it will go to her voicemail.

Only it doesn't. "Tills..."

I launch off my bed. "Madison!"

"Shhhh!" she scolds me. "Don't say that too loud."

"First of all are you okay?"

"Yes," she answers somberly.

"Okay good, because what the fuck do you think you're doing running away like this? Why didn't you tell me you were going!"

"I—I felt so guilty, Tillie."

"Madison," I sigh, my shoulders sagging. "I would have never been mad at you. I understand this stupid world more than you know. I would have understood," I repeat, my voice softer. "But what I don't understand is why you ran! Where are you?"

"In New Zealand with Jesse. You can't tell Bishop!"

"He already knows," I answer truthfully.

"He does?" Her voice cracks on the end.

"Yeah, and he's letting you go."

"Oh," she answers sadly. "I guess that's a good thing."

"No, it's not. The minute you realize you want to come home, you better come home. Because I want my friend back. I forgive you, it's all in the past. I never was mad at you in the first place."

"Oh no," Madison says. "That was just the beginning of our problems."

I lick my lips. "Can you give me something more on what happened with asshole?"

Silence. "He threatened to kill me, you, Bishop, Nate, everyone if I didn't go along with the video to make it look believable. So I took it." Her voice jolts and I know she's crying. "My heart, Tillie. Knowing that I was betraying Bishop and I couldn't do anything about it ripped me apart. I knew that any minute after it was done, Bishop was going to think I cheated." She sighs. "I don't know who he was working for or why he raped me. But when he finished, he called someone and told them that the deed was done and now they'd have to wait."

"God," I whisper. "I'm so sorry, Madison. I wish I could be there with you right now. I promise I'll get answers. These assholes will give me answers."

She chuckles. "You handle them all so much better than I ever did."

"Mads…" I whisper. "You're the fucking queen of the pack. You're Bishop fucking Vincent Hayes' lady. You underestimate your power."

"No," she says softly. "I overestimated it for too long. But I will come back one day."

"Good. Because I bought a house."

"You did?" She perks up. "Where?"

"Some fancy neighborhood in the suburbs. White picket fence and all. You'd be proud."

"I am proud."

"I need you back in my life," I sigh. "There's so much I've got to tell you."

"Well, I've got some time now?"

I snuggle into my bed. "Okay, so this bitch Valentina…"

Chapter Thirty-Eight

Two weeks later

Tillie

"I love that we're drinking out of mugs," Bailey says, sipping red wine. Purchasing and moving was easy. It seems the saying is true; money does talk.

"I know," I chuckle, looking around my lounge. "I still have to shop for the smaller things. I don't really drink wine, so it didn't come to me."

"Hey so…" Bailey murmurs, running her finger around the rim of her mug. "Have you heard from any of The Kings?"

I shake my head, tucking my legs under my ass. "No. I think they're all giving me the silent treatment."

Bailey laughs nervously. "Oh, I have a gift!"

"Oh, Bays, I can't take another exp—"

She hands me the box with Daemon's book. My eyes go to hers as I carefully take it from her. "Where'd you get this? I couldn't find it anywhere."

Bailey brushes my comment off, swallowing all of her wine in one gulp. "I figured it's important. You should read it tonight, and think again about coming to Nate's house warming. It won't be kicking off until probably after ten."

I look at the big clock that hangs on my pristine white walls. It's just after six. I smile, even though I know I won't be going. No way in hell.

"Thanks. But no. You have fun though!"

She gives me a hug and stands. "Try reading through that tonight. You might feel more insightful or something…" Then she leaves, and I'm left sitting there wondering how she knows about Daemon's book.

I flip through the pages, my fingers scanning over each image.

Picture after picture. I reach the end, where there's the baby rattle in the cell. I always thought he was giving me a clue to Micaela, but that was when I thought he was alive.

I tilt my head, looking closer at the image, then when I go to turn the last page, a photograph falls to my lap. I flip it over and pause, noticing it's the same image from the cabin.

"What?" I whisper, placing my wine onto the large coffee table and curling my knees under my butt. I flick back to the baby rattle and then look back at the picture.

I look closer.

This is the baby that Scarlet had said she wanted to raise.

Who is this baby girl? I swear if someone says it's me, I'm going to rage and burn this world down. I cannot take another fucking twist of parents.

I pick up my phone and dial Scarlet's number. She answers on the fourth ring.

"Tillie..."

"Scarlet, that little girl you told me about..."

Silence. "Yes?"

"Who was her mother? The woman Hector had an affair with?"

"Who do you think?" Scarlet answers calmly.

What has this book got to do with me. What are you trying to tell me, Daemon. My eyes close.

"It's Katsia, isn't it? My mother had another little girl..." But it wasn't Peyton, because we already know she wasn't Katsia's birth child.

"Correct. Think, Tillie... who could that little girl be?"

"I don't fucking know!" I yell, standing to my feet. I'm pacing back and forth on my white fur rug, adrenaline thrashing through my veins. *Who the fuck are you...*

I stop walking.

I stop breathing.

"Scarlet..." I whisper, blood draining from my body. "What color was her hair?"

Scarlet snickers. "So fucking smart, young queen. For her hair, was as white as snow."

The phone slips from my hands and without thinking, I snatch the keys to my car off the coffee table, running out the front door.

I don't care that I'm in yoga pants and a loose knit shirt. Or that I threw on the first sneakers at my front door.

I don't even care that all I know is Nate's street and not the number of his new house. I jump into my car and fire it to life, before skidding out of the driveway.

Chapter Thirty-Nine

Nate

Two things happened to me the day that Tillie left Perdita.

One, I realized that Brantley was right. I had to let her go. She needed to come back to me when she was fucking ready, and not because I'm forcing her to be in this life. In other cases, I'd be a selfish bastard and take her anyway, but with all the pain that this world has inflicted on her, I couldn't bring myself to force her to be here. I set her free. But mark my fucking words, the second she walks her ass back through any door of the house that I'm in, I'm calling it check-fucking-mate and stamping my name across her ass.

Bailey stumbles down the stairs, a bottle dangling between her fingers. "Nice house, Malum."

I ignore her, my eyes flying back outside as I watch as horny fucking college students dive into my lagoon-style pool that's outside my very fucking over the top mansion. The day I was told I had a daughter, was actually the day I started plans on building it. Took a while, but it's done now. Still some things needing to be put in, like the basketball court, and a place I've decided to call "The Den." Bishop and I have massive plans for it. Like a gentleman's club, with no fucking rules. It's where we're going to train the new generation of Kings, Abel included. It's going to be exclusive and fucking lethal.

From the foyer, the twin stairs lead up to the second level, that's wrapped in stained marble. The whole second level is rounded in a circle, with a railing that you can look downstairs from. It has ten bedrooms, a theater, a show garage, and a *room. The Room.* I built this house around that one room. The room that started the plans. If you know me well enough and look closely at this house, you'll see where I went dark. I started it happy with Micaela's room. Then it slowly went to shit and boom. The Den was built.

Everything spins around me, the alcohol pulsing through my system at a speed I can't catch up to. "Swervin" by A Boogie Wit da Hoodie starts playing and I lean my head back against the top of the sofa, closing my eyes. I usually rage when I'm this drunk, but I can't seem to find the energy to beat any of these fuckers tonight. I feel someone take a seat on my lap, wriggling.

My eyes fly open and I shove whoever it is off. The girl—who I don't fucking know—falls to the ground.

"Ouch, Nate!" She turns and I see that it's someone—I think—I've fucked with in the past. Her legs open slightly, and I see a flash of her pussy. Yeah, definitely remember that. I think. I'm drunk.

"Don't fucking touch me."

I shove through the crowd in my sitting room, half tempted to tell everyone to get the fuck out of my house and that I don't want any of them here when the front door flies open and everyone stops. She's like a fucking magnet for Kings, because they all slowly come into the sitting room, surrounding me.

I smirk devilishly, like I wasn't just brewing in my own salt with how things ended between her and I.

"Careful with that door, *Princessa*. It doesn't like being slammed half as much as you do."

She glares at me from all the way the fuck over there, and my head swims in all the scotch I consumed.

"Is it true?"

I pause. What exactly is she asking me? Did she work it out?

"Everyone out!" I snap at all the people in the lounge. They slowly pile out and make their way out to the back where the pool is. There's no way I'll be able to shut this party down right now, so I turn and look at Bishop. "Shut that fucking door and lock it."

"What are you talking about?" I answer her, but I'm pretty sure I slurred a few words in between. *Fuck.* I can't help but take in her fucking body. Even in yoga pants and a fucking granny cardigan that looks two sizes too large for her, she will still make every other girl walking this earth look like a solid *zero*. And that's being generous. She doesn't know this yet, but I haven't laid my hands on another girl since Micaela came into our lives. Never fucked Tate, even though I'm pretty sure, judging by her little cute confessions with her Bran Bran, she thinks I did, and fuck other girls often, but the truth is, I don't see any girls past her. Yeah, so I dabbled in pussy before, and between her when she left the first time, but since she came back, I've not.

Shit. I haven't fucked anyone since her. *What the fuck.*

She carefully steps farther inside, her eyes wild. She's the kind of wild you can't tame, but you wouldn't want to anyway, because her turbulent soul is reckless, desolate and raw. You wouldn't want her any other way, and if you did, well, fuck what you want.

"Is it true? Did Hector and Katsia have a baby girl..."

I slam my mouth closed, my eyes crashing into Bishop's before they swing back to her. "Yes."

She takes another step, her eyes narrowing. *Oh, she's fucking pissed.* "I have a half-sister?"

I hiss, baring my teeth as I take a swig of vodka. "Yes."

She's right in front of me now, looking up into my eyes. Her sweet little doe eyes momentarily distract me from her animosity that's throbbing off of her in waves. Then her eyes cut to Brantley.

"Who is the girl that lives with you, Bran Bran?"

Brantley's eyes blaze, and I watch as his demeanor changes. He doesn't like when Saint's name is brought up in a conversation. We all learned that the hard way.

"Brantley," Tillie whispers, her head bowing. "Who is she?"

Brantley softens, and then exhales, dropping down onto the sofa. "Saint," he clips out and then reaches for a random bottle of alcohol off the coffee table. He leans back into the sofa and perches one foot up. "And yeah, she's your half-sister."

Chapter Forty

Tillie

I have a half-sister. Someone I didn't know about—ever, and—I sink to the ground, fatigue settling into my bones.

"I'm tired."

Nate's shoes come into view. Nike Air Force Ones as white as his perfect teeth. He drops down, his fingers coming to my chin, tilting my face up to his.

"We only figured it out a couple weeks ago."

I snatch the bottle from him, bringing the rim to my mouth. "What does this mean?"

Nate sits on the floor opposite me and I see out of the corner of my eye as everyone scatters to relax. The music is still blaring outside.

"It means Daemon knew about her, probably all along."

"But why did he want me to find it? How would that have helped me?"

Nate chuckles. "He would have wanted you to know that you running Perdita wasn't your only option, that there was someone else who shares that responsibility with you."

I wince. Daemon. Sweet, beautifully haunted Daemon. Always there to look out and watch out for me, even from his grave.

"Which would never fucking happen, just to be clear," Brantley growls.

I bring my eyes up to his. "How long have you known?"

Brantley licks his lip, his eyes never moving from mine. "All her life. Dad bought her when she was two years old. She's lived with us since. I'm guessing your imagination can fill in the rest, what with everyone's knowledge of Lucian Vitiosis."

I pale. "Brantley... what did you do to that poor girl..."

He rolls his eyes. "She's not my fucking slave or anything. She gets the best of fucking everything. She couldn't go to school, so we hired tutors. Ones that I approved of. Her life before we took her, though, Tillie, it wasn't fucking good. And when Dad was alive, it wasn't much better, until I put a stop to it when she was thirteen."

My eyes glass over. "She looks so young and...pure."

Brantley's eyes drift over my head as he loses focus. "Yeah. I know. She's younger than you, though. Not by much."

"Her name is Saint?" I ask, tilting my head.

"Yeah. I named her."

I study Brantley's posture, how he positions himself in a defensive stance while we speak about her. Yeah, I wouldn't breathe near this girl without his permission. At all. It's frightening while being beautiful at the same time. To witness the scariest man I have ever met, ever known, with such a dark past and soul, soften toward a girl who is the opposite of him, is some sort of witchcraft.

"Okay. We don't need to talk about her anymore, but I do want to meet her..."

Brantley relaxes. "Yeah. Well, since everyone knows about her, and Nate is owned, I have no problem bringing her around."

"Aye!" Nate laughs, his head tilting back. "What, me? Little old me? You didn't want to bring her around because of *me*?"

Brantley rolls his eyes. "Don't fuckin' play dumb, Malum. Chicks fall to your cock. Though I knew she wouldn't, I couldn't risk killing you just in case you, or she, did."

"Mmm!" I whine, swiping my mouth after I take a sip of alcohol. "So Valentina staked her claim on you, since you're owned now?"

The room falls silent, all that's filling the space is the music from outside. When Nate doesn't answer me, I bring my eyes to his. My stomach flips at the way he's looking at me.

"What the fuck are you talking about?"

I don't want to admit that I want to know what happened when he and Bishop stayed behind, because that would show I care.

He props one knee up and rests his elbow on it, leaning his head back against the wall. He smirks. "You think I fucked Valentina when I stayed behind in Perdita..."

"—Okay," I hear Eli mutter from somewhere in the room. "I'm going to get pussy. Mommy and Daddy are fighting again."

"I don't even care," I answer with a level voice.

Nate reaches out and grabs my hand, tugging me forward. I end up on my knees in front of him as he looks up at me from sitting on the ground. His hand drifts up my cardigan and then he yanks me down so I'm face-to-face with him.

"Liar."

I search his eyes. "Does it matter?"

He chuckles. "Not fucking really."

I shove at his chest, pushing off him. "I don't even know why I bothered." He doesn't let me move so I shove harder until I'm back on my feet. I find Bishop. "You need to get in contact with Madison." Then I look at Brantley. "Thank you, Bran Bran. It's been fun."

Brantley's eyes shift to Nate desperately.

"I feel so much fucking better now that everything is deciphered. Only took a few murders, some hot sex, and losing my best friend, daughter, the man I fucking love, but whatever. Sayonara, bitches." I throw up deuces and turn, bearing straight for the front door. I need to run. One-thousand miles and clear my head.

"There's one little issue with your big dramatic exit, baby..." Nate murmur-slurs from behind me. Khalid's "OTW" thuds through the speakers.

I freeze, my fingers on the door handle. Slowly, I turn back around to face him, finding him a few steps in front of me.

"And what's that?" I ask, tilting my head.

"Just before you walked your little ass up in here, I made a promise to myself."

"Oh, you did, huh?" I humor him. "What was that promise?"

I'm tired and drained. I just want to finally mourn losing him. Losing him. I've never had to do it because we've always lingered together.

"Yeah." He smirks, taking a tentative step.

I step back.

He counters that by coming further.

My back slams against the door.

His hands fly up to either side of my head, his head dipping down to mine. He runs his nose tip over mine. "I promised myself that I'd let you go—until you walked your ass back into a house that I'm in, then I'm not letting you go. Ever."

I roll my eyes, shoving his hard chest, but he doesn't move. "Stop being ridiculous. I'm tired of the games."

His eyes narrow, then drop to my lips. "Not a game, baby. Gamechanger." He comes closer, his body pressing against mine and leans down, his lips floating across my ear. "I'll lock you in my room if I have to. You're not leaving me this time, or ever again."

I swallow. "I can't do this, Nate." I can feel all the emotions and feelings I have for him roaring to the surface. "I can't continue to love someone who isn't manufactured to love back. I can't fucking compete with other girls when it comes to your affection, and I can't fucking handle not having *all* of you!"

He slams me up against the door, his hands coming to my thighs. He lifts me off the floor and out of instinct, I wrap my legs around his lean waist. One hand rests on the front of my throat as his thumb caresses my collarbone. His other is wrapped around my lower back.

"One, you've never competed with *any fucking girl*. It's always been you and it makes me fucking testy hearing you say shit like that so I would advise that be the last time those words spill out from those lips, or I'll feel obliged to shove something else between them. Two, there is one person on this earth who gets all of me, Tillie. One fucking girl. And it's not the dispensable hos that have bounced on my dick. It's the one that fucking stole my heart, and lastly." He smirks, his lips brushing softly against mine. "I must have malfunctioned along the way somewhere, because I fucking love you."

I search his eyes when the first tear slips from the corner of mine. My heart feels like it's beating to a different tune now.

"What?"

He kisses me softly, his lips brushing against mine. I open my mouth to let him in further as his tongue touches mine. My stomach flips and my thighs clench. *He loves me.*

"Wait!" I stop, pushing at his chest. "You're drunk!"

He rolls his eyes.

The Kings in the background groan out loud. "For fuck's sake, Stuprum!" one of them curses.

Nate grins. "I'm not that drunk. Stop being difficult."

I wrap my fingers around the back of his neck and bring my nose tip to his. "I love you, too, but I have one condition for us going forward. You know, consider it a new trend, if you will. Our girl version of calling red."

Nate's eyes narrow, then he starts pressing small kisses over mine. "Anything."

Between kisses, I smirk. "We're going to visit the same tattoo artist that Madison and Bishop visited, and I'm claiming what's mine."

Nate bursts out laughing, his head tilting back as he lowers me to the ground. He takes my hand and kisses the front.

"Sure thing, baby. So where are you stamping your name?"

"That is not a thing," Brantley announces, flicking his finger between us.

"It actually is…" I raise my eyebrows in challenge.

"Says fucking who?" He glares at me.

"Says fucking me, and since I am royalty, what I say goes. Also, Madison agreed."

Brantley glares at Nate. "Tell her that it's not a thing."

Nate begins carrying me upstairs. "Oh, it's a thing, and tell everyone to get the fuck out of my house."

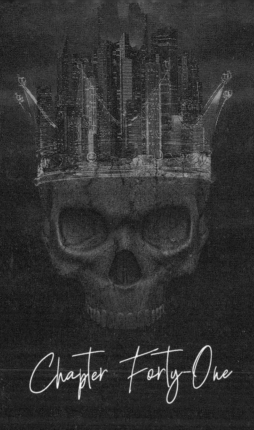

Chapter Forty-One

Tillie

Nate's bedroom bleeds opulence, the only kind that you could expect from him. I roll off his California king bed, dragging the sheet with me while leaving him completely naked behind.

I smirk, raking my hair out of my face as I make my way to the glass wall that is on the other side of his room. I find it interesting that they've all moved to NYC instead of staying in The Hamptons. Maybe it's a King thing. I run my fingertips over the walls. Dark grey with white trimmings. They almost look angry as they reach high up to the ceilings. The bathtub is behind a free-standing wall, along with a large shower head that stretches into a long rectangle. There are two walk-in wardrobes, one filled with all his clothes, and—I flick the light off, ducking into the other, where it's filled with some of my clothes.

"Shit that you left at Mom's."

"Oh," I whisper, not bothering to turn around to face him. "You just knew that I would take you back, huh?"

He chuckles, and I look over my shoulder to watch as he moves fluidly around the room, in all his naked glory. Muscles twitch with every movement and tattoos sprawl out everywhere with it. "Yeah, I did." He comes up behind me, wrapping his arms around my torso while hugging me into his chest. He bites on my neck roughly. "You're not a woman who can be owned. I knew that a long time ago. You may not belong to me, but you belong with me. And there ain't shit you can do about it."

I laugh, tilting my head as he drags his teeth over my shoulder. My eyes close as I fight the urge to moan.

He slaps my ass, pulling me out of my sex-induced haze. "I want to show you something before we leave."

"Before we leave?" I ask, tilting my head and watching as he turns the shower on. Steam instantly fills the room.

"Yeah," he smirks. "I promised you a fucking tattoo."

"And you really do want to?" I ask, an eyebrow cocked.

He glares at me. "Baby, I don't give a fuck. I would put your name across my head if I wanted to."

My eyes drop down his body, taking every single bit in. I grin when I get to the K I N G that sits over his pelvis. "I know just the thing."

"Yeah," he chuckles, slipping into the shower. "Bet you fucking do."

We wash up, in between the sex, and get changed in record time. I end up throwing on something of mine that he had brought here. Casual Vans, skinny jeans, and a leather jacket.

We're walking downstairs when he takes my hand and gestures down the elongated hallway. "When I built this house," he starts talking while leading me down. The walls drip in blood, the red a darker take in the very eccentric home. "I mean, when I started on the designs, it was when I first found out I had a daughter. I designed her room first and then built around it. That's why if you haven't noticed—"

"—the house changes in themes. Based on your mood," I finish for him, absently running my hand over the walls as we walk.

His fingers twitch in mine. "Exactly."

"What did you do with Micaela's room when she passed?"

He stops outside of a door and turns to face me. "If this is too much for you, I can change it. You can decide what to do with it. But for me, I figured this was what I wanted to do for now. A place we can go to feel her again when it starts to get numb."

Nate opens the door and I pause. The walls are pure white with Victorian style window panes that overlook the backyard of the house. There's a large purple rug in the middle of the floor and the walls are filled with large bookshelves, where all sorts of items sit inside little cubes.

"It's perfect..." I whisper, stepping farther into the room. "I love it." I turn around, flinging my arms around his neck and pulling him into me further. "Let's get that tattoo."

Chapter Forty-Two

Tillie
Two weeks later

"This is weird," Bailey murmurs, taking a seat beside me. It's Halloween, and the party in the cemetery is in full swing. I think it's the first time since we've all been back that I feel relaxed. After Nate's display of his love for me, we spent the following weeks deciding what to do about our two homes. Obviously, he trumped me on Micaela's room and the thought he put into his house, so we've decided to sit on mine. I refuse to sell it, it's too perfect. Maybe we could eventually rent it out to someone we know.

"I know." I shake my head, rubbing the palms of my hands down my legs. "I really miss Madison," I add when my eyes drift around everyone that's here.

Bailey hands me a glass of alcohol. "I hope I can meet her one day."

I stare at the glass.

"Here." She pushes the glass into my hands. I take it, placing the base onto my knees. The setup looks great. They've hung orange and yellow Jack-o'-lantern lights over the gravestones, and a DJ booth is set up near a large tomb.

"You'll meet her. I plan to drag her home soon."

Bailey laughs, her eyes flying around the place.

"Looking for Abel?" I tease, one quirked eyebrow.

Her face pales. "No. He hates me, and I hate him."

"Hate," I chuckle. "So much more complicated than its four letters."

Nate's arms snake around my neck from behind, and I tilt my head back to look up at him.

"Hey," I whisper, kissing his arm. "Are you having a good time?"

He runs his lips over my forehead. "I could be having a better time, but Hector is inside the house and wants to have a chat."

I groan, placing my glass onto the ground.

Brantley snickers. "Hector is scary as shit."

I laugh, turning around and lifting Nate's shirt, displaying his tattoo. "About as scary as this?"

Bailey chokes on her drink. "Holy shit. You actually put your name on him!"

I did. Above Nate's "King" tattoo over his pelvis, I signed *Tillie fucking Stuprum's* with a kiss. My lips and all. The artist had me kiss where I wanted it with red lipstick and then filled it all in. It's my favorite.

"Yes, I did, because he's my fucking King."

Nate grins, pulling me to stand up. "Damn straight."

"Okay. You guys are way too cute now. You need to go and sort Hector out."

I wave her off and follow Nate down the dark pathway. When we're halfway there, Nate picks me up by the backs of my thighs and flings me over his shoulder, slapping my ass.

"Nate!" I yell, tapping his back. "My stomach hurts!"

He laughs, slapping my ass again. "That's not all that's going to be hurting."

I bite down on the inside of my cheek as he carries me the rest of the way back to Brantley's house. Once we're inside, he gently sets me back to my feet and I shove him.

"Asshole. Stop manhandling me."

I slowly turn around to find the rest of The Kings, Hector, Scarlett, Elena and Joseph in the large sitting room.

"Stuprum," Hector announces, smiling at me.

I can't smile back.

He did plan to take my daughter. "Why?" I ask, tilting my head. "I know you didn't do it, but why did you plan to take her?"

He gestures to the sofa closest to his. I slowly sink into it, wrapping my hoodie around myself. "I know I don't have to explain to you how dangerous this world can be."

"Correct," I say, waiting for him to continue.

"The young man who raped Madison was a Lost Boy, Tillie. We've had issues happening on Perdita since before you came back. The problems that lie within that soil actually stem back to when your mother ran it into the ground. Your grandmother was nothing like your mother. She ruled Perdita strong, but even her strength had softness. Something I hadn't witnessed again, until you."

"—So you plan to steal my daughter?"

"—No," he interrupts. "That was not why."

"Then why!" I demand. "I need to know why."

Hector watches me carefully. "The Lost Boy who raped Madison was working with Peyton. Peyton had been working with people, not a lot, very few, to attempt to bring The Kings down. We're still not sure exactly what his intentions were by raping her, but we're hoping to talk to her at some point and gather all the information we need. We get enemies every decade or so, and then we kill them all until the next lot try." He sighs. "I ordered Khales to do it, because I knew that she would. I didn't know that she would take Peyton with her."

I won't cry again. I can't. "So why were you trying to take her?" I reach for my bracelet, fiddling with the strings.

"To show that you didn't have a weakness. Erase Micaela out of the picture—temporarily—and that leaves the hate tribe with nothing else to use, and lights a fire inside of you. I needed you to be focused and on fire to rule Perdita and help bring these fools down." He clears his throat, and I notice the fine wrinkles around his face. "Micaela was precious to our world. You have to believe that. She was a Stuprum. I would, and anyone in this world would do anything to protect one."

My eyes glass over. "You were trying to protect her."

"In his own way, Tillie, he was. I know it's hard to come to terms with," Bishop adds. "But he was trying to protect her, while also looking at something in his gain, i.e., you."

I sag back on the sofa, my eyes coming to Elena. "Secrets like this is why people die. Why they run away and why love is burned." I glare at Bishop. He winces and looks away.

"Hector?" I question. "Do we have any more enemies?"

"We will always have enemies, Tillie."

"Well can you kill them all in around eight month's time?"

Silence.

"Wait! What?" Nate comes to the front of me, dropping to the ground.

I search his eyes, reaching into my hoodie pocket and handing him a little white stick. "Surprise."

Nate's eyes fall to the pregnancy test, and I watch as a swim of emotions pass over his face.

Shit. What if this is too much and he's not ready? What if it's still too raw and close to Micaela. I hear gasps from behind us, but everyone in the room melts away.

Nate finally brings his eyes up to me, a smile spreading over his face. "Are you fucking kidding me?"

"Well, no, I—"

He pulls me into his chest, his arms wrapping around my back as he lifts my body from the floor. His hands come to my face as he gently places my feet back on the ground. "You make me the fucking happiest man in the world, Tillie." Then his hand comes down to the front of my belly. "We're having a baby?" he asks, searching my eyes for validation.

"Yes." I turn around to face Hector, who has a genuine smile on his face. "Please, Hector. Please don't—"

He hushes me with a flick of his wrist. "I swear to you on everything I stand by, that no harm will ever come to your baby, Tillie."

I bring my eyes back to Nate. "Can I trust him?"

Nate tilts his head over his shoulder to look at Bishop. "Yeah, babe. Yes, you can."

Elena comes over to me instantly, rubbing my back and I sift through everyone congratulating us. I didn't plan to blurt it out here, but I need everyone to know how serious I am. I also want reassurance that my baby will be guarded by the Godfather and his Kings.

I clear my throat. "I'm trusting you. All of you." Taking a few seconds to catch my breath, I make an effort to bring my eyes to each of them. "I'm trusting you with something that you have broken previously. I know it wasn't intentional, and I know that none of you actually did the act, but this world did. I can't blame it all on you, or on Nate, because this world is mine too, but I'm trusting you. Please don't break that trust."

"Little terror?" Brantley teases once the silence stretches out into awkward territory. "You will be the most protected woman, and that baby will be guarded by Hellhounds, I promise you. I *fucking* promise you."

I relax, my heart resting in my chest. *I trust him. I trust my Kings.* I may not completely trust Hector, but I know who my family are.

"I love you," I whisper to Brantley.

He blows me a kiss.

Then we all quiet as faint footsteps patter down the stairs. All of our eyes shoot to the entryway of the sitting room, waiting to see who it is that turns the corner.

Long white hair.

Pale, smooth skin.

Dark green doe eyes.

A fragile body held together by a yellow sundress hanging delicately from her frame.

"Hi," she announces softly. "I'm Saint."

ACKNOWLEDGMENTS

To my husband. For being a muggle.

To my kids, for being the best little assholes I could ever ask for.

To Sarah, for being my main girl. Not just in book life (glares), but in real life. You run my street team, handle everything that I cannot do, beta read my books, and still manage to be an amazing mum, wife, and work. You're so much more than you realize.

To Chantal, for being the best distraction I could have asked for.

clears throat *I'm not drunk enough for this....*

To Anne, for being my rock. Seriously. This bitch.

To Lyla, for being my best friend. You're one of the strongest girls I know. We've been through it all. Made mistakes together, made memories together, and cried together. I can't wait to walk behind you as you get married. I love you so much.

To Nichole, for being the best friend a girl could ask for. For drinking my problems away with me, and then curling up in my bed to kick back and Netflix and chill. Drunk. With chocolate wrappers everywhere. You. Are. A. Diamond.

To Leigh, for reminding me who I am when I forget sometimes. You have had my back more times than I can count. I will always have you.

To Jacq, you had me read the darkest series I've ever read and distracted me from my writing. But it was worth it and I love you.

To Charleigh. Seriously? I need Seb. You distracted me from writing also, in the best fucking way possible. Now, write that next book...

To Ellie, for being all that you are. Your skills are irreplaceable. YOU are irreplaceable.

To Petra, for being yourself. For cleaning through my words with a respectful hand.

To my street queens, I love you. Thank you for being everything that I could ever ask for in a loyal bunch of girls.

To my bloggers, thank you for taking the time to read and review my words. I appreciate you more than you could know.

To my readers, if I wrote a 100k novel on how much I love and appreciate all that you are, it still wouldn't be enough. Thank you for riding with me, staying with me, and joining me. You inspire me and keep me strong.

My Wolf Pack, you got the dedication, but again, *howls*

To CrossFit, because without you I would have committed first-degree murder.

To my haters, *waves* heeeyyyy, giirrrlll!

To my dog, Raze, for reminding me that I really should appreciate a clean yard...

Lastly, to anyone who is trying. The ones who are getting through but kicking off their worn shoes at the end of the day. I see you. I love you. And I acknowledge you. Stay strong.

Xo—Amo.